R.A. SALVATORE

Collector's THE *Edition*

HUNTER'S BLADES
TRILOGY

THE HUNTER'S BLADES TRILOGY
COLLECTORS EDITION

Cover art by Matthew Stewart
This Edition First Printing: January 2007
The Thousand Orcs First Printing: October 2002
The Lone Drow First Printing: October 2003
The Two Swords First Printing: October 2004

9 8 7 6 5 4 3 2 1

ISBN: 978-0-7869-4315-9
620-95973720-001-EN

U.S., CANADA,	EUROPEAN HEADQUARTERS
ASIA, PACIFIC, & LATIN AMERICA	Hasbro UK Ltd
Wizards of the Coast, Inc.	Caswell Way
P.O. Box 707	Newport, Gwent NP9 0YH
Renton, WA 98057-0707	GREAT BRITAIN
+1-800-324-6496	Save this address for your records.

Visit our web site at www.wizards.com

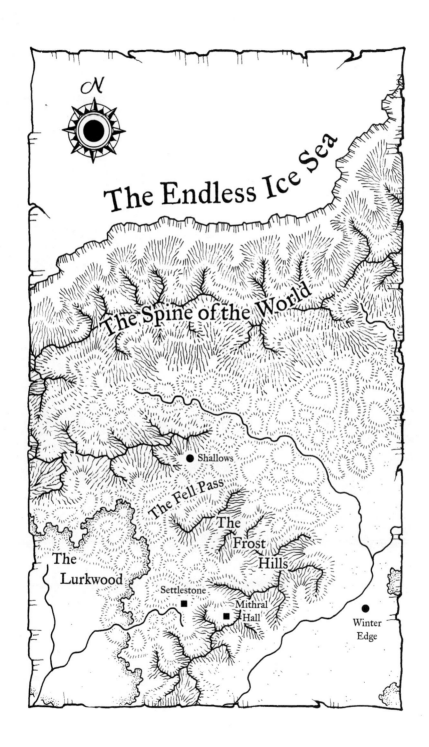

N

The Endless Ice Sea

The Spine of the World

● Shallows

The Fell Pass

The
Frost
Hills

The
Lurkwood

Settlestone
■

Mithral
Hall
■

● Winter
Edge

THE THOUSAND
THE HUNTER'S BLADES TRILOGY   BOOK I
ORCS

"Oh, well ye got to be pullin' harder than that!" Tred McKnuckles yelled to his team of two horses and three dwarves. "I'm hoping to be making Shallows afore the summer sun shines on me balding head!"

His voice echoed off the stone around them, a bellow befitting one of Tred's stature. He was stout, even as dwarves go, with a body that could take a beating and lumpy arms that could dish one out. He wore his yellow beard long, often tucked into the front of his huge belt, and kept a throwing hammer—commonly called "a dwarven arrow"—strapped on the back of each shoulder, ready for launch.

"It'd be easier if ye didn't have th' other horse sitting in the back o' the wagon, ye blasted fool!" one of the pulling dwarves yelled back.

Tred responded by giving him a crack on the rump with the whip.

The dwarf stopped, or tried to, but the fact that the wagon kept on rolling, and he was strapped into the yoke, convinced him that maybe it would be a good idea to continue moving his strong and stubby legs.

"Don't ye doubt that I'll be payin' ye back for that one!" he growled at Tred, but the other dwarves pulling, and the three others still sitting up on the wagon beside the boss dwarf, all just laughed at him.

They had been making fine progress since leaving Citadel Felbarr two tendays earlier, chancing the north run along the western face of the Rauvin Mountains. Breaking through to the flat ground, the group had done some minor trading and re-supplying at a large settlement of the Black Lion barbarian tribe. Named Beorunna's Well, it, along with Sundabar, Silverymoon, and Quaervarr, was a favored trading locale for the seven thousand dwarves of Citadel Felbarr. Typically, the dwarves' caravans would run to Beorunna's Well, swap their wares, then turn back to the south, to the mountains and their home, but this particular group had surprised the leaders of the barbarian settlement and had pressed on to the west-northwest.

Tred was determined to open up Shallows and the other smaller towns along the River Surbrin, running the western edge of the Spine of the

World, for trade. Rumors had it that Mithral Hall had for some unknown reason slowed its trade of late with the towns upriver, and Tred, ever the opportunist, wanted Felbarr to fill that void. Other rumors, after all, said that some pretty amazing gems and even a few ancient artifacts, thought to be dwarven, were being pulled from the shallow mines on the western edges of the Spine of the World.

The late winter weather had been quite favorable for the fifty mile run, and the wagon had rolled along without incident past the northern tip of the Moonwood and right to the foothills of the Spine of the World. The dwarves had gone a bit too far to the north, however, and so had turned south, keeping the mountains on their right. Still, the temperatures had remained relatively warm, but not so warm that they would destroy the integrity of the snow sheets and thus rain avalanches all about the trails. That same morning, though, an abscess had reared its ugly head on the hoof of one of the horses, and while the handy dwarves had been able to extract the stone the horse had picked up and drain the abscess, the horse was not yet ready to pull the laden wagon. It wasn't even walking very comfortably, so Tred had the team put the horse up on the back of the large wagon, then he split the other six dwarves into two teams of three.

They were quite good at it, and for a long time, the wagon had kept up its previous pace, but as the second team neared the end of its second shift, they were starting to drag.

"When're ye thinking we'll get that horse back in the harness?" asked Duggan McKnuckles, Tred's younger brother, whose yellow beard barely reached the middle of his chest.

"Bah, she'll be trotting along tomorrow," Tred answered with confidence, and all the others nodded.

None knew horses better than Tred, after all. In addition to being one of the finest blacksmiths in all of Citadel Felbarr, he was also the place's most prominent farrier. Whenever merchant caravans rolled into the dwarf stronghold, Tred would inevitably be called upon, usually by King Emerus Warcrown himself, to shoe all the horses.

"Might be that we should be putting up for the night then," said one of the dwarves pulling along in front. "Set a camp, eat us a good stew, and lighten that load we got by a keg o' ale!"

"Ho ho!" several of the others roared in agreement, as dwarves usually did when the possibility of consuming ale was mentioned.

"Bah, ye've all gone soft on me!" Tred pouted.

"Ye're just wanting to beat Smig to Shallows!" Duggan declared.

Tred spat and waved his hands. It was too obvious a protest. Everyone there knew it was true enough. Smig was Tred's greatest rival, two friends who pretended to hate each other, but who, in truth, only lived to outdo each other. Both knew that the small town of Shallows, with its trademark tower and renowned wizard, had seen an influx of people right before the winter—frontiersmen who would need fine weapons, armor, and horse-shoes—and both had heard King Warcrown's proclamation that he would be pleased to establish trading routes along the Spine of the World. Since the recapture of the dwarven citadel, which had been in orc hands for three centuries, the area west of Felbarr had calmed considerably, with the mountainous region to the east still buzzing with monstrous activity. There was an Underdark route to Mithral Hall, but none had been discovered thus far to open the lands north of Clan Battlehammer's stronghold. All of those accompanying Tred—his workers, including his brother Duggan, Nikwillig the cobbler, and the opportunistic brothers, Bokkum and Stokkum, who were carrying essential goods (mostly ale) for other Felbarr tradesmen—had eagerly signed on. The first caravan would be the most profitable one, taking their pick of the treasures garnered by the frontiersmen. Even more important than that, the first caravan would carry bragging rights and the favor of King Warcrown.

Right before the departure, Tred had engaged Smiggly "Smig" Stumpin in a good-natured drinking game, but not before he had paid one of the Moradin priests well for a potion that defeated the effects of alcohol. Tred figured that he and his had been out of Citadel Felbarr for a day and more before poor Smig had even awakened, and another day before the dwarf could shrink his head enough to get out the citadel's front door.

Tred would be damned if he'd let a little thing like an abscessed horse hoof slow them down enough for Smig to have a chance of catching up.

"Ye put up a trot for three more miles and we'll call it a good day," Tred offered.

Groans erupted all about him, even from Bokkum, who stood to lose the most profits by an early camp, and hence, more ale consumed and less to sell—though the betting was that he wouldn't end up selling it in Shallows anyway, and that he'd take it back for the celebration on the return journey.

"*Two* miles, then!" Tred barked. "Are ye wanting to share a camp this night with Smig and his boys?"

"Bah, Smig ain't even out yet," Stokkum said.

"And if he is, he and his got slowed plenty by the rock-fall we dropped in the path behind us," Nikwillig added.

"Two more miles!" Tred roared.

He cracked the whip again, and poor Nikwillig stood up very straight and managed to turn about enough to put a glower over the rugged driver.

"Ye hit me again and I'll be making ye a pair o' shoes ye won't soon be forgetting!" Nikwillig blustered.

His feet were digging little trenches as he got dragged along, and that only made Tred and the others laugh all the louder. Before Nikwillig could start his grumping again, Duggan kicked up a song about a mythical dwarven utopia, a great town in a deep mine that would please Moradin himself.

"Climb that trail!" Duggan crooned, and several looked at him, not sure if he was singing or ordering them around. "Break down that door!" Duggan went on, prompting Stokkum to yell out, "What door?"

But Duggan only continued, "Find that tunnel and run some more!"

"Ah, Upsen Downs!" Stokkum yelled, and the whole crew, even surly Nikwillig, couldn't resist, and broke into a rowdy, back-slapping song.

> "*Climb that trail*
> *Break down that door*
> *Find that tunnel*
> *and run some more*

> "*Cross the bridge of fiery glow*
> *Running deeper down below*
> *Make some smiles from those frowns*
> *Ye've found the town of Upsen Downs!*

> "*Upsen Downs! Upsen Downs!*
> *Ye've found the town of Upsen Downs!*
> *Upsen Downs! Upsen Downs!*
> *Make some smiles from those frowns.*

*"Ye've found the place o' the finest ale
With arm-sized pretzels that're never stale!
With big Chef Muglump and his coney stew
And Master Bumble with his forty brews!*

*"And in the holes ye can break the rock
and haul it up with yer tackle and block
Smelt it down and ye'll get it sold
Upsen Downs's got the finest gold!*

*"Upsen Downs! Upsen Downs!
Ye've found the town of Upsen Downs!
Upsen Downs! Upsen Downs!
Make some smiles from those frowns.*

It went on for many verses, and when the seven dwarves ran out of the formal lines of the old song, they just improvised, as they always did, with each piping in his own wants from such a remarkable place as Upsen Downs. That was the fun of the dwarven song, after all, and also a fairly subtle way for any perceptive dwarf to take a good measure of a potential friend or a potential foe.

Also, the song was a fine distraction, mostly for the three tugging the wagon along, backs bent and straining. They made fine progress through those minutes, bouncing along the rocky ground, the mountains rising up to their right as they moved south along the trail.

In the driver's seat, Tred called out names in order, bellowing for each to add the next verse. It went on smoothly, until he called out to his little brother Duggan.

The other five kept humming, providing the background, but they went through almost an entire verse, and there was still no response from Duggan.

"Well?" Tred asked, turning to regard his little brother and seeing a very confused look on Duggan's face. "Ye got to sing in, boy!"

Duggan looked at him curiously, confusedly, for a long moment, then quietly said, "I think I be hurt."

Only then did Tred look past that puzzled expression, moving his head back and taking a wider view of Duggan. Only then did Tred notice the spear sticking out of Duggan's side!

He gave a shriek, and the humming behind him stopped, with the two sitting in the back of the wagon turning to regard the slumping Duggan. Up front it quieted, too, but not completely, until a huge boulder whistled down, slamming the path right beside the three surprised dwarves and bouncing over them, clipping Nikwillig on the shoulder and knocking him silly.

The terrified horses broke into a gallop, and both the injured horse and poor Stokkum broke free of the rig, with Stokkum tumbling out onto the stony ground. Tred grabbed the reins hard, trying to slow the beasts, for his poor kinsmen up front were being tugged and dragged along, especially Nikwillig, who seemed unconscious.

Another boulder smashed down right behind the bouncing wagon, and a third hit the ground before the charging team. The horses veered wildly to the left, then tried to turn back to the trail on the right, putting the wagon up on two wheels.

"Move right!" Tred ordered, but even as he spoke the command, the wagon's left wheels buckled and the cart crashed down and flipped.

The horses broke free, then, taking the harness and the three strapped dwarves on a dead run down the rocky trail.

The two dwarves behind Tred went flying away—and Duggan was hardly aware of it—and Tred would have, too, except that his leg got hooked under the wagon seat. He felt the crunch of bone as the wagon came down atop him, then he got smacked on the head, and hard. He thought he had erupted into a bloody mess for a moment as the wagon continued its sidelong roll, but he had the fleeting notion that it was ale washing over him.

Luck alone extracted the dwarf from the crunching catastrophe, for he somehow wound up inside that decapitated keg. He went bounding and rolling away down the slope of the foothills. A rock stopped him abruptly, shattering the keg, and Tred went into a weird twisting somersault.

Tough as the stone around him, the dwarf struggled to his feet. One of his legs gave out under him, so he fell forward against the stone, stubbornly propping himself up on his elbows.

He saw them then, dozens and dozens of orcs, waving spears, clubs, and swords, swarming over the destroyed wagon and fallen dwarves. A pair of giants followed them down from the higher ground—not hill giants, as Tred would have expected, but larger, blue-skinned frost giants. He knew then that this was no ordinary band of raiders.

Slipping from consciousness, Tred kept enough of his wits about him to throw himself backward, falling into a roll down another slope, ending hard against another rock beneath a tangle of brambles. He tried to stand again but then tasted bloody dirt in his mouth.

Tred knew no more.

"Well, are ye alive, or ain't ye?" came a distant, gravelly voice.

Tred opened one eye, caked with blood, and through a haze saw the battered form of Nikwillig, crouched before the brambles and staring in at him.

"Good, so ye are," said Nikwillig and he slipped his arm in, offering Tred a hand. "Keep your arse low or the pickers'll be skinning it good."

Tred took that hand and squeezed it tightly but did not start out of the tangle.

"Where're the others?" he asked. "Where's me brother?"

"The orcs killed 'em all to death in battle," came the grim response, "and the pigs're not too far away. Damned horses dragged me a mile an' more."

Tred didn't let go, but neither did he start forward.

"Come on, ye dolt," Nikwillig scolded. "We got to get to Shallows and get the word spreadin' back to King Warcrown."

"Ye run on," Tred replied. "Me leg's all broke. I'll slow ye down."

"Bah, ye're talking like the fool I always knowed ye was!"

Nikwillig gave a great tug, dragging Tred right out from under the brambles.

"Bah, yerself!" Tred growled at him.

"And so ye'd be leaving me if it was th' other way around?"

That question hit home. "Get me a stick, ye stubborn old fool!"

Soon after, arm in arm, with Tred leaning on both Nikwillig and a stick, the two hardy dwarves ambled off toward Shallows, already plotting their revenge on the ambushing orc band.

They didn't know that another hundred such bands were out of their mountain holes and roaming the countryside.

PART ONE A LONGER ROAD THAN EXPECTED

When Thibbledorf Pwent and his small army of battle-ragers arrived in Icewind Dale with news that Gandalug Battlehammer, the First King and Ninth King of Mithral Hall, had died, I knew that Bruenor would have no choice but to return to his ancestral home and take again the mantle of leadership. His duties to the clan would demand no less, and for Bruenor, as with most dwarves, duties to king and clan usurp everything.

I recognized the sadness on Bruenor's face as he heard the news, though, and knew that little of it was in grieving for the former king. Gandalug had lived a long and amazing life, more so than any dwarf could ever hope. So while he was sad at losing this ancestor he had barely known, that wasn't the source of Bruenor's long look. No, what most troubled Bruenor, I knew, was the duty calling him to return to a settled existence.

I knew at once that I would accompany him, but I knew, too, that I would not remain for long in the safe confines of Mithral Hall. I am a creature of the road, of adventure. I came to know this after the battle against the drow, when Gandalug was returned to Clan Battlehammer. Finally, it seemed, peace had found our little troupe, but that, I knew so quickly, would prove a double-edged sword.

And so I found myself sailing the Sword Coast with Captain Deudermont and his pirate-chasing crew aboard Sea Sprite, with Catti-brie at my side.

It is strange, and somewhat unsettling, to come to the realization that no place will hold me for long, that no "home" will ever truly suffice. I wonder if I am running toward something or away from something. Am I driven, as were the misguided Entreri and Ellifain? These questions reverberate within my heart and soul. Why do I feel the need to keep moving? For what am I searching? Acceptance? Some wider reputation that will somehow grant me a renewed assurance that I had chosen well in leaving Menzoberranzan?

These questions rise up about me, and sometimes bring distress, but it is not a lasting thing. For in looking at them rationally, I understand their ridiculousness.

With Pwent's arrival in Icewind Dale, the prospect of settling in the security and comforts of Mithral Hall loomed before us all once more, and it is not a life I feel I can accept. My fear was for Catti-brie and the relationship we have forged. How would it change? Would Catti-brie desire to make a home and family of her own? Would she see the return to the dwarven stronghold as a signal that she had reached the end of her adventurous road?

And if so, then what would that mean for me?

Thus, we all took the news brought by Pwent with mixed feelings and more than a little trepidation.

Bruenor's conflicted attitude didn't hold for long, though. A young and fiery dwarf named Dagnabbit, one who had been instrumental in freeing Mithral Hall from the duergar those years ago, and son of the famous General Dagna, the esteemed commander of Mithral Hall's military arm, had accompanied Pwent to Icewind Dale. After Bruenor held a private meeting with Dagnabbit, my friend had come out as full of excitement as I had ever seen him, practically hopping with eagerness to be on the road home. And to the surprise of everyone, Bruenor had immediately put forth a special advisement—not a direct order, but a heavy-handed suggestion—that all of Mithral Hall's dwarves who had settled beneath the shadows of Kelvin's Cairn in Icewind Dale return with him.

When I asked Bruenor about this apparent change in attitude, he merely winked and assured me that I'd soon know "the greatest adventure" of my life—no small promise!

He still won't talk about the specifics, or even the general goal he has in mind, and Dagnabbit is as tight-lipped as my irascible friend.

But in truth, the specifics are not so important to me. What is important is the assurance that my life will continue to hold adventure, purpose, and goals. That is the secret, I believe. To continually reach higher is to live; to always strive to be a better person or to make the world around you a better place or to enrich your life or the lives of those you love is the secret to that most elusive of goals: a sense of accomplishment.

For some, that can be achieved by creating order and security or a sense of home. For some, including many dwarves, it can be achieved by the accumulation of wealth or the crafting of a magnificent item.

For me, I'll use my scimitars.

And so my feet were light when again we departed Icewind Dale, a hearty caravan of hundreds of dwarves, a grumbling (but far from miserable) halfling, an adventurous woman, a mighty barbarian warrior, along with his wife and child, and me, a pleasantly misguided dark elf who keeps a panther as a friend.

Let the snows fall deep, the rain drive down, and the wind buffet my cloak. I care not, for I've a road worth walking!

–Drizzt Do'Urden

1

ALLIANCE

He wore his masterwork plated armor as if it was an extension of his tough skin. Not a piece of the interlocking black metal was flat and unadorned, with flowing designs and overlapping bas-reliefs. A pair of great curving spikes extended from each upper arm plate, and each joint cover had a sharpened and tri-pointed edge to it. The armor itself could be used as a weapon, though King Obould Many-Arrows preferred the greatsword he always kept strapped to his back, a magnificent weapon that could burst into flame at his command.

Yes, the strong and cunning orc loved fire, loved the way it indiscriminately ate everything in its path. He wore a black iron crown, set with four brilliant and enchanted rubies, each of which could bring about a mighty fireball.

He was a walking weapon, stout and strong, the kind of creature that one wouldn't punch, figuring that doing so would do more damage to the attacker than to the attacked. Many rivals had been slaughtered by Obould as they stood there, hesitating, pondering how in the world they might begin to hurt this king among orcs.

Of all his weapons, though, Obould's greatest was his mind. He knew how to exploit a weakness. He knew how to shape a battlefield, and most of all, he knew how to inspire those serving him.

And so, unlike so many of his kin, Obould walked into Shining White, the ice and rock caverns of the mighty frost giantess, Gerti Orelsdottr, with his eyes up and straight, his head held high. He had come in as a potential partner, not as a lesser.

Taking his lead, Obould's entourage, including his most promising son Urlgen Threefist (so named because of the ridged headpiece he wore, which allowed him to head-butt as if he had a third fist), walked with a proud and confident gait, though the ceilings of Shining White were far from comfortably low, and many of the blue-skinned guards they passed were well more than twice their height and several times their weight.

Even Obould's indomitable nature took a bit of a hit, though, when the frost giant escort led him and his band through a huge set of iron-banded doors into a freezing chamber that was much more ice than stone. Against the wall to the right of the doors, before a throne fashioned of black stone and blue cloth, capped in blue ice, stood the giantess, the heir apparent of the Jarl, leader of the frost giant tribes of the Spine of the World.

Gerti was beautiful by the measure of almost any race. She stood more than a dozen feet tall, her blue-skinned body shapely and muscled. Her eyes, a darker shade of blue, focused sharp enough to cut ice, it seemed, and her long fingers appeared both delicate and sensitive, and strong enough to crush rock. She wore her golden hair long—as long as Obould was tall. Her cloak, fashioned of silver wolf fur, was held together by a gem-studded ring, large enough for a grown elf to wear as a belt, and a collar of huge, pointed teeth adorned her neck. She wore a dress of brown, distressed leather, covering her ample bosom, then cut to a small flap on one side to reveal her muscled belly, and slit up high on her shapely legs, giving her freedom of movement. Her boots were high and topped with the same silvery fur—and were also magical, or so said every tale. It was said they allowed the giantess to quicken her long strides and cover more ground across the mountainous terrain than any but avian creatures.

"Well met, Gerti," Obould said, speaking nearly flawless frost giant.

He bowed low, his plated armor creaking.

"You will address me as Dame Orelsdottr," the giantess replied curtly, her voice resonant and strong, echoing off the stone and ice.

"Dame Orelsdottr," Obould corrected with another bow. "You have heard of the success of our raid, yes?"

"You killed a few dwarves," Gerti said with a snicker, and her assembled guards responded in kind.

"I have brought you a gift of that significant victory."

"Significant?" the giantess said with dripping sarcasm.

"Significant not in the number of enemies slain, but in the first success of our joined peoples," Obould quickly explained.

Gerti's frown showed that she considered the description of them as "joined peoples" a bit premature, at least, which hardly surprised or dismayed Obould.

"The tactics work well," Obould went on, undaunted. He turned and motioned to Urlgen. The orc, taller than his father but not as thick of limb and torso, stepped forward and pulled a large sack off his back, bringing it around and spilling its gruesome contents onto the floor.

Five dwarf heads rolled out, including those of the brothers Stokkum and Bokkum, and Duggan McKnuckles.

Gerti crinkled her face and looked away.

"I would hardly call these gifts," she said.

"Symbols of victory," Obould replied, seeming a bit off-balance for the first time in the meeting.

"I have little interest in placing the heads of lesser races upon my walls as trophies," Gerti remarked. "I prefer objects of beauty, and dwarves hardly qualify."

Obould stared at her hard for a moment, understanding well that she could easily and honestly have included orcs in that last statement. He kept his wits about him, though, and motioned for his son to gather up the heads and put them back away.

"Bring me the head of Emerus Warcrown of Felbarr," Gerti said. "There is a trophy worthy of keeping."

Obould narrowed his eyes and bit back his response. Gerti was playing him and hard. King Obould Many Arrows had once ruled the former Citadel Felbarr, until a few years previous, when Emerus Warcrown had returned, expelling Obould and his clan. It remained a bitter loss to Obould, what he considered his greatest error, for he and his clan had been battling another orc tribe at the time, leaving Warcrown and his dwarves an opportunity to retake Felbarr.

Obould wanted Felbarr back, dearly so, but Felbarr's strength had grown considerably over the past few years, swelling to nearly seven thousand dwarves, and those in halls of stone fashioned for defense.

The orc king fought back his anger with tremendous discipline, not wanting Gerti to see the sting produced by her sharp words.

"Or bring me the head of the King of Mithral Hall," Gerti went on. "Whether Gandalug Battlehammer, or as rumors now say, the beast Bruenor once again. Or perhaps, the Marchion of Mirabar—yes, his fat head and fuzzy red beard would make a fine trophy! And bring me Mirabar's Sceptrana, as well. Isn't she a pretty thing?"

The giantess paused for a moment and looked around at her amused warriors, a wicked grin spreading wide on her fine-featured face.

"You wish to deliver a trophy suitable for Dame Orelsdottr?" she asked slyly. "Then fetch me the pretty head of Lady Alustriel of Silverymoon. Yes, Obould—"

"*King* Obould," the proud orc corrected, drawing a hush from the frost giant soldiers and a gasp from his sorely out-powered entourage.

Gerti looked at him hard then nodded her approval.

They let their banter go at that, for both understood the preposterous level it had reached. Lady Alustriel of Silverymoon was a target far beyond them. Neither would put her and her enchanted city off the extended list of potential enemies, though. Silverymoon was the jewel of the region.

Both Gerti Orelsdottr and Obould Many Arrows coveted jewels.

"I am planning the next assault," Obould said after the pause, again, speaking slowly in the strange language, forcing his diction and enunciation to perfection.

"Its scope?"

Obould shrugged and shook his head. "Nothing major. Caravan or a town. The scope will depend upon our escorting artillery," he ended with a sly grin.

"A handful of giants are worth a thousand orcs," Gerti replied, taking the cue a bit further than Obould would have preferred.

Still, the cunning orc allowed her that boast without refute, well aware of her superior attitude and not really concerned about it at that time. He needed the frost giants behind his soldiers for diplomatic reasons more than for practical gain.

"My warriors did enjoy plunking the dwarves with their boulders," Gerti admitted, and the giant to the side of the throne dais, who had been on the raid, nodded and smiled his agreement. "Very well, King Obould, I will spare you four giants for the next fight. Send your emissary when you are ready for them."

Obould bowed, ducking his head as he did, not wanting Gerti to see his wide grin, not wanting her to know how important her additions would truly be to him and his cause.

He came up straight again and stomped his right boot, his signal to his entourage to form up behind him as he turned and left.

"They are your pawns," Donnia Soldou said to Gerti soon after Obould and his orc entourage had departed.

The female dark elf, dressed head to toe in deep shades of gray and black, moved easily among the frost giants, ignoring the threatening scowls many of them assumed whenever she was about. Donnia walked with the confidence of the dark elves, and with the knowledge that her subtle threats to Gerti concerning bringing an army to wipe out every living creature in the Spine of the World who opposed her had not fallen on deaf ears. Such were the often true tactics and pleasures of the dark elves.

Of course, Donnia had nothing at all to back up the claim. She was a rogue, part of a band that included only four members. So when she threw back her cowl and shook her long and thick white hair into its customary place, thrown to the side so that the tresses covered half her face, including her right eye, she did so with an air of absolute certainty.

Gerti didn't have to know that.

"They are orcs," Gerti Orelsdottr replied with obvious disdain. "They are pawns to any who need to make them so. It is not easy to resist the urge to squash Obould into the rock, simply for being so ugly, simply for being so stupid . . . simply for the pleasure of it!"

"Obould's designs strengthen your own," Donnia said. "His minions are numerous. Numerous enough to wreak havoc among the dwarf and human communities of the region, but not so overwhelming as to engage the legions of the greater cities, like Silverymoon."

"He wants Felbarr, so that he can rename it the Citadel of Many Arrows. Do you believe that he can take so prosperous a stronghold and not invoke the wrath of Lady Alustriel?"

"Did Silverymoon get involved when Obould's kin sacked Felbarr the last time?" Donnia gave a chuckle. "The Lady and her advisors have enough to keep them concerned within their own borders. Felbarr will be isolated, eventually. Perhaps Mithral Hall or even Citadel Adbar will choose to send aid, but it will not be substantial if we create chaos in the neighboring mountain ranges and out of the Trollmoors."

"I have little desire to do battle with dwarves in their tiny tunnels," the frost giant remarked.

"That is why you have Obould and his thousands."

"The dwarves will slaughter them."

Donnia smiled and shrugged, as if that notion hardly bothered her.

Gerti started to respond, but just nodded her agreement.

Donnia held her smile, thinking that this was going quite well. Donnia and her companions had stumbled upon the situation at exactly the right time. The old Grayhand, Jarl Orel of the frost giants, was very near death, by all accounts, and his daughter was anxious to assume his mantle. Gerti was possessed of tremendous hubris, for herself and her race. She considered frost giants the greatest race of Faerûn, destined to dominate. Her pride and racism exceeded even that Donnia had seen from the matron mothers of her home city, Ched Nasad.

That made Gerti an easy mark indeed.

"How fares the Grayhand?" Donnia asked, wanting to keep Gerti's appetite whetted.

"He cannot speak, nor would he make any sense if he did. His reign is at its end in all ways but formal."

"But you are ready," Donnia assured the already self-assured giantess. "You, Dame Gerti Orelsdottr, will bring your tribes to the pinnacle of their glory, and woe to all of those who stand against you."

Gerti finally sat down upon her carved throne, resting back, but with her chin thrust high and strong, a pose of supreme pride.

Donnia kept her smile to herself.

"I hate them damn giants as much as I hate them damn dwarves," Urlgen proclaimed when he and the others were out of Gerti's caves. "I'd spit in Gerti's face, if I could reach it!"

"You keeps you words to youself," Obould scolded. "You said them giants helped in you's raid—didn't you like their bouncing boulders? Think it'll be easier like going after dwarf towers without those boulders softening them up?"

"Then why is we fighting the damn dwarves?" another of the group dared to ask.

Obould spun and punched him in the face, laying him low. So much for that debate.

"Well, let's see how much them giants'll be helping us then," Urlgen pressed. "Let's get them all out on a raid and flatten the buildings aboveground at Mirabar!"

A couple of the others bristled and nodded eagerly at that thought.

"Need I remind you of the course we have chosen?" came a voice from the side, very different from the guttural grunting of the orcs, more melodic and musical, though hardly less firm. The group turned to see Ad'non Kareese step out of the shadows, and many had to blink to even recognize how completely the drow had been hidden just a moment before.

"Well met, Sneak," said Obould.

Ad'non bowed, taking the compliment in stride.

"We met the big witch," Obould started to explain.

"So I heard," said the drow, and before Obould could begin to elaborate, Ad'non added, "All of it."

The orc king gave a chortle. "Course you's did, Sneak. Can get anywhere you wants, can't you?"

"Anywhere and anytime," the drow replied with all confidence.

Once he had been among the finest scouts of Ched Nasad, a thief and assassin with a growing reputation. Of course, that distinction had eventually led him to an ill-fated assassination attempt upon a rather powerful priestess, and the resulting fallout had put Ad'non on the road out of the city and out of the Underdark.

Over the past twenty years, he and his Ched Nasad associates, fellow assassin Donnia Soldou, the priestess Kaer'lic Suun Wett, and the newcomer, a clever fellow named Tos'un Armgo sent astray in the disastrous Menzoberranzan raid on Mithral Hall, had found more fun and games on the surface than ever they had known in their respective cities, and more freedom.

In Ched Nasad and in Menzoberranzan, the four had been hire-ons and pawns for the greater powers, except for Kaer'lic who had been fashioning a mighty reputation among the priestesses of the Spider Queen before disaster had blocked her path. Up among the lesser races, the four acted with impunity, ever with the threat that they were the advance for great drow armies, ready to sweep in and eliminate all foes. Even proud Obould and prouder Gerti Orelsdottr would shift uncomfortably in their respective seats at the slightest hint of that catastrophe.

"So we push up that course a bit," Urlgen argued against the drow. "Choice ain't you'ses, Sneak. Choice is Obould's."

"And Gerti's," the drow reminded.

"Bah, we can fool the witch easy enough!" Urlgen declared, and the others nodded and grunted their agreement.

"Fool her into bringing about complete destruction for her designs and for your father's," the drow calmly replied, ending the cheering session. Ad'non looked at Obould as he continued, "Small forays alone, for a long while. You asked my opinion, and I have not wavered on it for a moment. Small forays and with restraint. We draw them out, little by little."

"That might be taking years!" Urlgen protested.

Ad'non nodded, conceding the point.

"The minor skirmishes are expected and even accepted as an unavoidable by-product of the environment by all the folk of the region," he explained, as he had so often in the past. "A caravan intercepted here, a village sacked there, and none will get overly excited, for none will understand the scope of it. You can tickle the gold sacks of the dwarves, but prod your spear too deeply, move them beyond a reasonable response, and you will unite the tribes."

He stared hard at Obould and continued, "You will awaken the beast. Think of the three dwarf strongholds joined in alliance, supplying each other with goods, weapons and even soldiers through their connecting tunnels. Think of the battle you will face in reclaiming the Citadel of Many Arrows if Adbar lends them several thousand shield dwarves and Mithral Hall outfits them all in the finest of metals. Why, Mithral Hall is the smallest of the three, yet she fended the army of Menzoberranzan!"

His emphasis on that last word, a name to strike terror into the hearts of any who were not of Menzoberranzan—and in the hearts of a good many who *were* of the city—had a couple of the orcs shuddering visibly.

"And through it all, we must take care, wise Obould, not to invoke the wrath of Silverymoon, whose Lady is a friend to Mithral Hall," the drow advisor went on. "And we must never allow an alliance to form between Mithral Hall and Mirabar."

"Bah, Mirabar hates them newcomers!"

"True enough, but they do not fear the newcomer dwarves in any but economic ways," Ad'non explained. "They will fear you and Gerti with their very lives, and such fear makes for unexpected alliances."

"Like the one between me and Gerti?"

Ad'non considered that for a moment, then shook his head.

"No, you and Gerti understand that you'll both move closer to your goals by allying. You are not afraid, of course."

"Course not!"

"Nor should you be. Play the game as we've discussed, as you and I have planned it all along, my friend Obould." He moved closer and whispered so that only the orc king could hear. "Show why you are above the others of your race, why you alone might gather a strong enough alliance to reclaim your rightful citadel."

Obould straightened and nodded, then turned to his kinfolk and recited the litany that Ad'non had taught him for months and months.

"Patience . . ."

"I'll not even bother to ask how your parlay with Obould progressed," priestess Kaer'lic Suun Wett remarked when Ad'non finally arrived at the comfortable, richly adorned chamber off a deep, deep tunnel below the southernmost spurs of the Spine of the World, not far from the caverns of Shining White, though much deeper.

Kaer'lic was the most striking member of the group. Heavyset, which was very unusual for a dark elf, and with broad shoulders, Kaer'lic had lost her right eye in a battle when she was a young priestess nearly a century before. Rather than have the orb magically restored, the stubborn Kaer'lic had replaced it with a black, many-chambered eye pried from the carcass of a giant spider. She claimed the orb was functional and allowed her to see things that others could not, but her three friends knew the truth of it. Many times, Ad'non and Donnia had sneaked up on Kaer'lic's right side, completely undetected, for no better reason than to tease her.

Still, the two assassins had gone along with Kaer'lic's ruse to their newest companion for many tendays. Spiders, after all, made quite an impact on dark elves from Menzoberranzan, and Tos'un Armgo had remained suitably impressed for a long time, until Ad'non had finally let him in on the ruse—and that, only after the three long-term friends had come to understand that Tos'un was one who could be trusted.

Ad'non shrugged in response to Kaer'lic's remarks, telling the other three that it had gone exactly as they would all expect when dealing with an orc. Indeed, Obould was more cunning than his kind, but that wasn't really saying much by drow standards.

"Dame Gerti holds the course, as well," Donnia added. "She believes it to be her destiny to rule the Spine of the World and will follow any course that may lead her to that place."

"She might be right," Tos'un put in. "Gerti Orelsdottr is a smart one, and between Obould's masses and the stirring trolls from the moors, enough chaos might be created for Gerti to step forward."

"And we will be ready to profit, in material and in pleasure, whatever the outcome," Donnia said with a wry grin, one that was matched by her three friends.

'It amazes me that I ever considered returning to Menzoberranzan," Tos'un Armgo remarked, and the others laughed.

Donnia and Ad'non were staring rather intently at each other when that laughter abated. The lovers had been apart for several days, after all, and both of them found such talk of conquest, chaos and profit quite stimulating.

They practically ran out of the chamber to their private room.

Kaer'lic howled with renewed laughter as they departed, shaking her head. She was always more pragmatic about such needs, never reducing them to overpowering levels, as the two assassins often did.

"They will die in each others' arms," she remarked to Tos'un, "coupling and oblivious to the threat."

"There are worse ways to go, I suppose," the son of House Barrison Del'Armgo replied, and Kaer'lic laughed again.

These two were part-time lovers as well, but only part time, and not for a long, long time. Kaer'lic wasn't really interested in a partner, in truth, far preferring a slave to use as a toy.

"We should expand these raids to the Moonwood," she remarked lewdly. "Perhaps we could convince Obould to capture us a couple of young moon elves."

"A couple?" Tos'un said skeptically. "A handful would be more fun."
Kaer'lic laughed yet again.

Tos'un leaned back into the thick furs of his divan, wondering again how he could have ever even considered returning to the dangers discomforts and subjugation that he, as a male, could not avoid, along the dark avenues of Menzoberranzan.

NOT WELCOME

The wind howled down at them from the peaks to the north, the towering snow-capped Spine of the World Mountains. Just a bit farther to the south, along the roads out of Luskan, spring was in full bloom, fast approaching summer, but at the higher elevations, the wind was rarely warm, and the going rarely easy.

Yet it was precisely this course that Bruenor Battlehammer had chosen as the route back to Mithral Hall, walking east within the shadow of the mountains. They had left Icewind Dale without incident, for none of the highwaymen or solitary monsters that often roamed the treacherous roads would challenge an army of nearly five hundred dwarves! A storm had caught them in the pass through the mountains, but Bruenor's hearty people had trudged on, turning east even as Drizzt and his other unsuspecting friends were expecting to soon see the towers of Luskan in the south before them.

Drizzt had asked Bruenor about the unexpected course change, for though this was a more direct route, it certainly wouldn't be much quicker and certainly not less hazardous.

In reply to the logical question, Bruenor had merely snorted, "Ye'll see soon enough, elf!"

The days blended into tendays and the raucous band put more than a hundred and fifty difficult miles behind them. Their days were full of dwarven marching songs, their nights full of dwarven partying songs.

To the surprise of Drizzt, Catti-brie, and Wulfgar, Bruenor moved Regis by his side soon after the eastward turn. The dwarf was constantly leaning in and talking to the halfling, while Regis bobbed his head in reply.

"What's the little one know that we don't?" Catti-brie asked the drow as they flanked the caravan to the north, looking back on the third wagon, Bruenor's wagon, to see Bruenor and Regis engaged in one such discussion.

Drizzt just shook his head, not really sure of how to read Regis at all anymore.

"Well, I'm thinking we should find out," Catti-brie added, seeing no response forthcoming.

"When Bruenor wants us to know all the details, he will tell us," Drizzt assured her, but her smirk made it fairly clear that she wasn't buying into that theory.

"We've turned the both of them from more than one ill-aimed scheme," she reminded. "Are ye hoping to find out right before the cataclysm?"

The logic was simple enough, and in considering the pair on the wagon, and the fact that raucous and none-too-brilliant Thibbledorf Pwent was also serving Bruenor in an advisory position, the drow could only chuckle.

"And what are we to do?"

"Well, hot pokers won't get Bruenor talking, even against a birthday surprise," Catti-brie reasoned, "but I'm thinking that Regis has a bit lower tolerance."

"For pain?" Drizzt asked incredulously.

"Or for tricks, or for drink, or for whatever else might work," the woman explained. "Think I'll be getting Wulfgar to carry the little rat to us when Bruenor's off about other business tonight."

Drizzt gave a helpless laugh, understanding well the perils that awaited poor Regis, and glad that Bruenor had taken the halfling into his confidence and not him.

As with most nights, Drizzt and Catti-brie set a camp off to the side of the gathering of dwarves, keeping watch, and even more than that, keeping a bit of their sanity aside from Thibbledorf Pwent's antics and the Gutbuster's training. Pwent did come over and join the pair this night, though, walking right in and plopping down on a boulder to the side of their fire.

He looked at Catti-brie, even reached up to touch her long auburn hair.

"Ah, ye're looking good, girl," he said, and he dropped a sack of some muddy compound at her feet. "Ye be putting that on yer face each night afore ye go to sleep."

Catti-brie looked down at the sack and its slimy contents, then up at Drizzt, who was sitting on a log and resting back against a rock facing, his hands tucked behind his head, brushing wide his thick shock of white hair so that it framed his black-skinned face and his purple eyes. Clearly, the battlerager amused him.

"On me face?" Catti-brie asked, and Pwent's head bobbed eagerly. "Let me guess. It will make me grow a beard."

"Good and thick one," said Pwent. "Red to match yer hair, I'm hoping. Oh, a fiery one ye'll be!"

Catti-brie's eyes narrowed as she looked over at Drizzt once more, to see him choking back a chuckle.

"Make sure ye're not putting it up too high on yer cheeks, girl," the battlerager went on, and now Drizzt did laugh out loud. "Ye'll look like that durned Harpell werewolf critter!"

As he finished the thought, Pwent sighed and rolled his eyes longingly. It was well known that the battlerager had begged Bidderdoo Harpell, the werewolf, to bite him so that he too might be afflicted by the ferocious disease. The Harpell had wisely refused.

Before the wild dwarf could continue, the trio heard a movement to the side, and a huge form appeared. It was Wulfgar the barbarian, nearly seven feet tall, with a broad and muscled chest. He was wearing a beard to match his blond hair, but it was neatly trimmed, showing the renewed signs of care that had given all the friends hope that Wulfgar had at last overcome his inner demons. He carried a large sack over one shoulder, and something inside of it was squirming.

"Hey, what'cha got there, boy?" Pwent howled, hopping up and bending in curiously.

"Dinner," Wulfgar replied. The creature in the sack moaned and squirmed more furiously.

Pwent rubbed his hands together eagerly and licked his lips.

"Only enough for us," Wulfgar said to him. "Sorry."

"Bah, ye can spare me a leg!"

"Just enough for us," Wulfgar said again, putting his hand on Pwent's forehead and pushing the dwarf back to arm's length. "And for me to bring some leftovers to my wife and child. You will have to go and dine with your kin, I fear."

"Bah!" the battlerager snorted. "Ye ain't even kilt it right!"

With that, he stepped up and balled his fist, retracting his arm for a devastating punch.

"No!" Drizzt, Wulfgar, and Catti-brie all yelled together.

The woman and the drow leaped up and rushed in to intercept. Wulfgar, spinning aside, put himself between the battlerager and the sack. As he did, though, the sack swung out wide and bounced off the rock facing, drawing another groan from within.

"We're wanting it fresh," Catti-brie explained to the befuddled battlerager.

"Fresh? It's still kicking!"

Catti-brie rubbed her hands together eagerly and licked her lips, mimicking Pwent's initial reaction.

"It is indeed!" she said happily.

Pwent backed off a step and put his hands firmly on his hips, staring hard at the woman, then he exploded into laughter.

"Ye'll make a good dwarf, girl!" he howled.

He slapped his hands against his thighs and bounded away, back down the slope toward the main encampment.

As soon as he was gone, Wulfgar swung the sack over his shoulder and bent low, gently spilling its contents: one very irate, slightly overweight halfling dressed in fine traveling clothes, a red shirt, brown vest, and breeches.

Regis rolled on the ground, quickly regained his footing, and frantically brushed himself off.

"Your pardon," Wulfgar offered as graciously as he could while stifling a laugh.

Regis glared up at him then hopped over and kicked him hard in the shin—which of course hurt Regis's bare toes more than it affected the mighty barbarian.

"Relax, my friend," Drizzt bade him, stepping over and draping his arm over the halfling's shoulder. "We needed to speak with you, that is all."

"And asking is beyond your comprehension?" Regis was quick to point out.

Drizzt shrugged. "It had to be done secretly," he explained. Even as the words left his mouth Regis began to shrink back, apparently catching on.

"Ye been talking a lot with Bruenor of late," Catti-brie piped in, and Regis shrank back even more. "We're thinking that ye should be sharing some of his words with us."

"Oh, no," Regis replied, patting his hands in the air before him, warding them away. "Bruenor's got his plans spinning, and he will tell you when he wants you to know."

"Then there is something?" Drizzt reasoned.

"He is returning to Mithral Hall to become the king," the halfling replied. "That is something, indeed!"

"Something more than that," said Drizzt. "I see it clearly in his eyes, in the bounce of his step."

Regis shrugged. "He's glad to be going home."

"Oh, is that where we're going?" Catti-brie asked.

"You are. I am going farther," the halfling admitted. "To the Herald's Holdfast," he explained, referring to a renowned library tower located east of Mithral Hall and northwest of Silverymoon, a place the friends had visited years before, when they were trying to locate Mithral Hall so that Bruenor could reclaim the place. "Bruenor has asked me to gather some information for him."

"About what?" asked the drow.

"Gandalug and Gandalug's time, mostly," Regis answered, and while it seemed to the other three that he was speaking truthfully, they also sensed that he was speaking incompletely.

"And what might Bruenor be needing that for?" asked Catti-brie.

"I'm thinking that's a question ye should be asking Bruenor," came the gruff reply of a familiar voice, and all four turned to see Bruenor stride into the firelight. "Ye go grabbing Rumblebelly there, when all ye had to do was ask meself."

"And ye'd be telling us?" Catti-brie asked.

"No," said the dwarf, and three sets of eyes narrowed immediately. "Bah!" Bruenor recanted. "Hoping to surprise ye three is hoping for the impossible!"

"Surprise us with what?" asked Wulfgar.

"An adventure, boy!" the dwarf howled. "As great an adventure as ye've ever knowed."

"I've known a few," Drizzt warned, and Bruenor howled.

"Sit yerselfs down," the dwarf bade them, motioning to the fire, and all five sat in a circle about the blaze.

Bruenor pulled a bulging pack off his back. After dropping it to the ground he pulled it open to reveal packets of food and bottles of ale and wine.

"Though ye're fancying fresher food," he said with a wink to Catti-brie, "I was thinking this'd do for now."

They sorted out the meal, and Bruenor hardly waited for them to begin eating before he launched into his tale, telling them that he was truly glad they had pressed the issue, for it was a tale, a promise of adventure, that he desperately wanted to share.

"We'll be making the mouth o' the Valley of Khedrun tomorrow," he explained. "Then we're turning south across the vale, to the River Mirabar, and to Mirabar herself."

"Mirabar?" Catti-brie and Drizzt echoed in unison, and with equal skepticism.

It was hardly a secret that the mining city of Mirabar was no supporter of Mithral Hall, which threatened their business interests.

"Ye're knowing Dagnabbit?" Bruenor asked, and the friends all nodded. "Well, he's a few friends there who'll be giving us some information that we're wanting to hear."

The dwarf paused and hopped up, glancing all around into the darkness as if searching for spies

"Ye got yer cat about, elf?" the red-bearded dwarf asked.

Drizzt shook his head.

"Well, get her here, if ye can," Bruenor bade him. "Send her out about and tell her to drag in any who might overhear."

Drizzt looked to Catti-brie and to Wulfgar, then reached into his belt pouch and brought forth an onyx figurine of a panther.

"Guenhwyvar," he called softly. "Come to me, friend."

A gray mist began to swirl around the figurine, growing and thickening, gradually mirroring the shape of the idol. The mist solidified quickly, and the huge black panther Guenhwyvar stood there, quietly and patiently waiting for Drizzt's instructions.

The drow bent low and whispered into the panther's ear, and Guenhwyvar bounded away, disappearing into the blackness.

Bruenor nodded. "Them Mirabar boys're mad about Mithral Hall," he said, which wasn't news to any of them. "They're looking for a way to get back an advantage in the mining trade."

The dwarf looked around again, then bent in very close, motioning for a huddle.

"They're looking for Gauntlgrym," he whispered.

"What is that?" Wulfgar asked.

Catti-brie looked equally perplexed, though Drizzt was nodding as if it was all perfectly logical.

"The ancient stronghold of the dwarves," Bruenor explained. "Back afore Mithral Hall, Citadel Felbarr, and Citadel Adbar. Back when we were one big clan, back when we named ourselves the Delzoun."

"Gauntlgrym was lost centuries ago," Drizzt put in. "Many centuries ago. Beyond the memory of any living dwarves."

"True enough," Bruenor said with a wink. "Now that Gandalug's gone to the Halls of Moradin."

Drizzt's eyes widened—so did those of Catti-brie and Wulfgar.

"Gandalug knew of Gauntlgrym?" the drow asked.

"Never saw it, for it fell afore he was born," Bruenor explained.

"But," he added quickly, as the hopeful smiles began to fade, "when he was a lad the tales of Gauntlgrym were fresher in the mouths o' dwarves." He looked at each of his friends in turn, nodding knowingly. "Them Mirabar boys're looking for it under the Crags to the south. They're looking in the wrong place."

"How much did Gandalug know?" Catti-brie asked.

"Not much more than I knew about Mithral Hall when first we went a' lookin'," Bruenor admitted with a snort. "Less even. But it'll be an adventure worth making if we're finding the city. O, the treasures, I tell ye! And metal as good as anything ye've e'er seen!"

He went on and on about the legendary crafted pieces of the Gauntlgrym dwarves, about weapons of great power, armor that could turn any blade, and shields that could stop dragonfire.

Drizzt wasn't really listening to the specifics, though he was watching every movement from the fiery dwarf. By the drow's estimation, the adventure would be well worth the risks and hardships whether or not they ever found Gauntlgrym. He hadn't seen Bruenor this animated and excited in years, not since the first foray to find Mithral Hall.

As he looked around at the others, he saw the eager gleam in Catti-brie's green eyes and the sparkle in Wulfgar's icy blue orbs—further confirmation to him that his barbarian friend was well on the road to recovery from the trauma of spending six years at the clawed hands of the demon Errtu. The fact that Wulfgar had taken on the responsibilities of husband and father, Delly and the baby never far from him even in their present camp, was all the more reassuring. Even Regis, who had no doubt heard this tale many times already along the road, leaned in, drawn to the dwarf's tales of dungeons deep and treasures magical.

It occurred to Drizzt that he should ask Bruenor why they all had to go to Mirabar, where they wouldn't likely be welcomed. Couldn't Dagnabbit go in alone or with a small group, less conspicuously? The drow held his thoughts, though, understanding it well enough. He hadn't been with Bruenor in Icewind Dale when the first reports of antagonism from Mirabar had been sent to him from King Gandalug. He and Catti-brie had been sailing the Sword Coast at that time, but when they had found Bruenor back in Icewind Dale, the dwarf had pointed it out more than once, a simmering source of anger.

Openly, the Council of Sparkling Stones, the ruling council of Mirabar, comprised of dwarves and men, spoke warmly of Mithral Hall, welcoming their brothers of Clan Battlehammer back to the region. Privately, though, Bruenor had heard over the years many reports of more subtle derogatory comments from sources close to the Council of Sparkling Stones and Elastul, the Marchion of Mirabar. Some of the plots that had caused Gandalug headaches had been traced back to Mirabar.

Bruenor was going there for no better reason than to look some of the folk of Mirabar straight in the eye, to make a proclamation that the Eighth King of Mithral Hall had returned as the Tenth King, and he was one a bit more clued in to the subterfuge of the present day politics of the wild north.

Drizzt just sat back and watched his friends' continuing huddle. The adventure had begun, it seemed, and it was one the drow believed he would truly enjoy.

Or would he?

For something else occurred to Drizzt then, a memory quite unexpected. He recalled his first visit to the surface, a supposed great adventure alongside his fellow dark elves. Images of the slaughter of the surface elves swirled through his thoughts, culminating in the memory of a little elf girl he had smeared with her own mother's blood, to make it appear as if she too had been mortally wounded. He had saved her that terrible day, and that massacre had, in truth, been the first real steps for Drizzt away from his vile kinfolk.

And, all these years later, he had killed that same elf child. He winced as he saw Ellifain again, across the room in the pirate cavern complex, mortally wounded and pleased by the thought that in sacrificing herself, she had taken Drizzt with her. On a logical level, the drow could surely understand that nothing that had happened that day was his fault, that he could not have foreseen the torment that would follow that rescued child all these decades.

But on another level, a deeper level, the fateful fight with the anguished Ellifain had struck a deep chord within Drizzt Do'Urden. He had left Icewind Dale full of anticipation for the open road, and indeed, he was glad to be with his friends, traveling the wilds, full of adventure and excitement.

But the keen edge of a purpose beyond material gain, beyond finding ancient kingdoms and ancient treasure, had been dulled. Drizzt had never fancied himself a major player in the events of the wider world. He had contented himself in the knowledge that his actions served those around him in a positive way. From his earliest days in Menzoberranzan, he had held an innate understanding of the fundamental differences between good and evil, and he had always believed that he was a player for the side of justice and goodness.

But what of Ellifain?

He continued to listen to the excited talk around him and held fast his consenting smile, assuring himself that he would indeed enjoy this newest adventure.

He had to believe that.

There was nothing pretty about the open air city of Mirabar. Squat stone buildings and a few towers sat inside a square stone wall. Everything about the place spoke of efficiency and control, a no-nonsense approach to getting their work done.

To the sensibilities of a dwarf like Bruenor, that made Mirabar a place to be admired to a point, but to Drizzt and Catti-brie as they approached the city's northern gate, Mirabar seemed an unadorned blotch, uninteresting and unremarkable.

"Give me Silverymoon," Drizzt remarked to the woman as they walked along to the left of the dwarven caravan.

"Even Menzoberranzan's a prettier sight," Catti-brie replied, and Drizzt could only agree.

The guards at the north gate seemed an apt reflection of Mirabar's dour attitude. Four humans stood in pairs on opposite ends of sturdy metallic doors, halberds set on the ground and held vertically before them, silver armor gleaming in the early morning sun. Bruenor recognized the crest emblazoned on their tower shields, the royal badge of Mirabar, a deep red double-bladed axe with a pointed haft and a flaring, flat base, set on a black field. The approach of a huge caravan of dwarves, a veritable army, surely shook them all, but to their credit, they held their posture perfect, eyes straight ahead, faces impassive.

Bruenor brought his wagon around, moving to the front of the caravan, Pwent's Gutbusters running to keep their protective guard to either flank.

"Bring her right up afore 'em," Bruenor instructed his driver, Dagnabbit.

The younger, yellow-bearded dwarf gave a gap-toothed grin and urged his team on faster, but the Mirabar guards didn't blink.

The wagon skidded to a stop short of the closed doors and Bruenor stood up tall (relatively speaking) and put his hands on his hips.

"State your business. State your name," came a curt instruction from the inner guard on the right.

"Me business is with yer Council o' Sparkling Stones," Bruenor answered. "I'll be tellin' it to them alone."

"You will answer the appointed gate guard of Mirabar, visitor," the inner guard on the left hand side of the doors demanded.

"Ye think?" Bruenor asked. "And ye're wantin' me name? Bruenor Battlehammer's the name, ye durned fool. *King* Bruenor Battlehammer. Now ye go and run that name to yer council and we'll be seeing if they're to talk to me or not."

The guards tried to hold their posture and calm demeanor, but they did glance over at each other, hastily.

"Ye heard o' me?" Bruenor asked them. "Ye heard o' Mithral Hall?"

A moment later, one of the guards turned to the guard standing beside him and nodded, and that man produced a small horn from his belt and blew a series of short, sharp notes. A few moments later, a smaller hatch cunningly cut into the large portals, banged open and a tough-looking, many-scarred dwarf wearing a full suit of battered plate mail, ambled out. He too wore the badge of the city, emblazoned on his breastplate, as he carried no shield.

"Ah, now we're getting somewhere," Bruenor remarked. "And it does me old heart good to see that ye've a dwarf for a boss. Might be that ye're not as stupid as ye look."

"Well met, King Bruenor," the dwarf said. "Torgar Delzoun Hammerstriker at yer service." He bowed low, his black beard sweeping the ground.

"Well met, Torgar," Bruenor replied, offering a gracious bow of his own, something that he, as head of a nearby kingdom, was certainly not required to do. "Yer guards here serve ye well at blocking the way and better as fodder!"

"Trained 'em meself," Torgar responded.

Bruenor bowed again. "We're tired and dirty, though the last part ain't so bad, and looking for a night's stay. Might ye be opening the doors for us?"

Torgar leaned to one side and the other, taking a good look at the caravan, shaking his head doubtfully. His eyes went wide and he shook his head more vehemently when he glanced to his right, to see a human woman standing off to the side beside a drow elf.

"That ain't gonna happen!" the dwarf cried, pointing a stubby finger Drizzt's way.

"Bah, ye heard o' that one, and ye know ye have," Bruenor scolded. "The name Drizzt ringing any bells in yer thick skull?"

"It is or it ain't, and it ain't making no difference anyway," Torgar argued. "No damned drow elf's walkin' into me city. Not while I'm the Topside Commander of the Axe of Mirabar!"

Bruenor glanced over at Drizzt, who merely smiled and bowed deferentially.

"Not fair, but fair enough, so he's stayin' out," Bruenor agreed. "What about me and me kin?"

"Where're we to put five hunnerd o' ye?" Torgar asked sincerely, correctly estimating the force's size. He held his large hands out helplessly to the side. "Could send a bunch to the mines, if we let anyone into the mines. And that we don't!"

"Fair enough," Bruenor replied. "How many can ye take?"

"Twenty, yerself included," Torgar answered.

"Then twenty it'll be." Bruenor glanced at Thibbledorf Pwent and nodded. "Just three o' yers," he ordered, "and me and Dagnabbit makes five, and we'll be adding Rumblebelly . . ." He paused and looked at Torgar. "Ye got any arguing to do about me bringing a halfling?"

Torgar shrugged and shook his head.

"Then Rumblebelly makes six," Bruenor said to Dagnabbit and Pwent. "Tell th' others to pick fourteen merchants wanting to go in with some goods."

"Better to take me whole brigade," Pwent argued, but Bruenor was hearing none of it.

The last thing Bruenor wanted in this already tenuous circumstance was to turn a group of Gutbuster battleragers loose on Mirabar. In that event Mithral Hall and Mirabar would likely be at open war before the sun set.

"Ye pick the two goin' with ye, if ye're planning on going," Bruenor explained to Pwent, "and be quick about it."

A short while later, Torgar Delzoun Hammerstriker led the twenty dwarves through Mirabar's strong gate. Bruenor walked at the front of the column, right beside Torgar, looking every bit the road-wise, adventure-hardened King of Mithral Hall spoken of throughout the land. He kept his many-notched, single-bladed axe strapped on his back, but prominently displayed atop the foaming mug shield that was also strapped there. He wore his helmet, with one horn broken away, like a badge of courage. He was a king, but a dwarf king, a creature of pragmatism and action, not a flowered and prettily dressed ruler like those common among the humans and elves.

"So who's yer marchion these days?" he asked Torgar as they crossed into the city.

Torgar's eyes widened. "Elastul Raurym," he replied, "though it's no name ye need be thinking of."

"Ye tell him I'm wanting to talk with him," Bruenor explained, and Torgar's eyes widened even more.

"He's fillin' his meetings for the spring in the fall, for the summer in the winter," Torgar explained. "Ye can't just walk in and get an audience . . ."

Bruenor fixed the dwarf with a strong, stern gaze. "I'm not *gettin'* an audience," he corrected. "I'm *granting* one. Now, ye go and get a message to the marchion that I'm here for the talking if he's got anything worth hearing."

The sudden change in Bruenor's demeanor, now that the gates were behind him, clearly unsettled Torgar. His off-balance surprise fast shifted to a grim posture, eyes narrowing and staring hard at his fellow dwarf.

Bruenor matched that stare—more than matched it.

"Ye go an' tell him," he said calmly. "And ye tell yer council and that fool Sceptrana that I telled ye to tell him."

"Protocol . . ."

"Is for humans, elves, and gnomes," Bruenor interrupted, his voice stern. "I ain't no human, I sure ain't no elf, and I'm no bearded gnome. Dwarf to dwarf, I'm talking here. If yerself came to me Mithral Hall and said ye needed to see me, ye'd be seeing me, don't ye doubt."

He finished with a nod, and dropped his hand hard on Torgar's shoulder. That little gesture, more than anything previous, seemed to put the sturdy warrior at ease. He nodded, his expression grim, as if he had just been reminded of something very important.

"I'll be telling him," he agreed, "or at least, I'll be tellin' his Hammers to be tellin' him."

Bruenor smirked at that, and Torgar shuffled. Against the obvious disdain of the dwarf King of Mithral Hall, the inaccessibility of the Marchion of Mirabar to one of his trusted shield dwarf commanders did indeed seem a bit trite.

"I'll be tellin' him," Torgar said again, with a bit more conviction.

He led the twenty visitors away then to a place where they could stay the night, a large and unremarkable stone house with several sparsely furnished rooms.

"Ye can set up yer wagons and goods right outside," Torgar explained. "Many'll be comin' to see ye, I'm sure, 'specially for them little white trinkets ye got."

He pointed to one of the three wagons that had come in with the visitors, its side panels tinkling with many trinkets as it bounced along the rough ground.

"Scrimshaw," Bruenor explained. "Carved from knucklehead trout. Me little friend here's good at it."

He motioned to Regis, who blushed and nodded.

"Ye make any of the stuff on the wagon?" Torgar asked the halfling, and the dwarf seemed genuinely interested.

"A few pieces."

"Ye show me in the morning," Torgar asked. "Might that I'll buy a few."

With that, he nodded and left them, heading off to deliver Bruenor's invitation to the marchion.

"You turned him over quite well," Regis remarked.

Bruenor looked at him.

"He was ready for a fight when we first arrived," the halfling observed. "Now I believe he's thinking of leaving with us when we go."

It was an exaggeration, of course, but not ridiculously so.

Bruenor just smiled. He had heard from Dagnabbit of many curses and threats being hurled against Mithral Hall from Mirabar, and surprisingly (or not so, when he thought about it), more seemed to be coming from the dwarves of Mirabar than from the humans. That was why Bruenor had insisted on coming to this city where so many of his kinfolk were living in conditions and climate much more fitting to human sensibilities than to a dwarf's. Let them see a true dwarf king, a legend of their people come to life. Let them hear the words and ways of Mithral Hall. Maybe then, many of Mirabar's dwarves would stop whispering curses against Mithral Hall. Maybe then, the dwarves of Mirabar would remember their heritage.

"It's troubling ye that they wouldn't let ye in," Catti-brie remarked to Drizzt a short time later, the two of them on a high bluff to the east of the remaining dwarves and the caravan, overlooking the city of Mirabar.

Drizzt turned to regard her curiously, and saw sympathy etched on his dear friend's face. He realized that Catti-brie was reacting to his own wistful expression.

"No," he assured her. "There are some things I know I can never change, and so I accept them as they are."

"Yer face is saying different."

Drizzt forced a smile. "Not so," he said—convincingly, he thought.

But Catti-brie's returning look showed him that she saw better. The woman stepped back and nodded, catching on.

"Ye're thinking of the elf," she reasoned.

Drizzt looked away, back toward Mirabar, and said, "I wish we could have saved her."

"We're all wishing that."

"I wish you had given the potion to her and not to me."

"Aye, and Bruenor would've killed me," Catti-brie said. She grabbed the drow and made him look back at her, a smile widening on her pretty face. "Is that what ye're hoping?"

Drizzt couldn't resist her charm and the much-needed levity.

"It is just difficult," he explained. "There are times when I so wish that things could be different, that tidy and acceptable endings could find every tale."

"So ye keep trying to make them endings acceptable," Catti-brie said to him. "It's all ye can do."

True enough, Drizzt admitted to himself. He gave a great sigh and looked back to Mirabar and thought again of Ellifain.

Dagnabbit went out later that afternoon, the sun setting and a cold wind kicking up through the streets of the city. He didn't return until right before the dawn, and spent the day inside with Bruenor, discussing the political intrigue of the city and the implications to Mithral Hall, while the merchants and Regis worked their wagons outside.

Not many came to those wagons—a few dwarves and fewer humans—and most of those who did bargained for deals so poor that the Clan Battlehammer dwarves ultimately refused. The lone exception arrived soon after highsun.

"Well, show me yer work, halfling," Torgar bade Regis.

A dozen heads, those of Torgar's friends, bobbed eagerly behind him.

"Regis," the halfling explained, extending his hand, which Torgar took in a firm and friendly shake.

"Show me, Regis," the dwarf said. "Me and me friends'll need a bit o' convincing to be spendin' our gold pieces on anything ye can't drink!"

That brought a laugh from all the dwarves, Battlehammer and Mirabarran alike, and from Regis. The halfling was wondering if he should consider using his enchanted ruby necklace, with its magical powers of persuasion, to "convince" the dwarves of a good deal. He dismissed that thought almost immediately, though, reminding himself of how stubborn some dwarves could be against any kind of magic. Regis also considered the implications on the relationship between Mithral Hall and Mirabar should he get caught.

Still, soon enough it became apparent to Regis that he wouldn't need the pendant's influence. The dwarves had come well stocked with coin, and many of their friends joined them. The goods on the wagons, Regis's work and many other items, began to disappear.

From the window of the house, Bruenor and Dagnabbit watched the bazaar with growing satisfaction as dozens and dozens of new patrons, almost exclusively dwarves, followed Torgar's lead. They also noted, with a mixture of apprehension and hope, the grim faces of those others nearby, humans mostly, looking upon the eager and animated trading with open disdain.

"I'm thinking that ye've knocked a wedge down the middle o' Mirabar by coming here," Dagnabbit observed. "Might be that fewer curses'll flow from the lips o' the dwarfs here when we're on the road out."

"And more curses than ever'll be flowing from the mouths o' the humans," Bruenor added, and he seemed quite pleased by that prospect.

Quite pleased indeed.

A short while later, Torgar, carrying a bag full of purchases, knocked on the door.

"Ye're coming to tell me that yer marchion's too busy," Bruenor said as he answered the knock, pulling the door open wide.

"He's got his own business, it seems," Torgar confirmed.

"Bet he didn't answer yer knock," Dagnabbit remarked from behind Bruenor.

Torgar shrugged helplessly.

"How about yerself?" Bruenor asked. "And yer boys? Ye got yer own business, or ye got time to come in and share some drink?"

"Got no coins left."

"Didn't ask for none."

Torgar chewed his lip a bit.

"I can't be speaking as a representative o' Mirabar," he explained.

"Who asked ye to?" Bruenor was quick to reply. "A good dwarf's putting more into his mouth than he's spilling out. Ye got some tales to tell that I ain't heared, to be sure. That's more than worth the price o' some ale."

And so, with Torgar's agreement, they had a party that night in the unremarkable stone house on the windswept streets of Mirabar. More than a hundred Mirabarran dwarves made an appearance, with most staying for some time, and many sleeping right there on the floor.

Bruenor wasn't surprised to find the house surrounded by armed, grim-faced soldiers—humans, not dwarves—when daylight broke.

It was time for Bruenor and his friends to go.

Torgar and his buddies would find a bit of trouble over this, no doubt, but when Bruenor looked back at him with concern, the tough old veteran merely winked and grinned.

"Ye find yer way to Mithral Hall, Torgar Delzoun Hammerstriker!" Bruenor called back to him as the wagons began to roll back out the gates. "Ye bring all the friends ye want, and all the tales ye can tell! We'll find enough food and drink to make ye belch, and a warm bed for as long as ye want to warm yer butt in it!"

No one on the caravan from Icewind Dale missed the scowls the human guards offered at those dangerous remarks.

"You do like to cause trouble, don't you," Regis said to Bruenor.

"The marchion was too busy for me, eh?" Bruenor replied with a smirk. "He'll be wishing he met with me, don't ye doubt."

Drizzt, Catti-brie, and Wulfgar linked up with Bruenor's wagon when it and the others had rejoined the bigger caravan outside the city gates.

"What happened in there?" the dark elf asked.

"A bit o' intrigue, a bit o' fun," Bruenor replied, "and a bit o' insurance that if Mirabar e'er decides to openly fight against Mithral Hall, they'll be missing a few hunnerd o' their shorter warriors."

3

RETREAT INTO VICTORY

"Ye gotta keep running!" Nikwillig scolded Tred.

The wounded dwarf was slumped against a boulder, sweat pouring down his forehead and cheek, a grimace of pain on his face as he favored his torn leg.

"Got me in the knee," Tred explained, gasping between every syllable. "She's not holding me up no more. Ye run on and I'll give them puppies reason to pause!"

Nikwillig nodded, not in agreement of the whole proposal, but in determination concerning the last part. "Ye can't run, then we'll stop and fight," he answered.

"Bah!" Tred snorted at him. "Bunch o' worgs coming."

"Bunch o' dead worgs, then," Nikwillig answered with as much grit and determination as Tred had ever witnessed from him.

Nikwillig was a merchant more than a warrior, but now he was "showing his dwarf," as the old expression went. And in viewing this transformation, despite their desperate situation, Tred couldn't help but smile. Certainly if the situation had been reversed, with Nikwillig favoring a torn leg, Tred would never have considered leaving him.

"We're needin' a plan, then," said Tred.

"One using fire," Nikwillig agreed, and as he finished, a not-so-distant howl split the air and was answered several times. Still, in that chorus, both dwarves found a bit of hope.

"They're not coming in all together," Tred reasoned.

"Scattered," Nikwillig agreed.

An hour later, with the howling much closer, Tred sat beside a roaring fire, his burly arms crossed before him, his single-bladed, pointy-tipped axe set across his lap. His leg was glad of the reprieve, and his tapping foot alone betrayed his patient posture as he waited for the first of the worgs to make its appearance.

Off to the side, in the shadows behind a pile of boulders, an occasional crackle sounded. Tred winced and bit his bottom lip, hoping the rope held long enough against the weight of the withered but not yet felled pine.

When the first red eyes appeared across the way, Tred began to whistle. He reached to the side and scooped up a large pail of water, dumping it over himself.

"Ye likin' yer meat wet, puppies?" he called to the worgs.

As the huge wolves leaped into sight, he kicked at the closest edge of the fire, sending sparks and burning brands their way, momentarily stopping them. The action brought a cry of pain from the dwarf, as well. His torn leg could not hold him as he kicked out with the good one, and he went tumbling down to the side.

The chopped, dead tree came tumbling too, along the line the cunning dwarves had planned. The dried out old pine fell into the blazing fire, the wind of its descent sending sparks and dry needles rushing out to the side. More than one stung poor Tred, even igniting his beard a bit. He slapped the flickers out, stubbornly growled against his agony, and forced himself into a defensive posture.

Across the way, the rushing flames bit at the handful of worgs that had stepped into the clearing, sending them yelping and scrambling away, biting at sparking bits of fur. More came on, some even getting bit by the frenzy of their companions.

The dried pine went up in a fiery blaze between Tred and the wolves, but not before several dark forms leaped across or circumvented it.

Hands low on the handle, Tred slashed his axe across, batting aside the first flying wolf and sending it spinning to the ground. He reversed quickly, sliding his lead hand up the axe handle and setting it against his belt. As the second wolf leaped at him, it skewered itself on the axe's pointy tip. Tred didn't even try to slow that momentum, just held the flying wolf up high, guiding it over him. He brought his axe back at once, a ferocious downward chop that got the third charging worg right atop the head, smashing and splitting its skull, driving its front end down to the stone with its forelegs splaying out wide.

Nikwillig was beside him, sword in hand. When the next two worgs approached, one from either side, the dwarves turned back to back and fended the attacks.

Frustrated, the worgs circled. Nikwillig pulled a dagger from his belt and sent it flying into one worg's flank. The creature yelped and rushed off into the shadows.

Its companion quickly followed.

"First round's ours," Tred said, shying back as the heat from the burning tree became more intense.

"That pack's not wanting more of a fight," Nikwillig reasoned, "but more'll be catching us, don't ye doubt!"

He started away, pulling Tred along. Just out of the clearing, though, Tred stood taller and held his companion back.

"Unless we're catching them first," Tred said into Nikwillig's puzzled expression, when the merchant turned back to regard him. "Orcs're guiding the worgs," Tred reasoned. "No more orcs, no more worgs."

Nikwillig considered his friend for a few moments, looking mostly at Tred's torn leg, a clear indication that the pair could not hope to outdistance their pursuit. That seemed to leave only two choices before them.

And the first, leaving Tred behind, simply was not an option.

"Let's go find us some orcs," Nikwillig offered.

His smile was genuine.

So was Tred's.

They moved along as swiftly as they could, backtracking in a roundabout manner through the dark trees and rocky outcroppings, scrambling over uneven ground when they could find no trail. More often than not, Nikwillig was practically carrying Tred, but neither dwarf complained. The sound of worgs echoed all around them, but their diversion had worked, it seemed, throwing the pursuit off the scent and making more than a few of the creatures think twice about continuing their pursuit.

Sometime later, from a high vantage point, the dwarves spotted a few small campfires in the distance. Not one large encampment, it seemed, but several smaller groups.

"Their mistake," Tred remarked, and Nikwillig thoroughly agreed.

With a new goal in sight, the dwarves moved along at an even swifter pace. When his leg locked up on him, Tred merely hopped, and if he fell to the stone, which he often did, the tough dwarf merely pulled himself up, spat in his hand to clean off the new scrape, and scrambled forward. Down along one clear patch of ground, they encountered another wolf, but even as it bared its teeth and hunched its back in a threatening posture, Tred launched his axe into its flank, laying it low. Nikwillig was quick to the spot, finishing the beast before its yelps could alert the orc camp, which wasn't far away.

Soon after, and with the eastern sky brightening in the first signs of dawn, the pair crept up a small dirt banking and peered through the gap between a tree trunk and a boulder. A small campfire burned beyond, with a trio of orcs sitting around it and several more sleeping nearby. A single, injured worg sat beside the trio, snarling, growling, licking its wounds, and turning a hateful eye upon one of the orcs whenever it offered a berating curse at the inability of the worg and its companions to catch the fleeing dwarves.

Nikwillig put a finger to his pursed lips and motioned for Tred to stay put. He slipped off to the side, taking full advantage of the obvious fact that the confident orcs weren't expecting any unannounced visitors.

Tred watched his progress with a nod and a grin as Nikwillig belly-crawled to the edge of the encampment, putting his knife to fast work on one, then a second, sleeping orc. The observant dwarf saw the worg's head come up fast, though, and so he knew the game was up. With all the strength he could muster, Tred pulled himself up between the boulder and the tree.

"Well, ye wanted me, and so ye found me!" he roared.

The trio of orcs, and the worg, leaped up and gave a shout. Their third sleeping companion similarly started, but Nikwillig was already beside it, laying it low before it could even begin to respond.

The closest orc brandished a huge axe and charged headlong at Tred, coming in with a fancy, spinning maneuver that showed the creature was no novice with the weapon. But neither was he a profound thinker, obviously, for when Tred lifted his hand and hurled the stone he had picked up when he had announced himself, the orc was caught completely by surprise, and taken right in the face. The stunned orc stumbled forward, and Tred's swinging battle-axe promptly swatted it aside.

46

The other two orcs glanced around, only then realizing the devious work of Nikwillig, and the presence of the second dwarf.

"Two against two," Nikwillig said to them in the grunting Orcish tongue.

"We got wolfie!" one started to respond, but the battered worg apparently didn't agree, for it darted out of the camp and ran yelping along the dark trails.

One of the orcs tried to take the same course, leaping off to the side. Tred didn't hesitate, launching his axe at the fleeing creature. The spinning weapon didn't miss, but neither did it fully connect, tripping up the orc and slowing it as the handle tangled between its legs, but not hurting it much at all.

The second orc, seeing the obviously wounded dwarf standing there, apparently unarmed, howled and lifted its jagged sword. It charged in hard.

Nikwillig knew he couldn't get to Tred in time, so he went for the fallen orc first. Leaping upon the creature even as it started to rise, he bore it to the ground beneath his heavy boots. Nikwillig stomped and stabbed with his sword, trading a stinging hit from the orc's spear as it came around in exchange for a clear opening at the creature's chest. Nikwillig's shoulder stung from the stab, to be sure, but his sword opened the orc from breast to belly.

He heard Tred crying out for his brother then, with grunts between each shout. Nikwillig turned, expecting to see his friend in dire straits.

He let his weapon slide low, for Tred had the situation, and the orc, well in hand. He gripped the orc by the wrists, holding the creature's arms up high and out wide, and after every cry for his lost brother, Tred snapped his head forward and yanked the orc's arms out wider, the pair connecting forehead to face with each jolt.

The first few belts sounded loud and solid, bone on bone, but each succeeding smash made a crunchier sound, as if Tred was driving his forehead into a pile of dry twigs.

"I think ye can put it down now," Nikwillig remarked dryly after a few more thumps, the orc having long gone limp.

Tred grabbed the battered, dying creature by the collar with one hand and slapped his other hand hard into the orc's groin. A heave and a twist had the orc high over the powerful dwarf's head. With another call for his lost brother, Tred launched the orc down the bank behind him, to crash hard against a rock below.

"Lots of supplies," Nikwillig remarked, hopping about the camp.

"Damn orc sticked me," Tred replied.

Only then did his companion notice a new wound on the sturdy dwarf, a bright line of blood running from the side of Tred's chest. Nikwillig started for his companion, but Tred waved him back.

"Ye gather the supplies and we'll get going," he explained. "I'll dress it meself."

He did just that, and the pair were on their way soon after, Tred grunting in pain with every step, but otherwise offering not the slightest complaint.

He had lost a bucket of blood or more, and every time his foot slipped on a loose rock, the resulting lurch opened his newest wound anew, moistening his side with fresh blood. Still Tred didn't complain, nor did he slow Nikwillig's brisk pace. Their turn and attack had daunted the pursuit, it seemed, for few howls came rolling out to them on the night winds, and none of those were very close.

When Tred and Nikwillig crested a high ridge and looked far down upon a distant village—just a cluster of houses, really—they looked to each other with concern.

"We go in there and we might bring a horde o' orcs and wolfies on 'em," Tred reasoned.

"And if we don't go in, ye're gonna slow, and slow some more," Nikwillig replied. "We'll not be making Mithral Hall anytime soon, if we can even find our way to the place."

"Ye think they're knowin' how to fight?" Tred asked, looking back to the village.

"They're living in the wild mountains, ain't they?"

Simple enough, and true enough, and so Tred just gave a shrug and followed Nikwillig along the descending trail.

A wall of piled stones as tall as a man surrounded the cluster of houses, but it wasn't until the pair got very close that they noted any sentries. Even the two humans—a man and a woman—who finally peeked over the wall to call out to them didn't seem as if they were formal sentries. It was as if they simply happened to be walking by and noticed the dwarves.

"What are you two about?" came the woman's call.

"We'd be about to fall, I'd be guessin'," Nikwillig answered. He propped Tred up a bit to accentuate his point. "Ye got a warm bed and a bit o' hot stew for me injured kinfolk here?"

As if all of his energy had been given in the march, and his stubborn mind finally allowed his body the chance to rest, Tred fell limp and collapsed to the ground. Nikwillig guided him down as softly as possible.

There was no gate on that side of the village, but the woman and man came right out, scrambling over the wall and rushing to the dwarves. They, particularly the woman, went to work inspecting the injured dwarf, but they also both looked past the two dwarves, as if they expected an army of enemies to be chasing the battered duo in.

"You from Mithral Hall?" the man asked.

"Felbarr," Nikwillig answered. "We was headin' for Shallows when we got hit."

"Shallows?" the woman echoed. "Long way."

"Long chase."

"What hit you? Orcs?" asked the man.

"Orcs an' giants."

"Giants? Haven't seen any hill giants about in a long time."

"Not hill giants. Blue-skinned dogs. Lookin' pretty and hittin' ugly. Frost giants."

Both the man and woman looked up at him in concern, their eyes going wide. The folk of this region were not unfamiliar with trouble concerning frost giants. The old Grayhand, Jarl Orel, hadn't always kept his mighty people deep within the mountains over the decades, though thankfully, the frost giant forays hadn't been numerous. Still, any fight in any part of the area that included frost giants, perhaps the most formidable enemy in all the region next to the very occasional dragon, became news, dire news, the stuff of fireside tales and nightmares.

"Let's get him inside," the woman offered. "He's needing a bed and a hot meal. I can't believe he's even alive!"

"Bah, Tred's too ugly to die," Nikwillig remarked.

Tred opened a weary eye and slowly lifted his hand toward his friend's face, as if to pat him thankfully.

But as he got close, he pressed his index finger under his thumb, and flicked Nikwillig under the nose. Nikwillig fell back, grabbing his nose, and Tred settled back down, closing his eyes, a slight smile spreading on his crusty, pale face.

The folk of the small village, Clicking Heels, multiplied their guarding duties many times over, with a third of the two hundred sturdy folk working at a time as sentries and scouts in eight hour shifts. After two days recuperating, Nikwillig joined in those duties, bolstering the line, and even helping to direct the construction of some additional fortification.

Tred, though, was in no position to take part in anything. The dwarf slept through the night and through the day. Even after a couple of days, he woke only long enough to devour a huge meal the good folk of Clicking Heels were kind enough to supply. There was one cleric in the town, as well, but he wasn't very skilled at the magical part of his vocation and his healing skills, though he piled them on Tred, did little more good than the rest.

By the fifth day, Tred was up and about and starting to look and sound like his surly old self once more. By the end of a tenday, and still with no pursuit—giant, orc or worg—in sight, Tred was anxious to get moving.

"We're off to Mithral Hall," Nikwillig announced one morning, and the folk of Clicking Heels, humans all, seemed genuinely sorry to see the dwarves off. "We'll get King Gandalug to send some warriors up to check in on ye."

"King Bruenor, you mean," one of the villagers replied. "If he's returned to his folk from far off Icewind Dale."

"That right?"

"So we've heard."

Nikwillig nodded, offering a sigh for the loss of Gandalug before returning to his typically determined expression.

"King Bruenor then, as fair a dwarf as e'er there's been."

"I'm not sure he'll comply and send his soldiers, nor am I convinced that we need them," the man went on.

"Well, we'll tell him what's about and let him make up his own mind, then," Tred interjected. "That's why he's the king, after all."

That same morning, Tred and Nikwillig walked out of Clicking Heels, their steps strong once more, their packs full of supplies—good and tasty food and drink, not the slop they had stolen from the orcs. The folk had given them detailed directions to Mithral Hall as well, and so the dwarves were hopeful that they would find the end of this part of their journey soon enough. They intended to go to Mithral Hall, warn King Bruenor, or whomever it was leading their bearded kin, then get an escort from there through the connecting tunnels of the upper Underdark, back to their homes in Citadel Felbarr.

Even that wouldn't be the end of the road for Tred at least, for the tough dwarf had every intention of raising a band of warriors to head back out and avenge his brother and the others.

First things first, though, and that meant finding their way to Mithral Hall. Despite the directions, the dwarves found that no easy task in the winding and confusing mountain trails. A wrong turn along the narrow channels running through the stone often meant a long and difficult backtrack.

"It's the wrong damn stream," Tred grumbled one morning, the pair moving along steadily, but going south and east, whereas Mithral Hall was southwest of Clicking Heels.

"It'll wind back," Nikwillig assured him.

"Bah!" Tred snorted, shaking a fist at his companion.

They were lost and he knew it, and so did Nikwillig, whether he'd admit it or not. They didn't turn back, though. The road along the river had led them down a pair of very difficult descents that promised to be even more difficult climbs. To turn around after having gone so far seemed foolish.

They continued on, and when the stream took another unexpected dive over a waterfall, Tred grunted, grumbled, and climbed down the rocks to the side.

"Might be that it's time to think about going th' other way," Nikwillig offered.

"Bah!" was all that stubborn Tred would reply, and that grunt was exaggerated, for Tred hit an especially slick stone as he had waved his hand in a dismissive manner at Nikwillig.

He got down to the bottom faster at least.

They went on in silence after that and were looking about for a place to set camp when they crested one outcropping of huge cracked boulders to see the land fall away, wide and low before them, a huge valley running east and west.

"Big pass," Nikwillig remarked.

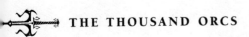

"One caravans might be using to get to Mithral Hall," Tred reasoned. "West it is!"

Nikwillig nodded, standing beside his companion, glad, as was Tred, to see that the going might be much easier the next day.

Of course, neither knew that they were standing on the northern rim of Fell Pass, the site of a great battle of old, where the very real and very dangerous ghosts of the vanquished lingered in great numbers.

CONFLICTING LOYALTIES

The dwarf councilor, Agrathan Hardhammer, shifted uneasily in his seat as the volume around him increased along with the agitation of the others, all human, in the room.

"Perhaps you should have granted him an audience," said Shoudra Stargleam, the sceptrana of the city.

Shoudra's bright blue eyes flashed as she spoke, and she shook her head, as she always seemed to be doing, letting her long dark hair fly wide to either side. Her hair was often the subject of gossip among the women of the city, for though Shoudra was in her thirties and had lived for all her life in the harsh, windblown climate of Mirabar, it held the luster and shine that one might expect on the head of a girl half Shoudra's age. In all respects, the sceptrana was a beautiful creature, tall and lithe, yet with deceptively delicate features. Deceptive, because though she was ultimately feminine, Shoudra Stargleam was possessed of a solidity, a formidability, that rivaled the strongest of Mirabar's men.

The fat man sitting on the cushioned throne, the Marchion of Mirabar, smirked at her and waved his hands in disgust.

"I had, and have, more important matters to attend to than to see to the needs of an unannounced visitor," the marchion said, staring hard at Agrathan as he spoke, "even if that visitor is the King of Mithral

Hall. Besides, is it not your duty, and not mine own, to negotiate trade agreements?"

"King Bruenor did not come here for any such purpose, by any reports," Shoudra protested, drawing another wave of Marchion Elastul's thick hands.

Elastul shook his head and looked about at his Hammers, his principal attendants, scarred old warriors all.

"Might that she should've met with Bruenor anyway," Djaffar, the leader of the group, remarked. He nudged the marchion's shoulder. "Shoudra's got a trick or two that could soften even a dwarf!"

The other three soldier-advisors and Marchion Elastul burst out in snickers at that. Shoudra Stargleam narrowed her blue eyes and assumed a defiant pose, crossing her arms over her chest.

To the side, Agrathan shifted again. He knew Shoudra could handle herself, and that she, like all the folk of Mirabar who had any access to Elastul, was used to the liberties of protocol often taken by the vulgar Hammers and by the marchion himself. His was an inherited position, unlike the elected councilors and sceptrana.

"He asked to see you, Marchion, not me and not the council," Shoudra reminded curtly, ending the snickers.

"And what am I to do with the likes of Bruenor Battlehammer?" Elastul replied. "Dine with him? Cater to him, and quietly explain to him that he will soon be irrelevant?"

Shoudra looked over at Agrathan plaintively, and the dwarf cleared his throat, drawing the marchion's attention.

"Ye wouldn't be doing well to underestimate Bruenor," Agrathan advised. "His boys're good at what they do."

"Irrelevant," Elastul said again, settling back comfortably. "That curiosity piece Gandalug is dead, may the stones powder his bones, and Bruenor is inheriting a kingdom on the decline."

Again, Shoudra looked over at Agrathan, this time wearing a doubting smirk, for she and the dwarf knew what was coming.

"More than two dozen metallurgists and alchemists." Elastul boasted. "I'm paying them well, and they'll be showing results soon enough!"

Agrathan lowered his eyes so that Elastul wouldn't see his doubting expression as the marchion went on to describe the most recent promises of those folks he had hired in an effort to strengthen the metal produced by Mirabar's mines. The metallurgists had been promising from the day they arrived, several years before, combinations of strength and flexibility beyond anything anyone in all the world could produce. Grand, and as far as Agrathan believed, empty claims all.

Agrathan hadn't worked the mines in over a century—since he had turned to the practice of preaching the word of Dumathoin—but as a priest of that dwarf god, a deity who was known as the Keeper of Secrets Under the Mountain, Agrathan firmly believed that the claims of the hired alchemists and metallurgists were not among those secrets. To Agrathan, if some magical way to enhance any metal wasn't among the secrets of Dumathoin, then it simply didn't exist.

The hired group was very good at what it did. What it did, as far as Agrathan was concerned, was keep the marchion curious and intrigued enough to keep the gold flowing, and that was all that was flowing. Mirabar boasted less than half the dwarves of Mithral Hall, just over two thousand, and several hundred of those were busy serving in the Axe, keeping the mines clear of monsters. The thousand who worked the mines could barely meet the quotas set out by the Council of Sparkling Stones each year and that from existing veins. Little exploration was being done at the deeper levels, where the dangers were greater, but so too were the true promises of better quality in the form of better ore.

The simple fact was that Mirabar couldn't afford to cut production long enough to seek out those better veins, so the marchion had fallen into the scam of these supposed specialists—with not a dwarf among them—who claimed to understand metals so well. Besides, to Agrathan's thinking, if there were such processes as the marchion believed, why hadn't they been put in practice centuries before? Why hadn't these metallurgists and alchemists reduced the dwarves of Mithral Hall, the dwarves of all the world, to positions of providing base material alone? They promised weapons, armor, and other metal goods strong enough to outshine anything Bruenor's folk might produce, and yet, if they knew of such secrets, if there were such secrets, then why weren't there weapons of legend that had been produced through such processes?

"Even if your specialists deliver their promises, we will still be far from making King Bruenor and Mithral Hall 'irrelevant'," Shoudra Stargleam replied, and Agrathan was glad that she was taking the lead. "They are out-producing us in volume more than three-to-two."

The marchion waved his hands at her. "There was nothing for me to say to Bruenor Battlehammer anyway. Why did he come here? Who invited him? Who asked . . ." He ended with a derisive snort.

"Perhaps we should not have allowed him entrance," Shoudra remarked.

Agrathan looked up at Elastul, guessing correctly the dangerous glare the marchion would be offering to Shoudra at that moment. When word that King Bruenor was at Mirabar's gate had been passed along, it had been Elastul's decision to let Bruenor and the others in. None on the council, or the sceptrana, had even been informed until the Clan Battlehammer dwarves had already set up their carts on Mirabar's streets.

"Yes, perhaps my faith in the loyalty of my citizens was misplaced," the marchion countered, harsh words aimed more at Agrathan, the dwarf knew, than at Shoudra. "I expected King Bruenor to find greater embarrassment than rejection by the ruler of the city. I expected the folk of Mirabar to know enough to not even bother with our guests."

Agrathan glanced over to see that the marchion was indeed staring directly at him as he spoke. No humans, after all, had gone to do business with Clan Battlehammer, only dwarves, and Agrathan was the highest-ranking dwarf in the city, the unofficial leader and voice of Mirabar's two thousand.

"Have you spoken with Master Hammerstriker?"

"What would ye have me say?" Agrathan asked.

While he was the accepted voice for the dwarves among the human leaders, that wasn't always the case among the Mirabarran dwarves themselves.

"I would have you remind Master Hammerstriker where his loyalties lie," the marchion replied. "Or where they *should* lie."

Agrathan worked hard to keep his expression placid, to hide the sudden storm welling inside of him. The loyalty of Torgar Delzoun Hammerstriker could not be questioned. The crusty old warrior had served the marchion, and the marchion before him, and before him, and before him, and before him, and before him, for longer than any human in the city could remember, longer than the long dead parents of the dead parents of any human in the city could have remembered. Torgar had been among the leading soldiers charging along the tunnels of the upper Underdark against monsters more foul than anything any of the marchion's Hammers—those elite advisors selected supposedly because of their glorious veteran warrior status—had ever known. When the orc hordes attacked Mirabar, a hundred and seventeen years past, Torgar and a very few other dwarves had held the eastern wall strong against the assault, fending off the hordes while the bulk of Mirabar's warriors had been engaged on the western wall, against what had proven to be no more than a feint by the enemy. In scars, wounds, and cunning victories, Torgar Delzoun Hammerstriker had earned his position as a leader among the Axe.

But even to Agrathan the marchion's words rang with a bit of truth. It wasn't a question of loyalty, as far as Agrathan was concerned, but rather one of judgment. Torgar and his fellows had not understood the implications of trading with their rivals from Mithral Hall or from subsequently socializing with them.

With that, Agrathan and Shoudra left the agitated marchion, walking side by side along the outer corridors of the palace and out into the pale sunlight of the late afternoon. A chill breeze was blowing, a reminder to the pair that in Mirabar, winter was never far away.

"You will approach Torgar with a bit more gentleness than Marchion Elastul showed?" Shoudra asked the dwarf, her smile one of genuine amusement.

As sceptrana, Shoudra was involved in signing trade agreements. With the rise of Mithral Hall, she too had suffered, or at least her work had. Shoudra Stargleam had taken it more in stride than many others in the city, though, including many of the dwarves. To her, the way to beat Mithral Hall was to increase production and find better ore for better product. To her, the rise of a trading rival should be the catalyst to make Mirabar stronger.

"I'll tell Torgar and his boys what I can, but ye know that one, and know that not many can be telling Torgar anything."

"He is loyal to Mirabar," Shoudra stated, and though Agrathan nodded, the expression on his face showed that he wasn't so certain of that anymore.

Shoudra Stargleam caught that look and stopped, and put her hand on Agrathan's shoulder to stop him as well.

"Is he loyal to city or to race?" she asked. "Does he consider the marchion his true leader or King Bruenor of Mithral Hall?"

"Torgar's fought well for every marchion since before yer parents were born, girl," Agrathan reminded her.

Shoudra nodded, but like Agrathan a moment earlier, she didn't seem overly convinced.

"They should not have gone to trade and drink with the visiting dwarves," Shoudra remarked.

She bustled her cloak in front of her and started on her way.

"Mighty temptations there. Good trade, good drink, and better stories. Are ye thinking that my folk aren't wanting to hear the Battle of Keeper's Dale? Are ye thinking that your own world would be a better place if the damn drow invaders had won at Mithral Hall?"

"Well, perhaps if the dark elves had inflicted a bit more damage before they had been chased off. . . ." Shoudra replied.

Agrathan snapped a scowl over her, but it was quickly defeated, for the woman was grinning mischievously even as she spoke the words.

"Bah!" Agrathan snorted.

"So by your reasoning, Mirabar owes a debt to Mithral Hall for their victory against the dark elves?" Shoudra asked.

Agrathan paused for a moment and thought long and hard on that one. In the end, he shrugged, not willing to make a commitment.

Shoudra grinned again and nodded, for it was obvious that the dwarf's heart was giving one answer and his pragmatic head, the part that owed loyalty to Marchion Elastul and Mirabar, was giving another. It wasn't a laughing matter, though. In fact, the notion that Agrathan, a major voice on the Council of Sparkling Stones, was apparently holding mixed feelings concerning Mithral Hall incited more than a little trepidation in the sceptrana. Agrathan had been one of the strongest voices of opposition to Mithral Hall, often relating the words of his more vocal dwarf constituents who wanted covert action to be taken against Clan Battlehammer. Agrathan had once outlined a plan for infiltrating the neighboring kingdom and slipping cooler-burning charcoal into their stores, weakening their smelting and shaping work.

Many times during council meetings Agrathan Hardhammer had himself exploded in tirades against the dwarves of Clan Battlehammer, but having seen them face-to-face, Shoudra was seeing the true depth of his, and his people's, resolve.

"Tell me, Agrathan, was that famous drow elf accompanying King Bruenor's caravan?"

"Drizzt Do'Urden? Yes, he was there, but they didn't let him into the city."

Shoudra looked at him curiously. Drizzt had made quite a reputation for himself in the North, even before his actions against his own people when they had attacked Mithral Hall. By all accounts, he was a hero.

"The Axe weren't about to let a cursed dark elf walk the streets, whatever his name," Agrathan said firmly, "but he was there. Torgar and some others saw him and that human girl that Bruenor is calling his own, along with that human boy that Bruenor is calling his own, off to the side, watching it all."

"Was he as handsome as they say?" Shoudra asked.

Agrathan turned an even bigger scowl over her, twisted into an expression of skepticism.

"He's a drow, ye damned fool!"

Shoudra Stargleam merely laughed, and Agrathan shook his hairy head.

They stopped their walk then, for they had come to Undercity Square, an open area between three buildings, one of them a large sectioned building where Shoudra kept her apartment. In the center of the triangular area was a descending stairway, which led to the most heavily guarded room in all of Mirabar, the main entrance to the Undercity—the real city as far as Agrathan and his kin were concerned—where the real work went on.

Shoudra bid the dwarf farewell and entered her house. Agrathan stood at the top of the stairway for a long, long while, more uncomfortable than he had ever been before entering the domain of Mirabar's two thousand dwarves. It was his solemn duty to go and deliver the marchion's message to Torgar and the others, but Agrathan knew his kin well enough to understand that the words would cause more than a little anger and division among the dwarves. Their emotions ran the gamut concerning Mithral Hall. Many of the Mirabarran dwarves had even called for confiscation of any Mithral Hall caravan moving west of Clan Battlehammer's domain, knowing full well that such an action might mean open warfare between the two cities. Others quietly remarked that their ancestors had lived in Mithral Hall with King Bruenor's predecessors, and that it had been a good life, as good a life as any dwarf could ever want.

Agrathan snorted—a "dwarven sigh," he called it—and thumped his way down the stairs, brushing past the many human guards in the upper chamber as he made his way to the lift. He waved away the attendant and worked the heavy ropes himself, lowering himself down hundreds of feet to a second well-guarded room, with all exits blocked by external portcullises and iron-bound doors. The guards there were all dwarves, some of the toughest of all the Axe.

"Ye go and put the word to all our kin in all the holes," Agrathan instructed them, "and to them working the walls up top. We're meeting after sunset in the Hall of All Fires, and I want every one of my boys there. Everyone!"

The guards opened one of the exits for Agrathan and he exited, head down and murmuring to himself, trying to discern the best way to handle this most delicate of situations.

Though he was more tactful than most, as was evidenced by his rank in a city that was dominated by humans, Agrathan was still a dwarf, and subtlety had never been his strong point.

The scene was never controlled and quiet in the Hall of All Fires when a significant number of Mirabar's dwarves were assembled, but that night, with nearly all of the city's two thousand in attendance and with the subject so controversial, the place was in absolute chaos.

"So now ye're to tell me whose story I can hear, and whose I can't?" Torgar Hammerstriker roared back at Agrathan. "It was a good bit o' ale, and a finer bit o' tales!"

Many of the dwarves who had accompanied Torgar to the Icewind Dale bazaar and later to the Clan Battlehammer reception shouted their agreement. One or two held up beautiful pieces of scrimshaw they had purchased from the traders, wonderful pieces gotten at better prices.

"I can resell this in Nesmé for ten times what I paid!" one industrious, red-bearded fellow declared. He jumped high onto a dark furnace, holding up his small statue—a scrimshaw depiction of a shapely barbarian woman—for all to see. "Ye tellin' me I can't be making good deals, priest?"

Agrathan slumped back a bit, not surprised by the reaction.

"I have come to deliver the words of Marchion Elastul, a reminder—and yes, a stern one—to us all that the dwarves of Clan Battlehammer are not friends to Mirabar. They take our trade—"

"Is there a one of us here who can rightly say that he's livin' better since they opened Mithral Hall again?" another dwarf cut the priest off. "Even wit' yer pretty statue, fat Bullwhip, ye're not to have a good year in the matter o' yer purse, now are ye?"

Many dwarves seconded that, cheering the agitated speaker on.

"We had better lives and bigger coins afore the damn Battlehammers came back in! And who invited them?"

"Bah! Ye're talking the part of a fool!" Torgar lashed out.

"Says the dwarf who looked to other councilors for a loan!" the fiery one shot back. "Ye needin' coin now, Torgar? Will King Bruenor's stories fill yer belly?"

Torgar climbed up to the raised area at the north end of the hall to stand beside Agrathan. He paused for a long while, looking to and fro, commanding everyone's attention.

"What I'm hearing here is jealous talk, plain and simple," he said, very calmly. "Ye're talking about Clan Battlehammer as if they've declared war upon us, when all they've done is open up mines that've been there, and been theirs, since afore Mirabar was Mirabar. They've a right to their homeland and a right to make it work. We're sittin' here making plans to bring 'em down, when it's seemin' to me that we should be making plans to bring ourselfs up!"

"They been stealin' our business!" someone yelled from the crowd. "Ye forgetting that part?"

"They been beatin' us," Torgar pointedly, and immediately, corrected. "They got better mines an' better metal, and they built themselves a strong reputation one dead orc, duergar, and stinkin' drow elf at a time. Ye can't be blamin' King Bruenor and his boys for working hard and fighting harder!"

The shouts erupted from every corner, many in agreement and many in dissent. A couple of fistfights broke out in various corners of the hall.

Up on the raised platform, Torgar and Agrathan stared hard at each other, and though neither had fully embraced the other's viewpoint on this matter only a few days before, their respective visions were crystallizing.

There came a shout from somewhere in the crowd, "Hey priestie, ye taking the side o' the humans over that o' yer kinfolk dwarfs?"

Both Torgar and Agrathan turned at once, and many others did as well. All the great meeting chamber went silent, dwarves stopping their fighting in mid-swing, for there it was, spelled out simply and to the point.

For Torgar, it was a moment of confusion and self-examination. Was it actually coming down to this, a choice between his dwarven kin of Mithral Hall and the joint community of Mirabar?

For Agrathan, leading member of the Council of Sparkling Stones, the choice was less fuzzy, for indeed, if that was the way that some of his kin chose to view things, then so be it. Agrathan's loyalties lay to Mirabar and to Mirabar alone, but when he looked at his counterpart, he saw that the marchion's remarks, which Agrathan had considered insulting, toward Torgar Delzoun Hammerstriker were not without merit.

Agrathan's faith in his community was a bit shaken a moment later, when the great gates of the Hall of All Fires swung wide and a large contingent of the Axe of Mirabar swept in, wading into the confused throng in a wedge formation, then forcefully widening their stance so that a huge triangular area of the room was quickly secured. In marched the marchion and several of the more stern councilors, along with the sceptrana.

"This is not the behavior the human folk of Mirabar expects from their dwarf comrades," Elastul scolded.

He should have left it at that, a quiet and calm reminder that the city had enough enemies without to worry about such squabbles within.

"Accept that Torgar Hammerstriker and those who accompanied him to the carts of Clan Battlehammer, and to the liars . . . er, the *bards* of the same clan erred, and badly, in their judgment," Elastul bluntly warned. "Beware, Master Hammerstriker, lest you lose your position in the Axe. For the rest of you, lured by ale and this creature, this false legend, who is Bruenor Battlehammer, remind yourselves where your loyalties lie, and remind yourselves as well that Clan Battlehammer threatens our city."

Elastul swiveled his head slowly, taking in all the gathering, trying to wilt them under his stern gaze. But these were dwarves, after all, and few wilted, and few of those who agreed with the marchion wagged their heads.

Many of those who disagreed stood a bit straighter and a bit taller, and in looking at his counterpart on the stage, Agrathan seriously wondered if Torgar was going to peel off his Axe insignia then and there and throw it at Elastul's feet.

"Disperse, I command you!" Marchion Elastul roared. "Back to your work, and back to your lives."

The dwarves did disperse then, and the marchion and his entourage, including the human soldiers, departed, with the sole exception of Shoudra Stargleam who stayed to speak with Agrathan.

"Well, ain't them the words of a true king," Torgar muttered as he walked past Agrathan, and he spat at the priest's feet.

"The marchion was ill-advised to be coming here like that now," Agrathan remarked to Shoudra when they were alone.

"Many of your peers on the council pressed him to action," Shoudra explained. "They feared that the visit of King Bruenor might be having an adverse affect on our dwarf citizens."

"It was," Agrathan said glumly, "and it is. Even more now."

Agrathan meant every word. He watched the remaining dwarves departing the hall or going back to stoke the furnaces that lined it. He noted their expressions, their deep-set scowls and angry eyes. Torgar's misjudgment had brought a rift in the clan, had put a wedge into the solid community.

Agrathan couldn't help but think that the marchion had just taken a sledge and smashed that wedge hard.

WHERE GHOSTS ROAM

The troupe crossed the bridge to the south of Mirabar, then followed the River Mirar to the east of the city for a tenday of easy marching. South of them loomed the tall trees of Lurkwood, a forest known to harbor many orc tribes and other unpleasant neighbors. To the north stood the towering mountains of the Spine of the World, their tops holding defiantly white against the coming summer season.

The grass grew tall around them, and dandelions dotted the rolling fields of the Valley of Khedrun, but the ever-vigilant dwarves were not lulled by the peaceful season and scenery. This far to the north, anywhere outside of a city had to be considered untamed land, so they doubled their guard every night, circled their wagons, and kept Drizzt, Catti-brie, and Wulfgar working the flanks. Guenhwyvar joined the trio in their scouting whenever Drizzt was able to summon her.

At the eastern end of the valley, with nearly a hundred miles between them and Mirabar, the River Mirar bent to the north, flowing from the foothills of the Spine of the World. The Lurkwood, meanwhile, also bent to the north, following the line of the river as if shadowing the water, several miles to the south.

"Ground's gonna get tougher," Bruenor warned them all as they set camp that night. "We'll be back in the foothills tomorrow by midday, and moving tight under the shadows o' the forest."

He looked around at his clan, to see every head nodding stoically.

"Next days'll be tougher," Bruenor told them, and not a one batted an eye.

They broke their gathering, and went back to their posts.

"The road's not so bad, by my measurin'," Delly Curtie said to Wulfgar when he joined her and Colson, their young daughter, at the small lean-to Delly had set beside a wagon. "No meaner than Luskan's streets."

"We've been fortunate so far," Wulfgar replied, holding his arms out to take Colson, whom Delly gladly gave over.

Wulfgar looked down at the tiny girl, the daughter of Meralda Feringal, the Lady of Auckney, a small town nestled in the Spine of the World not far to the west of the pass that had brought the troupe out of Icewind Dale. Wulfgar had rescued Colson from the trials of Lord Feringal and his tyrannical sister, retribution against the bastard child since Colson was not Feringal's daughter. The Lord of Auckney had thought Wulfgar the father, for Meralda had concocted a lie to protect the man's honor, claiming that she had been raped on the road.

But Wulfgar was not the father, had never known Meralda in that manner. Looking at Colson, though, at the tiny creature who had become so precious to him, he wished that he was. He looked up from Colson to see Delly staring at him lovingly, and he knew that he was a lucky man indeed.

"Ye going out with Drizzt and Catti-brie tonight?" Delly asked.

Wulfgar shook his head. "We're too close to the Lurkwood. Drizzt and Catti-brie can keep the watch well enough without me."

"Ye're staying close because ye're afraid for me and Colson," Delly reasoned, and Wulfgar didn't disagree.

The woman reached to take the baby back, but Wulfgar rolled his shoulder to block her hands, grinning at her all the time.

"Ye cannot be forsaking yer duties for me own sake," Delly complained, and Wulfgar laughed at her.

"This," he said, presenting the baby, then pulling her back in close when Delly reached for her, "is my duty, first and foremost. Drizzt and Catti-brie know it, too. We are close to the Lurkwood now, and that means close to orcs. You might be thinking that Luskan's streets are meaner than the wilds because you've not yet truly seen the wilds. If the orcs come upon us in numbers, the blood will flow. Orc blood, mostly, but with dwarf blood mixed in. You've never witnessed a battle, my love, and I hope it stays like that, but out here. . . ."

He let it go at that, shaking his head.

"And if the orcs come for us, ye'll be there keeping them off me and Colson," Delly reasoned.

Wulfgar, determined, looked at her then down at Colson who was sleeping angelically in his arms. His smile widened.

"No orc, no giant, no dragon will harm you," he promised the babe, lifting his eyes to include Delly as well.

Delly started to respond, and Wulfgar was sure she meant to offer one of her typically sarcastic remarks, but she didn't. She stopped short and just stood there staring at him, even offering a little nod to show that she did not doubt him.

As Bruenor had warned, the traveling got much more difficult the next day, with grassy meadows giving way to boulder-strewn trails climbing into the foothills. The ground was flatter to the south, but veering there would have put the dwarves into the thick underbrush and dangerous shadows of the Lurkwood, home to many unfriendly beasts. With so many sturdy dwarves in the caravan, Bruenor decided to keep them out in the open, to let any enemies understand the power of the force.

The dwarves did not complain, and when they came upon a gully or a particularly broken stretch over which the wagons could not roll, a host of dwarves moved up beside each cart, lifting it in their strong hands and carrying it across. That was their way, an attitude of logical stoicism and pragmatism that cut long tunnels through hard rock, one inch at a time.

Watching them at their march, Drizzt understood well the kind of determination and long-range thinking that had produced such beautiful and marvelous places as Mithral Hall. It was the same patience that had allowed one such as Bruenor to create Aegis-fang, to deliberately engrave perfect representations of the trio of dwarf gods on the hammer's head, where one errant scratch would have ruined the whole process.

Soon after the second day out of Khedrun Pass, with the trees of the Lurkwood so near that the group could hear birds singing in the boughs, a cry from the front confirmed Bruenor's other fear.

"Orcs outta the woods!"

"Form yer battle groups!" Bruenor called.

"Group One Left, make yer wedge!" Dagnabbit shouted. "One Right, square up!"

To the left, farthest from the woods, Drizzt and Catti-brie watched the precision of the veteran dwarf warriors and saw the small band of orcs rushing out of the forest, making for the lead wagons.

The orcs hadn't scouted their intended target properly, it seemed, for once they cleared the brush and saw the scope of the force allayed before them, they skidded to a stop and fell all over each other in fast retreat.

How different were their movements from those of the calm, skilled dwarves—well, almost all of the dwarves. Ignoring the calls of Bruenor and Dagnabbit, Thibbledorf Pwent and his Gutbusters assembled into their own formation, unique to their tactics. They called it a charge, but to Drizzt and Catti-brie it more resembled an avalanche. Pwent and his boys whooped, hollered, and scrambled headlong into the darkness of the forest shadows in pursuit of the orcs, leaping through the first line of brush with gleeful abandon.

"The orcs may have set a trap," Catti-brie warned, "showing us but a small part o' their force to drag us into their webs."

Cries resounded within the boughs, just south of the caravan, and flora and fauna, and orc body parts, began to fly wildly all about the area the Gutbusters had entered.

"Stupid orcs, then," Drizzt replied.

He started down from the higher ground, Catti-brie in tow, to join Bruenor. When they reached the king, they found him standing on his wagon bench, hands on his hips, and with groups of properly arrayed dwarves in tight formations all around him. One wedge of warriors passed skillfully by the defensive squares two others had assembled.

"Ain't ye going to join the fun?" Bruenor asked.

Drizzt looked back at the forest, at the continuing tumult, a volcano come to life, and shook his head.

"Too dangerous," the drow explained.

"Damn Pwent makes it hard to see the point o' discipline," Bruenor grumbled to his friends.

He winced, and so did Drizzt and Catti-Brie, and Regis who was standing near to Bruenor, when an orc came flying out of the underbrush to land face down on the clearer ground in front of the dwarves. Before any of Bruenor's boys could react, they heard a wild roar from back within the boughs, up high, and stared in blank amazement as Thibbledorf Pwent, high up in a tree, ran out to the end of one branch and leaped out long and far.

The orc was just beginning to rise when Pwent landed on its back, blasting it back down to the ground. Likely it was already dead, but the wild battlerager, with broken branches and leaves stuck all about his ridged armor, went into his devastating body shake, turning the orc into a bloody mess.

Pwent hopped up, then hopped all around.

"Ye can get 'em moving again, me king!" he yelled back to Bruenor. "We'll be done here soon enough."

"And the Lurkwood will never be the same," Drizzt mumbled.

"If I was a squirrel anywhere around here, I'd be thinking of making meself a new home," Catti-brie concurred.

"I'd pay a big bird to fly me far away," Regis added.

"Should we hold the positions?" Dagnabbit called to Bruenor.

"Nah, get the wagons moving," the dwarf king replied with a wave of his hand. "We stay here and we'll all get splattered."

Pwent and his boys, some hurt but hardly caring, rejoined their fellows a short while later, singing songs of victory and battle. Nothing serious emanated from this group. Their songs sounded more like the joyful rhymes of children at play.

"Watching Pwent makes me wonder if I wasted my youth with all that training," Drizzt said to Catti-brie later on, the pair patrolling with Guenhwyvar along the northern foothills again.

"Yeah, ye could've just whiled away the hours banging yer head against a stone wall, like Pwent and his boys did."

"Without a helmet?"

"Aye," the woman confirmed, keeping a straight face. "Though I'm thinking that Bruenor made him armor the poor wall. Protecting the structural integrity of the realm."

"Ah," said Drizzt, nodding, then just shaking his head helplessly.

No more orc bands made any appearances against the caravan throughout the rest of that day, nor over the next few. The going was difficult and slow, but still, not a dwarf complained, even when they had to spend the better part of a rainy day moving the remnants of an old rockslide from the trail.

As the days wore on, though, more and more rumbles began to filter through the line of wagons, for it became obvious to them all that Bruenor wasn't planning a turn to the south anytime soon.

"Orcs," Catti-brie remarked, examining the partial footprint in the dirt of a high trail. The woman looked up and all around, as if gauging the wind and the air. "Few days, maybe."

"At least a few," replied Drizzt, who was a short distance away, leaning on a boulder with his arms crossed over his chest, scrutinizing the woman's work as if he knew something that she did not.

"What?" the woman asked, catching the non-verbal cue.

"Perhaps I have a wider picture of it," Drizzt answered.

Catti-brie narrowed her eyes as she stared hard at the drow, matching his mischievous grin with a thin-lipped one of her own. She started to say something less than complimentary, but then caught on that perhaps the drow was speaking literally. She stood up and stepped back, taking in the area of the footprint from a wider viewpoint. Only then did she realize that the orc print was beside the mark of a much larger boot.

Much larger.

"Orc was here first," she stated without hesitation.

"How do you know that?" Drizzt wasn't playing the part of instructor here, but rather, he seemed genuinely curious as to how the woman had come to that.

"Giant might be chasin' the orc, but I'm doubting that the orc's chasing the giant."

"How do you know they weren't traveling together?"

Catti-brie looked back to the tracks. "Not a hill giant," she explained, for it was well known that hill giants often allied with orcs. "Too big."

"Mountain giant, perhaps," said Drizzt. "Larger version of the same creature."

Catti-brie shook her head doubtfully. Most mountain giants typically didn't even wear boots, covering their feet with skin wraps, if at all. The sharp definitions of the giant heel print made her believe that this particular boot was well made. Even more telling, the foot was narrow, relatively speaking, whereas mountain giants were known to have huge, wide feet.

"Stone giants might be wearin' boots," the woman reasoned, "and frost giants always do."

"So you think the giant was chasing the orc?"

The woman looked over at Drizzt again and shrugged. With it put so plainly—Drizzt apparently wasn't questioning her—she realized just how shaky that theory truly was.

"Could be," she said, "or they might've just passed this way independent of each other. Or they might be workin' together."

"A frost giant and an orc?" came the skeptical question.

"A woman and a drow?" came the snide response, and Drizzt laughed.

The pair moved on without much concern. The tracks were not fresh, and even if it was an orc or a group of orcs, and a giant or two besides, they'd think twice before attacking an army of five hundred dwarves.

It was slow and it was hot and it was dry, but no more monsters showed themselves to the force as the dwarves stubbornly made their way to the east. They climbed up one dusty trail, the sun hot on their backs, but when they crested the ridge and started down the backside, all the world seemed to change.

A vast, rocky vale loomed before them, with towering mountains both north and south. Shadows dotted the valley, and even in those places where there seemed no obstacle to block the sunlight, the ground appeared dull, dour, and somehow mysterious. Wisps of fog flitted about the valley, though there was no obvious water source, and little dew-catching grass could be seen.

Bruenor, Regis, Dagnabbit, and Wulfgar and his family led the way down the backside of the ridge to find Drizzt and Catti-brie waiting for their wagon.

"Ye're not likin' what ye're seein'?" Bruenor asked Drizzt, noticing a disconcerted expression on the face of the normally cool drow.

Drizzt shook his head, as if he couldn't put it into words.

"A strange feeling," he explained, or tried to.

He looked back toward the gloomy vale and shook his head again.

"I'm feelin' it too," Catti-brie chimed in. "Like we're bein' looked at."

"Ye probably are," Bruenor said.

He cracked the whip and sent his team, which also seemed more than a little skittish, moving down the trail. The dwarf gave a laugh, but those around him didn't seem so comfortable, particularly Wulfgar, who kept looking back at Delly and Colson.

"Your wagon should not be in the front," Drizzt reminded Bruenor.

"As I been telling him," Dagnabbit agreed.

Bruenor only snorted and drove the team on, calling back to the next wagons in line and to the soldiers flanking them.

"Bah, they're all hesitating," Bruenor complained.

"Can ye not feel it?" Dagnabbit asked.

"Feel it? I'm swimmin' in it, shortbeard! We'll put up right down there," he conceded, pointing to a flat, open area just below, about a third of the way down the side of the ridge, "then ye get 'em all about and I'll give them the tale."

"The tale?" Catti-brie asked, the same question that all the others were about to voice.

"The tale o' the pass," Bruenor explained. "The Fell Pass."

It was a name that meant little to Bruenor's Icewind Dale non-dwarf companions, but Dagnabbit blanched at the mention—as much as the others had ever seen a dwarf blanch. Still, Dagnabbit performed as instructed, and with typical efficiency, bringing the wagons in line from the ridge top to the plateau Bruenor had indicated. When the dwarves had finished their bustling and jostling, setting their teams in place and finding acceptable vantage points to hear the words of their leader, Bruenor climbed up on a wagon and called out to them all.

"Ye're smellin' ghosts, and that's what's got ye itching," he explained. "And ye should be smellin' ghosts, for the valley here is thick with them. Ghosts o' Delzoun dwarves, long dead, killed in battle by orcs." He swept his arm out to the east, to the wide pass opening before them. "And what a battle she was! Hunnerds o' yer ancestors died here, me boys, and thousands and thousands o' their enemies. But ye keep yerselfs strong in heart. We won the Battle o' Fell Pass, and so if ye're seeing any o' them ghosts down there on our way through, ye taunt it if it's an orc and ye bow to it if it's a dwarf!"

The other friends from Icewind Dale watched Bruenor with sincere admiration, noting how he added just the right inflections to his voice, and emphasis on key words to hold his clan in deep attention. He was acknowledging that there might be supernatural things down in the reputedly haunted valley, yet if there was an ounce of fear in Bruenor Battlehammer, he did not show it.

"Now we could've gone further south," he went on. "Coulda swung along the northern edge o' the Trollmoors and into Nesmé."

He paused and shook his head, then gave a great, "Bah!"

Drizzt and the others surveyed the audience, noting that many, many bearded heads were bobbing in agreement with that dismissive sentiment.

"But I knowed me boys'd have little trouble walking among the dead heroes of old," Bruenor finished. "Ye won't embarrass Clan Battlehammer. Now ye get yer teams moving. We'll bring the wagons in a tight double line across the pass, and if ye're seeing a dwarf of old, ye be remembering yer manners!"

The army swung into precise action, sorting the wagons and moving them along the trail, down to the floor of the wide pass. They tightened their ranks, as Bruenor had instructed, and rolled along two-by-two. Before the last of the wagons had even begun moving, one of the dwarves struck up a marching song, a heroic tale of an ancient battle not unlike the one that had taken place in Fell Pass. In moments, all the line had joined in the song, their voices strong and steady, defeating the chilling atmosphere of the haunted place.

"Even if there are ghosts about," Drizzt whispered to Catti-brie, "they'll be too afraid to come out and bother this group."

Just to the side of them, Delly was equally at ease with Wulfgar.

"And ye keep telling me how ugly the road can be," she scolded. "And here I was, all afraid."

Wulfgar gave her a concerned look.

"I never known a better place to be," Delly said to him. "And how ye could e'er have thought o' giving up this life for one in the miserable city, I'm not for knowing!"

"Nor are we," Catti-brie agreed, drawing a surprised look from the barbarian. She returned Wulfgar's stare with a disarming smile. "Nor are we."

The wind moaned—perhaps it was the wind, perhaps something

else—but the sound seemed like a fitting accompaniment to the continuing song. Many white stones covered the area—or at least, the dwarves thought they were stones at first, until one of them looked closer and realized that they were bones. Orc bones and dwarf bones, skulls and femurs, some laying out in the open, others half-buried. Scattered about them were pieces of rusted metal, broken swords, and rotted armor. It seemed like the former owners, of both bones and armor, might still be about as well, for sometimes the wisps of strange fog seemed to take on definitive shapes—that of a dwarf, perhaps, or an orc.

Clan Battlehammer, lost in the rousing song and following their unshakable leader, merely saluted the former and sang all the louder, growled away the latter and sang all the louder.

They set their camp that night, wagons circled, nervous horses brought right into the center, with a ring of torches all around the tight perimeter. Still the dwarves sang, to ward off the ghosts that might be lurking nearby.

"Ye don't go out this night," Bruenor instructed Drizzt and Catti-brie, "and don't bring up yer stupid cat, elf."

That brought him a couple of puzzled expressions.

"No plane-shifting around here," Bruenor explained. "And that's what yer cat does."

"You fear that Guenhwyvar will open a portal that unwelcome visitors might also use?"

"Talked to me priests and we're all agreein' it's better not to find out."

Drizzt nodded and settled back.

"All the more reason for me and Drizzt to go out and keep a scouting perimeter," Catti-brie reasoned.

"I ain't suggesting that."

"Why?"

"What do you know, Bruenor?" Drizzt prompted.

He moved in closer, and so did Catti-brie, and so did Regis, who was nearby and eavesdropping.

"She's a haunted pass, to be sure," Bruenor confided, after taking a moment to look all around.

"Full o' yer ancestors," said Catti-brie.

"Full o' worse than that," said Bruenor. "We're to be fine—too many of us for even them ghosts to be playing with, I'm guessing."

"Guessing?" Regis echoed skeptically.

Bruenor only shrugged and turned back to Drizzt.

"We're needin' to get an idea o' all the land about," he explained.

"You think that Gauntlgrym is near?"

Another shrug. "Doubtin' that—it'd be more toward Mirabar—but we're likely to find some clues here. That fight them centuries ago was going the orcs' way—a bad time for me ancestors—but then the dwarves outsmarted them . . . not a tough thing to do! There's tunnels all about this pass, and deep caves, some natural, others cut by the Delzoun. Me ancient kin interlocked them all and used them to supply, to bind their wounds, and to fix their weapons—and for surprise, for the dwarfs lured them stupid orcs in on what looked like a small group, and when them ugly beasts came charging, their tongues flapping outside their ugly mouths, the Delzoun popped up from trapdoors all about them, within their ranks.

"Was still a fierce fight. Them orcs can hit hard, no one's doubting, and many, many o' me ancestors died here, but me kin won out. Killed most o' them orcs and sent the others running back to their holes in the deeper mountains. Them caves are likely still down there, holding secrets I mean to learn."

"And holding nasties of many shapes and sizes," Catti-brie added.

"Someone's gotta clear them nasties away," Bruenor agreed. "Might as well be me."

"You mean *us*," Regis corrected.

Bruenor gave him a sly smile.

"You plan to find a way down there and take the army underground?" Drizzt asked.

"Nah. I'm plannin' on passing through, as I said. We'll go back to Mithral Hall and get through with the formalities, then we'll decide how many we should be bringing back out after the next winter blows past. We'll see what we can find."

"Then why go through here now?"

"Think about it, elf," Bruenor answered, looking around at the encampment, which seemed fairly calm and at ease, despite their location. "Ye look danger right in the face, at its worst—or what ye're thinking to be its worst—right up front, and ye're not to be caught off yer guard by fear no more."

Indeed, in looking around at the settled camp, Drizzt understood exactly what Bruenor was driving at.

The night was not completely restful, and more than once, a sentry team cried out, "Ghost!" and the dwarves and others scrambled.

There were sightings and shrieks from unseen sources out in the darkness. Despite their weariness from the road, the clan did not get a good night's sleep, but they were back on the move in the morning, singing their songs, denying fear as only a dwarf could.

"Dreadmont and Skyfire," Bruenor explained to his friends the next day, pointing out two mountains, one to the south and one to the north. "Markin' the pass. Ye take in every landmark, elf. I'll be needing yer ranger nose if we're finding a place worth a return visit."

That day went uneventfully, and the troupe passed another fitful, but not overly so, night and were back on the road before the dawn.

At mid-morning, they were rolling along at a brisk pace, singing their songs from front to back, the battleragers and other soldiers trotting along easily.

But then the wagon beside Bruenor's lurched suddenly, its back right wheel dropping, and its front left coming right off the ground. The horses reared and whinnied, and the poor drivers fought hard to hold it steady. Dwarves rushed in from the side, grabbing on, some trying to catch the cargo that was sliding off the back, sliding into a gaping hole that was opening in the ground like a hungry mouth.

Drizzt rushed across in front of Bruenor's wagon and darted back behind the frightened, rearing horses, who were being dragged back with the rest of the wagon. His scimitars flashed repeatedly, cutting loose the harness, saving the team.

Catti-brie ran past the drow, heading for the drivers, and Wulfgar leaped from Bruenor's wagon to join her.

The wagon fell backward into the hole, taking the two struggling dwarves and the woman who had rushed to rescue them into the darkness.

Without even hesitating, Wulfgar dived down to his chest at the lip of the hole and reached out, catching the remains of the horse harness in his powerful hands. The wagon wasn't falling free. If it had been, Wulfgar would have disappeared along with it. Rather, it was slipping down along a rocky shaft, and enough of its weight was supported from below so that Wulfgar somehow managed to tentatively secure it.

The growling barbarian nearly let go in shock when a diminutive figure ran past him and leaped headlong into the hole, and behind him, Drizzt did cry out for Regis. Then both noticed that the halfling was tethered, and with Bruenor standing secure on his wagon, holding the other end of the line.

"Got them!" came a cry from below.

Dagnabbit and several other dwarves joined Bruenor, taking up the line and locking it in place.

Catti-brie was the first to climb out along the lifeline, followed in short order by the two shaken and bruised but not badly hurt drivers.

"Rumblebelly?" Bruenor called when the other three were out with no sign of the halfling.

"Lots of tunnels down here!" came Regis's cry, cut short by a shriek.

That was all the dwarf team had to hear, and they began pumping their powerful arms, hoisting a very shaken Regis from the hole. Wulfgar could hold the wagon no longer. It went crashing down, disappearing from view, until the clatter of its descent became a distant thing.

"What'd ye see?" Bruenor and many others yelled at Regis, who was as white as an autumn cloud.

Regis shook his head, his eyes wide and unblinking. "I thought it was you," he said to one of the drivers. "I . . . I went to hand you the rope. It went right through . . . I mean, it didn't touch . . . I mean."

"Easy, Rumblebelly," Bruenor said, patting the halfling on the shoulder. "Ye're safe enough here and now."

Regis nodded but didn't seem convinced.

Off to the side, Delly gave Wulfgar a huge hug and kiss.

"Ye done good," she whispered to him. "If ye hadn't caught the wagon, then all three would've crashed down to their deaths."

Wulfgar looked past her to Catti-brie, who was standing comfortably in Drizzt's embrace but was looking Wulfgar's way and nodding appreciatively.

Surveying the scene, recognizing that many were thoroughly shaken, Bruenor Battlehammer walked over to the edge of the hole, put his hands on his hips, and yelled down, "Hey, ye damned ghosties! Ye got nothing more about ye than a wisp of smoke?"

A chorus of moans rolled out of the hole, and dwarves scrambled away.

Not Bruenor, though. "Oo, ye got me shaking in me boots now!" he taunted. "Well, if ye got something to say, then get up here and say it. Otherwise, shut yer traps!"

The moans stopped, and for a short, uncomfortable moment, not a dwarf moved or made the slightest sound, all of them wondering if Bruenor's challenge was about to be met by a wave of attacking ghosts.

As the seconds slipped by and nothing ominous crawled out of the hole, the troupe settled back.

"Ye get Pwent and his boys tethered together on long lines and out in front, stomping the ground as they go," Bruenor instructed Dagnabbit. "Don't want to be losin' any more wagons."

The team went back into action, and Drizzt moved near his dwarf friend.

"Challenging the dead?" he asked.

"Bah, they don't mean nothing with their booing and floating about. Probably don't even know they're dead."

"True enough."

"Mark well this spot, elf," Bruenor instructed. "I'm thinking that it might be a good place to start our hunt for Gauntlgrym."

With that, the unshakable Bruenor moved back to his wagon, patted Regis on the shoulder one more time, then led the clan forward as if nothing had happened.

"Roll on, Bruenor Battlehammer," Drizzt whispered.

"Don't he always?" Catti-brie asked, moving beside the drow and wrapping her arm comfortably around his waist.

It took them three days to cross the broken ground of the Fell Pass. The ghosts hovered around them every step of the way and the wind did not cease its mournful song. Some areas were relatively clear, but others were thick with remnants of that long-ago battle. The signs weren't always physical, often just a general feeling of loss and pain, a thick, tangible aura of a land haunted by many lost souls.

Late that third day, up high on one ridge, Catti-brie spotted a distant, welcomed sight, a silvery river running through the land to the east like a giant snake.

"The Surbrin," Bruenor said with a smile when she told him, and all heads about began to bob in recognition, for the great River Surbrin passed only a few miles to the east of Mithral Hall, and the dwarves had actually opened an eastern gate right along its banks. "Couple o' days and we'll be home," the dwarf explained, and a great cheer went up for King Bruenor, who had conquered the Fell Pass.

"I'm still not figuring why ye took us this way, if ye're just meaning to go home anyway," Catti-brie confided to the dwarf as the excitement continued around them.

"Because I'm coming back out here, and so're yerself, the elf, Rumblebelly, and Wulfgar if he's wanting it. And so're Dagnabbit and some o' me best shield dwarves. Now we're knowing the ground, and we learned it under the protection of an army. Now we can start our looking."

"Ye think the leaders in Mithral Hall are to let ye go out and run free?" Catti-brie asked. "Ye're their king, ye might be remembering."

"Are they to *let* me? Well, I'm their king, ye might be remembering," Bruenor shot back. "I'm not thinking that I'm needing anyone's permission, girl, and so what makes ye think I'm to be askin'?"

There wasn't really much that Catti-brie could say against that.

"Ain't ye supposed to be out hunting with Drizzt?" Bruenor asked.

"He took Regis with him today," Catti-brie answered, and she looked to the north, as if she expected to spot the pair running along a distant ridgeline.

"The halfling howl about going?"

"No. He asked if he could go."

"Still wonderin' what's got into Rumblebelly," Bruenor admitted with a shake of his hairy head.

Regis, once the lover of comfort, did indeed seem transformed. He had pressed on through the bitter cold of winter in the Spine of the World without complaint, indeed even lending rousing words for his friends. In every action, the halfling had tried to get involved, to somehow help out, whereas the Regis of old seemed amazingly adept at finding an out of the way shadow.

The change was somehow unsettling to Bruenor and to all the others, a shifting of the sand beneath the world as they had known it. At least it seemed to be shifting in a positive direction.

Not so far away, Wulfgar came upon Delly as she watched Catti-brie and Bruenor in their private discussion. The barbarian noted that his wife was focusing almost exclusively on Catti-brie, as if taking a measure of the woman. He walked up behind her and wrapped his huge arms around her waist.

"She is a fine companion," he said.

"I can see why ye loved her."

Wulfgar gently turned Delly around to face him. "I did not . . ."

"Oh, sure ye did, and stop trying to save me feelings!"

Wulfgar stammered over a couple of responses, not knowing how he should respond.

"She is a companion to me, on the road, in battle . . ."

"And in all yer life," Delly finished.

"No," Wulfgar insisted. "Once I thought that I desired such a joining, but now I see the world differently. Now I see you, and Colson, and know that I am complete."

"Who said ye weren't?"

"You just said . . ."

"I said that yer Catti-brie was a companion in all yer life, and so she is, and so ye're better off for it," Delly corrected. "Ye don't be puttin' her back from yerself for me own sake!"

"I do not wish to hurt you."

Delly turned around to regard Catti-brie.

"Nor does she. She's yer friend, and I'm liking it that way." She pulled away from Wulfgar but stood back and stared at him, a sincere smile wide on her pretty face. "To be sure, there's a part o' me fearing that ye'll want her for more than friendship. I can't be helping that, but I'm not to be giving in to it. I trust ye and trust in what me and ye have started here, but don't ye be putting Catti-brie away from yerself in trying to protect me, because that's not where she belongs. Most folks'd be glad to have a friend like her."

"And I am," Wulfgar admitted. He looked curiously at Delly. "Why are you saying this now?"

Delly couldn't suppress her telling grin.

"Bruenor's talking about coming back out here. He's hoping that ye'll be joining him."

"My place is with you and Colson."

Delly was shaking her head even as he started that predictable response.

"Yer place is with me and our girl when yer life permits. Yer place is on the road with Bruenor and Drizzt and Catti-brie and Regis. I'm knowing that, and it makes me love ye all the more!"

"Their road is a dangerous one," Wulfgar reminded.

"Then more the reason for ye to help them along it."

"They're dwarfs!" Nikwillig exclaimed, his voice breaking with excitement and relief.

Tred, who had not climbed the last part of the steep boulder tumble and so could not see the huge caravan rolling along the flat ground to the south, leaned back against a rock and put his head in his hands. His left leg was swollen and would not bend. He hadn't realized how badly it had been torn during their respite in the small village, and he knew that he would not be able to go on for much longer without some proper tending, maybe even some divine intervention, courtesy of a cleric.

Of course, Tred hadn't complained at all and had fought with every ounce of his strength to keep up with Nikwillig in their flight. It had been a strong and valiant run, but both dwarves knew they were nearing the end of their endurance. They needed a break, and apparently, one had found them.

"We can catch them if we angle out to the southeast," Nikwillig explained. "Ye up for one more run?"

"We need to make the run, we make the run," Tred said. "Ain't come this far to lay down and die."

Nikwillig nodded and turned around, gingerly beginning the steep descent. He stopped, though, freezing in place, his eyes locked across the way. Tred noted that look and followed that gaze to see a huge panther, black as the night sky, crouched on a ledge not so far away—not far enough away!

"Don't ye move," Nikwillig whispered.

Tred didn't even bother to answer, thinking exactly the same thing, though he understood that the great cat knew exactly where they were. He pondered what he might do if the cat sprang his way. How could he even begin to hurt that mass of muscle and claws?

Well, he decided, if it comes on, it goes away bloody.

The seconds slipped past, neither the cat nor the dwarves moving an inch.

With a growl that seemed a challenge, Tred pushed out from the wall to stand straight and strong and put his heavy axe up at the ready beside him.

The great panther looked his way but not threateningly. In fact, the cat seemed almost bored.

"Please don't throw that at her," came a voice from below and to the side, and the two dwarves glanced down to see a brown-haired halfling moving out onto an open, flat stone. "When Guenhwyvar gets an invitation to play, it's hard to stop her."

"That yer cat?" Tred asked.

"Not mine, no," the halfling answered. "She a friend and mastered by a friend, if you get my meaning."

Tred nodded. "Well, who are ye then?"

"I could be asking you the same question," the halfling answered. "In fact, I believe that I will."

"And ye'll be getting yer answer after we're getting ours."

The halfling bowed low. "Regis of Mithral Hall," he said. "Friend to King Bruenor Battlehammer, and scout for the caravan your friend sees below. Returning from Icewind Dale."

Tred relaxed, and so did Nikwillig.

"The King o' Mithral Hall keeps strange company," Tred remarked.

"Stranger than you would ever believe," Regis was quick to answer.

He glanced to the side, and so did both dwarves, to see a second dark figure, this one not feline, but a drow elf.

Tred nearly fell over. Above him, Nikwillig did slip a bit, barely catching a hold before he tumbled from the climb.

"You still have not told me your name," Regis reminded, "and I am guessing that you're not from around here if you've not heard of Drizzt Do'Urden and his panther Guenhwyvar."

"Wait, I heared o' him!" Nikwillig said from above Tred, and Tred looked up. "Bruenor's friend drow. Yeah, we heared o' that!"

"And pray tell us where you were when you heard," Drizzt prompted.

Nikwillig moved down fast, dropping beside Tred, and both dwarves set themselves more presentably, with Nikwillig brushing some of the road dust from his weathered tunic.

"Tred McKnuckles's me name," Tred announced, "and this's me friend Nikwillig, outta Citadel Felbarr and the kingdom o' Emerus Warcrown."

"Long way from home," Drizzt observed.

"Longer than ye're thinking," Tred answered. "Been a road o' orcs and giants, and one wrong trail leading to another wrong trail."

"A tale well worth hearing, I am sure," Drizzt replied, "but not here and not now. Let us get you down to Bruenor and the others."

"Bruenor's in that caravan?" Nikwillig asked.

"Returning from Icewind Dale to assume the throne of Mithral Hall, for word reached us that Gandalug Battlehammer is dead."

"Moradin put him to work at his anvil," said Tred, a customary blessing for dead dwarves.

Drizzt nodded. "Indeed. And may Moradin guide Bruenor well."

"And may Moradin, or whatever good god is listening, guide us well, back to the caravan," Regis reminded.

When Drizzt and the others regarded the halfling, they saw that he was looking around nervously, as if he expected that Tred and Nikwillig had led a host of giants to the ridge, giants that were preparing to rain stones on the five of them.

"Keep scouting, Guenhwyvar," Drizzt instructed, and he started toward the dwarves.

Both of the bearded fellows instinctively stiffened and the perceptive drow stopped his approach.

"Regis, you accompany them to Bruenor," Drizzt decided. "I will keep the perimeter with Guenhwyvar." He saluted the dwarves and slipped away, and both Tred and Nikwillig visibly relaxed.

"We're safe with Drizzt and Guenhwyvar flanking us," Regis assured the dwarves as he approached. "Safer than you can imagine."

Tred and Nikwillig looked at each other, then back at the halfling, and nodded, though neither seemed overly confident in Regis's words.

"Don't worry," the halfling said, offering an understanding wink. "You'll get used to him."

6

SMARTER THAN
AN ORC OUGHT

The arrival of the two dwarves brought much excitement to the village of Clicking Heels, and that deep into the wilds of the Spine of the World, excitement was not usually welcomed. After the two dwarves had gone on their way, the villagers settled back from the initial fear that they would be attacked and began to savor the story. Excitement within a larger cocoon of safety was always welcomed.

Still, the villagers of Clicking Heels were seasoned enough to not fall too deeply into that cocoon. They limited their out-of-town travel over the next few days and doubled the daytime watch and tripled the nighttime watch.

All through the nights, at short, regular intervals, the sentries would call out, "All clear!" from one checkpoint to another. Everyone kept his eyes peeled to the cleared ground around the village walls with that special vigilance that could only be learned through harsh experience.

Even toward the end of the first tenday after the dwarves' departure, the watch held strong and steady, with no slacking, no sleeping or even dozing along the wall.

Carelman Twopennies, one of the sentries that particular night seven days after Nikwillig and Tred had gone on their way, was tired, and so he wouldn't even lean against a pole for fear that he would nod off. Every time he heard the all clear call circling along the wall to his right, the man shook his head briskly and strained his eyes toward the dark field beyond his section of wall, ready for his turn to yell out.

Soon after midnight, the calls circling, Carelman did just that, and peering into the emptiness beyond, he was fairly certain that his impending call would be an honest one. When it came to his turn, he yelled out, or started to, "All clear!"

He heard a rush of air above him as the words began to leave his mouth, though, and was merely unfortunate enough to be standing in the way of the giant-thrown boulder, and so his "All clear!" came out as "All clea—*ugh!*"

He felt the explosion, for just an instant, then he was dead, lying on the ground beneath the rubble of the wooden parapet and the heavy stone.

Carelman Twopennies didn't hear the cries erupting around him or the subsequent explosions as heavy boulders smashed through the walls and buildings, softening the defenses of the small village. He didn't hear the shouts of alarm after that as a horde of orcs, many riding fierce worgs, swept down upon the battered town.

He didn't hear the deaths of his family, his friends, his home.

Marchion Elastul stroked his wild red whiskers, a movement that many dwarves took as a proud gesture, one used for showing off one's beard. Of course, Torgar wasn't overly impressed by the red whiskers of the human marchion, for no human could grow a beard to match the worst of dwarf beards.

"What am I to do with you, Torgar Hammerstriker?" Elastul asked.

Behind him, his four guardsmen, the Hammers, bristled and whispered amongst themselves.

"Didn't think ye was to do anything with me, your honorness," the dwarf answered. "Been going about me business in Mirabar since before ye was born and before yer daddy was born. I'm not needing ye to do much."

The marchion's sour look showed that he was not overly impressed with the statement or the not-so-subtle reminder that Torgar had been in service to Mirabar for a long, long time.

"It is just that heritage that brings me a quandary," Elastul explained.

"Quandary?" Torgar asked, and he scratched his own beard. "That a place where ye get both rocks and milk?"

The marchion's face screwed up with confusion.

"A dilemma," he explained.

"What is?" asked the dwarf.

Torgar worked hard to hide his grin. One thing he knew about humans was that they carried an internal superiority belief, and playing dumb was the easiest way a dwarf could deflect ire.

"What is what?" the marchion replied.

"Yeah, that."

"Enough!" the marchion cried. He was visibly trembling, to which Torgar only shrugged, as if he understood none of it. "Your actions present me with a dilemma."

"How's that?"

"The people of Mirabar look up to you. You're one of the most trusted commanders in the Axe, a dwarf of fine reputation and honor."

"Bah, Marchion Elastul, ye're bringing a blush to me bearded cheeks and to me other ones, as well." He finished the sentence by twisting to look over his shoulder. "Though I'm guessing them nether ones're becoming about as hairy as old age begins to set in."

Elastul looked as if he wanted to slap himself across the face, which pleased Torgar greatly.

The man gave a great sigh and started to respond, but the door to the audience chamber banged open and Sceptrana Shoudra Stargleam entered.

"Marchion," she greeted with a bow.

"We are discussing whether or not I should have you melt the Axe symbol off of Torgar's armor," the marchion replied, throwing aside Torgar's distracting remarks.

"We are?" the dwarf asked innocently.

"Enough!" Elastul scolded again. "You know well enough that we are, and you know well enough why I have summoned you here. To think that you, of all dwarves, would go consorting with our enemies."

Torgar held up his stubby-fingered hands, his expression going suddenly grim.

"Ye take care on who ye're calling our enemies," he warned Elastul.

"Need I remind you of the wealth that Bruenor Battlehammer and his dwarves have stolen from us?"

"Bah, they've stolen not a thing! I made me a couple o' pretty deals from where I'm looking."

"Not their caravan! Their mines to the east. Need I remind you of the drop in business since Mithral Hall's forges began to burn once more? Ask Shoudra there. She above all others can tell you of the difficulty in renewing contracts and attracting new buyers."

"True enough," the woman added. "Since the return of Mithral Hall, my job has become far more difficult."

"As have all of our jobs," Torgar agreed. "And that'll make us better, from where I'm looking."

"Clan Battlehammer is no friend of Mirabar!" Elastul declared.

"Nor are they our enemy," Torgar replied, "and ye should be careful afore ye go callin' them such."

The marchion came forward in his chair so suddenly that Torgar reflexively brought a hand up by his right shoulder, near to the hilt of the large axe he always kept strapped across his back, and that movement, in turn, made the marchion and his four Hammers start and widen their eyes.

"King Bruenor came in as a friend," Torgar remarked when things had settled a bit. "He came here on his way through, as a friend, and he was let in as a friend."

"Or to take a measure of his greatest rivals," Shoudra remarked, but Torgar just shrugged that thought away.

"And if ye're letting a dwarf legend into yer city, then how can ye be sayin' the dwarves o' yer city can't go and sit with him?"

"Many of the dwarves of my city are among the loudest voices for espionage against King Bruenor's Mithral Hall," Elastul reminded. "You have heard their calls for spies to go into Mithral Hall and find some way to shut down the forges, or to flood some of the more promising tunnels, or to place cheaper goods in among the armor and weapons Clan Battlehammer is sending out to market."

Torgar couldn't deny the truth of the marchion's words, nor the fact that he, himself, had uttered similar curses against Mithral Hall in the past, but that seemed different to him than this personal visit, a rant against a faceless rival. Torgar might not wish Clan Battlehammer well with their merchandising, but if an enemy came against Bruenor and his clan, Torgar would gladly lead a charge to assist them.

"Ye ever think that we might be going against Clan Battlehammer in the wrong way?" the dwarf asked. The marchion and Shoudra exchanged curious looks. "Ye ever think that we might be using their strengths and our own strength together to the benefit of us all?"

"What do you mean?" Elastul asked.

"They got the ore—better ore than we'll be findin' here if we dig a hunnerd miles down—and they got some great craftsmen, don't ye doubt, but so do we. Might that our best and their best could work with their good ore to make great pieces, while our apprentices and their apprentices, or a few who're too old to see it right or lift the hammer well enough, could work with the lesser ore in making the lesser pieces—railings and cart wheels instead o' swords and breastplates, if ye see me meaning."

The marchion's eyes went wide indeed, but not because he was the least bit intrigued by the suggestion of cooperation. Torgar saw that immediately and knew that he had crossed a line.

Trembling so badly that he seemed as if he might vibrate right out of his chair, Elastul forced himself, with great effort, to settle back. He shook his head, seeming too enraged to even speak a denial.

"Just a thought," Torgar remarked.

"A thought? Here is a thought—why don't we have Shoudra burn that axe from your breastplate? Why don't I have you dragged out and flogged publicly, perhaps even tried for treason against Mirabar? How dare you lead so many into the embrace of King Bruenor Battlehammer! How dare you bring comfort to our principle rival, a dwarf who leads a clan that has cost us piles of gold! How dare you represent any prospect of friendship between Mithral Hall and Mirabar, and how dare you suggest such a thing to me!"

Shoudra Stargleam came forward to the side of the marchion's throne. She put her hand on Elastul's arm, obviously trying to calm him. She looked to Torgar as she did and nodded toward the door to the room, motioning for him to make a fast exit.

But Torgar wasn't ready to leave just yet, not before he had the last word.

"Ye might be hatin' Bruenor and his boys, and ye might have reason," he said, "but I'm seein' it more as our own weakness than anything Bruenor and his boys did to us."

Marchion Elastul started to respond with another "how dare you," but Torgar kept on rolling.

"That's the way I'm seein' it," the dwarf stated flatly. "Ye want to take me Axe emblem, then take it, but if ye're thinking o' flogging me, then ye should be looking more closely at me kin."

With that threat hanging in the air, Torgar Delzoun Hammerstriker turned and stormed from the room.

"I will have his head on a pike!"

"Then you'll have two thousand shield dwarves running wild in Mirabar," Shoudra explained. She was still holding the man's arm and firmly. "I don't completely disagree with any of the things you say about Mithral Hall, good Elastul, but given the response from Torgar and many others, I wonder the wisdom of holding our present course of open animosity."

Elastul shot her an angry and threatening glower, the look alone reminding her that few on the Council of Sparkling Stones would side with her reasoning.

So Shoudra let him go and stepped back, bowing her head deferentially, while silently wondering how destabilizing King Bruenor's visit had truly been to Mirabar. If the marchion kept pushing this hard, the result could be disastrous for the ancient mining city.

Shoudra also silently applauded King Bruenor for his shrewd move of even showing up where he knew he would not be welcomed, but where he would neither be flatly rebuked. Yes, it was a cunning maneuver, and it seemed to the Sceptrana of Mirabar that her boss was playing right into Bruenor's hands.

"Prisoners?" Obould asked his son as they stood overlooking the ruins of Clicking Heels.

"Few left," Urlgen said with an evil grin.

"Ye're interrogating?"

Urlgen straightened, as if the thought hadn't occurred to him.

Obould gave a growl and slapped Urlgen on the back of his head.

"What we need to know?" the confused Urlgen asked.

"Whatever they can tell us to help us," Obould explained, speaking slowly and articulating each word carefully, as if he was addressing a toddler.

Urlgen snarled but didn't voice his displeasure. The insult had been earned, after all.

"Ye know how to interrogate?" Obould asked, and his son looked at him as if the question was purely ridiculous. "Just like torture," Obould explained anyway, "except ye ask them questions while ye play."

Urlgen's lips curled into a perfectly evil smile, and with a nod, he headed back into the village, where many of his warriors were already at play on the few unfortunate villagers who had not died in the attack.

An hour later, Urlgen caught up to his father, finding Obould at parlay with the giants who had helped in the raid, playing the political angles as always.

"Not all them dwarfs got killed when we hit them," Urlgen remarked, his tone a mixture of excitement for the chase, and disappointment.

"Dwarfs? There were dwarfs in that stupid little town?"

Urlgen seemed confused. "Not them dwarfs," he said. "Weren't none of them dwarfs."

Now Obould and the giants seemed confused.

"No dwarfs in the town," Urlgen stated clearly, trying to end the circular confusion. "When we hit them dwarfs a tenday ago, two got away."

It wasn't completely surprising to Obould, for they knew that some dwarves, at least, were running around the region. A band of orcs had been slaughtered not too far from this town, with tactics indicating a dwarven ambush.

"They come in there, and hurt," Urlgen explained.

"And they died in there?"

"Nope, kept runnin', looking for Mithral Hall, and were gone before we hit."

"How long?"

"Not long."

Obould wore an excited expression. "A fun hunt?" he asked the giants, and as one the great blue-skinned behemoths nodded.

But Obould's expression quickly changed as he remembered the warnings of Ad'non Kareese. "Small forays, and with restraint. We draw them out, little by little," the drow had said. Chasing these dwarves to the south would bring the force dangerously close to Mithral Hall, perhaps, and might incite a battle far beyond what Obould wanted.

"Nah, let 'em go," the orc king decided, and while the giants seemed to accept that readily enough, Urlgen's eyes popped open so wide that they seemed as if they would fall right out of his ugly head.

"Ye can't be . . ." the younger and rasher orc started to argue.

"I can be," Obould interrupted. "Ye let 'em make the hall, with their tales o' death and destruction, and the dwarfs there'll send out a force to investigate. That'd be a bigger and better fight."

Urlgen's smile began to widen once more, and Obould let him in on the rest of the reasoning, just for prudence. After all, any mention of Mithral Hall might send the young warriors charging headlong to the south.

"We get too close and start that fight, and some o' them dwarfs might get back home, and all the stinkin' Mithral Hall'll empty out on us, and that's a fight we're not wantin'!"

Despite the nods of agreement, even from sour Urlgen, Obould felt obliged to add, "Not yet."

THE TRAPPINGS OF ROYALTY

Bruenor purposely excluded Thibbledorf Pwent from the meeting with the two dwarves of Citadel Felbarr, knowing the gist of their story before-hand from Regis, and knowing that the battlerager would likely charge right off into the mountains to avenge their fallen Felbarr kin. And so Nikwillig and Tred recounted their adventures to a group that was comprised more of non-dwarves—Drizzt, Catti-brie, Wulfgar, and Regis—than dwarves.

"A fine escape," Bruenor congratulated when the pair had finished. "Ye done Emerus Warcrown proud."

Both Tred and Nikwillig puffed up a bit at the compliment from the dwarf king.

"What're ye thinking?" Bruenor asked, directing the question to Dagnabbit.

The younger dwarf considered the question carefully for a long while, then answered, "I'll take me a group o' warriors, including the Gutbuster Brigade, and backtrack the route to the Surbrin in the north. If we find the raiders, we'll crush 'em and come home. If not, we'll tack south along the river and meet up with ye in Mithral Hall."

Bruenor nodded throughout the recitation of the plan, expecting every word. Dagnabbit was good, but he was also predictable.

"I'd be likin' another shot at them killers," Tred interjected.

His words made Nikwillig, who obviously didn't share the sentiment, look more than a little uncomfortable.

"Forgettin' yer hurt leg?" Nikwillig remarked.

"Bah, Bruenor's priests done me good with their warm hands," Tred insisted, and to accentuate the point the dwarf stood up and began hopping around, and indeed, despite a wince or two, he seemed ready for the road.

Bruenor studied the pair for a moment.

"Well, we can't let ye both get killed, or yer tale'll not be told proper to Emerus Warcrown. So, ye can come on the hunt, Tred, and yerself, Nikwillig, will go back to Mithral Hall with the others."

"King Bruenor, yer words make ye sound like ye're headin' out on the hunt yerself," Dagnabbit remarked, drawing a hard stare from Bruenor.

Bruenor knew the expectations of those around him, particularly of Dagnabbit, who was sworn to secure his king's safety. He knew that the proper course for him, as King of Mithral Hall, would be to head south straightaway with the bulk of his force, back to the security of his king-dom, back where he could direct further counterstrikes in search of this marauding band of orcs and giants. That was what was expected of him, but the mere thought of it made Bruenor's gut churn.

He looked over at Drizzt with a pleading look, and the dark elf offered a slight, knowing nod in response.

"What're ye thinking, elf?" Bruenor asked.

"I would have an easier time finding the monsters than Pwent and his wild band," Drizzt replied. "An easier time even than good Dagnabbit here, though I doubt not his prowess at hunting orcs."

"Then ye come with me," Dagnabbit offered.

There was a slight crack in his voice, showing that he saw where this might be heading, and showing that he was not too pleased by the prospect.

"I will go," Drizzt agreed, "but with my friends around me. Those whom I have come to trust the most. Those who best recognize how to compliment my every move."

He nodded in turn to Catti-brie, to Wulfgar, and to Regis, then paused for a moment and turned directly to Bruenor—and nodded. A smile widened on the face of the dwarf king.

"No, no, no," Dagnabbit remarked immediately. "Ye cannot be taking me king into the wilds."

"I believe the choice is Bruenor's to make, my friend, not yours, and not mine," Drizzt replied. He returned Bruenor's grateful smile and asked the king, "One last hunt?"

"Who says it's the last?" came Bruenor's gruff reply.

The friends chuckled, then laughed all the harder when Dagnabbit stomped his heavy boot on the ground and exclaimed, "Dagnabbit!"

"Bah, but yerself can come along, ye dumb dwarf," Bruenor said to his young commander. "And yerself," he added, looking over at Tred, who nodded grimly.

"And ye bring some fighters with ye!" Dagnabbit insisted.

"Pwent and his boys," said Bruenor.

"No!" Dagnabbit shouted emphatically.

"But you just said . . ."

"That was afore I thinked yerself was goin'."

Bruenor patted his hands in the air to calm the excited dwarf.

"Not Pwent, then," he said, understanding his young commander's concern. Pwent could start a fight with a rock, so it was said in Mithral Hall, and hurt himself and everyone around him badly before he won the scuffle. "Ye pick the group yerself. Twenty o' yer best—"

"Twenty-five," Dagnabbit argued.

"Well, get 'em ready soon," Bruenor said to Dagnabbit, and to all of them. "I'm wanting to be on the road this same day. We got orcs and giants to squish!"

The dwarf looked around at all his friends and noted that Wulfgar's grin was not as wide as those of Drizzt, Catti-brie, and even Regis. Bruenor nodded his understanding to his adopted son, his implied permission for Wulfgar, now a father and a husband, to opt out of the hunt if he saw fit to do so.

Wulfgar tightened his jaw in response, returned the nod, and strode away.

"Ye can't be thinkin' what I'm thinkin' ye're thinkin'!" said Shingles McRuff.

He was one of the toughest looking critters in all of Mirabar, a short and exceedingly stout dwarf whose nasty attitude was always clearly shown on his ruddy, weathered face. He was missing an eye, and simply never bothered to fill in the empty socket, just covered it with an eye patch. Half of his black beard was torn away, the right side of his face showing as one big scar.

"Well, I'm thinkin' what I'm thinkin'," Torgar Hammerstriker replied, "and I'm not knowin' what ye're thinkin' I'm thinkin'!"

"Well, I'm thinkin' that ye're thinkin' o' leavin'," Shingles stated bluntly, and that got the attention of all the other dwarves in the crowded tavern in the highest subterranean level of the city. "Don't know what the marchion said to ye, bud, but I'm betting it ain't nothing next to what yer grandpa'd be sayin' to ye if yer grandpa was still here to be sayin' things to ye."

Torgar threw up his hands and waved away the words, and the looks of all the others.

At least he tried to, for several other dwarves moved in close, pulling up chairs, and more than one started the same question: "Ye heading out o' Mirabar, Torgar?"

Torgar ran his hands through his thick hair.

"Course I ain't, ye durned fools!" he said, rather unconvincingly. "Me father's father's father's father's father spent his days here."

Despite his bluster, even Torgar could recognize the hint of doubt in his own statements, and that made him ask himself if he really was thinking of leaving Mirabar. He was as mad as a demon at Elastul, to be sure, but was there really a notion, deep in his head and deep in his heart, that it might be time for him to end the Hammerstriker dynasty in Mirabar?

He ran his hands through his thick hair again, and again, and ended up shouting, "*Bah!*" in the faces of those around him.

He stood up so forcefully that his chair skidded out behind him, and he stomped away, grabbing a flagon of ale from the bar as he passed and tossing back a coin to the obviously amused tavern keeper.

Out in the cavern that housed the cluster of buildings in the First Below—the highest section of Mirabar's Undercity—Torgar looked all around him, noting the structures and noting the striations of the stone that housed them, stone so familiar to him that he felt as if it was a part of him, and of his heritage.

"Stupid Elastul," he muttered under his breath. "Stupid all o' ye, not seein' King Bruenor and his boys for the friends they be."

He walked away, unaware that his last statements had been overheard by several others, including Shingles, all huddled near the open window of the tavern.

"He's meanin' it," another dwarf remarked.

"And I'm thinkin' that he's gonna go," said another.

"Bah, whaddya know aside from which drink ye're drinkin'?" Shingles blustered at them. "If ye're even knowin' which drink ye're drinkin'!"

"I'm knowing!" shouted another dwarf, from across the way. "So I'm thinkin' that I'm not drinkin' enough o' what I'm drinkin'!"

That brought a roar, and cries of rounds from several parts of the tavern.

Shingles McRuff just grinned at them all, though, and kept looking out the window, though Torgar, his old buddy and comrade at arms, was long out of sight.

Despite his disclaimer and Torgar's denial, Shingles could not disagree with the consensus that Torgar was indeed serious about leaving Mirabar. The arrival of King Bruenor and the boys from Mithral Hall had put a face on a previously faceless enemy, a face that Torgar and many others had come to see as a friend. A rival, perhaps, but certainly no enemy. The treatment Elastul and the other leaders, mostly human, had shown to Bruenor and to the Mirabarran dwarves who had gone to hear Bruenor's tales or buy the wares from Icewind Dale had not set well with Torgar or with many others.

For the first time since the incident, Shingles McRuff seriously considered the recent events and the wider implications of them.

He didn't much like where his thoughts were suddenly, and already, leading him.

"Guilt's a funny thing, now ain't it?" Delly Curtie playfully asked Wulfgar when he returned to her and Colson at their wagon.

"Guilt?" came the skeptical response. "Or an understanding of my responsibilities?"

"Guilt," Delly answered without the slightest hesitation.

"In taking on a family, I accepted the responsibility of protecting that family."

"And what do ye think will happen to me and Colson surrounded by two hundred friendly dwarves? Ye're not abandoning us out in the wilds,

Wulfgar. We're going to safety. 'Tis yerself that's walking to danger!"

"And even in that, I am abandoning my respons—"

"Oh, don't ye start that again!" Delly interrupted, and loudly, drawing the attention of several nearby dwarves. "Ye do as ye must. Ye live the life ye were meant to live."

"You came all the way out here with me . . ."

"Livin' the life I'm choosin' to live," Delly explained. "I'm not wanting to lose ye—not for a moment—but I know that if ye abandon yer heart to stand with me and Colson all the day, then I've already lost ye. Come to Mithral Hall if that's what's truly in yer heart, me love, but if not, then get yerself out on the road with Bruenor and th' others."

"And what if I die out there, away from you?"

It was not a question asked out of fear, for Wulfgar was not afraid of dying out on the road. He was an adventurer, a warrior, and as long as he could hold faith that he was following the true course of his life, then whatever was put before him would be acceptable.

Of course, he wouldn't die on the road without a fight!

"I think about it all the time," Delly admitted, "because I'm knowin' that ye've got to be going. And if ye die on the road, then know that yer Colson will be proud o' her daddy. For a bit, I thinked about changing yer heart, about tricking ye into staying by me side, but that's not who ye are. I see it on yer face—a face that's smiling all the wider when the wild wind is blowin' across it. Me and Colson can accept whatever fate ye find at the end o' yer road, Wulfgar son of Beornegar, so long as ye're walking the road of yer heart."

She moved up close as she spoke, kneeling in front of the sitting Wulfgar and draping her arms over his shoulders.

"Just give an orc a good smack for me, will ya?"

Wulfgar was smiling then as he looked into her sparkling eyes—sparkling more than they ever had back in the days when Delly had worked in Arumn's tavern in the seedy bowels of Luskan. Something about the road, the fresh air, the adventure, the child, had gotten into the woman, and Delly seemed to grow more beautiful, more wholesome, more healthy with every passing day.

Wulfgar pulled her close and hugged her tightly. His thoughts went back to the day when Robillard had dropped him in the center of Luskan, presenting him with two choices: the road south and security beside Delly and Colson, or the road north, to join his friends in adventure. Hearing

Delly's words, the sincerity in her voice, the love and admiration accompanying it, Wulfgar was never more glad of his choice, of that northward turn, and never more sure of himself.

And never more in love with this woman who had become his wife.

"I will give him *two* good smacks for you," Wulfgar answered, and he moved in to kiss his wife.

"Nah," Delly said, pulling back teasingly. "Yer first one'll send him flyin' far enough."

She didn't move away again as Wulfgar's lips found hers, in a long and leading kiss, gentle at first but then pressing more urgently. The barbarian started to stand, easily lifting the lithe Delly up with him, guiding her to the privacy of their covered wagon.

Colson woke up then and started to cry.

Wulfgar and Delly could only laugh.

Thibbledorf Pwent hopped around, uttering a series of sounds that amply reflected his frustration and disappointment, and kicking at every stone he passed, even those far too big to be kicked. Still, if the tough dwarf felt any pain, he didn't show it much, just an occasional grunt within the steady stream of curses, and an added hop here or there after a particularly vicious kick at a particularly stubborn rock.

Finally, after circling King Bruenor for many minutes of random cursing, Pwent hopped to a stop, and put his stubby hands on his hips.

"Ye're going for a fight, and a fight's where me and me boys belong!"

"We're going to pay back a small band o' orcs and a couple o' giants," Bruenor corrected. "Won't be much of a fight, and even less o' one if Pwent and his boys are there."

"It's what we do."

"And too well!" Bruenor cried.

Pwent's eyes widened.

"Huh?"

"Ye durned fool!" Bruenor scolded. "Don't ye see that this'll be me last time? When we get back to Mithral Hall, I'll be the king again, and what a boring title that is!"

"What're ye talkin' about? Ye're the best king . . ."

Bruenor silenced him with a wave and an exaggerated look of disgust.

"Talkin' with lying emissaries, making pretty with fancy fool lords and fancier and more foolish ladies . . . Ye think I'll get to use me axe much in the next hunnerd years? Only if another army o' damned drow come a'knocking at our doors! So now I get the chance, one last chance, and ye're thinking to steal all me fun with yer killer band. And I thinked ye was me friend."

That set Pwent back on his heels, putting the whole situation in a light he had never begun to imagine.

"I am yer friend, King Bruenor," Pwent said somberly, as reserved as Bruenor or anyone else had ever seen him. "I'll be takin' me boys back to Mithral Hall to get the place ready for yer arrival."

He paused and offered Bruenor a sly wink—well, it was intended to be sly, at least, but from Pwent it just came out as an exaggerated twitch.

"And I'm hopin' ye won't be back anytime soon," Pwent went on, with more comprehension than Bruenor had expected. "Might be just one small band that hit the boys from Felbarr, but might be that ye'll find a bunch o' other small bands betwixt here and that one, and a bunch more on yer way back home. Good fighting, King Bruenor. May ye notch yer axe a thousand more times afore ye see yer shining halls once more!"

With great cheering and fanfare, promises of death to the orcs and giants, and eternal friendship between Mithral Hall and Citadel Felbarr, the band of Bruenor and his dear friends, along with Dagnabbit, Tred, and twenty-five stout warriors, moved off from the main group, turning north into the mountains. Dwarves were not a bloodthirsty race, but they knew how to celebrate when the occasion was a war against goblinkind and giantkin, their most hated of foes.

As for the friends, as one (even Regis!) they felt energized and refreshed to be on the road to adventure once again, and so the only regrets that fine morning were felt by those who had not been chosen to go.

For the dark elf, it was old times and new times all rolled together, the same camaraderie that had so enriched his life of recent years, his old band marching together into adventure in rugged lands, and yet, with a better understanding of each other and of their respective places in the world. The day was full of promise indeed!

What Drizzt Do'Urden did not understand was that he was walking headlong into the saddest day of his life.

PART TWO | UNWITTINGLY INTO A GIANT MOUTH

I am not afraid to die.

There, I said it, I admitted it . . . to myself. I am not afraid to die, nor have I been since the day I walked out of Menzoberranzan. Only now have I come to fully appreciate that fact, and only because of a very special friend named Bruenor Battlehammer.

It is not bravado that makes such words flow from my lips. Not some needed show of courage and not some elevation of myself above any others. It is the simple truth. I am not afraid to die.

I do not wish to die, and I hold faith that I will fight viciously against any attempts to kill me. I'll not run foolishly into an enemy encampment with no chance of victory (though my friends often accuse me of just that, and even the obvious fact that we are not yet dead does not dissuade them from their barbs). Nay, I hope to live for several centuries. I hope to live forever, with my dear friends all about me every step of that unending journey.

So, why the lack of fear? I understand well enough that the road I willingly walk—indeed, the road I choose to walk—is fraught with peril and presents the very real possibility that one day, perhaps soon, I, or my friends, will be slain. And while it would kill me to be killed, obviously, and kill me even more to see great harm come to any of my dear friends, I will not shy from this road. Nor will they.

And now I know why. And now, because of Bruenor, I understand why I am not afraid to die.

Before, I expected that my lack of fear was due to some faith in a higher being, a deity, an afterlife, and there remains that comforting hope. That is but a part of the equation, though, and a part that is based upon prayers and blind faith, rather than the certain knowledge of that which truly sustains me, which truly guides me, which truly allows me to take every step along the perilous road with a profound sense of inner calm.

I am not afraid to die because I know that I am part of a something, a concept, a belief, that is bigger than all that is me, body and soul.

When I asked Bruenor about this road away from Mithral Hall that he has chosen, I put the question simply: what will the folk of Mithral Hall do if you are killed on the road?

His answer was even more simple and obvious: they'll do better then than if I went home and hid!

That's the way of the dwarves—and it is an expectation they place upon all of their leaders. Even the overprotective ones, such as the consummate bodyguard Pwent, understand deep down that if they truly shelter Bruenor, they have, in effect, already slain the King of Mithral Hall. Bruenor recognizes that the concept of Mithral Hall, a theocracy that is, in fact, a subtle democracy, is bigger than the dwarf, whoever it might be, who is presently occupying the throne. And Bruenor recognizes that kings before him and kings after him will die in battle, tragically, with the dwarves they leave behind caught unprepared for his demise. But countering that seeming inevitability, in the end, is that the concept that is Mithral Hall will rise from the ashes of the funeral pyre. When the drow came to Mithral Hall, as when any enemy in the past ever threatened the place, Bruenor, as king, stood strong and forthright, leading the charge. Indeed, it was Bruenor Battlehammer, and not some warrior acting on his behalf, who slew Matron Baenre herself, the finest notch he ever put into that nasty axe of his.

That is the place of a dwarf king, because a dwarf king must understand that the kingdom is more important than the king, that the clan is bigger than the king, that the principles of the clan's existence are the correct principles and are bigger than the mortal coil of king and commoner alike.

If Bruenor didn't believe that, if he couldn't honestly look his enemies coldly in the eye without fear for his own safety, then Bruenor should not be King of Mithral Hall. A leader who hides when danger reveals itself is no leader at all. A leader who thinks himself irreplaceable and invaluable is a fool.

But I am no leader, so how does this apply to me and my chosen road? Because I know in my heart that I walk a road of truth, a road of the best intentions (if sometimes those intentions are misguided), a road that to me is an honest one. I believe that my way is the correct way (for me, at least), and in my heart, if I ever do not believe this, then I must work hard to alter my course.

Many trials present themselves along this road. Enemies and other physical obstacles abound, of course, but along with them come the pains of the heart. In despair, I traveled back to Menzoberranzan, to surrender to the drow so that they would leave my friends alone, and in that most basic of errors I nearly cost the woman who is most dear to me her very life. I watched a confused and tired Wulfgar walk away from our group and feared he was walking into danger from which he would never emerge. And yet, despite the agony of that parting, I knew that I had to let him go.

At times it is hard to hold confidence that the chosen fork in the road is the right one. The image of Ellifain dying will haunt me forever, I fear, yet I hold in retrospect the understanding that there was nothing I could have truly done differently. Even now knowing the dire consequences of my actions on that fateful day half a century ago, I believe that I would follow the same course, the one that my heart and my conscience forced upon me. For that is all that I can do, all that anyone can do. The inner guidance of conscience is the best marker along this difficult road, even if it is not foolproof.

I will follow it, though I know so well now the deep wounds I might find.

For as long as I believe that I am walking the true road, if I am slain, then I die in the knowledge that for a brief period at least, I was part of something bigger than Drizzt Do'Urden.

I was part of the way it should be.

No drow, no man, no dwarf, could ever ask for more than that.

I am not afraid to die.

—Drizzt Do'Urden

AROUND THE EDGES
OF DISASTER

"We're lost!" the yellow-bearded dwarf roared.

He took a threatening step forward, nearly tripping over his long, wagging beard. He was a square-shouldered creature, with hardly a neck to speak of, and a face full of exaggerated features: a huge nose, long and wide; a great mouth of large teeth showing under the pronounced yellow whiskers; and wild dark eyes set in wide sockets, seeming all the wilder as he wound up into one of his more animated moods. Though his heavy plate mail was lying by the bedrolls, he still wore his great helm, fashioned of metal and the towering antlers of a ten-point deer.

"How can we be lost, ye danged fool?" he said. "Ye got all them birds leadin' ye, don't ye?"

The other dwarf, his older brother, shrugged and gave a plaintive, "*Oooo*" sound.

He looked down at his feet, clad in sandals and not the typical heavy dwarven boots, and kicked a nearby rock, sending it bouncing into the brush.

"Ye said ye could get me there!" Ivan Bouldershoulder roared on. "A shortcut? Yeah, a danged shortcut that's got us somewhere. Near to Mithral Hall? No! But somewhere, and ye're right, ye stupid doo-dad, ye got us here fast!"

The blustering dwarf stood up straight and adjusted his battered chain mail jerkin, fixing the bandoleer of tiny crossbow bolts that crossed from his left shoulder to his right hip.

"Tick, tick, tick, boom," his brother warned for the hundredth time, waggling a finger at those special crossbow bolts, each fitted with a small vial of oil of impact.

In response, the angry Ivan drew out a handheld crossbow, an exact replica of the kind favored by the dark elves of the Underdark, and waggled it back at Pikel.

"Boom, yerself, ye stupid doo-dad!"

Pikel's eyes rolled up into his head and he whispered a quick chant. Before Ivan could tell him to knock it off, a small branch snapped down at the yellow-bearded dwarf's extended arm, enwrapping the wrist and tugging back up to put Ivan on the tips of his toes.

"Ye don't want to play like this," Ivan warned. "Not now."

"No boom," Pikel said firmly, waggling his finger like a scolding mother.

He seemed perfectly ridiculous, of course, as he usually did, with his long, green-dyed beard parted in the middle and pulled up over his large ears, then braided together with his long hair to run halfway down his back. He wore light green robes, layered and tied with a thick rope at his waist, and with voluminous sleeves that hung down over his hands if he held his arms at his side.

Ivan gave a little laugh, one that promised his older brother that he'd be meeting a fist very soon.

Pikel just ignored him and walked to the side of their small encampment, where a bowl of vegetable stew was boiling over the fire. The pair had been out of the Spirit Soaring cathedral in the mountains above the small town of Carradoon for more than a tenday, accepting Cadderly's invitation to them to represent him and his wife Danica and all the cathedral in the formal coronation of King Bruenor Battlehammer of Mithral Hall. Ivan and Pikel had been muttering about going to see Mithral Hall for years, ever since Drizzt Do'Urden and Catti-brie had come through the Spirit Soaring on the road to find a lost friend. With things settled comfortably along the Snowflake Mountains, and with the great event of Bruenor's forthcoming coronation, the time seemed perfect.

Just out of the Snowflake Mountains, their road barely begun, Pikel, who was a druid in his heart and in practice, had informed his brother that he could guide them more swiftly on their long journey. He could talk to animals after all, though he hardly seemed able to talk to anyone else except for Ivan, who understood his every grunt. He could predict the weather with a high degree of accuracy, and there was one more little trick up Pikel's wide sleeve, a mode of teleportation that druids understood, using the connectedness of trees to step into one and emerge through another, many miles away.

Ivan and Pikel had done just that, once thus far, and with more than a little complaining from Ivan, who thought the whole trip perfectly unnatural. They had come out into a deep, dark forest. At first, Ivan had figured that they had entered Shilmista, the elf woodland across the Snowflakes from Carradoon, but after a day of wandering in the dark place, both he and Pikel had come to realize that the tone of this particular forest was very different from the magical land ruled by Elbereth and his dancing kin. This forest, wherever it was and whatever it was, was darker and more foreboding than that airy forest of Shilmista. The wind held a deeper bite, as if they had gone further north.

"Ye gonna let me down?" Ivan called from his perch beneath the entrapping tree.

"Uh-uh."

Ivan gave a little chuckle, held his free hand out under the trapped arm and dropped the handheld crossbow to his own waiting grasp. He moved fast, bringing the weapon up to his face, hooking the bowstring under his top teeth and pushing it straight up until it clicked in the readied position, then he bit the weapon's handgrip, holding it in his mouth, while he reached down to pull a small dart from his bandoleer.

"*Oooo!*" Pikel howled when he noticed. He lifted a small log from beside the fire and uttered a quick chant, proclaiming it a "Sha-la-la," and charged for his brother.

Ivan calmly and deliberately set the quarrel in place on the crossbow, then took up the weapon, pointing it at the entangling branch. Realizing that the howling Pikel was too close, though, the yellow-bearded dwarf matter-of-factly lowered the weapon the charging Pikel's way and fired.

The quarrel hit Pikel's raised enchanted club squarely, the quarrel sticking home, then collapsing on itself. A blinding, concussive flash halted Pikel's charge, and left the stunned dwarf standing there, his beard and hair smoking on the right side, his right arm still upraised, but holding only a blackened stump instead of an enchanted cudgel.

"Oooo," the druid dwarf moaned.

"Yeah, and yer tree is next!" Ivan promised, and he put the crossbow back in his mouth, his hand going for another dart.

Pikel hit him with a flying tackle that became more of a *flying* tackle when the hugging dwarves flew backward, only to be pulled forward by the strong branch, and of course, to rebound backward again.

And so they went, bouncing back and forth, Pikel grabbing at the crossbow and at Ivan's pumping arm, and Ivan punching Pikel, though they were too tightly embraced for him to do any real damage. All the while, the stubborn branch held strong, and the two struggling dwarves only seemed to gain momentum on their back and forth and all-around ride.

They were nearing the highest point of one such bounce when Pikel's enchantment let go, sending a ball of Bouldershoulder soaring into the air, to land with a communal "*Oof,*" and go rolling away.

They rolled past the fire, very close, and Ivan yelped when he burned the tip of his nose. They crashed through the lean-to Pikel had constructed, sending twigs flying. At one point, Pikel managed to wriggle away enough to begin casting another enchantment, so Ivan slapped his strong hand over his brother's mouth. Pikel promptly bit him.

It would have gone on for many minutes—it usually did when the Bouldershoulder brothers were involved, but a low growl from the fire pit stopped both dwarves dead in their roll, each with a fist heading in strong for the other's face. As one, the prone brothers turned their heads, to see a large black bear pawing at the hot vegetable stew.

Ivan shoved Pikel away and leaped to his feet.

"Praise Moradin!" he yelled as he looked around for his mighty axe. "Got me a new cloak!"

Pikel's shriek rent the night air and silenced every night bird for a hundred yards around.

"Shut yer trap!" Ivan ordered.

He rushed out to the side, spying his weapon, and heard his brother chanting again as he started past. Ivan expected to get his with another relatively harmless but ultimately annoying trick of nature.

When the excited Ivan had his axe in hand, he turned back to the fire . . . to see Pikel sitting in front of the contented bear, resting comfortably against its thick fur.

"Ye didn't," Ivan moaned.

"Hee hee hee."

With a growl, Ivan lifted his arm and sent his axe twirling down to stick into the sod.

"Damned Cadderly," he bitched, for in Ivan's eyes, Cadderly had created a monster in Pikel.

It was Cadderly who had first made a pet of a wild animal, a white squirrel he had named Percival, of all things. Taking that cue, Pikel had become rather famous for the friends he had made (*infamous* to Ivan, who thought the whole thing quite embarrassing) at the Spirit Soaring cathedral, particularly among Cadderly and Danica's children. To date, those friends included a great eagle, a pair of bald-headed vultures, a weasel family, three chickens, and a stubborn donkey named Bobo.

And now a bear.

Ivan sighed.

The bear gave a soft moan and seemed to fall over, settling comfortably on the ground, where it started snoring almost immediately. So did Pikel.

Ivan sighed more deeply.

"I do not demand applause, no," the gnome Nanfoodle explained, his little arms crossed over his thin chest, one large foot tapping anxiously on the floor, "but it would be appreciated, yes!"

Standing at no more than three and a half feet, with a long, pointy, crooked nose, his head bald but for a semicircular mane of wild white hair that stuck straight out above his ears and all the way back around, Nanfoodle was not an imposing figure. He was, however, one of the most celebrated alchemists in the North, a fact that Elastul and Shoudra Stargleam knew well.

The Marchion of Mirabar began clapping, his smile wide and sincere, for Nanfoodle has just brought him a piece of specially treated metal, smelted and fashioned of ore taken from the mines just a tenday before. Coated with the new formula the ingenious gnome had concocted, this plate was stronger than the others made of the same batch.

To the side, the Sceptrana was too busy continuing her inspection of the various pieces to join in the applause, but she did offer an appreciative nod to the gnome, which Nanfoodle gladly accepted. The two were great friends and had been since before Elastul had hired Nanfoodle and brought him to Mirabar, mostly on the recommendation of Shoudra.

"And with your new treatment for the metals, our pieces will prove the best in the North," Elastul said.

"Well . . ." The gnome hesitated. "They will be better than they were, but . . ."

"But? There can be no 'buts,' my dear Nanfoodle. Sceptrana Shoudra has contracts to secure, and it will take the finest—not merely better, but the finest!—to reclaim much of the commerce lost in recent years."

"The ore from our rivals is richer, and their techniques impeccable," Nanfoodle explained. "My treatment will increase the strength and durability of our products by a fair amount, but I doubt that we'll outshine the ore of Mithral Hall."

Elastul seemed to collapse in his seat, his hands clenched at his side.

"But we have improved!" Nanfoodle said with great enthusiasm, hoping the emotion would prove infectious.

It didn't.

"I do believe that this is the first time any measurable improvement through alchemical treatments has ever been honestly noted," Shoudra Stargleam added, and she quietly tossed a wink Nanfoodle's way. "Despite the outlandish claims of many alchemists, there have been few—nay, not few, but *no*, improvements that are not magical in nature.

"And any improvement will help," Shoudra went on. "There are many previous clients who are on the borderline of decisions between Mirabar and Mithral Hall, and if we can improve our quality without raising our prices, then I believe I may sway more than a few our way."

Elastul did begin to brighten at that, even started to nod, but Nanfoodle chimed in, "Well . . ."

"Well?" the marchion asked suspiciously.

"The adamantine flakes needed in the treating solution do not come cheap," the gnome admitted.

Elastul dropped his head into his hands. Behind him, the four Hammers muttered a few select curses.

"You are using adamantine?" Shoudra asked. "I thought you were experimenting with lead."

"I was," the gnome answered. "And all of the blending formula was developed with lead as the additive base." He gave a shrug. "But that only weakened the end product, unfortunately."

"Wait," Elastul bade him with biting and obvious sarcasm. The marchion came up straight in his chair, his finger pointing as if he had suddenly caught on to the big picture. "You have found a way to blend the metals? And in doing so, if you use a stronger metal, you get a better product, but if you use a cheaper one, well, then you get a weaker product?"

"Yes, Marchion," Nanfoodle admitted, lowering his huge head against the biting sarcasm.

"Ever heard of *alloys*, dear Nanfoodle?"

"Yes, Marchion."

"Because I think you just re-invented them all over again."

"Yes, Marchion."

"How much am I paying you?"

"Enough," Shoudra Stargleam cut in, moving near to the marchion and dropping her hand on his forearm to calm him. "This may be the first step to a great benefit. If Nanfoodle's technique eases the expensive process, then it is not without benefit. In any case, this seems the first step on a potentially profitable road. A good start, I would say!"

Her exuberance did make the gnome stand a bit straighter, but Marchion Elastul merely offered a sarcastic smirk in response.

"Well, by all means, good Nanfoodle," he said. "Do not waste my time and coin in easing me along the whole of the process. Back to work, for you, and not to return until we are *much* farther along."

The gnome gave a curt bow and scampered out of the room. When he was gone, Marchion Elastul gave a great, frustrated roar.

"Alchemy is the science of boast," Shoudra said.

It was advice she had offered many times in the past. Elastul was spending huge sums on his team of alchemists and in truth, this was the greatest advance they had heard of thus far.

"This will not do," he said somberly, as if his anger had been thrown out in that previous roar. "King Bruenor walks into our city and sets it all into confusion. They are beating us with their ore and with their demeanor. This will not do."

"Our markets remain strong for all the items that do not need the fine and expensive Mithral Hall ore," Shoudra reminded. "Those items, the hoes and plows, the hinges and wheel strips, outnumber the swords and breastplates by far. Mithral Hall has cut down one portion of our business alone."

"The one portion that defines a mining city."

"True enough," Shoudra had to agree, but she merely shrugged.

She had never been overly excited about the return of the neighboring dwarven stronghold and had always figured that Clan Battlehammer were better neighbors than the previous inhabitants of the place, the evil grey dwarves.

"Their momentum mounts," Elastul said, and he seemed to be talking more to himself than to Shoudra. "King Bruenor, the legend, returns to them now."

"King Gandalug Battlehammer was fairly well known himself," Shoudra sarcastically replied. "Returning from the ages lost, and all."

Elastul shook his head with every word. "Not like Bruenor, who wrested back control of the hall in our time. With his strange friends and hearty clan, Bruenor reshaped the northland, and his return is significant, I fear. With Bruenor back on the throne, you will find an even harder time in securing the contracts we need to prosper."

"Not so."

"It is not a chance I wish to take," Elastul snapped. "Witness what his reputation alone did to shake our own city. A simple pass through, and half the dwarves are muttering his praises. No, this cannot stand."

He sat back and put a finger to his pursed lips. Behind them, a smile gradually widened, as if some devious plan was formulating.

Shoudra looked at him curiously and said, "You cannot be thinking . . ."

"There are ways to see that Mithral Hall's reputation drops a few notches."

"Ways?" an incredulous Shoudra asked.

"We have dwarves here who have befriended King Bruenor, yes? We have dwarves among us who now call the King of Mithral Hall their friend, and he returns the compliment."

"Torgar will commit no sabotage against Mithral Hall," Shoudra reasoned, seeing easily enough where this was leading.

"He will if he doesn't know he's doing it," Elastul said mysteriously, and for the first time since Nanfoodle had arrived with the initial, misguided news, the marchion's smile was wide and genuine.

Shoudra Stargleam just looked at the man doubtfully. She had often heard his devious plotting, for he spent a great portion of his time on his throne doing just that. Almost always, though, it was just his wishful thinking at work. Despite his bluster, and even more than that, the bluster of the four Hammers who always stood behind him, Elastul wasn't really a man of action. He wanted to protect what he had and even try to improve it in a safe and secure manner, such as hiring alchemists, but to go an extra step, to actually attempt sabotage against Mithral Hall, for example, and thus risk starting a war, simply was not the man's style.

It was entertaining to watch, though, Shoudra had to admit.

BECAUSE THAT'S
HOW WE DO IT

For Tred McKnuckles, the sight was as painful as anything he had ever witnessed. By his estimation, the people of Clicking Heels had treated him and Nikwillig with generosity and tender care, had jeopardized their own safety by getting into a conflict that had not even involved them. Nikwillig and he had done that to them by approaching their town, and they had reacted with more kindness and openness than a pair of lost dwarves from a distant citadel could have expected.

And now they had paid the price.

Tred walked about the ruins of the small village, the blasted and burned houses, and the bodies. He chased away the carrion birds from one corpse, then closed his eyes against the pain, recognizing the woman as one of the caring faces he had seen when he had first opened his eyes after resting against the weariness of the difficult road that had brought him there.

Bruenor Battlehammer watched the dwarf's somber movements, noting always the look on Tred's face. Before there had been a desire for vengeance—the dwarves' caravan had been hit and destroyed, and Tred had lost friends and a brother. Dwarves could accept such tragedies as an inevitability of their existence. They usually lived on the borderlands of the wilderness, and almost always faced danger of one sort or another, but the look on Tred's tough old face was somewhat different, more subdued, and in a way, more pained. A good measure of guilt had been thrown into the tumultuous mix. Tred and Nikwillig had stumbled into Clicking Heels on their desperate road, and as a result, the town was gone.

Simply, brutally, gone.

That frustration and guilt showed clearly as Tred made his way about the smoldering ruins, especially whenever he came upon one of the many orc corpses, always giving it a good kick in the face.

"How many're ye thinking?" Bruenor asked Drizzt when the drow returned from the outlying countryside, checking tracks and trying to get a clearer picture of what had occurred at the ruins of Clicking Heels.

"A handful of giants," the drow explained. He pointed up to a ridge in the distance. "Three to five, I would make it, based on the tracks and the remaining cairns of stones."

"Cairns?"

"They had prepared well for the attack," Drizzt reasoned. "I would guess that the giants rained boulders on the village in the dark of night, softening up the defenses. It went on for a long time, hours at least."

"How're ye knowing that?"

"There are places where the walls were hastily repaired—before being knocked down once more," the drow explained. He pointed to a remote corner of the village. "Over there, a woman was crushed under a boulder, yet the townsfolk had the time to remove the stone and drag her away. In desperation, as the bombardment continued, a group even left the village and tried to sneak up on the giants' position." He pointed up toward the ridgeline, to a boulder tumble off to the side of where he had found the giant tracks and the cairns. "They never got close, with a host of orcs laying in wait."

"How many?" Bruenor asked him. "Ye say a handful o' giants, but how many orcs came against the village?"

Drizzt looked around at the wreckage, at the bodies, human and orc.

"A hundred," he guessed. "Maybe less, maybe more, but somewhere around that number. They left only a dozen dead on the field, and that tells me that the villagers were completely overwhelmed. Giant-thrown boulders killed many and methodically tore away the defensive positions. A third of the village's fighting force were slaughtered out by the ridge, and that left but a score of strong, hearty frontiersmen here to defend. I don't think the giants even came into the town to join in the fight." His lips grew very tight, his voice very grave. "I don't think they had to."

"We gotta pay 'em back, ye know?"

Drizzt nodded.

"A hunnerd, ye say?" Bruenor went on, looking around. "We're out-numbered four to one."

When the dwarf looked back at the drow, he saw Drizzt standing easily, hands on his belted scimitars, a look both grim and eager stamped upon his face—that same look that inspired both a bit of fear and the thrill of adventure in Bruenor and all the others who knew the drow.

"Four to one?" Drizzt asked. "You should send half our force back to Pwent and Mithral Hall . . . just to make it interesting."

A crooked smile creased Bruenor's weathered old face. "Just what I was thinking."

"Ye're the king, damn ye! Ain't ye knowin' what that means?"

Dagnabbit's less than enthusiastic reaction to Bruenor's announcement that they would hunt down the orcs and giants to avenge the destruction of the town and the attack on Tred's caravan came as no surprise to the dwarf king. Dagnabbit was seeing things through the lens offered by his position as Bruenor's appointed protector—and Bruenor did have to admit that at times he needed protecting from his own judgment.

But this was not one of those times, as far as he was concerned. His kingdom was but a few days of easy marching from Clicking Heels, and it was his responsibility, and his pleasure, to aid in cleansing the region of foul creatures like orcs and renegade giants.

"One thing it means is that I can't be lettin' the damned orcs come down and kill the folks about me kingdom!"

"Orcs *and* giants," Dagnabbit reminded. "A small army. We didn't come out here to—"

"We come out here to kill them that killed Tred's companions," Bruenor interrupted. "Seems likely it's the same band to me."

To the side, Tred nodded his agreement.

"And a bigger band than we thinked," the stubborn Dagnabbit argued. "Tred was saying that there were a score and a couple o' giants, but 'twas more 'n that that leveled this town! Ye let me go back and get Pwent and his boys, and a hunnerd more o' me best fighters, and we'll go and get the durned orcs and giants."

Bruenor looked over at Drizzt. "Trail'll be cold by then?" he pleaded more than asked.

Drizzt nodded and said, "And we'll find little advantage in the way of surprise with an army of dwarves marching across the hills."

"An army that'll kill yer orcs and giants just fine," said Dagnabbit.

"But on a battlefield of their choosing," Drizzt countered. He looked to Bruenor, though it was obvious that Bruenor needed little convincing. "You get an army and we can, perhaps, find a new trail to lead to our enemies. Yes, we will defeat them, but they will see us coming. Our charge will be through a rain of giant boulders and against fortified positions—behind rock walls, or worse, up on the cliff ledges, barely accessible and easily defended. If we go after them now and hunt them down quickly and with surprise, then we will choose and prepare the battlefield. There will be no flying boulders and no defended ledges, unless we are the ones defending them."

"Sounds like ye're looking to have a bit o' fun," Catti-brie snidely remarked, and Drizzt's smile showed that he couldn't honestly deny that.

Dagnabbit started to argue, as was, in truth, his place in all of this, but Bruenor had heard enough. The king held up his hand, silencing his commander.

"Go find the trail, elf," he ordered Drizzt. "Our friend Tred's looking to spill a bit o' orc blood. Dwarf to dwarf, I'm owing him that."

Tred's expression showed his appreciation at the favorable end to the debate. Even Dagnabbit seemed to accept the verdict, and he said no more.

Drizzt turned to Catti-brie. "Shall we?"

"I was thinkin' ye'd never ask. Ye bringing yer cat?"

"Soon enough," Drizzt promised.

"Regis and I will run liaison between you and Bruenor," Wulfgar added.

Drizzt nodded, and the harmony of the group, with everyone understanding so well their place in the hunt, heightened Bruenor's confidence in his decision.

In truth, Bruenor needed that boost. Deep within him came the nagging worry that he was doing this out of his own selfish needs, that he might be leading his friends and followers into a desperate situation all because he feared, even loathed, the statesmanlike life that awaited him at the end of his road.

But, looking at his skilled and seasoned friends beginning their eager preparations, Bruenor shrugged many of those doubts aside. When they were done with this bit of business, when all the orcs and giants were dead or chased back into their deep holes, he'd go and take his place at Mithral Hall, and he'd use this impending victory as a reminder of who he was and who he wanted to be. There would be the trappings of bureaucratic process, the seemingly endless line of dignitary visitors who had to be entertained, to be sure, but there would also be adventure. Bruenor promised himself that much, thinking again of the secrets of Gauntlgrym. There would be time for the open road and the wind on his wild red beard.

He smiled as he silently made that promise.

He had no idea that getting what you wished for might be the worst thing of all.

"It's all rocks and will be a difficult track, even with so many of them," Drizzt noted when he and Catti-brie entered the rocky slopes north of the destroyed village.

"Or perhaps not," the woman replied, motioning for Drizzt to join her.

As he came beside her, she pointed down at a dark gray stone, at a patch of red marking its smooth surface. Drizzt went down to one knee, removed a leather glove and dipped his finger, then brought it up before his smiling face.

"They have wounded."

"And they're letting them live," Catti-brie remarked. "Civilized group of orcs, it seems."

"To our advantage," Drizzt remarked. He ended short and turned to see a large form coming around the bend.

"The dwarves are readied for the road," Wulfgar announced.

"And we've found them a road to walk," Catti-brie explained, pointing down to the stone.

"Orc blood or a prisoner's?" Wulfgar asked.

The question took the smiles from Drizzt and Catti-brie, for neither of them had even thought of that unpleasant possibility.

"Orc, I would guess," said Drizzt. "I saw no signs of mercy at the village, but let us move, and quickly, in case it is the other."

Wulfgar nodded and headed away, signaling to Regis, who relayed the sign to Bruenor, Dagnabbit, and the others.

"He seems at ease," Catti-brie remarked to Drizzt when Wulfgar had left them, the barbarian fading back to his position ahead of the dwarf contingent.

"His new family pleases him," Drizzt replied. "Enough so that he has forgiven himself his foolishness."

He started ahead, but Catti-brie caught him by the arm, and when he turned to face her, he saw her wearing a serious look.

"His new family pleases him enough that it does not pain him to see us together out here, hunting side by side."

"Then we can only hope to one day share Wulfgar's fate," Drizzt replied with a wry grin. "One day soon."

He started off, then, bounding across the uneven rock surfaces with such ease and grace that Catti-brie didn't even try to pace him. She knew the routine of their hunting. Drizzt would move from vantage point to vantage point all around her while she meticulously followed the trail, the drow serving as her wider eyes while her own were fixed upon the stone before her feet.

"Don't ye be too long in calling up yer cat!" she called to him as he moved away, and he responded with a wave of his hand.

They moved swiftly for several hours, the blood trail easy enough to follow, and by the time they found the source—an orc lying dead along the side of the path, which brought a fair bit of relief—the continuing trail lay obvious before them. There weren't many paths through the mountains, and the ground outside the lone trail stretching before them was nearly impossible to cross, even by long-legged frost giants.

They signaled back through their liaisons and waited for the dwarves then set camp there.

"If the trail does not split soon, we will catch up to them within two days," Drizzt promised Bruenor as they ate their evening meal. "The orc has been dead as long as three days, but our enemies are not moving swiftly or with purpose. They may even be closer than we believe, may even have doubled back in the hopes of finding more prey along the lower elevations."

"That's why I doubled the guard, elf," Bruenor replied through a mouth full of food. "I'm not looking to have a hunnerd orcs and a handful o' giants find me in me sleep!"

Which was precisely how Drizzt hoped to find the hundred orcs and the handful of giants.

They hustled along the next day, Drizzt and Catti-brie spying many signs of the recent passing, like the multitude of footprints along one low, muddy dell. In addition to showing the way, the continuing indications lent credence to Drizzt's estimate of the size of the enemy force.

The drow and Catti-brie knew that they were gaining, and fast, and that the orcs and giants were making no effort to conceal themselves or watch their backs for any apparent pursuit.

And why should they? Clicking Heels, like all the other villages in the Savage Frontier, was a secluded place, a place where, under normal circumstances, the complete disaster and destruction of the village might not be known by the other inhabitants of the region for tendays or months, even in the summertime when travel was easier. This was not a region of high commerce, except in the markets of places like Mithral Hall, and not a region where many journeyed along the rugged trails. Clicking Heels was not on the main road of commerce. It existed on the fringes, like a dozen or more similar communities, comprised mostly of huntsmen, that rarely if ever even showed up on any map.

These were the wilds, lands untamed. The orcs and giants knew all of this, of course, as Drizzt and Catti-brie understood, and so the couple didn't think it likely that their enemies would have sentries protecting their retreat from a village crushed with no survivors.

When the couple joined the dwarves for dinner that second evening, it was with complete confidence that Drizzt reasserted his prediction to Bruenor.

"Tell your fellows to sleep well," he explained. "Before the setting of tomorrow's sun, we will have first sight of our enemies."

"Then afore the rising o' the sun the next day after that, our enemies'll be dead," Bruenor promised.

As he spoke, he looked over at the dwarf he had invited to dine with him that night.

Tred replied with a grim and appreciative nod then dug into his lamb shank with relish.

The terrain was rocky and broken, with collections of trees, evergreens mostly, set in small protected dells against the backdrop of the increasingly towering mountains. The wind swept down and circled about, rebounding off the many mountainous faces. The winding paths of swift-running streams cascaded down the slopes, silver lines against a background of gray and blue. For the inexperienced, the mountain trails would be quietly deceiving, leading a traveler around, in, up, and down circles that ultimately got him nowhere near where he intended to be or taking him on a wide-ranging path that ended abruptly at a five-hundred-foot drop.

Even for Drizzt and his friends, so attuned with the ways of the wild, the mountains presented a huge challenge. They could pursue the orc force readily enough, for the correct trail was clearly marked to the trained eyes of the drow, but finding a way to flank that fleeing force as the trail grew fresher would not be so easy.

On one plateau of a particularly wide mountain, fed by many trails and serving as a sort of hub for them all, Drizzt found a tell-tale marker. He bent over a patch of mud, its edge depressed by the step of a recent boot.

"The print is fresh," he explained to Catti-brie, Regis, and Wulfgar. He rose up from his crouch, rubbing his muddied fingers together. "Less than an hour."

The friends glanced around, focusing mostly on the higher ridgeline that loomed to the north.

Catti-brie was first to catch sight of the movement up there, a hulking giant form gliding around a line of broken boulders.

"Time for Guenhwyvar," Wulfgar remarked.

Drizzt nodded and pulled the statue from his belt pouch, then placed it on the ground and summoned the magical panther to his side.

"We should pass word to Bruenor as well," the barbarian added.

"Ye do it," Catti-brie replied, speaking to Wulfgar. "Ye can get there quicker than the little one with yer longer legs."

Wulfgar nodded; it made sense.

"We'll better locate and assess the enemy while you fetch the dwarves," Drizzt explained. He glanced off at Regis, who was already moving—to the west and not the north. "Flanking?"

"I go this way, you go north, and she goes east," Regis explained.

His three friends smiled, glad to see a bit of the old Regis returned, for the giant they had spotted had been moving west to east and by going west, Regis was almost assuring that his two hunting friends would find the orc and giant band before he did.

"Guenhwyvar comes with me to the north, in a direct line toward the enemy," Drizzt explained. "She alone can run without inviting suspicion. We four will meet back here right before the sunset."

With final nods and determined looks, they split apart, each moving swiftly along the appointed trail.

It was a strange feeling for Regis, being out alone in the wilderness without Drizzt or any of the others protectively at his side. Back in Ten-Towns, the halfling had often ventured out of Lonelywood by himself, but almost always along familiar trails, particularly the one that would take him to the banks of the great lake Maer Dualdon and his favorite fishing hole.

Being alone in the wilds, with known, dangerous enemies not too far away, felt strangely refreshing. Despite his very real fears, Regis could not deny the surge of energy coursing through his diminutive body. The rush of excitement, the thrill of knowing that a goblin might be hiding behind any rock, or that a giant might even then be taking deadly aim at him with one of its huge boulder missiles. . . .

In truth, this wasn't an experience that Regis planned to make the norm of his existence, but he understood that it was a necessary risk, one leading to the greater good, and one that he had to accept.

Still, he wished he hadn't been the first to encounter the orcs, a group of a dozen stragglers lagging behind their main lines. Caught up in his own thoughts, the distracted halfling almost walked right into their midst before ever realizing that they were there.

Drizzt didn't like what he was seeing. High up on a rocky ledge, the drow lay flat on his belly peering over an encampment of several scores of orcs—what he had expected. Just beyond the camp, though, loomed a quartet of behemoths: huge frost giants, and not the dirty rogues one might expect to find consorting with orcs. These were handsome creatures, clean and richly dressed, adorned with ornamental bracelets and rings, and fine furs that were neither particularly new nor particularly weather-beaten.

The giants were part of a larger, more organized clan—obviously a part of the network the Jarl Grayhand, a name not unknown to Drizzt and the dwarves of Mithral Hall, had formed in this part of the Spine of the World.

If the old Grayhand was loaning some of his mighty warriors out to an orc clan, the implications might prove darker than one flattened village and an ambush on a band of dwarves.

Drizzt looked all around, wondering if there was a way for him to get closer to the giants, to try to overhear their conversation. He could only hope they'd be speaking in a language that he could comprehend.

The cover between him and the orc camp was not promising, though, nor was the climb down the almost sheer cliff facing. Beyond that, the sun was already hanging low in the sky, and he didn't have much time if he hoped to rejoin his friends in the appointed place at the appointed hour.

He lingered for many more minutes, watching from afar the limited interaction between the giants and orcs. His attention piqued when one large and powerful orc, wearing the finest garments of all the filthy band, and with a huge, decorated axe strapped across its back, approached the giant quartet. The orc didn't go in the hesitating manner of some of the others, who had been either bringing food to the behemoths or simply trying to navigate past them in as unobtrusive a manner as possible. This orc—and Drizzt understood that it had to the leader, or at least one of the leaders—strode up to the giants purposefully and without any apparent trepidation and began conversing in what seemed to be a jovial manner.

Engaged, straining to hear whatever tidbit he might, even if only a burst of laughter, Drizzt was hardly aware of the approach of an orc sentry until it was too late.

From one high vantage point, Catti-brie noted where the orcs and giants had stopped to set their camp, far to the west of where she had entered the higher, northern ridgeline. She realized that Drizzt was likely already surveying their encampment, and she could get there, but her estimate told her that she'd probably arrive on the spot just in time to accompany Drizzt, if they found each other, back to their assigned meeting spot. Thus, the woman spent her time running past the east end of the enemy encampment, checking the ground over which the orcs and giants would likely traverse in the morning—unless, of course, they decided to break camp early and march on through the night, which would favor the orcs, no doubt, though probably not be to the liking of the giants.

With the eye of a trained tactician, which she, as the adopted daughter of Bruenor Battlehammer, most certainly was, she looked for advantageous assault points. Bottlenecks in the trail, high ground where dwarves could send rocks and hammers spinning down at their enemies. . . .

Despite her many duties, the woman was the first of the four to return to the rendezvous point. Wulfgar returned soon after her with Bruenor, Dagnabbit, and Tred McKnuckles at his side.

"They have encamped almost directly north of this point," the woman explained.

"How many?" Bruenor asked.

Catti-brie gave a shrug. "Drizzt will know. I was searching the ground ahead to see where and how we might strike tomorrow."

"Ye find any good killin' spots?"

Catti-brie answered with a wicked smile, and Bruenor eagerly rubbed his hands together, then looked over at Tred and offered a nudge and a wink.

"Ye'll get yer payback, friend," the dwarf king promised.

As so often in the past, luck alone saved Regis. He skittered behind a convenient rock without notice from the group of orcs, who were engaged in an argument over some loot they had pilfered, probably from the sacked village.

They argued, pushed and shouted at each other, and deciding to divide the loot up privately amongst themselves, they suddenly quieted. Instead of continuing along the trail to join up with the larger band, they plopped themselves down right there, sending a couple ahead to fetch some food.

That afforded Regis a lovely eavesdropping position while they rambled on about all sorts of things, answering many questions for the halfling and leading him to ask many, many more.

Drizzt could not have been in a more disadvantageous situation, lying face down between a rise of stone and a boulder, peering over a ledge and with someone, something—likely an orc—moving up behind him. He ducked his head and shrugged the cowl of his cloak up a bit higher, hoping the creature would miss him in the dim light, but when the footsteps closed, the drow knew that he had to take a different course.

He shoved up to his knees and gracefully leaped to his feet from there, spinning around and drawing his scimitars, moving them as quickly as possible into a defensive position, trying to anticipate the attacker's thrust. If the creature had come straight on, Drizzt would have been caught back on his heels from the outset.

But the orc, and it was an orc, hadn't charged, and didn't charge. It stood back, hands upraised and waving frantically, having dropped its weapon to the ground at its feet.

It said something that Drizzt didn't completely comprehend, though the language was close enough to the goblin tongue, which the drow did know, for him to understand that there was some recognition there, spoken in an almost apologetic tone. It seemed as if the orc, recognizing a drow elf, feared that it was intruding.

The obvious fear didn't surprise Drizzt, for the goblinkin were usually terrified of the drow—as were most reasoning races—but this went beyond that, he sensed. The orc wasn't surprised, as if the appearance of a drow elf near to this force was not unexpected.

He wanted to question the creature further but saw a black flash to the side of the orc and knew his opportunity had passed.

Guenhwyvar came across hard and fast, in a great leap that put the panther about chest level with the orc.

"Guen, no!" Drizzt cried as the cat flew past.

The orc's throat erupted in blood and the creature went flying down to the stone. Drizzt rushed to it, turning it over, thinking to stem the flow of blood from its throat.

Then he realized that the orc had no throat left at all.

Frustrated that an opportunity had flitted away, but grateful that Guenhwyvar had seen the danger from afar and come rushing in to rescue him, Drizzt could only shake his head.

He hid the dead orc as well as possible in a crevice, and with Guenhwyvar at his side, he started back to the rendezvous, having discovered more questions than answers.

"Plenty of ground to shape to our liking," Catti-brie assured them all when they had reassembled on the plateau below the enemy's position. "We'll get the fight we want."

None disagreed, but Bruenor wore a concerned expression.

"Too many giants," he explained when all the others had focused on him. "Four'd make a good enough fight by themselves. I'm thinking we got to hit them afore the morning. Trim the numbers."

"Not an easy thing to do, if we're still wanting surprise tomorrow," Catti-brie added.

They bounced a few ideas back and forth, possible plans to lure out the giants, and potential areas where they could hit at the brutes away from the main force. There seemed no shortage of these, but getting them out wouldn't be an easy task.

"There may be a way . . ." Drizzt offered, the first words he had contributed to the planning.

Replaying the scene with the orc, the reactions of the creature toward him, Drizzt wondered if his heritage might serve him well.

They agreed on a place, and the six and Guenhwyvar, minus Drizzt, started away, while the drow moved back toward his last position overlooking the encampment. He stayed there for just a few moments, his keen eyes cutting the night and discerning an approach route toward the separate giant camp, and he was gone, slipping away as silently as a shadow.

"He'll bring 'em down from the right," Bruenor said when they reached the appointed ambush area.

The dwarf was facing a high cliff, with a rocky, broken trail running left and right in front of it before him.

"Can ye get up there, Rumblebelly?"

Regis, standing at the base of the cliff, was already picking his course. He had discerned a few routes already to the ledge he was hoping to reach, but he wanted an easier one for a companion who was not quite as nimble as he.

"You want to get in on the kill?" he asked Tred McKnuckles, who was standing beside him and looking more than a little overwhelmed by the frantic planning and implementation of the seasoned companions.

"What d'ya think?" the dwarf shot back.

"I think you should put that weapon on your back and follow me up," Regis replied with a wry grin, and without further ado, the halfling began his climb.

"I ain't no damn spider!" Tred yelled back.

"Do you want the kill or not?"

It was the last thing Regis meant to say, and the last thing he had to say, for Tred, grumbling and growling to make a robbed dwarf proud, began his ascent, following the exact course of footholds and handholds Regis had taken. It took him a long time to get to the ledge, and by the time he arrived, Regis was already sitting comfortably with his back against the wall, twenty-five feet above the ground.

"See if you can break off a large chunk of that rock," the halfling remarked, nodding to the side, where a fair-sized boulder had lodged itself on the ledge.

Tred looked at the solid stone, a thousand pounds of granite, doubtfully.

"Ye think ye can drop it off?" came a call from below from Catti-brie.

Regis moved forward to regard her, and Tred looked on even more doubtfully.

Catti-brie didn't wait for an answer but moved to the side to confer with Wulfgar. The barbarian rushed away, returning a few moments later with a long and thick broken branch. He positioned himself below the ledge, then reached up as far as he could, and when it was apparent that he still couldn't reach his companions with the branch, he tossed it up.

Regis caught it and pulled it up beside him. Smiling, he handed it to the bewildered Tred.

"You'll see," the halfling promised.

To the side, on another ledge at about the same height as Regis and Tred's, Guenhwyvar gave a low growl, and poor Tred seemed more unsettled than ever.

Regis just grinned and moved back into position to watch the trail behind.

When he heard them talking in a language that was close enough to Common to be understood, Drizzt's hopes for his plans climbed a bit. He was on the fringes of the encampment, out in the shadows behind a large rock. Neither the orcs nor the giants had set any guards, obviously secure in their victory.

The giants' conversation was small talk mostly, giving the drow no real information. That didn't concern him too much. He was more interested in finding a chance to approach one of them alone, to play his hunch that this group was somewhat familiar with dark elves.

He got his chance almost an hour later. One of the giants was snoring, a sound not unlike an avalanche. Another, the only female of the quartet, lay beside him, near sleep if not already so. The remaining two continued their conversation, though with the long lags of silence attributable to drowsiness. Finally, one of the pair stood up and wandered off.

Drizzt took a deep breath—dealing with creatures as formidable as frost giants was no easy task. In addition to their great size, strength, and fighting prowess, frost giants were not blathering idiots like their hill giant and ogre cousins. By all accounts, they were often quite sharp of mind, and not easily fooled. Drizzt had to count on his heritage, and the reputation that he hoped would precede him.

He crept in under cover of the shadows to within a few feet of the sitting behemoth.

"You missed some treasure," he whispered.

The giant, obviously sleepy, started a bit and fell back to one elbow, turning his head to regard the speaker as it asked, "What?"

Seeing the dark elf, the giant did move more ambitiously, snapping back up to a straight-backed position.

"Donnia?" it asked, a name that Drizzt did not recognize, except to recognize that it was indeed a name, a drow name.

"An associate," he replied quietly. "You missed a great treasure."

"Where? What?"

"At the village. A huge chest of gems and jewels, buried beneath one of the fallen buildings."

The giant looked around, then leaned in more closely.

"You offer this?" he asked suspiciously, so obviously not convinced that the drow, that *any* drow, would walk in and give such information away.

"I cannot carry so much," Drizzt explained. "I cannot carry one tenth of that which lies within. While I could ferry the treasure away one arm-load at a time, I suspect there is more still, buried beneath a slab I can't budge."

The giant looked around again, its movements showing that it was more than a little interested. Not far to the side, one of its companions snored, coughed, and rolled over.

"I will share with you, fifty-fifty, and with your kin, if you believe we need them," Drizzt said, "but not with the orcs."

A wicked smile that crossed the giant's face told Drizzt that his understanding of the race relationships within the enemy band was not far from the mark.

"Let us continue this discussion, but not here," Drizzt said, and he began fading back into the shadows.

The giant looked around yet again, then moved into a crouch and crept after him, following eagerly into the night, moving quietly along a rocky trail to a small clearing protected behind by a sheer cliff wall.

On a ledge on that wall, some ten feet above the head of the towering giant, two sets of curious eyes looked on.

"What will Donnia Soldou think of this?" the giant asked.

"Donnia need not know," Drizzt replied.

The giant's shrug told him much, told him that Donnia, whoever she might be, was not an overriding controlling force but more likely just an associate. That brought a bit of relief to the dark elf. He would hate to think that the orcs and giants were acting at the behest of a drow army.

"I will take Geletha with me," the giant announced.

"Your friend with whom you were speaking?"

The giant nodded. "And we take two shares, you take one."

"That hardly seems fair."

"You cannot move the slab."

"You cannot find the slab." Drizzt continued the banter, trying hard to keep the giant unsuspicious while his friends moved into their final positions.

He figured he wouldn't have to keep it up for long.

When a blue-streaking arrow shot out from behind him, zipped past, and thudded hard into the giant's chest, the drow was not surprised.

The behemoth groaned but was not badly hurt. Drizzt drew his scimitars and leaped around, turning to face Catti-brie's position, still playing the part of the giant's ally.

"Where did it come from?" he shouted. "Lift me that I might see."

"Straight ahead!" roared the great creature.

It started to bend to accommodate the drow, and Drizzt turned fast and ran up its treelike arm. His scimitars slashed hard across the behemoth's face, drawing bright lines of red.

The giant roared and grabbed at him, but the drow had already leaped away, with another blue-streaking arrow sizzling in behind him, slamming the giant yet again.

Shrugging it off, the behemoth continued to move toward Drizzt, until there came a sound like a log splitting. Bruenor Battlehammer's many-notched axe smashed the brute in the back of the knee.

The giant howled and lurched, grabbing the wound, and Catti-brie hit it again with an arrow, this time in the face.

Ignoring the hit as much as possible, the brute lifted a foot, obviously intending to smash Bruenor.

And it was hopping, as Dagnabbit rushed out and planted his warhammer right on top of the giant's set foot.

And a cry of "Tempus!" followed by a second warhammer, this one spinning through the air, changed that course.

Aegis-fang hit the behemoth in the chest, just below its neck, with a force that knocked the giant back against the wall. Wulfgar came in behind the hammer, recalling it magically to his grasp, then charged before the giant had recovered and launched a tremendous smash right into the giant's kneecap.

How the brute howled!

Catti-brie's next arrow hit it right in the face.

Up on the ledge, Tred, with the branch lever tucked tight over one shoulder, looked from the giant to Regis, his expression dumbfounded. He had battled giants before, on many occasions, but never had he seen one so battered so quickly.

He looked past Regis then to Guenhwyvar. The great panther crouched on a ledge to the side, watching the fight, but more than that, watching back toward the east, her ears perked up.

Regis held his hand out toward the ledge, indicating that the target behemoth was in position.

Tred gave a satisfied grunt and bore down on the displaced boulder, setting the lever more solidly and driving on. The rock tilted and tumbled, and the poor giant below, which was just then beginning to regain its senses and set some type of defense against the rushing onslaught of the drow, the barbarian, the woman, and the two fiery dwarves, got a thousand pounds of granite right on top of the head. The crunching sound from its neck echoed off the stone, as did the resounding crash as the boulder bounced away.

Regis gave Tred a salute for the fine shot, but the relief was short-lived, for only then did the halfling and the dwarf come to understand what had so piqued Guenhwyvar's interest and had kept the cat out of the fight. Another giant was charging down the path, and yet another one, a female, behind that.

Regis looked at Tred. "We could find another rock," he offered, just a hint of fear creeping into his voice.

Behind them, Guenhwyvar leaped onto the shoulder of the charging giant, and as it pounded on down the trail, Tred shrugged and did likewise, using the cat's distraction to get a clear shot at the giant's head with his mighty axe. No crack of stone against stone had ever sounded louder than the report of Tred's axe cracking into the giant's skull.

Regis winced and looked over.

"Or we could do that," the halfling remarked, though the dwarf couldn't hear him.

With great effort, Tred stubbornly hung on to the axe handle, hanging off the back of the giant's head. He rode the behemoth down as it stumbled to its knees, then down to the ground.

Tred rose from the dead behemoth's back and swung around to join the fray against the remaining beast—or tried to, then got jerked back around by his axe, which remained firmly embedded.

He heard a groan, from the side and down, and only then realized—and he was the only one of the band to notice—that Dagnabbit had been in an unfortunate position as the giant had slumped down and was buried beneath the behemoth's great weight.

Drizzt started the counterattack, charging up the path at the furious female frost giant. He saw the giant raise her arm to throw, a large stone in hand, and responded by calling upon his innate drow abilities, summoning a globe of darkness before the creature's face. The drow dived aside, frantically, and the hurled rock clipped the stone where he had been standing. Its rebound sent it skipping fast, brushing Wulfgar in the shoulder and sending him flying, then just missing Catti-brie, taking Taulmaril from her hands and bloodying her fingers. She fell to her knees, clutching her hands, her face locked in a grimace of pain.

Drizzt came in hard at the giant. The behemoth kicked across at him, and the drow went into a leaping, rolling somersault right over the flying foot, landing gracefully and spinning about, his deadly scimitars cutting two deep lines in the back of the huge calf.

Bruenor came in next and hard, driving in against the giant's other shin with his axe. The giant swatted him aside with a brutal slap, but the dwarf just accepted the bouncing ride along the rocks, regained his footing, adjusted his one-horned helmet, and wagged a finger back at the behemoth.

"Now ye're makin' me mad, ye overfed orc!"

The giant kicked at Drizzt again, but he was too quick for that, skipping aside time and time again, and spinning about to cut a wicked slash whenever presented an opening.

Apparently realizing that it was overmatched, the behemoth kicked one last time, shortening the blow in an effort not to thump the drow, but to just keep him at bay. The giantess turned to the south and started to run along the broken ground instead of the path, where her long legs would give her an advantage.

Or she tried to.

Aegis-fang whipped in, smashing the ankle of the giantess's trailing foot, driving that foot behind the other ankle and tripping the behemoth up.

She fell hard to the stone, her breath blasted out by the impact.

She tried to rise but had no chance. Drizzt was there, running up her back. And Guenhwyvar was there, leaping onto her shoulders and biting hard at the back of her neck. And Catti-brie was there, holding Khazid'hea, her devilishly sharp sword, gingerly in her injured grasp. And Bruenor was there with his axe, with Wulfgar behind him with the mighty warhammer back in his grasp.

And Tred came in, escorting a shaken, but not too badly hurt Dagnabbit.

Up on the ledge behind them, Regis watched and cheered. He called out when he noticed that the first felled giant was moving again, albeit groggily, the behemoth struggling to rise. Wulfgar rushed back and put Aegis-fang to swift and deadly work on the creature's huge head.

"I never seen nothing like it," Tred admitted as the band made their way back toward the main force of waiting dwarves.

"It's all about shaping the battlefield," Bruenor explained.

"And none do it better 'n King Bruenor!" Dagnabbit added.

"None, unless it's him," Bruenor replied, nodding his chin toward Drizzt, who was tending Catti-brie's hands as they walked.

She had at least one broken finger but seemed more than ready to continue.

There would be no rest for the band that night. There was another battlefield to properly shape, in preparation for an even larger fight.

NOT WELCOME

"Uh uh," Pikel said stubbornly, stamping his foot hard and standing before the wide oak, barring Ivan's way into the enchanted tree.

"What are ye saying?" Ivan shot back. "Ye openin' the door just to keep it blocked, ye dopey fool?"

Pikel pointed past his brother to the bear, which was sitting and watching, its expression forlorn.

"Ye ain't takin' the bear!" Ivan bellowed, and he came forward.

"Uh uh," Pikel said again, waggling his finger and shifting to fully block the way.

Nose to nose, Ivan glowered at his brother, but he heard the bear growling behind him soon enough and realized this next fight wouldn't be even.

"Ye can't be taking him," the yellow-bearded dwarf reasoned. "Ye might be breakin' up his bear family, and ye wouldn't want to be doing that!"

"Oooo," said Pikel, seeming caught off guard for just a second before his face brightened.

He came forward and whispered into Ivan's ear.

"How do ye know he ain't got no family?" Ivan roared in protest, and Pikel whispered some more.

"He told ye?" Ivan bellowed in disbelief. "The stupid bear told ye?

And ye're believing him? Ye ever think that he might be fibbing? That he might be telling ye that just to get away from his . . . cow or his doe or his . . . bearess, or whatever they're calling a she-bear?"

"Bearess, hee hee hee," said Pikel, and giggling, he whispered some more.

"He's a *she*-bear?" Ivan asked, and he glanced back. "How're ye knowin' it's a . . . never mind, don't ye be telling me. It ain't no matter, anyway. He-bear or she-bear, he . . . she . . . it, ain't goin'."

Pikel's face seemed to sink, his bottom lip getting pressed forward in a most pitiful pout, but Ivan held his ground. He wasn't about to do this strange tree-walking, unsettling under the best of conditions, with a wild bear beside him.

"Nope, it ain't," he said calmly. "And when we're missin' Bruenor's coronation, ye can tell Cadderly why. And when the winter's finding us out here, and yer friend's gone to sleep, ye watch me skin her for some warm blankets! And when . . ."

Pikel's low moan stopped his fiery brother's tirade, for Ivan surely recognized the defeat in Pikel's tone.

The green-bearded Bouldershoulder walked past Ivan and over to his bear. He spent a long while grooming the back of the gentle animal's ears, scratching and pulling ticks, and gently placing the insects down on the ground.

Of course, whenever he put down a bloated one, Ivan made a point of picking it up, holding it high, and popping it between stubby fingers.

A few moments later, Pikel's bear ambled away, and though Pikel remarked that he thought the creature was quite sad, Ivan frankly saw no difference. The bear was going on its way, and any way would have likely been good enough for the bear.

Pikel walked past Ivan again. He took up his newest walking stick and knocked three times on the trunk, then bowed low and reverently as he asked the tree's permission to enter.

Ivan didn't hear anything, of course, but apparently his brother did, for Pikel half-turned and held his arm out Ivan's way, inviting the yellow-bearded brother to lead the way.

Ivan deferred and responded by motioning for Pikel to go ahead.

Pikel bowed again and motioned for Ivan to lead.

Ivan deferred again and motioned more emphatically.

Pikel bowed yet again, still with complete calm, and motioned for Ivan to lead.

Ivan started to motion back yet again but changed his mind in mid-swing, and shoved his brother through instead, then turned and charged the tree.

To smack face-first into the solid trunk.

With his pale, almost translucent skin, and blue eyes so rich in hue they seemed to reflect the colors around him, the elf Tarathiel seemed a tiny thing. Though not very tall, he was lean and seemed all the more so with his angular features and long pointed ears. That was all an errant vision, though, for the elf warrior was a formidable force indeed and certainly would be seen as no tiny thing to any enemy tasting the bite of his fiercely-sharp, slender sword.

Crouching in the high, windblown pass, a day's flight from his home in the Moonwood, Tarathiel recognized the sign clearly enough. Orcs had been through. Many orcs, and not too long ago. Normally that wouldn't have concerned Tarathiel too much—orcs were a common nuisance in the wilds of the valley between the Spine of the World and the Rauvin Mountains—but Tarathiel had tracked the band, and he knew from whence they'd come. They'd come out of the Moonwood, out of his beloved forest home, bearing many, many felled trees.

Tarathiel gnashed his teeth together. He and his clan had failed, and miserably, in the defense of their forest home, for they had not even located the orcs quickly enough to chase them off. Tarathiel feared what that might mean for the near future. Would the lack of defense prompt the ugly brutes to return?

"If they do, then we will slaughter them," the moon elf remarked, turning to speak to his mount, who stood grazing off to the side.

The pegasus snorted in reply, almost as if he'd understood. He threw his head about and tucked his white-feathered wings in tighter over his back.

Tarathiel smiled at the beautiful creature, one of a pair he had rescued a few years earlier from these same mountains, after their sire and dam had been killed by giants. Tarathiel had found the felled pair, smashed down by thrown boulders into a rocky dell. He could tell from the dead mare's teats that she had recently given birth, and so he had spent the better part of a tenday searching the area before finding the pair of foals. That pair had done well in the Moonwood, growing strong and straight under the guidance—not the ownership—of Tarathiel's small clan. This one, which he had named Sunset because of the reddish tinges in his white hair all along his long, glistening mane, welcomed him as a rider. Tarathiel had named Sunset's twin Sunrise, because her shining white mane was highlighted by a brighter color red, a yellowish pink hue. Both pegasi were about the same height, sixteen hands, and both were well-muscled, with strong, thick legs and wide, solid hooves.

"Let us go and find these orcs and show them a little rain," the elf said slyly, tossing a wink at his mount.

Sunset, as if he had understood again, pawed the ground.

They were up in the air soon after, Sunset's huge, powerful wings driving hard or spreading wide to catch the updrafts off the mountain cliffs. They soon spotted the orc band, a score of the creatures, trudging along a trail higher up in the mountains.

So attuned were mount and rider that Tarathiel was easily able to guide Sunset with just his legs, swooping the pegasus down from on high, flashing through the air some fifty yards above the orcs. The elf's bow worked furiously, firing arrow after arrow down at the orcs.

They scrambled and shouted curses, and Tarathiel guessed that more got hurt by diving frantically behind rocks or over ridges than felt the sting of his arrows. He went up and around the bend and flew on for some distance before turning Sunset around. He wanted to give the orcs time to regroup, time to think that the danger had passed. And he wanted to come in faster this time. Much faster.

The pegasus climbed higher into the sky, then banked a sharp turnabout and went into a powerful dive, wings working hard. They came around the corner much lower, just above the reach of the orcs had any been carrying a pole arm or long spear. From that height, despite the swift flight, Tarathiel's bow rang true, plugging one unfortunate orc right in the chest, throwing it back and to the ground.

Sunset soared past, a host of thrown missiles climbing harmlessly into the air behind them.

Tarathiel didn't push his luck for a third run. He banked to the southeast and set off from the mountains, soaring fast for home.

"How was I to know yer stupid spell had run out?" Ivan bellowed against his brother's continuing laughter. The yellow-bearded dwarf rubbed some blood off his scraped nose. "I didn't see no stupid door when ye said there was a door, so how'm I to be knowing when the door that ain't there anyway ain't there no more?"

Pikel howled with laughter.

Ivan stepped forward and launched a punch, but Pikel knew it was coming, of course, and he snapped his head forward, dropping his cooking pot helmet into his waiting, and blocking, hand.

Bong! And Ivan was hopping about in pain once more.

"Hee hee hee."

Ivan recovered in a few moments and went hard for his brother, but Pikel stepped into the tree, disappearing from sight.

Ivan stopped short and settled his senses then jumped in behind his brother. The world turned upside down for the poor dwarf.

Literally.

Pikel's tree-transport was not an easy ride, nor was it a level or even upright one. The brothers were rushed along the root network, magically melded into the trees, flowing through the roots of one to the adjoining roots of another. They went up fast and dropped suddenly—Pikel howling "Weeee!" and Ivan trying hard to keep his stomach out of his mouth.

They spun corkscrew motions along one winding route, then went through a series of sharp turns so violent that Ivan bit the inside of one cheek then the other.

It went on for many minutes, and finally, mercifully, the brothers came out. Ivan, who had somehow caught up to and surpassed Pikel, stumbled face-down in the dirt. Pikel came out hard and fast behind him, landing right atop his brother.

It always seemed to happen exactly like that.

With a great heave, Ivan had his brother bouncing away, but even that shove did little to stop Pikel's continuing laughter.

Ivan leaped up to throttle him, or tried to, for he was too disoriented, too dizzy, and his stomach was churning a bit too much. He ambled a step forward, two to the side, then after a pause, a third and a fourth to the side, to bang against a tree. He almost caught himself but tripped over a root and went down to his knees.

Ivan looked up and started to rise, but a rush of dizziness held him there, clutching at his churning stomach.

Pikel, too, was dizzy, but he wasn't fighting it. Like one of Cadderly's little children, he was up and laughing, trying to walk a straight line and inevitably falling to the ground, enjoying every second of it.

"Stupid doo-dad," Ivan muttered before he threw up.

Tarathiel watched the play of Sunset and Sunrise, the pegasi obviously glad to be reunited. They trotted across the small lea, whinnying and playfully nipping at each other.

"You never grow tired of watching them," came a higher-pitched, beautifully melodic voice behind him.

He turned to see Innovindil, his dearest friend and lover, walking onto the lea. She was smaller than he, with hair as yellow as his was black, and eyes as strikingly blue. She had that look on her face that so enchanted Tarathiel, a smile just a little bit crooked on the left, rising up sharply there to give her a mysterious, I-know-more-than-you-know look.

She moved beside him, to take his waiting hand.

"You've been gone too long," she scolded.

She brought her free hand up and tousled Tarathiel's hair, then dropped it lower and gently caressed his slender, strong chest.

His expression, which had been soft and bright as he had observed the pegasi at play, and brighter still at Innovindil's approach, darkened.

She asked, "Did you find them?"

Tarathiel nodded and said, "A band of orcs, as we suspected. Sunset and I came upon them in the mountains to the north, dragging trees they felled from the Moonwood."

"How many?"

"A score."

Innovindil gave that wry smile. "And how many are now alive?"

"I killed at least one," Tarathiel replied, "and sent the others scrambling."

"Enough to make them reconsider any return?"

Again the elf nodded.

"We two could go out and find them again," Tarathiel offered, returning the smile. "It will take a day at least to catch up to them, but if we kill them all, we can be sure they will not return."

"I have a better way to spend the next few days," Innovindil replied. She moved closer and gently kissed her husband on the lips. "I'm glad you have returned," she said, her voice growing more husky, more serious.

"As am I," he agreed, with all his heart.

The pair walked off from the lea, leaving the two pegasi to their play. They headed in the direction of the small village of Moonvines, their home, the home of their clan.

They had barely left the lea, though, when they spotted a campfire in the distance.

A campfire in the Moonwood!

Tarathiel handed his bow over to Innovindil and drew out his slender sword. The two set out at once, moving with absolute silence through the dark trees. Before they had gotten halfway to the distant fire, they were met by others of their clan, also armed and ready for battle.

"Ye made a stew again!" Ivan bellowed. "Ain't no wonder me belly's always growling at me of late! Ye won't let me eat any meat!"

"Uh-uh," said Pikel, waggling that finger, a gesture that was growing more and more annoying to Ivan, spawning fantasies of biting that stubby and crooked finger off at the top knuckle. At least then, he'd have some meat, he mused.

"Well, I'm getting me some real food!" Ivan roared, hopping to his feet and hoisting his heavy axe. "And it'd be a lot easier on the deer, or whatever I'm findin', if ye'd use yer spells to hold the thing still so I can kill it clean."

Pikel crinkled his nose in disgust and stood tapping one foot, his arms crossed over his chest.

"Bah!" Ivan snorted at him, and he started away.

He stopped, seeing an elf perched on a branch before and above him, bow drawn back.

"Pikel," the dwarf said quietly, hardly moving, and hardly moving his lips. "Ye think ye might talk to this tree afore me?"

"Uh oh," came Pikel's response.

Ivan glanced back, to see his brother standing perfectly still, hands in the air in a sign of surrender, with several grim-faced elves all around him, their bows ready for the kill.

All the forest came alive around the brothers, elf forms slipping from every shadow, from behind every tree.

With a shrug, Ivan dropped his heavy axe over his shoulder and to the ground.

11

ON A FIELD
OF THEIR CHOOSING

They seemed nervous as they moved along the trail, a single giant among the horde, with the other three inexplicably missing.

Watching them from the boughs of an evergreen, concealed at a height just above the giant, Drizzt Do'Urden recognized that level of alertness clearly and knew that he and his friends would have to be even more precise. The giant was the key to it all, the drow recognized, and had explained as much to Dagnabbit and Bruenor when they were setting out the forces. With that belief firmly in hand, Drizzt had taken a bit of his own initiative, moving up ahead of the concealed dwarves. He was ready, with his formidable panther ally, to make what he hoped would be the decisive first strike.

The trail was clearly defined as it moved through the copse of trees in the small, sheltered dell. Drizzt held his breath and tightened against the trunk of the pine when the orcs wisely sent lead runners in to inspect the area. He was glad that he had convinced Bruenor and Dagnabbit to set the ambush just past that place.

The orc scouts milled about down below, slipping in and out of the shadows, kicking through leafy piles. A pair took up defensive positions, while another pair headed back out the way they had entered, signaling for the approach.

On came the caravan, marching easily and without too much apparent concern.

The lead orcs passed below Drizzt's position. He looked across the trail, to Guenhwyvar, motioning for the cat to be calm, but be ready.

More and more orcs filtered below, then came the giant, walking alone and with a great scowl upon his face.

Drizzt set himself upon the branch he had specifically selected, drawing out his scimitars slowly and keeping them low, under the sides of his cloak so that their gleaming metal and magical glow would not give him away.

The giant marched through, one long stride after another, eyes straight ahead.

Drizzt leaped out, landing on the giant's huge shoulder, his scimitars slashing fast as he scrambled away, leaping off the other side and into the second pine as the giant reached up to grab at him. The drow ranger hadn't done much damage—he hadn't intended to—but he did turn the behemoth, just enough, and got its arms, eyes, and chin moving upward.

When Guenhwyvar leaped out the other way, she had an open path to the giant's throat, and there she lodged and dug in, tearing and biting.

The giant howled, or tried to, and snapped his huge hands onto the cat. Guenhwyvar didn't relent, digging deeper, biting harder, tearing and crushing the behemoth's windpipe, opening arteries.

Below, the orcs scrambled to get out of the way of stomping boots and breaking branches.

"What's it?" one orc yelled.

"A damned mountain cat!" another howled. "A great black one!"

The giant finally tugged stubborn Guenhwyvar free, not even realizing that he was taking a good portion of his own neck along with the cat. With another great effort, the giant brought the cat in close, under his huge arms, and began to crush her. Guenhwyvar gave a loud, pitiful wail.

Drizzt, wincing at the sound, dismissed her to her astral home. The giant folded a bit more tightly, the panther it had been squeezing turning to insubstantial mist.

The behemoth reached up to his neck, patting the spurting blood wildly, frantically. He stumbled to and fro, scattering terrified orcs, before finally staggering to his knees, then falling down, gasping, into the dirt.

"It kilt the cat!" one orc yelled. "Buried the damned thing right under it!"

A couple of orcs rushed to aid the giant, but the floundering, terrified behemoth slapped them aside. Scores of orcs had their attention squarely on the prone behemoth, wondering if it would rise again.

Which is why they didn't notice the stealthy dark elf, slipping down the tree and into position.

Which is why they didn't notice the dwarves moving in a bit closer, hammers ready to throw, melee weapons in easy reach.

There was much yelling, screaming, suggestions and pleas from the confused orcs, when finally one turned enough to see the force creeping in against them. Its eyes went wide, it lifted its finger to point, and it opened its mouth to cry out.

That yell became a communal thing, as a score or more dwarves joined in the chorus, running forward suddenly, launching their first missile barrage, then wading in, axes, hammers, swords, and picks going to fast and deadly work.

In the back, one orc tried to direct the response—until a scimitar slashed into its back and through a lung. Off to the side, another orc took up the lead—until an arrow split the air, knocking into a tree beside its head. More concerned with its own safety than with organizing against the dwarves, the would-be leader ducked, scrambled, and simply ran away.

Just when those orcs closest to the dwarves seemed to begin some semblance of a defense, in came Wulfgar, his warhammer swatting furiously, slapping aside orcs two at a time. He took a few stinging hits but didn't begin to slow, and he didn't begin to lessen his hearty song to Tempus, his god of battle.

Off to the side of the battle, Catti-brie was both pained and overjoyed. She kept taking up her bow and lowering it in frustration. Her battered fingers simply would not allow for enough accuracy for her to dare shooting anywhere near to her friends. That, plus the fact that she had no idea where Drizzt might be in that morass of scrambling, screaming orcs.

It pained her greatly to be out of the fight, but she saw that it was going as well as they could have hoped. They had taken the orcs completely off their guard, and the fierce dwarves would not begin to relent such an advantage.

Even more brilliant and inspiring to Catti-brie were the movements of Wulfgar. He strode with confidence, such ferocity, with a surety of his every deadly strike. This was not the man she had been engaged to, who became unsure, fearful, and protective. This was not the man who had walked away from them when they had set out to destroy the Crystal Shard.

This was the Wulfgar she had known in Icewind Dale, the man who had charged gladly beside Drizzt into the lair of Biggrin. This was the Wulfgar who had led the barbarian countercharge against the minions of Akar Kessell back in that frozen place. This was the son of Beornegar, returned to them, and fully so, from the clutches of Errtu.

Catti-brie could not hide her smile as she watched him wade among the enemies, for she somehow instinctively knew that no sword or club would harm him this day, that somehow he was above the rest of them. Aegis-fang tossed orcs aside as if they were mere children, mere inconveniences. One orc rushed behind a sapling, and so Wulfgar growled more loudly, shouted more loudly, and swung more powerfully, taking out the tree and the huddling creature behind it.

By the time Catti-brie managed to tear her stare away from the man, the fight was over, with the remaining orcs, still outnumbering the dwarves at least three to one, fleeing in every direction, many throwing down their weapons as they ran.

Bruenor and Dagnabbit moved their troops fast and sure, to cut off as many as possible, and Wulfgar paced all fleeing near him, chopping them down.

Off to the other side, Catti-brie saw one group of three rush into the trees, and she lifted her bow but was too late to catch them with an arrow.

The shadows within the group of trees deepened, engulfed in magical darkness, and the ensuing screams told her that Drizzt was in there and that he had that situation well in hand.

One orc did come rushing out, running right toward her, and she lifted Taulmaril to take it down.

But then it fell, suddenly and hard, tripped up by a lump that appeared on the ground before it, and Catti-brie merely shook her head and grinned when she saw the diminutive form of Regis unfold and rise up. The halfling darted forward and swung his mace once and again, then winced back from the crimson spray, a sour look upon his face. He looked up, noted Catti-brie, and just shrugged and melted back into the grass.

Catti-brie looked all around, her bow ready if needed, but she put it up and replaced the arrow in her magical, always-full quiver.

The short and brutal fight was done.

In all Faerûn there was no tougher race than the dwarves, and among the dwarves there were few to rival the toughness of Clan Battlehammer—especially those who had survived the harshness of Icewind Dale—and so the battle was long over, and the dwarves had regrouped before several of them even realized that they had been injured in the battle.

Some of those wounds were deep and serious; at least two would have proven fatal if there had not been a pair of clerics along with the party to administer their healing spells, salves, and bandages.

Numbered among the wounded was Wulfgar, the proud and strong barbarian gashed in many places by orc weapons. He didn't complain any more than a reflexive grunt when one of the dwarves poured a stinging solution over the wounds to clean them.

"Are ye all right then?" Catti-brie asked the barbarian when she found him sitting stoically on a rock, waiting his turn with the overworked clerics.

"I took a few hits," he replied, matter-of-factly. "Nothing as hurtful as the chop Bruenor put on me when first we met, but. . . ."

He ended with a wide smile, and Catti-brie thought she'd never seen anything more beautiful than that in all her life.

Drizzt joined them then, nursing one hand.

"Clipped it on an orc's hilt," he explained, shaking it away.

"Where's Rumblebelly?" Catti-brie asked.

The drow nodded toward the place where Catti-brie had seen Regis trip up one orc.

"He won't end a fight without searching the bodies of the dead," Drizzt explained. "He says it's the principle of the thing."

They sat and talked for just a bit longer, before a louder argument off to the side drew their attention.

"Bruenor and Dagnabbit," Catti-brie remarked. "How am I guessin' what that's about?"

She and Drizzt rose to leave. Wulfgar didn't follow, and when they turned to question him, he waved them away.

"He's hurtin' a bit more than he's sayin'," Catti-brie remarked to Drizzt.

"But he could take a hundred times those wounds and still be standing," the drow assured her.

By the time they arrived, they had already discerned the cause of the argument, and it was exactly as Catti-brie had guessed.

"I'm heading for Mithral Hall when I'm telling ye I'm heading for Mithral Hall!" Bruenor roared, poking his finger hard into Dagnabbit's chest.

"We got wounded," Dagnabbit replied, staying strong to his unfortunate task of trying to protect the stubborn king.

Bruenor turned to Drizzt. "What're ye thinking?" he asked. "I'm sayin' we should move along from one town t' the next, all the way to Shallows. Wouldn't do to let 'em get run over without a warning."

"The orcs're dead and scattered," Dagnabbit put in, "and all their giant friends're lying dead too."

Drizzt wasn't sure he agreed with that assessment at all. The dress and cleanliness of the giants had told him that these were not rogues but were part of a larger clan. Still, he decided to keep that potentially devastating news to himself until he could gather more information.

"*These* orcs and *these* giants!" Bruenor bellowed before the drow could respond. "Might that there are more of 'em, running in packs all about!"

"Then all the more reason to go back, regroup, and get Pwent and his boys to join us," Dagnabbit replied.

"We take Pwent and his boys to Shallows and the last thing they'll be worryin' about're stupid orcs," Bruenor said.

Several around him, Drizzt included, caught on to the joke and appreciated the tension-breaking levity. Dagnabbit, his scowl as deep as ever, didn't seem to catch it.

"Well, ye're making more than a bit o' sense," Bruenor admitted a moment later. "The way I'm seein' it, we got a couple o' responsibilities here, and none I'm willing to ignore. We got to get our wounded back. We got to tell the folk o' the region about the danger and help 'em get prepared, and we got to get ourselves ready for fighting nearer to Mithral Hall."

Dagnabbit started to respond, but Bruenor stopped him with an upraised hand and continued on, "So let's send back a group with the wounded, and with orders to tell Pwent and his boys to lead a hunnerd to set up a base north o' Keeper's Dale. They can send another two hunnerd to block the low ground along the Surbrin north o' Mithral Hall. We'll make the rounds and work off that."

"A good plan, and I'm agreein'," said Dagnabbit.

"A good plan, and ye got no choice," Bruenor corrected.

"But . . ." Dagnabbit interjected, even as Bruenor turned to Drizzt and Catti-brie.

The dwarf king swung back to his commander.

"But ye're among them that's taking the wounded back to Mithral Hall," Dagnabbit demanded.

Drizzt was certain that he saw smoke coming out of Bruenor's ears at that remark and was almost as certain that he'd be spending the next few minutes pulling Bruenor off Dagnabbit's beard.

"Ye telling me to go and hide?" Bruenor asked, walking right up to the other dwarf, so that his nose was pressing against Dagnabbit's.

"I'm telling ye that it's me job to keep ye safe!"

"Who gived ye the job?"

"Gandalug."

"And where's Gandalug now?"

"Under a cairn o' rocks."

"And who's taking his place?"

"Yeah, that'd be yerself."

Bruenor assumed a bemused expression and posture, dropping his hands on his hips and smirking at Dagnabbit as if the ensuing logic should be perfectly obvious.

"Yeah, and Gandalug told me ye'd be saying this," Dagnabbit remarked, seeming defeated.

"And what'd he tell ye to tell me when I did?"

The other dwarf shrugged and said, "He just laughed at me."

Bruenor punched him on the shoulder. "Ye go and get things set up as I telled ye," he ordered. "Leave us with fifteen, not countin' me boy and girl, the halfling, and the drow."

"We gotta send at least one priest back with the hurt ones."

Bruenor nodded. "But we'll keep th' other."

With that settled, Bruenor joined Catti-brie and Drizzt.

"Wulfgar's among them wounded," Catti-brie informed him.

She led him back to where Wulfgar was still sitting on the rock, tying a bandage tight about one thigh.

"Ye wantin' to go back with the group I'm sending?" Bruenor asked him, moving over to better inspect the many wounds.

"No more than you are," Wulfgar replied.

Bruenor smiled and let the issue drop.

Later on, eleven dwarves, seven of them wounded and one being carried on a makeshift stretcher, started off for the low ground to the south, and the trails that would take them home. Fifteen others, led by Bruenor, Tred, and Dagnabbit, and with Drizzt, Catti-brie, Regis, and Wulfgar running flank, moved off to the northeast.

12

SPIN

"If they did not run away, the day was ours," Urlgen insisted to his fuming father. "Gerti's giants fled like kobolds!"

King Obould furrowed his brow and kicked the face-down body of a dead orc, turning it half up then letting it drop back to the dirt, utter contempt on his ugly face.

"How many dwarfs?" he asked.

"An army!" Urlgen cried, waving his arms emphatically. "Hundreds and hundreds!"

To the side of the young commander, an orc screwed up his face in confusion and started to say something, but Urlgen fixed the stupefied creature with a wicked glare and the warrior snapped his mouth shut.

Obould watched it all knowingly, understanding his son's gross exaggeration.

"Hundreds and hundreds?" he echoed. "Then Gerti's missing three would have done you's no good, eh?"

Urlgen stammered over a reply, finally settling on the ridiculous proclamation that his forces were far superior, whatever the dwarves' numbers, and that an added trio of giants would have indeed turned his tactical evasion into a great and sweeping victory.

Obould took note that never once had his son, there or when Urlgen had first arrived in the cavern complex, mentioned the words "defeat" or "retreat."

"I am curious of your escape," the orc king remarked. "The battle was pitched?"

"It went on for long and long," Urlgen proclaimed.

"And still the dwarfs did not encircle? You's got away."

"We fought our way through!"

Obould nodded knowingly, understanding full well that Urlgen and his warriors had turned tail and fled, and likely against a much smaller force than his son was indicating—likely against a force that was not even numerically equal to their own. The orc king didn't dwell on that, though. He was more concerned with how he might lessen the disaster in terms of his tentative and all-important alliance with Gerti.

Despite his bravado and respect for his own forces—orc tribes that had thrown their allegiance to him—the cunning orc leader understood well that without Gerti, his gains in the region would always be restricted to the most desolate patches of the Savage Frontier. He would be doomed to repeat the fiasco of the Citadel of Many Arrows.

Obould also knew that Gerti wasn't going to be pleased to learn that one of her giants was dead, lying amid a field of slaughtered orcs. With that unsettling thought in mind, Obould made his way to the fallen giant, the behemoth showing few wounds other than the fact that his throat was almost completely torn away.

He looked over at Urlgen, his expression puzzled, and offered a prompting shrug.

"My scouts said it was a big cat," his son explained. "A big black cat. Jumped from that tree to the throat. Killed the giant. Giant killed it."

"Where is it?"

Urlgen's mouth twisted, his formidable fangs pinching into his lower lip. He looked around at the other orcs, all of whom immediately began turning questioning looks at their comrades.

"Dwarfs musta taken it. Probably wanting its skin."

Obould's expression showed little to indicate that he was convinced. He gave a sudden growl, kicked the dead giant hard, and stormed away, furrowing that prominent brow of his and trying hard to figure out how he might parlay this disaster into some sort of advantage over Gerti. Perhaps he could shift the blame to the three deserters, explaining that in the future her giants would have to be more forthcoming of their intentions to the orcs they accompanied on raids like this.

Yes, that might work, he mused, but then a cry came in from one of the many scouts they had sent out into the surrounding areas. That call soon led to a dramatic redirection of thinking for the frustrated and angry orc king.

Soon after, Obould furrowed his brow even more deeply as he looked over the second scene of battle, where three giants—the missing three giants, including one of Gerti's dear friends—lay slaughtered. They weren't far from where Urlgen had set his camp the night before the catastrophic battle, and it was obvious to Obould that the trio were missing from the march because they had been killed before that last march began. He knew it would be obvious to Gerti, who surely would investigate if he pushed the issue that the disaster was more the fault of her giants than his orcs.

"How did this happen?" he asked Urlgen.

When his son didn't immediately respond, the frustrated Obould spun around and punched him hard in the face, laying him low.

"Obould is frightened," Ad'non Kareese announced to his three co-conspirators.

Ad'non had followed Obould's forces to both battlegrounds and had met with the orc king soon after, counseling, as always, patience.

"He should be," said Kaer'lic Suun Wett, and the priestess gave a little cackle. "Gerti will roll him into a ball and kick him over the mountains."

Tos'un joined in the priestess's laughter, but neither Ad'non nor Donnia Soldou seemed overly amused.

"This could break the alliance," Donnia remarked.

Kaer'lic shrugged, as if that hardly mattered, and Donnia shot her an angry look.

"Would you be content to sit in our hole in boring luxury?" Donnia asked.

"There are worse fates."

"And there are better," Ad'non Kareese was quick to put in. "We have an opportunity here for great gain and great fun, and all at a minimal risk. I prefer to hold this course and this alliance."

"As do I," Donnia seconded.

Kaer'lic merely shrugged and seemed bored with it all, as if it did not matter.

"What about you?" Donnia asked Tos'un, who was sitting off to the side, obviously listening and obviously amused, but giving little indication beyond that.

"I think we would all do well to not underestimate the dwarves," the warrior from Menzoberranzan remarked. "My city made that mistake once."

"True enough," agreed Ad'non, "and I must tell you that Urlgen's report of the size of the dwarven force seemed greatly exaggerated, given the battleground. More likely, the dwarves were greatly outnumbered and still routed the orcs—and killed four giants besides. Their magic may have been no less formidable."

"Magic?" Kaer'lic asked. "Dwarves possess little magic, by all accounts."

"They had some here, as far as I can discern," Ad'non insisted. "The orcs spoke of a great cat that felled the giant, one that apparently disappeared after doing its murderous business."

Off to the side, Tos'un perked up. "A *black* cat?"

The other three looked at the Menzoberranyr refugee.

"Yes," Ad'non confirmed, and Tos'un nodded knowingly.

"Drizzt Do'Urden's cat," he explained.

"The renegade?" Kaer'lic asked, suddenly seeming quite interested.

"Yes, with a magical panther that he stole from Menzoberranzan. Very formidable."

"The panther?"

"Yes, and Drizzt Do'Urden," Tos'un explained. "He is no enemy to be taken lightly, and one who threatens not only the orcs and giants on the battleground, but those quietly behind the orcs and giants as well."

"Lovely," Kaer'lic said sarcastically.

"He was among the greatest of Melee-Magthere's graduates," Tos'un explained, "and further trained by Zaknafein, who was regarded as the greatest weapons master in all the city. If he was at that battle, it explains much about why the orcs were so readily defeated."

"This one drow can sway the tide of battle against a host of orcs and a foursome of giants?" Ad'non asked doubtfully.

"No," Tos'un admitted, "but if Drizzt was there, then so was—"

"King Bruenor," Donnia reasoned. "The renegade is Bruenor's closest friend and advisor, yes?"

"Yes," Tos'un confirmed. "Likely the pair had some other powerful friends with them."

"So Bruenor is out of Mithral Hall and roaming the frontier with a small force?" Donnia asked, a wry smile widening on her beautiful face. "How fine an opportunity is this?"

"To strike a wicked blow against Mithral Hall?" Ad'non asked, following the reasoning.

"And to keep Gerti interested in pursuing our present course," said Donnia.

"Or to show our hand too clearly and bring the wrath of powerful enemies upon us," said the ever-cynical Kaer'lic.

"Why priestess, I fear that you have grown too fond of luxury, and too forgetting of the pleasures of chaos," Ad'non said, his growing smile matching Donnia's. "Can you really so easily allow this opportunity for fun and profit pass you by?"

Kaer'lic started to respond several times but retreated from every reply before she ever voiced it.

"I find little pleasure in dealing with the smelly orcs," the priestess said, "or with Gerti and her band, who think they are so positively superior, even to us. More pleasure would I find if we turned Obould against Gerti and let the giants and the orcs slaughter each other. Then we four could quietly kill all those left alive."

"And we would be alone up here, in abject boredom," said Ad'non.

"True enough," Kaer'lic admitted. "So be it. Let us fester this war between the dwarves and our allies. With King Bruenor out of his hole, we may indeed find an interesting course before us, but with all caution! I did not leave the Underdark to fall victim to a dwarven axe, or to the blade of a drow traitor."

The others nodded, sharing the sentiment, particularly Tos'un, who had seen so many of his fellows fall before the armies of Mithral Hall.

"I will go to Gerti and soften the blow of this present disaster," Donnia said.

"And I back to Obould," said Ad'non. "I will wait for your signal before sending the orc king to speak with the giantess."

They departed at once, eagerly, leaving Kaer'lic alone with Tos'un.

"We are winding our way into a deep chasm," the priestess observed. "If our allies betray us at the end of a dwarven spear, then our flight will by necessity be long and swift."

Tos'un nodded. He had been there once before.

Obould's every step was forced as he made his way through the caverns of Gerti's complex, very conscious of the many scowls the frost giant sentries were throwing his way. Despite Ad'non's assurances, Obould knew that the giants had been told of their losses. These creatures weren't like his own race, the orc king understood. They valued every one of their clan, every one of their kind. The frost giants would not easily dismiss the deaths of four of their kin.

When the orc king walked into Gerti's chamber, he found the giantess sitting on her stone throne, one elbow on her knee, her delicate chin in her hand, her blue eyes staring straight ahead, unblinking.

The orc walked up, stopping out of the giant's reach, fearing that Gerti would snap her hand out and throttle him. He resisted the urge to speak out about the disaster and decided that he would be better off waiting for Gerti to start the conversation.

He waited for a long, long while.

"Where are their bodies?" Gerti finally asked.

"Where they fell."

Gerti looked up at him, her eyes going even wider, as if her rage was boiling over behind them.

"My warriors can not begin to carry them," Obould quickly explained. "I will have them buried in cairns where they fell, if you desire. I thought you would wish to bring them back here."

That explanation seemed to calm Gerti considerably. She even rested back in her seat and nodded her chin at him as he finished his explanation.

"You will have your warriors lead my chosen to them."

"Course I will," said Obould.

"I was told that it is possible your son's rash actions may have brought powerful enemies upon the band," Gerti remarked.

Obould shrugged. "It is possible. I was not there."

"Your son survived?"

Obould nodded.

"He fled the fight, along with many of your kin."

There was no mistaking the accusatory edge that had come into Gerti's voice.

"They had only one of your kin with them when the battle was joined, and that giant went down fast," Obould was quick to reply, knowing that he could not let Gerti go down this road with him if he wanted to get out of that place with his head still on his shoulders. "The other three wandered off the night before without telling anyone."

From Gerti's expression, the orc recognized that he had parsed those words correctly, rightly redistributing the blame for the disaster without openly accusing the giants of any failings.

"Do we know where the dwarves went after the fight?"

"We know they did not head straight out for Mithral Hall," Obould explained. "My scouts have found no sign of their march to the south or east."

"They are still in our mountains?"

"I'm thinking that, yeah," said the orc.

"Then find them!" Gerti demanded. "I have a score to settle, and I always make it a point to pay my enemies back in full."

Obould fought the desire to let a grin widen on his face, understanding that Gerti needed this to remain solemn and serious. Still, containing the excitement building within him was no easy task. He could see from Gerti's eyes and could tell from the tone of her voice that this defeat would not hold for long, that she and her giants would become even more committed to the fight.

King Obould wondered if his dwarf counterpart had any idea of the catastrophe that was about to drop on him.

13

THERE, I SAID IT . . .

A slight shift of Torgar's head sent the heavy fist sailing past, and the dwarf wasted no time in turning around and biting the attacker hard on the forearm. His opponent, another dwarf, waved that bitten arm frantically while punching hard with the other, but tough Torgar accepted the beating and bit down harder, driving in close to lessen the impact of the blows.

Pushing, twisting, and driving on with his powerful legs, Torgar took his opponent right over a table and chair. The two of them crashed down hard, wood splintering around them.

They weren't the only dwarves in the tavern who were fighting. Fists and bottles flew wildly, foreheads pounded against foreheads, and more than one table or chair went up in the air, to come crashing down on an opponent's head.

The brawl went on and on, and the poor barkeep, Toivo Foamblower, gave up in frustration, falling back against the wall and crossing his thick forearms over his chest. His expression ranged from bemused to resigned, and he didn't get overly concerned for the damage to his establishment because he knew that the dwarves involved would be quick with reparations.

They always were when it came to taverns.

One by one the combatants left the bar, usually at the end of a foot or headfirst through the long-since shattered windows.

Toivo's grin grew as the crowd thinned to see that the one who had started it all, Torgar Hammerstriker, was still in the thick of it. That had been Toivo's prediction from the beginning. Tough Torgar almost never lost a bar brawl when the odds weren't overwhelming, and he-never ever lost when Shingles was fighting beside him.

Though not as quick as some others with his fists, the surly old Shingles knew how to wage a battle, knew how to keep his enemies off their guard. Toivo laughed aloud when one raging dwarf charged up to Shingles, raised bottle in hand.

Shingles held up one finger and put on an incredulous look that gave the attacker pause. Shingles then pointed at the upraised bottle and wagged his finger when the attacker saw that there were still some traces of beer inside.

Shingles motioned for the dwarf to pause and finish the drink. When he did, Shingles brought out his own full bottle, moved as if to take a deep swallow, then smashed it into his attacker's face, following it with a fist that laid the dwarf low.

"Well, throw 'em all out, then!" Toivo yelled at Torgar, Shingles, and a pair of others when the fight at last ended.

The four moved about, lifting semi-conscious dwarves, ally and enemy alike, and unceremoniously tossing them out the broken door.

The four remaining combatants started to make their way out then, but Toivo called to Torgar and Shingles and motioned them back to the bar where he was already setting up drinks.

"A reward for the show?" Torgar asked through fat lips.

"Ye're paying for the drinks and for a lot more than that," Toivo assured him. "Ye durned fool. Ye thinkin' to start trouble all across the city?"

"I ain't starting no trouble. I'm just sharing the trouble I'm seein'!"

"Bah!" the barkeep snorted, wiping a pile of broken glass from the bar. "What kind o' greetings did ye think Bruenor'd be getting from Mirabar? His hall's killin' our business."

"Because they're better'n us!" Torgar cried. He stopped short and brought a hand up to his stinging lips. "They're making the better armor and the better weapons," he said, more in control, and with a bit of a lisp. "The way to beat 'em is to make our own works better or to find new places to sell. The way to beat 'em is—"

"I'm not arguing yer point and not agreeing with ye, neither," Toivo interrupted, "but ye been running about shouting yer grief all over town. Ye durned fool, can ye be expectin' any less than ye're getting? Are ye thinking to raise all the dwarfs against the marchion and the council? Ye looking to start a war in Mirabar?"

"Course not."

"Then shut yer stupid mouth!" Toivo scolded. "Ye come in here tonight and start spoutin' yer anger. Ye durned fool! Ye know that half the dwarfs in here are watching their gold chests withering, and knowing well that the biggest reason for that's the reopening o' Mithral Hall. Are ye not to know that yer words aren't finding open ears?"

Torgar gave a dismissive wave and bent low to his drink, physically closing up as a reflection of his impotence against Toivo's astute observation.

"He's got a point," said Shingles beside him, and Torgar shot him a glare.

"I ain't tired o' the fighting," Shingles was quick to add. "It's just that we wasted a lot o' good brew tonight, and that can't be a good thing."

"They got me riled, is all," Torgar said, his tone suddenly contrite and a bit defeated. "Bruenor ain't no enemy, and making him one instead o' honestly trying to beat him and his Mithral Hall boys is a fool's road."

"And yerself ain't never been fond o' the folks up top. Not the marchion or the four fools that follow him about, scowling like they was some great warriors," Toivo said with more than a bit of sympathy. "Ain't that the truth?"

"If Mithral Hall was a human town, ye think the marchion and his boys would be so damned determined to beat 'em?"

"I do," Toivo answered without hesitation. "I just think Torgar Hammerstriker wouldn't care so much."

Torgar dropped his head to his arms, folded on the bar. There was truth in that, he had to admit. Somewhere deep inside him was the understanding that Bruenor and the boys from Mithral Hall were kin of the blood. They had all come from the Delzoun Clan, way back beyond the memories of the oldest dwarves. Mithral Hall, Mirabar, Felbarr . . . they were all connected by history and by blood, dwarf to dwarf. On a very basic level, it galled Torgar to think that petty arguments and commerce would come between that all-important bond.

Besides, given the evening he had spent with the visitors from Mithral Hall, Torgar had found that he honestly liked them.

"Well, I'm hopin' ye'll stop shouting so we can stop the fighting," Shingles said at length. He nudged Torgar, and gave the ringleader a wink when he looked up. "Or at least slow it down a bit. I'm not a young one anymore. This is gonna hurt in the mornin'!"

Toivo patted Torgar on the shoulder and walked off to begin his clean-up.

Torgar just lay there, head down on the bar all the night long. Thinking.

And wondering, to his own surprise, if the time was coming for him to leave Mirabar.

"Hope th' elf don't catch 'em and kill 'em tonight," Bruenor grumbled. "He'll take all the fun."

Dagnabbit fixed his king with a curious stare, trying hard to read the unreadable. There had only been a pair of tracks, after all, a couple of unfortunate orcs running scared from the rout. The last few days had been the same, chasing small groups, often just one or two, along this mountain trail or that. As Bruenor was complaining, more often than not, Drizzt, Catti-brie, Wulfgar, and Regis had come upon the fleeing creatures first and had them long dead before the main band ever caught up.

"Not many left for catching," Dagnabbit offered.

"Bah!" the dwarf king snorted, placing his empty bowl of stew on the ground beside him. "More'n half the hunnerd runned off and we ain't catched a dozen!"

"But every day's sending them that's left into deep holes. We ain't to chase 'em in there."

"Why ain't we?"

The simple question was quite revealing, of course, for Bruenor said it with a raging fire behind his fierce eyes, an eagerness that could not be denied.

"Why're ye out here, me king?" Dagnabbit quietly asked. "Yer dark elf friend and his little band can be doin' all that's left to be done, and ye're knowing it, too!"

"We got Shallows to get to and warn, along with th' other towns."

"Another task that Drizzt'd be better at, and quicker at, without us."

"Nah, the folk'd chase off the damned elf if he tried to warn 'em."

Dagnabbit shook his head. "Most about are knowing Drizzt Do'Urden, and if not, he'd just send Catti-brie, Wulfgar, or the little one in to warn 'em. Ye know the raiding band's no more, though more'n half did run off. Ye know they're scattering, running for deep holes, and won't be threatening anyone anytime soon."

"Ye're figuring that the raiding band's all there was," Bruenor argued.

"If there's more than that, then all the more reason for yerself to be back in Mithral Hall," said Dagnabbit, "and ye're knowin' that, too. So why're ye here, me king? Why're ye really here?"

Bruenor settled himself squarely on the log he had taken as a seat and fixed Dagnabbit with a serious and determined stare.

"Would ye rather be out here, with the wind in yer beard and yer axe in yer hands, with an orc afore ye to chop down, or would ye rather be in Mithral Hall, speakin' to the pretty emissaries from Silverymoon or Sundabar, or arguin' with some Mirabarran merchant about tradin' rights? Which would ye rather be doin', Dagnabbit?"

The other dwarf swallowed hard at the unexpected and direct question. There was a political answer to be made, of course, but one that Bruenor knew, and Dagnabbit knew, would ultimately be a lie.

"I'd be beside me king, because that's what I'm to do . . ." the young dwarf started to dodge, but Bruenor was hearing none of it.

"*Rather*, I asked ye. Which would ye rather? Ain't ye got no preferences?"

"My duty—"

"I ain't askin' for yer duty!" Bruenor dismissed him with a wave of his hand. "When ye're wanting to talk honestly, then ye come talk to me again," he blustered. "Until then, go and fetch me another bowl o' fresher stew, cuz this pot's all crusty. Do yer duty, ye danged golem!"

Bruenor lifted his empty bowl and presented it to Dagnabbit, and the younger dwarf, after a short pause, did take it. He didn't get up immediately, though.

"I'd rather be out here," Dagnabbit admitted. "And I'd take a fight with an orc over a day at the forge."

Bruenor's smile erupted beneath his flaming red beard.

"Then why're ye asking me what ye're asking me?" he asked. "Are ye thinkin' that I'm not akin to yerself? Just because I'm the king don't make me wanting any different from any other Battlehammer."

"Ye're fearing to go home," Dagnabbit dared to say. "Ye're looking at it as the end o' yer road."

Bruenor sat back and shrugged, then noticed a pair of purple eyes staring at him from the brush to the side.

"And I'm still thinking that I'm wanting more stew," he said.

Dagnabbit stared at him hard for a few moments, chewing his lip and nodding.

"I'm hoping that the durned elf don't kill 'em all tonight meself," he said with a grin, and he rose to leave.

As soon as Dagnabbit had walked off, Drizzt Do'Urden moved out of the brush and took a seat at Bruenor's side.

"Already dead, ain't they?" Bruenor asked.

"Catti-brie is a fine shot," the drow answered.

"Well, go and find some more."

"There will always be more," the drow replied. "We could spend all our lives hunting orcs in these mountains." He held a sly look over Bruenor until the dwarf looked back at him. "But you know that, of course."

"First Dagnabbit and now yerself?" Bruenor asked. "What're ye wantin' me to say, elf?"

"What's in your heart. Nothing more. When first we started on the road, you went with great anticipation, and a skip in your determined stride. You were seeing Gauntlgrym then, or at least the promise of a grand adventure, the grandest of them all."

"Still am."

"No," Drizzt observed. "Our encounter in Fell Pass showed you the trouble your plans would soon enough encounter. You know that once you get back to Mithral Hall, you'll have a hard time leaving again. You know they will try to keep you there."

"Few guesses, elf?" Bruenor said with a wave of his hand. "Or are ye just thinkin' ye know more than ye know?"

"Not a guess, but an observation," Drizzt replied. "Every step of the way out of Icewind Dale has been heavier than the previous one for Bruenor Battlehammer—every step except those that temporarily turn us aside from our destination, like the journey to Mirabar and this chase through the mountains."

Bruenor leaned forward and grabbed Dagnabbit's empty bowl. He gave it a shake, dunked it in the nearly-empty stew pot, then brought it in and licked the thick broth from his stubby fingers.

"Course, in Mithral Hall I might be getting me stew served to me in fine bowls, on fine platters, and with fine napkins."

"And you never liked napkins."

Bruenor shrugged, his expression showing Drizzt that he was certainly catching on.

"Appoint a steward, then, and at once upon your return," the drow offered. "Be a king on the road, expanding the influence of his people, and searching for an even more ancient and greater lost kingdom. Mithral Hall can run itself. If you did not believe that, you never would have gone to Icewind Dale in the first place."

"It's not so easy."

"You are the king. You define what a king is. This duty will trap you, and that is your fear, but it will only do so if you allow yourself to be trapped by it. In the end, Bruenor Battlehammer alone decides the fate of Bruenor Battlehammer."

"I'm thinkin' ye're making it a bit too easy there, elf," the dwarf replied, "but I'm not saying ye're wrong."

He ended with a sigh, and drowned it in a huge gulp of hot stew.

"Do you know what you want?" Drizzt asked. "Or are you a bit confused, my friend?"

"Do ye remember when we first went huntin' for Mithral Hall?" Bruenor asked. "Remember me trickin' ye by makin' ye think I was on me dyin' bed?"

Drizzt gave a little laugh—it was a scene he would never forget. They, leading the folk of Ten-Towns, had just won victory over the minions of Akar Kessell, who possessed the Crystal Shard. Drizzt had been taken in to Bruenor, who seemed on his deathbed—but only so that he could trick the drow into agreeing to help him find Mithral Hall.

"I did not need much convincing," Drizzt admitted.

"I thought two things when we found the place, ye know," said Bruenor. "Oh, me heart was pumping, I tell ye! To see me home again . . . to avenge me ancestors. I'm tellin' ye, elf, riding that dragon down to the darkness was the greatest single moment o' me life, though I was thinkin' it was the last moment o' me life when it was happening!"

Drizzt nodded and knew what was coming.

"And what else were you thinking when we found Mithral Hall?" he prompted, because he knew that Bruenor had to say this out loud, had to admit it openly.

"Thrilled, I was, I tell ye truly! But there was something else . . ." He shook his head and sighed again. "When we got back from the southland and me clan retook our home, a bit o' sadness found me heart."

"Because you came to realize that it was the adventure and the road more than the goal."

"Ye're knowin' it, too!" Bruenor blurted.

"Why do you think that I, and Catti-brie, were quick to leave Mithral Hall after the drow war? We are all alike, I fear, and it will likely be the end of us all."

"But what a way to go, eh elf?"

Drizzt gave a laugh, and Bruenor was fast to join in, and it seemed to Drizzt as if a great weight had been lifted off the dwarf's shoulders. But the chuckling from Bruenor stopped abruptly, a serious expression clouding his face.

"What o' me girl?" he asked. "What're ye to do if she gets herself killed on the road? How're ye not to be blaming yerself forever more?"

"It is something that I have thought of often," Drizzt admitted.

"Ye seen what it done to Wulfgar," said Bruenor. "Made him forget his place and spend all his time looking out for her."

"And that was his mistake."

"So, ye're saying ye don't care?"

Drizzt laughed aloud.

"Do not lead me to places I did not intend to go," he retorted. "I care— of course I do—but you tell me this, Bruenor Battlehammer, is there anyone in all the world who loves Catti-brie, or Wulfgar, more than yourself? Will you then put them in Mithral Hall and hold them safely there?

"Of course you would not," Drizzt continued. "You trust in her and let her run. You let her fight and have watched her get hurt—only recently. Not much of a father, if you ask me."

"Who asked ye?"

"Well, if you did . . ."

"If I did and ye telled me that, I'd kick ye in yer skinny elf arse!"

"If you did and I told you that, you'd kick empty air and wonder why a hundred blows were raining upon your thick head."

Bruenor scoffed and tossed his bowl to the ground, then pulled off his one-horned helm and began rapping hard on his head.

"Bah! Ye'd need more'n a hunnerd to get through this skull, elf!"

Drizzt smiled and didn't disagree.

Dagnabbit returned then to find his king in a fine mood. The younger dwarf looked at Drizzt, but the drow merely nodded and grinned all the wider.

"If we're wantin' to make Shallows in two days, we gotta set straight out," Dagnabbit remarked. "No more chasin' orcs after this group's dead."

"Then no more chasing orcs," said Drizzt.

Dagnabbit nodded, seeming neither surprised nor upset.

"Rushing me home, still," Bruenor said with a shake of his head, broth flying from his wild beard. He brought a hand up and wiped the beard down.

"Or we might be using Shallows as the front base," Dagnabbit offered. "Put a link line to Pwent an' his boys at both camps outside o' Mithral Hall, and spend the summer runnin' the mountains near to Shallows. The folks'll appreciate that, I'm thinking."

A look of astonishment melted into a smile on Bruenor's face.

"And I'm liking the way ye're thinking!" he said as he took the bowl for his third helping. "Making sure there's not too much for Rumblebelly when he gets in," Bruenor offered between gulps. "Can't let him get too fat again if we're walkin' mountain roads, now can we?"

Drizzt settled back comfortably and was quite pleased for his dwarf friend. It was one thing to know your heart, another thing to admit it.

And something altogether different to allow yourself to follow it.

Torgar walked his post on Mirabar's northern wall, a slight limp in his stride from a swollen knee he had suffered in the previous night's escapade. The wind was up strong this day, blowing sand all about the dwarf, but it was warm enough so that Torgar had loosened his heavy breastplate.

He was well aware of the many looks, scowls mostly, coming at him from the other sentries. His actions with Bruenor had resulted in downward spiral, with arguments growing across the city and with many fists being raised. Torgar was tired of it all. All he wanted was to be left alone to his duties, to walk the wall without conversation, without trouble.

When he noted the approach of a well-groomed dwarf wearing bright robes, he knew he wouldn't get his wish.

"Torgar Hammerstriker!" Councilor Agrathan Hardhammer called.

He moved to the base of the ladder leading to the parapet, hiked up his robes and began to climb.

Torgar kept walking the other way, looking out over the wall and feigning ignorance, but when Agrathan called again, more loudly, he realized that to delay would only bring him more frustration.

He paused and leaned his strong, bruised hands on the wall, staring out to the empty, open land.

Agrathan moved up beside him, and similarly leaned on the wall.

"Another battle last night," the councilor stated.

"When they're askin' for a fist, they're getting a fist," Torgar replied.

"And how many are ye to fight?"

"How many're needin' a good kick?"

He looked at Agrathan, and saw that the councilor was not amused.

"Yer actions're tearing Mirabar apart. Is that what ye're looking to do?"

"I'm not looking to do anything," Torgar insisted, and honestly. He turned to Agrathan, his eyes narrowing. "If me speaking me mind's doing what ye say, then the problem's been there afore I speaked it."

Agrathan settled more comfortably against the wall and seemed to relax, as if he was not disagreeing.

"Many of us have been shaking our heads at the Mithral Hall problem. Ye know that. We're all wishin' that our biggest rivals weren't Battlehammer dwarves! But they are. That's the way of it, and ye know it, and if ye keep pressing that point into everyone's nose, ye're to bend those noses out of shape."

"The rivalry and the arguin' are as much our own fault as the Battlehammers'," Torgar reminded. "Might that a deal benefiting us both could be fashioned, but how're we to know unless someone tries?"

"Yer words aren't without merit," the councilor agreed. "It's been suggested and talked about at the Sparkling Stones."

"Where most o' the councilors ain't dwarfs," Torgar remarked, and Agrathan fixed him with a cold stare.

"The dwarves are spoken for, and their thoughts are heard at council."

Torgar knew from the dwarf's look and icy tone that he had hit a nerve with Agrathan, a proud and long-serving councilor. He thought for a moment to take back his bold and callous statement, or at least to exclude his present company, but he didn't. He felt as if he was being carried away by an inner voice that was growing independent of his common sense.

"When ye joined the Axe of Mirabar, you took an oath," Agrathan said. "Are ye remembering that oath, Torgar Hammerstriker?"

Now it was Torgar's turn to issue a cold stare.

"The oath was to serve the Marchion of Mirabar, not the King of Mithral Hall. Ye might be wise to think on that a bit."

The councilor patted Torgar on the shoulder—many seemed to be doing that lately—and took his leave.

Torgar remembered his oath and weighed that oath against the realities of present day Mirabar.

14

THEY THOUGHT THEY
HAD SEEN IT ALL

"Well, ain't this a keg o' beer in a commode," Ivan grumbled.

He was moving around the small lea that the elves were using as a temporary prison for the two intruders. Using some magic that Ivan did not understand, the moon elves had coaxed the trees around the lea in close together, blocking all exits with a nearly solid wall of trunks.

Ivan, of course, was none too happy with that. Pikel reclined in the middle of the field, hands tucked comfortably behind his head as he lay on his back, staring up at the stars. His sandals were off and the contented dwarf waggled his stubby toes happily.

"If they hadn't taked me axe, I'd be making a trail or ten!" Ivan blustered.

Pikel giggled and waggled his toes.

"Shut yer mouth," Ivan fumed, standing with hands on hips and staring defiantly at the tree wall.

He blinked a moment later and rubbed his eyes in disbelief as one of the trees drifted aside, leaving a clear path beyond. Ivan paused, expecting the elves to enter through the breach, but the moments slipped past with no sign the their captors. The dwarf hopped about, started for the break, then skidded to a stop and swung around when he heard his brother giggling.

"Ye did that," Ivan accused.

"Hee hee hee."

"Well if ye could do that, then why've we been sitting here for two days?"

Pikel propped himself on his elbows and shrugged.

"Let's go!"

"Uh uh," said Pikel.

Ivan stared at him incredulously. "Why not?"

Pikel hopped to his feet and jumped all around, putting a finger to pursed lips and saying "*Shhhhhh!*"

"Who ye shushing?" Ivan asked, his expression going from angry to confused. "Ye're talking to the damned trees," he realized.

Pikel looked at him and shrugged.

"Ye're meaning that the damned trees'll tell the damned elfs if we walk outta here?"

Pikel nodded enthusiastically.

"Well, shut 'em up!"

Pikel shrugged helplessly.

"Ye can move 'em, and ye can walk through 'em, but ye can't shut 'em up?"

Pikel shrugged again.

Ivan stomped a boot hard on the ground. "Well, let 'em tell the elfs! And let them elfs try to catch me!"

Pikel put his hands on his hips and cocked his head to the side, his expression doubtful.

"Yeah, yeah," Ivan called to him, waving his hand and not wanting to hear any of it.

Of course he had no weapon. Of course he had no armor. Of course he had no idea of where he was or of how to get out of there. Of course he wouldn't likely get fifty feet into the forest before being recaptured, probably painfully.

But none of that really mattered to the outraged dwarf. He just wanted to do something, do *anything*, to stick his finger in the eyes of his captors. That was the way of dwarves, after all, and of Ivan beyond the norm for his taciturn race. It was better to head-butt your enemy, even if he was wearing a full-faced plated helmet, even if it was spiked, than to stand helplessly before him.

Determined, Ivan strode through the Pikel-made gap and down the forest trail.

Pikel sighed and moved to retrieve his sandals. Hearing a commotion beyond the lea, he merely shrugged yet again and fell back to the grass and stared up at the stars. Perfectly content.

"Never would I have believed that a dwarf could move a tree without using an axe," Innovindil remarked.

She stood at Tarathiel's side, on a low branch overlooking the lea, observing the brothers.

"He truly is possessed of druidic magic," Tarathiel agreed. "How is that possible?"

Innovindil giggled. "Perhaps the dwarves are moving to a higher state of consciousness, though it is hard to believe when you consider that one as the source."

Looking at Pikel and his waggling toes, Tarathiel found it hard to disagree with the last part of her statement.

The pair watched silently as Ivan stormed out of the meadow then patiently waited the few minutes it took for the struggling dwarf to be reunited forcibly with his brother, a trio of elves dragging him back.

"This could get dangerous," Innovindil remarked.

"We still can't be sure of their intentions," Tarathiel replied.

She had been pushing him all day to resolve the issue with the dwarves, leaning heavily in favor of escorting them to the edges of the Moonwood and letting them go.

"Then test him," Innovindil said, her tone showing that she had just found a revelation. "If he is a druid, as he seems, then there is one way to prove it. Let Pikel Bouldershoulder find his judge at Montolio's grove."

Tarathiel stroked his thin chin, a smile growing as he considered the words. Perhaps Innovindil was on to something, which really didn't surprise Tarathiel when he thought about it. Ever had Innovindil been the farsighted one, finding roads out of the darkest dilemmas.

He looked to her appreciatively, but she was eyeing the field, concern growing on her fair face. She nodded his way and bade him to follow, then hopped down from the branch and moved onto the field, where it looked like the confrontation between the yellow-bearded Bouldershoulder and the three elves might be about to explode.

"Hold fast, Ivan Bouldershoulder," she called, and the attention of all five turned to her. "Your ire is not justified."

"Bah!" the dwarf snorted, so predictably. "Ye're locking me in, elf? How'd ya think I'd take it?"

"And I am certain that if one of us went into your homeland, he would find himself welcomed with open arms," came the sarcastic reply.

"Probably would," Ivan retorted, offering a snort at Pikel, who merely giggled. "Cadderly's always been a soft one, even for a human!"

"Your *dwarven* homeland," the quick-on-her-feet Innovindil clarified.

"Nah," Ivan had to agree, "but why would an elf want to go there?"

"Why would a pair of dwarves walk out of a tree?" came the reply.

Ivan started to argue, but realized the futility of that.

"Point for yerself," he agreed.

"And how does a dwarf coax a tree to move aside?" the elf asked, looking at Pikel.

"Doo-dad," came the giggling response, with Pikel poking his thumb into his chest.

"Well, that is a common sight," Tarathiel said sarcastically.

"Nothing common about that one," Ivan agreed.

"So please excuse our confusion," said Innovindil. "We do not wish to hold you captive, Ivan Bouldershoulder, but neither can we readily dismiss you and your curious brother. You must appreciate that you have intruded into our home, and the security of that home remains above all else."

"I'll give ye that point, too," the dwarf replied, "but ye gotta be appreciatin' that I got better things to do than sit here and watch the stars. Damned things don't even move!"

"Oh, but they do," Innovindil enthusiastically replied, thinking she may have found a commonality, a way to thin the ice, if not break it all together.

Her hopes only grew when Pikel hopped up and gave an assenting squeal.

"Some do, at least," the elf explained.

She moved closer to Ivan and pointed to one particularly bright star, low on the horizon, just above the tree line. She continued for just a moment, until she took the time to look at Ivan and see him staring at her incredulously, hands on his hips.

"I think ye're missin' me point," he said dryly.

"True enough," the elf admitted.

"It ain't like we ain't been with elfs afore," Ivan explained. "Fought aside a whole flock o' them in Shilmista Forest, chasing off the orcs and goblins. They was glad for me and me brother!"

"Me brudder!" Pikel agreed.

"And perhaps we will come to be, as well," said Innovindil. "In truth, I predict exactly that, but I beg your patience. This is too important for us to make any hasty choices."

"Well, ain't that like an elf," Ivan replied with a resigned, but clearly accepting, sigh. "Seen one in Carradoon, gone to market to buy some wine. Took her time, she did, moving front to back and back to front across the winery, then course she bought the first bottle she'd seen."

"And that elf enjoyed the experience of the purchase, as we wish to enjoy the experience of learning about Ivan and Pikel Bouldershoulder," Innovindil explained.

"Ye'd be learning more if ye'd let us off this stupid field."

"Perhaps, and perhaps soon."

As she finished Innovindil glanced at Tarathiel, who obviously wasn't sharing her generous thoughts. She gave him a hard nudge in the ribs.

"We shall see," was all that he would admit, and that grimly.

Thibbledorf Pwent kicked a stone, launching it many feet through the air.

"Bruenor's expecting better of ye," scolded Cordio Muffinhead, the cleric who had accompanied the wounded back to Mithral Hall.

They had found Pwent and the Gutbuster Brigade camped along the high ground north of Keeper's Dale, the battlerager having gone back out after escorting the main force into Mithral Hall.

What a sight that meeting had been, with Cordio and the others waving frantically to slow down the insane charge of Pwent and his boys. The relief had been palpable when Cordio had at last been able to explain that Bruenor and the others were fine and were moving along a different and roundabout course on their way back to Mithral Hall, checking in with the various settlements, as a good king must now and again.

"If he's knowin' me at all, then he should be knowin' that I'm about to set off to find the fool!" Pwent argued.

"He's knowing that ye're a loyal warrior, who's to do what ye're told to do!" Cordio yelled back at him.

Pwent hopped aside and did a three-step to another stone, kicking it with all his strength. This one was much larger, though, and not quite detached from the ground, and so it hardly moved. Pwent did well to hide his newly-acquired limp.

"Ye got two camps to organize," Cordio said sternly. "Quit breakin' yer toes and get yer runners to Mithral Hall. Ye build a camp here and get one set up on the Surbrin, north o' the mines."

Pwent spat and grumbled, but he nodded and went to work, barking orders that sent the Gutbusters scrambling. That same day, what had been a casual camp awaiting Bruenor's return was transformed into a small fortress with walls of piled stones, perched on the north side of a mountain north of Keeper's Dale.

The next morning, two hundred warriors left Mithral Hall, heading north to join up with the Gutbusters, while at the same time a hundred and fifty warriors moved out of Mithral Hall's eastern gate and marched north along the banks of the Surbrin, laden with supplies for constructing the second forward outpost.

Thibbledorf Pwent immediately set his Gutbusters into a liaison mode, working the direct trails between the two camps.

It tormented Pwent to stay so far south and wait, but he did his job, though he continually sent scouting parties to the north and northeast, searching for some sign of his beloved, and absent, king. It remained foremost in his thoughts that Bruenor wouldn't have ordered the establishment of advanced camps unless he believed they might be needed.

That only made the waiting all the more unsettling.

"He truly is a druid?" Tarathiel asked, hardly believing his ears as a pair of his clan reported the news to him that Pikel's spells were not some trick, that the dwarf did indeed seem to have druidic magic about him.

Beside him, Innovindil could hardly contain her grin. She was truly enjoying these unexpected guests, and indeed, she had been spending quite a bit of time with Ivan, the surly one, who was about as perfectly dwarflike as any dwarf she had ever seen. She and Ivan had swapped many fine tales over the past few days, and though he remained a prisoner it was fairly obvious that Innovindil's contact with Ivan had brightened his mood and lessened the trouble he was causing.

Still, Tarathiel thought her a fool for bothering.

"He prays, sincerely so, to Mielikki," said one of the observers, "and there can be no doubt of his magical abilities, many of which could not be replicated by any cleric of a dwarf god."

"It makes little sense," Tarathiel remarked.

"Pikel Bouldershoulder makes little sense," said the other, "but he is what he appears to be, by all that we can discern. He is a woodland priest, a 'Doo-dad,' as he himself puts it."

"How powerful is his magic?" asked Tarathiel, who had always held druids in great respect.

The two observers looked at each other, their expressions showing clearly that this was a question they had feared.

"It is difficult to discern," said the first. "Pikel's magic is . . . sporadic."

Tarathiel looked at him curiously.

"He seems to throw it as he needs it," the other tried to explain. "Minor dweomers, mostly, though every now and again he seems possessed of a quite potent spell, one that would only be expected of a high-ranking druid, their equivalent of a high priest."

"It seems almost as if he has caught the goddess's fancy," said the first. "As if Mielikki, or one of her minions, has taken a direct interest in him and is watching over him."

Tarathiel paused a moment to digest the information, then said, "You still have not answered my question."

"He is no more dangerous than his brother, certainly," the first replied. "Surely no threat to us or to the Moonwood."

"You are certain?"

"We are," answered the second.

"Perhaps it is time for you to speak with the dwarves," Innovindil offered.

Tarathiel paused again, thinking. "Do you think Sunrise will bear him?" he asked.

"To Montolio's grove?"

Tarathiel nodded. "Let us see if the image of Mielikki's symbol will look kindly upon this 'Doo-dad' dwarf."

PART THREE
WHERE ONE ROAD ENDS

I have come to view my journey through life as the convergence of three roads. First is the simple physical path, through my training in House Do'Urden, to Melee-Magthere, the drow school for warriors, and my continued tutelage under my father, Zaknafein. It was he who prepared me for the challenges, he who taught me the movements to transcend the basics of the drow martial art, indeed to think creatively about any fight. Zaknafein's technique was more about training one's muscles to respond, quickly and in perfect harmony, to the calls of the mind, and even more importantly, the calls of the imagination.

Improvisation, not rote responses, is what separates a warrior from a weapons master.

The road of that physical journey out of Menzoberranzan, through the wilds of the Underdark, along the mountainous trails that led me to Montolio, and from there to Icewind Dale and the loved ones I now share, has intertwined often with the second road. They are inevitably linked.

For the second road was the emotional path, the growth I have come to find in understanding and appreciation, not only of what I desire to be and to have, but of the needs of others, and the acceptance that their way of looking at the world may not coincide with my own. My second road started in confusion as the world of Menzoberranzan came clear to me and made little sense to my views. Again it was Zaknafein who crystallized the beginning steps of this road, as he showed me that there was indeed truth in that which I knew in my heart—but could not quite accept in my thoughts, perhaps—to be true. I credit Catti-brie, above all others, with furthering this journey. From the beginning, she knew to look past the reputation of my heritage and judge me for my actions and my heart, and that was such a freeing experience for me that I could not help but accept the philosophy and embrace it. In doing so I have come to appreciate so many people of various races and various cultures and various viewpoints. From each I learn, and in learning, with such an open mind, I grow.

Now, after all these adventurous years, I have come to understand that there is indeed a third road. For a long time, I thought it an extension of the second, but now I view this path as independent.

It is a subtle distinction, perhaps, but not so in importance.

This third journey began the day I was born, as it does for all reasoning beings. It lay somewhat dormant for me for many years, buried beneath the demands of Menzoberranzan and my own innate understanding that the other two paths had to be sorted before the door to this third could truly open.

I opened that door in the home of Montolio deBrouchee, in Mooshie's Grove, when I found Mielikki, when I discovered that which was in my heart and soul. That was the first step on the spiritual road, the path more of mystery than of experience, more of questions than of answers, more of faith and hope than of realization. It is the road that opens only when the needed steps have been taken along the other two. It is the path that requires the shortest steps, perhaps, but is surely the most difficult, at least at first. If the three paths are each divergent and many-forked at their beginning, and indeed, along the way—the physical is usually determined by need, the emotional by want, the spiritual—?

It is not so clear a way, and I fear that for many it never becomes so.

For myself, I know that I am on the right path, but not because I have yet found the answers. I know my way is true because I have found the questions, specifically how, why, and where.

How did I, did anyone, get here? Was it by a course of natural occurrences, or the designs of a creator or creators, or are they indeed one and the same?

In either case, why am I here? Is there indeed even a reason, or is it all pure chance and randomness?

And perhaps the most important question to any reasoning being, where will my journey take me when I have shrugged off this mortal coil?

I view this last and most important road as ultimately private. These are questions that cannot be answered to me by anyone other than me. I see many people, most people, finding their "answers" in the sermons of others. Words sanctified by age or the perceived wisdom of authors who provide a comfortable ending to their spiritual journey, provide answers to truly troubling questions. No, not an ending, but a pause, awaiting the resumption once this present experience of life as we know it ends.

Perhaps I am being unfair to the various flocks. Perhaps many within have asked themselves the questions and have found their personal answers, then found those of similar ilk with whom to share their revelations and comfort. If that is the case, if it is not a matter of simple indoctrination, then I envy and admire those who have advanced along their spiritual road farther than I.

For myself, I have found Mielikki, though I still have no definitive manifestation of that name in mind. And far from a pause or the ending of my journey, my discovery of Mielikki has only given me the direction I needed to ask those questions of myself in the first place. Mielikki provides me comfort, but the answers, ultimately, come from within, from that part of myself that I feel akin to the tenets of Mielikki as Montolio described them to me.

The greatest epiphany of my life came along this last and most important road: the understanding that all the rest of it, emotional and physical—and material—is naught but a platform. All of our accomplishments in the external are diminished many times over if they do not serve to turn us inward. There and only there lies our meaning, and in truth, part of the answer to the three questions is the understanding to ask them in the first place, and more than that, to recognize their penultimate importance in the course of reason.

The guiding signs of the spiritual journey will rarely be obvious, I believe, for the specific questions found along the road are often changing, and sometimes seemingly unanswerable. Even now, when all seems aright, I am faced with the puzzle of Ellifain and the sadness of that loss. And though I feel as if I am on the greatest adventure of my life with Catti-brie, there are many questions that remain with me concerning our relationship. I try to live in the here and now with her, yet at some point she and I will have to look longer down our shared path. And both of us, I think, fear what we see.

I have to hold faith that things will clarify, that I will find the answers I need.

I have always loved the dawn. I still sit and watch every one, if my situation permits. The sun stings my eyes less now, and less

with each rising, and perhaps that is some signal that it, as a repre-
sentation of the spiritual, has begun to flow more deeply into my
heart, my soul, and my understanding of it all.

That, of course, is my hope.

–Drizzt Do'Urden

15

INTOLERANCE

"Ye're really meaning to do this?" Shingles asked Torgar when he found his friend, fresh off his watch, at his modest home in the Mirabar Undercity, stuffing his most important belongings into a large sack.

"Ye knowed I was."

"I knowed ye was talking about it," Shingles corrected. "Didn't think yer brain was rattled enough for ye to actually be doin' it."

"Bah!" Torgar snorted, coming up from his packing to look his friend in the eye. "What choice are they leavin' to me? Agrathan comin' to me on the wall just to tell me to shut me mouth . . . Shut me mouth! I been fightin' for the marchion, for Mirabar, for three hunnerd years. I got more scars than Agrathan, Elastul, and all four o' his private guards put together. Earned every one o' them scars, I did, and now I'm to stand quiet and hear the scolding of Agrathan, and that on me watch, with th' other sentries all lookin' and listenin'?"

"And where're ye to go?" Shingles asked. "Mithral Hall?"

"Yep."

"Where ye'll be welcomed with a big hug and a bottle o' ale?" came the sarcastic reply.

"King Bruenor's not me enemy."

"And not near the friend ye're thinkin'," Shingles argued. "He's to be wonderin' what bringed ye there, and he'll think ye a spy."

It was a logical argument, but Torgar was shaking his head with every word. Even if Shingles proved right on this point, the potential consequences still seemed preferable to Torgar than his present intolerable situation. He was getting up in years and remained the last of the Hammerstriker line, a situation he was hoping to soon enough correct. Given all that he had learned over the last few tendays of King Bruenor, and more importantly, of his own beloved Mirabar, he was thinking that any children he might sire would be better served growing up among Clan Battlehammer.

Perhaps it would take Torgar months, even years, to win the confidence of Bruenor's people, but so be it.

He stuffed the last of his items into the sack and hoisted the bulging bag over his shoulder, turning for the door. To his surprise, Shingles presented him a mug of ale, then held up his own in toast.

"To a road full o' monsters ye can kill!" the older dwarf said.

Torgar banged his mug against the other.

"I'll be clearing it for yerself," he remarked.

Shingles gave a little laugh and took a deep drink.

Torgar knew that his response to the toast was purely polite. Shingles's situation in Mirabar was very different than his own. The old dwarf was the patriarch of a large clan. Uprooting them for a journey to Mithral Hall would be no easy task.

"Ye're to be missed, Torgar Hammerstriker," the old dwarf replied. "And the potters and glass-blowers're sure to be losin' business, not having to replace all the jugs and mugs ye're breakin' in every tavern in town."

Torgar laughed, took another sip, handed the mug back to Shingles, and continued for the door. He paused just once, to turn and offer his friend a look of sincere gratitude, and to drop his free hand on Shingles's shoulder in a sincere pat.

He went out, drawing more than a few stares as he moved along the main thoroughfare of the Undercity, past dozens and dozens of dwarves. Hammers stopped ringing at the forges he passed. All the dwarves of Mirabar knew about Torgar's recent run-ins with the authorities, about the many fights, about his stubborn insistence that the visiting King Bruenor had been badly mistreated.

To see him determinedly striding toward the ladders leading to the overcity with a huge sack on his back. . . .

Torgar didn't turn to regard any of them. This was his choice and his journey. He hadn't asked anyone to join him, beyond his remark to Shingles a moment before, nor did he expect any overt support. He understood the magnitude of it all and quite clearly. Here he was, of a fine and reputable family who had served in Mirabar for centuries, walking away. No dwarf would undertake such an act lightly. To the bearded folk, the hearth and home were the cornerstone of their existence.

By the time he reached the lifts, Torgar had several dwarves following him, Shingles included. He heard their whispers—some of support, some calling him crazy—but he did not respond in any way.

When he reached the overcity, the late afternoon sun shining pale and thin, he found that word of his trek had apparently preceded him, for a substantial group had assembled, human and dwarf alike. They followed him toward the eastern gate with their eyes, if not their feet. Most of the remarks on the surface were less complimentary toward the wayward dwarf. Torgar heard the words "traitor" and "fool" more than a few times.

He didn't react. He had expected and already gone through all of this in his thoughts before he had stuffed the first of his clothes into the sack.

It didn't matter, he reminded himself, because once he crossed out the eastern gate, he'd likely never see or speak with any of these folks ever again.

That thought nearly halted him in his walk.

Nearly.

The dwarf replayed his conversation with Agrathan over and over in his mind, using it to bolster his resolve, to remind himself that he was indeed doing the right thing, that he wasn't forsaking Mirabar so much as Mirabar, in mistreating King Bruenor, and in scolding any who dared befriend the visiting leader, had forsaken him. This was not the robust and proud city of his ancestors, Torgar had decided. This was not a city determined to lead through example. This was a city on the decline. One more determined to bring down their rivals through deceit and sabotage than to elevate themselves above those who would vie with them for markets

Just before he reached the gate, where a pair of dwarf guards stood looking at him incredulously and a pair of human guards stood scowling at him, Torgar was hailed by a familiar voice.

"Do not be doing this," Agrathan advised, running up beside the stern-faced dwarf.

"Don't ye be tryin' to stop me."

"There is more at stake here than one dwarf deciding to move," the councilor tried to explain. "Ye understand this, don't ye? Ye're knowing that all your kinfolk are watching ye and that your actions are starting dangerous whispering among our people?"

Torgar stopped abruptly and turned his head toward the frantic Agrathan. He wanted to comment on the dwarf's accent, which was leaning more toward the human way of speaking than the dwarven. He found it curiously fitting that Agrathan, the liaison, the mediator, seemed to speak with two distinct voices.

"Might be past time the dwarfs o' Mirabar started asking them questions ye're so fearin'."

Agrathan shook his head doubtfully, gave a shrug and a resigned sigh.

Torgar held the stare for a moment longer, then turned and stomped toward the door, not even pausing to consider the expressions of the four guards standing there, or the multitude of folks, human and dwarf alike, who were following him, the horde moving right up to the gate before stopping as one.

One brave soul yelled out, "Moradin's blessings to ye, Torgar Hammerstriker!"

A few others yelled out less complimentary remarks.

Torgar just kept walking, putting the setting sun at his back.

"Predictable fool," Djaffar of the Hammers remarked to the soldiers beside him, all of them astride heavily armored war-horses.

They sat behind the concealment of many strewn rocks on a high bluff to the northeast of Mirabar's eastern gate, from which a lone figure had emerged, walking proudly and determinedly down the road.

Djaffar and his contingent weren't surprised. They had heard of the exodus only a few moments before Torgar had climbed the ladder out of the Undercity, but they had long-ago prepared for just such an eventuality. Thus, they had ridden out quietly through the north gate, while all eyes had been on the dwarf marching toward the eastern one. A roundabout route had brought them to this position to sit and wait.

"If it were up to me, I'd kill him here on the road and let the vultures have his rotting flesh," Djaffar told the others. "And good enough for the traitor! But Marchion Elastul's softer in the heart—his one true weakness—and so you understand your role here?"

In response, three of the riders looked to the fourth, who held up a strong net.

"You give him one chance to surrender. Only one," Djaffar explained.

The four nodded their understanding.

"When, Hammer Djaffar?" one of them asked.

"Patience," the seasoned leader counseled. "Let him get far from the gate, out of sight and out of their hearing. We have not come out here to start a riot, but only to prevent a traitor from bringing all of our secrets to our enemies."

The grim faces looking back at Djaffar assured him that these hand-picked warriors understood their role, and the importance of it.

They caught up to Torgar a short while later, with dusk settling thick about the land. The dwarf was sitting on a rock, rubbing his sore feet and shaking the stones out of his boots, when the four riders swiftly approached. He started to jump up, even reached for his great axe, but then, apparently recognizing the riders for who they were, he just sat back down and assumed a defiant pose.

The four warriors charged up and encircled him, their trained mounts bristling with eagerness.

A moment later, up rode Djaffar. Torgar gave a snort, seeming hardly surprised.

"Torgar Hammerstriker," Djaffar announced. "By the edict of Marchion Elastul Raurym, I declare you expatriated from Mirabar."

"Already done that meself," the dwarf replied.

"It is your intention to continue along the eastern road to Mithral Hall and the court of King Bruenor Battlehammer?"

"Well, I'm not for thinking that King Bruenor's got the time for seein' me, but if he asked, I'd be goin' to see him, yes."

It was all said so casually, so matter-of-factly, that the faces of the five men tightened with anger, which seemed to please Torgar all the more.

"In that event, you are guilty of treason to the crown."

"Treason?" Torgar huffed. "Ye're declarin' a war on Mithral Hall, are ye?"

"They are our known rivals."

"That don't make me goin' there treason."

"Espionage, then!" Djaffar yelled. "Surrender now!"

Torgar studied him carefully for a moment, showing no emotion and no indication of what might happen next. He did glance over at his heavy axe, lying to the side.

That was all the excuse the Mirabarran guards needed. The two to Torgar's left dropped their net between them and spurred their horses forward, running past on either side of the dwarf, plucking him from his seat and bouncing him down to the ground in the strong mesh.

Torgar went into a frenzy, tearing at the cords, trying to pull himself free, but the other two guards were right there, drawing forth solid clubs and dropping from their mounts. Torgar thrashed and kicked, even managed to bite one, but he was at an impossible disadvantage.

The soldiers had the dwarf beaten to semi-consciousness quickly, and managed to extricate him from the net soon after, unstrapping and removing his fine plate armor.

"Let the city find slumber before we return," Djaffar explained to them. "I have arranged with the Axe to ensure that no dwarves are on the wall this night."

Shoudra Stargleam was not truly surprised, when she thought about it, but she was surely dismayed that night. The sceptrana stood on her balcony, enjoying the night and brushing her long black hair when she noted a commotion by the city's eastern gate, of which her balcony provided a fine view.

The gates opened wide and some riders entered. Shoudra recognized Djaffar of the Hammers from his boastfully plumed helmet. Though she could make out few details, it wasn't hard for the Sceptrana to guess the identity of the diminutive figure walking behind the riders, stripped down to breeches and a torn shirt and with his hands chained before him, on a lead to the rear horse.

She held quiet but did nothing to conceal herself as the prisoner caravan wound its way right beneath her balcony.

There, shuffling along behind the four, and being prodded by the fifth, came Torgar Hammerstriker, bound and obviously beaten.

They hadn't even let the poor fellow put his boots on.

"Oh, Elastul, what have you done?" Shoudra quietly asked, and there was great trepidation in her voice, for she knew that the marchion might have erred and badly.

The knock on her door sounded like a wizard's thunderbolt, jarring Shoudra from her restless sleep. She leaped out of bed and scrambled reflexively to answer it, only half aware of where she was.

She pulled the door open, then stopped cold, seeing Djaffar standing there leaning on the wall outside her apartment. She noted his eyes, roaming her body head to toe, and became suddenly conscious of the fact that she was wearing very little that warm summer's night, just a silken shift that barely covered her.

Shoudra edged the door closed a bit and moved modestly behind it, peering out through the crack at the leering, grinning Hammer.

"Milady," Djaffar said with a tip of his open-faced helm, glinting in the torchlight.

"What is the hour?" she asked.

"Several before the dawn."

"Then what do you want?" Shoudra asked.

"I am surprised that you retired, milady," Djaffar said innocently. "It was not so long ago that I saw you, quite awake and standing on your balcony."

It all began to make sense to Shoudra then, as she came fully awake and remembered all that she had seen that far from ordinary night.

"I retired soon after."

"With many questions on your pretty mind, no doubt."

"That is my business, Djaffar." Shoudra made sure that she injected a bit of anger into her tone, wanting to put the too confident man on the defensive. "Is there a reason you disturb my slumber? Is there some emergency concerning the marchion? Because, if there is not . . ."

"We must discuss that which you witnessed from your balcony, milady," Djaffar said coolly, and if he was the slightest bit intimidated by Shoudra's powerful tone he did not show it.

"Who is to say that I witnessed anything at all?"

"Exactly, and you would do well to remember that."

Shoudra's blue eyes opened wide. "My dear Djaffar, are you threatening the Sceptrana of Mirabar?"

"I am asking you to do what is right," the Hammer replied without backing down. "It was under the orders of the marchion himself that the traitor Torgar was arrested."

"Brutally . . ."

"Not so. He surrendered to the lawful authority without a fight," Djaffar argued.

Shoudra didn't believe a word of it. She knew Djaffar and the rest of the four Hammers well enough to know that they loved a fight when the odds were stacked in their favor.

"He was brought back to Mirabar under the cover of darkness for a reason, milady. Surely you can understand and appreciate that this is a sensitive matter."

"Because the dwarves of Mirabar, even those who disagree with Torgar, would not be pleased to learn that he was dragged into the city in chains," Shoudra replied.

Though there was a substantial amount of sarcasm in her voice, Djaffar ignored it completely and merely replied, "Exactly."

The Hammer gave a wry smile.

"We could have left him dead in the wilderness, buried in a place where none would ever find him. You do understand that, of course, as you understand that your silence in this matter is of prime importance?"

"Could you have done all of that? In good conscience?"

"I am a warrior, milady, and sworn to the protection of the marchion," Djaffar answered with that same grin. "I trust in your silence here."

Shoudra just stared at him hard. Finally recognizing that he wasn't going to get any more of an answer than that, Djaffar tipped his helm again and walked away down the corridor.

Shoudra Stargleam shut her door, then turned her back and leaned against it. She rubbed her eyes and considered the very unusual night.

"What are you doing, Elastul?" she asked herself quietly.

In the room next to Shoudra's, another was asking himself that very same question. Nanfoodle the alchemist had been in Mirabar for several years but had tried very hard to keep away from the politics of the place. He was an alchemist, a scholar, and a gnome with a bit of talent in illusion magic, but that was all. This latest debacle, concerning the arrival of the legendary King of Mithral Hall, whom Nanfoodle had dearly wanted to go and meet, had him more than a bit concerned, however.

He had heard the loud knock, and thinking it was on his own door, had scrambled from his bed and rushed to answer. When he had arrived there, though, he already heard the voices, Shoudra and Djaffar, and recognized that the man had come to speak with her and not him.

Nanfoodle had heard every word. Torgar Hammerstriker, one of the most respected dwarves in Mirabar, whose family had been in service to the various marchions for centuries, had been beaten on the road and dragged back, secretly, in chains.

A shiver ran up Nanfoodle's spine. The whole episode, from the time they had learned that Bruenor Battlehammer was knocking on their gate, had him quite unhinged.

He knew that it would all come to no good.

And though the gnome had long before decided to remain neutral on anything politic, to do his experiments and take his rewards, he found himself at the house of a friend the next day.

Councilor Agrathan Hardhammer was not pleased by the gnome's revelations. Not at all.

"I know," Agrathan said to Shoudra as soon as she opened her door that next morning, the dwarf having gone straight from his meeting with Nanfoodle to the sceptrana's apartment.

"You know what?"

"What you know, about the treatment and return of a certain disgruntled dwarf. Torgar was dragged in by the Hammers last night, in chains."

"By one Hammer, at least."

"Djaffar, curse his name!" said Agrathan.

The dwarf's ire toward Djaffar surprised Shoudra, for she had never heard Agrathan speak of any of the individual Hammers at all before.

"Elastul Raurym is the source of the decision, not Djaffar or any of the other Hammers," she reminded.

Agrathan banged his head on the door jamb.

"He is blowing the embers hot in a room full of smokepowder," the dwarf said.

Shoudra did not disagree—to a point. She understood Agrathan's frustration and fears, but she also had to admit that she understood Elastul's reluctance in letting the dwarf walk away. Agrathan knew Mirabar's defenses as well as any and knew their production capacities and the state of their various ore veins as well. The sceptrana didn't honestly believe that it would ever come to war between Mithral Hall and Mirabar, but if it did. . . .

"I believe that Elastul felt he had no choice," Shoudra replied. "At least they did not murder the wayward dwarf on the road."

That statement didn't have the effect Shoudra had hoped for. Instead of calming Agrathan, the mere mention of that diabolical possibility had the dwarf's eyes going wide, and his jaw clenching tightly. He calmed quickly, though, and took a deep, steadying breath.

"It might have been the smarter thing for him to do," he said quietly, and it was Shoudra's turn to open her eyes wide. "When the dwarfs of Mirabar learn that Torgar's a prisoner in his own town, they're not to be a happy bunch—and they will learn of it, do not doubt."

"Do you know where they're keeping him?"

"I was hoping that you'd be telling me that very thing."

Shoudra shrugged.

"Might be time for us two to go and talk to Elastul."

Shoudra Stargleam did not disagree, though she understood better than Agrathan, apparently, that the meeting would do little to resolve the present problem. In Elastul's eyes, obviously, Torgar Hammerstriker had committed an act of betrayal, of treason even, and Shoudra doubted that the unfortunate dwarf would be seeing the world outside his prison cell anytime soon.

She did go with Agrathan to the marchion's palace, though, and the two were ushered in to Elastul's audience chamber forthwith. Shoudra noted that all of the normal guards and attendants in the room were absent, other than the four Hammers, who stood in their typical position behind the marchion. She also noted the look that Djaffar shot her way, one suggestive and uncomfortable, one that made her want to pull her robe tighter about her.

"What is the urgency?" the marchion asked at once, before any formal greetings. "I have much to attend this day."

"The urgency is that you've put Torgar Hammerstriker in prison, Marchion," Agrathan bluntly replied, and he added with great emphasis, "Torgar *Delzoun* Hammerstriker."

"He is not being mistreated," Elastul replied, and he added, "As long as he does not resist," when he took note of Shoudra's doubtful look.

"I have asked for, and expect, discretion on this matter," the marchion went on, obviously aiming this remark at Shoudra.

"She wasn't the one who told me," Agrathan answered.

"Then who?"

"Not important," the dwarf replied. "If you intend to hunt any who'd speak of this, then ye'd do better trying to hold water from dripping through your fingers."

Elastul didn't seem pleased at all by that remark, and he turned a frown upon Djaffar, who merely shrugged.

"This is important, Marchion," Agrathan said. "Torgar is not just any citizen."

"Torgar is not a citizen," Elastul corrected. "Not anymore, and by his own volition. I am charged with the defense of Mirabar, and so I have taken steps to just that effect. He is jailed, and he shall remain jailed until such time as he recants his position on this matter, publicly, and forsakes this ludicrous idea of traveling to Mithral Hall."

Agrathan started to respond, but Elastul cut him off.

"There is no debate over this, Councilor."

Agrathan looked to Shoudra for support, but she shrugged and shook her head.

And so it was. Marchion Elastul considered Mithral Hall an enemy, obviously, and every step he took seemed to ensure that his perception would become reality.

Both Agrathan and Shoudra hoped that Elastul understood fully the implications of this latest action, for both feared the reaction should the truth of Torgar's imprisonment become general knowledge around the city.

The dwarf's remark about hot embers in a smokepowder filled room seemed quite insightful to Shoudra Stargleam at that moment.

16

THE HERO

Catti-brie crept silently to the edge of the rocky lip, peering over. As she had expected, the orc's camp lay below her on a flat rock with strewn boulders all around it. There wasn't much of a fire, just a pit of glowing embers. The orc huddled close to it, blocking most of the glow.

Catti-brie scanned the area, allowing her eyes to shift into the spectrum of heat instead of light, and she was glad that she had her magical circlet with her when she spotted the soft glow of a second orc, not so far away, whittling away at a broken branch. She did a quick scan of the area then let her vision shift back to the normal spectrum. Her circlet was a marvelous item indeed, one that helped her to see in the dark, but it was not without its limitations. It operated far better underground, allowing her vision where she would have had none at all than under the night sky. When the stars were out or near the glow of a fire, the magical circlet often only added to the woman's confusion, distorting distances, particularly on heat-neutral surfaces such as broken stones.

Catti-brie paused and stood perfectly still, her eyes unblinking as they adjusted to the dim light. She had already picked a route that would take her down to the orc and had confirmed that route with the magical circlet, intending to go down and capture or slay the creature.

But now there were two.

Catti-brie reached instinctively for Taulmaril as she considered the new odds, but her hand stopped short of grabbing the bow that was strapped across her back. Her fingers remained swollen and bruised, with at least one broken. After practicing earlier that day, she knew she could hardly hope to hit the orcs from that distance.

She went to Khazid'hea instead. Her fabulous sword, nicknamed Cutter because of its fine and deadly blade, could shear through armor as easily as it could cut through cloth. She felt the energy, the eagerness, of the sentient, hungry sword as soon as her hand closed around the hilt. Khazid'hea wanted this fight, as it wanted any fight.

That pull only strengthened as she slowly and silently slid the sword out of its scabbard, holding it low behind the rocky barricade. Its fine edge could catch the slightest glimmer of light and reflect it clearly.

The sword's hunger called out to her, bade her to start moving down the trail and toward the first victim.

Catti-brie almost started away, but she paused and glanced back over her shoulder. She should go and get some of the others, she realized. Drizzt had gone off earlier, but her other friends could not be far away.

It is only a pair of orcs after all, and if you strike first and fast, it will be one against one, she thought—or perhaps it was her sword suggesting that thought to her.

Either way, it seemed a logical argument to Cattie-brie. She had never met an orc that could match her in swordplay.

Before she could further second-guess herself, Catti-brie slipped out from behind the rocky lip and started slowly and quietly down the nearest trail that would get her to the plateau and the encampment.

Soon she was at the orc's level and barely ten feet away. The oblivious creature remained huddled over the embers, stirring them occasionally, while its equally-oblivious companion continued its whittling far to the side.

She moved a half step closer, then another. Barely five feet separated her from the orc then. Apparently sensing her, the creature looked up, gave a cry—

—and fell over backward, rolling and scrambling as Catti-brie stuck it, once and again, before having to turn back to face its charging companion.

The second orc skidded to a stop when Khazid'hea flashed up before it in perfect balance. The orc stabbed viciously with its crude spear, but Catti-brie easily turned her hips aside. It struck again, to similar non-effect, then came forward, retracted suddenly, and thrust again, this time to the anticipated side.

The wrong side.

Catti-brie dodged the second thrust, then started to dodge the third, but stopped as the orc retracted, and dodged out the other way as the spear charged ahead.

She had her chance, and it was one she didn't miss. Across went Khazid'hea, the fabulous blade cleanly shearing the last foot off the orc's spear. The creature howled and jumped back, throwing the remaining shaft at the woman as it did, but a flick of Catti-brie's wrist had that spear shaft spinning off into the darkness.

She rushed ahead, sword leading, ready to thrust the blade into the orc's chest.

And she stopped, abruptly, as a stone whistled across, right before her.

And as she turned to face this newest attacker, she got hit in the back by a second stone, thrown hard.

And a third skipped by, and a fourth hit her square in the shoulder, and her arm, suddenly gone numb, slipped down.

Orcs crawled over the strewn rocks all around the encampment, waving their weapons and throwing more rocks to keep her dancing and off-balance.

Catti-brie's mind raced. She could hardly believe that she had so foolishly walked into a trap. She felt Khazid'hea's continuing urging to her to jump into battle, to slay them all, and wondered for a moment how much control she actually held over the ever-hungry sword.

But no, she realized, this was her mistake and not the weapon's. Normally in this position, she'd play defensively, letting her enemy come to her, but the orcs showed little sign of wanting to advance. Instead they bent to retrieve more stones and came up hurling them at her. She dodged and danced and got hit a few times, some stinging. She picked what she perceived to be the most vulnerable spot in the ring and charged at it, her sword flashing wildly.

It was pure instinct then for Catti-brie, her muscles working faster than her conscious thoughts could follow. Nothing short of brilliant, the woman parried a sword, an axe, and another spear—one, two, three—and still managed to step out to the side suddenly, stabbing an orc who had expected her to move forward. Clutching its belly, that one fell away.

And a second orc joined it, dropping to the stone and writhing wildly while trying to stem the blood flow from its slashed neck.

A twist of Catti-brie's wrist had the weapon of a third orc turned tip down to the stone, leaving her an easy opening for a deadly strike, but as Khazid'hea started its forward rush, a stone clipped the woman's already wounded hand, sending a burst of fiery pain up her arm. To her horror, before she even realized the extent of what had happened, she heard Khazid'hea go bouncing away across the stones.

A spear came out hard at her, but the agile woman turned fast aside, then grabbed it as it thrust past. A step forward, a flying elbow had the orc staggered, and she moved to pull free the weapon and make it her own.

But then a club cracked her between the shoulder blades and her arms went weak, and the spear-holding orc yanked back its weapon and stabbed ahead, gashing the woman across the hip and buttocks. She staggered forward and away, and somehow managed to slap her hand out and turn aside a slashing sword then do it again, though the second block had the tender skin of her palm opened wide.

Every movement was in desperation then, more desperate than Catti-brie had ever been. It occurred to her, somewhere deep in her swirling thoughts, how close to the edge of disaster she and her friends had been and for so long. She noted then, in a flash of clarity before the club hit her again, sending her stumbling to her knees as she tried to run across the camp and leap away into the dark night, how a single mistake could prove so quickly disastrous.

She went down hard to the stone and noted Khazid'hea, not so far away. It was out of her reach, might as well have been across the world, the woman realized as the orcs closed in. She rolled desperately to her back and began kicking out and up at them, anything to keep their weapons away.

"What is it, Guen?" Drizzt asked quietly

He came up beside the panther, whose ears were flattened as she stood perfectly still, staring out into the dark night. The drow crouched beside her and similarly scanned, not expecting to find any enemies about, for he had seen no orc sign at all that day or night.

But something was wrong. The panther knew it, and so did Drizzt. Something was out of place. He looked back down the mountainside, to the distant glow of Bruenor's camp, where all seemed quiet.

"What do you sense?" the drow asked the panther.

Guen gave a low, almost plaintive growl. Drizzt felt his heart racing, and he began looking desperately all around, scolding himself for going off on his own that afternoon, pushing farther into the mountains in an effort to try to spot the lone tower that marked the town of Shallows, and leaving his friends so far behind.

She did a fair job of keeping the orcs off of her for a long, long time, but the angle was too awkward, and the effort too great, and gradually Catti-brie's kicks slowed to inconsequential. She got kicked hard in the ribs, and she had no choice but to curl up and clutch at the pain. Tears flowed freely as the woman realized her error and the consequences of it.

She would never see her friends again. She would never laugh with Drizzt again, tease Regis again, or watch her father take his place as King of Mithral Hall.

She would never have children of her own. She would not watch her daughter grow to womanhood or her son to manhood. She would never hold Colson again or take heart at the smile that had so recently returned to Wulfgar's face.

Everything seemed to pause around her, just for a moment, and she looked up to see the biggest of the orc group towering over her at her feet, lifting a heavy axe in both its strong hands, while the others cheered it on.

She had no defense. She prayed it would not hurt too much.

Up went the axe, and down went the orc's head.

Down, driven down, right into its shoulders at the end of a warhammer's gleaming mithral head. The orc went into a short bounce, but didn't fall right back to the stone as Wulfgar slammed his powerful shoulder into it, launching it right over the prone woman.

With a roar, the son of Beornegar stepped forward, straddling Catti-brie with his strong legs, his powerful arms working mightily to send Aegis-fang sweeping back and forth and all about, driving back the surprised orcs. He clipped one, shattering its side, then stepped forward enough to nail a second with a sweep across its legs that upended it and dropped it howling to the stone. In a rage beyond anything that Catti-brie had ever before seen, a battle fury beyond anything the orcs had ever encountered, the barbarian crouched and turned around, launching Aegis-fang into the chest of the nearest orc, blasting it away. Unlike Catti-brie a few moments before, however, not an orc thought this monstrous human unarmed. Wulfgar charged right into them, ignoring the puny hits of their half-hearted swings and countering with punches that sent orcs flying away.

Catti-brie regained her wits enough to roll to the side toward her lost sword. She retrieved it and started to rise but could hardly find the strength. She stumbled again and thought her attempt would cost her her life and mock Wulfgar's desperate rescue, when an orc rushed beside her. A split second later, though, the woman realized that the creature wasn't trying to attack her but was simply trying to run away.

And why not, she realized when she looked back at Wulfgar. Another orc went flying off into the night, and another was up in the air at the end of one hand clutched tightly around its throat. The orc was large, nearly as wide as Wulfgar, but the barbarian held it aloft easily. The flailing creature couldn't begin to break his iron grasp.

Wulfgar warded off yet another pesky orc with his free hand. Aegis-fang returned to his grasp, and he gave a warding swing, then turned his attention back to the orc he held aloft. With a primal growl, his corded muscles flexed powerfully.

The orc's neck snapped and the creature went limp, and Wulfgar tossed it aside.

On he came, his rage far from abated, Aegis-fang chopping down orcs and scattering them to the night. Bones shattered under his mighty blows as he waded through their fleeing ranks like a thresher through a field of wheat.

And it was over so suddenly, and Wulfgar's arm went down to his side. Trembling visibly, his face appearing ashen even in the meager light, he strode to Catti-brie and reached down to her.

She took his hand with her own and a quick tug had her standing before him on legs that would hardly support her.

That didn't matter, though, for the woman simply fell forward into

Wulfgar's waiting grasp. He lifted her in his arms and hugged her close.

Catti-brie buried her face against the man's strong shoulder, sobbing, and Wulfgar crushed against her, whispering calming words in her ear, his own face lost in the her thick auburn hair.

All around them, the night creatures, stirred by the sharp ruckus of battle, gradually quieted and the orcs fled into the darkness, and the night slipped past.

17

MIELIKKI'S APPROVAL

While at first Tarathiel found the constant "*wheeee!*" of Pikel Boulder-shoulder annoying, he found that by the time he set Sunset down in the mountain forest and helped the dwarf off the pegasus's back, he had grown quite fond of the green-bearded fellow.

"Hee hee hee," Pikel said, glancing back many times at the pegasus as he followed Tarathiel along.

They had been up and flying for most of the day, and the afternoon light was beginning to wane.

"You are pleased by Sunset?" Tarathiel asked.

"Hee hee hee," Pikel answered.

"Well, I have something else, I hope, that I expect might please you equally," the elf explained.

Pikel looked at him curiously.

"We are nearing the home of a great ranger, now deceased," Tarathiel explained. "An enchanted and hallowed place that has come to be known as Mooshie's Grove."

Pikel's eyes widened so greatly that they seemed as if they would fall out of his head.

"You have heard of it?"

"Uh huh."

Tarathiel smiled and led on through the winding mountain trail, with tall pines all about, the wind swirling around them. They came to the diamond-shaped grove of trees and piled stone walls soon after, the place still looking as if the ranger Montolio was still alive and tending it. There was strong magic about the grove.

Tarathiel only hoped that the last inhabitant of the area he had known was still around. He had taken Drizzt Do'Urden there a few years before, as a measure of the unusual dark elf, and he and Innovindil had decided that a similar test might suit Pikel Bouldershoulder well.

The two went into the grove and walked around, admiring the elevated walkways and the simple, beautiful design of the huts.

"So, you and your brother were heading to the coronation of King Bruenor Battlehammer?" the elf asked to pass the time, knowing that Innovindil was similarly questioning the other brother back in the Moonwood.

"Yup yup," Pikel said, but he was obviously distracted, hopping about, scratching his head and nodding happily.

"You know King Bruenor well, then?"

"Yup yup," Pikel answered.

He stopped suddenly, looked at the elf, and blinked a few times.

"Uh uh," he corrected, and gave a shrug.

"You do not know Bruenor well?"

"Nope."

"But well enough to represent . . . what was his name? Cadderly?"

"Yup yup."

"I see. And tell me, Pikel," Tarathiel asked, "how is it that you have come by such druidic . . . ?"

His voice trailed off, for he noticed that Pikel was suddenly distracted, looking away, his eyes widening. Following the dwarf's gaze, Tarathiel soon enough understood that his question had fallen on deaf ears, for there, just outside the grove, stood the most magnificent of equine creatures in all the world. Large and strong, with legs that could shatter a giant's skull, and a single, straight horn that could skewer two men standing back to back, the unicorn pawed the ground anxiously, watching Pikel every bit as intently as the dwarf was regarding it.

Pikel put his arm above his head, finger pointing up, like his own unicorn horn, and began hopping all about.

"Be easy, dwarf," Tarathiel warned, unsure of how the magnificent, and ultimately dangerous, creature would respond.

Pikel, though, hardly seemed nervous, and with a shriek of delight, the dwarf went hopping across the way, tumbling over the stone wall that lined that edge of the grove, and rushed out toward the beast.

The unicorn pawed the ground and gave a great whinny, but Pikel hardly seemed to notice and charged on.

Tarathiel grimaced, thinking himself foolish for bringing the dwarf to the grove. He took up the chase, calling for Pikel to stop.

But it was Tarathiel who stopped, just as he was going over the stone wall. Across the small field, Pikel stood beside the unicorn, stroking its muscled neck, his face a mask of awe. The unicorn seemed a bit unsure and continued pawing the ground, but it did not ward Pikel away, nor did it make any move to rush off.

Tarathiel sat down on the wall, smiling and nodding, and very glad of that.

Pikel stayed with the magnificent unicorn for some time before the creature finally turned and galloped away. The enchanted dwarf floated back across the field, skipping so lightly that his feet didn't even seem to touch the ground.

"Are you pleased?"

"Yup yup!"

"I think it liked you."

"Yup yup!"

"You know of Mielikki?"

Pikel's smile nearly took in his big ears. He reached under the front of his tunic and pulled forth a pendant of a carved unicorn head, the symbol of the nature goddess.

Tarathiel had seen another wearing a similar pendant, though Pikel's was carved of wood while the other had been made of scrimshaw using the bones of the knucklehead trout of Icewind Dale.

"Will King Bruenor be pleased that one who worships the goddess is in his court?" Tarathiel asked, leading the conversation to a place he thought might prove revealing.

Pikel looked at him curiously.

"He is a dwarf, after all, and most dwarves are not favorably disposed toward the goddess Mielikki."

"*Pffft,*" Pikel scoffed, waving a hand at the elf.

"You believe I am wrong?"

"Yup yup."

"I have heard that there is another in his court so favorably disposed to Mielikki," Tarathiel remarked. "One who trained right here with Montolio the Ranger. A very unusual creature, not so much unlike Pikel Bouldershoulder."

"Drizzit Dudden!" Pikel cried, and though it took Tarathiel a moment to recognize the badly-pronounced name, when he did, he nodded his approval.

If the unicorn hadn't been proof enough, then Pikel's knowledge of Drizzt certainly was.

"Drizzt, yes," the elf said. "It was he I took out here, when first I found the unicorn. The unicorn liked him, too."

"Hee hee hee."

"Let us spend the night here," the elf explained. "We will set out as soon as the sun rises to return to your brother."

That thought seemed quite acceptable, even pleasing to Pikel Bouldershoulder. The dwarf ran off, searching all the grove, soon enough finding a pair of hammocks he could string up.

They spent a comfortable night indeed within the magical aura that permeated Mooshie's Grove.

"He knew Drizzt Do'Urden," Tarathiel said to Innovindil when the two met that following evening, to discuss their respective meetings with the unusual dwarf brothers.

"As did Ivan," Innovindil confirmed. "In fact, Drizzt Do'Urden and Catti-brie, Bruenor's adopted human daughter, are the ties between the priest Cadderly and Mithral Hall. All that Ivan and Pikel, and Cadderly, know of Bruenor they learned from that pair."

"Pikel believes that Drizzt will be with Bruenor," Tarathiel said somberly.

"If he returns to the region, we will learn the truth of Ellifain's current state, of being and of mind."

Tarathiel's eyes clouded over and he looked down. The life and fate of Ellifain Tuuserail was among the saddest and darkest tales in the Moonwood. Ellifain had been but a young child that fateful night, half a century before, when the dark elves had crept out of their tunnels and descended upon a gathering of moon elves out in celebration of the night. All were slaughtered, except for Ellifain, and the baby girl would have found a similar fate had it not been for the uncharacteristically generous action of a particular drow, Drizzt Do'Urden. He had buried the child beneath her dead mother, smearing her with her mother's blood to make it look like Ellifain, too, had been mortally wounded.

While Tarathiel and Innovindil and all the rest of the Moonwood clan had come to understand the generosity of Drizzt's actions and to trust in the remarkable dark elf's account of that horrible night, Ellifain had never gotten past that one terrible moment. The massacre had scarred the elf beyond reason, despite the best efforts of hired clerics and wizards, and had put her on a singular course throughout her adult life: to kill drow elves and to kill Drizzt Do'Urden.

The two had met face to face when Drizzt had once ventured through the Moonwood, and it had taken all that Tarathiel and the others could muster to hold Ellifain in check, to keep her from Drizzt's throat, or more likely, from death at the end of his scimitars.

"Do you think she will reveal herself in an effort to get at him?" Innovindil asked. "Is it our responsibility, in that case, to warn Drizzt Do'Urden and King Bruenor to take care of what elves they allow entry to Mithral Hall?"

Tarathiel shrugged in answer to the first question. A few years before, without explanation, Ellifain had disappeared from the Moonwood. They had tracked her to Silverymoon, where she was trying to hire a swordsman to serve as a sparring partner, with the requirement that he was skilled in the two long weapon style common among drow.

The pair had almost caught Ellifain on numerous occasions, but she had always seemed one step ahead of them. And she had disappeared, simply vanished, it seemed, and the trail soon grew cold. The elves suspected wizardly interference, likely a teleport spell, but they had found none who would admit to any such thing, and indeed, had found none who would even admit to ever meeting Ellifain, despite all their efforts and a great deal of offered gold.

The trail was dead, and the elves had hoped—they still did hope—that

Ellifain had given up her life-quest of finding and killing Drizzt, but Tarathiel and Innovindil doubted that to be the case. There was no reason guiding Ellifain's weapon hand, only unrelenting anger and a thirst for vengeance beyond anything the elves had ever known before.

"It is our responsibility as a neighbor to warn King Bruenor," Tarathiel answered.

"We hold responsibilities to dwarves?"

"Only because Ellifain's course, if she still follows it, is not one guided by any moral trail."

Innovindil considered his words for a few moments then nodded her agreement. "She believes that if she can kill Drizzt, she will destroy those images that haunt her every step. In killing Drizzt, she is striking back against all the drow, avenging her family."

"But if warned, and she reveals herself and her intent, he will likely slaughter her," Tarathiel said, and Innovindil winced at the thought.

"Perhaps that would be the most merciful course of all," the female said quietly, and she looked up at Tarathiel, whose face grew very tight, whose eyes narrowed dangerously.

But that expression softened in the face of Innovindil's simple logic, in the undeniable understanding that Ellifain, the true Ellifain, had died that night long ago on the moonlit field, and that this creature she had become was ultimately and inexorably flawed.

"I do not think that Ivan and Pikel Bouldershoulder are the ones to deliver such a message to King Bruenor," Innovindil remarked, and Tarathiel's dark expression brightened a bit, a smirk even crossing his face.

"Likely they would jumble the message and bring about a war between Mithral Hall and the Moonwood," he said with a forced chuckle.

"Boom!" Innovindil added in her best Pikel impression, and both elves laughed aloud.

Tarathiel's eyes went to the western sky, though, where the setting sun was lighting pink fires against a line of clouds, and his mirth dissipated. Ellifain was out there, or she was dead, and either way, there was nothing he could do to save her.

18

A CITIZEN IN
GOOD STANDING

It never took much to fluster the gnome, but this was more than his sensibilities could handle. He walked swiftly along the streets of Mirabar, heading for the connections to the Undercity, but not traveling in a direct line. Nanfoodle was trying hard—too hard—to avoid being detected.

He was cognizant of that fact, and so he tried to straighten out his course and settle his stride to a more normal pace. Why shouldn't he go into the Undercity, after all? He was the Marchion's Prime Alchemist, often working with fresh ore and often visiting the dwarves, so why was he trying to conceal his destination?

Nanfoodle shook his head and scolded himself repeatedly, then stopped, took a deep breath, and started again with a more normal stride and an expression of forced calm.

Well, a calm expression that lasted until he considered again his course. He had told Councilor Agrathan of Torgar's imprisonment and had thought to let his incidental knowledge of the situation go at that, figuring that he had done his duty as a friend—and he truly felt that he was a friend—of the dwarves. However, with so much time behind them and no apparent action coming on Torgar's behalf, Nanfoodle had come to realize that Agrathan had taken the issue no further than the marchion. Even worse, to the gnome's sensibilities, Mirabar's dwarves were still under the impression that Torgar was on the road to, or perhaps had even arrived at, Mithral Hall. For several days, the gnome had wrestled with his conscience over the issue. Had he done enough? Was it his duty as a friend to tell the dwarves, to tell Shingles McRuff at least, who was known to be the best friend of Torgar Hammerstriker? Or was it his duty to the marchion, his employer and the one who had brought him to Mirabar, to keep his mouth shut and mind his own business?

As these questions played yet again in poor Nanfoodle's thoughts, the gnome's strides became less purposeful and more meandering, and he brought his hands together before him, twiddling his thumbs. His eyes were only half-open, the gnome exploring his heart and soul as much as paying attention to his surroundings, and so he was quite surprised when a tall and imposing figure stepped out before him as he turned down one narrow alleyway.

Nanfoodle skidded to an abrupt stop, his gaze gradually climbing the robed, shapely figure before him, settling on the intense eyes of Shoudra Stargleam.

"Um, hello Sceptrana," the gnome nervously greeted. "A fine day for a walk it is, yes?"

"A fine day *above* ground, yes," Shoudra replied. "Can you be so certain that the Undercity is similarly pleasant?"

"The Undercity? Well, I would know nothing about the Undercity . . . have not been down there with the dwarves in days, in tendays!"

"A situation you plan to remedy this very day, no doubt."

"W-why, no," the gnome stammered. "Was just out for a walk. Yes, yes . . . trying to sort a formula in my head, you see. Must toughen the metal . . ."

"Spare me the dodges," Shoudra bade him. "So now I know who it was who whispered in Agrathan's ear."

"Agrathan? The Councilor Hardhammer, you mean?"

Nanfoodle realized how unconvincing he sounded, and that only made him seem more nervous to the clever Shoudra.

"Djaffar was a bit loud in the hallway on the night when Torgar Hammerstriker was dragged back to Mirabar," Shoudra remarked.

"Djaffar? Loud? Well, he usually is, I suppose," Nanfoodle bluffed, thinking himself quite clever. "In any hallway, I would guess, though I've not seen nor heard him in any hallway that I can recall."

"Truly?" Shoudra said, a wry grin widening on her beautiful face. "And yet you were not surprised to hear that Torgar Hammerstriker was dragged back to Mirabar? How, then, is this not news to you?"

"Well, I . . . well . . ."

The little gnome threw up his hands in defeat.

"You heard him, that night, outside my door."

"I did."

"And you told Agrathan."

Nanfoodle gave a great sigh and said, "Should he not know? Should the dwarves be oblivious to the actions of their marchion?"

"And it is your place to tell them?"

"Well . . ." Nanfoodle gave a snort, and another, and stamped his foot. "I do not know!"

He gnashed his teeth for a few moments, then looked up at Shoudra, and was surprised to see an expression on her face that was quite sympathetic.

"You feel as betrayed as I," he remarked.

"The marchion owes me, and you, nothing," the woman was quick to respond. "Not even an explanation."

"Yet you seem to think that we owe him something in return."

Shoudra's eyes widened and she seemed to grow very tall and terrible before the little gnome.

"You owe to him because he *is* Mirabar!" she scolded. "It is the position, not the man, deserving and demanding of your respect, Nanfoodle the Foolish."

"I am not of Mirabar!" the gnome shot back, with unexpected fury. "I was brought in for my expertise, and I am paid well because I am the greatest in my field."

"Your field? You are a master of illusion and a master of the obvious all at once," Shoudra countered. "You are a carnival barker, a trickster and a—"

"How dare you?" Nanfoodle yelled back. "Alchemy is the greatest of the Arts, the one whose truths we have not yet uncovered. The one that holds the promise of power for all, and not just a select few, like those powers of Shoudra and her ilk, who guard mighty secrets for personal gain."

"Alchemy is a means to make a few potions of minor magic, and a bit of powder that blows up more often on its creator than on its intended target. Beyond that, it is a sham, a lie perpetrated by the cunning on the greedy.

You can no more strengthen the metal of Mirabar's mines than transmute lead into gold."

"Why, from the solid earth I can create hungry mud at your feet to swallow you up!" Nanfoodle roared.

"With water?" Shoudra calmly asked, the simple reply taking most of the bluster from the excited gnome, visibly shrinking him back to size.

He started to reply, stammering indecipherably, and just gave a snort, and remarked, "Not all agree with your estimation of the value of alchemy."

"Indeed, and some pay well for the unfounded promises it offers."

Nanfoodle snorted again. "The point remains that I owe nothing to your marchion beyond my position to him as my employer," he reasoned, "and only as my *current* employer, as I am a free-lance alchemist who has served many well-paying folks throughout the wide lands of the North. I could walk into Waterdeep tomorrow and find employ at near equal pay."

"True enough," Shoudra replied, "but I have not asked you for any loyalty to Elastul, only to Mirabar, this city that you have come to name as your home. I have been watching you closely, Nanfoodle, ever since Councilor Agrathan came to me with his knowledge of the imprisonment of Torgar. I have replayed many times my encounter with Djaffar, and I know whose door it is that abuts my own. You are out this day, walking nervously, meandering your course, which is obviously to the mines and the dwarves. I share your frustration and understand well that which gnaws at your heart, and so, since Councilor Agrathan has taken little action, you have decided to tell others. Friends of Torgar, likely, in an effort to start some petition against the marchion's actions and get Torgar freed from his cell, wherever that may be."

"I have decided to tell the friends of Torgar only so that they might know the truth," Nanfoodle admitted, and corrected. "What actions they might take are their own to decide."

"How democratic," came the sarcastic reply.

"You just said you share my frustrations," Nanfoodle retorted.

"But not your foolishness, it would seem," Shoudra was quick to respond. "Do you truly understand the implications? Do you truly understand the brotherhood of dwarf to dwarf? You risk tearing the city asunder, of setting human against dwarf. What do you owe to Mirabar, Nanfoodle the Illusionist? And what do you owe to Marchion Elastul, your employer?"

"And what do I owe to the dwarves I have named as my friends?" the little gnome asked innocently, and his words seemed to knock Shoudra back a step.

"I know not," she admitted with a sigh, one that clearly showed that frustration she had spoken of.

"Nor do I," Nanfoodle agreed.

Shoudra straightened herself, but she seemed not so tall and terrible to Nanfoodle, seemed rather a kindred soul, befuddled and unhappy about the course of events swirling around her and outside of her control.

She dropped a hand on his shoulder, a gesture of sympathy and friendship, and said quietly, "Walk lightly, friend. Understand the implications of your actions here. The dwarves of Mirabar are on the fine edge of a dagger, stepping left and right. They among all the citizens bear the least love and the most loyalty to the present marchion. Where will your revelations leave them?"

Nanfoodle nodded, not disagreeing with her reasoning, but he added, "And yet, if this city is all you claim it to be, if this wondrous joy of coexistence that is Mirabar is worthy of inspiring such loyalty, can it suffer the injustice of the jailing of Torgar Hammerstriker?"

Again, his words seemed to set Shoudra back on her heels, striking her as profoundly as any slap might. She paused, closed her eyes, and gradually began to nod.

"Do what you will, Nanfoodle, with no judgment from Shoudra Stargleam. I will leave your choice to your heart. None will know of this conversation, or even that you know of Torgar—not from me, at least."

She smiled warmly at the little gnome, patted him again on the shoulder, and turned and walked away.

Nanfoodle stood there, watching her depart and wondering which course would be better. Should he return to his apartment and his workshop and forget all about Torgar and the mounting troubles between the dwarves and the marchion? Or should he continue as he had intended, knowing full well the explosive potential of his information, and tell the dwarves the truth about the prisoner in the marchion's jail?

No question of alchemy, that most elusive of sciences, had ever perplexed the gnome more than this matter. Was it his place to start an uproar, perhaps even a riot? Was it his place, as a friend, to sit idly by and allow such injustice?

And what of Agrathan? If the marchion had convinced the dwarf councilor to remain silent, as seemed obvious, was Nanfoodle playing the part of the righteous fool? Agrathan must know more than he, after all. Agrathan's loyalty to his kin could not be questioned, and Agrathan had apparently said nothing about Torgar's fate.

Where did that leave Nanfoodle?

With a sigh, the little gnome turned back and started walking for home, thinking himself very foolish and very uppity for even beginning such a course. He had barely gone ten strides, though, when a familiar figure crossed before him, and paused to say hello.

"Greetings to you, Shingles McRuff," Nanfoodle responded, and he felt his stomach turn and his knees go weak.

His short legs churning, Councilor Agrathan burst into Marchion Elastul's audience chamber completely unannounced and with several door guards hot on his heels.

"They *know!*" the dwarf cried, before the surprised marchion could even inquire about the intrusion, and before any of the four Hammers who were standing behind Elastul could scold him for entering without invitation.

"They?" Elastul replied, though it was obvious to all that he knew exactly of whom Agrathan was speaking.

"Word's out about Torgar," Agrathan explained. "The dwarves know what you did, and they're none too happy!"

"Indeed," Elastul replied, settling back in his throne. "And how is it that your people know, Councilor?"

There was no mistaking the accusation in his tone.

"Not from me!" the dwarf protested. "You think I'm pleased by this development? You think it does my old heart good to see the dwarves of Mirabar yelling at each other, throwing words and throwing fists? But you had to know they would learn of this and soon enough. You cannot keep such a secret, Marchion, not about one as important as Torgar *Delzoun* Hammerstriker."

His emphasis on that telling middle name, a distinguished title indeed among the dwarves of Mirabar, had Elastul's eyes narrowing dangerously. Elastul's middle name, after all, was not Delzoun, nor could it be, and to all the marchions of Mirabar, humans all, the Delzoun heritage could be both a blessing and a curse. That Delzoun heritage bound the dwarves to this land, and this land bound them to the marchion. But that Delzoun heritage also bound them to a commonality of their own race, one *apart* from the marchion. Why was it, after all, that every time Agrathan spoke of the weight of Elastul's decision to imprison the traitor Torgar, he used, and emphasized, that middle name?

"So they know," Elastul remarked. "Perhaps that is the proper thing, in the end. Surely most of the dwarves of Mirabar recognize Torgar Hammerstriker as the traitor that he is, and surely many of those same dwarves, merchants among them, craftsmen among them, understand and appreciate the damage the traitor might have caused to us all if he had been allowed to travel to our hated enemies."

"Enemies?"

"Rivals, then," the marchion conceded. "Do you believe that Mithral Hall would not welcome the information that the traitor dwarf might have offered?"

"I am not certain that I believe that Torgar would have offered anything other than his friendship to King Bruenor," Agrathan replied.

"And that alone would be worthy of hanging him," Elastul retorted.

The Hammers laughed and agreed, and Agrathan paled, his eyes going wide.

"You can't be thinking. . . ."

"No, no, Councilor," Elastul assured him. "I have not constructed any gallows for the traitor dwarf. Not yet, at least. Nor do I intend to. It is as I told you before. Torgar Hammerstriker will remain in prison, not abused, but surely contained, until such time as he sees the truth of things and returns to his own good senses. I'll not risk the wealth of Mirabar on his judgment."

Agrathan seemed to calm a bit at that, but the cloud did not leave his soft (for a dwarf, at least) features. He stroked his long white beard and paused for a bit, deep in thought.

"All that you say is true," he admitted, his vernacular becoming more sophisticated as he calmed. "I do not deny that, Marchion, but your reason, for all of its worth, does little to alleviate the fires burning brightly beneath this very room. The fires in the hearts of your dwarf subjects—in a good number of them, at least, who named Torgar Delzoun Hammerstriker as a friend."

"They will come to their senses," Elastul replied. "I trust that Agrathan, beloved councilor, will convince them of the necessity of my actions."

Agrathan stared at Elastul for a long time, his expression shifting to one of simple resignation. He understood the reasoning, all along. He understood why Torgar had been taken from his intended road, and why he had been jailed. He understood why Elastul considered it up to him to calm the dwarves.

That didn't mean that Agrathan believed he had any chance of succeeding, though.

"Well good enough for him, I'm saying," one dwarf cried, and banged his fist on the wall. "The fool would o' telled them all our tricks. If he's to be a friend o' Mithral Hall, then throw him in a hole and leave him there!"

"The words of a fool, if ever I heared 'em," yelled another.

"Who ya callin' a fool?"

"Yerself, ye fool!"

The first dwarf charged forward, fists flying. Those around him, rather than try to stop him, came forward right beside him. They met the name-caller and his friends of similar mind.

Toivo Foamblower leaned back against the wall as the fight exploded around him, the fifth fight of that day in his tavern, and this one looking as if it would be the largest and bloodiest of them all.

Out in the street, just beyond his windows, a score of dwarves were fighting with a score of dwarves, rolling and punching, biting and kicking.

"Ye fool, Torgar," Toivo muttered under his breath.

"And ye bigger fool, Elastul!" he added as he dodged a living missile that soared over him, smashing the wall and a sizeable amount of good stock before falling to the floor, groaning and bitching.

It was going to be a long night in the Undercity. A long night indeed.

The scene was repeated in every bar along the Undercity and in the mines, where miner squared off against miner, sometimes with picks raised, as the news of the imprisonment of Torgar Hammerstriker spread like wildfire among the dwarves of Mirabar.

"Good for Elastul!" was shouted all along the dwarven enclaves, only to be inevitably refuted by a shout of "Damn the marchion!"

Raised voices, predictably, led to raised fists.

Outside Toivo's tavern, Shingles McRuff and a group of friends confronted a host of other-minded dwarves, the group spouting the praises of the man who had "stopped the traitor afore he could betray Mirabar to Mithral Hall."

"Ye're seeming a bit happy that Elastul's quick to jail one o' yer own," Shingles argued. "Ye're thinking it a good thing to have a dwarf rotting in a human jail?"

"Might be that I'm thinking it a good thing to have a traitor to Mirabar rotting in a Mirabar jail!" retorted the other dwarf, a tough-looking character with a black beard and eyebrows so bushy that they nearly hid his eyes. "At least until we've built the dog a proper gallows!"

That brought applause from the dwarves behind him, roars of anger from those beside Shingles, and an even more direct opposition response from old Shingles himself in the form of a well-aimed fist.

The black-bearded dwarf hopped backward beneath the weight of the blow, but thanks to the grabbing arms of his companions, not only didn't he fall, but he came rushing right back at Shingles.

The old dwarf was more than ready, lifting his fists as if to block the attack up high, then dropping to his knees at the very last second and jamming his shoulder into the black-bearded dwarf's waist. Up scrambled Shingles, lifting the outraged dwarf high and launching him into his fellows, then leaping in right behind, fists and feet flying.

Battling dwarves rolled all about the street, and the commotion brought many doors swinging open. Those dwarves who came to view the scene wasted little time in jumping right in, flailing away, though in truth they often had little idea which side they were joining. The riot went from street to street and snaked its way into many houses, and more than one had a fire pit overturned, flames leaping to furniture and tapestries.

Amidst it all, there came the blaring of a hundred horns as the Axe of Mirabar charged down from above, some on the lifts, others just setting ropes and swinging over, trying to get down fast before the rioting swept the whole of the Undercity into disaster.

Dwarf against dwarf and dwarf against man, they battled. In the face of the battle joined by humans, some with weapons drawn, many of the dwarves who had initially opposed Shingles and his like-minded companions changed sides. To many of those in the middle ground concerning the arrest of Torgar, it then became a question of loyalty, to blood or to country.

Though nearly half of the dwarves were fighting beside the Axe, and though many, many humans continued to filter down to quell the riot, it took hours to get the supporters of Torgar under control. Even then, the soldiers of the marchion were faced with the unenviable task of containing more than a hundred prisoners.

Hundreds more were watching them, they knew, and the first sign of mistreatment would likely ignite an even larger riot.

To Agrathan, who came late upon the scene, the destruction along the streets, the bloodied faces of so many of his kin, and even more than that the expressions of sheer outrage on so many, showed him the very danger of which he had warned the marchion laid bare. He went to the Axe commanders one by one, pressing for lenience and wise choices concerning the disposition of the prisoners, always with a grim warning that though the top was on the boiling kettle, the fire was still hot beneath it.

"Keep the peace as best ye can, but not a swing too far," Agrathan warned every commander.

After reciting that speech over and over, after pulling one angry guard after another off a prisoner, the exhausted councilor moved to the side of one avenue and plopped down on a stone bench.

"They got Torgar!" came a voice he could not ignore.

He looked up to see a bruised and battered Shingles, who seemed more than ready to break free of the two men who held him and start the row all over again.

"They dragged him from the road and beat him down!"

Agrathan looked hard at the old dwarf, gently patting his hands in the air to try to calm Shingles.

"Ye knew it!" Shingles roared. "Ye knew it all along, and ye're not for caring!"

"I care," Agrathan countered, leaping up from the bench.

"Bah! Ye're a short human, and not a thing more!"

As he shouted the insult, the guards holding Shingles gave a rough jerk, one letting go with one hand to slap the old dwarf across the face.

That was all the opening he needed. He accepted the slap with a growing grin then leaped around, breaking completely free of that one's grasp. Then, without hesitation, he launched his free fist hard into the gut of the soldier still holding him, doubling the man over and loosening his grasp. Shingles tore free completely, twisting and punching to avoid the grasp of the first man.

The soldier backed, calling for help, but Shingles came in too fast, kicking the man in the shin, and snapping his forehead forward and down, connecting solidly—too solidly—on the man's codpiece. He doubled over and dropped to his knees, his eyes crossing. Shingles came back around wildly, charging for the second soldier.

But when that soldier dodged aside, the dwarf didn't pursue. Instead he continued ahead toward his true intended target: poor Councilor Agrathan.

Agrathan had never been a fighter of Shingles's caliber, nor were his fists near as hard from any recent battles as those of the surly miner. Even worse for Agrathan, his heart wasn't in his defense nearly as much as Shingles's was in his rage.

The councilor felt the first few blows keenly, a left hook, a right cross, a few quick jabs, and a roundhouse that dropped him to the ground. He felt the bottom of Shingles's boot as the dwarf, lifted right off the ground by a pair of pursuing guards, got one last kick in. Agrathan felt the hands of a human grabbing him under the arm and helping him to his feet, an assist the dwarf roughly pushed away.

Gnashing his teeth, wounded inside far more than he could ever be outside, Councilor Agrathan stormed back for the lifts.

He knew that he had to get to the marchion. He had no idea what he was going to say, had no idea even what he expected or wanted the marchion to do, but he knew that the time had come to confront the man more forcefully.

19

MORTAL WINDS
BLOWING

"In all the days of all my life, I have never felt so mortal," Catti-brie said to the whispering wind.

Behind and below her, the dwarves, Regis, and Wulfgar went about their business preparing supper and setting up the latest camp, but the woman had been excused from her duties so that she could be alone to sort through her emotions.

And it was a tumult of emotions beyond anything Catti-brie had ever known. Her last fight had not been the first time the woman had been in mortal peril, surely, and not even the first time she had been help-less before a hated enemy. Once before, she had been captured by the assassin, Artemis Entreri, and dragged along in his pursuit of Regis, but in that instance, as helpless as she had felt, Catti-brie had never really expected to die.

Never like she had felt when caught helpless on the ground at the feet of the encircling, vicious orcs. In that horrible moment Catti-brie had seen her own death, vividly, unavoidably. In that one horrible moment, all of her life's dreams and hopes had been washed away on a wave of . . .

Of what?

Regret?

Truly, she had lived as fully as anyone, running across the land on wild adventures, helping to defeat dragons and demons, fighting to reclaim Mithral Hall for her adoptive father and his clan, chasing pirates on the open seas. She had known love.

She looked back over her shoulder at Wulfgar as she considered this.

She had known sorrow, and perhaps she had found love again. Or was she just kidding herself? She was surrounded by the best friends that anyone could ever hope to know, by an unlikely crew that loved her as she loved them. Companions, friends. It had been more than that with Wulfgar, so she had believed, and with Drizzt . . .

What?

She didn't know. She loved him dearly and always felt better when he was beside her, but were they meant to live as husband and wife? Was he to be the father of her children? Was that even possible?

The woman winced at the notion. One part of her rejoiced at the thought, and believed it would be something wonderful and beautiful. Another part of her, more pragmatic, recoiled at the thought, knowing that any such children would, by the mere nature of their heritage, remain as outcasts to any and all save those few who knew the truth of Drizzt Do'Urden.

Catti-brie closed her eyes and put her head down on her bent knees, curling up as she sat there, high on an exposed rock. She imagined herself as an older woman, far less mobile, and surely unable to run the mountainsides beside Drizzt Do'Urden, blessed as he was with the eternal youth of his people. She saw him on the trails every day, his smile wide as he basked in the adventure. That was his nature, after all, as it was hers. But it would only be hers for a few more years, she knew in her heart, and less than that if ever she was to become with child.

It was all too confusing, and all too painful. Those orcs circling her had shown her something about herself that she had never even realized, had shown her that her present life, as enjoyable as it was, as wild and full of adventure as it was, had to be (unless she was killed in the wilds) a prelude to something quite a bit different. Was she to be a mother? Or an emissary, perhaps, serving the court of her father, King Bruenor? Was this to be her last run through the wilds, her last great adventure?

"Doubt is expected after such a defeat," came a voice behind her, soft and familiar.

She opened her eyes and turned to see Wulfgar standing there, just a bit below her, his arms folded over the bent knee of his higher, lead leg.

Catti-brie gave him a curious look.

"I know what you are feeling," the barbarian said quietly, full of sincerity and compassion. "You faced death, and the looming specter warned you."

"Warned me?"

"Of your own mortality," Wulfgar explained.

Catti-brie's expression turned to incredulity. Wasn't Wulfgar stating the obvious?

"When I fell with the yochlol . . ." the barbarian began, and his eyes closed a bit in obvious pain at the memory. He paused and settled, then opened his eyes wide and pressed on. "In the lair of Errtu, I came to know despair. I came to know defeat beyond anything I had ever imagined, and I came to know both doubt and regret. For all that I had accomplished in my years, in bringing my people together, and into harmony with the folk of Ten-Towns, in fighting beside you, my friends, to rescue Regis, to reclaim Mithral Hall, to . . ."

"Save me from the yochlol," Catti-brie added, and Wulfgar smiled and accepted the gracious compliment with a slight nod.

"For all of that, in the lair of Errtu, I came to know an emptiness that I had not known to exist until that very moment," the barbarian explained. "As I looked upon what I believed to be the last moments of my existence, I felt strangely cold and dissatisfied with my lack of accomplishments."

"After all that you did accomplish?" the woman asked skeptically.

Wulfgar nodded. "Because in so many other ways, I had failed," Wulfgar answered, looking up at her. "In my love for you, I failed. And in my own understanding of who I was, and who I wanted to be, and what I wanted and needed for a life that I might know when the windy trails were no longer my home . . . I had failed."

Catti-brie could hardly believe what she was hearing. It was as if Wulfgar was looking right through her, and pulling her own words out.

"And you found Colson and Delly," she said.

"A fine start, perhaps," Wulfgar replied.

His smile seemed sincere, and Catti-brie returned that smile, and they went quiet for a bit.

"Do you love him?" Wulfgar asked suddenly, unexpectedly.

Catti-brie started to answer with a question of her own, but the answer was self-evident as soon as she truly considered his words.

"Do you?" she asked instead.

"He is my brother, as true to me as any could ever be," Wulfgar answered without the slightest hesitation. "If a spear were aimed for Drizzt's chest, I would gladly leap in front of it, even should it cost me my own life, and I would die contented. Yes, I love him, as I love Bruenor, as I love Regis, as I love . . ."

He stopped there, and simply shrugged.

"As I, too, love them," Catti-brie answered.

"That is not what I mean," Wulfgar replied, not letting the dodge go past. "Do you love him? Do you see him as your partner, on the trails and in the home?"

Catti-brie looked at Wulfgar hard, trying to discern his intent. She saw no jealousy, no anger, and no signal of hopes, one way or the other. What she saw was Wulfgar, the true Wulfgar, son of Beornegar, a caring and loving companion.

"I do not know," she heard herself saying before she ever really considered the question.

The words caught her by surprise, hung in the air and in her thoughts, and she knew them to be true.

"I have felt your pain and your doubts," Wulfgar said, his voice going even softer, and he moved to her and braced her shoulders with his hands and lowered his forehead against hers. "We are all here for you, in any manner that you need. We, all of us, Drizzt included, are first your friends."

Catti-brie closed her eyes and let herself sink into that comforting moment, losing herself in the solidity of Wulfgar, in the understanding that he knew her pain, profoundly, that he had climbed from depths that she could hardly imagine. She found comfort in the knowledge that Wulfgar had returned from hell, that he had found his way, or at least, that he was walking a truer road.

She, too, would find that path, wherever it led.

"Bruenor told me," Drizzt said to Wulfgar when the drow returned from his extended scouting of the mountains to the northeast.

The drow dropped a hand onto his friend's shoulder and nodded.

"It was a rescue not unlike one of those Drizzt Do'Urden has perfected," Wulfgar replied, and he looked away.

"You have my thanks."

"I did not do it for you."

The simple statement, spoken simply, without obvious malice or anger, widened Drizzt's purple eyes.

"Of course not," he agreed.

The dark elf backed away, staring hard at Wulfgar, trying to find some clue as to where the barbarian's thoughts might be.

He saw only an impassive face, turned toward him.

"If we are to go thanking each other every time one of us stays the weapon hand an enemy has aimed at another, then we will spend our days doing little else," Wulfgar said. "Catti-brie was in trouble, and I was fortunate enough—we were all fortunate enough—to have come upon her in time. Did I do any more or less than Drizzt Do'Urden might have done?"

The perplexed Drizzt said, "No."

"Did I do more, then, than Bruenor Battlehammer might have done, had he seen his daughter in such mortal peril?"

"No."

"Did I do more, then, than Regis would have done, or at least, would have tried to do?"

"I have taken your point," Drizzt said.

"Then hold it well," said Wulfgar, and he looked away once more.

It took Drizzt a few moments to finally catch on to what was happening. Wulfgar had seen his thanks as condescending, as if, somehow, he had done something beyond what the companions would expect of each other. That notion hadn't sat well on the big man's shoulders.

"I take back my offer of thanks," Drizzt said.

Wulfgar merely chuckled.

"Perhaps, instead, I offer you a warm welcome back," Drizzt added.

That turned Wulfgar to him, the barbarian throwing a puzzled expression his way.

Drizzt nodded and walked away, leaving Wulfgar with those words to consider. The drow turned his gaze to a rocky outcropping to the south of the encampment, where a solitary figure sat quietly.

"She's been up there all the day," Bruenor remarked, moving beside the drow. "Ever since he brought her back."

"Lying at the feet of outraged orcs can be an unsettling experience."

"Ye think?"

Drizzt looked over at his bearded friend.

"Ye gonna go to her, elf?" Bruenor asked.

Drizzt wasn't sure, and his confusion showed clearly on his face.

"Yeah, she might be needin' some time to herself," Bruenor remarked. He looked back at Wulfgar, drawing the drow's gaze with his own. "Not exactly the hero she'd expected, I'd be guessin'."

The words hit Drizzt hard, mostly because the implications were forcing him to emotional places to which he did not wish to venture. What was this about, after all? Was it about Wulfgar rescuing his former and Drizzt's present love? Or was it about one of the companions rescuing another, as had happened so many times on their long and trying road?

The latter, Drizzt decided. It had to be the latter, and all the rest of it was emotional baggage that had no place among them. Not out where an orc or giant seemed crouched behind every boulder, ready to kill them. Not out where such distractions could lead to incredible disaster. Drizzt nearly laughed aloud as he considered the swirl of thoughts churning within him, including those same protective feelings toward Catti-brie for which he had once scolded a younger Wulfgar.

He focused on the positive, then, on the fact that Catti-brie had survived without serious wounds, and on the fact that this stride Wulfgar had taken, this act of courage and strength and heroism, would likely move him further along his road back from the pits of Errtu's hell. Indeed, in looking at the barbarian then, moving with confidence and grace among the dwarves, a calm expression upon his face, it seemed to Drizzt as if the last edges of the smoke of the Abyss has washed clean of his features.

Yes, Drizzt decided, it was a good day.

"I saw the tower of Shallows at midday," the drow told Bruenor, "but though I was close enough to see it clearly, even to make out the forms of the soldiers walking atop it, I believe we have a couple of days' march ahead of us. I was on the edge of a long ravine when I glimpsed it, one that will take days to move around."

"But the town was still standing?" the dwarf asked.

"Seemed a peaceful place, with pennants flying in the summer breeze."

"As it should be, elf. As it should be," Bruenor remarked. "We'll go in and tell 'em what's been what, and might that I'll leave a few dwarves with 'em if they're needing the help, and—"

"And we go home," said Drizzt, studying Bruenor as he spoke, noting clearly that the dwarf wasn't hearing those words as any blessing.

"Might be other towns needin' us to check in on them," Bruenor huffed.

"I am sure that we can find a few if we look hard enough."

Bruenor either missed the sarcastic grin on Drizzt's face or simply chose to ignore it.

"Yup," the dwarf king said, and he walked away.

Drizzt watched him go, but his gaze was inevitably drawn back up to the high outcropping, to the lone figure of Catti-brie.

He wanted to go to her—desperately wanted to go and put his arms around her and tell her that everything was all right.

For some reason, though, Drizzt thought that would be ultimately unfair. He sensed that she needed some space from him and from everyone else, that she needed to sort through all the emotions that her close encounter with her own mortality had brought bubbling within her.

What kind of a friend might he be if he did not allow her that space?

Wulfgar was with the main body of dwarves that next day on the road, helping to haul the supplies, but Regis remained outside the group, moving along the higher trails with Drizzt and Catti-brie. He spent little time scouting for enemies, though, for he was too busy watching his two friends, and noting, very definitely, the change that had come over them.

Drizzt was all business, as usual, signaling back directions and weaving around with a sureness of foot and a speed that the others, save Guenhwyvar who was not even there this day, could not hope to match. The drow was pretending as if nothing had happened, Regis saw clearly, but it was just that, a pretense.

His zigzagging routes were keeping him closer to Catti-brie, the halfling noted, constantly coming to vantage points that put him in sight of the woman. Truly, the drow's movements surprised Regis, for never before had he seen Drizzt so protective.

Was it protectiveness, the halfling had to wonder, or was it something else?

The change in Catti-brie was even more obvious. There was a coolness about her, particularly toward Drizzt. It wasn't anything overtly rude, it was just that she was speaking much less that day than normally, answering his directions with a simple nod or shrug. The incident with the orcs was weighing heavily on her mind, Regis supposed.

He glanced back at the dwarven caravan then looked all around, ensuring that they were secure for the time being—no sign of any orc or giant had shown that day—then he scrambled forward along the trail, catching up to Catti-brie.

"A chill in the wind this morning," he said to her.

She nodded and kept looking straight ahead. Her thoughts were inward and not on the trail before her.

"Seems that the cold has affected your shoulder," Regis dared to remark.

Catti-brie nodded again, but then she stopped and turned deliberately to regard him. Her stern expression did not hold against the cherubic halfling face, one full of innocence, even though it was obvious that Regis had just made a remark at her expense.

"I'm sorry," the woman said. "A lot on me mind is all."

"When we were on the river, on our way to Cadderly, and the goblin spear found my shoulder, I felt the same way," Regis replied, "helpless, and as if the end of my road was upon me."

"And more than a few have noted the change that has come over Regis since that day."

It was Regis's turn to shrug.

"Often in those moments when we think all is lost," he said, "many things . . . priorities . . . become clear to us. Sometimes, it just takes a while after the incident to sort things out."

Catti-brie's smile told him that he had hit the mark.

"It's a strange thing, this life we've chosen," Regis mused. "We know that the odds tell us without doubt that we'll one day be killed in the wilds, but we keep telling ourselves that it won't be this day at least, and so we walk farther along that same road.

"Why does Regis, no friend of any road, take that walk, then?" Catti-brie asked.

"Because I've chosen to walk with my friends," the halfling explained. "Because we are as one, and I would rather die out here beside you than learn of your death while sitting in a comfortable chair—especially when such news would come with my feelings that perhaps if I had been with you, you would not have been killed."

"It is guilt, then?"

"That, and a desire not to miss the excitement," Regis answered with a laugh. "How much grander the tales are than the experiences. I know that from listening to Bruenor and his kin exaggerating every thrown punch into a battering ram of a fist that could level a castle's walls, yet even knowing it, hearing those tales about incidents that did not include me, fill me with wonder and regret."

"So ye've come to admit yer adventurous side?"

"Perhaps."

"And ye're not thinking that ye might be needing more?"

Regis looked at her with an expression that conveyed that he was not sure what "more" might mean.

"Ye're not thinking that ye might want a life with others of yer own ilk? That ye might want a wife and some . . ."

"Children?" the halfling finished when Catti-brie paused, as if she could not force the word from her lips.

"Aye."

"It has been so many years since I've even lived among other halflings," Regis said, "and . . . well, it did not end amicably."

"It's a tale ye've not told."

"And too long a tale for this road," Regis replied. "I don't know how to answer you. Honestly. For now, I've got my friends, and that has just seemed to be enough."

"For now?"

Regis shrugged and asked, "Is that what's troubling you? Did you find more regrets than you expected when the orcs had encircled you and you thought your life to be at its end?"

Catti-brie looked away, giving the halfling all the answer he needed. The perceptive Regis saw much more than the direct answer to his question. He understood the source of many of those regrets. He had been watching Catti-brie's relationship with Drizzt grow over the last months, and while the sight of them surely did his romantic heart good, he knew that such a union, if it ever came to pass, would not be without its troubles. He knew what Catti-brie had been thinking when the orcs hovered over her. She had been wondering about children, her children, and it was obvious to Regis that children were nothing Drizzt Do'Urden could ever give to her. Could a drow and human even bear offspring?

Perhaps, since elves and humans could, and had, but what fate might such a child find? Was it one that Catti-brie could accept?

"What will you do?" the halfling asked her, drawing a curious look.

Regis nodded ahead on the trail, to the figure of Drizzt walking toward them. Catti-brie looked at him and took a deep breath.

"I will walk the trails as scout for our group," the woman answered coolly. "I will draw Taumaril often and fire true, and when battle is joined I'll leap in with Cutter's gleaming edge slashing down our foes."

"You know what I mean."

"No, I do not," Catti-brie answered.

Regis started to argue, but Drizzt was upon them then, and so he bit back his retort.

"The trails are clear of orc-sign," the drow remarked, speaking haltingly and looking from Regis to Catti-brie, as if suspicious of the conversation he was so obviously interrupting.

"Then we will make the ravine before nightfall," Catti-brie replied.

"Long before, and make our turn to the north."

The woman nodded, and Regis gave a frustrated, *"Hrmmph!"* and walked away.

"What troubles our little friend?" Drizzt asked.

"The road ahead," the woman answered.

"Ah, perhaps there is a bit of the old Regis within him yet," Drizzt said with a smile, missing the true meaning of her words.

Catti-brie just smiled and kept walking.

They made the ravine soon after and saw the gleaming white tower that marked the town of Shallows—the tower of Withegroo Seian'Doo, a wizard of minor repute. Hardly pausing, the group moved along its western edge until long after the sun had set. They heard the howls of wolves that night, but they were far off, and if they were connected in any way to any orcs, the companions could not tell.

They rounded the ravine the next day, turning to the east and back toward the south and took heart, for still there was no sign of the orcs. It seemed as if the group that had hit Clicking Heels might be an isolated one, and those who had not fallen to the vengeful dwarves had likely retreated to dark mountain holes.

Again they marched long after sunset, and when they camped, they did so with the watch fires of Shallows's wall in sight, knowing full well that their own fires could be seen clearly from the town.

Drizzt was not surprised to find a pair of scouts moving their way under the cover of darkness. The drow was out for a final survey of the area when he heard the footfalls, soon coming in sight of the creeping men. They were trying to be quiet, obviously, and having little fortune, almost constantly tripping over roots and stones.

The drow moved to a position to the side of the pair behind a tree and called out, "Halt and be counted!"

It was a customary demand in these wild parts. The two humans stumbled again and fell to low crouches, glancing about nervously.

"Who is it who approaches the camp of King Bruenor Battlehammer without proper announcement?" Drizzt called.

"King Bruenor!" the pair yelled together, and at each other.

"Aye, the lord of Mithral Hall, returned home upon news of the death of Gandalug, who was king."

"He's a bit far to the north, I'm thinking," one man dared reply.

The pair kept hopping about, trying to discern the speaker.

"We're on the trail of orcs and giants who sacked a town to the south and west," Drizzt explained. "Journeying to Shallows, fair Shallows, to ensure that the folk are well, and well protected, should any monsters move against them."

One man snorted, and the other yelled back, "Bah! No orc'll e'er climb the wall of Shallows, and no giant'll ever knock it down!"

"Well spoken," Drizzt said, and the man assumed a defiant posture, standing straight and tall and crossing his arms over his chest. "I take it that you are scouts of Shallows, then?"

"We're wanting to know who it is setting camp in sight of our walls," the man called back

"Well, it is as I told you, but please, continue on your way. You will be announced to King Bruenor. I am certain that he will gladly share his table this night."

The man eased from his defiant posture and looked to his friend, the two seeming unsure.

"Run along!" Drizzt called.

And he was gone, melting into the night, running easily along the rough ground and quickly outdistancing the men so that by the time they at last reached the encampment, Bruenor and the others were waiting for them, with two extra heaping plates set out.

"Me friend here told me ye'd be in," Bruenor said to the pair.

He looked to the side, and so did the scouts, to where Drizzt was dropping the cowl of his cloak, revealing his dark heritage.

Both men widened their eyes at the sight, but then one unexpectedly cried out, "Drizzt Do'Urden! By the gods, but I wondered if I'd ever meet the likes of yerself!"

Drizzt smiled—he couldn't help it, so unused was he to hearing such warm greetings from surface dwellers. He glanced at Bruenor, and noted Catti-brie standing beside the dwarf and looking his way, her expression curious, a bit confused, and a bit charmed.

Drizzt could only guess at the swirl of emotions behind that look.

20

SHARP TURN
IN THE ROAD

They moved along the paths of the Moonwood easily, with Tarathiel, astride Sunset, leading the way. The bells of his saddle jingled merrily, and Innovindil walked with the dwarf brothers right behind. The sky was gray, and the air stifling and a bit too warm, but the elves seemed in a fine mood, as did Pikel, who was marveling at their winding trail. They kept coming upon seeming dead ends and Tarathiel, who knew the western stretch of the Moonwood better than anyone alive, would make a slight adjustment and a new path would open before him, clear and inviting. It almost seemed as if Tarathiel had just asked the trees for passage, and that they had complied.

Pikel so loved that kind of thing.

Among the four, only Ivan was in a surly mood. The dwarf hadn't slept well the previous night, awakened often by Elvish singing, and while Ivan would join in any good drinking song, any hymn to the dwarf gods (which was pretty much the same thing), or songs of heroes of old and treasures lost and treasures found, he found the Elvish styling little more than whining, pining at the moon and the stars.

In fact, over the past few days, Ivan had had about enough of the elves altogether and only wanted to be back on the road to Mithral Hall. The yellow-bearded dwarf, never known for his subtlety, had related those emotions to Tarathiel and Innovindil often and repeatedly.

The four were moving out to the west from the region where the elves of the Moonwood made their main enclave and just a bit to the north, where the ground was higher and they would likely spot the snaking River Surbrin. The dwarves could then use the river as a guide on their southerly turn to Mithral Hall. Tarathiel had explained that they had about a tenday of traveling ahead of them—less, if they managed to float some kind of raft on the river and glide through the night.

Pikel and Innovindil chatted almost constantly along the trail, sharing information and insights on the various plants and animals they passed. Once or twice, Pikel called a bird down from a tree and whispered something to it. The bird, apparently understanding, flew off and returned with many others, lining the branches around the foursome and filling the air with their chirping song. Innovindil clapped her hands and beamed an enchanted smile at Pikel. Even Tarathiel, the far more serious of the two elves, seemed quite pleased. Ivan missed it all, though, stomping along, grumbling to himself about "stupid fairies."

That, of course, only pleased the elves even more—especially when Pikel convinced the birds to make an amazingly accurate bombing run above his brother.

"Think ye might be lending me yer fine bow?" the disgruntled Ivan asked Tarathiel. The dwarf glared up at the branches as he spoke. "I can get us a bit o' supper."

Tarathiel's answer was a bemused smile, which only widened when Pikel added, "Hee hee hee."

"We shan't be accompanying you two to Mithral Hall," Tarathiel explained.

"Who was askin' ye?" Ivan grumbled in reply, but when the two elves fixed him with surprised and a bit wounded looks, the dwarf seemed to retract a bit. "Bah, but why'd ye want to go and stay with a bunch of dwarfs anyway? Course ye could, if ye're wanting to, and me and me brother'd make sure that ye was treated as well as ye treated us two in yer stinkin . . . in yer pretty forest."

"Your compliments roll as freely as a frozen river, Ivan Boulder-shoulder," Innovindil said in a deceivingly complimentary tone.

She tossed a wink to Tarathiel and Pikel, who giggled.

"Aye," said Ivan, apparently not catching on.

He smirked and looked hard at the elf.

"We have much to discuss with King Bruenor, though," Tarathiel remarked then, bringing the conversation back to the issue at hand. "Perhaps you will bid him to send an emissary to the Moonwood. Drizzt Do'Urden would be welcomed."

"The dark elf?" Ivan balked. "Couple o' moon elves like yerselves asking me to ask a drow to walk into yer home? Ye best be careful, Tarathiel. Yer reputation for hospitality to dwarfs and dark elfs might not be sittin' well with yer kin!"

"Not to dark elves, I assure you," the elf corrected, "but to that one dark elf, yes. We would welcome Drizzt Do'Urden, though we have not named him as a friend. We have information regarding him—information that will be important to him and is important to us."

"Such as?"

"That is all that I am at liberty to say at this time," Tarathiel replied. "I'd not burden you with such a long and detailed story to bring to King Bruenor. Without knowledge of that which came before, you would not understand enough to properly convey the information."

"It is out of no mistrust of you two that we choose to wait for King Bruenor's official emissary," Innovindil was quick to add, for a scowl was growing over Ivan's face. "There is protocol that must be followed. This message we ask you to deliver is of great importance, and we let you go with complete confidence that you will not only deliver our words to King Bruenor, but deliver them with our sense of urgency in mind."

"Oo oi!" Pikel agreed, punching a fist into the air.

Tarathiel started to second that, but he stopped suddenly, his expression growing very serious. He glanced around, then at Innovindil, then slid down from his winged mount.

"What's he seein'?" Ivan demanded.

Innovindil locked stares with Tarathiel, her expression growing equally stern.

Tarathiel motioned for Ivan to be quiet then moved silently to the side of the trail, bending low to the ground, head tilted as if he was listening. Ivan started to say something again, but Tarathiel held up a hand, silencing him.

"Oooo," said Pikel, looking around with alarm.

Ivan hopped about, seeing nothing but his three concerned companions.

"What'd ye know?" he asked Tarathiel, but the elf was deep in thought and did not reply.

Ivan rushed across to Pikel and asked, "What'd ye know?"

Pikel crinkled his face and pinched his nose.

"Orcs?" Ivan cried.

"Yup yup."

In a single movement, Ivan pulled the axe from his back and turned, feet set wide apart in solid balance, axe at the ready before him, eyes narrowed and scouring every shadow.

"Well, bring 'em on, then. I'm up for a bit o' chopping afore another long and boring road!"

"I sense them, too," Innovindil said a moment later.

"Dere," Pikel added, pointing to the north.

The two elves followed his finger, then looked back at him, nodding.

"Our borders have seen orc incursions of late," Innovindil explained. "This one, as the others, will be repelled. Trouble yourselves not with these creatures. Your road is to the west and the south, and there you should go and quickly. We will see to the beasts that dare stain the Moonwood."

"Uh-uh," Pikel disagreed, crossing his burly, hairy arms over his chest.

"Bah!" Ivan snorted. "Ye're not for throwin' us out afore the fun begins! Ye call yerselfs proper hosts and ye're thinking o' chasin' us off with orcs needin' killing?"

The two elves looked to each other, honestly surprised.

"Yeah, I know, and no, I'm not liking ye," Ivan explained, "but I'm hatin' yer enemies, so that's a good thing. Now, are ye to make a friend of a dwarf and let him chop an orc or fifty? Or are ye to chase us off and hope we're remembering the words ye asked us to deliver to King Bruenor?"

Still the elves exchanged questioning glances, and Innovindil gave a slight shrug, leaving the decision to Tarathiel alone.

"Come along, then," the elf said to the brothers. "Let us see what we can learn before rousing my people against the threat. And do try to be quiet."

"Bah, if we're too quiet, might be that the orcs'll just wander away, and what good's that?"

They moved a short distance before Tarathiel motioned for them to stop and bade them to wait. He climbed onto the pegasus, found a run for Sunset, and lifted into the air, rising carefully in the close quarters, up and out to the north.

He returned almost immediately, setting down before the three, motioning for them to hold silent and to follow him. Up to the north a short distance, the elf led them to the top of a ridge. From that vantage point, Ivan saw that the mystical tree-attuned senses of his companions had not led them astray.

There, in a clearing of their own making, was a band of orcs. It was a dozen at least, perhaps as many as a score, weaving in and out of the shadows of the trees. They carried large axes, perfect for chopping the tall trees, and more importantly (and explaining why Tarathiel had been so quick to return with Sunset) and more atypically, they also each had a long, strong bow.

"I saw them from afar," Tarathiel explained quietly to the other three as they crouched at the ridge top. "I do not believe that they spotted me."

"We must get word to the clan," Innovindil said.

Tarathiel looked around doubtfully. They had been traveling for a couple of days. While he realized that his people would move much more quickly with such dire news as orc intruders, and without having a pair of dwarves slowing them down, he didn't think that they would get there in time to catch the orcs in the Moonwood.

"They must not escape," the elf said grimly, thoughts of the last band retreating into the mountains still fresh in his mind.

"Then let's kill 'em," Ivan replied.

"Three to one," Innovindil remarked. "Perhaps five to one."

"It'll be quick, then," Ivan replied.

He took up his heavy axe. Beside him, Pikel fished his cooking pot out of his sack, plopped it on his head, and agreed, "Oo oi!"

The elves looked to each other with obvious confusion and surprise.

"Oo oi!" Pikel repeated.

Tarathiel looked at Innovindil for his answer.

"It has been a long time since I have had a good fight," she said with a wry grin.

"Only a dozen—ye'll have longer to wait for any real fight," Ivan said dryly, but the elves didn't seem to pay his remark much heed.

Tarathiel looked over at Ivan and asked, "Where will you fit in?"

"In the middle o' them, I'm hoping," the dwarf answered, pointing toward the distant orcs. "And I'm thinking me axe'll be fitting in real well between them orcs' eyeballs."

That seemed simple enough, and so Tarathiel and Innovindil looked to Pikel, who merely chuckled, "Hee hee hee."

"Don't ye be frettin' about me brother," Ivan explained. "He'll find a way to do his part. I'm not knowin' how—I'm usually not knowin' how even after the fightin's over—but he does, and he will."

"Good enough, then," said Tarathiel. "Let us find the best vantage point for launching our strike."

He moved to Sunset and whispered something into the pegasus's ear, then started away while Sunset walked off in another direction. Innovindil went next, moving as silently as her elf partner. Then came Ivan and Pikel, crunching away on every dry leaf and dead stick.

"Vantage point," Ivan huffed to his brother. "Just walk in, say yer howdies, and start killing!"

"Hee hee hee," said Pikel.

Innovindil also wore a smile at that remark, but it was one edged with a bit of trepidation. Confidence was one thing, carelessness quite another.

With the elves guiding them, and despite the noisiness of the dwarves, the foursome came to the edge of a rocky clearing. Across the way, the orcs were at their work, some chopping hard at one tree, others holding guiding ropes tied off along the higher branches.

"We will hit at them after they have retired," Tarathiel quietly explained. "The sun is high. It should not be long."

Pikel's face grew very tight, though, and he shook his head.

"He's not for watching them cut down a tree," Ivan explained, and the elves looked to each other doubtfully.

Pikel opened a pouch, revealing a cache of bright red berries. His expression grew very serious and very stern. With a grim nod to the others, he walked up to a nearby oak, the widest tree around, and put his forehead against its thick trunk. He closed his eyes and began muttering under his breath.

Still muttering, he stepped *into* the tree, disappearing completely.

"Yeah, I know yer feelings," Ivan whispered to the two elves, who were standing dumbfounded, their mouths hanging open. "He does it all the time."

Ivan's gaze went up to the branches, and he pointed and said, "There."

Pikel exited the trunk some twenty feet above the ground, moving out on a branch that overhung the rocky field.

"Your brother is a curious one," Innovindil whispered. "Many tricks."

"We may need them," Tarathiel added.

He was looking doubtfully at the dozen or more orcs, all with bows on their backs or lying within easy reach. Looking up at Pikel, though, he knew that the dwarves weren't likely to wait, whatever he suggested, so he went into a crouch and began surveying the battlefield, then motioned to Innovindil to fan out to the side.

Ivan walked right between them, crunching through the trees, axe in hand, stepping onto the edge of the clearing.

"Can't be hitting anything that moves, now can ye?" he taunted loudly.

The chopping stopped immediately. All sound from the other side of the clearing halted, and the orcs turned as one, their yellowish, bloodshot eyes wide.

"Well?" Ivan called to them. "Ain't ye never looked death in the eye before?"

The orcs didn't charge across the way. They began to move slowly, deliberately, with a couple barking orders.

"Them're the leaders," Ivan whispered back to the concealed elves. "Pick yer shots."

The orcs never blinked, never took their eyes off the spectacle of the lone dwarf standing barely twenty feet from them, as they slowly began to collect their bows, to string the weapons and bring them up to the ready.

The leaders continued to talk to the others, and it was obvious that they were calling for a coordinated barrage, bidding those already prepared to fire to hold their shots.

The elves fired first, a pair of arrows soaring out from the brush to strike true across the way, Tarathiel's taking one leader in the throat, Innovindil's catching another in the belly, sending it squirming to the ground.

At that same moment, the air before Ivan seemed to warp like a ripple on a pond, and that wave rushed across the clearing as the orcs let fly.

Arrows warped even as they cleared the bows, bending like the strands of a willow tree and flying every which way but straight. Except for one, from the trees to the side, that soared in at Ivan.

The dwarf saw it in time, though, and he jerked down, bringing his axe up to the side and, fortunately, in line with the missile. It clipped the blade, then Ivan's armored shoulder, staggering the dwarf to the side but doing no real damage against the armor he wore.

"Get 'em all, ye durned fool!" Ivan scolded his brother, who giggled from the boughs above him.

Across the way, the orcs looked at their bows as if deceived and saw that most of those, too, had warped under the druidic magic wave, and so they threw them down, drew out swords and spears, and charged wildly.

Two more barely began their run before elven arrows dropped them.

Ivan Bouldershoulder resisted the urge to counter with his own charge, and the urge to look up and make sure that his scatterbrained brother was still paying attention.

Another pair of elven arrows soared off, and Tarathiel and Innovindil leaped out beside Ivan, each drawing a slender sword and a long dirk.

The orcs closed, leaping stones and scrambling over boulders, and howling their guttural battle cries.

Handfuls of bright red berries flew out over Ivan and the elves, enchanted missiles that popped loudly and sparked painfully as they hit. Dozens of little bursts settled in and around the charging orcs. The enchanted bombs did little damage, but brought about massive confusion, an opening that neither Ivan nor the elves missed.

Ivan pulled a hand axe from his belt and flung it into the face of the nearest orc, then drew a second and cut down an orc to the side. Out he charged with a roar, his large axe going to work immediately on one stumbling monster, halting its charge with a whack in the chest, then flying wide as Ivan spun past, coming in hard and chopping the creature on the back of the neck.

But it was the movement of the elves, and not ferocious Ivan, that elicited the sincerely impressed "Oooo" from Pikel up above.

Standing side by side, Tarathiel and Innovindil brought their weapons up in a flowing cross before their chests, rising past their faces and going out at the ready to either side, so that Tarathiel's right arm crossed against Innovindil's left, forearm to forearm. They held that touch as they went out against the charge, moving as if they were one, flowing back and forth and turning as they went, Tarathiel crossing behind Innovindil, coming around to the female's right and shifting past, so that they were touching right forearm to right forearm, right foot to right foot, heel against toe.

Not understanding the level of the joining, an orc rushed in at

Tarathiel's seemingly exposed back, only to find Innovindil's blade waiting for it, turning its spear aside with ease. Innovindil didn't finish the move, though, but rather went back to an orc that was still off-balance from Pikel's bomb barrage. The elf slid the blade easily through the orc's exposed ribs as it stumbled past. She didn't have to finish that move either, for Tarathiel had understood everything she had accomplished in the parry as surely as if he had done the movement himself. He just reversed his grip on the dirk in his left hand, and while still parrying the blade of the orc he was fighting before him with his sword, he thrust out hard behind, stabbing the attacking spear wielder in the chest.

In a single, fluid movement, Tarathiel extracted the dagger and flipped it into the air, catching it by the tip, then brought his arm toward the orc before him as if he meant to throw the dirk.

The orc flinched, and Tarathiel rotated away.

Innovindil came across, her long sword slashing the confused orc's throat.

Tarathiel stopped the rotation first and dropped his sword arm down and around, hooking his still-moving partner around the waist. He pulled hard, lifting Innovindil off the ground, pulling her over his hip, and whipping her across before him, her feet extended and kicking at the orc that had come in at Tarathiel.

She didn't score any hits on that orc—she wasn't really trying to—but her weaving feet had the creature reacting with its short, hooked blade, striking at her repeatedly and futilely.

As Innovindil rolled across his torso, Tarathiel reached across with his left hand, and she hooked her right elbow over it, and he stopped his rotation completely, except with that arm, playing with Innovindil's momentum to send her spinning out to his left.

At the same time, as soon as she had cleared the way, the male struck out with his right arm, his sword arm. The poor orc, still trying to catch up to Innovindil, never even saw the blade coming.

Innovindil landed lightly, her momentum and spin bringing her right across the path of another orc, her blades slashing high, stabbing low.

In that one short charge and spin, the elves had five orcs dead or dying.

"Oooo," said Pikel, and he looked down at the berries in his hand doubtfully.

Then he caught a movement to the side, moving through the brush, and saw a pair of orcs lifting bows.

He threw before they could fire, the two dozen little explosions making the orcs jump and jerk, stinging and blinding them.

Pikel's arms went out that way, his fingers waggling, calling to the brush around the pair of orcs. Vines and shrubs grabbed at the creatures, and at a third, Pikel realized with a giggle, for he heard the unseen orc roaring in protest below its trapped companions.

Ivan didn't have the grace or coordination of the warrior elves, and in truth, their deadly dance was impressive to the dwarf. Amusing, but impressive nonetheless.

What he lacked in grace, the yellow-bearded dwarf more than made up for in sheer ferocity, though. Rushing past the orc he had chopped down, he met the charge—and hard—of another, accepting a shield rush and setting his legs powerfully. He didn't move. The orc bounced back.

Ivan chopped that leading shield arm hard, his axe creasing the shield, even digging into the arm strapped under it. He jerked the weapon free immediately, lifting the orc into a short turn and forcing it to regain its balance. The dwarf struck again, this time getting the axe head past the blocking shield, chopping hard on the orc's shoulder.

The wounded creature stumbled back, but another rushed past it, and a third behind that.

Ivan was already moving, taking one step back and dropping low. He grabbed up a rock and threw it hard as he came up, thumping the closest orc in the chest, staggering it. As its companion came past it on its left, Ivan went past it on the right. His axe took the stunned orc in the gut, lifting it into the air and dropping it hard on its back.

The second orc skidded to a stop and started to turn—and caught Ivan's axe, spinning end over end, right in the chest.

Ivan, orcs in hot pursuit, charged right in, bowling over the creased orc as it fell and collecting his axe on the way. He kept running to a nearby boulder and leaped up and rolled over it, landing on his feet and falling back against it.

Orcs split around the boulder, charging on, and expecting that Ivan had run out the other side.

His axe caught the first coming by on the left, then went back hard to the right, smashing the lead orc from there as well.

Ivan hopped out behind the backhand, ready to fight straight up, but he found the work ending fast, as elven blades, already dripping orc blood, caught up to his pursuers.

There, facing the dwarf from either side of the boulder, stood Tarathiel and Innovindil. Much passed between the three at that moment, a level of respect that none of them had expected.

Ivan broke the stare first, glancing around, noting that no orcs were in the area except for dead and dying ones. He heard the clatter of the remaining creatures fleeing in the distant trees.

"Got me eight," Ivan announced.

He looked to the orc he had hit with the backhand, blunt side of his axe. It was hurt and dazed, and trying to rise, but before the dwarf could make a move toward it, Tarathiel's sword sliced its throat.

The dwarf shrugged. "All right, seven and a half," he said.

"And yet, I would reason that the one among us who scored the fewest kills was the most instrumental in our easy victory," said Innovindil.

She looked up to the tree to where Pikel had been sitting. A movement to the side turned her gaze, and those of Ivan and Tarathiel, to a tangle of brush from which Pikel was emerging, bloody club in hand and a wide grin on his face.

"Sha-la-la," the dwarf explained, holding forth the enchanted club. He held up three stubby fingers. "Tree!" he announced.

There came a movement behind him. Pikel's smile disappeared, and the dwarf spun around, his club smashing down.

The three across the way winced at the sound of shattering bone, but then Pikel came back up, his smile returned.

"Not quite done?" Ivan asked dryly.

"Tree!" came Pikel's enthusiastic reply, three fingers pointed up into the air.

The day was warm and sunny when the four companions came to the northwestern corner of the Moonwood. From a vantage point up high on a ridge, Tarathiel pointed out the shining line of the River Surbrin, snaking its way along the foothills of the Spine of the World to the west, flowing north to south.

"That will bring you to the eastern gates of Mithral Hall," Tarathiel explained. "Near to it, at least. I suspect you will find your way to the dwarven halls easily enough."

"And we trust that you will deliver our message to King Bruenor and the dark elf, Drizzt Do'Urden," Innovindil added.

"Yup," said Pikel.

"We'll tell 'em," said Ivan.

The elves looked at each other, neither expression holding any doubt at all. The four parted as friends, with more respect between them, particularly from Ivan and Tarathiel, than they had ever expected to find.

PART FOUR THE TURN IN THE ROAD

W e have to live our lives and view our relationship in the present. That is the truth of my life with Catti-brie, and it is also my fear for that life. To live in the here and now, to walk the wind-swept trails and do battle against whatever foe opposes us. To define our cause and our purpose, even if that purpose is no more than the pursuit of adventure, and to chase that goal with all our hearts and souls. When we do that, Catti-brie and I are free of the damning realities of our respective heritage. As long as we do that, we can live our lives together in true friendship and love, as close as two reasoning beings could ever be.

It is only when we look further down the road of the future that we encounter troubles.

On the mountainous trails north of Mithral Hall, Catti-brie recently had a brush with death and more poignantly, a brush with mortality. She looked at the end of her life, so suddenly and brutally. She thought she was dead, and believed in that horrible instant that she would never be a mother, that she would bear no children and instill in them the values that guide her life and her road. She saw mortality, true mortality, with no one to carry on her legacy.

She did not like what she saw.

She escaped death, as she has so often done, as I, and all of us, have so often done. Wulfgar was there for her, as he would have been for any of us, as any of us would have been for him, to scatter the orcs. And so her mortality was not realized in full.

But still the thought lingers.

And there, in that clearer understanding of the prospects of her future, in the clearer understanding of the prospect of our future, lies the rub, the sharp turn in our adventurous road that threatens to spill all that we have come to achieve into a ravine of deadly rocks.

What future is there between us? When we consider our relationship day by day, there is only joy and adventure and excitement; when we look down the road, we see limitations that we, particularly Catti-brie, cannot ignore. Will she ever bear children? Could she even bear mine? There are many half-elves in the world, the product of mixed heritage, human and elf, but half-drow? I have never heard of such a thing—it was rumored that House Barrison Del'Armgo fostered such couplings, to add strength and size to their warrior males, but I know not if that was anything more than rumor. Certainly the results were not promising, even if that were true!

So I do not know that I could father any of Catti-brie's children, and in truth, even if it is possible, it is not necessarily a pleasant prospect, and certainly not one without severe repercussions. Certainly I would want children of mine to hold so many of Catti-brie's wonderful qualities: her perceptive nature, her bravery, her compassion, her constant holding to the course she knows to be right, and of course, her beauty. No parent could be anything but proud of a child who carried the qualities of Catti-brie.

But that child would be half-drow in a world that will not accept drow elves. I find a measure of tolerance now, in towns where my reputation precedes me, but what chance might any child beginning in this place have? By the time such a child was old enough to begin to make any such reputation, he or she would be undoubtedly scarred by the uniqueness of heritage. Perhaps we could have a child and keep it in Mithral Hall all the years.

But that, too, is a limitation, and one that Catti-brie knows all too well.

It is all too confusing and all too troubling. I love Catti-brie—I know that now—and know, too, that she loves me. We are friends above all else, and that is the beauty of our relationship. In the here and in the now, walking the road, feeling the wind, fighting our enemies, I could not ask for a better companion, a better compliment to who I am.

But as I look farther down that road, a decade, two decades, I see sharper curves and deeper ravines. I would love Catti-brie until the day of her death, if that day found her infirm and aged while I was still in the flower of my youth. To me, there would be no burden, no longing to go out and adventure more, no need to go out and find a more physically compatible companion, an elf or perhaps even another drow.

Catti-brie once asked me if my greatest limitation was internal or external. Was I more limited by the way people viewed me as a dark elf, or by the way I viewed people viewing me? I think that same thing applies now, only for her. For while I understand the turns our road together will inevitably take, and I fully accept them, she fears them, I believe, and more for my sensibilities than for her own. In three decades, when she nears sixty years of age, she will be old by human standards. I'll be around a hundred, my first century, and would still be considered a very young adult, barely more than a child, by the reckoning of the drow. I think that her brush with mortality is making her look to that point and that she is not much enjoying the prospects—for me more than for her.

And there remains that other issue, of children. If we two were to start a family, our children would face terrific pressures and prejudices and would be young, so very young, when their mother passed away.

It is all too confusing.

I choose, for now, to walk in the present.

Yes, I do so out of fear.

—Drizzt Do'Urden

THE AURA
OF BEING KING

Even after the greeting by the guards sent out from Shallows, the response from the town the following morning, when the King of Mithral Hall and his entourage walked through the front gate of the walled town, stunned the group.

Trumpeters sounded from the parapets and from the top of the lone tower that stood along the northern wall of the small town. Though none of the trumpeters was very good, and none dressed in the shining armor one might expect from the court of a larger city like Silverymoon, Bruenor was certain that he had never heard anyone play with more heart.

All the people of the village, more than a hundred, encircled the area beyond the gate, clapping and waving and throwing petals. There were more women than Bruenor had expected from a frontier town and even a few children, including a couple of babies. Perhaps he should be spending quite a bit of time out of Mithral Hall and watching over these developing towns, Bruenor mused. It was not an unpleasant thought. In just looking at the place, it seemed to him as if Shallows was trying hard to become a regular town, a settled place, instead of the pocket of rogues and outlaws he had always thought it and all the other towns of the Savage Frontier to be. He considered his former home then, Ten-Towns, and recalled the evolution of those ten cities into something far more settled than they had been when he had first arrived in Icewind Dale those centuries before.

The dwarf, leading the procession, paused and looked around, past the many cheering people to their sturdy houses. Most were made of stone with supporting wooden frames, and all were built solid, as if the inhabitants meant to be there for a while. Bruenor nodded his silent approval, his gaze gradually moving to the single tower that so clearly marked the town. It was a thirty-foot gray cylinder, flying a pennant of a pair of hands surrounded by golden stars on a red background. A wizard's emblem, obviously, and when the crowd before him parted and a white-bearded old man walked through, dressed in a tall and pointy hat and bright red robes emblazoned in golden stars, it wasn't hard for the dwarf to make the connection.

"Welcome to my humble town, King Bruenor of Mithral Hall," the man said, walking up to stand right before Bruenor. He swept off his hat and fell into a grand bow. "I am Withegroo Seian'Doo, the founder of Shallows and present liege. This honor is unexpected but surely not unwelcome."

"Me greetings to yerself, Withe . . ."

"Withe*groo*."

"Withegroo," Bruenor finished. "And I'm not yet King Bruenor—well, not yet again, if ye get me meaning."

"It was with great sadness that I and my fellow townsfolk here heard of the passing of your ancestor, Gandalug."

"Yep, but the old one had himself a few good centuries, and I'm not thinking we can be askin' for more than that," Bruenor replied.

He looked around, to see the cheery and sincere smiles of the townsfolk, and he knew that he could be at ease there, that he and his friends, even Drizzt who was standing right behind him, were indeed welcomed guests in Shallows.

"Got the word in the west," the dwarf explained. "In Icewind Dale, where me and a few o' me friends were making our homes."

"Did you get lost on your journey home to Mithral Hall?"

Bruenor shook his head.

"Found me a couple o' friends from Felbarr," he explained, and he turned and indicated Tred, who gave an uncomfortable though still gracious bow. "They'd found themselves a bit o' trouble with some orcs."

He noted a shadow cross over Withegroo's wrinkled old face and long, hawkish nose. The man's enormous ears twitched beneath the bristles of his wild white hair, which was sticking out in every direction under the bent brim of his red hat.

Bruenor matched that look with a grave one of his own.

"Ye know the town o' Clicking Heels?" he asked somberly.

Withegroo looked around, to see several of his townsfolk nodding.

"Well, it ain't no more," Bruenor said bluntly. "Orcs 'n giants laid it to waste. Killed them all."

Groans, gasps, and whispers sprang up all around the courtyard.

"We been chasin' the dogs and killed more than a few," Bruenor went on quickly, wanting to put a better light on the tragedy. "Left a handful o' giants and near to a hunnerd orcs layin' dead in the mountains, but we thought it smart to come in here and make sure that Shallows was standing strong."

"Stronger than you can imagine," Withegroo replied.

He stood up straight and tall—and he was tall, well over six feet, tall enough to look Wulfgar in the eye without bending back his head. Unlike Wulfgar, though, the man was stick lean and couldn't have weighed more than half the barbarian's three hundred pounds.

"We have suffered the likes of orcs and giants many times," the wizard continued, "but not once have any crossed the line of our strong walls."

"Old Withegroo lays 'em dead with his lightning!" one man shouted from the side, and others immediately took up the chorus of cheers for the wizard.

Withegroo smiled, somewhat sheepishly, somewhat pridefully, and turned to them, patting his hands humbly to silence the growing chorus.

"I do what I can," the wizard said to Bruenor, turning back to face the dwarf. "I am no novice to battle, and I made my name and my fortune adventuring in dark caves filled with all sorts of beasts."

"And ye bought yerself a town," Bruenor remarked, with no sarcasm in his tone.

"I built myself a tower," the wizard corrected. "I thought this a fine place to live out my days, in study and recollections of adventures past. These good folk"—he turned and swept his hand across the crowd—"found me, one by one and family by family. I believe they recognized the value of having so striking a landmark as my tower in their intended settlement—brings in the dwarf traders, you see."

He ended with an exaggerated wink, which brought a smile to Bruenor's face.

"Bet they weren't minding having a wizard lookin' over them, throwing a few bolts o' lightning at any monsters venturing too close, either," the dwarf said to Withegroo, who took the compliment in stride.

"I do what I can."

"I'm bettin' ye do."

"Well," the wizard said with a deep breath, setting an abrupt change in the conversation. "You have come to check in on us, and an honor it is, King—or soon to be King—Bruenor Battlehammer. You can see that we are secure and strong, but I beg you, do not take quick leave of us. The walls of Shallows and the houses alike are of stone, and may seem cold—though not to a dwarf!—but they mask hearths of warmth and the voices of those with many adventures to share." He stepped back and looked up, addressing the whole company. "You are welcome, one and all. Welcome to Shallows!"

And with that, a great cheer went up form all the townsfolk, and Bruenor motioned for his road-weary group to disperse and relax.

"A bit better welcome than we received from Mirabar," Drizzt remarked to Bruenor, Catti-brie, Regis, and Wulfgar when the dwarf king moved away from Withegroo to rejoin his closest friends.

"Yeah, Mirabar," Bruenor grumbled. "Remind me to knock that place down."

"Not a sign o' orc about," Catti-brie said, "and a town with strong walls and stronger folk, and a wizard backing them. . . ."

She nodded her approval.

"And a southern road awaiting us," Wulfgar put in.

"But not right yet," said Catti-brie. "I'm thinking we should stay on a bit, just to be sure they're safe."

"Ye got a feeling, do ye?" Bruenor asked.

Catti-brie looked around, and despite the festivities, the laughter, and the seemingly normal scene, a cloud crossed her face.

"Yeah, I got it, too," said Bruenor. "But not to worry. We'll be checkin' all the land, and we'll take our march to the Surbrin in the east. Tred's telling me there's a couple more towns down that way. Let's see how many o' the folk in the region are as welcoming to King Bruenor and his friends."

He looked at Drizzt and pointedly added, "All his friends."

The drow shrugged as if it did not matter, and in truth, it did not.

"There are ten thousand more in dark holes who will be led if they believe that they will find greater glory," Ad'non Kareese said to his three companions.

He had just returned from a scouting circuit of the region between the dark elves hideaway and Gerti's complex, including a pair of visits with other minor monster kings: an orc who knew of Obould and a particularly wretched goblin.

"Twenty thousand," Donnia corrected, "at least. The mountain caverns crawl with the little beasts, and the only thing that keeps them in there is their own stupidity and fear. If Obould and Gerti claim this prize, the head of the king of the dwarven stronghold, then we will coax more than a few, I am certain."

"To what end?" Kaer'lic interjected doubtfully. "Then we will only have to look at the beasts scurrying about the surface."

"In chaos we find comfort," Tos'un put in with a wry grin.

"Spoken like a dolt from Menzoberranzan," said Kaer'lic, which only made Tos'un smile even wider.

"To your own tests of worthiness, then," Tos'un replied. "In chaos we find wealth. In chaos we find enjoyment."

Kaer'lic shrugged and didn't argue.

"I have already made some connections with the leaders of the various goblin and orc tribes and have heard hints of one that holds great ties to the more formidable beasts of the Trollmoors to the south," Ad'non remarked.

"Beware the boasts of goblins," said Donnia. "They would tell you that the mountain giants bow to them if they thought you would be impressed."

"Their tunnels stretch long," Ad'non replied.

"I am willing to believe that we can do this," said Tos'un, "and willing to believe that we will enjoy it greatly. I was the biggest doubter when we first tried to tie Obould to Gerti, and I was certain that the giantess would throttle the wretched orc when she learned of the loss of four of her kin, yet look where we are. Obould's scouts are everywhere, running the mountains, tracking this band that we believe contains King Bruenor himself. Once he is found, and Gerti takes her revenge. . . ."

"We can rally thousands to Obould's side," said Ad'non. "We can create a dark swarm that will cover the land for miles around!"

"And?" Kaer'lic asked dryly.

"And let them kill the dwarves, the humans, and each other," Ad'non replied. "And we will be there, always one step behind, yet always one step ahead, to collect our due at every turn."

"And to thoroughly enjoy the spectacle of it all," Donnia added with a wicked grin.

Kaer'lic accepted that reasoning and nodded her approval.

"Be certain that our allies are warned of the presence of a drow who is not a friend," the priestess advised.

She sat back as the others began formulating plans for their next moves. Kaer'lic did like the excitement, but there were other matters that concerned her more. She thought back to some experiences she had faced before finding her two, then three companions, when she had been out of her Underdark city on a mission for the ruling priestesses.

In those thoughts, Drizzt Do'Urden surely came to mind more than once, for he was not the first traitor to Lolth and drow ways that Kaer'lic the Terrible had faced.

It wasn't that she had any particular hatred or vendetta against Drizzt, of course—Tos'un would more likely harbor such resentments, she supposed—but the ever-plotting priestess had to wonder how it would all play out. Would she find unexpected opportunities to pay back old debts? Might the reputation of one renegade drow be put in good service to the Spider Queen, and even more importantly, to a priestess who had fallen out of favor with the goddess?

She smiled and looked around at the other three, all seeming so much more eager to play this out than was she.

Kaer'lic the Terrible, ever the patient one.

They heard the trumpets, and though they were somewhat dim-witted, one of the orc band made the connection between that heralding sound and the troupe they had been tracking.

From across the ravine, the orcs had the same view of Withegroo's tower as Drizzt and his friends had enjoyed only the day before.

Wicked grins splayed on their misshapen, tusked mouths, the orc patrol rushed away, back up into the foothills to where Urlgen, son of Obould, waited.

"Bruenor in the town," the patrol leader informed the tall, cruel orc leader.

Urlgen curled his torn lip, welcoming the information. The orc needed to redeem himself, and nothing short of the death of Bruenor Battlehammer would suffice. Obould blamed him, and so did Gerti, and for any creature living in the cold mountains at the end of the Spine of the World, having those two angry with him was not a good thing.

But they had King Bruenor within their grasp, at rest in a remote town and with little understanding of the catastrophe that was about to befall him.

Urlgen dispatched his messengers with all speed and with orders to press Obould to move quickly. They had the rat in the trap and Urlgen did not want him to slip out.

The orc was exhausted, having spent day after day in rallying others to his cause. Still, King Obould knew that he had to make this journey personally and not deliver the news that Bruenor had been found through any messenger.

He found Gerti sitting on the very edge of her throne, her blue eyes narrow and dangerous, her posture that of a predator anxious to spring.

"You have located King Bruenor and those others who murdered my kin?" she asked before the orc king could even offer a formal greeting.

"A small town," Obould replied. "The one with the lone tower."

Gerti nodded her recognition. With its singular tower, Shallows was quite distinct in this region of abandoned, simple villages and underground dwarven or goblinkin strongholds.

"And you have prepared your forces?"

"An army is out and running already," Obould answered.

Gerti's eyes widened and she seemed about to explode.

"Only to circle south," the orc quickly explained. "The ground is flat and easy to cross there, and King Bruenor must be held in the town."

"They are out to seal the road and nothing more?"

"Yes."

Gerti nodded to one of her attendants, a massive, muscular frost giant clad in shining metal armor and holding the largest, nastiest spear Obould had ever seen. The warrior immediately returned the nod with a bow and started out of the room.

"Yerki will lead my forces," Gerti explained. "They are ready to march at once."

"How many?" the orc had to ask.

"Ten," Gerti replied.

"And a thousand orcs," Obould added.

"Then our contributions to the downfall of King Bruenor Battle-hammer are about the same," remarked the superior-minded giantess.

Obould almost blurted a sarcastic response, but he remembered where he was and how easy it would be for any of Gerti's associates to smash him, and he just chuckled instead.

With her eyes still focused, narrow again and deadly serious, Gerti didn't join in his mirth.

"We must be away at once," Obould explained, shifting the subject a bit. "Three days running to the town."

"Make it in two," Gerti said.

Obould nodded, bowed, and turned around, hustling away from the giantess, but she stopped him as he was about to exit the cave, calling out his name.

The orc turned to face the power that was Gerti.

"Do not fail me . . . again," the giantess warned, putting emphasis on that last, damning word.

But Obould stood tall and straight and didn't back away from Gerti's imposing stare at all. He had ten giants at his disposal. Ten giants!

And a thousand orcs!

TOO CLEAR
A WARNING

Ivan had at first scoffed at Pikel's suggestion that they ride the currents of the River Surbrin to Mithral Hall's eastern gates, but after they set their camp the third night out of the Moonwood, with the river right below them, Pikel surprised his brother by sneaking away in the dark to collect fallen logs. By the time Ivan's snores had turned to the roaring yawns of morning, his green-bearded brother had fashioned a fair-sized raft of notched, interlocking logs, tied together by vines and rope.

Ivan's first reaction, of course, had been one of doubt.

"Ye fool, ye'll get us both drowned to death!" he said, hands on hips, feet wide-spaced, as if expecting Pikel to take the insult with typical grace and leap upon him.

Pikel only laughed and launched the raft. It bobbed in a shallow ebb pool at the river's edge in perfect balance and hardly dipped at all when Pikel hopped aboard.

With a lot of coaxing and many reminders of sore feet, Ivan finally joined his brother on the craft, "just to give it a test!" Before Ivan announced his final intent, Pikel paddled the raft out into the main currents, where it drifted easily.

Ivan's protests were lost in the sheer comfort of the journey, an easy glide. Pikel had fashioned the raft beautifully, creating a couple of amazingly comfortable seats, and even stringing a small hammock at one end of the craft.

Ivan didn't have to ask where his brother had learned to make such things. He knew that Pikel's weird druidic magic had been involved—obviously so! Some of the wood, like the chair he had taken as his own, seemed shaped, not carved, and the oar Pikel was using was covered in designs of leaves and trees so intricate that it would have taken a skilled woodcarver a tenday to fashion it. Pikel had done it in a single night.

They made great time that first day on the Surbrin, and on Pikel's suggestion, they continued right through the night. What a pleasant experience it was, particularly for Pikel, to be gliding on the easy currents under the canopy of twinkling stars. Even Ivan, so much the true dwarf, gained a bit more respect for elves under that amazing summer sky, or at least, he admitted some understanding (to himself!) of the elves' love of stars.

The second day, the river edged closer to the towering mountains, running the line along the eastern edge of the Spine of the World. Shining walls of gray stone, spattered with green foliage and streaks of white, marked the right bank, and sometimes both sides, as the river wove in and out of the rocky terrain. It didn't seem to bother Pikel in the least, but it made Ivan fall more on his guard. They had recently battled orcs, after all, and wouldn't this landscape make for a wonderful ambush?

At Ivan's insistence, they put up on the riverbank that second night, and in truth, the river was becoming a bit too unpredictable and rushed for travel in the dark anyway. Besides, the dwarves needed to re-supply.

Rain found them the next day, but it was a gentle one mostly, though it soaked them and made them miserable. At least the mountains retreated somewhat, the riverbank to the east falling away, and the mountain slopes on the west becoming more rounded and gently up-sloping.

"Think we'll find 'em today?" Ivan asked early on.

"Yup yup," Pikel replied.

Both dwarves retreated into thoughts of the real reason for their journey out of the Spirit Soaring cathedral. They had come to see Mithral Hall, to see King Bruenor's coronation. The prospect of viewing great dwarven halls, something neither of the brothers had done since their youngest years, far more than a century before, incited great joy in Ivan. His mind thought back to the most distant of his memories, to the sound of hammers ringing on metal, the smell of coal and sulfur and most of all mead. He could see again the strong, tall columns that supported the greatest chambers of his own home and believed that those of legendary Mithral Hall would probably exceed even those magnificent works by far.

Yes, to Ivan's thinking, as much as he loved Cadderly, Danica, and the kids, it would be grand to be among his own kind again, and in a place fashioned to the tastes of dwarves.

He looked over at Pikel as he considered his anticipation and wondered, hoped, that perhaps being in a place like Mithral Hall might go a long way into guiding the "doo-dad" back to his true heritage. If Pikel could fashion such work as this raft out of wood, Ivan had to wonder how magnificent his art might be when working with the true dwarven materials of stone and metal.

Of course, Ivan's budding fantasy would have been more convincing to him if, in the middle of his contemplations, Pikel hadn't summoned down a large and incredibly ugly bird to his upheld forearm, then engaged in a long and seemingly detailed conversation with the creature.

"Talkin' to yer own level?" Ivan asked dryly when the vulture flew away.

Pikel turned to his brother with a surprisingly serious expression, then pointed to the western bank and began steering the raft that way.

Ivan knew better than to argue. His often silly brother had proven too many times that the information he could garner from animals could prove vital. Besides, the river was getting a bit more vigorous and Ivan longed to put his feet on solid ground once more.

As soon as they had the boat beached, Pikel grabbed his large sack of supplies, plopped his cooking pot over his head, and leaped away, rushing for the higher ground away from the riverbank. Ivan caught up to him a short time later, on a rocky mound.

Pikel pointed to the southwest, to a cluster of activity against the backdrop of the gray mountains.

"Dwarfs," Ivan remarked.

He narrowed his eyes and shielded them from the glare with his hand. He nodded, affirming his own observation. They were indeed dwarves, and had to be from Mithral Hall, all rushing around, apparently working on defensive fortifications.

He looked back to his brother but found Pikel already moving, cutting a straight line for the construction. Side-by-side they ran along the gently sloping ground, first down then up a steep trail.

A short time later came a roaring command, "Halt and be known! Be liked or be skewered!"

The brothers, understanding the seriousness of that tone, skidded to a stop before the closed iron gates set at the front of a stone wall.

A burly red-bearded dwarf in full battle-mail rushed out through those gates.

"Well, ye don't look like orcs and ye don't smell like orcs," he said.

"Though I'm not for certain what yerself looks and smells like," he added, scrutinizing Pikel.

"Doo-dad," Pikel remarked.

"Ivan Bouldershoulder at yer service, and I'm thinking ye must be in service to King Bruenor. This is me brother Pikel. We're coming outta Carradoon and the Snowflake Mountains, sent by High Priest Cadderly Bonaduce to serve as witnesses to the new king's coronation."

The soldier nodded, his expression showing that while he might not have understood all that Ivan had just said, he seemed to get the gist of it and seemed to think it a perfectly reasonable explanation.

"Cadderly's a friend o' that drow elf that runs about with yer soon-to-be king," Ivan explained, drawing a knowing nod from the soldier. "He's still soon-to-be, ain't he?"

The soldier's expression turned sour for just a moment, his crusty features tightening, then widened in understanding.

"We ain't crowned him yet, as he ain't been in from Icewind Dale."

"We feared we'd miss him," Ivan said.

"Ye would've if he'd've come right in," the soldier explained, "but him and his found orcs on the road and're chasin' them down and putting them back in their filthy holes."

Ivan nodded with sincere admiration.

"Good king," he said, and the soldier beamed.

"Small band and nothin' more, so it won't be long," the soldier explained. He turned to the side and motioned for the brothers to come along. "We're a bit short o' the ale out here," he explained. "Come out fast from the halls to set the camp, while our brothers are up there on the west, setting another."

"Just a small band?" Ivan asked skeptically.

"We're not for taking any chances, Ivan Bouldershoulder," the soldier explained. "We been fighting much o' late, and not too far from our memories are them damned drow coming up from their deep holes.

I'm not knowing this Carradoon or them Snowflake Mountains ye're mentioning, but up here's a wild land."

"We just got done fighting a few orcs ourselfs," Ivan replied. He turned to the river and nodded his bearded chin to the east. "Out in the Moonwood. Me brother put us a bit outta the way."

"Oo," said Pikel, hardly taking the blame in stride.

"Yeah yeah, ye got us up here quick, even if ye did land us in a nest o' elves!" Ivan admitted, and turned back to the soldier. "Orcs crawling everywhere, are they? Well, then I guess we come to the right place!"

It was spoken like a true dwarf, and the soldier appreciated the sentiment enough to slap Ivan on the shoulder.

"Let me see what ye're buildin'," Ivan offered. "Might know a trick or two from the south that ye ain't heared of here."

"Ye heading out?" came a soft voice, one that Drizzt Do'Urden surely welcomed.

He looked up from the small pouch he was preparing for the road to see Catti-brie's approach. The two had said little over the past few days. Catti-brie had retreated within herself, for private contemplations that Drizzt wasn't sure he understood.

"Just ensuring that the orcs were indeed chased away," the drow answered.

"Withegroo's got patrols out."

Drizzt offered a doubting smirk.

"Yeah, I was thinking the same thing. They're knowing the ground, at least."

"As I soon will."

"Let me get me bow, and I'll take yer flank," the woman offered.

Drizzt looked up. "It is a dark night," he said.

Looking as if she had just been slapped, Catti-brie also let her gaze move about before settling it enough to stare back at Drizzt.

"I got me a little headpiece here for just such an occasion," she remarked.

From her belt pouch she brought forth the cat's-eye circlet that she often wore, one that magically conveyed heightened vision in very low light.

"Not as keen as a drow's eyes," Drizzt remarked. "The ground is rocky and likely treacherous."

Catti-brie started to argue, to remind him that the circlet had served her even in the Underdark, and that this had never been an issue between them before, but Drizzt interrupted her before she could even get started.

"Remember the rocky climb outside of Deudermont's house?" he asked. "You hardly managed it. After the rain, the rocks here are no doubt equally slick."

Again, Catti-brie looked as if he had just slapped her. His words were true enough. She could not pace him in the daylight, let alone in the dark of night, but was he saying that she would slow him down? Was he, for the first time since his foolish decision to go to Menzoberranzan alone, forsaking the help of his friends?

He nodded, offered the thin veil of a smile, slung his pack over his shoulder, and rose, turning away.

Catti-brie caught him by the arm, forcing him to turn and face her.

"Ye know I can do this," she said.

Drizzt looked at her hard and long. His stern expression melted away into a nod.

"There is no better partner in all the world," he admitted.

"But ye want to go out alone this night," Catti-brie stated more than asked.

Again the drow nodded.

Catti-brie pulled him close into a hug, and it was one of warmth and love, with just a bit of sadness.

Drizzt went out from Shallows soon after. Guenhwyvar was not with him, but he had the figurine close and knew that the cat would be available to his call should he need her. Barely fifty feet from the torchlit gate, the drow melted into the shadows, becoming one with the dark of night.

He saw the patrols from Shallows several times in the night and heard them long before they came into view. Drizzt avoided them easily every time. He did not want company, but his inner turmoil did little to dull his focus. Out there, in the dark, he was hunting as only a skilled drow might do, roaming the trails and the woods as silently as a shadow. He expected to find nothing, but he was seasoned enough to understand that those honest expectations would lean him toward the precipice of disaster if he embraced them too deeply.

Thus he was not surprised when he found orc-sign. Prints showed themselves to Drizzt's keen drow eyes amidst a circle of sitting stones. They were fresh, very recent, yet there was no sign of any campfire or of any residue from a torch. Night had been on for some time, and all of the patrols from Shallows were human in make-up, and all of them were carrying torches.

But someone had been there, someone human-sized or close to it, and someone traveling in the dark of night without any apparent light source. Given all the recent events, the fact that these were orcs—from the tracks, the drow figured there were two of them—was not hard to determine.

Neither was the trail. The creatures were moving quickly and without much regard to their tracks. Within half an hour's time, Drizzt knew that he had closed considerably.

He did not for a moment wish that Catti-brie or any of the others were at his side. He did not for a moment turn his thoughts away from the task at hand, from the dangers and needs of that very second.

Under the cover of a low tree branch, the drow spotted them. A pair of orcs, crouched on a nearby ridgeline, peered around some lilac bushes toward the distant and well-lit town of Shallows.

Step-by-step, each foot meticulously placed before the other, the drow closed.

Out came his scimitars, and the orcs nearly jumped out of their boots, turning to see curving blade tips in close to their throats. One threw up its hands, but the other, stupidly, went for its weapon, a short, thick sword.

It got the blade out, even managed a quick thrust, but Drizzt's left hand worked a circle around the weapon, turning it down and out wide, while his right hand held his other scimitar poised for a kill on the other orc.

He could easily have killed the attacking orc at that moment—after the turning parry, he had an open strike to the creature's chest—but he was more interested in prisoners than corpses, so he brought his scimitar in against the creature's ribs, hoping the threat alone would end the fight.

But the orc, stubborn to the end, leaped back—right over the north side of the ridge, which was, in fact, a thirty foot cliff.

Holding his scimitar in tight against the second creature, Drizzt skittered up to the cliff edge. He saw the orc bounce once off a rocky protrusion, go into a short somersault, and smash hard onto the stone below.

The other orc bolted away.

Again, Drizzt could have killed it, but he stayed his hand and took up a swift pursuit.

The orc went for the trees, rushing around strewn rocks, falling down one descent and scrambling up the backside. It glanced back many times during its wild flight, thinking and hoping that it had left the dark elf far behind.

But Drizzt was merely off to the side, easily pacing the creature. As it veered around one tree—the same tree from which Drizzt had been watching the pair a few moments earlier—the drow took a more direct route. Leaping onto a low branch, Drizzt ran with perfect balance and the lightest of steps along the limb. He hopped around the trunk to a branch heading out the other way, similarly traversed it, and fell into a roll at its end that landed him on the ground. The dark elf crouched down on one knee, with both blades pointed back at the rushing orc that was now heading straight for him.

The orc shrieked and swerved, and Drizzt feigned a double thrust that sent the creature turning off balance.

Drizzt retracted the blades immediately and spun around, kicking out his trailing foot into the orc's trailing foot as it skittered, forcing its legs crossed and sending it sprawling face down to the rocky ground.

Not really hurt, the orc flattened its hands on the ground and started to push back up, but a pair of scimitar blades touching against the base of its skull convinced it that it might be better to lie still.

Torchlight and noises in the distance told Drizzt that the commotion had roused one of the patrols. He called out to them, bringing them to his side, then bade them to take the prisoner to King Bruenor and Withegroo while he scouted out the rest of the area.

The look on Bruenor's face when Drizzt returned to Shallows some hours later puzzled the drow. Drizzt had expected either frustration from the dwarf because the orc wouldn't talk, or more likely, simple anger, the continuation of the feelings about the tragedy at Clicking Heels.

What he saw on his red-bearded friend's face, though, was neither. Bruenor's look was more tentative in quality, his skin ashen.

"What do you know?" the drow asked his friend, sliding into a seat beside Bruenor, in front of a blazing hearth in the house the folk of Shallows had given them to use.

"He says there's a thousand out there," Bruenor explained somberly. "Says that the orcs 'n giants are all about and ready to squish us flat."

"A ruse to force a lenient hand from his captors," Drizzt reasoned.

Bruenor didn't seem convinced.

"How far'd ye go out, elf?"

"Not very," Drizzt admitted. "I merely ran the town's perimeter, looking for any small bands that might bring havoc."

"Orc says the lands south o' here're crawling with its dirty kinfolk."

"Again, it is a cunning lie, if it is a lie."

"Nah," said Bruenor. "The orc would o' said the north then. That'd be more believable and harder to make sure of. Putting them in the flatlands to the south makes the truth a patrol away. Besides, the squealing pig wasn't in any flavor to be thinking beyond them words that were coming outta its mouth, if ye get me meaning."

A shudder coursed Drizzt's spine as he did, indeed, get the dwarf's meaning.

"Spoke pretty quick, he did," said Bruenor. The dwarf reached over the low arm of his chair and brought up a flagon of ale, moving it to his waiting lips. "Looks like we might be gettin' a bit more fighting afore we find our way back to Mithral Hall."

"That displeases you?"

"Course not!" Bruenor was quick to retort. "But a thousand's a lot o' orcs!"

Drizzt gave a comforting laugh, reached over and patted Bruenor's arm.

"My dear dwarf," he said, "you and I both know that orcs can't count!"

The drow sat back in his chair, pondering the potentially devastating news.

"Perhaps I should be out again at once," he said.

"Rumblebelly, Wulfgar, and Catti-brie are already on their way," Bruenor explained. "The town's sent scouts o' their own, and old Withegroo's promising to use some magic eyes. We'll know afore the turn o' dark if the orc was squealin' the truth or telling lies."

It was true enough, Drizzt realized, and so he rested back again. He let his lavender eyes close, glad to be among such capable friends, particularly if there was any truth at all to the orc's dire tale.

"And I got Dagnabbit working hard on plans for getting us all outta here if there's too many or for holding off whatever might come if there's not," Bruenor rambled on, oblivious to his friend's descent into deep, deep rest. "Might be that we'll find ourselfs a bit o' fun! Ye can't be guessin' how glad I am that I didn't let them talk me into going straight to me home, elf! Aye, this is what any good dwarf's livin' for—a chance to smash an orc face! Aye, and don't ye doubt that I'll be getting me share o' kills. Don't ye doubt it for a minute! I'll be gettin' more than yerself or me girl or me boy all put together."

He lifted his mug in a toast to himself.

"Got room for a hunnerd more notches on me axe, elf! And that's just on the sharpened side!"

23

SWORD AGAINST
SWORD

They were frontiersmen, hunters and by brutal experience, warriors. Not a man or woman of Shallows was unfamiliar with the use of a blade, nor were any inexperienced in killing. Orcs and goblins were all too common in the wilds.

The folk of Shallows knew well the habits of the creatures from the dark mountain holes, knew well the tendencies and the tricks of the wretched orc-kin.

Too well.

The scouting party out of Shallows was not too wary that night, despite the warnings from King Bruenor and his friends, and the tale of the disaster at Clicking Heels. Even as Drizzt was returning with the captured orc, a force of a dozen strong warriors was departing Shallows's southern gate, moving fast along ground comfortably familiar.

They spotted orc-sign soon after and agreed that it was two or three of the creatures at the most. Eager for some sport, the band deserted their information gathering mission and went on the hunt instead, coming down one fairly steep trail into a shallow, boulder-strewn dell. They knew they were close. Every sword, axe, and spear came out at the ready.

The point woman motioned back for the main group to hold fast, then she fell to her belly and started to crawl about a pair of boulders. A wide grin was on her face, for she expected the duo or trio of orcs to be waiting on the other side of that very rock, oblivious to the fact that they were about to die.

Her grin disappeared as she came around the far side to see not two, not three, but a score of the humanoid creatures, standing ready, weapons drawn.

Confident that she had not been seen but knowing well that her band had been spotted long before—likely as they were descending into the dell—the woman edged back around the boulders and turned into a sitting position. She was thinking to ward her friends away, or at least to assemble them in some kind of defensive position. She started to motion for them to do just that, swinging her arm up from pointing at them to showing the ridge behind.

She froze. Her face, gone stern from its previous smile, slipped into an expression of sheer dread. There, up on the ridge behind her fellows, the woman saw the unmistakable forms of many, many enemies.

A cry from back there, from the trailing human scout, confirmed the horror, and the other members of the party swung around.

A horde of orcs came down fast, howling with every step.

The woman started to scramble up to go and join her companions, but she fell back at the sound of footsteps rushing around and coming over the boulders. The score of orcs went right past her, bearing down on their prey, and the woman knew that her friends were doomed to a man.

Too many enemies, she knew. Too many.

She fell back, recoiling instinctively from the horrible screams of agony that began to erupt all over the bloody battlefield. She saw one man go up several feet into the air at the end of a trio of orc spears. Howling and kicking, he somehow managed to fall back to his feet and somehow hold his balance, though he was surely mortally wounded.

He stood determinedly—until a group of orcs leaped atop him, smashing him down.

The woman melted back, crawling between the paired boulders, squeezing into the dark place underneath their abutting overhangs. She tried to control her breathing, tried to stifle the shrieks welling up within her. From under the stones she could not see the battlefield, but she could hear it well enough. Too well.

She lay there in the dark, terrified, for a long, long while after the cries had abated. She knew that at least one man had been dragged off as a prisoner.

But there was nothing she could do.

She lay there, praying every minute that some orc wouldn't happen by and notice her, and she held back her tears as the long night passed.

Overwhelmed and trembling, sheer exhaustion overcame her.

The sound of birds awakened her the next morning. Still terrified, it took every ounce of willpower she could muster to crawl out of that small cubby-hole. Coming out the way she had gone in, but feet first, was no easy task, physically or emotionally. Every inch that she moved out made her feel more vulnerable, and she almost expected a spear to be thrust into her belly at any time.

When she had to blink away the bright sunlight, she gradually managed to sit up.

There she saw the bodies of her companions, hacked apart—an arm here, a head lying over there. The orcs had slaughtered them, had mutilated them.

Gasping for breath, the woman tried to turn to her side and stand, but stopped halfway and fell to her knees, falling forward to all fours and vomiting.

It took her a long time to manage to stand, and a long time to wander past the carnage of those who had been her companions, her hunting partners, her friends. She didn't pause to reassemble any corpses, to look for lost limbs or lost heads, to count the bodies to try to determine how many, if any, had been taken off as prisoners.

It didn't seem to matter then, for she knew beyond doubt that any who had been dragged away were already dead.

Or wished they were.

She came up out of the dell slowly, cautiously, but no sign of the orc ambush group was to be found. The first step over that lip came hard to her, as did the second, but each subsequent stride moved more quickly, more determinedly, until she was running flat out across the mile of ground she needed to cover to get back to her home.

"It ain't right, I tell ye!" yelled one dwarf, who was a bit too full of the mead. The feisty fellow stood up on his chair and pounded his fist on the table in frustration. "Ye just can't be forgetting all the years! All the damned years! More'n any o' yerselfs'll e'er know!"

He ended by wagging an accusing finger at a group of humans seated at a nearby table in the crowded tavern.

Over at the bar, Shingles watched the spectacle with resignation, and he even gave a knowing nod of what was soon to come, when one the humans wagged a finger back at the drunk dwarf and told him to "sit down and shut his hairy mouth."

Was there anyone in Mirabar whose knuckles were not bruised from recent fights?

"Not another one, I pray," came a quiet voice to the side.

Shingles turned to regard the dwarf who had taken the stool beside him. The old dwarf nodded and lifted his mug to second the sentiment, but he stopped before the mug even lifted from the bar.

"Agrathan?" Shingles asked in surprise.

Councilor Agrathan, dirty and disguised, put a finger to pursed lips, motioning for old Shingles to calm down.

"Aye," he said quietly, looking around to make certain that none were watching. "I heard that trouble was brewing on the streets."

"Trouble's been brewing since yer fool marchion hauled Torgar Hammerstriker back from the road," Shingles pointed out. "Been a dozen fights every day and every night, and now the fool humans are coming down here, and doin' nothing but causing more trouble."

"Those in the city above have come to view this as a test of loyalty," the councilor explained.

"To blood or to town?"

"To town, which to them is of utmost importance."

"Ye're speakin' like a human again," Shingles warned.

"I'm just telling ye the truth of it," Agrathan protested. "If ye don't want to be hearing that truth, then don't be asking!"

"Bah!" Shingles snorted. He buried his face with the mug, swallowing half its contents in one big gulp. "What about the loyalty of the marchion to the folk o' Mirabar? Ain't that countin' for nothing?"

"Elastul's thinking that he did right by the folk of Mirabar by preventing Torgar from going to Mithral Hall, taking our secrets along with him," Agrathan replied, an argument that Shingles and all the others had heard countless times since Torgar's imprisonment.

"More years than ye'll know from the time yer mother dropped ye to the time they plant ye in the ground!" the drunk dwarf at the table shouted even more loudly and more vehemently.

He was wagging a fist at the men, not just a finger. He threw back his chair and staggered toward the men, who rose as one, along with many other humans in the establishment—and along with many, many dwarves, including the drunk's companions, who rushed to hold the drunk back.

"And more years than the marchion's to rule and to live, and more than the ten marchions before him and a good number yet to come," Shingles added privately to Agrathan. "Torgar and his kin been serving since Mirabar's been Mirabar. Ye just can't be throwing a fellow like that in yer jail and not expecting to stir the folk."

"Elastul remains firm that he did the right thing," Agrathan answered.

For just a moment, Shingles thought he caught a look of regret cross the councilor's face.

"I hope ye're telling him that he's a fool, then," Shingles bluntly replied.

Agrathan's expression went to a stern look.

"Ye should be watching your words concerning our leader," the councilor warned. "I took an oath of loyalty to Mirabar and one to Elastul when I took my place at the table of the Sparkling Stones."

"Are ye threatening me, Agrathan?" Shingles quietly and calmly asked.

"I'm advising you," Agrathan corrected. "Many ears are out and about, don't doubt. Marchion Elastul's well aware that there might be trouble."

"More trouble than Mirabar would e'er've knowed if he just let Torgar alone," Shingles grumbled.

Agrathan gave a great sigh. "I come to you to ask ye to help me calm things down a bit. The place is on the edge of a fall. I can smell it."

Even as he finished, the drunken dwarf broke free of his comrades and launched himself at the humans, beginning a brawl that quickly escalated.

"Well?" Agrathan yelled at Shingles as the place began to erupt. "Are you with me or against me?"

Shingles sat calmly, despite the tornado exploding into fury all around him. So there it was, presented calmly, a choice that he had been mulling over for a month. He looked around at the growing fight, man against dwarf and dwarf against dwarf. Of late, Shingles had been playing the part of the calming voice in these nightly brawls, had been taking a diplomatic route in the hopes that Elastul's imprisonment of Torgar would prove a temporary thing, maybe even that Elastul would come to see that he had erred in capturing Torgar in the first place.

"I'm with ye if ye can tell me truly that Elastul'll be lettin' Torgar out soon," he answered.

"The condition hasn't changed," Agrathan replied. "When Torgar denounces his road, Torgar walks free."

"Won't happen."

"Then he won't walk free. Elastul's not moving on this one."

A body came crashing past, flopping over the bar between the pair so quickly that neither was really sure if it had been a human or a dwarf.

"Are you with me or against me?" Agrathan asked again, for the fight was at the critical moment, obviously, just about to get out of control.

"Thought I gived ye me answer three tendays ago," Shingles replied.

As a reminder, he balled up his fist and laid Agrathan low with a single heavy punch.

For all the like-minded dwarves in the tavern that night, those on the line of divided loyalties, Shingles's action came as a signal to fight. For all those, human and dwarf, of the opposite mind, the punch thrown by this leader of Torgar's supporters was a call to arms.

Within seconds, everyone in the tavern was into it, and it began to spill onto the streets. Out there, of course, more were drawn in, mostly dwarves, and more on Shingles's side than opposing.

As the fight tilted Shingles's way, the Axe of Mirabar arrived in force, brandishing weapons and telling the dwarves to disperse. This time, unlike all the previous, the dwarf supporters of Torgar Hammerstriker were ready to take their case to a higher authority.

Many ran off at the first sign of the Axe, only to return in full battle gear, wearing mail and with weapons drawn, in numbers far greater than the ranks of the policing Axe. In the ensuing standoff, more and more of Shingles's allies ran to get their gear, as well, and many of those dwarves opposing Shingles threw insults freely, or warned against the action.

But surprisingly few would go to that next level and take up arms against their kin.

The standoff held for a long time, but as the dwarves' numbers increased—one hundred, two hundred, four hundred—the predominantly human soldiers of the Axe began to shrink back toward the lifts that would take them back to the overcity.

"Ye're not wanting this fight," Shingles called to them. He had taken his position at the front center of the mob of dwarves. "Not over that one dwarf ye got jailed."

"The marchion's word . . ." the leader of the Axe contingent yelled back.

"Won't be much good if ye're all dead, now will it?" Shingles interrupted.

He could hardly believe he was speaking those words aloud, could hardly believe that he, and those following him, were taking this road. It was a path that would lead to the overcity, certainly, and likely right out of the city. This wasn't like the initial riot, which was based solely on shock and sheer emotion. The tone was different. This was a revolt more than a riot.

"Seems ye got yer choice, boys," Shingles bellowed. "Ye want to fight us, then fight us, but one way or th' other, we're gettin' Torgar back among them where he's belongin'!"

As Shingles finished, he noticed the bloodied Agrathan standing off to the side, looking at him plaintively, a desperate expression begging him to reconsider this most dangerous course.

As he finished, the dwarves behind him, hundreds strong, gave out a round of wild cheers and began to move inexorably forward, like a great, unstoppable wave.

The doubt was easily recognizable on the faces of the Mirabarran soldiers, as clear as was the resolve stamped upon the grim face of every dwarf marching behind Shingles.

It wasn't much of a battle, there in the Undercity, in the great corridor just off the lift area. A few hits were traded, a couple of them serious, but the Axe gave way, running back to the room with all the lifting platforms and barring the doors. Shingles's dwarves pounded on them for a bit, but in an orderly fashion, they followed their leader down another side corridor, one that would get them to the surface along a winding, sloping tunnel.

Agrathan, his face bloody and bruised, stood before them, alone.

"Do not do this," the councilor pleaded.

"Get outta our way, Agrathan," Shingles told him, firmly but with a measure of respect. "Ye tried yer way in getting Torgar out—I know ye did—but Elastul's not for listening to ye. Well, he'll be listening to us!"

The cheers behind Shingles drowned out Agrathan's responses and told the councilor beyond all doubt that the dwarves would not be deterred.

He turned and ran along the tunnel ahead of the marching mob, who took up an ancient war song, one that had rung out from Mirabar's walls many times over the millennia.

That sound, as much as anything else, nearly broke Agrathan's heart.

The councilor rushed through the positions of the Axe warriors at the tunnel's exit in the overcity, bidding the commanders to wield their force judiciously.

Agrathan ran on, down the streets toward Elastul's palace.

"What is it?" came a cry behind him and to the side.

He didn't slow, but turned his head enough to see Sceptrana Shoudra Stargleam coming out of one avenue, waving for him to wait for her. He kept running and motioned for her to catch up instead.

"They are in revolt," Agrathan told her.

Shoudra's expression after the initial shock showed that she was not so surprised by the news.

"How serious are they?" she asked as she ran along beside Agrathan.

"If Elastul will not release Torgar Hammerstriker, then Mirabar will know war!" the dwarf assured her.

Djaffar was waiting for the pair when they arrived at Elastul's palace. He leaned on the door jamb, seeming almost bored.

"The news beat you here," he explained.

"We must act, and quickly!" Agrathan cried. "Assemble the council. There is no time to spare."

"The council need not get involved," Djaffar began.

"The marchion has agreed to the release?" Shoudra cut in.

"This is a job for the Axe, not the council," Djaffar went on, seeming supremely confident. "The dwarves will be put down."

Agrathan trembled as if he would explode—and he did just that, leaping at the Hammer and putting a lock on the man's throat, pulling Djaffar down to the ground.

A bright flash of light ended that, blinding both combatants, and in the moment of surprise, the Hammer managed to pull away. Both looked to Shoudra Stargleam, the source of the magic.

"The whole of the city will act thusly," the woman said sourly.

Even as she finished the sound of battle, of metal on metal, rang out in the night air.

266

"This is the purest folly!" Agrathan cried. "The city will tear apart because of—"

"The actions of one dwarf!" Djaffar interrupted.

"The stubbornness of Elastul!" Agrathan corrected. "Show us to him. Will he sit there quiet in his house while Mirabar burns down around him?"

Djaffar started to respond, his expression holding its steady, sour edge, but then Shoudra intervened, stepping up to the man and fixing him with an uncompromising glower. She walked right by him into the house.

"Elastul!" Shoudra called loudly. "Marchion!"

A door to the side banged open and the marchion, flanked by the other three Hammers, swept into the foyer.

"I told you to control them!" Elastul yelled at Agrathan.

"Nothing will control them now," the dwarf shot back.

"Nothing short of the Axe," Djaffar corrected.

"Not even yer Axe!" Agrathan cried, his voice taking on an unmistakable reversion to his Dwarvish accent. "Torgar's part o' that Axe, or have ye forgotten? And five hundred of me . . . of *my* people count among the two thousand of your ranks. You'll have a quarter that won't fight with you, if you're lucky, and a quarter that will join the enemy if you're not."

"Get out there," Elastul told Agrathan, "and speak to them. Your people are sorely outnumbered here, good dwarf. Would you have them slaughtered?"

Agrathan trembled visibly, his lips chewing on words that would not come. He turned and ran out of the house, following the volume of the battle, which predictably led him toward the town's jail.

"The dwarves are more formidable than you believe," Shoudra Stargleam told Elastul.

"We will defeat them."

"To what end?" the Sceptrana asked. It was hard to deter Elastul on such a matter by reasoning concerning losses to his soldiers, since his own safety didn't really seem to be at stake, but by changing the subject to the not-so-little matter of profits, she quickly gained the marchion's attention. "The dwarves are our miners, the only miners we have capable of bringing up proper ore."

"We'll get more," the marchion retorted.

Shoudra shot him a doubtful look.

267

"What would you have me do?"

"Release Torgar Hammerstriker," the Sceptrana replied.

Elastul winced.

"You have no choice. Release him and set him on the road. He'll not go alone, I know, and the loss to Mirabar will be heavy, but not all the dwarves will depart. Your reputation will not deter other dwarves, perhaps, from coming into the city. The alternate course is one of a bloody battle where there will be no winners, with naught but a shattered Mirabar in its wake."

"You overestimate the loyalty of dwarf to dwarf."

"You underestimate it. To a dwarf, any dwarf, the only thing more precious than gold and jewels is kin. And they're all kin, Elastul, family of Delzoun at their core. I say this as your advisor and as your friend. Let Torgar go, and quickly, before the battle mounts into a full riot, where all reason is flown."

Elastul lowered his gaze in thought, mulling it over with a range of expressions, anger to fear, washing over his face. He looked back up at Shoudra then at Djaffar.

"Do it," he commanded.

"Marchion!" Djaffar started to protest, but his retort was cut short by Elastul's uncompromising stance and expression.

"Do it now!" Elastul demanded. "Go and free Torgar Hammerstriker, and bid him to leave this city forever more."

"He may see your lenience as a reason for staying," Shoudra started to reason, wondering honestly if all of this might be used to further a deeper and better relationship between Elastul and the dwarves.

"He cannot stay and cannot return, under penalty of death."

"That may not prove acceptable to many of the dwarves," Shoudra pointed out.

"Then let those who agree with the traitor go with him," Elastul spat. "Let them go and die on the road to Mithral Hall, or let them get to Mithral Hall and infect it with the same disloyalty and feeble convictions that have too long plagued Mirabar!

"Go!" the marchion roared at Djaffar. "Go now and let us be rid of them!"

Djaffar gave a snarl, but he motioned for one of the other Hammers to accompany him and rushed out into the night.

With a look to Elastul, Shoudra Stargleam joined the Hammers.

The fight outside the jail was more a series of brawls than a pitched battle at the point where the three arrived, but the situation seemed to be fast degenerating, despite Agrathan's pleading efforts to calm the dwarves.

Several hundred were there in support of Shingles and Torgar, opposing perhaps twice that many soldiers of the Axe. Notably, no dwarves showed in the ranks of the Mirabarran garrison, though many dwarf Axe soldiers stood off to the side, arms crossed, faces dour and grim.

Shoudra looked over at Djaffar, who was regarding the dwarf non-combatants with open contempt.

"Do not even think of going against the marchion's orders," the sceptrana warned the stubborn Hammer, "and do not even think of delaying the release of Torgar in the hopes that this battle will erupt before us."

Djaffar turned a wry and wicked grin her way.

"I have spells prepared," Shoudra warned.

It was a bluff, but she didn't back away from the man an inch.

When that didn't work, she reminded, "It is a fight none in Mirabar can win. Look at them, Djaffar. Members of your own Axe stand to the side, torn in their loyalties."

Councilor Agrathan came over then, flustered and with his robes all twisted, as if someone had lifted him by the fine fabric and shook him all about (which, indeed, had happened).

"There's no talking to them!" the frustrated dwarf roared.

"Djaffar can talk to them," Shoudra explained, "for he has the news that Torgar is to be released." She looked over the Hammer, whose eyes had narrowed. "Immediately, on word from the marchion. Torgar will be set upon the road out of Mirabar, here and now, and with all of his personal items returned."

"Praise Dumathoin," Agrathan said with a great sigh of relief.

He rushed off to spread the news, using words, finally, to quell many of the mounting brawls.

"Be done with the foul Torgar, then!" Djaffar spat at Shoudra, an admission of defeat. "And let him be done with us. Let all his smelly little kin walk out with him, for all I care!"

Shoudra accepted that tantrum for what it was, never really expecting anything more than that from Djaffar of the Hammers.

Shoudra took center stage, commanding the attention of all by sending a magical burst of light up above her. All eyes upon her, she gave the announcement that so many of Mirabar's dwarves desperately wanted to hear.

When Torgar Hammerstriker walked out of the Mirabar jail a short while later, he did so to thunderous applause from Shingles and his supporters, mixed in with curses and jeers from many of the humans—and a few groans and mixed sounds from the Axe dwarves, still standing to the side.

Shoudra made her way to Torgar and found Agrathan there as well.

"You are not completely free in your choice of road," the sceptrana explained to the dwarf, her body language and tone telling him that she was no enemy, despite her words. "You are bid to depart the city at once."

"Already decided upon that," Torgar said.

"Give him the night, at least," Agrathan asked of Shoudra. "Allow him his farewells to those he will leave behind."

"I'm not thinking that he's leaving many behind worth saying farewell to," came a gruff voice, and the trio turned to see old Shingles, outfitted in traveling clothes and with a huge pack on his back, moving toward them.

When they looked past the old dwarf, they saw others similarly outfitted, and others across the great square, meeting runners bearing their supplies and traveling gear.

"Ye can't be doing this!" Councilor Agrathan protested, but his was the only protest, for when he looked to Shoudra, he saw her nodding with grim resignation.

Soon after, Torgar Hammerstriker left Mirabar for the last time, along with nearly four hundred dwarves, nearly a fifth of all the dwarves of Mirabar, many of whom had lived in the city for more than a century, and many from families who had served Mirabar since its founding. They all walked with their heads held high and with the conviction that they would not be ill-treated and would not be turned away by the King of Mithral Hall.

"I did not think this possible," Agrathan said to Shoudra as the pair, along with Djaffar, watched the departure.

"Rats leave the ship when it's taking water," Djaffar reminded. "They're seeing more riches in Mithral Hall, the greedy dogs."

"What they are seeing is the possibility that they will have a greater place among their own than we afford them in the city of Marchion Elastul," Shoudra corrected. "The greatest of riches is respect, Djaffar, and few in all Faerûn are more deserving of respect than the dwarves of Mirabar."

Agrathan almost cynically added, "The dwarves of Mithral Hall, you mean," but he bit the words back and reminded himself that he still had sixteen hundred dwarf constituents looking to him for leadership, particularly in this confusing time.

Agrathan knew that it would take a long time for Mirabar to shake off the stench of the recent events.

A very long time.

WITH SURPRISING SKILL

Drizzt, Catti-brie, Wulfgar, and Regis sat around a rough map Regis had drawn of the town and the surrounding area and upon which Drizzt had added detail. The mood was dour and fearful—not for themselves, but for the towns-folk. First the orc prisoner had mentioned a huge army encircling the town, then a woman who had been out on patrol had come in, battered and terrified, and report-ing that all the others were dead, wiped away by a powerful force of humanoids.

Though she was obviously unnerved, her words told of a well-coordinated group, a dangerous foe beyond the usual expectations.

None of the friends mentioned Clicking Heels that morning, but the images of that flattened town surely played upon all their minds. Shallows was larger than Clicking Heels and much better defended, with a wizard to help, but the signs were getting very dark.

Bruenor came in soon after, his face locked in a scowl.

"Stubborn bunch," the dwarf remarked, moving between Regis and Wulfgar and observing the map with an approving grunt.

"Withegroo cannot be dismissing the claims of the lone survivor," Drizzt came back. "They lost nearly one in ten this morning."

"Oh, he's believin' her, he is," Bruenor explained, "but him and the others're thinking that they're to pay back them that killed their kin. The folk of Shallows are up for a fight."

"Even if that fight's against a foe they can't be beating?" Catti-brie asked.

"Don't know that they're thinking such a foe's about," came Bruenor's response.

The words had barely left his lips when Drizzt and Catti-brie rose up, the woman reaching for her bow, Drizzt going for his cloak.

"I'll go, too," Regis offered.

Wulfgar rose and picked up Aegis-fang.

"The two of ye take the short perimeter," Catti-brie said. "I'll take one round out from there, and let Drizzt do the deep scouting."

"Should we wait for the cover of night?" Regis asked.

"Orcs're better at night than in the day," Catti-brie remarked.

"And we might not have that much time to spare," Drizzt added. He looked to Bruenor and said, "The townsfolk have to agree to let the weak and infirm leave, at least."

"Got Dagnabbit putting together plans for a run even now," the dwarf confirmed, "but I'm not thinking that many o' Shallows's folk'll be wantin' to go out. This is their place, elf, their home and the place of security they've known for many years. They're trusting in Withegroo, and he's one to be trustin', I don't doubt."

"I fear that he might be wrong this time," Drizzt replied. "Every sign darkens the possibilities. If the force allied against Shallows is as strong as indications are, then before too long the folk of the town may all wish that they had gone out."

"Go and see," Bruenor bade him. "I'll make 'em listen while ye're out. I'll get the horses ready and the wagons packed. I'll get me dwarfs in proper order and ready to roll out. I'll be talking with Withegroo again, right off, now that I can catch him alone and without them hollering fools wanting revenge here and now."

"Do ye think he'll hear ye?" Catti-brie asked.

Bruenor gave a shrug and an exaggerated wink, and said, "I'm the king, ain't I?"

On that lighter note, the four scouts rushed out of the building and out of the town. Wulfgar and Regis peeled away to high ground near to the town's walls. Catti-brie found a similar but more defensible vantage point a hundred yards farther out, and Drizzt rushed away from there.

Other scouting groups went out from Shallows as well, but none were nearly as organized, nor nearly as stealthy.

One such group, seven strong, passed Wulfgar and Regis just outside the town's southern gate.

"Well met again," the townsfolk greeted, pausing for just a moment.

"You would do well—better for your town—if you remained inside the walls, preparing defenses should the expected attack come," Wulfgar told the apparent leader: a young man, strong of limb and with a grim and angry expression locked upon his dark, strong features.

The man stopped, his six companions paused behind him, and he shot the barbarian a curious, somewhat angry look.

"We will discern the strength of our common enemy," Wulfgar explained, "and report fully to the town leaders. None can scout the trails better than Drizzt Do'Urden."

The man's look did not soften. It was almost as if he was taking Wulfgar's remarks as a personal affront.

"Every person out here is at risk," Wulfgar went on, not backing down an inch. "For Shallows to lose seven more able-bodied fighters now would not bode well."

The man's nostrils flared and his eyes widened, his expression intense indeed.

Regis motioned to him, bidding him to move off to the side.

"There are other considerations," the halfling remarked, and he offered a sidelong glance at Wulfgar as he spoke, even managing a little telling wink to his large friend.

The scout eyed the halfling suspiciously, but Regis only smiled innocently and turned, nodding for the man to follow. They held a short, private conversation off to the side, and the man from Shallows was smiling and nodding as he returned.

"Back to the town," he ordered his companions, sweeping past them and taking them up in his wake. "Our friends here are correct and we're splitting our forces apart before we even know what it is we're soon to fight."

There came some murmuring of dissent and confusion but the speaker was obviously the appointed and accepted leader, and the group started back the way they'd come.

"Do you never feel the slightest twinge of regret when employing your magical ruby?" Wulfgar asked Regis when the others had moved off.

"Not when it's for their own good," Regis replied, grinning from ear to ear. "We both heard that group coming from fifty feet away. I think the orcs would have, as well." He turned and looked out to the south. "And if there are nearly as many as we've been led to believe, I likely just saved those seven from death this day."

"A temporary reprieve?" Wulfgar asked, the jarring question catching Regis off his guard and stealing the smile from his cherubic face.

He and the barbarian looked at each other, but then Wulfgar looked past him, the barbarian's blue eyes widening.

Regis spun around, looking to the south once more, and there he saw Catti-brie running flat out toward them, waving her arms and her bow in the air.

Regis winced. Wulfgar leaped ahead as the woman staggered suddenly, grasping at her shoulder. Only then did Regis and Wulfgar understand that she was being pursued by archers.

Regis spun around and saw the seven scouts from Shallows rushing back his way.

"To the town!" he yelled to them. "To the town and man the walls. Have the gate ready to swing wide for us!"

By the time the halfling turned back, Catti-brie and Wulfgar had joined up and were both running back toward him, with Wulfgar supporting the wounded woman.

Behind them, coming out of the brush and around the rocks, rushed a horde of orcs.

Regis paused and watched, measuring the distance, and only then did he realize that he wouldn't be doing Wulfgar and Catti-brie much good if they had to sweep him up in their wake.

He turned and ran, reaching the gate at about the same time as his two friends. They scrambled in and the gate was closed and secured behind them, and after a cursory look at Catti-brie's wound, which was superficial, the three rushed for the ladders and the wall parapets.

The orcs came on, a great number indeed, and horns blew throughout the town, with folk rushing all around.

The wave didn't approach, though, but rather swung around in a fierce charge, howling all the louder as they ran back to the south.

"That would be Drizzt," Regis remarked.

"Buying us time," Catti-brie concurred.

She looked up at Wulfgar as she spoke, and he at her, both of them grim-faced and concerned.

The first boulder bounced across the stony ground and hit the town wall a few minutes after sunset. Surprisingly, it had come from the north, from across the narrow ravine.

Horns blew and the militiamen of Shallows rushed to their defensive positions, as did Dagnabbit's dwarves, and King Bruenor and his friends.

A second boulder bounced in, this time closer.

"Can't even see 'em!" Bruenor growled at his three friends as they stood along the northern wall, peering into the gloom.

"There!" Regis cried out, pointing to a boulder tumble.

The others squinted and could just make out the forms of giants across the way.

Catti-brie put her bow up immediately, taking aim, then lifting the angle to compensate for the great distance. She let fly, her arrow cutting a lightninglike line across the darkening sky.

She didn't hit a giant, but the flash at impact told her that she was in the general area at least. She lifted her bow, gritting her teeth against the pain in her fingers and shoulder, which had been creased by an orc's arrow. Before she let fly, though, she had to stop and grab onto Wulfgar, for all the wall was shaking then, hit by a thrown rock.

"Take cover!" came the cry from the lead sentry.

Catti-brie got her bow back up and fired off her second shot, but then she and all her friends were scrambling as one boulder smashed into the courtyard behind them and another landed short of the wall but skipped in hard. Another hit the wall squarely, and another hit the northeastern juncture then skipped along the eastern wall, clipping stones and soldiers.

"How many damned giants are there?" Bruenor asked as he and the others scrambled for cover.

"Too many," came Regis's answer.

"We gotta find a way to counter them," the dwarf king started to reason, but before he could gain any momentum for that thought, a cry from the southern wall told him and his friends that they had other more immediate problems.

By the time Bruenor, Wulfgar, Regis, and Catti-brie reached the southern wall to stand beside Dagnabbit and the other dwarves, the orcs' charge was on in full. The field before the city seemed black with the rushing horde, and the air reverberated with their high-pitched keening. Hundreds and hundreds came on, not slowing at all as the first barrage of arrows went out from Shallows's strong wall.

"This is gonna hurt," Bruenor remarked, looking to his friend and to Dagnabbit.

"Gonna hurt them orcs," Dagnabbit corrected with a grim nod. "We take the center!" he cried to his fifteen remaining warriors. "None come through that gate! None come over the wall!"

With cheers of "Mithral Hall!" and "King Bruenor!" Dagnabbit's well-drilled warriors clustered in the appointed area, the most vulnerable spot on Shallows's southern wall. As one, they took up their dwarven arrows and their well-balanced throwing hammers, and they crouched. The orcs were throwing spears and launching arrows of their own. The dwarves held their ground atop the wall until the last possible second, then leaped up and whipped their hammers into the leading edge of the orc throng, interrupting the charge.

Shallows's bowmen sent a volley out from the walls, and Catti-brie put the Heartseeker to devastating work, her streaks of arrow lightning cutting lines through the enemy ranks.

An agonized cry from behind told them all that one of the townsfolk had caught a giant-thrown rock, and the continuing explosions and ground-shaking made it clear that the giants hadn't let up their barrage in the least.

Dagnabbit's dwarves let fly a second volley before leaping from the wall into the courtyard to bolster the gate defenses, King Bruenor joining them. The bowmen and Catti-brie continued to drive into the orcs' ranks as the blackness closed.

Ropes and grapnels came up over the walls, many catching hold. The orcs, seemingly oblivious to the rain of death, leaped onto them and began scrambling up, while others below threw themselves at the gates, the sheer weight of the force bending the heavy locking bars.

"I wish Drizzt was here!" a terrified Regis cried.

"But he is not," Wulfgar countered, and the two shared a look.

With a growl of determination, Wulfgar nodded for the halfling to follow, and away they went, running along the parapet. The mighty barbarian grabbed grapnels and ropes, using his great strength to pull them free even if they were taut from the weight of orcs climbing on the other side.

At one point, an orc crested the wall just as Wulfgar reached for the supporting grapnel. The barbarian howled and spun. The orc roared and started to swing its heavy club.

And a silver-streaking arrow caught it in the armpit and blew it aside.

Wulfgar glanced back at Catti-brie for just a moment then pulled free the grapnel.

Another orc caught the wall-top as the barbarian tossed the rope back over. It started to pull itself up.

Regis's mace smashed it in the face once, then again.

"More to the east!" Wulfgar cried.

He rushed along to secure a breach where several orcs were even then coming over the wall, doing close battle with a group of Shallows's bowmen.

Regis started to follow but skidded to a stop as the reaching hands of another orc showed on the wall-top right before him. He lifted his mace, but he changed his mind and met the orc with a dazzling, spinning ruby instead.

The orc held in place, truly mesmerized by the spinning gem, its magic reaching out with promises and warm feelings. In a split second, the creature harbored no doubts that the halfling holding the amazing gemstone was its best friend.

"How strong are you?" Regis asked, but the orc didn't seem to understand.

"Strong?" the halfling said more forcefully, and he lifted one arm and made a muscle—not much of one, but a muscle nonetheless.

The orc smiled and grunted.

Regis motioned for it to slip back down, just a bit, and grab the rope again. The creature complied.

Then the halfling patted both his hands emphatically, gesturing for the orc to hold its place right there. Again it complied, and that one rope, at least, was blocked for the time being.

Regis glanced to the right to see Catti-brie staring at him in disbelief. He shrugged then turned back to the left, just in time to see Wulfgar lift an orc high overhead and throw it into a pair of others as they tried to get over the wall. All three fell back outside.

In other places the wall defense wasn't so secure, and orcs poured in, leaping down to the courtyard.

There, centering the defense, stood seventeen toughened dwarves—Dagnabbit and Bruenor among them. As the orcs came down, the dwarves swarmed over them, axes and hammers slashing and smashing.

Bruenor led that charge, hitting the first orc before it had even touched down from its leap. He caught it in the legs and sent it spinning right over, to land face down. Not bothering to finish the kill, the dwarf plowed on, shield-rushing a second orc as it hit the ground. The two of them came together with enough impact to rattle Bruenor's teeth.

The dwarf bounced back and shook his head fiercely, his lips wagging. He swung his axe reflexively across in front of him, thinking that the orc might even then be bearing down on him.

He hit only air, though, and when he recovered his wits a bit, he looked ahead to see that the orc hadn't taken the hit as well as he. The creature was sitting, leaning backward on stiffened arms, its head lolling side to side.

It hardly seemed fair to Bruenor, but war wasn't fair. He charged forward, past the orc, slowing only enough so that he could crease its skull with his heavy axe.

The sheer ferocity of the assault had caught Drizzt off his guard. Barely away from the group he had turned, the drow had been skipping down one descent when he had first caught sight of the charging orcs. Avoiding them had been easy enough, but by the time Drizzt had been able to scramble out of the bowl and head back toward Shallows, the leading edge of the assaulting force was far ahead of him. He saw his three friends in the distance, running back for the town. He saw Catti-brie get clipped by an arrow, and he breathed a great sigh of relief when she, escorted by Wulfgar and Regis, got behind the town's strong walls.

From the shadows of a tree, the drow watched the orc horde sweep past him. He knew he couldn't get back to the town to fight, and perhaps die, beside his friends.

A group of orcs passed below him, and he considered leaping in among them and slashing them down.

But he held his position in the tree, tight to the trunk. It occurred to him that these particular orcs he had chosen to avoid might be the ones who would slay one of his friends, but he dismissed that devastating thought at once, having no time for such distractions. The choices lay clear before him—he could either join in the battle, out there among the horde, or use the distraction of the battle to scout out the truth of their enemies.

The drow surveyed the sweeping lines of orcs, charging headlong for Shallows. How much could he really do out there? How many could he kill, and how much of an effect would a few less orcs really have on this fight?

No, Drizzt had to trust that his friends and the townsfolk would hold. He had to trust that this was likely an exploratory assault, the first rush, the test of defenses.

Shallows would be better off after that initial battle if they understood the true size and strength of their enemy, the location of the orc camps and their defenses.

As the last of the horde swept past beneath him, Drizzt dropped lightly from the tree and sprinted off, not back to the north and the town, but to the east, moving along behind the main bulk of the enemy force.

He could hardly lift his arms anymore, so many swings had he taken, so many orcs had he thrown, but Wulfgar pressed on with all the power he could muster, throwing himself against any and all who crested the southern wall.

Blood ran from a dozen wounds on Wulfgar, and on Regis, who fought valiantly, if less effectively, beside him, putting mace and gemstone to work. As one group of four orcs came over the wall simultaneously, Wulfgar looked back to his right, a silent plea for Catti-brie, but she was not there.

Panicked, the barbarian looked out over the wall, and the distraction as the orcs closed in nearly cost him dearly.

Nearly—but then an arrow sizzled down past him, clipping one orc and smashing into the stone with a blinding flash. Wulfgar glanced back over his shoulder, relief flooding through him as he noted Catti-brie in a new position at the top of the lone tower that so distinguished Shallows.

The woman let fly another arrow and nodded grimly at Wulfgar.

He turned back to meet the resumed charge, to sweep one orc away with his hammer, then he turned to Regis to help the halfling as another of the brutes bore down on him. The orc stopped suddenly, staring hard at a spinning ruby.

Wulfgar plowed ahead, shouldering the nearest orc back over the wall, but taking a stinging hit from the other's club. Grunting away the pain, Wulfgar took another hit—a solid blow to the forearm—but he rolled his arm around the weapon and pulled it in close, tucking it under his arm and moving nose to nose with the wretched orc.

The creature started to bite at him, or tried to, but Wulfgar snapped his forehead into the orc's face, flattening its nose and dazing it enough for him to shove it back from him. Knowing the creature was stunned, he released his hold on the club and grabbed the front of the orc's dirty leather armor instead. A quick turn and a heave had that orc flying out of the town.

Turning for the orc Regis had entranced, Wulfgar glanced back up at the tower, where Catti-brie and a couple of the town's archers were launching arrow after arrow into the throng beyond the wall.

Wulfgar paused, noting another presence up there. It was the old wizard Withegroo. The man was chanting and waving his arms.

"It's breaking in!" came a dwarf's cry from the courtyard below.

Wulfgar snapped his gaze that way to see Bruenor and his kin running roughshod over the orcs in the courtyard, scrambling back to reinforce the gate.

Out of the corner of his eye, though, he saw a small flare come out from above, a tiny ball of fire gracefully arcing out over the wall.

He felt a flash of heat as Withegroo's fireball exploded.

That shock snapped the orc standing before Regis out of its enchantment, and before the halfling could react, the creature stabbed straight out at him.

With a yelp, Regis fell back into the courtyard.

Wulfgar leaped upon the orc, bearing it down to the ground beneath him. Face down, the orc managed to push up to its elbows, but Wulfgar had it by the head then with both hands. With a roar of outrage, the barbarian drove the creature's head down to the stone parapet, again and again, even after the orc stopped fighting, even after the once solid skull became a misshapen, crushed, and bloody thing.

He was still bashing the orc down when a strong hand grabbed him by the shoulder.

Wulfgar spun frantically, angrily, but held back when he saw Bruenor staring down at him.

"They've run off, boy," the dwarf explained, "and I'm thinking that one's not to be causing us no more trouble."

Wulfgar rose, shoving the orc down one final time.

"Regis?" he asked breathlessly.

Bruenor nodded to the courtyard. The halfling was sitting up halfway, though he hardly seemed conscious of the events around him. Blood showed at his side and several dwarves tended him frantically.

"Bet that one hurt," Bruenor said grimly.

25

THE KEPT HALFLING

He felt as if he was awakening from a dream, a very bad dream. He felt a tightness in the side, but as he considered a sensation there, along his belly, Regis was very surprised that it didn't hurt much more.

The halfling's eyes popped open wide as the last scenes of battle—the orc thrusting its sword into his gut—played clearly in his mind. He had tried to jump back and had lost his footing almost immediately, falling from the wall.

Regis reflexively rubbed the back of his head—that fall had hurt! In retrospect, though, it had also likely saved his life. If he had been standing with his back to a wall, he'd have been thoroughly skewered, no doubt. He propped himself up on his elbows, recognizing the small side room to the cottage in Shallows. The light was dim around him, night had likely fallen in full outside.

He was alive and in a comfortable bed, and his wounds had been tended. They had turned back the orc tide.

Regis's wave of hope shook suddenly—as his body shook—when the thunderous report of a giant-hurled boulder slammed a structure somewhere nearby.

"Live to fight another day," the halfling mumbled under his breath.

He started out of the bed, wincing with each movement, but stopped when he heard familiar voices outside his small room.

"A thousand at the least," Drizzt said quietly, grimly.

Another rock shook the town.

"We can break through them," Bruenor answered.

Regis could imagine Drizzt shaking his head in the silence that ensued. The halfling crept out of his bed and to the door, which was open just a crack. He peered into the other room, to see his four companions sitting around the small table, a single candle burning between them. What struck the halfling most were the number of bandages wrapped around Wulfgar. The man had taken a beating holding the wall.

"We can't go north because of the ravine," Drizzt finally replied.

"And they've giants across it," Catti-brie added.

"A handful, at least," the drow agreed. "More, I would guess, since their bombardment has continued unabated for many hours now. Even giants get tired, and some would have to go and retrieve more rocks."

"Bah, they ain't done much damage," Bruenor grumbled.

"More than ye think," Catti-brie replied. "Now they're taking special aim at Withegroo's tower. Hit it a dozen times in the last hour, from what I'm hearing."

"The wizard showed himself in the last battle with the fireball," Drizzt remarked. "They will focus on him now."

"Well, here's hoping he's got more to throw than a single fireball, then," said Catti-brie.

"Here's hoping we all have more to give," Wulfgar chimed in.

They all sat quietly for a few moments, their expressions grim.

Regis turned around and leaned heavily on the wall. He was truly relieved that Wulfgar was alive and apparently not too badly hurt. He had feared the barbarian slain, likely while trying to defend him.

Of course it had come to this, the halfling realized. Ever since they had been fighting bandits on the road in Icewind Dale, Regis had been trying to fit in, had been trying to find a way where he would not only be out of harm's way but would actually prove an asset to his friends.

He had found more success than any of them had expected, particularly in the fight at the guard tower in the Spine of the World, when they had discovered the place overrun by ogres.

In truth, Regis was quite proud of his recent exploits. Ever since he had taken that spear in the shoulder on the river, when the friends were journeying to bring the Crystal Shard to Cadderly, Regis had come to view his place in the world a bit differently. Always before, the halfling had looked for the easy way, and in truth that was the way he most wanted to take even now, but his guilt wouldn't allow it. He had been saved that day on the river by his friends, by the same friends who had traveled halfway across the world to rescue him from the clutches of Pasha Pook, by the same friends who had carried him along, often literally, for so many years.

And so of late he had tried with all his might to find some way to become a greater asset to them, to pay them back for all they had done for him.

But never once had Regis believed that his luck would hold. He should have died atop that ogre tower in the Spine of the World, far to the west, and he should have died on the wall of Shallows.

His hand slipped down to his wounded belly as he considered that.

He turned around and peered out at the four friends again, the real heroes. Yes, he had been the one carried on the shoulders of the folk of Ten-Towns after the defeat of Akar Kessell. Yes, he had been the one who had ascended to a position of true power after the fall of Pook, though he had so quickly squandered that opportunity. Yes, he was spoken of by the folk of the North as one of the companions, but crouching there, watching the group, he knew the truth of it.

In his heart, he could not deny that truth.

They were the heroes, not he. He was the beneficiary of fine friends.

As he tuned back to the conversation, the halfling realized that his friends were talking of alternative plans to fighting, of sneaking the villagers away or of sending for help from the south.

The halfling took a deep and steadying breath, then stepped out into the room just as Bruenor was saying to Drizzt, "We can't be sparing yer swords, elf. Nor yer cat. Too long a run to Pwent. Even if ye could get there, ye'd not get back in time to do anythin' more then clean up the bodies."

"But I see no way for us to take a hundred villagers out of Shallows and run to the south," the drow replied.

He stopped short to regard Regis, as did the others.

"Ye're up!" Bruenor cried.

Catti-brie stood from her chair and moved to guide Regis to the seat, but the halfling, whose side was still stiff and tight, didn't really want to bend. Standing seemed preferable to sitting.

"Up halfway, at least," he answered Bruenor.

He winced as he spoke but waved Catti-brie away, motioning for her to keep her seat.

"You are made of tougher stuff than you seem, Regis of Lonelywood," Wulfgar proclaimed.

He held up a flagon in toast.

"And quicker feet," Regis replied with a knowing grin. "You don't believe that my descent from the wall was anything but intentional, do you?"

"A cunning flank!" Wulfgar agreed and all the friends shared a laugh.

It was a short-lived one, for the grim reality of the situation remained.

"We'd not get the folks of Shallows to follow us out in any case," Catti-brie put in when the conversation got back to the business at hand. "They're thinking to hold against whatever comes against them. They've great faith in themselves and their town and greater faith in their resident mage."

"Too much so, I fear," said Drizzt. "The force is considerable, and the giant bombardment could go on for days and days—there is no shortage of stones to throw in the mountains north of Shallows."

"Bah, they ain't doing much damage," Bruenor argued. "Nothing that can't be fixed."

"A townsman was struck and killed by a stone today," Drizzt answered. "Another two were hurt. We haven't many to spare."

Regis stepped back a bit and let the four ramble on with their defensive preparations. The idea of "ducking yer head and lifting yer axe," as Bruenor had put it, seemed to be the order of the day, but after the ferocity of the first attack, the halfling wasn't sure he agreed.

The giants hadn't crossed the ravine and yet the orcs had almost breached the wall, and the southern gates had been weakened by the press of enemies. While Shallows would continue to see a thinning of their forces as men and dwarves were injured, the orcs' numbers would likely grow. Regis understood the creatures and knew that others might be fast to the call if they believed victory to be imminent and riches to be split.

He almost announced then that he would take the initiative and leave Shallows for the south, that he would find a way to Pwent and the others and return beside a dwarven army. He owed his friends that much at least.

He almost announced it, but he did not, for in truth, the prospect of sneaking away to the south through an army of bloodthirsty orcs shook Regis to his spine. He would rather die beside his friends than out there, and even worse than dying would be getting captured by the orcs. What tortures might those beasts know?

Regis shuddered visibly, and Catti-brie caught the movement and offered a curious glance.

"I'm a bit chilled," Regis explained.

"Probably because you lost so much blood," said Drizzt.

"Get yerself back in yer bed, Rumblebelly," said Bruenor. "We'll take care o' keeping ye safe!"

Yes, Regis pondered, and the thought made him wince. They'd keep him safe. They were always keeping him safe.

They knew the second assault would come soon after sunset.

"They're being too quiet," Bruenor said to Drizzt. The pair was standing on the northern wall, peering out across the ravine to where the giant had been. "Restin' to come on, no doubt."

"The giants won't approach," Drizzt reasoned. "Not while the defense is still in place. They'll not face a wizard's lightning when they can strike from afar with complete safety."

"Complete?" Bruenor asked slyly, for he and Drizzt had just been discussing that very issue, and they had just come to the conclusion that Drizzt should go out and bring the fight to the giants or distract them from their devastating bombardment at least.

Now the drow was hesitating, and Bruenor knew why.

"We could use yer swords here, don't ye doubt," the dwarf said.

Drizzt eyed him curiously.

"But we'll hold without ye," Bruenor added. "Don't ye doubt that, either. Ye go and get 'em, elf. Keep their damned rocks off our heads and leave the little orcs to us."

Drizzt looked back to the north and took a deep breath.

"And now ye're asking all them questions in yer head again, ain't ye?" Bruenor remarked. "Ye're thinking that maybe ye were wrong in telling Catti-brie not to go. Ye're thinking that maybe ye were wrong in thinking to go out at all. Ye're thinking that everything ye're doing is wrong. But ye know better'n that, elf. Ye know where we're standing, and that's under the shadow o' flying rocks. As much as ye're thinking ye don't want to be away from yer friends, yer friends're thinking they don't want ye away."

Drizzt offered him a smile.

"Yet you believe that I have to go, as we discussed," he finished for the dwarf.

"We don't stop or at least slow them giants, and there's no Shallows to defend," the dwarf answered. "Seeming pretty simple from where I'm looking at it. Ye're the only one who can get across that ravine fast enough to make a difference, despite the arguing ye got from me girl when we decided ye should go."

At the mention of Catti-brie, Drizzt turned a bit and glanced back over his shoulder, up to the top of Withegroo's battered tower where the woman stood, bow in hand, looking out over the parapets. She glanced down at Drizzt and noticed his stare. She offered a wave.

"I'll not be away for long," the drow promised Bruenor, returning Catti-brie's wave with a salute of his own.

"Ye'll be as long as ye're needing to be," Bruenor corrected. "I'm thinking is ye can keep them giants off us through the next fight, we'll hold, and if we hold strong, then might be that them orcs'll give it up or break apart enough for us to get through and run to the south."

"Or at least to get some runners through with news for Thibbledorf Pwent," Drizzt added.

"Dagnabbit's working on that very thing," Bruenor assured him with a wink and a nod.

The dwarf didn't have to say any more. They both knew the truth of it. Shallows had to hold through the next couple of fights, either to weaken the orcs enough for a full breakout to the south or to make their enemies give up altogether.

As the bottom rim of the sun began to flirt with the western horizon, Drizzt went out over Shallows's wall, avoiding the northern gate, as he expected it was being watched. He slipped down beside the wider guard tower on the town's northwestern corner and moved off as stealthily as possible, rock to rock, brush to brush, belly-crawling across any open expanses. He made the lip of the ravine, and there he waited.

The dusk grew around him. He could hear the sounds of the stirring orcs to the south, and the grating of boulders being piled by the giants just a few hundred yards from his position, across the ravine. The drow pulled his cloak up tight around him and closed his eyes, falling into a meditative state, forcing himself to become the pure warrior. He had no honest idea of how he might divert the giants, though that was the goal his friends so desperately needed him to achieve.

The mere thought of those companions he had left behind shattered that meditative state and had Drizzt looking back over his shoulder at the battered town. The last image he had seen of Catti-brie, grim-faced and accepting, flashed over and over in his mind.

"Go," she had bade him earlier in the day when he had argued, for purely selfish reasons, against the course.

That was all she had said, but Drizzt knew better than to believe that other, darker thoughts weren't crossing her mind, as they surely were his own. They were going to try to hold the town, against the odds, and Drizzt and his friends had been forced to split up.

He had to wonder if he would ever see any of them alive again.

The drow let his forehead slip down to the earth, and he closed his eyes again. He wasn't scared—not for himself, at least—but he had seen the orc force, and he knew that there were several giants across the way. This band was organized, determined, and had them terribly outnumbered. Was this the end of his beloved band?

Drizzt lifted his head and stubbornly shook it, dismissing the question within a swirl of memories of other enemies overcome. Of the verbeeg lair with Wulfgar and Guenhwyvar. Of the fight to reclaim Mithral Hall. Of the wild chase on Calimport's streets to save Regis. And most of all, of the war with the army of Menzoberranzan, defending Mithral Hall against a terrible foe.

Then the dark elf couldn't even dwell on past victories, couldn't dwell on anything. He moved his consciousness purposefully across his limbs and torso, attuning himself, body and mind, into a singular warrior entity.

The sun dipped below the western horizon.

The Hunter moved over the lip of the ravine, sliding along the rock faces like the shadow of death.

It started almost exactly as the assault of the previous night, with giant boulders raining down across the town and a frenzied horde of orcs charging hard from the south. The defense followed much the same course, with Wulfgar centering the defense of the parapet and Bruenor's dwarves bolstering the gate.

This time, though, Bruenor was with his barbarian friend—and with Regis, who despite the advice of his friends that he should remain at rest, would not be left out.

On the tower behind the wall, Catti-brie sent the first responses out against the orc charge—a line of flashing arrows slashing across the southern fields—as much to put some light out there and mark the enemy advance as in hope of hitting anything.

When the orcs were but fifty feet from the wall, the other archers opened up. It was a devastating barrage made all the more powerful by one of Withegroo's fireballs.

Many orcs died in that moment, but the rest pressed on, rushing to the base of the wall and throwing their grapnels or setting ladders. One group bore a ram between two lines of orcs and pressed straightaway to the gate. Their initial hit almost took it down.

Bruenor, Regis, and Wulfgar met the first breach on that wall top. A pair of orcs scrambled onto the parapet, and Wulfgar caught one even as it spun over the wall, lifting it high, throwing it back outside, and taking one of its following companions down with it. Bruenor took a different tactic, coming in hard for the second orc even as it stood straight. The dwarf feigned high and ducked low, shouldering the orc across the knees and upending it. A twist and shove by the dwarf had the orc falling—not outside to join the one Wulfgar had thrown, but inside, to the courtyard, where Dagnabbit and the other dwarves waited.

As soon as the orc flew away, Bruenor hopped up. Regis rushed by him, or tried to, as another orc crested the wall, but the dwarf caught the halfling by the shoulder, pulled him back defensively, and stepped forward. A swipe of Bruenor's axe took that second orc down, and the dwarf's foam-emblazoned shield got a third, right on the head, as it too tried to come over.

Behind him, Regis tried to help, but in truth the halfling found himself more often ducking the back-swing of Bruenor's constantly chopping axe than any orc's weapon. Regis turned toward Wulfgar instead and found the barbarian in no less of a battle frenzy, whipping Aegis-fang back and forth with abandon, shoulder-blocking orcs back over the wall.

Regis hopped to and fro as more and more orcs tried to gain the wall, but he simply could not fit between or beside his ferocious friends.

One orc came up and over fast. Wulfgar, his hammer caught on another to the right side, just let go with his left hand and slapped the creature past him. The orc stumbled but caught itself and would have turned to attack the barbarian, except that Regis dived down low, cutting across its ankles and tripping it up.

The clever halfling got more than he bargained for, though, as the orc hooked him with its feet and pulled him along for the ride. Not wanting to take that fall again—and particularly not when he heard the gates groan in protest under yet another thunderous hit—Regis let go of his little mace and grasped desperately at the lip of the wall.

"Rumblebelly!" he heard Bruenor cry, his worst fears then realized.

He knew that he would be a distraction—a potentially deadly distraction—to his friends.

"Fight on!" the halfling cried back.

He let go, dropping the ten feet to the ground. He landed in a roll to absorb the blow, but nearly fainted as he came rolling across his wounded side. He was just to the west of the southern gate and saw that the gate was about to crash in. He grabbed his dropped mace and looked to the side to the grim-faced dwarves.

He knew he would be of no real help to them.

He knew what he had to do. He had known since he heard his friends remarking that they simply could not spare Drizzt's blades in the defense of the town.

Regis turned around and ran for the western wall. He heard Dagnabbit yell out to him to "Stand fast!" but he ignored the call, making the wall and turning north along it.

Soon he was on the parapet in the northwestern corner, the same place where Drizzt had gone out before him. Regis took a deep breath and looked back and up, to see Catti-brie staring at him incredulously.

He saluted her, then he willed his legs to move him over the wall.

"I am no evoker," Withegroo lamented after casting his fireball.

A few orcs had been killed, but unfortunately the rusty wizard hadn't put the blast where he had intended to, and he had done little more than momentarily delay the assault.

He leaned on the southern rim of his tower top, beside Catti-brie and a trio of other archers, and watched the battle unfold. He didn't have many effective spells to throw, so he knew he'd have to choose his castings carefully.

He saw a breach at the southeastern corner, orcs rolling up over the wall and leaping down to the courtyard below, and nearly threw one of a pair of lightning bolts he had prepared. He held the shot, though, seeing the dwarves of Mithral Hall rushing to the spot and overwhelming the orcs as they touched down.

Even as the old wizard breathed easier, he saw a second breach open up, a pair of orcs climbing onto the parapet in the southwestern corner. These didn't leap right down, but rather lifted heavy bows.

Withegroo beat one to the punch, waggling his fingers and sending a series of magical bolts out at the creature, burning it, staggering it, and ultimately dropping it to the stone.

Its companion responded by turning the bow up toward the tower top and letting fly a wild shot.

Before Withegroo could respond with a second spell, Catti-brie took aim on the orc and fired, her magical arrow snapping it down to the stone.

The wizard patted her shoulder, but she couldn't even pause long enough to acknowledge the teamwork. Too many other targets were already presenting themselves along the southern wall.

Then came the howls, to the east and to the west as the second wave came on, of scores and scores of orcs riding worgs.

Then came a heavier rain of boulders, ten at a time it seemed, falling heavily across the town.

Shallows shook under the weight of another battering blow to the southern gate. A hinge burst wide and one of the double-doors twisted inward.

He crossed the steep-sided and rocky ravine as quickly as possible, leaping from stone to stone and scrambling on all fours. As he came up the northern facing, he paused to look back at Shallows, and he knew then that his guess about the giants had been correct. They were more than five in number—likely twice that, at least. Since the beginning of the first assault, they had been taking turns throwing the rocks, conserving their strength, in shifts of two or three at a time.

But they were out in full as the assault escalated. The bombardment that echoed behind Drizzt Do'Urden was nothing short of spectacular, and devastating.

It pained Drizzt profoundly to think that his friends were in that town.

He shook the disturbing thought from his mind and pressed onward, scaling the rock face with the same sure-footed agility that had propelled him through the Underdark for all those years.

His mind whirled with all the possibilities, but he did find his center, his necessary meditative state. If there were a dozen giants up there, how might he begin to do battle with them? How might he engage them in any manner to distract them, to buy his friends and the other gallant defenders of Shallows some respite, at least, while they fended the town from the orc hordes?

As soon as Drizzt reached the lip of the ravine, he spotted the cluster of stones and the giants—nine by his count. The drow pulled the magical figurine from his pouch and brought forth his feline companion. He had Guenhwyvar rush off to the north and await his signal.

Drizzt reached for his scimitars then glanced back at Shallows. He wondered if there was some way he could get his friends out of there, but he quickly realized that even if Bruenor, Wulfgar, Catti-brie, and Regis were all beside him, they would find this enemy beyond even their skills. Nine giants, and not the more common and far less formidable hill giants, but nine cunning and mighty frost giants.

Drizzt corrected his count when he saw yet another moving in toward the band, carrying a bulging sack that the drow knew to be filled with rocks.

Could he, perhaps, lead his friends and the rest of Bruenor's dwarves out there? With Dagnabbit and Tred and the others, they might prepare a battlefield on which they could defeat the giants.

But considering the ravine he had just exited, the drow realized that line of reasoning to be one of folly. They could never get that group across the ravine in any short amount of time and without being detected—and how vulnerable they would be among the steep, sharp rocks down below with half a score of giants raining boulders on them.

Drizzt took a deep breath and forced himself to focus on the task at hand. He reached for his scimitars reflexively, but then moved his hands aside, leaving them in their sheaths. He had fooled the frost giants once before. . . .

"Hold!" he cried, walking to the edge of their position. "Another enemy has revealed itself to the north and west, not so far from here!"

The giants stared at him incredulously. Some looked to each other, and Drizzt recognized clearly the doubt stamped upon their faces.

"A second group of dwarves!" Drizzt cried, pointing out to the northwest. "A larger force, but one heading straight to reinforce Shallows, and one I am certain has not yet learned of your position out here."

"How many?" a giantess asked.

Drizzt noticed that some of the others were reaching for stones.

"Two score," the drow improvised, trying hard to put an urgent edge to his tone, to bring the obviously skeptical giants to action.

"Two score," one of the other giants echoed, and Drizzt noted clearly the dry edge in its tone.

He knew then, beyond any doubt, that his ploy would not work. Not this time, not on this group.

Drizzt was moving before the volley of rocks came at him, and that warrior reflex alone saved him from being battered to pulp then and there. He summoned a globe of darkness at his back as he rushed out of the boulder cluster then ran straight off to the rockier and more broken ground.

Half the giants gave chase.

In those first strides out of the cluster, all hope of deception flown, Drizzt fell into himself—into the warrior, into the Hunter. He was pure instinct, feeling the giants' movements around him before he saw them, sensing and anticipating his enemy.

He cut left and a boulder skipped past—one that would have crushed the life from him had he not veered off.

Cutting back to the right, he slipped into a narrow channel between two rock walls, brought up another globe of darkness, then leaped and scrambled over the wall to his right, rolling down behind a jut of stone.

He knew he couldn't sit and wait. It wasn't just about eluding the pursuit for self-preservation. It was about keeping the giants, as many as possible, away from their bombardment, and so, as the last of the chasing five rushed past, Drizzt sprang back the other way, managing to slash the trailing behemoth across the back as he went.

The giant gave a howl and its companions turned to follow.

Drizzt yelled for Guenhwyvar.

The mad rush throughout the stony mountainsides, one that would last all night long, was on.

The orcs poured through the breached gate like water, filling every opening, one after the other, in their lust to dive into a pitched battle.

Or at least, they started to.

From on high came the first and most devastating response, a blinding stroke of lightning slashing down past the startled Catti-brie, cutting before the startled Mithral Hall dwarves to explode against the metal gates in a multitude of bluish arcs.

Many orcs fell to Withegroo's stroke. Many were killed, others stunned and others blinded, and when Dagnabbit and Tred led the charge to secure the gate, the off-balanced and confused orcs proved easy prey.

Hammers thumped and axes chopped. Orcs squealed and bones shattered.

But the orcs still had the gate opened, and more poured in, pushing aside their smoking comrades, scrambling madly to get at the dwarves.

From the tower, Catti-brie sent a line of arrows at the blasted gates and the incoming orcs, but only for a moment. The wall top remained primary to her, where Wulfgar, Bruenor, and a handful of Shallows's townsfolk were fighting back a swarm of hungry attackers.

The dwarf and the barbarian quickly worked their way above the broken gate back-to-back. They turned, with Wulfgar facing out over the wall and Bruenor looking down at the mounting battle in the town's courtyard.

Catti-brie watched them curiously, then understood as Bruenor patted Wulfgar's broad back. With a cry to Clan Battlehammer, the soon-to-be Tenth King of Mithral Hall leaped down from on high, right into the midst of the swarming orcs.

"Bruenor," Catti-brie mouthed silently, desperately, for he disappeared almost at once in the swirling mob, almost as if he had leaped right into the mouth of a whirlpool.

The woman shook away the horrible image immediately and turned her attention back to the wall to Wulfgar, who was fast becoming a lone figure of defiance up there.

Catti-brie fired left of him, then right, each arrow taking down an orc as it tried to come over the wall. Her hand was aching badly, she could hardly draw the bowstring, but she had to, just as Wulfgar, with all his wounds and all his weariness, had to stand there and hold that wall.

She fired again, grimacing in pain, but scoring another hit. There was hardly any self-congratulation in that fact, though, for in looking at the wall, at the sheer number of orcs, Catti-brie wondered grimly if she could possibly miss.

He dived behind a rock, praying that the orcs were so concerned with the town that they had not seen him come out over the wall. He hunched lower, trembling with terror as worg-riding orcs swept past him, left and right, and others leaped the stone he was hiding behind—and leaped him as well.

He could only hope that he had gotten far enough from the wall so that when they were forced to stop, he could slip away.

It seemed that he had, for the worg-riders split left and right as they neared the wall, drawing out bows and sending arrows randomly over the wall.

Regis put his legs back under him and started to slowly rise.

He heard growling and froze, turning slowly, to see the bared fangs of a worg not three feet from his face. The orc atop it had its bow drawn, taking a bead on Regis's skull.

"I brought this!" Regis cried breathlessly, desperately, holding up his ruby and giving it a spin.

The halfling threw up his free arm to block as the worg's snapping jaw came for his face.

"I will sweep them from the wall!" Withegroo proclaimed in outrage as another of his townsmen went down under the press, far to Wulfgar's left.

The wizard waggled his fingers and swept his arms about, preparing to launch a second devastating lightning bolt. At that desperate moment, it certainly seemed as if Shallows needed one.

A rock hit the tower top and skipped across it, slamming the back of Withegroo's legs and crushing him against the tower's raised lip.

Catti-brie and the other archers rushed to him as he started to slump down, grimacing in agony, his eyes rolling up into his head.

More rocks hit the tower, the giants having apparently found the range, and it shuddered again and again. Another skipped across the top, to smash against the wall near the fallen wizard.

"We can't hold the tower!" one of the town's archers cried.

He and his companions pulled their beloved Withegroo from the trapping rock and gently lifted him.

"Come on!" the man cried to Catti-brie.

The woman ignored him and held her ground, keeping her focus on the wall and Wulfgar, who desperately needed her then. She could only hope that no rock would skip in behind her and take her down the same way.

Crying out for Mithral Hall and Clan Battlehammer—and with a lone and powerful voice yelling for his lost brother and Citadel Felbarr—the dwarves met the orcs pouring in through the gate and those coming down off the wall with wild abandon. At least it seemed to be that, though in truth the dwarves held their defensive formation strong, even in the midst of the tumult.

They saw Bruenor leap down from on high. Dagnabbit, spearheading the wedgelike formation, swung the group around to get to their fighting king.

Bruenor's many-notched axe swept left and right. He took a dozen hits in the first few moments after leaping from the wall but gave out twice that. While the orcs' blows seemed to bounce off of him without effect, his own swipes took off limbs and heads or swept the feet out from under one attacker after another.

The orcs pressed in on him, and he fought them back time and again, roaring his clan's name, spitting blood, taking hits with a smile and almost every time paying back the orc that had struck him with a lethal retort. Soon, with dead orcs piled around him, few others would venture in, and Bruenor had to charge ahead to find battle. Even then, the orcs gave ground before him, terrified of this bloody, maniacal dwarf.

The other dwarves were beside him, and Bruenor's exploits inspired them to even greater ferocity. No sword or club could slow them, no orc could stand before them.

The tide stopped flowing in through the battered and hanging gates. Amidst a shower of crimson mist and cries of pain and rage, the tide began to retreat.

None of the turn in the courtyard below would have mattered, though, if Wulfgar could not hold strong on the wall. Like a tireless gnomish machine, the barbarian swept Aegis-fang before him. Orcs leaped over the wall and went flying back out.

One orc came in hard with a shoulder block, thinking to knock Wulfgar back and to the ground, but the orc's charge ended as it hit the set barbarian. It might as well have tried to run right through Shallows's stone wall.

It bounced back a step, and Wulfgar hit it with a short right cross, staggering it. The orc went up in the air, grabbed by the throat with one hand. With seemingly little effort, Wulfgar sent it flying.

Behind that missile, though, the barbarian saw another orc, this one with a bow, aimed right for him.

Wulfgar roared and tried to turn, knowing he had no defense.

The orc flew away as a streaking arrow whipped past, burrowing into its chest.

Wulfgar couldn't even take the second to glance back and nod his appreciation to Catti-brie. Bolstered in the knowledge that she was still there, overlooking him, covering his flanks with that deadly bow of hers, the barbarian pressed on, sweeping another orc from the wall, and another.

The sudden blowing of many, many horns out across the battlefield did nothing to break the fanatic fury of the dwarves. They didn't know if the horns signaled the arrival of more enemies, or even of allies, nor did they care.

In truth, the dwarves, fighting for their clan, fighting for the survival of their king who stood tallest among them, needed no incentive and had no time for trepidation.

Only after many minutes, the orc mob thinning considerably, did they come to understand that their enemy was in retreat, that the town had held through the second assault.

Bruenor centered their line just behind the blasted gates, all of them breathing hard, all of them covered in blood, all of them looking around.

They had held, and scores of orcs lay dead or dying in and around the courtyard and the wall, but not a dwarf, not a defender in all the town, would consider the fight a victory. Not only the gates had been compromised, but the walls themselves had been badly damaged. In many places, mixed among the dead orcs, were the bodies of many townsfolk, warriors Shallows simply could not spare.

"They're gonna come back," Tred said grimly.

"And we're gonna punch 'em again!" Dagnabbit assured him, and he looked to his king for confirmation.

Bruenor returned that stare with one that showed a bit of uncharacteristic confusion on the crusty old dwarf king's intense face. He started some movement—it seemed a shrug—and he fell over.

With the battle ended, King Bruenor could no longer deny the wounds he had taken, including one sword stab when he had first leaped down from on high that had found a seam in his fine armor and slipped through to his lung.

Up above the fallen dwarf, Wulfgar slumped on the wall in complete exhaustion, and with more than a few wicked wounds of his own, oblivious to the fall of his friend down below—until, that is, he heard the shriek of Catti-brie. He glanced up to see the woman looking down from the tower, her gaze leading to the courtyard below him, her wide eyes and horrified expression telling him so very much.

26

PΘINT AND
CΘUNTERPΘINT

"Too many dead!" King Obould scolded his son, though not loudly, when he arrived on the scene south of Shallows and observed the body-strewn field.

Despite his obvious anger and disappointment at the course of the battle thus far and the resiliency of Shallows's defenders, Obould had brought several hundred more orcs with him. As he had gone about the caverns of the Spine of the World with news of the entrapment of the dwarf king of Mithral Hall, many tribes had been eager to join in the glory of the slaughter.

"The town is softened, and their dead lay thick about our own," Urlgen argued, his voice rising.

Obould shot Urlgen a threatening glare, then led his son's gaze to the three large orcs standing together off to the side, each a chief of his respective tribe.

"We think the wizard is dead," Urlgen went on. "A rock hit the top of his tower and he did nothing at the end of the battle."

"Then why did you run away?"

"Too many dead," Urlgen echoed sarcastically.

Obould's eyes narrowed into that particular look the orc king had, which told all standing near to him to dive for cover. Urlgen did no such thing, though. The young, strong upstart puffed out his chest.

"The town will not stand against the next attack," Urlgen insisted. "And now, with more warriors, we can finish them easily."

Obould was nodding with every word of the seemingly obvious assessment, but then he replied, "Not now."

"They are ripe!"

"Too many dead," said Obould. "Use the giants to knock down their walls with rocks. Use the giants to topple the tower. We chase them out or leave them nothing to hide behind. Then we kill them, every one."

"Half the giants are gone," Urlgen informed his father.

Obould's bloodshot eyes widened, his jaw going tight with trembling rage.

"Chasing a scout from the town," Urlgen quickly added.

"Half!"

"A dangerous scout," said Urlgen. "One who holds a black panther as a companion."

Urlgen's face eased almost immediately. Ad'non had warned them about Drizzt Do'Urden, as Donnia had warned the giants. Given everything the drow had told the orc king about this unusual dark elf, it seemed that having half the giants chasing him away might not be so bad a trade off.

"Tell the giants who remain to throw their stones," Obould instructed. "Big stones. And send arrows of fire into the town. Burn it and bash it! Stomp it down flat! And tighten the ranks around the enemy. No escape!"

Urlgen's tusky smile showed his complete agreement. The two orcs both looked back at the battered town with supreme confidence that Shallows would fall and that all within would soon enough be dead.

A boulder clipped the stone above him, bouncing wildly past and showering him with chips of broken stone.

Drizzt ducked his head against the stinging shower and doggedly went back to his work, tightening a belt around a twisted ankle. That done, he stood gingerly and shifted his weight to the wounded foot, nodding grimly when it would still support his weight.

Still, where to go?

The pursuit had been dogged, a handful of giants chasing him through the long night. He had used every trick he knew—backtracking and setting strategic globes of darkness, climbing one tree and rushing across its boughs to another and another, coming down far to the side and sprinting off in a completely different direction—but still the giants hounded him.

It occurred to Drizzt that someone was guiding them. Given his reception at the first giant camp, when they had thought him an ally of some unknown drow, he could render a guess as to who—or at least what—that someone might be.

As dawn broke over the eastern horizon, and with the unerring pursuit close behind, Drizzt realized that his greatest advantage was fast diminishing. He understood, too, that his companion needed to be sent away to her rest.

"Guen," he called softly.

A moment later the great panther leaped across the narrow channel above Drizzt, settling on a stone at his shoulder height, a few feet away.

"Rest easy and rest quickly," Drizzt bade the panther, willing her away. "I will need you again, and soon I fear."

The cat gave a low growl that blew away on the wind, as Guenhwyvar seemed to dissipate in the air, becoming less than substantial, becoming the grayish mist, then nothing tangible at all.

Loud voices from not too far behind told Drizzt that he had better get moving. He took some comfort in the fact that he had led so many giants away from the battle at Shallows, and indeed, he had taken them far to the northwest, to the rougher and higher rocky ground. Every once in a while, the drow came out on a high ridge that offered him a view of the distant, battered town, and each time he could only clutch at the hope that his friends were all right, that they had held strong, or perhaps even that they had found a way to slip out and make a run to the south.

A boulder skipped into the narrow channel then, followed by the roar of the giants, and Drizzt had no further time for contemplation. He darted off as quickly as his twisted ankle would allow, moving on all fours at times as he scaled the steep inclines.

He was tiring, though, and he knew it, and he knew, too, that giants did not tire as quickly as the smaller races. He couldn't keep up the run for much longer, if the pursuit remained so dogged, nor could he hope to turn and face his pursuers. If it was one giant, perhaps, or even two, he might try, but not this many. All his warrior skills wouldn't hold him for long against a handful of mighty frost giants.

He needed another solution, a different escape route, and he found it in the form of a dark opening among a tumble of boulders against one rocky cliff facing. At first he thought the cave within to be nothing more than the sheltered and darkened area formed by the formation of the rocks, but then he saw a deeper opening at the back of the alcove, a crack in the ground barely wide enough for him to slip through. He fell to his belly and peered in, breathed in. His Underdark senses told him that this was no little hole in the ground, but something large and deep.

Drizzt crawled back out and surveyed the area. Did he want to end the chase then and there? Could his friends afford for him to release the giants of their pursuit, when the behemoths would surely turn right back to their stone-throwing positions?

But what choice did he really have? This pursuit was going to end soon either way, he knew.

With a reluctant sigh, the drow slipped into the cave and moved a bit deeper into the darkness, then sat and listened, and let his eyes adjust to the dramatic shift of light.

Within minutes, he heard the giants milling around outside, and their grumbling told him that they knew exactly where he had gone. The light in the cave increased slightly as the boulder tumble outside was thrown away. After more angry grumbling, including a suggestion that they go and get some orcs or someone named Donnia—and Drizzt recognized that as a drow name—to pursue the drow into the cave, the hole was blocked by a giant's face. How Drizzt wished he had Catti-brie's bow in hand!

More roars of protest and grumbling ensued, but only briefly, and the cave went perfectly dark. The ground shook beneath Drizzt, as the giants piled stones over the opening, sealing him in.

"Wonderful," Drizzt whispered.

He wasn't really worried for himself, though, for he could tell from the feel of the air that he would find another way out of the cave. How long that might take, though, he could not guess.

He feared that by the time he got out and circled back to Shallows, there would be no town standing.

His left arm was all but useless. He knew that the bone had been shattered under the worg's tremendous bite, and the torn skin was taking on the unhealthy color of a dire infection, but he couldn't worry about that.

Regis pressed the charmed orc to urge the exhausted mount on faster, though he feared that he was pushing his luck more than pushing the obviously angry worg. With the limitations of their shared vocabulary, the halfling had somehow managed to convince the orc that he knew where they could find big treasure, and a horde of weapons for the other orcs, and so the dim-witted creature had beaten its worg into submission, and into letting go of Regis's shattered arm, and had forced the snarling and nipping creature to take a second rider on its broad back.

It certainly hadn't been a comfortable or comforting ride for Regis. Sitting before the big, smelly orc placed the halfling's dangling feet to the sides of the worg's neck—within nipping distance, he found out, whenever the great wolf slowed.

As they left the battlefield far behind that night and pressed on through the morning, the halfling had found the orc's resistance growing. He used his enchanted, mesmerizing ruby constantly on the orc, not ordering it but rather tempting it, again and again, with techniques the sneaky halfling had perfected on the streets of Calimport years before.

But even with the gemstone, Regis knew that he was on the edge of disaster. The worg could not be so tempted—certainly not as much as the taste of halfling flesh would tempt such a cruel creature—and the orc was not a patient thing. Even worse, several times, the halfling thought he would simply faint and fall off, for his shattered arm was shooting lines of burning, overwhelming, and disorienting pain through him.

He thought of his friends, and he knew that he could not falter, not for himself and not for them.

All Regis could think to do was to keep them running fast to the south and hope that some opportunity opened before him where he could kill the pair, or at least where he could slip away. And despite his trepidation, the halfling understood well that he could never have covered as much ground on foot as they had on the worg. When the dawn brightened the ground the next morning, they found that the mountains to the south, across the eastern stretches of Fell Pass, were much closer than those they had left behind.

The orc wanted to sleep, something that Regis knew he could not allow.

The halfling was sure that as soon as the brute closed its eyes, the worg would make a meal of him.

"Into the mountains," he told it with his halting command of the Orcish language. "We camp here and dwarves will find us."

Grumbling, the orc pressed the overburdened worg on.

As they came into the foothills, Regis watched every turn and every ridge, looking desperately for a place where he could make his escape. A small cliff face, perhaps, where he could quietly slip over and disappear into the brush below, or a river that might wash him far enough away from these two wretched companions.

He saw a couple of promising spots but let them pass by, too afraid to make such a break. He tried to bolster his resolve by reminding himself of the predicament of his friends to the north, but still he saw nothing that offered more than a fleeting hope.

Still, from the tone of the orc's complaints, Regis understood that he would have to do something soon.

"We gonna camp," the orc informed him.

Regis's eyes went wide and he looked around desperately for a way out. His darting eyes looked down to his small mace, belted at his hip.

He thought of taking it out then and there and smashing the worg atop the head. He couldn't get his hand to move to it, though, whatever the logic, for he knew beyond doubt that he would have to be perfect, and that the blow would have to fell the creature, which he sincerely doubted it would. Even without the wound to his arm, Regis was no match for a worg, and he knew it. He couldn't begin to hurt the thing before those snapping jaws found his throat.

The only thing keeping him alive was the orc, the worg's master.

The halfling nearly fell over when the orc stopped the mount suddenly, on a small and level landing along the mountainside. Regis remembered to leap off the worg's back only when the snarling creature turned and nipped at his foot. He ran to the side and the worg turned and darted at him, but the orc intercepted and scolded it, kicking it in the rump as it turned around.

The worg retreated across the way, looking back at Regis with its hateful eyes, a stare that told him that as soon as the orc fell asleep, the great wolf would have him dead.

He found his solution in the fact that this particular clearing was surrounded by trees. Deathly exhausted and afraid, and terribly sore from his ordeal, Regis moved to an appropriate tree and started to climb.

"Where you's going?" the orc demanded.

"I'll keep the first watch," Regis replied.

"The dog will watch." The orc indicated the worg, which looked at Regis and bared its filthy fangs.

"As will I!" the halfling insisted.

He scrambled up the tree as fast as his broken arm would permit, moving well out of the orc's reach as quickly as he could manage.

He found a nook and settled his back against the trunk, his legs stretched out over a branch, and tried to secure himself as much as possible. He thought to go down and prod the orc into moving along, but in truth, he knew that they all needed rest, particularly the worg—though if the thing fell over dead of exhaustion, the halfling wouldn't shed a tear.

Every few seconds, Regis glanced back to the north, toward distant Shallows, and thought of his friends.

He could only hope they were still alive.

"Three buildings burning strong," Dagnabbit informed Catti-brie and Wulfgar as they kept a vigil at Bruenor's bedside.

They had set up the infirmary in the low workmen tunnels beneath Withegroo's tower, a series of connecting passageways that allowed for inspections at key points of the tower's supporting base structure. This was actually the strongest section of the town, even stronger than the tower above, for the dwarves Withegroo had hired to build his tower had fashioned the tunnels first, reinforcing them against weather and enemies alike, for they alone had provided shelter during the months of the tower's construction.

Still, the cramped tunnels were hardly suited for their present purposes as makeshift bunkers. The friends were in the largest room—the only place that could rightly be called a room—and Wulfgar couldn't even stand up straight. He had to belly crawl through a ten-foot passageway to get in.

"The buildings are stone," Catti-brie argued.

"With a lot of wood support," said the dwarf. He moved beside Bruenor and sat down. "Giants threw a few firepots, and the rocks are coming in fast now."

"It's an organized group," said Wulfgar.

"Aye," Dagnabbit agreed, "and they're blocking all the south. We got no way out." He looked at Bruenor, so pale and weak, his broad chest barely rising with each breath. "Exceptin' that way."

Bruenor surprised them all, then, by opening one eye and even managing to turn his head toward Dagnabbit.

"Then ye take a bunch o' stinkin' orcs along for yer ride," the dwarf said, and he sank back into his bed.

Catti-brie was there in an instant, hovering over him, but after a quick inspection she realized that he had slipped off into that semi-conscious state once again.

"Where's Rockbottom?" she asked, referring to the one cleric who had remained with their group of dwarves when the expeditionary force had split.

"Tending Withegroo, though I'm thinking the old mage's about finished," Dagnabbit answered. "Rockbottom says he's done all he can for Bruenor for now, and he's thinking like I'm thinking that we're gonna be needin' that wizard to have any chance o' getting outta here."

Catti-brie bit back her urge to scream at poor Dagnabbit, for she realized that despite his seemingly callous attitude toward Bruenor, he was as torn up as she was about the dwarf king's predicament. Dagnabbit was above all else pragmatic, though. He was the commander of Mithral Hall's forces, and always followed the road that promised the best chance of positive result, whatever the emotional burden. Catti-brie understood that he was as angry and frustrated as she at their helplessness, at having to sit there and watch the life ebb out of Bruenor.

Dagnabbit moved to the side of Bruenor's bed and gently lifted the signature one-horned helm off the dwarf king's head, rolling it about in his hands.

"Even if we find a way outta here, I don't know if we can take him with us," the dwarf said quietly.

Wulfgar was up in an instant, towering over Dagnabbit despite his necessary crouch.

"You would leave him?" he roared incredulously.

Dagnabbit didn't shrink from the barbarian's wild stare. He looked from Bruenor to Wulfgar, then back to his beloved king.

"If bringing him means throwing out all chance of us running by them, yeah," he admitted. "Bruenor'd not want to go if going meant getting them he loves slaughtered, and ye're knowing that."

"Get Rockbottom back in here to tend to him."

"Rockbottom can't do a thing for him, and ye heared it yerself when last he was here," said Dagnabbit. "Damned orc got him good. He'll be needin' a bigger priest than Rockbottom, might be even that he'll be needin' a whole bunch o' priests."

Wulfgar started toward Dagnabbit, but Catti-brie grabbed him by the arms and forced him to stop and look at her. He saw only sympathy there, a complete understanding of, and agreement with, his frustrations.

"We'll make our choices as we see them," the woman said softly.

"If we are to run to the south, then I will carry Bruenor all the way to Mithral Hall," Wulfgar said, casting a stern look at Dagnabbit.

The commander didn't flinch, but he did, after a moment, nod.

"Well if ye do, then ye know that me and me boys'll do all we can to keep ye running and to keep them damned orcs off ye."

That calmed Wulfgar, even though he, Catti-brie, and Dagnabbit all knew that those were words of the heart, not of the mind. In truth, to all three, the point seemed moot anyway. A few scouts had dared to slip out of Shallows in the hours since the end of the second battle and the reports of the tightening ring of orcs showed no chance of any large-scale escape.

They were trapped, Bruenor was dying, Drizzt and Regis were both missing, and there was nothing they could do about it.

Punctuating that disturbing logic, another giant boulder smashed against the tower above them, and cries of "Fire! Fire!" echoed down the low tunnels leading to the small, smoky room.

"Town lost thirty in the fighting," Dagnabbit informed them. "Counting the twelve killed afore the first fight."

"Almost a third," said Catti-brie.

"And most o' them men—some o' their best fighters," said the dwarf. "Two o' me own are dead, another five down too hurt to fight. If they come on again, we'll be hard pressed to hold."

"We'll hold," Wulfgar said grimly.

"After seein' ye on the wall, I'm almost believing ye," the dwarf replied.

"Almost?" Catti-brie asked.

Dagnabbit, who had seen the extent of destruction to the fortifications above, could only offer a shrug in reply.

"We hold or we die," said Catti-brie.

"We gotta get out," Dagnabbit remarked.

"Or get help in," said Catti-brie. "Regis got over the wall, though I'm not for knowing if he's dead on the field outside, or if he's running for help." She looked to Wulfgar as she explained, "Right after he went over the wall, the orcs on worgs came charging in."

After the fight, the friends had searched the ground west of Shallows as much as possible, but had found no sign of Regis. That had brought them some hope, at least, but in truth, both of them feared the halfling captured or dead.

"Even if he got away, I'm not for hoping that'll do anyone but himself any good," said Dagnabbit. "How long will it take him to find Pwent? It'll take an army to get through to us, I'm thinking, and not just them Gutbusters. And how long will it take them to gather an army to our aid?"

"As long as it takes," said Wulfgar. "Until then, we must hold."

Dagnabbit started to reply, seeming as if to argue the point, but then he just blew a long sigh.

"Stay with King Bruenor," he bade Catti-brie. "If any're to keep his heart beating, it's yerself. Keep him warm, and wish him well from me and all me boys if he walks his journey to the other side."

He looked to Wulfgar.

"Help me and me boys fix what defenses we can?" he asked the man.

With a nod and a determined look to Catti-brie, the barbarian lifted his bloodied frame and crawled out of the small tunnel to begin the work of shoring up the defenses.

Such as they were.

He caught himself just as he was about to fall off of the branch, and when he realized that, when he realized where he was, the halfling had to spend a long moment telling his heart not to leap out of his chest. The fall probably wouldn't have been so bad, a few bruises and scratches, but Regis knew all too well what awaited him on the ground: a snarling, vicious worg.

He settled himself quickly and looked over the impromptu encampment. The orc was snoring contentedly between a pair of shading rocks, while the worg was curled right at the base of Regis's tree.

Wonderful, the halfling thought.

The sun was up and the day bright and warm, and Regis's heart told him that this was his last and only chance, that he had to find some way out of there. Would the orc still consider him a friend when it awoke? Would the gem-enhanced promises he had made of treasures and new weapons still hold strong in the dim-witted creature's thinking? If not, how could he use his ruby once again? How could he even get close enough to a hostile orc with that hungry worg wanting nothing more than to make a meal of him?

Regis put his head down and fought hard to hold back his sobs, for it seemed to him that it had all been for naught. He wished that he was back in Shallows with his friends, that if he was to die, as he surely believed he was, it would be with Bruenor and the others, with the friends who had walked the road beside him.

Not like this. Not torn apart by a cruel worg on a lonely mountain pass.

"Stop it!" Regis scolded himself, more loudly than he had intended.

Below him, the worg looked up, gave a long, low growl, then put its head back atop its paws.

"No time for self pity," the halfling whispered. "Your friends need you, Regis, so what are you going to do for them? Sit here and cry?"

No, he decided, and he sat up straighter and resolutely shook his head. Even that motion made his broken arm throb more. It was time to rouse the orc, to hope that the creature was still under the sway of the enchanted ruby, or to find some other way if it was not. If he had to fight them both, orc and worg, then he'd fight and be done with it. His friendship with those who had risked themselves time and again for his sake demanded no less.

Seeming taller, feeling taller, Regis rolled over the side of the branch and caught a foothold below, moving down the tree to a better vantage point where he could rouse the orc and judge its demeanor.

He stopped, though, and suddenly, his head snapping around, as something came bouncing into the encampment.

An old boot.

The worg leaped at it and tore at it with snapping jaws—and those jaws were snapping indeed, as a series of small explosions erupted from within the boot.

The worg yelped and howled, and leaped up into the air, doing a complete somersault.

The most curious looking creature Regis had ever seen rushed in to join the dance: a green-bearded dwarf wearing light green robes, open sandals on his dirty feet, and a cooking pot on his head. The dwarf ran right up to the worg and began waggling his fingers and his lips. The great wolf stopped its yammering and its hopping and froze in place, ears going back, eyes going wide.

With a sound that could only be described as a shriek, the worg put its tail between its legs and ran away.

"Hee hee hee," said the dwarf.

"What?" roared the awakened orc, its protesting cry cut short—as tended to happen when a battle-axe crushed the speaker's skull.

From behind the tumbling orc came a second dwarf, this one with a brilliant yellow beard, and dressed in more conventional dwarven attire—except for a tremendous helm that sported the huge antlers of a full-grown buck.

"Ye should o' killed the damned dog, too," the yellow bearded dwarf roared. "I'm hungry!"

As the green-bearded creature started wagging his finger in a scolding manner, Regis moved down the tree as quickly as his aching arm would permit.

"Who are you?" he called.

Both dwarves spun on him—and the yellow-bearded one almost launched his deadly axe Regis's way.

"No friend o' orcs . . . like yerself!" the yellow-bearded dwarf roared.

"No, no, no!" Regis insisted coming to the ground and waving his empty hand up in a sign of submission, his other arm tucked in close to his side. "I have come from the town of Shallows."

"Don't know it," said the yellow-bearded dwarf.

He looked to the other, who agreed with a "Nope, nope."

"And King Bruenor Battlehammer," Regis went on.

"Ah, now ye're talking!" said the dwarf with the yellow-beard. "Ivan Bouldershoulder at yer service, little one. And this's me brother—"

"Pikel!" Regis cried.

He had heard quite a bit about these two from Drizzt and Catti-brie, though in truth, no spoken words could do the specter of Pikel Boulder-shoulder justice.

"Aye," said Ivan, "and tell me, little one, how're ye knowin' that, and what're ye doing with the likes o' them two?"

"We have to hurry," Regis replied, urgency suddenly flying back into his tone. "Bruenor's in trouble—they all are!—and I have to get to Mithral Hall . . . no, to the camp that Thibbledorf Pwent was supposed to be building north of the hall."

"Yeah, that's where we're goin'," said Ivan. "To Pwent. We took a circular route, but a bird told me brother where they were at. We were just fixing to go there when another bird told me brother about the orc and his puppy."

"He talks to a lot of birds, does he?" Regis asked dryly.

"Aye, and to the trees. Come along and he'll get us there afore ye can ask me how."

"There is no time," Regis said to the Bouldershoulders, to Thibbledorf Pwent and to the other leaders at the second dwarven outpost, some twenty miles across uneven, rocky ground north of Keeper's Dale, the vale herald-ing the main entrance to Mithral Hall. "Bruenor and the others don't have the four extra days it will take for the runners to gather the army and return here."

"Bah, they'll do it in three!" one of the outpost bosses, a crusty little fellow named Runabout Kickastone, insisted. "Ain't ye never seen a mad dwarf run?"

"Three's three too many!" roared Pwent, who had been leaning toward the north ever since Regis and the Bouldershoulders had arrived with the dire news of Shallows's predicament.

Indeed, Thibbledorf Pwent had been leaning to the north since Bruenor had separated from him and sent him to the south.

"We only got a hunnerd!" said Runabout. "And from what the little one's saying, a hunnerd ain't to do much!"

"Ye got the Gutbusters!" Pwent roared right back. "Them orcs'll think they're outnumbered, don't ye doubt!"

"And you've got clerics," added Regis, who knew they had to be away at once, and who guessed easily enough that some of his friends were likely in desperate need of some healing magic.

Runabout sighed and looked around, planting his hands on his hips.

"We might be doin' some good if we can get to the town," he admitted. "Shorin' up defenses and healing them that's hurt and all that. Don't sound like we'll be getting there with any kind o' ease, though."

Off to the side, Pikel hopped over to Ivan and began whispering excitedly into his brother's ear. All the others turned to watch and listen, though they couldn't really make out any clear words or meanings.

"Me brother's got some berries that'll make ye walk longer and faster," Ivan explained. "Takin' away yer need to stop and eat or drink. That'll get us up there all the faster, with short camps."

"Getting up there's sounding like the easy part," the ever-doubting Runabout replied, and before he had even finished, Pikel hopped up to Ivan and put his lips near his brother's ear again.

Ivan's expression turned sour, his face full of doubt, and he began to shake his head, but as Pikel continued, ever more excitedly, the dwarf slowly settled and began to listen more intently.

Finally, Pikel hopped back and Ivan turned an incredulous stare upon him and asked, "Ye think?"

"Hee hee hee."

"What?" Thibbledorf Pwent, Regis, and Runabout all demanded at once.

"Well, me brother's got a plan," Ivan haltingly explained. "Crazy plan . . ."

"Yes!" said Pwent, punching his fist into the air.

"But a plan's a plan, at least," Ivan went on. He looked to Pikel and asked again, "Ye think?"

"Hee hee hee."

"Well?" prompted Runabout.

"Well, are we to stand here jawing or to get going?" Ivan shot right back. "Ye got a big, strong wagon?"

"Yes," Runabout answered.

"Ye got a lot o' wood? Especially them big logs ye been using to hold the stone walls in place?"

Runabout looked around and slowly nodded.

"Then get all yer wood and get yer biggest and strongest wagons, and get all yer boys into line on the road north," said Ivan.

"What about yer brother's plan?" Runabout asked.

"I'm thinkin' it'd be better if I tell ye on the way," Ivan responded. "Both because we can't be standing here talking while yer king's in trouble, and because . . ." He paused and looked at the giggling Pikel, then admitted, "Because when ye hear it, ye might think we'd've been better waiting for the army."

"Hee hee hee," said Pikel.

Within the hour, the hundred dwarves and Regis set out from the outpost, pulling huge wagons laden with tons of strong wood. Pikel wasn't pulling and wasn't even walking. Rather, the dwarf moved from wagon to wagon, working the wood with his druidic magic, considering each piece and how it might fit into his overall design, and giggling. Despite the gravity of the situation, despite the fact that they were walking into an obviously desperate battle, Pikel was always giggling.

WHEN HOPE
FADES

Catti-brie sat in the dim light of a single candle, staring at Bruenor, her beloved father, as he lay on the cot. His face was ashen, and it was no trick of the light, she knew. His chest barely moved, and the bandages she had only recently changed were already blood-stained yet again.

Another rock hit close outside, shaking the ground but not even stirring Catti-brie, for the explosions had been sounding repeatedly. The bombardment had increased in tempo and ferocity. Every twentieth missile or so was no rock but a burning fire pot that spread lines of devastation, often igniting secondary fires within the town. Three blazes had already been put out in the wizard's tower, and Dagnabbit had warned that the integrity of the structure had been compromised.

They hadn't moved Bruenor, though, for there was nowhere else to go.

Catti-brie sat and stared at her father, remembering all the good times, all the things he had done for her, all the adventures they had shared. Her mind told her that that was over, though her heart surely argued against that conclusion.

In truth, they were waiting for Bruenor to die, for when he took his last breath, they—all who remained—would crawl out of their holes and over the battered walls and make their desperate run to the south. That was their only hope, slim though it was.

But Catti-brie could hardly believe she was sitting there waiting for Bruenor to die. She could hardly accept that the toughened old dwarf's chest would sometime soon go still, that he would no longer draw breath. She had always thought he would outlive her.

She had witnessed his fall once before and had thought him dead, when he had ridden the shadow dragon down into the gorge in Mithral Hall. She remembered that heartbreak, the unbelievable hole she had felt in her heart, the sense of helplessness and the surreal nature of it all.

She was feeling that again, all of it, only this time the end would come before her eyes, undeniably and with no room for hope.

The woman felt a strong hand on her shoulder then and turned to see Wulfgar moving in beside her. He draped his arm across her shoulders, and she put her head on his strong chest.

"I wish Drizzt would return," Wulfgar remarked quietly, and Catti-brie looked at him. "And with Regis beside him," the barbarian said. "We should all be together for this."

"For the end of Bruenor's life?"

"For all of it," Wulfgar explained. "For the run to the south, or the last stand here. It would be fitting."

They said no more. They didn't have to. Each was feeling the exact same thing, each was remembering the exact same things.

Up above, the rain of boulders continued.

"How many orcs are there?" Innovindil asked Tarathiel.

The two elves were far from the Moonwood, flying through the night on their winged horses. She had to shout to be heard, and even then her voice carried thinly on the night breezes.

"Enough so that the security of our own home will surely be compromised," Tarathiel answered with all confidence.

They were in the foothills to the north of the town of Shallows, looking back at the hundreds of fires of orc camps and at the flames engulfing sections of the town, most notably the lone tower that so clearly marked the place.

The pair set down on one high ridge to better converse.

"We cannot help them," Tarathiel said to his more compassionate companion as soon as they set down and he could better see the look upon her fair face. "Even if we could get to the Moonwood and rouse all the clan, we'd not return in time to turn the tide of this battle. Nor should we try," he added, seeing her doubting expression. "Our first responsibility is to the forest we name as our home, and if this black tide turns to the east and crosses the Surbrin, we will know war soon enough."

"There is truth in your words," Innovindil admitted. "I wonder if we might go there, though, and perhaps pull some from the disaster before the darkness closes in over them."

Tarathiel shook his head and painted on an expression that showed no room for debate.

"Orc arrows would chase us every inch," he argued, "and if they brought down Sunrise and Sunset, what good would we do for anybody? Who would fly to the east and warn our people?"

He pressed on with the argument, though Innovindil didn't need to hear it. She understood her responsibilities, and just as importantly, her limitations. She knew that the catastrophe to the south was far beyond the ability of her and her friend, and all their clan, to correct.

It pained her, it pained them both, to watch the town of Shallows die, for though the elves of the Moonwood were no friends to any of the humans in the area, neither were they enemies.

They could only watch.

It was a difficult climb, made all the more so because of the swelling and soreness in his twisted ankle. Hand over hand, Drizzt pulled himself up the long and narrow natural chimney, chasing the last flickers of diminishing daylight up above.

Diminishing daylight.

The drow paused, more than halfway up the three hundred foot climb. The worse thing about the fading afternoon light above was that Drizzt knew it was not the day after he had first crawled into the cave, but was the day after that. The size of the caverns had truly surprised him. It was a vast underground network, and he had spent nearly two days wandering through it, looking for a way back to the surface. Following lighter air, the drow had found many dead ends, chutes and openings too small for him to exit through.

He was beginning to suspect that he had found another, but he continued his climb. Still, each foot traversed made it clearer to him that this too was a dead end. The light above had shone brilliantly when first he had seen it, a welcomed contrast to the darkness of the caverns, but that had been due to the angle of the sun, the drow realized, and not the width of the opening.

He continued up another hundred feet before he knew for certain that he would have to double back, that the opening would admit no more than an arm or perhaps his head.

With a quiet reminder to himself that his friends needed him, Drizzt Do'Urden started back down.

An hour later, he was walking as swiftly as his sore ankle and his sheer exhaustion would permit. He considered doubling back, moving all the way to where he had first entered the tunnels in the hope that he might move the barriers the giants had constructed there, but he shook that thought away.

The sun had long risen before the drow found the next opening, and this time the exit was large enough.

Drizzt came out into the daylight, blinking against the stinging brilliance, letting his eyes adjust as much as possible. Then he spent a long while studying the mountains around him, trying to find some recognizable landmark that would guide him back to Shallows. The angle was too different, though. Observing the sun told him east from west, and north from south, though, so he started south. He was hoping to hit the Fell Pass, and hoping that he would find his bearings once the ground had somewhat leveled out.

He tore a sleeve from his shirt and tightened the splint around his ankle, then trotted away, ignoring the pain. He watched the sun pass its zenith above him, then move to the western horizon and drop behind.

Hours later, he found the Fell Pass and recognized the ground.

He ran on to the east across the foothills, urgency growing with each stride. A short while later, he saw a distant glow against the lightening sky of the southeast. He rushed up over one hill, finding a better viewpoint and saw, in the distance, flames climbing into the night sky.

Withegroo's tower.

His heart pumping more out of fear than from exertion, Drizzt ran on. He saw a glowing ball sail across the sky, north to south. When it hit it burst into flame in the battered town.

Drizzt didn't veer to the south, instead charging straight for the giants' position, determined to deter them yet again. His hand went to his onyx figurine, though he didn't bring the panther to him just yet.

"Be ready, Guenhwyvar," he said quietly. "Soon we find battle."

Drizzt knew that fire in the night distorted distances greatly, and so he was not surprised at how long it took him to get back near the town and the attacking giants.

He moved to the northern rim of the ravine in clear sight of Shallows. He could see the defenders rushing around. The tower was burning, though not nearly as brightly as before, and most of the activity was centered around it.

The giants seemed to be concentrating on that particular target as well.

Drizzt took out the figurine and set it on the ground, determined to bring forth Guenhwyvar and charge straight on into the giant encampment. He paused, though, noting a familiar figure atop that burning tower.

Drizzt couldn't make out much, but one thing showed clearly to him: a one-horned helmet that he knew so very well.

"Defy them, Bruenor," the drow whispered, a wry grin on his face.

Almost in response, a series of missiles smashed against that tower, one clipping right near the brightest burning fires and sending a shower of sparks through the night sky.

There the dwarf remained, atop the structure, directing the forces on the ground.

Drizzt's smile widened, or started to, for then there came a loud groaning and scraping sound from the south. Eyes wide with horror, Drizzt watched the tower lean, watched the dwarf atop it scramble to the edge, diving desperately for the rim.

The tower toppled to the south, and half fell over, half crumbled, so that the poor doomed dwarf fell down amidst tons of crushing stone.

Drizzt didn't even realize his own movements, didn't even register that his legs hadn't supported him through that terrible sight, that he was sitting down on the stone.

He knew beyond any doubt that no one in all the world could have survived that catastrophe.

A chill rushed through him. His hands trembled and tears filled his violet eyes.

"Bruenor," he whispered over and over.

His hands reached out to the south, into the empty air, with nothing to hold on to.

28

BOWING BEFORE
THE WRONG GOD

She could see nothing, could feel only the pain of raw scrapes all around her arms and shoulders, and the discomfort of breathing in chunks of stony dust. She groped around in the darkness of the partially collapsed tunnel, searching desperately for her father.

Luck was with her, for the area around which Bruenor lay had survived the catastrophe almost intact. Catti-brie got up beside her father, gently running her hands over his face, then putting her ear low to his mouth, to find that he was still breathing, shallow though it was.

The woman turned around, trying to get her bearings, trying to figure out which way would provide the shortest route to the surface, though she wondered if she should even go to the surface at all. Had the orcs come on in full after the fall of Withegroo's tower, which surely had fallen? If so, she wondered if she would be better off staying there, in the dark, for as long as she could manage before trying to find a way out of the town altogether so she could head for the south.

That seemed the safer course, perhaps, but Wulfgar was up there, and Dagnabbit and the others were up there, and the townsfolk were up there, and if the orcs had indeed come on, the battle would be desperate.

Catti-brie crawled to the side of the small chamber and began to claw at the stone, digging free several chunks and a mound of dirt and stone dust. Her fingers bled but she pushed on. The ground above her groaned ominously, but she pushed on, ignoring the exhaustion that crept through her as the minutes passed.

She hit a rock too big for her to move. Undaunted, the woman started working at the side of the stone, and she jumped back as the rock suddenly shifted.

Morning light streamed in as the boulder went away, hoisted and tossed aside by the strong arms of Wulfgar.

He reached in for her and she gave him her hand and the barbarian gently pulled her from the small tunnel.

"Bruenor?" Wulfgar asked desperately.

"He's the same," Catti-brie replied. "The collapse didn't touch his room. Dwarves built it well."

As she finished, the woman looked around at the devastation. The tower had half fallen over and half collapsed in on itself, and it had taken out several buildings on its toppling descent, leaving a long line of rubble. She wanted to ask so many questions then, about who had survived and who had fallen, but she could find no words, her jaw just drooping open.

"Dagnabbit is gone," Wulfgar informed her. "Three other dwarves were lost with him, and at least five townsmen."

Catti-brie continued her scan, hardly believing the devastation that had befallen the town. Most of the buildings were down or badly damaged, and little remained of the wall. When the orcs came on—and she knew it would be soon since she could hear their horns blowing and drums beating in the south—there would be no organized defense, just fighting from street to street, and before the bitter end, from tunnel to tunnel.

She looked to Wulfgar and gathered strength from his stoic expression and his wide shoulders. He'd kill more than a few before the orcs finished him, Catti-brie knew, and she decided that she would too. A wry smile widened on her face, and Wulfgar looked at her curiously.

"Well, if it's to end, then it's to end in a blaze o' fighting!" she said, nodding and grinning.

It was either that or fall down and weep.

She put her hand on Wulfgar's shoulder, and he on hers.

"They're coming," came a voice behind them.

They turned to see Tred, battered and bloody, but looking more than ready for a fight. The dwarf stood sidelong, one hand hidden behind his back, the other holding his double-bladed axe.

Wulfgar pointed out several positions in a rough circle around the cave entrance leading back to Bruenor.

"We'll hold these four positions," he explained, "and fall back behind one pile after another to join up right here."

"And then?" asked Tred.

"We fall back into the caves, or what's left of them," the barbarian said. "Let the orcs crawl in and be killed until we are too weary to strike at them."

Tred looked around, then nodded his agreement though he understood, as they all did, the ultimate futility of it all. Certainly some orcs, thirsty for blood, would foolishly come into the caves after them, but soon enough the wicked creatures would realize that time was on their side, that they could just wait out the return of the defenders, or even worse, that they could start fires and smoke the defenders out of the caves.

"It'll be me honor to die beside yer King Bruenor and to die beside the fine children of the king. He was a fine and brave one, that Dagnabbit," Tred said somberly, glancing over at the long pile of broken stone. "Citadel Felbarr would've been proud to call him one of our own. I'm wishing we had the time to dig him out."

"It is a fitting grave," Wulfgar replied. "Dagnabbit stood tall and defied them, and at the moment of his fall he called to the dwarf gods. He knew that he had done well. He knew that he had honored his people and his race."

A solemn and silent moment passed, all three bowing their heads in deference to the fallen Dagnabbit.

"I got me some orcs to chop," Tred announced.

He saluted the pair and moved off, organizing the remaining few into battle groups to defend three of the positions.

Soon after, the bombardment increased once again but there was plenty of cover with so many piles of rubble, and there was little left to destroy. The giants' prelude seemed more an annoyance than anything else. The rain of boulders ended as the orcs, many riding worgs, came on, howling their battle cries.

Catti-brie started the fight for the defenders, popping up from behind the rubble pile and letting fly a streaking arrow that hit a worg squarely in the head, stopping it in its tracks and launching its rider through the air.

The woman let fly again to the side, for there was no shortage of targets with orcs swarming over the all but destroyed walls. She drove her arrows into their ranks, taking one, sometimes even two, down with every shot.

But still they came on.

"Stay with the bow," Wulfgar instructed her.

He rose up strong and tall and met the orcs' charge, Aegis-fang sweeping the leading orcs away, launching them through the air.

All around the pair, the defenders of Shallows rose to meet the charge, humans and dwarves fighting desperately side by side. For a while, it seemed as if no orc's blow could fell any of them, as if any hit they suffered was a minor thing, shrugged off and retaliated immediately and brutally. Bodies piled all around the four defended positions, and almost all of them at first were orc and worg.

The momentum couldn't hold, though, nor could the defense. The defenders, even in their desperate frenzy, knew it.

Wulfgar swept his warhammer tirelessly, battering through any defenses the orcs trying to stand before him could possibly manage. Occasionally one of the creatures managed to slip under the blow, or duck back from it, but before the orc could them come on, a streaking silver arrow drove it down.

Catti-brie put Taulmaril up again and again, her enchanted quiver never emptying. Whenever she could manage, she aimed for a worg instead of an orc, considering the snarling wolves to be the more dangerous foe. Most of the time, though, the woman didn't even bother to aim, nor did she have to.

Even with that devastating line of fire, and with Wulfgar fighting more brilliantly and brutally than she had ever witnessed, the orcs, like the incoming tide, began to press in, swarming through holes.

Catti-brie let fly an arrow, put another up and spun around, blasting away an orc point-blank. Another was there, though, and she had to take up her bow like a staff and fend the creature off.

A second joined it, and she almost yelled for Wulfgar. Almost, but she held her words, realizing that any distraction to him would surely bring about his swift downfall. The woman whipped Taulmaril out before her viciously, back and forth, forcing the two orcs back. She dropped the bow and in the same fluid movement brought forth Khazid'hea, her fine-edged sword.

The orcs pressed on, a thrusting spear coming in hard at her right. A downward parry sheared the spear's tip cleanly off, and the orc, surprised by the lack of any real impact with the parry, overbalanced just a bit.

Enough for Catti-brie to turn her hand over and stab out quickly, taking the creature in the chest.

Back came Khazid'hea, just in time to ring against the heavy blade of the second orc's sword. One on one, this creature would be no match for Catti-brie.

But two others joined it, on either side, and Catti-brie was working furiously to fend off the trio. Behind her, she heard an impact, followed by Wulfgar's grunt.

But she couldn't help him, and he couldn't help her.

Catti-brie worked her blade all the more ferociously, turning aside thrust after stab after slash. Frustration grew within her, for she was making no headway, and she was working far too hard to maintain the pace.

The orc before her and to the right moved suddenly, and in a way she could not have anticipated. At first, she thought the creature was charging her, but quickly she realized that it was just flying by, launched at the end of a heavy dwarven axe. Tred stepped forward behind it, launching a back-hand that doubled over the second of the trio, the one standing right before Catti-brie. The woman reacted quickly, diverting all of her attention to the orc on her left. She came forward suddenly, turned Khazid'hea over the orc's sword and down. The orc, both weapons down low, charged forward, trying to bowl her over, but the woman nimbly side-stepped the charge then stepped right past the orc. As the blades disengaged, she flipped her grip around and stabbed out behind her, severing the creature's spine.

"Defenses falling!" Tred cried, running to join the battered Wulfgar and nearly getting his head torn off by one of Aegis-fang's wild swings. "We're backing to the hole!"

Wulfgar grunted his accord and swiped away yet another orc, then fell back behind the rubble barricade.

A worg came flying over it, leaping for his throat.

Catti-brie, her bow retrieved, took the wolf in the flank, the powerfully enchanted arrow throwing it out to the side, quite dead.

She looked up to see a horde of others charging in, though, and expected they would be overwhelmed quickly. She heard a noise behind her on the ground and turned to see old Withegroo, his features gaunt and strained. He could hardly stand, his body trembling from the exertion of even being upright, but the look in his eyes was not dull, and he moved his lips with determination wrought of sheer rage.

His fireball stopped the charge of worg and orc, and brought the defenders a little more time, but the exertion cost Withegroo dearly. He managed a smile as he launched his devastating bomb, then he looked at Catti-brie and winked.

He fell over, and before she even went to him the woman knew that he was dead.

Withegroo's blast had defeated the charge of one flank, but the orcs did not scramble from the magical display. The dwindling defenders backed and backed some more, and when they heard horns blowing in the south they knew it was more orcs joining the already overwhelming odds.

Or were those horns some other signal? the defenders had to wonder, as the press suddenly lightened. They were practically backed to the end of the line by then, with several already forced down into the tiny tunnels.

The defenders of Shallows regrouped in a tight ring and battled on. Before long, Catti-brie and Wulfgar were back to their original defensive position, and this time with few orcs standing before them.

Still the horns blew in the south, and as the fighting subsided, Wulfgar dared to run to the highest mound he could find and peered out that way.

"What in the Nine Hells?" he called.

Tred, Catti-brie, and a few others joined him, and their incredulity was no less intense. There, rolling north and pulled by a strange looking team of more than twenty straggly mules, came a huge wooden totem. It was a gigantic statue of an orc face, but with a singular, grotesque eye.

"Gruumsh," Tred McKnuckles said. He spat upon the ground as if the mere mention of the orc god put a foul taste in his mouth. "They're bringing their clerics up," he reasoned. "A ceremony for their final victory, I'm guessin'."

The orcs that had been battling only moments before, filled the field to the south of the town, all pointing and cheering, many falling to their knees, prostrating themselves before the image of their revered, and feared, god.

Across the ravine, Drizzt heard the horns, though from his low vantage point creeping in on the giants' position, he couldn't see what the fuss was about. Even the giants standing up above him were talking excitedly, confused and pointing out to the south.

Drizzt spotted Guenhwyvar across the way, moving in for an attack. He caught the cat's attention with a wave of his hand, and motioned for her to hold her position. He looked around, wondering how he could find a better vantage point without being seen. He started out but stopped almost immediately. The giants, not so startled anymore, were conversing angrily. He couldn't understand very much of what they were saying, but he recognized that they were somewhat put off by the orcs—he heard something about the orc priests stealing all their glory.

A flicker of hope came to Drizzt that perhaps their enemies were about to split ranks, though he knew it was likely far too late to make any real difference.

The driver, huddled under heavy robes, cracked his whip above the long line of pulling beasts, and the dirty and shaggy creatures tugged harder, propelling the huge wagon and great statue of Gruumsh One-Eye, god of the orcs, along the sloping and rocky ground.

All of the orcs had turned their attention from Shallows, and the tiny pocket of hopelessly outnumbered defenders, to this new arrival. They bowed and fell to their knees in droves beside the wagon's course.

"What is this?" one orc commander asked the leader of the army, Urlgen, son of Obould.

Urlgen considered the strange scene with a perfectly confused expression, his tusks chewing at his lips.

"Obould has brought many allies," was all he could say, and all he could think.

Was his father elevating the glory of this attack? Was he tying the attacks directly to some edict of the orc god's?

Urlgen didn't know, and like the rest of his army his movements crept him closer to the great rolling statue. Unlike most of the others, though, Urlgen didn't focus entirely on that idol. He considered the curious team, perhaps the most unkempt and straggly looking team of . . . of what?

Urlgen didn't even really know what the creatures were. Mules? Small oxen? Rothé, perhaps, taken from the corridors of the Underdark?

From there, the unusually smart orc scrutinized the drivers. One was taller and broader than the other, though both were short by orc standards. Perhaps the second—more a passenger than a driver, he seemed—was a child, but Urlgen couldn't really tell, since both wore heavy cloaks that included wide, low cowls.

The wagon rolled to a stop some hundred or so feet from the town, which Urlgen thought rather foolish, since it left them in range of that horrible human woman and her nasty bow. The orc leader glanced back that way, and he did see several of the defenders watching, as were his own minions.

The larger driver stood up and lifted his arms above his head. The sleeves of his cloak slipped down to reveal gnarly hands and a hairy forearm that didn't seem very orclike.

Before anyone could truly take note of that, though, the driver grabbed a lever of some kind located on the front of the statue, right below the tusk-filled mouth.

He said something that sounded like, "Hee hee hee," and yanked the lever down.

"Well, here's one less priest for the damned Gruumsh," Catti-brie said with bitter determination.

She lifted Taulmaril and leveled it the driver's way, but Tred grabbed her arm and stayed the shot.

"One won't be makin' any difference," he said, "and something's not right about all this besides."

Catti-brie started to ask what he meant, but in truth she could sense it too. Something about the team and the drivers struck her as odd, even from a distance.

Her eyes widened when she heard the grinding sound that followed the orc shaman's pull of the lever, and they widened some more as the great statue seemed to grow, then split apart, the four sides breaking in the middle and falling out to form four wide planks.

Out onto those planks, from the hollow inside of the statue, ran dwarves—many dwarves—in the full battle array of the unmistakable Gutbusters!

One in particular led the way, wearing black, ridged armor and a helmet with a spike that was half again the height of the dwarf wearing it.

"It's Pwent!" Catti-brie cried.

Even as she spoke, Thibbledorf Pwent leaped out, roaring and flailing. He ducked his head with perfect timing to skewer one orc as he landed atop another, smashing it to the ground. Catti-brie lost sight of him then but winced anyway, for she knew his technique. She knew that he was jostling about wildly atop the orc, his sharpened armor shredding it.

His boys followed with equal abandon, running to the end of a plank and leaping wildly atop the confused throng of orcs. One after another they went, dwarven catapult balls raining death from on high. Even more dwarves appeared a moment later, throwing off camouflaging blankets that someone must have enchanted to make them look like a team of mules, and charging out from the yokes. How many fine targets they found in those first confusing seconds, with so many orcs kneeling on the ground, bowing forward.

The massacre became a fight soon after, but even then the orcs were outmatched. Many were running, caught by surprise, and as was typical for any goblinkin, ranks broke apart at the first sign of retreat.

The dwarven ranks stayed tight and strong and swept toward the town, with groups breaking away at the slightest sign of pursuit to chase off the orcs.

"Ye Battlehammers was always known for yer timing!" Tred McKnuckles cried, then he yelped and leaped aside as a great rock smashed down and bounced past.

"Damn giants again!" the dwarf cried.

Catti-brie ran to the remnants of the northern wall and lifted her bow.

"Move as you shoot!" Wulfgar warned, and indeed, as soon as the first arrow made its way out across the ravine, a volley of great stones came in at the position where the arrow had been fired.

It did Drizzt Do'Urden's heart good to see those telltale arrows sailing across the ravine, but even that good news—that Catti-brie was apparently still fighting—did not distract him from his course. The giants had started their bombardment in full force again, and that, he knew, he could not allow. He called Guenhwyvar into action, then scrambled up to the side of the giants' position himself, moving high up on a pile of boulders unnoticed by the behemoths.

The drow advanced without a sound, leaping out and crossing behind one giant, his scimitars slashing hard. He hit the ground running, executing a perfect double stab at the back of another's knee, and kept right on going, around the rocks on the other side.

Giants turned to follow, and one lifted its arms to throw a stone at the fleeing drow.

Instead of executing the throw, the giant caught a flying panther in its face—all six hundred pounds of raking claws. Guenhwyvar went for the eyes, not the kill, and scraped them deep, blinding the giant before leaping aside.

All the giants were scrambling, but Drizzt held no illusions that he and Guenhwyvar could keep them occupied for long. Nor did he think that he could possibly kill many, even any, of them, but maybe he and the panther could blind a few or get a few to chase them away.

He came back around the rocks the same way he had gone in and did indeed catch the closest giant off its guard, managing another few nasty stabs before scrambling the other way. The pursuit was better this time, though—was too good—with giants flanking both ways and another pair pursuing directly.

Drizzt moved to put his back to a wall, ready to make a final, desperate stand.

The nearest giant charged in.

Before it got to Drizzt, though, the behemoth winced and grabbed at its neck. As it spun around, the dark elf clearly saw the feathered fletching of a pair of arrows buried in the giant's neck. Drizzt's jaw dropped open when the brute moved just a bit to the side.

There, up above him to the north, sat a pair of elves astride flying horses.

The giants scrambled.

Drizzt rushed out to the side, stabbed yet another, then kept on running, leaping past some boulders. Few giants paid him any heed, though. A couple off to the side were still futilely trying to keep up with Guenhwyvar as the panther leaped all around them. Several of the others were moving fast for more rocks—to throw at the elves, obviously.

Drizzt couldn't let them get organized. He moved to the rock pile on the west. When one giant stooped and reached for a stone, he leaped out, slashing the behemoth hard across its fingers. The giant retracted the hand, and it, and a companion, gave chase on the drow.

This time Drizzt didn't turn and didn't slow, leading the giants off and yelling for Guenhwyvar to do the same across the way. The drow ranger saw a stone go flying into the air and heard the shriek of a pegasus a moment later, though when he looked to the north, both elves were still up there, flying around and firing their bows.

Drizzt sprinted out across some open ground, often glancing back at the destroyed town, hoping to catch some sign of his friends.

He saw nothing definitive, just a swarm of orcs charging for the town. Drizzt had to turn away, running to the north with a pair of giants close behind him.

"We got no time!" Thibbledorf Pwent cried, charging into Shallows. "Gather up yer things and yer wounded and follow me to the wagon!"

"We need a cleric!" Wulfgar yelled at him. "At once! We've wounded too badly hurt to be moved!"

"Then ye might need to leave 'em!" Pwent yelled back.

"One of them is Bruenor Battlehammer!" Wulfgar yelled back.

"*Cleric!*" yelled Pwent. "And get the one on the wagon with the green beard," the battlerager cried to another dwarf. "He's got more tricks than a den o' drunken wizards."

"Get 'em moving!" another dwarf cried. "Get the wounded on the wagon and get all the dead dwarfs ye can up there with 'em. We're not for leaving Battlehammers behind for the buzzards or the orcs!"

"How did ye find us so fast?" Catti-brie started to ask Pwent, but she stopped and smiled when she saw the obvious source of the daring rescue. The second driver, the little one, whom she recognized clearly once his cowl was pulled back. "Regis," the woman said.

With her heart busting, she moved to hug him but backed away quickly when she saw him wince as she put pressure against his arm.

"Someone had to feed the wolf," the halfling said with a sheepish shrug.

Catti-brie bent low and kissed him on the head, and Regis blushed deeply.

And they were moving, a whirlwind of scrambling dwarf warriors buzzing like a swarm of angry bees around the exhausted defenders of Shallows, a ragtag group. Of the hundred humans and twenty-six dwarves who had begun the defense of the town, less than a score were leaving of their own strength, and only another ten, Bruenor among them, were still drawing breath at all.

Hardly a victory.

29

WHERE ROADS MEET
AND ROADS DIVERGE

They ran in flanking lines left and right of the main wagons. Others pulled hard at the largest wagon—the orc god statue discarded—that bore the wounded, including King Bruenor Battlehammer. On the cart with him rode Regis, who was too injured to do much of anything else, and Pikel Bouldershoulder, the doo-dad, who used his enchanted berries and roots on Bruenor's wounds.

"He'll draw out the sickness," Ivan assured Wulfgar and Tred as they ran along behind that wagon. "Me brother's got some tricks, he does."

Wulfgar nodded grimly and took heart in the words, for Catti-brie had told him a short while before that Bruenor did seem to be resting more easily.

"Ain't that that's worrying me," Tred put in. "We're seeing orc sign all about, and if they come on now. . . ."

"They will be without their giant friends, who were left on the other side of the ravine," Wulfgar insisted.

"True enough," Tred admitted, though his dour expression did not brighten, "but I'm thinking we'll be finding a tougher fight with them orcs, even with yer boys from Mithral Hall here, when them orcs ain't so surprised that yer boys from Mithral Hall're here!"

There really wasn't much that Wulfgar could say against such logic.

He had seen the orc force, and he knew that those legions, despite being scattered and with many slaughtered outside of Shallows, would still prove overwhelming to this contingent in a level fight. Even as they had begun the run the previous day, they had all known that their only real hope was that the orcs had been too scattered to regroup in time to catch them before they reached the safety of Mithral Hall, or at least before they met up with the dwarven army rolling out of that fortress.

But already the signs were showing their hopes to be in vain. All through the night—in which the dwarves, utilizing more of Pikel's wondrous berries, had kept moving—they had heard the calls of worgs, left and right, shadowing them. Earlier the second day, they had caught sight of a dust cloud rising in the north, not so far behind, and they knew that they were being pursued.

Pwent had proposed a possible scenario to them that morning. The battlerager figured that the orc worg-riders would flank and circle in front of the dwarves, trying to slow their run, thus giving the pursuing main force time to catch up and overwhelm them. The dwarves had decided that if such a blockade had been formed, they would lower their heads and blast straight through it.

Wulfgar could only hope that it didn't come to that. They barely had enough to take turns pulling the wagon of wounded, and Pwent and his boys were reaching the end of their tolerance. Pikel's berries were amazing indeed, but they did not provide magical strength. They merely allowed the body to draw on its deeper resources. After the run to the north, the desperate fight, and the beginning of the run back to the south, Wulfgar could plainly see that those reserves were reaching their end. Even worse, those who had come from the prolonged defense of Shallows, himself included, were all carrying grievous wounds.

Another fight would likely be the end of all of them and at the least would eliminate any hope Wulfgar had of getting his beloved father back to Mithral Hall alive.

And so that afternoon, when scouts reported a growing cloud of dust to the west, the barbarian moved to the wagon to join Catti-brie, Regis, and Bruenor.

"That'll mark the end of it," Catti-brie remarked, staring out at the cloud.

Her demeanor, so removed from the ever-optimistic presence that

Wulfgar had always known, caught him off guard and surprised Regis as well.

"We'll fight them and beat them!" Regis replied. "And if more catch us, we'll fight them, too!"

"Indeed," Wulfgar agreed. "I would not see Aegis-fang in the hands of an orc, even if that means I must kill every orc in all the North. And I will see Bruenor back to Mithral Hall, where he will find his strength anew and resume the throne that is so rightfully his."

The words were empowering to both Regis and Catti-brie, and their appreciative looks to Wulfgar became grins and even laughter when Pikel Bouldershoulder chimed in with an enthusiastic "Oo oi!"

The dwarves closed ranks around the wagons, though they maintained their swift pace. Pwent began directing his charges, moving his most seasoned fighters to the delicate areas of defense, and calling out to his boys to be ready. At one point, he moved beside the wagon.

"There'll be a few hunnerd of 'em, judging by what me scouts're seeing," the battlerager explained. He added with an exaggerated wink, "Nothing me and me boys can't handle."

Wulfgar nodded, as did the others, but they all knew the truth of the matter. Being intercepted by several hundred orcs would be bad enough, but even if they could indeed win out against such odds, they would find themselves caught by an equal or larger group from behind because of the inevitable delay.

"Take up your bow," Wulfgar bade Catti-brie as he handed her Taulmaril. "Shoot well."

"Perhaps I could go out under a flag of truce and speak with them," Regis offered, pointedly pulling the enchanted ruby pendant over his shirt collar.

Wulfgar shook his head.

"They'd have ye dead even if ye managed to snare a few o' them with yer lies," Catti-brie remarked.

"Promises, not lies," Regis corrected.

He shrugged helplessly and looked down at the ruby then tucked it away.

The dwarven ranks tightened. It was obvious that they had been spotted by the intercepting force, and their choices were few. A turn to the east would likely put them into another group of orcs, and to stop and try to form some semblance of defense might bring the pursuing orcs upon them as well.

They plowed ahead, gripping weapons in one hand, wagon yokes in the other.

"We gotta make that ridge afore 'em!" Thibbledorf Pwent cried to his fellows, pointing ahead to some higher ground.

The dwarves responded by lowering their aching shoulders even more and charging on. They reached the base of the ridge and started up the slope, hardly slowing.

But they didn't get there first.

"The wing is not broken, but it is bruised badly and will not carry Sunset for any distance," Innovindil told Tarathiel when he and Sunrise returned to her in the mountain cave, some miles north east of the place where they had battled the giants.

Even with the glancing hit by the thrown rock, they had managed to outdistance the pursuing giants and had been fortunate to find a cave where they could put up for the time being.

"The giants have given up the chase, I believe," Tarathiel replied. "They will not find us."

"But neither will we get back to the Moonwood anytime soon," Innovindil reasoned, "or at least, not both of us."

Her expression as she finished was as clear a signal to Tarathiel that she wanted him to climb onto Sunrise and fly off for home as if she had spoken the words directly.

"I am not certain that our report to our people would be complete enough to properly prepare them for what is to come," he replied somberly.

"What have you seen?"

Tarathiel's expression held a grim edge.

"They are crawling out of their holes," he told her, "all to the north and the west. The orcs and goblins are rising as one, and we have seen that the giants, too, are with them. I fear that the force that sacked the town of Shallows is but a small portion of what we will discover."

"Then all the more reason for you to fly to our people."

Tarathiel looked to his mount and seemed, for just a moment, to be leaning that way, but then he looked back at his companion and stood resolute.

"I'll not leave you," he said. "The elves of the Moonwood will not be caught off their guard, whether I fly there or not."

Innovindil started to argue but changed her mind almost immediately. She did not want to be left out there alone, however brave she might sound. She did not know the region as did Tarathiel, and she truly feared for Sunrise. Though the pegasus would survive the wound, it had been so valiant in holding its position above the giants through the pain and shock that the elf had no intention of allowing Sunrise to do anything but heal, even if protecting the pegasus was at the cost of her own life. She knew that Tarathiel felt the same way.

"And we have something else to learn, and now may be our only chance to do so," Tarathiel added after a short pause.

"You believe that the dark elf escaped the fight with the giants," Innovindil reasoned.

"It is possible that Ellifain is out there, as well."

"It is probable that Ellifain is dead," said Innovindil, and Tarathiel could only nod.

Initial shock, the adrenaline of an approaching, desperate battle, fast shifted to confusion among the ranks of the battleragers and the others in the fleeing caravan, for there, on the ridge before them, stood dwarves—a host of dwarves—and arrayed with the colors not of Mithral Hall, but with the axe symbol of Mirabar.

"Who are ye, and what're ye about?" the lead dwarf cried, and he lifted his helm back off his face.

"Torgar!" Regis cried, surely recognizing the dwarf.

A perplexed expression came over the dwarf's face, and he motioned to his fellows to spread wide, left and right. He, along with several others, came down to the ragtag group.

"Well, yer King Bruenor's got our weapons, and so's Mithral Hall, whatever his fate," Torgar proclaimed when Wulfgar and the others filled him in on the desperate battle and the retreat to Mithral Hall. "We come out to ask King Bruenor for his friendship, and now I'm thinking we can prove our own to him and his. Ye just keep on yer run and me and mine'll follow ye close."

"Ye let me and me own run with ye, Torgar o' Mirabar," Thibbledorf Pwent cut in as he stepped forward, showing his ridged, bloodstained armor in all its gory glory. "We give them orcs a reason to run!"

"Luck has shone upon us," Wulfgar whispered to Catti-brie a moment later, as the five hundred reinforcements found positions around the retreating caravan.

They both looked to Bruenor and to Pikel, still tirelessly tending the dwarf king and the other wounded. Apparently sensing their looks, Pikel turned to regard them and offered a wink and a hopeful nod.

Catti-brie couldn't help but smile but then couldn't help but look back to the north.

"You're thinking of Drizzt," Wulfgar observed.

"As soon as we get Bruenor back to Mithral Hall, we'll head out to find him," Regis said, joining in on the conversation.

Catti-brie shook her head with even greater resolve. "He will see to himself and trust that we will see to our safety and the security of Mithral Hall. When his job is done out there, he will come home."

Both Wulfgar and Regis looked at her with surprise, but both inevitably agreed. Without information to the contrary, they knew they had to trust in Drizzt, and in truth, who in all the world was better suited to survive in the hostile environment of the orc-infested North? More practically, none of them were really fit to head back out. Certainly Regis was in no shape to be walking a dangerous road anytime soon.

Catti-brie continued to stare to the north, and without even realizing it, she began chewing nervously on her bottom lip.

Wulfgar grabbed her forearm and gave a gentle, comforting squeeze.

"Elastul told you?" Nanfoodle asked Shoudra when the two met up in the corridor of their building a few nights later.

"He instructed me to go with you," Shoudra replied, her tone making it clear that she was none too pleased with the order.

"He has erred and continues to do so," the little gnome said. "First he chases Bruenor off, then imprisons Torgar, and now . . ."

"This is hardly the same thing," said Shoudra.

"Is it so different? Will the remaining dwarves in Mirabar be pleased when they learn of our antics in Mithral Hall? Do we even have a hope of succeeding there, given that more than four hundred of Mirabar's dwarves will precede our arrival?"

"Elastul is counting on just that fact to gain us the confidence of Bruenor and his kin."

"To what end? Treachery?" asked the glum gnome.

Shoudra started to respond, but just shrugged. "We will see what we find when we arrive in Mithral Hall," she said after a moment's reflection.

Nanfoodle considered her words and her demeanor for a moment, then his face brightened.

"I plan to follow your lead in the cavern of Clan Battlehammer," he said, "even if that lead diverges from the edicts of Marchion Elastul."

Shoudra looked around cautiously, her expression bidding the gnome to speak no more of such foolishness.

In her own heart, though, the Sceptrana did not disagree. Elastul's edict had been direct and simple: Go to Mithral Hall and check on the traitor dwarves, and while they're there, do some serious damage to their rival's operations.

Better, Shoudra thought, that they go to Mithral Hall to reach out to King Bruenor through Torgar Hammerstriker and the others. After the disaster that had befallen Mirabar, they might find a new and stronger alliance with their fellow mining city, one that would benefit them all.

She could only sigh and wish things were different, though, for she knew Elastul well enough to understand the absurdity of even hoping that she could realize such an outcome.

EPILØGUE

With every stone he turned, Drizzt Do'Urden held his breath, expecting to find one of his friends buried beneath it. The destruction of Shallows had been complete by his estimation. He had no idea what the pile of shaped wood on the field just south of the town might be, but he supposed that the orcs had brought great siege engines with them in the final assault.

Not that they had needed any, given the damage the giants had wrought upon the town.

He took heart at the many dead orcs and worgs littered about the scene, but the fact that many had died right at the entrance to the substructure tunnels, logically the last line of defense, told him that the end had surely been bitter.

He found no bodies in those tunnels, at least, lending him some hope that his friends had been captured and not killed.

And he found a familiar one-horned helmet.

Hardly finding the strength to bend without falling over, the drow touched the crown of Bruenor Battlehammer and gently lifted it, turning it over in his hands. He had hoped that his eyes had deceived him from across the ravine that terrible night, when the flaming tower had fallen. He had hoped that Bruenor had somehow been able to leap away and escape the catastrophe.

The drow forced himself to look around, to poke at the rubble near to the helmet. There, under tons of stone, he found the end of a crushed hand, a gnarled, dwarf's hand.

So, he believed, he had found Bruenor's grave.

And were Wulfgar and Regis buried there too? And what of Catti-brie?

The images that flitted about in his whirling thoughts weighed heavily on Drizzt Do'Urden. He remembered thinking it would be better to adventure on the open road—even if it were to cost him his life, even if it were to cost Catti-brie's life—than to live a life in one secure place.

How hollow those thoughts felt to him in that terrible moment.

Strangely, he thought of Zaknafein then, of his family and his days in Menzoberranzan, of the tragedies that had marked his early life. He thought of Ellifain too, of all that he had tried to do for her that fateful night under the stars, and of her ultimate end.

He thought of his friends, some surely lost, and likely all dead, and was stabbed by the futility of it all. For all his life since his days with Zaknafein, his departure from Menzoberranzan, his days with Montolio and with the friends he had come to love above all others in Icewind Dale, Drizzt Do'Urden had followed a line of precepts based upon discipline and ultimate optimism. He fought for a better world because he believed that a better world could and would be made. He had never held any illusions that he would change the whole world, of course, or even a substantial portion of it, but he had always held strongly that fighting to better just his own little pocket of the world was a worthwhile course.

And there was Ellifain. And there was Bruenor.

He looked down at the helmet and rolled it over in his hands.

In all likelihood he had lost every close friend he had ever known.

Except for one, the drow realized when Guenhwyvar stirred beside him.

Three days later, Drizzt Do'Urden sat on the rocky slopes of a mountain, listening to the cacophony of horns around him and watching the progression of lines of torches moving along nearly every mountain trail. All that had happened had been but a prelude, he understood then. The orcs were massing, bringing a fair number of goblins along with them, and even worse, they had allied with the frost giants in greater numbers than any could have anticipated.

What had gone from a raid on a caravan from Citadel Felbarr had escalated to the sacking of two towns and to a threat to every life in the North. In just watching the progression, Drizzt could see that Mithral Hall itself would soon be threatened.

And, he believed, Mithral Hall was a leaderless place.

In truth, though, none of that realization sank very deeply into the thoughts and heart of Drizzt Do'Urden that dark night on a mountain slope, and when he saw the campfire of a small off-shoot of the massing humanoid force not too far away, all thoughts of anything but the immediate situation flew from him.

The drow produced his onyx figurine and called forth Guenhwyvar, then drew out his scimitars and started his slow walk toward the encampment. He didn't blink; his face showed no emotion at all.

It was time to go to work.

THE LONE
DROW

THE HUNTER'S BLADES TRILOGY   BOOK II

"The three mists, Obould Many-Arrows," Tsinka Shrinrill shrieked, her eyes wide, eyeballs rolling about insanely. She was in her communion as she addressed the orc king and the others, lost somewhere between the real world and the land of the gods, so she claimed. "The three mists define your kingdom beneath the Spine of the World: the long line of the Surbrin River, giving her vapors to the morning air; the fetid smoke of the Trollmoors reaching up to your call; the spiritual essence of your long-dead ancestors, the haunting of Fell Pass. This is your time, King Obould Many-Arrows, and this will be your domain!"

The orc shaman ended her proclamation by throwing up her arms and howling, and those many other mouths of Gruumsh One-Eye, god of orcs, followed her lead, similarly shrieking, raising their arms, and turning circles as they paced a wider circuit around the orc king and the ruined wooden statue of their beloved god.

The ruined *hollow* statue used by their enemies, the insult to the image of Gruumsh. The defiling of their god.

Urlgen Threefist, Obould's son and heir to the throne, looked on with a mixture of amazement, trepidation, and gratitude. He had never liked Tsinka—one of the minor, if more colorful shamans of the Many-Arrows tribe—and he knew that she was speaking largely along the lines scripted by Obould himself. He scanned the area, noting the sea of snarling orcs, all angry and frustrated, mouths wide, teeth yellow and green, sharpened and broken. He looked at the bloodshot and jaundiced eyes, all glancing this way and that with excitement and fear. He watched the continual jostling and shoving, and he noted the many hurled insults, which were often answered by hurled missiles. Warriors all, angry and bitter—as were all the orcs of the Spine of the World—living in dank caves while the other races enjoyed the comforts of their respective cities and societies. They were all anxious, as Urlgen was anxious, pointy tongues licking torn lips. Would Obould reshape the fate and miserable existence of the orcs of the North?

Urlgen had led the charge against the human town that had been known as Shallows, and he had found a great victory there. The tower of the powerful wizard, long a thorn in the side of the orcs, was toppled, and the mighty wizard was dead, along with most of his townsfolk and a fair number of dwarves, including, they all believed, King Bruenor Battlehammer himself, the ruler of Mithral Hall.

But many others had escaped Urlgen's assault, using that blasphemous statue. Upon seeing the great and towering idol, most of Urlgen's orc forces had properly prostrated themselves before it, paying homage to the image of their merciless god. It had all been a ruse, though, and the statue had opened, revealing a small force of fierce dwarves who had massacred many of the unsuspecting orcs and sent the rest fleeing for the mountains. And so there had been an escape by those remaining defenders of the dying town, and the fleeing refugees had met up with another dwarf contingent—estimates put their number at four hundred or so. Those combined forces had fended off Urlgen's chasing army.

The orc commander had lost many.

Thus, when Obould had arrived on the scene, Urlgen had expected to be berated and probably even beaten for his failure, and indeed, his vicious father's immediate responses had been along those very lines.

But then, to the surprise of them all, the reports of potential reinforcements had come filtering in. Many other tribes had begun to crawl out of the Spine of the World. In reflecting on that startling moment, Urlgen still marveled at his father's quick-thinking response. Obould had ordered the battlefield sealed, the southern marches of the area cleared of signs of any passage whatsoever. The goal was to make it seem as if none had escaped Shallows—Obould understood that the control of information to the newcomers would be critical. To that effect, he had put Urlgen to work instructing his many warriors, telling them that none of their enemies had escaped, warning them against believing anything other than that.

And the orc tribes from the deep holes of the Spine of the World had come running to Obould's side. Orc chieftains had placed valuable gifts at Obould's feet and had begged him to accept their fealty. The pilgrimages had been led by the shamans, so they all said. With their wicked deception, the dwarves had angered Gruumsh, and so many of Gruumsh's priestly followers had sent their respective tribes to the side of Obould, who would lead the way to vengeance. Obould, who had slain King Bruenor Battlehammer, would make the dwarves pay dearly for their sacrilege.

For Urlgen, of course, it had all come as a great relief. He was taller than his father, but not nearly strong enough to openly challenge the mighty orc leader. Add to Obould's great strength and skill his wondrously crafted, ridged and spiked black battle mail, and that greatsword of his, which could burst into flame with but a thought, and no one, not even overly proud Urlgen, would even think of offering challenge for control of the tribe.

Urlgen didn't have to worry about that, though. The shamans, led by the gyrating priestess, were promising Obould so many of his dreams and desires and were praising him for a great victory at Shallows—a victory that had been achieved by his honored son. Obould looked at Urlgen more than once as the ceremony continued, and his toothy smile was wide. It wasn't that vicious smile that promised how greatly he would enjoy torturing someone. Obould was pleased with Urlgen, pleased with all of it.

King Bruenor Battlehammer was dead, after all, and the dwarves were in flight. And even though the orcs had lost nearly a thousand warriors at Shallows, their numbers had since swollen several times over. More were coming, too, climbing into the sunlight (many for perhaps the first time in their lives), blinking away the sting of the brightness, and moving along the mountain trails to the south, to the call of the shamans, to the call of Gruumsh, to the call of King Obould Many-Arrows.

"I will have my kingdom," Obould proclaimed when the shamans had finished their dance and their keening. "And once I am done with the land inside the mountains and the three mists, we will strike out against those who encircle us and oppose us. I will have Citadel Felbarr!" he cried, and a thousand orcs cheered.

"I will send the dwarves fleeing to Adbar, where I will seal them in their filthy holes!" Obould went on, leaping around and running along the front ranks of the gathered, and a thousand orcs cheered.

"I will shake the ground of Mirabar to the west!" Obould cried, and the cheers multiplied.

"I will make Silverymoon herself tremble at the mention of my name!"

That brought the greatest cheers of all, and the vocal Tsinka grabbed the great orc roughly and kissed him, offering herself to him, offering to him Gruumsh's blessing in the highest possible terms.

Obould swept her up with one powerful arm, crushing her close to his side, and the cheering intensified yet again.

Urlgen wasn't cheering, but he was surely smiling as he watched Obould carry the priestess up the ramp to the defiled statue of Gruumsh. He was thinking how much greater his inheritance would soon become.

After all, Obould wouldn't live forever.

And if it seemed that he might, Urlgen was confident that he would find a way to correct that situation.

PART ONE   EMOTIONAL ANARCHY

I did everything right.

Every step of my journey out of Menzoberranzan was guided by my inner map of right and wrong, of community and self-lessness. Even on those occasions when I failed, as everyone must, my missteps were of judgment or simple frailty and were not in disregard of my conscience. For in there, I know, reside the higher principles and tenets that move us all closer to our chosen gods, closer to our definitions, hopes, and understandings of paradise.

I did not abandon my conscience, but it, I fear, has deceived me.

I did everything right.

Yet Ellifain is dead, and my long-ago rescue of her is a mockery.

I did everything right.

And I watched Bruenor fall, and I expect that those others I loved, that everything I loved, fell with him.

Is there a divine entity out there somewhere, laughing at my foolishness? Is there even a divine entity out there, anywhere?

Or was it all a lie, and worse, a self-deception?

Often have I considered community, and the betterment of the individual within the context of the betterment of the whole. This was the guiding principle of my existence, the realization that forced me from Menzoberranzan. And now, in this time of pain, I have come to understand—or perhaps it is just that now I have forced myself to admit—that my belief was also something much more personal. How ironic that in my declaration of community, I was in effect and in fact feeding my own desperate need to belong to something larger than myself.

In privately declaring and reinforcing the righteousness of my beliefs, I was doing no differently from those who flock before the preacher's pulpit. I was seeking comfort and guidance, only I was looking for the needed answers within, whereas so many others seek them without.

By that understanding, I did everything right. And yet, I cannot dismiss the growing realization, the growing trepidation, the growing terror, that I, ultimately, was wrong. For what is the point if Ellifain is dead, and if she existed in such turmoil through all the short years of her life?

For what is the point if I and my friends followed our hearts and trusted in our swords, only for me to watch them die beneath the rubble of a collapsing tower?

If I have been right all along, then where is justice, and where is the reciprocation of a grateful god?

Even in asking that question, I see the hubris that has so infected me. Even in asking that question, I see the machinations of my soul laid bare. I cannot help but ask, am I any different than my kin? In technique, surely, but in effect? For in declaring community and dedication, did I not truly seek exactly the same things as the priestesses I left behind in Menzoberranzan? Did I, like they, not seek eternal life and higher standing among my peers?

As the foundation of Withegroo's tower swayed and toppled, so too have the illusions that have guided my steps.

I was trained to be a warrior. Were it not for my skill with my scimitars, I expect I would be a smaller player in the world around me, less respected and less accepted. That training and talent are all that I have left now; it is the foundation upon which I intend to build this new chapter in the curious and winding road that is the life of Drizzt Do'Urden. It is the extension of my rage that I will turn loose upon the wretched creatures that have so shattered all that I held dear. It is the expression of what I have lost: Ellifain, Bruenor, Wulfgar, Regis, Catti-brie, and, in effect, Drizzt Do'Urden.

These scimitars, Icingdeath and Twinkle by name, become my definition of myself now, and Guenhwyvar again is my only companion. I trust in both, and in nothing else.

—Drizzt Do'Urden

1

ANGER'S REMINDER

Drizzt didn't like to think of it as a shrine. Propped on a forked stick, the one-horned helmet of Bruenor Battlehammer dominated the small hollow that the dark elf had taken as his home. The helm was set right before the cliff face that served as the hollow's rear wall, in the only place within the natural shelter that got any sunlight at all.

Drizzt wanted it that way. He wanted to see the helmet. He wanted never to forget. And it wasn't just Bruenor he was determined to remember, and not just his other friends.

Most of all, Drizzt wanted to remember who had done that horrible thing to him and to his world.

He had to fall to his belly to crawl between the two fallen boulders and into the hollow, and even then the going was slow and tight. Drizzt didn't care; he actually preferred it that way. The total lack of comforts, the almost animalistic nature of his existence, was good for him, was cathartic, and even more than that, was yet another reminder to him of what he had to become, of whom he had to be if he wanted to survive. No more was he Drizzt Do'Urden of Icewind Dale, friend to Bruenor and Catti-brie, Wulfgar and Regis. No more was he Drizzt Do'Urden, the ranger trained by Montolio deBrouchee in the ways of nature and the spirit of Mielikki. He was once again that lone drow who had wandered out of Menzoberranzan.

He was once again that refugee from the city of dark elves, who had forsaken the ways of the priestesses who had so wronged him and who had murdered his father.

He was the Hunter, the instinctual creature who had defeated the fell ways of the Underdark, and who would repay the orc hordes for the death of his dearest friends.

He was the Hunter, who sealed his mind against all but survival, who put aside the emotional pain of the loss of Ellifain.

Drizzt knelt before the sacred totem one afternoon, watching the splay of sunlight on the tilted helmet. Bruenor had lost one of the horns on it years and years past, long before Drizzt had come into his life. The dwarf had never replaced the horn, he had told Drizzt, because it was a reminder to him always to keep his head low.

Delicate fingers moved up and felt the rough edge of that broken horn. Drizzt could still catch the smell of Bruenor on the leather band of the helm, as if the dwarf was squatting in the dark hollow beside him. As if they had just returned from another brutal battle, breathing heavy, laughing hard, and lathered in sweat.

The drow closed his eyes and saw again that last desperate image of Bruenor. He saw Withegroo's white tower, flames leaping up its side, a lone dwarf rushing around on top, calling orders to the bitter end. He saw the tower lean and tumble, and watched the dwarf disappear into the crumbling blocks.

He closed his eyes all the tighter to hold back the tears. He had to defeat them, had to push them far, far away. The warrior he had become had no place for such emotions. Drizzt opened his eyes and looked again at the helmet, drawing strength in his anger. He followed the line of a sunbeam to the recess behind the staked headgear, to see his own discarded boots.

Like the weak and debilitating emotion of grief, he didn't need them anymore.

Drizzt fell to his belly and slithered out through the small opening between the boulders, moving into the late afternoon sunlight. He jumped to his feet almost immediately after sliding clear and put his nose up to the wind. He glanced all around, his keen eyes searching every shadow and every play of the sunlight, his bare feet feeling the cool ground beneath him. With a cursory glance all around, the Hunter sprinted off for higher ground.

He came out on the side of a mountain just as the sun disappeared behind the western horizon, and there he waited, scouting the region as the shadows lengthened and twilight fell.

Finally, the light of a campfire glittered in the distance.

Drizzt's hand went instinctively to the onyx figurine in his belt pouch. He didn't take it forth and summon Guenhwyvar, though. Not that night.

His vision grew even more acute as the night deepened around him, and Drizzt ran off, silent as the shadows, elusive as a feather on a windy autumn day. He wasn't constricted by the mountain trails, for he was too nimble to be slowed by boulder tumbles and broken ground. He wove through trees easily, and so stealthily that many of the forest animals, even wary deer, never heard or noted his approach, never knew he had passed unless a shift in the wind brought his scent to them.

At one point, he came to a small river, but he leaped from wet stone to wet stone in such perfect balance that even their water-splashed sides did little to trip him up.

He had lost sight of the fire almost as soon as he came down from the mountain spur, but he had taken his bearings from up there and he knew where to run, as if anger itself was guiding his long and sure strides.

Across a small dell and around a thick copse of trees, the drow caught sight of the campfire once more, and he was close enough to see the silhouettes of the forms moving around it. They were orcs, he knew at once, from their height and broad shoulders and their slightly hunched manner of moving. A couple were arguing—no surprise there—and Drizzt knew enough of their guttural language to understand their dispute to be over which would keep watch. Clearly, neither wanted the duty, nor thought it anything more than an inconvenience.

The drow crouched behind some brush not far away and a wicked grin grew across his face. Their watch was indeed inconsequential, he thought, for alert or not, they would not take note of him.

They would not see the Hunter.

The brutish sentry dropped his spear across a big stone, interlocked his fingers, and inverted his hands. His knuckles cracked more loudly than snapping branches.

"Always Bellig," he griped, glancing back at the campfire and the many forms gathered around it, some resting, others tearing at scraps of putrid food. "Bellig keeps watch. You sleep. You eat. Always Bellig keeps watch."

He continued to grumble and complain, and he continued to look back at the encampment for a long while.

Finally, he turned back—to see facial features chiseled from ebony, to see a shock of white hair, and to see eyes, those eyes! Purple eyes! Flaming eyes!

Bellig instinctively reached for his spear—or started to, until he saw the flash of a gleaming blade to the left and the right. Then he tried to bring his arms in close to block instead, but he was far too slow to catch up to the dark elf's scimitars.

He tried to scream out, but by that point, the curved blades had cut two deep lines, severing his windpipe.

Bellig clutched at those mortal wounds and the swords came back, then back again, and again.

The dying orc turned as if to run to his comrades, but the scimitars struck again, at his legs, their fine edges easily parting muscle and tendon.

Bellig felt a hand grab him as he fell, guiding him down quietly to the ground. He was still alive, though he had no way to draw breath. He was still alive, though his lifeblood deepened in a dark red pool around him.

His killer moved off, silently.

"*Arsh,* get yourself quiet over there, stupid Bellig," Oonta called from under the boughs of a wide-spreading elm not far to the side of the campsite. "Me and Figgle is talking!"

"Him's a big mouth," Figgle the Ugly agreed.

With his nose missing, one lip torn away, and green-gray teeth all twisted and tusky, Figgle was a garish one even by orc standards. He had bent too close to a particularly nasty worg in his youth and had paid the price.

"Me gonna kill him soon," Oonta remarked, drawing a crooked smile from his sentry companion.

A spear soared in, striking the tree between them and sticking fast.

"Bellig!" Oonta cried as he and Figgle stumbled aside. "Me gonna kill you sooner!"

With a growl, Oonta reached for the quivering spear, as Figgle wagged his head in agreement.

"Leave it," came a voice, speaking basic Orcish but too melodic in tone to belong to an orc.

Both sentries froze and turned around to look in the direction from whence the spear had come. There stood a slender and graceful figure, black hands on hips, dark cape fluttering out in the night wind behind him.

"You will not need it," the dark elf explained.

"Huh?" both orcs said together.

"Whatcha seeing?" asked a third sentry, Oonta's cousin Broos. He came in from the side, to Oonta and Figgle's left, the dark elf's right. He looked to the two and followed their frozen gazes back to the drow, and he, too, froze in place. "Who that be?"

"A friend," the dark elf said.

"Friend of Oonta's?" Oonta asked, poking himself in the chest.

"A friend of those you murdered in the town with the tower," the dark elf explained, and before the orcs could even truly register those telling words, the dark elf's scimitars appeared in his hands.

He might have reached for them so quickly and fluidly that the orcs hadn't followed the movement, but to them, all three, it simply seemed as if the weapons had appeared there.

Broos looked to Oonta and Figgle for clarification and asked, "Huh?"

And the dark form rushed past him.

And he was dead.

The dark elf came in hard for the orc duo. Oonta yanked the spear free, while Figgle drew out a pair of small blades, one with a forked, duel tip, the other greatly curving.

Oonta deftly brought the spear in an overhand spin, its tip coming over and down hard to block the charging drow.

But the drow slid down below that dipping spear, skidding right in between the orcs. Oonta fumbled with the spear as Figgle brought his two weapons down hard.

But the drow wasn't there, for he had leaped straight up, rising in the air between the orcs. Both skilled orc warriors altered their weapons wonderfully, coming in hard at either side of the nimble creature.

Those scimitars were there, though, one intercepting the spear, the other neatly picking off Figgle's strikes with a quick double parry. And even as the dark elf's blades blocked the attack, the dark elf's feet kicked out, one behind, one ahead, both scoring direct and stunning hits on orc faces.

Figgle fell back, snapping his blades back and forth before him to ward off any attacks while he was so disoriented and dazed. Oonta similarly retreated, brandishing the spear in the air before him. They regained their senses together and found themselves staring at nothing but each other.

"Huh?" Oonta asked, for the drow was not to be seen.

Figgle jerked suddenly and the tip of a curving scimitar erupted from the center of his chest. It disappeared almost immediately, the dark elf coming around the orc's side, his second scimitar taking out the creature's throat as he passed.

Wanting no part of such an enemy, Oonta threw the spear, turned, and fled, running flat out for the main encampment and crying out in fear. Orcs leaped up all around the terrified Oonta, spilling their foul foods—raw and rotting meat, mostly—and scrambling for weapons.

"What'd you do?" one cried.

"Who got the killing?" yelled another.

"Drow elf! Drow elf!" Oonta cried. "Drow elf kilt Figgle and Broos! Drow elf kilt Bellig!"

Drizzt allowed the fleeing orc to escape back within the lighted area of the camp proper and used the distraction of the bellowing brute to get into the shadows of a large tree right on the encampment's perimeter. He slid his scimitars away as he did a quick scan, counting more than a dozen of the creatures.

Hand over hand, the drow went up the tree, listening to Oonta's recounting of the three Drizzt had slain.

"Drow elf?" came more than one curious echo, and one of them mentioned Donnia, a name that Drizzt had heard before.

Drizzt moved out to the edge of one branch, some fifteen feet up from the ground and almost directly over the gathering of orcs. Their eyes were turning outward, to the shadows of the surrounding trees, compelled by Oonta's tale. Unseen above them, Drizzt reached inside himself, to those hereditary powers of the drow, the innate magic of the race, and he brought forth a globe of impenetrable darkness in the midst of the orc group, right atop the fire that marked the center of the encampment. Down went the drow, leaping from branch to branch, his bare feet feeling every touch and keeping him in perfect balance, his enchanted, speed-enhancing anklets allowing him to quickstep whenever necessary to keep his feet precisely under his weight.

He hit the ground running, toward the darkness globe, and those orcs outside of it who noted the ebon-skinned figure gave a shout and charged at him, one launching a spear.

Drizzt ran right past that awkward missile—he believed that he could have harmlessly caught it if he had so desired. He greeted the first orc staggering out of the globe with another of his innate magical abilities, summoning purplish-blue flames to outline the creature's form. The flame didn't burn at the flesh, but made marking target areas so much easier for the skilled drow, who, in truth, didn't need the help.

They also distracted the orc, with the fairly stupid creature looking down at its flaming limbs and crying out in fear. It looked back up Drizzt's way just in time to see the flash of a scimitar.

Another orc emerged right behind it and the drow never slowed, sliding down low beneath the orc's defensively whipping club and deftly twisting his scimitar around the creature's leg, severing its hamstring. By the time the howling orc hit the ground, Drizzt the Hunter was inside the darkness globe.

He moved purely on instinct, his muscles and movements reacting to the noises around him and to his tactile sensations. Without even consciously registering it, the Hunter knew from the warmth of the ground against his bare feet where the fire was located, and every time he felt the touch of some orc bumbling around beside him, his scimitars moved fast and furious, turning and striking even as he rushed past.

At one point, he didn't even feel an orc, didn't even hear an orc, but his sense of smell told him that one was beside him. A short slash of Twinkle brought a shriek and a crash as the creature went down.

Again without any conscious counting, Drizzt the Hunter knew when he would be crossing through to the other side of the darkness globe. Somehow, within him, he had registered and measured his every step.

He came out fast, in perfect balance, his eyes immediately focusing on the quartet of orcs rushing at him, his warrior's instincts drawing a line of attack to which he was already reacting.

He went ahead and down, meeting the thrust of a spear with a blinding double parry, one blade following the other. Either of Drizzt's fine scimitars could have shorn through the crude spear, but he didn't press the first through and he turned the second to the flat of the blade when he struck. Let the spear remain intact; it didn't matter after his second blade, moving right to left across his chest, knocked the weapon up high.

For Drizzt's feet moved ahead in a sudden blur bringing him past the off-balance orc, and Twinkle took it in the throat.

Drizzt continued without slowing, every step rotating him left just a bit, so that as he approached the second orc, he turned and pivoted completely, Twinkle again leading the way with a sidelong slash that caught the orc's extended sword arm across the wrist and sent its weapon flying. Following that slash as he completed the circuit, his second scimitar, Icingdeath, came in fast and hard, taking the creature in the ribs.

And the Hunter was already past.

He went down low, under a swinging club, and leaped up high over a thrusting spear, planting his feet on the weapon shaft as he descended, taking the weapon down under his weight. Across went Twinkle, but the orc ducked. Hardly slowing, Drizzt flipped the scimitar into an end-over-end spin, then caught the blade with a reverse grip and thrust it out behind him, catching the surprised club-wielder right in the chest as it charged at his back.

At the same time, the drow's other hand worked independently, Icingdeath slashing the spear-wielding orc's upraised, blocking arm once, twice, and a third time. Extracting Twinkle, Drizzt skipped to the side, and the dying orc stumbled forward past him, tangling with the second, who was clutching at his thrashed arm.

The Hunter was already gone, rushing out to the side in a direct charge at a pair of orcs who were working in apparent coordination. Drizzt went down to his knees in a skid and the orcs reacted, turning spear and sword down low. As soon as his knees hit the ground, though, the drow threw himself into a forward roll, tucking his shoulder and coming right around to his feet, where he pushed off with all his strength, leaping and continuing his turn. He went past and over the surprised pair, who hardly registered the move.

Drizzt landed lightly, still in perfect balance, and came around to the left with Twinkle leading in a slash that had the turning orcs stumbling even more. His weapons out wide to their respective sides, Drizzt reversed Twinkle's flow and brought Icingdeath across the other way, the weapons crossing precisely between the orcs, following through as wide as the drow could reach. A turn of his arms put his hands atop the weapons, and he reversed into a double backhand.

Neither orc had even managed to get its weapon around enough to block either strike. Both orcs tumbled, hit both ways by both blades.

The Hunter was already gone.

Orcs scrambled all around, understanding that they could not stand against that dark foe. None held ground before Drizzt as he rushed back the way he had come, cleaving the head of the orc with the torn arm, then dashing back into the globe of darkness, where he heard at least one of the brutes hiding, cowering on the ground. Again he fell into the world of his other senses, feeling the heat, hearing every sound. His weapons engaged one orc before him; he heard a second shifting and crouching to the side.

A quick side step brought him to the fire, and the cooking pot set on a tripod. He kicked out the far leg and rushed back the other way.

In the blackness of his magical globe, the one orc standing before him couldn't see his smile as the other orc, boiling broth falling all over it, began to howl and scramble.

The orc before him attacked wildly and cried for help. The Hunter could feel the wind from its furious swings.

Measuring the flow of one such over-swing, the Hunter had little trouble in sliding in behind.

He went out of the globe once more, leaving the orc spinning down to the ground, mortally wounded.

A quick run around the globe told Drizzt that only two orcs remained in the camp, one squirming on the ground, its lifeblood pouring out, the other howling and rolling to alleviate the burn from the hot stew.

The slash of scimitars, perfectly placed, ended the movements of both.

And the Hunter went out into the night in pursuit, to finish the task.

Poor Oonta fell against the side of a tree, gasping for breath. He waved away his companion as the orc implored him to keep running. They had put more than a mile of ground between them and the encampment.

"We got to!"

"*You* got to!" Oonta argued between gasps.

Oonta had crawled out of the Spine of the World on the orders of his tribe's shaman, to join in the glory of King Obould, to do war with those who had defaced the image of Gruumsh on a battlefield not far from that spot.

Oonta had come out to fight dwarves, not drow!

His companion grabbed him again and tried to pull him along, but Oonta slapped his hand away. Oonta lowered his head and continued to fight for his breath.

"Do take your time," came a voice behind them, speaking broken Orcish—and with a melodic tone that no orc could mimic.

"We got to go!" Oonta's companion argued, turning to face the speaker.

Oonta, knowing the source of those words, knowing that he was dead, didn't even look up.

"We can talk," he heard his companion implore the dark elf, and he heard, too, his companion's weapon drop to the ground.

"I can," the dark elf replied, and a devilish, diamond-edged scimitar came across, cleanly cutting out the orc's throat. "But I doubt you'll find a voice."

In response, the orc gasped and gurgled.

And fell.

Oonta stood up straight but still did not turn to face the deadly adversary. He moved against a tree and held his hands out defenselessly, hoping the deathblow would fall quickly.

He felt the drow's hot breath on the side of his neck, felt the tip of one blade against his back, the other against the back of his neck.

"You find the leader of this army," the drow told him. "You tell him that I will come to call, and very soon. You tell him that I will kill him."

A flick of that top scimitar took Oonta's right ear—the orc growled and grimaced, but he was disciplined and smart enough to not flee and to not turn around.

"You tell him," the voice said in his ear. "You tell them all."

Oonta started to respond, to assure the deadly attacker that he would do exactly that.

But the Hunter was already gone.

2

GRIT AND GUTS

The dozen dirty and road-weary dwarves rumbled along at a great pace, leaping cracks in the weather-beaten stone and dodging the many juts of rock and ancient boulders. They worked together, despite their obvious fears, and if one stumbled, two others were right there to prop him up and usher him on his way.

Behind them came the orc horde, more than two hundred of the hooting and howling, slobbering creatures. They rattled their weapons and shook their raised fists. Every now and then, one threw a spear at the fleeing dwarves, which inevitably missed its mark. The orcs weren't gaining ground, but neither were they losing any, and their hunger for catching the dwarves was no less than the terrified dwarves' apparent desperation to get away. Unlike with the dwarves, though, if one of the orcs stumbled, its companions were not there to help it along its way. Indeed, if a stumbling orc impeded the progress of a companion, it risked getting bowled over, kicked, or even stabbed. Thus, the orc line had stretched somewhat, but those in the lead remained barely a dozen running strides behind the last of the fleeing dwarves.

The dwarves moved along an ascending stretch of fairly open ground, bordered on their right, the west, by a great mountain spur, but with more open ground to their left. They continued to scream and run on, seeming

362

beyond terror, but if the orcs had been more attuned to their progress and less focused on the catch and kill, they might have noticed that the dwarves seemed to be moving with singular purpose and direction even though so many choices were available to them.

As one, the dwarves came out from the shadows of the mountain spur and swerved between a pair of wide-spaced boulders. The pursuing orcs hardly registered the significance of those great rocks, for the two boulders were really the beginning of a channel along the stony ground, wide enough for three orcs to run abreast. To the vicious creatures, the channel meant only that the dwarves couldn't scatter. And so focused were the orcs that they didn't recognize the presence of side cubbies along both sides of that channel, cunningly hidden by stones, and with dwarf eyes peering out.

The lead orcs were long into the channel, with more than half the orc force past the entry stones, when the first dwarves burst forth from the side walls, picks, hammers, axes, and swords slashing away. Some, notably the Gutbuster Brigade led by Thibbledorf Pwent, the toughest and dirtiest dwarves in all of Clan Battlehammer, carried no weapons beyond their head spikes, ridged armor, and spiked gauntlets. They gleefully charged forth into the middle of the orc rush, leaping onto the closest enemies and thrashing wildly. Some of those same orcs had been caught by surprise by that very same group only a tenday earlier, outside the destroyed town of Shallows. Unlike then, though, the orcs did not turn wholesale and run, but took up the fight.

Even so, the dwarves were better armored and better equipped to battle in the tight area of the rocky channel. They had shaped the ground to their liking, with their strategies already laid out, and they quickly gained an upper hand. Those at the front end, who had come out closest to the entry to the channel, quickly set a defense. Their escape rocks had been cleverly cut to all but seal the channel behind them, buying them the time they needed to finish off those orcs in immediate contact and be ready for those slipping past the barricade.

The twelve fleeing decoys, of course, spun back at once into a singular force, stopping the rush of the lead orcs cold. And those dwarves in the middle of the melee worked in unison, each supporting the other, so that even those who fell to an orc blow were not slaughtered while they squirmed on the ground.

Conversely, those orcs who fell, fell alone and died alone.

"Yer boys did well, Torgar," said a tall, broad dwarf with wild orange hair and a beard that would have tickled his toes had he not tucked it into his belt. One of his eyes was dull gray, scarred from Mithral Hall's defense against the drow invasion, while the other sparkled a sharp and rich blue. "Ye might've lost a few, though."

"Ain't no better way to die than to die fightin' for yer kin," replied Torgar Hammerstriker, the strong leader of the more than four hundred dwarves who had recently emigrated from Mirabar, incensed by Marchion Elastul's shoddy treatment of King Bruenor Battlehammer—ill treatment that had extended to all of the Mirabarran dwarves who dared to welcome their distant relative when he had passed through the city.

Torgar stroked his own long, black beard as he watched the distant fighting. That most curious creature, Pikel Bouldershoulder, had joined in the fray, using his strange druidic magic to work the stones at the entrance area of the channel, sealing off the rest of the pursuit.

That was obviously going to be a very temporary respite, though, for the orcs were not overly stupid, and many of the potential reinforcements had already begun their backtracking to routes that would bring them up alongside the melee.

"Mithral Hall will not forget your help here this day," the old, tall dwarf assured Torgar.

Torgar Hammerstriker accepted the compliment with a quiet nod, not even turning to face the speaker, for he didn't want the war leader of Clan Battlehammer—Banak Brawnanvil by name—to see how touched he was. Torgar understood that the moment would follow him for the rest of his days, even if he lived another few hundred years. His trepidation at walking away from his ancestral home of Mirabar had only increased when hundreds of his kin, led by his dear old friend Shingles McRuff, had forced Marchion Elastul to release him and had then followed him out of Mirabar, with not one looking back. Torgar had known in his heart that he was doing the right thing for himself, but for all?

He knew then, though, and a great contentment washed over him. He and his kin had come upon the remnants of King Bruenor's overwhelmed force, fleeing the killing ground of Shallows. Torgar and his friends had held the rear guard all the way back to the defensible point on the northern slopes of the mountains just north of Keeper's Dale and the entrance to Mithral Hall. During their flight back to Bruenor's lines, the dwarves had found several skirmishes with pursuing orcs, and even one that included a few of the orcs unusual frost giant allies. Staying the course and battling without complaint, they had, of course, received many thanks from their fellow dwarves of Mithral Hall and from Bruenor's two adopted human children, Wulfgar and Catti-brie, and his halfling friend, Regis. Bruenor himself had been, and still was, far too injured to say anything at all.

But those moments had only been a prelude, Torgar understood. With General Dagnabbit dead and Bruenor incapacitated and near death, the dwarves of Mithral Hall had called upon one of their oldest and most seasoned veterans to take the lead.

Banak Brawnanvil had answered that call. And how telling that Banak had asked Torgar for some runners to spring his trap upon some of the closest of the approaching orc hordes. Torgar knew there and then that he had done right in leading the Mirabarran dwarves to Mithral Hall. He knew there and then that he and his Delzoun dwarf kin had truly become part of Clan Battlehammer.

"Signal them running," Banak turned and said to the cleric Rockbottom, the dwarf credited with keeping Bruenor alive in the subchambers of the destroyed wizard's tower in Shallows through those long hours before help had arrived.

Rockbottom waggled his gnarled fingers and uttered a prayer to Moradin. He brought forth a shower of multicolored lights, little wisps of fire that didn't burn anything but that surely got the attention of those dwarves stationed near to the channel.

Almost immediately, Torgar's boys, Pwent's Gutbusters, the other fighters, and the brothers Bouldershoulder came scrambling over the sides of the channel, along prescribed routes, leaving not a dwarf behind, not even the few who had been sorely, perhaps even mortally, wounded.

And another of Pikel's modifications—a huge boulder almost perfectly rounded by the druid's stoneshaping magic—rumbled out of concealment from behind a tumble of stones near the mountain spur. A trio of strong dwarves maneuvered it with long, heavy poles, bending their shoulders to get it past bits of rough ground, and even up one small ascent. Other dwarves ran out of hiding near the top of the channel, helping their kin to guide the boulder so that it dropped into the back end of the channel, where a steeper incline had been constructed to usher it on its way.

The rumbling, rolling boulder shook the ground for great distances, and the remaining orcs in the channel issued a communal scream and fell all over each other in retreat. Some were knocked to the ground, then flattened as the boulder tumbled past. Others were thrown down by their terrified kin in the hopes that their bodies would slow the rolling stone.

In the end, when the boulder at last smashed against the channel-ending barricades, it had killed just a few of the orcs. Up higher on the slope, Banak, Torgar, and the others nodded contentedly, for they understood that the effect had been much greater than the actual damage inflicted upon their enemies.

"The first part of warfare is to defeat yer enemies' hearts," Banak quietly remarked, and to that end, their little ruse had worked quite well.

Banak offered both Torgar and Rockbottom a wink of his torn eye, then he reached out and patted the immigrant from Mirabar on the shoulder.

"I hear yer friend Shingles's done a bit of aboveground fighting," Banak offered. "Along with yerself."

"Mirabar is a city both above and below the stone," Torgar answered.

"Well, me and me kin ain't so familiar with doing battle up above," Banak answered. "I'll be looking to ye two, and to Ivan Bouldershoulder there, for yer advice."

Torgar happily nodded his agreement.

The dwarves had just begun to reconstitute their defensive lines along the high ground just south of the channel when Wulfgar and Catti-brie came running in to join Banak and the other leaders.

"We've been out to the east," Catti-brie breathlessly explained. A half foot taller than the tallest dwarves, though not nearly as solidly built, the young human did not seem out of place among them. Her face was wide but still delicate; her auburn hair was thick and rich and hanging below her shoulders. Her blue eyes were large even by human standards, certainly much more so than the eyes of a typical dwarf, which seemed always squinting and always peeking out from under a furrowed and heavily haired brow. Despite her feminine beauty, there was a toughness about the woman, who was raised by Bruenor Battlehammer, a pragmatism and solidity that allowed her to hold her own even among the finest of the dwarf warriors.

"Then ye missed a good bit o' the fun," said an enthusiastic Rockbottom, and his declaration was met with cheers and lifted mugs dripping of foamy ale.

"Oo oi!" agreed Pikel Bouldershoulder, his white teeth shining out between his green beard and mustache.

"We caught 'em in the channel, just as we planned," Banak Brawnanvil explained, his tone much more sober and grim than the others. "We got a few kills and sent more'n a few runnin' . . ."

His voice trailed off in the face of Catti-brie's emphatic waves.

"You used yer decoys to catch their decoys," the woman explained, and she swept her arm out to the east. "A great force marches against us, moving south to flank us."

"A great force is just north of us," Banak argued. "We seen it. How many stinking orcs are there?"

"More than you have dwarves to battle them, many times over," explained the giant Wulfgar, his expression stern, his crystal blue eyes narrowed. More than a foot taller than his human companion, Wulfgar, son of Beornegar, towered over the dwarves. He was slender at the waist, wiry, and agile, but his torso thickened to more than a dwarf's proportions at his broad chest. His arms were the girth of a strong dwarf's leg, his jaw firm and square. Those features of course brought respect from the tough, bearded folk, but in truth, it was the light in Wulfgar's eyes, a warrior's clarity, that elicited the most respect, and so when he continued, they all listened carefully. "If you battle them on two flanks, as you surely will should you stay here, they will overrun you."

"Bah!" snorted Rockbottom. "One dwarf's worth five o' the stinkers!"

Wulfgar turned to regard the confident cleric, and didn't blink.

"That many?" Banak asked.

"And more," said Catti-brie.

"Get 'em up and get 'em moving," Banak instructed Torgar. "Straight run to the south, to the highest ground we can find."

"That'll put us on the edge of the cliff overlooking Keeper's Dale," Rockbottom argued.

"Defensible ground," Banak agreed, shrugging off the dwarf's concerns.

"But with nowhere to run," Rockbottom reasoned. "We'll be putting a good and steep killing ground afore our feet, to be sure."

"And the flanking force will not be able to continue far enough south to strike at us," Banak added.

"But if we're to lose the ground, then we've got nowhere to run," Rockbottom reiterated. "Ye're puttin' our backs to the wall."

"Not to the wall, but to the cliff," Torgar Hammerstriker interjected. "Me and me boys'll get right on that, setting enough drop ropes to bring the whole of us to the dale floor in short order."

"It's three hunnerd feet to the dale," Rockbottom argued.

Torgar shrugged as if that hardly mattered.

"Whatever you're to do, it would be best if you were doing it fast," Catti-brie put in.

"And what're ye thinking we should be doing?" Banak replied. "Ye seen the orc forces—are ye not thinking we can make a stand against them?"

"I fear that we might be wise to go to the edge of Keeper's Dale and beyond," said Wulfgar, and Catti-brie nodded, in apparent agreement with him. "And all the way to Mithral Hall."

"That many orcs?" asked another visitor to Mithral Hall who had been caught up in the battle, the yellow-bearded Ivan Bouldershoulder, Pikel's tougher and more conventional brother. The dwarf pushed his way through his fellows to move close to the leaders.

"That many orcs," Catti-brie assured him. "But we cannot be going all the way into Mithral Hall. Not yet. Bruenor's the king of more than Mithral Hall now. He went to Shallows because his duty took him there, and so ours tells us that we cannot be running all the way into our hole."

"Too many'll die if we do," Banak agreed. "To the highest ground, then, and let the dogs come on. We'll send them running, don't ye doubt!"

"Oo oi!" Pikel cheered.

All the other dwarves looked at the curious little Pikel, a green-haired and green-bearded creature who pulled his beard back over his ears and braided it into his hair, which ran more than halfway down his back. He was rounder than his tough brother, seeming more gentle, and while Ivan, like most dwarves, wore a patchwork of tough and bulky leather and metal armor, Pikel wore a simple robe, light green in color. And where the other dwarves wore heavy boots, protection from a forge's sparks and embers, and good for stomping orcs, Pikel wore open-toed sandals. Still, there was something about the easygoing Pikel, who had certainly shown his usefulness. The idol that had gotten the rescuers close to Shallows had been his idea and fashioned by his own hand, and in the ensuing battles, he had always been there, with magic devilish to his enemies and comforting to his allies. One by one, the other dwarves offered him a smile appreciative of his enthusiasm.

For with the arrival of Wulfgar and Catti-brie and the grim news from the east, their own enthusiasm had inevitably begun to wane.

The dwarves broke camp in short order, and not a moment too soon, for barely had they moved up and over the next of the many ridgelines when the orc force to the north started its charge and the flanking force from the east began to sweep in.

Nearly a thousand dwarves rambled across the stones, legs churning tirelessly to propel them up the sloping ground of the mountainside. They crossed the three thousand foot elevation, then four thousand, and still they ran on and held their formation tight and strong. Now taller mountains rose on the east, eliminating any possible flanking maneuver by the orcs, though the force behind them continued its pursuit. The dwarves moved more than a mile up and were gasping for breath with every stride, but still those strides did not slow.

Finally Banak's leading charges came in sight of the last expanse, and to the lip of the cliff overlooking Keeper's Dale, the abrupt ending of the slope where it seemed as if the stone had just been torn asunder. Spreading out below them, fully the three hundred feet down that Rockbottom had described, lay Keeper's Dale, the wide valley that marked the western approach to Mithral Hall. A mist hung in the air that morning, creeping around the many stone pillars that rose from the nearly barren ground.

With discipline so typical of the sturdy dwarves, the warriors went to work sorting out their lines and constructing defensive positions, some building walls with loose stone, others finding larger boulders that could be rolled back upon their enemies, and still others marking all the best vantage points and defensive positions and determining ways they might link those positions to maximum effect. Torgar, meanwhile, brought forth his best engineers—and there were many fine ones among the dwarves of Mirabar—and he presented them with the problem at hand: the quick transport of the entire dwarf force to the floor of Keeper's Dale, should a retreat be necessary.

More than a hundred of Mirabar's finest began exploring the length of the cliff face, checking the strength of the stone and seeking the easiest routes, including ledges where the descending dwarves might pause and switch to lower ropes. Within short order, the first ropes were set, and Torgar's engineers slid down to find a proper resting ground where they might set the next relays. It would take four separate lengths at the lower points and at least five at the higher, and that daunting prospect would have turned away many in despair.

But not dwarves. Not the stubborn folk who might spend years digging a tunnel only to find no precious ore at its end. Not the hearty and brave folk who put hammer to spike in unexplored regions of the deepest holes, not even knowing if any ensuing sparks might set off an explosion of dangerous gasses. Not the communal folk who would knock each other over in trying to get to kin in need. To the dwarves who formed King Bruenor's northern line of defense, those of Mithral Hall and Mirabar alike, their common pre-surname of Delzoun was more than a familial bond, it was a call to honor and duty.

One of the descending engineers got caught on a jag of stone, and in trying to extricate himself, slipped from the rope and tumbled from the cliff, plummeting more than two hundred feet to his death. All the others paused and offered a quick prayer to Moradin, then went back to their necessary work.

Tred McKnuckles tucked his yellow beard into his belt, hoisted his overstuffed pack onto his shoulders, and turned to the tunnel leading west out of Mithral Hall.

"Well, ye coming?" he asked his companion, a fellow refugee from Citadel Felbarr.

Nikwillig assumed a pensive pose and stared off absently into the dark tunnel.

"No, don't think that I be," came the surprising answer.

"Ye going daft on me?" Tred asked. "Ye're knowin' as well as meself's knowin' that Obould Many-Arrows's got his grubby fingers in this, somewhere and somehow. That dog's still barking and still bitin'! And ye're knowing as well as meself's knowing that if Obould's involved, he's got his eyes looking back to Felbarr! That's the real prize he's wanting, don't ye doubt!"

"I ain't for doubting none o' that," Nikwillig answered. "King Emerus's got to hear the tales."

"Then ye're going."

"I ain't going. Not now. These Battlehammers saved yer hairy bum, and me own as well. Here's the place where there's orcs to crush, and so I'm stayin' to crush some orcs. Right beside them Battlehammers."

Tred considered Nikwillig's posture as much as his words. Nikwillig had always been a bit of a thinker, as far as dwarves went, and had often been a bit unconventional in his thinking. But this reasoning against returning to Citadel Felbarr, with so much at stake, struck Tred as beyond even Nikwillig's occasional eccentricity.

"Think for yerself, Tred," Nikwillig remarked, as if he had read his companion's puzzled mind. "Any runners to Felbarr'll do, and ye know it."

"And ye think any runners'll be bringing King Emerus out o' Citadel Felbarr to our aid if we're needin' it? And ye're thinking that any runners'll convince King Emerus to send word to Citadel Adbar and rally the Iron Guard of King Harbromm?"

Nikwillig shrugged and said, "Orcs're charging out o' the north and the Battlehammers are fighting them hard—and two o' Felbarr's own, Tred and Nikwillig, are standing strong beside Bruenor's boys. If anything's to get King Emerus up and hopping, it's knowin' that yerself and meself've decided this fight's worth fighting. Might be that we're making a bigger and louder call to King Emerus Warcrown by staying put and putting our shoulders in Bruenor's line."

Tred stared long and hard at the other dwarf, his thoughts trying to catch up with Nikwillig's surprising words. He really didn't want to leave Mithral Hall. Bruenor had charged headlong into danger to help Tred and Nikwillig avenge those human settlers who'd died trying to help the two wayward dwarves and to avenge Tred and Nikwillig's dead kin from Felbarr, including Tred's own little brother.

The yellow-bearded dwarf gave a sigh as he looked back over his shoulder, at the dark upper-Underdark tunnel that wound off to the west.

"Might that we should go find the runt, Regis, then," he offered. "Might that he'll find one to get to King Emerus with all the news."

"And we're back out with Bruenor's human kids and Torgar's boys," said Nikwillig, not backing down from his eager stance one bit.

Tred's expression shifted from curious to admiring as he looked over Nikwillig. Never before had he known that particular dwarf to be so eager for battle.

To tough Tred's thinking, the timing for Nikwillig's apparent change of heart couldn't have been better. The yellow-bearded dwarf's resigned look became a wide smile, and he dropped the heavy pack off his shoulder.

"I would ask of your thoughts, but I see no need," Wulfgar remarked, walking up to join Catti-brie.

She stood to the side of the scrambling dwarves, looking down the slope—not at the massing orcs, Wulfgar had noted, but to the wild lands beyond them. Catti-brie brushed back her thick mane of hair and turned to regard the man, her blue eyes, much darker and richer in hue than Wulfgar's crystalline orbs, studying him intently.

"I, too, wonder where he is," the barbarian explained. "He is not dead—of that I am certain."

"How can you be?"

"Because I know Drizzt," Wulfgar replied, and he managed a smile for the woman's sake.

"All of us would've perished had not Pwent come out," Catti-brie reminded him.

"We were trapped and surrounded," Wulfgar countered. "Drizzt is neither, nor can he easily be. He is alive yet, I know."

Catti-brie returned the big man's smile and took his hand in her own.

"I'm knowing it, too," she admitted. "Only if because I'm sure that me heart would've felt the break if he'd fallen."

"No less than my own," Wulfgar whispered.

"But he'll not return to us soon," Catti-brie went on. "And I'm not thinking that we're wanting him to. In here, he's another fighter in a line of fighters—the best o' the bunch, no doubt—but out there. . . ."

"Out there, he will bring terrible grief to our enemies," Wulfgar agreed. "Though it pains me to think that he is alone."

"He's got the cat. He's not alone."

It was Catti-brie's turn to offer a reassuring smile to her companion. Wulfgar clenched her hand tighter and nodded his agreement.

"I'll be needin' the two o' ye to hold the right flank," came a gruff voice to the side, turning the pair to see Banak Brawnanvil, the cleric Rockbottom, and a pair of other dwarves marching their way. "Them orcs're coming," the dwarf warlord asserted. "They're thinking to hit us quick, afore we dig in, and we got to hold 'em."

Both humans nodded grimly.

Banak turned to one of the other dwarves and ordered, "Ye go and sit with Torgar's engineers. Tell 'em to block their ears from the battle sounds and keep to their work. And as soon as they get some ropes all the way to the dale floor, ye get yerself down 'em."

"B-but . . ." the dwarf sputtered in protest.

He shook his head and wagged his hands, as if Banak had just condemned him. Banak reached up and slapped his hand over the other dwarf's mouth, silencing him.

"Yer own mission's the toughest and most important of all," the warlord explained. "We'll be up here smacking orcs, and what dwarf's not loving that work? For yerself, ye got to get to Regis and tell the little one we're needing a thousand more—two thousand if he can spare 'em from the tunnels."

"Ye're thinking to bring a thousand more up the ropes to strengthen our position?" Catti-brie asked doubtfully, for it seemed that they really had nowhere to put the extra warriors.

Wulfgar cast her a sidelong glance, noting how her accent had moved back toward the Dwarvish with the addition of Banak's group.

"Nah, we're enough to hold here for now," Banak explained. He let go of the other dwarf, who was standing patiently, though he was beginning to turn a shade of blue from Banak's strong grasp. "We got to, and so we will. But this orc we're fighting's smart. Too smart."

"You're thinking that our enemy will send a force around that mountain spur to the west," Wulfgar reasoned, and Banak nodded.

"More o' them stinking orcs get into Keeper's Dale afore us, and we're done for," the dwarf leader replied. "They won't even be needing to come up for us, then. They can just hold us here until we fall down starving." Banak fixed the appointed messenger with a grim stare and added, "Ye go and ye tell Regis, or whoever's running things inside now, to send all he can spare and more into the dale, to set a force in the western end. Nothing's to come in that way, ye hear me?"

The messenger dwarf suddenly seemed much less reluctant to leave. He stood straight and puffed out his strong chest, nodding his assurances to them all.

Even as he sprinted away for the cliff face, a cry went up at the center of the dwarven line that the orc charge was on.

"Ye get back to Torgar's engineers," Banak instructed Rockbottom. "Ye keep 'em working through the fight, and ye don't let 'em stop unless them orcs kill us all and come to the cliff to get 'em!"

With a determined nod, Rockbottom ran off.

"And ye two hold this end o' the line, for all our lives," Banak asked.

Catti-brie slid her deadly bow, Taulmaril the Heartseeker, from off her shoulder. She pulled an arrow from her quiver and set it in place. Beside her, Wulfgar slapped the mighty warhammer Aegis-fang across his open palm.

As Banak and the remaining dwarf wandered off along the assembling line of defense, the two humans turned to each other, offered a nod of support, then turned all the way around—

—to see the dark swarm coming fast up the rocky mountain slope.

3

BONES AND STONES

King Obould Many-Arrows at once recognized the danger of this latest report filtering in from the mountains to the east of his current position. Resisting his initial urge to crush the head of the wretched goblin messenger, the huge orc king stretched the fingers of one hand, then balled them into a tight fist and brought that fist up before his tusked mouth in his most typical posture, seeming a mix between contemplation and seething rage.

Which was pretty much the constant emotional struggle within the orc leader.

Despite the disastrous end to the siege at Shallows, when the filthy dwarves had snuck onto the field of battle within the hollowed out statue of Gruumsh One-Eye, the war was proceeding beautifully. The news of King Bruenor's demise had brought dozens of new tribes scurrying out of their holes to Obould's side and had even quieted the troublesome Gerti Orelsdottr and her superior-minded frost giants. Obould's son, Urlgen, had the dwarves on the run—to the edge of Mithral Hall already, judging from the last reports.

Then came reports that some enemy force was out there, behind Obould's lines. An encampment of orcs had been thrashed, with most slaughtered and the others scattered back to their mountain holes. Obould understood well the demeanor of his race, and he knew that morale was everything at that crucial moment—and usually throughout an entire campaign. The orcs were far more numerous than their enemies in the North and could match up fairly well one-against-one with humans and dwarves, and even elves. Where their incursions ultimately failed, Obould knew, lay in the often lacking coordination between orc forces and the basic mistrust that orcs held for rival tribes, and oftentimes held even within individual tribes. Victories and momentum could offset that disadvantage of demeanor, but reports like the one of the slaughtered group might send many, many others scurrying for the safety of the tunnels beneath the mountains.

The timing was not good. Obould had heard of another coming gathering of the shamans of several fairly large tribes, and he feared that they might try to abort his invasion before it had really begun. At the very least, a joined negative voice of two-dozen shamans would greatly deplete the orc king's reinforcements.

One thing at a time, Obould scolded himself, and he considered more carefully the goblin messenger's words. He had to find out what was going on, and quickly. Fortunately, there was one in his encampment at the time who might prove of great help.

Dismissing both the goblin and his attendants, Obould moved to the southern edge of the large camp, to a lone figure that he had kept waiting far too long.

"Greetings, Donnia Soldou," he said to the drow female.

She turned to regard him—she had sensed his approach long before he had spoken, he knew—peering at him under the low-pulled hood of her magical *piwafwi,* her red-tinged eyes smiling as widely and wickedly as her tight grin.

"You have claimed a great prize, I hear," she remarked, and she shifted a bit, allowing her white hair to slip down over one of her eyes.

Mysterious and alluring, always so.

"One of many to come," Obould insisted. "Urlgen is chasing the dwarves back into their hole, and who will defend the towns of the land?"

"One victory at a time?" Donnia asked. "I had thought you more ambitious."

"We cannot run wildly into Mithral Hall to be slaughtered," Obould countered. "Did not your own people try such a tactic?"

Donnia merely laughed aloud at the intended insult, for it had not been "her" people at all. The drow of Menzoberranzan had attacked Mithral

Hall, to disastrous results, but that was hardly the care of Donnia Soldou, who was not of, and not fond of, the City of Spiders.

"You have heard of the slaughter at the camp of the Tribe of Many Teeth?" Obould asked.

"A formidable opponent—or several—found them, yes," Donnia replied. "Ad'non has already started for the site."

"Lead me there," Obould instructed, his words obviously surprising Donnia. "I will witness this for myself."

"If you bring too many of your warriors, you will inadvertently spread the news of the slaughter," Donnia reasoned. "Is that your intent?"

"You and I will go," Obould explained. "No others."

"And if these enemies that massacred the Tribe of Many Teeth are about? You risk much."

"If these enemies are about and they attack Obould, then *they* risk much," Obould growled back at her, eliciting a smile, one that showed Donnia's pearly white teeth in such a stark contrast to the ebon hue of her skin.

"Very well then," she agreed. "Let us go and see what we might learn of our secretive foe."

The site of the slaughter was not so far away, and Donnia and Obould came upon the scene later that same day to find not only Ad'non Kareese, but Donnia's other two drow companions, Kaer'lic Suun Wett and Tos'un Armgo, already moving around the place.

"A couple of attackers, and no more," Ad'non explained to the new-comers. "We have heard of a pair of pegasus-riding elves in the region, and it is our guess that they perpetrated this slaughter."

As Ad'non spoke those words, his hands worked the silent hand code of the drow, something that Donnia, but not Obould, could understand.

This was the work of a drow elf, Ad'non quickly flashed.

Donnia needed to know nothing more, for she and her companions were aware that King Bruenor of Mithral Hall kept company with a most unusual dark elf, a rogue who had abandoned the ways of the Spider Queen and of his dark kin. Apparently, Drizzt Do'Urden had escaped Shallows, as they had suspected from the stories told by Gerti's frost giants, and apparently, he had not returned to Mithral Hall.

"Elves," King Obould echoed distastefully, and the word became a long drawn-out growl, with the powerful orc bringing his clenched fist up before him once again.

"They should not be so difficult to find if they are flying around on winged horses," Donnia Soldou assured Obould.

The orc king continued to utter a low and seething growl, his red-veined eyes glancing about the horizon as if he expected the pegasi riders to come swooping down upon them.

"Pass this off to the other leaders as an isolated attack," Ad'non suggested to the orc. "Donnia and I will ensure that Gerti does not become overly concerned."

"Turn fear into encouragement," Donnia added. "Offer a great bounty for the head of those who did this. That alone will place all the other tribes at the ready as they make their way to your main forces."

"Most of all, the fact that this was a small group attacking by ambush, as it certainly seems to be, lessens the danger to others," Ad'non went on. "These orcs were not vigilant, and so they were killed. That has always been the way, has it not?"

Obould's growl gradually decreased, and he offered an assenting nod to his drow advisors. He moved off then to inspect the campsite and the dead orcs, and the drow pair joined their two companions and did likewise.

No surface elf, Ad'non's fingers flashed to his three drow companions, though Kaer'lic Suun Wett wasn't paying attention and actually drifted away from the group, moving outside the camp. *The wounds are sweeping and slashing in nature, not the stabs of an elf. Nor were any killed by arrows, and those surface elves who went against the giants north of Shallows fought them with bows from on high.*

Tos'un Armgo moved around the bodies, bending low and examining them the most carefully of all.

"Drizzt Do'Urden," he whispered to the other three, and as Obould moved back toward him, he silently flashed, *Drizzt favors the scimitar.*

Kaer'lic returned soon after Obould, the plump priestess's fingers signing, *Cat prints outside the perimeter.*

Drizzt Do'Urden, Tos'un signaled again.

From a ridge to the northeast, Urlgen Threefist watched the great dark mass of orcs sweeping up the ascent. He had the dwarves pinned against the cliff and wanted nothing more than to push them into oblivion. Urlgen respected the toughness and work ethic of dwarves enough to understand that their defenses would strengthen by the hour if he let them sit up there. However, his own force was hardly prepared for such an attack; no reinforcements of giants had even caught up to the orc hordes yet, and many of those in the ranks were very new to the crusade and probably still confused about their order of battle and the hierarchy of leadership.

Urlgen's forces would strengthen in number, in weapons, and in tactics soon enough, but so too would the dwarves' defenses.

Weighing both and still stinging from the unexpected breakout at Shallows, the orc leader had sent the waves ahead. At the very least, he figured, the attacks would keep the dwarves from digging in even deeper.

Still, the orc leader grimaced when the leading edge of his rolling masses neared the lip of the ascent, for the dwarves leaped out in fury and fell over them from on high. Thrown rocks and rolling boulders led the way, along with those same devastating, streaking silvery arrows that had so stung Urlgen's forces at Shallows. Urlgen knew that orcs were dying by the dozen. As panic overcame many of those who survived the initial barrage, their disorientation and terror made the dwarves' countercharge all the more effective, allowing the vicious bearded folk to slice into the humanoid lines.

Those orcs turning in retreat only hindered the reinforcing back ranks from getting into the fray, and the confusion opened even more opportunities for the aggressive dwarves.

And still those arrows reached out, and in conjunction with that archer, a towering figure on the eastern end of the dwarf position swept orcs away with impunity.

"What we gonna do?" a skinny orc asked Urlgen, the creature running up and hopping all around frantically. "What we gonna do?"

Another of the gang leaders came rushing over.

"What we gonna do?" he parroted.

And a third charged over, shouting, "What we gonna do?"

Urlgen continued to watch the wild battle up the rocky slope. Dwarves were falling, but most who did were landing on the bodies of many orcs. Melee was fully joined, and Urlgen's orcs seemed no closer to forming into any acceptable formations, while the dwarves had grouped neatly into two defensive squares flanking a spearheading wedge. As that wedge charged forward, its wide base smoothly linked with the corners of each square, and those squares pivoted perfectly. One line of each square broke free to link up fully with the wedge, thus turning it into a defensive square, while the flanking dwarves reconfigured their ranks into more offensive formations.

To Urlgen, their movements were a thing a beauty, exhibiting the very same discipline that he and his father had tried hard to instill in their orc hordes. Given the one-sided slaughter, though, his soldiers obviously had a long way to go.

So mesmerized was Urlgen with the paradelike maneuvers of the seasoned dwarves that for many moments he hardly noticed the three orc commanders dancing around him and shouting, "What we gonna do?"

Finally their questions registered once more, as did the realization that the dwarves were turning the battle into a clear rout.

"Retreat!" Urlgen ordered. "Brings them back! Brings them all back until Gerti's giants get here."

Over the next few minutes, watching the relay of the order and the response to it, it occurred to Urlgen that his soldiers were much better at retreating than they were at charging.

They left many behind in their run back down the stones—stones that were slippery with blood. Scores lay dead or dying, screaming and groaning, until the closest dwarves walked over and shut them up forever with a heavy blow to the head.

But there were dead dwarves among those reddened stones, and orcs, by nature, hardly cared for their own losses. Urlgen nodded his acceptance. His forces would grow and grow, and he meant to keep throwing them at the dwarves until exhaustion killed them if the orcs could not. The orc leader knew what lay over the ridge behind the dwarves.

He knew he had them cornered. Either many more dwarves were going to have to pour out of Mithral Hall and take a roundabout route east or west to try to rescue that group, or the dwarves there were going to have to abandon their defensive position and break out on their own. Either way, Urlgen's lead strike force would have more than fulfilled Obould's vision for them.

Either way, Urlgen's stature among the swelling band of orcs would greatly increase.

"We know it was Drizzt Do'Urden, yet we tell Obould that surface elves were the cause," Tos'un Armgo said to his three drow companions as they retired to a comfortable cave to digest the latest developments.

"Thus leading Obould to even greater hatred for the surface elves," Donnia replied, her lips curling up in a delicious smile, one side of it almost reaching the cascading layers of white hair that crossed diagonally down her sculpted black face.

"He needs little urging in that direction," Kaer'lic remarked.

"More important, we delay Obould from believing that there are drow elves working against him," said Ad'non Kareese.

"He knows of Drizzt already, to some degree," Kaer'lic reasoned.

"Yes, but perhaps we can alleviate the problem of the rogue before it swells to proportions that enrage Obould against us," said Ad'non. "He does seem to think in terms of race, and not individuals."

"As does Gerti," said Kaer'lic. "As do we all."

"Except for Drizzt and his friends, it would seem," Tos'un said, the simple and obvious statement making them all gape.

The four drow rested back for just a moment, each looking to the others, but if there was any significant philosophical epiphany coming to the group, it was quickly buried under the weight of pragmatism and the needs of the present.

"You believe that we should do something to eliminate the threat of Drizzt Do'Urden?" Kaer'lic asked Ad'non. "You consider him to be our problem?"

"I consider that he could grow to become our problem," Ad'non corrected. "The advantages of eliminating him might prove great."

"So thought Menzoberranzan," Tos'un Armgo reminded. "I doubt the city has recovered fully from that folly."

"Menzoberranzan fought more than Drizzt Do'Urden," Donnia put in. "Would not Lady Lolth desire the demise of the rogue?"

As she asked the question, Donnia turned to Kaer'lic, the priestess of the group, and both Ad'non and Tos'un followed her lead. Kaer'lic was shaking her head to greet those inquisitive stares.

"Drizzt Do'Urden is not our problem," said Kaer'lic, "and we would do well to stay as far from his scimitars as possible. Sound reasoning is always Lady Lolth's greatest demand of us, and I would no more wish to leap into battle against Drizzt Do'Urden than I would to lead Obould's charge into Mithral Hall. That is not why we instigated all of this. You remember our desires and our plan, do you not? My enjoyment, such as it is, will not end at the tip of one of Drizzt Do'Urden's scimitars."

"And if he seeks us out?" asked Donnia.

"He will not, if he knows nothing about us," Kaer'lic replied. "That is the better course. My favorite war is one I watch from afar."

Donnia's sour expression as she turned to Ad'non was not hard to discern. Nor was Ad'non's responding disappointment.

But Kaer'lic had an ally, and a most emphatic one.

"I agree," Tos'un offered. "Since his days in Menzoberranzan, Drizzt Do'Urden has been nothing but a difficult and often fatal problem to those who have tried to go against him. In my wanderings of the upper Underdark after the disaster with Mithral Hall, I heard various and scattered tales about the repercussions within Menzoberranzan. Apparently, soon after my city's attack on Mithral Hall, Drizzt returned to Menzoberranzan, was captured by House Baenre, and was placed in their dungeons."

Astonished expressions followed that tidbit, for the mighty and ruthless House Baenre was well known to drow across the Underdark.

"And yet, he has returned to his friends, leaving catastrophe in his wake," Tos'un went on. "He is almost a cruel joke of Lady Lolth, I fear, an instrument of chaos cloaked in traitorous garb. More than one in Menzoberranzan has remarked on his belief that Drizzt Do'Urden is secretly guided by the Lady of Chaos for her pleasure."

"If we served any other goddess, your words would be blasphemous," Kaer'lic replied, and she gave a chuckle at the supreme irony of it all.

"You cannot believe . . ." Donnia started to argue.

"I do not have to believe," Tos'un interrupted. "Drizzt Do'Urden is either much more formidable than we understand, or he is very lucky, or he is god-blessed. In any of those cases, I have no desire to hunt him down."

"Agreed," said Kaer'lic.

Donnia and Ad'non looked to each other once more, but merely shrugged.

"It's a fine game, this," Banak Brawnanvil said to Rockbottom, who stood beside him as he directed the formations of his forces. "Except that so many wind up dead."

"More orcs than dwarves," Rockbottom pointed out.

"Not enough of one and too many o' the other. Look at them. Fighting with fury, taking their hits without complaint, willing to die if that's the choice o' the gods this day."

"They're warriors," Rockbottom reminded. "Dwarf warriors. That's meaning something."

"Course it is," Banak agreed. "Something."

"Yer plan's got them orcs on the run," Rockbottom observed.

"Not any plan of me own," the dwarf leader argued. "Was that Bouldershoulder brother's idea—the sane one, I mean—along with the help of Torgar of Mirabar. We found ourselfs some fine friends, I'm thinking."

Rockbottom nodded and continued to watch the beautifully choreographed display of teamwork, the three interlocking formations rolling down the slope and sweeping orcs before them.

"A child of some race or another will come here in a few hundred years," Banak remarked a short time later. He wasn't even watching the fighting anymore, but was more focused on the bodies splayed across the stones. "He'll see the whitened bones of them fighting for this piece of high ground. They'll be mistaken for rocks, mostly, but soon enough, one might be recognized for what it is, and of course that will show this to be the site of a great battle. Will those people far in the future understand what we did here? Or why we did it? Will they know our cause, or the difference of our cause to that o' the invading orcs?"

Rockbottom stared long and hard at Banak Brawnanvil. The tall and strong dwarf had been an imposing figure among the dwarves of Clan Battlehammer for centuries, though he usually kept himself to the side of the glory, and rarely offered his strategies for battle unless pressed by Bruenor or Dagna, or one of the other formal commanders. The other side of Banak, though, was what really separated him from others of the clan. He had a different way of looking at the world, and always seemed to be viewing current events in the context with which they might be seen by some future historian.

A shriek to the right had them both looking that way, to see the superb coordination and harmony of Wulfgar and Catti-brie as they held fast the flank. Orcs came up at them haphazardly, and many fell to the woman's deadly bow and her unending supply of arrows. Those that managed to escape sudden death at the end of a missile likely soon wished they had been hit, for they wound up before the great barbarian Wulfgar and his devastating hammer, the magnificent Aegis-fang, crafted by Bruenor Battlehammer himself. Even as Banak and Rockbottom focused on the pair, Wulfgar smashed one orc so hard atop its head that its skull simply exploded, showering the barbarian and those other orcs scrambling in with blood and brains.

An arrow whistled past Wulfgar to take down a second orc, and a great sweep of Aegis-fang had the remaining two stumbling, one falling to the ground, the other dancing out wide.

Catti-brie got the second one; a chop of Aegis-fang finished the one on the ground.

"Them two are making tales that'll live through the centuries," Rockbottom remarked.

"To some point," said Banak, "then they will fade."

Rockbottom looked at him curiously, surprised by his glum attitude.

"On his way home," Banak explained, "King Bruenor marched through Fell Pass."

Rockbottom nodded his understanding, for he had been on that caravan.

"Find any bones there?" Banak asked.

"More than ye can count," the cleric replied.

"Ye think that any of them fighting that long-ago battle in Fell Pass stood above the others, in bravery and might?"

Rockbottom considered the question for just a moment, before offering a shrug and an agreeing nod.

"Ye know their names?" Banak asked. "Ye know who they were and what they were about? Ye know how many orcs and other monsters they killed in that battle? Ye know how many held the head of a friend as he died?"

The point hit Rockbottom hard. He looked back to the main battle, where the dwarves were routing the orcs and sending them running.

"No pursuit down the slope!" Banak ordered.

"We've got them scared witless," Rockbottom quietly advised.

"They're witless anyway," said the dwarf warlord. "They only came on to draw us from our preparations. That preparation's not to wait while we chase a ragtag band around the mountains. We bring our boys all back and get back to work. This was a skirmish. The big fight's yet to come."

Banak looked back over his shoulder to the cliff area, and hoped that the engineers had not slowed in their work with the rope ladders to the floor of Keeper's Dale.

"Just a skirmish," he reiterated even as the fighting diminished and many of the dwarves began to turn their precise formations back toward his position.

He saw the dead and wounded lying around the blood-soaked stones.

He thought of the bones that would soon enough litter that ground, as thick and as quiet as rocks.

THE SELECTION PROCESS

His trail always seemed to lead him back to that spot. For Drizzt Do'Urden, the devastated rubble of Shallows served as his inspiration, his catalyst to allow the Hunter to fill his spirit with hunger for the hunt. He moved around the broken tower and ruined walls, but rarely did he go to the south of the town. It had taken him several days to muster the nerve to venture past the ruined idol of the foul orc god. As he had feared, he had found no sign of escaping survivors.

Drizzt soon started to visit that place for different purposes. On every return, he hoped he might find some orcs milling around the strewn dead, seeking loot perhaps.

Drizzt thought it would be fitting for him to slaughter orcs in the shadow of the devastation that was Shallows.

He thought he had found his opportunity upon his approach that afternoon. Guenhwyvar, beside him, was clearly on edge, a sure sign that monsters were about, and Drizzt noted the movements of some creatures around the ruins as he moved along the high ground across the ravine north of the town—the same high ground from which the giants had bombarded Shallows as a prelude to the orc assault.

As soon as he got a clear view of the ruins, though, Drizzt understood that he would not be doing any battle there that day. There were indeed orcs in Shallows—thousands of orcs—several tribes of the wretches encamped around the shattered remains of that great wooden statue south of the town's ruined southern wall.

Beside him, Guenhwyvar lowered her ears and issued a long and low growl.

That brought a smile to the dark elf's face—the first smile that had found its way there in a long time.

"I know, Guen," he said, and he reached over and riffled the cat's ear. "Hold patience. We will find our time."

Guenhwyvar looked at him and slowly blinked, then tilted her head so he could scratch a favored spot along her neck. The growling stopped.

Drizzt's smile did not. He continued to scratch the cat, but continued, too, to look across the ravine, to the ruins of Shallows, to the hordes of orcs. He replayed his memories over and over, recalling it all so vividly; he would not let himself forget.

The image of Bruenor tumbling in the tower ruins. The image of giants heaving their great boulders across the ravine at his friends. The image of the orc hordes overrunning the town. None of it had been asked for. None of it deserved.

But it would be paid back, Drizzt knew.

In full.

"King Obould knows of this travesty?" asked Arganth Snarrl, the wide-eyed, wild-eyed shaman of the orc tribe that bore his surname. With his bright-colored feathered headdress and tooth necklace (with specimens from a variety of creatures) that reached below his waist, Arganth was among the most distinctive and colorful of the dozen shamans congregated around the ruined Gruumsh idol, and with his shrieking, almost birdlike voice, he was also the loudest.

"Does he understand, does he? Does he? Does he?" the shaman asked, hopping from one of his colleagues to the next in rapid succession. "I do not think he does! No, no, because if he does, then he does not place this . . . this . . . this, blasphemy in proper order! More important than all his conquests, this is!"

"Unless his conquests are being delivered in the name of Gruumsh," shaman Achtel Gnarlfingers remarked, the interruption stopping Arganth in his tracks.

Achtel's dress was not as large and attention-grabbing as Arganth's, but it was equally colorful, with a rich red traveling cloak, complete with hood, and a bright yellow sash crossing shoulder to hip and around her waist. She carried a skull-headed scepter, heavily enchanted to serve as a formidable weapon, from what Arganth had heard. Even more than that, the priestess with the shaggy brown hair carried tremendous weight simply because she represented the largest of the dozen tribes in attendance, with more than six hundred warriors encamped in the area under her dominion.

The colorful priest stared wide-eyed at Achtel, who did not back down at all.

"Which Obould does do," Arganth insisted.

"We march for the glory of Gruumsh," another of the group agreed. "The One-Eye desires the defeat of the dwarves!"

That brought a cheer from all around, except for Arganth, who stood there staring at Achtel. Gradually, all eyes focused on the trembling figure with the feathered headdress.

"Not enough," Achtel insisted. "King Obould Many-Arrows marches for the glory of King Obould Many-Arrows."

Gasps came back at him.

"That is our way," Arganth quickly added, seeing the dangerously rising dissent and the sudden scowling of dangerous Achtel. "That is always our way, and a good way it is. But now, with the blasphemy of this idol, we must join the two, Obould and Gruumsh! Their glory must be made as one!"

The other eleven shamans neither cheered nor jeered, but simply stood there, staring at the volatile shaman of Snarrl.

"Each tribe?" one began tentatively, shaking his head.

The orc tribes had come to Obould's call—especially after hearing of the fall of King Bruenor Battlehammer, who had long been a reviled figure—but the armies remained, first and foremost, individual tribes.

Arganth Snarrl leaped up before the speaker, his yellow-hued eyes so wide that they seemed as if they would just roll from their sockets.

"No more!" he yelled, and he jumped wildly all about, facing each of the others in turn. "No more! Tribes are second. Gruumsh is first!"

"Gruumsh!" a couple of the others yelled together.

"And Gruumsh is Obould?" Achtel calmly asked, seeming to measure every movement and word carefully—more so than any of the others in attendance, certainly.

"Gruumsh is Obould!" Arganth proclaimed. "Soon to be, yes!"

He ended in a gesticulating, leaping and wildly shaking dance around the ruined idol of his god-figure, the hollowed statue the dwarves had used as a ruse to get amidst Obould's forces. With imminent victory in their grasp, overrunning Shallows, the ultimate, despicable deception of the wretched dwarves had salvaged some escape from what should have been a complete slaughter.

To use the orc god-figure for such treachery was beyond the bounds of decency in the eyes of those dozen shamans, the religious leaders of the more than three thousand orcs of their respective tribes.

"Gruumsh is Obould!" Arganth began to chant as he danced, and each shaman in turn took up the cry as he or she fell into line behind the wildly gesticulating, outrageously dressed character.

Except for Achtel. The thoughtful and more sedentary orc stepped back from the evocative dance and observed the movements of her fellow shamans, her doubts fairly obviously displayed upon her orc features.

All the others knew of her feelings on the matter and of her hesitation in counseling her chieftain to lead her tribe out of its secure home to join in the fight against the powerful dwarves. Until then, none had dared to question her in that decision.

"You must get better," Catti-brie whispered into her father's ear. She believed that Bruenor did hear her, though he gave no outward sign, and indeed, had not moved at all in several days. "The orcs think they've killed you, and we can't be letting that challenge go unanswered!" the woman went on, offering great enthusiasm and energy to the comatose dwarf king.

Catti-brie squeezed Bruenor's hand as she spoke, and for a moment, she thought he squeezed back.

Or she imagined it.

She gave a great sigh, then, and looked to her bow, which was leaning up against the far wall of the candlelit room. She would have to be out again soon, she knew, for the fighting up on the cliff would surely begin anew.

"I think he hears you," came a voice from behind Catti-brie, and she managed a smile as she turned to regard her friend Regis.

Truly, the halfling looked the part of the battered warrior, with one arm slung tight against his chest and wrapped with heavy bandages. That arm had fended the snapping maw of a great worg, and Regis had paid a heavy price.

Catti-brie rolled up from her father's side to give the halfling a well-deserved hug.

"The clerics haven't healed it yet?" she asked, eyeing his arm.

"They've done quite a bit, actually," Regis answered in a chipper tone, and to show his optimism, he managed to wriggle his bluish fingers. "They would have long ago finished their work on it, but there are too many others who need their healing spells and salves more than I. It's not so bad."

"You saved us all, Rumblebelly," Catti-brie offered, using Bruenor's nickname for the somewhat chubby halfling. "You took it on yerself to go and get some help, and we'd have been dead soon enough if you hadn't arrived with Pwent and the boys."

Regis just shrugged and even blushed a bit.

"How do we fare up on the mountain?" he asked.

"Fair," Catti-brie answered. "The orcs chased us right to the edge, but we got more than a few in a trap, and when they came on in full, we sent them running. Ye should see the work of Banak Brawnanvil, Ivan Bouldershoulder, and Torgar Hammerstriker of Mirabar. They had the dwarves turning squares and wedges every which way and had the orcs scratching their heads in confusion right up until they got run over."

Regis managed a wide smile and even a little chuckle, but it died quickly as he looked past Catti-brie to the resting Bruenor.

"How is he this day?"

Catti-brie looked back at her father and could only offer a shrug in reply.

"The priests do not think he'll come out of it," Regis told her, and she nodded for she had of course heard the very same from them.

"But I think he will," Regis went on. "Though he'll be a long time on the mend, even still."

"He'll come back to us," Catti-brie assured her little friend.

"We need him," Regis said, his voice barely a whisper. "All of Mithral Hall needs King Bruenor."

"Bah, but that's no attitude to be takin' at this tough time," came a voice from out in the hallway, and the pair turned to see a bedraggled old dwarf come striding in.

They recognized the dwarf at once as General Dagna, one of Bruenor's most trusted commanders and the father of Dagnabbit, who had fallen at Shallows. The two friends glanced at each other and winced, then offered sympathetic looks to the dwarf who had lost his valiant son.

"He died well," Dagna remarked, obviously understanding their intent. "No dwarf can ask for more than that."

"He died brilliantly," Catti-brie agreed. "Shaking his fist at the orcs and the giants. And how many felt the bite of his anger before he fell?"

Dagna nodded, his expression solemn.

"Banak's got the army out on the mountain?" he asked a moment later, changing both his tone and the grim subject with a burst of sudden energy.

"He's got it well in hand," Catti-brie answered. "And he's found some fine help in the dwarves from Mirabar and in the Bouldershoulder brothers, who have come from the Spirit Soaring library in the Snowflake Mountains."

Dagna nodded and mumbled, "Good, good."

"We'll hold up there," Cattie-brie said.

"Ye best," said Dagna. "I've got more than I can handle in securing the tunnels. We're not to let our enemies walk in through the Underdark while they're distracting us up above."

Catti-brie stepped back and looked to Regis for support. She had expected that, somewhat, for when Banak's couriers had come in with requests that a second force be sent forth from Mithral Hall to secure the western end of Keeper's Dale, their reception had been less than warm. Clearly there was a battle brewing about whether to fall back to Mithral Hall and hold the fort or to go out and meet the surface challenge of the orc hordes.

"They're getting their ropes down to the dale so that Banak can get them all out o' there?" Dagna asked.

"They've several rope ladders to the valley floor already," Catti-brie answered. "And Warlord Banak's ordered many more. Torgar's engineers are putting the climbs together nonstop. But Banak's not thinking to come down anytime soon. If we can assure him that Keeper's Dale is secure behind him, he'll stay up on that mountain until the orcs find a way to push him off."

Dagna grumbled something unintelligible under his breath, and though Catti-brie and Regis couldn't make it out, it was fairly obvious that the crusty old warrior dwarf wasn't thrilled with that prospect.

"We've got the right three directing the forces out there," Catti-brie assured him.

"True enough," Dagna admitted. "I sent Banak Brawnanvil out there meself, and I knowed there'd be none better among all the ranks o' Clan Battlehammer."

"Then give him the support he needs to hold that ground."

Dagna looked long and hard at Catti-brie, then shook his head. "Choice ain't me own to make," he replied. "Clerics asked me to direct the defense o' the tunnels, and so I am. They're not asking me to steward Bruenor's crown."

As he finished, he glanced over at Regis, and Catti-brie followed his gaze to her little friend, who suddenly seemed embarrassed.

"What do ye know?" the woman quietly asked the halfling.

"I-I told them it sh-should be you," Regis stammered. "Or Wulfgar, if not you."

Catti-brie turned her confused expression over Dagna, then back to the halfling.

"Yourself?" she asked Regis. "Are ye telling me that you've been asked to serve as Steward of Mithral Hall?"

"He has," Dagna answered. "And meself's the one who nominated him. With all me respect, good lady, for yerself and yer stepbrother, we're all thinking that none knew Bruenor's thoughts better than Regis here."

Catti-brie's expression as she turned back to regard Regis was more amused than angry. She lifted her head just a bit so that she could peek over the low collar of the halfling's shirt, looking toward a certain ruby pendant the halfling always wore. The implications of her questioning stare were clear enough and almost as obvious as if Catti-brie had just asked the halfling aloud if he had used his ruby pendant to "persuade" some of those deciding upon the matter of who should be steward in Bruenor's absence.

Regis's sudden gulp was even louder.

"You've got the word as king, then?" Catti-brie asked.

"He's got the primary vote," Dagna corrected. "The king's over there, lest ye're forgetting."

The crusty old dwarf pointed his chin Bruenor's way.

"Over there, and soon enough to join us again," Catti-brie agreed. "Until then, Steward Regis it is."

From somewhere down the hall came a call for Dagna, and the old dwarf gave a few "bahs" and excused himself, which was exactly what Catti-brie wanted, for she needed to have a few words in private with a certain little halfling.

"I-I've done nothing untoward," Regis stammered as soon as he was alone with Catti-brie, and the way the blood drained from the halfling's face showed that he understood her every concern.

"No one said you did."

"They asked me to serve Bruenor," Regis went on unsteadily. "How could I say no to that? You and Wulfgar will stay out and about, and who knows when Drizzt will return?"

"The dwarves wouldn't follow any of us three, anyway," Catti-brie agreed. "They'll take to a halfling, though. And everyone knows that Bruenor took Regis into his confidence all the way back from Icewind Dale. A good choice, I'd say, in Steward Regis. I've no doubt that you'll do what's best for Mithral Hall, and that's the point, after all."

Regis seemed to steady a bit, and even managed a smile.

"And what's good for Mithral Hall right now is for Steward Regis to get a thousand more dwarves out and in position to defend Keeper's Dale in the western edge," Catti-brie said. "And another two hundred running supplies, Mithral Hall to Keeper's Dale, and Mithral Hall to Warlord Banak and the force up on the mountain."

"We haven't got that many to spare!" Regis protested. "We're maintaining two groups outside the mines already, with those holding defense along the Surbrin in the east."

"Then bring that second group in and close the eastern gate," Catti-brie reasoned. "We know we're in for a fight up on the mountain, and if the orcs get around us into Keeper's Dale, Banak's to lose his whole force."

"If the orcs float down the Surbrin . . ." Regis started to warn.

"Then one well-positioned scout will see them," Catti-brie answered. "They'll be moving near to striking distance of some of our allies then as well."

Regis considered the logic for a short while, then nodded his agreement.

"I'll bring most of them in," the halfling said, "and send out the force through Keeper's Dale. Do we really need a thousand in the west? That many?"

"Five hundred at the least, by Banak's estimation," Catti-brie explained. "Though if they're left alone for a bit and can get the defenses up and in place, then we can cut that number considerably."

Regis nodded.

"But I'll not deplete the defenses of the mines," he said. "If the orcs are striking aboveground, then we can expect trouble below as well. Bruenor's got a responsibility to the folks of the land around, I agree, but his first duty is to Mithral Hall."

Catti-brie glanced past Regis, to the very still form of her beloved adoptive father.

She managed a wistful smile as she whispered, "Agreed."

The black foot came down softly, toes touching the dirt and stone, weight shifting gradually, ever so gradually, to allow for continued perfect balance and complete silence. A shift brought the next foot out in front, to repeat the stealthy stride.

He moved through the largest of the dozen separate encampments around the field of Shallows, slipping in and out of the predawn shadows with the skill that only a drow warrior—and only the best of the drow warriors—could possibly attain. He moved within a few strides of one group of oblivious orcs as they argued over something that didn't concern him in the least.

He slipped to the side of a tent then went in and silently through it, passing right between a pair of snoring orcs. Using a fine-edged scimitar, he cut a slice in the back flap, and quiet as a slight breeze, the dark elf moved back out.

Normally, he would have paused to slaughter those sleeping two, but Drizzt Do'Urden had something else in mind, something that he didn't want to compromise for lesser trophies.

For there sat a larger and more decorated tent in the distance, its deerskin flaps covered in sigils and murals representing the orc god. A trio of heavily armed guards paced around its entryway. There lay the leader of the tribe, Drizzt reasoned, and that tribe was the largest by far of those assembled.

The Hunter moved along, light-stepping and quick-stepping, always in balance, always at the ready, scimitars drawn and moving in harmony with his body as he strode and rolled, dipping back and stepping forward suddenly. It would not do for him to merely hold the weapons at his sides, he knew, for he wore the enchanted bracers around his ankles, speeding his stride, and in crossing so rapidly past so many cubbies and blind corners, the drow had to be ready to strike with precision in an instant. So the curving blades did a dance around him as his legs propelled him across the encampment, inexorably toward that large, decorated tent.

Within the cover of a lean-to just across from the large tent's entrance and its three orc guards, Drizzt slid his scimitars away. He had to be fast and precise, and he had to pick his moment carefully.

He looked around, waiting for another group of orcs to walk farther away.

Satisfied that he had a few moments alone, he casually rested his hands on the pommels of his belted weapons and strode across the way, smiling and with an unthreatening posture.

The orc guards, though, tensed immediately, one clutching his weapon more tightly, another even ordering Drizzt to stop.

The drow did halt, and locked the image of them into his sensibilities, noting their exact placement, counting the number of strides that would bring him before them, one after another.

The orc in the middle kept on talking, ordering, and questioning, and Drizzt just held his ground, smiling.

Just as one of the other orcs turned as if to move into the great tent, the drow reached into his innate magical powers and dropped a globe of darkness upon the trio. Even as he summoned it, Drizzt was moving, hands and feet. His scimitars appeared in his hands before he had taken two strides, and he was into the darkness before the orcs even realized that the world had suddenly gone black. Drizzt veered left first, still holding fast to the image of the three and confident that none had begun to move.

Twinkle came across at neck height, turning an intended cry for help into a gurgle.

A spin had both blades cutting down the second guard and a sudden forward rush out of that spin propelled the drow straight into the third, again with his blades finding the mark. He bowled over that third orc, the creature falling right through the tent flap, and Drizzt stepping in right across it, exiting the area of darkness.

Several startled faces looked back at him, including that of a red-cloaked female shaman.

Unfortunately, she was across the room.

Not slowing in the least, Drizzt rushed the closest orc, severing its upraised, blocking arm and quick-stepping past it while thrusting his other scimitar into its belly.

A table was set between Drizzt and the next in line on that right-hand side of the tent. The orc fell behind the table, using it to slow the drow's progress—or thinking to, for Drizzt went over it as if it wasn't even there. His foot came up to kick aside the small stool the orc thrust his way.

As that orc fell to the slashing blades, the Hunter spun around, bringing both his weapons across defensively, one following the other, and the first turned the tip of a flying spear while the second knocked the clumsily-thrown missile completely aside.

But the other orcs were organizing and setting their defenses, and the shaman was casting a spell.

Drizzt called upon his innate magical abilities yet again, but paused enough to mouth, *"olacka acka eento."*—a bit of arcane-sounding gibberish.

He even tossed one of his blades into the air and waggled his fingers dramatically to heighten the ruse. The shaman took the bait, and where the room had been in a ruckus and growing louder, suddenly all was silent.

Completely and magically silent, as the shaman predictably used the most efficient spell in her clerical arsenal to prevent attacks of wizardry.

That spell didn't prevent Drizzt's innate magic, though, and so the shaman was suddenly covered in purplish-glowing flames that outlined her form clearly, making her an easier target.

Drizzt didn't stop there, bringing forth another globe of impenetrable darkness right before the orc warriors who were even then bearing down upon him.

He summoned a second globe for good measure, to ensure that the whole of the large tent was filled with darkness and confusion, and he fell even more deeply into the Hunter.

He couldn't hear a thing and couldn't see a thing, and so he played by touch and instinct alone. He went into a spinning dance, his blades whipping all around him, setting a defense, and every so often he came out of it with one blade or the other stabbing forward powerfully or bringing it in a sudden and wide slashing sweep.

And whenever he sensed the presence of an orc in close quarters—the smell of the creature, the hot breath, or a slight brush—he struck fast and hard, scimitars coming to bear with deadly accuracy, finding holes in any offered defense simply because Drizzt knew the height of his opponents and understood their typical offered posture, defensive or attacking.

He worked his way straight across the room, then back toward the center tent pole, using that as a pivot.

He would have been surprised, had he not been in that primal and reactive mode, when a spell burst forth, countering his darkness with magical light.

Orcs were all around him, and all surprised—except for the shaman, who stood at the back wall of the tent, her eyes glowing fiercely, her body still outlined in the drow's faerie fire, her fingers waggling in yet another casting.

Those surprised orcs closest to Drizzt's right fell fast and fell hard, and the drow spun back to the left to meet the advance of some others, his weapons rolling over and over furiously, slapping away defenses, stinging arms and hands, and driving the entire remaining quartet of warriors back.

He slowed suddenly, feeling as if his arms were leaden, as a wave of magical energy flowed through him. He knew the spell instinctively, one that could paralyze, and had he not been within the hold of the Hunter at that time, where instinct and primal fury built for him a wall of defense, his life would have swiftly ended.

As it was, the drow's defenses became sluggish for a moment, so much so that a club came in from the side and smacked him hard in the ribs.

Very hard, but the Hunter felt no pain.

A globe of darkness engulfed him again, and he went right at the attacker, accepting a second hit, much less intense, and returning it with a trio of quick stabs and a slash, and any of the four attacks could have alone laid the orc low.

The enchantment of magical silence expired or was dismissed, and the Hunter's ears perked up immediately, registering the movements of those orcs nearby and hearing, too, the incantation of the troublesome shaman. He brought his scimitars into sudden crossing diagonal slashes before him, winding them around in a loop to continue the rolling movements, then used that to get between a pair of orcs. On one downward roll, the drow used his building momentum to leap forward and out, turning a complete somersault and landing lightly on his feet in a short run out of the darkness.

Right behind him came a burst of sharp sound, as if the air itself exploded, and the drow fell into a stagger and nearly went to the floor.

And if that spell had done that much to him, Drizzt could well understand its effect on the orcs behind him!

He caught himself, pivoted, and went right back into the darkness, blades slashing wildly. He hit nothing, for as he had expected, the orcs were down, but he really didn't want to hit anything. Rather, he stopped short and cut a right angle to his left, then burst out of the darkness once more, right in front of the shaman, who was waggling her fingers yet again.

Twinkle took those fingers.

Icingdeath took her head.

Hearing a tremendous commotion back the other way, the Hunter ran right past the falling shaman to the wall of the tent. His fine blades slashed down, and he squeezed through.

He ran off across the encampment, and orcs scrambled to get out of his way even as the screams continued to grow from the main tent behind him. He picked his path carefully, running from shadow to shadow at full bent.

Soon he was running clear, his enchanted anklets speeding him on his way to the rougher ground to the east and north of the town.

He had killed only a handful of orcs, but Drizzt was certain that he had brought great distress to his enemies that day.

5

THE WIDER WORLD

Shoudra Stargleam moved back toward the light of her campfire. The woman, the Sceptrana of Mirabar and a fairly adept wizard as well, had gone out to search for some roots and mushrooms to use as components for a new spell she was researching. In the verdant land south of Fell Pass, she had found exactly what she was looking for, in great abundance, and so her arms were full, wrapped around the rolled up side of her dress.

She was about to call out to her traveling companion to bring her a sack when she caught sight of him—and all that came out of her mouth was a giggle. For the little gnome cut quite a figure as he sat huddled before the fire, rubbing his hands before him. He had his cloak tight around him, the hood up and pulled far forward.

But not forward enough to hide Nanfoodle's most prominent feature, his long and crooked snout.

"If you lean in much closer, you will burn the hair out of your nose," Shoudra managed to say as she moved into the perimeter of fallen logs they had set around the fire.

"A chill wind tonight," the gnome replied.

"Unseasonably so," Shoudra agreed, for it was still summer, though fall was fast approaching.

"Which'll of course, only adds to the misery of the open road," Nanfoodle muttered.

Shoudra giggled again and took a seat opposite him. She started to unroll the side of her stuffed dress but paused when she caught the gnome staring at her shapely leg. She thought it perfectly ridiculous, of course; Shoudra was a statuesque woman, which made her leg alone taller than little Nanfoodle. She held the pose anyway, and even turned her leg just a bit to give Nanfoodle a better view, and watched his jaw drop open.

Eventually, the gnome glanced up enough to see Shoudra staring at him, an amused smile on her beautiful face.

Nanfoodle blinked repeatedly and cleared his throat, shuffling around as if he had misplaced something. Watching his every move, Shoudra unrolled her skirt and guided the roots and mushrooms gently to the ground.

"Do you find the road so miserable, truly?" she asked a few moments later, as she began separating the various components by type and size. "Do you not find it invigorating?"

Nanfoodle crossed his arms before him and huddled closer to the fire.

"Invigorating?" he echoed incredulously.

"Have you no sense of adventure then, my good Nanfoodle?" Shoudra asked. "Have you become so tame from your years and years in front of beakers and solutions that you've forgotten the thrill of roasting a goblin with a fireball?"

Nanfoodle fixed her with a curious stare.

"The Nanfoodle I met those years ago in Baldur's Gate could weave a spell or two, if I remember correctly," Shoudra remarked.

"Nothing as crude as a fireball, surely!" the gnome protested with a dismissive wave of his little hand. "Bah, a fireball! Next you will recount your glory at bringing forth a bolt of lightning. No, no, Shoudra. I prefer the magic of the mind to the blast and burn of elemental forces."

"Ah, yes," Shoudra replied. "Of course. I should have better recognized the link between illusion magic and alchemy."

How Nanfoodle's eyes widened at that! He had been hired by Marchion Elastul of Mirabar, Shoudra's superior, to bring his alchemical brilliance to the aid of their inferior ore in their trade war against Mithral Hall. Many times had he suffered the dry wit of Shoudra Stargleam on those occasions when he had to report his progress to the marchion, for alchemy was an imprecise and trial-and-error science. Unfortunately for Nanfoodle, his efforts in Mirabar had been almost exclusively of the error variety.

Something that Shoudra rarely failed to point out.

"What do you imply?" the gnome asked evenly.

Shoudra laughed and went back to separating her mushrooms.

"You do not believe in alchemy at all, do you?"

"Have I ever made a secret of that?"

"Yet, were you not the one who gave my name to Marchion Elastul?" Nanfoodle asked. "I was under the impression that he had learned of my growing reputation from none other than Shoudra Stargleam."

"I have no use for alchemy," Shoudra explained. "I never said that I have no use for, nor care for, Nanfoodle Buswilligan."

After a moment of quiet, the woman glanced up to see Nanfoodle staring at her curiously.

"If Marchion Elastul was so determined to throw his coin away on fool's gold, then why not have some of it go to Nanfoodle, at least?" Shoudra explained with a wry grin.

The alchemist nodded, but his perplexed expression showed her that he really didn't seem to know whether to thank her or berate her.

She liked it that way.

"We eat the food and yet our load increases," the gnome remarked, staring sourly at Shoudra's growing component collection.

"Our load?" came the sarcastic response. "A single mushroom would seem to be a load for poor little Nanfoodle." She ended by playfully throwing a small white-capped mushroom across the fire. Nanfoodle's hand came up to block it, but he merely deflected the item, which bounced from his hand to thump against his long nose, drawing yet another laugh from Shoudra.

Scowling and muttering under his breath, Nanfoodle deliberately reached down and picked up the missile, then regarded it for a moment, still muttering, before throwing it back.

Shoudra had her defenses set, her hands up in front of her, except that not one, but a half dozen identical mushrooms suddenly flew her way.

"Well done!" she congratulated as the real missile bounced off her forehead, the illusionary ones flying right through her, and she laughed all the louder.

"One should be careful not to raise the ire of Nanfoodle," the gnome boasted, and he puffed out his chest, which almost tightened his small cloak around him.

"I have a few here we can use to dress our dinner," the woman remarked, and she held up both hands full of mushrooms and various roots. "If you eat enough—and that has never seemed to be a problem for you!—our load will lighten."

Nanfoodle started to offer a reply, but the sound of hoofbeats stopped him short and turned both him and Shoudra to regard the road that passed just south of their camp.

"The rider has seen our fire!" the gnome said with alarm.

He fell back to the shadows, seeming to retreat even more under his cloak, and he began chanting and waggling his fingers almost immediately.

Shoudra watched the gnome with some amusement, but then focused on the road. She wasn't overly afraid, for she was a seasoned adventurer and could stand her ground with weapon and with spell.

But then everything seemed to go out of focus, as if some enchantment had engulfed the camp, and Shoudra gave a slight cry and started to dive aside.

Started to, for she quickly enough realized that the spell was not the work of an enemy, but of Nanfoodle. She glared at the gnome, who just looked at her from under the cowl of his hood, grinning from ear to ear. He placed a finger over his lips, bidding her to silence.

Up bounded the horse, a large and muscular bay stallion, bearing a tall human rider in a weather-beaten gray cloak. The man pulled his mount up short, then dismounted with practiced ease. He walked before the horse and patted the dust from his cloak, then bowed politely—bowed to a tree a couple of feet to the side of Nanfoodle.

The rider seemed to be of middle age, perhaps forty years, but was in fine physical shape, and his hair was still mostly black, with a bit of gray showing at the edges. He wore a broadsword on his left hip and a dagger on his right, and he had his right hand resting on that smaller weapon as he approached, in a position that seemed one of convenience to the untrained eye. To a seasoned adventurer like Shoudra, though, the man's posture was one of readiness. She could tell from the angle of his settled right arm that he could bring his hand around in an instant, drawing forth and launching the dagger in a single fluid movement.

"Well met, good gnome," the tall man said to the tree, and Shoudra had to fight hard to stop from giggling.

She looked to Nanfoodle, who was grinning even wider and more emphatically trying to silence her. The little one began waggling his fingers once more.

"I am Galen Firth of Nesmé," the man introduced himself.

"And I am Nanfoodle, principal alchemist of the Marchion of Mirabar," the tree answered through the power of the illusionist gnome's spell. "Pray tell us, good sir, your business in these parts. You are a long way from home."

"As are you," Galen commented.

"Indeed, but it was our camp which was violated," Nanfoodle's chosen tree replied.

Galen bowed again.

"Grim news from Nesmé," he remarked. "The bog blokes and the trolls have marched upon us. Our situation is grim—I do not know if my people hold on even as we speak."

"We can turn fast for Mirabar!" came a voice from the side, Shoudra's voice, and the woman moved toward Galen.

His gig up, Nanfoodle waggled his fingers and dispelled the grand illusion, leaving Galen Firth to blink repeatedly as he tried to get his bearings.

"I am the Sceptrana of Mirabar," Shoudra explained when Galen focused on her at last. "Let us turn for Mirabar immediately, that I can persuade Marchion Elastul to rouse the guard to your aid."

"Riders are well on their way to your Marchion," Galen explained, and he continued to blink and look around. "My course is Mithral Hall and the court of King Bruenor Battlehammer."

The man finally focused on the real Nanfoodle, looking from the gnome to the area of illusion, as if he was still trying to figure out what had just happened, and why he was talking to and bowing before a tree.

"Mithral Hall is our destination as well," came Nanfoodle's voice from the back of the camp, and the gnome came forward under Galen's scrutinizing glare. "Forgive the misdirection illusion that greeted you, good rider of Nesmé. One cannot be too careful, after all."

"Indeed," said Galen. "Especially where illusionists are concerned."

Nanfoodle grinned and bowed.

"Your horse shines with sweat," Shoudra remarked. "He cannot run much farther this night. Come, share our evening meal with us and tell us your tale of Nesmé more completely. We will accompany you with all haste to find King Bruenor, and I will add what weight I can to the urgency of your cause."

"That is most generous, Sceptrana," Galen replied.

He moved to the side and tethered his horse.

"This is not good," Nanfoodle whispered to Shoudra while they were alone by the fire.

"I only hope the Marchion is more sympathetic to Nesmé's plight than he has shown toward outsiders of late," Shoudra replied.

"King Bruenor will send aid," Nanfoodle reasoned, and Galen Firth, heading into the camp by then, heard him.

"I can only hope that King Bruenor's memory is short concerning slights," Galen admitted, drawing curious looks from both.

"He came through the region of Nesmé some years ago," the newcomer explained as he took an offered seat on a log beside the fire. "I fear that my patrol did not treat him very well." He gave a little sigh and lowered his eyes, but then quickly added, "It was not King Bruenor who instilled our doubts and fear, but his traveling companion, a drow elf."

"Drizzt Do'Urden," Shoudra remarked. "Yes, I expect that the company Bruenor keeps is off-putting to many people."

"I am hoping that the dwarf will see beyond our past indiscretion," said Galen, "and recognize that it is in his best interests to bolster Nesmé in her time of need."

"From all that we know of King Bruenor, we would expect no less," Nanfoodle put in, and Shoudra nodded her agreement.

Galen Firth nodded as well, but his expression held grim.

The night deepened around them, and given Galen's news of Nesmé, the darkness seemed all the more intimidating.

"A big well-done for yer friend Rumblebelly," Banak Brawnanvil said to Catti-brie as he and a group of others looked over the rope-strewn cliff facing down into Keeper's Dale, to see a substantial dwarf force moving east-to-west across the valley.

"He's one to count on," Catti-brie remarked.

"Oo oi!" Pikel Bouldershoulder seconded.

"Well, I feel better knowing the dale's secure behind us," Ivan Bouldershoulder joined in. "But I'm still thinking that the ridge to the west is a problem in the making."

All eyes turned to the north and west as Ivan reminded them, to view that one long mountain spur, the only higher ground in the region that seemed at all accessible.

"The orcs have been hunting beside giants," Ivan added. "They might be thinking to put a few o' them up there."

"Giants couldn't reach us from up there," Banak answered, the same reply he had offered earlier in their strategy discussions. "Long way off."

"Still a good place for them to hold," Ivan countered. "Even if they just put a few scouts up there, it will give them a fine view of the entire battlefield."

"It is good ground," agreed Torgar Hammerstriker.

"Yer scouts get back from the ridge yet?" Banak asked.

"It's clear so far," Torgar reported. "Me boys said the place is full of tunnels. Quite a network, as far as they could tell. They're guessing that some would lead up to the high ground."

"Probably," said Ivan.

"Let me take a hunnerd," Torgar offered. "I'll go and hold those tunnels."

"And if they find out ye're there?" Banak asked. "Them orcs might come on ye in full. I'm not for losing a hundred!"

"Ye won't," Torgar assured him. "There's an entry into the tunnels way back near to the Keeper's Dale cliff, just down to the west o' here. We'll get in fast and get out faster, if need be."

Banak looked to Ivan for some answers, then to Catti-brie and Wulfgar.

"Catti-brie and I will move to the tunnel entrance and serve as liaison," Wulfgar offered.

Banak looked back out over his current defenses. They had turned the orcs back twice, though the second assault had been nowhere as determined as the first. The orc leader had simply come on again with his forces to disrupt the work of the dwarves, Banak understood, and he was quite a bit impressed by the unusual display of tactics.

Still, that second assault had done little to disrupt the dwarves' preparations, for Banak's warriors had repelled it with ease, and with many never stopping the rock chopping and stone piling. The battlefield was nearly shaped, with solid walls of piled stones forcing any orc charge into a bottleneck. Given that and the fact that the engineers were done with their initial rope work along the cliff face, Banak knew that he could spare a hundred dwarves, even two hundred, without compromising his position.

For if the orcs came on, a large number of the dwarves would have to simply stand behind their fighting kin, missing all the fun.

"Take half of yer own and sweep those tunnels clear," Banak instructed Torgar. "And get a good look at what's to the north once ye get up atop them rocks, will ye?"

"I'll paint ye a picture," Torgar said with a wide grin.

"Hee hee hee," said Pikel.

"And if they come against ye with too much, ye get yerself and yer boys out o' there," Banak instructed. "I don't want to be telling King Bruenor that I lost all his new recruits before they even got themselves into his halls!"

"Ye're not to be losing Torgar and the boys from Mirabar to a bunch of smelly orcs!" Torgar insisted.

"Even if they bring a hundred giants beside them!" agreed Shingles McRuff, the old and grizzled dwarf standing beside Torgar.

Shingles gave a wink at Banak, then dropped a friendly hand hard onto Torgar's shoulder. Torgar's look told all the onlookers that the two were good old friends indeed. In fact, Shingles had been a friend of Torgar's family long before Torgar had seen his first sunrise over Mirabar, and that was centuries gone by.

When the Marchion of Mirabar had treated Torgar so shabbily, blaming him for the warm reception some of Mirabar's dwarves had given to Bruenor, Shingles had been the first to Torgar's side, and had, in fact, been the one to organize the exodus that had taken more than four hundred of Mirabar's finest dwarves out of the city and onto the road to Mithral Hall.

And there they were, a long way from their old home but with their new home in sight across Keeper's Dale. Before they had ever gotten near to Mithral Hall, they had chanced upon the caravan fleeing the disaster of Shallows with the wounded King Bruenor. Torgar, Shingles, and the Mirabarran dwarves had fought a rearguard for that caravan and had performed brilliantly.

Even with all the fighting, even with the orc hordes pressing down upon them, not one of the Mirabarran dwarves had shown the slightest inclination to turn back to their old city in the west.

Not one.

And soon after Torgar's meeting with Banak, with the potentially dangerous duty offered before them, not one backed away from volunteering to spearhead the push into the tunnels of the mountain spur.

Torgar left it to Shingles to pick the half who would accompany him.

The expressions on the faces of the three guests showed that the leader sitting on Mithral Hall's throne before them was not exactly who or what they had expected.

But Regis did not shrink away in the face of those obvious doubts.

"I am the Steward of Mithral Hall," he explained, "serving in the name and interests of King Bruenor."

"And where is your king?" asked Galen Firth, his tone a bit abrupt and impatient.

"Recovering from grievous wounds," Regis admitted, and how he hoped his description was correct. "He was on the front end of the fighting you heard when you were escorted across Keeper's Dale."

Galen started to respond again, but Regis came forward and put on as stern an expression as he could muster with his cherubic features.

"I have heard rumors as to whom you three are," said the halfling, "who come here unbidden—but surely not unwelcome!—in this dangerous time. Before I answer any more of your understandable questions, I would know the truth from you, of who you are and why you have come."

"I am Galen Firth of the Riders of Nesmé," said Galen, and his mention of the riders brought a hint of a scowl to the halfling's face. "Come to bid King Bruenor to send aid to my besieged town. For the trolls have arisen out of their moors. We are sorely pressed!"

Regis brought a hand up to rub his chin, and he glanced to the Battlehammer dwarves standing a bit off to the side. They were a long way from Nesmé; could he dare to send any of Bruenor's clan so far and into such exposure? He offered Galen a nod, for he had nothing more to give just then.

"And you are the Sceptrana of Mirabar," Regis remarked, turning from Galen to Shoudra. "Such was told to me, and I recognize you in any case from my recent visit to your town."

"Your scrimshaw has become quite a novelty in Mirabar, good Steward Regis," Shoudra said politely, and she bowed low. "Shoudra Stargleam at the service of Mithral Hall. This is my assistant, Nanfoodle Buswilligan."

"At the service of Mithral Hall?" Regis echoed. "Or come to check on your wayward dwarves?"

The gnome at Shoudra's side bristled, but the sceptrana merely smiled all the wider.

"I pray that Torgar fares well," she replied, and if she was bothered at all by the emigration of Torgar and his band of dwarves, neither her tone nor her expression showed it.

"But you have not come to join him," said Regis.

Shoudra chuckled at the seemingly absurd notion and said, "I do not agree with Torgar's choice, nor with those who accompanied him away from Mirabar, but it was I who convinced Marchion Elastul that he must allow the dwarves to leave, if that was their decision. It was a sad day in Mirabar when Torgar Hammerstriker and his kin departed."

"When they came to Mithral Hall," Regis reminded. "And Mithral Hall has accepted them as brothers, a bond forged in battle from the day we first met up with Torgar in the mountains and valleys north of here. They are of Clan Battlehammer now. You know this?"

"I do, and though it pains me greatly, I accept it," Shoudra finished with another bow.

"Then why have you come?"

"I beg of your pardon, Steward Regis," Galen Firth interrupted, "but I have not come to witness an argument over the disposition of purposefully misplaced dwarves. My town is besieged, my business urgent." Some of the dwarves at the side of the room began to mutter and shift uneasily as Galen's voice steadily rose in ire. "Could you not continue your discussion with Sceptrana Shoudra at a later time?"

Regis paused and stared at the tall man for a long time.

"I have heard your request," the halfling said, "and deeply regret the situation in Nesmé. I too have some experience with the foul creatures of the Trollmoors, having come through that place in our search to find and reclaim Mithral Hall."

He fixed Galen with a look that told the man in no uncertain terms that he remembered well the shabby treatment the Riders of Nesmé had offered to Bruenor and the Companions of the Hall on that long-ago occasion.

"But you cannot expect me to throw wide the gates of Mithral Hall and empty the place of warriors with a horde of orcs and giants pressing us across the northland," Regis went on, and he gave a glance at the dwarves and took comfort in their assenting nods. "Your situation and request will be discussed at length, and in short order, but before I adjourn this meeting I wish to have all the facts open before me concerning the disposition of all of Mithral Hall's guests, that I might bring all options to the council."

"Decisive action is necessary!" Galen argued.

"And I have not the power to give you that which you desire!" Regis yelled right back. He came forward out of the throne and stood upon the dais, which allowed him to almost look the tall man in the eye. "I am not King Bruenor. I am not the king of anything. I am a steward, an advisor. I will discuss your situation in detail with the dwarves who better understand what Mithral Hall could or could not do to aid Nesmé in her time of need, particularly when we, too, are in a time of need."

"Then my business now, at this meeting, is at its end?" Galen asked, not blinking as he matched Regis's stare.

"It is."

"I will take my leave, then," said Galen. "Am I to presume that Mithral Hall will offer me a place of respite, at least?"

That last "at least" had Regis narrowing his brown eyes.

"Of course," he said, though his jaw hardly moved to let the words escape.

The halfling turned to the side and nodded. A pair of dwarves moved up to flank Galen. The man gave a bow that was more curt than polite and moved off, his heavy boots emphatically thumping against the stone floor.

"He is fearful for the fate of his town, is all," Shoudra remarked when Galen had left.

"True enough," Regis agreed. "And I certainly understand his fears and impatience. But the folk of Clan Battlehammer do not consider Nesmé to be much of a friend, I fear, for Nesmé has never shown much friendship to the folk of Mithral Hall. When we came looking for the Hall those many years ago, we encountered a group of the Riders of Nesmé just outside of the Trollmoors. They were in dire straits, under assault by a band of bog blokes. Bruenor didn't hesitate to go to their rescue—neither did Wulfgar, nor Drizzt. We saved their lives, I believe, and were soundly rebuffed in return."

"Because of the drow elf," Shoudra said.

"True enough," Regis sighed. He gave a little shrug as he settled back in his chair. "That in itself wasn't such a problem. It has happened often and will again."

His obvious reference to the treatment the caravan out of Icewind Dale had received at Mirabar's gate, where Drizzt Do'Urden had not been allowed entrance, had the woman and the gnome looking to each other with a bit of embarrassment.

"After the reclamation of Mithral Hall, Settlestone was rebuilt," the halfling went on. "By Uthgardt warriors, not dwarves."

"I remember Berkthgar the Bold and his people," said Shoudra.

"The community was promising early on," said Regis. "We were all hopeful that the barbarians from Icewind Dale would flourish here. But while they maintained a close relationship with Mithral Hall, their primary goods—furs—were of little use to the dwarves who lived underground, where the temperature remains nearly constant. If Nesmé, the closest neighbor of Berkthgar's people, had welcomed them with trade, Settlestone might still thrive today. Instead, it is just another abandoned ruin along the mountain pass."

"The people of Nesmé lead a difficult existence," Shoudra remarked. "They suffer on the very edge of the dangerous moors, in nearly constant battle. They have learned through tragic experience that they must rely upon themselves most of all, oftentimes only upon themselves. Not a family in Nesmé has not known the tragedy of loss. Most have witnessed at least one of their loved ones being carried off by horrid trolls."

"It's all true," Regis admitted. "And I do understand. But I could not pledge any help to Galen. Not now. Not with Bruenor lying near death and the orcs pressing us to our gates."

"Offer him a sanctuary, then," Shoudra suggested. "Tell him that if his people are overrun, they should turn to Mithral Hall, where they will find friendship, comfort, and shelter."

Regis was nodding before she ever finished, for that was exactly along the lines he had been thinking.

"Perhaps we might find some spare warriors to return with him to

Nesmé, as well," the halfling said. He paused for a moment, then gave a little snort. "Here I am, begging advice from a visitor. A fine steward am I!"

Shoudra started to reply, but Nanfoodle cut in, "The finest leaders are those who listen more than they talk."

That brought a smile to Shoudra and to Regis, but the halfling asked, "Does that show wisdom? Or trepidation?"

"For one whose actions greatly affect others, they are one and the same," Nanfoodle insisted.

Regis pondered that remark, and took some comfort in it. However, the finest leader Regis had ever known was none other than Bruenor Battlehammer, and if the dwarf was ever unsure of a decision, even the boldest of decisions, he surely had never shown it.

THE RECKLESS ONE

"He is sure to get himself killed," Tarathiel whispered to Innovindil as the two lithe and small figures lay on a flat overhang, looking down at the returning Drizzt Do'Urden. The drow was clearly limping and favoring his right hip.

"His determination borders on foolishness," Innovindil replied. She looked at her companion. Their eyes were quite similar in color—rich blue—but looked very different in their respective faces, for while Innovindil's hair was golden, Tarathiel's was as black as a raven's wing. "Never have I seen one so singularly . . . angry."

The elf pair had been keeping an eye on Drizzt ever since the sacking of Shallows. In that fight, when Drizzt had been across the ravine distracting the giant bombardiers, Tarathiel and Innovindil had flown in to his aid. Up high on their pegasi, Sunset and Sunrise, the elves believed that Drizzt had seen them, though he had made no move to find them subsequent to that one incident.

Not so with the elves. Both were skilled trackers, and Tarathiel had found Drizzt again soon after the fateful fight—mostly by following the trail of dead orcs the drow was leaving in his wake. In the two tendays since Shallows's fall, Drizzt had struck at orc camps and patrols nearly every day. The latest attack, against one of the great tribes that had recently arrived on the scene at Shallows, showed that he was growing bolder—dangerously so.

Still, he was winning, and to Tarathiel and Innovindil, that was an admirable thing.

"He lost friends at Shallows," Tarathiel reminded her. "The orcs claim that Bruenor Battlehammer fell there."

Innovindil looked down at the drow warrior. He had undressed then and was cleaning his latest wound—one of many—in a small brook near to his meager shelter of piled boulders.

"He is not one I would desire as an enemy," she whispered.

Tarathiel turned to her as he considered her words, and the implication they clearly held for another of the clan. As soon as they had heard that Bruenor Battlehammer was returning to Mithral Hall, with Drizzt Do'Urden beside him, Tarathiel and Innovindil had welcomed the chance to meet with Drizzt. For one of their own, poor lost Ellifain, had gone off after the drow, seeking revenge for a dark elf raid that had occurred decades before, when Ellifain had been just an infant. Ellifain's entire family had been slaughtered in that terrible raid, and Drizzt Do'Urden had been among the raiders.

But Drizzt had not partaken of that slaughter, the elves knew, and in fact, had saved Ellifain by splashing her with her own mother's blood and hiding her beneath her mother's corpse. To Tarathiel and Innovindil, and all the other elves of the Moonwood, Drizzt Do'Urden was more hero than villain, but poor Ellifain had never been able to get past her grief, had never been able to view the noble drow ranger as anything more than a lie.

Despite all their efforts to educate and calm Ellifain, she had gone off from the Moonwood a couple of years previous in search of her revenge. Tarathiel and Innovindil had tracked her and chased her, determined to stop her, but the trail had gone stone cold in Silverymoon.

Drizzt was back in the area, though, and very much alive. What might that bode for Ellifain?

Innovindil had thought to go right down and speak with Drizzt about that very thing when first they'd located him, but Tarathiel, after observing the drow for a short while, had advised against that course. From all appearances, Drizzt Do'Urden seemed to Tarathiel to be an unknown entity, a wild card, a creature existing purely within his rage and survival instincts.

He wasn't even wearing boots as he set out each day across the unforgiving stony ground, and on the two occasions in which Tarathiel had witnessed Drizzt in battle, the drow seemed something beyond a conscious and cautious warrior. Tarathiel had seen Drizzt taking hits without a flinch and had seen him lop the heads from enemies without the slightest hesitation or expression of regret.

In many ways, the drow reminded him of that Moonwood friend he had recently lost, that young elf maiden so full of anger that she was blind to anything else in all the world.

"We must speak with him before he is slain," Tarathiel said suddenly.

His callous words, spoken so matter-of-factly, turned Innovindil's surprised look his way. For the tone of Tarathiel's words made it clear that he considered the outcome, that Drizzt would be slain, an inevitability. Tarathiel felt the intensity of her gaze and returned her concern with a simple shrug.

"Is his quest murderous or suicidal?" Tarathiel asked. "Or both, perhaps?"

"Then perhaps we should dissuade him of this course."

Tarathiel gave a little laugh and looked back to the distant Drizzt, who had stopped washing by then and had moved into a slow and steady series of stretching and balancing movements, focusing most of his movements on his wounded right hip. Stretching out the bruise, likely.

"He might know of Ellifain," Innovindil went on.

"And if he has faced Ellifain and defeated her, then what will he make of us two when we walk in upon him?"

"You are not a complete stranger to Drizzt Do'Urden," Innovindil argued. "Did he not convince you of his goodness those years ago when he crossed through the Moonwood? Did not the goddess Mielikki grant him a visit by her unicorn before your very eyes?"

It was all true, of course, but somehow in looking at that angry creature exercising below him, Tarathiel couldn't help but feel that it was not the same Drizzt Do'Urden he had once met.

His balance held perfectly, with not a tremor of muscle or sudden shift of his planted left foot. Slowly, Drizzt let his horizontally extended right leg flow through its full range of motion, front to back and back to front. He kept it up high, stretching his hamstring and other muscles as he worked through the tightening sensation within his right hip.

It truly surprised him to realize how hard he had been struck in that last fight, and he feared that he might have a broken bone.

Gradually, as the drow worked through his range of motion, his fears lessened. He found no impediment to his movement other than the ache and realized no overly sharp pains.

Drizzt had survived another encounter intact, fortunately so, and if any second-guesses about his decision to go into that large camp flitted through his thoughts, they were quickly dismissed by the drow's imagining of the scene he had left behind. He had delivered a blow to the orcs that would not be soon forgotten.

But it was not enough, the Hunter knew.

Not nearly enough.

Drizzt looked up at the midmorning sky and calculated when he might bring Guenhwyvar back to his side. The panther needed her rest on the Astral Plane, but she would be ready to resume her hunt soon, Drizzt knew, and the thought brought a wicked grin to his ebon-skinned face.

The orcs might be scrambling to find him, and if they were, he and Guenhwyvar would surely find a few wayward creatures to slaughter.

Drizzt's attention shifted quickly from that pleasant thought to consider the two elves who were up on the flat rock watching him.

Yes, the Hunter knew of them, for in that state, Drizzt was too attuned to his environment to miss even that stealthy pair. He didn't know who they might be, but given his last, tragic encounter with a surface elf, he wasn't pleased by the possibilities.

"It was drow!" the orc protested, as vigorously as he dared. "I seen drow!"

Arganth Snarrl leaped over to stand before the insistent orc, the shaman's huge tooth necklace swinging around wildly, and even slapping across the face of the upstart.

"You seen drow?" the shaman asked.

"I just told you!" the orc protested.

Arganth ignored the reply and spun around to regard the other shamans, all gathered at the scene of Achtel's demise.

"Did Ad'non Kareese do this?" one of the other shamans asked, his brutish face full of outrage.

Arganth searched about for some answer, not wanting to reduce the drama of the murder—a mystery that the volatile shaman desired to exploit for his own ends. Achtel, after all, had been the sole quiet opposition among the gathered shamans to Arganth's insistence that King Obould should be viewed as one with Gruumsh. Not willing to relinquish the independence of her powerful tribe, Achtel had privately questioned some of the other shamans concerning the wisdom of Arganth's unification desires.

Achtel wasn't just dead, she seemed to have been singled out. For Arganth, the answer was obvious: Achtel's impudence had angered Gruumsh One-Eye, whose vengeance had been swift and uncompromising. Of course, Arganth was also wise enough to recognize that if the other shamans somehow connected Obould's drow friends to the murder of Achtel, then they might come to suspect some nefarious organization, working to persuade through terror—which was, after all, the orc way.

"Not Ad'non," the orc witness dared to put in. "It was the . . . one."

The suddenly husky tone of his voice as he uttered that peculiar phrase told the others exactly of whom he was speaking. Word had been filtering throughout the ranks of all the orcs and giants who had come out of their mountain holes that a lone drow, an ally of dead King Bruenor, was working behind their lines, and to deadly effect.

"The Drizzit," Arganth said in low and threatening tones. "Gruumsh has used our enemy against our enemy."

"Achtel was our enemy?" asked one of the other shamans.

"Achtel denied the joining of his spirit to King Obould's body," Arganth explained. "It is clear before us. This sign cannot be denied!"

Murmurs erupted all around him as soon as he widened the investigation to encompass his political aspirations, but most of those murmuring orcs were also nodding their agreement.

"Obould is Gruumsh!" Arganth dared to declare.

Not a protesting word came back at him.

"He wastes little time," Innovindil said to Tarathiel when she caught up to him around the backside of a copse of trees on the mountain slopes overlooking the region where Drizzt Do'Urden had taken up his shelter.

"Is he out again already?" Tarathiel asked, and he looked up at the sky, confirming that it was still a couple of hours to sunset. "I would have thought he would need to rest his hip."

"He brought in the panther," Innovindil explained.

Tarathiel nodded and looked again at the sky, his blue eyes glowing in the light.

"I fear he has erred," said the elf. "His hip is more injured than he realizes—if the wound upsets his balance. . . ."

Innovindil drew forth her slender sword and shrugged. She turned toward the path that would put them on the trail of the dark elf.

"Perhaps I should follow alone," Tarathiel offered. "On Sunrise, and high above the hunting cat."

Innovindil stared at him hard.

"Sunset is not yet ready to carry you," Tarathiel reasoned. "Soon, perhaps, but not yet."

Innovindil had little to offer in the way of an argument to that. In the fight with the giants north of Shallows, her pegasus had been struck in the wing, causing a deep bruise and laceration. Sunset seemed well on the mend, for pegasi were resilient creatures, but Tarathiel's assessment was correct, she knew, and she would not dare ask the mount to climb into the sky, particularly not with her added weight.

But she had no intention of being excluded.

"What a fine target you will make in the afternoon sky," she said. "Or perhaps you will still be airborne when the sun does set, leaving your steed blind and soaring about the mountain spurs."

"I only fear that we might encounter the panther as it moves about Drizzt," Tarathiel explained. "I have little desire for a battle with that creature!"

"It will not come to that if we are cautious," Innovindil insisted.

She motioned toward the path. Tarathiel was by her side in a moment, and the two rushed off, their footfalls silent, their senses trained. Soon enough, they had the trail of Drizzt and Guenhwyvar.

The orcs were so thick about the region that Drizzt and Guenhwyvar had already found a band of them with the sun still hanging in the western sky.

"Gerti says," one of the creatures complained, scooping a bucket in the cold waters of a fast-rushing mountain spring. "Gerti says!"

"How do we know what Gerti says, and what them giants says Gerti says?" another bitched, and he too sloshed a bucket through the water.

"Gerti talks too much," a third chimed in.

"Gerti," Drizzt whispered to Guenhwyvar. "A giant?"

The intelligent panther, seeming to understand every word, lowered her ears flat to her head. Thinking it wise to better assess the strength of the group, Drizzt motioned for Guenhwyvar to circle off to the right, while he went left. Sure enough, within a couple of minutes time, the drow found a frost giant, reclining on the river stones around a bend, head back to bask in the late afternoon sun. Her heavy boots sat on the bank, one upright, the other bent over in half, and her huge cleaver rested there as well. Oblivious to all the world she seemed as she splashed her bare feet in the icy water.

Drizzt spotted Guenhwyvar across the river and motioned to her, then to the relaxing giantess.

The Hunter went back over the rocks to the spot around the bend where the handful of orcs were still at work—they seemed to be filling a wide and shallow pit. A fire burned nearby, with rocks piled all around. Every now and then, an orc would kick one of those heated stones into the watery shallow.

"A bathtub?" Drizzt whispered under his breath.

The drow dismissed the thought as unimportant and narrowed his focus to the task at hand. He subconsciously rubbed his wounded hip as he surveyed the lay of the land, taking note of possible escape routes, for the orcs more than for himself, and searching among the up-and-down terrain to try to guess if other orc bands might be in the immediate area.

A growl from beyond the bend, followed by a scream of surprise, ended that search and sent the Hunter leaping from the stones and sprinting toward the orcs. As one the pig-faced creatures howled, tossing buckets aside.

One sprinted out to the right, along the river, but Drizzt, his feet sped by the enchanted anklets, caught it quickly and sliced it down. He turned fast—and nearly stumbled as a sharp pain rolled out from his hip—and charged back toward the main group.

The closest pair lifted spears to slow his charge, but he skidded down to his knees before them, then came up fast as they adjusted the angle of

their weapons. Two fast strides had Drizzt rushing out to the left, and a pair
of spears came slashing across that way to fend.

Except that the Hunter had already reversed his direction back to
the right and had started down low for just an instant, just long enough
to bring the two spears into a second dip as the orcs tried to reverse their
momentum.

Drizzt leaped up and forward, double-kicking left and right, hitting one
orc squarely in the face and clipping the other's forearm as it let go of its
spear and moved to block. The Hunter came down lightly on one pointed
foot—and again came a wave of pain from that hip. He turned immediately
into a spin, scimitars flying out wide.

Both orcs fell away, lines of bright red appearing on each.

The Hunter ran past, into the next orc in line. A twist, a turn, a feint,
then a second, had the orc turning every which way as the drow ran right
past it. A flip of the wrist and reversed stab took the confused creature in
the spine. On Drizzt went, not even slowing as a tremendous roar came from
around the bend, followed by the splashing of the running giantess.

She came around the bend, stumbling across the many large, slick river
stones, her hands up by her face, trying to pull the stubborn panther free.

The Hunter dispatched another orc with a double-thrust low that had
the creature leaping back, then stumbling forward in the inevitable overbal-
ance. The drow followed with a pair of twisting uppercuts, one right behind
the other, that took the creature about the face and neck. Before the dying
orc even fell, the Hunter had turned, focusing on the giantess.

He saw Guenhwyvar finally come away from the behemoth's torn face,
go up in the air over the staggering giantess's head, then go flying away. He
heard the plaintive, wounded roar and felt, for just a moment, the panther's
agony.

But he was the Hunter, not Drizzt, and he didn't move immediately
for the figurine to dismiss the pained cat back to the Astral Plane and her
peace. Instead, scimitars high, he took the opening on the horribly wounded
and obviously blinded giantess, rushing in and stabbing her hard about the
belly and back, running around to keep her turning. Always one step ahead
of her, the Hunter scored again and again, and when the stubborn giantess
finally went down to her knees in the river, he took up the attacks even more
ferociously, finding her neck with every strike.

Blood flew wildly, inciting nothing but an even deeper rage within the

Hunter. He bashed and slashed with abandon, even as the giantess fell face down into the water. His surroundings didn't matter to him. He saw the fall of Ellifain at the end of one scimitar, saw Bruenor ride that burning tower down to the ground. And he fought those images with all his heart and soul, battered them away by cracking one blade after another against the giantess's thick skull. She became the focus of all that rage; for those few seconds of pure intensity, Drizzt Do'Urden broke free of his turmoil.

The wail of broken Guenhwyvar brought him from his frenzy, though, and shot through his heart with a stab of profound guilt. The panther lay on the river's far bank, struggling to get clear of the water's incessant pull with her shaking front paws, while her rear haunches lay limp and twisted, her pelvic area shattered by the giantess's strong grip.

Behind her came another group of orcs, spears raised and some already throwing for the panther.

"Go home, Guen," Drizzt called softly, lifting the onyx figurine from his belt pouch. He knew that she would heal well on the Astral Plane, knew that no injuries Guenhwyvar received on this plane of existence could ever truly harm her.

Still, she felt pain, a searing agony that rode her wail to Drizzt's heart.

A spear soared in for her, the shot true.

But it passed through as the panther faded and became a swirling gray mist drifting away and dissipating to nothingness.

The orcs shifted direction, coming fast for the drow standing mid-stream. He hardly registered them at first, still hearing Guenhwyvar's cry, still feeling the weight of her pain.

He glanced up at the closing orcs and tried to use that pain to shift back to his rage, to let free the Hunter once more. Behind him, he heard more of the brutes.

He raised his scimitars; in glancing around, he understood just how badly he was outnumbered. Too badly, likely.

The Hunter merely smiled—

—then charged through a rain of flying spears, his scimitars slashing before him to take the missiles from the sky. He dodged and turned, his senses falling so keenly into the sounds around him that he knew without looking when one of the spears from behind would catch him and he was able to react, a quick turn in perfect balance, to parry it aside.

He went out of the river along a run of five slick stones, his bare feet not slipping an inch on any of the sure-footed strides. He hit the rocky and sandy bank in a dead run, then threw himself aside into a sudden roll, and back up and forward, and to the side once more.

Through the orc ranks he went, scimitars cutting the way. His hands worked in a blur as his feet stepped forward and sideways, toes ahead, toes turned, every step sure and fast, his weight shifting effortlessly to stay over his pumping legs.

His momentum only gradually began to falter; he kept up the run for a long, long while. But at every turn, the orcs were there, pressing back at him, swinging clubs and swords, stabbing spears. Twinkle and Icingdeath rang repeatedly against metal and wood, taking blades high or low, or pushing them out wide so that Drizzt could step through.

But the orcs weren't stupid creatures, nor were they cowardly. They took their losses but kept their formations, groups working in concert to lock down every possible escape route the rogue drow might find.

Finally, the exhausted drow found himself in a shallow dell, over a sandy bluff twenty feet away from the river. Ringed by orcs, but with not a one within striking distance, he fell into a defensive stance, scimitars ready to intercept any forthcoming missile.

One of the orcs barked a command at him, a word that he thought meant "surrender." That one would die first, the Hunter decided. His feet shifted under him. Orcs all around feigned a charge or a throw but held back to their tight ranks.

The Hunter wanted them to move first, to present him an opening.

They would not.

The Hunter dashed out to the side, against the orc line, weapons working in a blaze. But the orcs held firm, their defenses tight and coordinated.

Again he went at them and again was repulsed.

They were gaining confidence, he realized from their wide, toothy smiles, and he knew, too, that their confidence was well founded. There were too many. His rage had carried him to a place beyond his abilities.

If only they would break the circle!

A commotion to the side had him spinning, weapons coming up to block. The orcs weren't coming his way, though, and many from that side weren't even looking at him any longer. He watched in shared confusion with them as their back ranks scrambled and fell, as orcs shoved orcs aside frantically.

The wave cut right through the perimeter, and a pair of slender forms emerged into the dell before the Hunter. Dressed in white tunics and tan breeches, with forest green cloaks flying behind them, the two were joined, forearm to forearm as they came in, and each used the other to heighten his or her balance as they moved in a whirlwind of a sword dance. Long and thick hair, black and yellow, flew out behind as they crossed around each other repeatedly, always maintaining the slightest contact, each altering the attack angles independently but in perfect harmony with the movements and choices of the other.

One went around and down low, and the orcs closest responded accordingly—except that the leading elf (and they were indeed surface elves, Drizzt recognized) simply rotated along past them, while his partner came in hard and high, above the set defenses. Orcs screamed and orcs fell, and more orcs tried to press in.

They fell, too.

The Hunter forced himself free of the amazing spectacle, a dance as graceful and perfect as anything he had ever before witnessed. He purposely put his back to the spinning pair, refusing to be distracted, and he charged into the nearest orcs, who suddenly and quite understandably seemed more intent upon running away

He caught a few and slew them, and many more went howling in flight across the trails. The threat gone, and the battle won. He turned to face his unknown allies, offering a salute to them with one scimitar.

The male of the group, breathing heavily but wearing an easy smile, similarly saluted with his bloody sword.

And he nearly knocked the drow over with a simple statement, "Well met again, Drizzt Do'Urden."

7

BEYOND THE
BOUNDS OF TIME

"I have heard of your citadel," Nanfoodle said to Nikwillig.

The gnome was wandering the grounds outside of Mithral Hall's western gate when he came upon his fellow visitor to the Battlehammer stronghold sitting on a flat stone in Keeper's Dale. They could hear the fighting up above them in the north.

"Me kinsman Tred's up there now," Nikwillig remarked.

"You fear for him," reasoned the gnome.

"For Tred?" came the laughing response. "Nah, never that. Nikwillig's the name here, little one, and who might yerself be?"

"Nanfoodle Buswilligan at your service, good dwarf," the gnome answered with a polite bow. "A visitor to Mithral Hall, as are you."

"Ye come from Silverymoon?"

"Mirabar," Nanfoodle answered. "I serve as Marchion Elastul's Principal Alchemist."

"Alchemist?" Nikwillig echoed, and his tone clearly showed that he didn't hold much faith in that particular art. "Well, what's an alchemist doing out on the wider roads?"

That question set off warning bells in Nanfoodle's head and reminded him that perhaps he should not be so forthcoming, given his true mission. Certainly Torgar and the others from Mirabar knew the truth of his position in that city, but why make the information so readily available?

"Better that yer marchion sent a war advisor, I'm thinking," the dwarf added.

"Ah, but we did not know that Mithral Hall was at war," Nanfoodle answered, and coincidentally, at that moment, horns blew up above, followed by the rousing cheers of another dwarf charge. "I came with the sceptrana, following the exodus of many of Mirabar's dwarves."

"I heard about that," Nikwillig replied. He turned to the cliff behind him and nodded. "Torgar and his boys're up there now, from what I'm hearing."

"Doing Mirabar proud, though they are not of Mirabar any longer."

"Ye come to coax them back, did ye?"

Nanfoodle shook his head.

"To check on them," said the gnome. "Too see that their journey went well and that their reception here was appropriate. There are bridges to be rebuilt—animosity serves neither Mirabar nor Mithral Hall."

How Nanfoodle wished that he could believe in those words as he spoke them!

"Ah," Nikwillig mumbled. "Well, no worry then. No better hosts in all the world than King Bruenor and his kin, unless of course one goes to Citadel Felbarr and the court of King Emerus Warcrown."

"They have treated you and your friend well?"

"How do ye think King Bruenor got himself knocked silly?" Nikwillig said. "He was hunting the band of orcs and giants that hit me and Tred. We paid them back, too, we did, though in the end too many of the stinking orcs came onto the field. Aye . . . no better friend than Bruenor Battlehammer."

"How will your king react to this attack?" Nanfoodle asked, genuinely curious.

The gnome had always recognized the bond between dwarves—and had been among the loudest voices warning Marchion Elastul and his advisors that he might be erring greatly in his treatment of Torgar Hammerstriker. It touched Nanfoodle to hear this dwarf of Citadel Felbarr, the closest dwarven stronghold to Mithral Hall and certainly a trading rival, speaking so highly of Bruenor and his kin.

The gnome glanced up the tall cliff, thinking that Tred was up there battling, risking his life for a kingdom that was not his own. And that Torgar was up there, and Shingles McRuff as well, no doubt fighting with all the fury they would muster in defending Mirabar herself.

Nanfoodle began to ask another question, but the dwarf perked up suddenly and looked past him. Nikwillig hopped down and pushed past the gnome to intercept a dwarf wearing long robes.

"What of King Bruenor then?" Nikwillig asked. "Ye been with him?"

The dwarf, young in appearance but looking quite weary and worn, straightened his shoulders and his robes and tucked his brown beard into the belt sash.

"Hello once again, Nikwillig of Citadel Felbarr," he said.

"This is me new friend, Nanfoodle," Nikwillig introduced, pulling the gnome forward.

"Of Mirabar, yes," the dwarf replied, and he gave Nanfoodle's small hand a solid grasp and shake. "Cordio Muffinhead at yer service."

"Priest of Moradin," the gnome observed, and Cordio bowed deeply.

"And yes, I've just come from the side of King Bruenor, where yet again today, meself and several others have exhausted our magical energies on his behalf."

"To gain?" Nikwillig asked.

"So we were thinking," the despondent cleric replied. "King Bruenor uttered some words earlier, and we thought he'd found his way back to us. But he was calling to his father and his father's father, warning them of the shadow."

"The shadow?" Nanfoodle asked.

"The shadow dragon, perhaps," Cordio added.

"King Bruenor was seeing in the past," Nikwillig explained. "Far in the past, before Clan Battlehammer got chased away from Mithral Hall, to wander and settle in Icewind Dale."

"Where I was born," Cordio said. "I never knew Mithral Hall until King Bruenor took it back. What a fight that was, I tell ye! I was there all the way, fighting right beside Dagnabbit, finest young warrior in all the clan."

"Dagnabbit fell at Shallows," Nikwillig explained to Nanfoodle, and the gnome offered a deferential nod at Cordio.

"Lost me a good friend that dark day," Cordio admitted. "But he died fighting orcs—no dwarf could ever be wanting a better way to go."

Cordio turned around and stepped away from the flat stone. Many other dwarves were in the area, ferrying supplies—both up the rope ladders to Banak Brawnanvil and his boys and out to the west where a force was digging in for the defense of Keeper's Dale. Other dwarves coming back from the wall in the north ferried the wounded and dead.

"Been a long and bloody history in these lands," Cordio remarked. "Lots o' dead dwarves."

"More dead orcs," Nanfoodle reminded. "And more dead goblins."

That brought a grin to the weary cleric, and Nikwillig clapped Cordio warmly on the shoulder.

"The most dwarves o' Mithral Hall that ever died in one place at one time, died right about where ye're sitting," Cordio explained to Nanfoodle.

"In the fight with the drow?" Nikwillig asked.

"Nah," answered the cleric. "Long before that. Way back afore me father's father's father's time. Way back when Gandalug was just a boy."

That news brought wide eyes from both of Cordio's listeners. Gandalug Battlehammer had become quite a legend in Mirabar and Citadel Felbarr, and everywhere else in the North. He had been the proud and revered King of Mithral Hall centuries before, but he had been magically imprisoned and wound up in the clutches of Matron Mother Baenre of Menzoberranzan. When the drow had come against Mithral Hall a decade before, Bruenor had slain Baenre and had freed Gandalug. And Bruenor had returned to Icewind Dale, which had been his home for centuries, giving Mithral Hall back to his returned ancestor.

"Gandalug told me so much of them old days," Cordio Muffinhead went on, and his gray eyes seemed to look off in the distance, across space and time. "He oft walked with me out here in Keeper's Dale. The dale wasn't a valley in his childhood, but this whole place . . ." He paused and swept his short arms out to encompass the whole of the rocky dale. "This whole place was the grand entryway of Mithral Hall, and what a foyer it was! With great towers. . . ." He laughed and pointed to some of the closer obelisks that so dotted the floor of Keeper's Dale. "Every one o' them was covered in carvings, ye know. Grand carvings. Battles of old, even the finding of Mithral Hall. Ye can't see 'em now—wind's taken them and scattered them to the bounds o' time.

"Like the dead, ye know? Scattered and gone when we're not remembering them anymore." Cordio gave a helpless little chuckle and added, "I'm not thinking to let Gandalug or Dagnabbit go that way for a bit!"

Nanfoodle sat quietly, staring at that most unusual dwarf and at the effect his words were obviously having on Nikwillig. Their bond struck the gnome profoundly. As thick as a dwarven handshake, it seemed, or as a mug of the mead the dwarves passed off as holy water.

Nikwillig inquired as to what could have so caused the complete destruction of an area as large as Keeper's Dale, and in looking around, what most struck Nanfoodle was the lack of rubble and broken stones.

"Flight o' dragons?" Nikwillig asked, and Nanfoodle answered "No" even before Cordio could.

Both dwarves looked at the gnome.

"Ye've heard the story?" Cordio asked.

"They had tunnels below here," Nanfoodle reasoned. "Mines. And they hit some hot air."

He didn't have to explain to either of the dwarves, who had spent years and years working in tunnels, about the dangers and potential catastrophe of "hot air," or natural gas deposits. Any dwarf would babble on for hours about the dangers of their tunnels or the deeper Underdark, of goblins and displacer beasts, of drow and shadow dragons. Few spoke openly about hot air, though, for it was a killer they could not smash with a hammer or chop with an axe.

Nanfoodle could only imagine the height of catastrophe that had shaped Keeper's Dale. It must have been quite a flow of hot air to get up there so completely and in so short a span of time as to go undetected until it was too late. The gnome could imagine those last frantic moments—perhaps the dwarves had at last detected the invisible killer. And the explosion, a clean puff of fiery orange and the grating of stone being torn apart. The area all around Keeper's Dale was littered with boulders. Nanfoodle had a better idea of what had put them there.

"No mines below Keeper's Dale now," Cordio Muffinhead remarked. "We shut them down centuries ago. Sealed them good!"

Nanfoodle nodded his agreement. Before going out there, he had wandered around the great Undercity of Mithral Hall, with the lines of forges and the many entryways for carts filled with ore coming in from all the working mines. There were many maps down there, old and new, and in recalling some of them, it seemed to Nanfoodle indeed that the western gate to Mithral Hall was the westernmost point below, as well as above.

Their thoughts were interrupted then by renewed shouts and sounds of battle from up on the cliff to the north. Cordio Muffinhead glanced that way and gave a great sigh.

"I must go and take my rest," he remarked. "My powers will be needed all too soon, I fear."

"Damn orcs," muttered Nikwillig.

Nanfoodle eyed the Felbarr dwarf for a long while, then meandered back to the gate and into Mithral Hall. He headed for the Undercity and the maps, wanting to view them again in light of Cordio's tale.

Regis was surprised to see Torgar Hammerstriker awaiting an audience later that day.

"Well met, Steward," the dwarf from Mirabar greeted with a low bow. "The battle goes well?"

Torgar gave a shrug and replied, "Orcs ain't really throwing much our way. They're more thinking to knock down our defenses and stop us from digging in too deep, is me own guess."

"While they bring up allies," Regis reasoned and Torgar nodded.

"Group o' giants been seen moving this way."

"I'm surprised that you've come down then."

"Just for a bit," said Torgar. "Just to see yerself in private. I'm moving me Mirabar dwarfs off to Banak's left flank when darkness falls. We're to hold the tunnels beneath the mountain spur."

"We've protected the backside, the western end of Keeper's Dale, as much as we can," Regis explained. "Every dwarf but the necessary workers in Mithral Hall are out on the fronts now, but I couldn't send too many out. We have reports of trouble in Nesmé, not too far to the southwest, and there are tunnels connecting to our mines from there."

"Protect the hall at all costs," Torgar agreed. "Them who're outside will run back in, if they're needing to."

Regis replied with a warm smile, for he was truly glad to hear even more approval of his decisions. This mantle of steward weighed heavily upon him, even though he realized that the true leaders of Mithral Hall in Bruenor's absence, the toughened Battlehammer dwarves, wouldn't let him do anything they didn't agree with.

"And I come down here to talk to yerself about protecting yer hall," Torgar went on. "Ye've got more visitors from Mirabar, so's been told to me."

"The sceptrana herself, and a gnome companion," Regis confirmed.

"Good enough folk, mostly," said Torgar. "But keep yer head that

Mirabar's in desperate straits now that me and so many o' me kin've walked away. Nanfoodle's a clever one, and Shoudra's got some powerful magic at her disposal."

"You believe they were sent here to do more than check up on your welcome?"

"I'm not for knowing," Torgar admitted. "But when I heard from Catti-brie that they'd come in, first thing I thought was that them two are worth watchin'."

"From afar," Regis agreed, and Torgar nodded again.

"Whatever ye're thinking is best, Steward Regis," he said, and the halfling could hardly hold back from wincing at the open recitation of his title. "I just figured it'd be best for me to come to yerself direct and let ye know me feelings."

"And it is appreciated, Torgar," Regis quickly replied. "More than you can understand. You and your boys from Mirabar have already proven your-selves as friends of the hall, and I expect that Bruenor will have more than a little to say to you all when he awakens. He does like to personally greet the newest members of his clan, after all."

Regis knew that he had worded that perfectly when he saw the smile beam out from Torgar's hairy face. The dwarf nodded and bowed, then moved off, leaving Regis with his warning.

What to do about Shoudra and Nanfoodle? the halfling wondered. Regis had been taken by their warmth and openness in his meeting with them, and certainly, they seemed to be reasonable enough folks. But the Steward of Mithral Hall could not ignore the possibility of mischief, not when such mischief could prove absolutely disastrous for Clan Battlehammer.

"You understand that you did not come down here alone," Shoudra Stargleam remarked to Nanfoodle when she caught up to the gnome along the floor of the Undercity.

Hammers rang out all around them and smoke filled the uncomfort-ably warm air, for every furnace was fully stoked, every anvil engaged. To the side, great whetstones spun unceasingly, weapon after weapon running across them, honing the fine edges so that they could be delivered back to the forces engaged with the orcs.

"They are unobtrusive enough," the gnome replied, referring to the dwarf pair who had quietly shadowed his every movement through the tunnels. Nanfoodle wiped the sweat from his face, then pulled off his red robe and began to cross it over his forearm. Noting the soot that had already settled upon the fine garment, the gnome crinkled his long nose, brushed the robe, then reversed it back to its weathered brown. "Could we expect anything else?"

"Of course not," Shoudra agreed. "And I do not complain of our treatment here, certainly. Steward Regis is a fine host. But if we are to carry out our designs, we might need a bit of deceptive magic. Easily enough accomplished."

The sceptrana narrowed her gaze as she scrutinized Nanfoodle's sour expression.

With a shrug, the gnome continued on his way, Shoudra falling into step beside him.

"Why here?" she asked. "Would we not have a better opportunity in the lower transfer rooms, where the separated ore awaits delivery?"

Still the sour expression, and Nanfoodle noticeably increased his pace.

"Or have you perhaps forgotten why we ventured here to Mithral Hall?" Shoudra asked bluntly.

"I have forgotten nothing," Nanfoodle snapped back.

"Second thoughts, then?"

"Have you noted the treatment Mithral Hall has afforded Torgar and the others?"

"Regis needs the warriors," Shoudra replied. "Torgar was a convenient addition."

Nanfoodle stopped and stared hard at her.

The sceptrana smiled helplessly back. Of course the gnome was right, she knew. Torgar and the other dwarves of Mirabar were helping the cause, and in a vital role, and it was just that vital role that proved Nanfoodle's point. Bruenor's clan had taken the Mirabarran dwarves at their word and on their honor, without question. Especially in such dangerous times, that was no small thing.

"You have made a friend in the other visitor to Mithral Hall, I have heard," she remarked as Nanfoodle started on his way once more.

"Nikwillig of Citadel Felbarr—a place that is as much a rival to

Mithral Hall as is Mirabar, surely," the gnome explained. "Have you heard his tale?"

"You will tell me that Bruenor fell avenging him," Shoudra predicted, for she had indeed.

They came up to a large wood and stone table then, its front side holding a rack of pigeon holes and each with a rolled parchment inside. Nanfoodle bent low, reading the descriptions, then he pulled forth a map and unrolled it on the sloping tabletop. A quick perusal brought a frustrated sigh, and the gnome bent low again, seeking a second map.

"None are better at shaping an axe blade, but one would think that these dwarves would know how to label a simple map!" he complained.

Shoudra put her hand on his shoulder, drawing his attention.

"We are being observed, you understand," she said.

"Of course."

"Then what are you doing?"

Nanfoodle drew out the second map and stood straight, spreading it over the first one before him.

"Trying to determine how I might aid in the cause of Clan Battlehammer," the gnome said matter-of-factly.

Shoudra's hand slapped down on the center of the map.

"Bruenor fought for the dwarves of Felbarr," the gnome responded. "Bruenor himself! Fighting for a rival. Would Marchion Elastul think of such a thing?"

"Is it our place to judge?"

"Is it not?"

Shoudra glared at her diminutive companion—or tried to, for in truth, she had a hard task in defending their mission. They had come to use Nanfoodle's alchemical potions to secretly ruin a great deal of Mithral Hall's ore, that Clan Battlehammer would produce a batch of inferior works—perhaps enough to weaken Mithral Hall's reputation with the merchants of the North, thus affording Mirabar an upper hand in the trade war.

"How petty are we two, Shoudra?" Nanfoodle quietly asked. "The marchion pays me well, 'tis true, but how am I to ignore that which I see about me? These dwarves follow a course of justice, first and foremost. They welcomed Torgar and the wayward pair from Felbarr with open hearts."

"Dwarf to dwarf," came the skeptical reply.

"And dwarf to gnome, and dwarf to sceptrana," Nanfoodle countered. "Consider our welcome here compared to that which Elastul afforded King Bruenor."

"You are beginning to sound a bit too much like Torgar Hammerstriker," the tall and beautiful woman remarked.

"You did not disagree with Torgar."

"Not with his greeting of King Bruenor, no," Shoudra admitted. "But with his abandonment of Mirabar? I do indeed disagree, Nanfoodle. I am glad of our reception, do not doubt, and I harbor no ill will toward Bruenor and his clan, but I am first and foremost the Sceptrana of Mirabar, and there remains my first loyalty."

"Do not ask me to poison their metal," Nanfoodle pleaded. "Not now . . . I beg you."

Shoudra stared at him for a few moments, then backed away, removing her hand from the map.

"No, of course not," she agreed, and Nanfoodle gave a great sigh of relief. "Our actions would do more than wound them in trade, but would likely cost the lives of many now engaged with the foul orcs. Clearly Elastul would agree with our decision to abort the mission . . . for now."

Nanfoodle nodded and smiled, but his expression told Shoudra clearly that he, like her, did not believe that last statement in the least. Shoudra knew—and it truly pained her to know—that Marchion Elastul would insist on attacking the ore even more aggressively if he thought it might bring even greater catastrophe upon Mithral Hall.

"So tell me what you are looking for, and what you plan to do?" she asked the gnome, and she peered at the map over his shoulder, recognizing it at once as the westernmost reaches of Mithral Hall, the gate at Keeper's Dale and the tunnels below.

"I do not yet know," Nanfoodle admitted. "But I will see what I can see and try to find a way to use my expertise to the benefit of the cause."

"Seeking a better offer from King Bruenor?" Shoudra asked with a wry grin.

Nanfoodle started to protest, until he noted her expression.

"I have been here but a couple of days and already I feel as if Mithral Hall is more my home than Mirabar ever was," he admitted.

Shoudra didn't argue the point. She wasn't quite as enamored of the place, for the whole of it was below ground, but she certainly understood the gnome's feelings.

"You should study beside me," Nanfoodle said, turning his attention back to the map. "Your skills with magic could prove of great value to Clan Battlehammer in this dark time."

Again, despite herself, Shoudra didn't argue the point.

Exhausted and with several new wounds to attend, Catti-brie was barely back into Mithral Hall that night when she heard the commotion of the clerics rushing to her father's side. The woman dropped her cloak, her bow, and even her sword belt right there in the hallway and sprinted off to the room, to find her father's bed surrounded by a handful of priests and Pikel Bouldershoulder. All of them were chanting, praying, and one by one they placed their hands gently on Bruenor's chest and released their healing magic.

Halfway through the process, Bruenor actually moved a bit and even coughed, but then he settled quickly back into his completely sedentary state.

Cordio Muffinhead and Stumpet Rakingclaw, the two highest ranking clerics, took a moment to examine Bruenor, then looked around and nodded with satisfaction. They had staved off another potential disaster, had once again brought Bruenor back from the very brink of death.

Catti-brie spent more time looking at the priests then, than at her resting father. Several leaned on the edge of Bruenor's bed, obviously spent, and though they had performed another apparent miracle, not a one of them seemed overly pleased—not even the perpetually happy Pikel.

They began to filter out then, moving past Cathi-brie, most of them patting her on the shoulder as they passed.

"Every day we come to him. . . ." Cordio Muffinhead remarked when he and Catti-brie were alone in the room.

Catti-brie moved to her father's side and knelt by the bed. She took his hand in her own and squeezed it to her breast. How cool he felt, as if the energy of his life had diminished to almost nothingness. She gave a cursory glance around the room, to the many candles and the warm furnishings, trying to remind herself that this was a very different place than the cramped, dark, and wet tunnels beneath the ruins of Withegroo's crumbled tower in Shallows. Surely it was more comfortably furnished and ventilated, and gently lit, but to Catti-brie, it didn't seem all that different. The focus of the young woman could not be the furnishings, nor the light, but on, always on, the central figure that lay so very still in the middle of the room.

In looking at him at that moment, Catti-brie was reminded of another friend lying close to death. Back in the west, along the Sword Coast, she and the others had found Drizzt in such a state, lying mortally wounded on one side of the room with Le'lorinel—Ellifain—that most tragic of elves, similarly slashed on the other. Drizzt had begged her to save Ellifain instead of him, to use the one magical potion available to them to heal the elf's wounds and not his own.

Bruenor had been the one to dismiss that thought out of hand, and so Drizzt had survived. Still, Catti-brie and the others had been given a difficult choice at that moment, and they had acted for their own personal needs and for the greater good—fortunately, the two had seemed congruous.

But what about now? Were their personal, perhaps even selfish, desires making them all follow a course that was not for the greater good?

The heroics of the clerics were keeping Bruenor alive—if what he was now could even be considered alive. Every day, often more than once, they had to rush in and put forth their greatest healing efforts just to bring him back to that comatose state of near-death.

"Should we just let ye go?" the woman asked Bruenor quietly.

"What was that ye say?" asked Cordio, hustling over beside her.

Catti-brie looked up at the dwarf, studied his concerned expression, and smiled and said, "Not a thing, Cordio. Was just calling to my father."

She looked back at Bruenor's grayish face and added, "But he's not hearing me."

"He knows ye're here," the dwarf whispered, and he put his hands on the back of the woman's shoulders, offering her his strength.

"Does he? I'm not thinking it so," Catti-brie replied. "Might that that's the problem. Have ye lost all of your heart and hope?" she asked Bruenor. "Are you thinking me dead, and Wulfgar and Regis and Drizzt all dead? The orcs won at Shallows, from what you know, didn't they?"

She stared at Bruenor a moment longer, then looked up at Cordio, and his expression was all the agreement she needed.

"Is he all right?" came a call from the door, and the two looked to see Regis come running into the room, Wulfgar close behind.

Cordio assured them that Bruenor was fine, then took his leave, but not before bowing low to Catti-brie's side and offering her a kiss on the cheek.

"Keep talking to him, then," the dwarf whispered.

Catti-brie squeezed Bruenor's hand all the tighter and focused all of her senses on that hand, seeking some return grasp, some tiny hint that Bruenor felt her presence.

Nothing. Just the cool, seemingly inanimate skin.

The woman took a deep breath, gave another squeeze, then forced herself back to her feet and turned around to regard her friends.

"We've got some choices we're needing to make," she said, holding her voice steady with great determination.

Wulfgar looked at her curiously, but Regis, more familiar with all that was going on within the hall, offered a loud sigh.

"The priests grow more and more frustrated," he said.

"And they're needed elsewhere, as much as here," Catti-brie made herself admit, though every word stung her profoundly. She looked back at poor Bruenor, his breath coming so shallow that she couldn't even see the rise and fall of his chest. "We have wounded with injuries that can be tended."

"Do you believe they will leave their king?" Wulfgar asked, with a hint of anger edging his tone. "Bruenor *is* Mithral Hall. He brought his clan back here and brought them back to prominence. They owe him all of their efforts and more."

"And do you think Bruenor would want that?" Regis asked before Catti-brie could reply. "If he knew that others were suffering, perhaps even dying, because so many priests were stuck here time after time, holding him alive when he had so little life left in him, he would not be pleased."

"How can you speak such words?" Wulfgar shouted back. "After all that Bruenor has—"

"None of us love him less than yourself," Catti-brie interrupted. She moved right up to Wulfgar and pushed his pointing, accusing fingers aside, battling with him for a moment before wrapping her arms around him and pulling him close. "Not me, and not Rumblebelly."

She finished by hugging Wulfgar even tighter, and he didn't resist.

"None of us can serve in his stead," Regis remarked. "I am Steward of

Mithral Hall, but that is only because I speak for Bruenor. I cannot speak without Bruenor—not to Clan Battlehammer."

"Nor can I, and not Wulfgar nor Drizzt," Catti-brie agreed, finally letting go and stepping back from the overwhelmed barbarian. "Only a dwarf can serve as King of Mithral Hall, but I'm thinking that we three, as Bruenor's family and friends, will have a large say in who succeeds him. We owe it to Bruenor to choose well."

"It would have been Dagnabbit, I think," said Regis.

"His father, then?" Catti-brie asked, and though she had incited it, she could hardly believe that they were discussing such grim business.

Regis shook his head and replied, "Dagna wouldn't take it . . . as he refused the stewardship. We should speak with him, of course, but he's shown little interest."

"Then who?" asked Wulfgar.

"Cordio Muffinhead has been an amazing leader among the dwarves in the hall," Regis remarked. "He has organized the defense of the lower tunnels brilliantly, as well as putting all of the priests into balanced shifts to handle the wounded and Bruenor."

"But Cordio's not a Battlehammer," Catti-brie reminded them. "And never has a priest led Mithral Hall."

"The Brawnanvil's are the closest cousins of Bruenor," said Wulfgar. "And surely none has distinguished himself any greater than Banak in the fighting outside the hall."

The other two thought on that for a moment, then each nodded their agreement.

"Banak, then," said Regis. "If he survives the war with the orcs."

"And if . . ." Catti-brie started to add, but the words caught in her throat, and she turned back to regard Bruenor.

They would recommend Banak as the new King of Mithral Hall, but only, of course, after her father, the dear old dwarf who had taken her in as an orphaned child and raised her with dignity and hope, had passed on from the world of flesh and blood.

PART TWO LOOKING IN THE MIRROR

I erred, as I knew I would. Rationally, in those moments when I have been able to slip away from my anger, I have known for some time that my actions have bordered on recklessness, and that I would find my end out here on the mountain slopes.

Is that what I have desired all along, since the fall of Shallows? Do I seek the end of pain at the end of a spear?

There is so much more to this orc assault than we believed when first we encountered the two wayward and wounded dwarves from Citadel Felbarr. The orcs have found organization and cooperation, at least to an extent that they save their sharpened swords for a common enemy. All the North is threatened, surely, especially Mithral Hall, and I would not be surprised to learn that the dwarves have already buttoned themselves up inside their dark halls, sealing their great doors against the assault of the overwhelming orc hordes.

Perhaps it is that realization, that these hordes threaten the place that for so long was my home, that so drives me on to strike against the raiders. Perhaps my actions are bringing some measure of discomfort to the invaders, and some level of assistance to the dwarves.

Or is that line of thinking merely justification? Can I admit that possibility to myself at least? Because in my heart I know that even if the orcs had retreated back to their holes after the fall of Shallows, I would not have turned back for Mithral Hall. I would have followed the orcs to the darkest places, scimitars high and ready, Guenhwyvar crouched beside me. I would have struck hard at them, as I do now, taking what little pleasure seems left in my life in the warmth of spilling orc blood.

How I hate them.

Or is it even them?

It is all too confusing to me. I strike hard and in my mind I see Bruenor atop the burning tower, tumbling to his death.

I strike hard and in my mind I see Ellifain falling wounded across the room, slumping to her death.

I strike hard, and if I am lucky, I see nothing—nothing but the blur of the moment. As my instincts engulf my rational mind, I am at peace.

And yet, as those immediate needs retreat, as the orcs flee or fall dead, I often find unintended and unwelcome consequences.

What pain I have caused Guenhwyvar these last days! The

panther comes to my call unerringly and fights as I instruct and as her instincts guide. I ask her to go against great foes, and there is no complaint. I hear her wounded cry as she writhes in the grip of a giant, but there is no accusation toward me buried within that wail. And when I call upon her again, after her rest in the Astral Plane, she is there, by my side, not judging, uncomplaining.

It is as it was in the Underdark those days after I walked out of Menzoberranzan. She is my only contact to the humanity within me, the only window on my heart and soul. I know that I should be rid of her now, that I should hand her over to one more worthy, for I have no hope that I will survive this ordeal. How great it wounds me to think of the figurine that summons Guenhwyvar, the link to the astral spirit of the panther, in the clutches of an orc.

And yet, I find that I cannot make that trip to Mithral Hall to turn over the panther to the dwarves. I cannot walk this road without her, and it is a road I am unable to turn from.

I am weak, perhaps, or I am a fool. Whichever the case, I am not yet ready to stop this war I wage; I am not yet ready to abandon the warmth of spilled orc blood. These beasts have brought this pain upon me, and I will repay them a thousand thousand times over, until my scimitars slip from my weakened grasp and I fall dying to the stone.

I can only hope that Guenhwyvar has gone beyond the compulsion of the magic figurine, that she has found some free will against its pressure. I believe that she has, and that if an orc pries the figurine from my dead body and somehow discovers how to use it, he will bring to his side the instrument of his death.

That is my hope at least.

Perhaps it is another lie, another justification.

Perhaps I am lost in a web of such soft lies too deep to sift through.

I know only the pain of memory and the pleasure of the hunt. I will take that pleasure, to the end.

—Drizzt Do'Urden

POSTURING

Drizzt stared hard at the elf who had just spoken his name. A flicker of recognition teased the drow, but it was nothing tangible, nothing he could hold onto.

"We have some salves that might help with your wound," the elf offered.

He took a step forward—and Drizzt backed away an equal step.

The elf stopped his approach and held up his hands.

"It has been many years," said the elf. "I am pleased to see that you are well."

Drizzt couldn't completely suppress his wince at the irony of that statement, for he felt anything but "well." The reference that he had met the elf before had his thoughts shifting away from that, however, as he tried hard to place the speaker. He had known few surface elves in his years out of the Underdark. Not many were in Ten-Towns, though Drizzt hadn't been close to many of the folk of the towns, anyway, preferring to spend his hours with the dwarves or out on the open tundra.

As soon as he thought of Ellifain, though, that poor troubled elf who had pursued him to the end of the world, and to the end of her life, Drizzt made the connection.

"You are of the Moonwood," he said.

440

The elf glanced at his female companion, bowed, and said "Tarathiel, at your service."

It all came flooding back to Drizzt then. Years before, on his journey back to the Underdark, he had traveled through the Moonwood and had met up with the clan of Ellifain. This elf, Tarathiel, had led him away, had even allowed him to ride on of the elf clan's fine horses for a bit. Their meeting had been brief and to the point, but they had left with mutual respect and a bit of trust.

"Forgive my poor memory," Drizzt replied.

He wanted to express his gratitude for Tarathiel's former generosity and to thank the pair for coming to his aid in the recent fight, but he stopped. Drizzt found that he simply did not want to begin that conversation. Did the pair know of Ellifain's pursuit of him and attack upon him? Could he tell them about Ellifain's fate, slain at the end of the very scimitars Drizzt even then held at his sides?

"Well met again, Tarathiel," Drizzt said, somewhat curtly.

"And Innovindil," Tarathiel remarked, motioning to his beautiful and deadly partner.

Drizzt offered her a somewhat stiff bow.

"The orcs are fast returning," Innovindil remarked, for she alone had been looking around during the brief exchange. "Let us go somewhere that we might better speak of the past, and of the present danger that engulfs this region."

The two started off and motioned for Drizzt to hurry to keep up, but the drow did not.

"We cannot give our enemies a single target of pursuit," Drizzt said. "Perhaps our paths will meet again."

He gave another bow, slid his scimitars away, and rushed off in the opposite direction.

Tarathiel started after Drizzt and started to call out, but Innovindil caught him by the arm.

"Let him go," Innovindil whispered. "He is not ready to speak with us."

"I would know about Ellifain," Tarathiel protested.

"He knows of us now," Innovindil explained. "He will seek us out when he is ready."

"He should be warned of Ellifain at least."

Innovindil shrugged as if it didn't matter.

"Is she anywhere about?" she asked. "And if so, will her pursuit of Drizzt Do'Urden overrule all sensibility? The land is thick with more immediate enemies."

Tarathiel continued to look after the departing drow and still leaned that way, but he didn't pull away from Innovindil's insistent hold.

"He will seek us out, and soon enough," Innovindil promised.

"You sound as if you know him," Tarathiel remarked.

He turned to regard his companion, to find that she, too, was staring off in the direction of the departing drow.

Innovindil slowly nodded.

"Perhaps," she replied.

Urlgen Threefist watched the latest wave of his shock troops, goblins mostly, charging up the sloping stone ground, throwing themselves with abandon at the dwarven defenses. The orc leader ignored the sudden shift from battle cry to wail of agony, focusing his attention on the defenders of the high ground.

The dwarves moved with great precision, but their lines wove a bit more slowly now, the orc leader believed, as if their legs were growing weary. Urlgen's lip curled back from his tusked mouth in a wicked smile. They should be tired, he knew, for he would allow them no rest. By day, he hit them with his orc forces and by night, his goblin shock troops. Even in those hours of retreat and regroup, the dwarves could not rest, for their defenses were not fully in place.

Flashes to the right side of the dwarven line, ahead to Urlgen's left, drew the tall orc's attention. Once again the dwarves had anchored their line with a marvelous pair of warriors, a huge human, strong as a giant, and an archer woman whose magical bow had devastated the extreme of Urlgen's left flank on every attack. They were two of Shallows's survivors, Urlgen knew, for he remembered well those silvery lines of death—the shining magical arrows—and the barbarian who had inspired terror among his ranks back at the doomed town. The great warrior had held the center of Shallows's wall single-handedly, scattering the attackers with impunity. His fists struck as hard as iron weapons, and that hammer of his had swept orcs from the wall two or three at a time.

Urlgen noted that fewer of the goblins seemed anxious to come in from that angle. His force was more constricted toward the center and right.

But still that magical bow fired off shot after shot, and Urlgen had no doubt that the barbarian warrior would find enemies to slaughter.

Soon enough, the assault stalled, and the disorganized and over-whelmed goblins came running back down the stony slope. Perhaps as a sign of their growing exhaustion, the dwarves did not pursue nearly as far as on the previous attacks, and Urlgen took faith that he was wearing them down.

That notion had the tall orc looking back over his shoulder, back to the wide lands north of his position. Reports had come in of the great gathering of orc tribes. His father's ranks were swelling. But where were they?

Urlgen was torn about the implications of that question. On the one hand, he understood that he simply didn't have the numbers at his disposal to dislodge the dwarves, and so he wanted those hordes to come forth and help him to push the ugly creatures right off the cliff face and back into their filthy hole at Mithral Hall. But on the other hand, Urlgen wasn't overly thrilled at the prospect of being rescued by his arrogant father, and even less by the thought of Gerti Orelsdottr coming in with the large remaining force of her giants and devastating the dwarves before him.

Perhaps it would be better if things continued as they were, for more warriors were filtering into Urlgen's force every day. Despite the hundreds of orcs and goblins dead on the mountain slope, Urlgen's army was actually larger than when he had first cornered the dwarves.

He couldn't risk a straight-out charge to push the dwarves off.

But attrition was on his side.

She started to draw her bow, but the creature was too close. Always ready to improvise, Catti-brie just flipped the weapon in her hand, bring-ing it up high before her where she caught it by the end in both hands and swept it out, swatting the pesky goblin across the face.

The goblin stumbled backward but was hardly felled by the blow. At last seeing an apparent opening in the defenses of that terrible pair, it and its companions howled and charged the woman.

But Catti-brie had dropped her bow and drawn out Khazid'hea, and the sentient, fine-edged blade felt eager in her hands. She met the goblin charge with one of her own, slashing across, then stabbing ahead, once and again. Khazid'hea, nicknamed Cutter, lived up to its reputation, slicing through anything the goblins put in it way: spears, a feeble wooden shield, and more than one arm.

The goblin press continued forward, more out of momentum than any eagerness to engage the warrior, but Catti-brie did not back down. A backhand severed a spear tip before the thrusting weapon got close; a turn down had the overbalancing creature throwing its feet out behind it, but a sudden reverse brought Khazid'hea straight up, slicing the goblin's face in half.

Well done! the sword telepathically communicated.

"Glad to be of such service," Catti-brie muttered.

She forced the sword across, then slid out to the side, sensing a presence coming fast for her back.

With perfect timing, Wulfgar rushed past her and headlong into the front of the charging goblin group. Hardly slowing, he ran over the first two in line, kicking them aside as he passed, and swept another couple from out before him with mighty Aegis-fang. It was his turn to pause, and he did so, bringing his hammer around and up high so that Catti-brie could charge past under his upraised arms, Cutter stabbing repeatedly.

Within a matter of a few moments, the goblins understood their doom, and those closest to the powerful pair fell all over each other and trampled down those behind them in their frenzy to get away.

All the goblins were running then, from one end to the other along the dwarven line. Wulfgar gave pursuit, catching one by the back of the neck in one hand. With a growl, the barbarian put the creature up high, and when it tried to resist, when it tried to swing its club out behind at the man, Wulfgar gave it such a vicious shake that its lips flapped loudly and its body jerked wildly, so much so that its club went flying away. Then the goblin followed, as Wulfgar threw it high and far, and over the lip of the small ravine that marked the end of the dwarven line.

The barbarian turned around to see Catti-brie leveling Taulmaril, and he walked back to join the woman as she put a few shots out among the retreating goblins.

"My damned sword's complaining," Catti-brie said to him. "Wants to be out, fighting and killing enemies." She gave a chortle. "Killing enemies and friends alike, for all Cutter's caring!"

"I fear that it will get all that it desires and more," Wulfgar replied.

"The wretches don't even care that we're slaughtering them," said Catti-brie. "They're coming up here for no better reason than to keep us tired, and we're killing them one atop the next."

"And in the end, they will have this ridge," Wulfgar remarked.

He put his arm on Catti-brie's shoulder as he glanced back, drawing the woman's gaze with his own.

The dwarves were already clearing their wounded, loading them onto stretchers lashed to the rope ladders and sending them down the cliff face using blocks-and-tackle. Only the most grievously wounded of the dwarves were going, of course, since the tough warriors weren't easily to be taken out of battle, but still, more than a few went over the cliff, sliding down to waiting hands in Keeper's Dale.

Other dwarves who were leaving the battlefield had been lined up off to the side, and there was no hurry to evacuate that group, for they were beyond the help of any priests.

"With the enchanted quiver, I can keep shooting Heartseeker day and night," Catti-brie observed. "I'll not run short of arrows. Not like Banak's charges, though, for his line's to thin and thin. We'll be getting no help from below, for they're working hard to secure the lower halls and tunnels, the eastern gate, and Keeper's Dale."

"He would do well to have a quiver like yours," Wulfgar agreed, "only one that produces dwarf warriors instead of magical arrows."

Catti-brie barely managed a smile at the quip, and in looking at Wulfgar, she knew that he hadn't meant the statement humorously, anyway.

Already the stubborn dwarves were back to their other work, building the defensive positions and walls, but it seemed to Catti-brie that the hammers swung a bit more slowly.

The orcs and goblins were wearing them down.

The monsters didn't care for their dead.

He came to the lip of the huge boulder silently, on bare feet and with an easy and balanced stride. Drizzt went down to his belly to peer over and spotted the cave opening almost immediately.

As he lay there watching, the female elf walked into sight, leading a pegasus. The great steed had one wing tied up tight against its side, but that was no effort to hobble the winged horse, Drizzt knew, but rather some sort of sling. The creature's discomfort seemed minimal, though.

As Drizzt continued to watch, the sun sliding to the horizon behind him, the female elf began to brush the glistening white coat of the pegasus, and she began to sing softly, her voice carrying sweetly to Drizzt's ears.

It all seemed so . . . normal. So warm and quiet.

The other pegasus came into view then, and Drizzt ducked back a little bit as Tarathiel flew the creature down across the way, beyond his partner. As soon as the steed's hooves touched stone, Tarathiel dismounted with a graceful movement, putting his left leg over the saddle to the right before him, then turning sidesaddle and simply rolling over into a backward somersault. He landed in easy balance and moved to join his companion—who promptly tossed him a brush so that he could groom his mount.

Drizzt watched the pair for a bit longer with a mixture of bitterness and hope. For in them, he saw the promise of Ellifain, saw who she might have become, who she *should* have become. The unfairness of it all had the drow clenching his hands at his sides, had him gnashing his teeth, had him wanting nothing more than to run off right then and find more enemies to destroy.

The sun dipped lower and twilight descended over the land. Side by side, the two elves led their winged horses into the cave.

Drizzt rolled onto his back, marking the first twinkling stars of the evening. He rubbed his hands across his face and thought again of Ellifain, and thought again of Bruenor.

And he wondered once more what it was all about, what worth all the sacrifice had been, what value was to be found in his adherence to his moral codes. He knew that he should go right off for Mithral Hall, to find out which of his friends, if any, had survived the orc victory at Shallows.

But he could not bring himself to do that. Not now.

He knew, then, that he should crawl off his rock and go and speak with those elves, with Ellifain's people, to explain her end and express his sorrow.

But the thought of telling Tarathiel such grim news froze him where he lay.

He saw again the tower falling, saw again the death of his dearest friend.

The saddest day of Drizzt's life played out so clearly and began to pull him down into the darkness of despair. He rose from the boulder, then, and rushed off into the deepening gloom, running the mile or so to his own tiny cave shelter, and there he sat for a long while, holding the one-horned helmet he had retrieved from the ruins.

The sadness deepened as he turned that helmet in his hands. He felt the blackness rising up around him, grabbing at him, and he knew that it would swallow him and destroy him.

And so Drizzt used the only weapon he possessed against such despair. He wanted to bring in Guenhwyvar, but he could not, for the panther had not rested long enough, given the wounds the giant had inflicted.

And so the Hunter went out alone into the dark of night to kill some enemies.

9

WITH GRUUMSH WATCHING

King Obould built a wall of tough guards all around him as he made his way through the vast encampment at the ruins of Shallows. The great orc was tentative that day, for the ripples emanating from the murder of Achtel were still flowing out among the gathering and Obould had to wonder if that backlash would turn some of the tribes against him and his cause. The reactions of the orcs guarding the region's perimeter had been promising, at least, with several falling flat before Obould and groveling, which was always welcomed, and all the others bowing low and staying there, averting their eyes to the ground whenever they reverently answered the great orc king's questions. As one, the sentries had directed Obould to seek out Arganth Snarrl.

The spectacular shaman was not difficult to locate. With his wild clothing and feathered headdress, the cloak he had proffered from dead Achtel, and his continual gyrations, Arganth commanded the attention of all around him. Any trepidation Obould held that the charismatic shaman might pose some rivalry to him were dispelled almost immediately when he came in sight of the shaman. The shaman caught sight of Obould and fell flat to his face as completely and as surely as if he had been felled by a giant-thrown boulder.

"Obould Many-Arrows!" Arganth shrieked, and it was obvious that the shaman was literally crying with joy. "Obould! Obould! Obould!"

Around Arganth, all the other orcs similarly prostrated themselves and took up the glorious cry.

Obould looked to his personal guards curiously and returned their shrugs with a suddenly superior look. Yes, he was enjoying it! Perhaps, he mused, he should demand more from those closest around him. . . .

"Are you Snarrl? Arganth Snarrl?" the king asked, moving up to tower over the still gyrating, facedown shaman.

"Obould speaks to me!" Arganth cried out. "The blessings of Gruumsh upon me!"

"Get up!" King Obould demanded.

When Arganth hesitated, he reached down, grabbed the shaman by the scruff of his neck and jerked him to his feet.

"We have awaited your arrival, great one," Arganth said at once, and he averted his eyes.

Obould, falling back off balance a bit, realizing then that such apparent overblown fealty could be naught but a prelude to an assassination, grabbed the shaman's chin and forced him to look up.

"We two will speak," he declared.

Arganth seemed to calm then, finally. His red-streaked eyes glanced around at the other prone orcs, then settled back to meet Obould's imposing stare.

"In my tent, great one?" he asked hopefully.

Obould released him and motioned for him to lead the way. He also motioned for his guards to stay on alert and to stay very close.

Arganth seemed a completely different creature when he and Obould were out of sight of the rest of the orcs.

"It is good that you have come, King Obould Many-Arrows," the shaman said, still holding a measure of reverence in his tone, but also an apparent inner strength—something that had been lacking outside. "The tribes are anxious now and ready to kill."

"You had a . . . problem," Obould remarked.

"Achtel did not believe, and so Achtel was murdered," said Arganth.

"Believe?"

"That Obould is Gruumsh and Gruumsh is Obould," Arganth boldly stated.

That put the orc king back on his heels. He narrowed his dark eyes and furrowed his prominent brow.

"I have seen this to be true," Arganth explained. "King Obould is great. King Obould was always great. King Obould is greater now, because the One-Eye will be one with him."

Obould's expression did not lose its aura of obvious skepticism.

"What sacrilege was done here by the dwarves!" Arganth exclaimed. "To use the idol!"

Obould nodded, beginning to catch on.

"They defiled and desecrated Gruumsh, and the One-Eye is not pleased!" Arganth proclaimed, his voice rising and beginning to crack into a high-pitched squeal. "The One-Eye will exact vengeance upon them all! He will crush them beneath his boot! He will cleave them with his great-sword! He will chew out their throats and leave them gasping in the dirt!"

Obould continued to stare and even brought his hand up in a wave to try to calm the increasingly animated shaman.

"His boot," Arganth explained, pointing to Obould's feet. "His great-sword," the shaman went on, pointing to the massive weapon strapped across Obould's strong back. "Obould is the tool of Gruumsh. Obould is Gruumsh. Gruumsh is Obould! I have seen this!"

Obould's large and ugly head tilted as he scrutinized the shaman, seeking even the slightest clue that Arganth was taunting him.

"Achtel did not accept this truth," Arganth went on. "Gruumsh did not protect her when the angry drow arrived. The others, they all accept and know that Obould is Gruumsh, I have done this for you, my king . . . my god."

The great orc king's suspicious look melted into a wide and wicked grin.

"And what does Arganth want in return for his service to Obould?"

"Dwarf heads!" the shaman cried without the slightest hesitation. "They must die. All of them! King Obould will do this."

"Yes," Obould mused. "Yes."

"Will you accept the blessings of Gruumsh, delivered through the hand of Arganth and the other gathered shamans?" the orc priest asked, and he seemed to shrink down a bit lower as he dared ask anything of Obould, his gaze locked on the floor.

"What blessings?"

"You are great, Obould!" Arganth shrieked in terror, though there was no overt accusation in Obould's questioning tone.

"Yes, Obould is great," Obould replied. "What blessings?"

Arganth's bloodshot eyes sparkled as he answered, "To Obould we give the strength of the bull and the quickness of the cat. To Obould we give great power. Gruumsh will grant this. I have seen it."

"Such spells are not uncommon," Obould answered sharply. "I would demand no less from—"

"No spell!" Arganth interrupted, and he nearly fainted dead away when he realized that he had done so. He paused for along moment, apparently hoping that the great orc would not crush him. "A spell to give, yes, but forevermore. Obould is Gruumsh. Obould will be strong—stronger!" he quickly and enthusiastically added when the scowl began to spread over Obould's ugly face. "The god-blessing of Gruumsh is a rare and beautiful gift," Arganth explained. "Not in a hundred years has it been granted, but to you, great Obould, it will be. I have seen this. Will you accept and join us in ceremony?"

Obould stared long and hard at the shaman, having no idea what he might be referring to. He had never heard of any "god-blessing of Gruumsh" before. But he could tell that Arganth was afraid and full of sincere respect. The priests had always favored Obould before. Why should they not when he made every conquest with his obligatory dedication to the great One-Eye?

"Obould will accept," he told Arganth, and the shaman nearly did a back flip in his excitement.

Obould was quick to sober him, grabbing him by the collar and lifting him easily right from the ground, then pulling him in close so that he could smell the king's hot breath.

"If I am disappointed, Arganth, I will stake you to a wall and I will eat you, starting at your fingers and working my way up your arm."

Arganth nearly fainted dead away again, for it was often rumored that Obould had done just that to other orcs on several occasions.

"Do not disappoint me."

The shaman's response might have been a "yes," or might have been a "no." It didn't really matter to Obould, for the mere tone of it, a simple and pitiful squeak, confirmed all the orc king needed to know.

"Am I doing them honor?" Drizzt asked Guenhwyvar.

He sat on the boulder that formed half of his new home, rolling the one-horned helmet of Bruenor over in his delicate fingers. Guenhwyvar lay beside him, right up against him, staring out over the mountainous terrain. The wind blew strongly in their faces that evening and carried a bit of a chill

"I know that I escape my pain when we are in battle," the drow went on.

His gaze drifted past the helmet to the distant mountains. He was speaking more to himself than to the cat, as if Guenhwyvar was really a conduit to his own conscience.

Which of course, she had always been.

"As I focus on the task at hand, I forget the loss—it is a moment of freedom. And I know that our work here is important to the dwarves of Mithral Hall. If we keep the orcs off-balance, if we make them fear to come out of their mountain holes, the press against our friends should lessen."

It all made perfect sense of course, but to Drizzt, the words still sounded somewhat shallow, somewhat of a rationalization. For he knew beneath the surface that he should not have stayed out there, not immediately, that despite the obvious signs that none had escaped, he should have gone straightaway from Shallows to Mithral Hall. He should have gone for his own sensibilities, to confirm whether or not any of his dear friends had escaped the onslaught, and he should have gone for the sake of the surviving dwarves of Clan Battlehammer, to bear witness to the fall of their king and to coordinate his subsequent movements with their own defenses.

The drow dismissed his guilt with a long sigh. Likely the dwarves had buttoned up the hall behind their great doors of iron and stone. The orcs would bring great turmoil to the North, no doubt, particularly to the myriad little towns that dotted the land, but Drizzt doubted that the humanoids would pose much of a real threat to Mithral Hall itself, even with the loss of King Bruenor. The dark elves of Menzoberranzan had attempted to wage such a war, after all, and with far greater resources and greater access through the many Underdark tunnels, and they had failed miserably. Bruenor's people were a resilient and organized force, indeed.

"I miss them, Guenhwyvar," the drow whispered, and the panther perked up at the resumption of talk, turning her wide face and soft eyes over her friend. "Of course I knew this could happen—we all knew it. In fact, I expected it. Too many narrow escapes and too many lucky breaks. It had to end, and in this type of a fall. But I always figured that I would be the first to fall, not the last, that the others would witness my demise, and not I, theirs."

He closed his eyes and saw again the fall of Bruenor, that terrible image burned indelibly into his mind. And again he saw the fall of Ellifain, and in many ways, that faraway battle wounded him even more deeply. For the fall of Bruenor brought him personal pain, but it was in accordance with those principles that had so guided Drizzt for all of his life. To die in defense of friend and community was not so bad a thing, he believed, and while the disaster at Shallows wounded his heart, the disaster along the Sword Coast, in the lair of Sheila Kree, wounded more, wounded the very foundation of his beliefs. Every memory of the fall of Ellifain brought Drizzt back to that terrible day in his youth, when he had first ventured onto the surface along with a raiding party that had attacked and slaughtered a group of innocent surface elves. That had been the first real trial, the first life-and-death trial, of his principles that Drizzt Do'Urden had ever faced. That fateful night so long ago, his first night under the stars, had changed Drizzt's perceptions indelibly. That fateful night had indeed been the beginning of the end of his existence in Menzoberranzan, the moment when Drizzt Do'Urden had truly come to see the evil of his people, an evil beyond redemption, beyond tolerance, beyond anything Drizzt could hope to combat.

Zaknafein had nearly killed him for that wretched surface raid, until he had learned that Drizzt had not really partaken of the killings and had even deceived his companions and the Spider Queen herself by allowing the elf child to live.

How it had pained Drizzt those years before, when he had ventured through the Moonwood to happen upon Ellifain and her people, only to find the grown elf child out of her mind with rage and so obviously distorted.

And in the battle along the Sword Coast, for him to inadvertently slay her!

On so many levels, it seemed to Drizzt that Ellifain's death had mocked his principles and had made so much of his life, not a lie, but a fool's errand.

The drow rubbed his hands over his face, then dropped one atop Guenhwyvar, who had lain her head upon his leg by then, and was breathing slowly and rhythmically. Drizzt enjoyed those moments with Guenhwyvar, when they were not engaged in battle, when they could just rest and enjoy the temporary peace and the mountain breezes. The instincts of the Hunter understood that he should dismiss the cat, to allow her to rest in her Astral home. For she would be needed more desperately when orcs and giants were about.

But Drizzt, and not the Hunter, so torn and internally battling at that moment, could not listen to that pragmatic alter ego.

He closed his eyes and thought of his friends—and not of their fall. He saw again the uncomplicated Regis on the banks of Maer Dualdon, his fishing line stretched out to the dark waters before him. He knew that the hook wasn't baited, and that the line was nothing more than an excuse to simply relax.

He saw again Bruenor, grumping about the caves surrounding Kelvin's Cairn, shouting orders and banging his fists—and all the while winking at Drizzt to let him know that the gruff facade was just that.

He saw again the young boy that was Wulfgar, growing under the tute-lage of both Drizzt and Bruenor. He remembered the fight in the verbeeg lair, when he and Wulfgar had charged in headlong against a complex full of powerful enemies. He remembered the battle with Icingdeath in the ice cave, when a clever and lucky Wulfgar had brought down the icicle roof to defeat the dragon.

He saw again Catti-brie, the young girl who had first greeted him on the slopes of Kelvin's Cairn. The young woman who had first shown him the truth of his life on the surface, in a faraway southern desert. The woman who had stayed beside him, through all his doubts and all his fears, through all his mistakes and all his triumphs. When he had foolishly returned to Menzoberranzan in an effort to free his friends of the shackles of his legacy, Catti-brie had braved the Underdark to rescue him from the drow and from himself. She was his conscience and always told him when she thought he was wrong, but more than that, she was his friend and never really judged him. With a gentle touch, she could take away the shivers of doubt and fear. With a glance from those enticing blue eyes, she could look into his soul and see the truth of his emotions, busting any facade he might have painted upon his face. With a kiss on his cheek, she could remind him that he had his friends around him, always and evermore, and that in light of those friends, nothing could truly wound him.

In light of those friends. . . .

That last thought had Drizzt's head slumping to his hands, had his breath coming in shorter, forced gasps, and had his shoulders bobbing with sobs. He felt himself sinking into a grief beyond anything he had ever known, felt himself falling into a dark and empty pit, where he was helpless.

Always and evermore? Ellifain? Were those the lies of Drizzt Do'Urden's life?

He saw Zaknafein fall into the acid. He saw Withegroo's tower, that awful tower, crumble to dust and flames.

He fell deeper, and he knew only one way to climb out of that pit.

"Come, Guenhwyvar," the Hunter said to the panther.

He rose on steady legs, and with steady hands, he drew forth his scimitars. The Hunter's eyes scanned the distance, moving below the twinkling stars and their invitation to painful introspection to the flickers of campfires and the promise of battle.

The promise of revenge.

Against the orcs.

Against the lies.

Against the pain.

Thousands of orcs gathered around the broken statue of Gruumsh One-Eye one dark night, staying respectfully back as they had been instructed by their respective spiritual leaders. They whispered among themselves and bullied for position that they might witness the miraculous event. Those scuffles were kept to a minimum, though, for the shamans had promised that any who distracted the proceedings would be offered as sacrifice to Gruumsh. To back up their threat, the shamans had more than a dozen unfortunate orcs already in custody, allegedly for crimes committed out on the battlefield.

Gerti Orelsdottr was there that night as well, along with nearly a hundred of her frost giant kin. She kept her enclave even farther back from the statue, wanting to witness the supposed miracle that had the orcs in such a state of frenzy, but not wanting to give it too much credence by the weight of her immediate presence.

"Detached amusement," she had instructed her kin. "Watch it with little outward concern and detached amusement."

Another two sets of eyes were also witnessing the event. Kaer'lic Suun Wett and Tos'un Armgo at first remained near to Gerti's group—and indeed had met with the frost giantess earlier in the evening—but soon they inched closer, the drow cleric in particular wanting to get a better view.

The call for silence went out from those shamans near to the statue, and those orcs who did not immediately obey were quickly warned, usually at the end of a spear tip and often with a painful prod, by the many soldiers of Obould who were scattered throughout the throng.

Many shamans, Tos'un communicated to Kaer'lic, using the silent drow language of intricate hand movements.

A great communal spell, Kaer'lic explained. *It is not so uncommon a thing among the drow, but rarely have I heard of the lesser races employing such a tactic. Perhaps this ceremony is as important as the orcs have hinted.*

Their powers are not great! Tos'un argued, emphatically grabbing his thumb at the end of his statement.

Individually, no, Kaer'lic agreed. *But do not underestimate the power of shamans joined. Nor the power of the orc god. Gruumsh has heard their call, perhaps.*

Kaer'lic smiled as she noted Tos'un shift uncomfortably, his hands sliding near to the twin weapons he had sheathed on his hips.

Kaer'lic was not nearly as concerned. She knew Obould's designs, and she understood that those designs were not so different from her own or those of her companions or those of Gerti. This would not be a ceremony that turned the orcs against their allies, she was certain.

Her thoughts were cut short as a figure dramatically appeared atop the ruined idol of the orc god. Wearing dead Achtel's red robes and his typical ceremonial headdress, Arganth Snarrl leaped up to the highest point on the broken statue and thrust his arms up high, a burning torch in each hand, flames dancing in the night wind. His face was painted in reds and whites and a dozen toothy bracelets dangled from each arm.

He gave a sudden shrill cry and thrust his arms even higher, and two dozen other torches soon flared to life, in a ring around the statue.

Kaer'lic carefully eyed the holders of these lower torches, shamans all, and painted and decorated garishly to an orc. The drow had never seen so many orc shamans in one place, and given the typical stupidity of the brutish race, she was surprised that so many were even clever enough to assume that mantle!

Up on the statue, Arganth began to slowly turn around. In response, those shamans on the ground began to move slowly around the perimeter of the statue, each turning small circles within the march around the larger circle. Gradually Arganth began to increase the pace of his turn, and those below similarly began to move faster, both in their own circles and in their larger march. That march became more animated with each step, becoming more of a dance. Torches bobbed and swayed erratically.

It went on for many minutes, the shamans not seeming to tire in the least—and that alone told perceptive Kaer'lic that there was some magic afoot. The drow priestess narrowed her eyes and began scrutinizing more closely.

Finally, Arganth stopped all of a sudden, and those below stopped at precisely the same moment, simply freezing in place.

Kaer'lic sucked in her breath—only a heightened state of communion could have so coordinated that movement. With the synchronicity of a practiced dance team—which of course they were not, for the shamans were not even of the same tribes, for the most part, and hadn't even known each other for more than a few days—the group swayed and rotated, gradually coming to stand straight, torches held high and steady.

And Obould appeared. As one, the crowd, including Kaer'lic and her drow associate, including Gerti and her hundred giants, gasped.

The orc king was naked, his muscular frame painted in bright colors, red and white and yellow. His eyes had been lined in white, exaggerating them so that it seemed to every onlooker as if Obould was scrutinizing him specifically, and the crowd reflexively shrank back.

As she collected her wits about her, Kaer'lic realized how extraordinary the ceremony truly was, for Obould was not wearing his magnificent masterwork armor. The orc king had allowed himself to be vulnerable, though he hardly appeared helpless. His torso rippled with every stride, and his limbs seemed almost as if his muscles were stretched too tightly, the sinewy cords standing taut and straight. In many ways, the powerful orc seemed every bit as imposing as if he had been fully armed and armored. His face contorted as his mouth stretched in a wide and threatening growl, as his intensity heightened so that it seemed as if his mortal coil could not contain it.

Up above, Arganth dropped one torch to the horizontal, then swept it before him. The first orc prisoner was dragged out before Obould and forced to his knees by the escorting guard.

The creature whined pitifully, but its squeals were quickly drowned out by the shamans, who began chanting the name of their god. That chant moved outward, to encompass the front ranks of the crowd, and continued to spread back through all the gathering until thousands of orc voices joined in the call to Gruumsh. So hypnotic was it that even Kaer'lic caught herself mouthing the name. The drow glanced around nervously, hoping that Tos'un had not seen, then she smiled to see him similarly whispering to the orc god. She gave him a sharp elbow to remind him of who he was.

Kaer'lic looked back to the spectacle just as Arganth shrieked and brought his two torches in a fast and definitive cross before him, and the crowd went suddenly silent. Looking down to Obould, Kaer'lic saw that he had produced a great blade from somewhere. He slowly raised it high above his head. With a cry, he brought it flashing down, lopping the head from the kneeling orc.

The crowd roared.

The second orc prisoner was dragged in and brought to his knees beside the decapitated corpse of the first.

And so it went, the process of chanting and beheading repeated through the ten prisoners, and each execution brought a greater cry for the glory of Gruumsh than the previous.

And each made Obould seem to stand just a bit taller and stronger, his powerful chest swelling more tightly beneath his stretched skin.

When the killings were finished, the shamans began their circular dance once more, and all the crowd took up the chant to the great One-Eye.

And another creature was brought forth, a great bull, its legs hobbled by strong chords. The orc soldiers surrounding the creature prodded it with their spears and gave it no leeway whatsoever, marching it before their magnificent king.

Obould stared hard at the bull for a long while, the two seeming to fall into some sort of a mutual trance. The orc king grasped the bull by the horns, the two standing motionless, just staring.

Arganth came down from on high, and all the shamans moved around him and surrounded the bull. They began their spellcasting in unison, invoking the name of Gruumsh with every sentence, seeking the blessings of their god.

Kaer'lic recognized enough of the words to know the general spell, an invocation that, temporarily, greatly increased the strength of the recipient. There was a different twist to that one, though, the drow understood, for its intensity was so great that she could feel the magical tingling even from a distance.

A series of weird, multicolored lights, green and yellow and pink, began to flow around the bull and Obould. More and more of the lights began to emanate from the bull, it seemed. Those lights ran forward to engulf and immerse themselves in the orc king. Each one seemed to take a bit of strength from the animal, and soon it stood on trembling legs, and each one seemed to make Obould just a bit more formidable

It ended, and only then did Kaer'lic even recognize that during the process, the bindings had been cut away from the bull, so that the only thing holding it was Obould, one hand grasped upon each horn.

All fell silent, a great hush of anticipation quieting the crowd.

Obould and the creature stared at each other as the moments slipped by. With sudden strength and speed, the orc king brought his hands around, twisting the bull's head upside down. Reversing his grips, the orc king completed the circuit, bringing the poor creature's head around a full three hundred and sixty degrees.

Obould held that pose for a long moment, still staring at the bull. He let go, and the bull fell over.

Obould thrust his arms to the sky and cried out, "Gruumsh!"

A wave of energy rolled out from him across the stunned and silent crowd.

It took Kaer'lic a moment to realize that she had been knocked to her knees, that all around her were similarly kneeling. She glanced back at the frost giants, to see them on their knees as well, and none of them, particularly Gerti, looking overly pleased by that fact.

Again the shamans went into their wild dance around the broken statue, and not a one in the crowd dared to rise, though every voice immediately joined in the chanting.

It stopped again, abruptly.

A second creature was brought forth, a great mountain cat, held around the neck by long noose poles. The creature growled as it neared Obould, but the orc king didn't shy from it at all. He even bent forward, then fell to all fours, staring the cat in the eye.

The attendants loosened their nooses and removed the poles, freeing the beast.

The stare went on, as did the anticipating hush. The cat leaped forward, snapping and roaring, claws raking, and Obould caught it in his hands.

The great cat's claws couldn't dig in against Obould's flesh.

The great cat's teeth could find no hold.

Obould rose up to his full height and easily brought the squirming, thrashing cat up high above his head.

The orc king held that pose for a long moment, then called out again to Gruumsh and began to move about, his feet gaining speed with every stride, his balance holding perfect with every turn and every leap. He stopped in the middle of the frenzied movement and gave a great and sudden twist. The cat cried out, then fell silent and limp. Obould tossed its lifeless body to the ground beside the dead bull.

The crowd began to roar. The shamans began to sing and to dance, their circle bringing them around the orc king and the dead prisoners and animals.

Arganth moved inside the ring, then he ordered the culmination of the dance. The leading shaman began to sway rhythmically, whispering an incantation that Kaer'lic could not hear.

The ten headless orcs stood up and marched in silent procession to form two ranks behind Obould.

Again Arganth fell into his spellcasting, and suddenly, both the bull and the mountain cat sprang up, very much alive.

Very much alive!

The confused and frightened creatures leaped about and ran off into the night. The orcs cheered, and Obould stood very calm.

Kaer'lic could hardly draw her breath. The animation of the corpses did not seem like such a tremendous feat—certainly nothing she had expected from an orc shaman, but nothing too great in magical power—but the resurrection of the animals! How was that possible, coming from an orc?

And Kaer'lic knew, and Kaer'lic understood. Gruumsh had attended the ceremony, in spirit at least. The orc cry to their god had been answered, and the One-Eye's blessing had been instilled in Obould.

Kaer'lic saw that clearly in scrutinizing the calm orc king. She could feel the gravity of him, even from afar, could recognize the added, supernatural strength and speed that had been placed within his powerful frame.

The dwarves had erred, and badly, she knew. Their ruse in using the image of Gruumsh to so deceive his minions had brought upon them the wrath of the orc god—in the form of King Obould Many-Arrows.

Suddenly, Kaer'lic Sun Wett was very much afraid. Suddenly, she knew, the balance of power among those united in battling the dwarves had shifted.

And not for the better.

1o

WHEN THE TUTORED
STEPS FORTH

"It was impressive," Kaer'lic Suun Wett somberly admitted.

Beside her, Tos'un scoffed, and across from her, both Donnia and Ad'non sat very still, their mouths agape.

"They are mere orcs," said the castoff of House Barrison Del'Armgo. "It was all illusion, all emotion."

For a moment, it seemed as if Kaer'lic would reach over and smack Tos'un, for her face grew very tight, her muscles very taut.

"Of course," Donnia agreed with a dismissive chuckle. "The mood, the throng—the ceremony was amplified by the intensity of the—"

"Silence!" Kaer'lic demanded, so forcefully that both Donnia and Ad'non slipped hands quietly to their respective weapons. "If we underestimate Obould now, it could prove disastrous. This shaman, Arganth of tribe Snarrl . . . he was inspired. Divinely inspired."

"That is quite a claim," Ad'non quietly remarked.

"It is something I have witnessed before, in a ceremony in which several yochlol appeared," Kaer'lic assured him. "I recognized it for what it was: divine inspiration." She turned to Tos'un. "Are you normally so easily deceived that you can now convince yourself that you did not see what you did indeed see?"

"I understand the trick of the mood," Tos'un hesitantly replied.

"The bull's head was twisted right around," Kaer'lic scolded him and reinforced to the others. "The creature was dead, then it was not, and this sort of resurrection is simply beyond the powers of orc shamans."

"Normally so, yes," said Ad'non. "Perhaps it is Arganth whom we should not underestimate."

Shaking her head with every word, Kaer'lic replied, "Arganth is indeed worthy, relative to his heritage. He is frenetic in his devotion to Gruumsh and handled the coincidental death of Achtel quite cleverly. But if he was possessed of priestly powers sufficient to resurrect the two dead animals, then he could have overwhelmed Achtel and her doubts long before her untimely death. He did not do that—did not even attempt to do it."

"You believe Achtel's death a fortunate coincidence?" Donnia asked.

"She was killed by Drizzt Do'Urden," answered Kaer'lic. "There can be no doubt. He was witnessed, right down to his scimitars. He slew her and rampaged through the camp and off into the night. I would doubt him to be an instrument of Gruumsh. But Arganth played it that way to the dimwitted orcs, much to his credit and much to his success."

"And now we know that Drizzt has allied with the surface elves," Tos'un remarked.

"To what extent?" asked Donnia, who, despite the reports of the fight at the river, was not so convinced.

"That is secondary," Kaer'lic pointedly reminded. "Drizzt Do'Urden is not our concern!"

"You keep saying that," Ad'non interrupted.

"Because it seems as if you do not understand it," the priestess replied. "Drizzt is not our problem, nor are we his unless he learns of our existence. He is Obould's problem and Gerti's problem, and we would do well to let them handle him. Particularly now that Obould has been gifted by Gruumsh."

A couple of snorts accompanied that claim from the still-doubting duo across from Kaer'lic.

"Underestimate him at your peril now," Kaer'lic replied to those scoffs. "He is stronger—visibly so—and he is possessed of great quickness. Even Tos'un, who believes he was tricked, cannot deny these things. Obould is far more formidable."

Tos'un reluctantly nodded his agreement.

"Obould was always formidable," Ad'non replied. "Even before this ceremony, I had little desire to wage battle with him openly. And surely none of us wishes to do battle with Gerti Orelsdottr. But did the shamans make the orc king brighter and more clever? I hardly think so!"

"But they gave him, above all else, the confidence of a mandate and the supreme confidence of knowing that his god was with him on his endeavors," Kaer'lic pointed out. "Do not miss the significance of these two gains. Obould will be possessed of no insecurity now, of no inner doubts that we might exploit to our wishes. He walks with confidence, with strength, and with surety. He will look more carefully at our every word that contradicts his instincts, and even more carefully at our suggestions that run tangentially to his previously decided course. He is a stronger and swifter running current now, one that will be more difficult to deflect along our desired course."

The doubting smirks became scowls, and quickly so.

"But I believe that we have already set the river's course in proper flow," Kaer'lic went on. "We need not manipulate Obould any longer, for he is determined to execute the very war we desired—and now he seems more able to do it."

"We become detached and amused onlookers?" Tos'un asked.

Kaer'lic shrugged and replied, "Not such a bad fate."

Across the way, Donnia and Ad'non exchanged doubting glances, and Ad'non shook his head.

"There is still the matter of Gerti," he reasoned. "And this ceremony for Obould will likely put the giantess even more on her guard. Seeing the growth of Obould might bring cohesion to the orc tribes, but it will likely instill grave doubts in Gerti. For all the power you believe the orc king has gained, he will need Gerti's giants to seal the dwarves back in their holes and ravage the countryside."

"Then we must make certain that Gerti continues to follow Obould," said Tos'un.

The other three turned somewhat sour looks upon him, silently berating him for his lack of understanding. He took their expressions with proper humility. He was the youngest of the group, after all, and by far the least experienced in such matters.

"No, not follow," Donnia corrected. "We need to make her continue to travel the course beside him and to make sure that he still understands that he is walking beside her, and not leading her."

The others nodded; it was a subtle distinction, but a very important one.

Ad'non and Donnia went out as soon as the sun had set, exiting the deep cave the group had taken as their temporary residence, not too far to the east of the ruins of Shallows. The two dark elves blinked repeatedly as they came to the surface, for though no moon was up, the relative light of the surface night remained at first uncomfortable.

Donnia looked out to the east, beyond the steep slopes and cliffs, to see the Surbrin winding its way south, starlight sparkles dancing around the rushing waters. Beyond that lay the darkness of the Moonwood, Donnia knew, where more elves resided. As far as the four drow knew, only a couple had involved themselves in the affairs of Obould since the orc king, at the drow's bidding, had not yet crossed the Surbrin with any substantial numbers.

"Perhaps they will come forth from their forest home," Ad'non said to Donnia, reading her mind and her desires.

The male drow grinned wickedly and gave a low laugh.

They both hoped that the elves would come forth in force, Donnia knew. Obould could handle a small clan, and how sweet it would be to see some faeries lying dead at orc feet. Or even better—dare she even hope?—to have faeries taken as prisoners and handed over to Donnia and her band for their pleasures.

"Kaer'lic's continuing fear of Drizzt is disturbing," Ad'non remarked.

"Tos'un names the rogue as formidable."

"Indeed, and I do not doubt our Menzoberranyr friend at all in that regard," said Ad'non. "Still. . . ."

"Kaer'lic seems more fearful of everything lately," Donnia agreed. "She verily trembled when she spoke of Obould. A mere orc!"

"Perhaps she has been away from our people for too long. Perhaps she needs to revisit the Underdark—back to Ched Nasad, possibly, or even Menzoberranzan, if Tos'un can smooth our way in."

"Where we would be homeless rogues until one matron mother or another saw fit to offer us shelter—in exchange for slavish fealty," Donnia said sourly, and Ad'non could only shrug at that distinct possibility.

"Kaer'lic would not be pleased if she knew our intent this night," Donnia remarked a moment later.

Again Ad'non shrugged and said, "I answer not to Kaer'lic Suun Wett."

"Even if her reasoning is sound?"

Ad'non paused and considered the words for a long while.

"But we are not seeking Drizzt Do'Urden in any case," he said at length.

It was true enough, if only technically so. The pair had made up their minds to investigate the troubles Obould's rear lines had been experiencing over the past couple of tendays. Of course they knew that Drizzt Do'Urden was central to those troubles, but it was not he who had lured the two drow out of their deep holes—both because of Kaer'lic's reasoning and Tos'un's warnings, and because, as far as Donnia and Ad'non were concerned, there was better prey to hunt.

A pair of surface elves, seen by Gerti's giants riding winged horses—wouldn't those mounts be fine trophies!

Within the hour, the pair were at the scene of the last assault, near to the smaller river within the mountains. Orc bodies still littered the ground, for no one had bothered to bury them. Following the path of the massacre, the two soon had Drizzt's route of battle discerned, and the bodies of many orcs in a circle around one point showed them where the two surface elves had joined the fray.

More than a score dead, and only three blades engaged, Donnia flashed with silent hand signals, taking care to hold her silence.

Most felled by Drizzt, no doubt, before the other two even arrived, came Ad'non's answer.

They tarried around the battleground for quite a while, trying to learn as much as they could, both from the pattern of the dead to the types of wounds, about the fighting styles of those engaged. More than once, Donnia flashed to Ad'non a signal revealing her admiration for the sword work, and more than once, Ad'non agreed. And, with the night almost half over, the pair went out from the immediate area, working about the perimeter and beyond for some sign of passage.

To their surprise and delight, they found a trail easily enough and knew from the footprints and the bent blades of grass that it had been made by at least two of the three enemies.

The surface elves, Ad'non flashed. *I would have expected them to better cover their tracks.*

Unless they were not making the trail for the orcs, Donnia reasoned. *Few orcs could follow these subtle signs, I expect, though to our trained eyes they seem obvious.*

To our trained eyes and to those of Drizzt Do'Urden, perhaps? asked Ad'non's fingers.

Donnia grinned and bent low to study one particular stretch of brush. Yes, it made perfect sense to her. The trail seemed obvious to the keen eyes and tracking skills of the trained dark elves, but surely it was nothing that any orcs would find and follow. And yet, with her experiences concerning surface elves, Donnia knew that it was a clumsy passage, at best. The more she looked, the more Ad'non's subtle suggestion that the trail had been left on purpose for Drizzt rang true to her. The elves thought their enemies to be orcs, goblins, and giants, and thought that a dark elf was numbered among their allies. The orcs who had witnessed the massacre had indeed noted that the surface elves and the dark elf had parted ways immediately following the fighting; perhaps the surface elves wanted to make sure that Drizzt Do'Urden knew how to find them should he need them.

Shall we go and find our pleasure? Ad'non's fingers waggled.

Donnia brought her hands up before her, a movement of accentuation and exclamation, and tapped the outsides of her thumbs together.

Indeed!

Tension hung thick in the air by the time Kaer'lic and Tos'un entered Obould's great tent. One glance at Gerti, the giantess sitting cross-legged (which still put her head near to the arched deerskin ceiling) between a pair of grim-faced guards, told the two drow that the meeting had not gone well to that point.

"Nesmé has been overrun in the south," Gerti resumed as soon as the two newcomers took their places across from her and to Obould's right. "Proffit and his wretched trolls have made more progress than we and in a shorter time."

"Their enemies were not nearly as formidable as ours," Obould countered. "They battled humans in open villages, while we try to dislodge dwarves from their deep holes."

"Deep holes?" Gerti roared. "We have gotten nowhere near to Mithral Hall yet. All you and your worthless son have encountered are minor settlements and a small force of dwarves on open ground! And Urlgen has not even been able to push a minor force over the cliff face and back to Mithral

Hall. This is not victory. It is standstill, and all the while, Proffit the wretch marches from the Trollmoors!"

Proffit? Tos'un signed to Kaer'lic, spelling the unknown name phonetically.

Leader of the trolls, Kaer'lic replied, an assumption, of course, for she really had little knowledge of what was happening in the southland.

Kaer'lic turned her full attention back to the giantess and orc leader as she signed, though, and the expression on Obould's face rang out bells of alarm.

"King Obould's son claims the head of Bruenor Battlehammer as a trophy," the drow female interjected, trying to diffuse the situation.

Kaer'lic was only beginning to understand the depth of the change in the orc king, and it occurred to her that with his newfound confidence and prowess, Obould might not be above challenging Gerti or siccing his legions upon her and her minions.

"*I* have not seen any Battlehammer head," Gerti sharply replied.

"His fall was witnessed by many," Kaer'lic pressed. "As the tower fell."

"My giants claim no small part in that kill."

"True enough," Kaer'lic replied before Obould could explode—as he surely seemed about to do. "And so our victories to date at least equal those of this troll . . . Proffit?"

"Proffit," Obould confirmed. "Who has bound the trolls and bog blokes under his command. Who has led them from the Trollmoors in greater numbers than ever before."

"He will squeeze Mithral Hall from the south?" Kaer'lic asked.

Obould leaned forward and dropped his chin in his hand, mulling it over.

"Better from the tunnels," Tos'un reasoned, and the eyes of the three leaders turned over him.

"Let Proffit keep the pressure on the dwarves," the drow went on. "Let him and his minions keep them fighting in their tunnels after we seal them in Mithral Hall. We will raze the land and claim our boundaries and turn our attention to the beleaguered dwarves."

Kaer'lic's face remained impassive, but she did flash a signal of gratitude to Tos'un for his clever thinking.

"The fall of Nesmé and the presence of the trolls will more likely incite

Silverymoon to action," Kaer'lic added. "That, we do not want. Let them go underground and do battle with Mithral Hall, as the son of Barrison Del'Armgo suggests. Perhaps then our greater enemies will think that Proffit and his wretched creatures have retreated back to the Trollmoors, where even Lady Alustriel would not go in pursuit."

Obould was nodding, slightly, but what caught Kaer'lic's attention most was the scowl stamped upon Gerti's face and the set of her blue eyes that never once left the specter of King Obould. There was more going on than the lack of recent progress in the march to Mithral Hall, Kaer'lic understood. First and foremost, Gerti was seething about the apparent transformation of Obould. Was it jealousy? Fear?

For a moment, the notion terrified Kaer'lic. A rift between the giants and the orcs at such a critical juncture could allow the dwarves to regroup and wipe out their gains.

It was but a fleeting thought, though, for it occurred to Kaer'lic that watching the giants and orcs turn against each other might be as fine a show as watching their combined forces rolling over the dwarves.

"The suggestion intrigues me," Obould said to Tos'un. "We will speak more on this. I have sent word to Proffit to turn east to the Surbrin and north to Mithral Hall's eastern gate, where we will meet with him as we chase the dwarves into their hole."

"We must go straight to the south and push the resistance from in front of your worthless son," Gerti demanded. "Urlgen's forces are being slaughtered, and while it pains me not at all to see orcs and goblins shredded, I fear that the losses are too great."

A look of utter contempt came over Obould at those remarks, and Kaer'lic immediately began preparing a spell that would provide cover so that she and Tos'un could flee should the orc king launch himself at Gerti.

But to his credit, Obould settled back, staring hard at the giantess.

"My ranks have swelled threefold since the fall of Shallows," the orc king reminded her.

"The dwarves are slaughtering your son's forces," Gerti replied.

"And the dwarves are taking heavy losses in the process," said the orc king. "And they are growing weary, with few to replace them on the battle line, while fresh warriors join Urlgen's ranks every day. If more giants joined in the fray, the dwarf losses would increase even more."

"I do not sacrifice my warriors."

Obould began to chuckle and said, "Giants will die in this campaign, Dame Orelsdottr."

The sheer power of his tone had Kaer'lic tilting her head to study his every movement. Clearly the ceremony had done something to Obould, had instilled in him the confidence to deal with Gerti in a manner even beyond that which the drow cleric had anticipated.

"The choice remains yours to make," Obould went on. "If you fear losses, then retreat to the Spine of the World and the safety of Shining White. If you wish the rewards, then press on. The Battlehammers will be beaten back into their hole, and the Spine is ours. Once secured, we will flush the dwarves from that hole, and Mithral Hall will be renamed the Citadel of Many-Arrows."

That bit of news brought surprise to everyone in the room who was not an orc. Since the day she had met Obould, Kaer'lic had seen in him a singular desire: to retrieve lost Citadel Felbarr. Had he abandoned that course in favor of the closer dwarven settlement of Mithral Hall?

"And how will King Emerus Warcrown react to this?" Gerti said slyly, picking up on the same discrepancy and not-so-subtly reminding Obould of that other goal.

"We cannot cross the Surbrin," Obould countered without the slightest hesitation. "I'll not allow the greater powers of the North to ally against us—not now. Citadel Felbarr will send aid and warriors to Clan Battlehammer, of course, but when Mithral Hall is lost to them, with King Bruenor dead, the dwarves in the east will more likely welcome the refugees of Mithral Hall to their own deep holes. Then, once the adjoining tunnels are secured, our victory is complete and all the land from the mountains to the Surbrin, south to the Trollmoors, will be ours."

A smaller bite, Tos'un signaled to Kaer'lic.

A wiser course, Kaer'lic flashed back. *Obould seeks more than vengeance and battle now. He seeks victory.*

The notion astonished Kaer'lic even as her delicate fingers communicated it to Tos'un. While quite worthy among his inferior kin, Obould had always seemed to Kaer'lic so much less refined than that. From the day she'd met him, the orc king had spoken almost exclusively of retaking Citadel Felbarr, which, with the reclamation of Mithral Hall and the solidification of the alliances between the dwarven triumvirate—Mithral Hall, Citadel Felbarr, and Citadel Adbar—seemed completely unattainable.

Even in fostering this alliance and campaign, the four plotting dark elves had always assumed that Obould would reach for that goal, to abject disaster. Kaer'lic and her associates had never considered any real and lasting victory, but rather a simple state of resulting chaos from which they could find enjoyment and profit.

Had the shaman Arganth's ceremony granted some sort of greater insight to the orc king? Had the dwarves' blasphemy with the idol of Gruumsh brought the possibility of true and lasting victory to Obould and his swelling ranks of minions?

Kaer'lic took care not to let those thought spiral out of control, reminding herself that they were but orcs, after all, whatever their numbers. All she had to do was look at the simmering hatred in Gerti's eyes to recognize that Obould's designs could splinter and shatter at any moment.

"We seal the region under our domain at the onset of winter," Obould explained. "Put the dwarves in their hole and secure all the land above to the corner of the mountain range. We will fight through Mithral Hall's tunnels throughout the winter."

"The dwarves will prove more formidable in their underground halls," Kaer'lic said.

"But how long will they deign to remain there in battle?" Obould asked. "King Bruenor is dead, and they will have no trade unless they try to break out."

It made a lot of sense, Kaer'lic had to admit to herself, and the thought was both optimistic and fear-inspiring. Perhaps Obould was making too much sense. Ever skeptical of the entire endeavor, the drow priestess could see both a higher potential climb and a higher potential fall.

The worst part of it was her confirmation that King Obould had suddenly become much less malleable to the designs and deceptions of the dark elves.

That could make him dangerous.

Kaer'lic looked at Gerti and recognized that the giantess was thinking along pretty much the same lines.

11

UNSHACKLING

In a rare moment of respite, the exhausted Wulfgar leaned back against a boulder and stared out over Keeper's Dale, his gaze drawn to the western gates of Mithral Hall.

"Thinking of Bruenor," Catti-brie remarked when she joined him.

"Aye," the big man whispered. He glanced over at the woman and nearly laughed at the sight, though it would have been a chuckle of sheer resignation and nothing out of true amusement. For Catti-brie was covered in blood, her blond hair matted to her head, her clothing stained, her boots soaked with the stuff. "Your sword cuts too deep, I fear," he said.

Catti-brie ran a hand through her sticky hair and gave a helpless sigh.

"Never thought I'd admit to being sick of killing orcs and goblins," she said. "And no matter how many we kill, seems there're a dozen more to take the place of each."

Wulfgar just nodded and gazed back across the valley.

"Regis has given the order to all the clerics now that Bruenor is not to be tended," Catti-brie reminded.

"Should we be there when he dies?" Wulfgar asked, and it was all he could do to keep his voice from breaking apart.

He heard the woman's approach but did not turn to her, afraid that if he looked into her eyes at that moment he would burst out in sobs. And that was something he could not do, something none of them could afford.

"No," Catti-brie said, and she dropped a comforting and familiar hand on Wulfgar's broad shoulder, then moved in closer to hug his head against her breast. "He's already lost to us," she whispered. "We witnessed his fall in Shallows. That was when our Bruenor died, and not when his body takes its last breath. The priests have been keeping him breathing for our own sake, and not for Bruenor's. Bruenor's long gone already, sitting around a table with Gandalug and Dagnabbit, likely, and grumbling about us and our crying."

Wulfgar put his own huge hand over Catti-brie's and turned to look at her, silently thanking her for her calming words. He still wasn't sure about all of it, feeling almost as if he was betraying Bruenor by not being by his side when he passed over to the other world. But how could Banak and the others spare him and Catti-brie at that point, for surely the efforts of the pair were doing much to bolster the cause?

And wouldn't Bruenor slap him across the head if he ever heard of such a thing?

"I can hardly say my farewells to him," Wulfgar admitted.

"When we thought you dead, taken by the yochlol, Bruenor fretted about for tendays and tendays," Catti-brie explained. "His heart was ripped out from his chest like never before." She moved around, placing one hand on either side of Wulfgar's face and staring at him intently. "But he did go on. And in those first days, with the murdering dark elves still thick about us, he let his anger lead the way. No time for mourning, he kept muttering, when he thought none were about to hear him."

"And we must be equally strong," Wulfgar agreed.

They had been over it all before, of course, saying many of the same words and with the same determination. Wulfgar understood that the need he and Catti-brie had to repeat the conversation came from deep-seeded doubts and fears, from a situation that had so quickly spun out of their control.

"Bruenor Battlehammer's rest with his ancestors," he continued, "will be easier indeed if he knows that Mithral Hall is safe and that his friends and family fought on in his name and for his cause."

Catti-brie kissed him on the forehead and hugged him close, and with a deep breath, Wulfgar let go of his pain—temporarily, he knew. All the world had changed for him, and all the world would change again, and not for the better, when they buried King Bruenor beside his ancestors.

Catti-brie's words made sense, and Wulfgar understood that Bruenor had died gloriously, as a dwarf ought to die, as Bruenor would have chosen to die, in the fight at Shallows.

That realization did make it a little easier.

Just a little.

"And what of you?" Wulfgar asked the woman. "You are so concerned with how everyone else might be feeling, and yet I see a great pain in your blue eyes, my friend."

"What creature would I be if losing the dwarf who raised me as his own child didn't wound me heart?" Catti-brie replied.

Wulfgar reached up and grabbed her firmly by the forearms.

"I mean about Drizzt," he said quietly.

"I do not think he's dead," came the emphatic reply.

Wulfgar shook his head with every word, agreeing wholeheartedly.

"Orcs and giants?" he said. "No, Drizzt is alive and well and likely killing as many of our enemies as this whole army of us are killing here."

Catti-brie's responding expression was more grit than smile as she nodded.

"But that is not what I meant," Wulfgar went on. "I know the confusion that you now endure, for it is clear to all who know you and love you."

"You're talking silliness," Catti-brie answered, and in a telling gesture, she tried to pull away.

Wulfgar held her firm and steady.

"Do you love him?" he asked.

"I could ask the same of Wulfgar, and get the same answer, I'm sure."

"You know what I mean," Wulfgar pressed. "Of course you love Drizzt as a friend, as I do, as Regis does, as Bruenor does. I knew that I would find my way from the drink and from my torment when I returned to you four, my friends. My true friends and family. And you understand that which I now ask. Do you love him?"

He let go of Catti-brie, and she did step back, though she didn't turn her eyes from his crystalline blue gaze and did not even blink.

"When you were gone . . ." she started to reply.

Wulfgar laughed at her obvious attempt to spare his feelings.

"This has nothing to do with me!" he insisted. "Except in the manner that I am to you a friend. Someone who cares very deeply for you. Please, for your own sake, do not avoid this. Do you love him?"

Catti-brie gave a deep sigh, and she did look down.

"Drizzt," she said, "is special to me in ways beyond that of the others of our group."

"And are you lovers?"

The blunt and personal question had the woman snapping her gaze back up at the barbarian. There was nothing but true compassion in his eyes, though, and so Catti-brie did not lash out.

"We spent years together," she said quietly. "When ye fell and were lost to us, me and Drizzt spent years together, riding and sailing with Deudermont."

Wulfgar smiled at her and held up his hand, gently telling her that he had heard enough, that he understood well her meaning.

"Was it love or friendship that guided your way through those years and those roads?" Wulfgar asked.

Catti-brie pondered that for a bit, glancing off into the distance.

"There was always friendship," she said. "We two never let go of that. Friendship and companionship above all else sustained me and Drizzt on the road."

"And now you're pained because it was more than that for you," Wulfgar reasoned. "And when you thought you were dead with those orcs, the sting was all the more because you've all the more to lose."

Catti-brie stood staring at him and making no move to answer.

"So tell me, my dear friend, are you ready to surrender that road?" Wulfgar asked. "Are you ready to forsake the adventures?"

"No more than Bruenor ever was!" Catti-brie snapped at him without the slightest bit of hesitation.

Wulfgar smiled widely, for it was all sorting out for him then, and he believed that he might be able to actually help his friend when she needed him.

"Do you wish to have children?" he asked.

Catti-brie stared at him incredulously.

"What kind of question is that for you to be asking me?"

"The kind a friend would ask," said Wulfgar, and he asked it again.

Catti-brie's stern gaze dissipated, and it was obvious to Wulfgar that she was really looking inward then, honestly asking herself that very same question for perhaps the first time.

"I don't know," she admitted. "I always thought it'd be an easy choice, and of course, I'd want to have some of me own. But I'm not so sure of meself, though I'm guessing that I'm running out of time to decide."

"And do you wish to have Drizzt's children?"

A look of panic came over the woman, her eyes going wide with apparent horror, but then softening quickly. She was torn, Wulfgar could clearly see, and had certainly expected. For this was the crux of it all, the rough rub in their relationship. Drizzt was a drow, and could Catti-brie honestly go down that path? Could she honestly have children who were half-drow in heritage? Certainly the answer here was twofold, a heartfelt yes and a logical no, and both were emphatic.

Wulfgar began to chuckle.

"You're mocking me," Catti-brie said to him, and Wulfgar noted that as she became agitated, she seemed to sound more like a dwarf!

"No, no," Wulfgar assured her, and he held up his hands defensively. "I was considering the irony of it all, and it amuses me that you are even listening to my words of advice. I, who have taken a wife from the most unlikeliest of places and who am raising a child that is neither mine nor that of my unlikely wife."

As that message sank in, a smile widened over Catti-brie's face as well.

"And we of a family with a dwarf father who raises two human children as his own," she replied.

"And should I begin to list the ironies of Drizzt Do'Urden?" Wulfgar asked.

Catti-brie's laughter had her holding her sides then.

"Can we be saying," she said, "that Regis is the most normal among us?"

"Then be afraid!" Wulfgar replied dramatically, and Catti-brie laughed all the harder. "Perhaps it is just those ironies about us that drive us on along this road we so often choose."

Catti-brie sobered a bit at that remark, then stopped her giggling, her expression going suddenly more grim—and Wulfgar understood that the conversation had led her right back to where they had started, right back to the state of Bruenor Battlehammer.

"Perhaps," the woman agreed. "Until now, with Bruenor gone and Drizzt out there alone."

"No!" Wulfgar insisted, and he came up from the rock, standing tall before her. "Still!"

Catti-brie sighed and started to reply, but Wulfgar cut her short.

"I think of my wife and child back in Mithral Hall," the warrior said. "Every time I walk out of there, I know that I might not see Delly and Colson again. And yet I go, because the road beckons me—as you yourself just admitted it so beckons you. Bruenor is gone, so we must accept, and Drizzt . . . well, who can know where the drow now runs? Who can know if an orc spear has found his heart and quieted him forever? Not I, and not you, though we both hold fast to our prayers that he is all right and will return to us soon.

"But even should he not, and even if Regis accepts a permanent position of steward, or counselor, perhaps, if Banak Brawnanvil becomes King of Mithral Hall, I will not forsake the road. This is my life, with the wind upon my face and the stars as my ceiling. This is my lot, to wage battle against the orcs and the giants and all others who threaten the good folk of the land. I embrace that lot and revel in it, and I shall until I am too old to run about the mountain trails or until an enemy blade lays me low.

"Delly knows this. My wife accepts that I will spend little time in Mithral Hall beside her." The barbarian gave a self-deprecating chortle and asked, "Can I really call her my wife? And Colson my child?"

"You're a good husband to her and a fine father to the little one."

Wulfgar gave a nod of thanks to the woman for those words.

"But still I will not forsake the road," he said, "and Delly Curtie would not have me forsake the road. That is what I have come to love most about her. That is why I trust that she will raise Colson in my absence, should I be killed, to be true to whomever it is that Colson is meant to be."

"True to her nature?"

"Independence is what matters," Wulfgar explained. "And it is more difficult by far to be independent of our own inner shackles than it is of the shackles that others might place upon us."

The simple words nearly knocked Catti-brie over. "I said the same thing to a friend of ours, once," she said.

"Drizzt?"

The woman nodded.

"Then heed your own words," Wulfgar advised her. "You love him and you love the road. Why does there need to be more than that?"

"If I'm wanting to have children of me own. . . ."

"Then you will come to know that, and so you will redirect the road of your life appropriately," Wulfgar told her. "Or it might be that fate intervenes, against all care, and you get that which you're not sure you want."

Catti-brie sucked in her breath.

"And would it truly be such a bad thing?" Wulfgar asked her. "To mother the child of Drizzt Do'Urden? If the babe was possessed of half his skills and but a tenth of his heart, it would be among the greatest of all the folk of the northland."

Catti-brie sighed again and brought a hand up to wipe her eyes.

"If Bruenor can raise a couple of human brats as troublesome as us. . . ." Wulfgar remarked with a smirk, and he let the thought hang in the air.

Catti-brie laughed and smiled at him, with warmth and gratitude.

"Take your love and your pleasure as you find it," Wulfgar advised. "Do not worry so much of the future that you let today pass you by. You are happy beside Drizzt. Need you know more than that?"

"You sound just like him," Catti-brie answered. "Only not when he was advising me, but when he was advising himself. You're asking me to go to the same place that Drizzt found, the same enjoyment in the moment and all the rest be damned."

"And as soon as Drizzt found that place, you began to doubt," Wulfgar said with a coy smile. "When he found the place of comfort and acceptance, all obstacles were removed, and so you put one up—your fears—to hold it all in stasis."

Catti-brie was shaking her head, but Wulfgar could tell that she wasn't disagreeing with him in the least.

"Follow your heart," the big man said quietly. "Minute by minute and day by day. Let the course of the river run as it will, instead of tying yourself up in fears that you may never realize."

Catti-brie looked up at him, her head beginning to nod. Glad that he had brought her some comfort and some good advice, Wulfgar bent over and kissed his friend on the forehead.

That elicited a wide and warm smile from Catti-brie, and she seemed to him, for the first time in a long time, to be at peace with herself. He had forced her emotions back into the present, he knew, and had released her from the fears that had taken hold. Why would she sacrifice her present joys—the wild road, the companionship of her friends, and the love of Drizzt—for fear of some uncertain future wishes?

He watched her continue to visibly relax, watched her smile become more and more genuine and enduring. He could see her emotional shackles falling away.

"When'd you get so smart?" she asked him.

"In Hell and out of it," Wulfgar replied. "In a hell of Errtu's making, and in a hell of Wulfgar's making."

Catti-brie tilted her head and stared at him hard.

"And are you free?" she asked. "Are you really free?"

Wulfgar's smile matched her own, even exceeded it, his boyish grin so wide and so sincere, so warm and, yes, so free.

"Let's go kill some orcs," he remarked, words that were truly comforting music to the ears of Catti-brie.

12

SUBTERFUGE

They swept across the vale between Shallows and the mountains north of Keeper's Dale like a massive earthbound storm, a great darkness and swirling tempest. Led by Obould-who-was-Gruumsh and anchored by a horde of frost giants greater than any that had been assembled in centuries, the orc swarm trampled the brush and sent the animals small and large fleeing before it.

For the first time in tendays, King Obould Many-Arrows met up with his son, Urlgen, in a sheltered ravine north of the sloping battleground where the dwarves had entrenched.

Urlgen entered the meeting full of fury, ready to demand more troops so that he could push the dwarves over the cliff and back into their holes. Fearing that Obould and Gerti would blame him for his lack of a definitive victory, Urlgen was ready to go on the offensive, to chastise his father for not giving him enough force to unseat the dwarves from the high ground.

As soon as he entered his father's tent, though, the younger orc's bluster melted away in confusion. For he knew, upon his very first glance, that the brutish leader sitting before him was not his father as he had known him, but was something more. Something greater.

A shaman that Urlgen did not know sat in place before, below, and to the side of Obould, dressed in a feathered headdress and a bright red robe.

To the side, against the left-hand edge of the tent, sat Gerti Orelsdottr, and she seemed to the younger orc leader not so pleased.

Mostly though, Urlgen focused on Obould, for the brash young orc was barely able to take his eyes off his father, off the bulging muscles of the intense orc's powerful arms, or the fierce set of Obould's face, seeming on the verge of an explosion. That was not so uncommon a thing with Obould, but Urlgen understood that the danger of Obould was somehow greater than ever before.

"You have not pushed them back into Mithral Hall," Obould stated.

Urlgen could not tell if the statement was meant as a mere recitation of the obvious or an indictment of his leadership.

"They are a difficult foe," Urlgen admitted. "They reached the high ground before we caught up to them and immediately set about preparing their defenses."

"And those defenses are now entrenched?"

"No!" Urlgen said with some confidence. "We have struck at them too often. They continue to work, but with arms weary from battle."

"Then strike at them again, and again after that," Obould demanded, coming forward suddenly and powerfully. "Let them die of exhaustion if not at the end of an orc spear. Let them grow so weary of battle that they retreat to their dark hole!"

"I need more warriors."

"You need nothing more!" Obould screamed right back at Urlgen, and he came right out of his seat then and put his face just an inch from his son's. "Fight them and stab them! Crush them and grind them into the stone!"

Urlgen tried hard to match his father's stare, but to no avail, for more than anger was driving the younger orc then. Obould had marched in with a force ten times the size of his own, and with a horde of giants beside him. One concentrated attack would force the dwarves into complete retreat, would chase them all the way back into Mithral Hall.

"I go east," Obould announced. "To seal the dwarves' gate along the Surbrin and chase them underground. There I will meet with the troll Proffit, who has overrun Nesmé, and I will arrange for him to begin the underground press upon our dwarf enemies."

"Let us close this western gate first," Urlgen suggested, but his father was snarling and shouting "No!" before he ever finished.

"No," Obould repeated. "It will not be enough to let these smelly dwarves run back into Mithral Hall. Not anymore. They have chosen to stand against us, and so they will die! You must hold them and batter at them. Keep them in place, but keep them weary. I return soon, and we will see to the end of them."

"I have lost hundreds," Urlgen protested.

"And you have hundreds more to lose," Obould calmly replied.

"My warriors will break rank and flee," Urlgen insisted. "They splash through the blood of their kin. They climb over orc bodies to get to the dwarves."

Obould let out a long, extended growl. He reached up and grasped Urlgen by the front of his tunic. Urlgen grabbed Obould's hand with both of his own, and tried to twist free, but with a flick of his wrist, Obould sent his startled son flying across the room to crash down by the flap of the tent.

"They will not dare flee," Obould insisted. He turned to the red-robed shaman as he spoke. "They will see the glory of Obould."

"Obould is Gruumsh!' Arganth Snarrl insisted.

Urlgen stared incredulously at his father, stunned by the sheer strength of Obould and the sheer intensity in his simmering yellow eyes. A glance to Gerti showed Urlgen that she was horrified by the display and similarly frustrated. Most of all, Urlgen recognized that frustration, and only then did it occur to him that Gerti had not said a word.

Gerti Orelsdottr, the daughter of the great Jarl Greyhand, who had always held the upper hand in all dealings with the orcs, had not said a word.

Like a great yawning river, the swarm of King Obould's orcs began their pivot and deliberate flow out to the east.

Urlgen Threefist, stung and afraid, watched the turn and march from a high ridge at the back of his own forces. His father had reinforced him, but with nothing substantial. Enough to hold on, enough to keep the dwarves under pressure, but not enough to dislodge them.

For suddenly King Obould didn't want to dislodge them. His reasoning had seemed sound—keep the dwarves fighting and separated so that they could completely cut them off and kill as many as possible before Mithral Hall's western door banged closed—but Urlgen could not dismiss the feeling that part of the delaying tactic was for no better reason than to push the credit for success squarely off of Urlgen's shoulders and squarely onto Obould's.

A noise from behind and below turned Urlgen from his contemplations.

"I feared you would not come," the orc said to Gerti as the giantess climbed up to stand just below him, which put her face level with his own.

"Was it not I who asked you to come out here at this time?" the giantess replied.

Urlgen bit back a sharp retort, for he still had not reconciled within himself the value of any dialogue with Gerti, whom he hated.

"You have come to fear my father," the orc did say.

"Can you state any differently?" Gerti asked.

"He has grown," Urlgen admitted.

"Obould seeks to dominate."

"King Obould," Urlgen corrected. "You would ask me to help the giants prevent the rise of the orcs?"

"Not of the orcs," Gerti clarified. "I would ask you, for the sake of Urlgen and not of Gerti, to check the rise of King Obould. Where will Urlgen fit in under the god-figure that Obould is fast becoming?"

In light of the weight of that question, Urlgen didn't question Gerti's omission of his father's title.

"Will Urlgen find any credit and glory?" Gerti asked. "Or will he serve as convenient scapegoat at the first sign of disaster?"

Urlgen's lip curled in a snarl, and as much as he wanted to lash out at the giantess (though of course he would never dare do anything of the sort!), his anger came more from the fact that Gerti's reasoning was sound than from the obvious insult to him. Obould was holding him from gaining a great victory there and, but should he fail, Urlgen held no doubts of the severity of his powerful father's judgment.

"What do you need from me?" Gerti surprised him by asking.

Urlgen glanced back at the marching thousands, then turned to Gerti once more, staring at her curiously, trying to read the message behind her words.

"When the time comes to destroy the dwarves before you, you wish to make certain that the orcs praise Urlgen," Gerti reasoned. "I will help you to do that."

Urlgen narrowed his eyes but was nodding despite his cynicism.

"And that the orcs praise Gerti," he remarked.

"If we share in Obould's glory, we will help ensure that we do not suffer all the blame."

It made sense, of course, but to Urlgen, it all seemed so surreal. He had never been close to Gerti in any form. He had often argued with his father against even enlisting the giants as allies. And for her part, Urlgen understood that Gerti despised him even more than she hated Obould and the other orcs. To Gerti, Urlgen had never been anything more than a wretch.

And yet, there they were, sharing plans behind the back of Obould.

Urlgen led Gerti's gaze to the south, to the steeply rising ground and the distant dwarven encampment.

"I need giants," he said. "To secure my lines and throw huge stones!"

"The high ground gives the dwarves the advantage of range," Gerti replied. "I will not see the orc bodies covered by those of my kin."

"Then what do you offer?" Urlgen asked, growing more and more frustrated.

Gerti and Urlgen both scanned the area.

"There," the giantess said, pointing to the high ridge far to the west. "From there, my kin will be out of the dwarves' range and on ground as high as that of our enemies. My kin will serve as your flank and your artillery."

"A long throw for a giant."

"But not for a giant-sized catapult," said Gerti.

"There are tunnels beneath the ridge," Urlgen explained. "The dwarves have taken them and secured them. It will be difficult to—"

"As difficult as arguing your cause when your father declares that you have failed?"

That straightened Urlgen, and straightened his thinking as well.

"Take the ridge, and I will give you the warriors to secure it and to strike out against the dwarves, for the glory of us both," Gerti promised.

"No easy task."

Gerti led Urlgen's gaze back up the slope, to the piles and piles of orc bodies rotting in the morning sun, letting the implication speak for itself.

"Bash! They're fightin' again, and we're stuck here watching!" the old dwarf Shingles McRuff grumbled to Torgar Hammerstriker.

Torgar moved to the opening in the ridge's eastern wall, overlooking the mountain slope that had served as battlefield for so many days. Sure enough, the charge was on again in full, with orcs and goblins running up the steep ascent, howling and hooting with every stride. A look back to the south told the dwarf that his kin were ready to meet that charge, their formations already composing, Catti-brie's devastating bow already sending lines of sizzling arrows streaming out at the oncoming horde. Every now and then, there came a small explosion among the front ranks of the charging orcs, and Torgar smiled, knowing that Ivan Bouldershoulder had put that clever hand crossbow of his to work.

Even though he held all confidence that Banak and the others would stave off the assault, Torgar was soon chewing his lower lip with frustration that he and half the dwarves of Mirabar could not stand beside them.

"They were needing us here," Shingles reminded Torgar, and he dropped his hand hard onto Torgar's strong shoulder. "We're serving King Bruenor well."

"In holding tunnels that ain't getting attacked," Torgar muttered.

The words had hardly left his mouth when shouts echoed back at him and Shingles from the deeper tunnels to the north.

"Orcs!" came the cry. "Orcs in the tunnels!"

Shingles and Torgar turned wide-eyed expressions at each other, both fast shifting into snarling battle rage.

"Orcs," they muttered together.

"Orcs!" Shingles echoed loudly, for the benefit of all those dwarves nearby, particularly those back toward the southern entrance. "Get yer axes up, boys. We got orcs to kill!"

With energy, enthusiasm, and even glee, the dwarves of Mirabar set off to predetermined positions to support those farther to the north, where, they learned almost immediately from ringing steel and cries of rage and pain, the battle had already been joined.

Torgar barked out orders with every stride, reminders that he knew he really didn't have to offer to his disciplined warriors. The Mirabarran dwarves understood their places, for in the days they had been in the tunnels, they had come to know every turn in every corridor and every chamber where defenses could be, and had been, set. Still, Torgar barked reminders, and he told them to fight for the glory of Bruenor Battlehammer and Mithral Hall, their new king, their new home.

Torgar had set the defenses purposefully, designing them with every intent that he and Shingles would not be left out of the fighting. The pair rushed down one descending corridor and came out onto a ledge overlooking an oval-shaped chamber, and below they found their first orcs, engaged with a force of more than a dozen Mirabarran dwarves.

Hardly slowing, Torgar leaped from the ledge, crashing in hard among the orc ranks, bringing a pair down beside him. He was up on his feet in an instant, his axe sweeping back and forth—but in control. Shingles was airborne by that time, along with several others who had followed the pair to that room.

Those dwarves up front pressed on more forcefully with the arrival of the reinforcements, hacking their way through orcs as they tried to link up with Torgar and the others. Almost immediately, the battle turned in favor of the dwarves. Orcs fell and orcs tried to flee, but they were held up by their stubborn kin trying to filter out of the tunnel and join in the fray.

"Kill enough and they'll run off!" Torgar roared, and of course, that was indeed the expectation when fighting orcs.

Many minutes later and with the floor covered in orc blood, the dwarves had reached the tunnel entrance, driving back the invaders. With Torgar centering them, the dwarves formed an arc around the narrow opening, so that many weapons could be brought to bear against any orc that stepped through. Surprisingly, though, the orcs still came through, one after another, taking hits and climbing over the fast-piling bodies of their fallen kin. On and on they came, and five orcs fell for every dwarf that was forced back with wounds.

"Damn stubborn lot!" Shingles cried at Torgar's side.

He accentuated his shout with a smash of his hammer that laid yet another brute low.

"Too stubborn," Torgar replied—quietly, though, and under his breath.

He didn't want the others to take note of his alarm. Torgar could hardly believe that orcs were still squeezing out of that tunnel. Every other one never even got a single step back into the room before being chopped down, but still they came.

Cries echoing from the tunnels near to them told Torgar that it was not a unique occurrence in that particular battle, that his boys were being hard-pressed at every turn.

More minutes passed, and more orcs crowded into the room, and more orcs died on the floor.

Torgar glanced back at the ledge, where an appointed dwarf was waiting.

"Position two!" he cried to the young scout and the dwarf ran off, shouting the call.

"Ye heard him!" Shingles cried to the others in the room. "Tighten it up!"

As he finished, Shingles spun around a large rock that had been set in place at the side of the tunnel entrance, bracing his back against the unsteady stone.

"On yer call!" Shingles cried.

Torgar pressed his attack on the nearest orc, shifting as he swung so that he could directly confront the next creature as it tried to come out of the tunnel. Behind him, his boys went into a frenzy, finishing those in the room.

As soon as he thought the door temporarily secured, Torgar shouted, *"Now!"*

A great heave by Shingles sent the rock falling across the door, and Torgar had to scamper back to avoid getting clipped.

"Go! Go! *Go!*" Shingles cried.

The dwarves gathered up their wounded and dead and retreated fast to the opposite end of the room and out to the south.

Before they could get through that other door, though, the orcs had already breached the makeshift barricade and a pair of spears arced out, one scoring a hit on poor Shingles.

"Ah, me bum!" he cried, grabbing at the shaft that was protruding from his right buttock.

Though he already had one unconscious dwarf over his other shoulder, Torgar hooked his dearest friend under the arm and pulled him along, out of the room and down the southern tunnel, where a series of stone drops had been set in place to slow any pursuit in just such a situation. All across the tunnel complex beneath the western ridge, the dwarves were forced into organized retreats, but they had been in the tunnels for several days and that was more than any dwarves ever needed to prepare a proper defense.

Torgar was back in battle soon enough, and even a limping Shingles returned to his side, hammer swinging with abandon. They and a handful of other dwarves had made a stand in a stalagmite-filled room that sloped up to the south behind them. Figuring to make the orcs pay for every foot of ground across the wide chamber, the dwarves battled furiously, and again, the orc blood began to flow and the orc bodies began to pile.

But still the stubborn creatures came on.

"Damn stupid lot!" Shingles cried out yet again.

Torgar didn't bother replying to the obvious or to the hidden message of his friend. They were beginning to catch on that the orcs meant to take the tunnels, whatever the cost. That troublesome thought only gained even more credence a few moments later when another group of dwarves unexpectedly crashed into the room from a western corridor.

"Giants!" they cried before Torgar could even ask them why they had abandoned the organized retreat that would have had them bypassing that chamber altogether. "Giants in the tunnels!"

"Giants?" Shingles echoed. "Too low for giants!"

The dwarves charged across and launched themselves into the fray, slaughtering the orcs that stood between them and Torgar's group.

"Giants!" one insisted when he came up before the leader.

Torgar didn't question him, for in looking over his shoulder, the dwarf leader saw the truth of the words in the form of a giant, a giantess actually, crouching, even crawling in places, to arrive at the entrance of the western corridor.

"Get that one!" Torgar demanded, eager to claim that greater prize.

His boys rushed past him, and past those who had just entered, lifting warhammers to throw and ignoring the warning cries of their newly arrived companions to stay back.

A dozen hammers went spinning across the expanse, and every throw seemed true—until the missile neared the pale, bluish-skinned creature and simply veered away.

"Magic?" Torgar whispered.

Almost as if she had heard him, almost as if she was mocking him, the giantess smiled wickedly and waggled her fingers.

Torgar's boys began their charge.

Then they were stumbling, slipping, and blinded, as a sudden burst of sleet filled the room, slicking up the floor.

"Close ranks!" Torgar shouted above the din of the magical storm.

A bright burst of fire appeared, reaching down from the chamber's ceiling and immolating a trio of dwarves who were trying to do just that.

"Run away!" yelled Shingles.

"No," Torgar muttered, and with rage burning in his eyes almost as brightly as the magical fire of the giantess, the refugee from Mirabar stalked through the sleet at the kneeling behemoth.

She looked at him, her eyes blazing with hatred, and she began to mutter yet another spell.

Torgar increased his stride into a run and lifted his axe. He roared above the din, denying the storm, denying his fear, denying all the magic.

Two strides away, he threw himself forward.

And he was hit by wracking pains, by a sudden, inexplicable magical grasp that closed upon his heart and stiffened him in midflight. He tried to bring his arms forward to strike with his axe, but they wouldn't move to his call. He could not get past that burst of agony, that grasp of ultimate pain.

Torgar smashed into the giantess, who didn't move an inch, and he bounced away. He tried to hold his balance for just a moment, but his legs were as useless as his arms. Torgar fell back several stumbling steps. He stared at the giantess curiously, incredulously.

Then he fell over.

Behind him, dwarves swarmed into the room, crying for their leader, bending their backs against the continuing sleet, and Gerti (for it was indeed Gerti herself who had entered the fray), her most powerful enchantments spent, wisely retreated, covering her departure by launching a host of orcs into the fray behind her.

Ignoring the pain in his rump, ignoring the fresh flow of blood down the back of his leg and the new wounds, Shingles scrambled to Torgar's side. He slapped Torgar hard across the face and shouted for him to wake up.

Gasping, Torgar did manage to look at his friend.

"Hurts," he whispered. "By Moradin, she's crushed me heart!"

"Bah, but yer heart's stone," Shingles growled at him. "So quit yer whinin'!"

And with that, Shingles hoisted Torgar over his shoulder and started back the other way, determinedly and carefully putting one foot in front of the other as he struggled up the icy slope with his dear friend.

They did get out of the room and out of many more, and while the fighting raged outside, the dwarves from Mirabar battled and battled for every inch of ground.

But stubborn indeed were the orcs, and willing to lose ten-to-one against their enemies. By the sheer weight of numbers, they gained ground, corridor to corridor and room to room.

Back near the southern end of the tunnel complex, Shingles reluctantly ordered the last and most definitive ceiling drops.

He told all his boys, even the wounded, "Ye dig in and be ready to die for the honor o' Mithral Hall. They took us in as brothers, and we'll not fail them Battlehammers now."

A cheer went up around him, but he could hear the shallowness of it. For nearly a third of their four hundred were down, including Torgar, their heart and soul.

But the dwarves did as Shingles ordered, without a word of complaint. The last ground in the tunnels, the first ground they had claimed in entering the complex, was the best prepared of all, and if the orcs meant to push them back out the exits near to the cliff overlooking Keeper's Dale, they were going to lose hundreds in the process.

The dwarves dug in and waited.

They propped those with torn legs against secure backing and gave them lighter weapons to swing, and waited.

They wrapped their more garish wounds without complaint, some even tying weapons to broken hands, and waited.

They kissed their dead good-bye and waited.

But the orcs, with three quarters of the ridge complex conquered, did not come on.

"The most stubborn they been yet," Banak observed when the orcs and goblins finally turned and retreated down the slope. For more than an hour they had come on, throwing themselves into the fray with abandon, and the last battle piled more orc and goblin bodies on the blood-slicked slope than all the previous fights combined. And through it all, the dwarves had held tight to their formations and tight to their defensible positions, and never once had the orcs seemed on the verge of victory.

But still they had come on

"Stubborn? Or stupid?" Tred McKnuckles replied.

"Stupid," Ivan Bouldershoulder decided.

His brother added, "Hee hee h—"

Pikel's laugh was cut short, and Banak's response did not get past his lips, for only then did they see the very telling movement in the west of Torgar's retreat, only then did they see the lines of wounded dwarves streaming out of the tunnels, those able enough carrying dead kin.

"By Moradin," Banak breathed, realizing then that the huge battle on the open slopes had been nothing more than a ruse designed to prevent reinforcements from flocking to Torgar's ranks.

Banak squinted, a prolonged wince, as the lines of limping wounded and borne dead continued to stream out from the southern entrance of the complex. Those dwarves had just joined Mithral Hall—most of them had never even seen the place that had drawn them from the safety of their Mirabar homes.

"The retreat's organized," Ivan Bouldershoulder observed. "They didn't get routed, just pushed back, I'm guessin'."

"Go find Torgar," Banak instructed. "Or whoever it is that's in charge. See if he's needing our help!"

With an "Oo oi!" from Pikel, the Bouldershoulders rushed off.

Tred offered a nod to Banak and ran right behind.

Two others came up to the dwarf leader at just that moment, grim-faced and covered in orc blood.

"What's the point of it?" Catti-brie asked, observing the lines. "They gave so many dead to take the tunnels, but what good are those tunnels to them anyway? None connect to Mithral Hall proper—not even close."

"But they don't know that," said Banak.

Catti-brie didn't buy it. Something else was going on, she believed, and when she looked at Wulfgar, she could see that he was thinking the same way.

"Let's go," Wulfgar offered.

"I got them Bouldershoulders and Tred going to Torgar now," Banak told him.

Wulfgar shook his head. "Not going to Torgar," he corrected. "There is nothing in those tunnels worth this to our enemies," he added, sweeping his arm out to highlight the sheer carnage about the mountain slopes.

Banak nodded his agreement but kept his real fear unspoken. It was coming clearer to him and to the others, he knew, why the orcs had so desperately played for those tunnels.

Giants.

Wulfgar and Catti-brie sprinted away, actually catching and passing by the three dwarves heading to find Torgar.

"We're going up top," Catti-brie explained to them.

"Then take me brother!" Ivan called. "He's more help out of doors than in."

"Me brudder!" shouted Pikel, and he veered from his dwarf companions toward the duo.

Without complaint, having long before learned to not underestimate and to appreciate the dwarf "doo-dad," Catti-brie and Wulfgar continued along. They got to the southern end of the ridge and began to scale, beside the tunnel entrance from which came the line of wounded.

"We're holding!" one badly injured but still-walking dwarf proudly called to them.

"We never doubted that ye would!" Catti-brie yelled back, allowing her Dwarvish accent to strike hard into her inflection. In response, the dwarf punched a fist into the air. The movement had him grimacing with pain, though he tried hard not to let it show.

Wulfgar led the way up the rocky incline, his great strength and long legs allowing him to scale the broken wall easily. At every difficult juncture, he stopped and turned, reaching down and easily hoisting Catti-brie up beside him. A couple of points presented a more difficult challenge concerning short Pikel, though, for even lying flat on the stone, Wulfgar couldn't reach back that low.

Pikel merely smiled and waved him back, then went into a series of gyrations and chanting, then stopped and stared at the flat stone incline, giggling all the while. The green-bearded dwarf reached forward, his hand going right into the suddenly malleable stone. He reshaped it into one small step after another. Then, giggling still, the dwarf simply walked up beside the two humans and motioned them to move along.

The top of the ridgeline was broken and uneven but certainly navigable, even with the wind howling across the trio, left to right. Downwind as they were of the western slopes, they actually caught scent of the enemy before ever seeing them.

They fell back behind a high jut and watched as the first frost giant climbed to the ridge top.

Catti-brie put up Taulmaril and took deadly aim, but Pikel grabbed the arrow, shook his hairy head, and waggled the finger of his free hand before her, then pointed out to the north.

Where more giants were coming up.

"One shot," Wulfgar whispered. He grasped Aegis-fang tightly. "Be running as you let fly."

"Ready," Catti-brie assured him, and she motioned for Pikel to let go of her arrow, then for him to be off.

With a porcine squeal, Pikel sprinted out from behind the jut, running full out to the south. The nearest giant howled and pointed and started to give chase.

But then a streaking arrow hit the behemoth in the chest, staggering him backward, and a spinning warhammer followed the shot, striking in almost exactly the same place. The giant staggered more and tumbled off the western side of the ridge.

Wulfgar and Catti-brie heard the roar but didn't see it, for they were already in a dead run. They caught up to Pikel near to the southern descent, and without a word, Wulfgar merely scooped the dwarf up in his powerful grasp and ran on, hopping from ledge to ledge all the way back to the ground. Soon after they came down, boulders began to skip all around them, and the trio worked hard to help those dwarves still in the area back into the shelter of the tunnel.

Not so far in, they rejoined Ivan and Tred, along with Shingles McRuff and a very shaken Torgar Hammerstriker.

"Casters," Shingles explained to them. "Giant witch reached out and nearly crushed me friend's heart!"

As he finished, he patted Torgar on the shoulder, but gently.

"Hurts," Torgar remarked, his voice barely audible. "Hurts a lot."

"Bah, ye're too tough to fall to a simple witch trick," Shingles assured his friend, and he started to slap Torgar again, but Torgar held up a hand to deny the blow.

"Giants up above," Wulfgar explained to the dwarves. "We should move in deeper in case they come down."

"They won't move south," Catti-brie reasoned. "They wanted the high ground, and so they got it."

"And them orcs ain't coming on anymore, neither," said Shingles. "We dropped the roof on them, but they could've gotten to us by now if they'd wanted to."

"They have what they came for," Catti-brie replied.

She glanced back to the southern exit, and all seemed calm again, the rock shower having ended. Still, Wulfgar and the others gave it some time before daring to exit the tunnel again. The long shadows of twilight greeted them, along with an unsettling quiet that had descended over the region.

Catti-brie looked back to the main dwarven force, far to the east.

"Too far for a giant's throw," she said, and she glanced back up at the ridge.

Wulfgar started up immediately, and the woman went right behind. Back on the ridge top, even in the deepening gloom of night, they quickly came to understand what the assault had been all about. Far to the north on the ridge, giants were hauling huge logs up the western slope, while others were assembling those logs into gigantic war engines. Catti-brie looked back to the dwarves' position, with alarm. The distance was too far for a giant's throw, indeed, but was it too far for the throw of a giant-sized catapult?

At that moment, it truly hit the woman just how much trouble they were in. For the orcs to sacrifice so many, for them to allow hundreds of their kin to be slaughtered simply to earn a tactical advantage in the preparation of the battlefield, revealed a level of commitment and cunning far beyond anything the woman had ever seen from the wretched, pig-faced creatures.

"Bruenor's often said that the only reason the orcs and goblins didn't take over the North was that the orcs and goblins were too stupid to fight together," the woman whispered to Wulfgar.

"And now Bruenor is dead, or soon will be," Wulfgar replied.

His grim tone confirmed to Catti-brie that he had come to fathom the situation along similar lines.

They were in trouble.

13

DEFINING THE BORDER

"By the gods, old William, ye could sleep the day away gettin' ready for yer nighttime rest," said Brusco Brawnanvil, first cousin to Banak, the war leader who was making his amazing reputation across the mountains to the west, on the other side of Mithral Hall.

"Yep," old William—Bill to his friends—HuskenNugget answered, and he let his head slide back to rest against the stone wall of the small tower marking the eastern entrance to the dwarven stronghold. Below their position, the Surbrin flowed mightily past, sparkling in the afternoon light.

Soon after the first reports had filtered back to Mithral Hall of monsters stirring in the North, a substantial encampment had been constructed just north of their current position, along the high ground of a mountain arm. But with the desperate retreat from Shallows and the advent of the war in the west, that camp had been all but abandoned, with only a few forward scouts left behind. The dwarves simply didn't have any to spare, and the orcs were pressing them hard in the mountains north of Keeper's Dale. Rumors from Nesmé had forced Clan Battlehammer to tighten the defenses of their tunnels as well, fearing an underground assault.

In the east, there was nothing but the dance of the Surbrin and the long hours of boredom, made worse for the veteran dwarves because of their knowledge that their kin were fighting and dying in the west.

Thus, with Banak, Pwent, and their charges—along with the dwarves of Mirabar—making their names in a heroic stand against the pursuing hordes, Brusco, Bill, and the others still in the east just closed their eyes and rested their heads and hoped there'd be orcs enough for them to kill before the war ended.

"Ain't seen Filbedo in a few days," Brusco remarked.

Bill cracked open one sleepy eye and said, "He went through to the west, and out across Keeper's Dale, from what I'm hearing."

"Aye, that he did," said Kingred Doughbeard, who was up above them in the tower, sitting beside the open trapdoor, his back resting along the waist-high wall that ringed the structure's top. "We're not to be relieved fifteen for fifteen no more. Only twenty-five of us left on this side o' the halls, so some'll be pulling shifts two times in a row."

"Bah!" Brusco snorted. "Wished they'd asked. I'd've gone off to the west!"

"So would us all," Kingred answered, and he gave a snort. "Exceptin' Bill there. Bill's just looking to sleep."

"Yep," Bill agreed. "And I'll take the two-times watch. Three times, if ye're wanting. Nine Hells, I'll stay out here all day and all the night."

"Snoring all the while," said Kingred.

"Yep," said Bill.

"Found himself a comfortable spot," Brusco remarked and Kingred laughed again.

"Yep," said Bill.

"Well, if ye're gonna sleep, then switch with Kingred," Brusco demanded. "Give me someone to roll bones with, at least."

"Yep," said Bill.

He yawned and somehow rolled to his side and up on his feet, then wearily began to climb.

The noise below, of Kingred, Brusco, and a couple of others they had coaxed from the tunnels to join in their gambling, did little to inhibit the ever-tired dwarf, and soon he was snoring contentedly.

Halfway up the outside wall of the tower, nestled in the dark crevice where the shaped tower edge met the natural stone of the mountain wall,

Tos'un Armgo heard the entire conversation. The drow paused at one comfortable juncture and waited, cursing silently—and not for the first time!—the absence of Donnia and Ad'non. They were the stealthy ones of the group, after all, whereas Tos'un was a mere warrior. At least, that's what Donnia and Ad'non were always insisting to him.

Kaer'lic had given Tos'un a few enchantments to help him as he ran forward scout for Obould, but still, he wasn't overly thrilled with being so exposed, out alone in a nest of tough dwarves.

Obould wasn't far behind, he told himself. Likely the orc and his minions would overrun the feeble defenses of the encampment to the north within a short time.

That notion made the drow take a deep breath and turn around, picking his handholds. The cursed, burning ball of fire in the sky had moved behind the mountains by this time, thankfully, extended long shadows over all the area on this eastern slope. Still, it was uncomfortably light by Tos'un's estimations.

But it was growing darker.

The time of the drow.

Brusco blew into his cupped hands, then shook them vigorously, rolling the bones around in the cup of his gnarly fingers and callused palms. Then he blew into them again and whispered a quick prayer to Dumathoin, the god of secrets under the mountain.

He repeated the process, and again, until the other dwarves around the cleared, rolling area began complaining, and one even cuffed him off the back of the head.

"Throw the damned things, will ye?"

Of course, the dwarf's annoyance had an awful lot to do with the fact that most of the silver pieces were set before Brusco by that point, as the dwarf had gotten onto a winning streak since sunset, some hours before.

"Gotta wait for good ol' Dum to tell me what's what," Brusco replied.

"Throw the damned things!" several shouted at once.

"Bah!" Brusco snorted and brought his hands back to roll.

And a horn blew, loud and clear and insistent, and all the dwarves froze in place.

"South?" one asked.

The horn blew again. Expecting it, they were able to discern that it had indeed come from the south.

"What d'ye see, Bill?" Kingred called up.

The others scrambled out of the tower, moving to higher points so that they could look for the signal fires from their watch-outposts in the southland.

"Bill?" Kingred called again. "Wake up, ye dolt! Bill!"

No answer.

And no snoring, Kingred realized, and there had been none for some time.

"Bill?" he asked again, more quietly and more concerned.

"What do ye know?" asked Brusco, running back in.

Kingred stared up, his expression speaking volumes to the other dwarf.

"Bill?" Brusco shouted.

He rushed to the ladder and began a fast climb.

"Trolls to the south!" came a cry from outside, from the distance. "Trolls to the south!"

Brusco paused on the ladder and thought, Trolls? What in the Nine Hells are trolls doing up here?

Another horn blew, from the north.

"Get to the crawls!" Brusco shouted down to Kingred. "Get 'em all to the crawls and get ready to shut 'em tight!"

Kingred scrambled out, and Brusco looked back up the ladder. He could see one of Bill's feet, hanging out over the open trapdoor.

"Bill?" he called again.

The foot didn't move at all.

A nauseous feeling came over Brusco then, and he forced himself up, slowly, hand over hand. Just below the lip, he slowly reached up and grabbed Bill's foot, giving it a tug.

"Bill?"

No movement, no response, no snoring.

And suddenly, Brusco was blind, completely in darkness. Instinctively, he simply let go and tucked, dropping to the stone floor and landing in a bumpy roll. By the time he came out of it, the veteran warrior had his sword in hand, and he was glad at least to find that he was not blind, that the spell that had dropped over him was an area of darkness and nothing that had actually affected his vision.

"Get in here!" he cried to his companions. "Magic! And something's got Bill!"

Other dwarves, led by Kingred, charged back into the tower.

"Set a catch blanket!" Brusco ordered.

He rushed back to the base of the ladder and started up again, moving much more quickly. The other dwarves grabbed a pair of blankets, doubling them up. Each taking a corner, they stretched it wide under the trapdoor.

They heard a commotion above, shouts from Brusco for Bill, and a grunt.

A dwarf came tumbling down, hitting the side of the blanket and rolling off to thud hard against the floor.

"Bill!" the four dwarves cried together, abandoning the blanket and rushing to their fallen comrade, a bright line of blood showing across his throat.

"Get him in to a priest!" one cried, and began to drag Bill away.

The dwarves rolled toward the door, then stopped and shouted for Brusco when they heard another commotion up above.

Brusco fell from the darkness, landing hard on the floor. He tried to stand and staggered to the side and would have fallen had not Kingred rushed over and caught him.

"Damned thing sticked me!" Brusco gasped.

He reached back and brought a blood-covered hand back in front. All strength left him then, and Kingred had to set himself firmly to hold the heavy dwarf up.

"A hand!" he called, and another dwarf rushed to the opposite side of the wounded Brusco.

"To the crawls," Brusco managed to remind them, coughing blood between each word.

By the time they got out of the small tower, two carrying Bill and two supporting Brusco, they caught sight of other companions charging up from the south and heard the calls of those rushing back from the north as well.

In the south, they shouted, *"Trolls!"*

From the north came the cries of, *"Orcs!"*

Kingred handed Brusco over fully to the other dwarf and sprinted ahead, drawing a hammer from his belt as he approached the huge iron doors of Mithral Hall. He went in hard, hammering away, once, twice . . . a pause, and a third time. He waited a few moments and banged out the coded signal again and again, and more emphatically when he thought he heard the locking bar being lifted behind the door.

The last thing he wanted at that moment was for those impregnable doors to open!

A grinding noise began off to the side of the main entrance and a small rock slid aside, revealing a dark crawl tunnel. In went the dwarves, one after another, with Kingred standing beside the tunnel, urging them on. Dwarves came from the north and from the south, each group barely outdistancing the advancing force—trolls in the south, orcs in the north. Kingred saw the truth of it; even though a second crawl tunnel had been opened, all the dwarves couldn't possibly get in ahead of the monsters. He almost called for his fellows to open the main doors then, but he held off the urge and bit back his fear. He and some others would have to stay out, would have to hold back the invaders to the bitter end.

Kingred took up his sword and strapped on a shield, and he continued to order those rushing up into the crawls.

"Go! Go! Go!" he called to them. "Keep yer butt down and keep yer butt moving!"

The trolls were the first monsters to arrive, their horrid stench filling Kingred's nostrils as he rushed out to meet them. His strong arms worked tirelessly, slashing away at the beasts, driving them back. A claw raked his shoulder, drawing a deep line, but he shrugged it off and turned, swinging, at that attacker. One after another, Kingred drove them back. Fighting like a dwarf possessed, a dwarf who knew that all, for him, was lost, Kingred growled and pressed on.

A great two-headed troll, as ugly as any creature Kingred had ever seen, as ugly a nightmare as Kingred had ever believed possible, shoved some of the other trolls out of the way and stepped up before him. Swallowing his fear, Kingred roared and charged headlong into the beast, but a huge spiked club whipped across to intercept and the dwarf was lifted from the ground and launched far, far away.

At that moment, the orcs arrived on the scene, sweeping down from the north, howling and hooting and throwing stones as they charged in with abandon.

"We got a dozen left out there!" cried Bayle Rockhunter, one of the inner gate guards. "Open them durned doors!"

The dwarf slapped a heavy pick across his hands and charged for the portal, and many others fell in behind him.

"It ain't to be done!" the wounded Brusco cried. "Ye know yer place!"

That reminder slowed the charge to the great doors—portals that were not to be opened in any event without express permission from the clan leaders back in the western reaches of the complex. The dwarves at the eastern gate were not an army by any means, but merely lookouts and sentries, holding the hall at all costs. Opening those doors would be engaging an apparently powerful force, one that could then flow into the hall.

But not opening those doors meant listening to their kin caught outside die.

"We can't be leaving them!" Bayle shouted back.

"Then ye're stealing all meaning from their deaths," Brusco responded, much more quietly.

That tone as much as the words themselves seemed to steal all the fire from the angry young dwarf.

"Hold the crawl tunnels open as long as ye can," another dwarf remarked.

Two score dwarves got into the safety of Mithral Hall that fateful evening, while some dozen stood with Kingred outside the crawl tunnels and the great, barred doors. Eventually, those inside reluctantly pulled the levers that dropped the counterweights that slid the stones back over the crawl entrances, sealing their kin outside, sealing their fate. Brusco and the others shut the crawl tunnels with heavy hearts and with promises that Kingred and the others wouldn't be forgotten, that songs would be written and sung, tavern to tavern.

King Obould, Gerti Orelsdottr, and Proffit the troll stood back from the tower and the doors, watching the work as giants, orcs, and trolls piled heavy stones before Mithral Hall's eastern entrance. All sound from inside the hall indicated that the dwarves were doing likewise, but Obould didn't want to take any chances. His goal had been to seal the eastern gates, and so he was doing just that.

"The land is ours to the Surbrin," the orc announced to his fellow leaders. From the shadows, Kaer'lic and Tos'un listened carefully.

He forgets that his son has not quite sealed in the dwarves, as yet, Kaer'lic flashed to her companion.

Tos'un appreciated the sarcasm, though he was more impressed with Obould's progress. Given the pressure that Urlgen was placing on Clan Battlehammer in the west, the victory had been all too easy. A few dead orcs, a few dead dwarves, and Obould controlled the western bank of the Surbrin, all the way from the Spine of the World to the end of the mountains south of Mithral Hall. With defensive positions already being constructed along the river north of their current position, that was no small thing.

"The dwarves will find another way out," Gerti remarked, and Tos'un could tell that she, like Kaer'lic, simply wanted to deflate the glorious orc king a bit.

Obould offered a quick scowl at the giantess but turned his attention to the two-headed troll, Proffit.

"You have done well," he congratulated. "Your march was impressive."

"Troll no . . ." said the left-side head.

". . . get tired," added the right.

"And so you will go right back to the south when we are finished here," Obould said, and both heads nodded.

"We stretch our line the length of the Surbrin," Obould explained to Gerti. "Hold our gains against any who would deny them. And our main force goes back to the west and north."

"And Proffit goes back to the Trollmoors?" Gerti asked.

Her disgust for the smelly troll was easy to see.

"To the tunnels in the south," Obould corrected. "Tunnels that connect to Mithral Hall. Proffit and his people will begin the battle for the dwarven stronghold within. We will defeat the dwarves without and claim our new kingdom."

He has a vision, Kaer'lic flashed.

Tos'un hid his smile, for he could tell that his companion was growing very uneasy with Obould. The four clever drow had incited all of it, but never had they actually believed that Obould would orchestrate something definitive and winnable! What would happen, Tos'un wondered (and he knew that his drow companions were also wondering), if the orc king managed to secure all the North between the Trollmoors and the Spine of the World, from the Surbrin to the Fell Pass? What would happen if, with such a base to serve as a kingdom, Obould did finally rout the dwarves from Mithral Hall? What would Silverymoon do? Or Mirabar? Or Citadel Adbar or Citadel Felbarr?

What could they do? More orcs were pouring forth from the mountains, by all reports. Had Tos'un and his companions inadvertently elevated Obould beyond their control?

An orc kingdom nestled within the various strongholds—human, dwarf, and elf. Would other tribes flock in to join in Obould's glory? Would Obould seek treaties, perhaps, and trade with the other cities?

It all seemed so preposterous to Tos'un, and also amusing. When he looked at Gerti, though, her expression grim even as she outwardly agreed with the orc king, the dark elf was reminded that there remained many potential pitfalls.

Only then did Tos'un realize that Kaer'lic was walking out to join the three leaders and that Obould was calling to him as well. He moved out beside the priestess of Lolth.

"You go with Proffit," Obould instructed the warrior of Barrison Del'Armgo.

"I?" Tos'un asked incredulously, and with more than a little revulsion at the less than appetizing thought.

"Proffit will travel the upper Underdark to do battle with the dwarves," Obould explained. "Much as your city did."

Tos'un looked at Kaer'lic with surprise, wondering how the orc king might have garnered that information.

It is for the best, Kaer'lic secretly flashed to him, alleviating all his doubts concerning the source.

"You know the tunnels leading to Mithral Hall," Obould reasoned to Tos'un. "You have been there."

"I know little," the drow argued.

"And that is more than anyone else," said Obould. "We must soon begin our attack within the hall, if the surface is to be secured. You will guide Proffit in this hunt."

There was no debate in Obould's tone, and when Tos'un started to argue anyway, Kaer'lic flashed an emphatic, *It is better!*

"I will go with him," Kaer'lic then announced. "I know some tunnels, and better for Proffit to have two dark elves directing his forces."

Obould nodded and turned to other matters, mostly the continuing sealing of the great doors.

Why have you done this? Tos'un's fingers asked Kaer'lic as the pair drifted back from the main conversation.

We should be away, came the reply.

What of Ad'non and Donnia?

Kaer'lic shrugged and replied, *They will fend for themselves. They always do. For now, it is best that we go to the south.*

Why?

Because Drizzt Do'Urden is in the north.

Tos'un stared curiously at his surprising companion. Kaer'lic had expressed great concern about Drizzt, but to go far away simply because the renegade drow was operating in the region? It made no sense.

He couldn't know Kaer'lic's suspicions, though. Ever since Tos'un had joined the band of renegades with his tales of Menzoberranzan's Mithral Hall disaster, Kaer'lic Suun Wett had feared that Drizzt Do'Urden might be something more than any of the Menzoberranyr drow had ever appreciated.

Beyond his fighting skills, there was something special about that particular renegade drow, something god-blessed. Kaer'lic had always been a clever one, but she almost hated her cunning, for in the grip of her suspicions, the drow priestess understood that she might be, in effect, condemning herself. Might that not be the price of enlightenment?

Unknown to her companions, the priestess of Lolth was convinced of something both unnerving and perfectly wicked: Drizzt Do'Urden had the favor of Lolth.

14

ELVEN GNATS

Weapons flying, feet flapping, the two orcs had no desire to continue any battle with the deadly elf warrior on his flying horse—seeing three of their kin already down and dead was more than enough for their cowardly sensibilities, so they threw their weapons and ran away, sprinting along the rocky trail and shouting for help.

Behind and above them came the elf, astride his beautiful white charger, great wings driving them on. The orcs couldn't outrun him, certainly, nor could they hide unless they found a way underground.

And they would not, the elf knew.

He brought Sunrise out to the left, herding the pair back on the main, narrow trail.

Oblivious to anything but the pegasus and the elf, the orcs willingly veered and ran on at full speed. They came around a bend, one behind the other, and charged up a slight incline around another boulder.

At least, they tried to get around the boulder.

The second elf appeared, as beautiful as she was deadly. She came out in a spin from the left, from behind the boulder. The lead orc gave a shriek and stopped cold, throwing its hands out before it, but the elf didn't even strike at it. She rolled right around it, using the orc as an optical barrier to its running partner. The second orc pulled up fast, seeing its companion unexpectedly stopped, and didn't even notice the lithe form coming around on its companion's right until it was too late.

A sword skewered the orc through the chest.

The first orc opened its eyes again, and thought it had survived the attack, that the female elf had somehow gone right past it. Apparently, not one to pause and consider such a fortunate turn, the orc started to run again.

It got almost one full step before a sword bit it in the kidney. It got almost a second full step before the blade struck again. It got almost a third full step before the deadly sword came in yet again, across the back of its neck.

"I'm beginning to understand why Drizzt Do'Urden enjoys this existence," Tarathiel remarked, walking his mount up beside Innovindil.

"I do not think he enjoys it," Innovindil replied. She looked out across the rocks and gave a whistle. Sunset appeared, trotting her way. "He is driven by rage and is beyond all joy. We saw that when we came to his aid. He could not even accept our generosity."

Tarathiel wiped his bloody sword on the ratty tunic of one felled orc. His partner was right, he knew. He had hoped to begin a relationship with the dark elf when he and Innovindil had come upon Drizzt at the river. Tarathiel had hoped to speak with him about Ellifain, to learn what he might about her or to warn Drizzt that she was beyond reason and hunting for him.

But their discussion that day had never gotten even close to that point, and for exactly the reasons Innovindil had just espoused.

"Somewhere deep inside him, he must take some pleasure at killing these foul creatures," Tarathiel did respond. "He must recognize that his actions are for the betterment of the world."

"Let us hope," said Innovindil, in a less-than-convincing tone.

She looked up and around as she spoke, as if scanning for some sign of Drizzt.

The two moved along soon after, knowing that other orcs were converging on the area, rushing to investigate the screams of the five orcs the elves had killed. They kept the pegasi on the ground for the most part, trotting along, but used the flying mounts to cross ravines and small cliff faces to discourage any pursuit. They held high confidence that the grounded orcs could not possibly catch up.

The elves didn't return directly to their cave that night, though, preferring to scout out even wider in search of more prey.

Drizzt might be acting out of rage, but for Tarathiel and Innovindil, there was indeed a sense of accomplishment and even pleasure at the sport. And there was no shortage of orcs to hunt.

Donnia didn't even have to signal her pleasure to Ad'non when the glow of warmth led them to the pile of manure, for her evil smile summed it up perfectly.

Ad'non's expression showed that he was no less pleased.

The drow could see that most of the heat was gone from the pile, and they had a point of reference so that they could use that to determine the time the manure had been there. Dark elves were taught to judge heat dissipation from droppings from an early age, and the pile was similar in texture and size to that typical of the rothé cattle the dark elves farmed in their underground cities.

The pair flashed coordinating messages, and they set off on a round-about path up the mountainside. Moving from bluff to bluff, from stone to stone, and from tree to tree, the pair made leap-frogging progress. Another pile of manure brought grins.

Then some more, down below them as they looked out from a flat stone.

Cave, Ad'non signaled, falling to his belly off to Donnia's right.

The two dark elves didn't know it, but they were atop the very same stone from which Drizzt had first glimpsed the cave of Tarathiel and Innovindil.

Donnia flicked a series of signals back to Ad'non, then slid forward on her belly to the very lip of the flat stone. A glance around and at Ad'non to ensure that he had his hand crossbow at the ready, and Donnia rolled right over the stone, holding securely to its lip, then skipping down the ten feet to hit the ground running across from the cave. At the side of the dark entrance, she drew out sword and hand crossbow.

Up above, Ad'non went over in a similar manner and quick-stepped his way to the wall opposite the entrance from Donnia.

Warm ashes within, Donnia flashed, a sure sign that the place was being used as a campsite.

Ad'non fell low and peered around, taking his time with the scan.

Empty, he silently told his companion. *But not deserted.*

Neither had to signal the other that they should set an ambush.

The drow elves moved around outside the cave, looking for some promising vantage points for an ambush. They didn't remain too close to the entrance, though, nor did they go in, showing proper respect for their dangerous adversaries. Soon after, Donnia stumbled upon something even more promising: a second cave.

This one is deeper, she signaled.

Ad'non came up to the lip of the small tunnel. He studied the descent within and the general angle of the corridor, then measured both against the location of the cave the surface elves were obviously using as a base. He motioned Donnia back, then fell to his belly and turned his head away as he gingerly slid his hand into the cave, delicate and practiced fingers working around the rim in search of any cunning traps. Gradually, Ad'non's arm went in deeper, feeling every inch.

With a glance at Donnia, the drow male slithered into the small hole, disappearing from view.

Donnia moved to the lip and glanced in just in time to see Ad'non's feet slip around the first bend in the corridor. With a look all around, she gently put one ear to the stone. The tapping of a predetermined code sent her into motion, falling flat and slipping in. The going was tight and tighter still when she worked around that first bend, and she came to a hole in the floor that could be negotiated only by going in head first, and blindly. Few rational creatures would have continued through such an uncomfortable obstacle, but to the dark elves, who had spent so many decades working through countless similar corridors in the honeycombed Underdark, it was not so daunting.

The corridor below the hole was a bit wider, though the ceiling was too low for Donnia to lift her head as she crawled along. It widened even more and opened into a higher chamber, and there she found her companion, sitting on a stone.

We should go down lower, Ad'non reasoned, and he motioned to the several choices offered to them: a pair of corridors winding out of the chamber, a wider area up a steep incline that seemed to extend over a wall of piled stones, and a broken-walled, rocky hole winding down deeper.

Donnia knew better than to argue with Ad'non concerning underground direction sense, for the scout had always shown a remarkable ability to navigate such tunnels. He was possessed of a keen instinct for that type of searching, as if he could innately sense the structure of any cave complex, as if he could somehow step back from the smaller areas visible to them at any given time and view the whole of the region. Perhaps it was the flow of the air or gradations of heat or light, but however he did it, Ad'non always seemed to follow the best course along a maze of tunnels.

And sure enough, after squeezing down the rocky shaft, crawling under a low overhang of rock and following yet another winding tunnel, the dark elves came into a small chamber. A slight breeze blew through the far wall. Not much of a wind, but one that sounded clearly to the keen ears of the drow.

Dead end? Donnia asked.

Ad'non signed her to be patient, then he moved to that far wall and began feeling along the stone. He looked back and grinned wickedly, and when Donnia rushed up to join him, she soon understood.

For they had come into a chamber adjacent to the cave the surface elves were using as their camp, and while there was no access between the chambers, the dark elves were able to work enough of the stone to give them a view of the other room.

They carefully replaced the stones and went back out into the night.

Drizzt went down to one knee and stared out across the early-morning landscape. Mist rose from the many mountain streams, dulling the sharp lines of ridges and outcroppings and adding a surreal quality to the morning light, dispersing it in a haze of orange and yellow. That mist dulled the sounds, too. The cry of birds, the rumble of loose stones, the babble of running water.

The scream of orcs.

Drizzt followed those screams out across a valley to another ridge across the way, and he made out the winged form of one pegasus, lifting into the air, then diving suddenly, and again, while its rider let fly a line of arrows from a longbow.

That would be Tarathiel, Drizzt supposed, for he was usually the one chasing the orcs into Innovindil's ambush.

Drizzt shook his head and gave a grin at their efficiency, for the pair had been out hunting before the last sunset and were out again at the first signs of dawn. He doubted that they had even returned to their cave during the night. He watched the chase a bit longer, then padded off softly for a secluded glade that he knew of nearby. Once there, he found a quiet place off to the side where he could watch the grassy area unnoticed, and he waited.

Sure enough, barely half an hour later, a pair of pegasi trotted onto the meadow, the two elves walking beside them and talking easily. The mounts needed to rest and to eat and needed to be wiped down as well, for their white coats glistened with sweat.

Drizzt had figured as much, and thus, he had expected the elf pair. Once again, the thought of going to them nagged at him. Was it not his responsibility to tell them of Ellifain and the tragedy in the west?

And yet, as the minutes passed, with Tarathiel and Innovindil untacking the pegasi, the drow did not move.

He watched their movements as they gently watered down the marvelous steeds with water from a nearby brook. He watched Tarathiel bring a bucket up before each pegasus in turn, gently stroking the sides of their heads as they bent low to drink. He watched Innovindil bring forth some type of root. She put it in her mouth and stood before her mount teasingly, and the pegasus reached out and took the root from her in what could only be described as a kiss. The stallion reared then, but not threateningly, and Innovindil merely laughed and did not move as the great equine creature waved its front hooves in the air before her.

Drizzt's hand went to his belt pouch and the onyx figurine at the sight of the intimate interaction, for the way Tarathiel and Innovindil acted with their pegasi seemed a deeper level than master and creature, seemed a friendship more than anything else. Drizzt above all others understood such a relationship.

Again the drow felt the urge to go to them, to talk to them and to tell them the truth. He paused and looked down, then closed his eyes and relived that fateful battle with the disturbed Ellifain. For many minutes, he sat there quietly, remembering the encounter and the one previous with Ellifain, in the Moonwood and with Tarathiel nearby. He understood the pain Tarathiel would feel upon hearing of Ellifain's fate, for he had seen the compassion Tarathiel had shown to the disturbed elf female.

He didn't want to bring that pain to those two.

But they had a right to know, and he a responsibility to tell them.

Yes, he had to tell them.

But when he looked up, the elves were already gone. Drizzt moved from his hiding place, a low crook on a tree nestled among several others. He went to the edge of the meadow, scanning, and he saw the pegasi lift into the air from over the other end.

Drizzt knew that they weren't going hunting. The mounts were too weary and so were the elves, likely. He watched their progress and figured their direction.

They were going back to their cave.

Drizzt wondered if he really had the strength to go to them and tell them his tale.

"We should return to the Moonwood and gather the clan," Tarathiel said to his companion as the two elves settled their pegasi outside the ante-chamber of their cave shelter.

"Are you ready to abandon Drizzt Do'Urden when you have not yet learned of Ellifain?" Innovindil replied.

"Soon," Tarathiel replied.

He began stripping off his bloodstained clothing and carefully hung his sword belt on a natural wall hook above his bedroll, then pulled off his tunic. Noticing a wound on his shoulder, he went back to the sword belt and reached into his pouch to produce a jar of salve.

Across from him, Innovindil was similarly stripping down and carefully laying out her dirty clothes.

"One scored a hit on you," she remarked, seeing the long scratch along Tarathiel's shoulder and upper arm.

"A branch, I believe," Tarathiel corrected, and he winced as he rubbed the cleansing salve over the wound. "During Sunrise's dive."

He replaced the top on the jar of salve and dropped it down to his bedroll, then pulled off his breeches and knelt down, straightening the blankets.

"Not too deep?" Innovindil asked.

"Not at all," came the assurance from Tarathiel, but the reply ended abruptly, and when Innovindil turned to regard him, she saw him crumple down on the bedroll.

"Are you that weary?" she asked lightheartedly, at first thinking nothing of it.

A few seconds slipped past.

"Tarathiel?" she asked, for he hadn't responded at all and lay very still. Innovindil moved over to him and bent low. "Tarathiel?"

A slight noise turned her head up to look at the back wall, and she spotted the hole in the stones and the small contraption—a hand crossbow—set in it.

The click of its release halted her questioning gasp, and she watched the small dart zoom across the short expanse. She tried to dodge but was too close. She threw her hand up instinctively to block, but the dart was already past that point—already past the waving hand and sticking deep into the base of her neck, just above her collarbone.

Innovindil staggered backward, her hand still held out before her. The hand was trembling, and violently, she realized only by looking at it. Even then the drow poison was coursing through her veins, numbing her extremities, dulling her thoughts. She realized she was sitting, though she hadn't intended to.

Then she was on her back, staring up at the ceiling of the cave. She tried to call out, but her lips wouldn't move to her command. She tried to turn her head to regard her companion, but she could not.

Behind the wall, Ad'non and Donnia exchanged grins and quickly moved away. They moved out of the back tunnel in a few moments' time and rushed around the hill to the front entrance of the cave. They each reached into their innate magic and summoned a globe of darkness, one over each of the pegasi milling around the entrance. The pegasi whinnied and stomped the ground in protest, and the dark elves rushed past them quickly.

Ad'non led the way up to the two paralyzed surface elves, Innovindil lying on her back before him and Tarathiel beyond her, crumpled in the fetal position.

"Beautiful, naked, and helpless," Ad'non remarked as he lewdly regarded the elf female.

With a wide grin and a quick glance back to Donnia, the drow crouched over and began stroking the elf's bare shoulder. Innovindil shuddered and jerked spasmodically, obviously trying to curl up and cower away from the touch.

That brought a chuckle from Ad'non, and from Donnia, who was enjoying the show.

"Beautiful, naked and helpless," Ad'non said again, and he glanced back at his drow companion. "Just the way I like my fairies."

PART THREE COURAGE AND COWARDICE

How strange it was for me to watch the two elves come to my aid that day at the river. How out of sorts I felt, and how off-balance. I knew the hunting pair were in the area, of course, but to actually confront them on such terms took me to places where I did not dare to venture.

Took me back to the cave in the west, where Ellifain, their friend, lay dead at the end of my bloody blade. How convenient the situation was to me in that moment of recognition, for there was truth in my advisement that we should flee along separate trails to discourage pursuit. There was justification in my reasoning.

But that cannot hide the truth I know in my own heart. I ran off down a different path because I was afraid, because courage in battle and courage in personal and emotional matters are often two separate attributes, and an abundance of one does not necessarily translate into an ample amount of the other.

I fear little from enemies. I fear more from friends. That is the paradox of my life. I can face a giant, a demon, a dragon, with scimitars drawn and enthusiasm high, and yet it took me years to admit my feelings for Catti-brie, to let go of the fears and just accept our relationship as the most positive aspect of my entire life.

And now I can throw myself into a gang of orcs without regard, blades slashing, a song of battle on my lips, but when Tarathiel and Innovindil presented themselves to me, I felt naked and helpless. I felt like a child again in Menzoberranzan, hiding from my mother and my vicious sisters. I do not think those two meant me any harm; they did not aid me in my battle just so they could find the satisfaction of killing me themselves. They came to me openly, knowing my identity.

But not knowing of my encounter with poor Ellifain, I am fairly certain.

I should have told them. I should have confessed all. I should have explained my pain and my regret, should have bowed before them with sorrow and humility, should have prayed with them for the safekeeping of poor Ellifain's spirit.

I should have trusted them. Tarathiel knows me and once trusted me with one of the precious horses of the Moonwood. Tarathiel saw the truth and believed that I had acted nobly on that long-ago night when the drow raiding party had crept out of the Underdark to slaughter Ellifain's clan. He would have understood my encounter with Ellifain. He would have seen the futility of my position and the honest pain within my heart and soul.

And he should know the fate of his old friend. By all rights, he and Innovindil deserve to know of the death of Ellifain, of how she fell, and perhaps together we could then determine why she fell. But I couldn't tell them. Not there. Not then. The wave of panic that rolled through me was as great as any I have ever known. All that I could think of was how I might get out of there, of how I might get away from these two allies, these two friends of dead Ellifain.

And so I ran.

With my scimitars, I am Drizzt the Brave, who shies from no battle. I am Drizzt who walked into a verbeeg lair beside Wulfgar and Guenhwyvar, knowing we were outmatched and outnumbered but hardly afraid! I am Drizzt, who survived alone in the Underdark for a decade, who accepted his fate and his inevitable death (or so I thought) rather than compromise those principles that I knew to be the true guiding lights of my existence.

But I am also Drizzt the Coward, fearing no physical challenge but unable to take an emotional leap into the arms of Catti-brie.

I am Drizzt the Coward, who flees from Tarathiel because he cannot confess. I am Drizzt, who has not returned to Mithral Hall after the fall of Shallows because without that confirmation of what I know to be true, that my friends are all dead, I can hold a sliver of hope that somehow some of them managed to escape the carnage. Regis, perhaps, using his ruby pendant to have the orcs carry him to waiting Battlehammer arms. Wulfgar, perhaps, raging beyond sensibility, reverting to his time in the Abyss and a pain and anger beyond control, scattering orcs before him until all those others ran from him and did not pursue.

And Catti-brie with him, perhaps.

It is all folly, I know.

I heard the orcs. I know the truth.

I am amazed at how much I hide behind these blades of mine. I am amazed at how little I fear death at an enemy's hands, and yet, at how greatly I fear having to tell Tarathiel the truth of Ellifain.

517

Still, I know that to be my responsibility. I know that to be the proper and just course.

I know that.

In matters of the heart, courage cannot overcome cowardice until I am honest with myself, until I admit the truth.

My reasoning in running away from the two elves that day in the river was sound and served to deflect their curiosity. But that reasoning was also a lie, because I cannot yet dare to care again.

I know that.

—Drizzt Do'Urden

15

TACTICAL DISADVANTAGE

Catti-brie threw her back against a flat stone, avoiding the rock that whistled across beside her, clipped the ground, and rebounded out over the drop to Keeper's Dale. The woman couldn't afford to watch that missile, though, for she was already being hard pressed by the pair of orcs that remained of the trio charging her position.

She had taken one of them down with Taulmaril, but then came the barrage from those distant giants on the western ridge. They couldn't reach the dwarves' position with any large stones, so they were throwing slabs of shale instead, the thin, sharp missiles catching drafts of air in wild and arcing spins. Most of the throws went far wild, spinning crazily, turning up on end and soaring far to one side or the other, but some cut in too close to be ignored.

Another arrow went up on the bowstring, and Catti-brie drew back just as the lead orc came around, the side of the stone, club raised, teeth bared.

She blew the creature away, her arrow blasting it right in the chest, lifting it from the ground and throwing it a dozen feet backward to the stone.

Instinctively, the woman dropped the bow straight down, caught it at its end and stabbed out with it behind her to intercept the attack of a second orc. The curve of the bow brought the free tip up under the orc's chin, and Catti-brie kept the pressure on as she turned around, reversing her grip and pressing forward. She had the orc straining to its tiptoes then, and it reached up to grab the bow and push it aside.

But Catti-brie moved more quickly, turning slightly and putting her back in tight against the stone, angling the bow out. She twisted and shoved, and the orc had to retreat and twist away.

Unfortunately for the orc, it happened to be standing on the edge of Keeper's Dale. It managed to grab the bow as it started to fall, forcing Catti-brie to let go. She grimaced as she saw Taulmaril go over the edge. She didn't dwell on the loss, but rather quickly drew out Khazid'hea and spun back to face the threat.

An ugly orc face greeted her, leering at her from across the flat stone. The creature did a feint to the right, and the woman sent her sword out that way. It went back to the left quickly, and Catti-brie reacted accordingly. The orc shifted fast back to center and moved as if to scramble over the stone.

But Catti-brie tired of the game and thrust straight ahead, her fabulous sword slicing through the stone and right through the chest of the orc up against it.

The creature's bloodshot eyes stared at her incredulously over the sheared rock.

"Ye almost fooled me," Catti-brie said with a wink.

Another orc leaped at her then, suddenly and without warning, coming in from far and wide.

No, not leaped, she realized as the flailing creature soared right past, soared right out over the drop to the dale.

Catti-brie understood as Wulfgar appeared, hammer in hand.

"Ready your bow," he bade her. "We are turning them yet again!"

Catti-brie held up her free hand helplessly and started to motion toward the cliff. But she just shrugged when she realized that Wulfgar wasn't watching, having already turned back to the main fight. She leaped ahead, scrambling to the top of the stone and away in fast pursuit of her barbarian friend.

Side by side, they waded into the closest group of orcs, Aegis-fang swiping back and forth, scattering the closest enemies.

Catti-brie darted out to the side, where an orc presented a shield against her. It was a feeble defense against Khazid'hea. The blade bit right through the wooden shield, right through the arm strapped against its other side, and right through the orc's chest.

Catti-brie slashed across to intercept the charge of a second creature, and the fine blade, so aptly nicknamed Cutter, sliced through bone and flesh and wood to tear free of its first victim. Turning it down, Catti-brie caught the second orc's thrusting spear and dropped its tip harmlessly. She snapped the blade back up with two quick stabs—two clean holes in the orc's chest. The creature staggered backward and tried to regroup, but the swiping Aegis-fang caught it in the back and sent it flying past Catti-brie.

She put Cutter into its side for good measure as it went by.

How fine I eat this night! came a thought in her mind.

Though the words hardly registered, the sensation of bloodthirst surely did. Before she could even consider the implications, before she even realized that the sentient sword had awakened and found its way into her conscious once more, the woman charged ahead, past Wulfgar, rushing with abandon into a throng of orcs.

Ferocity replaced finesse, with Cutter lashing out wickedly at anything that moved near. Out to the left she thrust, across her chest and through one shield and arm. A quick retraction and the blade slashed across in front of her, forcing the two orcs before her to stumble backward and taking the tip from the spear of another that was coming in from her right. Catti-brie turned her trailing foot and swung her hips, then charged out suddenly to the right, stabbing repeatedly, poking hole after hole into the curling and screaming orc.

Recognizing her vulnerability, the woman turned back to face the remaining two, and she dived aside as something flew past.

Aegis-fang, she realized when one of the two orcs seemed to simply disappear.

He shares our plate! Khazid'hea protested, and the sword compelled the woman to charge forward at the remaining orc.

Terrified, the creature threw its sword at her and turned and fled, and though the weapon smacked against her, it hardly slowed her. She caught the orc as it joined up with a pair of its fellows and still didn't slow, coming in with fury, stabbing and slashing. She took a hit and ignored the pain, willing to trade strike for strike, orc weapon against marvelous Khazid'hea.

The three were down, and Catti-brie ran on.

"Wait!" came a cry behind her.

It was Wulfgar's cry, but it seemed distant and not insistent. Not as insistent as the hunger in her thoughts. Not as insistent as the fire coursing through her veins.

Another orc fell before her. She hit another, thinking to rush past with a following stab on the creature behind it. But her strike was too strong, and the fine blade slashed through the orc's upper arm, severing the limb, then bit deeply into the creature's side, cutting halfway through its torso. There the blade halted and got stuck, for the momentum of the slash was stolen by too-eager Catti-brie, her weight coming past before she had finished the move. The dying orc flopped about and the woman nearly lost her grip on the blade. She turned and tugged fiercely, knowing she had to get it free, seeing the next creature barely feet away.

"Bah! Ye're taking all the fun!" that creature called at her.

Only then did Catti-brie stop struggling with the stuck sword. Only then did she realize that she had already reached the end of the dwarven line.

She offered a sheepish smile at the dwarf, keeping the thought private that if she hadn't accidentally caught her blade on the orc, that dwarf would likely have fallen to the hunger of Khazid'hea.

Spurred by that thought, the woman silently swore at the sword, which of course heard her clearly. She planted a foot on the dead orc and tried again to pull Khazid'hea free but was stopped by a large hand gripping her shoulder.

"Easy," Wulfgar bade her. "We fight together, side by side."

Catti-brie let go of the blade and stepped back, then took a long and steadying deep breath.

"Sword's hungry," she explained.

Wulfgar smiled, nodded, and said, "Temper that hunger with common sense."

Catti-brie looked back at the path of carnage she had wrought, at the sliced and slashed orcs, and at herself, covered head to toe in orc blood.

No, not all of it was orc, she only then realized and only then felt the burning pain. The thrown sword had opened a gash along her left arm, and she had another wound on her right hip and another where a spear tip had cut into her right foot.

"You need a priest," Wulfgar said to her.

Catti-brie, jaw clenched against the pain, stubbornly stepped forward and grabbed Khazid'hea's hilt. She roughly tore it free—and yet another fountain of orc blood painted her.

"And a bath," Wulfgar remarked, half in humor and half in sadness.

Banak Brawnanvil shoved two thick fingers into his mouth and blew a shrill whistle. The orcs were in retreat yet again, and the dwarves were giving chase, holding perfectly to their formations as they went. But those orcs were veering, Banak realized from his high vantage point back near the cliff face. They were sidling west in their run down the slope.

Banak whistled again and again and called for his nearby commanders to turn the dwarves around.

Before that order ever reached the pursuing force, though, all the dwarves, commander and pursuer alike, came to understand its intent and urgency. For in their bloodlust, the dwarves had moved too far to the north and west, too close to the high ridge and the waiting giants. As one, the formation skidded to a stop and swung around as giant boulders began to rain down upon them.

Their focused turn became an all-out retreat, and the orcs who had baited them turned as well, making the pursuers the pursued.

"Damned clever pigs," Banak grumbled.

"They've got the tactical advantage with them giants on the ridge," agreed Torgar, who stood at Banak's side.

That advantage was likely leading to complete disaster. Those orcs in pursuit, with the artillery support of the giants, would likely cut deep into the dwarven lines.

The two dwarf commanders held their breaths, praying that the errant band would get out of the giants' effective range and would then be able to offer some defense against the orcs. Banak and Torgar measured the ground, both calling out commands to support groups, moving all the remaining dwarves into position to catch and bolster their running kin.

Their plans took a sudden turn, though, as one group from the fleeing dwarves broke away from the main force, turning back upon the orcs with sudden ferocity.

"That'd be Pwent," Banak muttered.

Torgar tipped his helmet in admiration of the brave Gutbusters.

Pwent and his boys hit the orc line with abandon, and that line broke almost immediately.

The giants turned their attention to that particular area. Boulders rained down, but there were many more orcs than dwarves, a ratio of more than five to one—and that ratio held up concerning the numbers dropped by giant-thrown stones.

The pursuit was over and the main dwarven force was able to return to their defensive positions. All eyes turned back to the area of carnage, to see a group of Gutbusters, less than half of those who had bravely turned and charged, come scrambling out, running zigzags up the inclining stone.

Banak's charges cheered for them, urging them on, shouting for them to, "Run!" and, "Duck!" and, "Keep going!"

But rocks smashed among the zigzagging group, and whenever one of Pwent's boys went down, the cheering dwarves gave a collective groan.

One figure in particular caught the attention of the onlookers. It was Pwent himself, running up the slope with not one, but a pair of wounded dwarves slung over his shoulders.

The cheers went up for him, for "Pwent, Pwent, Pwent!"

He lagged behind, so he became the focus of the giants as well. Rocks smashed down all around him. Still he charged on, roaring with every step, determined to get his wounded boys out of there.

A rock hit the ground behind him and skipped forward, slamming him in the back and sending him flying forward. The wounded dwarves rolled off to either side, all three hitting the ground hard.

Up above, cheers turned to stunned silence.

Pwent struggled to get up.

Another stone clipped him and laid him face down.

Two figures broke out from the dwarf ranks then, running fast on longer legs, sprinting down the slope toward the fallen trio.

Amazingly, Pwent forced himself back up and turned to face the giants. He swung one arm up, slapping his other hand across his elbow so that his fist punched high in the air—as rude a gesture as he could offer.

Another boulder smashed the stone right in front of him, then bounced up over him and clunked down behind.

And there stood Pwent, signaling curses at the giants.

Catti-brie wished that she had her bow with her! Then, perhaps, she could at least offer some cover against that suicidal charge.

Wulfgar outdistanced her, his hands free, for he had left Aegis-fang back up with the dwarves.

"Get to Pwent!" the barbarian cried, and he veered for one of the two more seriously wounded warriors.

Catti-brie reached the stubborn battlerager and grabbed him by the still-cursing arm.

"Come on, ye dolt!" she cried. "They'll crush you down!"

"Bah! They're as stupid as they are tall!" Pwent shouted.

He pulled his arm from Catti-brie, hooked a finger of each hand into either side of his mouth, and pulled it wide, sticking out his tongue at the distant behemoths.

He sobered almost at once, though, and not from Catti-brie's continuing pleas, but from the specter of Wulfgar crossing before him, an unconscious dwarf over one shoulder. Pwent watched as Wulfgar moved to the second fallen Gutbuster, a huge hand clasping over the scruff of the dwarf's neck and hoisting him easily.

When Catti-brie tugged again, Pwent didn't argue, and the woman pulled him along, back up the slope. The rain of boulders commenced with full force, but luck was with the trio and their unconscious cargo, and Wulfgar was hardly slowed by the burden of the two injured dwarves. Soon enough, they were out of range of the boulders. The frustrated giants went back to their shale then, filling the air with spinning and slashing sharp-edged stones.

Dwarves cheered wildly as the group of five approached. As one, the hundreds lifted their arms in rude gestures and stood defiantly against the whizzing missiles of slate.

"Get yer bandages ready," Banak shouted to Pikel Bouldershoulder, who was off to the side, jumping around excitedly.

"Oo oi!" the dwarf yelled back, and he turned and lifted an arm in salute to Banak.

The slate flew past, taking Pikel's raised arm at the elbow. The green-bearded dwarf put on a puzzled look and stumbled forward, then shrugged as if he didn't understand.

And his eyes went wide as he saw the severed limb—*his* severed limb!—lying off to the side.

His brother Ivan slammed into him from the side, slapping a cloak tightly around Pikel's blood-spurting stump, and other dwarves nearby howled and rushed to help.

Pikel was sitting then, ushered down by his brother.

"Oooo," he said.

16

EMBRACING THE HUNTER

Ad'non Kareese's long, slender fingers traced a line down over Innovindil's delicate chin, down the moon elf's birdlike neck and to the base of her throat.

"Can you feel me?" the drow teased, though he believed, of course, that the paralyzed surface elf couldn't understand his language.

"Have your way with the creature and be done with her," Donnia said from behind him.

Ad'non smiled, keeping his head turned away from his companion so that she could not see the amusement he was taking at her obvious consternation. She understood his intended action as debasement more than any real emotional connection, of course—and as she was drow herself so she was certainly going to find her own pleasures with their paralyzed playthings—but still, there sounded a bit of unmistakable agitation around the edges of her voice.

Amusing.

"If I find you soft and warm, perhaps I will keep you alive for a while," Ad'non said to Innovindil.

He watched the surface elf's eyes as he spoke and could see that they were indeed reacting to the sound of his voice and the feel of his touch. Yes, she couldn't outwardly make any movements—the drow poison had done its job well—but she understood what was happening, understood what he was about to do to her, and understood that she had no chance to get out of it.

That made it all the sweeter.

Ad'non ran his hand lower, across the female's small breasts and down over her belly. Then he stood up and stepped back. He glanced back at Donnia, who stood with her arms crossed over her chest.

"We should drag them to a different cave," he said to his companion. "Let us keep them prisoner."

"Her, perhaps," Donnia replied, indicating Innovindil. "For that one, there will be only death."

It seemed fine enough to Ad'non, and he glanced back at the female elf and grinned.

And he couldn't see her—a ball of blackness covered her and her companion.

Never to be taken completely by surprise, the two dark elves swung around, Ad'non unsheathing his swords, Donnia drawing a blade and her hand crossbow. The form behind them, by the entrance, was easily enough distinguishable. It was a drow standing calmly, standing ready, scimitars drawn.

"Traitor!" Donnia growled, and she lifted her crossbow and fired.

Drizzt trembled with rage when he first entered the cave, seeing the two elves lying flat, and the two drow standing over them. He had known of the trouble before he'd ever come in, for the calls and stomping hooves of the pegasi outside had alerted him from some distance away. Without thinking twice, the drow ranger had broken into a run, leaping down the flat rock from which he'd often observed the area, and charging between the winged horses even as the darkness globes dissipated.

So alarmed was Drizzt that he hadn't even paused long enough to bring forth Guenhwyvar.

And he faced the drow pair.

He didn't even see the movement, but he heard the distinctive *click,* and remembered well enough that telltale sound. The ranger spun, pulling his cloak in a wide sweep around him.

His quick defense caught the dart in the swinging cloak, but even as the dart stuck in place, the second *click* sounded. Drizzt spun again, but the second dart got past the flying cloak and struck him in the hip.

Almost immediately, Drizzt felt the numbing chill of the drow poison.

He staggered back toward the exit and thought to call in Guenhwyvar. He couldn't reach for his belt pouch, though, for it was all he could do to hold fast to his weapons.

"How wonderful of you to join us, Drizzt Do'Urden," said the female drow who'd shot him.

Her words, spoken in the language of his homeland, brought him drifting back across the years, brought him back to images of Menzoberranzan and his family, of House Do'Urden and Zaknafein, of Narbondel glowing with heat and the great structures of the drow palaces, stalagmite and stalactite palaces, shaped and set with sweeping balconies and decorated with multicolored accents of faerie fire.

He saw it all so clearly—the early days beside his sisters and training with the weapons masters at Melee Magthere, the school for drow warriors.

The sound of metal clinking against stone woke him up, and only then did he realize that he was leaning heavily on the wall and that he had dropped one of his blades.

"Ah, Drizzt Do'Urden, I had hoped you would put up a better fight than this," said the male drow. The sound of his voice alone told Drizzt that his enemy was steadily approaching. "I have heard so much of your prowess."

Drizzt couldn't keep his eyes open. He felt the numbness flowing through his lower extremities so that he couldn't even feel the ground beneath his feet. The only reason he was still standing, he understood through the haze that was filtering his thoughts, was because of his angle against the wall.

The poison crept in, and so did the sword-wielding drow.

Drizzt tried to fight back against the numbness, tried hard to find his center, tried hard to shake his mind clear of the cloudy disorientation.

He could not.

"Now perhaps we have found a true plaything, Ad'non," he heard the drow female remark from somewhere so very, very distant.

"Too dangerous is this one, my dear Donnia," the male argued. "He dies quickly."

"As you will . . ."

Her voice trailed away, and it seemed to Drizzt as if he was falling far away, into a pit of blackness from which there could be no escape.

Wulfgar lay on the stone, peering down, trying to discern the best angle of approach toward the ledge where Taulmaril balanced precariously.

Behind him, Catti-brie tied a rope around her waist and checked the length of the cord.

"The devilish sword almost had me enthralled," the woman admitted as Wulfgar turned around and sat up facing her. "I've not felt its call so insistently in many months."

"Because you are tired," Wulfgar replied. "We're all tired. How many times have our enemies come at us? A dozen? They give us no rest."

"Just hit the damned thing with a rock, send it tumbling to the floor, and go get it," said Torgar, coming over with Shingles McRuff beside him.

Both of them were limping, and Shingles was holding one arm protectively close against his side.

"We've tried," Wulfgar replied.

"How is Pikel?" Catti-brie asked. "And Pwent?"

"Pwent's hopping mad," Shingles replied.

"Nothing new there," the woman remarked.

"And Pikel's said nothing but 'oooo' since he lost the arm," Shingles added. "I'm thinking it'll take him a bit afore he's used to it. Banak sent him down to Mithral Hall for better tending."

"He'll live, though, and that's more than many can say," added Torgar.

"Well, be quick about getting yer bow," Shingles said. "Might that we'll all be going inside the hall soon enough." He glanced back over his shoulder toward the distant ridge and the giants. "We can hold firm so far, as long as we're not stupid enough to chase the damned orcs back in range of the brutes. But they're bringin' up big logs and building giant-sized catapults. Once them things are throwing, we'll be fast out o' here."

Wulfgar and Catti-brie exchanged concerned looks, for neither had any answer to that logic.

"Banak would've called for the retreat to begin already," said Torgar, "except now we've got a force set west of Keeper's Dale, and he knows that if he surrenders this ground, they'll have the dickens getting back to the gate, since they'd be crossing the dale right under giant fire."

Again the two humans exchanged a concerned look. Their enemies had gained a huge tactical advantage, one that would drive the dwarves from the area, and yes, back into Mithral Hall. That much seemed certain.

What did that mean for all the other towns nearby?

What did that mean for Mithral Hall, with no surface trade and no way to get out in numbers sufficient to take back the land?

And for Wulfgar and Catti-brie, there remained one more nagging problem. If they were forced back underground, what did it mean for Drizzt Do'Urden? Would he ever be able to find his way back to them?

He saw Zaknafein falling into the acid pit.

He saw Ellifain falling against the wall.

He saw Bruenor falling atop a tower.

He felt the keen sting of each loss, the pain and the anger, and he did not push them away. No, Drizzt embraced them, called those emotions to him, basked in them and heightened them.

He imagined Regis being torn apart by orcs.

He imagined Wulfgar falling amidst a bloody sea of enemy spears.

He imagined Catti-brie, down and helpless, surrounded by enemies, bleeding from a hundred wounds.

He imagined, and those conjured images blended with the very real and painful images he had known in his life, the visions of sorrow and despair, the scenes of his life that had brought him to a place of emotional darkness.

He felt the Hunter rising within him. All the images ran together then, one long line of pain and loss and sorrow and regret, and most of all, of pure rage.

A sword stabbed in at Drizzt's left side, but the ring of metal on metal sounded clearly, a warning bell to his two attackers that their poison could not defeat the Hunter. For across came the backhand slash of a scimitar, in the blink of an astonished drow eye, whipping up and around in an instant to catch the thrusting sword and turn it up and out.

The second sword followed, predictably low, but even in anticipation of the coming blade and given the attack angle, the defender seemingly had no practical chance of either snapping down his first scimitar or of getting to his second, which lay on the floor.

But he was the Hunter, and not only did that first scimitar blade come back down, rapping the sword and driving it out to the right out in front of him as he turned, but the Hunter fell into a crouch with the parry, scooping up the fallen Twinkle. As he came up fast, blades working in perfect harmony, the retrieved scimitar came in and over the sword and rode it out even more.

That first scimitar reversed and snapped back up, hard, ringing the first sword again.

And so the attacker, Ad'non, stood helpless, swords out wide to either side, two deadly scimitars *inside* them.

A sudden and brutal ending, or so it would have been for the surprised Ad'non, had not his companion come in then hard at the Hunter's back. A sudden jerk shoved Ad'non's blades out even more, and he had to step back to hold any sort of defensive position. But he needed no defense at that moment, for the Hunter spun away from him, blades cutting the air in a protective weave before him as he turned left to right.

Donnia squealed at the surprising deflection of her sword, but the skilled female warrior followed the flow of the scimitars and quick-stepped in behind for a dagger thrust.

The Hunter's hip was already moving, keeping him out of reach.

And Drizzt spun again, defeating Ad'non's double-thrust, scimitars rolling up and across, hitting the swords a dozen times in rapid succession before he continued around, the whirling blades forcing that dirk back, then driving hard against Donnia's sword once more.

The Hunter continued to spin, rolling blades striking one side and the other, always coming around at the exact angle to intercept, as if the lone drow was anticipating each attack, as if he was seeing it before it ever began.

His attackers were not novices, though, and they had fought together many, many times. They kept opposite each other and kept their attacks coordinated—and they were expending far less energy than the spinning drow defender. Still, as they struck and leaped back, every thrust, high or low, left or right, was met by the ringing impact of a perfectly aimed scimitar.

Then, suddenly, the twirl stopped, and the pair attacked, but the Hunter went back around the other way. Again came the ring of metal on metal, two scimitars striking hard against three swords.

That spin ended almost immediately, though, leaving the Hunter side-long to both attackers.

In came Ad'non, double-thrust high.

The Hunter ducked below it and stabbed for the male's knees, then leaped straight up over Donnia's slashing sword as Ad'non retracted. Drizzt landed in a fast step toward Ad'non, snapping his scimitars up in a cross between Ad'non's leveled blades, stabbing them high until his arms crossed and the hilts caught at the blade, then snapping them out across again, out wide, nearly tearing the swords from Ad'non's grasp.

Ad'non threw himself backward, but so did the Hunter, leaping into a backward somersault right above and over the stabbing sword of Donnia. He landed lightly, still backstepping.

As he crossed over, defeating her attack, the dexterous Donnia flipped her dirk in her hand and whipped it at his chest.

But the defending drow's right scimitar snapped up to cleanly block, and before the deflected dirk could bounce away, the left-hand scimitar locked up under it, pinning it against the first blade for just a moment before slashing back to the left, redirecting the dirk into a swift flight at his retreating adversary. Ad'non desperately dived back and around but got clipped across the cheek as he tumbled away.

Donnia pressed the attack, drawing a whip from her belt as she thrust ahead with her sword.

That sword thrust never got close, as the Hunter's right reversed down and around, turning it, then lifting it as the left hand came back in, striking it again, lifting it higher. The right scimitar climbed that parrying ladder in turn, knocking it still higher.

Donnia accepted the blocks with only a minimal attempt to break free, for her second hand worked perfectly then, sending the whip in a teasing forward slide, then snapping it suddenly for the Hunter's face.

A scimitar picked it off, but it did not cut the enchanted whip, and the same magic that prevented the tear also reacted to Donnia's willful call, the living tentacle wrapping fast around the blade.

Her eyes blazing with apparent victory, the female yanked the scimitar free. She was surprised at how easily she got it from the strong drow—only until she realized that he had let it go, turning as he did and pulling his cloak from around his neck.

Ad'non came in hard from the side, but the Hunter quick-stepped ahead and to the opposite side, moving around Donnia to use her as a screen. As he went, he brought his cloak up above his head in a spin, and as Donnia snapped the whip, so he launched the cloak.

She felt her whip crack hard against his shoulder and got wrapped about the head by the flying cloak in return—which she accepted as more than an even trade.

Until she felt the sudden sting at the side of her neck, and she realized that her dart was hanging in that cloak and that the vicious and sneaky warrior had angled the throw perfectly to get its poisoned tip near to her.

With a shriek, the female fell back and threw aside the garment.

One scimitar against two swords, the Hunter still slapped and parried perfectly, never letting Ad'non get close to hitting. He backstepped as he parried, swiftly working his way in perfect balance to his lost scimitar.

Following that maneuver, Ad'non increased his attack, even went into a sudden and furious charge.

The Hunter leaped aside, to Ad'non's left, and the skilled killer redirected his left-hand blade out immediately, and when it got slapped aside, he followed with a thrust of the right.

That, too, was parried, and the Hunter turned inside both, putting his back to Ad'non. A quick double-pump of his arm brought his scimitar forward and back twice, brought its pommel hard into Ad'non's face—twice.

Staggered, the drow stumbled backward, his blades working furiously in desperate defense. They hit only air, though, and a look of abject terror flashed across the drow's face.

Except that the Hunter hadn't pursued. Instead, he'd turned and sprinted for his lost scimitar.

A globe of darkness covered him as he reached the blade, and he responded with one of his own, right where he remembered the female to be.

Grabbing up the scimitar, he went out furiously, diving into a roll, then charged right through the second globe, his own globe, sliding in low, blades working all around.

He came out to find the female sprinting across toward the male, who had warm blood trickling down his face.

Unafraid, the Hunter stalked in.

"Together and to the sides," the Hunter heard the male say, and Ad'non started to the left.

And the female felt at the side of her neck, a look of panic on her face.

The Hunter covered her in blue-glowing flames, harmless faerie fire that marked her as a clearer target.

As Ad'non charged, she turned and ran.

They worked their blades so quickly that the ring sounded as one long call. Ad'non stabbed with one sword then the other and got hit with a double-block left and a double-block right, each of his attacks being picked off by not one, but both of the Hunter's scimitars.

A slash across hit nothing but air as the Hunter ducked. A thrust flew freely as the Hunter deftly turned, and that blade got smacked hard on the retraction, nearly tearing it free of Ad'non's grasp.

"Donnia!" he screamed.

He growled and worked his own blades magnificently as a sudden series of diagonal slashes, tap-tapping each scimitar just enough to make it slide past him harmlessly. So fast did those scimitars come, though, that Ad'non was forced to steadily retreat and couldn't begin to think of any possible counters.

But those blades did gradually slow, leaving a slip of an opening.

One that Ad'non leaped through, offering a devastating double-thrust low.

Amazingly, the scimitars somehow fell into the only possible defense, double-cross-down, which left the two at a draw for that particular routine, so Ad'non thought. For Ad'non Kareese was not of Menzoberranzan and did not know that his foe, Drizzt' Do'Urden, had long-ago found the solution for the routine-end.

With amazing dexterity and balance, the Hunter's foot came up right between the crossed scimitars and smashed Ad'non squarely in the face, sending him staggering backward yet again.

He tried to mount a defense, but the scimitars led the way, batting his swords aside, and as he slammed hard against the wall, he could not block the diving, curved blade.

It hit him squarely in the chest, and he screamed.

And the Hunter growled, thinking the fight at its end.

But the scimitar did not penetrate! Nor did its sister blade score a mortal wound as it came in hard against Ad'non's side. Oh yes, the two blades had hurt the drow warrior, but neither had found its way in for the kill.

And suddenly, the Hunter was off-balance, was caught by surprise.

Across came a sword, knocking both scimitars aside, and the Hunter went into a spin, right-to-left. But Ad'non went to his right behind him, pressing the attack, forcing him to run past or get skewered.

But there was a wall there, Ad'non knew, and he smiled, for the devilish drow renegade had nowhere to go. In Ad'non charged, both blades going for the kill.

But the Hunter was not there.

Ad'non's blades clipped the bare stone, and he stopped suddenly, eyes wide.

"O cunning Drizzt," he said as he figured out that Drizzt had gone right over him, running up the wall and flipping a back somersault to stand behind him.

The scimitar came slashing across just above Ad'non's shoulder, cleanly lopping off his head.

Drizzt glanced across the way to the two paralyzed elves and even started toward them, just a step. But then, his anger far from sated, the Hunter ran out of the cave and off into the night. He paused and glanced around and saw the blue glow of his faerie fire along a slope to the west. His eyes cast determinedly as if set in stone, the Hunter drew forth his onyx figurine and called to Guenhwyvar.

The blue glow still showed when the great panther materialized beside him, and Drizzt pointed it out.

"Catch her, Guen," the drow instructed. "Catch her and hold her for me."

With a growl, the panther charged off into the night, gaining great expanses with every mighty leap.

17

STEWARDSHIP
AND ESPIONAGE

Regis squeezed Bruenor's hand and stared down at his friend, wondering if it would be last time he would see the dwarf king alive. Bruenor's breaths seemed more shallow to him, and the dwarf's color was even more grayish, as if he was made of stone. Stumpet and Cordio had told Regis that it likely wouldn't be much longer, and he could see that plainly.

"I owe you this," the halfling whispered, barely able to get his voice out through the lump in his throat. "We all do, and know as you rest that Mithral Hall will stand strong in your absence. I will not let this place fall."

The halfling gave another gentle squeeze, then laid the dwarf's hand down across his chest. For a moment, he saw no movement in Bruenor's chest, and he wondered if the dwarf had heard him and had at last let go.

But then Bruenor took a breath.

Not yet.

Regis patted the dwarf's hands and briskly walked out of the room, overcome and trying hard to bring himself emotionally back to center. He moved quickly along the tunnels, knowing that he was late for a meeting with Galen Firth of Nesmé. He still didn't know how he would handle the fierce warrior. What aid might he offer with Mithral Hall under such duress? The eastern door was sealed—the dwarves had even dropped the tunnels behind it to make sure that any enemies trying to come in that way would have to claw through more than twenty feet of stone.

Reports from the north were no more promising, for Banak Brawnanvil had sent word that he was not certain how long he could hold his position. The giants were setting catapults on the western ridge, and soon enough, Banak feared, his forces would be under terrible duress.

He had asked for Regis to swing the force that had settled in the western end of Keeper's Dale around to the north to overrun the ridge from the west, but the request had come with a caveat: *if* it was feasible. Even Banak, settled in an increasingly desperate situation, recognized the danger of following such a course. Not only would that be exposing one of his two remaining surface armies to a potentially devastating situation, but in moving them out of their defensive position in Keeper's Dale, Regis would be risking leaving a wide-open path to Mithral Hall's western gate.

And Nesmé was sorely pressed—likely even overrun—so the halfling had to keep the western approach protected from potential enemies moving up from the south.

Too many problems flitted through the halfling steward's mind. Too many issues confronted him. He hardly knew where he was half the time, and in truth, all he wanted was to go eat a big meal or two and settle down in a warm bed, with nothing troubling him more than the all-important decision of what he would choose to eat for breakfast.

With all of that weighing down his little shoulders, Regis started away. But he stopped and glanced back at the candlelit room where King Bruenor lay, and he remembered his words to his dying friend.

Regis straightened his shoulders immediately, bolstered by his sense of duty. His promise had not been idly given, and he did indeed owe Bruenor at least that much, and surely even more.

First things first, Regis decided, and he moved off more quickly and determinedly for his meeting with Galen Firth. He found the man in the appointed audience room, a smaller and more personable sitting area than the grand chamber. It was appointed with comfortable chairs—three padded ones with arm rests and wide-flaring backs—set on a thick-woven rug patterned in the foaming mug emblem of Clan Battlehammer. Completing the square of the sitting area was a stone hearth, wherein burned a small and cozy fire.

Despite the obvious comforts, Galen Firth was pacing, his hands behind his back, his fingers running all around, his eyes cast down at the floor. Regis had to wonder if this man was ever anything but agitated.

"Well met again, Galen Firth of Nesmé," the halfling steward greeted as he entered the room. "Forgive my tardiness, I beg, for there are many pressing problems all needing my attention."

"Your tardiness this day is more forgivable than the tardiness of Mithral Hall's answer to Nesmé's desperate call," the disagreeable man replied rather harshly.

Regis gave a sigh, walked past Galen and plopped himself down in one of the chairs. When the warrior made no move to join him in the sitting area, the halfling pointedly gestured to the seat directly across from him, to the right of the fire as his was to the left.

Never blinking and never taking his eyes from the halfling, the Rider of Nesmé moved to the chair.

"What would you have me do?" Regis asked as Galen at last sat down.

"Launch an army of dwarves to the aid of Nesmé, that we can drive the trolls back into their brackish waters and restore my town."

"And when this army marches south and a greater army of orcs and giants offers pursuit, then what would you have any of us do?" Regis reasoned, and Galen's eyes narrowed. "For that is what will happen, you do understand. The orcs press us on the north and have sealed the door to Mithral Hall on the east—you have heard of this latest battle, yes? I have one force up on the cliff north of Keeper's Dale waging battle daily against the orcs, but if the reports of the size of the attacking force in the east were anywhere near to accurate, my warriors will soon be even harder pressed and likely forced to forfeit the ground.

"You do not fully comprehend what is transpiring all around us, do you?" the halfling asked.

Galen Firth sat there staring, grim faced.

"It is no accident that Nesmé was attacked just now," Regis explained. "These enemy forces, north and south, have coordinated their movements."

"That cannot be!"

"Did you hear no details of the fall of Mithral Hall's eastern gate?"

"Few, nor do I care to—"

"The forces out there were besieged by giants and orcs from the north and by a host of trolls from the south," Regis interrupted, and Galen's bluster fell away as clearly as his suddenly drooping jaw.

"It would seem that our common enemies are sweeping all the land from the Surbrin to Nesmé, from the Trollmoors to the Spine of the World," Regis went on. "That leaves only a handful of settlements, Mithral Hall, and Nesmé to stop them, unless we can elicit help from the neighboring lands."

"Then you admit that we must join our forces," Galen reasoned. "Then you see the wisdom of sending a force fast for Nesmé."

"I do," said Regis, "and I do not. We must stand together, and so we shall, but I believe your desire to hold our ground at Nesmé is ill considered. Mithral Hall will hold, but outside of our gates, all is lost—or soon shall be."

"What foolishness is this?" Galen Firth demanded, leaping from his chair, his eyes ablaze with anger.

"We fight for every inch of ground," Regis countered, and his voice didn't waver in the least, nor did he tense up or shy away from the imposing man. "And when we cannot hold, we retreat into the defensible tunnels of Mithral Hall. From here, we keep the lines of tunnels open to Citadel Felbarr; they will be our eyes, ears, and mouth to the outside world. From here, we continue to implore Silverymoon and Sundabar to mobilize their forces. I already have emissaries hurrying along their way through tunnels to find Lady Alustriel of Silverymoon and the leaders of Sundabar. From here, we hold the one remaining fortress against the onslaught of monstrous enemies."

"While my people die?" Galen Firth spat.

"No," said Regis. "Not if we can help them. From the moment you arrived, I had dwarf scouts striking out to the southwest, underground, seeking a course to Nesmé. Their progress has been strong, and I expect that they will find an exit to the surface near enough to your town to join up with your people."

"Then send an army, and let us drive the trolls back!"

"I will send what I can spare, but I expect that will be far fewer than needed for the task you espouse," said Regis.

"Then what?" the warrior's voice suddenly mellowed, and he even slumped back in the chair.

He turned his head and rested his chin in his hand, staring into the flames.

"Let us find your people and help them as we may," Regis explained. "We will fight beside them, if that remains a viable option. And if not, or when it becomes not, we will retreat, with your people in tow, back into the Underdark and back to Mithral Hall. Though my dwarves will not be able to defeat our enemies aboveground, I have little doubt that they can hold their own tunnels against pursuing monsters."

Galen Firth said nothing, just kept staring into the fire.

"I wish I could offer more," Regis went on. "I wish I could empty Mithral Hall and charge south to overrun the trolls. But I cannot, and you must understand."

Galen sat there quietly for a long while, then turned to Regis, his features softened.

"You truly believe that the orcs and giants work in concert with the Trollmoors trolls?"

"The fall of the eastern gate would indicate as much," the halfling replied.

"And it tells, too, that my people are in dire trouble," Galen said. "If the trolls had enough strength to send a force as far east and north as your gates on the Surbrin. . . ."

"Then tarry no more," Regis said. He reached into his vest and produced a rolled parchment, tossing it across to the man. "Take that to the Undercity and Taskman Bellows. The expedition is outfitting even now and will be ready to march this very day."

Again Galen Firth paused, staring at the parchment, then back at Regis as he slowly climbed out of the chair once more. He said nothing more, but his nod held enough appreciation for Regis to see that the man understood the reasoning, even if he did not necessarily agree.

He gave a slight bow and left the room and the halfling steward breathed a sigh of relief, thinking he had one less issue pressing.

Regis slid back in his chair and turned to the fire, but before he could even begin to relax, a knock on the door turned him back.

"Enter, please," he said, expecting it to be a returned Galen Firth.

The door pushed open and in walked a soot-covered dwarf, Miccarl Ironforge by name, one of Mithral Hall's best blacksmiths. So dirty was this one that the color of his wide, short beard (rumored to be red) was impossible to tell. He wore a thick leather apron and a black shirt with only one sleeve, covering his left arm completely and sewn as one with a heavy heat-resistant glove. His bare right arm, streaked with soot, was nearly twice the girth of his left, muscled from years and years of lifting heavy hammers.

"The gnome again?" Regis asked.

Miccarl had sought him out twice before in the last tenday, offering reports that their little visitor from Mirabar had been acting overly curious in snooping around the Undercity.

"The little one's been in the maps again," Miccarl explained.

"Same maps?"

"Western tunnels—mostly unused."

"Where is he now?"

"Last I saw was him moving down those same tunnels," Miccarl explained. "I'm thinking that he's thinking he's found something there."

"And what might be there?"

"Nothing that I'm knowing, nor that anyone else's knowing. Them tunnels been mostly sealed for a few hunnerd years, unless them duergar that took the hall with the dragon opened them—and none who've been down that way since our return ever found anything."

"Then what? A way out—a way to bring an army from Mirabar in?" Regis asked. "Ore that could be stolen for Mirabar's forges?"

"Nothing there—not even good ore," Miccarl answered. "Never was nothing there but shale and coal for the forges. If the little one's come all the way to find a source for that, then he's a bigger fool than ye know, for there's not much worth in the stuff and Mirabar's already got more than she'd ever need."

"Tunnels to Mirabar?"

Miccarl snorted and said, "We got enough already known. We could get far west of here in a day's time and be aboveground beyond the reach of our enemies and well on our way to Mirabar. The little one's got to know that."

"Then what?" Regis asked again, but quietly, and more to himself than to the dwarf.

What might Nanfoodle be doing? As he pondered the possibilities, the halfling's hand instinctively went up to the chain around his neck.

"Find Nanfoodle and bid him join me," Regis instructed the dwarf.

"Aye," Miccarl readily agreed. "Ye wanting me to drag him or knock him black and carry him?"

"I'm wanting you to coerce him," Regis replied. "Tell him that I have some news for Mirabar and need his advice forthwith."

"Not as much fun," Miccarl muttered, and he left.

A procession of informants followed the departure of the blacksmith, with news from the east and news from the west, with reports about the fighting outside and from the progress in securing and scouting the tunnels. Regis took it all in, paying strict attention, weighing all the possibilities, and mostly, formulating a line of questions for his dwarf advisors. He recognized that he was more the synthesizer of information than the decision maker, though he found that his advice was carrying more and more weight as the dwarves came to trust his judgment.

That pleased him and frightened him all at the same time.

His dinner was delivered to him in the same room, coming in alongside yet another messenger, one reporting that the expedition of fifty dwarves had set off for the south with Galen Firth.

Regis invited the dwarf to join him, or started to, but then Miccarl Ironforge appeared at the door.

"More work," Regis explained to the first messenger.

The halfling gave an apologetic shrug and motioned to the plates of food set on the small table between the chairs.

"Yup," replied the dwarf, and he stepped over, piled a few pounds of meat on a plate and filled the largest flagon to its tip with mead.

He gave a nod to Regis, which sent some mead spilling over the front of the flagon, then took his leave.

In walked Miccarl and Nanfoodle.

"Got work to do," the sooty blacksmith explained, and after moving over to similarly outfit himself with meat and mead for the trek back to the Undercity, he too took his leave.

"Sit and eat and drink," Regis offered to the gnome.

"They left little," Nanfoodle remarked with a grin, but even as he spoke the words, a pair of dwarves entered with refills of both food and drink.

Both the halfling and the gnome, not to be outdone by any dwarf, began their long, hearty meal.

"I am told you have news of Mirabar, or for Mirabar," Nanfoodle said between gulps of the golden liquid. "Master Ironforge was not explicit."

"I have a request for Mirabar," Regis explained between bites. "You understand the weight of our present dilemma, I hope."

"Many monsters, yes," Nanfoodle replied, and he took another bite of lamb and another gulp of mead.

"More than you know," Regis replied. "Pressing all the region. No doubt word has already reached your marchion from besieged, and perhaps already overrun, Nesmé. I know not how long we might hold any presence on the surface, and so Mirabar must mobilize her forces."

"For the good of Mithral Hall?" asked the gnome.

So surprised was he that a bit of mead fell out of his mouth as he blurted the words. He quickly dabbed it up with his napkin and took another big swallow.

"For the good of Mirabar," Regis corrected. "Are we to assume that these monsters will end their march here?"

It seemed to him that the gnome was growing a bit more concerned, and in his nervousness, Nanfoodle seemed to be taking more and more drink and less and less food. That was good, Regis thought, and so he kept the conversation going for some time, detailing the fall of the eastern gate and the fears that the trolls of the south had joined with the orcs and giants from the north, or perhaps that the groups had been working in concert all along. He spared no detail at all, drawing out the conversation for as long as possible, and letting Nanfoodle drink more and more mead.

At one point, when the servers arrived with even more food and drink, Regis called one over and whispered into his ear, "Cut the next bit of drink with Gutbuster." The halfling glanced at the gnome, trying to get a measure of his present sensibilities. "Twenty-to-one mead," he explained to the server, not wanting to knock the poor gnome unconscious.

An hour later, Regis was still talking, and Nanfoodle was still drinking.

"But you and your sceptrana claim that you came here to check on Torgar and to strengthen the bond between our towns," Regis said suddenly, and with increased volume. He had been steering the conversation that way for a bit, moving away from the particulars of the monsters and the fighting and toward the issue of relations between Mirabar and Mithral Hall. "That is true, is it not?"

Nanfoodle's eyes opened wide—or at least, as wide as the somewhat inebriated gnome could open them.

"W-well . . . yes," Nanfoodle sputtered. "That is why we came here, after all."

"Indeed," said Regis.

He shifted forward in his chair, leaning near to Nanfoodle. He fished his necklace out of the front of his vest and fiddled with the ruby pendant, sending it into a little spin.

"Well, we all want that, of course," the halfling said, and he noted that Nanfoodle had glanced at the ruby and up, and again at the ruby. "Better relations, I mean."

"Yes, yes, of course," said the gnome, his eyes more and more focused on the tantalizing spin of the enchanted ruby pendant.

Regis would never have tried it on the gnome normally. Nanfoodle was a brilliant alchemist, so Torgar and Shingles McRuff had told him, and also was known to dabble in illusionary magic. Add to that obvious intelligence the natural resistance of a gnome to such enchantments as the ruby might cast, and the pendant would never have been effective.

But Nanfoodle was drunk.

He didn't even turn his eyes from the pendant anymore, obviously mesmerized by its continuing sparkling and spinning.

"And do you seek those relations in the westernmost tunnels of Mithral Hall?" Regis asked casually.

"Eh?" Nanfoodle remarked.

"You were there, were you not?" Regis pressed, but quietly so, not wanting his suspicions to break the charm. "In the western tunnels, I mean. You have been going there quite a bit, from what I hear. The dwarves find that curious, even amusing, for there is nothing down there . . . or is there?"

"Sealed tunnels, pitch-washed," Nanfoodle answered absently.

"Then what importance might they offer to your mission in coming all this way?" the halfling asked. "Since you came to check on Torgar, did you not? And to better the relationship between Mirabar and Mithral Hall?

Nanfoodle gave a snort and a shake of his head.

"If only that were so," said the gnome.

Regis froze in place, resisting the urge to fall back in his chair. He gave the pendant another spin.

"Indeed, if only!" he enthusiastically agreed. "So tell me, good gnome, why have you really come?"

The hair on the back of Shoudra Stargleam's neck rose inexplicably when a dwarf informed her that her friend was sitting with Steward Regis, and had been for more than two hours. The sceptrana moved along the corridors, half-running and often slowing as she tried to sort things out. Why was she so bothered and nervous, after all, for wasn't Nanfoodle a reliable companion?

She came into an anteroom where a trio of dwarves stood calmly, each holding a nasty-looking polearm.

"Well met yerself," one of them said to Shoudra, and he motioned for the door to the audience room.

A second dwarf, standing beside the door, pushed it open, and Shoudra heard laughter from within and saw the glow of a comfortable fire. Still, she didn't calm down; something wasn't sitting well with her. She moved to the opening and peered in to see Nanfoodle laughing stupidly on one cushy chair, while a more sober Regis, his wounded arm back in its supporting sling, sat across from him.

"So nice of you to join us, Sceptrana Shoudra," the halfling said, and he motioned to the empty chair.

Shoudra took one step into the room, then jerked suddenly as the door slammed behind her.

"Nanfoodle and I were just discussing the disposition of the relationship between our respective communities," Regis explained, and again he indicated the empty chair to the unmoving sceptrana.

Shoudra hardly heard him, for her attention followed her scan around the room. The walls were all hung with tapestries, save the one that held the hearth, and the heavy hangings were not flat against the wall. Shoudra's gaze went lower, and she noted the toes of more than one pair of boots below the bottom fringe.

Slowly, the sceptrana turned her gaze to Regis.

"It is an interesting relationship, don't you agree," the halfling said, and there was no missing the sudden change in his tone.

"One we hope to strengthen," Shoudra replied, her gaze going to the obviously drunk Nanfoodle.

"Truly?" Regis asked.

Shoudra turned back to him.

"To strengthen our relationship by weakening Mithral Hall's ore?" the halfling asked, and he pulled a large pouch out from behind him on the chair and tossed it on the floor at Shoudra's feet.

Shoudra slowly bent and retrieved the pouch but didn't even have to open it to know what was inside: Nanfoodle's weakening solution.

The sceptrana turned her stunned expression over the gnome, who burst out in great laughter and nearly fell off the chair.

"My new friend Nanfoodle told me everything," Regis stated.

He snapped his fingers in the air, and the tapestries were pulled aside, revealing a trio of grim-faced dwarves. The door behind Shoudra opened as well, and the sceptrana knew that polearms were aimed at her back.

"He has told me," Regis went on, "of how you came here on orders of the marchion to sabotage our ore. Of how Mirabar intended to wage a trade war upon Mithral Hall through such means, to ruin our reputation and steal our customers."

Shoudra began to shake her head.

"You must understand . . ." she started.

"Understand?" Regis interrupted. "Weakened metal in our hands as we battle the orc hordes? Weakened metal on the barricades we construct to keep the monsters out of our halls? What is there to understand, Sceptrana?"

"We didn't know you were at war!" Shoudra blurted.

"Oh, then of course your spying and espionage are not so important!" came the halfling's sarcastic reply.

"No, you must understand the temperament of Marchion Elastul," Shoudra tried to explain. She moved beside Nanfoodle as he spoke and casually draped an arm across his shoulders. "This is his . . . his way. Marchion Elastul fears Mithral Hall, and so he instructed Nanfoodle and I to come here and learn if Torgar was divulging the secrets of Mirabar. You must admit that Mithral Hall has gained a sudden advantage in the trade war, with four hundred of Mirabar's dwarves deserting our city to come to yours."

"Yes, a tremendous advantage with hordes of orcs knocking on our doors."

"We did not know." Shoudra took a deep breath and went on, "And I doubt that Nanfoodle or I would have had the heart to cause any mischief even if there was no war. Neither of us approve of the marchion's tactics here, nor of his disposition concerning King Bruenor and Mithral Hall. We two seek a better way."

"You would say that now, of course," Regis interrupted.

Shoudra closed her eyes and blew a long sigh, then began muttering under her breath.

"Take them and lock them away—and separately," Regis instructed.

The six dwarves advanced on the pair, but then they were gone, winking out of sight.

"The door!" Regis cried, and the dwarf closest the exit rushed back and slammed the portal shut.

Shoudra and a very surprised-looking Nanfoodle appeared suddenly on the far side of the room, and the dwarves hooted and charged.

They disappeared again, reappearing a few moments later in front of the hearth.

"She's casting again! Stop her!" Regis cried, noting Shoudra's renewed chant.

"Watch for fireballs!" cried the dwarf by the door.

He pulled it open, and Shoudra and Nanfoodle appeared right there, as fortune would have it. The dwarf fell away with a shriek.

Nanfoodle giggled stupidly, and Shoudra yanked him out of the room and into a run through the anteroom and out into the corridor, chased every step by the shouting dwarves.

"You silly gnome!" Shoudra scolded, and Nanfoodle giggled even more.

With the dwarves gaining and Nanfoodle lagging, Shoudra gave an exasperated growl and scooped Nanfoodle up.

They went through a door, which Shoudra shut and promptly barred, and out the other side of the room into another corridor. On they ran for the western gate, cries of alarm sounding all around them.

Soon the dwarves had them located once more, a dozen shouts echoing down every side passage they crossed. Finally, the pair turned into the long main corridor, which ended on a wide landing lined by statues of the kings of Mithral Hall. A descending staircase beyond that landing led to a smaller room and across that the last rays of daylight were streaming through the great hall's open western doors.

Doors that weren't to remain open for long, Shoudra realized, for dwarves down there were already pushing aside the doorstops, while others were forming a defensive line across the opening.

"Well, they got us," Nanfoodle said with a chuckle. "Time for torture!"

"Shut up, you fool," Shoudra scolded.

She looked all around, then at the last moment, tugged Nanfoodle into the shadows behind the nearest statue. And not a moment too soon, for a group of dwarves came charging through the moment they were out of sight, all of them shouting to, "Hold the door!" or, "Bar the way!"

Nanfoodle started to cry out in response, but Shoudra clamped a hand over his mouth and held him tight. She took a deep breath and gathered her courage, then she peeked out at the outside door and the area beyond. After finally calming the drunken gnome, the sceptrana began to cast another spell.

She whispered out a chant and the tips of her two index fingers began to glow bright blue. With them, the sceptrana then drew out the lines of a door in the air.

"There!" came a shout—Regis's shout, and Shoudra glanced back to see the halfling and a group of dwarves charging her way.

Without hesitation, the sceptrana hoisted Nanfoodle once more, and as the great western doors of Mithral Hall banged closed, she carried Nanfoodle through her portal.

The dimensional door closed right behind her, and Shoudra breathed a sudden sigh of relief to realize that she and her companion were outside the closed doors, standing alone in Keeper's Dale.

"You got so many tricks," Nanfoodle squeaked, and he laughed again.

Shoudra's eyes shot darts at the foolish alchemist.

"More than you know," she promised.

She hoisted him higher and moved off to the side of the gates, to a hollow area already dark with shadows.

There, the glum Shoudra sat, but not until she had forced Nanfoodle down to the ground. He tried to rise, but Shoudra dropped both of her legs over him, pinning the unsteady gnome.

He started to protest, but Shoudra flicked her finger against the underside of his long and pointy nose.

"Hey!" Nanfoodle cried.

"Shhh," Shoudra insisted, putting her finger over her pursed lips. In a voice low and threatening, she added, "You be quiet, or I'll make you quiet. I've a few magic tricks left."

Those words seemed to take a bit of the drunk off Nanfoodle. He swallowed loudly and said no more.

They sat there as afternoon turned to twilight and twilight to night.

And Shoudra had no idea what they were going to do.

THE FRIENDSHIP DARE

Drizzt pulled himself up over the dark stone and dexterously moved his foot atop the abutment. He started to leap over, quickly sorting out his landing area, but he relaxed and paused, noting that Guenhwyvar had the situation completely under control.

There stood the female drow, weapons in hand, but talking to the cat, bidding Guenhwyvar to back off and not kill her.

"Perhaps if you threw your weapons to the ground, Guenhwyvar would not seem so hungry," Drizzt called down, and he was surprised at how easily the little-used drow language came back to him.

"And when I do, you will instruct your panther to slay me," came the reply.

"I could instruct her so right now," Drizzt argued, "and could be down beside her quickly enough, I assure you. Your choices are few. Surrender, or fight and die."

The female glanced up at him—even from a distance, he could see her sneer—but then she looked back at Guenhwyvar and angrily threw her sword and dagger to the ground.

Guenhwyvar continued to circle her but did not advance.

"What is your name?" Drizzt asked, scrambling over the stone and picking a rocky path down to the small stone hollow where the cat had cornered the female.

"I am of family Soldou," the female replied tentatively. "Is that a name known to you?"

"It is not," Drizzt announced, suddenly right behind her, having fast-stepped around the bowl, out of sight. The suddenness of his arrival startled the female. "And in truth, your surname is not important to me. Not nearly as important as your purpose in being here."

Slowly, the female turned to face him. She was quite pretty, Drizzt noted, with her hair parted so that long strands covered half her face, including one of her reddish eyes—not the spidery bloodshot lines he often saw in orcs, but a general reddish hue.

"I escaped the Underdark much as you did, Drizzt Do'Urden," she answered, and though he did well to hide it, the references to him, the apparent knowledge of his course, did indeed surprise Drizzt. "If you knew of family Soldou, you would understand that we lost favor with the Spider Queen, by choice. As one, we forsook that wicked demon queen, and so we were destroyed almost to a one."

"But you got out?"

"Here I stand."

"Indeed, and in company quite fitting a follower of Lolth," Drizzt remarked, and he brought Twinkle up in a flash, the edge of the blade resting against the side of the female's neck.

She didn't flinch.

"Only so that I could survive," the female tried to explain. "I came out and still have not adapted to this fiery orb that burns its way across the high ceiling."

"It takes time."

"I found the other drow—his name is Ad'non—"

"Was," Drizzt corrected, and he shrugged.

The female didn't flinch.

"I would have killed him soon enough anyway," she went on. "I could not tolerate his vileness any longer. As soon as he stripped down to take advantage of the paralyzed elf, I meant to run him through."

Drizzt nodded, though of course he did not believe a word of it. For a supposed convert against the drow nature, she seemed quite willing to put a dart or two into him, after all.

"You still have not told me your name."

"Donnia," she answered, and Drizzt was somewhat relieved that she had not lied to him on that, at least. He had heard the male call her by name, after all. "I am Donnia Soldou, who seeks the blessing of Eilistraee."

That reference put Drizzt somewhat off his center, obviously so.

"You have heard of the Lady of the Dance?"

"Rumors," said Drizzt.

He believed that the female was lying, of course, but still, he couldn't help but be intrigued, for he had indeed heard whispers of the goddess Eilistraee and her followers—supposedly drow of like heart to his own.

"I am sorry that I turned on you in the cave of the elves," Donnia went on. She lowered her gaze. "You must understand that my companion was a powerful warrior and that I was alive only by his good graces. If he suspected that I was a traitor, he would have long-ago killed me."

"And you found no opportunities in all this time to be rid of him?"

Donnia stared up at him.

"Or is he not the only companion you have found?"

"Only Ad'non," Donnia said. "Well, Ad'non and his friends, the giants and the orcs. He has been here for many years, a rogue not unlike yourself—though his intent is far different. He haunts the tunnels among the upper Underdark and about the Spine of the World, finding his pleasures where he can."

"Then why did you not rid yourself of him and be on your way?" Drizzt asked.

Donnia nodded and rubbed a hand across her face.

"Then I would have been alone," she whispered. "Alone and up here, in this place I do not know. I was weak, Drizzt Do'Urden. Can you not understand?"

"I can indeed," Drizzt admitted.

He sheathed Icingdeath and moved Twinkle from Donnia's neck. With his free hand he began patting the female down. He found a dagger at her belt and took it away, along with her hand crossbow and a belt pouch filled with darts. One of those darts came out quickly and quietly, the ranger sliding it into his belt. Drizzt patted lower, along her leg, and noted the slightest lump at the top of one of her soft boots. He purposely ignored that bulge as he slid his hand down across her ankles. It was a knife, of course, and he made it look like he had just missed it in his inspection.

"Your weapons are drow-made," he remarked, tossing the discovered dagger and hand crossbow to the ground beside the sword and the other dagger. "They will do you little good up here if you plan to remain under the light of the sun." He slid Twinkle into its sheath. "Come along then," he instructed, and he started away, pointedly walking right past the discarded weapons.

He looked back at Donnia as he did, and noting that she wasn't paying him any heed at the moment, he hooked the hand crossbow with his foot and brought it up fast to catch it with his free hand and hook it on his belt.

"Come along," he instructed her once more, and he started away.

He heard Donnia suck in her breath slightly as she moved past the pile of weapons, and he knew what she was thinking. She believed that he was testing her, that he was ready to pull forth his blades and defend should she grab at one of those discarded weapons.

When they crossed by, the weapons still in their pile, Drizzt knew that Donnia believed she had passed that test. Little did she understand that first opportunity to be no more than a ruse.

"Guenhwyvar," the ranger called, baiting the trap all the more sweetly. "Too long have you tarried here. Go home now, I bid!"

Drizzt glanced sidelong at Donnia, watching her as she observed the great panther begin stalking in a circle, round and round until Guenhwyvar's lines blurred and she became a drifting gray mist, initially in the shape of a cat, but then drifting apart to nothingness.

"Guenhwyvar's time here is limited," Drizzt explained. "She tires easily and must return to her Astral home to rejuvenate."

"A marvelous companion," Donnia remarked.

"One of three," Drizzt replied. "Or five, if you count the pegasi, and I assure you that they should be counted."

"You are allied with the surface elves then?" Donnia asked, and before Drizzt could answer, she added, "That is good—they are fine companions for one of our kind who has forsaken the Spider Queen."

"Mighty companions," Drizzt agreed. "The female is a high priestess of an elf god, Corellon Larethian. She will wish to speak with you, no doubt, to determine your veracity."

He noted the slight hesitation in Donnia's step as she moved along right behind him.

"She has spells she will cast upon you," Drizzt pressed. "But fear not, for they are merely to detect if you are lying. Once she has seen the truth of Donnia Soldou . . ."

He ended his words with a sudden spin left to right, drawing Icingdeath from the sheath on his right hip as he turned. As he expected, the panicked Donnia was coming at him, dagger drawn from her boot and arm extended.

Drizzt's leading right hand slapped down over Donnia's wrist and turned her stabbing blade up high and wide, and in rushed the scimitar to poke hard against the female's ribs, drawing a long gash. Donnia spun and scrambled away, but not before she got hit again across the extended arm, hard enough so that she let go of her blade. Clutching her right arm and holding it in tight against the wound to her right side, Donnia stumbled.

Drizzt ran past her.

"All of it a lie—as if I should have ever expected anything else from a drow!" he cried, and he rushed to the side as Donnia veered.

"I will have the truth now, or I will have your head!" Drizzt demanded. "Why are you here? And how many of our kin are in your band?"

"Hundreds!" Donnia yelled at him, and still she scrambled, looking for some escape. "Thousands, Drizzt Do'Urden! And all of them with the edict to bring your head to the Spider Queen!"

Drizzt rushed to block the way before her, and Donnia summoned a globe of darkness around him.

She charged right into it, guessing correctly that he would go out one side or the other. She got past and rushed out of the darkness, coming to the lip of a long drop. Without hesitation, the drow leaped out, again bringing forth the innate magic of her station and race. Before she had plummeted twenty feet, she was drifting down slowly.

"You so disappoint me," she heard Drizzt say behind and above her, and she sensed sincerity in his voice, as if perhaps he truly wanted to believe her tale.

And indeed, he had wanted to believe her. How badly Drizzt wanted to find a drow companion! Another of like mind to him to share his adventures, to truly understand the solitude that was ever in his heart.

Donnia had barely gotten the smile onto her face when she heard the click of a hand crossbow from behind and above, and she felt the sudden sting atop her shoulder. She held her place in midair, counteracting the pull of the ground completely with the levitation. Then she stared at the dart and felt the poison beginning to seep into her shoulder.

She was motionless, helpless, hanging there.

Drizzt looked down at her and sighed deeply. He dropped the hand crossbow—Donnia's own hand crossbow that he had scooped up from the pile as they had set out—and watched it drop past her, down, down, the two hundred feet to shatter on the stones below.

Drizzt fell into a crouch and put his head in his hand. He didn't look away, though, determined to bear witness.

The levitation soon expired and the paralyzed Donnia dropped. She couldn't even scream out as she fell, for her vocal chords could not function against the potent poison.

Drizzt looked away at the last second, not wanting to watch her hit. But then he looked back, to see the drow female splayed across the stones, warm blood pooling around her.

The ranger sighed again, though he wasn't really surprised it had ended like that. Still, the one emotion that dominated Drizzt Do'Urden at that moment was anger, just anger, at the futility of it all.

He gathered himself up a few moments later, reminding himself that Tarathiel and Innovindil were likely still fairly helpless in their cave, and he started back at a fast run. He found them safe and sound, and even beginning to move a bit once more.

Innovindil was reaching for her clothing as Drizzt entered, so he promptly retrieved the items and gave them over, then moved back near the entrance and began cleaning up the mess that was Ad'non.

"Well met again, Drizzt Do'Urden," Tarathiel said to him. "And a most fortunate meeting it is, for us at least."

"You have dealt with the remaining drow?" Innovindil asked.

"She is dead," Drizzt confirmed, his tone somber. "She fell from a cliff face."

"Did it pain you to kill them?" Innovindil asked.

Drizzt's head snapped around at her, his eyes narrow.

"Did it?" Innovindil asked again, not backing away at all.

Drizzt's visage softened.

"It always does," he admitted.

"Then your soul is intact," Tarathiel remarked. "Be afraid when the killing no longer affects you."

How profound that simple remark seemed to Drizzt at that moment, to the creature who seemed to be caught somewhere between his true self and the Hunter. Certainly he felt more soulless at those times when he was the Hunter. The deaths didn't bother him in that mode. He had felt nothing but the satisfaction of victory when he had beheaded Ad'non, but the death of Donnia had stung more than a little. There had to be some middle ground, Drizzt knew, a place where he could fight as the Hunter and yet hold on to his soul. He thought back across the years and believed that he had found that place before. He could only hope that he would find it again.

Drizzt rummaged through Ad'non's pockets, searching for some clue as to who the dark elf might be and why he was there. He found little, other than a few coins that he did not recognize. One other thing did catch his eye though: the fine light gray silk shirt that Ad'non wore under his cloak. That shirt had stopped Drizzt's scimitars; he could see the indentation marks where his fine blades had struck hard. Furthermore, though the area all around the corpse was deep in blood, none of it seemed to touch Ad'non's shirt.

"Strong magic," Innovindil remarked, and when Drizzt looked to her, she motioned for him to take the shirt as his own. "To the victor. . . ." she recited.

Drizzt began removing the shirt. His own chain mail, forged by Bruenor, was in sore need of repair, with many broken links, and some of them rubbing him uncomfortably.

"We are most grateful," Tarathiel remarked. "You understand that, of course?"

"I could not let them harm you, as I believe you would have come to my aid—indeed, as you have come to my aid," Drizzt replied.

"We are not your enemies," Tarathiel said, and the tone of his voice made Drizzt pause and consider him.

"I have never desired the enmity of any surface elf I have ever known," Drizzt replied, both his tone and his words leading.

He didn't miss the movement as Innovindil and Tarathiel exchanged concerned glances.

"We must tell you that you have made an enemy of one," Innovindil admitted. "Through no fault of your own."

"You remember Ellifain," Tarathiel added.

"Keenly," Drizzt assured him, and he sighed and lowered his gaze. "Though when I last met her, she was called Le'lorinel and was masquerading as a male."

Again the two elves looked to each other, Tarathiel nodding.

"That was how she evaded us in Silverymoon," he said to his partner.

"She came after you," Innovindil reasoned. "We knew that such was her course, though we knew not where you might be. We tried to stop her—you must believe us when we tell you that Ellifain was beyond reason and was acting on her own and against the wishes of our people."

"She was beyond reason," Drizzt agreed.

"And you met her in battle?" Tarathiel quietly asked, his voice full of concern.

Drizzt glanced up at him but lowered his eyes almost immediately and sighed yet again.

"I had no desire to . . . had I known, I would have . . ." he stammered. He took a deep breath and looked directly at the pair. "I caught up to her in the company of some thieves that I and my companions were pursuing. I had no idea of who she was—or even that she was a 'she'—when we joined in combat. It was not until . . ."

"Until you struck the killing blow," Tarathiel reasoned, and Innovindil looked away.

Drizzt's responding silence spoke volumes.

"I feared that it would end this way," Tarathiel said to Drizzt. "We tried to save Ellifain from herself—no doubt you did as well, or that you would have, had you known."

"But she was full of a rage that transcended all rationality," Innovindil added. "With every tale we heard about your exploits in the service of the goodly races, she grew even more outraged, convinced that it was all a lie. Convinced that Drizzt Do'Urden was all a lie."

Drizzt didn't blink as he responded, "Perhaps I am."

"Is that what you believe?" Innovindil asked, and Drizzt merely shrugged.

"We do not judge you harshly for defending yourself against Ellifain," Tarathiel remarked.

"It would change nothing if you did," said Drizzt, and that seemed to take the pair off their balance a bit.

"And so we can fight together in our common cause," Tarathiel went on. "Side-by-side."

Drizzt stared at him for a short while, then looked back at Innovindil. It was a tempting offer, but it entailed a commitment that Drizzt was not yet ready to take. He looked back to Tarathiel and shook his head.

"I hunt alone," he explained. "But I will be there to support you if I may, in times when you are in need."

He gathered up the marvelous silken shirt then and started to go.

"We will always be in need of your help," Tarathiel said from behind him. "And would you not be stronger if . . ."

"Let him go," Drizzt heard Innovindil remark to her companion. "He is not yet ready."

The next morning, Drizzt Do'Urden sat on a bluff looking back at the area of the elves' cave, mulling over the generous offer Tarathiel had given him. He had just admitted to killing their friend and kin, and yet, neither had judged him at all harshly.

It put a whole new light on the unfortunate Ellifain incident for Drizzt Do'Urden, but he just wasn't certain of how that light might yet shine.

And he was confronted with the prospect of new friendship, of new allies, and while the thought tempted him on a very basic level, it also frightened him profoundly.

He had known great friends once and the greatest allies anyone could ever hope to command.

Once.

So he sat and he stared, torn apart inside, wondering what might be and what should be.

Always, always, he found the image of the blasted tower tumbling, taking Bruenor down with it.

Drizzt felt an urgent need to go back to his own cave then, to feel the one-horned helmet, to smell the scent of Bruenor, and to remember his lost friends. He started off.

Before the end of the day, though, he was drawn back to that bluff, looking across the stones to the lair of Innovindil and Tarathiel.

He watched with great interest as one of the pegasi swooped past, bearing Tarathiel down to the cave entrance. To his surprise, the elf dismounted and did not go right in, but rather, ran out his way and called to him.

"Drizzt Do'Urden!" Tarathiel cried. "Come! I have news that concerns us all!"

Despite his reservations, despite the deep pain that pervaded his every fiber, Drizzt found himself trotting along to join the pair.

"Yet another tribe crawls from its dark hole," Innovindil said to Drizzt when he entered the cave. "Tarathiel has seen them marching along the foothills of the Spine of the World."

"You called me in to tell me of orcs in the area?" Drizzt asked incredulously. "There is no shortage of—"

"Not just any orcs, but a new tribe," Tarathiel interrupted. "We have seen them flocking to this cause, one tribe after another. Now we have found a group that has not yet linked up."

"If we strike at them hard, they might go back to their holes," Innovindil explained. "That would be a great victory to our cause." When Drizzt didn't overtly react, she added, "It would be a great victory for those dwarves defending Mithral Hall."

"How many?" Drizzt heard himself asking.

"A small tribe—perhaps fifty," Tarathiel replied.

"The three of us are to kill fifty orcs?" Drizzt asked.

"Better to kill ten and turn the other forty around," Tarathiel replied.

"Let them whisper in their tunnels about certain death awaiting any who go to the call of the orc leader," Innovindil added.

"The orcs and giants have amassed a great army," Tarathiel explained. "Thousands of orcs and hundreds of giants, we fear, and truthfully, our efforts against such a great army will prove a minor factor in the end result. But the more ominous cloud for those in the region, the dwarves of Mithral Hall, the elves of the Moonwood, the people of Silverymoon, are the seemingly limitless reinforcements pouring out of the Spine of the World."

"Tens of thousands more orcs and goblins may flock to the call of whoever it is who leads this army," Innovindil put in.

"But perhaps we can stem that flow of vermin," said Tarathiel. "Let us turn back the orcs, that they warn their fellows about leaving the mountains. Our kills could be multiplied many times over concerning monsters who choose not to join in." He paused and stared hard at Drizzt.

"This is, perhaps, our chance to make a real difference in this war. Just we three."

Drizzt couldn't deny the potential of Tarathiel's plan.

"Quickly, then," Tarathiel remarked when it became obvious that Drizzt wasn't going to argue. "We must hit them before they travel far from the caves, before the fall of night."

Drizzt marveled at how precisely the two elves angled their descending mounts, putting themselves in line with the setting sun as they approached the orc force.

Beside the drow, Guenhwyvar gave an anxious growl, but Drizzt held her back.

In came the two elves and their winged mounts, and their bows began to hum. And the orcs began to shriek and to point up to the sky.

"Now, Guen," Drizzt whispered, and he turned the panther loose.

Guenhwyvar bounded away along a line north of the orcs, while Drizzt sprinted off the other way, hemming the tribe on the south. He found his first battle soon after, even as orcs across the way screamed out in terror at the sight of Guenhwyvar. Drizzt leaped atop a boulder and stood staring down at a pair of orcs who had taken cover from the elves' arrow barrage. He waited for them to finally look up before dropping between them.

Out went Twinkle, a killing blow to his left, while he turned Icingdeath to the flat side as he slapped hard at the orc on his right, sending the creature scrambling away.

Behind him and to his left, the pegasi set down, and the two elves let fly another round of arrows, then leaped free and drew their weapons.

"For the Moonwood!" Drizzt heard Tarathiel cry.

Despite the urgent moment, Drizzt Do'Urden was wearing a grin when he came out hard from behind that boulder, leaping into a devastating spin at the closest ranks of orcs.

At his side, Tarathiel and Innovindil linked arms and went into their deadly dance.

The orcs fell back. One tried to call out commands for them to regroup, but Drizzt immediately engulfed the creature in a globe of darkness.

Another shouted out a command—right before a flying Guenhwyvar buried it.

Within moments, the orcs were running back the way they had come, and when the last rays of daylight winked out, they were still running, and still with Guenhwyvar flanking them on the left and Drizzt on the right and Tarathiel and Innovindil and their powerful mounts pressing them from behind.

Soon after, Drizzt watched the last pair run into a dark, wide cave. He charged up behind them, calling out threats. When one slowed and started to glance back, he rushed ahead and cut the creature down.

Its companion did not look back.

Nor did any others of the tribe.

Drizzt stood in the cave entrance, hands resting against his hips, staring down the deep tunnel beyond.

Guenhwyvar padded up beside him, and soon he heard the clopping of pegasi hooves.

"Exactly as I had hoped," Tarathiel remarked, dismounting and moving to stand beside Drizzt.

He lifted a hand and patted the drow on the shoulder, and though he did flinch a bit initially, Drizzt did not pull away.

"Our technique will only strengthen with practice," Innovindil said as she walked up on Drizzt's other side.

The drow looked deeply into her eyes and saw that she had just challenged him yet again, had just invited him yet again.

He did not openly deny her, nor did he pull away when she moved very close to his side.

19

SETTLING INTO
THE ORC KING'S SHADOW

The work along the western bank of the Surbrin moved at a frenetic pace, with orcs and giants constructing defensive fortifications at all of the possible fords near the southern edge of the mountains around the closed gate of Mithral Hall. King Obould deemed one crossing particularly dangerous, where the river was wide and shallow and an entire army could cross in short order. And so Obould set most of his orcs into action, bringing tons of stones down to the water and packing them tightly together, then filling in with tons of sand, forming a levy that tightened up the river and deepened and strengthened the flow.

Not to be outdone, and taking no chances, Gerti Orelsdottr ordered her giants to ensure that the dwarven gate would not soon be opened, at one point even bringing a landslide down from the mountains. She would not have Clan Battlehammer sneaking out at her backside!

The work went on day and night, with high walls quickly constructed at every crossing point. Giants piled boulders suitable for bombardment at every outpost, ready to meet any crossing with heavy resistance, and orcs similarly filled rooms with hastily made spears. If reinforcements meant to come across the Surbrin, Gerti and Obould meant to make them pay dearly for the ground.

The two leaders met every night, along with Arganth, who was fast becoming Obould's principal advisor. The discussions were usually civil, a discourse about how to best and quickly secure their gains, but it did not escape Gerti's notice that Obould was leading the way at every turn, that his plans made great sense, that his vision had suddenly clarified to a keen and attainable edge. Thus, when the giantess was leaving the nightly meetings, she was usually in a foul mood, and increasingly, she went into the meetings gnashing her teeth.

So it was that night a tenday after the fall of Mithral Hall's eastern gate.

"We must move back to the west," Gerti began, the litany she spoke to open every meeting of late. "Your son remains locked in a stalemate with the dwarves, and he has not the giant allies he needs to dislodge them."

"You are in a hurry to chase them into Mithral Hall?" Obould casually asked.

"One less problem for us when we do."

"Better to let attrition take a heavy toll on them while we have them out here in the open," the orc king reasoned. "Deplete the resources they would employ against Proffit and his smelly trolls."

The notion of the orc king referring to any other race as "smelly" struck Gerti as laughable, but she was in no mood for mirth.

"Do you believe that a few trolls will chase Clan Battlehammer from its ancestral home?" she scoffed.

"Of course Proffit will not succeed," Obould admitted. "But we do not need him to succeed. He will soften them and tighten the noose around them. The tighter we squeeze them in their tunnels, the better the resolution."

"That we wipe them from the North?" Gerti asked, a bit confused, for it did not seem to her that Obould was moving along that line, though it had always before been his stated intent.

"That would be wonderful," the orc king remarked. "If we can. If not, perhaps with their outer doors sealed and pressed in the tunnels, Clan Battlehammer will seek to negotiate a settlement."

"A treaty between conquering orcs and dwarves?" Gerti asked incredulously.

"What is their option?" asked Obould. "Will they carry on their trade through tunnels to Silverymoon and Felbarr?"

"They might."

"And when we at last locate and drop those tunnels?" Obould asked, seeming perfectly confident in that. "Will the dwarves follow the way of that wretched Do'Urden creature and begin doing trade with the drow of the Underdark?"

"Or perhaps they will do nothing of the sort," Gerti argued. "Surely Mithral Hall is self-contained and self-sustaining. Clan Battlehammer may be content to remain in their hole for a century, if necessary." She leaned forward over her crossed legs. "Your kind has never been known for its long-term resolve, Obould. Orc conquests are usually short-lived affairs, and more often than not, lost by the warring of other orcs."

That particular reference was purposely worded and aimed to sting Obould, for not long in the past the orc king had made a great conquest indeed, sweeping the dwarves from Citadel Felbarr and renaming it the Citadel of Many-Arrows. But then had come the inevitable squabbling, orc against orc, and the dwarves under King Emerus Warcrown had wasted little time in chasing Obould's distracted and chaotic invaders back out. Gerti had launched her not-too-subtle reminder of that disaster just to drop her counterpart's mounting ego a few pegs. The giantess was surprised, though, and more than a little disappointed, at how composed Obould remained.

"True enough," the orc king even admitted. "Perhaps we have learned from our mistakes."

Gerti honestly wanted to ask that strange creature who he truly was and what he had done with that sniveling fool, Obould.

"When the region is secured and our numbers great enough, we will build orc cities," Obould explained, and he seemed to be looking far away then, as if he was visualizing that of which he spoke. "We will find our own commerce and trade and seek out surrounding towns to join in."

"You will send an emissary to Lady Alustriel and Emerus Warcrown seeking trade agreements?" Gerti blurted.

"Alustriel first," Obould calmly replied. "Ever has Silverymoon been known for tolerance. I expect that King Warcrown will need more persuading."

He looked directly at Gerti and grinned wickedly, his tusks curling over his upper lip.

"But we will have barter," Obould asked, "will we not?"

"What goods might you produce that they cannot get elsewhere?"

"We will hold the key to Clan Battlehammer's freedom," Obould explained. "Perhaps we allow for the reopening of the eastern door of Mithral Hall. Perhaps we even construct a great bridge at that point over the Surbrin. We allow Mithral Hall to trade openly and aboveground once again, and all for a tithe, of course."

"You have gone mad," Gerti snapped at him. "Dwarves fall before orc blades! King Bruenor himself was killed by your son's charges. Do you believe they will so quickly forget?"

"Who can know?" the orc king said with a shrug, and he seemed to hardly care. "They are just the options, all the more possible because of our successes. If all this land becomes an orc stronghold, will the peoples of the region band together and fight us? How many thousands will they sacrifice? How long will they hold their resolve when their kin die by the score? By the hundred, or thousand? And all of that with the option of peace honestly offered to them."

"Honestly?"

"Honestly," Obould replied. "We cannot take Silverymoon, or Sundabar, if all my kin and all your kin and all the trolls of the Trollmoors banded together. You know this as I know this."

The admission nearly had Gerti choking with disbelief, for she had known that truth from the beginning, of course, but had never believed that Obould would ever truly understand his real limitations.

"Wh-what about Citadel Felbarr?" she did manage to stammer, hoping once more to throw the orc king off his guard.

"We will see how far our victories take us," Obould replied. "Perhaps Mithral Hall will be conquered—that is no less a prize than Felbarr. Perhaps even the Moonwood will fall to us in the months it will take to secure any peace. We will be in need of lumber, of course, and not so that we might dance about the living trees as do the foolish elves."

He looked to the side again, as if staring far away, and gave a little guttural chuckle.

"We get too far ahead of ourselves," the orc king remarked. "Let us secure what we now have. Close the Surbrin to those who would support Mithral Hall. Let Proffit work his disaster in the southern tunnels, and let Urlgen then drive the dwarves fully into their hole and close the western door. Then we might decide our next march."

Gerti settled back against the wall of the stone room and stared at her counterpart and at the smug shaman sitting next to him. She resisted the urge to reach out and crush the life out of Arganth, though she dearly wanted to do just that, if only because he was such an ugly little wretch.

And she wondered, honestly, if she should spring forward and crush the life out of Obould first. The creature who was sitting before her was constantly amazing her, was constantly putting her off her balance. He was not the sniveling orc who had once brought her dwarf heads as a present. He was not the overreaching and doomed-to-disaster warrior leader whom she had played as an ally out of amusement. Obould was biding his time over in the west against the dwarves, sacrificing short-term gain and swift victory for a long-term benefit. What orc ever thought like that?

It seemed to Gerti as if Obould honestly had it all planned out, and even more amazing, it seemed as if he had a real chance of succeeding. What she had to wonder, however, was what plans the orc king might have in store for her.

"They smell like rothé dung in fetid water," Tos'un complained.

Despite her generally foul mood, Kaer'lic Suun Wett didn't argue the point—her nose wouldn't let her.

"And Proffit is the smelliest of the bunch," Tos'un rambled on.

Kaer'lic shot him a look reminding him that they were two drow amidst an army of trolls and that it might not do well to so openly insult the leader of the brutes.

"Perhaps that is how he got so elevated," Tos'un added, amusing himself, Kaer'lic figured, for she found nothing at all amusing about their current state of affairs. Particularly concerning her own state of indecision.

Tos'un continued to grumble and began to stalk around. He stopped suddenly and took a closer look at the small cave Kaer'lic had taken for her temporary shelter. Glyphs and runes had been etched here and there, and the priestess's ceremonial robes were set out.

When Tos'un turned to more closely scrutinize her, she did not hide the fact that she had been beginning to change into those garments when he had burst in.

"This is not a ceremonial day, is it?" the male asked.

"No," the priestess answered simply.

"Then you are communing . . . perhaps to locate our lost companions?"

"No."

"To gain spells that will help us with the trolls?"

"No."

"Am I to guess every possible purpose, then? Or is it that you would not tell me in any case?"

"No."

Tos'un paused and studied her, obviously not quite sure of where that last answer fit in exactly.

"Your pardon, high priestess," he said with clear sarcasm, and he dipped a bow that was full of his frustration. "I forget my place as a mere male."

"Oh, shut up," Kaer'lic replied, and she moved toward her vestments and began further disrobing. "I am as confused as you are," she admitted.

She gave a little laugh as she considered that—why shouldn't she tell Tos'un the truth, after all, since he was the only drow companion she was going to know for some time?

"It does not surprise me that Ad'non and Donnia sneaked away," Tos'un said.

"Nor does it surprise me," Kaer'lic replied. "My confusion has nothing to do with them."

"Then what? Obould?"

"He would be part of it, yes," said the priestess. "As would be whatever intervention his brutish god offered."

"It was an impressive ceremony."

Kaer'lic turned on him suddenly, caring not at all that she was stripped to the waist.

"I fear that I have angered Lolth," she admitted.

It didn't seem to sink into Tos'un at first, and he started to respond. But then, with her continuing stare, the weight of her words nearly bowled the male over. He glanced around, as if expecting some creature of the Abyss to leap out of the shadows and devour him then and there.

"What does that mean?" he asked, his voice shaky.

"I do not know," Kaer'lic replied. "I do not even know if I am correct in my assessment."

"Do you think the intervention of Gruumsh One-Eye to be—"

"No, it was before that ceremony," Kaer'lic admitted.

"Then what?"

"I fear it is because of your advice," Kaer'lic honestly replied.

"Mine?" the male protested. "What have I done that holds any sway to the Spider Queen? I have offered nothing—"

"You suggested that we would be better served in avoiding Drizzt Do'Urden, did you not?"

Tos'un rocked back on his heels, his eyes darting around, seeming like a trapped animal.

"I fear that I am trapped within a web of my own suspicions," said Kaer'lic. "Perhaps my unwillingness to engage the traitor, as you advised, has cost me Lolth's favor, but in truth, I fear that going against Drizzt Do'Urden and slaying him would anger the Spider Queen even more!"

Tos'un looked as if a slight breeze would have knocked him over.

"She denies you communion?"

"I am afraid to even try," the priestess admitted. "It is possible that my own fears work against me here."

"Your fears of Drizzt?" he asked, shaking his head, so obviously at a complete loss.

"Long ago, I came to some conclusions concerning the renegade of House Do'Urden," Kaer'lic explained. "Even before I knew of Matron Baenre's march against Mithral Hall. The name of Drizzt was not unknown to us even before you joined our little band. So many of our priestesses have come to errant presumptions concerning that one, I fear . . . and I believe. They see him as an enemy of the Spider Queen."

"Of course," said Tos'un. "How could he be anything but?"

"He is a facilitator of chaos!" Kaer'lic interrupted. "In his own beautiful way, Drizzt Do'Urden has brought more chaos to your home city than perhaps any before him. Would that not be the will of Lolth?"

Tos'un's eyes widened so much that it seemed as if they might simply roll out of their sockets.

"You believe the road of Drizzt Do'Urden to be Lolth-inspired?" he asked.

"I do," said Kaer'lic, and she turned away. "Clever Kaer'lic! To see the irony of the rebel. To imagine the beauty of Lolth's design."

"It does make sense," the other drow admitted.

"And either way, whether my guess is correct or not, I am trapped by my own cleverness," said Kaer'lic.

Tos'un moved around to stare at her curiously.

"If I am wrong," the priestess explained, "then we should have engaged the renegade with all our powers, as I believe Ad'non and Donnia now seek to do. If I am right, then I have exposed a design that is far beyond . . ."

Her voice trailed away.

"If you are right, the mere fact that you have solved the riddle of Drizzt brings weakness to Lady Lolth's designs," the male reasoned.

"And we cannot know."

Tos'un began shaking his head and trembling.

He said, "And you told me."

"You asked."

"But . . ." the male stammered. "But . . ."

"We do not know anything," Kaer'lic reminded him, holding up her hand before the quivering fool to calm him. "It is all speculation."

"Then let us break free of these wretched trolls and seek Drizzt out, that we might learn the truth," Tos'un offered.

"To reveal my discovery fully?"

Tos'un seemed to quickly come to see her point, his sudden, apparent eagerness fast wilting.

"Then what?" he asked.

"Then I will seek my answers as we travel with Proffit," Kaer'lic explained. "I must find my heart for the call to the handmaidens, though I fear the machinations of Lady Lolth and the fate that awaits those who seek to look through her plans."

"The Time of Troubles marked the greatest chaos in Menzoberranzan," he told her. "When House Oblodra, fortified by their psionic powers when the magic of all others seemed to fail about them, aspired to the mantle of First House and nearly won it. Of course, Lady Lolth then returned to the pleas of Matron Baenre . . . never have I seen such a catastrophe as that which befell the Oblodrans!"

Kaer'lic nodded, for the male had told her and her fellows that story before, in great and gory detail.

"It is a confusing time," she said again. "If my fears of Lolth's purpose concerning Drizzt Do'Urden weren't enough, we witness a rare display of true orc shaman might."

"You fear Obould," Tos'un stated more than he asked.

"We would be wise to stay wary of that one," Kaer'lic replied, not denying a thing. "And not because he is suddenly so much physically stronger and so much quicker. No, we must watch Obould carefully because, so suddenly, he is right!"

"Perhaps we were wrong in our estimation of the gifts Gruumsh has placed on that one. Perhaps the shamans imbued him with more than muscle and agility," Tos'un reasoned. "Is it possible that the ceremony gave to him the gift of insight as well?"

"At the least, he learned well his priorities," said Kaer'lic. "Forgoing his anger and hunger for a level of reason beyond anything I ever expected of the pig-faced creature. Consider this mission we find ourselves along—consider how easily and completely Obould is using Proffit and his trolls. If Obould can secure the area and keep the flow of orcs and goblins coming strong from the mountains, all the while holding firm his alliance with Proffit, then there is every reason to believe that he might just succeed in creating an orc nation in the North. Is it possible that Obould will bring his people to parity with Silverymoon and Sundabar, that he will force treaties, perhaps even trade agreements?"

"They are orcs!" Tos'un protested.

"Too smart for orcs, suddenly," lamented Kaer'lic. "We would do well to carefully watch these developments and to take no course contrary to Obould for the time being."

Once again, both Kaer'lic and Tos'un found themselves back on their heels at the observation; the two had been over it all before, but every time, they came to the same inescapable conclusion, and both were amazed.

"I wish that Ad'non and Donnia had not gone running off," Tos'un lamented. "It would be best if we were all together now."

"To retreat?"

"If it comes to that," the warrior from House Barrison Del'Armgo admitted. "For where and how shall we fit into Obould's kingdom?"

"From afar, in any case," Kaer'lic answered. "But fear not, for we shall find our fun. Even if Obould's vision comes to pass and he secures the realm he will claim as his own, how long will the orc kingdom hold? How long did it hold when Obould had Citadel Felbarr in his grasp? They will fall apart soon enough, do not doubt, and we will find enjoyment throughout the process, so long as we are cunning and careful."

Her own lack of confidence as she spoke that thought struck the blustering priestess profoundly. Was she uncomfortable because of her fears concerning the ultimate power behind the renegade Do'Urden? Or had the orc ceremony so unsettled her? Kaer'lic had to wonder if her lack of confidence was well founded, and directly proportional to her growing confidence in Obould's capabilities.

"And our enjoyment now?" Tos'un asked sarcastically.

"Yes, the trolls smell terribly," Kaer'lic replied. "But let us lead them as we were asked, through the tunnels toward Mithral Hall. You and I stay out of the way and out of the fighting—let the trolls and the dwarves slaughter each other with abandon. What do we care which side emerges victorious?"

Tos'un considered the words for a few moments, then nodded his agreement. He looked around at the hastily decorated chamber.

"Do you think you will find your confidence in Lolth's graces once more?" he asked.

"Who can know Lolth's will?" Kaer'lic said, with more than a little defeat obvious in her tone. "The enigma of the renegade Do'Urden troubles me greatly. In this time of chaos, I am the main representative of Lady Lolth and in the face of great presence of Gruumsh One-Eye. If through my cleverness or folly, I have compromised my own position in this, I have removed Lady Lolth from a deserved position in this delicious conquest."

"Or is there a personal remedy?" Tos'un remarked with a sly grin.

"I am not yet ready to embrace that notion and go chasing after Drizzt Do'Urden," Kaer'lic replied. "If Lolth is angry with me for my suspicions of her intentions concerning the rogue, then I will need guidance, and I will need to be well equipped with her blessing."

Tos'un nodded and glanced around once more.

"I wish you well in your search," he said. He turned to leave, adding, "for both our sakes."

Kaer'lic appreciated that last remark and felt better about her decision to reveal her weakness to the warrior. Normally, a dark elf would never offer advantage to another dark elf, fearing a dagger in the back. Might Tos'un figure to gain favor with Lolth by killing Kaer'lic? The priestess pushed that unsettling notion aside, reminding herself that their little band wasn't typical for the drow. The four of them were more reliant on each other than normal, for defense, for profit, and yes, even for companionship. How horrible the journey would be for her if Tos'un was not beside her. And he felt the same way, she knew, and that had guided her instincts that it would be acceptable to reveal the truth to him.

Because if it was personal, if Lolth was angry at her for purposefully turning away from Drizzt Do'Urden, then she would need Tos'un's assistance—and Ad'non's and Donnia's as well, if the renegade's reputation was to be believed.

Yes, Kaer'lic was thinking very much along the same lines as Tos'un. She wished those other two had not run off.

"What is it?" Gerti asked as she entered the wide cave beside the river that Obould had taken as his temporary quarters. The orc king sat on a stone to one side, his head resting in one hand and a look of concern on his brutish face—more concern than Gerti had seen since that troublesome ceremony.

"News from the north," Obould replied. "The Red Slash emerged from the Spine of the World to join in our cause."

His word choice alone reminded Gerti that he was not the same orc king who had often before come sniveling into her cave.

Obould looked up at her and said, "They were turned back."

"Turned back?" Gerti asked, and her voice turned snide. "Have your people already reverted to their self-destructive ways? Are they preparing the way for a counterattack before victory has even been achieved?"

"They were turned back by elves," Obould sourly replied, and he glared at the giantess, as open a threat as Gerti had ever seen from any orc.

"The elves have crossed the Surbrin?" the giantess asked, but not with too much concern.

"They were turned back by a *pair* of elves . . . and a drow," Obould clarified. "Does that ring familiar?"

"These Red Slash orcs—a small tribe?"

"Does it matter?" Obould replied. "They will run back into the tunnels now, and alert any others who were considering coming out to join with us."

"But Arganth spreads the word of the glory of Obould," said Gerti, "and Obould is Gruumsh, yes?"

As Obould narrowed his eyes, Gerti knew that he had caught on to the underpinnings of sarcasm in her voice, and she was glad of that. She might not overtly go against him just then, but she was more than willing to let him know that she remained less than impressed.

"Do not underestimate the advantages that Arganth and his shamans have brought to us," Obould warned.

"To us, or to Obould?"

"To both," the orc said definitively. "Their call sounds deep in the tunnels. I have brought forth perhaps fifteen thousand orcs, and thousands of goblins as well, but there are ten times those numbers still available to us if we can coax them forth. We cannot have these puny enemies turning the retreat of a few into a tactical advantage for our enemies."

Gerti wanted to argue of course—mostly because she just wanted to argue with everything Obould said—but she found that she really could not find flaws in the logical reasoning. "What will you do?" she heard herself asking.

"The preparations here are well underway, so we will take the bulk of our force and march off at once, back to the west and the north," Obould announced. "We will send some to reinforce Urlgen so that he can continue the fight on the north ridge for as long as the dwarves are foolish enough to stay and battle. Whatever his losses, we can afford them much more easily than the dwarves can afford theirs.

"I had planned to swing immediately around to the west," Obould went on, "and close the vice on the place the dwarves call Keeper's Dale, driving them into Mithral Hall. But first I will go north with Arganth and some others to see to this problem."

Gerti eyed him suspiciously, trying not at all to hide her trepidation.

"I expect that you will afford me a few of your kin for my journey," Obould answered that look. "You can come along or not, at your pleasure. Either way, I will have a pair of elf heads and a drow's to hang on the sides of my carriage."

"You do not have a carriage," the giantess remarked.

"Then I will build one," Obould replied without missing a beat.

Gerti didn't answer but merely turned and exited, and that act alone signified to her the change that had come over her relationship with Obould. Always before, it had been the orc king coming to Shining White, her icy mountain home, to speak with her, but lately, she more often than not seemed the visitor in Obould's growing kingdom.

With that unsettling thought reverberating within her as she walked out into the daylight, the giantess also heard the orc king's dismissive, "you can come along or not, at your pleasure," echoing in her mind.

Gerti pointedly reminded herself that she could not afford to let Obould move her too far to the margins. Her thoughts began to crystallize around the realization that if the orc king's confidence continued to grow into such impertinence, she might have to kill him. The timing would be everything, the giantess realized. She had to let Obould play his hand out, let him chase the dwarves into the tunnels and begin the full-fledged flushing of Clan Battlehammer, and let him stand as the center point of war with the larger communities in the North, if it came to that.

If there was to be a fall, Gerti wanted Obould to take it. If there was to be only glory and gain, then she would have to give Obould his fall and step into the vacated position.

The giantess would enjoy crushing the life out of the impertinent and ugly orc.

She had to keep telling herself that.

DELAYING THE INEVITABLE

"That's it then? We just leave?" Nanfoodle asked Shoudra.

The little gnome assumed a defiant posture, folding his little arms over his chest and tapping his foot impatiently, his toes, which could not be seen, flapping the front of his red robes.

"You would have us go back in there after your revelations to Steward Regis?" the sceptrana returned, pointing back over Nanfoodle's shoulder at the closed door of Mithral Hall. "I prefer to report in person to Marchion Elastul, if you please, and not simply by having my disembodied head delivered to him on a Clan Battlehammer platter!"

Nanfoodle's bluster did diminish a bit at the reminder that he had been the one to betray them, and his foot stopped tapping quite so insistently.

"It . . . it was the truth," he stammered. "And when they hear the whole truth, they will understand—I never meant to follow through with Marchion Elastul's stupid mission anyway."

"So just march in and tell that to Regis," Shoudra offered. "I am certain he will believe you."

Nanfoodle muttered under his breath and went back into his defiant mode.

"Of course we cannot go back in there!" said the gnome. "Not yet. We have to prove ourselves to the dwarves—and why should we not? We did come here under false pretenses and with nefarious designs. So let us show them the truth of Nanfoodle and Shoudra and of how the truth is different from that of Marchion Elastul."

"Well said," Shoudra remarked, her sarcasm still dripping. "Shall we go and destroy the orc hordes? Perhaps we can return to the halls before the afternoon beer and cookies . . ."

She stopped, seeing Nanfoodle's eyes go wide and for a moment, she thought he was staring incredulously at her. But then Shoudra heard the wailing behind her and she spun around to see a trio of dwarves approaching from the north. Two flanked the green-bearded one in the center, the dwarf on Pikel Bouldershoulder's right holding him under the shoulder, while the dwarf on his left, his brother Ivan, held a blood-soaked cloth up to the stump that remained of his left arm.

"Oooo," Pikel whined.

Nanfoodle and Shoudra rushed across the expanse to meet up with the trio.

"Oooo," said Pikel.

"They got me brother good," Ivan bellowed. "Took his arm off clean with that slate them giants're chucking. Damned unlucky shot!"

"They've got the high ground now, and once they get their war engines built, there will be many more coming down," said the other dwarf supporting Pikel. "This wound'll be a little one compared to what we're soon to see."

The trio hustled by, heading straight for the door, and Shoudra and Nanfoodle wisely moved farther out of the way.

"We cannot abandon them in this dark hour," Nanfoodle insisted.

Shoudra peeked around a boulder as the great doors opened and the trio were hustled inside. The sceptrana fell back quickly, though, for a couple of dwarf guards came out and began glancing all around.

"What would you have us do, Nanfoodle the alchemist," she replied, putting her back to the stone and seeming, in that dark moment, as if she truly needed it for support. "Perhaps we can join with the orcs, and you can poison their weapons with your concoction."

It was meant as a joke, of course, but Nanfoodle seemed to brighten suddenly as he stared at Shoudra. He snapped his stubby fingers in the air.

"We just might do that!" he declared.

He started away toward the north, staying close to the cover of the uneven, broken wall.

"What are you talking about?" Shoudra demanded, pacing him easily.

"They need us up there, so let us go and see where we might fit in," the gnome replied.

Shoudra grabbed him by the shoulder and halted him.

"Up there?" she echoed, pointing up to the top of the northern cliff. "Up there, where the battle rages?"

Nanfoodle fell back into his cross-armed, toe-tapping stance.

"Up there," he answered.

Shoudra scoffed.

"You know that I am right in this," the gnome argued. "You know that we owe it to Clan Battleham—"

"We *owe* it to Clan Battlehammer?" the sceptrana asked.

"Yes, of course," said Nanfoodle, and it was his turn to bathe his words in sarcasm. "We owe them nothing. Not even in common cause against monstrous armies. Not even though they might be the only thing standing between these orc and giant hordes and Mirabar herself! Not even because they have offered Torgar Hammerstriker and his followers the friendship of brothers. Not even because they welcomed us into their homes, trusting us even though they had no sound reason to. Not even because—"

"Enough, Nanfoodle," said Shoudra, and she waved her hands in surrender. "Enough."

The tall, beautiful woman gave a long sigh as she looked back up at the high cliff and at the lines of rope ladders hanging down, crossing from ledge to ledge.

"Up there," she stated more than asked.

"Perhaps you have a spell that will carry us up to them?" the gnome asked hopefully.

Shoudra looked back at him and shook her head.

His look was crestfallen, but that was quickly pushed aside by renewed determination as little Nanfoodle the alchemist led the way to the base of the cliff and the nearest rope ladder. He gave one look over at Shoudra, and he began to climb.

It took the pair more than an hour to get up the side of the cliff, pausing to rest at every available ledge. When they finally did near the top, the first faces that greeted them were not dwarves', to their surprise.

"Regis sent you?" Catti-brie asked, peering over at the two.

She reached her hand down toward Nanfoodle, while Wulfgar fell flat beside her and extended his strong arm to Shoudra.

"We came on our own," Shoudra answered as she climbed up and brushed herself off. "We were preparing to leave—back home to Mirabar—but thought to check in and see if we might be of some use up here."

"We can use all the help we can find," Wulfgar answered. He turned and stepped aside, giving the pair a wide view of the lands below them to the north, where the vast orc and goblin army was regrouping. "They have come at us regularly, several times each day."

Lowering her gaze to encompass the descending ground between the dwarves and the orcs, Shoudra could see the truth of the barbarian's words, as evidenced by the scores of hacked orc and goblin bodies. Blood was so thick about the battleground by that point that it seemed as if the gray stone itself had taken on a deeper, reddish hue.

"We're killing them twenty to one," Catti-brie remarked. "And still they're coming."

Shoudra glanced over at Nanfoodle, who nodded grimly.

"We will help where we may," the sceptrana assured the two human children of King Bruenor.

"Ye'd be helping more if ye might be finding a way to take out them giants," came the call of a dwarf, Banak Brawnanvil, as he stalked over to greet the pair of new recruits.

He turned as he approached, motioning back to the ridge in the distant west, a mountain arm running north-south.

"They cannot reach us with their stones," Catti-brie explained. "But they've improvised well, hurling flat pieces of—"

"Slate," Shoudra finished, nodding. "We met up with the unfortunate Bouldershoulder down in Keeper's Dale."

"Poor Pikel," said Catti-brie.

"The giants will become more of a problem than that soon enough," Banak put in.

He didn't elaborate, but he didn't have to, for as she scanned the giants' position far to the northwest, Shoudra could see the great logs that had been brought up to the ridge, some of them already assembled into wide bases. No stranger to battle, Shoudra Stargleam could guess easily enough what the behemoths might be constructing.

"The slate is troublesome and unnerving," Wulfgar explained. "But in truth, they cannot often get the soaring pieces anywhere near to us, despite Pikel's misfortune. But once they assemble and sight in those catapults, we will have little cover from the barrage."

"And I'm thinking that they'll have a couple up and launching tomorrow," Banak added.

"Their advantage will drive you from the cliffs," Nanfoodle reasoned, and no one disagreed.

"Well, we're glad to have ye, for as long as we can have ye," Banak said suddenly and enthusiastically, brightening the dampened mood. He turned to Wulfgar and Catti-brie. "The two of ye show them about so they might figure how they'll best fit in."

Despite the many forays by their enemies, the dwarves had done a fine job of creating defensive positions, Shoudra and Nanfoodle quickly realized. Their walls were neither high nor thick, but they were well angled to protect from flying slate and well designed to allow for the bearded warriors to move from position to position along the trenches created behind them. Most of all, the dwarves had forced a series of choke points up near the cliff, areas where the orc advantage in numbers would be diminished by lack of room. Shoudra could well imagine that the last orc charge, if designed to drive the dwarves over the cliff, would prove very costly to the aggressors.

And the dwarves were preparing for the eventuality of that retreat as well. With several hundred to evacuate, it seemed clear to Shoudra that many would be killed on the journey down the rope ladders—taken down by missiles from above and perhaps tumbling away when ropes were slashed. Shoudra recognized many of the dwarves, Mirabar engineers, hard at work on the answer to that dilemma. They were digging a tunnel, a slide actually, with a wide hopper area leading to a narrower channel that wound down within the stone, paralleling the descent of the cliff itself.

"Would you even fit down there?" Shoudra asked the huge Wulfgar.

"They've set drop-ropes as well," the barbarian explained. "The slide is for those last dwarves leaving."

"Ye think ye got a spell or two to grease the run?" came a familiar voice from out of the hole.

Nanfoodle fell flat and peered in to see Shingles McRuff climbing up from the darkness.

"It is good to see you well," Shoudra said when the dwarf emerged from the hole.

"Well enough, I suppose," Shingles replied. "But we lost many kin when them ugly orcs took the tunnels in the west."

"Tunnels?"

"Under the ridge," Catti-brie explained. "Torgar, Shingles, and the others from Mirabar tried to hold them, but the onslaught was too great." The woman glanced over at the dirty dwarf. "But more orcs died than dwarves, to be sure," she added, and Shingles managed a smile.

"Tunnels under the ridge?" Nanfoodle inquired.

"A fair network," Shingles explained. "Not too wide and not too many, but running one end to the other."

Nanfoodle's expression suddenly became very intrigued, and he looked up at Shoudra.

"And no easy access up to the ridge," Catti-brie remarked, "if you're thinking we should fight our way back in there and rush up at the giants."

Nanfoodle merely nodded and began tapping his finger against his chin. He moved off for a moment and glanced back over the cliff at Keeper's Dale.

"What's he thinking?" Shingles asked.

"With him, who can tell?" came Shoudra's answer, given with a shrug. "Pray tell me, my old friend, how fares Torgar?"

"He's well," Shingles reported.

He looked down to the northeast, to a group of dwarves holding a tight formation behind a low wall, ready to spring up and counter any orc charge. Studying the group, Shoudra thought she could make out the familiar figure of Master Hammerstriker, whose actions in Mirabar carried effects for them all that seemed to go on and on.

"Well as can be," Shingles added. "He's not much happy about losing the tunnels."

"Too many orcs," Catti-brie said. "And too many giants, and some with dark magic. The Mirabarran dwarves did well to hold as long as you did."

"Yeah, yeah," came Shingles's dismissive answer.

"Perhaps you'll get the chance to take it back," Nanfoodle offered, rejoining the group.

"Might that we will, but I'm not for seeing any reason," Shingles replied. "Won't do us much good in getting rid o' them giants, and them giants're the big trouble now. Can't see how we're to stop 'em."

Nanfoodle looked at Shoudra, who gave a great sigh and walked off a couple of steps to the northwest, cupping her hand over her eyes and looking off at the high ridge.

"Solutions are often complicated," Nanfoodle said, and the gnome was grinning widely. "Unless you follow them logically, one little step at a time."

"What're you thinking?" Catti-brie asked.

"I am thinking that I have been presented a problem. One in need of a solution in short order." Still smiling, the gnome turned back to Shoudra—to her back, actually, for she continued her scan of the ridge. "And what are you thinking, Shoudra?" he asked.

"I am thinking that I know what you can do to metal, my friend," the sceptrana answered. "Would you have a similar solution for wood?"

Nanfoodle looked back to the puzzled expressions of Catti-brie, Wulfgar, and Shingles.

He offered them another wide smile.

The feeling of flying was strange indeed to Wulfgar—almost as much so as the spell Shoudra had cast upon him so that he could see in the night as well as any elf. He was the only one enchanted with the power of flight—the others were simply levitating—so he was the guiding force, pulling them all across the broken terrain of the mountain ridge.

He kept glancing back at them, though since they were invisible, he couldn't see them or the tow ropes. He knew they were there, for he could feel the resistance on the separate ropes from all four: Catti-brie, Torgar, Shoudra, and Nanfoodle.

Remembering Shoudra's warning that magical flight was unpredictable, Wulfgar set down as soon as it seemed to him that the remaining run to the giants and their war engines was smooth enough to easily traverse. He set himself firmly and ducked low, understanding that the levitating foursome would continue to fly past him. One by one, he caught them and broke their momentum as their different lengths of rope played out to the end, and though all of them did their best to remain quiet against the tug, there came a slight grunt from Nanfoodle that had them all holding their breath.

The giants didn't seem to notice.

It took the five a short while to untangle and untie themselves and get together, for only Shoudra and Nanfoodle, enchanted with spells of magical vision, could see the others. Finally, they were all settled behind a small jut.

"We were wise in coming out," Shoudra whispered. "The giants' catapults are nearing completion."

"I will need five minutes," Nanfoodle whispered in reply.

"Not so long a time," said Shoudra.

"Longer than you think, with a score of giants about," Catti-brie whispered.

Nanfoodle set off then, and Shoudra guided her three invisible companions around to the east of the giants, to a defensible position.

"Just say when to go," Catti-brie offered.

"As soon as you attack, the invisibility spell will dissipate," Shoudra reminded her.

In response, Catti-brie lifted Taulmaril over the lip of the jut, settling the bow into the general direction of the closest group of giants. Only then did she realize that she couldn't rightly aim the invisible weapon, for she had no reference points with which to sight it in.

"You two here, then," Shoudra agreed. "You will hear the first sounds soon enough." The sceptrana took Torgar's hand and led him away, circling even more to the east and north of the giant encampment.

"I'd be feeling a bit more comforted if I could see you ready beside me," Catti-brie whispered to Wulfgar.

"Right here," he assured her.

He went silent and so did she, for a giantess moved very near to their position.

Many minutes slipped past in tense silence, broken only by the hum of the wind whistling through the many broken stones. Even the wind was not loud that night, as if all the world was hushed in anticipation.

And it began. Catti-brie and Wulfgar jumped back in surprise at the abrupt commotion off to the north, a great din that sounded as if an entire dwarf army had gone on the attack. The giants reacted at once, leaping up and turning that way.

Catti-brie let the nearest of the behemoths get a few long strides farther away, then let fly a sizzling blue bolt, slamming the giantess right in the center of her back. She howled and had just started to turn when Aegis-fang smacked her across the shoulder, sending her sprawling to the stone.

"To the glory of Moradin!" came a great roar, a magically enhanced blast of Torgar's voice, Catti-brie realized.

Then came a lightning bolt, splitting the darkness and sending a handful of giants tumbling aside.

Catti-brie let fly another arrow into the giantess, and as soon as his magical warhammer reappeared in his waiting hand, Wulfgar launched it at the next nearest giant, who was turning to see to his fallen companion.

More cries to the dwarf god echoed from the north, another lightning bolt lit up the night, then came a sudden storm, a downpour of sleet pelting the stones near to Wulfgar and Catti-brie.

The woman hardly slowed her shooting, letting fly arrow after arrow, and many giants turned and charged at her position.

And many giants slipped on the slick stones. One nearly navigated his way all the way to the jut, but Aegis-fang smashed him in the chest. Though the giant seemed to handle the heavy blow well, he staggered backward under its weight, his feet sliding out from under him.

Catti-brie hit him in the face with an arrow as he sat there on the wet and shiny stones.

A great hand appeared right in front of her, the scrambling giantess finally crawling to the other side of the jut. She pulled herself up with a roar, and Catti-brie was suddenly falling away.

It wasn't from anything the giantess had done, though, the woman soon realized. Wulfgar had tossed her aside, taking her place, and as the giantess's head came up over the jut, the barbarian gave a roar to his god of war and brought Aegis-fang sweeping down from on high.

Catti-brie winced at the sharp retort, a sound like stone clacking against stone, and the giantess disappeared from view.

But more were coming, as fast as they could manage across the slippery surface. Others took a different tack, finding stones and sending them sailing at the pair. It was Catti-brie's turn to pull Wulfgar aside, as she dived behind the cover of the jut, catching him by his thick shock of blond hair and forcing him down beside her. And not a moment too soon, for barely had the barbarian hit the ground when a boulder smashed the tip of the jut and went rebounding past.

The two quickly untangled, trying to regroup, and both cried out in surprise as a blue line appeared in the darkness, running straight up to a height of about six feet. That line widened and stretched, forming a doorway of light, and through it stepped Shoudra and Torgar.

"Just run!" Shoudra cried, pulling at Catti-brie as she began her sprint to the south.

"Nanfoodle?" Catti-brie cried.

"Just run!" Shoudra insisted.

And there seemed no other choice, for the giants were closing and were soon to be out of the icy area, and more rocks began to skip all around them.

They scrambled and they tumbled, and whenever one fell, the others hoisted him up and pulled him along. At one point, a rather wide and seemingly bottomless chasm, Wulfgar grabbed Catti-brie and tossed her across. A protesting Torgar got the treatment next, then Shoudra. With giant-thrown rocks cracking the stone all around him, Wulfgar made the leap himself.

On they ran, too afraid to even look back. Gradually, the bombardment thinned and the yells of outrage behind them diminished to nothingness.

Huffing and puffing, the foursome pulled up behind a wall of stone.

"Nanfoodle?" Catti-brie asked again.

"If we're lucky, the giants never even knew he was there," Shoudra explained. "He has potions that should allow him easy escape."

"And if we're not lucky?" Wulfgar asked.

Shoudra's grim expression was all the answer he needed. Wulfgar had seen enough of giants in his day, and enough of frost giants in particular, to understand the odds Nanfoodle would face if they noticed him.

"I don't know . . . that we killed any . . . but there's one . . . giantess who is sure to be . . . wishing we hadn't come," Catti-brie remarked between gasps.

"I am sure that my lightning stung a few," Shoudra added. "But I doubt I did any serious harm to any."

"But that wasn't the point, now was it?" Torgar reminded them. "Come on, let's get off these rocks before the next orc charge. I didn't get no swings at the damned giants, but I mean to have me a few orcs' heads!"

He stomped off, and the others followed, all of them nursing more than a few cuts and bruises from their nighttime run, and all of them glancing back repeatedly in hopes of seeing their gnome companion.

They should have been looking ahead instead, for when they arrived back at the main encampment, they found Nanfoodle resting against a stone, an oversized pipe stuffed into his mouth, his smile stretching wide to either side.

"Should be an interesting morning," the gnome remarked, grinning from ear to ear.

Soon after dawn the next day, the first giant barrage began—almost.

All the dwarves watched as in the distance, a pair of great catapults, baskets piled with stones, bent back, giants straining to set them.

From below, the orcs howled and began their charge, thinking to catch the dwarves vulnerable under the giant-sized volley.

Beams creaked . . . and cracked.

The giants tried to release the missiles, but the catapults simply fell to pieces.

All eyes in the area turned to Nanfoodle, who whistled and pulled a vial out of his belt pouch, holding it up before him and swishing greenish liquid around inside it.

"A simple acid, really," he explained.

"Well, ye bought us some time," Banak Brawnanvil congratulated the fivesome, and he looked down the slope at the stubbornly charging orcs. "From them giants, at least."

The dwarf ran off then, barking orders, calling his formations into position.

"They'll need many new logs if they hope to reconstitute their war engines," Nanfoodle assured the others.

Of course, none of them were surprised later that same day, when scouts reported that new logs were already being brought in to that north-western ridge.

"Stubborn bunch," the little gnome observed.

21

TWO HELMETS

The diamond edge held his gaze, its glaring image crystallizing his thoughts.

Drizzt sat in his small cave, Icingdeath laid out before him, Bruenor's lost helmet propped on a stick to the side. Outside, the morning shone bright and clear, with a brisk breeze blowing and small clusters of white clouds rushing across the blue sky.

There was a vibrancy in that wind, a sense of being alive.

To Drizzt Do'Urden, it shamed him and angered him all at the same time. For he had gone there to hide, to slide back into the comfort of secluded darkness—to put his feelings behind a wall that effectively denied them.

Tarathiel and Innovindil had assaulted that wall. Their forgiveness and apology, the beauty of their fighting dance, the effectiveness of their actions beside him, all showed Drizzt that he must accept their invitation, both for the sake of the cause against the invading orcs and for his own sake. Only through them, he knew, could he begin to sort out the darkness of Ellifain. Only through them might he come to find some closure on that horrible moment in the pirate hideout.

But seeking those answers and that closure meant moving out from behind the invulnerable wall that was the Hunter.

Drizzt's gaze slipped away from the diamond edge of Icingdeath to the one-horned helmet.

He tried to look away almost immediately, but it didn't matter, for he wasn't really looking at the helmet. He was watching the tower fall. He was watching Ellifain fall. He was watching Clacker fall. He was watching Zaknafein fall.

All that pain, buried within him for all those years, came flooding over Drizzt Do'Urden there, alone in the small cave. Only when the first line of moisture slid down his cheek did he even realize how few tears he had shed over the years. Only when the wetness crystallized his vision did Drizzt truly realize the depth of the pain within him.

He had hidden it away, time and again, beneath the veil of anger in those times when he became the Hunter, when the pain overwhelmed him. And more than that—more subtly but no less destructive, he only then realized—he had hidden it all away beneath the veil of hope, in the logical and determined understanding that sacrifices were acceptable if the principles were upheld.

Dying well.

Drizzt had always hoped that he would die well, battling evil enemies or saving a friend. There was honor in that, and the truest legacy he could ever know. Had anyone died more nobly than Zaknafein?

But that didn't alleviate the pain for those left behind. Only then, sitting there, purposefully tearing down the wall he had built of anger and of hope, could Drizzt Do'Urden begin to realize that he had never really cried for Zaknafein or for any of the others.

And under the weight of that revelation, he felt a coward.

It started as the slightest of movements, a jerk of the drow's slender shoulders. It sounded as a small gasp at first, a mere chortle.

For the first time, Drizzt Do'Urden didn't let it end at that point. For the first time, he did not let the Hunter build a wall of stone around his heart, nor let the justifications of principle and purpose dull the keen edge of pain. For the first time, he did not shy from the emptiness and the helplessness; he did not embrace them, but neither did he run.

He cried for Zaknafein and for Clacker. He cried for Ellifain, the most tragic loss of all. He considered the course of his life—but not with lament, stubbornly throwing aside all the typical regrets that he should have turned his friends from the course into the mountains, that he should have ushered them straight to Mithral Hall. They had walked with eyes wide. All of them, knowing the dangers, expecting the inevitable. Circumstance and bad luck had guided Drizzt's journey to that fallen tower and to the helmet of his lost friend. His journey had taken him to the saddest day of his life, to a moment of the greatest loss he could possibly know. In an instant, he had lost almost everything dear to him: Bruenor, Wulfgar, Catti-brie, and Regis.

But he had not cried.

He had run away from the pain. He had built the wall of the Hunter, the justification being that he would continue the fight—heighten it—and pay back his enemies.

There was truth in that course. There was purpose and there was, undeniably, effectiveness.

But there was a price as well, Drizzt understood on a very basic level, as the wall fell down and the tears flowed. The price of his heart.

For to hide away behind the stone of anger was to deny, as well, the pleasures of being alive. All of that separated him from the orcs he killed. All of that gave true purpose to waging the war, the difference between good and evil, between right and wrong.

All of that had blurred with the fall of Ellifain.

All of that blended within the veil of the Hunter.

Drizzt thought of Artemis Entreri then. His arch-nemesis, his . . . alter ego? Was that Hunter within Drizzt in truth who Entreri was, a man so full of pain and anguish that he denied his own heart? Was Drizzt destined to follow that uncaring road?

Drizzt let the tears flow. He cried for them all, and he cried for himself, for the profound loss that had so emptied the joy from his heart. Every time the anger welled, he threw it back down. Every time he visualized his blades taking the head from an orc, he instead forced forth the image of Catti-brie smiling, or of Bruenor tossing him a knowing wink, or of Wulfgar singing to Tempus as they trotted along the mountain trails, or of Regis lying back, fishing line tied to his toe, on the banks of Maer Dualdon. Drizzt forced the memories to come forth, despite the pain.

He was hardly conscious of the deepening shadows of nightfall, and he lay there, somewhere between sleep and memory throughout the night.

By the time morning dawned once more, Drizzt had at last found the strength to take the first steps along a necessary road to follow the elves, who had moved their encampment. To accept their invitation to join with them in common cause.

He put away his scimitars and took up his cloak, then paused and looked back.

With a bittersweet smile on his face, Drizzt reached in and lifted Bruenor's helmet from the supporting stick. He rolled it over in his hands and brought it close so that he could again catch Bruenor's scent. Then he put it in his pack and started away.

He paused only a couple of steps out from the entrance, though, and nearly laughed aloud when he looked down at his callused feet.

A moment later, the drow held his boots in his hand. He considered putting them on, but then just tied them together by the laces and slung them over one shoulder.

Perhaps there was a happy medium to be found.

At the same time Drizzt was rolling Bruenor's helmet over in his hands, another, not so far away, was likewise studying a different armored headpiece. That helm was white as bone and resembled a skull, though with grotesquely elongated eyes. The "chin" of the helmet would hang down well over Obould's own chin, offering protection for his throat. The elongated eye holes were the most unique part of the design, though, for they were not open. A glassy substance filled them, perfectly translucent.

"Glassteel," Arganth explained to the great orc. "No spear will pierce it. Not even a great dwarven crossbow could drive a bolt through it."

Obould growled softly in admiration as he rolled the helmet over in his hands. He slowly brought it up and fitted it over his head. It settled low, right to his collarbones.

Arganth held up a scarf, laced with metal.

"Wrap this around your neck and the helmet will settle upon it," the shaman explained. "There will be no opening."

Behind the glassteel, Obould narrowed his eyes. "You doubt my ability?" he demanded.

"There can be no opening," Arganth bravely replied. "Obould is the hope of Gruumsh! Obould is chosen."

"And Gruumsh will punish Arganth if Obould fails?" the orc king asked.

"Obould will not fail," the shaman replied, dodging the question.

Obould let it go at that and considered instead the seemingly endless line of precious gifts. Every time he clenched his fist, he could feel the added strength in his arms; every easy step he took across the broken ground reminded him of the additional balance and speed. Beneath his plate mail he wore a light shirt and breeches, enchanted, so said the shamans, to protect him from fire and ice.

The shamans were making him impregnable. The shamans were building around him a failsafe armor.

But he could not let that notion permeate his thoughts, Obould understood, or he would inevitably relax his guard.

"Does it please you?" Arganth asked, his excited voice nearly a squeal.

Still growling, Obould removed the helm and took the metal-laced scarf from the shaman.

"Obould is pleased," he said.

"Then Gruumsh is pleased!" Arganth declared.

He danced away, back to the waiting cluster of shamans, who all began talking excitedly. No doubt pooling their thoughts toward a new improvement for their god-king, Obould realized. The orc king gave a grating chuckle. Always before, he had demanded devotion and exacted it with fear and with muscle. But the growing fanaticism was something completely different.

Could any king hope for more?

But such fanaticism came with expectations, Obould understood, and he looked around at the dark mountains. They had forced marched north in short order, through the day and through the night, because a threat loomed before his grand design.

Obould meant to eliminate that threat.

A quick glance to the west told Tarathiel that he was pushing his luck, for the sun's lower rim was almost to the horizon and his and Innovindil's camp was some distance away. When the sun went down, he'd have to bring

Sunrise to the ground, for flying around in the dark of night was no easy task, even with the elf and his keen eyesight guiding the pegasus.

Still, the elf's adrenaline was pumping with the thrill of the hunt—he had a dozen orcs running scared along the mountain trail below him—and even more so that day because he knew that Drizzt Do'Urden was about. After their joint efforts in turning the orc tribe back to the Spine of the World, the drow had gone off again, and Tarathiel and Innovindil hadn't seen him for a few days. Then Tarathiel, out hunting alone, had spotted Drizzt moving along a trail toward the cave he and Innovindil were using as their new base. Drizzt had offered a wave; not much of an assurance, of course, but Tarathiel had noticed a couple of hopeful signs. Drizzt was carrying the helmet of his lost friend—Tarathiel had spotted its one remaining horn poking out of the drow's shoulder pack—and perhaps even more notably, Drizzt was carrying his boots.

Had his resistance to the advances of the two elves begun to break down?

Tarathiel meant to return to Innovindil, and hopefully Drizzt, with news of another victory, albeit a minor one. He meant to have at least four kills under his belt that day before going home. He already had two, and with a dozen targets still scrambling below him, it did not seem unlikely that he would get his wish.

The elf settled more comfortably in his saddle and leveled his bow for a shot, but the orcs cut down into a narrow stone channel, dropping from sight. Tarathiel brought Sunrise around, sweeping over that crevice, and saw that the creatures were still running. He circled his pegasus and came in over the channel, following the line, looking for a shot.

His bow twanged, but off the mark as both the channel and the targeted orc cut to the right. Again the elf had to circle, so that he didn't overfly the group.

He was back in sight shortly, and his arrow struck home, marking his third kill. Again, he then had to fly his mount in a wide circle. Tarathiel glanced west at the lowering sun as he did and realized that he didn't have too much time remaining.

Again he bore down on the fleeing orcs. The channel descended along the mountainside and cut sharply between two high juts of stone, where the ground opened up beyond. Tarathiel told himself that he'd catch them as they exited the crevice and seek out whichever one scattered in the general direction of his cave.

Smiling widely, eager for that last kill, Tarathiel brought Sunrise soaring through the gap.

And as he did, two long poles rose up before him, crossing diagonally and going upright to either side. It wasn't until Sunrise plowed right in that the elf even realized that a net had been strung to the poles.

The pegasus let out a shocked whinny and it and Tarathiel balled up, wings folding under the press. They continued forward for just a bit as the poles crossed again behind them, netting them fully, and the whole trap slid down to the ground.

Tarathiel twisted and slipped underneath Sunrise as soon as they touched down, using the free area beneath the pegasus to draw out his sword and begin cutting at the net. With a few links severed, the elf scrambled out. He looked around, expecting enemies to be fast closing.

He sucked in his breath, seeing that the netting poles had been held not by orcs, but by a pair of frost giants.

They weren't approaching, though, and so Tarathiel spun around and went to fast work on the net, trying desperately to free Sunrise.

He stopped when torches flared to life around him. He stopped and realized the completeness of this trap.

Slowly the elf moved away from the struggling pegasus, walking a defensive circle around Sunrise, sword out before him as he eyed the torchbearers, a complete circle of ugly orcs. They had set him up, and he had fallen for it. He had no idea how he could possibly get himself and Sunrise out of there. He glanced back at the pegasus to see that Sunrise was making some progress in extracting himself—but certainly not quickly enough. The elf had to get back and cut more of the netting, he knew, and he turned.

Or started to.

There before him, emerging from the line of orcs, came a creature of such stature and obvious power that Tarathiel found he could not turn away. Suited in beautifully crafted, ridged and spiked plate mail and a skull-shaped white helmet with elongated eyes and shining teeth, the large orc stepped out from the line. Tarathiel noted the carved hilt of a huge sword protruding up diagonally from behind the brute's right shoulder.

"Obould!" the other orcs began to chant. "Obould! Obould! Obould!"

It was a name that Tarathiel, like every other worldly creature across the Silver Marches surely knew, the name of an orc king who had brought a powerful dwarven citadel to its knees.

Tarathiel wanted to turn back for Sunrise and the net. He knew he had to, but he could not. He could not tear his eyes away from the spectacle of King Obould Many-Arrows.

The burly orc strode toward Tarathiel, reaching up his thick right arm to grasp the carved hilt. Slowly, the orc extended his arm, drawing up the greatsword. He lifted the weapon clear of its half-sheath, to a horizontal position above his head. Still stalking in, hardly slowing, not changing his expression one bit (as far as Tarathiel could see through the huge eye holes), the determined creature swept the weapon down to his side.

The blade flamed to life.

Tarathiel moved his free left hand to the small of his back, to the hilt of a throwing dagger. He had to finish the orc quickly, he understood, to stun the onlookers and buy himself time to get back to Sunrise. He forced aside his fears and studied the incoming orc, looking for an opening, any opening.

Only its bloodshot eyes appeared vulnerable—not an easy throw, but to Tarathiel, a necessary one.

He slid the dagger free of his belt and casually lowered his arm to his side, concealing the weapon behind his hand, with its blade running up behind his arm.

Obould was barely fifteen feet away by then and showed no sign of slowing, no sign of speaking. The orc took another long stride.

Tarathiel's arm snapped forward, the small dagger spinning out.

Obould didn't move fast to dodge or block, but he did stiffen suddenly, staring without a blink.

Tarathiel started to break to the side at once, back toward Sunrise, thinking that his missile would surely drop the brute. But even as he took the first step away, the elf noted the impact. The dagger's tip clipped against the translucent shield of glassteel and ricocheted harmlessly aside.

Beneath the skull teeth of that awful helmet, King Obould widened his grin and gave an eager growl.

Tarathiel stopped in his tracks and spun back to face the orc's sudden charge. He ducked the orc's surprisingly swift one-armed cut of the great-sword, feeling the heat of its flames as it passed above him. Ahead stepped the elf, his own sword stabbing hard for Obould's belly.

But the orc didn't jump back, again trusting in his armor, and instead caught up his own sword in both hands and came over and down diagonally back the other way.

Tarathiel's sword did connect, but before he could slip it around in search of an opening or drive it in harder to test the plate, he found himself leaping aside, spinning as he went, every muscle working to keep him away from the orc's mighty sword.

As he turned his back to Obould, before completing the spin, the elf quick-stepped straight away. He felt the pursuit, felt the hunger of his adversary, and suddenly completed the spin, reversing direction and ducking into a squat as he flashed past the lumbering Obould. The elf turned again and drove his sword hard into Obould's lower back. The orc howled as he spun to catch up, his greatsword splitting the air with a *swoosh* of flame and ferocity.

Tarathiel didn't leave his feet, didn't even move his feet, as he threw himself backward, arms flying out wide to either side. Down he tumbled, the deadly fiery sword passing above his chest and face as he fell nearly horizontal. And, with an amazing display of agility and leg strength, the elf popped right back up to the vertical, his sword stabbing ahead once and again.

Sparks flew from the orc king's black armor as the fine elven blade struck hard, but if either of the strikes had hurt Obould, the orc didn't show it.

Again, that greatsword came across, and again, Tarathiel fell back, coming out of the stiff movement with a wise backstep. Obould didn't overswing again and had his sword in stubborn pursuit.

But Tarathiel had one advantage, his quickness, and he knew that if he did not err, he could stay away from that terrible sword. He had to bide his time, to take his opportunities where he found them, and hope to wear down the great orc. He had to fight defensively, always one step ahead of his opponent, until the weight of that massive sword began to take a toll on Obould's strong arms, forcing them down so that Tarathiel could find some weakness in that suit of armor, find some place to score a mortal wound on the orc.

Tarathiel understood all of that immediately, but a glance to the side, where Sunrise was still struggling under the net, reminded him that time was a luxury he could not afford.

On came Obould, driving the elf. Then the elf went suddenly out to the side, spinning and turning around that stabbing greatsword. As he sensed that mighty weapon coming back in pursuit, the elf fell flat to the ground and scrambled suddenly at the orc's thick legs, driving in hard, thinking to trip him up.

He might as well have tried to knock over a pair of healthy oaks, for Obould didn't budge an inch, and the impact against the orc's legs left the elf's shoulders numb.

Tarathiel did well to emotionally dismiss the surprise, to continue moving around the orc king's legs, angling to ensure that he gave no opening for that pursuing sword. He came back to his feet, falling into a defensive stance as Obould came around to face him.

With a sudden roar, the orc came on, and again, Tarathiel was dancing and dodging, searching for some opening, searching for some sign that Obould was tiring.

Surprisingly, though, the orc only seemed to be gaining momentum.

Innovindil looked with some distress at the dipping sun, knowing that Tarathiel should have arrived by then. She had moved out to join him, guessing the general area where he would herd any potential enemies and figuring that she would find some way to assist in his hunt.

But there had been no sign.

And the sun was going down, which would likely ground the pegasus.

"Where are you, my love?" the female whispered to the night breeze.

She caught the movements of a dark figure off to the north of her position and smiled, somewhat comforted by the knowledge that Drizzt Do'Urden was flanking her hunt.

She told herself that Tarathiel had to be close and quickly reminded herself of all those times when her bold companion had run off into the night in pursuit of fleeing orcs. How Tarathiel loved to kill orcs! Innovindil gave a helpless and exasperated sigh, silently promising herself that she would scold him for worrying her so. She moved on, heading up the side of one ridge so that she could get a better view of the ground to the northwest.

She heard the chanting, like the low rumbling of a building thunderstorm. "Obould! Obould! Obould!" they said in the communal croaking voice, and even though she did not at first recognize the reference and the name, Innovindil understood that there were orcs around—too many orcs.

Normally, that notion would not have fazed the elf. Normally, she would have then simply figured that Tarathiel was in hiding nearby, probably gaining a fair estimate of the nearby force, probably even finding some weaknesses among the orc ranks that they two could exploit. But for some reason, Innovindil had the distinct feeling that something was amiss, that Tarathiel was not safe and secure behind a wall of mountain stone.

Perhaps it was the insistent tone of the chanting, "Obould! Obould!" with an undercurrent that seemed hungry and elated all at the same time. Perhaps it was just the lengthening shadows of a dark night. Whatever the reason, Innovindil found herself moving once more, running as fast as she could manage across the broken and rocky slope, veering inevitably toward that distant chanting.

When she at last crested the ridge in the north, coming over and continuing down the other side across the craggy rocks, the elf's heart dropped. For there in the rocky vale before her flickered the torches of scores of orcs, all in a wide ring, all chanting.

Innovindil did recognize the name, and before she could even fully register the implications. Her eyes scanned across the lines, toward the center of the circle, and her heart fell away. For there was Tarathiel, dodging and diving, always a fraction of a step ahead of a fiery greatsword. And there behind him in the shadows was Sunrise, struggling, pinned by a net.

Gasping for breath, Innovindil fell back against the stone, mesmerized by the dance of the combatants and by the spectacle of the onlookers. Her love, her friend, dived and rolled, spun a beautiful turn, and rushed in hard, his sword flashing, sparks flying.

Then he was diving again, the greatsword slashing across just above him.

Innovindil looked around the orc ring, trying to find some way she could penetrate it, some way she could get down there beside Tarathiel. She silently cursed herself for leaving Sunset back at their new cave, and she considered rushing back to gather up the flying steed.

But could Tarathiel possibly hold out for that long?

Innovindil started back up to the south, then she paused and turned back to the north. She realized that she had no other option, and so she spun again to the south and her cave, looking back and praying to the elf gods to protect Tarathiel.

She stopped suddenly, mesmerized once more by the intensity of the fight, the dance. Tarathiel went by Obould and stabbed hard, and the greatsword flashed down across in front of the backing elf. Innovindil blinked—and she understood that Tarathiel had, too—when that sword-fire suddenly blinked out.

Innovindil's eyes bulged as her mouth widened in a silent scream, recognizing that the blackout had frozen Tarathiel's eye for just an instant, the last flash of fire holding his attention and making him think that the blade was still down low.

But it was not.

It was up high again and back the other way.

"Obould! Obould! Obould!" the orcs chanted for their mighty and cunning leader.

The burly orc leaped forward and brought his sword down and across in a great diagonal swipe.

Tarathiel leaped back as well, and when he didn't fly away, Innovindil believed for a moment that he must have somehow backed out of range. She knew that to be impossible, but he was still standing there before the orc king.

How had the strike missed?

It hadn't. It couldn't have.

Not breathing, not moving, Innovindil stared down at Tarathiel, who stood perfectly still, and even from a distance, she could tell that he wore a perplexed look.

The sword had not missed; the mighty cut had slashed through Tarathiel's collarbone and down and across, left to right, to come out just under his ribs on the other side. Still staring, he just fell apart, his torso sliding out to the left, his legs buckling under him.

"Obould! Obould! Obould!" the orcs screamed.

Innovindil screamed as well. She leaped away, charging down the rocky slope, drawing forth her slender sword.

Or trying to, for then she got tackled from the side, and before she hit the ground, before she could cry out in surprise, a slender but strong hand clamped hard across her mouth. She struggled futilely for a moment before finally recognizing the voice whispering into her ear.

Drizzt Do'Urden stayed tight against her on the ground, holding her, telling her that it would be all right, until at last her muscles relaxed.

"There's nothing to do," the drow said over and over again. "Nothing we can do."

He pulled Innovindil up into a sitting position against him and together they looked down on the rocky vale, where the orc king, his sword aflame once more, stalked around the halved body of Tarathiel, where more netting was being thrown over poor Sunrise, holding the pegasus down, where scores of orcs and more than a few giants cheered and danced in the torchlight.

The couple sat there for a long, long time, staring in disbelief, and despite Drizzt holding her as tightly as he could, Innovindil's shoulder bobbed with great sobs of despair and grief.

She couldn't see it, for her eyes were transfixed on the horrible scene before her, but behind her, Drizzt, too, was crying.

PART FOUR | WHEN DARKNESS FALLS

I watched the descent of Obould's sword.

With my heart undefended, risking friends once more, I watched, and again my heart was severed.

All is a swirl of confusion again, punctuated by pinpricks of pain that find my most vulnerable and sensitive areas, stinging and burning, flashing images of falling friends. I can build the stone wall to block them, I know, in the form of anger. To hide my eyes and hide my heart—yet I am not sure if the relief is worth the price.

That is my dilemma.

The death of Tarathiel was about Tarathiel. That is obvious, I know, but I must often remind myself of that truth. The world is not my playground, not a performance for my pleasure and my pain, not an abstract thought in the mind of Drizzt Do'Urden.

Bruenor's fall was more poignant to Bruenor than it was to me. So was Zaknafein's to Zaknafein, and that of all the others. Aside from that truth, though, there is my own sensibility, my own perception of events, my own pain and confusion. We can only view the world through our own eyes, I think. There are empathy and sympathy; there is often a conscious effort to see as a friend or even an enemy might—this is an important element in the concept of truth and justice, of greater community than our own wants and needs. But in the end, it all, for each of us, comes back to each of us individually, and everything we witness rings more important to each of us than to others, even if what we witness is a critical moment for another.

There is an undeniable selfishness in that realization, but I do not run away from that truth because there is nothing I, or anyone, can do about that truth. When we lose a loved one, the agony is ours as well. A parent watching his or her child suffer is in as much pain, or even more, I am sure, than the suffering child.

And so, embracing that selfishness at this moment, I ask myself if Tarathiel's fall was a warning or a test. I dared to open my heart, and it was torn asunder. Do I fall back into that other being once more, encase my spirit in stone to make it impervious to such pain? Or is this sudden and unexpected loss a test of my spirit, to show that I can accept the cruelty of fate and press on, that I can hold fast to my beliefs and my principles and my hopes against the pain of those images?

I think that we all make this choice all the time, in varying degrees. Every day, every tenday, when we face some adversity, we find options that usually run along two roads. Either we hold our course—the one we determinedly set in better and more hopeful times, based on principle and faith—or we fall to the seemingly easier and more expedient road of defensive posture, both emotional and physical. People and often societies sometimes react to pain and fear by closing up, by sacrificing freedoms and placing practicality above principle.

Is that what I have been doing since the fall of Bruenor? Is this hunting creature I have become merely a tactic to forego the pain?

While in Silverymoon some years ago, I chanced to study the history of the region, to glance at perspectives on the many wars faced by the people of that wondrous community throughout the ages. At those times when the threatened Silverymoon closed up and put aside her enlightened principles—particularly the recognition that the actions of the individual are more important than the reputation of the individual's race—the historians were not kind and the legacy did not shine.

The same will be said of Drizzt Do'Urden, I think, by any who care to take notice.

There is a small pool in the cave where Tarathiel and Innovindil took up residence, where I am now staying with the grieving Innovindil. When I look at my reflection in that pool, I am reminded, strangely, of Artemis Entreri.

When I am the hunting creature, the reactionary, defensive and closed-hearted warrior, I am more akin to him. When I strike at enemies, not out of community or personal defense, not out of the guiding recognition of right and wrong or good and evil, but out of anger, I am more akin to that closed and unfeeling creature I first met in the tunnels of duergar-controlled Mithral Hall. On those occasions, my blades are not guided by conscience or powered by justice.

Nay, they are guided by pain and powered by anger.

I lose myself.

I see Innovindil across the way, crying still for the loss of her dear Tarathiel. She is not running away from the grief and the loss.

She is embracing it and incorporating it into her being, to make it a part of herself, to own it so that it cannot own her.

Have I the strength to do the same?

I pray that I do, for I understand now that only in going through the pain can I be saved.

—Drizzt Do'Urden

THE CALL OF
DESPERATE TIMES

"Uh oh," Nanfoodle whispered to Shoudra.

When the sceptrana looked his way, the little gnome motioned his chin toward a group of dwarves holding a conversation near the lip of the cliff. Torgar and Shingles were there, as well as Catti-brie, Wulfgar, Banak, and Tred of Citadel Felbarr. Tred had just returned from Mithral Hall with word of Pikel, no doubt, and also of the duo from Mirabar.

At around the same time Banak and the others all turned to regard the gnome and Shoudra, and their expressions spoke volumes.

"Time for us to go," Shoudra whispered back, and she grabbed Nanfoodle's shoulder.

"No," the gnome insisted, pulling away. "No, we will not flee."

"You underestimate—"

"We helped them in their dilemma here. Dwarves appreciate that," Nanfoodle said, and he started off toward the group.

"I thought it from the first," Torgar Hammerstriker said when Nanfoodle arrived, Shoudra moving cautiously behind. "Ye still can't see the truth o' that damned marchion."

"We didn't flee, did we?" Nanfoodle replied.

"Ye'd probably be smart in keeping yer mouth shut, little one," offered Shingles, and his tone wasn't threatening as much as honest, even sympathetic. "Ye've got yerself in enough trouble by-the-by. These folk'll treat ye fair and put ye on yer way back home soon enough."

"We could be well on our way home already, if that was the course we chose," Nanfoodle stubbornly replied. "But we did not."

"Because ye're a dolt?" Torgar remarked.

"Because we believed we could be useful," Nanfoodle countered.

"To us or to them orcs?" Banak Brawnanvil put in. "Ye came here to ruin our metal, so ye told Steward Regis yerself."

"That was before we knew of the orc army," Nanfoodle explained.

He tried to focus and find his center, tried to calm his breathing, telling himself to trust in the truth.

"And that's making it any better?" Banak demanded.

"We came here under orders to do exactly what you have stated," Shoudra Stargleam admitted. She came forward to stand beside Nanfoodle and managed to release herself from Banak's imposing stare long enough to shoot her little friend a comforting look. "Your departure brought great fear and distress to Mirabar," she went on, addressing Torgar directly. "And weakened our city greatly."

"That's not me problem," the stubborn dwarf answered.

"No, it is not," Shoudra admitted. "It is the duty of the marchion to protect his people."

"He'd do better protecting them if he could tell the difference between friends and enemies," Torgar shot back, poking a stubby finger Shoudra's way.

The sceptrana held her hands up to calm him, patting them in the air.

"This is not the time to rehash the debate," she said.

"Good a time as any, as far as I'm seein' it," said Torgar.

"We came here not to sabotage . . ." the sceptrana began.

"The little one admitted it," said Tred, who had brought the news up to the cliff.

". . . but to investigate," Shoudra went on. "We had to know if there was any danger to Mirabar—surely you can understand that. Perhaps the emigrating dwarves harbored resentment that would bring them back upon our city, with a host of Battlehammers behind them."

"Ye're talking stupid," said Torgar.

Shoudra started to respond, then sighed and nodded.

"I am telling you things from the perspective of Marchion Elastul, who is charged with the security of Mirabar," she explained.

"Like I said," came Torgar's dry reply.

"Barring any imminent threat to Mirabar—which Nanfoodle and I did not expect to find—we would never have used the formula. In fact, it was that same formula that Nanfoodle used to destroy the giant catapults. Have you so quickly forgotten our help?"

"Course we ain't," said Banak. "Which makes this news all the more painful. We're in a war here, so ye come here as friends or ye come here as enemies. Ain't no middling ground when the blood is flowing."

"We are here as friends," Nanfoodle said without hesitation. "We could have run home, but we did not. We were free in Keeper's Dale and would have been long off to the west before any word came out of Mithral Hall had we chosen to flee. But how could we, when we knew that you were fighting our common enemy up here? How could we when we knew that we could bring valuable assistance to your cause? Judge not my drunken words to Regis—never did I desire to poison Mithral Hall's metal. It is a mission I resisted every step out of Mirabar, and one that I only embarked upon with the intention of turning aside its course. And no less can be said of Shoudra Stargleam, who has ever been a friend of Torgar Hammerstriker and Shingles McRuff."

Banak, Tred, Catti-brie, and Wulfgar all turned to the Mirabarran dwarves, and the pair nodded their agreement with Nanfoodle's assessment.

"Then what would ye have me do, little one?" Banak asked. "Let ye run free down the road to Mirabar?"

Nanfoodle looked to Shoudra, then, smiling, back at the dwarf.

"No," he insisted. "Take me to Regis that I might make my case. In chains, if you must."

He held out his hands to the dwarf, who pushed them aside.

"Ye helped us here. Ye bought us needed time," Banak said. "If ye're wanting to run, now's the time for it. We'll look away long enough for ye to be long gone."

Again Nanfoodle glanced at Shoudra before eyeing the dwarf directly.

"If we thought we could be of no more assistance, we would accept your generous offer, good dwarf." Nanfoodle glanced back to the ridge, where new logs were already piling up, and said, "You must deal with those giants, and I think I can help. So no, I will not leave at this time and will accept the judgment of Steward Regis."

"Sounds like the little one's got a plan," said Catti-brie.

Nanfoodle's smile widened even more.

Regis sat back in his comfortable chair, dropped his chin into one hand and stared down at the many maps and diagrams Nanfoodle had spread out on the floor.

"I don't understand," he admitted, and he looked to Shoudra.

The sceptrana seemed equally perplexed and could only shrug in response.

"Is he always this abstract?" the halfling asked.

"Always," Shoudra admitted.

In the chair beside Regis, Ivan Bouldershoulder pored over a group of other diagrams Nanfoodle had given him, and it took him some time to realize that the other three were staring his way.

"Easy enough," the dwarf told them, particularly Regis. "The box at least. Simple enough contraption."

"The open-ended metal cylinders will prove no more complicated," Nanfoodle said.

"Agreed, except for the number ye're wanting," said Ivan, and he looked to Regis. "Ye'd have to set every furnace in Mithral Hall working day and night to get it done in time."

Regis shook his head, seeming more perplexed than negative.

"If I am right . . ." Nanfoodle started to say.

"You don't even know if those tunnels are open," Regis replied. "Nor do you know what you'll find if they are."

"Then let me go and look, at least," said the gnome.

"I can't commit my smiths to the task until we're sure," the steward replied.

Despite the denial, or more so because of the wording of the denial, Nanfoodle's grin nearly took in his abundant ears.

"Yes, go," Regis relented. He looked down at the mass of maps and diagrams and shook his head in disbelief and open skepticism. "It seems a fool's errand, but we have nothing better."

Nanfoodle bowed, again and again, as if he was bobbing with happiness—as indeed he usually was when someone in power offered him the opportunity to chase down another of his often wild proposals. Eventually, he managed to turn back to Ivan, whose reputation as a craftsman had long preceded him to Mithral Hall.

"You will construct the box?" he asked.

"Got all I need," said the dwarf. "Except this flame water potion."

"Leave that to me, when the time is near," Nanfoodle assured him. The brightness on the gnome's face dimmed then, as he added, "Where might I find your brother?"

"Sitting in the dark," Ivan replied. "And I'm wishing ye luck on getting him to go tunneling with ye. He's not much in the mood for anything right now."

"We shall see," said Nanfoodle.

"With your permission, I will return to Master Brawnanvil," Shoudra put in then.

"I feel the fool for trusting you after what he admitted to me," Regis said to her. "I should throw you both in chains and have Marchion Elastul pay a high ransom for your safe return."

Shoudra smiled at him and said, "But you will not."

"Go to Banak," Regis said with a wave of his little hand.

Shoudra started out of the room but paused and looked back as the gracious steward added, "And thank you."

As she left the room, the sceptrana told herself pointedly that when she returned to Mirabar, she would oppose Marchion Elastul's every move against this neighbor and ally.

As he moved up to the door, Nanfoodle heard the soft, "Oooo" and winced in sympathy for the poor dwarf. The gnome lifted his fist to knock but held back and slowly dropped that hand to the dragon-shaped doorknob and quietly turned the latch. The perfectly balanced and well-oiled portal made not a sound as it swung open.

There sat Pikel in the middle of the floor, head down, his remaining hand absently drawing designs on the stone floor of the room. So distracted and distraught was the green-bearded dwarf that he didn't even look up as Nanfoodle approached, moving right beside him. Every now and then, the dwarf gave another plaintive, "Oooo."

"Does it still hurt?" Nanfoodle quietly asked.

Pikel looked up at him.

"Uh uh," he said, and he waved his stumped forearm in Nanfoodle's direction.

"Then you are sad," Nanfoodle said, and Pikel looked at him as if that should be obvious enough. "Do you believe that you have nothing to offer to Clan Battlehammer now?"

"Eh?" the green-bearded dwarf replied.

He held up his hand and waggled his fingers.

"You are still able to cast your spells then?"

"Yup yup," said Pikel.

"What are you doing there on the floor?" the gnome asked.

He came forward and leaned over the still-sitting Pikel—to see that the dwarf wasn't just sliding his hand over the stone in swirling designs, he was actually swirling the stone itself around. A grin widened on Nanfoodle's face, for that was exactly one of the purposes he had in mind for Pikel Bouldershoulder.

Nanfoodle moved around in front of Pikel and squatted down to look the dwarf directly in the eye.

"Your brother is working for me," he said.

"Eh?"

"I needed a craftsman, an engineer," Nanfoodle explained. "I was told that Ivan was among the best."

"Yup. Hee hee, me brudder."

"And Regis was very interested in telling Ivan to help me because he understands that my plan could well change the battle raging up on top of the cliff." He paused and studied the dwarf to make sure that he had Pikel's attention. "You want to help them, yes?"

Pikel's expression was perfectly perplexed.

"Yup yup."

"You see, I have many different needs right now," Nanfoodle tried to explain. "Important things must be done, but many of the tasks are a bit different than the dwarves could normally offer. Oh, there are a few that Steward Regis knew who might be able to assist me with one task or another, but there was only one name that came through repeatedly, for every task."

"Pikel?" the dwarf asked, pointing to himself—with a finger that was covered in fast-hardening stone.

"Pikel," Nanfoodle confirmed. He pointed down to the designs on the floor. "For that, and because I need help from animals—they won't be injured, I assure you. Not if we are smart and quick."

"Hee hee hee."

It did Nanfoodle's heart good to see that he had brought a smile to the despondent dwarf's face. Pikel seemed such a gentle soul to him; the mere thought of such a person suffering so grievous an injury pained Nanfoodle greatly. But Nanfoodle also understood that Pikel's pain was more emotional than physical, and that, in such cases as his, a person's self-worth was often the greatest casualty.

"Come on," he cheerfully offered to the dwarf, extending his hand to help Pikel to his feet. "We have much to do."

"Ye're pulling me beard," said Wocco Brawnanvil, brother of Brusco and proud cousin of Mithral Hall's heroic war commander.

"I ain't, and if I was, ye'd be kneeling, don't ye doubt," Ivan Bouldershoulder replied.

"This little gnome's a troublesome one, then," said Wocco. "He's not for building them damn arky-busses, is he? Heared them things blow up in yer face more'n they boom yer enemies."

"Nah, none o' them," Ivan confirmed.

Wocco and all the other blacksmiths standing around him breathed a sigh of relief. Ivan thought discretion necessary. If those dwarves, miners all, understood what Nanfoodle had in mind, they wouldn't be pleased.

"So ye're just wanting a tube of metal?" another dwarf asked.

"But all gotta be the same diameter," Ivan replied.

"And length?"

"Long as ye can make 'em."

The blacksmiths all looked around at each other.

"And Regis wants us doing this?" one asked.

"Got his mark, don't it?" Ivan asked, pointing to the parchment he had handed over, complete with diagrams and instructions and the signature of the Steward of Mithral Hall.

"*All* the forges?" one of them asked.

"We got lots of weapons to fix, with the fighting up above," Wocco explained. "We're behind already, after outfitting the band Regis sent running down the southern tunnels."

"This comes first," said Ivan. "Bah, if ye're quick about it and make a proper mold, ye'll put them out a dozen at a time!"

Again the blacksmiths looked around at each other, but a couple, at least, were nodding.

"How many ye need?" asked Wocco.

"Just ye keep making them," said Ivan.

He grinned and pulled out another rolled parchment, opening it wide for the other dwarves to see. It contained a diagram, one far more complicated than the instructions for the simple rolled metal tubes.

"And I'm working with impact oil," Ivan said with a snicker.

"Boom?" asked Wocco.

"I'm hopin' I don't slip with me hammer," Ivan said with a laugh, and the others joined in.

"Boom!" several said together.

Wocco lifted the parchments in salute, then motioned for his companions to follow him back to the lines of forges.

Ivan, whose work would be much more delicate, turned and moved off the other way, back to the smaller work area Regis had afforded him near the audience chambers.

He did pause long enough to look across the Undercity to the northwest, to the doors blocking the little-used tunnels, and his smile fast faded. Pikel was down there, with Nanfoodle.

Ivan could only hope that his brother would be all right, and that he would find his heart again, and his laugh.

Pikel held his shortened arm up and the small bird sitting on it shifted nervously. The dwarf druid brought the delicate creature in close and whispered reassuring words, then lowered the arm and started off down the side passage, which was lit with a soft, reddish glow.

"You are sure of this?" Nanfoodle asked the dwarf. "I have little in the way of weaponry about me and am not even certain that my more potent spells would affect such creatures."

In response, Pikel looked back at Nanfoodle and scrunched up his face, closing his eyes tight, a reminder that the gnome had insisted that they use no fire in the potentially disastrous tunnels.

"Yes, but . . ." Nanfoodle started to protest.

Pikel just gave a, "Hee hee hee," and started away.

Nanfoodle turned back to the five dwarf warriors assigned as escort and merely shrugged, and so did they, seeming more amused than worried.

"Just bugs, little one," one of the group explained. "Big bugs, but bugs all the same."

To reassure the gnome, the group presented their weapons, including the two enchanted, glowing long swords that had been providing all of their light.

They didn't need those weapons, though, for Pikel had little trouble in persuading the potential enemies that there was no battle to be found, and soon after, all seven were riding rather than walking, atop large beetles with red-glowing glands. Fire beetles, they were called, often coveted by Underdark adventurers for those helpful glands, which would retain their glow for days after the creature had been slain. Of course, there was even more practicality in Pikel's method, because the living beetles never stopped providing the light.

All along the tunnels, the green-bearded dwarf communicated to his new "friends" with a series of clicks and pops, and he even (so he said) managed to glean a bit of useful information out of the giant insects.

Whether or not that claim was true, the dwarf did lead the party to a most curious tunnel, sloping down to the north and reeking of a particularly nasty odor. Streaks of color lined the dark walls, though it was hard to distinguish its true hue in the red light.

"Yellow," Nanfoodle told them, for the gnome knew the smell of sulfur. "Keep a careful watch on your bird, Pikel. You don't want him to fall over dead."

Pikel gave a squeak of protest and brought the brave little bird up close to his face. Almost immediately, the bird began to panic, and Pikel whispered into its ear and sent it flying back up to clearer air.

Beside him, Nanfoodle understood the positive sign, and he pressed on through the reek.

The tunnel ended in a wide, high chamber full of stalagmites that narrowed as they rose, then widened again as they joined with the great stalactites hanging down from above. A haze filled the room, and even the sturdy dwarves had to pull the cloths Pikel had prepared up before their faces.

"Gonna lose me breakfast," one announced, and the others all nodded in agreement.

Nanfoodle, though, was simply too excited to consider such possibilities. He urged his beetle mount up ahead, then quickly dismounted and moved between the pillars of stone to the edge of an underground pool.

His smile erupted when he at last managed to peer through the haze, to see the source of that sulfuric fog, for the water roiled and bubbled, a sure sign of gasses escaping.

"If you lit a torch in here, we would all be incinerated," the gnome somberly announced.

"Hope that breakfast wasn't too spicy, then," chortled one dwarf, motioning over to another who was on his hands and knees gagging.

Those who were able moved up beside Nanfoodle to view the spectacle.

"The gas we need is invisible and has no odor," the gnome explained.

"Could o' fooled me," said one dwarf.

"No no," the gnome explained. "It mixes with other gasses in the pressure below. But you see how it escapes?" he asked, pointing to the bubbles. "Yes, yes, it is all in place."

"Got no idea what ye're talking about, gnome," said a dwarf. "But ye found it, yep? So now we can be leaving?"

"In a few moments," Nanfoodle replied. "We have to know the texture of the stone. We must be prepared when we return, for this will be no easy task."

He looked to Pikel, who was already falling within himself, eyes closed, arms waving.

The dwarf finished, giggled, and lay down, then simply melted into the stone, disappearing from view.

"That one's just not right," muttered a thoroughly shaken dwarf.

"Shut yer trap and get on yer beetle," another sarcastically remarked.

"Doo-dad. . . ." said a third, shaking his head.

Nanfoodle just smiled through it all.

A short while later, Pikel's form reappeared in the stone, like a bas relief carved into the floor. He came forth fully and hopped up, brushing himself off.

"Whew!" he said.

"How thick?" the excited Nanfoodle asked.

Pikel tapped himself on the head three times.

"Fifteen feet," Nanfoodle muttered.

"How'd he know that?" one dwarf asked another.

"Three Pikels deep," reasoned another.

"Ye're scarin' me, gnome," a third remarked.

"Can we get through that much?" Nanfoodle asked Pikel, ignoring the others.

"Hee hee hee," said the green-bearded dwarf.

23

ELF MUSING,
GIANT FEARS

Drizzt sat on a high stone on the eastern slope, watching as the sky brightened before him, as pinks and violets grew from the deep blue of predawn. He was glad when he heard the soft footfalls of Innovindil behind him, for it was her first journey out of the cave since Tarathiel's fall, two days before.

She walked up beside him and leaned on the stone.

"It will be a beautiful dawn," she said.

"They all are," Drizzt replied. "Even when the clouds lay thick about the horizon, the glow of the sun is a most welcomed sight to my Underdark weary eyes."

"Even after all these years?"

Drizzt looked over at Innovindil, at the warmth of her elf features—seeming less angular in the soft, predawn light—and at the depth of her blue eyes. Dawn was a time befitting her beauty, he thought. The softness and the quiet. The opposite of the hardened warrior he had witnessed in battle. Only then, in that flavor, did Drizzt truly begin to appreciate her depth.

"How old are you?" he asked before he could even consider the propriety of the question.

"This time marks the end of my third century," she answered. "Tarathiel was older than I, by many decades."

"That seems inconsequential to us of elf heritage."

Drizzt closed his eyes as he spoke, considering his own statement. What was waiting for him in his second century of life? he wondered. Was each existence among the shorter lived races a replay of the previous? A simple continuation?

He glanced at the sunrise and wondered, hoped, that perhaps it was not, that perhaps each "existence" as measured by the life span of a human or even a dwarf, would instead place layers upon knowledge already gained. He looked down at Innovindil, hoping that perhaps there might be some clue to be found in the depths of her eyes, but he found her smiling widely at him, a look that seemed almost condescending.

"You do not understand what it is to be an elf, do you?" she asked him.

Drizzt just stared at her. He understood what she was hinting at and even believed that there was more than a little truth in her words.

"You left the Underdark when you were but a child," Innovindil went on.

"Not so young."

"But never trained in the perspectives of elven culture," Innovindil said.

Drizzt shrugged and had to agree, for in his time in Menzoberranzan, he had spent his hours training to fight and to kill.

"And up here," she went on, "you have mostly been in the company of shorter-lived races."

"Bruenor counts his age in centuries, as do you," Drizzt reminded.

"Dwarves do not have an elf's perspective."

"You speak as if it is a tangible thing."

Drizzt paused then, as did Innovindil, for the eastern sky brightened with brilliant pinks and purples. The dawn came on gloriously, for there were just enough clouds, all drifting in distinct clusters and lines, to catch the morning rays and reflect them in myriad hues and textures.

"Was the beauty of that sunrise a tangible thing?" Innovindil asked.

Drizzt smiled and surrendered with a sigh.

"You must come to understand what it is or what it will be to live for several centuries, Drizzt Do'Urden," she said. "For your own sake, should you be fortunate enough to dodge your enemies and see those long years.

You have picked your friends among the lesser races, and you must understand the implications of those choices."

"Lesser . . ." Drizzt started to ask, but Innovindil cut him short by explaining, "Lesser-*lived* races."

Drizzt started to respond again, but he fell silent and let his gaze drift back to the east. He concentrated on the beauty of the continuing sunrise, trying to hide behind it and not show the pain that had come into his heart.

"What is it?" Innovindil pressed him.

He held silent. He felt Innovindil's hand softly touch his shoulder, and he couldn't deny that her warm touch was drawing him away from the wall of anger that was building again around his heart.

"Drizzt?" she asked quietly.

"Good friends," he said, his voice quavering.

Innovindil's hand continued to hold him until he at last turned to regard her.

"More than friends?" she asked.

Drizzt's lips went very tight.

"The daughter of Bruenor," Innovindil reasoned. "You love the human daughter of Bruenor Battlehammer, the one named Catti-brie."

Drizzt swallowed hard.

"Loved," he corrected.

It was Innovindil's turn to put on a curious look.

"She fell at Shallows, with Bruenor, Wulfgar, and Regis," Drizzt mustered the strength to say. "I picked my friends and could not have found better companionship, but . . ."

His voice cracked apart, and he turned fast back to the dawn, locking himself into the spectacle of colors, even held his stare against the sting of the rising sun itself, as if its burn on his sensitive eyes could somehow block out the other, more profound pain.

Innovindil squeezed his shoulder hard and asked, "Do you question your choice?"

"No," Drizzt insisted without the slightest hesitation.

"And your choice to love a human?"

"Was I wrong for that?" Drizzt asked. His defiance melted suddenly, and he asked again, more quietly, as if searching for an honest answer, "Was I wrong for that?"

Drizzt had to pause then and take a deep breath, and another, and he turned back to the rising sun, his eyes moist from more than the bright light's sting.

"Do you think it unwise for an elf, who might live for seven or more centuries, to fall in love with a human who will not know the end of one?" Innovindil asked him. "Do you think it a terrible notion that if you had children with a human, they would age and die before you?"

Drizzt winced at both questions.

"I do not know," he admitted, his voice barely a whisper.

"Because you do not know what it is to be an elf," Innovindil said with certainty.

Drizzt looked back at her and asked, "You say that I was wrong?"

But Innovindil's smile disarmed his ire.

"Our curse is to outlive so many of those we will know and love," she said. "I have known two human lovers."

Drizzt eyed her, not knowing what to make of the admission.

"The first man I fell in love with was a human, and he was not a young man, by human counting," Innovindil went on, and it was her turn to look to the rising sun. "He was a good man, a wizard of great talent, if little ambition." She gave a wistful chuckle. "But how I loved him—as greatly as I have ever loved anyone. I buried him when I was still a child by an elf's counting—younger even than you are now. How that pained me. . . .

"Nearly a century passed before I was able to dare to love another human," the elf went on, still staring to the east, not blinking at all.

"And he died as well," Drizzt reasoned.

"But not before we had three wonderful decades together," Innovindil replied, her smile widening. She paused for a long while, then turned and looked directly at Drizzt once more. "You really do not understand what it is to be an elf, Drizzt Do'Urden, because no one has shown you."

Her tone told Drizzt clearly that her words were an offer.

But could he dare to take her up on that offer? Could he dare to leave his heart open wide once more, where it would possibly get seared yet again?

"We have business to attend," the drow announced, his voice strong and determined. "Tarathiel's death will not go unavenged."

"You will kill the orc who slew him?"

"On my word," Drizzt declared through clenched teeth.

It took him a while to realize that Innovindil was staring at him hard.

He turned to her, his determination ebbing as he looked into her wide-eyed, angry glare.

"That is our purpose then?" Innovindil asked. "To avenge Tarathiel?"

"Is it not?"

"It is not!" the elf growled at him, and she seemed to grow tall and terrible, seemed to rise up and tower over Drizzt. "Our purpose—my purpose—is not a journey of hatred and vengeance."

Drizzt shrank back from her.

"Not while Sunrise is held captive by such unmerciful and brutal masters," Innovindil explained. She settled back then and seemed herself once more. "I will not let my anger get in the way of my purpose, Drizzt Do'Urden. I will not let anger cloud my vision or turn me one step to the side of the path I must take. Sunrise is my charge—I will not fail him to satiate my anger."

She looked at Drizzt for a moment longer, then turned and walked back to the cave.

Leaving Drizzt alone on the rock in the slanting rays of early morning.

"He cut the elf in half," the giant, one of two who had come in to see their dame, told Gerti. "He wields that sword with the strength of *Tierlaan Gau*," he added, using the giants' name for members of their race.

Gerti Orelsdottr tightened her jaw. Obould had won again, an impressive show in front of creatures who already thought him a god.

"What of the drow and the other elf?"

"Of Drizzt Do'Urden, we have heard nothing . . . perhaps," the giant replied, and he turned and looked to his partner, also recently returned from the incidents up north.

"Perhaps?"

"A body was found," the giant explained.

"That of a drow," said the other.

"Drizzt?"

"Donnia Soldou," the first giant replied, and Gerti's eyes widened.

"Dead among the rocks," the other giant added. "Murdered by fine blades."

Gerti mulled over the words for a bit. Had Donnia met up with Drizzt? Or perhaps with the surface elves? Gerti couldn't help but chuckle as she considered that perhaps Donnia had angered her own three companions. That was the thing about drow, was it not? They were so often busy killing each other that they could never manage any real conquests.

"I will miss her," Gerti admitted. "She was . . . amusing."

The other two relaxed, obviously relieved that Gerti wasn't taking the death of Donnia very hard.

"Obould slew one of the elves that has been terrorizing the region," the giantess stated.

"And captured his winged horse," the scout reported.

Again Gerti's eyes went wide.

"A pegasus? Obould is in possession of a pegasus?"

"We would have preferred to kill it," the scout explained. "That elf and his beast made up half the pair who assaulted us in the fight at Shallows."

"A bit of horseflesh would taste good," said the other.

Gerti thought it over for a moment, then said, "You should have slaughtered the creature. While Obould was battling the elf, you should have walked over and crushed its head!"

The two looked startled, but Gerti pressed on, "They are creatures of beauty, yes, and I would favor one for myself. But I do not wish to see King Obould Many-Arrows flying about above the battlefields, calling out orders to his charges. I do not wish to see him up on high, riding about, godlike."

"W-We did not know," the scout stammered.

"We could not have killed the winged beast, in any case," said the other. "We would have been battling scores of orcs had we tried."

Gerti dismissed them both with a wave and turned away, her mind whirling from the surprising news. Obould was the hero once more, which would be beneficial in bringing forth more of the orc and goblin tribes. His glory had bound them together.

But where did that glory leave her? Beneath him on the field while he soared around on his winged steed?

A horn brought the giantess from her contemplations, and she turned north to see the returning host of orcs, King Obould walking at their head.

"Walking," she whispered, thinking that a good thing.

She caught sight of the pegasus, moving along to the side, bound and hobbled by short ropes tied leg to leg. Indeed it was a beautiful creature, majestic and with a brilliant white coat and mane. Too wondrous for the likes of an orc, to Gerti's thinking. She decided right then that she would demand the pegasus in time—true, she could never ride it, but what a wonderful addition to Shining White such a magnificent beast would prove!

As the column neared, Obould motioned for his charges to continue, then he veered toward Gerti, the miserable Arganth trotting along at his heels.

"We found just one," he told her. "But that one will be enough to bring the orcs from the tunnels."

"How can you know?" Gerti asked, and she wasn't looking at the orc king but rather at the pegasus as it was pulled past on her distant right.

"Yes, a mount for a king," Obould remarked. "We have begun the breaking. I will fly the beast when that bitch Alustriel of Silverymoon comes pleading that we do not continue our march."

Gerti glanced back as the pegasus moved past, and she could clearly see the signs of the brutal orc breaking. Whip marks marred the pegasus's white coat. Every time the steed tried to lift its head proudly, the orc tugging it along yanked down on the lead, and the horse bowed. Gerti could only imagine the bite of the nasty bit the orc must be using to so bend the powerful pegasus.

"I have been informed of Donnia's demise," Gerti said, turning back to the orc king.

"Dead and rotting on the mountainside," said Obould.

"Then Drizzt Do'Urden is still around, and other elves, no doubt."

Obould nodded and shrugged as if it didn't really matter.

"We will stay in the region for a while," he explained, "to better coax out any tribes who choose to join us. Arganth will lead some back into the northern tunnels to better spread the word of my victory and to give hope to the orcs. Perhaps we will find Drizzt Do'Urden and the other elf or elves, and they too will fall to my blade. If they are wise, they will flee across the Surbrin and back into the Moonwood, though perhaps they will not be safe there, either."

Behind Obould, Arganth snickered.

Gerti studied the orc king carefully. Was his dimwit resurfacing? Would he begin to believe the accolades others were putting on his shoulders and change his mind about securing the borders of his planned kingdom? Gerti knew that crossing the Surbrin would prove a huge, and likely fatal, error.

Despite herself, she hoped Obould would do it.

"My king," Arganth Snarrl said from behind. "Methinks you should go south to your son and be done with the dwarves."

"You question me?"

"No, my king, no!" Arganth said, bowing repeatedly. "I fear . . . Drizzt Do'Urden and the elf's companion are still about . . . there is . . ."

Obould glanced back at Gerti, then turned back to Arganth, looking somewhat confused. He gave a sudden, great belly laugh.

"You fear for my safety?"

"Obould is Gruumsh!" Arganth said, and he fell flat to the ground. "Obould is Gruumsh!"

"Get up!"

Arganth jumped to his feet but continued to genuflect.

"Were you afraid when I battled the elf?" Obould asked.

"No, my king! He was nothing against you!"

"But Drizzt Do'Urden. . . ."

"Is nothing to you, my king!" Arganth screeched. "Not in fair battle. But he is drow. He will cheat. He will come in when you are asleep, methinks. I fear—"

"Silence!" growled Obould.

Arganth gave a whine and seemed as if he would faint away.

Obould turned back to Gerti, his face a mask of anger.

Gerti couldn't hide her amusement, and didn't even try to.

"Forgive me, my king," Arganth whispered, moving up behind Obould.

A backhand slap sent the fool flying away.

"I do not fear this rogue drow, nor a host of the elf's companions," the orc told Gerti. "If all the Moonwood came forth to avenge their dead, I would rush to that battle eagerly."

And die horribly, Gerti thought and hoped.

"We already have enough resources to put the dwarves in their hole and to defend the Surbrin," the giantess remarked.

"Not yet," Obould replied. "I want them to pay in deep pools of blood for trying to hold ground against Urlgen. Let him continue the battle outside of Mithral Hall a while longer. Proffit will need time to being the press from the south."

"You will find little hunting in this region beyond Drizzt and any other elves who might be around. The humans are all dead or have wisely fled."

Obould stared at her for a short while, then just muttered under his breath, "I will consider our movements," and walked away.

Gerti nearly slugged him as he passed, for merely presuming to count her and her giants into his considerations. How dare he act as if his decisions would so affect her? How dare he . . .

Gerti let her bluster die away, a private admission that, just then at least, she would be wise to perhaps play along with Obould. The sheer number of followers he had amassed could press her giants greatly should she make an enemy of him.

The giantess glanced around at the hundreds of orcs and the handful of giants. It struck her then that she had unwisely spread out her forces, with so many working along the Surbrin and the score she had given to Urlgen.

Hopefully that fool of an orc had used those giants as intended and had already driven the dwarves back into Mithral Hall.

Gerti wanted the glory to begin to spread out, instead of simply falling onto Obould's broad shoulders at every point.

She'd find out soon enough, she learned a short while later, when word reached her of Obould's decision to return to the south and Urlgen's battlefield.

24

ON FLEETING HOPES

Regis ruffled the pile of papers—scouting reports—then pushed them all aside. Up on the cliff, Banak was holding strong. But how? Or the better question, why? The force of orcs and giants—to say nothing of the trolls!—that had closed the eastern gate of Mithral Hall had by all accounts been huge. Fortifications were being constructed all around the fords of the Surbrin and yet the bulk of the monstrous forces had departed, with the trolls marching south and the main force of orcs turning back to the north. If that main force linked up with the orcs opposing Banak, then the valiant dwarf and his charges would be pushed over the cliff to Keeper's Dale and all the way back into Mithral Hall. There could be no doubt.

The question nagged at Regis's thoughts: Why hadn't the orcs already done that?

The halfling looked up to Catti-brie, who sat across the way. He started to say something, but her expression caught him and held him in place. She seemed relaxed, physically at least, leaning back in the soft chair, her legs crossed at the knee, her head turned to the side and looking off into nowhere, one hand up, one finger absently playing about her chin and lips. Exhaustion was written across her face, a mask of weariness but also of resolve.

Regis looked closer, noticed the bruises on her hand, the small cuts on her extended finger, rubbed raw from the draw of her powerful bow. He noted the dried blood in her auburn hair, the streaks and clumps. And most of all, he noted the look in her blue eyes, the quiet determination, but undercut by something darker, some sense that, for all their efforts, they could not prevail.

"They are fortifying the western bank of the Surbrin," the halfling informed her, and Catti-brie slowly turned her head to regard him. "Every ford and shallow."

"To keep the elves in the Moonwood and Alustriel in Silverymoon," Catti-brie replied. "To keep Felbarr from joining."

"Felbarr's soldiers will come through the tunnels," Regis corrected.

"Aye, but then if they're to go up and fight, they'll be filtering in beside Clan Battlehammer's own. We'll put no vice on the orcs if we're all coming out the same hole."

"It will fall to the humans, then," said Regis. "To Alustriel and Silverymoon, and to the folk of Sundabar, if they can be raised. We need them."

He heard the pain in his own voice, the realization that crossing the Surbrin would likely take a terrible toll on those hoped-for allies.

"The orcs're counting on the pain of the Surbrin defenses to keep them at bay," Catti-brie said, as if she had read the halfling's mind.

"Some advisors have hinted that I should reopen an eastern exit and strike at the Surbrin fortifications from behind. We could sneak a few hundred dwarves out, and that few hundred could cause more damage than an army of ten thousand across the river."

Catti-brie's expression immediately turned doubtful.

"We would need to coordinate it precisely with the arrival of any allies, of course," the halfling clarified. "Else the beasts would chase us back in and just rebuild their defenses."

Catti-brie began to shake her head.

"You do not agree?"

"You've more than a thousand up with Banak and thousands more digging in on the west end of Keeper's Dale," she explained. "We're hearing the sounds of trolls in the southern tunnels, and you've got dwarves running south to find if any're surviving Nesmé."

"We cannot spare five hundred at this time," Regis replied.

"Even if we could . . ." Catti-brie said, her voice halting, and still shaking her head.

"What do you know?"

"It seems amiss . . ." the woman started and stopped with a sigh. "They could put us in our hole, but they're not."

Regis heard the words clearly and let them echo in his thoughts. It was such a simple truth, but one whose significance seemed to have escaped them all. Indeed, it seemed obvious that the orcs could have chased Banak from the cliff and all of them back into Mithral Hall. The enemy numbers were too great, too overwhelming. And yet, not only were the dwarves still dug in strongly up on that cliff, but they had set another defense in the west and were now considering a third surface foray, back to the east.

"We're being baited," Regis heard himself saying, and he could hardly believe the words as they left his mouth. He came forward in his chair, eyes wide with the terrible recognition. "They're forcing us to fight on terms more favorable to them."

"The hundreds of orc and goblin dead on the slopes in the north wouldn't be agreeing with you," Catti-brie replied. "Banak's slaughtering them."

Then Regis was the one shaking his head.

"They're accepting the losses for the sake of the bigger gain," he explained. "We kill a thousand, two thousand, ten thousand, but they can replace them. Our replacements come harder, and keeping us fighting aboveground continues the clarion call to the neighboring communities to come forth and join in the battle."

It made sense to Regis. The orcs were driving the issue to the bitter end. That great force that had marched back to the north after sealing Mithral Hall's eastern gate would indeed turn their sights upon Banak and drive the dwarves into their hole. But by that time, Silverymoon and perhaps Sundabar would have played their hands, would have come forth or not. And all on terms favorable to the orcs and giants. Regis fell back in his seat, running his chubby fingers through his curly brown hair.

"The orcs want us to stay out there," he said.

"So you're thinking we should come in?"

Regis pondered Cattie-brie's words for a moment, then stared at the woman in confusion.

"We cannot ignore the damage Banak is inflicting," he said. "And there

are reports of refugees making their way to the west, north of the battle."
He paused and riffled through a pile of parchments, looking for the report
that indicated such an emigration. "If we break off the fighting, any left in
the area will be without hope, for the orcs could turn their full attention
against them."

"That would include Drizzt," Catti-brie remarked, and the thought had
Regis stammering as he tried to continue.

"Don't fret," Catti-brie offered. "The choice won't be your own for
long. Banak's thinking he's got less than a tenday before the giants bring
their catapults to bear—and we won't be stopping them this time. Once
those great engines of war begin throwing, he'll have to retreat or be wiped
out."

"And if they get the high ground above Keeper's Dale, we'll have no
choice but to come inside. All of us," Regis said.

"And if they're thinking of coming in behind us, we'll cut them down,"
Catti-brie grimly offered.

It seemed a hollow potential to Regis, though, understanding that all of
it—the fighting and the timing—was being controlled by their enemies.

Catti-brie pulled herself out of her chair.

"I'm to be heading back to Banak," she stated.

She pulled up Taulmaril from the side of her chair and slung the bow
over her shoulder in a determined and even angry motion. But Regis could
see the weariness creeping behind that determination.

Before the woman even turned to leave, there came a knock on the door,
and in walked the two emissaries from Mirabar, the gnome's arms filled
with dozens of rolled parchments.

"We can do it," Nanfoodle declared before anyone even had the chance
for proper greetings. "We can do it!"

"Do it?" Catti-brie asked, turning to Regis.

Regis held up his hand to stop the questions from the woman.

"As you suspected?" the halfling asked the gnome.

"Of course," said Nanfoodle. "And fortune is with us, for the deposit is
under the northern edges of Keeper's Dale and close enough to open tunnels
so that we will not need to dig through much stone at all."

"What's the little one talking about?" Catti-brie quietly demanded.

Nanfoodle bobbed over, a more somber Shoudra in tow.

"With the help of Pikel Bouldershoulder, we can string the metal tubes in short order," Nanfoodle explained. "Within a single day, if you offer enough dwarves to aid us."

"Tubes?" Catti-brie asked, and she looked from Nanfoodle to Shoudra, who merely shrugged, then back to Regis.

"What do you know of it?" Regis asked the sceptrana.

"I know that Nanfoodle is excited by the prospects," Shoudra replied, stating the obvious, for the little gnome was bobbing about, hopping from foot to foot.

"We can do it, Steward Regis," Nanfoodle insisted. "Only give the word and I will commence the organization of the workers. Twenty should accomplish the task, along with Pikel, Ivan, and myself. More than that would likely get in each others' way! Ha ha!"

"Regis?" Catti-brie demanded more insistently.

The halfling put his palms over his eyes and blew a deep sigh. He was surprised by the gnome's success in finding the gasses, and not necessarily pleasantly surprised. For despite Nanfoodle's obvious exuberance, that new development only upped the stakes for troubled Regis. True, he had diverted his forges to satisfy the gnome's requirements for "tubes," but that action had involved little real risk, after all. To move forward with the gnome's planning, the halfling steward would have to order dwarves into dangerous battle, with the risks much greater to all of them, particularly to Banak and his forces on the northern cliff.

And what would happen if Nanfoodle proved correct and brought his plan to fruition?

A shudder coursed through Regis's spine, and he turned to Catti-brie. "Can we take the tunnels underneath the ridge again?"

"Below the giants?"

"That ridge, yes."

The woman looked again at the gnome, curiously, then sat back and considered the problem. She had no idea of how determinedly the orcs were holding those tunnels, with the giants in place above. Likely the resistance would be greatly diminished, since the strategic importance of the labyrinth seemed negligible.

"I would expect that we could," she answered.

Nanfoodle gave a little squeal and punched his fist into the air.

"Won't be an easy fight, though," the woman added, just to dampen the little one's spirits a bit.

Regis looked from Nanfoodle to Shoudra and back again, then back at Shoudra, his eyes asking her quite clearly to help him, to tell him if he could really trust the gnome's wild planning. The woman, apparently catching the cue, gave the slightest of nods.

"How long before those giant catapults come to bear?" the halfling asked Catti-brie again.

"Within the tenday," she replied. "Might be as few as three days."

"Then go to Banak and prepare a force. Get me the tunnels back the morning after next," the steward instructed. "Nanfoodle will send up specifics this very afternoon."

"Ivan Bouldershoulder will meet you up there with instructions," the gnome put in.

"You think ye might be telling me what this is all about?" Catti-brie asked.

Regis looked to the other two again, then he snorted and shrugged.

"I'm afraid to do that," he admitted. "You would not believe me, and if you did, you might just cut me down where I sit."

All eyes went to Nanfoodle then, the obvious architect of all of it all.

"We can do it," the little gnome assured them.

Tred McKnuckles came upon Torgar Hammerstriker and Ivan Bouldershoulder shortly after hearing that Banak had put out a call for volunteers to go and retake the tunnels beneath the western ridge. The pair were distracted as Tred approached, and so they did not seem to notice him. Their attention was fixed upon a small box held by Torgar, one side of it as shiny as any mirror, the other three, and top and bottom, smooth wood.

"Well met," the dwarf of Citadel Felbarr greeted the pair.

"And to yerself," said Ivan.

Torgar nodded and smiled, then went back to inspecting the box.

"Is yerself to lead the fight for the tunnels?" Tred asked Torgar. "Might that I could be joinin' ye?"

"Aye, and aye," Torgar replied. "We'll be going in the morning to drive them smelly orcs out. Me and me boys'll welcome yer company."

"Any word on why?" Tred asked. "I'm not thinkin' we can get to them stinking giants from the holes beneath 'em."

Torgar and Ivan exchanged a grin, and Torgar held up the box.

"Here's why," he explained.

Tred reached for it, but Torgar pulled it back.

"Handle it carefully," the dwarf warned.

"Full o' the oil from me darts," Ivan explained, and he slipped his hand under his bandoleer of explosive crossbow darts and held it forward. "And a concoction the little gnome made—bottle of firewater that blows up when it touches the air."

Tred scrunched up his face and retracted his hand.

"We're going in with bombs, then?" Tred asked.

"Nah, we'll use our axes and hammers to be rid of the durned orcs," said Torgar. "The bombs're for later."

Tred looked curiously from dwarf to dwarf, but both of them merely shrugged and returned his expression.

"It's all beyond us," Torgar admitted. "But Banak's wanting them tunnels taken, and so we're for taking them. We'll see what magic the gnome's got later on."

"Could be worse," Ivan put in. "Least we're getting to smash some orcs."

"Always a good thing," Torgar agreed, and Tred nodded.

"Eleven-hunnerd more feet!" Wocco Brawnanvil cried when Nanfoodle laid out the diagrams before him.

"Eleven hundred and thirty," Nanfoodle corrected.

"Ye'll tie up all the forges for another tenday, ye stupid gnome!"

"Another tenday?" asked the gnome. "Oh no, I need this tomorrow—all of it. My assistants will be pulling it right out of the cooling troughs, piece by piece."

Wocco sputtered for several moments, his flapping lips forming curse after curse, but his incredulity beating every word back before it could get out.

"Seven foot lengths," he finally managed to say. "It's a hunnerd and fifty pieces!"

"A hundred and sixty-two," Nanfoodle corrected. "With half of one left over."

"We can't be doing that!"

"You have to," the gnome countered. "If this was a merchant's order needing to be filled, you would pump those furnaces hot and get the job done."

"Merchants're paying," Wocco dryly answered.

"And so am I," Nanfoodle insisted.

"And what's yer pay, little one?"

"A score of giants," Nanfoodle answered with a great flourish, for he saw that he had many of the other blacksmiths watching him. "A score, I say, and victory for Banak Brawnanvil and Mithral Hall. I offer you nothing less than that, good Master Brawnanvil."

"We build weapons for that," came the smithy's protest.

"This is a weapon," Nanfoodle assured him. "As great a weapon as you've ever built. A hundred and sixty-two. You can do this."

Wocco glanced over at the other blacksmiths.

"It's a lot o' metal," one of the smiths remarked.

"It'll take more than half our stores," said another.

"Much more," a third put in.

"You can do this," Nanfoodle said again to Wocco. "You must do this. Time is running out for Banak and his forces. Would you fail them and have them pushed over the cliff?"

That hit a nerve, the gnome saw immediately, for Wocco puffed out his chest and tightened his jaw, his wide mouth puckering up into an angry pout.

For a moment, Nanfoodle thought the dwarf would surely punch him, but the gnome did not back away an inch, and even added, "This is Banak's only chance to hold out against the hordes. Without your superior efforts here, he will be forced into a disastrous retreat."

Wocco held the pose but did not come forward to throttle the gnome, and gradually, the dwarf's anger seemed to melt into resolve. He looked to the other blacksmiths.

"Well, ye heared him. We got work to do." Wocco turned back to Nanfoodle and said, "Ye'll get yer hunnerd and sixty-two and a few extra for good measure, in case yer own measure weren't so good."

As the chief blacksmith stormed back to his forge, Nanfoodle settled back against the table. He moved to begin collecting his many diagrams but stopped and brought his hand to cover his eyes, overwhelmed suddenly.

He could hardly believe that he was really doing it, that the dwarves were trusting him enough to take such a risk.

He hoped that trust wasn't misplaced, for he understood that he was reaching to the ends of common sense, and though he had so vigorously defended his plans to Regis, Shoudra, Wocco Brawnanvil, and all the others, he had to privately admit that his words were stronger than his thoughts.

Nanfoodle sincerely hoped he didn't destroy all of Mithral Hall.

25

SILENCING THE CHEERS

"Obould is Gruumsh!" Arganth Snarrl shouted at the tribe of orcs exiting the tunnel along the eastern side of one mountain. "He killed the elf demon—all of us witnessed this great victory! He is the chosen! He will lead us to glory!"

The dozen of his comrades behind the shaman took up the chant, and those orcs coming out from their mountain homes glanced around but gradually came to similar chanting.

"He is a dangerous one," Innovindil remarked to Drizzt, the two of them crouched behind a low wall of stone off to the side. They had been listening to Arganth for some time and were both somewhat overwhelmed by the sheer intensity of the orc shaman in his praise for Obould.

"He truly believes that Obould is the avatar of his vile god," Drizzt replied.

"Then he will watch his vile god die."

Innovindil hadn't turned to face Drizzt as she spoke the angry vow, but he could feel the intensity in her eyes and heart as she spat every word. He thought to point out to her that she had scolded him for just the same angry attitude not so long before, bidding him to look past his thirst for vengeance. But crouching behind and to the side of the elf, looking down at her fair profile, Drizzt could recognize the pain there. Of course she was hurting.

And despite her wise words to him, that pain could slip past her guard and bring her uncharacteristic moments of weakness. Drizzt, who had recently witnessed the fall of a dear friend, could surely understand.

"The orc king has gone south with his force, but this one remains," Drizzt remarked.

"To rouse the rabble who crawl out of their mountain holes," said Innovindil.

"We cannot underestimate the importance of that," said Drizzt. "And this one is close to Obould—he may have information."

Innovindil turned around and looked up at the drow, and her expression told him that she understood his reasoning completely.

"They will likely camp within the tunnels," she said.

Drizzt looked to the east and agreed, for already the lighter blue of dawn was blossoming beyond the horizon. Also, while the new orc additions had come forth from the tunnel, they hadn't come out very far.

"They will not move off until late afternoon, likely," said Innovindil.

Drizzt scanned the area, then patted Innovindil's shoulder and motioned for her to follow him off to the side.

"Let us go underground before them and learn our way around," he explained. "We will take the shaman while he sleeps. There is much I wish to hear from that one."

The two drow moved swiftly along the tunnels, their keen eyes scanning every crevice, every jut, every uneven grade, in the darkness. Well in advance of Proffit's lumbering trolls, Kaer'lic and Tos'un paused many times and listened—and more often than not, found their scouting inhibited by the ruckus of the trolls.

They do roll along, Kaer'lic's fingers flashed to her partner, and she gave a disgusted shake of her face.

Eager for dwarf blood, came Tos'un's response. *Will Proffit be so eager to meet with dwarven fire? For the bearded folk know how to battle trolls!*

Before Kaer'lic could begin to signal her agreement, she caught a whisper of noise reverberating through the stone. Her fingers stopped abruptly, and she left one extended to signal her companion to silence, then she eased her head against the stone. Yes, there it was, unmistakably so, the march of heavy dwarven boots.

Tos'un came up beside her.

Our friends again? his fingers asked.

Kaer'lic nodded.

"A sizable force," she whispered. "Two score or more, I would guess."

How far? asked Tos'un's fingers.

Kaer'lic paused and listened for a moment, then shook her head.

Not far . . . she started to sign.

But parallel, Tos'un's movements interrupted. *And who knows where these tunnels might intersect?*

One thing is certain, Kaer'lic replied, *our enemies are heading past us to the south. Back toward the Trollmoors.*

Reinforcements for Nesmé? asked Tos'un.

Kaer'lic looked back at the stone wall, her expression doubtful.

"Ornamental, if so," she whispered. "A gesture by Mithral Hall, perhaps, to show support for their neighbors."

Sounds echoed down the corridor behind them as the trolls closed ground. The two drow looked at each other, each silently asking the same question.

"Proffit will wish to chase the dwarves down, but the diversion will cost Obould the desired pressure on the dwarves underground, perhaps for several days," reasoned Tos'un.

That possibility didn't bother Kaer'lic greatly, as she let her expression show.

"We might perhaps find some enjoyment if the dwarf band is not so large," Tos'un went on, a smile widening on his face.

"Run along with all speed and find a place where we might cross over to the tunnels used by our enemies," Kaer'lic instructed. "Better to pursue them out to the south than to backtrack and hope to find their tunnel's exit on the cursed surface."

Tos'un gave a deferential nod, then turned to leave.

"With all care!" Kaer'lic called after him.

The drow priestess found that her own words surprised her. Were those not the words of a friend? And since when did Kaer'lic Suun Wett consider anyone a friend? Donnia and Ad'non had been her companions for years, and never once in all the trials of their journeys did she ever so dramatically warn them to take care. On several occasions she had believed one or the other dead, and never once had she wept, or even really cared, beyond her own inevitable needs. Why, then, had she just been so insistent with Tos'un?

Because she was afraid, she realized, and because she feared that she was vulnerable. And with Donnia and Ad'non off who-knew-where, Tos'un was her only real companion.

The stench of troll began to grow around her as Proffit and his band closed in, and that only reinforced for the priestess the value of her lone drow companion. She'd hardly find life tolerable without Tos'un.

For a long, long while, Kaer'lic stared at the dark tunnel down which Tos'un had disappeared, pondering that realization.

Though he had tried to become a creature of the surface, as soon as he moved deep into the gloom of the tunnels, Drizzt Do'Urden realized just how much he remained a denizen of the Underdark. Beside him, Innovindil moved with an elf's grace, but in the tunnels, it was not nearly as fluid and easy a stride as the dark elf's. In the Underdark, Drizzt was as much superior to her as she was to him in the open daylight.

They made their way across some broken ground and up into a natural chimney, branching off the main corridor of the complex. In looking at Innovindil as they set themselves, Drizzt could see her reservations. And why not? He had placed them in the center of the main corridor, and if the orcs did come in, they would surely pass that way in force and would even possibly camp in that very spot, perhaps right below the pair.

But Drizzt merely looked back to the tunnel below and hid his smile. Innovindil did not understand the level of stealth a drow in such places could achieve. She didn't understand that even if the orcs set their main encampment right below the natural chimney, the drow could slip down among them with ease.

He did look back at Innovindil then, offering her an assuring nod, and the two sat still and quiet, letting the minutes slip past.

Drizzt's sensitive eyes showed him that the gloom lessened just a bit; the heightening of morning outside, he knew. Soon after, there came the shuffling of orc feet and the procession began below them. Drizzt estimated that perhaps two dozen orcs had come in, and as they moved past, he motioned for Innovindil to hold her place, then crept down the chute, head first, spider-like. Pausing for a moment to listen, he poked his head out into the corridor and scanned both ways. The orcs had moved deeper in, but not far. They were milling around, he could hear, likely setting their camp.

Back up he went.

"Two hours," Drizzt whispered into Innovindil's ear.

The patient elf nodded. The two settled in more comfortably, and to Drizzt's surprise, Innovindil pulled him close to her so that his head was resting comfortably against her bosom. As he relaxed, she gently stroked his long and thick white hair, and even kissed him once atop the head.

It was a comfortable place and a tender sharing, and Drizzt allowed himself to relax more than he had in a long, long while.

The two hours passed all too swiftly for him then, but he was able to pull himself from his zone of comfort and rouse the hunting instincts within. Again, he motioned to his companion to hold her place, and again, he went down the chute, head first.

The corridor was clear. Drizzt hooked strong fingers on the lip of the chimney chute, then rolled himself over, dropping silently to a standing position in the tunnel. He drew out his blades, crept along deeper into the complex, and found the orc camp soon after, set in the corridor and in a pair of small chambers to the side.

The twisting and uneven corridor offered him a plethora of vantage points as he studied his enemies. A few were awake, milling around a small cookfire, and a couple were off to the side, against the far wall, eating and talking. Beyond them was an opening, leading into a slightly higher chamber wherein several orcs snored. Across the way sat the other chamber, with more sleeping brutes. Drizzt did spot one orc dressed in a garb that seemed to mark him as a shaman, but it was not *the* shaman, not that Arganth creature who seemed so valuable to King Obould.

The drow slid his scimitars away and crept closer, looking for an oppor-tunity. Many minutes passed, but finally the camp settled down a bit more, with all but a couple of the orcs lying back and closing their eyes. Drizzt didn't hesitate. He pulled his cloak tight around him and crept in closer, moving in the shadows on the wall opposite the small cookfire—which was really no more than a few glowing embers by then. He paused just past that main area until those orcs still talking seemed more distracted, then he slipped right by them and into the small room across the way.

He saw Arganth, sleeping soundly.

Back out again, the drow reversed his movements and went back to the chimney, where he found Innovindil waiting. He considered the setup once again, then offered her his plan using short whispers, stopping often to listen and ensure that he had not alerted any nearby enemies. He considered then that perhaps he should try to teach Innovindil the drow sign language, and the thought nearly had him laughing aloud.

He had tried to teach the language to Regis once, but the halfling's stubby fingers, despite his exceptional dexterity, simply could not form the proper letters—Drizzt had explained that the movements seemed as if Regis was speaking with a lisp! He had tried to teach Catti-brie the signals as well and had succeeded to a very small degree, but even a human as clever as Catti-brie simply didn't have the necessary finger coordination. But Innovindil would possess the nimbleness, he was sure. Perhaps when they had more time together, he would show her.

"You may have trouble getting out afterward," the elf replied when Drizzt finished explaining his plan.

Drizzt was touched that her only concern seemed to be with his safety—particularly considering that if things went accordingly, she was the one who would be pursued by most of the orcs.

They went back out into the night then, to ensure that the orc tribe that had come out of the mountains hadn't camped too close.

Then they were back into the tunnels, just around the bend from the nearest point of the orc encampment. They exchanged pats on the shoulder and nods, then Drizzt slipped ahead, mimicking his earlier movements. It took some time, for the group seated by the opposite room were stirring and arguing, but the stealthy drow finally managed to get into the chamber with Arganth and several others.

One by one, he slit their throats, leaving only the lead shaman alive.

Arganth was rudely awakened, a hand over his mouth and a scimitar tip up tight against his back.

"If you squirm in the least, I will cut out your heart," Drizzt promised, his voice merely a buzzing in the terrified shaman's ear.

He pulled Arganth back against the wall and down to the floor, shielding himself with the shaman in case any should look in. He even managed to hook a filthy blanket and pull it up over them somewhat as a further precaution.

Drizzt waited. He had told Innovindil to give him plenty of time to get the shaman nabbed.

A shriek told him that the elf had gone to work.

Outside the small chamber, orcs began to scramble all around, some running past to Drizzt's right, deeper into the tunnels but most heading the other way, or scrambling around. One came to the entryway and called out for help, but of course, none in the room moved or responded. Drizzt grabbed Arganth all the tighter and slumped lower beneath the blankets.

Another shriek outside told him that Innovindil had scored a second hit with her bow.

A few moments later, the drow wriggled his legs under him and yanked Arganth to his feet, then dragged the shaman to the door. Drizzt saw his moment and slipped out, moving to the left, deeper into the tunnels. He slipped into a side passage as soon as one presented itself, and he pulled Arganth into a sheltered cubby.

He waited once more, as the sounds in the main corridor lessened. He waited a few moments longer, then moved his prisoner back out, and managed to get past the orc encampment without seeing a living enemy. Drizzt noted that three orcs were dead in the corridor, shot down by Innovindil.

The drow and his prisoner got all the way out into the night, and only then did Drizzt release the shaman.

"If you cry out, I will cut out your throat," he promised, and he knew from the responding expression that the clever Arganth had understood every word.

"Obould will ki—" the shaman started to say, but he went silent when a scimitar's fine edge flashed up against his throat.

"Yes . . . Obould," Drizzt replied. "We will speak about Obould at length, I promise you."

"I will tell you nothing!"

"I beg to differ." The scimitar went in even tighter. "I don't think that you want to die."

At that, Arganth put on a weird smile and, surprisingly, pressed even tighter against the blade.

"Gruumsh is with me!" he proclaimed, and he suddenly threw himself forward.

But Drizzt was quicker, retracting the scimitar and bringing his other one from its sheath and across, pommel leading. It smacked against

Arganth's skull, and he crumbled to the ground. He tried to move and tried to cry out, but Drizzt hit him again, and again, until he went very still.

Cursing under his breath, Drizzt slipped his blades away and scooped the shaman up over his shoulder, then ran off into the night.

He was relieved to find Innovindil back at their cave, as they had arranged. Her expression didn't change a bit as the drow dumped the unconscious shaman at her feet.

"You killed three in the cave," he told her.

"And several more outside," she answered, and she looked up at him grimly. "I would have killed them all had their pursuit been more dogged."

Drizzt let it go; he didn't want to raise Innovindil's ire at that time. He methodically went about tying up Arganth, then dragged the shaman to the wall and propped him into a sitting position.

"He will give us the information we need to avenge Tarathiel," Drizzt said.

His mention of the dead elf brought a pained grimace to fair Innovindil.

"And to help defeat this scourge of orcs," she did manage to reply, her voice soft, almost breaking.

"Of course," Drizzt said, offering a smile.

Arganth stirred a bit, and Drizzt kicked him hard in the shin. It was time to talk.

"The Nesmé dogs are scattered," said one of Proffit's heads.

"And running," added the other.

"And hiding," they both said together.

Kaer'lic looked from one to the other and back again, trying not to let on how unsettling it truly was in dealing with that ugly, two-headed beast.

"Perhaps the dwarves seek them," the drow replied.

"Then we follow dwarves," said Proffit's first head.

"And kill them," the second added.

"And squish them," the first put in.

"And eat them," they both decided.

"Just a small group of trolls should stay for eating dwarves and Nesmé dogs," the first head explained. "The rest go on to start the fight inside Mithral Hall."

Kaer'lic hid her grimace.

"But there were scores and scores of dwarves, perhaps," she replied. "A formidable force. We would be foolish to underestimate them."

"Hmm," the troll's heads pondered.

"Better that we all follow the dwarves out to the south," Kaer'lic reasoned. "Let us eat well, then turn back for Mithral Hall."

"But Obould. . . ."

"Is not here," Kaer'lic interrupted. "Nor has he begun to pressure Mithral Hall in any real way. We have time to finish this band of dwarves and the Nesmé dogs, then turn back and begin the war inside Mithral Hall."

For a moment, the drow considered explaining to Proffit that Obould was using him, was throwing his trolls into the fray inside the Clan Battlehammer tunnels knowing full well that their losses would be horrendous and without any real plan to come in support from the upper gates. The drow resisted the temptation, though, realizing that an angry two-headed troll would be likely to strike out at anything convenient—including a lone drow priestess. Besides, as much as Kaer'lic was becoming wary of Obould, she didn't think the pressure on Clan Battlehammer would be a bad thing. And if a few score trolls got slaughtered in the process, where would be the loss?

Proffit started to respond—to agree, Kaer'lic knew—but he stopped short as another figure came into sight, trotting easily down the passageway.

"We can rotate over to the tunnel the dwarves used not too far from here," Tos'un explained to them. "The joining corridor will be tight for our friends, but they will get through."

He looked at the gigantic Proffit as he said that, and his expression was less than complimentary.

Of course, the dim-witted troll didn't catch the subtle look.

"Off we go then," Kaer'lic remarked. "We'll follow them right out and, hopefully, to the Nesmé refugees, and . . ." she paused and looked over at Tos'un, "we'll eat well."

Her drow companion screwed up his face with disgust, but both of Proffit's heads were laughing, and both of his toothy mouths were drooling.

Such a thoroughly disgusting creature, Kaer'lic signaled to Tos'un. *But useful indeed in angering Obould.*

Tos'un's answer came in the sudden flash of nimble fingers. *A worthy cause, then.*

26

ÐURNEÐ GNØME

Regis gave a resigned sigh and dropped the parchment that the scout had just delivered. He watched it float down, gliding left then right before landing on the edge of his desk and hanging there precariously. How fitting, the halfling thought, for it was just one more troubling document in a pile of worry. The scout had come from the south to report that some trolls had turned around in apparent pursuit of Galen Firth and the band Regis had sent to the aid of Nesmé.

The halfling's instincts told him to muster an army and go retrieve the fifty dwarves.

But how could he? He had nearly a thousand still up on the cliff fighting with Banak and another even larger group settled into the western reaches of Keeper's Dale, holding Banak's flank and the course to Mithral Hall's western door. Those limited numbers of dwarves still within Mithral Hall proper had more than enough to keep them busy, between patrolling the tunnels, ferrying supplies up to and bringing wounded down from Banak—and replacing his losses—and running the forges nonstop, crafting the items for Nanfoodle.

A sour look crossed Regis's face when he thought of those forges, and for a moment he considered shutting Nanfoodle's crazy scheme down then and there. He could free up some dwarves at least and send them off to the south.

Another sigh escaped the halfling's lips, and he dropped his face into his palms. Hearing a rap on his door, he rubbed his face briskly, looked up, and bid the knocker to enter.

In came a dwarf arrayed in battle gear, except that his head was wrapped with a bandage instead of encased in a helmet.

"Fighting's begun in the tunnels under the giant ridge," the dwarf reported. "Banak told me to tell yerself."

"When you came down to get your wounds tended," Regis reasoned.

"Bah, just a scratch," said the dwarf. "Came down to get some long spears so we can build a few new defenses."

He nodded and started back out.

"How goes the fighting in the tunnels?" Regis asked after he recovered from the dwarf's statement.

The warrior looked much worse than he was letting on. One side of the head-wrap was dark with blood and his armor showed dozens of tears and dents. The dwarf turned back.

"Ye ever try to push an enemy outta a tunnel?" he asked. "An enemy that's dug in and ready for ye?"

Regis tried not to grimace as he shook his head. The dwarf just nodded grimly and walked away.

That brought yet another sigh from Regis, but not until the dwarf had closed the door—he didn't want to show any outward display of despair or weakness after all. But it was getting to him, truly wearing at his emotional edges. Dwarves were fighting and dying, and ultimately, it was his decision to keep them there. As steward, the halfling could recall Banak and his forces, could bring all of Clan Battlehammer and all of the newcomers to the halls back within the defenses of Mithral Hall itself. Let the orcs try to move them out then! And given his own revelation that this continuing battle might be exactly what the orcs were hoping for, perhaps recalling the forces would be the most prudent move.

But such a move would, in effect, be handing all the region over to the invading orcs, would be abandoning Mithral Hall's standing as the primary kingdom in their common cause of the defense of the goodly folk in the wild lands beneath the shadows of the eastern stretches of the Spine of the World.

It was all too confusing and all too overwhelming.

"I am no leader," Regis whispered. "Curse that I was put in this role."

The moment of despair passed quickly, replaced by a wistful grin as Regis imagined the answer Bruenor would have had for him had he heard him utter those words.

The dwarf would have called him Rumblebelly, of course, and would have backhanded him across the back of his head.

"Ah, Bruenor," Regis whispered. "Will you just wake up then and see to these troubles?"

He closed his eyes and pictured Bruenor, lying so still and so pale. He went to Bruenor each night, and slept in a chair right beside the dwarf king's bed. Drizzt was nowhere around, and Catti-brie and Wulfgar were both tied up with Banak in the fighting, but Regis was determined that Bruenor would not die without one of his closest companions beside him.

The halfling both feared and hoped for that moment. He couldn't understand why Bruenor was even still alive, actually, since all the clerics had told him that the dwarf would not survive more than a day or so without their tending—and that had been several days before.

Stubborn old dwarf, Regis figured, and he pulled himself out of his chair, thinking to go and sit with his friend. He usually didn't visit Bruenor that early in the evening, certainly not before he had taken his supper, but for some reason, Regis felt that he had to go there just then. Perhaps he needed the comfort of Bruenor's company, the reminder that he was the dwarf king's closest friend, and therefore was correct in accepting the call as Steward of Clan Battlehammer.

Or maybe he could simply find strength in sitting next to Bruenor, recalling as he often did his old times beside the toughened dwarf. What an example Bruenor had been for him all those years, standing strong when others turned to flee, laughing when others crouched in fear.

As he was moving through the door, another thought struck Regis and took from him every ounce of comfort that the notion of going to Bruenor had seeded within his heart and mind.

Perhaps, he suddenly realized, he had felt the need to go to Bruenor because somehow Bruenor's spirit was calling out to him, telling him to get to the king's bedside if he truly wanted to be there when his friend breathed his last.

"Oh no," the halfling gasped, and he ran off down the corridor as fast as his legs would carry him.

The speed of his approach and the unusually early arrival time in

Bruenor's chamber brought to Regis an unexpected enlightenment, for as he moved through the door, he found not only Bruenor Battlehammer, lying still as death on the bed, but another dwarf crouching over him, whispering prayers to Moradin.

For a moment Regis thought that the priest was helping to usher Bruenor over to the other side and that perhaps he had arrived too late to witness his friend's passage.

But then the halfling realized the truth of it, that the priest, Cordio Muffinhead, was not saying good-bye but was casting spells of healing upon Bruenor.

Wide-eyed, wondering if Bruenor had done something to elicit such hope as healing spells, Regis bounded forward. His sudden movement alerted Cordio to his presence, and the dwarf looked up and fell back, sucking in his breath. That nervous movement clued Regis in that his hopes were for naught, that something else was going on there.

"What are you about?" the halfling asked.

"I come to pray for Bruenor's passing every day," the dwarf gruffly replied, a half-truth if Regis had ever heard one.

"To ease it, I mean," Cordio tried to clarify. "Praying to Moradin to take him gently."

"You told me that Bruenor was already at Moradin's side."

"Aye, and so his spirit might be—aye, it . . . it must be," Cordio stammered. "But we're not for wanting the body's passing to be a painful thing, are we?"

Regis hardly heard the response, as he stood there considering Bruenor, considering his friend who should have died days before, soon after he gave the order to the priests to let him be.

"What are you about, Cordio?" the halfling started to ask, but he stopped short when another rushed into the room.

"Steward's comi—" Stumpet Rakingclaw started to say, until she noted that Regis was already in the room.

Her eyes went wide, and she seemed to mutter some curse under her breath as she stepped back.

"Aye, Cordio Muffinhead," Regis remarked. "Steward's coming, so end your spells of healing on King Bruenor and be gone quick."

He turned on Cordio as he spoke the accusation, and the dwarf did not shrink back.

"Aye," Cordio replied, "that would've been close to Stumpet's own words, had ye not been in here."

"You're healing him," Regis accused, engulfing them both in his unyielding glare. "Every day you come in here and cast your magic into his body, preserving his life's breath. You won't let him die."

"His body's here, but his spirit's long gone," Cordio replied.

"Then let him die!" Regis ordered.

"I cannot," said Cordio.

"There is no dignity!" the halfling yelled.

"No," Cordio agreed. "But Bruenor's got his duty now, and I'm seeing that he holds it. I cannot let King Bruenor's body pass over."

"Not yet," said Stumpet.

"But you are the ones who told me that you cannot bring him back, that soul and body are far separated and will not hear the call of healing powers," the halfling argued. "Your own words brought forth my decision to let Bruenor go in peace, and now you defy my order?"

"King Bruenor cannot fully join his ancestors until the fighting's done," Cordio explained. "And not for Bruenor's sake—this's got nothing to do with Bruenor."

"It's got to do with the king, but not the dwarf," Stumpet added. "It's got to do with them who're out there fighting for Mithral Hall, fighting under the name o' King Bruenor Battlehammer. Ye go and tell Banak Brawnanvil that Bruenor's dead and see how long his line'll hold against the orc press."

"This ain't for Bruenor," said Cordio. "It's for them fighting in Bruenor's name. Ye should be understanding that. Mithral Hall's needing a *king*."

Regis tried to find an argument. His lips moved, but no sound came forth. His eyes were drawn low, to the specter of Bruenor, his friend, the king, lying so pale and so still on the bed, his strong hands drawn up one over the other on his once-strong chest.

"No dignity. . . ." the halfling did whisper, but the complaint sounded hollow even to him.

Bruenor's life had been about honor, duty, and above all else, loyalty. Loyalty to clan and to friend. If staying alive meant helping clan and friend, even if it meant great pain for Bruenor, the dwarf would put an angry fist in the eye of anyone who tried to stop him from performing that duty.

It pained Regis to stand there staring at his helpless friend. It pained Regis to think that those clerics were going against the wishes of Catti-brie and Wulfgar, the two who held the largest claim over the fate of their adoptive father.

But the halfling could find no argument against the logic of Cordio and Stumpet's reasoning. He glanced at the two dwarves and without either affirming or denying their work, he put his head down and walked out of the room, yet another weight on his burdened shoulders.

The two heavy iron tubes clanged down to the stone floor and bounced around for a moment until Nanfoodle finally managed to corral them and hold them steady. The gnome huffed and puffed after carrying the two lengths all the way from the forges. He didn't sit back and rest, but instead adjusted the metal tubes so that they were set end to end.

Pikel Bouldershoulder looked at the items curiously, then down at the pile of mud set before his crossed legs. The enchantment would soon fade on the mud, he knew, reverting it to its former solidity. The green-bearded dwarf scooped a handful and slid over to the two pipes, then lifted the end of one and examined it.

"Heh," he said appreciatively, noting that the dwarves had put a lip on either end of each piece.

He waved Nanfoodle over to his side, and the gnome took up the other tube and carefully held it up to the end Pikel had elevated.

Pikel helped press them together, and Nanfoodle quickly wrapped the area of the joint round and round with a strip of cloth. Pikel brought his hand in, slopping the mud all around the joint, all over the cloth wrap. He worked the mud around, then he and Nanfoodle carefully laid the two pieces back on the floor. Nanfoodle quickly gathered some small stones and buffered them against the curving sides of the two pieces, securing them in place while Pikel's stone hardened.

And harden it did, sealing the two pieces together into a single length.

"Sssss," Pikel explained, pointing down at the joint, and he pinched his nose.

"Yes, it will leak if we leave it as is," Nanfoodle agreed. "But we shall not."

He rushed out and returned a few moments later bearing a heavy bucket, the handle of a wide brush protruding over its lip. Setting the bucket down, Nanfoodle lifted the brush, which was dripping with heavy black tar. Again, the gnome bent low to the joint, washing over it with the tar.

"No ssssss," he said to Pikel, waggling his finger in the air.

"Hee hee hee," the green-bearded dwarf agreed.

It did Nanfoodle's heart good to see Pikel in such fine spirits. Since the loss of his arm, the dwarf had been sullen, and even less talkative than usual. Nanfoodle had watched him carefully, though, and had come to the conclusion that Pikel's despair was wrought more from being helpless in the face of the current adversity than in his own sudden disadvantage.

Engaging the green-bearded dwarf so completely in his plan—and indeed, Pikel was the best suited of all for such a task—had brought energy back to the dwarf and had rekindled the dwarf's wide smile. Sitting there with his stone-turned-to-mud, Pikel even offered the more-than-occasional "Hee hee hee."

"They're fighting up above," Nanfoodle remarked.

"Oooo," Pikel replied.

He started to rise and turn, as if he meant to run right off to the battlefield.

"The tunnels under the giants," Nanfoodle explained, grabbing Pikel's arm and holding him in place. "If we are fortunate, the battle will be over before we could even get up to join it. But we cannot ask our friends to hold those tunnels for long—doing so will deplete Banak's resources greatly."

"Oooo."

"Only we can help alleviate that, Pikel," Nanfoodle said. "Only you and I, by working hard and working fast."

He glanced down at the lengths of metal tubing.

"Uh huh," Pikel agreed, and he fell back to work, gathering up his large bucket of mud, which was fast turning back to its previous solid state.

Nanfoodle nodded and took a deep breath. It was indeed time to begin in earnest. He considered the course he had to lay out and quickly estimated the maximum number of dwarves he could press into service before creating a situation with simply too many workers. Regis would be easy to convince, the gnome understood, for up above, the truly brutal work, the clearing of the tunnels, was already underway.

Nanfoodle imagined some of the scenes of battle that were no doubt occurring even then.

A shudder coursed his short spine.

"Damned archers!" Tred McKnuckles cried.

He fell to the side of the tunnel, throwing himself behind a rock. The dwarves had easily enough gained the outer areas of the tunnels, the southern stretches nearest to Keeper's Dale, but as they had moved in deeper, the resistance had grown more and more stubborn. Tred's group, which included Ivan Bouldershoulder and Tred's Felbarr friend Nikwillig, had hit fortified resistance along one long and narrow tunnel.

A short distance from them, the orcs had dug in behind a wall of piled stones and held several vantage points from which they could fire their bows and throw their light spears.

"Torgar's pressing on to our left," Ivan, who had similarly dived for cover on the opposite side of the corridor, called back to Tred. "He'll move past us to the wider halls. He's to be needing our support!"

"Bah!" Tred snorted, and he determinedly leaped out from behind the rock—and promptly got hit by a trio of arrows that had him slumping back from where he'd started.

"Ah, ye fool!" Ivan cried.

"That one's hurtin'," Tred admitted, clutching at one of the quivering arrow shafts.

"We'll get ye outta here!" Ivan promised.

Tred held up his hand and shook his head, assuring the other dwarf that he was all right.

"We gotta get 'em pushed back," the Felbarr dwarf called back.

"Nine Hells!" spouted a frustrated Ivan.

He pulled a crossbow quarrel from his bandoleer and eyed it carefully. His friend Cadderly had designed those bolts, with Ivan's help. Solid on both ends, they were partially cut out in the middle, designed to hold a small vial in their cubby. That vial was full of enchanted oil, designed to explode under the impact of the dart's collapse.

Ivan fitted the bolt to his small hand crossbow—another design that he and Cadderly had worked to perfection—then fell flat to his belly, eased himself out, and launched the missile down the corridor.

Without much force behind it, for it was merely a hand crossbow after all, the bolt looped down toward the orcs. It hit one of the rocks that formed their barricade and collapsed on itself. The oil flashed and exploded, blowing away a piece of the rocks.

"Let me chip away at their walls," Ivan called to Tred. "We'll send them pigs running!"

He fitted another bolt and let it fly, and another small explosion sounded down the tunnel.

And the tunnel began to tremble.

"What'd ye do?" a wide-eyed Tred asked.

Ivan's eyes were no less open.

"Damned if I'm knowing!" he admitted as the thunder began to grow around them. Ivan looked down at his bandoleer, and even pulled forth another dart. "Just a little thing!" he cried, shaking his head, and he looked back down toward the orcs.

He realized only then that the reverberations were behind his position, not in front.

"Tweren't me, then!" Ivan howled, and he looked back in alarm.

"Bah! Cave-in!" cried Tred, catching on. "Get 'em out! Get 'em all out!"

But it wasn't a cave-in, as the two dwarves and their companions learned a moment later, when the leading edge of the thunder-makers came around the corner behind them, charging up the tunnel with wild abandon.

"Not a collapse!" one dwarf further down the corridor called.

"Gutbusters!" cried another.

"Pwent?" Ivan mouthed at Tred, and both wisely rolled back tighter against their respective wall.

His answer came in one long, droning roar: the cry of sheer outrage, the scraping of metal armor, and the stamp of heavy boots. The column rushed past him, Thibbledorf Pwent in its lead, and bearing before him a great, heavy tower shield. Arrows thunked into that shield, and one skipped past, catching Pwent squarely in the shoulder. That only made him yell louder and run faster, leaning forward eagerly.

Orc bows fired repeatedly, and orc spears arced through the narrow passage, but the Gutbusters, be it from courage or stupidity, did not waver a single step. Several took brutal hits, shots that would have felled an ordinary dwarf, but in their heightened state of emotion, the Gutbuster warriors didn't even seem to feel the sting.

Pwent hit the rock barricade at a dead run, slamming against it, and the dwarves behind him hit him at a dead run too, driving on, forming a dwarven ramp over which their buddies could scramble.

And the wall toppled.

A few orcs remained, some firing their bows, some just swatting with flimsy weapons, others drawing swords.

The Gutbusters responded heart and soul, leaping onto their enemies, thrashing them with wickedly ridged armor, skewering them with head spikes, or slugging them with spiked gauntlets.

By the time Ivan helped the stung Tred hobble down to the toppled barricade, no orcs remained intact, let alone alive.

"Gotta take 'em fast and not let 'em shoot ye more'n a few times," the smelly Thibbledorf Pwent explained.

He seemed oblivious to the fact that a pair of arrows protruded from one of his strong shoulders.

"Get that tend—" Ivan started to say to him, but he was interrupted by a cry from farther along, calling out another barricade.

"Get 'em boys!" howled Pwent. *"Yaaaaaaaaaaa!"*

He kicked the broken stones off of his shield and yanked it up. With a chorus of cheering all around him, Pwent set off again at a dead run.

"Hope we don't get to the wider areas too much afore Torgar," Ivan remarked.

Tred just snorted and shook his head, and Ivan helped him along.

Far down from the fighting, in the sulfuric chamber beneath the northern floor of Keeper's Dale, Nanfoodle, Pikel, and a host of dwarves had gathered, heavy cloths over their faces, protecting them from the nasty stench.

Pikel crouched in a pit that had been carved on the edge of the yellowish water. He was mumbling the words of a spell, waving his hand and his stump of an arm over the stone. Beside him, one burly dwarf held a long metal tube vertically, its bottom end capped with a spearlike tip. Pikel finished the spell and fell back, nodding, and the dwarf plunged the long tube into the suddenly malleable stone. Burly arms pressed on, sliding the metal down through the mud, until more than half its length had disappeared.

"Hit rock," he explained.

Pikel nodded and smiled as he looked at Nanfoodle, who breathed a sigh of relief. It would be the trickiest part of all, the gnome believed. First, with Pikel's help, they had excavated ten feet of stone, leaving a thin wall of about five feet to the trapped gasses. There was little room for error.

They waited until the enchanted mud turned back to stone, and on a nod from the gnome, a pair of mallet-wielding dwarves stepped forward and began tapping at the top of the tube.

Nanfoodle held his breath—he knew that one spark could prove utterly disastrous, though he hadn't shared that little tidbit with any of the others.

He didn't breathe again properly until one of the hammering dwarves remarked, "We're through."

The other dwarf, again on a nod from the gnome, pulled out a knife and cut the tie that was holding the spear tip tight against the bottom lip, allowing it to fall away, and almost immediately both the dwarves spat and waved their hands before them as a deeper stench came flowing through the tube.

Pikel gave a little squeal of delight and ran forward, capping the end with a gummy substance Nanfoodle had prepared, then falling down and further sealing the tube in place with more stone-turned-to-mud.

"Craziest damned thing I ever seen," one dwarf off to the side remarked.

"Durned gnome," another answered.

Beneath his cloth veil, Nanfoodle merely smiled. He couldn't really even disagree with their assessment. On his word alone, the dwarves had strung a line of metal out of the chamber, along several tunnels, and through another ten feet of stone to the floor of Keeper's Dale. On his word alone, other dwarves had taken that line all the way to the base of the cliff, more than fifty feet farther to the north and twice that to the east. On his word alone, still more dwarves were even then continuing the line up the side of the cliff—two or three hundred feet up—securing the tubes end to end with a series of metal pins so that Pikel could later seal them together with his stone-turned-to-mud.

Pikel went back to work, with all the dwarves in tow, some carrying buckets of mud, others carrying buckets of sealing pitch. While the pit had been carved, the green-bearded dwarf had connected nearly all of the underground tubes, and so within the matter of an hour, the crew was back above ground, crawling their way across Keeper's Dale to the base of the cliff. Pikel had become quite proficient at his work by that time, even perfecting the technique for "elbowing" the stone joint when the tubes had to turn a corner.

Nanfoodle led a second crew all along the joined metal line, painting more pitch on any possible weak areas and propping stones against the metal to further secure it. There was no room for error, the gnome understood, particularly in those stretches underground.

Every so often, the gnome went back to the sulfuric chamber, just to make sure that the critical first tube was still solidly in place.

Just to reassure himself that he wasn't completely out of his mind.

After Pwent's dramatic victory at the barricade, the battling dwarves had the majority of the tunnels beneath the giant-held ridge secured within another hour, forcing the remaining orcs to the very northern end of the complex. Not wanting to delay much further than that, Torgar ordered the area sealed off (which greatly disappointed Pwent, of course), his engineers dropping a wall of stone before their enemies. Inspecting the cave-in, Torgar declared the complex won.

The work was only beginning, though. The dwarves rushed back out of the tunnel's southern end, back near Keeper's Dale, and replaced weapons on their belts as they took up buckets of dark and sticky pitch. As part of Torgar's troupe went back underground, buckets and brushes in hand, another part began stringing the come-alongs and ropes down to the floor of Keeper's Dale. Within a short expanse of time, a bucket brigade had begun, with tar-filled pails coming up the ropes and empty buckets moving back down for refilling.

Inside, the dwarves worked to seal every crack and crevice they could find, plastering the walls and ceiling with the sticky substance.

Using the designs offered by Nanfoodle, other dwarves secured themselves to the long ropes with harnesses and eased down the cliff face, taking up equidistant positions from the canyon floor all the way to the top. They began hammering in eyelet supports, building a straight line of supporting superstructure from floor to ledge.

Torgar, Ivan, and Tred—who continued to stubbornly wave away any who thought to tend his wounds—began to inspect the region near the center of the tunnels within the ridgeline, seeking the thinnest area of stone blocking the way to the east and the continuing battlefield. Torgar moved along deliberately, tapping the stone with a small hammer and listening carefully for the consistency of the ring. Convinced he had found an optimal spot, Torgar sent his diggers to work, and the team quickly bored a hole out to the east, breaking through the line of the stony ridge so that they could feel the open air upon them.

"That wide enough?" Torgar asked.

Ivan held up the small box he had constructed to Nanfoodle's specifications, with its mirrored side.

"Looks like it'll fit," he answered.

He moved close and held the box up tight. The diggers went back to work at once, shaping the hole so that it would be a better and more secure fit, then they moved back and Ivan squeezed in as far as he could, pressing the box, mirror facing outward, as far to the edge as possible.

"Seal it tight in place," Torgar instructed his team, and he and the other two leaders moved back the other way.

"What's that durned gnome thinking?" Tred asked.

"Couldn't begin to tell ye," Torgar admitted. "But Banak told me to take the damned tunnels, so I taked the damned tunnels."

"That ye did," said Ivan. "That ye did."

"And good'll come of it," Tred offered with a nod.

"Aye," agreed Ivan. "These Battlehammers know how to win a fight."

Torgar patted his companions in turn, and it struck Ivan then how ironic it was that he, Torgar, and Tred had been given charge of so important a mission as retaking the cave complex, in light of the fact that not one of them was of Bruenor's clan.

The stomping of battlerager boots interrupted that thought, and their conversation. The three turned to see Thibbledorf Pwent leading his troops at a swift pace back to the south.

"Fighting's startin' again outside," Pwent explained to the three as he passed. He called back to his team, "Hurry up, ye dolts! We're missing all the fun!"

With a great cheer, the Gutbuster Brigade charged past.

"Glad he's on our side," Tred remarked, drawing a chortle from both of his companions.

Before the next dawn, with fighting continuing along the sloping ground to the east and with Tred sent along for some priestly tending, Torgar and Ivan stood at the edge of the southernmost of the complex tunnels, right near the lip of the cliff drop to Keeper's Dale.

"We spill good dwarf blood just to close it all off," Torgar remarked with a frustrated sigh.

"I'm thinking the gnome's meaning to stink them giants off the ridge," Ivan replied. He kicked at the length of tubing that had been laid down from the cliff face to inside the tunnel itself. "He's for bringing up the stink."

Before the pair, a group of dwarves worked fast, piling rocks all around the center reaches of the long metal tube, carefully placing the stones so that they supported each other without putting any pressure on the metal pipe.

"Have to be a pretty good stink," said Torgar, "to chase giants off the ridge."

"Me brother says it's a good one," Ivan explained.

As the workers scurried to the side, he nodded to the dwarf engineers standing to either side of the tunnel, warning them away. Torgar and Ivan took up heavy mallets and simultaneously knocked out wooden supports that had been set in place, and the end of the rocky tunnel collapsed, burying the entrance and the middle sections of the tubing.

"Seal it up good," Ivan explained to his workers. "Wash it all with pitch, pile it with dirt, then wash it all again. We're not wanting any of that stink backing up on us."

The dwarves nodded and went to work without complaint.

Ivan returned the nod, then glanced back over the cliff facing, at the line of harnessed dwarves hanging all the way down to the floor of the dale. Other ropes brought buckets of muddy stone and still others hauled length of the metal tubing.

So much metal tubing.

"Durned gnome," Ivan remarked.

27

CONSCIENCE DECISIONS

"How fortunate for you that those giants decided to join with you," Obould remarked to Urlgen when he caught up to his son at the rear of Urlgen's encampment. As he spoke, the orc king directed Urlgen's attention to the western ridgeline, where Gerti's frost giant warriors were busily reconstructing their catapults. "Good fortune that this group happened your way."

Neither Urlgen nor Gerti, who was standing beside Obould, missed the orc king's sarcasm, nor his clear inference that he knew Gerti and Urlgen had tried to circumvent his control of the situation.

"I did not refuse valuable help," Urlgen replied, glancing at Gerti for support more than once.

"Valuable in scoring a victory without Obould?" the orc king bluntly asked, and both Urlgen and Gerti bristled and shifted nervously. "And still, even with the assistance of, what—a score of frost giants?—the dwarves remain."

"I will drive them from the cliff!" Urlgen insisted.

"You will do as you are instructed!" Obould countered.

"You would deny me this victory?"

"I would deny you a minor victory when a greater one is within our grasp," Obould explained. "Have everything in place to drive the dwarves from the cliff. I will quietly double your forces, out of sight of the foolish dwarves. After that, Gerti and I will march southwest and attack the dale below from the west. Then you can drive the dwarves from the cliff. They will have nowhere to run."

He looked from Urlgen to Gerti, who was clearly angry and just as clearly perplexed as she surveyed the ridgeline to the west.

"This should have been ended long ago," the giantess admitted, addressing Urlgen more than Obould. "Explain this delay."

"Two days ago the catapults were ready to finish the task," Urlgen growled back at her. "But our enemies came against them, and your giants failed to defend the war engines. It will not happen again."

"But there are reports that the dwarves retook the tunnels beneath the catapults," Gerti reminded, for word of the recent battle had been filtering through the camp all the day long.

"True," Urlgen admitted. "They have lost dwarves in retaking tunnels that were not worth defending. By the time they can dig through the thick stone to attack the giants, the battle outside will be long over.

"But that doesn't even seem to be their intent," he went on. "They fill the tunnels with stink—too great a stink for us to counterattack, and so great that your giants complain of it. Look on them closely, and you will see that they wear veils over their faces to ward the stench."

"Will an odor drive them from the ridge?" Obould asked.

"It is an inconvenience and nothing more," Urlgen explained. "The dwarves have assured that we cannot attack them through those tunnels. They believe they have protected their flank, but it was not an attack we would make anyway. Their fight in the tunnels has brought them no relief, and no victory."

Obould squinted his bloodshot eyes and stared at the ridge. In any event, it seemed as if the catapults were nearly completed and that work was continuing on them at a steady pace.

"We have a ten-mile march to wage the fight west of the dale," Obould explained. "When battle sounds in the southwest, begin your drive against the dwarves. Engage them fully and to the end. Drive them from the cliff into my waiting army, and they will be destroyed, and Mithral Hall will never again realize its present glory."

Urlgen glanced again at Gerti and seemed more than a little shaken.

"All glory to Obould," the younger orc said, rather unconvincingly.

"Obould is Gruumsh," the orc king corrected. "All glory to Gruumsh!"

With that, and with a warning snarl at both his son and the giantess, King Obould walked away.

"His army has grown many times over," Gerti explained to Urlgen. "He will more than double your force. You'll not even need my warriors and the catapults."

"The smell of dwarven trickery will not force them from the ridge," Urlgen assured her. "Let the catapults throw their stones and crush the dwarves. Perhaps we can direct some throws over the cliff and near to Obould's march, eh?"

"Take care your words," Gerti warned.

But there was no hiding the smile that showed her to be somewhat entertained by the mere notion of "accidentally" squishing King Obould Many-Arrows beneath a giant boulder. She glanced over at the departing orc king, that arrogant little wretch who was so controlling the entirety of the campaign.

Her smile widened.

"His zeal is religious in nature," Innovindil explained to Drizzt after hours of nearly fruitless interrogation of the captured shaman. "He will tell us nothing. He fears not pain nor death—not if it is in the name of his cursed god-figure."

Drizzt leaned back against the cave wall and considered the truth of Innovindil's reasoning. He had learned that Obould had marched south—but he had all but figured that out previous to capturing the shaman, anyway. The only other tidbit that seemed even remotely useful was the admission by Arganth that it was Obould's own son, Urlgen, who had sacked Shallows and was pressing the dwarves in a fierce battle just north of Mithral Hall.

"Are you ready to go to the south?" Innovindil quietly asked the drow. "Are you ready to face the surviving dwarves of Mithral Hall and confirm your fears?"

Drizzt rubbed his hands over his face and pushed away the awful image of Withegroo's tumbling tower. He knew what he was going to hear when he went to Mithral Hall.

And he didn't want to hear it.

"Let us go south, then," the drow answered. "We have business with this King Obould and have a loyal pegasus depending upon our every move. I mean to get that mount back and mean to pay Obould back for his actions."

Innovindil was smiling then, and nodding. Drizzt glanced to the side, to the opening of the side chamber that held the shaman.

"What do we do with that one?" he asked. "He will surely slow us down."

Without saying a word, Innovindil stood, gathered up her bow, and walked to the entrance of the side chamber.

"Innovindil?" Drizzt asked.

She fitted an arrow to her bowstring.

"Innovindil?"

Drizzt jerked in shock as the elf drew back and let fly, and let fly again, and a third time.

"I show them more mercy than they would show to us, by making the kill swift and clean," the elf replied, her voice perfectly impassive.

She glanced at Drizzt, and they both heard a moan coming from the chamber. Without a word, Innovindil dropped her bow aside and drew out her slender sword, then stalked into the side chamber.

Her actions bothered Drizzt. He thought back briefly to a goblin he had once known, a misunderstood slave who had been wrongfully beaten and murdered by his human master.

But the drow shook that image away. The creature they had captured was not like that goblin. A fanatical follower of an evil god, the orc shaman had lived to destroy, to pillage, to burn, and to conquer. Drizzt knew that Innovindil's assessment of the situation, that she had shown more mercy than the orcs ever would, was perfectly correct.

He began gathering up their things, preparing to break camp. It was time to head south.

Past time, perhaps.

Regis sat in the dark, recalling old times with his friend Bruenor. How many days they had shared back in Icewind Dale. How many times Bruenor had found him on the banks of Maer Dualdon, casually fishing, or at least pretending to. Bruenor had berated him—Regis could hear the words in his ears even then.

"Bah, Rumblebelly! Ye do the laziest job ye can find, and ye don't even do that with any heart!"

A smile creased the halfling's face as he recalled that Bruenor would often then plop down beside him on the lakeside, to "show him how to do it."

A great way to enjoy those precious few warm days in Icewind Dale.

Bruenor was still alive. Regis suspected that Cordio and Stumpet were still going to him in the quiet night, casting their preserving healing spells upon him. They weren't going to follow his orders on that issue—they had made that fairly clear—and Regis's position as steward offered him little leverage against two of Mithral Hall's leading priests.

In a way, Regis was glad that they were making the choice for him. He didn't know if he could find the heart to once again demand that Bruenor be allowed to die.

But still, the halfling could not bring himself to fully agree with the assessment of the two stubborn clerics, that for the sake of Mithral Hall, Bruenor had to be kept alive. They argued the symbolism of Bruenor Battlehammer, but it seemed obvious to Regis that Bruenor wasn't a king to anyone then.

No king would lie there if he knew that all his minions were in dire battle, that so many were falling wounded or dead.

"There has to be an answer," Regis muttered softly in the dark room.

He rolled up to a sitting position and stared into the darkness. There had to be more options.

Regis straightened suddenly as his thoughts wound around and coalesced, drawing new patterns in his mind. He considered Cordio's words, and Stumpet's. He considered his old friend Bruenor and all the times they had once shared. He thought of the dwarf's stubbornness, of his pride, of his loyalty and generosity.

There in the darkness, Regis found the answer, found the joining of his heart and his mind.

With more determination and fire in his belly than the unsure halfling had known in a long, long time, Regis, Steward of Mithral Hall, stormed out of his room and across the dwarven complex to find Cordio Muffinhead.

NANFOODLE'S DRAGON

"Keep the squares tight!" Banak Brawnanvil yelled to his forces—his *depleted* forces.

Not only had attrition begun to take a real toll on the dwarf defenders, but Banak had several dozen of his dwarves off the lines and working with Nanfoodle. They were further securing the pieces of metal tubing that were running from the tunnels beneath Keeper's Dale all the way up the side of the cliff face. That left the dwarf warlord fighting defensively, warding the newest vicious attack, but withholding any counterstrikes.

Banak's dwarves were holding well and would continue to hold, as far as the orcs were concerned. But the dwarf warlord kept glancing to his left, to the northwestern ridge and the giants busily completing the assembly on their great catapults. Every so often, a flash of white from the far ridge caught Banak's attention. Reports from his scouts said that Nanfoodle's stink was thick around the behemoths, crawling up through the rocks and settling like a fetid yellow cloud upon the ridge. But to Banak's dismay, that discomfort hadn't driven the giants away. They had wrapped their large faces in treated cloth and had methodically continued, and were continuing, their work.

"We're running out o' time, Banak," came a voice from the side.

The warlord turned to regard Ivan Bouldershoulder.

"We'll hold them back," Banak replied.

"Bah, them orcs're nothing," said tough Ivan. "But the little trickster's trick ain't working. By yer own eyes, ye can seem them giants still at their work. Catapults'll be up and throwin' before the sun's next rising. From that angle, they'll flatten us to the stone."

Banak rubbed his bleary eyes.

"We might want to be dropping down to the dale," Ivan offered.

Banak shook his head.

"Little one's still working on it," he huffed. "I've got a hunnerd dwarves working with him."

"He's only securing the line, from what I'm hearing," Ivan countered.

He motioned for Banak to follow and started off to the west, toward the line of dwarves hanging along the cliff facing down to Keeper's Dale. They came in sight of Nanfoodle and Ivan's brother in short order, standing atop the cliff, looking over reams of parchments and diagrams. Every so often, Nanfoodle would lean out a bit and holler down the line, telling the dwarves to re-tar the joints—all the joints.

"This'll make the smell so bad them giants can't stay up?" Banak asked when he and Ivan neared the pair.

Nanfoodle looked up at him, and the blood drained from the clearly worried gnome's face.

"Easy, little one," Banak offered. "Yer stink's slowing them at least, and we're grateful to ye for that."

"They're not even supposed to smell it!" Nanfoodle shouted.

"Ptooey!" Pikel spat in agreement.

Ivan looked at his brother and shook his head.

"We're not supposed to be stinking up the ridge," Nanfoodle tried to explain. "That means that the hot air . . . the pitch was supposed to seal the tunnels . . . we need to build this level of concentration . . ."

He stammered and stuttered and held up a sheet parchment scribbled with numbers and formulae that Banak couldn't begin to decipher.

"Ye got what he's saying?" Banak asked Ivan.

"Giants shouldn't be stinking," Ivan clarified.

"But then they'd be building their war engines without any hindrance at all," the warlord reasoned.

"Yup," Ivan agreed.

"But then . . ." Banak started, but he stopped and shook his head.

He gave Nanfoodle a confused look out of the corner of his eye, then shook his head again as he looked down at the many dwarves working on securing the line of metal tubes tight to the cliff—dwarves who could have been strengthening the defensive squares that were even then holding the line against the pressuring orcs.

With a snort, Banak moved back toward the area of battle.

"No, he doesn't understand," Nanfoodle pleaded to Ivan.

The yellow-bearded dwarf patted his gnarled hands in the air to calm the little one.

"And he never will," Ivan replied.

"The stink should not have escaped," Nanfoodle frantically tried to explain.

"I know, little one," Ivan assured him.

"Boom," Pikel quietly muttered.

"We needed to contain it, to thicken it . . ." Nanfoodle pressed.

"I know little one," Ivan interrupted, but Nanfoodle rambled along.

"The stench would never push them away—in the tunnels, maybe, where the concentration is greater . . ."

"Little one," Ivan said, and when Nanfoodle rambled on, he repeated his calm call again and again, until finally he caught the excited gnome's attention.

"Little one, I built yer box," Ivan reminded him.

He patted Nanfoodle on the shoulder, then hustled after Banak to help direct the battle.

Ivan glanced to the west as he departed, not to the ridgeline, but beyond it, where the sun had set and the twilight gloom was completing its hold on the land. Then he did lower his gaze to encompass the ridgeline and the dark silhouettes of the great working giants.

Ivan knew that their troubles would multiply before the next rising sun.

"The dwarves' plans did not work, boss," one of the orc undercommanders said to Urlgen.

The pair as standing in the center of the two armies at Urlgen's command: his own, which was continuing the battle up the slope against the dwarves; and those on loan from his father, who were still encamped and out of sight of their enemies.

Urlgen was looking to the west, to the ridge and the giants. The hourglass was flowing on the battle, as word had arrived from Obould that the assault in the west would begin in full at dawn. For Urlgen, that meant that he had to push those dwarves over the cliff, and doing that would be no easy task without the giant catapults.

"They will be ready," the orc undercommander remarked.

Urlgen turned to face him.

"The dwarves and their stink have not stopped the giants," the undercommander asserted.

Urlgen nodded and looked back to the west. He had assurances from the giants that the catapults would begin their barrage before the dawn.

Back in the north, the battle continued, not in full force, for that was not Urlgen's intent, but strongly enough to prevent the dwarves from retreating in full. He had to keep them there, engaged, until his father sealed off any possible escape.

The orc leader issued a low growl and curled his fists up at his side in eager anticipation. The dawn would bring his greatest victory.

He couldn't help but glance back nervously at the western ridge as he considered that without the giant catapults, his task would be much more difficult.

Nikwillig rolled the small mirror over and over in his hands. He glanced to the west and the ridge, then to the east and the taller peaks. He focused on one smaller peak at the edge of the cliff, a short but difficult climb. That was where he had to go to catch the morning rays. Returning from that place, should Banak lose, would prove nearly impossible.

"What am I hearing?" he heard Tred call to him, drawing him from the unsettling thought.

Nikwillig observed the swift approach of his Citadel Felbarr companion.

"What am I hearing?" Tred demanded again, storming up right before the seated Nikwillig.

"Someone's got to do it."

Tred put his hands on his hips and looked all around at the continuing bustle of the encampment. He had just come back from the fighting, dragging a pair of wounded dwarves with him, and he meant to get right back into the fray.

"I was wondering why ye weren't with us on the line," he said.

"I'm more trouble than help down there, and ye know it," said Nikwillig. "Never been a warrior."

"Bah, ye were doing fine!"

"It's not me place, Tred. Ye know it, too."

"Ye could've gone running back to King Emerus then, with news," Tred answered. "I bid ye to do just that—was yer own stubbornness that kept us both here!"

"And we belong here," Nikwillig was quick to reply. "We're owing that much to Bruenor and Mithral Hall. And to be sure, they're glad that Tred was up here fighting beside them."

"And Nikwillig!"

"Bah, I ain't killed an orc yet and would've been slain more than once if not for yerself and others pulling me out o' the fight."

"So ye're choosin' this road?" came the incredulous question.

"Someone's got to do it," Nikwillig said again. "The way I'm seeing it, I might be the most expendable one up here."

"What about Pikel?" Tred asked. "Or the durned gnome Nanfoodle—yeah, was his crazy idea in the first place."

"Pikel probably can't even make the climb with his one arm. And Nanfoodle might be needed here—ye know it. Pikel, too, since he's been so important to it all so far. Nah, Tred, shut up yer whining. This's a good job for meself and ye know it. I can do this as well as any, and I'll be the least missed here."

Tred started to argue, but Nikwillig rose up before him, his stern expression stealing the blustery dwarf's words.

"And I'm wanting to do it," Nikwillig declared. "With all me heart and soul. Now I'm paying back the Battlehammers for their help."

"Ye might find a tough time in getting back. In getting anywhere."

"And if that's true, then yerself and all them standing here will have hard a tough time of it, too," said Nikwillig. He gave a snort and a sudden burst of laughter. "Yerself's about to charge down headlong into a sea of smelly orcs, and ye're fearing for me?"

When he heard it put that way, Tred, too, gave a little laugh. He reached up and patted his longtime companion on the shoulder.

"I'm not liking that we might be meeting our ends so far apart," he said.

Nikwillig returned the pat, and the look, and said, "Nor am I. But I been looking to make meself as helpful as can be, and this job's perfect for Nikwillig." Again, Tred started to protest—reflexively, it seemed—but again, Nikwillig cut him short.

"And ye know it!" Nikwillig said flatly.

Tred went quiet and stared at his friend for a long moment, then gradually admitted as much with a hesitating nod.

"Ye be careful."

"Are ye forgetting?" Nikwillig replied with a wink. "I'm knowing how to run away!"

A shout from down the slope caught their attention then. The orcs had breached the dwarven line right between the two defensive squares—not seriously, but enough to put a few of the bearded folk in apparent and immediate danger.

"Moradin, put yer strength in me arms!" Tred howled, and he charged headlong down the slope.

Nikwillig smiled as he watched his friend go, then he turned back to the east and the dark silhouettes of the imposing mountains. He glanced back one more time to take his bearings and to better mark the critical area of the mountain spur, then, without another word, he tucked the mirror safely into his pack and trudged off on what he figured would be the last journey of his life.

Several hours later, the sky still dark but the eastern rim holding the lighter glow of the approaching dawn, word filtered up to Banak that an orc force had been spotted in the southwest, fast approaching the dwarf positions on the western edge of Keeper's Dale. The dwarf quickly assembled his leaders, along with Nanfoodle, Pikel, and Shoudra Stargleam, who had been the bearer of the information, having scouted the western reaches personally with her magical abilities.

"It is a sizable force," Shoudra warned them. "A great and powerful army. Our friends will be hard-pressed to hold out for very long."

The dispiriting news had all the dwarves glancing around to one another.

"Are ye saying that we should run down the cliff now and be done with it?" Banak asked.

Shoudra had no answer to that, and Banak turned to Nanfoodle.

"I'm hoping to steal a victory here," he explained. "But we're not to do that if them giants start throwing their boulders across our flank. It comes down to yer plan, gnome."

Nanfoodle tried to look confident—futilely.

"If we gotta leave, then we gotta leave," Banak said to them all. "But I'm thinkin' we need to hurt these pig orcs, and bad."

Thibbledorf Pwent growled.

"They're coming soon," Ivan Bouldershoulder put in. "They're stirring in the north, getting ready for another charge."

"Because they know the giants will soon begin their barrage," Wulfgar reasoned.

"But if them giants ain't throwing. . . ." Banak said slyly.

Again he turned to Nanfoodle, guiding the eyes of all the others to the gnome as well.

"Oo oi!" Pikel cheered in support of the hunched little alchemist.

"Is it gonna work?" Banak asked.

"Oo oi!" Pikel said again, punching his one fist into the air.

"The smell was not supposed to . . ." Nanfoodle started to reply, but then he stopped and took a deep breath. "I do not know," he admitted. "I think . . ."

"Ye *think?*" Banak berated. "Ye got more than a thousand dwarves up here, little one. Ye think? Do we hold the fight or get down now?"

Poor Nanfoodle had no idea how to answer and couldn't begin to take that heavy responsibility upon his tiny shoulders.

"Oo oi!" cried Pikel.

"It's gonna work," Ivan added.

"So we should stay?" Banak asked.

"That's yer own choice to make," Ivan replied. "But I'm thinking them giants're gonna be wishing we'd turned tail and run!"

He stepped over and patted Nanfoodle on the shoulder.

"Oo oi!" cried Pikel.

"Orcs're coming again," said another dwarf, Rockbottom the cleric. "Big charge this time."

"Good enough. I was gettin' bored!" said Thibbledorf Pwent, who was already covered in blood and gore from the evening's fighting—some of it his own, but most of it that of his unfortunate enemies.

"Dawn's another hour away," Ivan remarked.

"Less than that from Nikwillig's perch, if he got there," said Catti-brie.

"We got to hold then," Banak decided.

He turned to Nanfoodle and nodded, as much a show of support for the gnome's outrageous scheme as he could muster at that grim time. Banak was gambling a lot, and he knew it, and so did everyone else around him. With the giants throwing their boulders and the press of the orcs, the dwarves would have a difficult time getting over that cliff face and down to Keeper's Dale. If Shoudra's reports and assessment were correct, getting down to Keeper's Dale might prove to be the least of their problems and the worst of their decisions.

"Drive them back, Thibbledorf Pwent," Banak instructed. "Ye hold them pigs off us."

In response, Pwent held up a bulging wineskin, tapped it to his forehead in salute, and ran along to join his bloody and battered Gutbusters.

All eyes again went to Nanfoodle, who seemed to shrink under the press of those concerned gazes. His plan had to work, but the signs were not promising.

Soon enough, the sounds of battle again echoed up the slope as Pwent led the dwarves' counterassault.

Soon after that, the sounds of another battle echoed up from below, from the western reaches of Keeper's Dale.

And soon after that, the first of the giant catapults let fly. A huge boulder smashed and bounced across the back edge of the dwarven line, right along the cliff face.

"Ye got yer skins?" Thibbledorf Pwent asked his gathered Gutbusters as they circled back up and regrouped. To a dwarf, they produced the bulging bladders. "Some o' ye won't be needing them," he added solemnly. "And might be that some won't be able to get to them, but ye know yer place!"

As one, the Gutbusters cheered and roared.

"Get in and break their lines," the fierce dwarf instructed. "Drive them back and take yer dead place!"

Down went the force, another furious charge that slashed through the orc ranks. No defensive measure there, Pwent led his forces down the slope farther than any dwarves had previously gone, shattering the orc line and their supporting allies. Their goal was to cause more confusion than actual damage—no easy mind set for the carnage-hungry Gutbuster Brigade—and that's what they did.

The orc assault fell apart, with many forced to turn back and retreat before regrouping.

Thibbledorf Pwent kept his formation tight, not allowing the customary Gutbuster pursuit. He raised his waterskin in salute and reminder to the others. Then he found a broken weapon he could later use, offering a wink to those nearby so they would understand his intent.

Like an ocean tide, the orcs rolled back and gathered strength for the next wave. And during that brief lull, more of the giant catapults began heaving huge boulders through the predawn sky. Few had the range at first, and so the initial volleys were not so effective, but all the dwarves understood how quickly that might all change.

"We got to hold the east!" Tred cried at the others, mostly to Wulfgar, who had pretty much been anchoring that end of the line from the very beginning.

Wulfgar looked at him grimly, and that response alone quieted the Felbarr dwarf, reminding him of what he had known all along: that Nikwillig would have a hard time getting back to them.

Banak paced nervously around the cliff ledge, looking down to the southwest as often as he was looking at the raging battle down the slope to the north.

This is it, he thought.

It was the culmination of all his efforts and of all of his enemies' efforts. The orcs were closing their vice, north and west, as the giants were softening up the rear of Banak's position.

A boulder slammed down not so far away and bounced right past Banak, nearly clipping him off the cliff.

The tough dwarf didn't flinch, just continued his pacing, his eyes more and more going to the brightening eastern sky.

"Come on then, Nikwillig of Felbarr," he whispered, and even as he spoke the words, he saw the flash of a distant mirror, catching the first rays of dawn on the other side of the eastern ridge.

Others noted the same thing, some pointing excitedly to the east. Catti-brie came running Banak's way from the east, bow in hand, as did Nanfoodle, Shoudra, and Pikel, coming in fast from the west.

"Sight it, sight it," Shoudra coaxed quietly, watching the distant mirror.

Nanfoodle clenched his hands before him, hardly drawing breath.

"There!" Catti-brie said, pointing to the ridge, where the reflection of Nikwillig's roving sunbeam at last caught a second mirror, turning it to blazing brilliance. The woman lifted her bow.

Banak held his breath, as did the others.

Below them, the battle raged, orcs swarming up the slope in greater numbers than before. An all-out assault, it seemed, and all around their position came the calls for retreat, even some terrified shouts for the dwarves to retreat all the way, to get down to Keeper's Dale.

"What're we doing, then?" Catti-brie asked, glancing, as were all the others, over at Nanfoodle.

Nanfoodle began to huff and puff, unable to catch his breath, and for a moment it seemed as if he would simply fall over. He glanced over to regard Pikel, who was sitting next to the tubing near one wide joint.

Nanfoodle found strength in that image, in the giddy confidence of the green-bearded dwarf.

The gnome took a deep breath and nodded to Pikel.

"Oo oi!" Pikel Bouldershoulder cried.

The druid waved his hand over the stone that joined the tubes, then pressed against the suddenly malleable stone, crushing it flat and sealing off the flow.

Another deep breath and another gulp, and Nanfoodle forced himself to steady.

"Shoot straight!" he yelled, and he whimpered and cast himself aside.

Catti-brie leveled Taulmaril, sighting in the shining mirror—the reflector Ivan had placed on the side of the box that had been set in the ridge.

More giant boulders crashed down—several dwarves cried out in terror as the great rocks smashed across the dwarven line.

Catti-brie pulled back, but the eastern mirror held by distant Nikwillig shifted a bit and the reflector in the ridge went suddenly dark.

The woman held her posture, held her breath, and held her bow ready.

"Breach!" came the cry of a dwarf from below and to the north.

"Shoot it, then!" Banak implored her.

She didn't breathe and didn't let fly, waiting, waiting, trusting in Nikwillig. She saw his reflected sunbeam crawling around the dark stones of the ridge, seeking its target.

"Come on then," Shoudra whispered. "Sight it."

Banak ran away from them.

"Fall back!" he yelled down to those engaged in battle. "Form a second line!" he cried to those reserves up nearer to the cliff—reserves who were scrambling around, trying to find cover from the increasing catapult barrage.

Catti-brie put it all out of her mind, holding herself perfectly still and ready, and focusing on that reflected sunbeam—only on that crawling line of light.

There came a flash in the darkness of the western ridge.

Taulmaril hummed, the silver-streaking arrow soaring out across the many yards. The woman fired a second and a third off at once, aiming for the general area.

She needn't have bothered, for that first shot had struck the mark, smashing through the glass of the mirror, then driving home into the piece of wood set in place behind it. The force of the blow drove the wood back, collapsing the large vial and the enchanted and explosive oil burst to life.

For a brief instant, nothing happened, then . . .

BOOM!

All the west lit up as if the sun itself had leaped out from behind that ridge. Flames shot out from every crack in the mountain spur, side, and ceiling, jumping up past the stunned giants and their great war engines, leaping higher than any flames any of the awestricken onlookers had ever seen. A thousand feet into the air went the orange fires of Nanfoodle, turning night to daylight and carrying dust and stone and huge boulders high into the sky with them.

The flames lasted only a brief instant, the gases burning themselves out in one concussive blast, and the onlookers gaped and gasped. And a hot wave of shocking force rolled over them, over Catti-brie, Shoudra, and Nanfoodle, over squealing Pikel and wide-eyed Banak, over the battling warriors, dwarf and orc alike, throwing them all to the ground.

Within that hot wave of air came the debris, tons and tons of stones small and large sweeping across the battlefield slope. Since the main reaches of the slope were farther to the north, the orc hordes took the worst of it, with hundreds laid low in a single burst of power.

Back in the west, the ridge, once so evenly distributed, seemed a jagged and torn line. Catapults and giants alike—those few that were still somehow in place—were aflame, the war engines falling to pieces, the behemoths leaping wildly about.

Nanfoodle pulled himself off the ground and stood staring stupidly to the west.

"Remember that fireball you described to me from your visit to the mage faire those years ago?" he asked the equally stricken Shoudra.

"Elminster's blast, yes," the stunned woman replied. "The greatest fireball ever thrown."

Nanfoodle snapped his little fingers in the air and said, "Not any more."

"Oo oi!" Pikel Bouldershoulder squealed.

29

SHOCKWAVES

The gallant Sunset did not complain as he wound his way above the mountains with two riders sitting astride his strong back. Innovindil guided the pegasus from the front perch, with Drizzt sitting right behind her, his arms tight around her waist.

For Drizzt, flying was among the most amazing and wonderful experiences he had ever known. His traveling cloak and long white hair alike flew out behind him, waving in the wind, and he had to squint against the rush of air to keep his tears from flying. Though he was astride a mount and moving not of his own volition, the drow felt a profound sense of freedom, as if escaping the bounds of earth was somewhat akin to escaping the bounds of mortality itself.

Early on in the flight, he had tried to speak with Innovindil, but the wind was too loud around them, so that they had to shout to be heard at all.

And so Drizzt just rested back and enjoyed the ride, the rush of air and the predawn chill.

They were traveling south, far behind the mass of King Obould's army. Their destination weighed heavily upon Drizzt, though he had found some respite from his fears, at least, in the wondrous pleasures offered by the journey on the winged horse. They knew not what they might find as they approached Mithral Hall. Would Obould have the dwarves sealed away, with no chance for Drizzt and Innovindil to sneak through to communicate with Bruenor's kin? Would the dwarves be holding strong against the invaders, leaving Drizzt and Innovindil a field of torn orc corpses to cross? With so many possibilities spread wide before them, Drizzt had managed to settle back from them all, to simply enjoy the sensation of flight.

Ahead and to the right of the pair and their mount lay the soft darkness of predawn, but to the left, the east, the sky showed the pale blue of morning, above the pink rim created by the approach of the rising sun. Drizzt watched in awe as the red-glowing sun crested the horizon, the first streaks of dawn reaching out from the east.

"Beautiful," he muttered, though he knew that Innovindil could not hear him.

From that high vantage point, Drizzt followed the brightening line of morning as it spread east to west. He turned far ahead of it to catch one last glimpse of the departing night.

And there was daylight, so suddenly, everywhere at once! No, not daylight, Drizzt realized, but an orange glow, an orange flame leaping high into the sky, a fire so great that it brightened the landscape before him instantaneously. Into the air the fire leaped, so far up that the two pegasus-riding elves had to crane their necks and look up to see its apex.

Sunset pawed at the empty air and whinnied, and Innovindil, equally stunned and confused, eased the reigns and bade the mount to descend.

"What in all the world?" the female cried.

Drizzt started to similarly cry out, but then the hot shockwave of the explosion reached out to them, buffeting them with its winds, nearly dislodging both of them. The wind carried dust and small debris far from the fireball, and all three, elf, drow, and pegasus, squinted against the sting.

Down, down they went, Sunset frantic to get to the ground. Innovindil held tight and helped guide him, but Drizzt took the moment to survey the region lit up by the fast-dissipating fireball, to note the swarm of crawling forms. In that brief instant, the drow saw the distant battlefield, recognized the slope leading to the lip of Keeper's Dale, and knew at once that the dwarves were fiercely fighting.

"What in all the world?" a desperate Innovindil asked again as they touched down on solid ground. "Have they wakened a dragon, then?"

Drizzt had no answers for her, for never in all his life had he witnessed such a blast. His immediate thoughts conjured an image of one Harkle Harpell, a most eccentric and dangerous wizard, and Harkle's family of equally crazy mages. Had the Harpells come to Mithral Hall's aid once again, bearing new and uncontrollable magic?

But none of it made any sense to Drizzt, and he had nothing to answer Innovindil's wide-eyed and desperate stare.

"What have they done?" the elf asked.

Drizzt stammered and shook his head, then just offered, "Let us go and see."

The orc ranks flattened like tall grass before a gale. Those fortunate enough to escape the punch of flying debris went down hard anyway, blown from their feet by a shockwave the likes of which they had never imagined possible.

Urlgen, too, went flying down to the stone, but the proud and strong orc did not cry out in fear, nor did he cower. He climbed right back to his feet against the flush of heat and the last waves of the blast and surveyed the battlefield.

There he saw a squirming mass of stunned orcs and dwarves. The tall orc shook his head in disbelief and confusion. He glanced over at the blasted ridge, to see one giant rushing around to and fro, waving its arms, the whole of it immolated by bright flames.

As life itself seemed to return to the battlefield and to the orcs around Urlgen, he heard terrified cries and shrieks, and only then did he understand the true danger of that horrific blast. He had lost some orcs, to be sure, and his giant flank was no more, but the real danger presented itself far above the orc commander's position, as the dwarves regrouped quickly and began a devastating charge against his confused and scattering forces.

Urlgen shook his head and thought, It isn't supposed to go this way!

The shouts to retreat and run away echoed all around him, and for an instant, Urlgen almost conceded to them, almost ordered his warriors to run away.

Almost, but then he considered the bigger picture and the gains his father would even then be making down in the southwest. Urlgen had planned to soften the dwarves for a bit longer, to use the giants and his original force to shape the battlefield without the possibility of the dwarves escaping. Then he would send in the reinforcements his father had given to him and overwhelm the dwarves.

That had all changed in the instant of that terrible explosion.

With a roar that echoed above the din of scrambling orcs, Urlgen demanded and commanded attention. He ran along parallel to the battlefield, intercepting retreating orcs and turning them around—by sheer will and threat forcing them back into the fight.

And all the while, he shouted out to those reserves he had to that point kept hidden from the dwarves' view, turning loose the whole of his force in one great and sweeping charge.

"Kill them all!" the tall orc commanded.

As the swarm gradually swung around to reengage the charging dwarves, Urlgen lifted his fists, spiked gauntlets high, and for the first time, rushed into battle. It was all-or-nothing for him, he knew. He would win there, decisively, or all would be lost. He would forevermore be crushed under the mantle of his glorious father—if his glorious father even spared his life.

Banak Brawnanvil sucked in his breath when he saw the orc horde pivot and swing around. His boys had fared far better than the orcs in Nanfoodle's blast, and all the lower slopes were littered with orc dead. But his boys were still outnumbered—and outnumbered many times over as a second group charged in from behind the original orc ranks.

Banak growled. Given the effectiveness of the explosion, he had wanted to break out and join the definitive battle that would push the orcs back from Mithral Hall.

"Hit them hard and retreat to hold the line!" Banak called to his nearby commanders.

As he watched the full charge of orcs from below, though, it seemed apparent that there was a different tone to their charge, a different intent and intensity. The veteran dwarf began to understand almost immediately that his enemies did not mean to hit and run again. The old dwarf chewed his lip, considered the strength of his enemies, and considered his options.

"Come on, then," he muttered under his breath.

He set his feet firmly under him, determined to hold strong. That determination shifted none-too-subtly a moment later, though, from sheer dwarf grit to almost desperate need, when scouts out to the west shouted back along the line that there was fighting in the southwest, along the western edge of Keeper's Dale.

Banak found a vantage point and peered into the growing light in the southwest. As he noted the scope of the battle and the size of the opposing orc force, he nearly fell over.

"By Moradin, ye hold them," the old dwarf whispered, barely able to get the words out.

He looked back to the north, where the momentum of the wake of Nanfoodle's blast had played out, where the press of orcs was flowing up at him, driving the dwarves back toward their defensive positions. Then he glanced back to the southwest and the growing sounds of battle.

He surmised at once the orc plan.

He saw at once the danger.

With a determined grunt, the warlord forced himself to look back to the devastation of the western ridge. The orc plan had been a good one, well coordinated to not only win the ground, but to slaughter the dwarves to a warrior as well. Nanfoodle's explosion alone had bought him some breathing room, some time—perhaps enough to escape.

"Moradin be with ye, little one," Banak said, aiming the words at the distant gnome, who was too far away to hear.

The battle sounds to the southwest increased suddenly, dramatically, and Banak glanced back to see that a horde of giants had joined in with his enemies.

"Moradin be with us all," the dwarf mouthed.

The main dwarven line broke and retreated, as ordered, running flat out for their defensive positions atop the slope. Arrows and hammers came out over them in support, slowing the orcs that nipped at their heels every step.

Many of the dwarves were not fast returning, though. More than a few were dead, laid low by orc spears, or by the flying debris of Nanfoodle's momentous blast. Many more, well over a hundred others, lay splayed across the stones, covered in blood.

Not from wounds, though, but from torn waterskins. Thibbledorf Pwent and his Gutbusters, which included more than a few very recent recruits, had used the cover of the explosion to splash themselves with blood and fall "dead" to the ground. Some, like Pwent himself, accentuating the wounds by strategically placing broken weapons against them. Now they lay there, perfectly still as hordes of orcs ran past them, sometimes stepping all over them.

Pwent opened one eye and did well to hide his smile.

He leaped up and punched a spiked gauntlet right through the face of the nearest, surprised orc. He yelled out at the top of his lungs, and up came his Gutbusters as one, right in the middle of the confused enemy.

"Buy 'em time!" the toughened leader cried out, and the Gutbusters did just that, launching into a frenzy, slugging and slashing with abandon, tackling orcs and convulsing atop them, their ridged armor plates gashing their enemies to pulp.

Thibbledorf Pwent stood at their center, directing the battle through example more than words. For there was no overreaching plan. The last thing Pwent wanted was to create an atmosphere of coordination and predictability.

Mayhem.

Simple and beautiful mayhem. The call of the Gutbusters, the joy of the Gutbusters.

THE LAY OF BRUENOR

Watching the countercharge—thousands of orcs streaming up in blood-thirsty rage—Banak Brawnanvil understood that it was over. It would be the last battle on that ground, win or lose, press through or retreat. In realizing the sheer size of that orc force, with so many charging up in reinforcement, the dwarf wasn't thrilled with the prospects.

The sound of fighting behind and below him soon had him rushing back to join some of the others at the cliff ledge.

And there, the old dwarf saw nothing but doom.

The dwarves on the western edge of Keeper's Dale had broken ranks already. And how could they not? For the force arrayed against them was huge, larger than anything Banak had ever seen in all his years.

"How many orcs?" he asked breathlessly, for surely the spectacle of that arrayed force had stolen Banak's strength. "Five thousand? Ten thousand?"

"They'll sweep the dale in short order," Torgar Hammerstriker warned.

And that would be it, Banak knew.

"Get 'em down," Banak ordered, and he had to forcefully spit the dreaded words through his gritted teeth. "All of them. We make for the dale and the halls."

An order to retreat was nothing that the dwarves of Clan Battlehammer, nor of Mirabar, were used to hearing, and for a moment, all the commanders near to Banak stared at him open-mouthed.

"The giants're dead!" one protested. "Gnome blew up the ridge, and . . ."

But as the reality settled upon them, as they all came to see the truth of the orc press from the north and the rout behind them in the dale, that was the only dissenting voice. Before the grumbling dwarf had ever finished the statement, Torgar and Shingles, Ivan and Tred, and all the others were rushing out among their respective groups calling for and organizing a full retreat from the cliff.

The warlord ignored the protestor and turned his attention down the northern slopes, to where Thibbledorf Pwent and his Gutbusters were causing havoc across the center of the orc press. The old dwarf nodded his appreciation—their sacrifice was buying him precious time to get away.

"Fight hard, Pwent," he muttered, as unnecessary a cheer as could be spoken.

"Go! Go! Go!" Banak prodded those dwarves moving to the drop-ropes. "Don't ye slow a bit till ye've hit the floor o' Keeper's Dale!"

Banak watched the dwarves who had met the front end of the orc charge form into tighter squares and begin their pivot back up the slopes.

"We gotta break their front ranks to give them who're coming last time to get over," he heard Tred shout out from somewhere below and to the right.

In response to that call came two familiar forms, Wulfgar and Cattibrie, sprinting down the slope, driving the left flank of the orc line before them.

Banak held his breath. Tred's assessment was on target, he understood. If they could not break the orc momentum, could not turn the front ranks around in at least a short retreat and regroup, then many dwarves would die that day.

Behind him again, he heard several dwarves bickering, arguing that they weren't about to run away while their kin were fighting. Banak turned on them powerfully, eyes blazing with fury.

"Get ye down!" he shouted above the commotion of the argument, and all eyes turned his way.

"Go!" the old dwarf commanded. "Ye dolts, we're all to run, and them behind ye can't start until ye're off!"

One of the group punched another and roughly pushed him toward the edge and one of the drop-ropes.

"Ain't never left a friend," the dwarf continued to grumble, but he did indeed take up the rope in his strong hands and roll off the ledge.

Looking back at the furious battle, then farther down to where Pwent and his boys had been seemingly boxed in, Banak could certainly understand that sentiment.

"Crush them!" King Obould cried to his charges, urging them forward. The orc king didn't stand back and issue the order, but rather charged up toward the front ranks, prodding the orcs on, kicking aside the dead and wounded orcs who had already tried the devastating dwarven defenses.

Obould cursed his luck—his very first assault would have overwhelmed those walls and fortifications, he believed, except that the ground had violently lurched beneath them, followed by a hail of stones from up above. The orc king had no idea what in the world might have happened up there, but just then, it wasn't his concern.

Just then, he was focused on one goal alone.

"Crush them!" he cried again.

The orc king continued to push his way forward, crossing to the leading ranks. He came up against the front dwarven wall, sweeping his greatsword before him to knock aside the many prodding dwarven polearms. A couple avoided his wild parry, though, and the dwarves redirected the weapons quickly to stab at the great orc.

Those weapons of Mithral Hall, fine as they were, barely scratched the orc king's magnificent armor, and he barreled ahead, cutting a downward slash with his sword, igniting its flame as he did. One unfortunate dwarf popped up at that moment and had his head cleaved in half. Obould's sword drove down farther, crashing against the top of the stone wall and knocking out a sizeable chunk of it.

The orc king smashed again and again, sweeping that area clean. He leaped up, clearing the four vertical feet to the wall top.

And there he stood, flaming sword braced against one hip and angled diagonally upward out to the side, his other hand outstretched and clenched.

Arrows and crossbow bolts came at him and bounced away. Nearby dwarves scrambled, bringing their weapons to bear, smacking at the great orc's feet to try to dislodge him.

"Crush them!" Obould screamed, and he didn't budge an inch.

Bolstered by his display, the orcs swarmed the wall, and terrified of the display, the dwarves hesitated. To Obould's far right came a wedge of roaring giants, heaving boulders at the fortifications and charging in with abandon.

Beneath his skull-faced helmet, the orc king grinned wickedly. He had suspected that his bold attack would force Gerti and her reluctant kin into full action.

The front fortifications gave way before the swarm. The dwarves broke ranks and fled, and those who were not quick enough were pulled down by the throng and crushed into the stone.

Obould held his spot on the high ground, roaring, sword aflame, fist clenched. He glanced back up to the cliff in the northeast and wondered again about that tremendous explosion. But the implications did not hold his attention for long, for he looked back to his own overwhelming force and the growing rout in the west. Even if Urlgen failed him in the north, Obould knew that he would win the day in Keeper's Dale.

Close the door, the orc king mused, and let those dwarves trapped aboveground try to find their way home.

Drizzt couldn't see the front lines of the fighting, but he knew from the logjam of orc warriors in the middle and back of their ranks that the dwarves near to the cliff were putting up strong resistance. He could also see a commotion only a hundred yards or so south of his position, in the middle of the orc horde. As he watched one orc spinning up into the air, blood flying from multiple wounds, the drow figured that Thibbledorf Pwent was likely involved.

Drizzt didn't even allow himself a grin, for he was approaching the rear of the orc line and had drawn the attention of many of the stragglers.

"They will test you," he said to his companion, who stumbled before him, her arms bound behind her. "You must trust in me."

Innovindil tripped and fell, and Drizzt grimaced against his instinctual response, denying even the slightest hint of it, and let her go down hard. He grabbed her by the shoulder and roughly pulled her back to her feet—and again fought against his reflexive urge to wince when he saw the welt on her face.

It was the way it had to be.

Drizzt pushed her ahead, and she nearly stumbled down again, then he prodded her with one of his drawn blades. Orcs came in at the pair, yellow eyes wide, teeth bared, weapons ready. One moved right up before Innovindil, who looked down.

"A prisoner for Urlgen," Drizzt growled in his coarse command of Orcish.

"For Urlgen!" he reiterated powerfully when the orc made a move Innovindil's way.

"A prisoner from Donnia," the drow added, when doubting looks came back at him from many angles.

The orc in front motioned to another, who charged up behind Innovindil and tugged at her arms, checking the bonds. Drizzt slapped him away, after letting him see that the ties were authentic.

"For Urlgen!" he shouted yet again.

Whether in another test or just out of spite, the orc in front stabbed forward suddenly with its spear, right for the surface elf's gut.

Around went Drizzt, rolling around Innovindil's hip, scimitars slashing, taking the spear out wide with three quick hits.

The drow spun again, shouting, "For Urlgen!" with his scimitars working in a circular blur.

The orc flinched again and again, and fell back.

The drow settled before the elf, scimitars at his side.

The orc looked at him, then looked down at its own torso, cut and bleeding in more than a dozen bright and deep lines. Then it fell over.

"Take me to Urlgen!" Drizzt demanded of the others, "Take me!"

The drow moved behind Innovindil, pushing her forward with all speed, and the orc ranks parted before them like the waters of a lake before the prow of a fast sailing ship.

Up the slope they went, drawing stares from all around—but few of those orcs wanted to be anywhere near to them, Drizzt noted hopefully.

His eyes were soon enough drawn forward, up the slope, to the spectacle of one tall orc barking orders and roughly shoving aside any creatures who got too close to him.

The leader. Obviously the leader.

Drizzt began to fall into himself, finding his center, finding his anger, finding the primal creature that resided within his mortal coil, that instinctive Hunter, then moving through the Hunter and into the realm of pure concentration. With the swarm around him, he held little hope that he and Innovindil could get out of it, and given that, the drow had chosen to simply ignore the throng.

He took a quick look at Innovindil, her blue eyes set as if in stone, staring with abject hatred at the orc leader, at the son of the beast who had so brutally taken her Tarathiel from her.

Before they had come in with their ruse, Innovindil had exacted Drizzt's promise that Urlgen, son of Obould, was hers to kill.

The sounds of battle echoed all around them, the cries of the orc leader cut the air, and the orcs pressed on up the slope, where the stubborn dwarves held their ground.

And Drizzt Do'Urden tuned it out, focusing instead on a singular image.

A tower crumbling, burning, falling, and a dwarf rushing around on its tilting top, crying orders to the last.

The Hunter reached for Guenhwyvar.

They knew they had to hold. For the sake of their kin atop the cliffs, the dwarves had to fend the charging hordes. Where would Banak Brawnanvil run if they were forced back into Mithral Hall?

The defenders of western Keeper's Dale knew that truth keenly and used it to bolster their every moment of doubt. There was no choice; they had to hold.

But they could not, and their more immediate choice, up and down the length of their line, quickly became a simple decision to fall back or die where they stood. Many chose the latter, or the latter found them, while others did indeed fall back to the next defensible position. But the orc horde pursued, rolling along, smashing through every wall and swarming around every obstacle.

Like driftwood on an incoming tide, the dwarves fell back.

They sent runners to the base of the northern cliffs, shouting up for Banak to retreat in full, and indeed, their hopes were bolstered in seeing the first dwarves coming down the rope ladders. Immediately, those at the base began setting up a plan for defending the area, waving in the dwarves coming down the ropes to quickly join in.

Other dwarves sprinted farther to the east, shouting out to those guards near to Mithral Hall's doors, warning of the impending disaster.

Soon enough, all the remaining Keeper's Dale defenders were in sight of those great western doors, and every valiant effort to turn and make a stand was overrun, pushing them ever farther to the west.

They were almost level with the drop ropes from above when they made yet another determined stand, knowing that if they were pushed any farther, Banak's retreat would find a swift end.

"The hall's opening!" one dwarf cried, looking back and pointing to the wall.

Every dwarf in the line found a moment to glance back that way, to see indeed the great doors of Mithral Hall opening to their call for help. Out came reinforcements, scores of their kin, many still wearing their black-smith aprons or still dressed in common clothing instead of battle mail. Out came every remaining dwarf, it seemed, even many of the wounded who should have stayed in bed.

They all came to the call of distress; they all charged forth from the safety of their tunnels to aid in the battle.

Certainly there were not nearly enough reinforcements to win the day, nor even enough, it seemed, to begin to slow the orc rout.

But there was among the ranks of newcomers one dwarf in particular who could not be ignored, and whose presence could not be measured in the form of just another singular warrior.

For a dwarf larger than life centered that reinforcing line.

For Bruenor Battlehammer centered that reinforcing line.

Banak gnashed his teeth as he surveyed the scene below, hardly believing how fast the defenders of Keeper's Dale were being overrun and pushed back, hardly believing the sheer scope and ferocity of the newly arrived orc army.

The old dwarf broke his ranks and sent his charges over the ledge, scrambling like ants down the many rope ladders. It was a decision made on the fly, committed to in the blink of an eye, and when it was done, the order given, Banak could not help but second-guess himself.

For he could see the dark tide flowing west to east across Keeper's Dale. Would any of his fleeing dwarves even reach the floor of the dale before the darkness had crossed by? If they did, would they be able to mount a defense as more and more got down beside them?

The alternative, Banak Brawnanvil knew, would be abject dis-aster, perhaps a complete slaughter of all those brave souls entrusted to his care.

He continued to shout support at the retreating dwarves. He yelled down to Pwent and his boys to fight their way back up to the cliff, and he personally moved to the escape route of last resort: the drop chute Torgar's engineers had manufactured.

Wulfgar and Catti-brie met him there, just ahead of Torgar, Tred, and Shingles.

"The two of ye be on yer way," Banak instructed the two humans, one of whom was far too large to attempt the narrow chute. "Get to the ropes and get yerselfs down."

"We'll go when Pwent returns," Catti-brie said.

To accentuate her point, she lifted Taulmaril and sent a sizzling arrow sailing away at the orc throng. It disappeared into the morass, but none watching had any doubt that it had to have found a deadly mark on one creature or another.

Wulfgar, meanwhile, pulled two long drop ropes in closer to their position, setting them and looping them over and over to make them impossible to untie and more difficult to cut.

"Ye don't be stupid," Banak argued. "Ye're the children o' King Bruenor, and as such, ye're sure to be needed inside the hall."

"As we're needed up here right now," said Wulfgar.

"We'll go when Pwent returns," Catti-brie reiterated. She let fly again. "And not a moment before."

Banak started to argue but cut himself short, unable to counter the simple logic of it. He, too, would be an important voice in Mithral Hall after that day, of course, and yet he too, had no intention of going anywhere until the Gutbusters began their drop down the escape chute.

He stepped out in front of Catti-brie, Torgar and Shingles on his left, Tred and Ivan Bouldershoulder, who joined in after seeing a reluctant Pikel off along the ropes, on his right.

"Use me head to sight yer bow," Banak said to Catti-brie.

She did just that and cut down the closest of a group of orcs charging their way.

Her movements of grace and fluidity contrasted sharply with Urlgen's sudden, herky-jerky lunges and punches.

Innovindil glided around him, launching a series of thrusts and sweeping sword attacks, most designed merely to set the large orc up for a sudden and devastating finish.

Urlgen turned with her, his heavily armored arms swiping across and picking off each attack, his feet turning and keeping him always on balance as the elf swirled around him, circling continually to his right.

Then she was gone, reversing her movement back to the left, turning a complete circuit to gain momentum, and redirecting that newfound momentum into a single thrust for the orc's heart.

But Urlgen, son of Obould, saw the move coming and had it countered before it ever began. As soon as he lost sight of the elf, the orc turned his hips appropriately and brought his arms swinging down and across his body. That thrust, which would have skewered almost any orc, got nowhere close to hitting.

Innovindil didn't let her surprise show on her face, nor did she relinquish the attack and fall back to regroup. She didn't have the time for that, she knew, for Drizzt Do'Urden was working furiously around her, leaping and spinning, his deadly scimitars slashing down any nearby orcs who dared approach. Across from him, equally effective as she protected Innovindil's other flank, the mighty black panther reared and sprang. She came up before one orc who was scrambling desperately to get away and swiped off its face with one powerful claw, then charged back the other way, bowling over yet another orc.

Those two brave friends were giving her the battle, Innovindil knew, but time was not on their side.

She pressed the attack more furiously, stabbing left, right, and center in rapid succession. Sparks flew as her sword struck hard against one metal bracer, and a second, and again as both bracers crossed over her blade, driving it down and just to the side of Urlgen's left hip.

And the orc countered, not by raising his arms to the offense, but by living up to the reputation of his name, Threefist. He leaned over the blocked sword and snapped his forehead down. Though Innovindil was agile enough to shift her head away from a direct hit, even a glancing blow from the orc's metal head plate had her stumbling backward, dazed.

Instinct alone had her sword flailing before her, fending the heavy punches of the orc's spiked gauntlets. Only gradually did Innovindil collect her wits enough to get her feet firmly under her and solidify both her stance and her defenses. She fought the orc back to even footing.

"Lesson learned," she muttered under her breath, and she vowed that she'd watch for that devastating head-butt more closely.

Upon a stone did Bruenor make his stand.

His legs widespread and planted, his many-notched axe held high, the King of Mithral Hall called for his kin, called for all the Delzoun dwarves, to hold firm. And there did the dwarves of Clan Battlehammer rally. Whether by luck or by the guarding hands of his ancestors and his god, no spear found Bruenor that day.

With the swirling orc sea around him, he stood, a beacon of hope for the dwarves, a testament to sheer determination. Spears thrust and flew his way, orc hands grabbed at his sturdy legs, but none could uproot King Bruenor. A flying club smashed him in the face, opening a long wound, closing one eye.

Bruenor roared through it.

An orc saw the opportunity to get up beside the dwarf, slamming hard with a warhammer.

Bruenor took the hit and didn't flinch, then chopped the orc away with a deadly slash of his axe.

Another orc was up beside him and another and another, and for a moment, it seemed as if the dwarf king would be buried where he stood.

But they went flying away, one after another, thrown by the strength and determination of Bruenor Battlehammer, who would not fall, who would not fail. Blood ran freely from many wounds, some obviously serious. But Bruenor's roar was not in pain nor in fear. It was a denial, stubborn and strong, determined beyond mortal bounds.

Never did Delzoun hearts so swell with pride as on that day, as on that stone, when King Battlehammer cried!

There was no choice before them. To retreat past Bruenor meant to abandon those hundreds of dwarves even then crawling down the cliff face. Better to die, by all measures of dwarven logic, than to forsake kin.

Bruenor reminded them of that. His presence alone, somehow risen from his deathbed, reminded them all of who they were, of what they were, and of what, above all else, mattered: kin and kind.

And so the retreating dwarves did pivot as one, did dig in their heels and press back against the onslaught, matching spear with hammer and axe, matching orc bloodlust with dwarf determination.

And there, around the stone upon which stood the King of Mithral Hall, the orc wave broke and was halted.

Shoulder to shoulder and with Banak Brawnanvil in their middle, the five dwarves met the tip of the orc ranks with sheer fury, leaping in as one and pounding away with hammer and axe. Behind them, Catti-brie worked Taulmaril to devastating effect, coordinating her shots with Wulfgar as he ran back and forth along the short defensive line, preventing any orcs from getting behind the fighting fivesome.

"Pwent, ye hurry! All the boys're down!" Banak shouted to the very depleted group of Gutbusters who were finally making some headway in their desperate attempt to reach him and the drop chute.

Banak couldn't even see if Pwent was alive among that group.

"Girl, ye bring yer fire to bear!" Ivan Bouldershoulder shouted back to Catti-brie.

"Go," Wulfgar bade her, assuring her that he had the situation in hand.

Indeed it seemed as if he did, for no orcs wanted anything to do with the terrible barbarian warrior.

Catti-brie sprinted ahead, coming to a stop right behind Ivan. She took quick note of the situation ahead, of the group of orcs who had turned around in an attempt to seal off the retreat of the bloodied Gutbusters.

Up came Taulmaril, the Heartseeker, and sizzling lines of silver raced out from the line of five dwarves. Catti-brie worked left and right, not daring to shoot straight down the center for fear that her enchanted arrows would blow right through some orcs and into the retreating dwarves. She found her rhythm, swinging left and right, left and right, each shot slicing down to devastating effect. Those orcs in between the continuing lines of deadly arrows found no reinforcements to bolster their barricade against the fury of the Gutbusters, and seeing that reality, the Gutbusters themselves reacted, tightening their ranks and spearheading their way up the slope.

"Now get ye over that cliff!" Banak demanded of Catti-brie and Wulfgar when the line closed. "We got us a faster way down!"

Reluctantly, but unable to argue the logic, Catti-brie ran up to Wulfgar and the pair charged back to the cliff face. They shouldered their weapons, took up their respective ropes, and went over side by side, sliding down the face of the cliff.

They heard the Gutbusters leaping into the drop chute above them and took satisfaction in that. They heard Banak calling frantically for his fellows to go.

And they heard orcs, so many orcs.

Wulfgar's rope jolted suddenly, and again, and Catti-brie reached out for him, and he for her.

His rope fell away, cut from above.

Obould did not see his forces stall around the stone upon which stood King Bruenor, for his attention had been drawn to the side by that point, to the defensive stand in the north, where dwarves were fast descending.

The dwarves were making a stubborn stand, to be sure, but Obould's numbers should have swept them away.

But then a fireball exploded in the midst of his line. And, inexplicably, another charging group ran off to the side and began fighting against . . . against nothing, the orc king realized, or against each other, or against the stones.

A quick scan showed Obould the truth of it, that two others, a human woman and a gnome, had joined in the defensive stand, waggling their fingers and launching their magic. More dwarves came down from above, leaping to the dale floor, pulling free their weapons, and throwing themselves in to bolster the defensive line.

His orcs were going to break ranks!

A bolt of blue lightning flashed through the throng and a dozen orcs fell dead and a score more flopped on the ground, stunned and shocked.

The real beauty of his plan, to not simply push the dwarves into their holes but to slaughter the whole of the force up above, began to unravel before Obould's angry eyes. With a roar, he denied that unacceptable turn. With a growl and a fist clenched so tightly that it would have crushed solid stone, the great orc king began his own charge to that northern wall, determined to turn the tide yet again.

The dwarves were not going to escape his trap. Not again.

Banak went into the hole head first and last, after having forcibly thrown the exhausted and bloody Thibbledorf Pwent in before him. He expected to fall into the steep slide, but he had barely gotten into the hole when he got hung up.

Only then did the old dwarf realize that he had a spear sticking out of his back, and that it was stuck on the stone.

Orcs crowded around the hole above him, whacking at his feet, prodding down with their nasty spears.

Banak kicked furiously, but he knew he was dead, knew that there was no way he could extricate himself.

But then a hand grabbed him by the collar and the smelly Pwent clawed back up before him.

"Come on, ye dolt!" Pwent yelled.

"Spear," Banak tried to explain, but Pwent wasn't even listening, was just tugging.

A searing eruption of fire burned suddenly in poor Banak's back as the spear twisted around, and he gave a howl of agony.

And Pwent tugged all the harder, understanding that there was no choice, no option at all.

The spear shaft snapped and Banak and Pwent fell free, sliding down the steep, turning chute Torgar's engineers had fashioned. They came into a straight descent then and fell through an opening, dropping several feet onto a pile of hay that had been strategically placed in the exit chamber. Of course by that point, most of the hay had been scattered by those coming down earlier, and the two dwarves hit hard and lay there groaning.

Rough hands grabbed them, ignoring their cries of pain. For they had no time to concern themselves over wounds.

"Close the chute!" Pwent cried, but too late, for down dropped a pursuer, a small goblin who had likely been thrown down as leading fodder by the bullying orcs. The creature landed right atop the still prone Banak, who gave another agonized groan.

Pwent rolled back and drove his spiked gauntlet through the stunned goblin's face, and shouted again for the others to close the chute.

Torgar Hammerstriker was already moving. He shoved a lever, releasing a block, then reached up and guided the block plate into position beneath the chute. The top side of the block plate was set with long spikes, and they claimed their first victim almost as soon as the chute was closed, an orc or goblin dropping hard atop it and impaling itself.

The dwarves were too busy to relish in that kill, though, grabbing their two fallen comrades up, ushering Pwent along and carrying the seriously wounded Banak. The escape chamber opened onto a ledge about a quarter of the way down the cliff, where more rope ladders were in place. Many of the Gutbusters were already well on their way down the ladders, rushing to join the critical battle at the base of the cliff.

As soon as he saw that spectacle below, Thibbledorf Pwent shook away his dizziness—or embraced it, for it was often hard to distinguish which with Pwent!—and scrambled over the ledge and down the ropes.

"I got him first," Ivan Bouldershoulder insisted.

He carefully lifted Banak up over his shoulder and moved to the rope ladder. Tred went over the cliff side before him, offering assistance from below.

Torgar and Shingles drew out their weapons and stood guard at the entrance to the escape room, ready to protect their departing friends should the chute's block plate fail and the orcs come down at them. Not until Ivan and the others were far below, moving to the second series of lower rope ladders did the pair from Mirabar turn and flee.

He grabbed for her, instinctively, as she reached out for him. They caught each other by the wrists and held fast as the barbarian fell away, then rolled around, rebounding off the stone of the cliff face. The jolt of his weight almost dislodged the woman from her rope, but she stubbornly held on, grasping with all of her strength and determination.

Wulfgar's rope fell past, slapping over the big man, and again, he nearly broke free of Catti-brie's grasp.

But she wouldn't let him go. Her arms stretched, her muscles ached, her shoulders felt as if they would simply pop out of joint.

But she wouldn't let go.

Wulfgar looked up at her, his eyes wide with fear—as much for her, she knew, as for himself, for it seemed that he would indeed dislodge her and drop them both to their deaths.

But she wouldn't let go. For all her life, at the cost of her life, Catti-brie was not going to let her friend fall.

It seemed like minutes, though in truth, it had all occurred in the span of a split second. Finally, Wulfgar caught Catti-brie's rope with his free hand and pulled himself in tight.

"Go!" Catti-brie prompted as soon as she got her wits back about her, as soon as she understood that if his rope had been cut, hers would likely go next.

Wulfgar went down hand-over-hand, verily running down the thick line. He reached a ledge and scrambled onto it, then set himself as solidly as the footing would allow.

Catti-brie came down fast behind, but not fast enough, as her rope, too, came free and she dropped. Wulfgar caught her and pulled her in, and the both of them pressed themselves flat against the cliff.

"Not yet halfway," Wulfgar said a moment later.

He motioned across to the other side of the small ledge, where the next descending ladders were set.

Drizzt double-stabbed, then stepped forward, driving on and forcing the orc to go tumbling backward, thus hindering any approach by those others near it.

The drow turned away immediately, rolling around, scimitars flying widely but not wildly, every strike in complete control, every cut working to fend any interference from the onlookers to the spectacle of Innovindil's battle with their leader.

The drow turned again, taking in the scene across the way, where Guenhwyvar leaped onto an orc and suddenly sprang away to bury another.

Drizzt eyes scanned over to the main fight as he turned to meet the charge of two more, and in that instant scan, he noted that Urlgen was pressing his elf friend hard, that she had stumbled backward. He had to go to her, but he could not as an orc pair pressed in.

"Fall into your anger!" he cried to Innovindil. "Remember Tarathiel! Remember your loss and embrace the pain!"

With every word he cried, the drow had to swipe or parry with his blades, working furiously to keep back the press of increasingly emboldened orcs.

"Find a place of balance," he tried to explain to Innovindil. "A balance between your anger and your determination! Use the pain to focus!"

He was asking her to become the Hunter, he knew. He was asking her to forsake her reason at that moment and fall into a more primal state, a state of feeling, of emotion and fear. As she had worked to coax him from that anger, so he tried to moved her toward it.

Was there any other way?

Drizzt let go of his fears for his friend and let himself fall even more fully into the Hunter. The orcs pressed in, and his scimitars went into a frenzied dance, driving them back, cutting them down.

Despite her suddenly desperate situation, despite the press of that ferocious orc and the tumult of the crowding monsters all around her, Innovindil did hear the words of Drizzt Do'Urden.

Her sword worked furiously, fending blow after blow as the wild orc came at her, his spiked gauntlets swinging wildly. Her feet worked with equal desperation, trying to keep under her as she was forced to dodge and to back away. She tried to find her rhythm, but the orc's fighting style was unconventional at best, with attacks quickly re-angled to punch through any opening she presented. Innovindil had no doubt that she could gradually come to a point of understanding and logical counter, but she knew that she had no such luxury of time.

Thus, she followed the words of Drizzt Do'Urden, who was battling so brilliantly to keep the others away. She allowed her mind to wander the road of memory, to Tarathiel's horrible fall. She felt her anger rising and channeled it into determination.

Out left went her sword, cutting short a hooking right hand, and back fast to center to block a left jab.

Innovindil put her conscious thoughts aside, fell into the flow and the feeling of the fight. Sparks flew as she connected with a fist, and again as the orc blocked her own thrust with a second metal gauntlet.

She worked with sudden intensity, taking the fight back to him, and at last discerned a pattern to his counters and his blocks.

He was setting her up for a head-butt, she realized, looking for that killing opening.

Innovindil rolled with the punches and the continuing flow, fell deeper into her instinctual self, catching herself somewhere between rage and complete concentration.

She ducked one blow and seemed to fall almost completely off her balance, lunging to the side so violently that her free hand slapped against her doeskin boot. In came the orc's counter punch—one that could have truly hurt her. But it was not aimed for her, and she understood that. Rather, Urlgen was going for her sword, striking it hard and knocking it aside.

Presenting him with that opening.

He darted ahead, his strong back snapping his head forward.

Innovindil threw her free hand up across her forehead to block and felt the sudden impact driving down through her hand and smashing against her skull. Back she skittered, trying to hold her balance, but stumbling down to a sitting and vulnerable position.

But Urlgen wasn't pursuing, for he had driven his head down not only onto the elf's blocking hand, but onto the small knife she had cleverly pulled out from her boot, impaling himself up to its crosspiece. The orc staggered back, the hilt of the knife protruding from his forehead like some strange unicorn horn. His black gauntlets waved in the air, and he turned around and around, head thrown back, pommel high in the air.

In that moment of distraction, when all the orcs nearby stared incredulously at their leader, Drizzt Do'Urden rushed to Innovindil and roughly pulled her to her feet, then pushed her ahead, to the north, and took up the run. The drow cut back and forth in front of the stumbling, still-dazed Innovindil, his scimitars clearing the way. When they came upon a particularly dense group of enemies, Guenhwyvar leaped by the pair, launching herself full force into the crowd, scattering them and taking them down.

Drizzt sprinted by, pulling Innovindil behind him. He took out a slender rope and thrust its other end into her hand, and that tactile feel brought her somewhat back to her sensibilities, reminding her of her duties. She urged Drizzt to press on, then brought a free hand to her lips and blew a shrill whistle.

Down they ran, angling to a flat area to the side, and, coming in low under the rising sun, they saw their one hope: a winged horse fast descending.

Sunset touched down and charged across the stone, scattering orcs before his run. Drizzt and Innovindil moved to intercept, one on either side, a rope strung before them. Sunset accepted the hit as he ran into the rope, and both drow and elf used the sudden pull to move them aside the pegasi's flanks, ducking under the high-held wings. Innovindil went up first, Drizzt leaping right behind her, as Sunset never slowed in his run. His wide wings beat the air, and he sprang away, half-running, half-flying, moving out of range of any pursuit.

"Go home, Guenhwyvar!" Drizzt cried out to the panther, who was still scattering orcs, still battling fiercely.

Up into the air they went, climbing fast to the north. Spears reached up at them, but few got close to hitting the mark, and those who did were knocked away by the scimitars of the drow. Finally, they were safely out of range, and Drizzt looked back to the diminishing battle.

The orcs were right up to the cliff, by then, and the drow understood that the dwarves had been pushed over into Keeper's Dale.

Had he gotten up into the sky only a minute before, he might have noted the telltale silver flash of Taulmaril.

Shoudra Stargleam's eyes glowed with determination as she watched her fireball engulf a handful of orcs, sending them scurrying about, all aflame.

The sorceress launched a second strike to devastating effect, a burning bolt of lightning that dropped a line of orcs at the center of their press.

More than one dwarf glanced back her way to nod in appreciation, which only spurred the proud and noble sceptrana on even more. She was a Battlehammer then, by all measure, fighting as fiercely as if Mithral Hall was her home and the dwarves all around her, her kin.

Beside her, little Nanfoodle worked his wonders, confusing an entire company of orcs with an illusion that had them charging face first into the cliff wall.

"Well done," Shoudra congratulated him.

She followed his mind attack with a physical blast of lightning that scattered the confused group and laid many low. Shoudra threw a wink Nanfoodle's way, then glanced up nervously at the cliffs, where dwarves continued their descent. Behind her, she heard those first who had come down forming up the defensive plan that would take them all to Mithral Hall's grand doors.

But they had to hold out until all were down.

The sceptrana turned away and sucked in her breath as one dwarf up ahead of her fell back, a spear deep in his chest. With no reserves immediately available to fill the gap, the sceptrana stepped forward, extending one arm and calling forth a burst of magical missiles that drove the orcs back. So many more came on, though.

Shoudra breathed a sigh of relief as a pair of dwarves scrambled past her, one going to his wounded kin, the other taking the downed dwarf's position at the low stone wall.

The orcs came on.

Looking all around to find the most effective area for her blasts, Shoudra's attention was caught and held by the spectacle of a single orc, a huge, armored creature swinging a sword nearly as tall as she at the end of one strong arm. He waded through his own ranks, orcs scrambling to get out of his way, stalking determinedly for the wall.

A crossbow bolt whistled out and smacked hard against his metal breastplate, but it did not penetrate and did not slow him in the least. In fact, he even sped up his rush, leaping forward into a roaring run.

Shoudra brought forth her magical power and struck him head-on with a lightning bolt, one that lifted him from his feet and threw him back into the throng. Figuring him dead, the sceptrana turned her attention back to the throng pressing the dwarves, and she ignited another fireball just forward of the dwarven line, so close that even the dwarves felt the rush of heat.

Again, flaming orcs scrambled and fell burning to the ground, but through that opening came a familiar figure, that great orc carrying a huge greatsword.

Shoudra's eyes widened when she saw him, for no orc could so readily accept the hit of one of her lightning blasts!

But it was the same orc, she knew, and he came on with fury, plowing over any orcs who could not scramble out of his way, reaching the wall and dwarven line in a rush, his sword slashing across, scattering the dwarves. He dropped his shoulder and plowed on, driving right through the hastily built rock wall, knocking heavy stones aside with ease.

Dwarves went at him, and dwarves went flying away, slashed by the sword, swatted with his free arm, even kicked high into the air.

And all the while, Shoudra suddenly realized, he was looking directly at her.

On came the mighty orc, and Nanfoodle gave a shriek. Shoudra heard the gnome quickly casting, but she knew instinctively that he would not divert that beast. She brought her hands up before her, thumbs touching tip to tip.

"Be gone, little demon," she said, and a wide arc of orange flames erupted from her fingers.

The sceptrana turned, using the distraction to get out of the way, but then she got punched—or thought it was a punch. She tried to move, but her feet skidded on the stone, and she was strangely held in place. She looked back, and she understood, for it was no punch that had hit her, but the thrust of a greatsword. Shoudra looked down to see less than half of that blade remaining before her chest; she knew that it had gone right through her.

Still with only the one mighty hand holding the sword, the orc lifted Shoudra Stargleam up into the air.

She heard Nanfoodle shriek, but it was somehow very far away.

She heard the dwarves cry out and saw them scrambling, in fear, it seemed.

She saw a sudden flash of silver and felt the jerk as the great orc staggered backward.

Her legs looped within the coils of the drop rope, Catti-brie hung upside down, reloading her bow, letting fly another shot at the monstrous beast who held Shoudra aloft. Her first arrow had struck home, right in the thing's chest, and had knocked the orc backward a single step.

But it had not penetrated.

"Get him away!" Catti-brie yelled to Wulfgar.

The barbarian had leaped to the ground and was even then bearing down on the orc. He cried out to Tempus and brought his hammer to bear—brought his whole body to bear—throwing himself at the orc, trying to knock it aside.

Suddenly Wulfgar was flying backward, blocked, stopped and thrown back by a swipe of the great orc's arm. The great barbarian, who had taken hits offered by giants, staggered back and stumbled to the ground.

The orc lifted his arm higher, presented the squirming Shoudra up into the air, and roared. The sword came to fiery life, and Shoudra howled all the louder. The mighty orc jerked his arm side to side.

Shoudra Stargleam fell apart.

Catti-brie hit the beast with another arrow, and a third, but by that last shot, he wasn't even staggering backward from the blows anymore. He turned and started toward Wulfgar.

The spinning Aegis-fang hit him hard. The orc stumbled back a few steps, and almost fell to the ground.

Almost.

On came the beast, charging Wulfgar with abandon.

The barbarian recalled Aegis-fang to his hand and met that charge with another cry to his god, and a great swipe of his mighty hammer. Sword against hammer they battled, two titans standing tall above the onlookers.

Down came Aegis-fang, smashing hard against the orc's shoulder, sending him skidding to the side. Across came the flaming greatsword, and Wulfgar had to throw his hips back, barely getting out of reach.

The orc followed that wide slash by leaping forward even as Wulfgar came forward behind the blade, and the two collided hard, muscle against muscle.

A heavy punch sent Wulfgar flying away, had him staggering on the stones, barely able to keep his feet.

The orc pursued, sword in both hands, leaping in for the killing blow that the barbarian couldn't begin to block.

An arrow hit the orc in the face, spraying sparks across the glassteel, but he came on anyway and cleaved at the barbarian.

At least, the orc thought it was the barbarian, for where force and fire had failed, Nanfoodle had succeeded, misdirecting the blow with an illusionary Wulfgar, to the swift demise of a second orc who happened to be standing too close to King Obould's rage.

Catti-brie leaped down to the stone, caught up Wulfgar under one arm, and shoved him away.

The orc moved to catch them—or tried to, for suddenly the stone around his feet turned to mud, right up to his ankles, then turned back to stone.

"Bad orc!" cried a green-bearded dwarf, and he poked the fingers of his one hand in Obould's direction.

The furious orc king roared and squirmed, then reached down and punched the stone. Then, with strength beyond belief, he tore one foot free.

"Oooo," said the green-bearded dwarf.

Down came more help then, in the form of the Gutbusters, falling all around the pair, leaping into battle. Any who got near to the great orc, though, fell fast and fell hard.

Down came Torgar and Tred, Shingles and Ivan, and the wounded Banak, sweeping up Catti-brie and Wulfgar, the stunned and crying Nanfoodle, and all the others in their wake as they ran flat out across Keeper's Dale, angling for the doors of Mithral Hall.

Only then did Catti-brie notice the pillar of strength that stood supporting the routed dwarves in the wider battle, the indomitable power of her own father, legs planted firmly upon a tall stone, axe sweeping orcs away, dwarves rallying all around him.

"Bruenor," she mouthed, unable to even comprehend how it could be, how her father could have arisen once more.

Out toward the center of the dale, Bruenor marked well the run of Banak's retreat and of his own son and daughter—and glad he was to see them alive.

His forces had held strong, somehow, against the overwhelming odds, had stemmed the undeniable tide.

At great cost, the dwarf king knew, and he knew, too, that that orc sea would not be denied—especially since the giants were fast approaching, bolstering the orc lines.

From up on his rock, the dwarf king called for a retreat, told his boys to turn and run for the doors. But Bruenor didn't move, not an inch, until the others had all broken ranks.

His axe led the way as he chased after them. He felt the spears and swords reaching out for him, but there were no openings within the fury that was Bruenor Battlehammer. He spun and he dodged. He fled for the doors and stopped suddenly, reversing his course and chopping down the closest orc, and sending those others nearby into a terrified retreat.

He ushered all behind him as the doors drew near, refusing to break and flee until all were within. He fought with the strength of ten dwarves and the heart of a thousand, his many notched axe earning more marks that day than in many years previous. He piled orc bodies around him and painted all the ground a bloody red.

And it was time to go, he knew, and those holding the door called out to him. A swipe of his axe drove back the orc wall before him, and Bruenor turned and sprinted.

Or started to, for there behind him stood an orc, spear coming forward at an angle that Bruenor could not hope to fend. Seeing his doom, the dwarf king gave a howl of denial.

The orc lurched over backward and a spike drove out through its chest. A helmet spike, Bruenor realized as Thibbledorf Pwent stood straight behind his attacker, lifting the orc up in the air atop his head.

Before Bruenor could utter a word, Pwent grabbed him by the beard and yanked him into a stumbling charge that brought him into the hall.

And so Thibbledorf Pwent was the last to enter the dwarven stronghold that fateful day, the great doors booming closed behind him, the dead orc still flopping about atop his helmet, impaled by the long spike.

31

THROUGH THE BODIES

It hadn't been the victory he had hoped to achieve, for most of Clan Battlehammer's dwarves, even those from atop the cliff, had gotten back into the safety of Mithral Hall. Worse still for King Obould, there could be little doubt of the identity of the dwarf leader who had emerged to bolster the retreat. It had been King Bruenor, thought dead and buried in the rubble of Shallows.

The Battlehammer dwarves had chanted his name when he'd charged from the hall, and the sudden increased ferocity and stubbornness of their defense upon the red-bearded dwarf's arrival left little real doubt for Obould about the authenticity of their leader.

The orc king made a mental note to speak with his son about that curious turn of events.

Despite the unexpected arrival, despite the dwarves' success in retreating from the cliffs, Obould took satisfaction in knowing that the dwarves could not claim a victory there. They had been pushed into their hall, with little chance of getting out anytime soon—even then, Gerti's giants were hard at work sealing the hall's western doors. The orc losses in Keeper's Dale had been considerable, but there was no shortage of dwarf dead lying among that carnage.

"It was Bruenor!" came the predictable cry of Gerti Orelsdottr, and the giantess stormed up to the orc king. "Bruenor himself! The King of Mithral Hall! You claimed he was dead!"

"As I was told by my son, and your own giants," Obould calmly and quietly reminded her.

"The death of Bruenor was the rallying cry, dog!"

"Lower your voice," Obould told the giantess. "We have won here. This is not the moment to voice our fears."

Gerti narrowed her eyes and issued a low growl.

"You did not lose a single giant," Obould reminded her, and that seemed to take the wind out of Gerti's bluster. "The Battlehammer dwarves are in their hole, their numbers depleted, and you did not lose a single giant."

Still staring hard at the orc king and still snarling, she walked off.

Obould's gaze went up the cliff face, and he thought of the tremendous explosion that had heralded the beginning of the battle and the shower of debris that had followed. He hoped that his claim to Gerti was correct. He hoped that the fight atop the cliff had been a success.

If not, Obould decided, he would murder his son.

Her face wet with sweat and tears, blood and mud, Catti-brie fell to her knees before her father and wrapped him in a tight hug.

Bruenor, his face scarred and bloody, with part of his beard ripped away and one eye swollen and closed, lifted one arm (for the other hung limply at his side) and returned the hug.

"How's it possible?" Banak Brawnanvil asked.

He stood with many others in the entry hall, staring incredulously at their king, returned from death itself, it seemed.

" 'Twas Steward Regis who found the answer," said Stumpet Rakingclaw.

"Was him who showed us the way," agreed Cordio Muffinhead.

He walked over and slapped Regis so hard on the shoulder that the halfling stumbled and nearly dropped from his feet.

All eyes, particularly those of Wulfgar and Catti-brie, fell over Regis, who seemed uncharacteristically embarrassed by all the attention.

"Cordio woke him," he offered sheepishly.

"Bah! Was yer own work with yer ruby," Cordio explained. "Regis called to Bruenor through the gem. 'No real king'd lie there and let his people fight without him,' he said."

"You said the same thing to me some days ago," said Regis.

But Cordio just laughed, slapped him again, and continued, "So he went into that body and found the spark o' Bruenor, the one piece left o' the king keeping his body breathing. And Regis told him what was going on. And when me and Stumpet went back to our healing spells, Bruenor's spirit was back to catch 'em. His spirit heard our call as sure as his body was taking the physical healing. Come straight from Moradin's side, I'm guessing!"

Everyone turned to regard Bruenor, who just shrugged and shook his head. Cordio became suddenly solemn, and he moved up before the dwarf king.

"And so ye returned to us when we were in need," the cleric said quietly. "We pulled ye back for our own needs, and true to yer line, ye answered them. No dwarf can deny yer sacrifice, me king, and no dwarf could ever ask more o' ye. We're in now, and the halls're closed to our enemies. Ye've done yer duty to kin and clan."

All around began to murmur and to look on more closely. They quieted almost immediately, many holding their breath, as Cordio's intent became clearer.

"Ye've come to us, returned from Moradin's own halls," the cleric said to Bruenor, and he brought his hands up before the dwarf king to offer a blessing. "We can'no compel ye to stay. Ye've done yer duty, and so ye've earned yer rest."

Eyes went wide all around. Wulfgar had to grab Catti-brie, who seemed as if she would just fall over. In truth, the barbarian needed the support every bit as much as she.

For it seemed like Cordio's words were affecting Bruenor greatly. His eyes were half-closed, and he leaned forward, shoulders slumped.

"Ye need feel no more pain, me king," Cordio went on, his voice breaking.

He reached up to support Bruenor's shoulder, for indeed it seemed as if the dwarf would tumble face down.

"Moradin's welcomed ye. Ye can go home."

The gasp came from Regis, the sobs from everywhere around.

Bruenor closed his eyes.

Then Bruenor opened his eyes, and wide! And he stood straight and fixed the priest with the most incredulous look any dwarf ever offered.

"Ye dolt!" he bellowed. "I got me home surrounded by stinkin' orcs and giants, and ye're telling me to lie down and die?"

"B-but . . . but . . ." Cordio stammered.

"Bah!" Bruenor snorted. "No more o' the stupid talk. We got work to do!"

For a moment, no one moved or said anything, or even breathed. Then such a cheer went up in Mithral Hall as had not been known since the defeat of the drow those years before. They had been chased in, yes, and could hardly claim victory, but Bruenor was with them again, and he was fighting mad.

"All cheers for Bruenor!" one dwarf cried, and the throng erupted. "Hero of the day!"

"Who fought no more than the rest of ye," Bruenor shouted them down. "Was one of us alone who found the way to call me home."

And his gaze led those of all the others to a particular halfling.

"Then Steward Regis is the hero of the day!" one dwarf cried from the back of the hall.

"One of many," Wulfgar was quick to reply. "Nanfoodle the gnome facilitated our retreat from above."

"And Pikel!" Ivan Bouldershoulder put in.

"And Pwent and his boys," said Banak. "And without Pwent, King Bruenor'd be dead on our doorstep!"

The cheers went up with each proclamation.

Bruenor heard them keenly and let them continue, but he did not join in any longer. He still wasn't quite sure of what had happened to him. He recalled a feeling of bliss, a sense of complete peace, a place he never wanted to leave. But then he had heard a cry of help from afar, from a familiar halfling, and he walked a dark path, back to the realm of the living.

Just in time to jump into the fight with both feet. It would take some time to sort through the fog of the battle and measure their success or failure, Bruenor knew, but one thing was certain at that moment: Clan Battlehammer had been pushed back into Mithral Hall. Whatever the count of the dead, orc and dwarf, it had not been a victory.

Bruenor knew that he and his kin had a lot of work to do.

In the corridor running off the main entry chamber, Nanfoodle sat against the wall and wept.

Wulfgar found him there, among the many wounded and the many dwarves attending to them.

"You did well today," the barbarian said, crouching down beside the gnome.

Nanfoodle looked up at him, his face streaked with tears, and with more still rolling down his cheeks.

"Shoudra," he whispered and he shook his head.

Wulfgar had no answer to that simple remark and the horrific images it conjured, and so he patted the gnome on the head and rose. He brought a hand up tenderly to his ribs, wondering how bad he had been hurt by that tremendous blow the mighty orc had delivered.

But then all thoughts of pain washed away from the barbarian as he spotted a familiar figure rushing down the corridor toward him.

Delly ran up and wrapped her husband in a tight hug, and as soon as they were joined, all strength seemed to leave the woman, and she just melted into Wulfgar's strong chest, her shoulders bobbing with sobs.

Wulfgar held her tight.

From the entrance to the corridor, Catti-brie witnessed the scene and smiled and nodded.

In Keeper's Dale, Obould had lost orcs at somewhere around a four-to-one pace to the dying dwarves, an acceptable ratio indeed against a dug-in and battle-hardened defender. No one could question the cost of that victory, given the gains they had achieved.

Up there, though, without even getting any real body counts, Obould understood that the dwarves had slaughtered Urlgen's orcs at a far higher ratio, perhaps as sorely as twenty-to-one.

The ridge was gone, and all but one of the giants who had been up there were dead, and that one, who had been thrown several hundred feet by the monstrous explosion, would likely soon join his deceased companions.

Obould wanted nothing more than to call his son out for that disaster and to slaughter the fool openly before the entire army, to lay all the blame at Urlgen's deserving feet.

"Go and find my son!" he commanded all of those around him, and his crooked teeth seemed locked together as he spat the words. "Bring Urlgen to me!"

He stormed around, looking for any sign of his son, kicking dead bodies with nearly every stride. Only a few moments later, an orc ran up and nervously bowed over and over again, and explained to the great orc that his son had been found among the dead. Obould grabbed the messenger by the throat and with just that one strong hand, lifted him into the air.

"How do you know this?" he demanded, and he jerked the orc back and forth.

The poor creature tried to answer, brought both of its hands up and tried to break the choking grip. But Obould only squeezed all the harder, and the orc's neck snapped with a sharp retort.

Obould snarled and tossed the dead messenger aside.

His son was dead. His son had failed. The orc king glanced around to measure the reaction of those cowering orcs nearby.

A few images of Urlgen flashed through Obould's thoughts, and a slight wave of regret found its way through the crust of the vicious orc's heart, but all of that quickly passed. All of that was fast buried under the weight of necessity, of the immediate needs of the moment.

Urlgen was dead. Given that, Obould knew that he had to focus on the positive aspects of the day, on the fact that the dwarves had been dislodged from the cliff and forced back into Mithral Hall. It was a critical moment for his forces and the course of their conquest, he understood. He had his kingdom overrun, from the Spine of the World to Mithral Hall, from the Surbrin to Fell Pass. Little resistance remained.

He had to maintain his force's enthusiasm, though, for the inevitable counterstrike. How he wished that Arganth was there, proclaiming him to be Gruumsh.

Soon after, though, Obould learned that Arganth was dead, killed by an elf and a drow.

"This is unacceptable!" Gerti growled at the orc king as night encompassed the land and the weary army continued its work of reorganizing.

"Nineteen of yours fell, but thousands of mine," the orc countered.

"Twenty," said Gerti.

"Then twenty," Obould agreed, as if it didn't matter.

Gerti scowled at him and asked, "What weapon did they use? What magic so sundered that mountain arm? How did your son let this happen?"

Obould didn't blink, didn't shrink in the least under the giantess's imposing stare. He turned and walked away.

He heard the telltale noise of a sword sliding free of its sheath and moved completely on instinct, drawing forth his own greatsword as he swung around, bringing his blade across to parry the swipe of Gerti's huge weapon.

With a roar, the giantess came on, trying to overwhelm the orc king with her sheer size and strength. But Obould brought his sword to flaming life and slashed it across at Gerti's knees. She avoided the cut, turning sidelong and lifting her leg away from the fires.

Obould barreled in, dipping his shoulder against her thigh and driving on with supernatural strength.

To Gerti's complete surprise, to the amazement of all in attendance—orc, goblin, and giant alike—the orc king muscled Gerti right off the ground. With a great heave, he sent her flopping through the air to land hard and unceremoniously on the ground, face down.

She started to rise but wisely stopped short, feeling the heat of a fiery greatsword hovering above the back of her neck.

"All that is left here are the dwarven tunnels," Obould told her. "Go and defend the Surbrin or take your dead and retreat to Shining White." Obould bent low and whispered, so that only Gerti could hear, "But if you forsake our road now, know that I will visit you when Mithral Hall is mine."

He backed away then and allowed Gerti to scramble back to her feet, where she stood staring down at him with open hatred.

"Enough of this foolishness, giantess," Obould said loudly, so that those few astonished onlookers could hear. "We are both angered and sorrowful. My own son lies among the dead.

"But we have won a great victory this day!" the orc king proclaimed to the throng. "The cowardly dwarves have run away and will not soon return!"

That brought cheering.

Obould walked around, his arms raised in victory, his flaming sword serving as a focus of their collective glory. Every so often, though, the orc did glance back at Gerti, letting her alone see the continuing hatred and threat in his jaundiced and bloodshot eyes.

For Gerti, there was only uncertainty.

From a distance, another watched the celebration of the victorious orcs and saw that flaming sword lifted high in glory. Satisfied that he had done his duty well and that his work had been of a great benefit to the retreating dwarves, Nikwillig of Citadel Felbarr settled back against the cold stone and considered the distant glow of the setting sun.

His vantage point had allowed him a view of the general course of the battle not only up there, but down in Keeper's Dale, and he knew that the dwarves had been driven underground.

He knew that he had nowhere to run.

He knew that he would soon have nowhere to hide.

But so be it, the dwarf honestly told himself. He had done his duty. He had helped his kin.

EPILØGUE

"He will know that his son is dead by now," Drizzt remarked.

He was brushing Sunset, paying particular care to the many scratches the pegasus had suffered in the flight from the orc army.

"Then perhaps he will come to us," the elf replied, "and save us the trouble of hunting him down."

Drizzt's concern at Innovindil's grim tone washed away when he considered her wide grin. He watched her walking toward him—he couldn't pull his eyes away. She had taken off her battle gear and was dressed in a simple light blue gown of thin, nearly sheer material that rested smoothly against her every curve. Behind her, the last rays of day leaped forth from the horizon, backlighting the elf in a heavenly glow, surrounding her beautiful hair in soft yellow hues.

"You brought forth my anger," Innovindil reminded him.

"I have found a place of . . . concentration," Drizzt tried to explain, shaking himself from the spectacle of the elf. "A state of mind that is clearer. When I left my homeland, I traveled alone through the dark ways of the Underdark. For ten years, I wandered, mostly alone." He gave a grin and produced the onyx figurine. "Except for Guenhwyvar."

"If the Underdark is as I have heard, then you should not have survived."

"Nor would I have, even with Guen, had I not found the Hunter."

"The Hunter?"

"That place of concentration," Drizzt explained. "A place within my heart and mind where rage transforms into focus."

"Most would argue that rage is blinding."

"And so it can be," Drizzt agreed. "If it is not in control."

"And so you become this creature of focus and rage . . ."

"And the cost is heavy, I have come to know," Drizzt added. "The cost is joy and hope. The cost is . . ."

"Love?"

"I do not know," Drizzt admitted. "Perhaps there is room within for all that I must be."

"Room for Drizzt, and for the Hunter?"

The drow merely shrugged.

"We have much to do," Innovindil told him. "With the dwarves' retreat, all the North is imperiled. Who will rouse the forces of the land against Obould if not Drizzt and Innovindil?"

Drizzt nodded in agreement and added in all seriousness, "Should we rouse the world against him before or after we kill him?"

The thought brought a grim smile to Innovindil's fair face, creating a most amazing paradox to the lavender eyes of the drow. Beautiful and terrible all at once, she seemed, the warmest of friends and the deadliest of enemies.

"We gotta get back," Dagna grumbled. "Them trolls're heading for the halls, not to doubt!"

"We cannot!" Galen Firth shouted. "Not now! My people are nearby—somewhere."

He stopped and looked around, as did many of the others, at the muddy landscape, the few scraggly trees and the ground torn by battle and the march of many great trolls, as Galen Firth had warned upon his arrival to Mithral Hall. The band had been near to the southern tunnel exits when they'd realized the truth of the Nesmé rider's words, when a band of ugly and smelly trolls had struck hard at them.

Quick thinking and quicker feet had gotten the dwarves away, the band scrambling down a tunnel that was too low for the large trolls to pursue. That long tunnel, first completely of stone and rising and turning to stone and earth, had taken them to the edge of the Trollmoors and somewhere to the east of Nesmé, by Galen Firth's reckoning.

Grim-faced, Dagna stared hard at the animated Galen and gradually came to understand the man's point of view. As Dagna felt that his duty was to return to Regis and warn Mithral Hall, so Galen Firth fiercely believed that his course was to search there, to find his people and help them to safety. Dagna couldn't ignore that plea. He had been sent there to help the rider from Nesmé do just that.

"I'll give ye three days o' hunting," Dagna conceded. "After that, me and me boys gotta turn back fast for Mithral Hall. Them trolls didn't keep up the chase—they're heading for me home."

"You do not know that."

"I feel it," Dagna countered. "In me old bones, I can feel the threat to me kinfolk. What're Trollmoors trolls doing in tunnels?"

"Perhaps they chased the folk of Nesmé underground."

Dagna nodded and hoped that Galen Firth was right, that the trolls were not marching on Mithral Hall but were merely finishing their business there.

"Three days," he said to the man.

Galen Firth nodded his agreement, and fifty dwarves gathered up their packs and weapons. They had run flat out for hours, and that after a day of hard marching. The sun was sinking fast in the west, the long shadows reaching out to darken all the land.

But it was not the time for rest.

"The elf's out there," Bruenor muttered over and over.

Gathered beside him, Regis, Catti-brie, Wulfgar, and some of the other leaders just sat quietly and let all the information sink in. They had told him of the flight from Shallows, the fall of Dagnabbit, the unexpected rescue from Mirabar's refugees, and all the fighting that had followed.

"Well, we got to set our defenses all about, above at the gates and below in the tunnels," the dwarf king said at length. "No telling where them pigs'll hit at us."

"Or if they will," put in Regis, and all eyes turned to him. "What is their plan? Do they wish to try to complete their victory? They know the cost will be great."

"Or what else, then?" asked Bruenor.

Regis shook his head, closed his eyes, and let it all settle in his thoughts. The orcs that had driven them into the hall were different, he understood. They had acted cleverly at every turn. They had acted more like an army with a purpose than the typically vicious mob one associated with goblinkin.

"Whether it's the giants," said Regis, "or this orc of renown Obould Many-Arrows. . . ."

"Curse his name!" spat Tred McKnuckles.

"Yerself and yer kin o' Felbarr know him, to be sure," Bruenor said to Tred. "Are ye thinking he's to come crashing in?"

Tred gave a snort and shrugged.

"If he's thinking to, then he's thinking to have all his fellows slaughtered," promised Banak Brawnanvil, who wasn't sitting, but rather lying on a cot set in the side of the room.

Even with all the work Cordio and the others had done on him, the tough old dwarf was far from healed, for the orc spear had bitten him deep indeed. Despite his physical infirmity, there seemed no quit in the old dwarf, though.

Others seconded that sentiment.

"Any word from the south?" Bruenor asked, turning to Regis.

"Not from Dagna, no," the halfling replied, and he glanced around, somewhat sheepishly. It had been his decision to send the dwarves off with Galen Firth, after all. "But there is some fighting in the lower tunnels. Trolls have come forth, and in force."

"We'll hold them," Banak promised. "Pwent and his boys went down to join in the fighting. Pwent likes trolls, he says, because their pieces wiggle even after ye cut 'em off!"

Bruenor nodded, taking it all in. Mithral Hall had held strong against an onslaught of dark elves; he was confident that no orcs, even with the aid of trolls and frost giants, could ever hope to dislodge Clan Battlehammer.

They had much to do in strengthening their defenses, in licking their wounds and organizing their forces, but Bruenor took heart that in his absence, Mithral Hall had been well guided.

But while his confidence in his clan and home held strong, the other issue, that of a lost friend, played heavily on the crusty dwarf's heart.

"The elf's out there," he muttered again, shaking his head. His face brightened as he looked to Catti-brie, Wulfgar, and Regis in turn. "But I'm knowing a way out o' here and a way to get him back in."

"Ye cannot be thinking o' going out there!" Cordio Muffinhead scolded, and he stormed up to Bruenor's side. "Ye just got back to us, and ye're not for wandering—!"

He almost finished the sentence, until Bruenor's backhand sent him stumbling against the wall.

"Ye hear me, and ye hear me good," Bruenor told them all. "I seen the other side now, and I'm back with a mouth full o' spit on this. Ye call me yer king, and yer king I'll be—but I'm a king doing things me own way."

Bruenor looked back to his three dear friends and added, "The elf's still out there."

"Then maybe we should go get him," Regis replied.

Catti-brie and Wulfgar exchanged determined looks, then turned to regard Regis and Bruenor.

So it was agreed.

On a high bluff on a windblown mountainside, the dark elf watched the sunset. He wondered about the personal relevance of that image, of the light sinking behind a dark line. The change of day and, perhaps, of a chapter in the life of Drizzt Do'Urden.

He was an elf, yes, as Innovindil had reminded. He would see many sunsets, unless an enemy blade laid him low.

Merely thinking of that very real possibility forced a resigned grin to the drow's lips. Perhaps it would be such for him, as it had been for his friends, as it had been, before his very eyes, for poor Tarathiel. But it would not happen, he vowed silently then and there, until he had paid back the ugly orc, Obould Many-Arrows.

For all of it.

THE TWO
SWORDS

THE HUNTER'S BLADES TRILOGY   BOOK III

PRELUDE

The torchlight seemed such a meager thing against the unrelenting darkness of the dwarven caves. The smoky air drifted around Delly Curtie, irritating her eyes and throat, much as the continual grumbling and complaining of the other humans in the large common room irritated her sensibilities. Steward Regis had graciously given over a considerable suite of rooms to those seemingly ungrateful people, refugees all from the many settlements sacked by brutish King Obould and his orcs in their southern trek.

Delly reminded herself not to be too judgmental of the folk. All of them had suffered grievous losses, with many being the only remaining member of a murdered family, with three being the only remaining citizens of an entirely sacked community! And the conditions, as decent as Regis and Bruenor tried to make them, were not fitting for a human.

That thought struck hard at Delly's sensibilities, and she glanced back over her shoulder at her toddler, Colson, asleep—finally!—in a small crib. Cottie Cooperson, a spindly-armed woman with thin straw hair and eyes that drooped under the weight of a great loss, sat beside the sleeping toddler, her arms crossed tightly over her chest as she rocked back and forth, back and forth.

Remembering her own murdered baby, Delly knew.

That horrific thought sobered Delly, to be sure. Colson wasn't really Delly's child, not by birth. But she had adopted the baby girl, as Wulfgar had adopted Colson and in turn had taken on Delly as his traveling companion and wife. Delly had followed him to Mithral Hall willingly, eagerly even, and had thought herself a good and generous person in granting him his adventurous spirit, in standing beside him through what he had needed without regard for her own desires.

Delly's smile was more sad than joyous. It was perhaps the first time the young woman had ever thought of herself as good and generous.

But the dwarven walls were closing in on her.

Never had Delly Curtie imagined that she could harbor wistful memories of her street life in Luskan, living wild and on the edge, half-drunk most of the time and in the arms of a different man night after night. She thought of clever Morik, a wonderful lover, and of Arumn Gardpeck, the tavernkeeper who had been as a father to her. She thought of Josi Puddles, too, and found in those recollections of his undeniably stupid grin some measure of comfort.

"Nah, ye're being silly," the woman muttered under her breath.

She shook her head to throw those memories aside. This was her life now, with Wulfgar and the others. The dwarves of Clan Battlehammer were goodly folk, she told herself. Often eccentric, always kind and many times simply and playfully absurd, they were a lovable lot beneath their typically gruff exteriors. Some wore outrageous clothing or armor, others carried strange and ridiculous names, and most wild and absurd beards, but the clan showed Delly a measure of heart that she had never before seen, other than from Arumn perhaps. They treated her as kin, or tried to, for the differences remained.

Undeniably so.

Differences of preference, human to dwarf, like the stifling air of the caves—air that would grow even more stagnant, no doubt, since both exterior doors of Mithral Hall had been closed and barricaded.

"Ah, but to feel the wind and sun on my face once more!" a woman from across the common room shouted, lifting a flagon of mead in toast, as if she had read Delly's every thought.

From all across the room, mugs came up in response and clanged together. The group, almost all of them, were well on their way to drunkenness yet again, Delly realized. They had no place to fit in, and their drinking was as much to alleviate their helpless frustration as to dull the horrible memories of Obould's march through their respective communities.

Delly checked on Colson again and filtered about the tables. She had agreed to tend to the group, calling upon her experiences as a serving wench in Luskan. She caught bits of conversation wherever she passed, and every thought found a hold on her, and bit at what little contentment remained within her heart.

"I'm going to set up a smithy in Silverymoon," one man proclaimed.

"Bah, Silverymoon!" another argued, sounding very much like a dwarf with his rough dialect. "Silverymoon's nothing but a bunch of dancing elves. Get ye to Sundabar. Ye're sure to find a better livelihood in a town of folk who know proper business."

"Silverymoon's more accepting," a woman from another table argued. "And more beautiful, by all tellings."

Those were almost the very same words that Delly had once heard to describe Mithral Hall. In many ways, the Hall had lived up to its reputation. Certainly the reception Bruenor and his kin had given her had been nothing short of wonderful, in their unique, dwarven way. And Mithral Hall was as amazing a sight as Luskan's harbor, to be sure. Yet it was a sight that quickly melted into sameness, Delly had come to know.

She made her way across the room, veering back toward Colson, who was still sleeping but had begun that same scratchy cough that Delly had been hearing from all the humans in the smoky tunnels.

"I'm right grateful enough to Steward Regis and King Bruenor," she heard one woman say, again as if reading her very thoughts, "but here's no place for a person!" The woman lifted her flagon. "Silverymoon or Sundabar, then!" she toasted, to many cheers. "Or anywhere else ye might be seeing the sun and the stars!"

"Everlund!" another man cried.

In the stark crib on the cold stone floor beside Delly Curtie, Colson coughed again.

Beside the baby girl, Cottie Cooperson swayed.

PART ONE
ORC AMBITIONS

I look upon the hillside, quiet now except for the birds. That's all there is. The birds, cawing and cackling and poking their beaks into unseeing eyeballs. Crows do not circle before they alight on a field strewn with the dead. They fly as the bee to a flower, straight for their goal, with so great a feast before them. They are the cleaners, along with the crawling insects, the rain, and the unending wind.

And the passage of time. There is always that. The turn of the day, of the season, of the year.

When it is done, all that is left are the bones and the stones. The screams are gone, the smell is gone. The blood is washed away. The fattened birds take with them in their departing flights all that identified these fallen warriors as individuals.

Leaving the bones and stones, to mingle and mix. As the wind or the rain break apart the skeletons and filter them together, as the passage of time buries some, what is left becomes indistinguishable, perhaps, to all but the most careful of observers. Who will remember those who died here, and what have they gained to compensate for all that they, on both sides, lost?

The look upon a dwarf's face when battle is upon him would argue, surely, that the price is worth the effort, that warfare, when it comes to a dwarven nation, is a noble cause. Nothing to a dwarf is more revered than fighting to help a friend; theirs is a community bound tightly by loyalty, by blood shared and blood spilled.

And so, in the life of an individual, perhaps this is a good way to die, a worthy end to a life lived honorably, or even to a life made worthy by this last ultimate sacrifice.

I cannot help but wonder, though, in the larger context, what of the overall? What of the price, the worth, and the gain? Will Obould accomplish anything worth the hundreds, perhaps thousands of his dead? Will he gain anything long-lasting? Will the dwarven stand made out here on this high cliff bring Bruenor's people anything worthwhile? Could they not have slipped into Mithral Hall, to tunnels so much more easily defended?

And a hundred years from now, when there remains only dust, will anyone care?

I wonder what fuels the fires that burn images of glorious battle into the hearts of so many of the sentient races, my own paramount

among them. I look at the carnage on the slope and I see the inevitable sight of emptiness. I imagine the cries of pain. I hear in my
head the calls for loved ones when the dying warrior knows his
last moment is upon him. I see a tower fall with my dearest friend
atop it. Surely the tangible remnants, the rubble and the bones, are
hardly worth the moment of battle, but is there, I wonder, something less tangible here, something of a greater place? Or is there,
perhaps—and this is my fear—something of a delusion to it all that
drives us to war, again and again?

Along that latter line of thought, is it within us all, when the
memories of war have faded, to so want to be a part of something
great that we throw aside the quiet, the calm, the mundane, the
peace itself? Do we collectively come to equate peace with boredom
and complacency? Perhaps we hold these embers of war within us,
dulled only by sharp memories of the pain and the loss, and when
that smothering blanket dissipates with the passage of healing time,
those fires flare again to life. I saw this within myself, to a smaller
extent, when I realized and admitted to myself that I was not a being
of comfort and complacency, that only by the wind on my face, the
trails beneath my feet, and the adventure along the road could I truly
be happy.

I'll walk those trails indeed, but it seems to me that it is another
thing all together to carry an army along beside me, as Obould has
done. For there is the consideration of a larger morality here, shown
so starkly in the bones among the stones. We rush to the call of
arms, to the rally, to the glory, but what of those caught in the path
of this thirst for greatness?

Who will remember those who died here, and what have they
gained to compensate for all that they, on both sides, lost?

Whenever we lose a loved one, we resolve, inevitably, to never
forget, to remember that dear person for all our living days. But we
the living contend with the present, and the present often commands
all of our attention. And so as the years pass, we do not remember
those who have gone before us every day, or even every tenday. Then
comes the guilt, for if I am not remembering Zaknafein my father,
my mentor, who sacrificed himself for me, then who is? And if no
one is, then perhaps he really is gone. As the years pass, the guilt

will lessen, because we forget more consistently and the pendulum turns in our self-serving thoughts to applaud ourselves on those increasingly rare occasions when we do remember! There is always the guilt, perhaps, because we are self-centered creatures to the last. It is the truth of individuality that cannot be denied. In the end, we, all of us, see the world through our own, personal eyes.

I have heard parents express their fears of their own mortality soon after the birth of a child. It is a fear that stays with a parent, to a great extent, through the first dozen years of a child's life. It is not for the child that they fear, should they die—though surely there is that worry, as well—but rather for themselves. What father would accept his death before his child was truly old enough to remember him?

For who better to put a face to the bones among the stones? Who better to remember the sparkle in an eye before the crow comes a'calling?

I wish the crows would circle and the wind would carry them away, and the faces would remain forever to remind us of the pain. When the clarion call to glory sounds, before the armies anew trample the bones among the stones, let the faces of the dead remind us of the cost.

It is a sobering sight before me, the red-splashed stones.

It is a striking warning in my ears, the cawing of the crows.

—Drizzt Do'Urden

FOR THE LOVE OF ME SON

"We must be quicker!" the human commented, for the hundredth time that morning, it seemed to the more than two-score dwarves moving in a line all around him. Galen Firth appeared quite out of place in the torchlit, smoky tunnels. Tall even for a human, he stood more than head and shoulders above the short and sturdy bearded folk.

"I got me scouts up ahead, working as fast as scouts can work," replied General Dagna, a venerable warrior of many battles.

The old dwarf stretched and straightened his still-broad shoulders, and tucked his dirty yellow beard into his thick leather girdle, then considered Galen with eyes still sharp, a scrutinizing gaze that had kept the dwarves of Clan Battlehammer ducking defensively out of sight for many, many decades. Dagna had been a well-respected warcommander for as long as anyone could remember, longer than Bruenor had been king, and before Shimmergloom the shadow dragon and his duergar minions had conquered Mithral Hall. Dagna had climbed to power through deed, as a warrior and field commander, and no one questioned his prowess in leading dwarves through difficult conflicts. Many had expected Dagna to lead the defense of the cliff face above Keeper's Dale, even ahead of venerable Banak Brawnanvil. When that had not come to pass, it was assumed Dagna would be named as Steward of the Hall while Bruenor lay near death.

Indeed, both of those opportunities had been presented to Dagna, and by those in a position to make either happen. But he had refused.

"Ye wouldn't have me tell me scouts to run along swifter and maybe give themselves away to trolls and the like, now would ye?" Dagna asked.

Galen Firth rocked back on his heels a bit at that, but he didn't blink and he didn't stand down. "I would have you move this column as swiftly as is possible," he replied. "My town is sorely pressed, perhaps overrun, and in the south, out of these infernal tunnels, many people may now be in dire jeopardy. I would hope that such would prove an impetus to the dwarves who claim to be our neighbors."

"I claim nothing," Dagna was fast to reply. "I do what me steward and me king're telling me to do."

"And you care not at all for the fallen?"

Galen's blunt question caused several of the nearby dwarves to suck in their breath, aimed as it was at Dagna, the proud dwarf who had lost his only son only a few tendays earlier. Dagna stared long and hard at the man, burying the sting that prompted him to an angry response, remembering his place and his duty.

"We're going as fast as we're going, and if ye're wanting to be going faster, then ye're welcome to run up ahead. I'll tell me scouts to let ye pass without hindrance. Might even be that I'll keep me march going over your dead body when we find yerself troll-eaten in the corridors ahead. Might even be that yer Nesmé kin, if any're still about, will get rescued without ye." Dagna paused and let his glare linger a moment longer, a silent assurance to Galen Firth that he was hardly bluffing. "Then again, might not be."

That seemed to take some of the steam from Galen, and the man gave a great "harrumph" and turned back to the tunnel ahead, stomping forward deliberately.

Dagna was beside him in an instant, grabbing him hard by the arm.

"Pout if ye want to pout," the dwarf agreed, "but ye be doing it quietly."

Galen pulled himself away from the dwarf's vicelike grasp, and matched Dagna's stare with his own glower.

Several nearby dwarves rolled their eyes at that and wondered if Dagna would leave the fool squirming on the floor with a busted nose. Galen hadn't been like that until very recently. The fifty dwarves had accompanied him out of Mithral Hall many days before, with orders from Steward Regis to do what they could to aid the beleaguered folk of Nesmé. Their journey had been steady and straightforward until they had been attacked in the tunnels by a group of trolls. That fight had sent them running, a long way to the south and out into the open air on the edges of the great swamp, the Trollmoors, but too far to the east, by Galen Firth's reckoning. So they had started west, and had found more tunnels. Against Galen's protests, Dagna had decided that his group would be better served under cover of the westward-leading underground corridors. More dirt than stone, with roots from trees and brush dangling over their heads and with crawly things wriggling in the black dirt all around them, the tunnels weren't like those they'd used to come south from Mithral Hall. That only made Galen all the more miserable. The tunnels were tighter, lower, and not as wide, which the dwarves thought a good thing, particularly with huge and ugly trolls chasing them, but which only made Galen spend half his time walking bent over.

"Ye're pushing the old one hard," a young dwarf, Fender Stouthammer by name, remarked when they took their next break and meal. He and Galen were off to the side of the main group, in a wider and higher area that allowed Galen to stretch his legs a bit, though that had done little to improve his sour mood.

"My cause is—"

"Known to us, and felt by us, every one," Fender assured him. "We're all feeling for Mithral Hall in much the same way as ye're feeling for Nesmé, don't ye doubt."

The calming intent of Fender didn't find a hold on Galen, though, and he wagged his long finger right in the dwarf's face, so close that Fender had to hold himself back from just biting the digit off at the knuckle.

"What do you know of my feelings?" Galen growled at him. "Do you know my son, huddled in the cold, perhaps? Slain, perhaps, or with trolls all about him? Do you know the fate of my neighbors? Do you—"

"General Dagna just lost his boy," Fender interrupted, and that set Galen back a bit.

"Dagnabbit was his name," Fender went on. "A mighty warrior and loyal fellow, as are all his kin. He fell to the orc horde at Shallows, defending his king and kin to the bitter end. He was Dagna's only boy, and with a career as promising as that of his father. Long will dwarf bards sing the name of Dagnabbit. But I'm guessing that thought's hardly cooling the boil in old Dagna's blood, or hardly plastering the crack in his old heart. And now here ye come, ye short-livin', cloud-sniffin' dolt, demanding this and demanding that, as if yer own needs're more important than any we dwarves might be knowing. Bah, I tried to take ye in stride. I tried to see yer side of the fear. But ye know, ye're a pushy one, and one that's more likely to get boot-trampled into the stone than to ever see yer home again if ye don't learn to shut yer stupid mouth."

The obviously flabbergasted Galen Firth just sat there for a moment, stuttering.

"Are you threatening me, a Rider of Nesmé?" he finally managed to blurt.

"I'm telling ye, as a friend or as an enemy—choice is yer own to make—that ye're not helping yerself or yer people by fighting with Dagna at every turn in the tunnel."

"The tunnel. . . ." the stubborn man spat back. "We should be out in the open air, where we might hear the calls of my people, or see the light of their fires!"

"Or find ourselves surrounded by an army o' trolls, and wouldn't that smell wonderful?"

Galen Firth gave a snort and held up his hand dismissively. Fender took the cue, rose, and started away.

He did pause long enough to look back and offer, "Ye keep acting as if ye're among enemies, or lessers. If all the folk o' Nesmé are as stupid as yerself—too dumb to know a friend when one's ready to help—then who's to doubt that the trolls might be doing all the world a favor?"

Galen Firth trembled, and for a moment Fender half expected the man to leap up and try to throttle him.

"I came to you, to Mithral Hall, in friendship!" he argued, loudly enough to gain the attention of those dwarves crowded around Dagna in the main chamber down the tunnel.

"Yerself came to Mithral Hall in need, offerin' nothing but complaints and asking for more than we could give ye," Fender corrected. "And still Steward Regis, and all the clan, accepted the responsibility of friendship—not the burden, but the responsibility, ye dolt! We ain't here because we're owing Nesmé a damned thing, and we ain't here asking Nesmé for a damned thing, and in the end, even yerself should be smart enough to know that we're all hopin' for the same thing here. And that thing's finding yer boy, and all the others of yer town, alive and well."

The blunt assessment did give Galen pause and in that moment, before he could decide whether to scream or to punch out, Fender rolled up to his feet, offered a dismissive, "Bah!" and waved his calloused hands the man's way.

"Ye might be thinking to make a bit less noise, yeah?" came a voice from the other direction, that of General Dagna, who glared at the two.

"Get along with ye, then," Fender said to Galen, and he waved at him again. "Think on what I said or don't—it's yer own to choose."

Galen Firth slowly moved back from the dwarf, and toward the larger gathering in the middle of the wider chamber. He walked more sidelong than in any straightforward manner, though, as if warding his back from the pursuit of words that had surely stung him.

Fender was glad of that, for the sake of Galen Firth and Nesmé Town, if for nothing else.

Tos'un Armgo, lithe and graceful, moved silently along the low corridor, a dart clenched in his teeth and a serrated knife in his hand. The dark elf was glad that the dwarves had gone back underground. He felt vulnerable and exposed in the open air. A noise made him pause and huddle closer to the rocky wall, his limber form melting into the jags and depressions. He pulled his *piwafwi*, his enchanted drow cloak that could hide him from the most scrutinizing of gazes, a bit tighter around him and turned his face to the stone, peering out of the corner of only one eye.

A few moments passed. Tos'un relaxed as he heard the dwarves back at their normal routines, eating and chatting. They thought they were safe back in the tunnels, since they believed they had left the trolls far behind. What troll could have tracked them over the last couple days since the skirmish, after all?

No troll, Tos'un knew, and he smiled at the thought. For the dwarves hadn't counted on their crude and beastlike enemies being accompanied by a pair of dark elves. Tracking them, leading the two-headed troll named Proffit and his smelly band back into this second stretch of tunnel, had been no difficult task for Tos'un.

The drow glanced back the other way, where his companion, the priestess Kaer'lic Suun Wett waited, crouched atop a boulder against the wall. Even

Tos'un would not have seen her there, buried under her *piwafwi*, except that she shifted as he turned, lifting one arm out toward him.

Take down the sentry, her fingers flashed to him in the intricate sign language of the drow elves. *A prisoner is desirable.*

Tos'un took a deep breath and instinctively reached for the dart he held clenched in his teeth. Its tip was coated with drow poison, a paralyzing concoction of tremendous power that few could resist. How often had Tos'un heard that command from Kaer'lic and his other two drow companions over the last few years, for he among all the group had become the most adept at gathering creatures for interrogation, especially when the target was part of a larger group.

Tos'un paused and moved his free hand out where Kaer'lic could see, then answered, *Do we need bother? They are alert, and they are many.*

Kaer'lic's fingers flashed back immediately, *I would know if this is a remote group or the forward scouts of Mithral Hall's army!*

Tos'un's hand went right back to the dart. He didn't dare argue with Kaer'lic on such matters. They were drow, and in the realm of the drow, even for a group who was so far removed from the conventions of the great Underdark cities, females ranked higher than males, and priestesses of the Spider Queen Lolth, like Kaer'lic, ranked highest of all.

The scout turned and slid down lower toward the floor, then began to half walk, half crawl toward his target. He paused when he heard the dwarf raise his voice, arguing with the single human among the troop. The drow moved to a properly hidden vantage point and bided his time.

Soon enough, several of the dwarves farther along told the two to be quiet, and the dwarf near to Tos'un grumbled something and waved the human away.

Tos'un glanced back just once, then paused and listened until his sensitive ears picked out the rumble of Proffit's closing war party.

Tos'un slithered in. His left arm struck first, jabbing the dart into the dwarf's shoulder as his right hand came across, the serrated knife cutting a very precise line on the dwarf's throat. It could easily have been a killing blow, but Tos'un angled the blade so as not to cut the main veins, the same technique he had recently used on a dwarf in a tower near the Surbrin. Eventually his cut would prove mortal, but not for a long time, not until Kaer'lic could intervene and with but a few minor spells granted by the Spider Queen save the wretched creature's life.

Though, Tos'un thought, the prisoner would surely wish he had been allowed to die.

The dwarf shifted fast and tried to cry out, but the drow had taken its vocal chords. Then the dwarf tried to punch and lash out, but the poison was already there. Blood streaming from the mortal wound, the dwarf crumbled down to the stone, and Tos'un slithered back.

"Bah, ye're still a bigmouth!" came a quiet call from the main group. "Keep still, will ya, Fender?"

Tos'un continued to retreat.

"Fender?" The call sounded more insistent.

Tos'un flattened against the corner of the wall and the floor, making himself very small and all but invisible under his enchanted cloak.

"Fender!" a dwarf ahead of him cried, and Tos'un smiled at his cleverness, knowing the stupid dwarves would surely think their poisoned companion dead.

The camp began to stir, dwarves leaping up and grabbing their weapons, and it occurred to Tos'un that Kaer'lic's decision to go for a captive might cost Proffit and his trolls dearly. The price of the drow's initial assault had been the element of surprise.

Of course, for the dark elf, that only made the attack all the more sweet.

Some dwarves cried out for Fender, but the shout that rose above them all came from Bonnerbas Ironcap, the dwarf closest to their fallen companion.

"Trolls!" he yelled, and even as the word registered with his companions, so did the smell of the wretched brutes.

"Fall back to the fire!" General Dagna shouted.

Bonnerbas hesitated, for he was but one stride from poor Fender. He went forward instead of back, and grabbed his friend by the collar. Fender flopped over and Bonnerbas sucked in his breath, seeing clearly the line of bright blood. The dwarf was limp, unfeeling.

Fender was dead, Bonnerbas believed, or soon would be.

He heard the charge of the trolls then, looked up, and realized that he would soon join Fender in the halls of Moradin.

Bonnerbas fell back one step and took up his axe, swiping across viciously and cutting a deep line across the arms of the nearest, low-bending troll. That one fell back, stumbling to the side and toppling, but before it even hit the floor it came flying ahead, bowled over by a pair of trolls charging forward at Bonnerbas.

The dwarf swung again, and turned to flee, but a clawed troll hand hooked his shoulder. Bonnerbas understood then the frightful strength of the brutes, for suddenly he was flying backward, spinning and bouncing off legs as solid as the trunks of tall trees. He stumbled and fell, winding up on his back. Still, the furious dwarf flailed with his axe, and he scored a couple of hits. But the trolls were all around him, were between him and Dagna and the others, and poor Bonnerbas had nowhere to run.

One troll reached for him and he managed to swat the arm with enough force to take it off at the elbow. That troll howled and fell back, but then, even as the dwarf tried to roll to his side and stand the biggest and ugliest troll Bonnerbas had ever seen towered over him, a gruesome two-headed brute staring at him with a wide smile on both of its twisted faces. It started to reach down, and Bonnerbas started to swing.

As his axe flew past without hitting anything, the dwarf recognized the dupe, and before he could bring the axe back over him, a huge foot appeared above him and crashed down hard, stomping him into the stone.

Bonnerbas tried to struggle, but there was nothing he could do. He tried to breathe, but the press was too great.

As the trolls pushed past the two fallen dwarves, General Dagna could only growl and silently curse himself for allowing his force to be caught so unawares. Questions and curses roiled in his mind. How could stupid, smelly trolls have possibly followed them back into the tunnels? How could the brutes have scouted and navigated the difficult approach to where Dagna had thought it safe to break for a meal?

That jumble quickly calmed in the thoughts of the seasoned commander, though, and he began barking orders to put his command in line. His first thought was to move back into the lower tunnels, to get the trolls bent over even more, but the dwarf's instincts told him to stay put, with a ready fire at hand. He ordered his boys to form up a defensive hold on the far side of the cooking fire. Dagna himself led the countercharge and the push, centering the front line of five dwarves abreast and refusing to retreat against the troll press.

"Hold 'em fast!" he cried repeatedly as he smashed away with his warhammer. "Go to crushing!" he told the axe-wielding dwarf beside him. "Don't yet cut through 'em if that's giving them a single step forward!"

The other dwarf, apparently catching on to the reasoning that they had to hold the far side of the fire at all costs, flipped his axe over in his hand and began pounding away at the closest troll, smashing it with the flat back of the weapon to keep it at bay.

All the five dwarves did likewise, and Galen Firth ran up behind Dagna and began slashing away with his fine long sword. They knew they would not be able to hold for long, though, for more trolls crowded behind the front ranks, the sheer weight of them driving the force forward.

Thinking that all of them were doomed, Dagna screamed in rage and whacked so hard at the troll reaching for him that his nasty hammer tore the creature's arm off at the elbow.

The troll didn't seem to even notice as it came forward, and Dagna realized his error. He had over-swung the mark and was vulnerable.

But the troll backed suddenly, and Dagna ducked and cried out in surprise, as the first of the torches, compliments of Galen Firth, entered the fray. The man reached over and past the ducking Dagna and thrust the flaming torch at the troll, and how the creature scrambled to get back from the fire!

Trolls were mighty opponents indeed, and it was said—and it was true—that if you cut a troll into a hundred pieces, the result would be a hundred new trolls, with every piece regenerating into an entirely new creature. They had a weakness, though, one that every person in all the Realms knew well: fire stopped that regeneration process.

Trolls didn't like fire.

More torches were quickly passed up to Dagna and the four others and the trolls fell back, but only a step.

"Forward, then, for Fender and Bonnerbas!" Dagna cried, and all the dwarves cheered.

But then came a shout from the other side of "Trolls in the tunnels!" and another warning shout from directly behind Dagna.

All the tunnels were blocked. Dagna knew at once that his dwarves were surrounded and had nowhere to run.

"How deep're we?" the general shouted.

"Roots in the ceiling," one dwarf answered. "Ain't too deep."

"Then get us through!" the old dwarf ordered

Immediately, those dwarves near to the center of the tightening ring went into action. Two braced a third and lifted him high with his pickaxe, and he began tearing away at the ground.

"Wet one down!" Dagna yelled, and he knew that it was all he had to say to get his full meaning across to his trusted comrades.

"And tie him off!" came the appropriate addition, from more than one dwarf.

"Galen Firth, ye brace the hole!" Dagna roared at the human.

"What are you doing?" the man demanded. "Fight on, good dwarf, for we've nowhere to run!"

Dagna thrust his torch forward and the troll facing him hopped back. The dwarf turned fast and shoved at Galen.

"Turn about, ye dolt, and get us out o' here!"

A confused Galen did reluctantly turn from the fight just as daylight appeared above the area to the left of the cooking fire. The two dwarves supporting the miner gave a great heave, sending him up, where he caught on and scrambled onto the surface.

"Clear!" he reported.

Galen understood the plan then, and rushed to the hole, where he immediately began hoisting dwarves. After every one he had to pause, though, for the dwarves up above began handing down more wood for the fire.

Dagna nodded and urged his line on, and the five fought furiously and brilliantly, coordinating their movements so that the trolls could not advance. But neither did the dwarves gain any ground, and Dagna knew in his heart that his two companions, Fender and Bonnerbas, were surely dead.

The tough old dwarf pushed the grim thoughts from his mind, and didn't even begin to let them lead him back down the road of grief for his lost boy. He focused on his anger and on the desperate need, and he forged ahead, warhammer and torch flailing. Behind him, he felt the heat increasing as his boys began to strengthen the fire. They'd need it blazing indeed if they meant to get the last of the group clear of the tunnels and up into the open air.

"Down in front!" came a call aimed at Dagna and his line.

As one the five dwarves sprang ahead and attacked ferociously, forcing the trolls to retreat a step. Then again as one they leaped back and dropped to the ground.

Flaming brush and logs flew over their heads, bouncing into the trolls and sending them into a frenzied scramble to get out of the way.

Dagna's heart fell as he watched the effective barrage, though, for beyond that line of confusion lay two of his kin, down and dead, he was sure. He and the other four fell back, then, moving right to the base of the hole, just behind Galen, who continued to ferry dwarves up.

The tunnel grew smokier and smokier with every passing second as more brush and logs came down the chute. A dwarven brigade carried the timber to the fire. The brush—branches of pine, mostly—flared up fast and furious to be rushed across to drive back whatever trolls were closest, while the logs were dropped onto the pile, replacing already flaring logs that were scooped up and hurled into the enemy ranks. Gradually, the dwarves were building walls of fire, sealing off every approach.

Their ranks thinned as more scrambled up to the surface, as Galen tirelessly lifted them into the arms of their waiting kin. Then the scramble became more frantic as the dwarves' numbers dwindled to only a few.

The dwarf beside Dagna urged him to go, but the crusty old graybeard slapped that notion aside by slapping the other dwarf aside—shoving him into Galen Firth's waiting arms. Up and out he went, and one by one, Dagna's line diminished.

Up came a huge flaming brand—Galen passing it to Dagna—and the old dwarf took the heavy log, handing back his hammer in exchange. He presented the log horizontally out before him and charged with a roar, barreling right into the trolls, the flames biting his hands but biting the trolls worse. The creatures fell all over each other trying to get back from the wild dwarf. With a great heave, Dagna sent the flaming log into them. Then he turned and fled back to where Galen was waiting. The human crouched, with his hands set in a clasp before him. Dagna hopped onto those waiting hands, and Galen turned, guiding him directly under the hole, then heaved him up.

Even as Dagna cleared the hole, and Galen instinctively turned to meet the troll charge he knew must be coming, dwarf hands reached into the opening and clasped tightly onto Galen's forearms.

The man went into the air, to shouts of, "Pull him out!"

His head and shoulders came out into the open air, and for a moment, Galen thought he was clear.

Until he felt clawed hands grab him by the legs.

"Pull, ye dolts!" General Dagna demanded, and he rushed over and grabbed Galen by the collar, digging in his heels and tugging hard.

The man cried out in pain. He lifted a bit out of the hole, then went back in some, serving as the line in a game of tug-of-war.

"Get me a torch!" Dagna cried, and when he saw a dwarf rushing over with a flaming brand he let go of Galen, who, for a moment, nearly disappeared into the hole.

"Grab me feet!" Dagna ordered as he went around Galen.

The moment a pair of dwarves had him securely about the ankles, the general dived face first into the hole behind the struggling Galen, his torch leading—and drawing a yelp from Galen as it brushed down behind him.

Galen frantically shouted some more as the torch burned him about the legs, but then he was free. The dwarves yanked both Galen and Dagna from the hole. Dagna held his ground as a troll stood up, reaching for the opening. The old dwarf whacked away with the torch, holding the creature at bay until his boys could get more substantial fire to the hole and dump it down.

Heavier logs were ferried into position and similarly forced down, blocking the opening, and Dagna and the others fell back to catch their collective breath.

A shout had them up and moving again, though, for the trolls had not been stopped by the clogged and fiery exit. Clawed hands rent the ground as the trolls began to dig escape tunnels of their own.

"Gather 'em up and get on the move!" Dagna roared, and the dwarves set off at a great pace across the open ground.

Many had to be helped, two carried even, but a count showed that they had lost only two: Fender and Bonnerbas. Still, not a one of them wanted to call that encounter a victory.

BONES AND STONES

Decay and rot had won the day, creeping around the stones and boulders of the bloody mountainside. Bloated corpses steamed in the cool morning air, their last wisps of heat flowing away to insubstantiality, life energy lost on the endless mitigating mourn of the uncaring wind.

Drizzt Do'Urden walked among the lower reaches of the killing field, a cloth tied across his black-skinned face to ward the stench. Almost all of the bodies on the lower ground were orcs, many killed in the monumental blast that had upended the mountain ridge to the side of the main area of battle. That explosion had turned night into day, had sent flames leaping a thousand feet into the air, and had launched tons and tons of debris across the swarm of monsters, mowing them flat under its press.

"One less weapon I will have to replace," said Innovindil.

Drizzt turned to regard his surface elf companion. The fair elf had her face covered too, though that did little to diminish her beauty. Above her scarf, bright blue eyes peered out at Drizzt and the same wind that carried the stench of death blew her long golden tresses out wildly behind her. Lithe and graceful, Innovindil's every step seemed like a dance to Drizzt Do'Urden, and even the burden of mourning, for she had lost her partner and lover, Tarathiel, could not hold her feet glumly to the stone.

Drizzt watched as she reached down to a familiar corpse, that of

Urlgen, son of Obould Many-Arrows, the orc beast who had started the awful war. Innovindil had killed Urlgen, or rather, he had inadvertently killed himself by slamming his head at hers and impaling it upon a dagger the elf had snapped up before her. Innovindil put a foot on the bloated face of the dead orc leader, grasped the dagger hilt firmly in hand, and yanked it free. With hardly a flinch, she bent further and wiped the blade on the dead orc's shirt, then flipped it over in her hand and replaced it in the sheath belted around her ankle.

"They have not bothered to loot the field, from dead dwarves or from their own," Innovindil remarked.

That much had been obvious to Drizzt and Innovindil before their pegasus, Sunset, had even set them down on the rocky mountain slope. The place was deserted, fully so, even though the orcs were not far away. The couple could hear them in the valley beyond the slope's crest, the region called Keeper's Dale, which marked the western entrance to Mithral Hall. The dwarves had not won there, Drizzt knew, despite the fact that orc bodies outnumbered those of his bearded friends many times over. In the end, the orcs had pushed them from the cliff and into Keeper's Dale, and back into their hole in Mithral Hall. The orcs had paid dearly for that piece of ground, but it was theirs. Given the sheer size of the orc force assembled outside the closed door of Clan Battlehammer's stronghold, Drizzt simply couldn't see how the dwarves might ever win the ground back.

"They have not looted only because the battle is not yet over," Drizzt replied. "There has been no pause until now for the orcs, first in pushing the dwarves back into Mithral Hall, then in preparing the area around the western gates to their liking. They will return here soon enough, I expect."

He glanced over at Innovindil to see her distracted and standing before the remains of a particularly nasty fight, staring down at a clump of bodies. Drizzt understood her surprise before he even went over and confirmed that she was standing where he had watched the battleragers, the famed Gutbuster Brigade, make a valiant stand. He walked up beside the elf, wincing at the gruesome sight of shredded bodies—never had there been anything subtle about Thibbledorf Pwent's boys—and wincing even more when he caught sight of more than a dozen dead dwarves, all tightly packed together. They had died, one and all, protecting each other, a fitting end indeed for the brave warriors.

"Their armor . . ." Innovindil began, shaking her head, her expression caught somewhere between surprise, awe, and disgust.

She didn't have to say anything more for Drizzt to perfectly understand, for the armor of the Gutbusters often elicited such confusion. Ridged and overlapping with sharpened plates, and sprouting an abundance of deadly spikes, Gutbuster armor made a dwarf's body into a devastating weapon. Where other dwarves charged with pickaxes, battle-axes, warhammers, and swords held high, Gutbusters just charged.

Drizzt thought to inspect the area a bit more closely, to see if his old friend Thibbledorf might be among the dead, but he decided against that course. Better for him, he thought, to just continue on his way. Counting the dead was an exercise for after the war.

Of course, that same attitude allowed Drizzt to justify his inability to return to Clan Battlehammer and truly face the realization that his friends were all gone, killed at the town of Shallows.

"Let us get to the ridge," he said. "We should learn the source of that explosion before Obould's minions return here to pick the bodies clean."

Innovindil readily agreed and started toward the blasted line of stone.

Had she and Drizzt moved only twenty more paces up toward the lip of Keeper's Dale, they would have found another telltale formation of bodies: orcs, some lying three in a row, dead and showing only a single burned hole for injuries.

Drizzt Do'Urden knew of a weapon, a bow named Taulmaril, that inflicted such wounds, a bow held by his friend Catti-brie, whom he thought dead at Shallows.

The dwarf Nikwillig sat on the east-facing side of a mountain, slumped against the stone and fighting against such desperation and despair that he feared he would be frozen him in place until starvation or some wayward orc took him. He took comfort in knowing that he had done his duty well, and that his expedition to the peaks east of the battlefield had helped to turn the tide of the raging conflict—at least enough so that Banak Brawnanvil had managed to get the great majority of dwarves down the cliff face and safely into Mithral Hall ahead of the advancing orc horde.

That moment of triumph played over and over in the weary dwarf's mind, a litany against the pressing fears of his current predicament. He had climbed the slopes higher than the combatants while the field of battle remained blanketed in pre-dawn darkness, had turned his attention, and the mirror he carried, to the rising sun. He had angled a reflected ray from that mirror back against the slope of the ridge across the way, until he had located the second mirror placed there, brilliantly illuminating the target for Catti-brie and her enchanted bow.

Then Nikwillig had watched darkness turn to sudden light, a flare of fire that had risen a thousand feet over the battlefield. Like a ripple in a pond or a burst of wind bending a field of grass, the waves of hot wind and debris had rolled out from that monumental explosion, sweeping the northern reaches of the battlefield where the majority of orcs were beginning their charge. They had gone down in rows, many never to rise again. Their charge had been all but stopped, exactly as the dwarves had hoped.

So Nikwillig had done his job, but even when he'd left, hoping for exactly that outcome, the Felbarran dwarf had known his chances of returning were not good. Banak and the others certainly couldn't wait for him to scramble back down—even if they had wanted to, how would Nikwillig have ever gotten through the swarm of orcs between him and the dwarves?

Nikwillig had left the dwarven ranks on a suicide mission that day, and he held no regrets, but that didn't dismiss the very real fears that huddled around him as the time of his death seemed near at hand.

He thought of Tred, then, his comrade from Felbarr. They, along with several companions, had started out on a bright day from the Citadel of King Emerus Warcrown not so long ago in a typical merchant caravan. While their route was somewhat different than the norm, as they tried to secure a new trading line for both King Emerus and their own pockets, they hadn't expected any real trouble. Certainly, they never expected to walk into the front scouts of the greatest orc assault the region had seen in memory! Nikwillig wondered what might have happened to Tred. Had he fallen in the vicious fight? Or had he gotten down into Keeper's Dale and into Mithral Hall?

The forlorn dwarf gave a helpless little laugh as he considered that Tred had previously decided to walk out of Mithral Hall and return home with the news to Citadel Felbarr. Toughened, war-hardened, and battle-eager Tred had thought to serve as emissary between the two fortresses and in the ultimate irony, Nikwillig had dissuaded him.

"Ah, ye're such the fool, Nikwillig," the dwarf said into the mournful wind.

He didn't really believe the words even as he spoke them. He had stayed, Tred had stayed, because they had decided they were indebted to King Bruenor and his kin, because they had decided that the war was about the solidarity of the *Delzoun* dwarves, about standing together, shoulder-to-shoulder, in common cause.

No, he hadn't been a fool for staying, and hadn't been a fool for volunteering, insisting even, that he be the one to go out with the mirror and grab those first rays of dawn. He wasn't a warrior, after all. He had walked willingly and rightly into this predicament, but he knew that the road ahead was likely to come to a fast and vicious ending.

The dwarf pulled himself to his feet. He glanced back over his shoulder toward Keeper's Dale, and again dismissed any thoughts of going that way. Certainly that was the closest entrance to Mithral Hall and safety, but to get to it meant crossing a massive orc encampment. Even if he somehow managed that feat, the dwarves were in their hole and those doors were closed, and weren't likely to open anytime soon.

So east it was, Nikwillig decided. To the River Surbrin and hopefully, against all odds, beyond.

He thought he heard a sound nearby and imagined that an orc patrol was likely watching him even then, ready to spring upon him and batter him to death. He took a deep breath. He put one foot in front of the other.

He started his dark journey.

Drizzt and Innovindil veered to the south as they headed for the blasted ridge, angling their march so that they came in sight of Keeper's Dale right near to the spot where the line of metal tubes had been placed by the dwarves. That line ran up from the ground to the entrance of the tunnels that wound beneath what was once a ridgeline. Of course neither of them understood what that pipeline was all about. Neither had any idea that the dwarves, at the instructions of Nanfoodle the gnome, had brought natural gasses up from their underground entrapment, filling the tunnels beneath the unwitting giants and their catapults.

Perhaps if the pair had been granted more time to ponder the pipeline, to climb down the cliff and inspect it more closely, Drizzt and Innovindil would have begun to decipher the mystery of the gigantic fireball. At that moment, however, the fireball seemed the least of their issues. For below them swarmed the largest army of orcs either had ever seen, a virtual sea of dark forms milling around the obelisks that marked Keeper's Dale. Thousands, tens of thousands, moved down there, their indistinct mass occasionally marked by the larger form of a hulking frost giant.

As he scanned across the throng, Drizzt Do'Urden picked out more and more of those larger monsters, and he sucked in his breath as he came to realize the scope of the army. Hundreds of giants were down there, as if the entire population of behemoths from all the Spine of the World had emptied out to the call of King Obould.

"Have the Silver Marches known a darker day?" Innovindil asked.

Drizzt turned to regard her, though he wasn't sure if she was actually asking him or simply making a remark.

Innovindil swung her head to meet his lavender-eyed gaze. "I remember when Obould managed to rout the dwarves from Citadel Felbarr," she explained. "And what a dark day that was! But still, the orc king seemed to have traded one hole for another. While his conquest had played terribly on King Emerus Warcrown and the other Felbarran dwarves, never was it viewed as any threat to the wider region. The orc king had seized upon an unexpected opportunity, and so he had prevailed in a victory that we all expected would be short-lived, as it was. But now this. . . ." Her voice trailed off and she shook her head helplessly as she looked back to the dale and the massive orc army.

"We can guess that most of the dwarves of Clan Battlehammer managed to get back into their tunnels," Drizzt reasoned. "They'll not be easily routed, I assure you. In their chambers, Clan Battlehammer once repulsed an attack by Menzoberranzan. I doubt there are enough orcs in all the world to take the hall."

"You may be right, but does that even matter?"

Drizzt looked at the elf curiously. He started to ask how it might not matter, but as he came to fully understand Innovindil's fears, he held the question in check.

"No," he agreed, "this force Obould has assembled will not be easily pushed back into their mountain holes. It will take Silverymoon and Everlund, and perhaps even Sundabar . . . Citadels Felbarr and

Adbar, and Mithral Hall. It will take the Moonwood elves and the army of Marchion Elastul of Mirabar. All the north must rally to the call of Mithral Hall in this, their hour of need."

"And even in that case, the cost will prove enormous," Innovindil replied. "Horrific." She glanced back to the bloody, carcass-ridden battlefield. "This fight here on the ridge will seem a minor skirmish and fat will the crows of the Silver Marches be."

Drizzt continued his scan as she spoke, and he noted movement down to the west, quickly discerning it as a force of orcs circling up and out of Keeper's Dale.

"The orc scavengers will soon arrive," he said. "Let us be on our way."

Innovindil stared down at Keeper's Dale a bit longer.

"No sign of Sunrise," she remarked, referring to the pegasus companion of Sunset, and once the mount of Tarathiel, her companion.

"Obould still has him, and alive, I am sure," Drizzt replied. "Even an orc would not destroy so magnificent a creature."

Innovindil continued to stare and managed a little hunch of her shoulders, then turned to face Drizzt directly again. "Let us hope."

Drizzt rose, took her hand, and together they walked down toward the north, along the ridge of blasted and broken stones. The explosion had lifted the roof of the ridge away, leaving a scarred ravine behind. Every now and again, the couple came upon the remains of a charred giant. In one place, they found a burned out catapult, somehow still retaining its shape despite the tremendous blast.

Their discoveries prompted more questions than they answered, however, leaving the pair no clue whatsoever as to what might have caused such a cataclysm.

"When we at last find our way into Mithral Hall, you can ask the dwarves about it," Innovindil said when they were far from the field, on an open plateau awaiting the return of the winged Sunset.

Drizzt didn't respond to the elf's direct implication that he would indeed soon return to the dwarven stronghold—where he would have no choice but to face his fears—other than to offer a quiet nod.

"Some trick of the gods, perhaps," the elf went on.

"Or the Harpells," Drizzt added, referring to a family of eccentric and powerful wizards—too powerful for their own good, or for the good of those around them, in most cases!— from the small community of

Longsaddle many miles to the west. The Harpells had come to the aid of Mithral Hall before, and had a long-standing friendship with Bruenor and his kin. Drizzt knew enough about them to realize that if anyone might have inadvertently caused such a catastrophe as befell the ridge, it would be that strange clan of confused humans.

"Harpells?"

"You do not want to know," Drizzt said in all seriousness. "Suffice it to say that Bruenor Battlehammer has made some unconventional friends."

As soon as he had spoken the words, Drizzt recognized the irony of them, and he managed a smile to match Innovindil's own widening grin as he glanced at her.

"We will know soon enough on all counts," she said. "For now, we have duties of our own to attend."

"For Sunrise," Drizzt agreed and he shook Innovindil's offered hand. "And for vengeance. Tarathiel will rest easier when Obould Many-Arrows is dead."

"Dead at the tip of a sword?" Innovindil asked, putting a hand to the hilt of her own weapon. "Or at the curve of a scimitar?"

"A scimitar, I think," Drizzt answered without the slightest hesitation, and he looked back to the south. "I do intend to kill that one."

"For Tarathiel, and for Bruenor, then," said Innovindil. "For those who have died and for the good of the North."

"Or simply because I want to kill him," said Drizzt in a tone so cold and even that it sent a shiver along Innovindil's spine.

She could not find the voice to answer.

PASSION

With a growl that seemed more anger than passion, Tsinka Shinriil rolled Obould over and scrambled atop him.

"You have put them in their dark hole!" the female shaman cried, her eyes wide—so wide that the yellow-white of her eyes showed clearly all around her dark pupils, giving her an expression that seemed more a caricature of insanity than anything else. "Now we dig into that hole!"

King Obould Many-Arrows easily held the excited shaman at bay as she tried to engulf him with her trembling body, his thick, muscular arms lifting her from the straw bed.

"Mithral Hall will fall to the might of Obould-who-is-Gruumsh," Tsinka went on. "And Citadel Felbarr will be yours once more, soon after. We will have them all! We will slay the minions of Bruenor and Emerus! We will bathe in their blood!"

Obould gave a slight shrug and moved the shaman off to the side, off the cot itself. She hit the floor nimbly, and came right back, drool showing at the edges of her tusky mouth.

"Is there anything Obould-who-is-Gruumsh cannot conquer?" she asked, squirming atop him again. "Mithral Hall, Felbarr . . . Adbar! Yes, Adbar! They will all fall before us. Every dwarven stronghold in the North! We will send them fleeing, those few who we do not devour. We will rid the North of the dwarven curse."

Obould managed a smile, but it was more to mock the priestess than to agree with her. He'd heard her litany before—over and over again, actually. Ever since the western door of Mithral Hall had banged closed, sealing Clan Battlehammer into their hole, Tsinka and the other shamans had been spouting preposterous hopes for massive conquests all throughout the Silver Marches and beyond.

And Obould shared that hope. He wanted nothing more than to reclaim the Citadel of Many Arrows, which the dwarves had named Citadel Felbarr once more. But Obould saw the folly in that course. The entire region had been alerted to them. Crossing the Surbrin would mean engaging the armies of Silverymoon and Everlund, certainly, along with the elves of the Moonwood and the combined forces of the *Delzoun* dwarves east of the deep, cold river.

"You are Gruumsh!" Tsinka said. She grabbed Obould's face and kissed him roughly. "You are a god among orcs!" She kissed him again. "Gerti Orelsdottr fears you!" Tsinka shrieked and kissed him yet again.

Obould grinned, rekindling the memory of his last encounter with the frost giant princess. Gerti did indeed fear him, or she certainly should, for Obould had bested her in their short battle, had tossed her to the ground and sent her slinking away. It was a feat previously unheard of, and only served to illustrate to all who had seen it, and to all who heard about it, that King Obould was much more than a mere orc. He was in the favor of Gruumsh One-Eye, the god of orcs. He had been blessed with strength and speed, with uncanny agility, and he believed, with more insight than ever before.

Or perhaps that new insight wasn't new at all. Perhaps Obould, in his current position, unexpectedly gaining all the ground between the Spine of the World, the Fell Pass, the River Surbrin, and the Trollmoors with such ease and overwhelming power, was simply viewing the world from a different, and much superior, position.

"... into Mithral Hall ..." Tsinka was saying when Obould turned his attention back to the babbling shaman. Apparently noting his sudden attention, she paused and rewound the thought. "We must go into Mithral Hall before the winter. We must rout Clan Battlehammer so the word of their defeat and humiliation will spread before the snows block the passes. We will work the dwarven forges throughout the winter to strengthen our armor and weapons. We will emerge in the spring an unstoppable force, rolling across the northland and laying waste to all who foolishly stand before us!"

"We lost many orcs driving the dwarves underground," Obould said, trying to steal some of her momentum. "The stones are colored with orc blood."

"Blood well spilled!" Tsinka shrieked. "And more will die! More must die! Our first great victory is at hand!"

"Our first great victory is achieved," Obould corrected.

"Then our second is before us!" Tsinka shouted right back at him. "And the victory worthy of He-who-is-Gruumsh. We have taken stones and empty ground. The prize is yet to be had."

Obould pushed her back out to arms' length and turned his head a bit to better regard her. She was shaking again, though be it from passion or anger, he could not tell. Her naked body shone in the torchlight with layers of sweat. Her muscles stood on edge, corded and trembling, like a spring too tightly twisted.

"Mithral Hall must fall before the winter," Tsinka said, more calmly than before. "Gruumsh has shown this to me. It was Bruenor Battlehammer who stood upon that stone, breaking the tide of orcs and denying us a greater victory."

Obould growled at the name.

"Word has spread throughout the land that he lives. The King of Mithral Hall has risen from the dead, it would seem. That is Moradin's challenge to Gruumsh, do you not see? You are Gruumsh's champion, of that there is no doubt, and King Bruenor Battlehammer champions Moradin. Settle this and settle it quickly, you must, before the dwarves rally to Moradin's call as the orcs have rallied to Obould!"

The words hit Obould hard, for they made more sense than he wanted to admit. He wasn't keen on going into Mithral Hall. He knew that his army would suffer difficult obstacles every inch of the way. Could he sustain such horrific losses and still hope to secure the land he meant to be his kingdom?

But indeed, word had spread through the deep orc ranks like a wind-swept fire across dry grass. There was no denying the identity of the dwarf who had centered the defensive line in the retreat to the hall. It was Bruenor, thought dead at Shallows. It was Bruenor, returned from the grave.

Obould was not so stupid as to underestimate the importance of that development. He understood how greatly his presence spurred on his own warriors—could Bruenor be any less inspiring to the dwarves? Obould hated dwarves above all other races, even elves, but his bitter experiences at Citadel Felbarr had given him a grudging respect for the stout bearded folk. He had taken Felbarr at an opportune moment, and with a great deal of the element of surprise on his side, but now, if Tsinka had her way, he would be taking his forces into a defended and prepared dwarven fortress.

Was any race in all of Toril better at defending their homes than the dwarves?

The drow, perhaps, he thought, and the notion sent his contemplations flowing to events in the south, where two dark elves were supposedly helping ugly Proffit and his trolls press Mithral Hall from the south. Obould realized that that would be the key to victory if he decided to crash into Mithral Hall. If Proffit and his smelly beasts could siphon off a fair number of Bruenor's warriors, and any amount of Bruenor's attention, a bold strike straight though Mithral Hall's closed western door might gain Obould a foothold within.

The orc king looked back at Tsinka and realized that he was wearing his thoughts on his face, so to speak. For she was grinning in her toothy way, her dark eyes roiling with eagerness—for conquest, and for Obould. The great orc king lowered his arms, bringing Tsinka down atop him, and let his plans slip from his thoughts. He held onto the image of dead dwarves and crumbling dwarven doors, though, for Obould found those sights perfectly intoxicating.

The cold wind made every jolt hurt just a little bit more, but Obould gritted his teeth and clamped his legs more tightly against the bucking pegasus. The white equine creature had its wings strapped tightly back. Obould wasn't about to let it get him up off the ground, for the pegasus was not broken at all as far as the orcs were concerned. Obould had seen the elf riding the creature, so easily, but every orc who'd climbed atop the pegasus had been thrown far away, and more than one had subsequently been trampled by the beast before the handlers could get the creature under control.

Every orc thus far had been thrown, except for Obould, whose legs clamped so powerfully at the pegasus's sides that the creature had not yet dislodged him.

Up came the horse's rump, and Obould's body rolled back, his neck painfully whipping and his head turning so far over that he actually saw, upside down, the pegasus's rear hooves snap up in the air at the end of the buck! His hand grabbed tighter at the thick rope and he growled and clamped his legs against the mount's flanks, so tightly that he figured he would crush the creature's ribs.

But the pegasus kept on bucking; leaping, twisting, and kicking wildly. Obould found a rhythm in the frenzy, though, and gradually began to snap and jerk just a little less fiercely.

The pegasus began to slow in its gyrations and the orc king grinned at his realization that the beast was finally tiring. He took that moment to relax, just a bit, and smiled even more widely as he compared the pegasus's wild gyrations to those of Tsinka the night before. A fitting comparison, he lewdly thought.

Then he was flying, free of the pegasus's back, as the creature went into a sudden and violent frenzy. Obould hit the ground hard, face down and twisted, but he grunted it away and forced himself into a roll that allowed him to quickly regain some of his dignity, if not his feet. He looked around in alarm for just a moment, thinking that his grand exit might have lessened his image in the eyes of those nearby orcs. Indeed, they all stared at him incredulously—or stupidly, he could not tell the difference—and with such surprise that the handlers didn't even move for the pegasus.

And the equine beast came for the fallen orc king.

Obould put a wide grin on his face and leaped to his feet, arms wide, and gave a great roar, inviting the pegasus to battle.

The steed stopped short, and snorted and pawed the ground.

Obould began to laugh, shattering the tension, and he stalked right at the pegasus as if daring it to strike at him. The pegasus put its ears back and tensed up.

"Perhaps I should eat you," Obould said calmly, walking right up to the beast and staring it directly in the eye, which of course only set the pegasus even more on edge. "Yes, your flesh will taste tender, I am sure."

The orc king stared down the pegasus for a few moments longer, then swung around and gave a great laugh, and all the orcs nearby took up the cheer.

As soon as he was confident that he had restored any lost dignity, Obould turned back to the pegasus and thought again of Tsinka. He laughed all the louder as he mentally superimposed the equine face over that of the fierce and eager shaman, but while the snout and larger features greatly changed, it seemed to him that, other than the white about the edges of Tsinka's iris, their eyes were very much the same. Same intensity, same tension. Same wild and uncontrollable emotions.

No, not the same, Obould came to recognize, for while Tsinka's gyrations and sparkling eyes were wrought of passion and ecstasy, the winged horse's frenzy came from fear.

No, not fear—the notion hit Obould suddenly—not fear. It was no wild animal, just captured and in need of breaking. The mount had been ridden for years, and by elves, riders whose legs were too spindly to begin to hold if the pegasus didn't want them to stay on.

The pegasus's intensity came not from fear, but from sheer hatred.

"O, smart beast," Obould said softly, and the pegasus's ears came up and flattened again, as if it understood every word. "You hold loyalty to your master and hatred for me, who killed him. You will fight me forever if I try to climb onto your back, will you not?"

The orc king nodded and narrowed his eyes to closely scrutinize the pegasus.

"Or will you?" he asked, and his mind went in a different direction, as if he was seeing things from the pegasus's point of view.

The creature had purposefully lulled him into complacency up there on its back. It had seemingly calmed, and just when Obould had relaxed, it had gone wild again.

"You are not as clever as you believe," Obould said to the pegasus. "You should have waited until you had me up into the clouds before throwing me from your back. You should have made me believe that I was your master." The orc snorted, and wondered what pegasus flesh would taste like.

The handlers got the winged horse into complete control soon after, and the leader of the group turned to Obould and asked, "Will you be riding again this day, my god?"

Obould snickered at the ridiculous title, though he wouldn't openly discourage its use, and shook his head. "Much I have to do," he said.

He noted one of the orcs roughly tying the pegasus's back legs together.

"Enough!" he ordered, and the orc gang froze in place. "Treat the beast gently now, with due respect."

That brought a few incredulous expressions.

"Find new handlers!" Obould barked at the gang leader. "A soft touch for the mount now. No beatings!"

Even as he spoke the words, Obould saw the error of distracting the crew, for the pegasus lurched suddenly, shrugging a pair of orcs aside, then kicked out hard, scoring a solid hit on the forehead of the unfortunate orc who had been tying its hind legs. That orc flew away and began squirming on the ground and wailing piteously.

The other orcs instinctively moved to punish the beast, but Obould overruled that with a great shout of, *"Enough!"*

He stared directly at the pegasus, then again at the orc leader. "Any mark I find on this beast will be replicated on your own hide," he promised.

When the gang leader shrank down, visibly trembling, Obould knew his work was done. With a sidelong look of contempt at the badly injured fool still squirming on the ground, Obould walked away.

The surprise on the face of the frost giant sentries—fifteen feet tall, handsome, shapely behemoths—was no less than Obould had left behind with his orc companions when he'd informed them, to the shrill protests of Tsinka Shinriil among others, that he would visit Gerti Orelsdottr alone. There was no doubt about the bad blood between Gerti and Obould. In their last encounter, Obould had knocked the giantess to the ground, embarrassing and outraging her.

Obould kept his head high and his eyes straight ahead—and he wasn't even wearing the marvelously protective helmet that the shamans had somehow fashioned for him. Giants loomed all around him, many carrying swords that were taller than the orc king. As he neared the entrance to the huge cave Gerti had taken as temporary residence far south of her mountain home, the giant guards shifted to form a gauntlet before him. Two lines of sneering, imposing brutes glared down at him from every angle. As he passed them, the giants behind him turned in and followed, closing any possible escape route.

Obould let his greatsword rest easily on his back, kept his chin high, and even managed a grin to convey his confidence. He knew that he was surrendering the high ground, physically, but he knew, too, that he had to do just that to gain the high ground emotionally.

He noted a flurry of commotion just inside the cave, with huge shapes moving this way and that. And when he entered, his eyes adjusting to the sudden change of light as daylight diminished to the glow of just a few torches, he found that he didn't have to search far to gain his intended audience. Gerti Orelsdottr, beautiful and terrible by frost giant standards, stood at the back, eyeing him with something that seemed a cross of suspicion and contempt.

"It would seem that you have forgotten your entourage, King Obould," she said, and it seemed to Obould that she had weighted her voice with a hint of a threat.

He remained confident that she wouldn't act against him, though. He had defeated her in single combat, had, in effect, shamed her, and greater would her shame be among her people if she set others upon him in retribution. Obould didn't completely understand the frost giants, of course—his experiences with them were fairly limited—but he knew them to be legitimate warriors, and warriors almost always shared certain codes of honor.

Gerti's words had many of the giants in the room chuckling and whispering.

"I speak for all the thousands," the orc king replied. "As Dame Orelsdottr speaks for the frost giants of the Spine of the World."

Gerti straightened and narrowed her huge blue eyes—orbs that seemed all the richer in hue because of the bluish tint to the giantess's skin. "Then speak, King Obould. I have many preparations before me and little time to waste."

Obould let his posture relax, wanting to seem perfectly at ease. From the murmurs around him, he took satisfaction that he had hit just the right physical timbre. "We have achieved a great victory here, Dame Orelsdottr. We have taken the northland in as great a sweep as has ever been known."

"Our enemies have barely begun to rise against us," Gerti pointed out.

Obould conceded the point with a nod. "Do not deny our progress, I pray you," he said. "We have closed both doors of Mithral Hall. Nesmé is likely destroyed and the Surbrin secured. This is not the time for us to allow our alliance to . . ." He paused and slowly swiveled his head so that he spent a moment looking every giant in the room directly in the eye.

"Dame Orelsdottr, I speak for the orcs. Tens of thousands of orcs." He put added weight into that last, impressive, estimate. "You speak for the giants. Let us go to parlay in private."

Gerti assumed a pose that Obould had seen many times before, one both obstinate and pensive. She put one hand on her hip and turned, just enough to let her shapely legs escape the slit in her white dress, and she let her lips form into a pucker that might have been a pout and might have been that last moment of teasing before she reached out and throttled an enemy.

Obould answered that with a bow of respect.

"Come along," Gerti bade him, and when the giant nearest her started to protest, she silenced him with one of the fiercest scowls Obould had ever seen.

Yes, it was going splendidly, the orc king thought.

At Gerti's bidding, Obould followed her down a short corridor. The orc took a moment to study the walls that had been widened by the giants, obviously, with new cuts in the stone clearly showing. The ceiling, too, was much more than a natural formation, with all the low points chipped out so that the tallest of Gerti's minions could walk the length of the corridor without stooping. Impressive work, Obould thought, especially given the efficiency and speed with which it had been accomplished. He hadn't realized that the giants were so good at shaping the stone quickly, a revelation that he figured might be useful if he did indeed crash the gates into Mithral Hall.

The chamber at the end of the hall was obviously Gerti's own, for it was blocked by a heavy wooden door and appointed with many thick and lush bearskins. Gerti pointedly kicked several aside, leaving a spot of bare stone floor, and indicated that to be Obould's seat.

The orc king didn't question or complain, and was smiling still when he melted down to sit cross-legged, drawing out his greatsword as he descended. Its impressive length would not allow him to sit in that position with it still on his back. He lay the blade across his crossed legs, in easy reach, but he relaxed back and kept his hands far from it, offering not the slightest bit of a threat.

Gerti watched his every move closely, he recognized, though she was trying to feign indifference as she moved to close the door. She strode across the room to the thickest pile of furs and demurely sat herself down, which still had her towering over the lower-seated and much smaller orc king.

"What do you want of me, Obould?" Gerti bluntly asked, her tone short and crisp, her eyes unblinking.

"We were angered, both of us, at the return of King Bruenor and the loss of a great opportunity," Obould replied.

"At the loss of frost giants."

"And orcs for me—more than a thousand of my kin, my own son among them."

"Are not worth a single of my kin to me," Gerti replied.

Obould accepted the insult quietly, reminding himself to think long-term and not jump up and slaughter the witch.

"The dwarves value their kin no less than do we, Dame Orelsdottr," he said. "They claim no victory here."

"Many escaped."

"To a hole that has become a prison. To tunnels that perhaps already reek with the stench of troll."

"If Donnia Soldou and Ad'non Kareese were not dead, perhaps we could better sort out information concerning Proffit and his wretches," said Gerti, referring to two of the four drow elves who had been serving as advisors and scouts to her and to Obould, both of whom had been found dead north of their current position.

"Do you lament their deaths?"

The question gave Gerti pause, and she even betrayed her surprise with a temporary lift of her evenly trimmed eyebrows.

"They were using us for their own enjoyment and nothing more, you know that of course," Obould remarked.

Again, Gerti cocked her eyebrow, but held it there longer.

"Surprised?" the orc king added.

"They are drow," Gerti said. "They serve only themselves and their own desires. Of course I knew. Only a fool would have ever suspected differently."

But you are surprised that I knew, Obould thought, but did not say.

"And if the other two die with Proffit in the south, then so much the better," said Gerti.

"After we are done with them," said Obould. "The remaining drow will prove important if we intend to break through the defenses of Mithral Hall."

"Break through the defenses?"

Obould could hardly miss the incredulity in her voice, or the obvious doubt.

"I would take the hall."

"Your orcs will be slaughtered by the thousands."

"Whatever price we must pay will be worth the gain," Obould said, and he had to work hard to keep the very real doubts out of his voice. "We must continue to press our enemies before they can organize and coordinate their attacks. We have them on their heels, and I do not mean to allow them firm footing. And I will have Bruenor Battlehammer's head, at long last."

"You will crawl over the bodies of orcs to get to him, then, but not the bodies of frost giants."

Obould accepted that with a nod, confident that if he managed to take the upper tunnels of Mithral Hall, Gerti would fall into line.

"I need your kin only to break through the outer shell," he said.

"There are ways to dislodge the greatest of doors," an obviously and suddenly intrigued Gerti remarked.

"The sooner you crack the shell, the sooner I will have King Bruenor's head."

Gerti chuckled and nodded her agreement. Obould realized, of course, that she was likely more intrigued by the prospect of ten thousand dead orcs than of any defeat to the dwarves.

Obould used the great strength in his legs to lift him up from his seated position, to stand straight, as he swept his sword back over his shoulder and into its sheath. He returned Gerti's nod and walked out, holding fast to his cocky swagger as he passed through the waiting lines of giant guards.

Despite that calm and confident demeanor, though, Obould's insides churned. Gerti would swing into swift action, of course, and Obould had little doubt that she would deliver him and his army into the hall, but even as he pondered the execution of his request, the thought of it gnawed at him. Once again, Obould envisioned orc fortresses dotting every hilltop of the region, with defensible walls forcing any attackers to scramble for every inch of ground. How many dwarves and elves and humans would have to lie dead among those hilltops before the wretched triumvirate gave up their thoughts of dislodging him and accepted his conquest as final? How many dwarves and elves and humans would Obould have to kill before his orcs were allowed their kingdom and their share of the bounty of the wider world?

Many, he hoped, for he so enjoyed killing dwarves, elves, and humans.

As he exited the cave and was afforded a fairly wide view of the northern expanses, Obould let his gaze meander over each stony mountain and windblown slope. His mind's eye built those castles, all flying the pennants of the One-Eyed God and of King Many-Arrows. In the shadows below them, in the sheltered dells, he envisioned towns—towns like Shallows, sturdy and secure, only inhabited by orcs and not smelly humans. He began to draw connections, trade routes and responsibilities, riches and power, respect and influence.

It would work, Obould believed. He could carve out his kingdom and secure it beyond any hopes the dwarves, elves, and humans might ever hold of dislodging him.

The orc king glanced back at Gerti's cave, and considered for a fleeting moment the possibility of going in and telling her. He even half-turned and started to take a step that way.

He stopped, though, thinking that Gerti would not appreciate the weight of his vision, nor care much for the end result. And even if she did, Obould realized, how might Tsinka and the shamans react? Tsinka was calling for conquest and not settlement, and she claimed to hold in her ears the voice of Gruumsh himself.

Obould's upper lip curled in frustration, and he let his clenched fist rise up beside him. He hadn't lied to Gerti. He wanted nothing more than to hold Bruenor Battlehammer's heart in his hands.

But was it possible, and was the prize, as he had claimed, really worth the no-doubt horrific cost?

4

A KING'S EYE VIEW

To all in the chamber, the torchlight did not seem so bright, its flickering flames did not dance so joyously. Perhaps it was the realization that the doors were closed and that the meager light was all that separated the whole of the great dwarven complex of Mithral Hall from absolute darkness. The dwarves and others could get out, of course. They had tunnels that led to the south and the edge of the Trollmoors, though there had reportedly been some fighting down there already. They had tunnels that would take them as far west as Mirabar, and right under the River Surbrin to the east, to places like Citadel Felbarr. None of those were easy routes, though, and all involved breaking into that vast labyrinth known as the Underdark, the place of dark denizens and untold horrors.

So Mithral Hall seemed a darker place, and the torches less inviting, and less frequent. King Bruenor had already ordered conservation, preparing himself for what surely seemed to be a long, long siege.

Bruenor sat on a throne of stone, thickly padded with rich green and purple cloth. His great and wild beard seemed more orange than red under the artificial lighting, perhaps because those long hairs had become noticeably more infested with strands of gray since the dwarf king's ordeal. For many days, Bruenor had lain close to death. Even the greatest clerics of Mithral Hall had only thought him alive through their nearly continual healing spells, cast upon a body, they believed, whose host had forsaken it. Bruenor, the essence of the dwarf, his very soul, had gone to his just reward in the Halls of Moradin, by the reckoning of the priests. And there, so it was supposed, Regis the halfling steward had found him, using the magic of his enchanted ruby pendant. Regis had caught what little flicker of life remaining in Bruenor's eyes and somehow used the magic to send his thoughts and his pleas for Bruenor to return to the land of the living.

For no king would lie so still if he knew that his people were in such dire need.

Thus had Bruenor returned, and the dwarves had found their way home, albeit over the bodies of many fallen comrades.

Those gray hairs seemed to all who knew him well to be the only overt sign of Bruenor's ordeal. His dark eyes still sparkled with energy and his square shoulders promised to carry the whole of Mithral Hall upon them, if need be. He was bandaged in a dozen places, for in the last retreat into the hall, he had suffered terrible wounds—injuries that would have felled a lesser dwarf—but if any of those wounds caused him the slightest discomfort, he did not show it.

He was dressed in his battle-worn armor, creased and torn and scratched, and had his prized shield, emblazoned with the foaming mug standard of his clan, resting against the side of his throne, his battle-axe leaning atop it and showing the notches of its seasons, chips from stone, armor, and ogre skulls alike.

"All who seen yer blast just shake their heads when they try to describe it," Bruenor said to Nanfoodle Buswilligan, the gnome alchemist from Mirabar.

Nanfoodle stepped nervously from foot to foot, and that only made the stout dwarf lean closer to him.

"Come on now, little one," Bruenor coaxed. "We got no time for humility nor nervousness. Ye done great, by all accounts, and all in the hall're bowing to ye in respect. Ye stand tall among us, don't ye know?"

Nanfoodle did seem to straighten a bit at that, tilting his head back slightly so that he looked up at the imposing dwarf upon the dais. Nanfoodle twitched again as his long, crooked, pointy nose actually brushed Bruenor's similarly imposing proboscis.

"What'd ye do?" Bruenor asked him again. "They're saying ye brought hot air up from under Keeper's Dale."

"I . . . *we* . . ." Nanfoodle corrected, and he turned to regard some of the others, including Pikel Bouldershoulder, the most unusual dwarf who had come from Carradoon on the shores of faraway Impresk Lake.

Nanfoodle nodded as Pikel smiled widely and punched his one fist up into the air, mouthing a silent, "Oo oi!"

The gnome cleared his throat and turned back squarely upon Bruenor, who settled back in his chair. "We used metal tubing to bring the hot air up from below, yes," the gnome confirmed. "Torgar Hammerstriker and his boys cleared the tunnels under the ridge of orcs and painted it tight with pitch. We just directed the hot air into those tunnels, and when Catti-brie's arrow ignited it all . . ."

"*Boom!*" shouted Pikel Bouldershoulder, and all eyes turned to him in surprise.

"Hee hee hee," the green-bearded Pikel said with a shy shrug, and all the grim folk in the room joined in on the much-needed laugh.

It proved a short respite, though, the weight of their situation quickly pressing back upon them.

"Well, ye done good, gnome," Bruenor said. "Ye saved many o' me kin, and that's from the mouth o' Banak Brawnanvil himself. And he's not one to throw praise undeserved."

"We—Shoudra and I—felt the need to prove ourselves, King Bruenor," said Nanfoodle. "And we wanted to help, any way we could. Your people have shown such generosity to Torgar and Shingles, and all the other Mirabarran—"

"Mirabarran, no more," came a voice, Torgar's voice, from the side. "We are Battlehammer now, one and all. We name not Marchion Elastul as our enemy, unless an enemy he makes of us, but neither are we loyal to the throne of Mirabar. Nay, our hearts, our souls, our fists, our hammers, for King Bruenor!"

A great cheer went up in the hall, started by the dozen or so formerly Mirabarran dwarves in attendance, and taken up by all standing around the room.

Bruenor basked in that communal glow for a bit, welcoming it as a needed ray of light on that dark day. And indeed, the day was dark in Mithral Hall, as dark as the corridors of the Underdark, as dark as a drow priestess's heart. Despite the efforts, the sacrifice, the gallantry of all the dwarves, of Catti-brie and Wulfgar, despite the wise choices of Regis in his time as steward, they had been put in their hole, sealed in their tunnels, by a foe that Mithral Hall could not hope to overcome on an open field of battle. Hundreds of Bruenor's kin were dead, and more than a third of the Mirabarran refugees had fallen.

Bruenor had entertained a line of important figures that day, from Tred McKnuckles of Felbarr, stung by the loss of his dear friend Nikwillig, to the Bouldershoulder brothers, Ivan and the indomitable Pikel, giggling always and full of cheer despite the loss of his arm. Bruenor had gone to see Banak Brawnanvil, the warcommander who had so brilliantly held the high ground north of Keeper's Dale for days on end against impossible odds. For Banak could not come to him. Sorely wounded in the final escape, insisting on being the last off the cliff, Banak no longer had any use of his legs. An orc spear had severed his backbone, so said the priests, and there was nothing their healing spells could do to fix it. He was in his bed that day, awaiting the completion of a comfortable chair on wheels that would allow him a bit of mobility.

Bruenor had found Banak in a dour mood, but with his fighting spirit intact. He had been more concerned about those who had fallen than with his own wounds, as Bruenor expected. Banak was a Brawnanvil, after all, of a line as sturdy as Battlehammer's own, strong of arm and of spirit, and with loyalty unmatched. Banak had been physically crippled, no doubt, but Bruenor knew that the warcommander was hardly out of the fight, wherever that fight may be.

Nanfoodle's audience marked the end of the announced procession that day, and so Bruenor dismissed the gnome and excused himself. He had one more meeting in mind, one, he knew, that was better made in private.

Leaving his escort—Thibbledorf Pwent had insisted that a pair of Gutbusters accompany the dwarf king wherever he went—at the end of one dimly lit corridor, Bruenor moved to a door, gently knocked, then pushed it open.

He found Regis sitting at his desk, chin in one hand the other holding a quill above an open parchment that was trying to curl against the press of mug-shaped paperweights. Bruenor nodded and entered, taking a seat on the edge of the halfling's soft bed.

"Ye don't seem to be eatin' much, Rumblebelly," he remarked with a grin. Bruenor reached under his tunic and pulled forth a thick piece of cake. He casually tossed it to Regis, who caught it and set it down without taking

760

a bite. "Bah, but ye keep that up and I'm to call ye Rumblebones!" Bruenor blustered. "Go on, then!" he demanded, motioning to the cake.

"I'm writing it all down," Regis assured him, and he brushed aside one of the paperweights and lifted the edge of the parchment, which caused a bit of the recently placed ink to streak. Noting this, Regis quickly flattened the parchment and began to frantically blow upon it.

"Ain't nothing there that ye can't be telling me yerself," Bruenor said.

Finally, the halfling turned back to him.

"What's yer grief then, Rumblebelly?" asked the dwarf. "Ye done good—damn good, by what me generals been telling me."

"So many died," Regis replied, his voice barely a whisper.

"Aye, that's the pain o' war."

"But I kept them out there," the halfling explained, leaping up from his chair, his short, stocky arms waving all around. He began to pace back and forth, muttering with every step as if trying to find some way to blurt out all of his pain in one burst. "Up on the cliff. I could have ordered Banak back in, long before the final fight. How many would still be alive?"

"Bah, ye're asking questions that ain't got no answers!" Bruenor roared at him. "Anyone can lead the fight the day after it's done. It's leading the fight *during* the fight that's marking yer worth."

"I could have brought them in," the halfling stated. "I should have brought them in."

"Ah, but ye knew the truth of the orc force, did ye? Ye knew that ten thousand would add to their ranks and sweep into the dale from the west, did ye?"

Regis blinked repeatedly, but did not answer.

"Ye knew nothing more than anyone else, Banak included," Bruenor insisted. "And Banak wasn't keen on coming down that cliff. In the end, when we learned the truth of our enemy, we salvaged what we could, and that's plenty, but not as much as we wanted to hold. We gived them the whole of the northland don't ye see? And that's nothing any Battlehammer's proud to admit."

"There were too many . . ." Regis started, eliciting another loud "Bah!" from Bruenor.

"We ran away, Rumblebelly! Clan Battlehammer retreated from orcs!"

"There were too many!"

Bruenor smiled and nodded, showing Regis that he had just been played like a dwarven fiddle. "Course there were, and so we took what we could get, but don't ye ever think that running from orcs was something meself'd order unless no other choice was afore me. No other choice! I'd've kept Banak out there, Rumblebelly. I'd've been out there with him, don't ye doubt!"

Regis looked up at Bruenor and gave a nod of appreciation.

"Questions for us now are, what next?" said Bruenor. "Do we go back out and fight them again? Out to the east, mayhaps, to open a line across the Surbrin? Out to the south, so we can sweep back around?"

"The south," Regis muttered. "I sent fifty to the south, accompanying Galen Firth of Nesmé."

"Catti-brie told me all about it, and in that, too, ye did well, by me own reckoning. I got no love for them Nesmé boys after the way they treated us them years ago and after the way they ignored Settlestone. Bunch o' stoneheads, if e'er I seen a bunch o' stoneheads! But a neighbor's a neighbor, and ye got to help do what ye can do, and from where I'm seeing it, ye did all that ye could do."

"But we can do more now," Regis offered.

Bruenor scratched his red beard and thought on that a moment. "Might that we can," he agreed. "A few hundred more moving south might open new possibilities, too. Good thinking." He looked to Regis as he finished, and noted happily that the halfling seemed to have shaken off his burden then, an eager gleam coming back into his soft brown eyes.

"Send Torgar and the boys from Mirabar," Regis suggested. "They're a fine bunch, and they know how to fight aboveground as well as below."

Bruenor wasn't sure if he agreed with that assessment. Perhaps Torgar, Shingles, and all the dwarves of Mirabar had seen enough fighting and had taken on enough special and difficult assignments already. Maybe it was time for them to take some rest inside Mithral Hall proper, mingling with the dwarves who had lived in those corridors and chambers since the complex had been reclaimed from Shimmergloom the shadow dragon and his duergar minions years before.

Bruenor gave no indication to Regis that he was doubting the wisdom of the suggestion, though. The halfling had proven himself many times over in the last tendays, by all accounts, and his insight and understanding was a resource Bruenor had no intention of squashing.

"Come along, Rumblebelly," he said with a toothy grin. "Let's go see how Ivan and Pikel are getting on. Might be that they know allies we haven't yet considered."

"Cadderly?"

"Was thinking more of the elves of the Moonwood," Bruenor explained. "Seems them two came through there on their way to Mithral Hall. I'm thinking it'd be a good thing to get them elves putting arrows and magic across the Surbrin to soften our enemy's entrenchment."

"How would we get word to them?" Regis asked. "The elves, I mean. Do we have tunnels that go that far east and north?"

"How'd Pikel get him and Ivan there in the first place?" Bruenor replied with an exaggerated wink. "By Ivan's telling, it's got something to do with trees and roots. We ain't got no trees, but we got plenty o' roots, I'm thinking."

Regis put on his best Pikel voice when he replied, "Hee hee hee."

Tred McKnuckles emphatically raised a finger to his pursed lips, reminding the dwarven catapult team that silence was essential.

Bellan Brawnanvil mimicked the movement back to Tred in agreement and tapped his sideslinger pull crew to ease up on their movements as they worked to set the basket. Mounted on the side of the jamb of a hallway door, the sideslinger catapult served as the staple war engine of the outer defenses of Mithral Hall. Its adjustable arm length made it the perfect war engine to fit any situation, and in the east, so close to the great flowing river that the stones continually hummed with the reverberations of its currents, the catapults were front-line and primary. For just beyond the group's present position in the eastern reaches of the complex, the tunnels dived down into the wilds of the Underdark. Even in times of peace, the eastern sideslingers were often put to use, chasing back umber hulks or displacer beasts, or any of the other dark denizens of those lightless corridors.

By his own request, Tred had come down for duty right after the door to Keeper's Dale had been sealed, for the position oversaw those tunnels that connected Mithral Hall, through the upper Underdark, to Citadel Felbarr, Tred's home. From that very spot, a location where an ironbound door that could be quickly and tightly sealed, emissaries from Steward Regis had gone out to gain audience with King Emerus Warcrown of Citadel Felbarr, to tell Emerus the tale of Tred and Nikwillig, and his missing caravan.

Tred had remained there for many hours, taking double shifts, and staying even when he was not on watch. The only time he'd gone back to the main halls of Clan Battlehammer's complex had been that very day, for he had been summoned to meet with King Bruenor. He had just returned from that meeting, to find his companions all astir at reports of movement in the east.

Tred stood with them anxiously and thought, Is this the front end of yet another attack by Obould's masses? Some monstrous Underdark creature coming forth in search of a meal? The return of the emissaries, perhaps?

Beyond the door, the tunnel sloped down into a roughly circular natural chamber that branched off in several directions. Ready to turn that chamber into a killing ground, the dwarves opposite the sideslinger readied several kegs of highly flammable oil. At the first sign of trouble, the dwarves would lead, rolling the barrels down into the lower room, contents spilling on the floor, then the sideslinger would let fly a wad of burning pitch.

Bellan Brawnanvil signaled Tred and the barrel-rollers that the catapult was ready, and all the dwarves hushed, more than one falling to the floor and putting an ear to the stone.

They heard a sound below, from one of the tunnels off the circular chamber.

A barrel was silently brought into place at the top of the ramp and an eager young dwarf put his shoulder behind it, ready to send it bouncing down.

Tred peered anxiously around the door jamb above that barrel, straining his eyes in the darkness. He caught the flicker of torchlight.

So did the dwarf behind the barrel, and he gave a little yelp and started to shove.

But Tred stopped him before he ever began, waggling a finger at him and fixing him with a scowl. A moment later, all were glad that he did, for they heard, "Bah, ye great snorter of pig-sweat, ye turned us all about again!"

"Did not, yer mother's worst mistake! This ain't no chamber we been through."

"Been through and been out four times, ye dolt!"

"Ain't not!"

Tred and the dwarves around him grinned widely.

"Well, if ye been through four times, then ye been through with a lot less racket than ye're making now, ye fat-bellied bearded bunch o' archery targets!" Tred hollered.

Below him, the chamber went silent, and the light quickly flickered out.

"Oh, so now ye're the sneaky things?" Tred asked. "Step up and be recognized, be ye Warcrown or Battlehammer!"

"Warcrown!" came a shout from below, a voice that sparked some recognition in Tred.

"Battlehammer!" said another, and the dwarves in the room recognized it as Sindel Muffinhead, one of the emissaries sent out by Steward Regis, a young acolyte, and expert pie baker, who named the now famous Cordio as his older brother.

Torches flared to life below and several figures moved into sight, then began stomping up the ramp. As they neared, Tred noted an old friend.

"Jackonray Broadbelt!" he called. "Been a halfling's meal and more since I last seen ye!"

"Tred, me friend!" replied Jackonray, leading the way into the room for his seven companions, including Sindel, but not the other emissary.

Jackonray wore heavy armor with dark gray metal plates set on thick leather. His helm was bowl-shaped and ridged, and topped a shock of gray hair that reached out wildly from beneath its metal hem. Jackonray's beard was not so unkempt, though, and was streaked with hair the color of gold and lines the color of silver, braided together to give the dwarf a very distinctive and distinguished appearance. In accord with his surname, his girdle was wide and decorated with sparkling jewels. He rested the elbow of his weapon arm on it as he continued, "Sorry I am to hear o' yer brother." He patted Tred hard on the shoulder with a hand that seemed as hard as stone.

"Aye, Duggan was a good friend."

"And a loyal companion. A tribute to yer family."

Tred reached up and solemnly squeezed Jackonray's thick and strong arm.

"Ye come from King Emerus, then, and with good news, I'm thinking," Tred remarked a moment later. "Let's get ye to King Bruenor."

"Aye, straightaways."

The pair and Sindel moved off at a swift pace, the other Felbarran dwarves falling in line behind them. As they wound through the more populated reaches of Mithral Hall, more than a few Battlehammer dwarves took up the march, as well, so that by the time they crossed through the great Undercity and climbed along the main tunnels leading to Bruenor's chamber, nearly fifty dwarves formed the procession, many of them chatting amongst themselves, exchanging information about their respective strongholds. Other runners went far ahead to announce them to Bruenor long before they arrived.

"Where's Nikwillig, then?" asked Jackonray, rolling along at Tred's side.

"Still out there in the North," Tred explained, and there was no mistaking the sudden graveness to his tone. "Nikwillig went out to the mountains in the east to send back a signal, and he knew in doing it that he'd not easily get back into Mithral Hall. Felt he—we, owed it to Bruenor, since he done so much to help us avenge our lost kin."

"Seems proper," said Jackonray. "But if he's not in now, he's likely dead."

"Aye, but he died a hero," said Tred. "And no dwarf's ever asking more than that."

"What more than that might ye ask?" asked Jackonray.

"Here, here," added Sindel.

When the troupe arrived at Bruenor's audience chamber door, they found it wide open, with the dwarf king inside on his throne, awaiting their arrival.

"King Bruenor, I give ye Jackonray Broadbelt," Tred said with a bow. "Of the Hornriver Broadbelts, first cousins to King Emerus Warcrown himself. Jackonray here's King Warcrown's own nephew, and a favored one at that. Sixth in line for the throne, by last count, behind King Emerus's five sons."

"Sixth or twenty-fifth, depending upon King Warcrown's disposition," Jackonray said with a wink. "He's one for keeping us guessing."

"Aye, and a smart choice that's always been," said Bruenor.

"Yer ambassadors're telling me King Emerus that ye've come against Obould Many-Arrows," Jackonray said.

"One and the same, by all I'm hearing."

"Well, King Bruenor, know that Obould's a smart one, as orcs go. Ye take great care in handling this snortsnout."

"He sealed me and me kin inside the hall," Bruenor explained. "Shut the east door by the Surbrin."

"Felbarr scouts have seen as much," Jackonray said. "And them giants and orcs're building defenses all along the river's western bank."

"And they drove me kin in from the western door, in Keeper's Dale," Bruenor admitted. "I'd not thought that Clan Battlehammer could be put underground by a bunch o' stinkin' orcs, but what a bunch it is. Thousands and thousands."

"And led by one that knows how to fight," said Jackonray. "Know in yer heart, King Bruenor, that if Obould's got ye in here, then Obould's thinking to come in after ye."

"That'll cost him."

"Dearly, I'm sure, good King Bruenor."

"They been fighting in the south tunnels a bit already," Bruenor reported. "With smelly trolls and not orcs, but the battling's not so heavy."

Jackonray stroked his silver and gold beard. "Lady Alustriel of Silverymoon's been sending out the word of a wide push from the Trollmoors. One that's threatened all the lands south of here. It's as big a fight as we thought we'd ever be seeing, don't ye doubt. But know that Obould's not to let it sit, and not to let you sit. By all me experience in fighting that dog, and I've had more than ye know, if there's fighting in the south, then prepare for something bigger from the north, east, or west. Obould's got you in a hole, but he's not to let you stay, even if it costs him every orc, goblin, and giant he can find."

"Stupid orcs," Tred muttered.

"Aye, and that's just why they're so dangerous," Bruenor said. He looked from the two dwarves to his own advisors, then back at Jackonray directly. "Well, then, what's coming from Felbarr?"

"I appreciate yer bluntness," Jackonray said with another low bow. "And I'm here to tell ye not to doubt us. Felbarr's behind ye to the last, King Bruenor. All our gold and all our dwarves. Right now we got hundreds working the tunnels under the Surbrin, securing the line all the way from Mithral Hall to Felbarr. We'll have them open and secure, don't ye doubt."

Bruenor nodded his gratitude, but at the same time motioned with his hand that he wanted to hear more.

"We'll set it as a trade and supply route," Jackonray went on. "King Emerus told me to tell yerself that we'll work as agents for Mithral Hall in yer time o' need, no commission taken."

That brought a concerned look to Bruenor's face, and it was a look mirrored on all the Battlehammers in attendance.

"Ye're to need to get yer goods to market, and so we'll be yer market," Jackonray stated.

"Ye're sounding like we're to give Obould all that he's got and let him keep it," Bruenor voiced.

For the first time since the meeting commenced, Jackonray seemed a bit less than sure of himself.

"No, we're not for that, but King Emerus is thinking that it's to take some time to push the orcs back," Jackonray explained.

"And when time's come to do the pushing?"

"If it comes to fighting, then we'll shore up yer ranks, shoulder to shoulder," Jackonray insisted. "Know in yer Delzoun heart, King Bruenor, that Felbarr's with ye, dwarf to dwarf. When the fighting's starting, we'll be with ye. And not just Felbarr, don't ye doubt, though it'll take Citadel Adbar longer to mobilize her thousands."

The show of solidarity touched Bruenor deeply, to be sure, but he didn't miss the equivocation to Jackonray's remark. The other leaders of the region had taken note of the orc march, indeed, but there was apparently some discussion going on about what they should, or even could, do about it.

"In the meanwhile, we'll get those tunnels opened and safe for ye to move yer goods through to Felbarr and out to market," Jackonray offered, and Bruenor, who hadn't even entertained such a thought, who hadn't even begun to resign himself to that grim possibility, merely nodded.

"That orc was something . . . beyond any orc," Wulfgar remarked. With a frame closer to seven feet than six, and hardened in the wilderness of the tundra of Icewind Dale, the barbarian was as strong as any man, and so he thought, stronger than any orc. But the brutish creature who had cut Shoudra Stargleam in half had taught Wulfgar better, tossing the barbarian aside with a shrug. "It was as if I was pushing against a falling mountainside."

Catti-brie understood his shock and distress. It wasn't often that Wulfgar, son of Beornegar, had been bested in a test of sheer strength. Even giants had not thrown him aside with such seeming ease. "They're saying it was Obould Many-Arrows, himself," she replied.

"He and I will meet again," Wulfgar vowed, his crystalline blue eyes sparkling at the thought.

Catti-brie limped up beside him and gently brushed his long blond hair from the side of his face, forcing him to turn and look at her directly.

"You don't be doing anything foolhardy," she said softly. "We'll get Obould, don't you doubt, but we'll get him in the proper order of business. We'll get him as we'll get all of them, and there's no room for personal vengeance here. Bigger stakes than pride."

Wulfgar snickered and smiled. "True enough," he replied, "and yet, you're not believing the words any more than you're expecting me to believe them. You want that ugly one in your bow-sight again, as much as I want him now that I understand what to expect from him."

Catti-brie tried hard not to smile back at the barbarian, but she knew that her rich blue eyes were shining as brightly as Wulfgar's. "Oh, I'm wanting him," she admitted. "But not so much with me bow."

She led his gaze with her own down to the fabulous sword sheathed on her left hip. Khazid'hea, "Cutter," as it was called, a name that surely fit. Catti-brie had put that blade through solid stone. Could any armor, even the wondrous suit encasing Obould Many-Arrows, turn its keen edge?

Both of them seemed to realize then that they were but inches apart, close enough to feel the warmth of each other's breath.

Catti-brie broke the tension first, reaching up and playfully tousling Wulfgar's wild shock of hair, then hopping up to her tip-toes and giving him a kiss on the cheek—the kiss of a friend, and nothing more.

In its own way, that was a defining moment for her.

Wulfgar's reciprocating grin, though, seemed a bit less than certain.

"So we're thinking we should be getting scouts out through the chimneys," came a voice from behind Catti-brie, and she turned around to see her adoptive father Bruenor entering the room, Regis in tow. "We got to know what our enemies are thinking if we're to counter them properly."

"They're orcs," Wulfgar said. "Betting would say that they're not thinking much."

His attempt at humor would have been more successful if that last maneuver of the orc army had not been so fresh in all their minds, the deceptive swing behind the mountain spurs to the west that brought the bulk of their force in behind Banak's charges, nearly spelling disaster for the dwarves.

"We can't be knowing a thing about them orcs unless we're seeing it ourselfs," Bruenor remarked. "I'm not for underestimating this one again."

Regis shifted uncomfortably.

"I'm thinking that we scored a bigger victory than we realized," Catti-brie was quick to remark. "We won the day out there, though our losses surely hurt."

"Seems to me like we're the ones in our hole," Bruenor replied.

"But it's seeming to me that we could not've done better," reasoned the woman, and she looked directly at the halfling, her expression showing her approval. "If we'd've come right in, then we'd not now know what's come against us. What straights might we soon find ourselves in if you had acted otherwise, if we had run from the ridge straightaway? Would we truly understand the size and ferocity of the force that's arrayed against us? Would we have delivered so powerful a blow against our enemy? They've come to fight us, and so we'll be fighting, don't you doubt, and better that we understand what we're fighting, and better that we've laid so many low already. Thanks to Nanfoodle and the others, we've killed them as overwhelmingly as we could ever have hoped thus far, even if all the fighting had been in our own defended tunnels."

"Ye got the right way o' seeing things, girl," Bruenor agreed after a pause to digest the reasoning. "If they're thinking to come in against us, at least now we're knowing what they got to throw our way."

"So hold our heads high and hold our weapons all the tighter," Wulfgar chimed in.

"Oo oi!" said Regis, and everyone looked at him curiously.

"What's that meaning, anyway?" asked Catti-brie.

Regis shrugged. "Just sounded right," he explained, and no one disagreed.

TOO HIGH A CEILING

Galen Firth paced furiously, every stride showing his mounting impatience. He muttered under his breath, taking care to keep his curses quiet enough so that they wouldn't disturb the dwarves, who were huddled together in a great circle, each with his arms over the shoulders of those beside him. Heads down, the bearded folk offered prayers to Moradin for the souls of Fender and Bonnerbas. They had run a long way from the hole they had cut out of the tunnels to escape the troll ambush, but they were still outdoors, sheltered within a copse of fir trees from a heavy rain that had come up.

When the dwarves had finished—*finally* finished, to Galen's thinking—General Dagna wasted no time in marching over to the human.

"We'll be considering our course this night," the dwarf informed him. "More'n a few're thinking it's past time we got back into tunnels."

"We just got chased out of tunnels," Galen reminded him.

"Aye, but not them kind o' tunnels. We're looking for tunnels deep, tunnels o' worked stone—tunnels to give a dwarf something worth holding onto. No trolls're gonna push Battlehammer dwarves out of stone tunnels, don't ye doubt!"

"You're forgetting our course and our reason for being here."

"Them trolls're onto us," Dagna replied. "They'll catch up to us soon enough, and ye know it."

"Indeed, if we continue to stop and pray every . . ." Galen's voice trailed off as he considered Dagna's expression and realized that he was going over the line.

"I'll forgive ye that, but just this once," the dwarf warned. "I'm knowin' that ye're hurting for yer losses. We're all knowin' that. But we're running out o' time. If we're staying here much longer, then don't ye be thinking we'll find our way back to our home anytime soon."

"What do you mean to do?"

Dagna turned around slowly, surveying the landscape. "We'll head west, to that high ridge there," he said, pointing to a line of elevated ground some miles distant. "From there we'll take us the best look we can find. Might be that we'll see yer people. Might be that we won't."

"And if we don't, then you intend to turn back for Mithral Hall."

"No other choice's afore me."

"And where for Galen, then?" the man asked.

"Wherever Galen's choosing to go," Dagna answered. "Ye've proven yerself in a fight, to me and me boys. They'll keep ye along, and not a one's to complain. But it might be that ye cannot do that. Might be that Galen's got to stay and look, and die, if that's to be. Might be that Galen's doing better by his folk if he goes off to Silverymoon or some other town that's not being pressed by orcs and can spare more of an army. Choice is yer own."

Galen rubbed a hand over his face, feeling stubble that was fast turning into a thick beard. He wanted to yell and scream at Dagna, truly he did, but he knew that the dwarf was offering him all that he could under the present conditions. Somehow, the trolls were dogging them, and would find them again. How many times could Dagna and his small force hope to escape?

"We begin our march to the ridge this very night?"

"See no reason to be waiting," Dagna replied.

Galen nodded and let it go at that. He got his gear collected and his boots tightened as the dwarves formed up for their march. He tried to focus on the present, on the duty before him, for he knew that if he tried to think ahead, his resolve would likely crumble. For every question in Galen Firth's life at that point seemed to begin with, "What if?"

"I will not tolerate a retreat into the tunnels until we have discovered the disposition of my people!" Galen Firth grumbled as he pulled himself over the last rise of rock to the top of the windswept ridgeline. The man brushed himself off and stared at Dagna, looking for some reaction to his insistence, but found the dwarf strangely distracted, and looking off toward the southwest.

"Wha—?" Galen asked, the word catching in his throat as he turned to follow the dwarf's line of sight, to see the light of fires—campfires, perhaps—in the distance.

"Might be we done just that," Dagna said.

More dwarves came up around them, all hopping and pointing excitedly to the distant lights.

"Durn fools to be lighting so bright a burn with trolls all about," one dwarf remarked, and others nodded their agreement, or started to, until Dagna, noting the erratic movements of the flames, cut them short.

"Them fires're against the trolls!" the general realized. "They got themselves a fight down there!"

"We must go to them!" cried Galen.

"A mile. . . ." a dwarf observed.

"Of tough ground," another added.

"Mark the stars and run on, then!" General Dagna ordered.

The dwarves lined up the fires with the celestial constants, and began to stream fast down the back side of the ridge. Galen Firth sprinted off ahead of the pack, foolishly so, for his human eyes weren't very good in the darkness. Before he'd gone half a dozen strides, the man tripped and stumbled, then ran face long into a tree branch and staggered backward. He would have fallen to the ground had not Dagna arrived with open arms to catch him.

"Ye stay right beside me, long legs," the dwarf ordered. "We'll get ye there!"

With their short, muscled legs, dwarves were not the fastest runners in the Realms, but no race could match their stamina and determination. The force rolled past and over rocks and logs, and when one tripped, others caught him, up righted him, and kept him moving swiftly along his way.

They charged along some lower ground, splashed through some unseen puddles and scrambled through a tangle of birch trees and brush, a snarl that got so thick at one point that several dwarves brought forth their axes and began chopping with abandon. As they came through that last major obstacle, the lights of the fires clearly visible directly ahead, Galen Firth began to hear the cries of battle. Shouts for support and calls of pain and rage split the night, and Galen's heart sank as he realized that many of those calls were not coming from warriors, but from women, children, and elderly folk.

He didn't know what to expect when he and Dagna crashed through the last line of brush and onto the battlefield, though he surely expected the worst scenario, a helter skelter slaughter ground with his people trapped into small groups that could offer only meager resistance. He began to urge Dagna to form up a defensive ring, a shell of dwarves to protect his people, but when they came in sight of the actual fighting, Galen's words caught in his throat, and his heart soared with renewed hope.

His people, the hearty folk of Nesmé, were fighting hard and fighting well.

"They're in a double ellipse," one dwarf coming in behind remarked, referring to a very intricate defensive formation, and one, Galen knew, that the riders of Nesmé had often employed along the broken, tree-speckled ground north of the Trollmoors. In the double ellipse, two elongated rings of warriors formed end-to-end with a single joining point between them. Worked harmoniously, the formation was one of complete support, with every angle of battle offering a striking zone to more defenders than attackers. But it was also a risky formation, for if it failed at any point, the aggressors would have the means to isolate and utterly destroy entire sections of the defending force.

So far, it seemed to be holding, but barely, and only because the defenders employed many, many flaming torches, waving them wildly to fend off the trolls and their even more stupid partners, the treelike bog blokes.

"Dead trees must fall!" Galen shouted when he realized that the common allies of the wretched trolls were among the attackers. For bog blokes resembled nothing more than a small and skeletal dead tree, with twisted arms appearing as stubby limbs.

As he spoke, the man noted one part of the Nesmé line in serious jeopardy, as a pair of young men, boys really, fell back before the snarling and devastating charge of a particularly large and nasty troll. Galen broke away from the dwarves and veered straight for the troll's back, his sword leading. He hit the unwitting creature at a full run, driving his sword right through the beast and making it lurch forward wildly. To their credit, the two young men didn't break ranks and flee, but just dodged aside of the lurching troll, then came right back in beside its swiping arms, smacking at it with their torches, the fires bubbling the troll's mottled green and gray skin.

Galen pulled his blade free and spun just in time to fend off the clawing hands of another troll, and another that came in beside it. Hard-pressed, and with the troll he had skewered behind him hardly out of the fighting, Galen feared that he would meet an abrupt end. He breathed a bit easier when the troll before him and to his left lurched over suddenly and tumbled away. As it fell, a heavy dwarven axe came up over its bending head and drove it down more forcefully. That dwarf pressed on, right past Galen to take on the wounded beast behind the man, while another dwarf leaped into view atop the fallen troll, using it as a springboard to launch him headlong into the other troll standing in front of Galen. His flying tackle took the beast around the waist, and as he swung about, the dwarf twisted his body to give him some leverage across the troll's lower half. The dwarf tugged mightily with his short, muscled arms, his momentum taking him right past the surprised troll. When the diminutive bearded warrior used that momentum, combined with his powerful arms, he compelled the troll to follow, the creature rolling right over him as he fell.

"Give me yer torch!" Galen heard the first dwarf cry to someone in the defensive line.

Galen turned and glanced over his shoulder to consider that scene, then fell back with a yelp as a torch flew right past his face. He followed the line of the fiery weapon, left to right, to the waiting hand of the complimenting dwarf, who caught it deftly and quickly inverted it. As the troll below that dwarf rolled around to counter the attack, the dwarf put that flame into its eye, and stuffed it right into the troll's mouth as the creature opened its jaws wide to let out an agonized roar. The troll flailed wildly and the dwarf went flying away, but he landed nimbly on his steady feet and brought a warhammer up before him in a single fluid movement.

Other enemies moved to engulf the dwarf and Galen, but Dagna and his boys were there first, fiercely supporting their comrades. They formed into a tight fighting diamond quickly to Galen's right, and to the man's left, the remaining dwarves similarly formed up. The two groups quickly pivoted to bring their lines together.

"Yer folks ain't no strangers to battle, I'm thinking!" General Dagna remarked to Galen. "Go on, then," Dagna offered, "join with yer folk. Me and me boys're here for ye, don't ye doubt!"

Galen Firth spun around and smashed the stubborn troll behind him yet again, then rushed past the falling beast to find a place in the human defensive line. He knew that at least some of the Riders must be among the group, for its coordination was too great for untrained warriors alone.

He spotted the central figure of the defenders even as that young man noted him, and Galen's gaze grew more stern. The young warrior seemed to melt back under that glare. Galen sprinted past his townsfolk, moving to the joint between the two coordinated defensive formations.

"I will assume the pivot," he said to the apparent leader.

"I have it secured, Captain Firth," the man, Rannek by name, replied.

"Move aside!" Galen demanded, and Rannek fell back.

"Tighten the ranks!" Galen called across the Nesmé position. "Bring it in closer so our dwarven allies can facilitate our retreat!"

"Good choice," muttered General Dagna, who had watched the curious exchange between the two men. Even with the arrival of two score dwarf warriors, the group of humans could not hope to win out against the monstrous attackers. Already the fires were dying low in several spots along the line, and wherever that happened, the fearsome trolls were fast to the spot, clawed hands striking hard and with impunity. For trolls did not fear conventional weapons. Cutting a troll to pieces, after all, only increased the size of its family.

"Form up, boys!" Dagna called. "Double ranks! Three sides o' chopping!"

With a communal roar, the disciplined dwarves spun, jumped, tumbled, and hopped into proper formation, forming a triangle whose each tip was tightly packed with the fiercest warriors. Clan Battlehammer called that particular formation the "splitting wedge" because of its ability to maneuver easily against weak spots in their enemy's line, shifting the focus of its offensive push. Dagna stayed in the middle of the formation, directing, rolling the dwarves like a great killing machine along the perimeter in support of the human line. They did an almost complete circuit, driving back the trolls with torches and splitting bog blokes like firewood with great chops of heavy axes. On Dagna's sudden order, and with stunning precision, one tip broke away and rushed past the human line to the north, back toward the higher ground, pummeling the few trolls blocking that particular escape route.

"To the north!" Galen Firth cried to his charges, seeing the plan unfolding. He shoved those people nearest him that direction, urging them on.

Across from him, Rannek did likewise, and between the two, they had the bulk of the human force moving in short order.

Dagna watched the haphazard movements, trying hard to time his own pivots to properly cover the rear of the retreat. He noted the two men working frantically, one seeming a younger version of the other, but with the calm one would expect of a trained and veteran soldier. He also noted that Galen Firth pointedly did not glance at his counterpart, did not acknowledge the man's efforts at all.

Dagna shook his head and focused again on his own efforts.

"Damn humans," he muttered. "Stubborn lot."

"The rescue mission succeeds," Tos'un Armgo remarked as he and Kaer'lic watched the continuing battle from afar.

"For now, perhaps," the priestess replied.

Tos'un read the nonchalance clearly in her tone, and indeed, why should Kaer'lic, and why should he, really care whether or not a group of humans escaped the clutches of Proffit's monstrous forces?

"The dwarves will turn for home now, likely," the male drow said. As he finished, he glanced over his shoulder to the bound and gagged Fender. With a sly grin, the drow kicked the dwarf hard in the side, and Fender curled up and groaned.

"That is but a small number of Nesmé's scattered refugees, by all reports," Kaer'lic countered. "And these frightened humans know that they have kin in similar straights all across the region. Perhaps the dwarves will link with this force in an effort to widen the rescue mission. Would that not be the sweetest irony of all, to have our enemies gather together for their ultimate demise?"

"Our enemies?"

The simple question gave Kaer'lic pause, obviously.

"In a choice between humans and trolls, even dwarves and trolls, I believe that I would side against the trolls," the male drow admitted. "Though now, the promise of finding a vulnerable wayward human is a tempting one that I fear I will not be able to resist."

"Nor should you," the priestess said. "Take your pleasures where you may, my friend, for soon enough, striking at the enemy will likely mean crossing lines of wary and battle-ready dwarves."

"Perhaps that pleasure might involve a few vulnerable orcs, as well."

Kaer'lic gave a little laugh at the thought. "I would wish them all, orc, troll, dwarf, human, and giant alike, a horrible death and be done with it."

"Even better," Tos'un agreed. "I do hope that the dwarves decide to remain in the southland openly and with a widening force. Their presence will make it easier for us to persuade Proffit to remain here."

The words silenced Tos'un even as he spoke them, and seemed to have a sobering effect upon Kaer'lic, as well. For that was the gist of it, the unspoken agreement between the two dark elves that they really did not want to wander the tunnels leading back to the north and the main defenses of Mithral Hall. They had been sent south by Obould to guide Proffit through that very course, to urge the trolls on as the monsters pressured the dwarves in the southern reaches of the complex. But the thought of going against fortified dwarven positions and into a dwarven hall accompanied by a horde of stupid brutes was not really an appealing one, after all.

"Proffit will turn his eyes to the north, as Obould bade him," Tos'un added a moment later.

"Then you and I must convince him that the situation here is more important," Kaer'lic replied without hesitation.

"Obould will not be pleased."

"Then perhaps Obould will slay Proffit, or even better, perhaps they will slaughter each other."

Tos'un smiled and let it go at that, perfectly comfortable with the role that he and his three drow companions had made for themselves. Prodding Obould and Gerti Orelsdottr to war from the beginning, the drow had never really concerned themselves with the outcome. In truth, they hadn't a care as to which side emerged victorious, dwarf or orc, as long as the drow found some excitement, and some profit, in the process. And if that process inflicted horrific pain and loss to the minions of Obould, Gerti, and Bruenor Battlehammer alike, then all the better!

Of course, neither Kaer'lic nor Tos'un knew then that their two missing companions, Donnia Soldou and Ad'non Kareese, lay dead in the north, killed by a rogue drow.

They found their first break in a shallow cave tucked into a rocky cliff behind a small pond more than an hour later, and there, too, their first opportunity to bandage wounds and determine who was even still among their continually thinning ranks. Nesmé had been an important town in the region for many generations, strong and solid behind fortified walls, the vanguard of the Silver Marches against intrusions from the monsters of the wild Trollmoors. That continual strife and diligence had bred a closeness among the community of Nesmians so that they felt every loss keenly.

The day had brought more than a dozen deaths, and had left several more people missing—a difficult loss for but one band of less than a hundred refugees. And given the seriousness of the wounds that many resting in that shallow cave had suffered, that number of dead seemed sure to rise through the remaining hours of the night.

"Daylight ain't no friend o' trolls, even in tracking," Dagna said to Galen Firth when he met the man at the cave entrance a short while later. "Me boys're covering the tracks and killing any trolls and blokes wandering too close, but we're not to sit here for long without them beasties coming against us in force."

"Then we move, again and again," Galen Firth said.

Dagna considered the man's tone—determination and resignation mingled into one—as much as his agreement.

"We'll cross shadow to shadow," Galen went on. "We'll find their every weakness and hit them hard. We'll find all the remaining bands of my townsfolk and meld them into a singular and devastating force."

"We'll find tunnels, deep and straight, and run headlong for Mithral Hall," General Dagna corrected, and Galen Firth's eyes flashed with anger.

"More of my people are out there. I will not forsake them in their time of desperation."

"Well, that's for yerself to decide," said Dagna. "I come here to see how I might be helping, and so me and me boys did. I left six more dead back there. That's eight o' fifty, almost one in six."

"And your efforts saved ten times the number of your dead. Are not ten of Nesmé's folk worth a single dwarf's life?"

"Bah, don't ye be putting it like that," Dagna said, and he gave a great snort. "I'm thinking that we're all to be slaughtered in one great fight if we make a single mistake. More than two score o' me boys and closer to a hunnerd o' yer own folk."

"Then we won't make a mistake," Galen Firth said in a low and even tone.

Dagna snorted again and moved past the man, knowing that he wouldn't be getting anything settled that night. Nor did he have to, for in truth, he had no idea of where the force might even find any tunnels that would take them back to Mithral Hall. Dagna knew, and so did Galen, that this band would be moving out of necessity and not choice over the next hours, and even days, likely, so arguing about courses that might not ever even become an option seemed a rather silly thing to do.

Dagna crossed by the folk of Nesmé, accepting their kind words and gratitude, and offering his own praise for their commendable efforts. He also found his own clerics hard at work tending the wounded, and he offered a solid pat on each dwarf shoulder as he passed. Mostly, though, Dagna studied the humans. They were indeed a good and sturdy folk, in the tough general's estimation, if a bit orc-headed.

Well, he supposed, orc-headed only if Galen Firth is an accurate representative of the community.

That notion had Dagna moving more purposefully among the ranks, seeking out a particular man whose actions had stood above the norm back on the battlefield. He found that man at the very back of the shallow cave, reclining on a smooth, rounded stone. As he approached, Dagna noted the man's many wounds, including three fingers on his left hand twisted at an angle that showed them to certainly be broken, and a garish tear on his left ear that looked as if the ear might fall right off.

"Ye might want to be seeing the priests about them fingers and that ear," Dagna said, moving up before the man.

Obviously startled, the warrior quickly sat up and straightened his battered chain and leather tunic.

"Dagna's me name," the dwarf said, extending his calloused hand. "General Dagna o' Mithral Hall, Warcommander to King Bruenor Battlehammer."

"Well met, General Dagna," the man said. "I am Rannek of Nesmé."

"One o' them Riders?"

The man nodded. "I was, at least."

"Bah, ye'll get yer town back soon enough!"

The dwarf noted that his optimism didn't seem to lift the man's expression, though he suspected, given the reception Galen Firth had offered Rannek back at the battlefield, that the dourness wasn't precipitated by the wider prospects for the town.

"Ye done well back there," Dagna offered, eliciting a less-than-resounding shrug.

"We fight for our very existence, good dwarf. Our options are few. If we err, we die."

"Ain't that the way of it?" asked the dwarf. "In me many years, I've come to see the truth in the notion that war's the time for determining the character of a dwarf. Or a man."

"Indeed."

Dagna's eyes narrowed under his bushy and prominent eyebrows. "Ye got nearly a hunnerd o' yer kin in here looking to ye. Ye're knowing that? And here ye be with a face showing defeat, yet ye got most o' yer folk out o' what them trolls suren thought to be the end o' yer road."

"They'll be looking to Galen Firth, now that he has returned," said Rannek.

"Bah, that's not a good enough answer."

"It is the only answer I have," said Rannek.

He slid off the rounded stone, offered a polite and unenthusiastic bow, and moved away.

General Dagna heaved a resigned sigh. He didn't have time for this. Not now. Not with trolls pressing in on them.

"Humans. . . ." he muttered under his breath, giving a shake of his hairy head.

"They are helpless and they are scattered," Kaer'lic Suun Wett said to the giant two-headed Proffit soon after the human band had temporarily escaped from the troll and bog bloke pursuit. "The hour of complete domination over all the region is at hand for you. If you strike at them now, hard and relentlessly, you will utterly destroy all remnants of Nesmé and any foothold the humans can dare hope to hold in your lands."

"King Obould wants us in the tunnels," one of Proffit's heads replied.

"Now!" the other head emphatically added.

"To help with Obould's victory in the north?" Kaer'lic said. "In lands that mean nothing to Proffit and his people?"

"Obould helped us," Proffit said.

"Obould showed Proffit the way out, with all the trolls behind him," the other head added.

Kaer'lic knew well enough what Proffit was referring to. It had been none other than Donnia Soldou, in fact, who had orchestrated the rise of Proffit, through the proxies of King Obould. All that Donnia had hoped was that Proffit and his force of brutish trolls would cause enough of a distraction closer to the major human settlements to keep the bigger players of the region, primarily Lady Alustriel of Silverymoon, from turning her eyes and her formidable armies upon Obould.

Of course at that time, Kaer'lic and the other dark elves had no idea of how fast or how high King Obould would rise. The game had changed.

"And Proffit helped Obould close the back door of Mithral Hall," Kaer'lic reminded.

"Tit," said one head.

"For tat," the other added with a rumbling chuckle.

"But dwarves are left," said the first.

"To," said the other.

"Kill!" they both shouted together.

"Dwarves of Mithral Hall to kill, yes," agreed Kaer'lic. "Dwarves who are stuck in a hole and going nowhere. Dwarves who will still be there waiting to be killed when Proffit has done his work here."

The troll's heads looked at each other and nodded in unison.

"But the humans of Nesmé are not so trapped," Tos'un Armgo put in, right on cue, as he and Kaer'lic had previously decided and practiced. "They will run far away, out of Proffit's reach. Or they will bring in many, many friends, and when Proffit comes back out of the tunnels, he may find a huge army waiting for him."

"More."

"To."

"Kill!" the troll said, both heads grinning stupidly.

"Or too many to kill," Tos'un argued after a quick, concerned glance at Kaer'lic.

"The human friends of Nesmé will bring wizards with great magical fires," Kaer'lic ominously warned.

That took the stupid and eager smile from Proffit's faces.

"What to do?" one head asked.

"Fight them now," said Kaer'lic. "We will help you locate each human band and to position your forces to utterly destroy them. It will not take long, and you can go into the tunnels to fight the dwarves confident that no force will mobilize against you and await your return."

Proffit's two heads bobbed, one chewing its lip, the other holding its mouth open, and both obviously trying to digest the big words and intricate concepts.

"Kill the humans, then kill the dwarves," Kaer'lic said simply. "Then the land is yours. No one will bother to rebuild Nesmé if everyone from Nesmé is dead."

"Proffit likes that."

"Kill the humans," said the other head.

"Kill the dwarves," the first added.

"Kill them all!" the second head cheered.

"And eat them!" yelled the first.

"Eat them all," Kaer'lic cheered, and she motioned to Tos'un, who added, "Taste good!"

Tos'un offered a shrug back at Kaer'lic, showing her that he really had no idea what to add to the ridiculous conversation. It didn't really matter anyway, because both dark elves realized soon enough that their little ploy had worked, and so very easily.

"I remember when Obould was as readily manipulated as that," Kaer'lic said almost wistfully as she and Tos'un left Proffit's encampment.

Tos'un didn't disagree with the sentiment. Indeed, the world had seemed so much simpler a place not so very long ago.

6

FORWARD THINKING ORC

"All the anger of the day," Tsinka Shinriil said as she ran her fingers over Obould's massive shoulder. "Let it lead you now." Then she bit the orc on the back of his neck and began to wrap her sinewy arms and legs around him.

Feeling the tautness of her muscles against him, Obould was again reminded of the wild pegasus. Amusing images floated through his mind, but he pushed them away as he easily moved the amorous shaman aside, stepping out into the center of his tent.

"It is much more than a stupid creature," he remarked, as much to himself as to Tsinka. He turned to see the shaman staring at him, her bewildered expression so much in contrast to her trembling and naked form.

"The winged horse," Obould explained. Tsinka slumped down on a pile of furs. "More than a horse . . . more than the wings . . ." He turned away, nodding, and began to pace. "Yes . . . that was my mistake."

"Mistake? You are Gruumsh. You are perfect."

Obould's grin became an open snicker as he turned back to her and said, "I underestimated the creature. A pegasus, so it would seem, is much more than a horse with wings."

Tsinka's jaw drooped. Obould laughed at her.

"A horse might be clever, but this creature is more," said Obould. "It is wise. Yes! And if I know that . . ."

"Come to me," Tsinka bade him, and she extended her arm and struck a pose so exaggerated, so intentionally alluring, that Obould found it simply amusing.

He went to her anyway, but remained quite distracted as he thought through the implications of his insight. He knew the disposition of the pegasus; he knew that the creature was much more than a stupid horse with wings, for he had come to recognize its stubbornness as loyalty. If he knew that, then the pegasus's former masters surely knew it, and if they knew it, then there was certainly no way that they would let the imprisonment stand.

That thought reverberated through Obould, overshadowing every movement of Tsinka, every bite, every caress, every purr. Rather than diminish in the fog of lust, the images of elves sweeping down to rescue the pegasus only gained momentum and clarity. Obould understood the true value of the creature his minions had captured.

The orc king gave a great shout, startling Tsinka. She froze and stared at him, her eyes at first wild and showing confusion.

Obould tossed her off to the side and leaped up, grabbing a simple fur to wrap around himself as he pushed through the tent flap and out into the encampment.

"Where are you going?" Tsinka shrieked at him. "You cannot go!"

Obould disappeared behind the tent flap as it fell back in place.

"You must not go out without your armor!" cried Tsinka. "You are Gruumsh! You are the god! You must be protected."

Obould's head poked back in, his eyes and toothy grin wide.

"If I am a god . . ." he started to say, but he left the question there, letting Tsinka reason it out for herself. If he was a god, after all, then why would he need armor?

"Sunrise," Innovindil said breathlessly when at long last she saw the marvelous winged horse.

Behind her, over the rocky bluff and down the back slope of the mountain spur, Sunset pawed the ground and snorted, obviously aware that her brother and companion was down there in the grassy vale.

Innovindil hardly heard the pegasus behind her, and hardly noticed her dark elf companion stirring at her side. Her eyes remained locked on the pegasus below, legs bound as it grazed in the tall brown grass. The elf couldn't block out recollections of the last time she had seen Sunrise, caught under a net, nor those images that had accompanied that troubling scene. The death of her lover Tarathiel played out so clearly in her mind again. She saw his desperate war dance against Obould and that sudden and stunning end.

She stared at Sunrise and blinked back tears.

Drizzt Do'Urden put a hand on her shoulder, and when Innovindil finally managed to glance over at him, she recognized that he understood very clearly the tumult within her.

"I know," the drow confirmed. "I see him, too."

Innovindil silently nodded.

"Let us find a way to take a giant stride toward avenging Tarathiel," Drizzt said. "Above all else, he would demand that we free Sunrise from the orcs. Let us give his spirit some rest."

Another silent nod, and Innovindil looked back down at the grassy vale. She didn't focus on the pegasus, but rather on the approach routes that would bring them near to the poor creature. She considered the orc guards milling about, counting half a dozen.

"We could swoop in fast and hard upon Sunset," she offered. "I drop you down right behind Sunrise and cover your movements as you free our captured friend."

Drizzt was shaking his head before she ever finished. He knew that the large enemy encampment was just over the low ridge on the other side of the vale.

"Our time will be too short," he replied. "If we alert them before we even arrive on the scene, our time to free Sunrise and be away will be shorter still. Frost giants can throw boulders a long, long way, and their aim is usually true."

Innovindil didn't argue the point. Her own thinking, in fact, had been moving along those same lines even as she was offering her suggestion. When she looked back at Drizzt, she rested more easily, for she could see the dark elf's eyes searching out every approach and weighing every movement. Innovindil had already gained tremendous respect for the dark elf. If anyone could pull off the rescue, it was Drizzt Do'Urden.

"Tell Sunset to be ready to come to your whistle," the drow said a few moments later. "Just as when we . . . when *you*, killed Obould's murderous son."

Innovindil slid back from the ridge, belly-crawling over the far side to Sunset. When she returned a few moments later, she was greeted by a smiling Drizzt, who was waving his hand for her to follow. He slithered over the stones as easily as a snake, Innovindil close behind.

It took the pair nearly half an hour to traverse the mostly open ground of the mountain's eastern slope. They moved from shadow to shadow, from nook to jag to cranny. Drizzt's path got them to the valley floor just north of the field where Sunrise grazed, but still with fifty yards of open ground between them and the pegasus. From that better vantage point, they noted two more orc guards, bringing the number to eight.

Drizzt pointed to himself, to Innovindil, then to the tall grass, and moved his hand in a slithering, snakelike fashion. When the elf nodded her understanding and began to crouch, the drow held up his hand to stop her. He started to work his fingers in the silent drow code, but stopped short in frustration, wishing that she could understand it.

Instead, Drizzt twisted his face and pushed his nose up, trying to look very orclike. Then he indicated the tall grass again and gave an uncertain shrug.

Innovindil winked in reply, to show that she had taken his meaning, and as she went back into her crouch, she produced a dagger from her boot and brought it up to her mouth. Holding it between clenched teeth, the elf went down to her belly and moved out of the trees and to the edge of the grass. She glanced back at Drizzt, indicating with her hand that she'd go out to the right, moving west of Sunrise's position.

The drow went into the grass to her left, similarly on his belly, and the two moved along.

Drizzt took his movements in bursts of ten elbow-steps, slowly and methodically creeping through the grass, then pausing and daring to lift his head enough to take note of the closest orc guard. He wanted to veer off and go right to that one, to leave it dead in the grass, but that was not the point of their mission. Drizzt fought aside his instinctive rage, against the Hunter within him that demanded continual retribution for the death of Bruenor and the others. He controlled those angry instincts and reminded himself silently that Sunrise was depending on him, that the ghost of Tarathiel, another fallen friend, demanded it of him.

He veered away from the orc guard, swerving wide enough to avoid detection and putting himself back in line to approach Sunrise from the east. Soon he was inside the orc guard perimeter. He could hear them all around, chattering in their guttural language, or kicking at the dirt. He heard Sunrise paw the ground and was able to guess that he was still about twenty-five feet from the steed. That distance would likely take him longer than the hundred-plus feet he had come from the trees, he knew, for every movement had to be silent and carefully made so as to not disturb the grass.

Many minutes passed Drizzt by as he lay perfectly still, then he dared to place one elbow out in front of him and propel himself a foot forward. He moved slightly back to the west as he made his way, closing the ground, he hoped, between himself and Innovindil.

A footstep right before him froze him in place. A moment later, through the grass, he saw a strong, thick orc leg, wrapped in leather and furs.

He didn't dare draw breath.

The brutish creature called to its friends—something in its native language spoken too quickly for Drizzt to decipher. The drow did relax just a bit, though, when he heard other orcs respond with a laugh.

The orc walked along to the west, moving out of Drizzt's way.

The dark elf paused a bit longer, giving the creature time to completely clear and also making sure that it did not take note of Innovindil.

Satisfied, he started to move along once more, but then stopped in surprise at a sudden whinny from Sunrise. The pegasus reared and snorted, front hooves thumping the ground hard. The winged horse neighed again, loudly and wildly, and bucked, kicking the air so forcefully that Drizzt clearly heard the crack of hooves cutting the air.

The drow dared lift his head—and quickly realized his mistake.

Behind him, up in the trees from which he and Innovindil had just come, he heard the shout of an orc lookout. Before him, the eight guards began to close ranks, and one called out.

A noise to the side turned the drow that way—to see more orcs charging over the distant ridgeline.

"A trap," he whispered under his breath, hardly believing it possible.

To his other side, he caught a burst of movement as Innovindil came up fast behind an orc guard. Her hand, so deceptively delicate, flashed around the surprised creature's face and pulled its head back, while her other hand came around the other way, the knife's edge drawing a red line on the creature's exposed neck.

The next nearest orc gave a shout and charged as its companion tumbled down, clutching its mortal wound.

Innovindil's hand snapped forward, launching the already bloody dagger at the incoming orc. With wild gyrations, hands flailing, the orc managed to avoid the missile, but the clever elf was really just looking for a distraction. In a fluid movement, she drew forth her sword and dived into a forward roll, closing the ground between herself and the dodging orc. She came up to her feet gracefully, still moving forward, sword leading and scoring a solid strike into the orc's chest.

But three others charged in at her.

Drizzt called upon his innate drow abilities and put a globe of magical darkness in their path, then leaped up and raced to intercept. One of the orcs managed to stop short of the enchanted area, while another simply roared and charged in headlong, and the third veered off to the side.

"Coming through!" the drow warned his companion, and even as he finished, the charging orc burst out the other side of the darkness globe, barely two strides from the elf.

But Drizzt's warning was enough for Innovindil, and she had her sword angled up before her. As the orc came in hard, spear leading, she parried the tip aside.

The orc barreled on, trying to bury her beneath its larger frame, but at the last moment, Innovindil fell to all fours, turning sidelong to the brute. Despite all its efforts, the orc couldn't slow and couldn't turn, and it tripped against her and tumbled into a somersault over her.

Innovindil couldn't get back to her feet in time, though, and had to block the sword strike from the next incoming brute from one knee. The orc pressed in harder, chopping viciously at her from varying angles with the sword. The elf had to work her blade frantically to deflect each strike.

She gave a shout as another form rushed past her, and it took her a long moment to even realize that it was Drizzt Do'Urden, and another moment to take a measure of the orc that had been pressing her. It was back a few steps suddenly, holding its sword in trembling fingers. As Innovindil watched, red lines of blood thickened on its face and neck.

"They were in wait for us!" Drizzt called to her, rushing past her again, moving behind her to meet the orc she had tripped up as it stood straight.

The orc thrust its spear at his new foe, and hit nothing but air. The perfectly-balanced, quick-moving drow easily slid back and to the side. Then Drizzt came ahead behind that stab, faster than the orc could begin to expect. The orc had never battled the likes of Drizzt Do'Urden before, nor had it ever seen a drow move in battle, let alone a drow wearing enchanted anklets that magically enhanced his foot-speed.

Rolling scimitars descended over the helpless creature, slashing line after line across its face and chest. It dropped its spear and tucked its arms in tight, trying somehow to fend off the attacks, but the drow's fine blades methodically continued their deadly work.

Drizzt had hit the retreating orc perhaps two dozen times, then he jumped up and kicked the creature in the chest for good measure, and also to use that movement to reverse his momentum and direction.

All thoughts of that orc flew from his mind as he turned around to see Innovindil backing from the remaining four guards. Many, many more orcs were closing ground left, right, and center across the field. Shouts from the trees told Drizzt that the humanoids were behind him as well, and there were louder shouts from not so far away.

"Get to Sunrise!" Innovindil shouted at Drizzt as he rushed up beside her, contacting her right arm with his left. He offered her an assuring look. He had seen Innovindil and Tarathiel fighting like that, and he and the elf had practiced the technique over the past few days.

Innovindil's doubting expression betrayed her.

"We have no choice," Drizzt pointed out.

He rolled ahead of the elf to meet the charge of the nearest orc. His scimitars worked furiously, batting at the creature's weapon, then cutting below its attempted parry, but at a shortened angle that could not reach the orc. The orc didn't realize that, however, as the drow spun past. In fact, the orc never began to understand the drow's intent, never began to recognize that the drow had worked his routine and sidelong retreat for no better reason that to set the orc up for the elf who was rolling in behind.

All the orc ever figured out was that an elven sword through the ribs hurt.

Already engaged with another orc, Drizzt hardly noted the grunt and fall of the first. He held complete confidence in Innovindil, though, and understood that if there was a weak link in the fighting chain that he and the elf had become, it was he. And so Drizzt fought with even more ferocity, scimitars working in a blur, batting away weapons and forcing awkward dodges, setting up the victims for Innovindil as she came in fast and hard behind him just as he was fast in behind her, going with all speed at those orcs Innovindil had left vulnerable for him.

Across the field the dancing duo went, moving in tight circles, rolling one upon the other and inexorably toward the trapped pegasus. But with every turn, every different angle coming clearly into his view, Drizzt understood that they would not rescue Sunrise that day. They had underestimated their enemy, had taken the scene of the pegasus grazing beside its handlers at face value.

Three more orcs were down. A fourth fell to Drizzt's double slash, a fifth to Innovindil's fast turn and stab at a creature that was still watching Drizzt turning aside.

When he came around the next time, Drizzt went down to his knees, avoiding an awkward cut from an orc sword. Rather than seizing the opportunity to strike at that overbalanced orc, the drow used the moment of respite to bring forth his onyx figurine. Guenhwyvar had not been gone from his side for long enough, he knew, but he had no choice and so he summoned the panther from her Astral home.

He went back to his feet immediately, blades working furiously to regain the edge against increasingly organized attacks. Behind him and Innovindil as they turned on their way, a gray mist began to take shape and solidify.

One orc noted that distinctive feline shape and slashed at the mist, its sword crossing through without finding a hold. The frustrated orc growled and reversed its cut, but the mist became more corporeal and a powerful cat's paw batted the sword aside before it could gain any momentum. Back legs twitching easily, the panther flew into the orc's face, laying it low, and a quick rake left the brute howling and squirming on the field while mighty Guenhwyvar sprang away to find her next victim.

Even the panther would not be nearly enough, though, Drizzt knew, as many more orcs came into view, swarming the field from . . .

"Every angle," he said to his companion. "No clear route."

"Every angle but one," Innovindil corrected, and gave a shrill whistle.

Drizzt nodded his understanding at once, and as Innovindil went for the thin rope she kept hooked on her belt, the drow increased his tempo, fighting furiously beside her, forcing the orcs to fall back. He called for his panther to coordinate with him, to keep one flank clear while he assaulted the other.

Innovindil had a lasso up spinning hard a moment later, building momentum. Then Sunset appeared in a powerful stoop, coming over the rocky ridge from which Innovindil and Drizzt had first observed the captive Sunrise. The pegasus came down in a rush—a giant-thrown boulder hummed in the air, narrowly missing the equine beast—and leveled out fifteen feet above the grass, soaring past the surprised orcs too quickly for their clumsily thrown spears to catch up.

The well-trained pegasus lowered her head as she crossed above Innovindil, who launched her lasso perfectly, then held on, hooking her foot into a loop at the bottom of the twenty-foot length of rope. The pegasus immediately turned upward as she soared along, dragging the elf.

Innovindil took a stinging hit as she barreled through the nearest orcs, for one spear was angled just right to slice her hip. Fortunately for the elf, though, that was the only weapon that came to bear as she crashed among the scrambling brutes. Then she was up above them, spinning along as Sunset's mighty wings beat furiously to gain speed and height.

Dazed from slamming against so many, and with her hip bleeding, Innovindil kept the presence of mind to hold fast and begin her climb.

Drizzt was too engaged to follow her movements, and he winced more than once as more boulders cut the air above him. Rage propelling him, the drow went into a sudden charge, bursting through the orc ranks and finally getting beside Sunrise.

The pegasus's front hooves were firmly staked. There was no way Drizzt was going to easily free him. And no way for him to get away, it seemed, for the orcs had him fully ringed, shoulder to shoulder in an unbroken line. From somewhere behind those ranks, the drow heard Guenhwyvar cry out in pain, a call so plaintive that he quickly dismissed the panther.

He scrambled across the area around Sunrise, charging for the orc ranks, then reversing direction to come back to the pegasus. It all seemed too eerily familiar to him, even more so when the orcs began to chant, "Obould! Obould! Obould!"

The drow remembered Tarathiel's last fight, remembered the brutish warrior who had slain his elf friend. He had vowed to avenge that death. But he knew beyond all doubt that it was not the time nor the place. He saw the orcs parting at one point and caught a glimpse of the bone-white helm of his adversary.

Drizzt's knuckles whitened with eagerness as he clenched his scimitars. How he longed to put those fine blades to use on the skull of King Obould Many-Arrows!

But there were shamans among the orc ranks, he noted—if he gained advantage on Obould, could he hope to inflict a mortal wound that would not be quickly healed? If he drove the orc king back to disadvantage, would not the orc horde fall over him?

He didn't want to look up and tip his hand for his one hope, but his lavender eyes did glance upward more than once. He noted Innovindil, like a kite string as she and Sunset disappeared behind some trees, and knew beyond doubt that when he saw her again, she would be astride the pegasus.

The bone white helmet bobbed behind the front ranks, closer, and the volume and tempo of the chanting steadily increased.

Drizzt snapped his head around, as if nervously, but really so that he could cover another quick glance upward.

He caught the movement, the shadow. Again he tightened his hands on his scimitars, wanting nothing more than to sink one of those fine blades deep into Obould's chest.

He turned suddenly and leaped upon Sunrise's strong back, and the pegasus bristled and tried to stamp and turn.

"Will you kill me, Obould?" the drow cried as he stood tall upon the pegasus's back, and from that vantage point, he could see the orc king's head and upper body clearly, the bone helmet with its elongated eyes, the last vestiges of daylight glinting off the translucent lenses. He saw the orc's magnificent black armor, all ridged, and that amazing greatsword, which Drizzt knew the orc king could cause to burst into flame with but a thought.

He saw the foe and Drizzt had to wonder if he could hope to beat Obould even in a different circumstance, even if he and the brute faced each other on neutral ground and without allies to be found.

"Are you mighty enough to defeat me, Obould?" he called in defiance anyway, for he knew that he had to make himself the focus, had to keep all eyes upon him and had to convince the orc king not to order its orcs to simply swarm him. "Come along, then," the drow boasted, and he flipped one of his scimitars in the air, deftly catching it by the hilt as it came around. "Long have I desired to see my blades stained red with your flowing blood!"

The last ranks of orcs parted then, leaving the line between Drizzt and Obould clear, and the drow had to consciously force himself to draw breath and to hold steady on his high perch. For the sheer presence of Obould assaulted him, the weight and balance of the creature, the solidity of form and the easy manner with which the king slowly moved his heavy sword with only one hand as if it was as light as an elven walking stick.

"I need you, Sunrise," the drow muttered quietly. "Lift me high, I beg, that I might find my way back to you."

A quick glance skyward showed Drizzt the return and dive of Innovindil and Sunset, but coming in much higher, the fine rope flowing below.

"Not now, Obould!" Drizzt screamed, startling many orcs, and he quick-stepped back to Sunrise's broad rump and kicked the pegasus.

Sunrise bucked on cue and Drizzt sprang away, using the lift to launch him high into the air. He snapped his scimitars away as he rose, twisting and turning to line himself up with the approaching rope.

"Another time, Obould!" he cried as he caught the rope with one hand some twenty feet from the ground. "You and I, another time!"

The orc king roared and his minions launched spears, stones, and axes up into the air.

But again they could not properly lead the swift-moving target, and Drizzt secured his hold, the wind snapping in his ears.

From his high vantage point he saw the giants, as did Innovindil and Sunset, obviously, for the pegasus veered as the boulders came sailing out.

They climbed higher into the fast-darkening sky, and avoided the barrage enough to get up over the ridge and to safety, both Drizzt and his elf companion having gained new respect for their cunning adversary.

Down on the field, Obould watched them disappear with as much amusement as disappointment.

Another time, indeed, he knew, and he was not the least bit afraid.

Around him, the orcs cheered and hooted.

Before him, Sunrise continued to buck and to whinny, and the pegasus's handlers moved in fast, whips in hand to control the beast.

Obould roared at them to steal their momentum.

"With ease and soft hands!" he demanded.

The next day, barely after the sun had cleared the eastern horizon, those handlers came to Obould.

"The beast was not hurt, god-king," the lead handler assured him. "The beast is ready to be ridden."

With Tsinka Shinriil on his arm, nibbling at his ear, Obould grinned widely at the handler.

"And if the beast throws me again, I will cut off your head," he promised, and Tsinka snickered.

The handler paled and shrank back.

Obould let him squirm uncomfortably for a few moments. The orc king had no intention of going to the captured pegasus that day, or ever again. He knew that he could never ride the beast safely, and knew, too, that he would never again be able to use the pegasus to lure his enemies in close. In short, the winged horse had outlived its usefulness to him—almost.

It occurred to the orc king that there might be one last service the captured pegasus could perform.

7

AS GRUUMSH WILLS

"They won't come on, I tell ye, for them trolls in the south've run off," said Cordio, who was fast being recognized as one of Mithral Hall's leading priests, and leading voices in their difficult struggle.

"Moradin tell ye that, did he?" Bruenor came right back.

"Bah! Got nothing to do with that," Cordio answered. "I'm using me own thinking here, and not needin' more'n that. Why'd them trolls back out o' the tunnels if them orcs're meaning to press in? Even orcs ain't that stupid. And this one, Obould, been showing himself smarter than most."

Bruenor looked from the priest to Cordio's patient, Banak Brawnanvil, still unable to walk or even stand after taking an orc spear in the back on his retreat from the ridge north of Keeper's Dale.

"I ain't so sure," the wise old warrior dwarf answered. "Trolls could come back at any time, of course, and ye're guessing that Obould even knows them trolls've left. We got no eyes out there, King Bruenor, and without them eyes, I ain't for putting the safety o' Mithral Hall on a guess."

Bruenor scratched his hairy head and tugged on his red beard. His gray eyes went from Banak to Cordio, then back to Banak.

"He's coming in," Bruenor decided. "Obould's not to let this stand. He took Felbarr once, and he's wanting nothing more than to do it again. And he's knowing that he ain't to get there unless he comes through Mithral Hall. Sooner or later, he's coming in."

"I'm guessing sooner," said Banak, and he and Bruenor both turned to Cordio.

The dwarf priest held up his hands in surrender. "I'll argue all the day long on how ye might be bandaging a wound, but ye're the warcommanders. Cordio's just one to clean up after yer messes."

"Well, let's make this mess one for Obould's shamans to clean," said Bruenor.

"The boys're already making them top halls ready for defense," Banak assured him.

"I got an idea of how we might give Obould's shamans some extra work," the dwarf king remarked, heading for the corridor. He pulled Banak's door open wide, then looked back, grinning. "All the clan's owing to ye, Banak Brawnanvil. Them boys from Mirabar're thinking yerself to be a demigod."

Banak stared at his king stoically, though a bit of moisture was indeed beginning to glisten at the corners of his dark eyes.

Bruenor kept staring hard at the wounded warcommander. He reached down and snapped open his thick belt, and with one quick motion, pulled it off. He wrapped the leather around his hand locking the buckle, a thick, carved mithral clasp adorned with the foaming mug standard of the clan, across his knuckle. Still looking Banak in the eye, Bruenor grabbed and secured the door with his free hand then hit it with a solid left cross. He pulled the door open a bit wider, so that Banak and Cordio could see his work: the indent of the Battlehammer foaming mug.

"We're gonna fill that with silver and gold," Bruenor promised, which was the highest honor a king of Mithral Hall could bestow upon any of his subjects. With that, Bruenor nodded and left, closing the door behind him.

"I'm thinking that yer king's a bit fond of ye, Banak Brawnanvil," said Cordio.

Banak slumped back, resting flat on his back. "Or he's thinking I'm all done for."

"Bah!"

"Ye get me fixed then, ye durned fool," Banak demanded.

Cordio exhaled and took a long pause, then muttered, "By Moradin's blessing," under his breath.

And truly the priest hoped that Moradin was paying attention and would grant him the power to alleviate some of Banak's paralysis, at least. A dwarf as honored and respected as Banak should not be made to suffer such indignity.

Obould stood up high on the rocky bluff, overlooking the work. Orcs scrambled all around Keeper's Dale, sharpening weapons and practicing tight and fast strike formation, but the majority of the important work was being done not by orcs, but by Gerti's giants. Obould watched a procession of more than a dozen behemoths enter the western end of the dale, dragging a huge log with ropes as thick as an orc's chest. Other giants worked on the stone wall around the closed western doors, tossing aside debris and checking the strength of the mountain above the portal. Still other giants tied off and hammered logs on tall towers set on either side of the doors, and a third that rose up a hundred feet, which was located straight back from the iron-bound western gates of Clan Battlehammer's hall.

Obould scanned higher up on the mountain above the doors, at his many scouts scrambling over the stones. Foremost in his mind was the element of surprise. He didn't want any dwarf eyes peering out at the preparations in the dale. Tsinka and the other shamans had assured him that the dwarves would never expect the assault. The bearded folk were tied up in the south with Proffit's trolls, they presumed, and like those dwarves in Citadel Felbarr years before, they held too much confidence in the strength of their iron portals.

The orc king moved down the rocky slope, seeing Gerti standing among some of her giantkin, poring over parchments spread on a tall wooden table. The giantess looked from the parchments to the work on the towers and the huge log sliding across the stone floor of the dale, and grinned. The giant beside her pointed down to the parchment, nodding.

They were good at this, Obould knew, and he gained confidence with every stride.

"Mighty doors," he said to Gerti as he approached.

Gerti shot him a look that seemed somewhere between incredulity and disgust. "Anything a dwarf can build, a giant can knock down," she replied.

"So we shall soon see," the orc king responded with a low and respect-ful bow. He moved closer and those giants near to Gerti stepped aside, granting them some privacy.

"How far into Mithral Hall will your giants travel?" Obould asked her.

"*Into* Mithral Hall?" came her scoffing reply. "We are not built for dirty, cramped dwarven tunnels, Obould."

"The ceiling of the entry hall is high, by all that I have heard."

"I told you that we would knock down the door, and so we shall. Once the portal falls, let your orcs run into the killing chambers of King Bruenor."

"The treasures of Mithral Hall are considerable, so it is said," Obould teased.

"Treasures that I have already earned."

Obould bowed again, not as low, and not as respectfully. "Your giants will be of great help to my warriors in that entry hall," he said. "Help us to secure our foothold. From there, my warriors will spread like thick smoke throughout the tunnels, routing the dwarves."

Gerti's sly smile showed that she wasn't so sure of that.

"Then you and your kin can go to the Surbrin, as we agreed," said Obould.

"I will go to the Surbrin as *I* determine," Gerti retorted. "Or I will not. Or I will go back to Shining White, or to Silverymoon, if I feel so inclined to take the city of Lady Alustriel. I am bound by no agreements to Obould."

"We are not enemies, Dame Orelsdottr."

"Keep it that way, for your own sake."

Obould's red-streaked yellow eyes narrowed for just an instant, tipping off the giantess to the simmering rage within him.

"I wish for your giants to accompany the lead ranks through the entry hall," said Obould.

"Of course you do. You have no warriors who can approach their strength and skill."

"I do not ask this without recompense."

"You offer me the treasures of Mithral Hall?" asked Gerti. "The head of King Battlehammer, whom you already claimed dead?"

"The pegasus," Obould blurted, and for a brief moment, he saw a tell-tale flash of intrigue in Gerti's blue eyes.

"What of it?"

"I am not so foolish as to try to ride the creature, for it is not an unthinking beast, but a loyal friend to the elf I destroyed," Obould admitted. "I could eat it, of course, but would not any horse do as well? But you believe it to be a beautiful creature, do you not, Dame Orelsdottr? A fitting trophy for Shining White?"

"If you have no use for it—"

"I did not say that," Obould interrupted.

"You play a dangerous game."

"I make an honest offer. Send your giants in beside my orcs to crush the initial defenses of Mithral Hall. Once we have pushed the dwarves to the tighter tunnels, then leave the hall to me and go your own way, to the Surbrin or wherever you choose. And take with you the winged horse."

Gerti held a defiant pose, but the sparkle in her eyes betrayed her interest.

"You covet that creature," Obould said bluntly.

"Not as much as you believe."

"But your giants will charge into the hall beside my orcs."

"Only because they do so enjoy killing dwarves."

Obould bowed low once again and let it go at that. He didn't really care why Gerti sent her forces in there, as long as she did.

"Hee hee hee."

Ivan couldn't help but smile at his brother's continuing glee. Pikel hopped all about the upper western chambers of Mithral Hall, chasing behind Nanfoodle mostly. King Bruenor had come to the pair immediately following his discussion with Cordio and Banak. Convinced that the orcs would try to break into the hall, Bruenor had commissioned the two unconventional characters, the dwarf "doo-dad" as Pikel described himself, and the gnome alchemist, to help in setting unconventional and unpleasant surprises for the invaders. Of course, Nanfoodle had immediately set the best brewers of Mithral Hall to work in concocting specific formulas of various volatile liquids. All of the rarest and most expensive ingredients were even then being poured into vats and beakers. On Bruenor's instructions, Nanfoodle's team was holding nothing back.

Ivan followed behind the pair, carefully and gently carrying one such large pail of a clear liquid. He tried very hard not to let the volatile fluid slosh about, for in that pail was the same liquid that was held in a small vial in each of his hand crossbow darts. "Oil of Impact," it was commonly called, an exotic potion that exploded under the weight of concussion. Ivan's crossbow darts had been designed to collapse in upon themselves on impact, compressing the chamber and vial, and resulting in an explosion that would then drive the tip through whatever barrier it had struck. Given the force of those explosions using only a few drops of the oil of impact, the dwarf couldn't even begin to guess what clever Nanfoodle had in mind for so much of the potent mix.

"Right there," Nanfoodle instructed a pair of other dwarves who had been put in his charge. He pointed to a flat wall in the western entry chamber, to the side of the doors that led into the main upper level corridors. He motioned for Ivan to bring the pail up, which Ivan did, to the continuing "hee hee hee" of his brother Pikel.

"Would you be so kind as to go and inquire of Candles how he fares in his work?" Nanfoodle asked, referring to a thin, squint-eyed dwarf named Bedhongee Waxfingers, nicknamed Candles because of his family's line of work.

Ivan gently set the bucket on the floor before the wall and glanced back at the other two helpers, both of who were carrying brushes. "Aye, I'll go," he said, looking back at the gnome. "But only because I'm wanting to be far from here when one o' them dolts kicks the bucket."

"Boom!" said Pikel.

"Yeah, boom, and ye're not knowing the half of it," Ivan added, and he started away.

"What were the dimensions again?" Nanfoodle asked him before he had taken two strides.

"For Candles? Two dwarves abreast and one atop another," Ivan replied, which meant five feet wide and eight high.

He watched Nanfoodle motion to the pair with the brushes.

"Durned gnome," he muttered, and he left the chamber.

Barely in the hallway, he heard Nanfoodle lift his voice in explanation: "Bomblets, Pikel. No big explosions in here, of course—not like what we did outside."

"Boom!" Pikel replied.

Ivan closed his eyes and shook his head, then moved along more swiftly, thinking it prudent to put as much ground between himself and Nanfoodle as possible. Like most dwarves, Ivan applauded clever engines of war. The Battlehammer sideslinger catapults and "juicer," a rolling cart designed to flatten and crush opponents, were particularly impressive. But Nanfoodle's work assaulted Ivan's pragmatic dwarven sensibilities. Outside, in the battle for the ridge, the gnome had brought trapped subterranean gasses up under a ridgeline held by frost giants, and had blown the entire mountain spur to pieces.

It occurred to Ivan that while Nanfoodle's efforts might help secure Mithral Hall, it was also quite possible that he would destroy the whole complex in the process.

"Not yer business," the dwarf grumbled to himself. "Ye're the warrior, not the warcommander."

He heard his brother laughing behind him. More often than not, Ivan knew all too well, that laugh didn't lead to good things. Images of flames leaping a thousand feet into the air and the rubble of a mountain ridge flying wide filled his thoughts.

"Not the warcommander," he muttered again, shaking his head.

"Ye're doing great, Rumblebelly," Bruenor prompted.

Regis shifted at the unexpected sound, sending a small avalanche of soot tumbling back on his friend, who was climbing the narrow chimney behind him. Bruenor grumbled and coughed, but offered no overt griping.

"You're certain this will get us out?" Regis asked between his own coughs.

"Used it meself after ye all left me in here with the stinking duergar," Bruenor assured him. "And I didn't have the climbing tools, either! And carried a bunch o' wounds upon me battle-weary body! And . . ."

He rambled on with a string of complaints, and Regis just let them float by him without landing. Somehow having Bruenor below him, ranting and raving, brought the halfling quite a bit of comfort, a clear reminder that he was home. But that didn't make the climb any easier, given Regis's still-aching arm. The wolf that had bitten him had ground its teeth right into his bone, and even though tendays had passed, and even though Cordio and Stumpet had cast healing spells upon him, he was a battered halfling indeed.

He knew the honor Bruenor had placed upon him in asking him to lead the way up the chimney, though, and he wasn't about to slow down. He let the cadence of Bruenor's grumbling guide him and he reached up, hooked his fingers on a jag in the rough stone and hauled himself up another foot. Over and over, he repeated the process, not looking up for many minutes.

When he finally did tilt his head back, he saw at last the lighter glow of the nighttime sky, not twenty feet above him.

Regis's smile faded almost immediately, though, as he considered that there could be an orc guard out there, standing ready to plunge a spear down atop his head. The halfling froze in place, and held there for a long while.

A finger flicked against the bottom of his foot, and Regis managed to look down into Bruenor's eyes—shining whiter, it seemed, for the dwarf's face was completely blackened by soot. Bruenor motioned emphatically for Regis to continue up.

Regis gathered his nerve, his eyes slowly moving up to the starlight. Then, with a burst of speed, he scrambled hand over hand, not letting himself slow until he was within reach of the iron grate, one bar missing from Bruenor's climb those years ago. With a determined grunt, his courage mounting as he considered the feat of his dwarf friend in escaping the duergar, Regis moved swiftly, not pausing until his upper half was right out of the chimney. He paused there, half in and half out, and closed his eyes, waiting for the killing blow to fall.

The only sound was the moan of the wind on the high mountain, and the occasional scraping from Bruenor down below.

Regis pulled himself out and climbed to his knees, glancing all around.

An amazing view greeted him from up on the mountain called Fourthpeak. The wind was freezing cold and snow clung to the ground all around him, except in the immediate area around the chimney, where warm air continued to pour forth from the heat of the great dwarven Undercity.

Regis rose to his feet, his eyes transfixed on the panoramic view around him. He looked to the west, to Keeper's Dale, and the thousands of campfires of Obould's great army. He turned around and considered the eastern stretches below him, the dark snaking line of the great River Surbrin and the line of fires on its western bank.

"By Moradin, Rumblebelly," Bruenor muttered when he finally got out of the hole and stood up to survey the magnitude of the scene, of the campfires of the forces arrayed against the goodly folk of the Silver Marches. "Not in all me days have I seen such a mob of foes."

"Is there any hope?" Regis asked.

"Bah!" snorted the toughened old king. "Orcs're all! Ten to one, me dwarves'll kill 'em."

"Might need more than that," the halfling said, but wisely under his breath so that his friend could not hear.

"Well, if they come, they're coming from the west," Bruenor observed, for that was obviously the region of the most densely packed opposition.

Regis moved up beside him, and stayed silent. They had an hour to go before the first light of dawn. They couldn't really go far, for they needed the warmth of the chimney air to help ward the brutal cold—they hadn't worn too many layers of clothes for their tight climb, after all.

So they waited, side by side and patiently. They each knew the stakes, and the bite of the wind was a small price to pay.

But the howls began soon after, a lone wolf, at first, but then answered again and again all around the pair.

"We have to go," Regis said after a long while, a chorus of howls growing closer by the second.

Bruenor seemed as if made of stone. He did move enough to glance back to the east.

"Come on, then," the dwarf prodded, speaking to the sky, calling for the dawn's light.

"Bruenor, they're getting close."

"Get yerself in the hole," the dwarf ordered.

Regis tugged his arm, but he did not move.

"You don't even have your axe."

"I'll get in behind ye, don't ye doubt, but I'm wanting a look at Obould's army in the daylight."

A howl split the air, so close that Regis imagined the wolf's hot breath on his neck. His arm ached from memory alone, and he had no desire to face the gleaming white fangs of a wolf ever again. He tugged more insistently on Bruenor's arm, and when the dwarf half-turned, as if moving toward the chimney, the halfling scrambled belly down to the ground and over the lip.

"Go on, then," Bruenor prompted, and he turned and squinted again to the west.

The air had grown a bit lighter, but Bruenor could still make out very little in the dark vale. He strained his eyes and prayed to Moradin, and eventually made out what looked like two great obelisks.

The dwarf scratched his head. Were the orcs building statues? Watch towers?

Bruenor heard the padded footsteps of a canine creature not far away, and still staring down into the dale, he bent low, scooped up a loose stone, and pegged it in the general direction of the noise.

"Go on, then, ye stupid puppy. Dog meat ain't to me liking, to yer own good!"

"Bruenor!" came Regis's cry from the chimney. "What are you doing?"

"I ain't running from a few skinny wolves, to be sure!"

"Bruenor. . . ."

"Bah!" the dwarf snorted. He kicked at the snow, then turned around and started for the chimney, to Regis's obvious relief. The dwarf paused and looked back one more time, though, concentrating on the tall, dark shapes.

"Towers," he muttered, and shook his hairy head. He hopped into the hole, catching the remainder of the grate to break his fall.

And it hit him.

"Towers?" he said. He lifted himself up and glanced to the side at a movement, to see the glowing eyes of a wolf not ten strides away. "O, ye clever pig-face!"

Bruenor dropped from sight.

He prodded Regis to hurry along all the way down the chimney, realizing then that his precious Mithral Hall was in more danger than he had imagined. He had wondered whether Obould would try to come in through lower tunnels, or perhaps make one of his own, or whether he would try to crash through the great iron doors.

"Towers. . . ." he muttered all the way down, for now he knew.

The next morning, a tree appeared atop the mountain called Fourthpeak, except that it wasn't really a tree, but a dwarf disguised as a tree by the druidic magic of the strange Pikel Bouldershoulder. A second tree appeared soon after, farther down the mountain slope to the west, and a third in line after that. The line of "new growth" stretched down, dwarf after dwarf, until the leading tree had a clear vantage point of the goings-on in Keeper's Dale.

When reports began filtering back to Mithral Hall about the near-readiness of the giant towers and the ghastly, ram-headed battering pole that would be suspended and swung between those obelisks, the work inside the hall moved up to a frenetic pace.

There were two balconies lining the large, oval entry hall of the western reaches of the dwarven complex. Both had crawl tunnels connecting them back to corridors deeper within the complex, and both provided fine kill areas for archers and hammer-throwers. On the westernmost side of one of these balconies, the dwarves constructed a secret chamber, large enough to hold a single dwarf. From out its top, they ran some of the same metal pipes that Nanfoodle had used to bring the hot air up on the northern ridgeline, securing them tight against the ceiling and carrying the line out to the center of the large oval chamber. A heavy rope was then threaded through the piping, secured on a crank within the small secret chamber and dangling out the other end of the pipe, nearly to the floor, some thirty to forty feet below.

All across the reaches of that chamber, the dwarves built defensive positions, low walls over which they could fend off attackers, and which afforded them a continual line of retreat back into the main corridor in the east. They coordinated those junctures in the many walls with drop-points along the ledge above. Under the watchful eye of none other than Banak Brawnanvil, the teams practiced their timing continually, for those below knew that their brethren above would likely be their only chance of getting out of the chamber alive. To further hinder their enemies, the industrious Battlehammer gang placed hundreds of caltrops just inside the great doors, some fashioned purposely and many others nothing more than sharp pieces of scrap metal—waste brought up from the forges of the Undercity.

Outside that expected battlefield, the work was no less intense. Forges glowed, great spoons in brew barrels constantly stirred, sharpening stones whirred, smithy hammers pounded away, and the many pottery wheels spun and spun and spun.

The crowning moment came late one afternoon, when a procession of dwarves carried a large, layered circular bowl into the chamber. More than fifteen feet across, the contraption was all of beaten metal, layered in fans and hooked together on a center pole that rose up just a couple of feet and ended in a sturdy eyelet. Through this, the dwarves tied off the dangling rope.

Nanfoodle nervously checked the trip-spring mechanism on the center pole several times. The tension had to be just right—not so loose that the weight of the bowl's contents could spring it, and not so tight that the drop wouldn't trigger it. He and Ivan Bouldershoulder had done the calculations more than a dozen times, and their confidence had been high.

Had been.

In looking around at all the curious dwarves, Nanfoodle realized just how much was at stake, and the thought had his little knees clicking together.

"It'll work," Ivan promised him, the dwarf bending in low and whispering in his ear. He gently took Nanfoodle's shoulder and ushered the gnome back, then motioned to the helpers who had come in behind the pair, gently pushing a wide cart full of ceramic balls.

The dwarves began placing the delicate orbs inside the bowl of the contraption, along set ridges, all of which ended with a curled lip of varying angles.

When that work was done, the dwarves up above shoved a long handle into the crank in the secret cubby and began lifting the contraption from the floor, drawing the rope slowly and evenly. Other dwarves climbed ladders beside the bowl as it rose, slowly rotating it through its climb.

"Get a ladder and smooth the edges," Ivan ordered as the whole disk was locked into place up near the ceiling, for though the bottom of the bowl had been painted to make it look like the stone of the ceiling, once it was in place, he could see where improvements might be made.

"It'll work," the yellow-bearded Bouldershoulder said again to Nanfoodle, who was staring up nervously.

The gnome looked to Ivan and managed a meager smile.

Up on the ledge, Bruenor, Regis, Catti-brie, and Wulfgar watched the work with a mixture of hope and sheer terror. The two humans had already witnessed one of Nanfoodle's surprises, and both figured that one incident had made enough of an impression to foster grandiose stories for a lifetime.

"I'm not for liking yer choice," Bruenor said to Regis. "But I'm respecting yer decision, and respecting yerself more and more, little one."

"I'm not for liking my choice, either," Regis admitted. "But I'm no warrior, and this is my way of helping."

"And how are you to get out of there if we don't retake the hall?" Catti-brie asked.

"Would that question be any different if a dwarf was accepting the duty?" the halfling shot right back.

Catti-brie thought on that for a moment, then just said, "Maybe we can catch an orc and trick it into pulling the pin."

"Yeah, that'd work," Bruenor said. Beneath his sarcastic quip, the other three caught the slightest of quivering in his voice, a clear sign that he, like the others, realized that this might be the last time they saw their halfling friend.

But then, if they failed in this, they would all likely die.

"I'm wanting you two up on the other ledge," Bruenor said to his two human children. "Right near the escape corridor."

"I was thinking to fight on the floor," Wulfgar argued.

"The walls're too short for ye, and what a fine target ye'll be making for our enemies, standing twice a dwarf's height down there," Bruenor answered. "No, ye fight on the ledge, the two o' ye together, for that's when ye're at yer best. Hold all yer shots, bow and hammer, for any giants, should they come in, and keep yerselves at the escape tunnel."

"So that we might be the first to leave?" Catti-brie asked.

"Aye," the dwarf admitted. "First out and not bottlenecking the low crawl for me kin."

"If that's the reasoning, then shouldn't we be last?" Wulfgar asked, tossing a wink at Catti-brie as he did.

"No, ye go first and ye go early, and that's the end of it," said Bruenor. "Ye got to be near the tunnel, as ye'll both be needing that tunnel to fall back from sight, for ye can't get as low as me boys that'll be up there with ye. Now stop yer arguing with me and start sorting out yer tactics."

The dwarf turned to Regis and asked, "Ye got enough food and water?"

"Does he ever?" Catti-brie asked.

Regis grinned widely, his dimpled cheeks climbing high. He patted his bulging backpack.

"Should be today," Bruenor told him. "But ye might have a bit of a wait."

"I will be fine, and I will be ready."

"Ye know the signal?"

The halfling nodded.

Bruenor patted him on the shoulder and moved away, and with a grin and helpless shrug to his friend, Regis moved inside the secret cubby, pulled the stone-shaped door closed and bolted it on the inside. A pair of dwarves moved right up to the closed portal and began working its edges with mud and small stones, sealing the portal and also blending it in to the surrounding wall so perfectly that a trained elf thief would have a hard time spotting the door if he'd been told exactly where to find it.

"And you'll be on the floor, of course?" Catti-brie asked Bruenor.

"Right in the middle of the line's me place." He noted Catti-brie's scowl and added, "Ye might want to dip yer bow every now and then to clear the way if ye see that I'm attracting a bit too much orc attention."

That brought a light to the woman's face, a clear reminder that whether up on the ledge or down on the floor, they were in it together.

"We're gonna make 'em pay for every inch o' ground," Bruenor told his charges when word came down the chimneys that the towers were completed in Keeper's Dale, and that great lengths of rope were being strung. It took quite a while for that word to run up the dwarven "tree" line, down the chimney to the Undercity, then back up the corridors to the entry hall, though, and so the words had just left Bruenor's mouth when the first thunderous smash hit the great iron doors. All the chambers shook under the tremendous weight of that blow, and more than one dwarf staggered.

Those closest to the doors immediately moved to inspect the damage, and with just that one blow, cracks appeared in the stone supporting the massive portals.

"Won't take many," the lead engineer closest the doors called.

He and his group moved back fast, expecting the second report—which shook the chamber even more. The doors cracked open under the great weight. More than one set of eyes went up nervously to the ceiling and the delicate bowl contraption.

"It'll hold," Bruenor shouted from the front rank in the center of the dwarven line, directly across the hall from the doors. "Don't ye be looking up! Our enemies're coming in through the doors in the next hit or two.

"Girl!" he called up to Catti-brie. "Ye set yer sights on that center line in the doors and if it opens and an ugly orc puts its ugly face against it, ye take it down hard! All of ye!"

The great ram swung in again, slamming the iron, and the doors creaked in some more, leaving a crack wide enough to admit an orc, if not a giant. Just as Bruenor had predicted, enemies did come against the portals, hooting, shouting, and pressing. One started through, then began to jerk in place as a barrage of arrows and crossbow bolts met it.

The orcs behind the unfortunate point pushed it in and to the floor, and hungrily crowded against the open slot.

More arrows and bolts met them, including a silver-streaking arrow that sliced right through the closest creature and several behind it, lessening the press for a moment.

Then the ram hit again, and the right-hand door busted off its giant top hinge and rolled inward, creaking and groaning as the metal of the bottom hinge twisted. Chunks of stone fell from above, smashing the first ranks of orcs, but hardly slowing the flood that followed.

The orcs poured in, and the dwarves howled and set themselves against the charge. The broken door twisted and settled back the other way, crashing down upon many of the unfortunate orcs and somewhat slowing the charge.

Missiles rained down from on high. A heavy warhammer went spinning among the throng, splitting the skull of one orc. As the charge neared the first of the newly-constructed low walls, dwarves sprang up from behind it, all of them leveling crossbows and blasting the closest rank of enemies. Bows fell aside, the dwarves taking up long spears and leveling them at the charging throng. Those orcs in front, pressed by the rolling wave behind, couldn't hope to slow or turn aside.

As one, Banak's well-drilled team let go of their spears and took up their close-combat weapons. Sword, axe, and hammer chopped away wildly as the orc wave came on. From above, a concentrated volley devastated the second rank of enemies, allowing the dwarves a chance to retreat back beyond the second wall.

The scene would repeat itself in ten-foot sections, wall to wall, all the way back to Bruenor's position.

"Wulfgar! Girl!" Bruenor cried when a larger form appeared in the broken doorway. Even as he spoke, a magical arrow from Catti-brie's Taulmaril zipped out for the hulking giant form, followed closely by a spinning warhammer.

The orcs made the second wall, where many more died.

But the monstrous wave rolled on.

Regis curled up and blocked his ears against the screaming and shouting that reverberated across the stones. He had seen many battles—far too many, by his estimation—and he knew well the terrible sounds. And it always sounded the same. From the street fights in Calimport to the wild battles he had seen in Icewind Dale, both against the barbarians of the tundra and the goblinkin, to the battles to retake and hold onto the coveted mines of Mithral Hall, Regis had been assailed by those same sounds over and over again. It didn't matter if the wails came from orcs or dwarves or even from giants. As one, they split the air, carrying waves of agony on their shrill notes.

The halfling was glad to be in his sealed compartment where he did not have to witness the flowing blood and torn bodies. He took faith that his role was an important one for the success of the dwarves' plan, that he was contributing in a great way.

For the time being, though, he wanted to put all those thoughts out of his head, wanted to put everything out of his mind and just lay in the near-absolute blackness of the sealed cubby. He closed his eyes and blocked his ears, and wished that it was all far, far away.

"Giant!" Wulfgar said to Catti-brie, who was kneeling on the balcony beside him. As he spoke, the huge form crossed over the lighter area of the fallen door and into the chamber, spurring orcs on before it. With a roar to his god of war, Wulfgar brought his warhammer up over his shoulder, then rolled his arms around to straighten them, putting the hammer directly in line behind his back.

"Tempus!" he cried again, and he leaned his tall frame back, then began a rolling movement that seemed to start as his knees, his back arcing and swaying forward, huge shoulders snapping ahead as his arms came up over his head, launching mighty Aegis-fang into an end-over-end flight across the room.

Catti-brie targeted quickly upon Wulfgar's call and let fly, her arrow easily outdistancing the warhammer to strike the giant first, right in the upper arm. The behemoth cried out and straightened, squaring up to the pair on the ledge right as the warhammer slammed in, taking it squarely in the face with a tremendous slapping sound.

The giant staggered. Another arrow hit it in the torso, then a third, and Wulfgar, the enchanted warhammer magically returned to his grasp, yelled out for Tempus again and launched the missile.

The giant turned and stumbled back toward the door.

The hammer pounded in right against its bending back, launching it forward and to the floor, where it crushed an unfortunate orc beneath its tumbling bulk.

"More of 'em," Catti-brie remarked as another, then another huge form crossed the leaning door.

"Just keep a line of arrows then," Wulfgar offered, and again his hammer appeared magically in his grasp. He started to take aim at one of the new adversaries, but then saw the wounded giant stubbornly trying to rise again. Wulfgar adjusted his angle, roared to his war god, and let fly. The hammer hit the giant right on the back of the skull as it tried to rise, with a crack that sounded like splitting stone. The behemoth went down fast and hard and lay very still.

Two other giants were in the foyer, though, the lead one accepting a hit from Catti-brie's devastating bow, and dodging fast as a second arrow sped by, the enchanted missile slicing right into the stone wall. Another behemoth appeared at the doorway and held there, and a moment later, the bombardiers on the balcony understood the tactic. For that giant turned fast and tossed something to the farthest one in the hall, who caught it and swiveled about, tossing it to the leading brute.

Another arrow from Catti-brie stung that behemoth but did not drop it, and when it turned around to face the ledge, its arms went up high, holding a huge boulder, and it let fly.

"Run away!" cried the dwarf to Wulfgar's left, and he grabbed the barbarian by the belt and tugged him aside.

Wulfgar twisted, off-balance, and tumbled to the balcony behind the dwarf. Only as he landed hard and managed to glance back did Wulfgar come to realize that the dwarf had saved his life. The giant-thrown boulder smashed hard against the front of the balcony and skipped upward, slamming into the wall at the side of the exit tunnel.

It rebounded from there back to the balcony, and Wulfgar could only look on in horror as it crushed down upon his dear friend.

"Clear the hall!" came a voice above the tumult of battle, the voice of Bruenor Battlehammer who centered the line of dwarves on the floor, ushering his retreating kin out. "Give us time, archers!"

"Special arrows!" cried dwarves all along both balconies.

As one the crossbowmen reached for their best quarrels, tipped with a metal that burned like a flaring star when touched to flame. Torchbearers ran the length of the archer lines, while cries went out to concentrate the killing area.

Flaring quarrel after quarrel soared down to the center rear of the entry hall, to the region just before the unmoving Bruenor Battlehammer and his elite warriors, the Gutbuster Brigade, as they held the last line of retreat.

"Now go!" Bruenor cried as the orc ranks shook apart under the glare of the magnesium bolts and the shrieks of unbelievable agony from those who had been struck.

"Block it!" Bruenor cried.

Up on the ledge above him, a dwarf tugged hard at Wulfgar, pulling him away from the boulder that had fallen on Catti-brie.

"We need ye now!" the dwarf cried.

Wulfgar spun away, his blue eyes wet with tears. He was part of a team who were supposed to definitively finish the retreat, one of four assigned to lift the vat of molten metal and pour it down before the escape corridor, buying the fleeing Bruenor and the Gutbusters some time.

Wulfgar, full of rage, changed that plan. He pushed the dwarves aside and wrapped his arms around the vat, then hoisted it and quick-stepped to the edge of the balcony, roaring with every step.

"He can't be doing that," one dwarf muttered.

But he was.

At the edge, the barbarian dropped the vat and tipped it, glowing molten metal pouring down upon the orcs.

A boulder slammed the ledge right below him and the force of the blow threw him aside, stumbling, as pieces of stone broke away below him.

With one last look back to Catti-brie, Wulfgar fell from the ledge, tumbling right after the heavy metal vat.

8

GALEN'S STAND

General Dagna exhaled deeply, his whole body finally seeming to relax. Good news at last, he thought, for one of his scouts had returned with word that tunnels had been found leading straight and deep to the north, back to Mithral Hall, in all likelihood.

For more than a tenday, Dagna, his forty remaining dwarves, and Galen Firth and his human refugees had been moving fast across the muddy, scraggly terrain, collecting remnants of the scattered folk of Nesmé. They had more than four hundred Nesmians in tow, but less than half were battle-capable, and many were wounded.

Worse, their enemies had been dogging their every step, nipping at them in scattered attacks. The skirmishes had diminished to nothing over the past couple of days, but the nagging thought remained with Dagna that those fights had not been so haphazard, that perhaps they were a coordinated effort toward a larger goal. In fact, it occurred to Dagna, though he did not mention it to Galen Firth, that the last couple of bands of refugees, mostly women, children, and very old folk, had been left alone by the trolls purposely. The apparently cunning trolls seemed to recognize that Dagna and Galen would absorb the refugees, and that those less able would surely slow them all down and drain their resources. Dagna recognized that he and his comrades were, in effect, being herded. The wise old dwarf warcommander understood the ways of battle enough to realize that time was working against him and his impromptu army. Tough as the humans were showing themselves to be, and determined as Galen Firth might be, Dagna believed in his heart that if they couldn't find their way out of there, they would all soon be dead.

Finally on that cold and rainy day had come the welcomed news of a potential escape route, and one through tunnels, where Dagna knew that he and his boys could be much more effective in slowing the powerful trolls. He found Galen Firth a short while later, and was surprised to see that the man was as excited as he.

"Me scouts're back," Dagna said in greeting.

"As are my own," Galen replied with equal enthusiasm.

Dagna started to explain about the tunnel, thinking that perhaps Galen had heard a similar tale, but the man wasn't listening, he realized, and indeed, Galen soon began talking right over him.

"Our enemies are weak between here and Nesmé," Galen explained. "A thin line, with no support to be found anywhere around the town."

"The *ruins* of Nesmé, ye mean," Dagna corrected.

"Not so ruined. Battered yes, but still defensible."

The dwarf paused for a moment and let those words digest. "Defensible?"

"Behind our walls, we are formidable, good dwarf."

"I'm not for doubting that, but are ye forgetting that yer enemy already chased ye out from behind those walls once?"

"We weren't properly prepared for them."

"Yer forces were many times yer present number!"

"We can hold the town," Galen insisted. "Word has gone out to Everlund, Mirabar, and Silverymoon. Surely help will soon arrive."

"To bury yer bones?" Dagna said, and Galen scowled at him. "Ye can't be thinking to move closer to the Trollmoors with an army o' bog blokes and trolls on yer heels."

"Army? The fighting has lessened since our escape from the trolls," Galen argued. "We have reason to believe that many of our enemies have gone into tunnels heading for Mithral Hall."

"Aye, tunnels to Mithral Hall," said Dagna. "Which is why I come to ye this day. We found the way back, deep and quiet. We can make the tunnels afore the morrow and be well on our way."

"Have you not listened to a word I've said?"

"Have ye yerself heared them words?" Dagna replied. "Ye're for walking out from the protection o' the mountains onto open ground where yer enemies can sweep upon ye. Ye're to get yer people slaughtered."

"I am to save Nesmé."

"Nesmé's gone!"

"And would you so quickly abandon Mithral Hall, General Dagna?"

"Mithral Hall's not gone."

It was Galen Firth's turn to pause and take a deep breath against the unrelenting pragmatism of General Dagna. "I am of the Riders of Nesmé," he explained slowly and calmly, as if reciting a vow he had made many times before. "My life has been given to the protection of the town, wholly so. We see a way back to our homes. If we get back behind our city wall—"

"The damned trolls'll catch ye there and kill ye."

"Not if many have turned their eyes to the north, as we believe."

"And ye'd be willing to risk all yer kinfolk on that belief?"

"Help will come," Galen declared. "Nesmé will rise again."

Dagna locked stares with the man. "Me and me boys're heading for the tunnels and back to Mithral Hall. Ye're welcomed to join us—Steward Regis's offered his hand. Ye'd be wise to take it."

"If we go home—to *our* homes, good dwarf!—will Mithral Hall not offer us the support we need?"

"Ye're asking me to follow ye on a fool's errand!"

"I am asking you to stand beside your neighbors as they defend their homes from a common enemy."

"You cannot be serious," came another voice, and both Dagna and Galen Firth turned to see Rannek moving to join them. The young man's stride was purposeful and determined. "We have a way to the north, underground where our allies can better protect us."

"You would abandon Nesmé?"

Rannek shook his head vigorously. "I would secure the wounded and those who cannot fight, first and foremost. They are the cause of the Riders, not empty buildings and walls that can be rebuilt."

"Rannek now determines the course of the Riders? Rannek the watchman?"

Dagna watched the exchange carefully, and noted how the younger man seemed to lose all momentum so suddenly.

"I speak for the Riders and I speak for all the folk of Nesmé," Galen Firth went on, turning back to the dwarf. "We see an opportunity to return to our homes, and we shall seize it."

"A fool's errand," said Dagna.

"Can you say with certainty that these tunnels you have found will be any less filled with enemies? Can you be so certain that they will even usher us to Mithral Hall? Or might it be that we go underground, flee from the region, only to have the armies of Mirabar, Silverymoon, and Everlund arrive? What then, General Dagna? They will find no one to rescue and no town to help secure. They will believe they are too late and turn for home."

"Or turn north to the bigger fight that's facing Clan Battlehammer."

"That would be your hope, wouldn't it?"

"Don't ye be talking stupid," Dagna warned. "We come all the way down here, I put ten of me boys in the Halls o' Moradin, and all for yer own sake."

Galen Firth backed off just a bit, and even dipped the slightest of bows.

"We are not unappreciative of your help," he said. "But you must understand that we are as loyal to our home as Clan Battlehammer is to Mithral Hall. By all reports, the way is nearly clear. We can fight our way to Nesmé with little risk and it is unlikely that our enemies will be able to organize against us anytime soon to try to expel us once more. By that time, help will arrive."

The dwarf, hardly convinced, crossed his hairy arms over his chest, his muscles tense and bulging around the heavy leather bracers adorning each wrist.

"And what of the remaining refugees who are still out there?" Galen Firth went on. "Would you have us abandon them? Shall we run and hide," he asked, turning quickly to Rannek, "while our kin cower in the shadows with no hope of finding sanctuary?"

"We do not know that more are out there," Rannek offered, though his voice seemed less than sure.

"We know not if there are none," Galen Firth retorted. "Is my life worth that chance? Is your own?" The fierce veteran turned back on Dagna. "It is," Galen answered his own question. "Come with us if you will, or run and hide in Mithral Hall if that is your choice. Nesmé is not yet lost, and I'll not see her lost!"

With that, Galen turned and stormed away.

Dagna tightened the cross of his arms over his chest and stared at Galen as he departed for a long while before finally turning back to Rannek.

"A fool's errand" he said. "Ye're not for knowing where them trolls're hiding."

Rannek didn't offer any answers, but Dagna understood that the man knew that it wasn't his place to answer. When Galen Firth declared that he spoke for the folk of Nesmé, he was speaking truthfully. Rannek had been given his say, short though it had been, but it was settled.

The young warrior's expression revealed his doubts, but he offered only a bow, then turned and followed Galen Firth, his commander.

A short while later, as twilight began its descent over the land, Dagna and his forty dwarves stood high on the side of a hillock, watching the departing march of Galen Firth and his four hundred Nesmians. Every bit of common sense in the old dwarf told him to let them go and be done with it. Turn about and head into the tunnels, he told himself over and over.

But he didn't give that command as the minutes passed and the black mass of walking humans receded into the foggy shadows of the marshland north of Nesmé.

"I'm not for liking it," Dagna offered to those dwarves around him. "The whole thing's not looking right to me."

"Ye might be thinking a bit too much favor on the cunning of trolls," a dwarf near the old veteran remarked, and Dagna certainly didn't dismiss the comment.

Was he giving the trolls too much credit? The patterns of the escape thus far and the disposition of those refugees they had acquired had led him to consider the trap he might be laying if he was the one chasing the fleeing humans. But he was a dwarf, a veteran of many campaigns, and his enemies were trolls, hulking, stupid, and never strong on tactics.

Maybe Galen Firth was right.

But still the doubts remained.

"Let's follow 'em just a bit, for me own peace o' mind," Dagna told his fellows. "Put a scout left, put a scout right, and we'll all come up behind, but not close enough so that the durned fool Galen can see us."

Several dwarves grumbled at that, but not loudly.

"They coming, little dwarfie," an ugly troll, gruesome even by troll standards, said to the battered dwarf who lay on the ground below it. "Just like them drow elves said they would."

Another troll giggled, which sounded like a group of drunken dwarves forcing spit up from their lungs, and the pair leaned in close against the muddy bank, peering out through the scraggly brush that further camouflaged their position.

Below them, one heavy foot on his chest, poor Fender Stouthammer could hardly draw breath, let alone do anything to help. He wasn't gagged, but couldn't make any sounds other than a wet wheeze, the result of the male drow's clever work with his blade.

But neither could Fender just lie there. He had heard the drow telling the trolls that they would soon have all the refugees and the stubborn dwarves in their grasp. Fender had lain helpless throughout the last days watching those two dark elves orchestrate the movements of the trolls and the bog blokes. A clever pair, the dark elves had assured the biggest and ugliest of the trolls, a two-headed monstrosity named Proffit, that the stupid humans would walk right into their trap.

And there they were, not so far from the abandoned city of Nesmé, cleverly hidden in a long trench to the north of the west-marching humans, while on the right, their comrades, the treelike bog blokes, lay in wait.

The troll pinning Fender started laughing even harder and began jumping up and down, each descent crunching the dwarf a little deeper into the muck.

Reacting purely on instinct, thinking he would be crushed to death, Fender quickly reached out and grabbed an exposed tree root, then rolled back, pulling the soft wood out with him. As the troll came down the next time, its foot settled on the root instead of the dwarf, and to Fender's relief, the troll seemed not to notice—the root had about the same give, he figured.

Not pausing to savor in his minor victory, Fender bent the root so that it would remain sticking out far enough to accommodate the troll, then rolled back the other way, coming up to all fours as he wound about. He crept off quietly behind a line of equally distracted trolls, but couldn't begin to imagine how he might escape.

Because he could not, Fender Stouthammer admitted to himself. There was no way for him, battered as he was, to hold any hope of getting free of the wretched trolls.

"Next best thing, then," the dwarf silently mouthed and he moved into position at the base of the most gently sloping region of the trench, and near to a series of roots that climbed all the way to the crest, some eight feet from the muddy bottom. With a deep breath and a moment of regret for all those hearty friends and family he'd not ever see again, Fender exploded into motion, running up the root line, hand over hand.

He counted on surprise, and so he had it as he crossed out of the pit and away from the nearest, startled troll. Back behind him, he heard the hoots of his guards, and the growing rumble of outrage.

Fender sprinted for all his life, and more importantly for the lives of all those humans unwittingly approaching the designated kill zone. He tried to scream out to warn them off the trolls, but of course he could not, and he waved all the more frantically when several of the leading men began rushing his way.

Fender did not have to look behind him to know that the trolls had come out in pursuit, for he saw the humans blanch and skid to a stop as one. He saw their eyes go wide with shock and horror. He saw them start to back-pedal, then turn and run off shouting in terror.

"Run on," Fender gasped. "Run far and run free."

He felt as if he had been punched hard in the back then, his breath blasted away. He didn't go flying away, though, and strangely felt no pain. When he looked down to his own chest, he understood, for the thick and sharpened end of a heavy branch protruded from between his breasts.

"Oh," Fender remarked, probably the loudest vocalization he had managed since his throat had been cut.

Then he fell over, hardly free, but satisfied that he had properly executed the next best thing.

Stupid trolls, Tos'un Armgo's fingers flashed to Kaer'lic in the silent hand code of the dark elves. *They cannot be trusted to guard a single wounded prisoner!*

Equally disgusted, Kaer'lic held her tongue and watched the unfolding events. Already, the humans were in full and furious retreat, running back to the east. From her high vantage point in the north, Kaer'lic began to nod with renewed hope as the human line predictably began to veer south, away from the charging trolls.

"Is he dead?" Kaer'lic asked, motioning toward the dwarf.

As she spoke, though, Fender squirmed.

"Run for the cover of the trees," the drow priestess said. The copse was comprised of three bog blokes—which very much resembled dead, wintry trees—for every real tree. "Yes, there you will find wood with which to burn the trolls!"

Kaer'lic's wide smile met a similarly knowing one from her partner, for he too recognized the certain doom looming before the ragtag bunch.

But Tos'un's growl stole her mirth, and she followed his scowl back to the east-northeast, where a second force appeared, sweeping down a rocky slope, whooping for war, rattling weapons, and calling out to the dwarf gods Moradin, Clangeddin, and Dumathoin.

Then, amazingly, the dwarves all joined voice in song, a single refrain repeated over and over again, "Along our wake ye people flee. We'll hold 'em back and get ye free!"

Over and over again they sang it out, more emphatically at every juncture when it seemed as if the folk of Nesmé wouldn't veer back to the northeast.

"They've seen the truth of the bog blokes," Kaer'lic observed.

Tos'un gave a derisive laugh and replied, "Of all the races on and under Toril, are any less adept at holding a simple trap than smelly trolls?"

"Any that were less adept than trolls likely were exterminated eons ago."

"What now?"

"Watch the fun," the priestess replied. "And go fetch that fallen dwarf. Perhaps Lady Lolth will grant me the power I need to keep him alive, so that we might find more enjoyment from him before we kill him."

Dagna's scouts had picked the perfect route for intercepting the chase. The dwarves came down from on high, their short, strong legs gaining momentum as they rambled down the slope. They rushed past the fleeing Nesmians to the left, to a dwarf hollering angrily at those few human warriors who seemed ready to turn and join in the dwarves' charge.

Dagna led his boys right around the humans, hardly slowing as they met the charge of the trolls. Axes, swords, and hammers chopping, they slashed through the front ranks. Those leading trolls who were still standing turned around to fight their new, closer enemies.

Thus, by their own tactics, the dwarves found themselves surrounded almost immediately. There was no despair at that realization, however, for that was exactly as they, to a dwarf, had planned. They had stopped the troll charge in its tracks, and had given the Nesmians a free run.

They knew the cost.

And accepted it with a song of battle on their lips.

Not one of Dagna's boys came off that field alive.

"Look how easily Proffit's fools are distracted!" Kaer'lic said. "They turn on a force of two score, while twenty times that number run away!"

"They'll not escape," replied Tos'un, who had climbed a tree above Kaer'lic and the panting Fender, which afforded him a wider range of view. "The bog blokes outpace them from the south. Already the humans see that they will be caught. Many of their males are forming a defense."

Kaer'lic looked up to her companion, but her smile became a curious frown, for high above Tos'un, the priestess saw a line of fire streaking across the sky west to east, descending as it went. As the fiery object crossed over Tos'un, Kaer'lic began to make out its shape. It was some kind of a cart, a chariot perhaps, pulled by a team of fiery horses.

Tos'un glanced up, too, as did everyone on the field.

Down the chariot swooped, cutting low over the humans, many of whom fell to the ground in fear, but with others suddenly cheering.

Then, just south of the cluster of humans, great fireballs erupted, flames leaping into the night sky.

"The bog blokes!" Tos'un cried out.

East of his position, the humans started on their run once more.

Her long silvery hair flying out behind her, Lady Alustriel of Silverymoon held the reigns of her magically-created chariot of fire in one hand and waved the other hand in a series of movements that brought another tiny pill of glowing flame to her grasp. She veered the chariot for a run over the largest remaining cluster of bog blokes and tossed the pill upon them as she passed.

The fireball erupted in their midst, the hungry flames biting at the barklike skin of the creatures.

Alustriel banked to get a view of the scene below, and saw that the humans were well on their way again, and that the remaining bog blokes seemed too busy getting away from burning kin to offer any more pursuit. Alustriel's heart sank more than a little when she glanced back to the west, for the battle was all but over, with the trolls overwhelming the dwarves.

Her admiration for Clan Battlehammer only grew that dark night, not only for the actions of that particular brave force, but for even sending any warriors south at such a dark time. Word had come to Silverymoon from Nesmé of the rise of the Trollmoors, and further information had filtered down through King Emerus Warcrown of Citadel Felbarr detailing the march of Obould Many-Arrows. Alustriel had set off at once to survey the situation.

She knew that Mithral Hall was under terrible duress. She knew that the North had been swept by the ferocious orc king and his swarm of minions, and that the western bank of the Surbrin had been heavily fortified.

She knew that she had done little to help that situation, but in looking at the fleeing, desperate Nesmians, she took comfort that she had helped a bit at least.

9

DISPUTING DIVINE
INTERVENTION

Wulfgar flailed his arms and tried to twist as he fell from above, hoping to get away from the area of confusion, where orcs screamed in agony and ran all around, where molten metal glowed angrily, and where the vat bounced down hard. He couldn't change his angle of descent, but was fortunate to have instinctively pushed out when first he fell. He came down hard atop a group of unsuspecting orcs, burying them beneath his bulk.

They only partially broke the fall of nearly two dozen feet, though, and Wulfgar hit hard, twisting and slamming painfully as he and the orcs below him went down to the floor. Burning pain assailed him from many places—he figured that more than one bone had cracked in that fall—but he knew he had no time to even wince. Screaming indecipherably, the barbarian put his feet under him and forced himself up, flailing wildly with fist and hammer, trying to keep the closest orcs at bay.

He stumbled for the exit corridor where he knew Bruenor and the others were making their last stand in the great hall, but many orcs stood between him and that door. Any hopes he had that the confusion caused by the molten metal and the heavy vat would allow him to break free dissipated quickly as the orcs reacted to him, prodding at him from every direction. He felt a stab in his shoulder and twisted fast, snapping a flimsy spear's head right off. Aegis-fang swung around hard, cracking an orc in the side with a blow heavy enough to send it flying into a second, and to send both of them tumbling over a third.

A spear hit Wulfgar in the buttocks, and one of the orcs lying on the floor near to him bit him hard on the ankle. He kicked and thrashed, he swung his hammer and shouldered his way forward, but against increasing resistance.

He couldn't make it, nor could the dwarves hope to get to him.

To the side of Wulfgar's position, a group of orcs moved cautiously toward a single door, not knowing whether it blocked yet another corridor or a second room. Fearing that enemies were waiting just beyond the closed portal, the orcs called to one of the frost giants, inviting it to crash through.

The giant wore a frown at first, lamenting that it could not get to the fallen human—the one, it knew, who had killed its friend with that terrible warhammer—in time to claim the kill. But when it noted the orcs pointing excitedly at the door, the behemoth curled up its lips and launched into a short run, bending low. The giant slammed into the door that was not a door, shouldering it, thinking to smash it into the room.

Except that there was no room, and it was no door.

It was wax, mostly, formed into the shape of a door and set not against a corridor or room opening, but against solid stone—a section of wall that had been thoroughly soaked with explosive oil of impact.

The fake door crashed in hard and the wax disintegrated under the force of the sudden and devastating explosion. The many pieces of sharpened metal concealed within the wax blew free, blasting outward in a line across the room.

The giant bounced back, what was left of its face wearing an expression of absolute incredulity. The behemoth held its arms wide and looked down at its shredded body, at the heavy clothing and flaps of skin wagging freely from head to toe, at the lines of blood dripping everywhere.

The giant looked back helplessly, and fell dead.

And all around it in that line of devastating shrapnel, orcs tumbled, shrieked, and died.

Across the eastern end of the great hall, the fighting stopped, dwarves and orcs alike turning back to gawk at the swath of death the exploding door cut through the line of orcs and another pair of unfortunate giants. Alone in the crowd, one warrior kept on fighting, though. Too blinded by pain and anger to even hear the blast and the screams, Wulfgar gained momentum, swatting with abandon, growling like an animal because he had not the sensibility remaining to even form the name of his god.

He stumbled as much as he intentionally moved forward, crashing through the lines of distracted orcs. He hardly heard the next loud report, though the sudden vibration nearly knocked him from his feet as a large rock crashed down behind him, clipping one orc and smashing a second. Had he turned back, had his sensibilities not been shattered by the pain, emotional and physical, Wulfgar would have recognized that particular boulder.

But he didn't look back, just drove forward. With the help of the distraction from the door blast, he managed to plow through to Bruenor's ranks. Dwarves surged out all around him, swarming behind him like a mother's loving arms and gathering him into the tunnel before them.

"Aw, get him to the priests," Bruenor Battlehammer said when he finally got the chance to take a good look at his adopted son.

Spear tips and orc arrows protruded from the barbarian in several places, and those represented only a fraction of the battered man's visible wounds. Bruenor knew well that Wulfgar likely had many more injuries he could not see.

The dwarf king had to move past his fear for his boy, and quickly, for the organized retreat reached a critical juncture that required absolute coordination. Bruenor and his warriors kept up the stubborn fight, but at the same time began to flow backward from the wider chamber, tightening the line appropriately as they melted into the single escape corridor.

Those in the first few ranks held tight their formations, but those farther back from the fighting broke and ran, clearing the way for the flight that would soon follow.

Farther back, in hidden side rooms, engineers held their positions at peg-and-crank mechanisms.

Bruenor stayed in the center of the trailing line of flight, face to face with the pursuing orcs. His axe added more than a few notches that day, creasing orc skulls. With every step he took backward, the dwarf king had to battle against his outrage that the filthy beasts had come into his sacred halls, and had to remind himself that he would fall back on them before the turn of day.

When his line passed the assigned point, Bruenor called out and his voice was joined by the shouts of all those around him.

The engineers pulled their pegs, literally dropping the ceiling of the corridor back toward the great entry hall. Two huge blocks of stone slid down, filling the corridor, crushing flat the unfortunate orcs beneath them and sealing off a score of their comrades, those closest to Bruenor's boys, from their swarming kin in the foyer.

The outraged dwarves made fast work of the trapped orcs.

Any joy that Bruenor had at the successful evacuation and upon learning that Wulfgar's injuries were not too serious, was short-lived, though. A few moments later, Bruenor's retreat route intersected with that of the dwarves fleeing the ledge, dwarves who carried Catti-brie tenderly in their arms.

Tucked into the secret cubby, Regis rubbed his chubby hands over his face, as if trying to brush away his mounting fear. He glanced up often to the light streaming in through a neatly-blown hole in the solid stone wall of his hiding place. Regis had heard the blast, and knew it to be the trapped wax door. Apparently, one of the projectiles had been deflected—off an orc skull, he hoped—and had rocketed up high, cracking through the outer stone wall of the cubby and splitting the air barely an inch in front of the poor halfling's face. Every so often, Regis glanced across at the other, far more substantial stone wall, where the projectile, a metal sling bullet, could be seen embedded in the rock.

The halfling fought hard to keep his breathing steady, realizing that the last thing he could afford was for orcs to discover him. And they had come up to the ledge, he knew, for he could hear their grunting and their large feet slapping on the stone behind him.

"Five hours," he silently mouthed, for that was the planned pause before the counterattack. He knew that he should try to get some sleep, then, but he could smell the orcs nearby and simply couldn't relax enough to keep his eyes closed for any length of time.

The dwarves gathered around Bruenor could hear the tentativeness in his every word.

"But will it keep on rolling?" the dwarf king asked the engineers standing beside a modified version of a "juicer," a heavy rolling ram designed to squish the blood out of orcs and the like by pressing them against a wall. Unlike the typical Battlehammer juicers, which were really no more than a cylinder of stone on a thick axle with poles behind so the dwarves could rush it along, the new contraption had been given a distinct personality. Carved wooden likeness of dwarves upon battle boars, the handiwork of Pikel Bouldershoulder, stood out in front of the main body of the one-ton battering ram, and below them was a skirt of metal, fanning out like a ship's prow. An "orc-catcher," Nanfoodle had named it, designed to wedge through the throng of enemies like a spear tip, throwing them aside.

The whole of the thing was set upon well-greased metal wheels, lined in a thin, sharpened ridge that would simply cut through any bodies the catcher missed. Handles had been set for twenty dwarves to push, and as an added bonus, Nanfoodle had geared the boar-riding statues to an offset on the axle, so that the six wooden dwarf "riders" would seem to be charging, leaping over each other in a rolling motion.

"They'll stop it eventually," Nanfoodle reasoned. "More by the pile of their dead, I would guess, than by any concerted effort to halt the thing. Once the dwarves get this contraption rolling, it would take a team of giants to slow it!"

Bruenor nodded and kept moving, studying the device from every conceivable angle.

He had to keep moving, he knew. He had to keep studying and thinking of the present crisis.

His two children had been hurt.

Wincing with every movement, Wulfgar swung his wolf-hide cloak across his shoulders and managed to bring his right arm back far enough to get behind the mantle and wrap it around him, covering his strong chain shirt of interlocking mithral links.

"What're ye doing?" Delly Curtie asked him, coming back into the room after settling Colson in her bed.

Wulfgar looked back at her as if the answer should be obvious.

"Cordio said ye wasn't to be going back today," Delly reminded him. "He said ye're too hurt."

Wulfgar shook his head and clasped the wolf-hide surcoat closed. Before he finished, Delly was at his side, tugging at one arm.

"Don't go," she pleaded.

Wulfgar stared down at her incredulously. "Orcs are in Mithral Hall. That cannot hold."

"Let Bruenor drive them out. Or better, let us thicken the walls before them, and leave them in empty chambers."

Wulfgar's expression did not straighten.

"We can go out the tunnels to Felbarr," Delly went on. "All of the clan. They'll be welcomed there. I heard Jackonray Broadbelt say as much when he was talking to the folk chased down from the northland."

"Perhaps many of those folk would be wise to go," Wulfgar admitted.

"Not one's intending to make Felbarr a home. They're all for Silverymoon and Everlund and Sundabar. Ye've been to Silverymoon?"

"Once."

"Is it as beautiful as they say?" Delly asked, and the sparkle in her eyes betrayed her innermost desire, showing it clearly to Wulfgar, whose own blue eyes widened at the recognition.

"We will visit it," he promised, and he knew, somehow, that "visiting" wasn't what Delly had in mind, and wouldn't be nearly enough to assuage her.

"What are you saying?" he demanded suddenly.

Delly fell back from the blunt statement. "Just want to see it, is all," she said, lowering her gaze to the floor.

"Is something wrong?"

"Orcs're in the hall. Ye said so yerself."

"But if no orcs were in the hall, you would still wish to go to Silverymoon, or Sundabar?"

Delly kicked at the stone, her hesitance seeming so completely out of character that the hair on the back of Wulfgar's strong neck began to bristle.

"What kind of life is a child to get if all she's seeing are her parents and dwarves?" Delly dared to ask.

Wulfgar's eyes flared. "Catti-brie had such an upbringing."

Delly looked up, her expression hardly complimentary.

"I have no time to argue about this," Wulfgar said. "They are bringing the juicer into position, and I will hold my place behind it."

"Cordio said ye shouldn't go."

"Cordio is a priest, and always erring on the side of caution regarding those he tends."

"Cordio is a dwarf, and wanting all who're able up there killing orcs," Delly countered, and Wulfgar managed a smile. He figured that if it were not for Colson, Delly would be marching out beside him to battle.

Or maybe not, he realized as he looked at her more closely, at the profound frown that was hidden just below the surface of her almost-impassive expression. He had hardly seen her since the conflict had begun, since they had separated on the road from Icewind Dale back to Mithral Hall. Only then did he realize how lonely she likely was, down there with dwarves too distracted by pressing issues to hold her and comfort her.

"We will go see Silverymoon when this is over. And Sundabar," he offered.

Delly looked back down, but gave a slight nod.

Wulfgar winced again, and it was from more than physical pain. He believed his own words and had no time for petty arguments. He walked over and bent low, stiffly, from the pain, to give Delly a kiss. She offered only her cheek for the peck.

By the time he had crossed out of the room, though, Wulfgar the warrior, son of Beornegar, son of Bruenor, a champion of Mithral Hall, had put Delly and her concerns out of his mind.

"We have breached the hall!" Tsinka shrieked.

Obould smirked at her, thinking that the shaman had forgotten how to speak without raising her voice several octaves. All around them, orcs cheered and hopped about, punching their fists in defiance. The grand entry hall was theirs, as well as a complex of rooms both north and south of that huge foyer. The eastern corridor had been sealed by heavy blocks, but if they had been able to breach the magnificent western doors of Mithral Hall, could any of them believe the impromptu barriers would pose any substantial obstacle?

Lines of orcs marched past, dragging dead companions out into Keeper's Dale where they were tossing them onto a gigantic pyre for burning. The line seemed endless! In the few minutes of battle in the hall, the rain of death from above and the stubborn defensive stance of the dwarves, more than three hundred orcs had died. Traps, including that devastating explosion, the source of which Obould was still to discern, had taken more than a score. What other tricks might Bruenor Battlehammer have in store, the orc king wondered. Was this entire section of Mithral Hall rigged to explode, like the mountain ridge up the northern cliff beyond Keeper's Dale?

Had they even killed any dwarves in the fight? Obould was certain they had taken down a few, at least, but so coordinated was the dwarves' retreat that not a body had been left behind.

Beside him, Tsinka rambled on in her shrill tone, replaying the events with a heroic spin. She spoke of the glory of Gruumsh and the coming sweep of Clan Battlehammer from their ancient homeland, and all the orcs near to her screamed with equal glee and enthusiasm.

Obould wanted to throttle the shaman.

The voice of Gerti Orelsdottr, obviously not happy with events, distracted him from the maniacal cheering. Four giants had died in the fight, with two others seriously wounded and scarred, and Gerti never took well to losing one of her precious kin. While he was growing tired of Gerti's continual whining, Obould knew that he would need the giantess and her forces if they were to prod farther into the hall, and even if they were to continue to hold their position along the River Surbrin. As much as he hated to admit it, Obould's current vision of his kingdom included Gerti Orelsdottr.

The orc king looked back to Tsinka. Could she even grasp the trials ahead of them? Did she even understand that they could not lose orcs by the hundreds for every room's gain into Mithral Hall? Or that even if they managed to chase the Battlehammers out at such a horrendous cost, Citadels Felbarr and Adbar and the cities of Silverymoon and Everlund would certainly come back at them?

"Gruumsh! Gruumsh! Gruumsh!" Tsinka began to chant, and the orcs near to her took it up at the top of their lungs.

"Gruumsh! Gruumsh! Gruumsh!"

The sound poured in through the hole in the cubby and reverberated off the stones, filling the space and flooding poor Regis's ears. The whole orc nation seemed to be sitting on the halfling's shoulders, screaming in victory, and Regis reflexively curled and brought his hands up to cover his ears. The volume only seemed to increase despite his cover, though, as the orcs began to stamp their feet, the whole of the great hall shaking under their collective exultation.

Regis curled tighter to try to block it out. He almost expected Gruumsh to walk into the hall and reach through the small hole to pull him out. His jaw chattered so badly that his teeth hurt and his ears throbbed under the assault.

"Gruumsh! Gruumsh! Gruumsh!"

To his horror, Regis found himself yelling to counter the awful sound. His frightened reaction proved most fortunate for the defenders of Mithral Hall, for the halfling snapped his hands from his ears to his mouth just in time to hear a different sound behind the chanting.

Dwarven horns, low and throaty, winded from somewhere deeper in the complex.

It took Regis a long moment to even register them, and another moment to recognize the signal.

He grabbed the peg lever with both hands and yanked it back, releasing the crank. He held it back for a count of two, then shoved it forward.

The wheel spun for those two seconds, the rope winding out, through the top of the cubby and the metal piping set along the ceiling. Outside in the great entry hall, the umbrellalike contraption dropped, then stopped suddenly with an abrupt jerk as the halfling's movement re-pegged the crank. The jolt cracked the hinges holding the various layers of the bowl-shaped hopper, inverting them one after another even as the whole of the contraption, reacting to the untwisting of the heavy rope, began to turn.

Ceramic balls rolled out from the center, down prescribed tracks of metal that ended in upward curls of varying elevations. With the turning movement and the differing angles of release, the rolling balls leaped from the contraption in a manner well-calculated to spread the "bombing" out across the maximum area.

Each of the ceramic balls was filled with one of two potions. Some were filled with bits of sharpened metal and the same oil of impact that had blown apart the wax door, while others held a more straightforward concoction of volatile liquid that exploded upon contact with air.

Bursts of shrapnel and mini-fireballs erupted all across the orc throng.

Chants of "Gruumsh!" became muffled grunts as bits of metal tore through porcine lungs, and were surpassed by shrieks of agony as flames bit at other orcs.

"A thousand wounds and a few deaths." That was how Ivan Bouldershoulder and Nanfoodle the gnome had aptly explained the effects of the umbrella contraption to Bruenor and the others.

And that was exactly what Bruenor wanted. The dwarves of Clan Battlehammer knew orcs well enough to understand the level of confusion and terror they'd created. Farther back in the complex, great levers, larger versions of the one Regis had used, were yanked back, releasing massive counterweights chained to the blocks that had been dropped to seal the tunnels into the entry hall.

The first movement came far to the back of the dwarven line. Lowering their shoulders, the dwarves grunted and shoved, starting the massive juicer on its roll. How greatly their efforts increased when Wulfgar appeared among their ranks, taking his place on the higher handles that had been put in just to accommodate him.

"Go! Go! Go!" the warcommanders yelled to the leading line of dwarves as the rolling juicer came into view, rumbling down the hall. The lead unit, cavalry on fierce war pigs, swept out in front of the juicer and charged down the hall even as the blocks began to rise. Beside them, Pikel Bouldershoulder waggled the fingers of his one hand and waved dramatically, conjuring a mist that seemed to rise from the very stones, obscuring the air at the end of the corridor and in the closest areas of the great foyer.

Beyond the block, confusion dominated the hall, with dozens of small fires keeping the orcs rushing every which way. Others thrashed wildly in fear and pain. Some saw the coming charge, though, and shouted for a defensive stand.

The dwarves on the war pigs howled to Moradin and kicked their mounts into a swifter run, but then, as they neared the opening, they slowed suddenly, tugging back their reins. They turned aside as one, skidding into the many alcoves that lined the hall.

The orcs closest the corridor still saw cavalry charging, though, or thought they did, for in the mist they couldn't really discern the difference between real pigs and the carved figures on the front of the juicer. So they set their spears and grouped in tight formation against the charge . . .

. . . and were swept aside by the rolling tonnage of the dwarven war engine.

Into the hall went Wulfgar and the dwarves, plowing ahead and tossing orcs aside with abandon. Behind them came the war pig cavalry, fanning out with precision and to great effect against the supporting orcs, those that did not have the long spears to counter such a charge.

Up above, as similar blocking stones were lifted by counterweights, Bruenor and other dwarves roared out onto the ledges, finding, as they had anticipated, more orcs staring back dumbfounded into the chaos of the foyer than orcs ready to defend. Bruenor, and Pwent and his Gutbusters, gained a foothold on the main ledge. With sheer ferocity they dislodged the orcs one after another. Within moments, the balcony was clear, but Pwent and his boys had prepared for that foregone conclusion well. Some of the Gutbusters had come out onto the ledge already in harnesses, roped back to weighted cranks. As soon as the ledge began to clear, the lead-liners, as Pwent had called them, simply leaped off, the counterbalanced cranks slowing their descent.

But not slowing them too much. They wanted to make an impression, after all.

The rest of the Gutbusters sprang upon the ropes to get down to the real action, and Bruenor did as well, turning the captured balconies over to lines of crossbow-armed dwarves pouring out through the small tunnels.

Confusion won those early moments, and it was something that Bruenor and his boys were determined to push through to the very end. More and more dwarves rolled in or came down from above, thickening and widening the line of slaughter.

Crossbowdwarves picked their targets carefully back by the entryway from Keeper's Dale, looking for any orcs barking orders.

"Leader!" one dwarf cried, pointing out to one orc who seemed to be standing taller than his fellows, perhaps up on a stone block so that he could better direct the fighting.

Twenty dwarves turned their crossbows upon the target, and on the order of "Fire!" let fly.

The unfortunate orc commander, shouting for a turn for defense, was suddenly silenced—silenced and shattered as a barrage of bolts, many of them packed with oil of impact, shredded his body.

The orcs around him howled and fled.

As Bruenor, Wulfgar, and all the floor fighters made their way across the foyer, out of the corridor came the most important dwarves of all. Engineers rambled out, bearing heavy metal sheets that could be quickly assembled into a killing pocket, a funnel-shaped pair of walls to be constructed inside the foyer near the broken doors. Lined on top with spear tips and cut with dozens of murder holes, the killing pocket would cost their enemies dearly if the orcs launched a counter charge.

But the work had to be done fast and it had to be done with perfect timing. The first pieces, those farthest back from Keeper's Dale, were set in place behind the leading edge of the dwarves' charge. If the orcs had countered quickly enough, perhaps with giant support, the dwarves caught in front of those huge metal wall sections would have been in a sorry position indeed.

It didn't happen, though. The orc retreat was a flight of sheer terror, taking all the surviving orcs right out of Mithral Hall, surrendering ground readily.

In the span of just a few minutes, scores of orcs lay dead and the foyer was back in Bruenor's hands.

"Turn them back! Lead them back!" Tsinka Shinriil pleaded with Obould. "Quickly! Charge! Before the dwarves fortify!"

"Your orcs must lead the way," Gerti Orelsdottr added, for she wasn't about to send her giants charging in to set off the no-doubt cunning traps the dwarves still had in place.

Obould stood outside of Mithral Hall's broken doors and watched his greatest fears come to fruition.

"Dwarves in their tunnels," he whispered under his breath, shaking his head with every word.

Tsinka kept shouting at him to attack, and he almost did it.

The visions of his kingdom seemed to wash away under rivers of orc blood. The orc king understood that he could counter the attack, that the sheer weight of his numbers would likely reclaim the entry hall. He even suspected that the dwarves were ready for such an eventuality, and would retreat again in a well-coordinated, pre-determined fashion.

Twenty orcs would die for every dwarf that fell, much like the first assault.

A glance to the side showed Obould the massive, still-smoldering mound of dead from the initial break-in.

Tsinka yelled at him some more.

The orc king shook his head. "Form defensive lines out here!" he shouted to his commanders and gang leaders. "Build walls of stone and hide behind them. If the dwarves try to come forth from their halls, slaughter them!"

Many of the commanders seemed surprised by the orders, but not a one had the courage to even begin to question King Obould Many-Arrows, and few of them wanted to charge back into the dwarven tunnels anyway.

"What are you doing?" Tsinka shrieked at him. "Kill them all! Charge into Mithral Hall and kill them all! Gruumsh demands—"

Her voice cut off suddenly as Obould's hand clamped hard around her throat. With just that one arm, the orc king lifted the shaman from the ground and brought her up very close to his scowling face.

"I grow weary of Tsinka telling me the will of Gruumsh. I am Gruumsh, so you say. We do not go back into Mithral Hall!"

He looked around at Gerti and the others, who were staring at him skeptically.

"Seal the doors!" Obould ordered. "Put the smelly dwarves in their smelly hole, and let us keep them there!" He turned back to Tsinka. "I will not throw orcs onto dwarven spears for the sake of your orgy. Mithral Hall is an inconvenience and nothing more—if we choose to make it that way. King Bruenor is soon to be insignificant, a dwarf in a covered hole who cannot strike out at me."

Tsinka's mouth moved as she tried to argue, but Obould clamped just a bit tighter, turning her whispers into a gasp.

"There are better ways," Obould assured her.

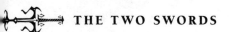

He tossed her down and she stumbled back a few steps and fell onto her behind.

"If you wish to live to see those ways, then choose your words and your tone more wisely," Obould warned.

He turned on his heel and moved away.

PART TWO DWARF AMBITIONS

From a high ridge east of Keeper's Dale, I watched the giants construct their massive battering ram. I watched the orcs practice their tactics—tight lines and sudden charges. I heard the awful cheering, the bloodthirsty calls for dwarf blood and dwarf heads, the feral screams of battle lust.

From that same ridge, I watched the huge ram pulled back by a line of giants, then let loose to swing hard and fast at the base of the mountain on which I stood, at the metal doorway shell of Mithral Hall. The ground beneath my feet shuddered. The booming sound vibrated in the air.

They pulled it back and let fly again and again.

Then the shouts filled the air, and the wild charge was on.

I stood there on that ridge, Innovindil beside me, and I knew that my friends, Bruenor's kin, were battling for their homeland and for their very lives right below me. And I could do nothing.

I realized then, in that awful moment, that I should be in there with the dwarves, killing orcs until at last I, too, was cut down. I realized then, in that awful moment, that my decisions of the last few tendays, formed in anger and even more in fear, betrayed the trust of the friendship that Bruenor and I had always held.

Soon after—too soon!—the mountainside quieted. The battle ended.

To my horror, I came to see that the orcs had won the day, that they had gained a foothold inside Mithral Hall. They had driven the dwarves from the entry hall at least. I took some comfort in the fact that the bulk of the orc force remained outside the broken door, continuing their work in Keeper's Dale. Nor had many giants gone in.

Bruenor's kin were not being swept away; likely, they had surrendered the wider entry halls for the more defensible areas in the tighter tunnels.

That sense of hope did not wash away my guilt, however. In my heart I understood that I should have gone back to Mithral Hall, to stand with the dwarves who for so long had treated me as one of their own.

Innovindil would hear nothing of it, though. She reminded me that I had not, had never, fled the battle for Mithral Hall. Obould's son was dead because of my decision, and many orcs had been turned back to their holes in the Spine of the World because of my—of our, Innovindil, Tarathiel and myself—work in the north.

It is difficult to realize that you cannot win every battle for every friend. It is difficult to understand and accept your own limitations, and with them, the recognition that while you try to do the best you can, it will often prove inadequate.

And so it was then and there, on that mountainside watching the battle, in that moment when all seemed darkest, that I began to accept the loss of Bruenor and the others. Oh, the hole in my heart did not close. It never will. I know and accept that. But what I let go then was my own guilt at witnessing the fall of a friend, my own guilt at not having been there to help him, or there to hold his hand in the end.

Most of us will know loss in our lives. For an elf, drow or moon, wild or avariel, who will see centuries of life, this is unavoidable—a parent, a friend, a brother, a lover, a child even. Profound pain is often the unavoidable reality of conscious existence. How less tolerable that loss will be if we compound it internally with a sense of guilt.

Guilt.

It is the easiest of feelings to conjure, and the most insidious. It is rooted in the selfishness of individuality, though for goodly folks, it usually finds its source in the suffering of others.

What I understand now, as never before, is that guilt is not the driving force behind responsibility. If we act in a goodly way because we are afraid of how we will feel if we do not, then we have not truly come to separate the concept of right and wrong. For there is a level above that, an understanding of community, friendship, and loyalty. I do not choose to stand beside Bruenor or any other friend to alleviate guilt. I do so because in that, and in their reciprocal friendship, we are both the stronger and the better. Our lives become worth so much more.

I learned that one awful day, standing on a cold mountain stone watching monsters crash through the door of a place that had long been my home.

I miss Bruenor and Wulfgar and Regis and Catti-brie. My heart bleeds for them and yearns for them every minute of every day.

But I accept the loss and bear no personal burden for it beyond my own emptiness. I did not turn from my friends in their hour of need, though I could not be as close to them as I would desire. From across that ravine when Withegroo's tower fell, when Bruenor Battlehammer tumbled from on high, I offered to him all that I could: my love and my heart.

And now I will go on, Innovindil at my side, and continue our battle against our common enemy. We fight for Mithral Hall, for Bruenor, for Wulfgar, for Regis, for Catti-brie, for Tarathiel, and for all the goodly folk. We fight the monstrous scourge of Obould and his evil minions.

At the end, I offered to my falling friends my love and my heart. Now I pledge to them my enduring friendship and my determination to live on in a manner that would make the dwarf king stare at me, his head tilted, his expression typically skeptical about some action or another of mine.

"Durned elf," he will say often, as he looks down on me from Moradin's halls.

And I will hear him, and all the others, for they are with me always, no small part of Drizzt Do'Urden.

For as I begin to let go, I find that I hold them all the tighter, but in a way that will make me look up to the imagined halls of Moradin, to the whispered grumbling of a lost friend, and smile.

—Drizzt Do'Urden

10

THE UNEXPECTED TURN

He heard a horn blow somewhere far back in the recesses of his mind, and the ground beneath him began to tremble. Shaken from Reverie, the elves' dreamlike, meditative state, Drizzt Do'Urden's lavender eyes popped open wide. In a movement that seemed as easy as that blink, the drow leaped up to his feet, hands instinctively going to the scimitars belted on each hip.

Around a boulder that served as a windbreak in their outdoor, ceiling-less camp came Innovindil, quick-stepping.

Beneath their feet, the mountain itself trembled. Off to the side, Sunset pawed at the stone and snorted.

"The dwarves?" Innovindil asked.

"Let us hope it is the dwarves," Drizzt replied, for he didn't want to imagine the hellish destruction that rumbling might be causing to Clan Battlehammer if Obould's minions were the cause.

The two sprinted away, full speed down the side of the rocky slope. No other race could have matched the pace of the fleet and balanced elves, drow and moon. They ran side by side, leaping atop boulders and skipping over narrow cracks deep beyond sight. Arm-in-arm they overcame any natural barriers, with Drizzt hoisting Innovindil over one short stone wall, and she turning back to offer him a complimentary hand up.

Down they ran, helping each other every step. They came to one smooth and steeply declining slope that ended in a sheer drop, but rather than slow their swift run as they approached that cliff, they put their heads down and sped on. For at the base of that slope, overlooking the cliff, was a small tree, and the pair came upon it in turn. Drizzt leaped and turned, his torso horizontal. He caught the tree with outstretched arms and swung around it, using its strength to veer his run to the side.

Innovindil came right behind with a similar movement and the two ran on along the ledge. They moved to the same vantage point they had taken to witness Obould's break-in to Mithral Hall, a high, flat stone on a westward jut that afforded them a view of most of the dale, excepting only the area right near the great doors of the hall.

Soon the pair could hear screams from below, and Drizzt's heart leaped when he came to recognize that they were the cries of orcs alone.

By the time Drizzt and Innovindil got to their lookout spot, orcs were pouring from the broken doors, running back out into Keeper's Dale in full flight. Flames sprouted on some, flickering orange in the diminishing daylight, and others staggered, obviously wounded.

"The dwarves fight back," Innovindil observed.

Drizzt's hands went to his scimitar hilts and he even started away, but Innovindil grabbed him by the shoulder and held him steady.

"As you did for me when Tarathiel was slain," she explained into his scowl when he turned to regard her. "There is nothing we can do down there."

Looking back, Drizzt knew she was right. The area of the dale closest the doors was a swaying sea of orc warriors, shouting and shoving, some running for the broken doors, others running away. Giants dotted that sea, like tall masts of an armada, closing cautiously. Echoing from the entry hall came the unmistakable sounds of battle, a cacophony of screams and shouts, the clang of metal, and the rumble of stonework.

A giant staggered out, scattering orcs before it.

Up on the stone, Drizzt punched his fist in victory, for it quickly became apparent that the dwarves were winning the day, that Obould's minions were being rudely evicted from Mithral Hall.

"They are giving ground," Innovindil called to him. He turned to see that she had moved far to the side, even climbing down over the lip of the flat stone perch to gain an even better vantage point. "The dwarves have gained the door!" she called.

Drizzt punched his fist again and silently congratulated the kin of King Bruenor. He had seen their mettle so many times up in the cold and harsh terrain of Icewind Dale, and in the war against his kin from Menzoberranzan. Thus, when he considered his former companions, he realized that he should not be surprised at the sudden turn of events. Still, it boggled even Drizzt to think that such an army as Obould's had been turned back in so efficient a manner.

Innovindil came up beside him a short while later, when the fighting had died down somewhat. She took his arm in her own and leaned in against him.

"It would seem that the orc king underestimated the strength of King Bruenor's kin," she remarked.

"I am surprised that they turned back against the orcs in this manner," Drizzt admitted. "The tunnels beyond the entry halls are tighter and more easily held."

"They do not want the stench of orcs in their halls."

Drizzt merely smiled.

For a long time, the pair stood there, and when they at last settled in for the remainder of the night, they did so right there on that flat stone, both eager to see what the orcs might do to counter the dwarves' charge.

As the slanting rays of the rising sun fell over them and past them to illuminate the dale below a couple of hours later, both elves were a bit surprised to see that the orcs had moved back from the doors, and seemed in no hurry to close in again. Indeed, from everything Drizzt and Innovindil could tell, it appeared as if the orcs and giants were taking up their own defensive positions. The elves watched curiously as gangs of orcs carted heavy stones in from the mountainsides, piling them near other teams who were fast at work in constructing walls.

Every now and then a giant would take one of those stones, give a roar of defiance, and launch it at the door area, but that, it seemed, was the extent of the monstrous counterattack.

"When have you ever known orcs to so willingly surrender ground, except in full retreat?" Drizzt asked, as much to himself as to his companion.

Innovindil narrowed her blue eyes and more closely studied the dale below, looking for some clue that there was something going on beneath the seemingly unconventional behavior by the brutish and aggressive monsters.

For all she could tell, though, the orcs were not gathering for another charge, nor were they breaking ranks and running away, as so often happened. They were digging in.

Delly Curtie crept up to the slightly opened door. She held her boots in her hand for she did not want them to clack against the hard stone floor. She crouched and peered in and wasn't surprised, but was surely disappointed, to see Wulfgar sitting beside the bed, leaning over Catti-brie.

"We drove them back," he said.

"I hope more got killed than got away," the woman replied in a voice still weak. She had to swallow hard a couple of times to get through that single sentence, but there was little doubt that she was steadily and greatly improving. When they had first taken Catti-brie down from the ledge, the clerics had feared that her injuries could prove fatal, but instead they had all they could handle in keeping the woman in her bed and away from the fighting.

"I hit a few for you," Wulfgar assured her.

Delly couldn't see his face, but she was certain that the smile flashed on Catti-brie's face was mirroring Wulfgar's own.

"Bet ye did," Catti-brie replied.

Delly Curtie wanted to run in and punch her. It was that simple. The pretty face, the bright smile, the sparkle in her rich blue eyes, even in light of her injuries, just grated on the woman from Luskan.

"Talking like a dwarf again, pretty one?" Delly said under her breath, noting that Catti-brie's accent, in her stark time of vulnerability, seemed more akin to the tunnels of Mithral Hall than the more proper speech she had been using of late. In effect, Catti-brie was talking more like Delly.

Delly shook her head at her own pettiness and tried to let it go.

Wulfgar said something then that she did not catch, and he began to laugh, and so did Catti-brie. When was the last time Delly and Wulfgar had laughed like that? Had they ever?

"We'll pay them back in full and more," Wulfgar said, and Catti-brie nodded and smiled again. "There is talk of breaking out through the eastern door, back toward the Surbrin. Our enemies are stronger in the west, but even there their ranks are diminishing."

"Swinging to the east?" Catti-brie asked.

Delly saw Wulfgar's shoulders hunch up in a shrug.

"Even so, they do not believe that they can get in that way, and they cannot expect that we can break out," Wulfgar explained. "But the engineers insist that we can, and quickly. They'll probably use one of Nanfoodle's concoctions and blow up half the mountain."

That brought another shared laugh, but Delly ignored that one, too intrigued by the possibilities of what Wulfgar was saying.

"Citadel Felbarr will support us across the Surbrin," he went on. "Their army now marches for the town of Winter Edge, just across the river and to the north. If we can establish a foothold from the eastern door to the river and establish a line of new warriors and supplies from across the river, Obould will not push us into the hall again."

And all those people from the north will get their wish and be gone from Mithral Hall, Delly silently added.

She watched as Catti-brie managed to prop herself up, wincing just a bit with the movement. She flashed that perfect smile again, the light of it searing Delly's heart.

For she knew that Wulfgar was similarly grinning.

She knew that the two of them shared a bond far beyond any she could ever hope to achieve with the man who called himself her husband.

"They will not break out without great cost," Obould told those gathered around him, the leading shamans and gang bosses, and Gerti Orelsdottr and a few of her elite frost giants. "They are in their hole, and there they will stay. We will not relent our efforts to fortify this dale. As the dwarves built their inner sanctum to cost an invader dearly, so this dale will become our first line of slaughter."

"But you will not go back in?" Gerti asked.

Across from her, Tsinka Shinriil and some of the other shamans growled at the thought, and King Obould gave them a sidelong glance.

"Let them have their hole," he said to Gerti. "I . . . we, have all this." He swept his muscular arm out wide, encompassing all the mountains and wide lands to the north.

"What about Proffit?" Tsinka dared to ask. "We put him into the southern tunnels to fight the dwarves. The trolls await our victory."

"May he find success, then," said Obould, "but we will not go in."

"You abandon an ally?"

Obould's scowl told everyone present that Tsinka was approximately one word from death at that moment.

"Proffit has found more gain that he could ever have hoped to achieve," said the orc king. "Because of Obould! He will fight and win some tunnels, or he will be pushed back to the Trollmoors where his strength has never been greater." Obould's red-streaked yellow eyes narrowed dangerously and a low growl escaped his torn lips as he added, "Have you anything more to say on this?"

Tsinka shrank back.

"You will end it here, then?" Gerti asked.

Obould turned to her and said, "For now. We must secure that which we have gained before we move further against our enemies. The danger now lies mostly in the east, the Surbrin."

"Or the south," Gerti said. "There are no great rivers protecting us from the armies of Everlund and Silverymoon in the south."

"If they come at us from the south, Proffit will give us the time we need," Obould explained. "The enemies we must expect are Adbar and Felbarr. Dwarf to dwarf. If they can breach the Surbrin, they will try to cut our lines in two."

"Do not forget the tunnels," one of Gerti's giant aides added. "The dwarves know the upper layers of the Underdark. We may find them climbing out of holes in our midst!"

All eyes went to the confident Obould, who seemed to accept and appreciate the warning.

"I will build a watchtower on every hill and a wall across every pass. No kingdom will be better fortified and better prepared against attack, for no kingdom is so surrounded by enemies. Every day that passes will bring new strength to Obould's domain, the Kingdom of Dark Arrow." He stood up tall and stalked about the gathering. "We will not rest our guard. We will not turn our eyes aside, nor turn our weapons upon each other. More will join our ranks. From every hole in the Spine of the World and beyond, they will come to the power of Gruumsh and the glory of Obould!"

Gerti stood up as well, if for no better reason than to tower over the pompous orc.

"I will have the foothills to the Trollmoors, and you will have the Spine of the World," Obould assured her. "Treasure will flow north as payment for your alliance."

The ugly orc gave a toothy grin and clapped his hands together hard. A group of orcs soon approached from the side of the gathering, leading the hobbled pegasus.

"It is not a fitting mount," Obould said to Gerti. "An unreliable and stupid beast. A griffon, perhaps, for King Obould, or a dragon—yes, I would like that. But not a soft and delicate creature such as this." He looked around. "I had thought to eat it," he joked, and all the orcs began to chuckle. "But I see the intrigue in your eyes, Gerti Orelsdottr. Our perceptions of ugliness and beauty are not alike. I suspect that you consider the beast quite pretty."

Gerti stared at him skeptically, as if she expected him to then walk over and cut the pegasus in half.

"Whether you think it ugly or pretty, the beast is yours," Obould said, surprising all those orcs around him. "Take it as a trophy or a meal, as you will, and accept it with my gratitude for all that you have done here."

No one in attendance, not even Gerti's close frost giant friends, had ever seen the giantess so perfectly unnerved, excepting that one occasion when Obould had bested her in combat. At every turn, the orc king seemed to have Dame Orelsdottr off-balance.

"You think it ugly so you offer it to me?" Gerti balked, stumbling through the convoluted rebuttal, and without much heart, obviously.

Obould didn't bother to answer. He just stood there holding his smile.

"The winter winds are beginning to blow high up in the mountains," Gerti said clumsily. "Our time here is short, if we are to see Shining White again before the spring."

Obould nodded and said, "I would ask that you leave some of your kin at my disposal along the Surbrin through the season and the next. We will continue to build as the winter snows protect our flank. By next summer, the river will be impervious to attack and your giants can return home."

Gerti looked from Obould to the pegasus several times before agreeing.

The mountainside south of Mithral Hall's retaken western door was more broken and less sheer than the cliffs north of that door or those marking the northern edge of Keeper's Dale, so it was that approach Drizzt and Innovindil chose as their descent. Under cover of night, moving silently as only elves could, the pair picked their careful path along the treacherous way, inching toward Mithral Hall. They knew the dwarves had the door secured once more, for every now and then a ballista bolt or a missile of flaming pitch soared out to smash against the defenses of Obould's hunkering force.

Confident that they could get into the hall, Drizzt realized that he was out of excuses. It was time to go home and face the demons of sorrow. He knew in his heart that his hopes would be dashed, that he would learn what he already knew to be true. His friends were lost to him, and a few hundred yards away as he picked his path among the stones, lay the stark truth.

But he continued along, Innovindil at his side.

They had left Sunset up on the mountaintop, untethered and free to run and fly. The pegasus would wait, or would flee if necessary, and Innovindil held all confidence that she would find her again when she called.

About a hundred and fifty feet above the floor of Keeper's Dale, the pair ran into a bit of a problem. Leading the way, Drizzt found that he was out of easy routes to the bottom, and could see no way at all for him and Innovindil to get down there under cover.

"They've got a fair number of sentries set and alert," Innovindil whispered as she moved down in a crouch beside him. "More orcs and more alert than I'd have expected."

"This commander is cunning," Drizzt agreed. "He'll not be caught unawares."

"We cannot get down this way," Innovindil surmised.

They both knew where they had gone wrong. Some distance back, they had come to a fork in the ravinelike descent. One path had gone almost straight down to the ridge above the doors, while the one they had opted to take had veered to the south. Looking at the doors, the pair could see that other trail, and it seemed as if it could indeed take them low enough for a final, desperate run to the dwarven complex.

Of course, they came to see the truth of it: if they went in, they wouldn't have an easy time getting out.

"We cannot backtrack and come back down the other way before the dawns light finds us," Drizzt explained. "Tomorrow, then?"

He turned to see a very serious Innovindil staring back at him.

"If I go in, I am abandoning my people," she replied, her voice even more quiet than the whispers of their conversation.

"How so?"

"How will we get back out when there seems no concealed trail to the valley floor?"

"I will get us out, if we have to climb the chimneys of Bruenor's furnaces," Drizzt promised, but Innovindil was shaking her head with every word.

"You go tomorrow. You must return to them."

"Alone?" Drizzt asked. "No."

"You must," said Innovindil. "We'll not get to Sunrise anytime soon. The pegasus's best chance might well be a parlay from Mithral Hall to Obould." She put her hand on Drizzt's shoulder, moved it up to gently stroke his face, then let it slip back down to the base of his neck. "I will continue to watch from out here. From afar, on my word. I know that you will return, and perhaps then we will have a means to retrieve lost Tarathiel's mount and friend. I cannot allow Obould to hold so beautiful a creature any longer."

Again her delicate hand went up to gently brush Drizzt's face.

"You must do this," she said. "For me and for you. And for Tarathiel."

Drizzt nodded. He knew that she was right.

They started back up the trail, thinking to return to a hidden camp, then take the alternate route when the sun began to dip below the western horizon once more.

The night was full of the sound of hammers and rolling stones, both inside the hall and outside in Keeper's Dale, but it was an uneventful night for the couple, lying side by side under the stars in the cool autumn wind. To his surprise, Drizzt did not spend the hours in fear of what the following night might bring.

At least, not concerning his friends, for his acceptance was already there. He did fear for Innovindil, and he looked over at her many times that night, silently vowing that he would come back out as soon as he could to rejoin her in her quest.

Their plans did not come to fruition, though, for under the bright sun of the following morning, a commotion in Keeper's Dale brought the two elves to their lookout post. They watched curiously as a large caravan comprised mostly of giants—almost all of the giants—rolled out to the west away from them, moving to the exit of Keeper's Dale. Some orcs traveled along with them, most pulling carts of supplies.

And one other creature paced in that caravan, as well. Even from a distance, the sharp eyes of Innovindil could not miss the glistening white coat of poor Sunrise.

"They break ranks?" she asked. "A full retreat?"

Drizzt studied the scene below, watching the movements of the orcs who were not traveling beside the giants. The vast bulk of the monstrous army that had come to Keeper's Dale was not on the move. Far from it, construction on defensive barriers, walls low and high, continued in full.

"Obould is not surrendering the ground," the drow observed. "But it would seem that the giants have had enough of the fight, or there is somewhere else where they're more urgently needed."

"In either case, they have something that does not belong to them," said Innovindil.

"And we will get him back," Drizzt vowed.

He looked down at the path that would likely get him to the western doors of Mithral Hall, the path that he had decided to walk that very night so that he could settle the past and be on with the future.

He looked back to the west and the procession, and he knew that he would not take that path to the doors that night.

He didn't need to.

He looked to his companion and offered her a smile of assurance that he was all right, that he was ready to move along.

That he was ready to bring Sunrise home.

11

STUMBLING

Dizzy and weak with hunger, his extremities numb, his fingers scraped and twisted from a dozen falls as he tried to make his way down the difficult mountain terrain, Nikwillig stubbornly put one foot in front of the other and staggered forward. He wasn't even sure where he was going anymore—just forward. A part of him wanted to simply lie down and expire, to be rid of the pain and the emptiness, both in his belly and in his thoughts.

The past few days had not been kind to the poor dwarf from Citadel Felbarr. His food was gone, though there was plenty of water to be found. His clothing was torn in many places from various falls, including one that had him bouncing thirty feet down a rocky slope. That fall had left him senseless for nearly an hour, and had also left him weaponless. Somewhere in the descent, Nikwillig had dropped his short sword, and as luck would have it, the weapon had bounced into a narrow ravine, a deep crack really, between two huge slabs of solid stone. After he'd gathered his sensibilities, the dwarf retraced his steps and had actually found the weapon, but alas, it lay beyond his short reach.

He had fetched a small branch and tried again, using the stick to try to maneuver the sword at a better angle for grabbing. But the sword slipped from its unexpectedly precarious perch, clanking down to the deeper recesses of the cavity.

With a helpless shrug, Nikwillig, who had never been much of a fighter anyway, had let it go at that. He didn't much care for the idea of being unarmed in hostile territory, with ugly orcs all around him, but he knew there was nothing more he could do.

So as he had done after watching Nanfoodle's explosion and the dwarves' retreat, Nikwillig of Felbarr just shrugged with resignation. He continued on his way, moving generally east, though the trails were taking him more north than he had hoped.

A few days later, the dwarf just stumbled along almost blindly. He kept repeating "Surbrin" over and over as a reminder, but most of the time, he didn't even know what the word meant. A dwarf's stubbornness alone kept him in motion.

One foot in front of the other.

He was on flatter ground, though he hardly knew it, and his progress was steady if not swift. Early in his journey, he had moved mostly at night, hiding in shallow caves during the daylight hours, but eventually it all seemed the same.

It didn't matter. Nothing mattered, except putting one foot in front of the other and repeating the word, "Surbrin."

Suddenly, though, something else did matter.

It came to Nikwillig on the breeze. Not a sight, nor a sound, but a smell. Something was cooking.

The dwarf's stomach growled in response and he stopped his march, a moment of clarity falling over him. In mere seconds, his feet were moving again, of their own accord, it seemed. He veered to the side—he knew not whether it was left or right, or what direction. The aroma of cooking meat pulled him inexorably forward, and he leaned as he walked, and began licking his cracked, dirty lips.

His sensibilities clarified further when he came in sight of the cooking fire, and of the chef, with its sickly dull orange skin, shock of wild black hair, and protruding lower jaw.

Nothing could sober a dwarf like the sight of a goblin.

The creature seemed oblivious to him. It hunched over the spit, pouring some gravy from a stone bowl.

Nikwillig licked his lips again as he watched the thick liquid splatter over the juicy dark meat.

Leg of lamb, Nikwillig thought and it took every ounce of control the battered dwarf could muster to not groan aloud, and not rush ahead blindly.

He held his ground long enough to glance left and right. Seeing no other monsters about, the dwarf launched into a charge, lowering his head and running straight for the unwitting goblin chef.

The goblin straightened, then turned around curiously just in time to catch a flying dwarf in the shoulder. Over the pair flew, upsetting the spit and scattering bits of the fire. They crashed down hard, the hot gravy flying wildly, most of it splashing the goblin in the face. The creature howled from the burns and tried to cover up, but Nikwillig grabbed it by its skinny throat with both hands. He lifted up and slammed down several times, then scrambled away, leaving the goblin whimpering and curling in the dirt.

The leg of lamb, too, had landed on the ground and rolled in the dirt, but the dwarf didn't even stop to brush it clean. He grabbed it up in both hands and tore at it eagerly, ripping off large chunks of juicy meat and swallowing them with hardly a chew.

A few bites in, Nikwillig paused long enough to catch his breath and to savor the taste.

Shouts erupted all around him.

The dwarf staggered up from his knees and began to run. A spear clipped his shoulder, but it skipped past without digging in. Good sense would have told Nikwillig to throw aside the meat and run full out, but in his famishment, the dwarf was far from good sense. Clutching the leg of lamb to his chest as dearly as if it was his only child, he charged along, weaving in and out of boulders and trees, trying to keep as much cover between him and the pursuing monsters as possible.

He came out the side of a small copse and skidded to a stop, for he found himself on the edge of a low but steep descent. Below him, barely fifty feet away, the broad, shining River Surbrin rolled along its unstoppable way.

"The river . . ." Nikwillig muttered, and he remembered then his goal when he had left his perch high on the mountain ridge north of Mithral Hall. If only he could get across the river!

A shout behind him sent him running again, stumbling down the slope—one step, two. Then he went down hard, face first, and tucked himself just enough to launch himself in a roll. He gathered momentum, but did not let go of his precious cargo, rolling and bouncing all the way down until he splashed into the cold water.

He pulled himself to his feet and staggered to the bank and tried to run along.

Something punched him hard in the back, but he only yelled and continued his run.

If only he could find a log. He'd drag it into the river, and freezing water be damned, he'd grab onto it and push himself out from the bank.

Some trees ahead looked promising, but the shouts were sounding closer and Nikwillig feared he would not make it.

And for some reason he did not immediately comprehend, his legs were moving more slowly, and were tingling as if they were going numb.

The dwarf stopped and looked down, and saw blood—his own blood—dripping down to the ground between his widespread feet. He reached around and only then did he understand that the punch he'd felt had been no punch at all, for his hand closed over the shaft of a goblin spear.

"O Moradin, ye're teasing me," Nikwillig said as he dropped to his knees.

Behind him, he heard the hoots and shouts of charging goblins.

He looked down at his hands, to the leg of lamb he still held, and with a shrug, he brought it up and tore off another chunk of meat.

He didn't swallow as fast, though, but chewed that bite and rolled it around in his mouth, savoring its sweetness, its texture, and the warmth of it. It occurred to him that if he had a mug of mead in his other hand that would be a good way for a dwarf to die.

He knew the goblins were close, but was surprised when a club smacked him off the back of the head, launching him face down in the dirt.

Nikwillig of Citadel Felbarr tried to concentrate on the taste of the lamb, tried to block out the pain.

He hoped that death would take him quickly.

Then he knew no more.

FOOL ME ONCE, SHAME ON ME, FOOL ME TWICE . . .

"You cannot even think of continuing back toward Nesmé," Rannek scolded after he had taken Galen Firth off to the side of the main encampment.

They had run for many hours after the heroic intervention of General Dagna and his dwarves, going back to the foothills in the north near where the dwarves had found the tunnels that would take them to Mithral Hall.

"Would you make the sacrifice of those fifty dwarves irrelevant for the sake of your pride?" Rannek pressed.

"You are one to be speaking of pride," Galen Firth replied, and his adversary did back down at that.

But only for a moment, then Rannek squared his shoulders and puffed out his broad chest. "I will never forget my error, Galen Firth," he admitted. "But I will not complicate that error now by throwing our entire force into the jaws of the trolls and bog blokes."

"They were routed!" Galen yelled, and both he and Rannek glanced back to the main group to note several curious expressions coming back at them. "They were routed," he said again, more quietly. "Between the dwarves' valiant stand and Alustriel's firestorm, the enemy forces were sliced apart. Did they even offer any pursuit? No? Then is it not also possible that the monsters have gone home to their dung-filled moor? Are you so ready to run away?"

"And are you truly stupid enough to walk back into them? Care you not for those who cannot fight? Should our children die on your gamble, Galen Firth?"

"We do not even know where the caves are," Galen argued. "We cannot simply wander the countryside blindly and hope we find the right hole in the ground."

"Then let us march to Silverymoon," offered Rannek.

"Silverymoon will march to us," Galen insisted. "Did you not see Alustriel?

Rannek chewed his lip and it took all of his control not to just spit on the man. "Are you that much the fool?" he asked. "The ungrateful fool?"

"I am not the fool who put us out here, far from our homes," Galen answered without hesitation, and in the same calm tone that Rannek had just used on him. "That man stands before me now, errantly thinking he has the credibility to question me."

Rannek didn't blink and didn't back down, but in truth, he knew that he had no practical answer to that. He was not in command. The beleaguered folk of Nesmé would not listen to him over the assurances and orders of the proven Galen Firth.

He stared at the man a while longer, then just shook his head and turned away. He didn't allow his grimace to stop the smooth flow of his departure when he heard Galen Firth's derisive snort behind him.

The next dawn made the argument to Galen Firth that Rannek had been unable to make, for the scouts from the refugee band returned with news that a host of trolls was fast closing from the south.

Watching Galen Firth as he heard that grim report, Rannek almost expected the man to order the warriors to close ranks and launch an attack, but even the stern and stubborn Galen was not that foolhardy.

"Gather up and prepare to march, and quickly," he called to those around him. He turned to the scouts. "Some of you monitor the approach of our enemies. Others take swift flight to the northeast. Find our scouts who are searching for the tunnels to Mithral Hall and secure our escape route."

As he finished, the man turned a glare over Rannek, who nodded in silent approval. Galen Firth's face grew very tight at that, as if he took the expression as a smarmy insult.

"We will lure our enemies into a long run, and circumvent them so that we might reclaim our home," Galen stubbornly told his soldiers, and Rannek's jaw dropped open.

Having grown adept at running, the Nesmé band was on the move in minutes, and in proper formation so that the weakest were well supported near the center of the march. Few said anything. They knew that trolls were in close pursuit, and that that day could mark the end of all their lives.

They came to higher and more broken ground by mid-morning, and from an open vantage point, Galen, Rannek, and some others got their first look at the pursuing force. It seemed to be trolls exclusively, for nowhere among the approaching mob did they see the treelike appendages of bog blokes. Still, there were more than a few trolls down there, including several very large specimens and some of those sporting more than one head.

Rannek knew that they had done right in retreating, as he had suggested many hours before. Any satisfaction he took from that was lost, though, in his fears that they would not be able to outrun that monstrous force.

"Keep them moving as fast as possible," Galen Firth ordered, his voice grave and full of similar fears, Rannek knew, whether Galen would admit them or not—even to himself. "Have we found those tunnels yet?"

"We've found some tunnels," one of the other men explained. "We do not know how deep they run."

Galen Firth pinched his lip between his thumb and index finger.

"And if we run in before we know for certain, and run into a dead end. . . ." the man went on.

"Hurry, then," Galen ordered. "Stretch lines of scouts into the tunnel. We seek one that will loop around and bring us out behind our pursuing enemies. We will have to either run by or run in—there will be no time to dally!"

The man nodded and rushed away.

Galen turned to regard Rannek.

"And so you believe that you were right," he said.

"For what that's worth," Rannek replied. "It does not matter." He looked back at the pursuing force, drawing Galen's eyes with his own. "Never could we have anticipated such dogged pursuit from an enemy as chaotic and undisciplined as trolls! In all my years . . ."

"Your years are not all that long," Galen reminded him. "Thus were you fooled that night you headed the watch."

"As you were fooled now into thinking the pursuit would not come," Rannek shot back, but the words sounded feeble even to him, and certainly Galen's smug expression did little to give him any thought that he had stung the man.

"I welcome their pursuit," Galen said. "If I'm surprised, it is pleasantly so. We run them off, farther from Nesmé. When we get behind our walls once more, we will find the time we need to fortify our defenses."

"Unless there are more trolls waiting for us there."

"Your failure has led you to a place where you overestimate our enemy, Rannek. They are trolls. Stupid and vicious, and little more. They have shown perseverance beyond expectation, but it will not hold."

Galen gave a snort and started away, but Rannek grabbed him by the arm. The Rider turned on him angrily.

"You would gamble the lives of all these people on that proposition?" Rannek asked.

"Our entire existence in Nesmé has been a gamble—for centuries," Galen replied. "It is what we do. It is the way we live."

"Or the way we die?"

"So be it."

Galen yanked himself free of Rannek's grasp. He stared at the man a while longer, then turned around and started shouting orders to those around him. He was cut short, though, almost immediately, for somewhere among the lines of refugees, a man shouted, "The Axe! The Axe of Mirabar is come!"

"All praise Mirabar!" another shouted, and the cheer was taken up across the gathering.

Rannek and Galen Firth charged through the throng, crossing the crowd to get a view of the source of the commotion.

Dwarves, dozens and dozens of dwarves, marched toward them, many of them bearing the black axe of Mirabar on their shields. They moved in tight and disciplined formation, their ranks holding steady as they crossed the broken ground in their determined advance.

"Not of Mirabar," one scout explained to Galen, huffing and puffing with every word, for he had run all the way back to precede the newcomers.

"More of Clan Battlehammer, they claim to be."

"They wear the emblem of Mirabar's famed Axe," said Galen.

"And so they once were," the scout explained. He stopped and stepped aside, watching with the others as the dwarves closed.

A pair of battle-worn dwarves approached, one with a thick black beard and the other ancient and one of the ugliest dwarves either man had ever seen. He was shorter and wider than his companion, with half his black beard torn away and one eye missing. His ruddy, weathered face had seen the birth and death of centuries, the humans easily surmised. The pair approached Galen's position, guided by yet another of the scouts the Nesmians had sent forth. They walked up before the man and the younger dwarf dropped the head of his heavy warhammer on the stone before him, then leaned on it heavily.

"Torgar Delzoun Hammerstriker of Clan Battlehammer at yer service," he said. "And me friend Shingles."

"You wear the symbol of Mirabar, good Torgar," said Galen. "And glad we are to have your service."

"We were of Mirabar," Shingles offered. "We left to serve a king of more generous heart. And so ye see the end of that, for here we are, to support ye and support General Dagna, who came out here with ye."

Several of the nearby humans looked to each other with concern, expressions that were not lost on the dwarves.

"I will tell you of Dagna's fall when the time permits a tale that would do him justice," Galen Firth said, straightening his shoulders. "For now, our enemies close fast from behind. Trolls—many trolls."

Most of the dwarves mumbled to each other about "Dagna's fall," but Torgar and Shingles kept their expressions stoic.

"Then let's get to the tunnels," Torgar decided. "Me and me boys'll do better against the gangly brutes when they're bending low so as not to bump their ugly heads on the ceiling."

"We fight them there and push them back," Galen agreed. "Perhaps we can break them and gain a path through their lines."

"Through?" asked Torgar. "Mithral Hall's at the other end of them tunnels, and that's where we're for."

"We have word that Silverymoon will soon join in the fight," Galen explained, and no one around him dared point out that he was stretching the truth quite a bit. "Now is the day of our victory, when Nesmé will be restored and the region secured!"

The dwarves both looked at him curiously for a moment, then looked to each other and just shrugged.

"Not to matter," Shingles said to Torgar. "Either choice we're to make, we're to make it from the tunnels."

"So to the tunnels we go," the other dwarf agreed.

"Side run's open!" came a relayed shout along the dwarven line.

"Torch 'em!" Shingles cried.

Twenty dwarves from the second rank rushed forward, flaming torches in hand, and as one they threw the fiery brands over Shingles and the first line of fighters, who were engaged heavily with the leading lines of troll pursuit.

They had run down a long tunnel that spread into a wider chamber, and had made their stand at the funnel-like opening, allowing a score of dwarves to stand abreast, where only a few trolls could come through to battle them. The torchbearers aimed their flaming missiles at the narrower tunnel entrance, where several pieces of seasoned kindling, soaked with lamp oil, had been strategically placed.

The fires roared to life.

Trolls weren't afraid of much, but fire, which defeated their incredible regenerative powers, ranked foremost among that short list.

The torches loosened the pursuit considerably, and Shingles put his line, and those who had come behind, into a sudden, devastating charge, driving back those few trolls that had been caught on the near side of the conflagration. A couple were forced back into the flames, while others were chopped down and stabbed where they stood.

The dwarves broke and ran in perfect formation. The side passage had been declared open, and the refugees were already well on their way.

Yet again, for the third time that afternoon, Torgar's boys had fended off the stubborn troll pursuit.

The monsters would come on again, though, they all knew, and so those dwarves leading the line of retreat were busy inspecting every intersection and every chamber to see if they could find a suitable location for their next inevitable stand.

From the rear defensive ranks of the human contingent, Rannek watched it all with admiration and gratitude. He knew that Galen Firth was stewing about it all, for they had already eschewed a route that likely would have put them back outside ahead of the trolls, possibly with open ground to Nesmé.

But it was Torgar, not Galen, who was in control. Rannek and all the folk of Nesmé understood that much. For after hearing the details of Dagna's fall, Torgar had explained in no uncertain terms that the humans could run away from the dwarven escort if they so chose, but they would do so at their own risk.

"All glory to Dagna and Mithral Hall," Torgar had said to Galen and the others after hearing the sad story. "He goes to join his son in the Halls of Moradin, where a place of honor awaits."

"He tried to help us reclaim our home," Galen put in, and those words had drawn a look from Torgar that dwarves often reserved for orcs alone.

"He saved yer foolish arse," Torgar retorted. "And if ye're choosing to try to make that run again, then 'twas his mistake. But know ye this, Galen Firth o' Nesmé, Torgar and his boys ain't about to make that same mistake. Any ground we're holding, we're holding with tunnels to Mithral Hall at our back, don't ye doubt."

And that had been the end of it, and even overly proud Galen hadn't argued beyond that, and hadn't said a word of rebuttal to the other Nesmian warriors, either. Thus, Torgar had taken complete control, and had led them on their desperate chase. They ran until pursuit forced a stand then they shaped every encounter to be a quick-hitting deflection rather than a head on battle.

Rannek was glad of that.

13

ÐIVERGING RØAÐS

"Are we to follow the commands of an orc?" a large, broad-shouldered frost giant named Urulha asked Gerti as the procession of nearly a hundred of the behemoths made its way around the northern slopes of Fourthpeak, heading east for the Surbrin.

"Commands?" Gerti asked. "I heard no commands. Only a request."

"Are they not one and the same, if you adhere to the request?"

Gerti laughed, a surprisingly delicate sound coming from a giantess, and she put her slender hand on Urulha's massive shoulder. She knew that she had to walk gently with him. Urulha had been one of her father's closest advisors and most trusted guards. And Gerti's father, the renowned Orel the Grayhand still cast a long shadow, though the imposing jarl hadn't been seen among the frost giants in many months, and few thought he would ever leave his private chambers. By all reports, Orel was certainly on his deathbed, and as his sole heir, Gerti stood to inherit Shining White and all his treasures, and the allegiance of his formidable giant forces.

That last benefit of Orel's death would prove the most important and the most tentative, Princess Gerti had known for some time. If a coup rose against her, led by one of the many opportunistic giants who had climbed Orel's hier-archical ladder, then the result, at best, would be a split of the nearly unified forces. That was something Gerti most certainly did not want.

She was a formidable force all her own, skilled with her sword and with her arcane magic. Gerti could bring the power of the elements down upon any who dared stand against her, could blast them with lightning, fire, and storms of pelting ice. But just putting her hand on Urulha's massive shoulder reminded her pointedly that sometimes magic simply would not be enough.

"It is in our interest, at present at least, that Obould succeed," she explained. "If his army were to shatter now, who would stop the forces of Mithral Hall, Felbarr, Adbar, Silverymoon, Everlund, Sundabar, perhaps Mirabar, and who knows what other nation, from pressing the war right to our doorstep at Shining White? No, my good Urulha, Obould is the buffer we need against the pesky dwarves and humans. Let his thousands swarm and die, but slowly."

"I have grown weary of this campaign," Urulha admitted. "I have seen a score and more of my kin killed, and we know not the disposition of our brethren along the Surbrin. Might the dwarves of Felbarr have already crossed? Might another twenty of our kin lay dead at the smelly feet of the bearded creatures?"

"That has not happened," Gerti assured him.

"You do not know that."

Gerti conceded that point with a nod and a shrug. "We will go and see. Some of us, at least."

That surprising caveat got Urulha's attention and he turned his huge head, with its light blue skin and brighter blue eyes, to regard Gerti more directly.

Gerti returned his curious look with a coy one of her own, noticing then that Urulha was quite a handsome creature for an older giant. His hair was long, pulled back into a ponytail that left him a fairly sharp peak up high on his forehead, his hairline receding. His features were still strong, though, with high cheekbones and a very sharp and definitive nose. It occurred to Gerti that if her verbal persuasion did not prove sufficient to keep Urulha in line, she could employ her other ample charms to gain the same effect, and that, best of all, it would not be such an unpleasant thing.

"Some, my friend," she said quietly, letting her fingers trace up closer to the base of the large giant's thick neck, even moving her fingertips to brush the bare skin above his chain mail tunic. "We will send a patrol to the river—half our number—to look in on our missing friends, and to begin collecting them. Slowly, we will rotate the force north and back home. Slowly, I say, so that Obould will not think our movement an outright desertion. He expects that he will need to secure the river on his own, anyway, and with his numbers, it should be of little effort to convince him that he does not need a few giants.

"I wish to hold the alliance, you see," she went on. "I do not know what the response from the communities of our enemies will yet be, but I do not wish to do battle with twenty thousand orcs. Twenty thousand?" she asked with a snicker. "Or is his number twice or thrice that by now?"

"The orcs breed like vermin, like the mice in the field or the centipedes that infest our homes," said Urulha.

"Similar intelligence, one might surmise," said Gerti as her fingers continued to play along her companion's neck, and she was glad to feel the tenseness ease from Urulha's taut muscles, and to see the first hints of a smile widen on his handsome face.

"It is even possible that our usual enemies will come to see a potential alliance with us," Gerti added.

Urulha scowled at the notion. "Dwarves? You believe the dwarves of Mithral Hall, Citadel Felbarr, or Citadel Adbar will agree to work in concert with us? Do you believe that Bruenor Battlehammer and his friends will forget the bombardment that tumbled a tower upon them? They know who swung the ram that breached their western door. They know that no orc could have brought such force to bear."

"And they know they might soon be out of options," said Gerti. "Obould will dig in and fortify throughout the winter, and I doubt that our enemies will find a way to strike at him before the snows have melted. By then. . . ."

"You do not believe that Silverymoon, Everlund, and the three dwarven kingdoms can dislodge orcs?"

Gerti took his incredulity in stride. "Twenty thousand orcs?" she whispered. "Forty thousand? Sixty thousand? And behind fortified walls on the high ground?"

"And so Gerti will offer to aid the countering forces of peoples long our enemies?" Urulha asked.

Gerti was quick to offer a pose that showed she was far from making any such judgment.

"I hold open the possibility of gain for my people," she explained.

"Obould is no ally to us. He never was. We tolerated him because he was amusing."

"Perhaps he feels the same way toward us."

Again the disciplined Gerti managed to let the too-accurate-for-comfort comment slide off her large shoulders. She knew that she had to walk a fine line with all of her people as they made their way back to Shining White. Her giants and Obould had achieved victory in their press to the south, but for the frost giants had there been any real gain? Obould had achieved all he had apparently desired. He had gained a strong foothold in the lands of the humans and dwarves. Even more important and impressive, his call to war had brought forth and united many orc tribes, which he had brought into his powerful grasp. But the army, for all its gains, had found no tangible, transferable plunder. They had not captured Mithral Hall and its treasuries.

Gerti's giants were not like the minions of Obould. Frost giants were not stupid orcs. Winning the field was enough for the orcs, even if they lost five times the number of enemies killed. Gerti's people would demand of her that she show them why their march south had been worth the price of dozens of giants' lives.

Gerti looked at the line ahead, to the pegasus. Yes, there was a trophy worthy of Shining White! She would parade the equine creature before her people often, she decided. She would remind them of the benefits of removing the pesky Withegroo and the folk of Shallows. She would explain to them how much more secure their comfortable homeland was now that the dwarves and humans had been pushed so far south.

It was, the giantess realized, a start.

He was surprised by the softness as his consciousness began to creep forth from the darkness, for the dwarf had always expected the Halls of Moradin to be warm with fires but as hard as stone. Nikwillig stirred and shifted, and felt his shoulder sink into the thick blanket. He heard the crackle of leaves and twigs beneath him.

The dwarf's eyes popped open, then he squeezed them shut immediately against the blinding sting of daylight.

In that instant of sight, that snapshot of his surroundings, Nikwillig realized that he was in a thick deciduous forest and as he considered that, the poor dwarf became even more confused. For there were no forests near where he fell, and the last thing he ever expected in the Halls of Moradin were trees and open sky.

"En tu il be-inway," he heard, a soft melodic voice that he knew to be an elf's.

Nikwillig kept his eyes closed as he played the words over and over in his jumbled thoughts. A merchant of Felbarr, Nikwillig often dealt with folk of other races, including elves.

"Be-inway?" he mouthed, then, "Awake. *En tu il bi-inway . . .* he is awake."

An elf was talking about him, he knew, and he slowly let his eyelids rise, acclimating himself to the light as he went. He stretched a bit and a groan escaped him as he tried to turn in the direction of the voice.

The dwarf closed his eyes again and settled back, took a deep breath to let the pain flow out of him, then opened his eyes once more—and was surprised to find himself completely surrounded by elves, pale of skin and stern of face.

"You are awake?" one asked him, speaking the common language of trade.

"A bit of a surprise if I be," Nikwillig answered, his voice cracking repeatedly as it crossed through his parched throat. "Goblins got poor old Nikwillig good."

"The goblins are all dead," the elf on his right explained. That elf, apparently the leader, waved all but one of the others away, then bent low so that Nikwillig could better view him. He had straight black hair and dark blue eyes, which seemed very close together to the dwarf. The elf's angular eyebrows pinched together almost as one, like a dark V above his narrow nose.

"And we have tended your wounds," he went on in a voice that seemed strangely calm and reassuring, given his visage. "You will recover, good dwarf."

"Ye pulled me out o' there?" Nikwillig asked. "Them goblins had me caught at the river and . . ."

"We shot them dead to a goblin," the elf assured him.

"And who ye be?" asked Nikwillig. "And who be 'we'?"

"I am Hyaline of the Moonwood, and this is Althelennia. We crossed the river in search of two of our own. Perhaps you of Mithral Hall have seen them?"

"I ain't of Mithral Hall, but of Citadel Felbarr," Nikwillig informed them, and he took Hralien's offered hand and allowed the elf to help him up gingerly into a sitting position. "Got whacked by that Obould beast, and was Bruenor that rescued me and me friend Tred. Seen nothing of yer friends, sorry to say."

The two elves exchanged glances.

"They would be upon great flying horses," Althelennia added. "Perhaps you have seen them from afar, high in the sky."

"Ah, them two," said Nikwillig, and both elves leaned in eagerly. "Nope, ain't seen them, but I heard of them from the Bouldershoulder brothers who came through yer wood on the way to Mithral Hall."

The crestfallen elves swayed back.

"And the hall remains in Bruenor's hands?" asked Hralien at the very same time that Althelennia inquired about "a great fire that we saw leap into the western sky."

"Aye and aye," said the dwarf. "Gnomish fire, and one to make a dragon proud."

"You have much to tell us, good dwarf," said Hralien.

"Seems I'm owin' ye that much at least," Nikwillig agreed.

He stretched a bit more, cracked his knuckles, his neck, and his shoulders a few times, and settled in, putting his back to a nearby tree. Then he told them his tale, from his march with the caravan out of Citadel Felbarr those tendays before, to the disastrous ambush, and his aimless wandering, injured and hungry, with Tred. He told them of the generosity of the humans and the kindness of Bruenor Battlehammer, who found the pair as he was returning home to be crowned King of Mithral Hall once more.

He told them of Shallows and the daring rescue, and of the unexpected help from Mirabarran dwarves, moving to join their Battlehammer kin. He described the standoff above Keeper's Dale, going into great detail in painting a mental image of the piled orc bodies.

Through it all, the elves remained completely attentive, expressions impassive, absorbing every word. They showed no emotion, even when Nikwillig jumped suddenly as he described the explosion Nanfoodle had brought about, a blast so complete that it had utterly decapitated a mountain spur.

"And that's where it stands, last I noted," Nikwillig finished. "Obould put Bruenor in his hole in the west, and trolls, orcs, and giants put Bruenor in his hole in the east. Mithral Hall's a lone jewel in a pile o' leaden critters."

The two elves looked at each other.

Their expressions did not comfort the battered dwarf.

After more than a tenday, Drizzt and Innovindil found themselves along the higher foothills of the Spine of the World. Gerti and her nearly three-score giants had taken a meandering path back to the higher ground, but they had moved swiftly along that winding road. The journey had given the two elves a good view of the work along the Surbrin, and what they had seen had not been reassuring. All along the bank, particularly at every known ford and every other area that seemed possible for crossing, fortifications had been built and were being improved on a continual basis.

The pair tried to focus on their present mission to rescue Sunrise, but it was no easy task, especially for Innovindil, who wondered aloud and often if she should divert her course and cross the river from on high to warn her kinfolk.

But of course, the elves of the Moonwood carefully monitored the Surbrin, and they already knew what was afoot, she had to believe.

So she had kept to the course with Drizzt, the two of them holding close watch on Gerti's progress and looking for some opening where they could get to Sunrise. In all that time, though, no such chance had presented itself.

Once they were in the mountains, in more broken terrain, keeping up with the giants grew more difficult. On several occasions, Drizzt had brought in Guenhwyvar to run fast ahead and locate the band just to ensure that he and Innovindil were keeping some pace, at least.

"It is folly, I fear," Innovindil said to Drizzt as they camped one night in the shadows of a shallow overhang, with just enough cover for Drizzt to chance a small fire. Normally, he would not have done so, but though autumn had barely begun down in the south near Mithral Hall, up there, at so high an elevation, the wind was already carrying its wintry bite. "And while we run the fool's errand my people and your dwarves are under siege."

"You will not desert Sunrise while a hope remains," Drizzt replied with a wry grin, his expression as much as his words acting as a rather uncomplimentary mirror to the elf lass.

"You are just frustrated," Drizzt added.

"And you are not?"

"Of course I am. I am frustrated, I am angry, I am sad, and I want nothing more than to take Obould's ugly head from his shoulders."

"And how do you fight past such emotions, Drizzt Do'Urden?"

Drizzt paused before he answered, for he saw a shift in Innovindil's eyes as she asked that question, and noted a distinct shift in her tone. She was asking him as much for his own sake as for hers, he realized. So many times in their tendays together, Innovindil had turned to Drizzt and said something along the lines of, "Do you know what it is to be an elf, Drizzt Do'Urden?" Clearly, she expected to be a bit of a mentor to him concerning the elf experience, and they were lessons he was glad to learn. He noticed too, for the first time with her last question, that whenever Innovindil began her subtle tutoring, she finished the question by referring to him with his full name.

"In moments of reflection," he answered. "At sunrise, mostly, I talk to myself aloud. No doubt anyone listening would think me insane, but there is something about saying the words, about speaking my fears and pain and guilt aloud that helps me to work through these often irrational emotions."

"Irrational?"

"My racist beliefs about my own kind," Drizzt replied. "My dedication to what I know is right. My pain at the loss of a friend, or even of one enemy."

"Ellifain."

"Yes."

"You were not to blame."

"I know that. Of course I do. Had I known it was Ellifain, I would have tried to dissuade her, or to defeat her in a non-lethal manner. I know that she brought her death upon herself. But it is still sad, and still a painful thing to me."

"And you feel guilt?"

"Some," Drizzt admitted.

Innovindil stood up across the way and walked around the campfire, then knelt before the seated Drizzt. She brought a hand up and gently touched his face.

"You feel guilt because you are possessed of a gentle nature, Drizzt Do'Urden. As am I, as was Tarathiel, as are most of elvenkind, though we do well to hide those traits from others. Our conscience is our salvation. Our questioning of everything, of right and wrong, of action and consequence, is what defines our purpose. And do not be fooled, in a lifetime that will last centuries, some sense of purpose is often all you have."

How well Drizzt had known that truth.

"You speak your thoughts after the fact?" Innovindil asked. "You take your experiences and play them out before you, that you might consider your own actions and feelings in the glaring and revealing light of hindsight?"

"Sometimes."

"And through this process, does Drizzt internalize the lessons he has learned? Do you, in reaffirming your actions, gain some confidence should a similar situation arise?"

The question had Drizzt leaning back for a minute. He had to believe that Innovindil had hit upon something. Drizzt had resolved many of his internal struggles through his personal discussions, had come almost full circle, so he believed—until the disaster at Shallows.

He looked back at Innovindil, and noticed that she had moved very close to him. He could feel the warmth of her breath. Her golden hair seemed so soft in that moment, backlit by the fire, almost as if she was aglow. Her eyes seemed so dark and mysterious, but so full of intensity.

She reached up and stroked his face gently, and Drizzt felt his blood rushing. He tried hard to control his trembling.

"I think you a gentle and beautiful soul, Drizzt Do'Urden," she said. "I understand better this difficult road you have traveled, and admire your dedication."

"So you believe now that I know what it is to be an elf?" Drizzt asked, more to alleviate the sudden tension he was feeling, to lighten the mood, than anything else.

But Innovindil didn't let him go so easily.

"No," she said. "You have half the equation, the half that takes care to anticipate the long-term course of things. You reflect and worry, ask yourself to examine your actions honestly, and demand of yourself honest answers, and that is no small thing. Young elves react and examine, and along that honest road of self-evaluation, you will one day come to react to whatever is found before you in full confidence that you are doing right."

Drizzt leaned back just a bit as Innovindil continued to press forward, so that her face was barely an inch from his own.

"And the half I have not learned?" he asked, afraid his voice would crack with each word.

In response, Innovindil pressed in closer and kissed him.

Drizzt didn't know how to respond. He sat there passively for a long while, feeling the softness of her lips and tongue, her hand brushing his neck, and her lithe body as she pressed in closer to him. Blood rushed through him and the world seemed as if it was spinning, and Drizzt stopped even trying to think and just . . . felt.

He began to kiss Innovindil back and his hands started to move around her. He heard a soft moan escape his own lips and was hardly even conscious of it.

Innovindil broke the kiss suddenly and fell back, her arms coming out to hold Drizzt from pursuing. She looked at Drizzt curiously for just a moment, then asked, "What if she is alive?"

Drizzt tried to question the sudden shift, but as her inquiry hit him, his response was more stutter than words.

"If you knew that Catti-brie was alive, then would you wish to continue this?" Innovindil asked, and she might as well have added, "Drizzt Do'Urden," to the end of the question.

Drizzt's mind spun in circles. He managed to stammer, "B-but . . ."

"Ah, Drizzt Do'Urden," Innovindil said. She twirled, rising gracefully to her feet. "You spend far too much time in complete control. You consider the future with every move."

"Is that what it is to be an elf?" Drizzt asked, his voice dripping with sarcasm.

"It might be," Innovindil answered. She came forward again and bent low, looking at Drizzt mischievously, but directly. "In your experience, stoicism is what it is to be an elf. But letting go sometimes, my friend, that is what it is to be alive."

She turned with a giggle and stepped away.

"You pulled back, not I," Drizzt reminded, and Innovindil turned on him sharply.

"You didn't answer my question."

She was right and Drizzt knew it. He could only begin to imagine his torn emotions had they gone through with the act.

"I have seen you reckless in battle," Innovindil went on. "But in love? In life? With your scimitars, you will take a chance against a giant or ten! But with your heart, are you nearly as brave? You will cry out in anger against goblinkind, but will you dare cry out in passion?"

Drizzt didn't answer, because he didn't have an answer. He looked down and gave a self-deprecating chuckle, and was surprised when Innovindil sat down again beside him and comfortably put her arm around his shoulders.

"I am alone," the female elf said. "My lover is gone and my heart is empty. What I need now is a friend. Are you that friend?"

Drizzt leaned over and kissed her, but on the cheek.

"Happily so," he answered. "But am I your friend or your student, when you so freely play with my emotions?"

Innovindil assumed a pensive posture and a moment later answered, "I hope you will learn from my experiences, as I hope to learn from yours. I know that my life is enriched because of your companionship these last tendays. I hope that you can say the same."

Drizzt knew he didn't even have to answer that question. He put his arm around Innovindil and pulled her close. They sat there under the stars and let the Reverie calm them.

14

REGROUPING

A pall hung over the audience chamber at Mithral Hall. The orcs had been pushed out, the western entry seemingly secured. And because of their cleverness and the explosive potions of Nanfoodle, few dwarves had fallen in either the initial assault that had brought the orcs into the hall or the counterattack that had pushed them out.

But word had come from the south, both hopeful and tragic.

Bruenor Battlehammer stood tall in front of his throne then, commanding the attention of all, from the guards lining the room to the many citizens and refugees standing by the doors awaiting their audience with the king.

To the side of Bruenor stood Cordio and Stumpet, the two principle clerics of the clan. Bruenor motioned to them, and Cordio quickly dipped a large mug in the barrel of dwarven holy water, a very sweet honey mead. Attendants all over the hall scrambled to disseminate the drink, so that everyone in attendance, even the three non-dwarves—Regis, Wulfgar, and Nanfoodle—had mug in hand when Bruenor raised his in toast.

"And so does General Dagna Waybeard of Adbar and Mithral Hall join his son in the Halls of Moradin," Bruenor proclaimed. "To Dagna and to all who served well with him. They gave their lives in defense of neighbors and in battle with smelly trolls." He paused, then raised his voice to a shout as he finished, "A good way to die!"

"A good way to die!" came the thunderous response.

Bruenor drained his entire mug in one great gulp, then tossed it back to Cordio and fell back into his seat.

"The news was not all bad," said Banak Brawnanvil, sitting at his side in a specially constructed chair to accommodate legs that would no longer support him.

"Yeah?" said Bruenor.

"Alustriel was seen at the fight," said Banak. "No small thing, that."

Bruenor looked to the young courier who had brought the news from the south. When Bruenor had sent out the Mirabarran dwarves, he had stretched a line of communication all the way from Mithral Hall, a relay team of couriers so that news would flow back quickly. With the orcs back out of Mithral Hall, the dwarf king expected a very fluid situation and had no intention of being caught by surprise from any direction.

"Alustriel was there?" he pressed the courier. "Or we're *thinking* she was there?"

"Oh, they seen her, me king," said the dwarf, "come in on a flaming chariot, down from the sky in a ball of fire!"

"Then how did they know it to be her, through the veil of flames?" Nanfoodle dared to ask. He blanched and fell back, showing everyone that he was merely thinking aloud.

"Aye, that's Alustriel," Bruenor assured the gnome and everyone else. "I'm knowing a thing or two about the Lady of Silverymoon's fiery chariot."

That brought chuckles from the others around Bruenor, especially from the normally quiet Wulfgar, who had witnessed first-hand Bruenor's pilot- ing of Alustriel's magical cart. Far to the south and out on the sea, Bruenor had brought Alustriel's conjured chariot of flame streaking across the deck of a pirate ship, to ultimate disaster—for the pirates, of course.

"So she's knowing that a fight's afoot," Bruenor said, and he looked to the emissary from another outside kingdom.

"Citadel Felbarr would surely've telled her," Jackonray Broadbelt agreed. "We've got a good flow o' runners to Silverymoon and to Sundabar. Alustriel's knowing what's afoot, to be sure, if she joined in the fight in the south."

"But will she come on to the north with her forces, as she did when the drow marched against Mithral Hall?" asked Wulfgar.

"Might be that we should send Rumblebelly to her to find out," Bruenor said, throwing a wink at the barbarian as they both turned their looks over Regis.

The halfling didn't catch it, obviously, for he sat very still and very quiet, head down.

Bruenor studied him for just a moment, and recognized the source of his apparent dismay. "What'd'ye think, Rumblebelly?" he bellowed. "Ye think ye might use yer ruby there on Alustriel and get all o' Silverymoon marching to help us?"

Regis looked up at him and shrugged, and his eyes widened as he apparently only then registered the absurd question.

"Bah, sit yerself back," Bruenor said with a laugh. "Ye won't go using that magical pendant o' yers on the likes of Alustriel!"

Everyone around the dwarf king joined in the laughter, but Bruenor's expression took on a more serious look as soon as he had the cover of the mirth.

"But we'll be needin' to talk about Silverymoon, and yerself and me girl're the two who're best knowing the place. Ye go and sit with her, Rumblebelly. I'll get by to talk with ye two as soon as I'm done here."

Regis's relief at being dismissed from the large gathering was evident to anyone who bothered to glance his way. He nodded and hopped up, then swiftly walked out of the room, even breaking into a trot as he reached the doorway.

Regis found Catti-brie sitting up in bed, a sizable plate of food set out before her. Her smile at him as he entered was among the sweetest sights he had ever known, for it was full of eagerness and acceptance. It was a smile that promised better days and another fight—something that Regis had feared Catti-brie would never be able to hope for again.

"Stumpet and Cordio have been hard at work, I see," he remarked as he moved into the room and pulled up a small chair to sit beside the woman's bed.

"And Moradin's been good enough to hear their call, for healing the likes of me. Do ye . . . you think perhaps I have more dwarf in me than either of us are knowing?"

The halfling found her answer somewhat ironic, given her own mid-sentence correction of her dwarven dialect.

"When do you think you'll be out of here?"

"I'll be out of bed in less than a tenday," Catti-brie answered. "I'll be fighting again in two—sooner if I find I'm needed, don't you doubt."

Regis looked at her skeptically. "Is that your guess or Cordio's?"

Catti-brie waved the question away and went back to eating, and so Regis understood that the priests had likely given estimates of at least a month.

As she finished with one piece of fruit, Catti-brie leaned over the opposite side of the bed, where a pail sat for the refuse. When she did, the movement caused the blanket to ride up on the side closest Regis, affording him a clear view of her torn hip and upper leg.

The woman settled back before the halfling could replace his pained expression.

"The rock hit you good," Regis said, knowing there was no way to avoid it.

Catti-brie tucked the blanket back down under her side. "I'm fortunate that it bounced off the ledge and the wall first," she admitted.

"How serious was the damage?"

Catti-brie's face went blank.

Regis met that stare and pressed on, "How far will you recover, do they say? That hip was crushed, the muscles torn through. Will you walk again?"

"Yes."

"Will you run?"

The woman paused a bit longer, her face growing tight. "Yes."

It was an answer more of determination than expectation, Regis knew. He let it go and stiffened his resolve against the wave of pity that wanted to flood out of him. He knew very well that Catti-brie would hear none of that.

"Word has come from the south," Regis said. "Lady Alustriel has joined the fight, albeit briefly."

"But Dagna has fallen," Catti-brie replied, surprising Regis.

"Word of such things passes quickly through a dwarven community," she explained.

Regis quieted for a few moments so that they could both offer a silent prayer for the soul of the fallen dwarf.

"Do you think it will ever be the same?" he asked.

"I don't," replied Catti-brie, and the halfling's head snapped up, for that was not precisely the answer he had expected and wanted from the normally optimistic woman. "As it was not the same when we drove the dark elves back underground. This fight's sure to leave a scar, my friend."

Regis considered that for a moment, then nodded his agreement. "Obould stuck it in deep, and stuck it hard," he said. "Bruenor will be glad when he has that one's head piked out beyond the western door."

"It is not all bad, these changes . . ." said Catti-brie.

"Torgar's here with his boys," Regis was quick to put in. "And we're talking with Felbarr as never before!"

"Aye," said the woman. "And sometimes tragedy is the catalyst for those who are left behind, to change in ways they knew they should, but never found the courage to grasp."

Something about her tone and the faraway look in her eye told the halfling that many things were stirring behind the blue eyes of Catti-brie, and not all of them in accordance to that which he and the others would normally expect of her.

"We're trying to get some scouts out and about, up through the chimneys," he said. "We're hoping for word from Drizzt."

Catti-brie's face twitched a bit at the mention of the drow. Not a grimace, but enough of a movement to tell Regis that he had hit a sensitive subject.

Again Regis quickly changed the topic. What use in speculating about Drizzt, after all, when none of them knew anything definite, though all of them held the same hopes? Instead Regis talked of better days to come, of the inevitable defeat of Obould and his stupid orcs and the good times they'd have with the brave dwarves of Mirabar, the newest members of the clan. He talked of Tred and Citadel Felbarr, and promises of allegiance that ran deep on both sides of the Underdark tunnels. He talked of Ivan and Pikel, and of the Spirit Soaring, their cathedral home set high in the Snowflake Mountains above the town of Carradoon on Impresk Lake. He would go and see that wondrous place, he prompted repeatedly, drawing smiles from Catti-brie, and finally coaxing her into talking about it, for she and Drizzt had once visited Cadderly and Danica.

After an hour or so, there came a sharp knock on the door, and Bruenor came bounding in.

"Word's in from Felbarr," he announced before he even bothered to say hello. "Jackonray's runners come back with the news that Emerus Warcrown's marching!"

"They will arrive through the eastern tunnels?" Regis asked. "We must set a proper feast for a visiting king."

"Ain't about food this time, Rumblebelly," said Bruenor. "And not through any tunnels. King Emerus's got his boys spilling out aboveground. A great force, marching to the River Surbrin. Already their front runners are setting up camp at Winter Edge, just across the river. Townsfolk there ain't never had such company as they're seeing today!"

"You're breaking out the eastern door," Catti-brie said.

"We're crossing Garumn's Gorge with everything we've got," Bruenor replied, referring to the cavern and ravine that separated the eastern end of Mithral Hall from the rest of the complex. "We'll blow the side o' the mountain away before us, and come out in such a rush that them stupid orcs'll be jumping into the river to get away from us!"

"And we'll wave at each other across the river?" Regis remarked.

Bruenor scowled at him and said, "We're gonna set a hold on our side, and smash those orcs back to the north. Emerus is coming across—they're building the boats as they march. From the eastern doors to the river will become a part of Mithral Hall, walled and strong, and with a bridge that'll cross over and give our growing allies a clean route to join in the fight."

The bold plan stole any quips from Regis, and had both he and Catti-brie sitting quietly attentive.

"How long?" the halfling finally managed to ask.

"Three days," said Bruenor, and Regis's jaw dropped open.

"I'll be ready to go," Catti-brie remarked, and both dwarf and halfling turned to her in surprise.

"No ye won't," said her father. "Already been talking to Cordio and Stumpet. This is one ye're missing, girl. Ye get yerself healthy and ready to fight. We'll be needing ye, don't ye doubt, when we've got the hold and're trying to get the damn bridge built. Yer bow on a tower's worth a legion of ground fighters to me."

"Ye're not keeping me out o' the fight!" Catti-brie argued.

Regis nearly giggled at how dwarflike the woman suddenly seemed when her ire went up.

"No, I'm not," Bruenor agreed. "It's yer wound that's doing that. Ye can't even stand, ye unbearded girl gnome."

"I will stand!"

"And ye'll hobble," said Bruenor. "And ye'll have me and me boy Wulfgar, and Rumblebelly there, looking back for ye as often as we're looking ahead at the damned orcs!"

Catti-brie, sitting so bolt upright then that she was leaning forward at Bruenor, started to argue, but her words dissipated as she seemed to melt beck into her pillows. The intensity didn't leave her eyes—she so dearly wanted to fight—but it was clear that Bruenor's appeal to her on the grounds of how her stubbornness would affect those she loved had done the trick.

"Ye get well," Bruenor said quietly. "I promise ye girl that there'll be plenty more orcs looking for an arrow when ye're ready to come back in."

"What do you need me to do?" Regis asked.

"Ye stick with Jackonray," the dwarf king instructed. "Ye're me eyes and ears for Felbarr's worries. And I might be needing ye to look in on Nanfoodle and them Bouldershoulders, to tell me straight and without the gnome's winding words and Pikel's 'Boom!' what's really what in their progress on opening up that durned door. Them giants've put a hunnerd tons o' rock over them doors when we closed them, and we're needing to break through fast and strong to drive right to the Surbrin."

Regis nodded and hopped up, starting out of the room. He skidded to an abrupt halt even as he began, though, and turned back to regard Catti-brie.

"Better days are coming," he said to her, and she smiled.

It was the smile of a friend, but one who, Regis understood, was beginning to see the world through a different set of eyes.

15

ÐWARVEN FꝊRTITUÐE

The mob of trolls receded down the hill, sliding back into the bog and mist to lick their wounds, and a great cheer went up along the line of warriors both dwarf and human. They had held their ground again, for the third time that day, stubbornly refusing to be pushed back into the tunnels that loomed as black holes on the hillside behind them.

Torgar Hammerstriker watched the retreat with less excitement than his fellows, and certainly with less enthusiasm than the almost-giddy humans. Galen Firth ran along the human lines, proclaiming yet another victory in the name of Nesmé.

That was true, Torgar supposed, but could victory really be measured in terms of temporary advances and retreats? They had held, all three fights, because they had washed the leading trolls with a barrage of fiery logs. Looking back at their supply of kindling, Torgar hoped they had enough fuel to hold a fourth time. Victory? They were surrounded, with only the tunnels offering them any chance of retreat. They couldn't get any more fuel for their fires, and couldn't hope to break out through the ranks and ranks of powerful trolls.

"They're grabbing at every reason to scream and punch their fists in the air," Shingles McRuff remarked, coming up to stand beside his friend. "Can't say I blame 'em, but I'm not seeing how many victory punches we got left."

"Without the fires, we can no hold," Torgar agreed quietly, so that only Shingles could hear.

"A stubborn bunch o' trolls we got here," the old dwarf added. "They're taking their time. They know we got nowhere to run except the holes."

"Any scouts come back dragging logs?" Torgar asked, for he had sent several runners out along side tunnels, hoping to find an out of the way exit in an area not patrolled by their enemies, in the hope that they might be able to sneak in some more wood.

"Most're back, but none with any word that we've got trees to drag through. We got what we got now, and nothing more."

"We'll hold them as long as we can," Torgar said, "but if we don't break them in the next fight it'll be our last battle out here in the open."

"The boys're already practicing their retreat formations," Shingles assured him.

Torgar looked across his defensive line, to their partners in the struggle. He watched Galen Firth rousing his men once more, the tall man's seemingly endless supply of energy flowing out in one prompting cheer after another.

"I'm not thinking our boys to be the trouble," Torgar said.

"That Galen's no less stubborn than the trolls," Shingles agreed. "Might be a bit harder in convincing."

"So Dagna learned."

The two watched Galen's antics a bit longer, then Torgar added, "When we get the last line o' fires out at the trolls, and they're not breaking, then we're breaking ourselves, back into the tunnels. Galen and his boys can come if they want, or they can stay out here and get swallowed. No arguing on this. I'm not giving another o' Bruenor's war bands to Moradin to defend a human too stubborn or too stupid to see what's plain afore him. He runs with us or he stands alone."

It was a sobering order, and one that Torgar issued in a raised voice. There was no compromise to be found, all those dwarves around him understood. They would not make a gallant and futile last stand for the sake of Galen Firth and the Nesmians.

"Ye telled that all to Galen, did ye?"

"Three times," said Torgar.

"He hearing ye?"

"Dumathoin knows," Torgar answered, invoking to the dwarf god known as the Keeper of Secrets under the Mountains. "And Dumathoin ain't for telling. But don't ye misunderstand our place here in the least. We're Bruenor's southern line, and we're holding for Mithral Hall, not for Nesmé. Them folks want to come, we'll get them home to the halls or die trying. Them folks choose to stay, and they're dying alone."

It couldn't be more clear than that. But neither Torgar nor Shingles believed for a moment that even such a definitive stand would ring clearly enough in the thick head of Galen Firth.

The trolls wasted little time in regrouping and coming on once more as soon as the fires from the previous battle had died away. Their eagerness only confirmed to Torgar that which he had suspected: they were not a stupid bunch. They knew they had the dwarves on the edge of defeat, and knew well that the fiery barrage could not continue indefinitely.

They charged up the hill, their long legs propelling them swiftly across the sloping ground. They kept their lines loose and scattered—an obvious attempt to present less of an opportunity for targeting fiery missiles.

"Ready yer throws!" Shingles ordered, and torches were put to brands across the dwarven line.

"Not yet," Torgar whispered to his friend. "That's what they're expecting."

"And that's all we're giving."

But Torgar shook his head. "Not this time," he said. "Not yet."

The trolls closed ground. Down at the human end of the defensive line, fiery brands went flying out.

But Torgar held his missiles. The trolls closed.

"Running wedge!" Torgar shouted, surprising all those around him, even Shingles, who had fought so many times beside his fellow Mirabarran.

"Running wedge?" he asked.

"Send 'em out! All of 'em!" Torgar shouted. He lifted his warhammer high and yelled, "With me, boys!"

Torgar leaped out from behind the stony barricade, Shingles at his side. Without even bothering to look left or right, the dwarf charged down the hill, confident that his boys would not let him down.

And that confidence was well placed. The dwarves poured out like water, tumbling and rolling right back to their feet. In a few short strides, they were already forming their running wedge and by the time they hit the leading trolls, their formations were tight and well supported.

Torgar was, fittingly, first to engage. He led with a great sweep of his hammer, and the troll standing before him hopped back out of range, then came in fast behind the swipe. Apparently thinking it had the aggressive little creature vulnerable, the troll opened wide its mouth and lunged forward to bite at the dwarf.

Just as Torgar had hoped, for as his hammer cut the air before the beast, the dwarf, who hadn't put half the weight behind that swing as he had made it appear, yanked against the momentum and reversed the flow of the weapon, bringing it in close. He slid one hand up the shaft of the hammer as he moved one foot forward, turning almost sidelong to the troll, then thrust weapon's head straight out into the diving mouth of the troll. Teeth splintered and Torgar heard the crack of the troll's jawbone.

Not one to sit on his laurels, the dwarf yanked his hammer back, snapping it into a roll over his trailing right shoulder and letting go with his left hand. He caught the weapon down low with his left hand again as it came spinning up over his head, then chopped down with all his strength, every muscle in his body snapping, driving the hammerhead into the troll's brain.

The creature fell straight to the ground, squirming wildly, and Torgar just kicked it in the face as he barreled by.

"Clever dwarves," Kaer'lic Suun Wett remarked.

With Tos'un beside her, the drow priestess stood on a high, tree-covered bluff off to the side of the main action.

"They saw that the trolls were coming up widespread and gradually, trying to draw out their flaming brands," Tos'un agreed.

"And now they've sent those leading decoys running or to the ground, and not a brand have they thrown," said Kaer'lic.

The contrast between the dwarves' tactics and those of the humans standing beside them came crystal clear. While the dwarves had come out in a wild charge, the humans held their ground, and had indeed launched many of their fiery brands against the leading troll line.

"Proffit will exploit the human line and drive around to flank the dwarves," Kaer'lic said, pointing up that way.

Lower on the field, the disciplined dwarves had already turned around, having scattered the leading trolls. Their wedge retreated without a pivot, so that the dwarves at the trailing, widespread edges were the first back over the wall, and those dwarves wasted no time in stoking the fires and readying the barrage.

Kaer'lic growled and punched her fist into her open palm when she noted Proffit's forces closing in on the dwarves' retreat. The trolls had been clearly enraged by the brash charge of the bearded folk, and were rolling up the hill behind the retreating point of the wedge, grouped tightly.

Before those running dwarves even got over the wall, the barrage began, with dozens and dozens of burning logs spinning over the wall and out over the dwarves. So closely grouped, the trolls took hit after hit, and when the flames stuck on one, sending it up in a burst of fire, its close-standing comrades, too, felt the fiery bite.

"Fools," Kaer'lic grunted, and the priestess began muttering the words of a spell.

A moment later, a small geyser of water appeared among the trolls, dousing fires and buying them some freedom from the dwarves' volley. Kaer'lic finished her spell, muttered under her breath, and began to conjure some more water. How much easier it all would have been, she thought, had Proffit not allowed the pursuit and had instead sent the bulk of his minions at the western, human end of the defensive line. . . .

Even with the magical interference of an unexpected burst of water, the firestorm proved considerable and highly effective, sending troll after troll up in a blaze. But Torgar saw the truth of the situation before him. They had stung their enemies again, but their time of advantage was over. Their fuel was exhausted.

Torgar looked past the flames and flaming trolls, to the horde of enemies behind, lurking down the hill, patiently waiting for the fires to diminish.

"Ye hold 'em here as long as ye can, but not a moment longer," Torgar instructed Shingles.

"Where're ye going, then?" the old dwarf asked.

"Galen Firth's needing to hear this from me again, so that there's no misunderstanding. We're going when we're going, and if they're not going, then they're on their own."

"Tell him, and let him see yer eyes when ye tell him," Shingles said. "He's a stubborn one."

"He'll be a dead one, then, and so be it."

Torgar patted his old friend on the shoulder and trotted along to the west, moving behind his boys and encouraging them with every step. He soon came to the human warriors, all readying their weapons, for their fires were burning low out on the hill before them. The dwarf had little trouble finding Galen Firth, for the man was up on a stone, shouting encouragement and pumping his fist.

"Well fought!" he said to Torgar when he spotted the approaching dwarf. "A brilliant move to go out and attack."

"Aye, and a smarter move's coming soon," Torgar replied. "The one that's putting us back in the tunnels, not to come out again."

Galen's smile remained as he digested those words, coming down from the stone. By the time he was standing before Torgar, that smile had been replaced by a frown.

"They have not breached our line, nor shall they!"

"Strong words, well spoken," said Torgar. "And true in the first and hopeful in the second. But if we're waiting to see if ye're right or wrong on what's to come, and ye're wrong, then we're all dead."

"I long ago pledged my life to the defense of Nesmé."

"Then stand yer ground if that's yer choice. I'm here to tell ye that me and me boys're heading into the tunnels, and there we're to stay." Torgar was well aware of the many frightened looks coming in at him from all around at that proclamation.

"Ye'll want to tighten yer line, then," said Torgar. "If ye're that stubborn. Me thinking's that ye should be going into the tunnels with us—yer old ones and young afore us, and yer fighters beside us. That's me thinking, Galen Firth. Take it as ye will."

The dwarf bowed and turned to leave.

"I beg you to stay," Galen surprised him by saying. "As General Dagna decided to fight for Nesmé."

Torgar turned on him sharply, his heavy eyebrows furrowing and shadowing his dark eyes. "Dagna gave his life and his boys gave theirs because ye were too stubborn to know when to run," he corrected. "It's not a mistake I'm planning on making. Ye been told that we're going. Ye been invited to come. Choice is yer own, and not mine."

The dwarf was quick in moving off, and when Galen called to him again, he just continued on his way, muttering, "Durn fool," under his breath with every step.

"Wait! Wait!" came a cry from behind, one that did turn Torgar around. He saw another of the Nesmé warriors, Rannek, running along the line toward Galen Firth and pointing up at the sky. "Good dwarf, wait! It is Alustriel! Alustriel has come again!"

Torgar followed his finger skyward, and there in the dark sky the dwarf saw the streaking chariot of fire, coming in hard and fast.

At the same time, drumbeats filled the air, booming in from the southeast, and horns began to blow.

"The Silver Guard!" one man cried. "The Silver Guard of Silverymoon is come!"

Torgar looked at Galen Firth, who seemed as surprised as any, though he had been saying that such help would arrive from the beginning.

"Our salvation is at hand, good dwarf," Galen said to him. "Stay, then, and join in our great victory this night!"

"Lady Lolth, she's back," Tos'un groaned when he saw the telltale flash of fire sweeping out of the night sky.

"Obould's worst nightmare," Kaer'lic replied. "Alustriel of Silverymoon. A most formidable foe, so we have been told."

Tos'un glanced at Kaer'lic, the tone of her words showing him that she had taken that reputation as a challenge. She was staring up at the chariot, eyes sparkling, mouthing the words of a spell, her fingers tracing runes in the empty air.

She timed her delivery perfectly, casting just as Alustriel soared past, not so far overhead. The very air seemed to distort and crack around the flying cart, a resonating, thunderous boom that shook the ground beneath Tos'un's feet. Alustriel's disorientation manifested itself to the watching drow through the erratic movements of the chariot, banking left and right, back and forth, even veering sharply so that it seemed as if it might skid out of control in the empty air.

Kaer'lic quickly cast a second spell, and a burst of conjured water intercepted Alustriel's shaky path.

The chariot dipped, its flight disturbed. For a moment, the flames on the magical horse team winked out, and down they all went.

"To the glory of Lolth," Tos'un said with a grin as the chariot plummeted.

The two anticipated a glorious wreckage, the enjoyable screams of horses and driver alike, and indeed, when the flying carriage first hit, they realized more disaster than even they could imagine.

But not in the manner they had expected.

The flames came alive again when Alustriel's chariot touched down, bursting from the carriage and horses alike, and leaping out in a fireball that swept out to the sides, then rolled up over the chariot as it charged along.

Both drow had their mouths hanging open as they watched the driver regain control, as her chariot—rolling along instead of flying—cut a swath of destruction and death through Proffit's ranks. Alustriel banked to the south, a wide sweep that both drow understood was intended to turn her around so that she could find her magical attackers.

"She should be dead," Kaer'lic said, and she licked her suddenly dry lips.

"But she's not," said Tos'un.

The chariot went up in the air, then continued its turn, completing a circuit. The dark elves heard the sound of a larger battle to the east, and the sound of horns and drums.

"She brought friends," said Kaer'lic.

"Many friends," Tos'un presumed. "We should leave."

The dark elves looked at each other and nodded.

"Get the prisoner," Kaer'lic instructed, and she didn't even wait as Tos'un moved off toward the small hole where they had concealed poor Fender.

The two dark elves and their captive started away quickly to the west, wanting to put as much ground as possible between themselves and the fierce woman in the flying chariot.

From the joyous cries among the line of dwarves and humans in the north, to the gathering sounds of a great battle erupting in the east, to the sheer power and control of the woman in the chariot up above, they knew that the end had come for Proffit.

Lady Alustriel and Silverymoon had come.

The Silver Guard of Silverymoon charged into the troll ranks in tight formation, spears leveled, bows firing flaming arrows from behind their ranks. Watching from the higher ground, Torgar could only think of the initial engagement as a wave washing over a beach, so fully did the Silver Guard seem to engulf the eastern end of the troll ranks.

But then that wave seemed to break apart on many large rocks. They were trolls, after all, strong and powerful and more physically resilient than any creature in all the world. The roar of the charge became the screams of the dying. The tight formations became a dance of smaller groups, pockets of warriors working hard to fend off the huge, ugly trolls.

Fireballs erupted beyond the leading edge of the Silver Guard, as Silverymoon's battle wizards joined in the fray.

But the trolls did not break and run. They met the attack with savagery, plowing into the human ranks, crushing warriors to the ground and stomping them flat.

"Now, boys!" Torgar yelled to his dwarves. "They came to help us, and it's our turn to repay the favor!"

From on high came the dwarven charge, down the barren, rocky slope at full run. To their right, the west, came Galen and the humans, sweeping in behind the trolls as the monsters pressed eastward to do battle with the new threat.

Blood ran—troll, dwarf, and human. Troll roars, human screams, and dwarven grunts mingled in the air in a symphony of horror and pain. The drama played out, minute by minute, a hundred personal struggles within the greater overall conflict.

It was the end for so many that day, lives cut short on a bloody, rocky slope under a pre-dawn sky.

As the lines tightened, the wizards became less effective and it became a contest of steel against claw, of troll savagery against dwarf stubbornness.

In the end, it wasn't the weapons or the superior tactics that won the day for the dwarves and humans. It was the care for each other and the sense that those around each warrior would stand there in support, the confidence of community and sacrifice. The willingness to stand and die before abandoning a friend. The dwarves had it most of all, but so did the humans of Nesmé and Silverymoon, while the trolls fought singly, self-preservation or bloodlust alone keeping them in battle.

Dawn broke an hour later to reveal a field of blood and body parts, of dead men, dead dwarves, and burned trolls, of troll body pieces squirming and writhing until the finishing crews could put them to the torch.

Battered and torn, half his face gouged by filthy troll claws, Torgar Hammerstriker walked the lines of his wounded, patting each dwarf on the shoulder as he passed. His companions had come out from Mirabar behind him, and had known nothing but battle after vicious battle by the end of the first tenday. Yet not a dwarf was complaining, and not one had muttered a single thought about going back. They were Battlehammers now, one and all, loyal to kin and king.

The fights, to a dwarf, were worth it.

As he moved past the line of his fighters, Torgar spotted Shingles talking excitedly to several of the Silverymoon militia.

"What do ye know?" Torgar asked when he came up beside his old friend.

"I know that Alustriel's not thinking to move north against Obould," came the surprising answer.

Torgar snapped his gaze over the two soldiers, who remained unshaken and impassive, and seemed in no hurry to explain the surprising news.

"She here?" Torgar asked.

"Lady Alustriel is with Galen Firth of Nesmé," one of the soldiers asked.

"Then ye best be taking us there."

The soldier nodded and led them on through the encampment, past the piled bodies of Silverymoon dead, past the lines of horribly wounded men, where priests were hard at work in tending the many garish wounds. In a tent near the middle of the camp, they found Alustriel and Galen Firth, and the man from Nesmé seemed in as fine spirits as Torgar had known.

The two dwarves allowed the soldiers to announce them, then walked up to the table where Lady Alustriel and Galen stood. The sight of Alustriel did give stubborn Torgar pause, for all that he had heard of the impressive woman surely paled in comparison to the reality of her presence. Tall and shapely, she stood with an air of dignity and competence beyond anything Torgar had ever seen. She wore a flowing gown of the finest materials, white and trimmed in purple, and upon her head was a circlet of gold and diamonds that could not shine with enough intensity to match her eyes. Torgar could hardly believe the thought, but it seemed to him that next to Alustriel, even Shoudra Stargleam would be diminished.

"L-lady," the dwarf stuttered, bowing so low his black beard brushed the ground.

"Well met, Torgar Hammerstriker," Alustriel said in a voice that was like a cool north wind. "I was hoping to speak with you, here or in the inevitable meetings I will have with King Bruenor of Mithral Hall. Your actions in Mirabar have sent quite an unsettling ripple throughout the region, you must know."

"If that ripple slaps Marchion Elastul upside his thick skull, then it's more than worth it," the dwarf answered, regaining his composure and taciturn facade.

"Fair enough," Alustriel conceded.

"What am I hearing now, Lady?" Torgar asked. "Some nonsense that ye're thinking the battle done?"

"The land is full of orcs and giants, good dwarf," said Alustriel. "The battle is far from finished, I am certain."

"I was just told ye weren't marching north to Mithral Hall."

"That is true."

"But ye just said—"

"This is not the time to take the fight to King Obould," Alustriel explained. "Winter will fast come on. There is little we can do."

"Bah, ye can have yer army—armies, for where's Everlund and Sundabar?—to Keeper's Dale in a tenday's time!"

"The other cities are watching, from afar," said Alustriel. "You do not understand the scope of what has befallen the region, I fear."

"Don't understand it?" Torgar said, eyes wide. "I been fighting in the middle of it for tendays now! I was on the ridge with Banak Brawnanvil, holding back the hordes. Was me and me boys that stole back the tunnels so that damned fool gnome could blow the top off the mountain spur!"

"Yes, I wish to hear all of that tale, in full, but another time," Alustriel said.

"So how can ye be saying I'm not knowing? I'm knowing better than anyone!"

"You saw the front waves of an ocean of enemies," Alustriel said. "Tens of thousands of orcs have crawled out of their holes to Obould's call. I have seen this. I have flown the length and breadth of the battlefield. There is nothing the combined armies can do at this time to be rid of the vermin. We cannot send thousands to die in such an effort, when it is better to secure a defensive line that will hold back the orc ocean."

"Ye came out to help Galen here!"

"Yes, against a manageable enemy—and one that still tore deeply into my ranks. The trolls have been pushed back, and we will drive them into the moors where they belong. Nesmé,"—she indicated the map on the table—"will be raised and fortified, because that alone is our best defense against the creatures of the Trollmoors."

"So ye come to the aid of Nesmé, but not of Mithral Hall?" said Torgar, never one to hold his thoughts private.

"We aid where we can," Alustriel answered, remaining calm and relaxed. "If the orcs begin to loosen their grip, if an opportunity presents itself, then Silverymoon will march to Mithral Hall and beyond, gladly beside King Bruenor Battlehammer and his fine clan. I suspect that Everlund will march with us, and surely Citadels Felbarr and Adbar will not forsake their Delzoun kin."

"But not now?"

Alustriel held her hands out wide.

"Nothing ye can do?"

"Emissaries will connect with King Battlehammer," the woman replied. "We will do what we can."

Torgar felt himself trembling, felt his fists clenching at his sides, and it was all he could do to not launch himself at Alustriel, or at Galen, standing smugly beside her, the man seeming as if all the world had been set aright, since Nesmé would soon be reclaimed.

"There is nothing more, good dwarf," Alustriel added. "I can not march my armies into the coming snow against so formidable an enemy as has brought war against Mithral Hall."

"It's just orcs," said Torgar.

No answer came back at him, and he knew he would get none.

"Will you march with us to Nesmé?" Galen Firth asked, and Torgar felt himself trembling anew. "Will you celebrate in the glory of our victory as Nesmé is freed?"

The dwarf stared hard at the man.

Then Torgar turned and walked out of the tent. He soon made it back to his kinfolk, Shingles at his side. Within an hour, they were gone, into the tunnels and marching at double-pace back to King Bruenor.

16

SHIFTING SANDS
AND SOLID STONE

"The boys from Felbarr're in sight across the river," Jackonray Broadbelt excitedly reported to King Bruenor.

For several days, the dwarf representative from Citadel Felbarr had been watching intently for the reports filtering down the chimneys for just such word. He knew that his kin were on the march, that Emerus Warcrown had agreed upon a Surbrin crossing to crash a hole in the defensive ring the orcs were preparing and link up aboveground with Mithral Hall.

"Three thousand warriors," Jackonray went on. "And with boats to get across."

"We're ready to knock out the hole in the east," Bruenor replied. "We got all me boys bunched at Garumn's Gorge, ready to charge out and chase the stinkin' orcs from the riverbank."

The two dwarves clapped each other on the shoulder, and throughout the audience hall other dwarves cheered. Sitting near to Bruenor's dais, two others seemed less than enthusiastic, however.

"You'll get them out fast?" Regis asked Nanfoodle.

The gnome nodded. "Mithral Hall will come out in a rush," he assured the halfling. "But fast enough to destroy the river defenses?"

The same question echoed in Regis's thoughts. They had won over and over again, and even when they'd lost ground, the cost had been heavier for their enemies. But all that had been achieved through *defensive* actions.

What they planned was something quite different.

"What do ye know, Rumblebelly?" Bruenor asked a moment later, and Regis realized that he wasn't doing a very good job of keeping his fears off of his face.

"There are a lot of orcs," he said.

"Lot o' dead orcs soon enough!" declared Jackonray, and the cheering grew even louder.

"We have the hall back, and they're not coming in," Regis said quietly. The words sounded incredibly inane to him as he heard them come from his mouth, and he had no idea what positive effect stating the obvious might bring. It was simply a subconscious delaying tactic, he understood, a way to move the conversation in another, less excitable direction.

"And they're soon to be running away!" Bruenor shot back at him, and the cheering grew even louder.

There was no way to go against it, Regis recognized. The emotions were too high, the anger bubbling over into the ecstasy of revenge.

"We should take no chances," Regis said, but no one was listening. "We should move with care," he said, but no one was listening. "We have them held now," he tried to explain. "How long will their forces hold together out there in the cold and snow when they know that there is nowhere left for them to march? Without the hunger of conquest, the orc momentum will stall, and so will their hearts for battle."

Nanfoodle's hand on his arm broke the halfling's gaining momentum, for it made Regis understand that Nanfoodle was the only one who even realized he was talking, that the dwarves, cheering wildly and leaping about, couldn't even hear his whispered words.

"We'll get out fast," the gnome assured him. "These engineers are magnificent. They will make wide tunnels, do not fear. The Battlehammer dwarves will come against the orcs before the orcs know they are being attacked."

Regis nodded, not doubting any of those specifics, but still very uneasy about the whole plan.

A clap on his other shoulder turned him around, to see Wulfgar crouching beside him.

"It is time to turn the orcs back to the north," the big man said. "It is time to put the vermin back in their mountain holes, or in the cold ground."

"I just . . ." Regis started.

"It is the loss of Dagna," said Wulfgar.

Regis glanced up at him.

"You struck out forcefully and the cost was heavy," the barbarian explained. "Is it so surprising that you would be less eager to strike out again?"

"You think it was my fault?"

"I think you did the right thing, and everyone here agreed and agrees still," Wulfgar answered with a reassuring smile. "If Dagna could reach out from the Halls of Moradin, he would pick you up by the collar and send you running to lead the charge out the eastern doors." Wulfgar put his hand on the halfling's shoulder—and from shoulder to neck, Regis disappeared under that gigantic paw.

The halfling tuned back in to the wider conversation then, in time to hear Bruenor shouting orders to send signalers up the chimneys to the mountaintop, to tell the Felbarr boys across the river that it was time to send Obould running.

The cheering drowned out everything, and even Regis and Nanfoodle were swept up in it.

It was time to send Obould running!

"Before winter!" came the shout, and the roar that was heard in the common room of the human refugees was as loud as that of the dwarves above vowing vengeance on King Obould. Word had filtered down the corridors of Mithral Hall that Citadel Felbarr had come, and that King Bruenor and his dwarves were preparing to burst out of their imprisonment.

The River Surbrin would be secured—that much seemed certain—and the dwarves had promised to set up passage over the river to the lands still tamed. They would cross the Surbrin before winter.

"Never again will I be crawling into any tunnels!" one man shouted.

"But huzzah to King Bruenor and his clan for their hospitality!" shouted another and a great cheer went up.

"Silverymoon before the snow!" one shouted.

"Everlund!" argued another.

"There's word that Nesmé's looking for hearty souls," added another, "to rebuild what the trolls tore down."

Each city mentioned drew a louder cheer.

Each one stung Delly as acutely as the bite of a wasp. She moved through the crowd nodding, smiling, and trying to be happy for them. They had been through so much turmoil, had seen loved ones die and houses burned to the ground. They had trekked across miles of rocky ground, had suffered the elements and the fear of orcs nipping at their heels all the way to Mithral Hall.

Delly wanted to be happy for them, for they deserved a good turn of fortune. But when the news had come down that the dwarves were preparing the breakout in earnest, and that they expected to open the way for the refugees to leave, all Delly could think about was that soon she would again be alone.

She had Colson of course, and Wulfgar when he was not up fighting—which was rarely of late. She had the dwarves, and she cared for them greatly.

But how she wanted to see the stars again. And bask in the sun. And feel the wind upon her face. A wistful smile crossed her face as she thought of Arumn and Josi at the Cutlass.

Delly shook the nostalgia and the self-pity away quickly as she approached a solitary figure in the corner of the large room. Cottie Cooperson didn't join in the cheers that night, and seemed hardly aware of them at all. She sat upon a chair, rocking slowly back and forth, staring down at the small child in her arms.

Delly knelt beside her and gently put her hand on Cottie's shoulder.

"Ye put her to sleep again, did ye, Cottie?" Delly quietly asked.

"She likes me."

"Who would not?" Delly asked, and she just knelt there for a long time, rubbing Cottie's shoulder, looking down at the peaceful Colson.

The sounds of eager anticipation continued to echo around her, the shouts and the cheers, the grand plans unveiled by man after man declaring that he would begin a new and better life. Their resilience touched Delly, to be sure, as did the sense of community that she felt there. All those refugees from various small towns, thrown together in the tunnels of dwarves, had bonded in common cause and in simple human friendship.

Delly held her smile throughout, but when she considered the source of the cheering, she felt more like crying.

She left the room a short while later, Colson in her arms. To her surprise, she found Wulfgar waiting for her in their room.

"I hear ye're readying to break free of the hall and march to the Surbrin," she greeted.

The bluntness and tone set Wulfgar back in his chair, and Delly felt him watching her closely, every step, as she carried Colson to her small crib. She set the baby down and let her finger trace gently across her face, then stood straight and took a deep breath before turning to Wulfgar and adding, "I hear ye're meaning to go soon."

"The army is already gathering at Garumn's Gorge," the big man confirmed. "The army of Citadel Felbarr is in sight above, approaching the Surbrin from the east."

"And Wulfgar will be there with the dwarves when they charge forth from their halls, will he?"

"It is my place."

"Yer own and Catti-brie's," Delly remarked.

Wulfgar shook his head, apparently missing the dryness of her tone. "She cannot go, and it is difficult for her. Cordio will hear nothing of it, for her wounds have not yet mended."

"Ye seem to know much about it."

"I just came from her bedside," said Wulfgar as he moved toward Colson's crib—and as Delly moved aside, so that he did not see her wince at that admission.

Bedside, or bed? the woman thought, but she quickly shook the preposterous notion from her mind.

"How badly she wishes that she could join in the battle," Wulfgar went on. So engaged was he with Colson then, leaning over the side of the crib and waggling his finger before the child's face so that she had a challenge in grabbing at it, that he did not notice Delly's profound frown. "She's all fight, that one. I think her hatred of the orcs rivals that of a Gutbuster."

He finally looked up at Delly and his smile disappeared the moment he regarded the stone-faced woman, her arms crossed over her chest.

"They're all leaving," she answered his confused expression. "For Silverymoon and Everlund, or wherever their road might take them."

"Bruenor has promised that the way will be clear," Wulfgar answered.

"Clear for all of us," Delly heard herself saying, and she could hardly believe the words. "I'd dearly love to see Silverymoon. Can ye take me there?"

"We have already discussed this."

"I'm needing to go," Delly said. "It's been too long in the tunnels. Just a foray, a visit, a chance to hear the tavern talk of people like meself."

"We will break through and scatter the orcs," Wulfgar promised. He came up beside her and hugged her close in his muscular arms. "We will have them on the run before winter and put them in their holes before midsummer. Their day is past and Bruenor will reclaim the land for the goodly folk. Then we will go to Silverymoon, and on to Sundabar if you wish!"

He couldn't see Delly's face as he held her so closely.

He wouldn't have understood anything he saw there, anyway, for the woman was just numb. She had no answers for him, had not even any questions to ask.

Resignation smacked hard against impatience, and the woman couldn't find the heart to start counting the many, many days.

Feeling refreshed and confident that he would rouse Citadel Felbarr to Mithral Hall's aid, Nikwillig walked out of the Moonwood to the south, escorted by Hralien. They would strike southwest, toward the Surbrin, to gather needed information, and Hralien planned to return to the Moonwood after seeing Nikwillig safely on his way back to his dwarven home.

When the pair reached the Surbrin, they saw their enemies across the way, still building on the already formidable defenses. Picket walls of huge sharpened logs lined the western bank and piles of stones could be seen, ready to be thrown by the few giants they saw milling about, or by the many catapults that had been constructed and set in place.

"They're thinking to hold it all," Nikwillig remarked.

Hralien had no response.

The two moved back to the east soon after, marching long into the night and far from the riverbank. The next morning, they set off early, and at a swift pace. At noon, they came to the crossroads.

"Farewell, good dwarf," Hralien offered. "Your enemy is our enemy, of course, and so I expect that we might well meet again."

"Well met the first time," Nikwillig replied. "And well met the second, by Moradin's blessing."

"Yes, there is that," Hralien said with a grin. He clapped the dwarf on the shoulder and turned back to the north and home.

Nikwillig moved with a spring in his step. He had never expected to survive the battle north of Keeper's Dale, had thought his signaling mission to be suicidal. But, at long last, he was going home.

Or so he thought.

He came upon a high bluff as twilight settled on the hilly landscape, and from that vantage point, Nikwillig saw the vast encampment of an army far to the south.

An army he knew.

Citadel Felbarr was already on the march!

Nikwillig punched his fist in the air and let out a growl of support for his warrior kinfolk. He considered the ground between him and the encampment. He wanted to run right out and join them, but he knew that his weary legs wouldn't carry him any farther that night. So he settled down, thinking to get a short rest.

He closed his eyes.

And awoke late the next morning, with the sun nearing its apex. The dwarf leaped up and rushed to the southern end of the bluff. The army was gone—marching east, he knew. East to the river and the mighty defenses that had been set in place there.

The dwarf glanced all around, studying the ground, looking for some sign of his kin. Could he catch them?

He didn't know, but did he dare try it?

Nikwillig hopped in circles for many minutes, his mind spinning faster than his body ever could. One name kept coming back to him: Hralien.

He ran off the bluff soon after, heading north and not south.

17

OVEREAGER

Bruenor Battlehammer stood on the eastern gatehouse of the bridge at Garumn's Gorge, overseeing the preparations for the coming assault. The couriers scrambled, relaying messages and information from the engineers and the many scouts working the eastern slopes of the mountain, who shouted the information down the cooled chimneys to the great Undercity. The dwarf king was arrayed in full battle regalia, his shield emblazoned with the foaming mug standard of his clan and his well-worn, often chipped battle-axe slung casually over one shoulder—but without his signature helmet, with its one horn remaining.

Regis and Wulfgar were there by his side, as was Banak Brawnanvil, seated and strapped into a carriage set upon two sturdy poles. Four strong dwarves attended Banak, ready to carry him out onto the battlefield and into position where he could help direct the movements of the various dwarven regiments.

"Girl's gonna miss the fun this day," Bruenor remarked, referring to the notably absent Catti-brie. She had argued and argued to be a part of the battle, but Cordio and the other priests would hear none of it, and in the end, Wulfgar and Bruenor had quietly pointed out that her presence would more likely jeopardize those attending her than anything else.

"Fun?" Regis echoed.

He continued to stare to the east, where three high platforms had been built, each holding a train of ore carts, cranked up and locked in place at the top of a high rail ramp. The rails swept down across the remaining distance of the gorge ledge, then into the exit tunnels. The doors to those tunnels had been reopened, but the orcs, trolls, and giants had done a fair job of bringing down that side of the mountain, leaving the dwarves trapped in their hole. And so while the engineers had constructed the rails, miners had dug extensions on the escape tunnels, scraping right to the very outer edge of the landslide, so close to the open air that they often had to pause in their work and let noisy orc guards wander by.

"Fun in a Pwent kind o' way," Bruenor remarked with a snicker. "Durned crazy dwarf's arguing to sit atop the middle train instead of inside!" Bruenor offered a wink at Banak.

"He'd lead with his helmet spike, and probably take half the mountain with him," Banak added. "And he'd love every tumble and every rock that fell upon his too-hard head."

"Not to doubt," said Bruenor.

"The middle tunnel will prove the widest," Wulfgar said more seriously.

"Me and yerself'll lead the charge right behind the carts out that one, then," said Bruenor.

"I was thinking to go on the left," said Wulfgar. "The scouts report that the watchtower is well defended by our enemies. Taking that, and quickly, will be crucial."

"To the left, then. The both of us."

"You'll be needed in the center, directing," Regis said.

"Bah!" Bruenor snorted. "Pwent's starting the fight there, and Pwent don't take no directions. These boys'll get Banak out fast enough, and he'll call the orders to the river."

All three, dwarf, human, and halfling, looked to the injured Banak as Bruenor spoke, and none of them missed the expression of sincere gratitude the old warrior wore. He wanted to see the fight through, wanted to complete what he had started on the high ridge north of Keeper's Dale. As they all had learned with Pikel Bouldershoulder after the green-bearded dwarf had lost an arm, the physical infirmity would be minimized if the wounded could still contribute to the cause.

The conversation rambled along for some time, the four really talking about nothing important, but merely trying to pass away the tense minutes until the final words came up from the Undercity. Everyone at Garumn's Gorge wanted to just go, to burst out and be on with the battle. Seasoned veterans all, the Battlehammer dwarves knew well that those moments before a battle were usually the most trying.

And so it was with hopeful eyes that the four turned to see the courier running to them from the depths of Mithral Hall.

"King Bruenor," the dwarf gasped, "the scouts're saying that Felbarr's ready to cross and that most o' the damned orcs've gone down to the river."

"That's it, then," Bruenor told them all.

He gave a shrill whistle, commanding the attention of all nearby dwarves, then lifted his battle-axe into the air and shook it about.

Cheering started near him and rolled out to the edges of the gorge like a wave on a pond. Up above, warriors scrambled into the ore carts, packing in tightly, and pulled the thick metal covers over them, and just below them, engineers moved to the locking pins.

Wulfgar bounded off toward the left-hand tunnel, nearly running over Nanfoodle as the gnome rushed to join Bruenor, who was offering last-minute instructions to Banak.

"I wish we had some of that oil of impact remaining," the gnome moaned.

"Bah, the dwarves'll knock them walls out!" said Regis, using his best Bruenor imitation, and when Bruenor turned to regard him curiously, the halfling tossed him a reassuring wink.

It seemed that Regis had put his doubts aside, or at least had suppressed them since they were moot in any case, but before Bruenor could begin to discern which it might be, the pins were yanked free and the three large trains began to rumble down the tracks.

They came down from a height of more than fifty feet, picking up speed and momentum as they shot along the oiled rails into the low, narrow tunnels. So perfectly timed was the release, and so minimal the tolerance of each set of rails, that they rolled along side-by-side into their respective tunnels and all hit the outer shell of the mountain blockade within a blink of each other.

The screech of metal grinding on metal and stone, and the thunder of tumbling boulders, echoed back into the main chambers, eliciting a great war whoop from the gathered forces, who took up the charge.

Wulfgar led the way on the left, though he had to stoop nearly double to pass through the tight corridor. Before him lay bright daylight, for the train had blasted right through and had gone skidding and tumbling down beyond the exit. Already dwarves were scrambling out of that wreckage, weapons ready.

The barbarian came out into the open air and saw immediately that their surprise was complete. Few orcs were in the area, and those that were seemed more frightened than ready to do battle. Wulfgar ignored his instincts to go to the seemingly vulnerable train-riders, and instead cut a fast left and sprinted up a rocky slope toward the watchtower. The door was partially ajar, an orc moving behind it just as Wulfgar lowered his shoulder and barreled into it.

The orc grunted and flew across the room, arms and legs flailing. Its three companions in the room watched its flight, their expressions confused. They seemed hardly aware that an enemy had burst in, even when Aegis-fang swept down from on high, smashing the skull of the closest.

Wulfgar pivoted around that dead orc as it fell, and in his turn, sent his warhammer sweeping out wide. The targeted orc leaped and turned, trying to twist out of the way, but the warhammer clipped it hard enough to launch it into a spin, around and around, into the air, its flight ending abruptly at the tower's stone wall. Wulfgar strode forward, chopping at the third orc, who rushed away and out of reach. But the barbarian just turned the momentum of the hammer, launching it out left to right so that it cracked into the back of the orc who was pressed face-up against the wall, crushing its ribs and splitting its sides. The creature gasped and blood fountained from its mouth.

Wulfgar wasn't watching, though, certain that his hit had been fatal. He let go of Aegis-fang, confident it would return to his call, and charged ahead, swatting aside the spear of the remaining orc as it clumsily tried to bring the weapon to bear.

The huge barbarian stepped close and got his hand around the orc's neck, then pressed ahead and down, bending the creature over backward and choking the life out of it.

"Above ye!" a dwarf called in a raspy voice from the doorway.

Wulfgar glanced back to see Bill HuskenNugget, the lookout who had been in there when the tower had been taken. Bill had been downed with a poisoned dart, and simultaneously, his throat had been expertly cut, taking his voice, which was only beginning to heal. The retreating dwarves had thought Bill dead, but they'd dragged him along anyway, as was their custom—and a good thing they had, for he had awakened cursing in a whisper soon after.

Wulfgar's gaze went up fast, in time to see an orc in the loft above him launching a spear his way. The orc jerked as it threw, Bill's crossbow bolt buried in its side.

Wulfgar couldn't dive out of the way, so he reacted with a twist and a jerk, throwing his arm, still holding the dying orc by the throat, coming up to block. The dying orc took the spear in the back, and Wulfgar tossed the creature aside. He glanced back to Bill, who offered a wink, then he ran to the ladder and leaped, reaching up high enough to catch the lip of the loft. With his tremendous strength, the barbarian easily pulled himself up.

"Aegis-fang!" he cried, summoning the magical hammer into his hands.

Roaring and swinging, he had orcs flying from the loft in short order. Down below, the dwarves, including Bill and Bruenor, finished them up even as they hit the ground.

Wulfgar ran for the ladder to the roof, and nearly tripped as a small form came rushing past him. He wasn't even surprised to see Regis go out the loft's small window, nor was he surprised when he charged up the ladder and shouldered through the trapdoor—a trapdoor that had been weighted down with several bags of supplies—to see Regis peeking at him over the lip of the tower.

As soon as Wulfgar got the attention of all three orcs on the tower top, the halfling came over and sat on the crenellation. Regis picked out a target and let fly his little mace, the weapon spinning end-over-end to smack the orc in the face. The creature staggered backward, nearly tumbling over the parapet, and as it finally straightened, the halfling hit it with a flying body block. The orc went over the edge, to be followed by a second, thrown out by Wulfgar, and a third, leaping of its own volition in the face of the raging barbarian.

"Good place to direct!" Bruenor yelled, coming through the trapdoor. He ran to the southern edge of the tower top, overlooking the battlefield.

The wide smile on the fierce dwarf's face lasted until he looked to the east, to the river.

The jolt when they hit the stone wall rattled their teeth and compressed all eight of the dwarves in the ore cart into an area that two had fully occupied just a moment before. They weathered it, though, to a dwarf. And not just in that cart and in the other nine in the same train, but in the twenty carts of the other two trains as well.

Ivan and Pikel Bouldershoulder stretched and shoved with all their might, trying to keep the dwarves in their cart from crushing each other. The jolts continued, though, the iron carts twisting and straining. Rocks bounced down as the train rumbled about.

When it finally settled, Ivan was first to put his feet under him and strain his back against the dented cover of the cart. He pushed it open a bit, enough so that he could poke his head out.

"By Moradin!" he cried to his companions. "All of ye boys, push now and push hard!"

For Ivan saw that the plan had not worked quite so well, at least with their particular train. They had hardly cracked through the mountain wall, instead beginning an avalanche over them that had left the train half buried, twisted, and still blocking the tunnel exit so that the soldiers running behind could not easily get out.

Ivan grabbed at the twisted metal cart cover and shoved with all his strength. When that did nothing, he reached out over it and tried to pry away some of the heavy stones holding it down.

"Come on, lads!" he shouted. "Afore the damned orcs catch us in a box!"

They all began shoving and shouldering the metal cover, and it creaked open a bit more. Ivan wasted no time in squeezing out.

The view from that vantage point proved no more encouraging. Only two of the other nine carts were open, and the dwarves coming out were bleeding and dazed. Half the mountainside had come down upon them, it seemed, and they were stuck.

And to the east, Ivan saw and heard the charge of the orcs.

The yellow-bearded dwarf scrambled atop his damaged cart and pushed aside several stones, then reached back and tugged the cover with all his strength.

Out popped Pikel, then another and another, with Ivan shouting encouragement all the while.

The orcs closed.

But then a second roar came down from just north of their position, and Ivan managed to get a peek over a pile of rubble to see the countering charge of the Battlehammer dwarves. The center train and the northern one had pounded right through, exactly as planned, and the army was pouring out of Mithral Hall in full force, sweeping east and fanning south to form a perimeter around the catastrophe of the southernmost train. The fierce dwarves met the orc charge head on, axe against spear, sword against sword, in such a violent and headlong explosion that half the orcs and dwarves leading their respective charges were down in the first seconds of engagement.

Ivan leaped from the rubble and led the charge of those few among the dwarves of the southern train who could follow. Of the eighty in the carts of that southern train, less than a score came forth, the others out of the fight either because of serious injury or because they simply could not force open their twisted and buried carts.

By the time Ivan, Pikel, and the others joined in the fray, that particular orc charge had been stopped in its tracks. More and more dwarves poured forth; formations gathered and marched with precision to support the flanks and to disrupt the in-flow of orc warriors.

"To the river, boys!" came a shout from the front of the dwarven line, and Ivan recognized the voice of Tred. "The boys of Felbarr have come and they're needing us now!"

That, of course, was all the ferocious Battlehammers needed to hear, and they pressed all the harder, driving back the orcs and raising their cheers in the common refrain of, "To the river!"

The progress in the center and south proved remarkable, the dwarves crushing the resistance and making good speed, but from the tower top in the north, Bruenor, Wulfgar, and Regis were granted a different perspective on it all.

Regis winced and looked away as a giant boulder crashed into a raft laden with Felbarr dwarves, sending several sprawling into the icy waters and driving the side of the craft right under, swamping it.

The boats were putting in upstream, obviously, the Felbarr dwarves trying to ride the current with their own rowing to get them to the bank at the point of conflict. But the orcs and giants had some tricks to play. Sharpened logs met the dwarven rafts in the swift river current, catching against the sides of the craft and disrupting the rowing. And the barrage of boulders, giant thrown and catapult launched, increased with every passing second. Rocks hit the water with tremendous *whumps!* and sent up fountains of spray, or crashed into and through the dwarven boats.

Dozens of boats were in the water, each carrying scores of dwarves, and the three observers on the tower had to wonder if any of them would even get across.

Bruenor shouted down to his commanders on the ground, "Get to the durned river and turn to the north! We got to clear the bank along the north. Take 'em over the ridge," the dwarf king instructed Wulfgar. "We got to stop those giants!"

Wulfgar nodded and started down the ladder, but Regis just shook his head and said, "Too many," echoing all their fears.

Within minutes, the main thrust of the dwarven army had split the orc forces in half, spearheading right to the bank of the Surbrin. But as more and more dwarves rushed out to support the lines, so too were the orcs reinforced from the north. A great swarming mass rushed down over the mountain spur to join in the fight.

Bruenor and Regis could only look on helplessly. They would take the riverbank and hold it south of that spur, Bruenor could see, but they'd never get up north enough to slow the giant barrage and help the poor dwarves of Citadel Felbarr and their ill-advised crossing.

Another boulder smashed a raft, and half the dwarves atop it tumbled into the water, their heavy armor tugging them down to the icy depths.

Regis rubbed his plump hands over his face.

"By the gods," he muttered.

Bruenor punched his fist against the stone, then turned to the ladder and leaped down to the loft. In moments, he was outside with Wulfgar, calling every dwarf around him to his side, and he and the barbarian led the charge straight north, up the side of the mountain spur and beyond.

Regis screamed down to him, but futilely. The halfling could see the force over that ridge, and he knew that Bruenor and Wulfgar were surely doomed.

Out in the water, another boat capsized.

18

THE SKIN OF A
DWARF'S TOOTH

Nikwillig groaned and shouted as another of the rafts overturned, dumping brave dwarves to a watery death. He looked to his companion for some sign of hope.

Hralien, as frustrated as the dwarf, looked away, back to his warriors as they sprinted along the stones. They had located the sight of the most devastating volleys, where a trio of giants were having a grand time of it, throwing boulder after boulder as the defenseless dwarven crafts floated past.

Many times did the elf leader wave at his warriors for patience, but all of them, even Hralien, were anxious and angry, watching good dwarves so easily slaughtered. Hralien held them together in tight formation, though, and had them holding their shots until the giant trio was right below them.

The elf nodded and all his charges, three-score of the Moonwood's finest warriors, bent back their bows. Silent nods and hand signals had the groups split evenly among the respective targets, and a shout from Hralien set them in motion.

A score of arrows reached out for each of the unsuspecting giants, and before that devastating volley struck home, the skilled elves had put the next arrows to their bowstrings.

Sixty more streaked out, the hum of elven bows drowned out by the howls of screaming giants.

One of the three went down hard under that second volley, grasping at the shafts sticking from its thick neck. The other two staggered, but not toward their attackers. The behemoths had seen enough of the elven war party already. One ran flat out, back to the west, while the other, hit many times in the legs, struggled to keep up. The straggler caught the full force of the next volley, three-score arrows reaching out to sting it hard and send it tumbling to the stones.

All around the western riverbank, where there had been only glee at the easy slaughter of dwarves, came tumult and confusion. Giants howled and orcs, dozens and dozens of the creatures, scrambled to and fro, caught completely unawares.

"Press forward!" Hralien called down his line. "None get close enough that we must draw swords!"

Grim-faced to an elf, each adorned with identical silver helmets that had flared sides resembling the wings of a bird, and silver-trimmed forest green capes flapping in the breeze behind them, the moon elf brigade marched in a perfect line. As one they set arrows to bowstrings, as one they lifted and leveled the bows, with permission to seek out the best targets of opportunity.

Few orcs seemed interested in coming their way, however, and so those targets grew fewer and fewer.

The elves marched south, clouds of arrows leading their way.

Wulfgar led the charge over the mountain spur, where he and the dwarves were met immediately by a host of orcs rushing south to reinforce their line.

With Aegis-fang in hand the mighty barbarian scattered the closest monsters. A great one-armed swing of the warhammer, and he clipped a pair of orcs and sent them flying, then stepped ahead and punched out, launching a third into the air. Beside him, the dwarves came on in a wild rush, weapons thrusting and slashing, shouldering orcs aside when their weapons didn't score a hit.

"The high ground!" Wulfgar kept shouting, demanding of his forces that they secure the ridgeline in short order.

Up went Wulfgar, stone by stone. Down went the orcs who tried to stand before him, crushed to the ground or tossed aside. The barbarian was the first to the ridge top, and there he stood unmovable, a giant among the dwarves and orcs.

He called for the dwarves to rally around him, and so they did, coming up in scattered pockets, but falling into perfect position around him, the first arrivals supporting the barbarian's flanks, and those dwarves following supporting the flanks of their kin. Lines of dwarves came on to join, but the orcs were not similarly bolstered, for those monsters farther down the northern face of the mountain spur veered east or west in an effort to avoid this point of conflict, to avoid the towering and imposing barbarian and his mighty warhammer.

From that high vantage point, Wulfgar saw almost certain disaster brewing, for farther to the east, down at the riverbank, such a throng of orcs had gathered and were streaming south that it seemed impossible for the dwarves to hold their hard-fought gains. The dwarves, too, were at the river then, south of the spur, trying hard to fortify their tentative position.

If they lost at the riverbank, the brave Felbarrans in the river would have nowhere to land their rafts.

Looking out at the river, at the splashes of giant boulders and the flailing dwarves in the water, at the battered craft and the line of missiles reaching out at them, Wulfgar honestly wondered if holding the riverbank would mean anything at all. Would a single Felbarran dwarf get across?

Yet the Battlehammers had to try. For the sake of the Felbarrans, for the sake of the whole dwarven community, they had to try.

Wulfgar glanced back behind him, and saw Bruenor leading another force straight east along the base of the mountain spur, driving fast for the river.

"Turn east!" Wulfgar commanded his troops. "We'll make a stand on the high ground and make the orcs pay for every inch of stone!"

The dwarves around him cheered and followed, rushing down the rocky arm toward where it, too, spilled into the river. With only a hundred warriors total in that group, there was no doubt that they would lose, that they would be overwhelmed and slaughtered in short order. They all knew it. They all charged on eagerly.

They made their stand on a narrow strip of high, rocky ground, between the battleground south, where Bruenor had joined in the fighting and the dwarves were gaining a strong upper hand and the approaching swarm from the north.

"Bruenor will protect our backs!" Wulfgar shouted. "Set a defense against the north alone!"

The dwarves scrambled, finding all of the best positions which offered them some cover to the north, and trusting in King Bruenor and their kin to protect them from those orcs fighting in the south.

"Every moment of time we give those behind us is a moment more the Felbarrans have to land on our shore!" Wulfgar shouted, and he had to yell loudly to be heard, for the orc swarm was closing, screaming and hooting with every running stride.

The orcs came to the base of that narrow ridge in full run and began scrambling up, and Wulfgar and the dwarves rained rocks, crossbow bolts, and Aegis-fang upon them, battering them back. Those who did reach the fortified position met, most of all, Wulfgar the son of Beornegar. Like an ancient oak, the tall and powerful barbarian did not bend.

Wulfgar, who had survived the harshness of Icewind Dale, refused to move.

Wulfgar, who had suffered the torment of the demon Errtu, denied his fears, and ignored the sting of orc spears.

The dwarves rallied around him, screaming with every swing of axe or hammer, with every stab of finely-crafted sword. They yelled to deny the pain of wounds, the broken knuckles, the gashes, and the stabs. They yelled to deny the obvious truth that soon the orc sea would wash them from that place and to the Halls of Moradin.

They screamed, and their calls became louder soon after, as more dwarves came up to reinforce the line, dwarves who fought with King Bruenor—and King Bruenor himself, determined to die beside his heroic human son.

Behind them, a Felbarran raft made the shore, the dwarves charging off and swinging north immediately. Then a second slid in, and more approached.

But it wouldn't be enough, Bruenor and Wulfgar knew, glancing back and ahead. There were simply too many enemies.

"Back to the hall?" Wulfgar asked in the face of that reality.

"We got nowhere to run, boy," Bruenor replied.

Wulfgar grimaced at the hopelessness in the dwarf's voice. Their daring breakout was doomed, it seemed, to complete ruin.

"Then fight on!" Wulfgar said to Bruenor, and he yelled it out again so that all could hear. "Fight on! For Mithral Hall and Citadel Felbarr! Fight on for your very lives!"

Orcs died by the score on the northern face of that ridge, but still they came on, two replacing every one who had fallen.

Wulfgar continued to center the line, though his arms grew weary and his hammer swings slowed. He bled from a dozen wounds, one hand swelled to twice its normal size when Aegis-fang connected against an orc club too far down the handle. But he willed that hand closed on the hammer shaft.

He willed his shaky legs to hold steady.

He growled and he shouted and he chopped down another orc.

He ignored the thousands still moving down from the north, focusing instead on the ones within his deadly range.

So focused was he and the dwarves that none of them saw the sudden thinning of the orc line up in the north. None noted orcs sprinting away suddenly to the west, or groups of others simply and suddenly falling to the stone, many writhing, some already dead as they hit the ground.

None of the defenders heard the hum of elven bowstrings.

They just fought and fought, and grew confused as much as relieved when fewer and fewer orcs streamed their way.

The swarm, faced with a stubborn foe in the south and a new and devastating enemy in the north, scattered.

The battle south of the mountain spur continued for a long while, but when Wulfgar's group managed to turn their attention in that direction and support the main force of Battlehammers, and when the elves of the Moonwood, Nikwillig among them, came over the ridge and began offering their deadly accurate volleys at the most concentrated and stubborn orc defensive formations, the outcome became apparent and the end came swiftly.

Bruenor Battlehammer stood on the riverbank just south of the mountain spur, staring out at the rolling water, the grave for hundreds of Felbarran dwarves that dark day. They had won their way from Mithral Hall to the river, had re-opened the halls and established a beachhead from which they could begin their push to the north.

But the cost. . . .

The horrible cost.

"We'll send forces out to the south and find a better place for landing," Tred said to the dwarf king, his voice muted by the sobering reality of the battle.

Bruenor regarded the tough dwarf and Jackonray beside him.

"If we can clear the bank to the south, our boats can come across far from the giant-throwers," Jackonray explained.

Bruenor nodded grimly.

Tred reached up and dared pat the weary king on the shoulder. "Ye'd have done the same for us, we're knowing. If Citadel Felbarr was set upon, King Bruenor'd've thrown all his boys into fire to help us."

It was true enough, Bruenor knew, but then, why did the water look so blood red to him?

ART THREE | A WINTER RESPITE

D o you know what it is to be an elf, Drizzt Do'Urden?"
I hear this question all the time from my companion, who seems determined to help me begin to understand the implications of a life that could span centuries—implications good and bad when one considers that so many of those with whom I come into contact will not live half that time.

It has always seemed curious to me that, while elves may live near a millennium and humans less than a century, human wizards often achieve levels of understanding and power to rival those of the greatest elf mages. This is not a matter of intelligence, but of focus, it seems clear. Always before, I gave the credit for this to the humans, for their sense of urgency in knowing that their lives will not roll on and on and on.

Now I have come to see that part of the credit for this balance is the elven viewpoint of life, and that viewpoint is not one rooted in falsehood or weakness. Rather, this quieter flow of life is the ingredient that brings sanity to an existence that will see the birth and death of centuries. Or, if preferable, it is a segmented flow of life, a series of bursts.

I see it now, to my surprise, and it was Innovindil's recounting of her most personal relationships with partners both human and elf that presented the notion clearly in my mind. When Innovindil asks me now, "Do you know what it is to be an elf, Drizzt Do'Urden?" I can honestly and calmly smile with self-assurance. For the first time in my life, yes, I think I do know.

To be an elf is to find your distances of time. To be an elf is to live several shorter life spans. It is not to abandon forward-looking sensibility, but it is also to find emotionally comfortable segments of time, smaller life spans in which to exist. In light of that realization, for me the more pertinent question thus becomes, "Where is the range of comfort for such existences?"

There are many realities that dictate such decisions—decisions that, in truth, remain more subconscious than purposeful. To be an elf is to outlive your companions if they are not elves; even if they are, rare is the relationship that will survive centuries. To be an elf is to revel in the precious moments of your children—should they be of only half-elf blood, and even if they are of full blood—and to know that they may not outlive you. In that instance, there is only comfort in the profound and ingrained belief that having these children and these little pockets of joyful time was indeed a blessing, and that such a blessing outweighs the profound loss that any compassionate being would surely feel at the death of an offspring. If the very real possibility that one will outlive a child, even if the child sees the end of its expected lifespan, will prevent that person from having children, then the loss is doubly sad.

In that context, there is only one answer: to be an elf is to celebrate life.

To be an elf is to revel in the moments, in the sunrise and the sunset, in the sudden and brief episodes of love and adventure, in the hours of companionship. It is, most of all, to never be paralyzed by your fears of a future that no one can foretell, even if predictions lead you to the seemingly obvious, and often disparaging, conclusions.

That is what it is to be an elf.

The elves of the surface, contrary to the ways of the drow, often dance and sing. With this, they force themselves into the present, into the moment, and though they may be singing of heroes and deeds long past or of prophecies yet to come, they are, in their song, in the moment, in the present, grasping an instant of joy or reflection and holding it as tightly as any human might.

A human may set out to make a "great life," to become a mighty leader or sage, but for elves, the passage of time is too slow for such pointed and definitive ambitions. The memories of humans are short, so 'tis said, but that holds true for elves as well. The long dead human heroes of song no doubt bore little resemblance to the perceptions of the current bards and their audience, but that is true of elves, too, even though those elf bards likely knew the principals of their songs!

The centuries dull and shift the memories, and the lens of time alters images.

A great life for an elf, then, results either of a historical moment seized correctly or, more often, it is a series of connected smaller events that will eventually add up to something beyond the parts. It is a continuing process of growth, perhaps, but only because of piling experiential understanding.

Most of all, I know now, to be an elf is not to be paralyzed by a future one cannot control. I know that I am going to die. I know that those I love will one day die, and in many cases—I suspect, but do not know!—they will die long before I. Certitude is strength and suspicion is worthless, and worry over suspicion is something less than that.

I know, now, and so I am free of the bonds of the future.

I know that every moment is to be treasured, to be enjoyed, to be heightened as much as possible in the best possible way.

I know, now, the failing of the bonds of worthless worry.

I am free.

—Drizzt Do'Urden

19

QUIET TENDAYS

Winter had already settled in far to the north, on the higher foothills of the Spine of the World. Cold winds brought stinging sheets of snow, often moving horizontally more than vertically. Drizzt and Innovindil kept their cowls pulled low and tight, but still the crisp snow stung their faces, and the brilliance of the snowcap had Drizzt squinting his sensitive eyes even when the sun was not brightly shining. The drow would have preferred to move after dark, but it was simply too cold, and he, Innovindil, and Sunset had to spend the dark hours huddled closely near a fire night after night. He couldn't believe how dramatically the shift in the weather had come, considering that it was still autumn back in the region of Mithral Hall.

The going was slow—no more than a few miles a day at most, and that only if they were not trying to climb higher along the icy passes. On a few occasions, they had dared to use Sunset to fly them up over a particularly difficult ridge, but the wind was dangerously strong for even the pegasus's powerful wings. Beyond that, the last thing the pair wanted was to be spotted by Gerti and her army of behemoths!

"How many days have passed?" Drizzt asked Innovindil as they sat for a break and a midday meal one gray afternoon.

"A tenday and six?" the elf answered, obviously as unsure of the actual time they had spent chasing Gerti as was Drizzt.

"And it seems as if we have walked across the seasons," said the drow.

"Summer never comes to the mountains, and up here, autumn and spring are what we in the lower lands would call winter, to be sure."

Drizzt looked back to the south as Innovindil responded, and that view reminded him of just how high up they had come. The landscape opened wide before him, sloping down and spreading so completely that it appeared to flatten out below him. In viewing that, it occurred to Drizzt that if the ground was bare and less broken, he could start a round stone rolling there and it would bounce all the way to Mithral Hall.

"They're getting far ahead of us," Drizzt remarked. "Perhaps we should be on our way."

"They're bound for Shining White, to be sure," Innovindil replied. "We will find it, do not doubt. I have seen the giant lair many times from Sunset's back." She motioned to the northwest, higher up in the mountains.

"Will we even be able to get through the passes?" Drizzt asked, looking back up at the steel gray sky, clouds heavy with the promise of even more snow.

"One way or another," she said. The drow took comfort in Innovindil's clear determination, in her scowl that seemed every bit as forceful and stoic as his own. "They treat Sunrise lovingly."

"Frost giants appreciate beauty."

As do I, Drizzt thought but did not say. Beauty, strength, and heart combined.

He considered all of that as he looked at Innovindil, but the thought itself sent his mind rushing back to an image of another female companion he had once known. There were many similarities, Drizzt knew, but he needn't look farther than Innovindil's pointy ears and sharply angled eyebrows to remember that there were great differences, as well.

Innovindil pulled herself up from beside the low-burning fire and began collecting her pack and supplies.

"Perhaps we can put some distance behind us before the snow begins," she said as she strapped on her sword and dagger. "With this wind, we'll not move through the storm."

Drizzt didn't reply other than a slight nod, which Innovindil was too busy to even notice. The drow just watched her going about her tasks, enjoying the flow of her body and the sweep of her long golden hair as gusts of wind blew through.

He thought of his days immediately following the fall of Shallows, when he had hidden in a cave, rolling the one-horned helm of his dead friend in his hands. The emptiness of that time assailed him again, reminding him of how far he'd come. Drizzt had given in to the anger and the pain, had accepted a sense of complete hopelessness for perhaps the first time in all his life.

Innovindil and Tarathiel had brought him from that dark place, with patience and calm words and simple friendship. They had tolerated his instinctive defenses, which he'd thrown up to rebuff their every advance. They had accepted his explanation of Ellifain's death without suspicion.

Drizzt Do'Urden knew that he could never replace Bruenor, Catti-brie, Regis, and Wulfgar; those four were as much a part of who he was as any friend could ever hope. But maybe he didn't have to *replace* them. Maybe he could satisfy his emotional needs around the holes, if not filling in the holes themselves.

That was the promise of Innovindil, he knew.

And he was glad.

"Move swifter," Kaer'lic instructed in her broken command of the Dwarvish tongue. She had gleaned a few words of the language in her years on the surface, and with its many hard consonant sounds, the language bore some similarities to the drow's own, and even more to the tongue of the svirfneblin, which Kaer'lic spoke fluently. To get her point across, even if her words were not correct, the drow priestess kicked poor Fender on the back, sending him stumbling ahead.

He nearly fell, but battered though he was, he was too stubborn for that. He straightened and looked back, narrowing his gray eyes under his bushy brows in a threatening scowl.

Kaer'lic jammed the handle of her mace into his face.

Fender hit the ground hard, coughing blood, and he spat out a tooth. He tried to scream at the priestess, but all that came through his expertly slashed throat was a wheezing and fluttering sound like a burst of wind through a row of hanging parchments.

"With all care," Tos'un said to his companion. "The more you injure him, the longer it will take for us to be away." As he finished, the male drow glanced back to the south, as if expecting a fiery chariot or a host of warriors to rush over him. "We should have left the wretch with Proffit. The trolls would have eaten him and that would have been the end of it."

"Or Lady Alustriel and her army would have rescued him as they overran Proffit, and wouldn't he be quick in telling them all about a pair of dark elves roaming the land?"

"Then we should have just killed him and been done with it."

Kaer'lic paused and spent a moment scrutinizing her companion. She allowed her expression to show her disappointment in him, for truly, after all those years, she expected more from the warrior of House Barrison Del'Armgo.

"Obould will get nothing more from him than we have already gleaned," Tos'un said, his tone uncertain and revealing that he knew he was trying an awkward dodge. "And we will need no barter with the orc king—he will be glad that we have returned to him, even though the news we bear will hardly be to his liking."

"The news of Proffit's downfall and the reclamation of Nesmé will outrage him."

"But he is smart enough to separate the message from the messenger."

"Agreed," said Kaer'lic. "But you presume that King Obould is still alive, and that his forces have not been scattered and overrun. Has it occurred to you that perhaps we are returning to a northland where Bruenor Battlehammer is king once more?"

That unsettling thought had occurred to Tos'un, obviously, and he glanced past Kaer'lic and kicked poor Fender as the dwarf tried to rise.

"When I see Donnia again, I will slap her for leading us down this horrid road."

"*If* we see Donnia and Ad'non again, we will all need to find a new road to travel, I fear," Kaer'lic replied, emphasizing that important first word. "Or perhaps Obould continues to press and to conquer. Perhaps this is all going better than any of us ever dared hope, despite the setback along the northern banks of the Trollmoors. If Obould has secured Mithral Hall, will even Lady Alustriel find the forces to drive him out?"

"Is that event more desirable?"

The question seemed ridiculous on the surface, of course, but before Kaer'lic snapped off a retort, she remembered her last encounter with the orc king. Confident, dangerously so, and imperious, he hadn't asked her and

Tos'un to go south with Proffit. He had ordered them.

"We shall see what we shall see," was all the priestess replied.

She turned her attention back to Fender and jerked him upright from his crouch, then sent him on his way with a rough shove.

To the northeast, they could see the shining top of Fourthpeak, seeming no more than a day's march.

There lay their answers.

With pieces of orc still hanging from the ridges of his plate mail armor, it seemed hard to take Thibbledorf Pwent very seriously. But in a confusing time of regret and despair, Bruenor Battlehammer could have found no better friend.

"If we hold the riverbank all the way down to the south, then them Felbarrans and other allies might be getting across out o' the durned giants' range," Pwent calmly explained to Bruenor.

The two stood on the riverbank watching the work across the way on the eastern side, where the Felbarrans were already laying the foundation for a bridge.

"But will we be able to stretch our line?" Bruenor asked.

"Bah! Won't take much," came the enthusiastic reply. "Ain't seen no stupid orcs south o' here at all, and they can't be coming in from the west cause o' the mountain. Only way for them dogs to get down here is the north."

The words prompted both dwarves to turn and look up that way, to the mountain spur, the line of rocks sloping down to the river's edge. Many dwarves were up there, constructing a wall from the steep mountainside to the tower Wulfgar and Bruenor had taken. Their goal was to tighten the potential area of approach as much as possible so that the orc force couldn't simply swarm over them. Once that wall was set and fortified, the tower would serve as an anchor and the wall would be extended all the way to the river.

For the time being, the ridgeline east of the tower was dotted by lookouts, and held by the Moonwood elves, their deadly bows ready.

"Never thought I'd be happy to see a bunch o' durned fairies," Pwent grumbled, and a much-needed grin creased Bruenor's face, a grin all the wider because of the truth of those words. Had not Nikwillig led the Moonwood elves south in force, Bruenor doubted that the dwarves would have won the day. At best, they would have been able to somehow get back inside Mithral Hall and secure the tunnels. At worst, all would have been lost.

The scope of the risk they had taken in coming out had never truly registered to King Bruenor until that moment when he had been battling at the riverbank at the southern base of the mountain arm, centering the three groupings of dwarven forces. With Wulfgar north and Pwent and the main force south, Bruenor had been struck by how tentative their position truly had been, and only then had the dwarf king come to realize how much they had gambled in coming out.

Everything.

"How're the ferry plans coming along?" he asked, needing to move on, to look forward. It had been a victory, after all.

"Them Felbarrans're planning to string the raft so it's not free floating," Pwent explained. "Too much rough water south o' here to chance one getting away. We should be getting it up in two or three days. Then we can get them humans out o' the hall, and start bringing the proper stones across to start building this side o' the bridge."

"And bring King Emerus across," came another voice, and the two turned to see the approach of Jackonray Broadbelt, one arm in a sling from a spear stab he'd suffered in the fighting.

"Emerus's coming?" Bruenor asked.

"He lost near to a thousand boys," Jackonray said grimly. "No dwarf king'd let that pass without consecrating the ground."

"Me own priests've already done it, and the river, too," Bruenor assured him. "And the blessings of yer own and of Emerus himself will only make the road to Moradin's Halls all the easier for them brave boys that went down."

"Ye been there, so they're saying," said Jackonray. "Moradin's Halls, I mean. A palace as grand as the tales, then?"

Bruenor swallowed hard.

"Aye, me king looked Moradin in the eye and said, 'Ye send me back to kill them stinkin' orcs!'" Pwent roared.

Jackonray nodded and grinned wide, and Bruenor let it go at that. The tales of his afterlife were flying wildly, he knew, with Cordio and the other priests shouting them and embellishing them loudest of all. But for Bruenor, there was nothing more.

Just the tales. Just the suppositions and the grand descriptions.

Had he been at Moradin's side?

The dwarf king honestly did not know. He remembered the fight at Shallows. He remembered hearing Catti-brie's voice, as if from far, far away. He remembered a feeling of warmth and comfort, but all of it was so vague to him. The first clear image he could conjure after the disaster at Shallows had been the face of Regis, as if the halfling and his magical ruby pendant had reached right into his soul to stir him from his deep slumber.

"Who'd be missing that kind o' fun?" Pwent was asking when Bruenor tuned back into the conversation.

He realized that Jackonray was hardly listening, and was instead just standing and staring at Bruenor.

"We'll be honored to see yer great King Emerus," Bruenor assured him, and he saw the Felbarran relax. "He can say his farewells to his boys and give his honor to Nikwillig o' Felbarr, right after I'm giving him the honor of Mithral Hall. 'Twas Nikwillig who won the day, not to doubt."

"It's a meeting long overdue, yerself and King Emerus," Jackonray agreed. "And we'll get King Harbromm from Adbar down here soon enough. Let's see them stupid orcs stand against the three kingdoms!"

"*Kill 'em all!*" Pwent roared, startling his two companions and drawing the attention of everyone nearby, and being dwarves, they of course took up the cheer.

They were all cheering again, except for Cottie Cooperson, of course, who never even smiled anymore, let alone cheered. Word had come down the tunnels that the eastern gate was open and the way would soon be clear to ferry the refugees across the Surbrin and to the tamer lands southeast. Before winter, they would all be in Silverymoon. And from there, in the spring, they could go out, free of the dark stones of Mithral Hall.

Those cheers followed Delly Curtie as she carried Colson along the corridor from the gathering hall. Inside, she had been all smiles, offering support and shoulder pats, assuring Cottie that she'd rebuild her life and maybe even have more children. She had gotten only a broken and somewhat sour look in response, for the brief moment that Cottie had lifted her teary-eyed gaze from the floor.

Out there, Delly found it hard to break any kind of a smile. In there, she supported the cheers, but outside they cut at her heart. They would all be going across the Surbrin soon, leaving her as one of only four humans in Mithral Hall.

She managed to keep her expression stoic when she entered her private chambers to find Wulfgar inside, pulling a blood-stained tunic over his head.

"Is it yer own?" Delly asked, rushing to his side.

She held Colson tight against her hip with one arm, while her other hand played over the barbarian's muscular frame, examining him for any serious wounds.

"The blood of orcs," Wulfgar said, and he reached across and gently lifted Colson from the woman's grasp. His face lit up as he brought the toddler up high to stare into her eyes, and Colson responded with a giggle and a wriggle, and a face beaming with happiness.

Despite her dour mood, Delly couldn't hold back her warm smile.

"It's secured to the river, they're saying," she said.

"Aye, from the mountain to the river and all along to the south. Pwent and his gang are finishing up any pockets of orcs even now. There won't likely be any living by morning."

"And they'll be floating the ferry then?"

Wulfgar glanced away from Colson just long enough to show his curiosity at the woman's tone, and Delly knew that her voice had been a bit too eager.

"They will begin stringing the guide ropes tomorrow, yes, but I know not how long the process will take. Are the folk of the razed lands anxious to be on their way?"

"Wouldn't ye be, yerself, if Bruenor wasn't yer own father?"

Again Wulfgar turned to show her his perplexed expression. He started to nod, but just shrugged instead.

"You are no child of Bruenor," he remarked.

"But I am the wife of Wulfgar."

Wulfgar brought Colson down to his hip, and when the toddler whined and wriggled, he set her down to the floor and let her go. He came up straight before Delly, facing her directly, and placed his huge hands on her slender shoulders.

"You wish to cross the river," he stated.

"My place is with Wulfgar."

"But I cannot leave," Wulfgar said. "We have only begun to break free of Obould's grasp, and now that we have a way beyond Mithral Hall's doors, I must learn the fate of my friend."

Delly didn't interrupt him, for she knew all of it, of course, and Wulfgar was merely reaffirming the truth of the situation.

"When the Surbrin east of Mithral Hall is more secure, have King Bruenor find you a place working out there, in the sun. I agree that we are not built as dwarves."

"The walls're closing in tight on me."

"I know," Wulfgar assured her, and he pulled her close. "I know. When this is done—by summer, we hope—you and I will journey to all the cities you long to see. You will come to love Mithral Hall all the more if it is your home and not your prison." As he finished, he pulled her closer, wrapping his strong arms around her. He kissed her on top of her head and whispered promises that things would get better.

Delly appreciated the words and the gestures, though in her mind, they hardly diminished the echoes of the cheers of the people who would soon be leaving the smoky dark tunnels of King Bruenor's domain.

She couldn't tell that to Wulfgar, though, she knew. He was trying to understand and she appreciated that. But in the end, he couldn't. His life was in Mithral Hall. His beloved friends were there. His cause was there.

Not in Silverymoon, where Delly wanted to be.

20

A FRIENDLY DOSE OF REALITY

Two thousand mugs raised in toast, the dwarven holy water foaming over the sides. Two thousand Battlehammer dwarves, every dwarf that could be spared from the work out in the east or from the tunnels, cheered, "To the Mirabarran Battlehammers!" Then as one, they drained their mugs, and invariably splashed foam on beards yellow and red and white and orange and black and brown and silver and even green.

"Oo oi!" came the shout from Pikel Bouldershoulder as soon as the toast was finished.

That a non-Battlehammer and non-Mirabarran like Pikel had so perfectly accentuated the celebration of Bruenor's clan for the immigrants from Mirabar was a point not lost on Catti-brie. Sitting beside her father's dais, propped with fluffy pillows—of which there were very few in all the halls—the woman considered the unlikely collection represented in the gathering before her.

Most of the group were Bruenor's kinfolk, of course, some dwarves who had lived in Mithral Hall before the coming of Shimmergloom the shadow dragon, and others who had been raised as Battlehammers under the shadow of Kelvin's Cairn in Icewind Dale. Others were Felbarran, coming in from the east and seeming as much at home as the Battlehammers themselves. Torgar and his boys were all there, even the many who had been wounded in the fighting on the ridge north of Keeper's Dale or more recently in the fighting in the south. Ivan and Pikel Bouldershoulder were there, and though they weren't Battlehammers, every dwarf in the complex wanted them to become of the clan. Nanfoodle the gnome was there, along with Regis, Wulfgar, and Catti-brie.

So they were not all joined by blood, Catti-brie understood, but they were certainly all joined by cause and by common resolve. She glanced over at her father, sitting on his throne and draining another mug of mead, blessed as holy water by the priests. His toasts and his appreciation were genuine, she knew. He couldn't be happier or more full of gratitude concerning the arrival of Torgar, Shingles, and the boys from Mirabar. They had saved the day over and over again, from the northern stretches of the mountainous terrain to, apparently, the work in the south. They had fought brilliantly with Banak Brawnanvil north of Keeper's Dale, had pushed the entrenched orcs from the tunnels so that Nanfoodle could work his magic on the ridge. They had suffered terrible losses, but had done so with typical dwarven stoicism. The losses would be worth the victory, and nothing short of victory was acceptable.

It was all a reflection of her father, Catti-brie realized. Everything from Torgar's decision to leave Mirabar to Citadel Felbarr's bold, if ill-advised, attempt to cross the river was due in part to the character of Bruenor Battlehammer.

Catti-brie could only smile as she looked upon her dear father.

Eventually, her gaze went across the dais to Banak, lying more than sitting, propped in a carriage the woman feared would soon become his prison. He had given his body for the cause—even the optimistic Cordio doubted that the dwarf would ever walk again—and yet there he was, cheering and drinking and with a bright smile gleaming out from between the whiskers of his hairy old face.

It was a good day to be a Battlehammer, Catti-brie decided. Despite the tragedy in the eastern breakout and their precarious position between Mithral Hall and the Surbrin, despite the horde of orcs pressing in on them from every side and the terrible losses they all had suffered, friends and kin forever lost, it was a good day to be a Battlehammer.

She believed that with all her heart, and yet was not surprised at the feel of a teardrop running down her soft cheek.

For Catti-brie had come to doubt.

She had lost Drizzt, she believed, and only in that realization did the woman finally admit it all to herself. That she had loved him above all others. That he alone had made her whole and made her happy. So many problems had come between them, issues of longevity and children, and of the perceptions of others—there it was, all before her and hopelessly lost. All those imagined ills seemed so foolish, seemed the petty workings of confusion and self-destruction. When Catti-brie had been down on the ground and surrounded by goblins, when she had thought her life at its end, she had found an emptiness beyond anything she had ever imagined possible. The realization of her mortality had sent her thoughts careening along the notions of things that should have been. Lost in that jumble, she had pushed Drizzt away. Lost in that jumble, Catti-brie had forgotten that the future isn't a straight road purposely designed by the traveler. The future is made of the actions of the present, each and every one, the choices of the moment inadvertently strung together to produce the desired trail. To live each and every day in the best possible manner would afford her a life without regret, and a life without regret was the key to an acceptance of inevitable death.

And now Drizzt was lost to her.

In all her life, would Catti-brie ever heal that wound?

"Are you all right?"

Wulfgar's voice was soft and full of concern, and she looked up to see his blue eyes staring back at her.

"It's been a difficult time," she admitted.

"So many dead."

"Or missing."

The look on Wulfgar's face told her that he understood the reference. "We are able to go out again," he said, "and so we must hope that Drizzt will be able to come in."

She didn't blink.

"And if not, then we will go find him. You and I, Bruenor and Regis," the big man declared. "Perhaps we will even convince Ivan and Pikel to join in the hunt—the strange one talks to birds, you know. And birds can see all the land."

She still didn't blink.

"We will find him," Wulfgar promised.

Another cheer rose up in the hall, and Bruenor called upon Torgar to come forth and give a proper speech about it all. "Tell us what bringed ye here," the dwarf king prompted. "Tell us all yer journeys."

Wulfgar's grin disappeared as soon as he looked back at Catti-brie, for her expression was no less distant and detached, and no less full of pain.

"Do you need to leave?" he asked.

"I'm weary to the bone," she answered.

With great effort, the woman pulled herself out of her chair and leaned heavily on the crutch Cordio had made for her. She began to take a shuffling step forward, but Wulfgar caught hold of her. With a simple and effortless movement, the large man swept her into his arms.

"Where're ye going, then?" Bruenor asked from the dais. Before him, Torgar was giving his account to a thoroughly engaged audience.

"I'm needing a bit of rest, is all," said Catti-brie.

Bruenor held a concerned look for a few moments, then nodded and turned back to Torgar.

Catti-brie rested her crutch across her body and put her head on Wulfgar's strong shoulder. She closed her eyes and let him carry her from the celebration.

Delly Curtie approached the audience chamber with good intent, determined to try to fit in, in the place that Wulfgar would always call home. She told herself with every step that she had followed Wulfgar out of Luskan of her own accord, with her eyes wide open. She reminded herself that her responsibilities went far beyond the issues surrounding her relationship with a man who seemed more at home beside the dwarves than with his own race. She reminded herself of Colson, and the girl's well-being.

She would have to strike a middle ground, she decided. She would take Wulfgar out of Mithral Hall as often as possible, and would stay with the folk of the neighboring and predominantly human communities for extended periods.

She caught a quick glimpse of someone coming the other way through the maze of anterooms, and from the size alone, she knew it had to be Wulfgar. Her step lightened. She would make the seemingly untenable situation work.

As she came through a half-door and moved around one of the huge vats the clerics used for their brewing, Delly caught sight of him again, more clearly.

He didn't see her, she knew, because he was looking at the woman he was carrying.

Delly's eyes widened and she threw herself behind the brew barrel, putting her back to it and closing her eyes tightly against the sudden sting. She heard Wulfgar and Catti-brie pass by on the other side, and watched them exit the small room and continue on their way.

The woman exhaled and felt as if she was simply melting into the floor.

Lady Alustriel did not need to wait for the ferries to be running in order to cross the Surbrin. The tall and beautiful woman, as accomplished in the magic arts and in the arena of politics as anyone in all the world, brought her fiery conjured chariot down on a flat stretch of ground just outside the opened eastern door of Mithral Hall, sending dwarves scrambling for cover and bringing a chorus of cheers and salutes from the Moonwood elves who held firm in their position on the mountain spur.

Alustriel stepped from the chariot and dismissed it into a puff of smoke with a wave of her hand. She straightened her dark robe and brushed her long silver hair into place, at the same time fixing a properly somber expression onto her delicate but determined features. It would be no easy visit, she knew, but it was one she owed to her friend Bruenor.

With purpose in every stride, Alustriel moved to the door. The dwarf guards fell aside, gladly admitting her, while one ran ahead to announce her to Bruenor.

She found the dwarf king with two other dwarves and an elf, drawing up plans for King Emerus Warcrown's arrival. The four stood up at her entrance, even Bruenor dipping into a low and polite bow.

"Good King Bruenor," Alustriel greeted. "It is uplifting to see you well. We had heard rumors of your demise, and truly a pall had befallen the lands of goodly folk."

"Bah, got to tease 'em a bit, ye know," Bruenor replied with a wink. "Makes my arrival all the more stunning and inspiring."

"I doubt that Bruenor Battlehammer needs aid in that manner."

"Always the kind one, ain't ye?"

Alustriel offered a quiet nod.

"I give ye Jackonray and Tred of Felbarr," Bruenor explained, pointing out the dwarves, who both nearly fell over themselves trying to bow before the great Lady of Silverymoon. "And this one's Hralien of the Moonwood. Never thought me and me boys'd be so grateful to see a bunch o' elves!"

"We stand together," Hralien answered. "Or surely we shall all of us fall before the darkness that is Obould."

"Aye, and glad I am that ye decided to come, good lady," Bruenor told Alustriel. "Torgar o' Mirabar just returned from yer victory over them stinking trolls, and he's telling a tale that yerself and Sundabar've decided to stay back."

"His words are true, I fear," Alustriel admitted.

"Aye, ye're thinking to wait out the winter, and I'm not for arguing that," Bruenor said. "But we'd be smart to set our plans for the spring soon as we can. We'll have a gnome's puzzling of it to get five armies working right." He paused when he noticed that Alustriel was shaking her head with his every word.

"What're ye thinking?" Bruenor asked her.

"I have come to confirm what Torgar has already told to you, my friend," said Alustriel. "We will hold Obould where he is, but it is not the decision of Silverymoon, Everlund, and Sundabar to wage war against him at this time."

Bruenor was certain that his chin had hit the floor, so wide did his mouth fall open.

"I have over flown the region you intend as a battlefield, and I tell you that this orc king is a wise one. He is fortifying even now, digging in his warriors on every mountaintop and preparing every inch of ground for a stubborn defense."

"All the more reason we got to get rid of him here and now," Bruenor argued, but again Alustriel shook her head.

"The cost will be too great, I fear," she said.

"But ye ran to Nesmé's aid, didn't ye?" Bruenor couldn't completely eliminate the sarcastic tone from his voice.

"We put the trolls back in the moor, yes. But they were not nearly as formidable as the force that has arrayed against Mithral Hall from the north. Tens of thousands of orcs have flocked to Obould's call."

"Tens of thousands who'll turn their weapons against yerself and yer precious Silverymoon!"

"Perhaps," said Alustriel. "And in that event, they will face a stubborn and determined defense. Should Obould press on, he will fight in ground of our choosing and not his own. We will fight him from behind our walls, not assail him behind his."

"And ye're to leave me and me kin out here alone?"

"Not so," Alustriel insisted. "You have opened the way to the river—I wish that Silverymoon could have arrived in force to aid in that."

"A few hunnerd less Felbarrans'd be lying at the bottom of the river if ye had," Tred dared to say, and his tone made it clear to all that he was no more happy with Alustriel's surprising stance than was Bruenor.

"These are trying times," Alustriel offered. "I do not pretend to make them seem better than they are. I come to you now to deliver a suggestion and a promise from Silverymoon and from Sundabar. We will help you build the bridge across the Surbrin, and we will help you to defend it and to hold open the eastern door of Mithral Hall. I see that you are constructing fortifications on the mountain spur north of the door—I will send batteries of archers and catapults to aid in that defense. I will rotate wizards up there to stand shoulder to shoulder with your warriors, offering fireballs against any who dare come against you."

Bruenor's scowl did diminish a bit at that, but just a bit.

"You know me well, Bruenor Battlehammer," the Lady of Silverymoon said. "When the drow marched upon Mithral Hall, my city came to your side. How many of the Silver Guard fell in Keeper's Dale in that battle?"

Bruenor twitched, his expression softening.

"I wish as you wish, that Obould and his scourge of orcs could be wiped from the lands for all time. But I have seen them. You cannot imagine the enemy allied against you. If all the dwarves of Felbarr and Adbar, and all the warriors of Silverymoon, Everlund, and Sundabar were to come to your side, we would still have to kill our enemies five for every one of our own to begin to claim a victory. And even then Obould's forces swell daily, with more orcs pouring out of every hole in the Spine of the World."

"And even with that, ye're not thinking that he's meaning to stop where he is?" Bruenor asked. "If his forces are swellin', the longer we . . . the longer *you* wait, the bigger they swell."

"We have not abandoned you, my friend, nor would we ever," Alustriel said, and she took a step toward Bruenor and gently reached up to place her hand on his shoulder. "Every wound to Mithral Hall cuts deeply into the hearts of the goodly folk of all the region. You will be the spur, the one shining light in a region fallen to darkness. We will not let that light dim. On our lives, King Bruenor, my friend, we will fight beside you."

It was not what he wanted to hear from Lady Alustriel, but it seemed as if it was all he was going to get—and truly, it was a lot more than he had expected, given Torgar's sour account of Alustriel's intentions.

"Let us weather the winter," Alustriel finished. "And let us see what promise the spring brings."

21

GERTI'S DOORBELL

Snow whipped all around them, forcing both Drizzt and Innovindil to bend low and lean into the wind to stop from being blown right over. The drow led the way, moving as swiftly as he could manage, for the trail of the giants remained clear to see, but would not last for long, he knew. Drizzt continually worked his fingers in his sleeve, clenching and unclenching his fist in a futile attempt to hold off the freezing. Innovindil had assured him that Shining White, the home of Gerti, was not far away. The drow hoped that was true, for he wasn't sure how long he and Innovindil could continue in such a blizzard.

By mid-morning the trail was all but overblown and Drizzt kept moving as much on instinct as through his tracking abilities. He soldiered along as straight as he could manage, and veered from the course only when he came upon boulder tumbles or ravines that would have likely forced the giants' caravan aside.

Around one such boulder tumble, the drow saw that he was guessing right, for there in the middle of a shallow dell was a pile of manure, half-covered and still steaming in the new-fallen snow. Drizzt made for it and bent low over it. He brought a gloved hand down and separated the pieces, inspecting each.

"No blood in the stool," he told Innovindil when she crouched near him.

"Sunrise is eating well, despite the onset of deep winter," the elf agreed.

"Gerti is treating him as she would a valued pet," said the drow. "It bodes well."

"Except that we can be certain now that she will not easily give up the pegasus."

"Never was there any doubt of that," said Drizzt. "We came here to fight for our friend, and so we shall." He looked up at Innovindil's fair face as he spoke the pledge, and saw that she appreciated his words. "Come along," he bade her, and started on his way.

Innovindil gave a tug on Sunset's reins to prompt the pegasus along, and followed with a renewed spring in her step.

It didn't last long, though. The storm intensified, snow blowing across so fiercely that Innovindil and Drizzt could hardly see each other if they moved more than a few feet apart.

They got a bit of a reprieve when they passed around an eastern spur, for the wind was from the northwest and suddenly both of those directions were blocked by mountain walls. Drizzt put his back against the bare stone and exhaled.

"If we can find a suitable overhang, perhaps we should put up for the day until the storm blows over," he offered, and he was glad that he was able to lower his voice without the wind to intercept and dissipate it.

He took another deep breath and pulled the frozen cowl back from his face. He wiped the snow from his brow, chuckling helplessly when he realized that his eyebrows were iced over, and he looked at his companion to see that she was paying him no heed.

"Innovindil?" he asked.

"No need," the elf answered. "To camp, I mean."

She met Drizzt's gaze then motioned for him to look across the way.

The rock wall ran north for some distance, then bent back to the east. Along that facing, a few hundred yards from them, Drizzt saw a gaping darkness, a cave face in the stone.

"Shining White?"

"Yes," Innovindil answered. "An unremarkable entrance to a place rumored to be anything but."

The two stood there a while, catching their breath.

"A plan?" Innovindil finally asked.

"Sunrise is in there," Drizzt answered. "So we go in."

"Just walk in?"

"Swords drawn, of course." He turned to his companion and offered a grin.

He made it sound so simple, which of course it was. They had come for Sunrise, and Sunrise was inside Shining White, and so they collected themselves and moved along, staying close to the mountain wall where the snow had not piled.

A dozen feet or so before the closest edge of the cave entrance, Drizzt motioned for Innovindil to stay back and crept ahead. He came up straight at the edge of the cave, then slowly bent and turned and peeked in.

He slipped around the edge, inching into a tunnel that widened almost immediately to nearly twenty feet across. The drow froze, hearing deep and steady breathing from across the way. He quick-stepped across the tunnel to the other wall, then crept along to an alcove.

Inside, a seated giant leaned back against the wall, its hands tucked behind its head, lips flapping with every snore. A massive maul lay across its outstretched legs, the business end worked brilliantly into the design of an eagle's head, with the sharp, hooked beak comprising the back side of the head.

Drizzt crept in. He could tell that the behemoth was sleeping soundly, and recognized that he could move right up and open wide its throat before it ever knew he was there. To his surprise, though, he found himself sliding his scimitars away. Gently, but with great effort, he lifted the maul from the giant's lap, and the beast snorted and grumbled, bringing one hand down and turning sideways.

Drizzt moved out of the alcove and back to the cave entrance, where Innovindil and Sunset stood waiting.

"Fine weapon," he whispered, though it seemed as if he could hardly hold the maul.

"You killed its wielder?" asked the elf.

"Fast asleep, and no threat to us."

Innovindil's curious expression reminded Drizzt of his strange choice. Why hadn't he simply killed the giant; would that not be one less enemy to battle?

His answer was just a shrug, though, and he put a finger to pursed lips and bade the elf to quietly follow.

The three moved past the alcove on the opposite side of the corridor.

Many feet farther along, the tunnel turned sharply to the right, and there the roof climbed much higher as well. A short way from the trio beamed a natural skylight, some fifty feet or more from the floor, the gray light of the stormy day streaming in. The floor became slick and some areas lay covered in snow. Farther down, a pair of large doors loomed before them.

"Let us hope that they are not locked, and that they are well greased," Innovindil quietly remarked.

The three inched along, Sunset clip-clopping with every stride, the sharp echoes making the other two more than a little nervous. Both the drow and the elf entertained thoughts of leaving the pegasus outside, and would have had it not been for the brutal storm.

Drizzt put his ear to the door and listened carefully for a long while before daring the handle—or almost daring the handle. For as he reached up, the ring being more than two feet above his head, he noted that its inner edge was not smooth, with one particularly sharp lip to it. He retracted his hand quickly.

"Trapped?" Innovindil asked.

Drizzt motioned that he did not know. He pulled off his cloak, then loosened his enchanted, armored shirt so that he could pull one sleeve down over his hand. He reached up again and slowly grasped the handle. He could feel the sharp edge through the shirt, and he gingerly altered the angle of his grasp so that the trap, if that's what it was, would not press on his palm.

"Ready to fight?" he mouthed to his companion, and he drew out Icingdeath in his left hand. When Innovindil nodded, Drizzt took a deep breath and pulled the door ajar, immediately snapping his hand down across his body to Twinkle, sheathed on his left hip.

But the sight that greeted the two had their hands relaxing almost immediately. A warm glow washed out of the open door. Beyond the portal, that light reflected brilliantly off of a myriad of walls and partitions, all made of shining ice—not opaque and snowy, but clear and highly reflective. Images of a drow, an elf, and a pegasus came back at the companions from every conceivable angle.

Drizzt stepped in and found himself lost in a sea of reflected Drizzts. The partitions were barely wide enough to admit a giant and sorted in a mazelike manner that set off alarm bells in the wary drow's mind as soon as he recovered from the initial shock of it all. He motioned to Innovindil to quickly follow and rushed ahead.

"What is it?" the elf finally asked when she caught up to Drizzt as he paused at a four-way intersection of shiny ice walls.

"This is a defense," Drizzt replied.

He looked around, soaking it in, confirming his fears. He noted the bare stone floor, in such a sharp contrast to the walls, which seemed to have no stone in them. He looked up to the many holes in the high ceiling, set strategically from east to west along the southern reaches of the chamber, designed, he realized, to catch the sunlight from dawn to twilight. Then he sorted through his images, following the line across the breadth of the huge chamber. A single sentry at any point along the wall would easily know of the intruders.

Magic had created that hall of mirrors, Drizzt knew, and for a specific purpose.

"Move quickly," the drow said even as he started off.

He dipped and darted his way through the maze, trying to find side aisles that would reflect him in a confusing manner to any sentries. He had to hope that any guards who might be posted to watch over the hall were, like the one in the previous tunnel, less than alert.

No alarm horns had blown and no roars had come at him from afar. That was a good sign at least, he had to believe.

Around one sharp bend, the drow pulled up short, and Innovindil, leading Sunset right behind him, nearly knocked him forward onto his face.

Still Drizzt managed to hold back, absorbing the energy of the bump and skittering to the side instead of forward, for he did not want to take another step, did not want to step out onto the open, twenty-foot border of the eastern end of the cavern. That border was a river, and though it was iced over, Drizzt could clearly see the water rushing below the frozen surface.

Across the way and down to his left, the drow spotted another tunnel. He motioned for Innovindil to carefully follow, then inched down the bank, stopping directly across from the exit tunnel. Up above him, he saw a large rope dangling—high enough for a giant to reach, perhaps, so that it might swing across.

He heard Sunset clip-clopping back away from him and turned to see Innovindil astride the pegasus, angling to line him up for a straight run to the exit tunnel. With a grin, Drizzt sprinted back to her and clambered up behind her, and the elf wasted no time in putting Sunset into a quick run and a short leap, wings going out and beating hard. With grace more akin to a deer than a horse, Sunset alighted across the frozen river in the tunnel and Innovindil quickly pulled him up to a stop.

Drizzt was down in a flash, Innovindil following.

"Do you think they know we're here?" the moon elf asked.

"Does it matter?"

Now the corridors became more conventional, wide, high, and winding, maze-like, with many turns and side passages. The enormity of Shining White surprised Drizzt, and the enormity of their task became more than a little daunting.

"Guenhwyvar will smell Sunrise out," he said as he pulled out the figurine.

"More likely to smell your blood, I suspect," came an answer from a voice that was not Innovindil's, that was far too deep and resonant to belong to an elf.

Drizzt turned slowly, as did his companion, and Sunset pawed the stone.

A pair of frost giants stood calmly some twenty feet or so behind them, one with hands on her hips, the other holding a massive hammer in his right hand patting it onto his left.

"You bring a second pegasus for Dame Gerti," the female remarked. "She will be pleased—perhaps enough so to allow you a quick death."

Drizzt nodded and said, "Aye, we have come to please Gerti, of course. That is our greatest desire."

He slapped Sunset on the rump as he finished, and Innovindil went up astride the pegasus even as it leaped away.

Drizzt turned to follow, took a few steps, then, hearing the giants charging in behind, he cut a quick turn and charged at them, howling with fury.

"Drizzt!" Innovindil shouted, and he knew by her tone that she had concluded that he meant to engage the behemoths.

Nothing could have been farther from his thoughts.

He rushed at the one holding the hammer, and as it started to swing at him he cut to the right, toward the second giant.

The first was too clever to continue its attack—an attack that likely would have struck its companion. But as the female behemoth reached for Drizzt he turned anyway again, back toward the first, his feet, their speed enhanced by magical anklets, moving in a blur. He dived into a roll, turning sidelong as he went so that he came up short and cut back to his right, which sent him rushing right between the giants. Both of them lurched in to grab at him, and the female might have had him, except that the pair knocked heads halfway down.

Both grunted and straightened, and Drizzt ran free.

Barely ten strides down the next corridor, though, the drow heard the shouts of more giants, and he had to turn into yet another perpendicular corridor so that he didn't run headlong into a behemoth.

"No dead ends," the drow whispered—a prayer if he ever heard one— with every blind turn.

He soon came into a wider corridor lined on both sides with statues of various shapes and size. Most were of ice, though a few of stone. Some were giant-sized, but most reflected the stature of a human or an elf. The detailing and craftsmanship was as finely worked as dwarven stone, and the elegance of the artwork was not lost on the drow—the statues would not have seemed out of place in Menzoberranzan or in an elven village. He had little time to pause and admire the pieces, though, for he heard the giants behind him and in front, and horns blowing from deeper in the seemingly endless complex.

He pulled his cloak from his shoulders and cut to the side, toward a cluster of several elf-sized statues.

Innovindil could only hope that the floor stayed stone and was not glazed over with ice, for she could ill afford to allow Sunset to slow the run with giants scrambling all around her. She came upon corridor after corridor, turning sometimes and running straight at others, meaning to turn at some others and yet finding a group of enemies coming at her from that direction. . . . A blind run was the best the elf could manage. Or a blind flight, for every now and then she put the pegasus up into the air to gain speed. She had to take care, though, for airborne, Sunset could not navigate the sharp, right-angled turns. Innovindil watched ahead and behind, and looked up repeatedly. She kept hoping that the ceiling would open up before her so that she could lift Sunset into a short flight, perhaps one that would get them both out through a natural chimney or a worked skylight.

At one corner, the elf and her pegasus nearly slammed into the stone wall, for the angle of the turn proved to be more than ninety degrees.

Sunset skidded to a rough stop, brushing the stone as Innovindil brought the pegasus about.

Innovindil sucked in her breath as they realigned and she prompted the pegasus to run again, for that moment of stillness left her vulnerable, she knew.

And so she was only a little surprised when she saw a gigantic spear of ice—a long, shaped icicle—soaring at her from down the previous corridor. She ducked instinctively, and if she had not, she would have been skewered. Even with the near miss, the elf was almost dislodged, for the spear shattered on the stone above her and a barrage of ice chips showered over her.

Stubbornly holding her seat, Innovindil kicked her heels into Sunset's flank and bade him to run on. She heard a shout behind her and to the side, from whence the spear had come, and she understood enough of the frost giant language, which was somewhat akin to Elvish, to understand that a giantess was berating the spear thrower.

"Do you want to hurt Gerti's new pet?"

"The pegasus or the elf?" the giant answered, his booming voice echoing off the stone behind Innovindil.

"Both, then!" the giantess laughed.

For some reason, their tone made Innovindil think that catching the spear in her chest would have been preferable.

Two giants charged down the corridor, only occasionally glancing to either side until one suddenly lurched to the left and gave a victorious shout.

The other yelled, "Clever!" when it, too, noticed the cloak on the statue—a cloak not carved of stone, but flowing as only fabric could.

With a single stride to the side, the first giant brought a heavy club to bear, crushing down on the cloak. The ice statue beneath it exploded into a shower of shards and splinters.

"Oh, you broke Mardalade's work!" the other shouted.

"T-the drow?" the first stammered and dropped its club.

"Finds you quite amusing," came an answer from behind, and both giants spun around.

Drizzt, skipping down the other way, paused long enough to offer a salute, then a smile as he pointed back behind the behemoths.

Neither turned—until they heard the low growl of a giant panther.

The two giants spun and ducked as six hundred pounds of black-furred muscle leaped over them, cutting close enough so that both threw up their hands and ducked even lower, one falling to the stone.

Drizzt sprinted away. He used the moment of reprieve to try to sort out the maze of crisscrossing corridors. He listened carefully to the sounds all around him, too, trying to make some sense of them. Shouts from unrelated areas told him that Innovindil was still running, and gave him a fairly good idea of her general direction.

He sprinted away, back to the west, then north, then west again. He heard the clip-clop of the running pegasus as he approached the next four-way intersection, and ran harder, thinking to catch hold of his friend as she passed through, and leap up behind her.

But he slowed, quickly abandoning that notion. Better that the giants had two targets, he realized.

Innovindil and Sunset crossed in front of him, head down and flying fast, with the pegasus a few feet off the ground. Though he could not help but pause and admire the elf's handling of the winged horse, Drizzt clearly heard the approach of giants not far behind. He picked up his pace again, and as a pair of giants ran through the intersection in fast pursuit of the elf, Drizzt rushed out right behind them, and managed to slash one in the back of the leg as he passed, drawing a howl of pain.

That one stopped and the other slowed, both turning to regard the running dark elf.

The wounded one then fell flat to his face, as a great panther sprang against the back of his neck, then leaped away. Three more giants poured into the intersection, and all five shouted wildly.

"Left!"

"Right!"

"Straight ahead!"

"The elf, you fools!"

"The drow!"

And all of that, of course, only gave Drizzt and Innovindil a bit more breathing room.

Around and around they went, and Drizzt crossed corridors he recognized. At another intersection, he heard the clip-clop of Sunset's hooves again, and he got there first. Again he thought of jumping up astride the pegasus, and again he abandoned the notion, for still more giants bobbed along behind his fleeing companion.

Drizzt stood at the corner, leaning out enough so that Innovindil noticed him. He pointed across the way, to the tunnel on the approaching Innovindil's left. She responded by bringing Sunset over to the right, near Drizzt, in a wider banking turn.

"Right, left, second right, and straight to the river!" the drow shouted as she thundered past.

Drizzt ducked back behind the corner. He heard giants approaching from behind him, as well as the ones coming in pursuit of Innovindil; he glanced both ways repeatedly and nervously, hoping that Innovindil's pursuit would arrive first.

His relief was sincere and deep when he saw that they would. Still focusing on the pegasus-riding elf, the giants came on at full speed, and were caught by complete surprise when Drizzt leaped around the corner beside them and shouted at them.

They stopped and fell all over themselves trying to get at him, and he ran off back the way they had come, and the confusion of all the giants increased many times over when the group previously chasing Drizzt also scrambled into the intersection in a wild tangle.

Drizzt's smile widened; he couldn't deny that he was enjoying himself!

But then he was in a storm of pelting sleet, a small black cloud roiling at the ceiling high overhead and stinging him with hailstones as big around as his feet. The stone below him grew almost instantly slick and he went into a controlled slide, holding his precarious balance.

Of course, as soon as he hit a drier spot, his foot kicked out behind him and he had to fall into a roll. He looked back as he did, and noted one of the giantesses in the tumult of the intersection staring down his way and waggling her huge fingers once more.

"Oh, lovely," the drow said. He put his feet under him and ran off as fast as he could manage on the slippery floor.

He sensed the lightning bolt an instant before it flashed, and he dived down and to the side. His fall sped along as the bolt clipped him. He had to ignore the burning and numbness in his arm, though, for the giants—both groups—came on in fast pursuit.

Drizzt ran for his life, with all speed, hoping his guess of the layout was correct. He had sent Innovindil on a roundabout course that he hoped would get him to a specific intersection at the same time as the swifter pegasus. With the ice storm and the lightning bolt, that wouldn't happen even if his quick calculations had been correct.

He saw her cross the intersection before him, in a straight run for the frozen river and the escape tunnels. She looked back as he came out right behind her, following her course.

"Run on!" he cried, for he knew that she had no time to pause and wait. Giants were on his heels, including that nasty spellcaster—and wouldn't she love to have all the intruders in a line before her in a long, straight tunnel.

"Leap it! Fly across!" Drizzt implored Innovindil as she neared the frozen river, and she did, bringing Sunset into a quick flight that carried her to solid ground on the other side. No fool, she, the elf pulled up on the reins, then turned the pegasus aside and moved down the bank, just a few feet out of the tunnel's line of sight.

Drizzt came up on the river right behind her, the giants closing fast. Not even slowing in the least, the drow dived headlong, thinking to slide across and begin his run once more. He saw Innovindil as he hit the ice on his belly, the elf calling to him.

He heard a loud grunt from the other side, to his right and up above, and rolled onto his side just in time to see a huge rock soaring down at him, thrown by a giant who was perched upon a ledge.

"Drizzt!" Innovindil yelled.

The drow tucked and turned, and caught a handhold, for he could see that the rock's aim had been true. Slowing his progress, he avoided being crushed, but the rock hit the ice right in front of him and crashed through. The drow, helpless in his slide, went into the icy waters.

"Drizzt!" Innovindil yelled again.

Hanging by a finger, the cold current pulling at him relentlessly, Drizzt managed to offer her a single shrug.

Then he was gone.

INNER VOICES

Ye must do this, Delly Curtie told herself over and over again, every step of the way through the dwarven complex. As sure as she was that what she was doing was for the best—for everyone involved—Delly needed constant reminders and assurances, even from herself.

Ye cannot stay here, not a minute longer.

Bah, but she's not yer child anyway, ye silly woman!

It's for his own good more'n yer own, and she's a better woman than ye'd ever be!

Over and over, the woman played out all the rationalizations, a litany that kept her putting one foot in front of the other as she neared the closed door to Catti-brie's private room. Colson stirred and gave a little cry, and Delly hugged the girl tighter against her and offered a comforting coo.

She came up to the door and pressed her ear, then hearing nothing, pushed it open just a bit, paused, and listened again. She heard Catti-brie's rhythmic breathing. The woman had returned exhausted a short while before from the audience chamber, announcing that she needed some sleep.

Delly moved into the room. Her first emotions upon seeing Catti-brie swirled within her, a combination of anger and jealousy, and a desperate feeling of inferiority that gnawed at her belly.

No, ye put it all aside! Delly silently determined, and she forced herself closer to the bed.

She felt the doubts crawling up within her with every step, a cacophony of voices telling her to hold on to Colson and never let go. She looked down on Catti-brie as the woman lay there on her back, her thick auburn hair framing her face in such a manner as to make her appear small, almost childlike. Delly couldn't deny her beauty, the softness of her skin, the richness of her every feature. Catti-brie had lived a good life, but a difficult one, and yet, she seemed somehow physically untouched by the hardships—except for her current injury, of course. For all her battles and swordfights, not a blemish was to be found on the woman's face. For a brief moment, Delly wanted to claw her.

A very brief moment, and Delly drew a deep breath and reminded herself that her own nastiness was more a negative measure of herself than any measure of Catti-brie.

"The woman's not ever shown ye an angry look nor offered ye a harsh word," Delly quietly reminded herself.

Delly looked to Colson, then back to Catti-brie.

"She'll make ye a fine mother," she whispered to the baby.

She bent low, or started to, then straightened and hugged Colson close and kissed her atop the head.

Ye got to do this, Delly Curtie! Ye cannot be stealing Wulfgar's child!

But that was the thing of it, she realized. *Wulfgar's* child? Why was Colson anymore Wulfgar's child than Delly Curtie's? Wulfgar had taken the babe from Meralda of Auckney at Meralda's desperate request, but since Delly had joined up with him and Colson in Luskan, she, not Wulfgar, had been more the parent by far. Wulfgar had been off in search of Aegis-fang, and in search of himself. Wulfgar had been out for days at a time battling orcs. And all the while, Delly had held Colson close, had fed her and rocked her to sleep, had taught her to play and even to stand.

Another thought came to her then, bolstering her maternal uprising. Even with Colson in his care and Delly gone, would Wulfgar stop fighting? Of course not. And would Catti-brie abandon her warrior ways after her wounds healed?

Of course not.

Where did that leave Colson?

Delly nearly cried out at the desperate thought. She spun away from the bed and staggered a step toward the door.

You are entitled to the child, and to a life of your own making, said the voice in her head.

Delly kissed Colson again and stepped boldly across the room, thinking to walk away without looking back.

Should everything good happen to her? the voice asked, and the reference to Catti-brie was as clear to Delly as if it was her own inner voice speaking.

You give and give of yourself, but your own good intentions bring to you desperation, said the voice.

Aye, and empty tunnels o' dark stone, and not a one to share me thoughts, Delly answered, not even aware that she was having a conversation with another sentient being.

She reached the door then, but paused, compelled to look to the side. Catti-brie's gear was piled on a small bench, her armor and weapons covered by her worn traveling cloak. One thing in particular caught Delly's eye and held it. Peeking out from under the cloak was a sword hilt, fabulous in design and gleaming beyond anything Delly had ever seen. More beautiful than the shiniest dwarf-cut gem, more precious than a dragon's mound of gold. Before she even knew what she was doing, Delly Curtie slipped Colson down to the side, balancing her on one hip, and took a fast step over and with her free hand drew the sword out from under the cloak and out of its scabbard at the same time.

She instantly knew that the blade was hers and no one else's. She instantly realized that with such a weapon, she and Colson could make their way in a troubled world and that all would be right.

Khazid'hea, the sentient and hungry sword, was always promising such things.

She opened her eyes to see a comforting face staring back at her, crystal blue orbs full of softness and concern. Before she even fully registered who it was and where she was, Catti-brie lifted her hand to stroke Wulfgar's cheek.

"You will sleep your life away," the big man said.

Catti-brie rubbed her eyes and yawned, then allowed him to help her sit up in her bed.

"Might as well be sleeping," she said. "I'm not doing much good to anyone."

"You're healing so that you can join in the fight. That's no small thing."

Catti-brie accepted the rationale without argument. Of course she was frustrated by her infirmity. She hated the thought of Wulfgar and Bruenor, and even Regis, standing out there on the battle line while she slumbered in safety.

"How goes it in the east?" she asked.

"The weather has held and the ferry is functional. Dwarves have come across from Felbarr, bearing supplies and material for the wall. The orcs strike at us every day, of course, but with the help of the Moonwood elves, they have been easily repelled. They have not come on in force, yet, though we do not know why."

"Because they know we'll slaughter them all across the mountains."

Wulfgar's nod showed that he did not disagree. "We hold good ground, and each passing hour strengthens our defenses. The scouts do not report a massing of orcs. We believe that they too are digging in along the ground they have gained."

"It'll be a winter of hard work, then, and not much fighting."

"Readying for a spring of blood, no doubt."

Catti-brie nodded, confident that she'd be more than ready to go back out into the fighting when the weather turned warm.

"The refugees from the northern settlements are leaving even now," Wulfgar went on.

"The way out is safe enough to risk that?"

"We've got the riverbank for a mile and more to the south, and we've put the ferry out of throwing range of any giants. They'll be safe enough—likely the first of them are already across."

"How clear is it up there?" Catti-brie asked, not even trying to hold the concern out of her voice.

"Very. Perhaps too much so," Wulfgar answered, misreading her concern, and he paused, apparently catching on. "You wonder if Drizzt will find his way to us," he said.

"Or if we can find our way to him."

Wulfgar sat on the edge of the bed and stared at Catti-brie for a long, long while.

"Not so long ago you told me he wasn't dead," he reminded. "You have to hold onto that."

"And if I cannot?" the woman admitted, lowering her eyes for even voicing such a fear.

Wulfgar cupped her chin with his huge hand and tilted her head back so that she had to look him in the eye. "Then hold on to your memories of him, though I do not believe he is dead," he insisted. "Better to have loved . . ."

Catti-brie looked away.

After a moment of confusion, Wulfgar turned her back yet again. "It is better to have loved him and lost him than never to have known him at all," he stated, reciting one of the oldest litanies in all corners of the Realms. "You were lovers; there is nothing more special than that."

Telltale tears welled in Catti-brie's deep blue eyes.

"You . . . you told me . . ." Wulfgar stammered. "You said that in your years on the boat with Captain Deudermont . . ."

"I didn't tell you anything," she replied. "I let you assume."

"But . . ."

Wulfgar paused, replaying that conversation he and Catti-brie had shared during their trials out on the battle line with Banak. He had asked her pointedly about whether or not she and Drizzt had become more than friends, and indeed she had not answered directly, other than to refer to the fact that they had been traveling as companions for six long years.

"Why?" Wulfgar finally asked.

"Because I'm thinking myself the fool for not," Catti-brie said. "Oh, but we came close. We just never . . . I'm not wanting to talk about this."

"You wanted to see how I would react if I believed that you and Drizzt were lovers," Wulfgar said, and it was a statement not a question, indicating that he had it all figured out.

"I'll not deny that."

"To see if Wulfgar had healed from his torment in the Abyss? To see if I had overcome the demons of my upbringing?"

"Don't you get all angry," Catti-brie said to him. "Maybe it was to see if Wulfgar was deserving of a wife like Delly."

"You think I still love you?"

"As a brother would love a sister."

"Or more?"

"I had to know."

"Why?"

The simple question had Catti-brie rocking back in her bed. "Because I know it's farther along with me and Drizzt," she said after only a brief pause. "Because I know how I feel now, and nothing's to change that, and I wanted to know how it would affect yourself, above all."

"Why?"

"Because I'd not break up our group," Catti-brie answered. "Because we five have forged something here I'm not wanting to lose, however I'm feeling about Drizzt."

Wulfgar spent a long while staring at her, and the woman began to squirm under that scrutiny.

"Well, what're you thinking?"

"I'm thinking that you sound less like a dwarf every day," he answered with a wry grin. "In accent, I mean, but you sound more like a dwarf every day in spirit. It's Bruenor who's cursed us both, I see. Perhaps we are both too pragmatic for our own good."

"How can you say that?"

"Six years beside a man you love and you're not lovers?"

"He's not a man, and there's the rub."

"Only if your dwarven practicality makes it a rub."

Catti-brie couldn't deny his tone or his smile, and it infected her soon enough. The two shared a laugh, then, self-deprecating for both.

"We've got to find him," Wulfgar said at length. "For all our sakes, Drizzt must come back to us."

"I'll be up and about soon enough, and out we'll go," Catti-brie agreed, and as she spoke, she glanced across the way at her belongings, at the weathered traveling cloak and the dark wood of Taulmaril peeking our from under it.

At the scabbard that once held Khazid'hea.

"What is it?" Wulfgar asked, noticing the sudden frown that crossed the woman's face.

Catti-brie led his gaze with a pointing finger. "My sword," she whispered.

Wulfgar rose and crossed to the pile, pulling off the cloak and quickly confirming that, indeed, the sword was gone.

"Who could have taken it?" he asked. "Who would have?"

While Wulfgar's look was one of confusion and curiosity, Catti-brie's expression was much more grave. For she understood the power of the sentient sword, and she knew that the person who pulled Khazid'hea free of its scabbard had gotten more than he'd bargained for.

Much more.

"We have to find it, and we have to find it quickly," she said.

It is not for you, came the voice in Delly's head as she moved toward the waiting ferry. All around her dwarves worked the stone, smoothing the path from the door to the river and building their defenses up on the mountain spur. Most of the human refugees were already aboard the ferry, though the dwarf pilot had made it quite clear that the raft wouldn't put out for another few minutes.

Delly didn't know how to answer that voice in her head, a voice she thought her own.

"Not for me?" she asked aloud, quietly enough to not draw too much attention. She masked the ridiculous conversation even more by turning to Colson and acting as if she was speaking to the toddler.

Are ye daft enough to think ye should go back into the mines and live yer life with the dwarfs, then? Delly asked herself.

The world is wider than Mithral Hall and the lands across the Surbrin, came an unexpected answer.

Delly moved off to the side, behind the screen of a lean-to one of the dwarves had put together for the workers to take breaks out of the cold wind. She set Colson on a chair and started to set her pack down—when she realized that the second voice wasn't coming from in her head at all, but from the pack. Gingerly, Delly unwrapped Khazid'hea and once the bare metal of the hilt was in her hand that voice rang all the more clearly.

We are not crossing the river. We go north.

"So the sword's got a mind of its own, does it?" Delly asked, seeming more amused than concerned. "Oh, but ye'll bring me a pretty bit o' coin in Silverymoon, won't ye?"

Her smile went away as her arm came out, drifting slowly and inexorably forward so that Khazid'hea's tip slid toward Colson.

Delly tried to scream, but found that she could not, found that her throat had suddenly constricted. Her horror melted almost immediately, however, and she began to see the beauty of it all. Yes, with a flick of her hand she could take the life from Colson. With a mere movement, she could play as a god might.

A wicked smile crossed Delly's face. Colson looked at her curiously, then reached up for the blade.

The girl nicked her finger on that wickedly sharp tip, and began to cry, but Delly hardly heard her.

Neither did Delly strike, though she had more than a little notion to do just that. But an image before her, the bit of Colson's bright red blood on the sword, on *her* sword, held her in place.

It would be so easy to kill the girl. You cannot deny me.

"Cursed blade," Delly breathed.

Speak aloud again and the girl loses her throat, the sentient sword promised. *We go north.*

"You—" Delly started to say, but she bit the word off in horror. *You would have me try to get out of here to the north with a child in tow?* she silently asked. *We'd not get past the perimeter.*

Leave the child.

Delly gasped.

Move! the sword demanded, and never in all her life had Delly Curtie heard such a dominating command. Rationally, she knew that she could just throw the sword to the ground and run away, and yet, she couldn't do it. She didn't know why, she just could not do it.

She found her breathing hard to come by. A multitude of pleas swirled through her thoughts, but they wound in on themselves, for she had no real answer to the commands of Khazid'hea. She was shaking her head in denial, but she was indeed stepping away from Colson.

A nearby voice broke her from her torment momentarily, and Delly surely recognized that particular wail. She spun to see Cottie Cooperson moving toward the ferry, where the pilot was barking for everyone to hurry aboard.

We cannot leave her, Delly pleaded with the sword.

Her throat . . . so tender . . . Khazid'hea teased.

They will find the child and come for us. They will know that I did not cross the Surbrin.

When no rebuttal came back at her, Delly knew she had the evil sword's attention. She didn't really form any cogent sentences then, just rambled through a series of images and thoughts so that the weapon would get the general idea.

A moment later, Khazid'hea wrapped and tucked under her arm, Delly ran for the ferry. She didn't explain much to Cottie when she arrived and handed Colson to the troubled woman, but then she really didn't have to explain anything to Cottie, who was too wrapped up in the feel and smell of Colson to hear her anyway.

Delly waited right there, until the pilot finally shouted down at her, "Away we go, woman. Get yerself aboard!"

"What're ye about?" asked one of the other passengers, a man who often sat beside Cottie.

Delly looked at Colson, tears welling in her eyes.

She had a fleeting thought to tear out the toddler's throat.

She looked up at the pilot and shook her head, and as the dwarf tossed the ferry ropes aside, freeing the craft into the river, Delly stumbled off the other way, glancing back often.

But ten steps away, she didn't bother to even look back again, for her eyes were forward, to the north and the promises that Khazid'hea silently imparted, promises that had no shape and no definition, just a general feeling of elation.

So caught was Delly Curtie by the power of Khazid'hea that she gave Colson not another thought as she worked her way through the workers and the guards, stone by stone, until she was running free north along the riverbank.

"Halt!" cried an elf, and a dwarf sentry beside him echoed the shout.

"Stop yer running and be counted!" the dwarf cried.

More than one elf lifted a bow toward the fleeing figure, and dwarven crossbows went up as well. More shouts ensued, but the figure was out of range by then, and gradually the bows began to lower.

"What do ye know?" Ivan Bouldershoulder asked the dwarf sentry who had shouted out. Behind him, Pikel lifted his hand to the sky and began to chatter excitedly. The dwarf sentry pointed far to the north along the riverbank, where the figure continued to run away.

"Someone run out, or might that it was an orc scout," the dwarf replied.

"That was no orc," said the elf bowman beside them. "A human, I believe, and female."

"Elfie eyes," the dwarf sentry whispered to Ivan, and he gave an exaggerated wink.

"Or might be half-orc," Ivan reasoned. "Half-orc scout might've wandered in with the others from the northern towns. Ye best be tightening the watch."

The elf nodded, as did the dwarf, but when Ivan started to continue his line of thought, he got grabbed by the shoulder and roughly tugged back.

"What're ye about?" he asked Pikel, and he stopped and stared at his brother.

Pikel held tight to Ivan's shoulder, but he was not looking at his brother. He stared off blankly, and had Ivan not seen that druidic trick before, he would have thought his brother had completely lost his mind.

"Ye're looking through a bird's eyes again, ain't ye?" Ivan asked and put his hands on his hips. "Ye durned doo-dad, ye know that's always making ye dizzier than usual."

As if on cue, Pikel swayed, and Ivan reached out and steadied him. Pikel's eyes popped open wide, and turned and stare at his brother.

"Ye back?" Ivan asked.

"Uh-oh," said Pikel.

"Uh-oh? Ye durned fool, what'd ye see?"

Pikel stepped up and pressed his face against the side of Ivan's head, then whispered excitedly in Ivan's ear.

And Ivan's eyes went wider than those of his brother. For Pikel had been watching through the eyes of a bird, and that bird, on his bidding, had taken a closer look at the fleeing figure.

"Ye're sure?" Ivan asked.

"Uh huh."

"Wulfgar's Delly?"

"Uh huh!"

Ivan grabbed Pikel and tugged him forward, shoving him out toward the north. "Get a bird watching for us, then. We gotta go!"

"What're ye about?" the dwarf sentry asked.

"Where are you going?" echoed the elf archer.

"Go send the word to Bruenor," Ivan shouted. "Catch that ferry and search the tunnels, and find Wulfgar!"

"What?" dwarf and elf asked together.

"Me and me brother'll be back soon enough. No time for arguing. Go tell Bruenor!"

The dwarf sentry sprinted off to the south, and the Bouldershoulder brothers ran to the north, heedless of the shouts that followed them from the many surprised sentries.

MUTUAL BENEFIT

The storm had greatly abated, but the day seemed all the darker to Innovindil as she sat on Sunset staring back at the cave entrance to Shining White. From what she could tell the giants had pursued her as far as the inner door, and the sentry out in the corridor was still contentedly snoring when she and Sunset had galloped past.

The elf knew that she should be on her way and should not linger out there. She knew that giants could be creeping out of secret passageways onto ledges along the mountain wall, perhaps very near to her and up above. She feared that if she glanced right or left at any time, she might see a boulder soaring down at her.

But Innovindil didn't look to the sides, and did not prompt Sunset to move off at all. She just sat and stared, hoping against all logic that Drizzt Do'Urden would soon come running out of that cavern.

She chewed her lip as the minutes passed. She knew it could not be so. She had seen him go into the rushing river, swept away below a sheet of ice through which he could not escape. The river didn't flow out aboveground anywhere in the area, from what she could see and hear, so there was nothing she could do.

Nothing at all.

Drizzt was lost to her.

"Watch over him, Tarathiel," the elf whispered into the wind. "Greet him in fair Arvandor, for his heart was more for the Seldarine than ever for his dark demon queen." Innovindil nodded as she spoke those words, believing them in her heart. Despite the black hue of his skin, Drizzt Do'Urden was no drow, she knew, and had not lived his life as one. Perhaps he was not an elf in manner and thought, either, though Innovindil believed that she could have led him in that direction. But her gods would not reject him, she was certain, and if they did, then what use might she have for them?

"Farewell my friend," she said. "I will not forget your sacrifice, nor that you entered that lair for the sake of Sunrise, and for no gain of your own."

She straightened and started to twist, moving to tug the reins to the right so she could be on her way, but again she paused. She had to get back to the Moonwood—she should have done that all along, even before Tarathiel had fallen to Obould's mighty sword. If she could rally her people, perhaps they could get back to Shining White and properly rescue Sunrise.

Yes, that was the course before her, the only course, and the sooner Innovindil began that journey, the better off they would all be.

Still, a long, long time passed before Innovindil found the strength to turn Sunset aside and take that first step away.

He scrambled and clawed, kicked wildly, and flailed his arms as he tried desperately to keep his face in the narrow pocket of air between the ice and the cold, cold water. Instinct alone kept Drizzt moving as the current rushed him along, for if he paused to consider the pain and the futility, he likely would have simply surrendered.

It didn't really seem to matter, anyway, for his movements gradually slowed as the icy cold radiated into his limbs, dulling his muscles and weakening his push. With every passing foot and every passing second, Drizzt slowed and lowered, and he found himself gasping water almost constantly.

He slammed into something hard, and the current drove him atop it so that he was granted a reprieve for a few moments, at least. Holding his perch on the rock, the drow could keep his mouth in an air pocket. He tried to punch up and break through the ice, but his hand slammed against an unyielding barrier. He thought of his scimitars and reached down with one hand to draw out Twinkle. Surely that blade could cut through—

But his numb fingers couldn't grasp the hilt tightly enough and as soon as he pulled the scimitar free of its sheath, the current took it from his grasp. And as he lurched instinctively for the drifting and falling blade, Drizzt was swept away once more, turning as he went so that his head dipped far under the icy water.

He fought and he scrambled, but it was all for naught, he knew. The cold was taking him, permeating his bones and inviting him to a place of a deeper darkness than Drizzt had ever known. He wasn't seeing anything anymore in the black swirl of water, and even if there had been light, Drizzt would not have seen, for his eyes were closed, his thoughts turning inward, his limbs and sensibilities dying.

Distantly, the drow felt himself jostled about as the underground river turned and dipped. He crashed though a rocky area, but hardly felt anything as he bounced from one stone to the next.

Then the river dropped again, more steeply, as if plunging over a waterfall. Drizzt fell hard and landed harder and felt as if he had wedged up against the ice, his neck bent at an awkward angle. The cold sting knifed at his cheek and pressed inward.

Innovindil moved east from Shining White, keeping the higher mountains on her left and staying within the shadow of those peaks. For she knew she would need them to shelter her from the icy wind when night fell, and to shield the light of the campfire she would have to make.

She didn't dare bid Sunset to take to the air, for the gusts of wind could bring catastrophe. It occurred to her that perhaps she should turn south, running to the better weather and to the dwarves of Clan Battlehammer. Would they help her? Would they march beside her all the way to Shining White to rescue a pegasus?

Probably not, Innovindil knew. But she understood, though it surely pained her to admit it, that she would not likely get back to Shining White before the spring thaw.

She could only hope that Sunrise would last that long.

Drizzt's misperception surprised him when he realized he was not pressed up against the underside of the ice sheet, but was, rather, lying atop it. With a groan that came right from his aching bones, the drow opened his eyes and propped himself up on his elbows. He heard the rush of the waterfall behind him and glanced back that way.

The river had thrown him free when he'd come over that drop, and he had gone out far enough, just barely, to land upon the ice sheet where it resumed beyond the thrashing water.

The drow coughed out some water, his lungs cold and aching. He rolled over and sat on the ice, but spread right back out again when he heard it crackling beneath him. Slowly and gingerly, he crept toward the stone wall at the side of the river, and there he found a jag where he could sit and consider his predicament.

He really hadn't gone that far in his watery journey, he realized—probably not more than fifty feet or so from where he'd fallen through, not counting the two large steps downward.

Drizzt snapped his hands to his belt to feel Icingdeath, but not Twinkle, and he grimaced as he recalled losing the scimitar. He glanced back up at the waterfall wistfully, wondering how in the world he might retrieve the blade.

Then he realized almost immediately that it didn't really matter. He was soaking wet and the cold was going to kill him before any giants ever could. With that thought in mind, the drow forced himself up on unsteady feet and began inching along the wall, keeping as much of his weight as possible against the stone, and stepping from rock to rock wherever he found the opportunity. He traveled only a few hundred feet, the sound of the waterfall still echoing behind him, when he noted a side passage across the way, fronted by a landing that included a rack of huge fishing poles.

He didn't really want to move back into Shining White, but he saw no choice. He lay down on his belly on the ice, maneuvering himself so that he was clear of all the rocks poking up through it. Then he pushed off, sliding out across the frozen river. He scraped and crawled and managed to get across then he went up to the landing and beyond, moving along an upward-sloping tunnel.

A short while later, he went back on his guard, for the tunnels became wider and more worked, with ornate columns supporting their ceilings, many of which were frescoed with various designs and artwork. At one point, he ducked back just in time as a pair of giants ambled across an intersection not far ahead.

He waited for them to clear the way, and . . .

What? he wondered. Where was he to go?

The giants had crossed left to right, so Drizzt went to the left, moving as swiftly as his still numb and sorely aching legs would allow, knowing that he needed to get to a fire soon. He fought to keep his teeth from chattering, and his eyelids felt so very heavy.

A series of turns and corridors had him moving into the more populated reaches of the complex, but if the giants were at all bothered by the continuing cold, they certainly didn't show it, for Drizzt saw no sign of any fires anywhere. He kept going—what choice did he have?—though he knew not where, and knew not why.

A cry from behind alerted him that he had been seen, and the chase was on once more.

Drizzt darted around a corner, sprinted some thirty feet, then ducked fast around another turn. He ran on, down a corridor lined with statues, and one that he recognized! On the floor lay a broken statue, along with the drow's own traveling cloak. He scooped it as he passed, wrapped it tight around him, and sprinted on as more and more giants took up the chase. He had his bearings, and he looked to make every turn one that would take him closer to the exit.

But every turn was blocked to him, as giants paralleled him along tunnels running closer to the exit. He found every route of escape purposefully blocked. He was being herded. Drizzt couldn't stop, though, unless he planned to fight, for a pair of giants chased him every stride, closing whenever he slowed. He had to turn left instead of right, and so he did, cutting a tight angle around the next corner and running on for all his life. He turned the next left, thinking that perhaps he could double back on the pair chasing him.

That way, too, was blocked.

Drizzt turned right and rushed through some open doors. He crossed a large chamber, and the two giants within howled and joined in the chase. Through another set of doors, he came to the end of the hallway, though it turned both left and right. Thinking one way as good as the other, the drow banked left and ran on—right into another large room, one sporting a huge round table where a group of frost giants sat and played, rolling bones for piles of silver coins.

The table went over, coins and bones flying everywhere, as the behemoths jumped up to leap after the drow.

"Not good," Drizzt whispered through his blue lips and chattering teeth.

The next door in line was closed, and the drow hardly slowed, leaping hard against it, shouldering it in. He stumbled and squinted, for he had come into the brightest-lit room in the complex. He tried to reorient himself quickly, to put his feet under him and continue on his way.

Whichever way that might be.

For he had come into a large oval chamber, decorated with statues and tapestries. Heads of various monsters—umber hulks, displacer beasts, and even a small dragon among them — lined the walls as trophies. Drizzt knew he wasn't alone, but it wasn't until he noted the dais at the far end of the room that he truly appreciated his predicament. For there sat a giantess of extraordinary beauty, decorated with fabulous clothing and many bracelets, necklaces and rings of great value, and wearing a white gown of fabulous texture and fabric. She leaned back in her seat and crossed her bare and shapely legs.

"I do so love it when the prey delivers itself," she said in the common tongue, her command of it as perfect as Drizzt's own.

The drow heard the doors bang closed behind him, and one of the pursuing giants graced him with an announcement. "Here is the drow you wanted, Dame Orelsdottr," the giant said. "Drizzt Do'Urden is his name, I believe."

Drizzt shook his head and brought a hand up to rub his freezing face. He reached low with the other one, pulling forth Icingdeath—and as he did, he heard giant sentries to either side of him bristle and draw weapons. He looked left and right, noting a line of spears and swords all pointing his way.

With a shrug, the drow dropped his scimitar to the floor, put his foot atop it and slid it out toward Gerti.

"Not even a fight from the famed Drizzt Do'Urden?" the giantess asked.

Drizzt didn't answer.

"I would have expected more of you," Gerti went on. "To surrender before dazzling us with your blade work? Or do you believe that you spare your life by giving yourself up to me? Indeed you are a fool if you do, Drizzt

Do'Urden. Gather your scimitar if you will. Take up arms and at least try to fight before my soldiers crush the life out of you."

Drizzt eyed her hatefully, and thought to do as she asked. Before he could begin to calculate his chances of getting the blade and quick-stepping ahead to at least score a hit or two upon Gerti's pretty face, however, a low and feral growl from the side of the giantess caught his, and her attention.

Gerti turned and Drizzt leveled his gaze, and every giant in the chamber followed suit, to see Guenhwyvar perched on a ledge barely fifteen feet from Gerti, level with her pretty face.

The giantess didn't blink and didn't move. Drizzt could see her tightening her grip on the white stone arms of her great throne. She knew the panther could get to her before she could even raise her hands in defense. She knew Guenhwyvar's claws would tear at her blue and tender skin.

Gerti swallowed hard.

"Perhaps now you are more in the mood for a bargain," Drizzt dared to say.

Gerti flicked a hateful glance his way then her gaze snapped back to the threatening cat.

"She probably won't be able to kill you," Drizzt said, his freezing jaw hurting with every word. "But oh, will anyone ever look upon Dame Gerti Orelsdottr again and marvel at her beauty? Take out her pretty eye, too, Guenhwyvar," Drizzt added. "But only one, for she must see the expressions on the faces of those who look upon her scarred visage."

"Silence!" Gerti growled at him. "Your cat might wound me, but I can have you killed in an instant."

"And so we must bargain," Drizzt said without the slightest hesitation. "For we both have much to lose."

"You wish to leave."

"I wish to sit by a fire first, that I might dry and warm myself. Drow are not so comfortable in the cold, particularly when we are wet."

Gerti snorted derisively. "My people bathe in that river, winter and summer," she boasted.

"Good! Then one of your warriors can retrieve my other scimitar. I seem to have dropped it under the ice."

"Your blade, your fire, your life, and your freedom," Gerti said. "You ask for four concessions in your bargain."

"And I offer back your eye, your ear, your lips, and your beauty," Drizzt countered.

Guenhwyvar growled, showing Gerti that the mighty panther understood every word, and was ready to strike at any time.

"Four to four," Drizzt went on. "Come now, Gerti, what have you to gain by killing me?"

"You invaded my home, drow."

"After you led the charge against mine."

"So I free you and you find your elf companion, and again you invade my home?" Gerti asked.

Drizzt nearly fell over with relief upon learning that Innovindil had indeed gotten away.

"We will come back at you only if you continue to hold that which belongs to us," said the drow.

"The winged horse."

"Does not belong as a pet in the caves of frost giants."

Gerti snorted at him again, and Guenhwyvar roared and tamped down her hind legs.

"Surrender the pegasus to me and I will be on my way," said Drizzt. "And Guenhwyvar will disappear and none of us will ever bother you again. But keep the pegasus, kill me if you will, and Guenhwyvar will have your face. And I warn you, Gerti Orelsdottr, that the elves of the Moonwood will come back for the winged horse, and the dwarves of Mithral Hall will join them. You will find no rest with your stolen pet."

"Enough!" Gerti shouted at him, and to Drizzt's surprise, the giantess started to laugh.

"Enough, Drizzt Do'Urden," she bade him in quieter tones. "But you have asked me for something more; you have upped my end of the bargain."

"In return—" Drizzt started to reply, but Gerti stopped him with an upraised hand.

"Tell me not of any more body parts your cat will allow me to keep," she said. "No, I have a better bargain in mind. I will get your blade for you and let you warm before a great fire, all the while feasting on as much food as you could possibly eat. And I will allow you to walk out of Shining White—nay, to ride out on your precious winged horse, though it pains me to allow so beautiful a creature to wander away from me. I will do all this for you, and I will do more, Drizzt Do'Urden."

The drow could hardly believe what he was hearing, and that sentiment seemed common in that chamber, where many giants stood with their mouths drooping open in amazement.

"I am not your enemy," said Gerti. "I never was."

"I watched your people bombard a tower with great boulders. My friends were in that tower."

Gerti shrugged as if it did not matter and said, "I, we, did not begin this war. We followed an orc of great stature."

"Obould Many-Arrows."

"Yes, curse his name."

That raised Drizzt's eyebrows.

"You wish to kill him?" Gerti asked.

Drizzt didn't answer. He knew he didn't have to.

"I wish to witness such a battle," Gerti said with a vicious little grin. "Perhaps I can deliver King Obould to you, Drizzt Do'Urden. Would that interest you?"

Drizzt swallowed hard. "Now it would seem that you have upped your own end of the bargain even more," he reasoned.

"Indeed I have, so accept it with two promises. First, you will kill Obould. Then you will broker a truce between Shining White and the surrounding kingdoms. King Bruenor's dwarves will not seek retribution upon my people, nor will Lady Alustriel, nor any other allies of Clan Battlehammer. It will be as if the giants of Shining White never partook in Obould's war."

It took Drizzt a long time to digest the startling words. Why was Gerti doing this? To save her beauty, perhaps, but there was so much more going on than Drizzt could begin to understand. Gerti hated Obould, that much was obvious—could it be that she had come to fear him, as well? Or did she believe that the orc king would falter in the end, with or without her treason, and the result would prove disastrous for her people? Yes, if the dwarves of the three kingdoms joined with the folk of the three human kingdoms, would they stop with the orcs, or would they press on to exact revenge upon the giants as well?

Drizzt glanced around and noted that many of the giants were nodding and grinning, and those whispering amongst themselves all seemed in complete accord with Gerti's proposal. He heard naysayers, but they were not loud and dominant.

It began to make sense to Drizzt as he stood there shivering. If he won, then Gerti would be rid of a rival she surely despised, and if he lost, then Gerti would be no worse off.

"Orchestrate it," Drizzt said to her.

"Pick up your fallen scimitar, then, and dismiss your panther."

Alarms went off in Drizzt's head, suspicion twisting his black face. But Gerti seemed even more relaxed.

"Before all my people, I give you my word, Drizzt Do'Urden. Among the giants of the Spine of the World, our word is the most precious thing we own. If I deceive you now, would any of my people ever believe that I would not do the same to them?"

"I am no frost giant, so I am inferior in your eyes," Drizzt argued.

"Of course you are," Gerti said with a chuckle. "But that changes nothing. Besides, it will amuse me greatly to watch you battle King Obould. Speed against strength, a fighter's tactics against a savage fury. Yes, I will enjoy that. Greatly so." She finished and motioned toward the scimitar again.

Drizzt stared her in the eye for a long moment.

"Be gone, Guenhwyvar," he instructed.

The panther's ears flicked up and she turned to regard Drizzt curiously.

"If she betrays me, the next time you come to the material plane, seek her out and steal her beauty," Drizzt said.

"My word is not to be broken," said Gerti.

"Be gone, Guenhwyvar," Drizzt said again, and he stepped forward and retrieved Icingdeath. "Go home and find your rest, and rest assured that I will call upon you again."

24

AT THE BEHEST OF OTHERS

Drizzt led Sunrise out of Shining White the next morning, well aware that Gerti's giants were watching his every step. The air was calm and warmer, the sun shining brilliantly against the new-fallen snow.

The drow stretched and adjusted his clothing and cloak, and the belt that held both his scimitars once more. Not twenty steps from the front, he turned and looked back at Shining White, still amazed that Gerti had stayed true to her word, and that she had cut the deal with him in the first place. He took that as a hopeful sign regarding the future of the region, for Gerti Orelsdottr and her frost giant army apparently held no heart for continuing the war, and perhaps equally important, apparently held no bond of friendship with Obould Many-Arrows. Gerti wanted the orc king dead almost as much as Drizzt did, it seemed, and if that was true of the giantess, might it also be true of some of Obould's rival orc chieftains? Would attrition play on the massive army, defeating it where the dwarves could not?

That hopeful thought was quickly replaced by another, for Drizzt realized that if Gerti really could arrange for him to meet Obould, he could accelerate that disintegration of the invading force. Without the orc king as figurehead, the chaotic creatures would turn on each other, day after day and tenday after tenday.

Drizzt clenched his hands and rolled his fingers, flexing the muscles in his forearms, chasing the last vestiges of the river's cold bite from his bones. As Innovindil had killed Obould's son, so he would strike an even greater blow.

The thought of his elf companion had him shielding his eyes with one hand and scanning the sky, hoping to spot a flying horse. He wanted to spring upon Sunrise's back and put the pegasus up high to gain a wider view of the region, but Gerti had strictly forbidden that. In fact, Sunrise was wearing a harness that would prevent the pegasus from spreading wide his wings.

Gerti was offering a bargain, but she was doing it on her terms and with her guarantees.

Drizzt accepted that with a nod, and continued to scan the skies. He had the pegasus with him. He had his scimitar back from the cold waters, and he had his life. After the disaster of his foray into Shining White, those things were more than he had imagined possible.

And he might get a fight with the hated Obould. Yes, Drizzt realized, things had worked out quite well.

So far.

Gerti sat on her great throne eyeing the giants milling around in the audience chamber. She had surprised them all, she knew, and the looks that came her way reflected suspicion as much as curiosity. Gerti knew that she was gambling. Her father, the great Jarl Orel who had united the many families of giants in the Spine of the World under his iron-fisted rule, lingered near death, leaving Gerti as the heir apparent. But it would be the first transfer of power since the unification, and that, Gerti knew, was no small thing.

She had followed the advice of Ad'non Kareese and Donnia Soldou and had joined with Obould's grand ambitions, leading her people out of their mountain homes in forays that were initially intended to be low-risk and short-lived, quick strikes using orc fodder to bear the losses, and frost giants to collect the gains. Ironically, Obould's successes had upped the ante for Gerti, and dangerously so, she had come to understand as Obould had gained more and more power in their relationship. Obould was making her look small and insignificant to her minions, and that was something Gerti knew she could ill afford. And so she had orchestrated her abandonment of Obould. But even that, she knew, had been a risk. For if the orc king had continued his conquering ways, or even if he could simply solidify and hold onto his already considerable gains, Gerti's people would have paid an exaggerated price—more than thirty frost giants had died in the campaign—for relatively minor gains in loot. The price Gerti herself would also pay in terms of stature could not be ignored.

A lone drow had given her an opening to change the equation, and she considered her bargain with Drizzt to be less of a gamble than those around her understood. The price had been nothing more than relinquishing the pegasus—true, the winged horse seemed a shiny bauble, but it was hardly of practical use to her. The gain?

That was the one variable, and the only part of any of it that seemed a gamble to Gerti. For if Drizzt killed Obould, then Gerti's abandonment of the orc's cause would seem prudent and wise, and even more so if Drizzt then followed through with his promise to relay the giantess's desire for a truce to the formidable enemies that would no doubt rush in to expel the leaderless orcs from their conquered lands. Might Gerti then salvage some practical gains from that ill-advised campaign, perhaps even the opening of trading routes with the dwarves of Mithral Hall?

The danger lay in the very real possibility that Obould would slay Drizzt, and thus gain even more stature among his subjects, if that was possible. Of course, in that eventuality, Gerti could claim to the orc king that she had delivered Drizzt to him for just that purpose. Perhaps she could even spin it to make it seem as if she, and not Obould, was truly the puppet-master.

"The winged horse was more trouble than it was worth," Gerti said to a nearby giantess who flashed her one of those suspicious and curious looks.

"It was beautiful," the giantess replied.

"And its beauty would bring an unending string of elves to Shining White, seeking to free it."

More curious looks came at her, for when had Gerti ever been afraid of the lesser races entering Shining White?

"Do you really wish to have the elves with their stinging bows sneaking into our home? Or the cunning dwarves digging new tunnels to connect to our lesser-used ways, insinuating themselves among us, popping up by surprise and smashing their ugly little hammers into our kneecaps?"

She saw a few nods among the giants as she explained, and Gerti weighed the various looks carefully. She had to play it just right, to make her maneuvering seem clever without reminding them all that her initial blunder had brought all of the risk and trouble to them in the first place. It was all about the message, Gerti Orelsdottr had learned well from her wise old father, and that was a message she meant to tightly control over the next few tendays, until the pain of losses faded.

If Drizzt Do'Urden managed to kill Obould, that message would be easier to shape to her advantage.

The same storm that had dumped heavy snows on the mountains near Shining White swirled to the southeast, bringing high winds and driving, cold rain, and whipping the waters of the Surbrin so forcefully that the Felbarran dwarves tied the ferry up on the eastern bank and retreated into sheltering caves. As anxious as they were to be on their way to Silverymoon, the human refugees did not dare to try their luck in the terrible weather, and so they, too, put up in those caves.

Cottie Cooperson made herself as inconspicuous as possible, staying in the back and at the very edges of the firelight, with Colson fully wrapped in a blanket. The others soon learned of the child, of course, and questioned Cottie.

"What'd ye do to its mother?" one man asked, and he bent low and forced Cottie to look at him squarely, demanding an honest answer.

"I seen Delly handing the child to Cottie of her own accord," another woman answered for the poor and lost Cooperson lass. "Right at the dock, and she run off."

"Run off? Or just missed the ferry?" the suspicious man demanded.

"Run off," the woman insisted. "Of her own choosing."

"She wanted the child out of Mithral Hall while they're fighting," Cottie lied.

"Then the dwarves should know they've got an adopted granddaughter of King Bruenor among their passengers," the man reasoned.

"No!" shouted Cottie.

"No," added the supportive woman. "Delly's not wanting that stubborn fool Wulfgar to know of it, as he'd be wanting the child back."

It made no sense, of course, and the man stood and turned his glare over the other woman.

"Bah! What business is it o' yer own, anyway?" she asked.

"None," another man answered. "And no one's a better mother than Cottie Cooperson."

Others seconded that remark.

"Then it's our own secret, and no business to them grumpy dwarves," the woman declared.

"Ye think Wulfgar's to be seeing it that way?" the doubting man argued. "Ye want the likes o' that one and his fierce father chasing us across all the lands?"

"Chasing us to what end?" the woman beside Cottie replied. "To get his child back? Well then we'll give him the little girl back, and no one's to argue."

"He'll come with rage in his eyes," the man argued.

"And it'll be rage he'll have to put on his wife, from where I'm sitting," said another man. "She give the child to Cottie to care for, and so Cottie's to care for the girl. Wulfgar and Bruenor got no right to anything but appreciation in that!"

"Aye!" several others loudly agreed.

The doubting man stared at Cottie's allies long and hard, then turned back to Cottie herself, who was hugging Colson as warmly as any mother ever could hold her own child.

He could not deny that the sight of Cottie with the child warmed his heart. Cottie, who had been through so very much pain, seemed content for perhaps the first time in all their trials. Even with his fears for the vengeance of Wulfgar, the man could not argue against that simple truth. He gave an accepting smile and a nod.

All construction of defenses along the mountain spur slowed during those hours of the storm, and the rain and sleet pelted the elves and dwarves who walked their patrols. They even dared to lessen those watches, for no enemies would come against them in the gale—or so they believed.

Similarly, Ivan and Pikel Bouldershoulder found their progress slowed to a crawl. Pikel's animal friends, who had guided them far north of the dwarves' position in pursuit of Delly Curtie, were still hunting at the behest of the doo-dad, but with lower and shorter flights and with very limited visibility.

"Durned fool woman," Ivan grumbled over and over again. "What's she thinking in running out o' Mithral Hall?"

Pikel squeaked to show his own confusion.

Ivan kicked at a stone, silently questioning his own decision to chase her out. They were more than a day's march from the mountain spur, and likely well behind the orc lines, though they hadn't seen any of the wretches in their march.

The dwarf truly hoped that they would not have to resort to Pikel's "root-walking" tricks to get back to Bruenor's boys.

"Durned fool woman," he grumbled and kicked another stone.

Compelled by the ever-hungry Khazid'hea, Delly Curtie was among the very few creatures wandering around outside in the cold storm. Exhausted, soaking wet, cold and miserable, the woman never entertained a single thought of finding shelter and stopping her march, because the sword would not let such a notion filter through her mind.

Khazid'hea held her, fully so. Delly Curtie had become an extension of the sword. Her entire existence was focused upon pleasing Khazid'hea.

The sword was not appreciative.

For though Delly was a willing slave, she was not what Khazid'hea coveted most of all: a worthy wielder. And so as darkness fell over the land and Delly's eyes conveyed to the sword the image of a distant campfire, the weapon compelled her to move toward it with all speed.

For hours she walked, often falling and skinning her legs, one time slipping on an icy rock so that she slammed her head and nearly knocked herself unconscious.

What am I doing out here, anyway? I meant to go to Silverymoon, or Sundabar, and yet here I am, walking wild lands!

That flicker of cogent thought only made Khazid'hea reinforce its compulsion over her, dominating her and making her trudge along, one foot in front of the other.

Khazid'hea felt her fear some time later, when they heard the guttural voices of the encamped creatures, the language of orcs. But the vicious sword took that fear and transformed it, bombarding poor Delly with images of her child being massacred by those same orcs, turning her terror into red rage so completely that she was soon running headlong for the camp. Khazid'hea in hand she burst into the firelight, killing the nearest surprised orc with a single thrust of the fabulous blade, that drove its tip right through a blocking forearm and deep into the orc's chest.

Delly yanked the blade free and swiped wildly at the next orc in line, slashing a deep cut through the trunk of a hardwood tree as the creature ducked aside. She pursued wildly, stabbing and slashing, and the orc managed one block, which took the end off its simple spear, before falling back in fear.

Something hit Delly in the side, but she hardly felt it, so consumed was she, and she pressed forward and stuck the retreating creature in its ugly face again and again, slashing and beating it, sending lines of bright blood flying into the air. She tasted that blood and was too outraged and too consumed to be revolted.

Again something hit her in the side, and she whirled that way, thinking that an orc was punching at her. A moment of clarity led to a moment of confusion as the woman regarded her attacker, standing across the campfire from her, bow in hand.

Delly glanced down to her side, to see two arrows deeply embedded, then looked back in time to watch the orc pull back its bowstring once more.

Khazid'hea overwhelmed her with an image of that very orc biting out Colson's throat, and the woman shrieked and charged.

And staggered back from the weight of an arrow driving into her chest.

With a growl, Delly held her feet, glaring at the archer, stubbornly taking a step toward the orc. She never heard its companion creeping up behind her, never heard the sword rushing for her back.

She arched, eyes going to the night sky, and a moment of peace came over her.

She noticed Selûne then, gliding overhead, trailed by her glittering tears, through a patch of broken clouds, and she thought it a beautiful thing.

Khazid'hea fell from her grasp, its sharp tip digging into the ground so that it stayed upright, waiting for a more worthy wielder to take it in its grasp.

The sword felt its connection with Delly Curtie break completely and knew itself to be an orphan.

But not for long.

25

GERTI'S AMUSEMENT

Drizzt watched the approach of two of Gerti's messengers from a sheltered dell a mile to the east of Shining White's entrance. The drow had quickly learned the limits of Gerti's trust, for he had been told explicitly that he could not remove Sunrise's harness, and he knew well that his every move was being carefully monitored. If he tried to run away, the giants would rain boulders upon him and the pegasus.

The drow believed that Gerti trusted him, though, for why would she not? Certainly his desire to do battle with Obould was honestly placed and stated! No, all the "precautions" Gerti was taking were more a show for her own people, he understood—or at least, he had to believe. He had been around a wise leader all his life, a dwarf who knew what to do and how to present it—two very different things—and he understood the politics of his current situation.

Of course, Gerti might just be using him to get a chance at killing Obould, with no intention of ever letting Drizzt and Sunrise go after the battle, whatever the outcome. So be it, Drizzt had to accept, for he had really found no options in that chamber in Shining White. All had been lost, then she'd offered at least a glimmer of hope.

The two giants entered Drizzt's dell and tossed a bag of food and a waterskin at his feet.

"A substantial force of orcs is moving east of here, along the border of the mountains to a high pass," said one, a giantess of no small beauty.

"Sent by King Obould to aid in the construction of a large city he plans in that defensible place," the other added. Muscular and wide-shouldered even by the standards of his huge race, the male's face was no less handsome than that of his female companion, with light blue skin and silvery eyebrows that turned into a **V** whenever he furrowed his brow.

"Dark Arrow Keep," said the giantess. "You would do well to remember that name and relay it to your allies should you escape all of this."

The implications of the report were not really surprising to Drizzt. On his journey north to Shining White, he had seen clear signs that the orc king intended to dig in and hold his conquered ground. The construction of a major city, and one in the defensible high ground of the Spine of the World—from which more and more orcs continued to rally to his cause—seemed a logical course to that end.

"Obould is not with the caravan, though," the giantess explained. "He is moving from mountain to mountain, overseeing the work on many lesser keeps, and reminding the orcs who they serve."

"With his shamans," added the other. "And likely a pair of dark elves serve as his wider eyes—are they known to you?"

Drizzt's expression was all the answer the giants needed.

"You killed a pair of those drow, we know," the giant went on. "These two are, or were, their companions. They were sent to the south with the troll army, but they will return. They will hold a grievance toward Drizzt Do'Urden, no doubt."

"Murder and warfare are so common among my people that they just as likely won't," Drizzt replied, and he shrugged as if it didn't matter, for of course it did not. If the two drow were with Obould, then they were already his enemies.

"We will move in the morning," the giantess said. "Gerti hopes to meet up with Obould within three days."

She wants him dead before his grand designs can take real shape, Drizzt thought, but did not reply.

Every added bit of information about Obould's movements reinforced Gerti's deal with him. The giantess saw a war coming beyond anything in her power to influence. Or, in the absence of that war, she saw her own position greatly diminishing before the rise of King Obould Many-Arrows.

Delivering Drizzt to Obould might prove a gamble to Gerti, Drizzt understood, for it was likely that Obould's stature would only climb if he proved victorious. The fact that Gerti was willing to take that chance showed Drizzt just how desperate she was becoming.

Obould was taking full control, so Gerti believed that she had nothing to lose.

The drow thought it odd that his victory over Obould would so greatly benefit Gerti Orelsdottr, a giantess he would hardly claim as an ally in any cause. He remembered the bombardment of Shallows, the callous disregard Gerti's warriors had shown for the poor besieged people of the village as they had launched boulder after boulder their way.

Yet, if he proved victorious and killed Obould, and the orc forces began to scatter and turn on themselves in the absence of a strong leader, Drizzt was then bound to parlay on behalf of those same giants for a truce.

The drow nodded grimly and accepted the notion then in his heart, as he had previously accepted it in his thoughts when his very life had been at stake. Better for everyone if the war could simply end, if the dark swarm of orcs could be pushed back into their holes and the land reclaimed for the goodly folk. What gain would there be in then pursuing an attack upon Shining White, in which hundreds of dwarves and their allies would be slain?

"Are you ready to fight him?" the giantess asked, and when Drizzt looked at her, he realized he'd been so wrapped up in his thoughts that he'd missed the question the first few times she'd asked it.

"Three days," he agreed. "Obould will die in three days."

The giant and giantess looked to each other and grinned, then walked off.

Drizzt replayed his pledge many times, letting it permeate his bones and his heart, letting it become a litany against all the pain and loss.

"Obould will die in three days," he repeated aloud, and his lips curled hungrily.

The two giants down the trail to his right kept Sunrise under close guard, but they were not holding Drizzt's attention that cold and clear morning. Up to his left, on a barren and rocky hilltop, Gerti Orelsdottr and

King Obould stood in the sunlight, talking and arguing.

She had orchestrated all of it, had set Drizzt in place within an easy and swift climb to the appointed spot, then had brought Obould out here alone for a parlay.

The orc didn't seem suspicious at all to Drizzt, he appeared at ease and supremely confident. Obould had been a bit on his guard when he and Gerti first arrived at the hilltop, but after a few minutes of pointing and talking, the orc visibly relaxed.

They were discussing the construction of defenses, Drizzt knew. All the way out there, a full four days of marching south from Shining White, Drizzt had witnessed the unveiling of King Obould's grand designs. Many hilltops and mountainsides were under construction in the north, with rock walls taking shape and the bases of large keeps already set in place. On an adjoining mound to the one where the two principals stood, a hundred orcs toiled at the stone, preparing strong defenses.

Those sights only heightened Drizzt's sense of urgency. He *wanted* to kill Obould for what the orc had done to his friends and to the innocents of the North; he *needed* to kill Obould for the sake of those remaining. It was not the behavior that Drizzt had come to expect from an orc. Many times, even back in Menzoberranzan, he had heard others remark that the only thing truly subjugating goblinkind to the other races was the lack of cohesion on their part. Even the superior minded matron mothers of Menzoberranzan had remained leery of their goblin and orc slaves, knowing that a unified force of the monsters, weak as they might be individually, could prove to be an overwhelming catastrophe.

If Obould truly was that unifying force, at least in the Spine of the World, he had to die.

Many minutes passed, and Drizzt subconsciously grasped at his scimitar hilts. He glanced nervously at the adjoining hilltop, where several other orcs—shamans, they appeared—kept a watch on their leader, often moving to the closest edge and peering across at the two figures. Their interest had faltered over the past few minutes, but Drizzt knew that would likely be a temporary thing.

"Hurry up, Gerti," he whispered.

The drow stepped back into the shadows, startled, for almost as if she had heard his plea, Gerti turned away from Obould and stormed off, moving down the mountainside with swift, long strides.

So surprised was he that Drizzt nearly missed the moment. Obould, apparently caught off his guard by Gerti's sudden retreat, stood there gaping at her, hands on his hips, eyes staring out from behind that curious skull-like helm with its oversized, glassy goggles.

The drow shook himself from his hesitation and bounded up the slope, moving fast and silently. He came atop the hillock just a few strides from the orc, and thought for a moment to rush in and stab his enemy before Obould even knew he was there.

But the orc king spun on him, and Drizzt had skidded to a stop anyway.

"I had thought you would never dare to stand without an ally," the drow said, and his scimitars appeared in his hands—almost magically, it seemed, so fast and fluid was his movement.

A low growl escaped Obould's lips as he regarded the drow.

"Drizzt Do'Urden?" he asked, the growling rumble continuing through every syllable.

"It is good that you know my name," Drizzt answered, and he began to stalk to the side, Obould turning to keep him squarely in line. "I want you to know. I want you to understand why you die this morning."

So sinister was Obould's chuckle that it hardly deviated from the continuing growl. He reached his right hand up slowly and deliberately over his left shoulder, grasped the large hilt of his greatsword, and slowly drew it up. The top edge of his scabbard was cut halfway up its length, so as soon as the sword tip broke free of the sheath, Obould snapped the sword straight up then down and across before him.

Drizzt heard a shout from the other hillock, but it didn't matter. Not to him, and not to Obould. Drizzt heard a larger commotion, and glanced to see several orcs running his way, and several others lifting bows, but Obould raised his hand out toward them and they skidded to a stop and lowered their weapons. The orc king wanted the fight as much as he did.

"For Bruenor, then," Drizzt said, and he didn't piece together the implications of the scowl that showed in Obould's bloodshot yellow eyes. "For Shallows and all who died there."

He kept circling and Obould kept turning.

"For the Kingdom of Dark Arrows," Obould countered. "For the rise of the orcs and the glory of Gruumsh. For our turn in the sunlight that the dwarves, elves, and humans have too long claimed as their own!"

The words sent an instinctual shiver down Drizzt's spine, but the drow was too wrapped up in his anger to fully appreciate the orc's sentiment.

Drizzt was trying to take a complete measure of his enemy, trying to look over the orc's fabulous armor to find some weakness. But the drow found himself locked by the almost hypnotic stare of Obould, by the sheer intensity of the great leader's gaze. So held was he, that he was hardly aware that Obould had started to move. So frozen was Drizzt by those bloodshot eyes, that he only moved at the very last second, throwing his hips back to avoid being cut in half by the sidelong swipe of the monstrous sword.

Obould pressed forward, whipping a backhand slash, then pulling up short and stabbing once, twice, thrice, at the retreating drow.

Drizzt turned and dodged, his feet quick-stepping, keeping him in balance as he backed. He resisted the urge to intercept the stabbing and slashing sword with one of his own blades, realizing that Obould's strokes were too powerful to be parried with one hand. The drow was using the moments as Obould pressed his attack to fall into his own rhythm. As he sorted out his methods, he realized it would be better to hold complete separation. So he kept his scimitars out to the side, his arms out wide, his agility and feet alone keeping Obould's strikes from hitting home.

The orc king roared and pressed on even more furiously, almost recklessly. He stabbed and stepped ahead, whipped his sword out one way then rushed ahead in a short burst as he slashed across. But Drizzt was quicker moving backward than Obould was in coming forward, and the orc got nowhere close to connecting. And the seasoned drow warrior, his balance perfect as always, let the blade go by and reversed his momentum in the blink of a bloodshot eye.

He ran right past Obould, veering slightly as the orc tried to shoulder-block him. A double-stab drove both his scimitars against Obould's side, and when the armor stopped them, Drizzt went into a sudden half-turn, then back again, slashing higher, one blade after the other, both raking across the orc king's eye plate.

Obould came around with a howl, his greatsword cutting the air—but only the air, for Drizzt was well out of range.

The drow's smile was short-lived, however, when he saw that his strikes, four solid hits, had done nothing, had not even scratched the translucent eye plate of the skull-like helm.

And Obould was on him in a flash, forcing him to dive and dodge, and even to parry once. The sheer force of Obould's strike sent a numbing vibration humming through the drow's arm. Another opening presented itself and Drizzt charged in, Twinkle cutting hard at the grayish wrap Obould wore around his throat.

And Drizzt, scoring nothing substantial at all, nearly lost some of his hair as he dived forward, just under the tremendous cut of the heavy greatsword. It occurred to Drizzt as he came around to face yet another brutal assault that his openings had been purposefully offered, that Obould was baiting him in.

It made no sense to him, and as he threw his hips left and right and back, and even launched himself into a sidelong somersault at one point, he kept studying the brute and his armor, searching desperately for some opening. But even Obould's legs seemed fully entombed in the magnificent armor.

Drizzt leaped up high as the greatsword cut across below him. He landed lightly and charged forward at his foe, and Obould instinctively reacted by throwing his sword across in front of him.

The greatsword burst into flame, but the startled Drizzt reacted perfectly, slapping Icingdeath across it.

The magic of the scimitar overruled the fires of the greatsword, extinguishing them in a puff of angry gray smoke, and it was Obould, suddenly, who was caught by surprise, just as he had started forward to overwhelm the drow. His hesitation gave Drizzt yet another opening, and the drow took a different tact, diving low and wedging himself between the orc's legs, thinking to spin and twist and send Obould tumbling away.

How might the armored turtle fight while lying on its back?

That clever thought met with the treelike solidity of King Obould's legs, for though Drizzt hit the orc full force, Obould's foot did not slip back a single inch.

Though dazed, the drow knew he had to move at once, before Obould could bring the sword around and skewer him where he crouched. He started to go, and realized he was quick enough to escape that blade.

But so did Obould, and so the orc did not focus on his sword, but rather kicked out hard. His armored foot crunched into the drow's chest and sent Drizzt flying back ten feet to land hard on his back. Gasping for breath that would not come, Drizzt rolled aside just as Obould's sword came down, smashing the stone where he'd just been lying.

The drow moved with all speed, twisting and turning, putting his feet under him, and throwing himself aside to barely avoid another great slash.

He couldn't fully avoid a second kick as the orc went completely on the offensive. The clip, glancing at it was, sent him tumbling once more. The drow finally straightened out enough to throw himself into a backward roll that put him on his feet once more, squarely facing the charging orc.

Drizzt yelled and charged, but only a single step before he burst out to the side.

He couldn't win, so he ran.

Down the side of the stony hill he went, the shouts of the orcs form the other hill and the taunts of Obould chasing him every step. He cut a fast turn around a jag in the stone, wanting to get out of sight of the archers, then cut again onto a straight descending path. His heart leaped when he saw Sunrise waiting for him, pawing the ground. As he neared, he realized that the pegasus was no longer wearing the harness.

Sunrise started running even as Drizzt leaped astride, and only a few steps off, the horse leaped into the air and spread his great wings, taking flight.

Gerti led the barrage, launching a stone that soared high into the air, not far behind the flying horse and drow rider. Her dozen escorting giants let fly as well, filling the air with boulders.

Not one scored a hit on the drow, though, for Gerti's instructions had been quite clear. As the pegasus banked, the giantess managed to catch the drow's attention, and his slight nod confirmed everything between them.

"He failed us, so why not kill him?" the giant beside Gerti asked.

"His hatred for Obould will only grow," the giantess explained. "He will try again. His role in this drama is not yet done."

She looked back to the hillock as she spoke, to see Obould standing imperiously, his greatsword raised in defiance, and behind him, the shamans and other orcs howled for him, and for Gruumsh.

Gerti looked back to Drizzt and hoped her prediction would prove correct.

"Find a way to kill him, Drizzt Do'Urden," she whispered, and she recognized the desperation in her own voice and was not pleased.

PART FOUR THE BALANCE OF POWER

There is a balance to be found in life between the self and the community, between the present and the future. The world has seen too much of tyrants interested in the former, selfish men and women who revel in the present at the expense of the future. In theoretical terms, we applaud the one who places community first, and looks to the betterment of the future.

After my experiences in the Underdark, alone and so involved in simple survival that the future meant nothing more than the next day, I have tried to move myself toward that latter, seemingly desirable goal. As I gained friends and learned what friendship truly was, I came to view and appreciate the strength of community over the needs of the self. And as I came to learn of cultures that have progressed in strength, character, and community, I came to try to view all of my choices as an historian might centuries from now. The long-term goal was placed above the short-term gain, and that goal was based always on the needs of the community over the needs of the self.

After my experiences with Innovindil, after seeing the truth of friends lost and love never realized, I understand that I have only been half right.

"To be an elf is to find your distances of time. To be an elf is to live several shorter life spans." I have learned this to be true, but there is something more. To be an elf is to be alive, to experience the joy of the moment within the context of long-term desires. There must be more than distant hopes to sustain the joy of life.

Seize the moment and seize the day. Revel in the joy and fight all the harder against despair.

I had something so wonderful for the last years of my life. I had with me a woman whom I loved, and who was my best of friends. Someone who understood my every mood, and who accepted the bad with the good. Someone who did not judge, except in encouraging me to find my own answers. I found a safe place for my face in her thick hair. I found a reflection of my own soul in the light in her blue eyes. I found the last piece of this puzzle that is Drizzt Do'Urden in the fit of our bodies.

Then I lost her, lost it all.

And only in losing Catti-brie did I come to see the foolishness of my hesitance. I feared rejection. I feared disrupting that which we had. I feared the reactions of Bruenor and later, when he returned from the Abyss, of Wulfgar.

I feared and I feared and I feared, and that fear held back my actions, time and again.

How often do we all do this? How often do we allow often irrational fears to paralyze us in our movements. Not in battle, for me, for never have I shied from locking swords with a foe. But in love and in friendship, where, I know, the wounds can cut deeper than any blade.

Innovindil escaped the frost giant lair, and now I, too, am free. I will find her. I will find her and I will hold onto this new friendship we have forged, and if it becomes something more, I will not be paralyzed by fear.

Because when it is gone, when I lay at death's door or when she is taken from me by circumstance or by a monster, I will have no regrets.

That is the lesson of Shallows.

When first I saw Bruenor fall, when first I learned of the loss of my friends, I retreated into the shell of the Hunter, into the instinctual fury that denied pain. Innovindil and Tarathiel moved me past that destructive, self-destructive state, and now I understand that for me, the greatest tragedy of Shallows lies in the lost years that came before the fall.

I will not make that mistake again. The community remains above the self; the good of the future outweighs the immediate desires. But not so much, perhaps. There is a balance to be found, I know now, for utter selflessness can be as great a fault as utter selfishness, and a life of complete sacrifice, without joy, is, at the end, a lonely and empty existence.

–Drizzt Do'Urden

INTO THE BREACH
ONCE MORE

He knew that Innovindil had escaped, of course, but Drizzt could not deny his soaring heart one clear and calm afternoon, when he first spotted the large creature in the distance flying above the rocky plain. He put Sunrise into swift pursuit, and the pegasus, seeming no less excited than he, flew off after the target with all speed. Just a few seconds later, Drizzt knew that he, too, had been spotted, for his counterparts turned his way and Sunset's wings beat the air with no less fervor than those of Sunrise.

Soon after, both Drizzt and Innovindil confirmed that it was indeed the other. The two winged horses swooped by each other, circled, and came back. Neither rider controlled the mounts then, as Sunrise and Sunset flew through an aerial ballet, a dance of joy, weaving and diving side by side, separating with sudden swerving swoops and coming back together in a rush that left both Drizzt and Innovindil breathless.

Finally, they put down upon the stone, and the elf and the drow leaped from their seats and charged into each other's arms.

"I thought you lost to me!" Innovindil cried, burying her face in Drizzt's thick white hair.

Drizzt didn't answer, other than to hug her all the tighter. He never wanted to let go.

Innovindil put him out to arms' length, stared at him, shaking her head in disbelief, then crushed him back in her hug.

Beside them, Sunrise and Sunset pawed the ground and tossed their heads near to each other, then galloped off, leaping and bucking.

"And you rescued Sunrise," Innovindil breathed, again moving back from the drow—and when she did, Drizzt saw that her cheeks were streaked with tears.

"That's one way to explain it," he answered, deadpan.

Innovindil looked at him curiously.

"I have a tale to tell," Drizzt promised. "I have battled with King Obould."

"Then he is dead."

Drizzt's somber silence was all the answer he needed to give.

"I am surprised to find you out here," he said a moment later. "I would have thought that you would return to the Moonwood."

"I did, only to find that most of my people have marched across the river to the aid of Mithral Hall. The dwarves have broken out of the eastern gate, and have joined with Citadel Felbarr. Even now, they strengthen their defenses and have begun construction of a bridge across the River Surbrin to reconnect Mithral Hall to the other kingdoms of the Silver Marches."

"Good news," the drow remarked.

"Obould will not be easily expelled," Innovindil reminded him, and the drow nodded.

"You were flying south, then, to the eastern gate?" Drizzt asked.

"Not yet," Innovindil replied. "I have been scouting the lands. When I go before the assembly at Mithral Hall, I wish to give a complete accounting of Obould's movements here."

"And what you have seen is not promising."

"Obould will not be easily expelled," the elf said again.

"I have seen as much," said Drizzt. "Gerti Orelsdottr informed me that King Obould has sent a large contingent of orcs northeast along the Spine of the World to begin construction of a vast orc city that he will name Dark Arrow Keep."

"Gerti Orelsdottr?" Innovindil's jaw drooped open with disbelief as she spoke the name.

Drizzt grinned at her. "I told you I had a tale to tell."

The two moved to a quiet and sheltered spot and Drizzt did just that, detailing his good fortune in escaping the underground river and the surprising decisions of Gerti Orelsdottr.

"Guenhwyvar saved your life," Innovindil concluded, and Drizzt didn't disagree.

"And the frost giants showed surprising foresight," he added.

"This is good news for all the land," said Innovindil. "If the frost giants are abandoning Obould's cause, then he is far weaker."

Drizzt wasn't so certain of that estimation, given the level of construction on defensive fortifications he had witnessed in flying over the region. And he wasn't even certain that Gerti was truly abandoning Obould's cause. Abandoning Obould, yes, but the greater cause?

"Surely my people, the dwarves, and the humans will fare better against orcs alone than against orc ranks bolstered by frost giants," Innovindil said to the drow's doubting expression.

"True enough," Drizzt had to admit. "And perhaps this is but the beginning of the greater erosion of the invading army that we all believe will occur. Orc tribes, too, have rarely remained loyal to a single leader. Perhaps their nature will reveal itself in the form of battles across the mountaintops, orc fortress against orc fortress."

"We should increase the pressure on the pig-faced creatures," Innovindil said, a sly grin creasing her face. "Now is the time to remind them that perhaps they were not wise in choosing to follow the ill-fated excursion of Obould Many-Arrows."

Drizzt's lavender eyes sparkled. "There is no reason that we have to do all of our scouting from high above. We should come down, now and again, and test the mettle of our enemies."

"And perhaps weaken that resolve?" Innovindil asked, her grin widening.

Drizzt rubbed his fingers together. Fresh from his defeat at the hands of Obould, he was quite anxious to get back into battle.

Before the sun set that very same day, a pair of winged horses bore their riders above a small encampment of orc soldiers. They came down powerfully, side by side, and both drow and moon elf rolled off the back of their respective mounts, hit the ground running and in balance and followed the thundering steeds right through the heart of the camp, scattering orcs as they went.

Both Drizzt and Innovindil managed a few strikes in that initial confusion, but neither slowed long enough to focus on any particular enemy. By the time Sunset and Sunrise had gone out the other side of the small camp, the two elves were joined, forearm to forearm, blades working in perfect and deadly harmony.

They didn't kill all twenty-three orcs in that particular camp, though so confused and terrified were the brutes at the onset of battle, more intent in getting out of the way than in offering any defense, that the devastating pair likely could have. The fight was as much about sending a message to their enemies as it was to kill orcs. Through all the wild moments of fighting, Sunset and Sunrise played their role to perfection, swooping in and kicking at orc heads, and at one point, crashing down atop a cluster of orcs that seemed to be forming a coherent defensive posture.

Soon enough, Drizzt and Innovindil were on their mounts again and thundering away, not taking wing for twilight was upon them, but running off across the stony, snowy ground.

Their message had been delivered.

The orc stared down the end of its bloody blade, to its latest victim squirming on the ground. Three swipes had brought it down, had taken its arm, and had left long, deep gashes running nearly the length of the dying orc's torso. So much blood soaked the fallen orc's leather tunic that anyone viewing the creature would be certain that it had been cut more than three times.

That was the beauty of Khazid'hea, though, for the wicked sword did not snag on leather ties or bone, or even thin metal clasps. Cutter was its nickname, and the name the sentient sword was using when communicating with its current wielder. And Cutter was a name that newest wielder understood to be quite apropos.

Several orcs had challenged the sword-wielder for the blade. All of them, even a pair who attacked the sword-wielder together, and another orc thought to be the best fighter in the region, lay dead.

Is there anything that we cannot accomplish? the sword asked the orc, and the creature responded with a toothy smile. *Is there any foe we cannot defeat?*

In truth, Khazid'hea thought the orc a rather pitiful specimen, and the sword knew that almost all of the orcs it had killed in its hands might have won their battle had the sword-wielder been holding a lesser weapon. At one point against the most formidable of the foes, Khazid'hea, who was telepathically directing its wielder through the combat, had considered turning the orc the wrong way so that its opponent would win and claim the sword.

But for the moment, Khazid'hea didn't want to take those risks. It had an orc that was capable in combat, though minimally so, but was a wielder Khazid'hea could easily dominate. Through that orc, the sentient sword intended to find a truly worthy companion, and until one presented itself, the orc would suffice.

The sword imagined itself in the hands of mighty Obould Many-Arrows.

With that pleasant thought in mind, Khazid'hea contented itself with its current wielder.

The last fight, this last dead orc, marked the end of any immediate prospective challengers, for all the other orcs working at the defensive fortification had made it quite clear that they wanted nothing to do with the sword-wielder and his new and deadly toy. With that, Khazid'hea went back into its sheath, its work done but its hunger far from sated.

That hunger could never be sated. That hunger had made the sword reach out to Delly Curtie so that it could be free of Catti-brie, a once-capable wielder who would not see battle again anytime soon, though a war waged outside her door. That hunger had made Khazid'hea force Delly into the wild North, for the region beyond the great river was mired in peace.

Khazid'hea hated peace.

And so the sword became quite agitated over the next few days, when no orcs stepped forth to challenge the sword's current wielder. Khazid'hea thus began to execute its plan, whispering in the thoughts of the orc, teasing it with promises of supplanting Obould.

Is there anything we cannot do? the sword kept asking.

But Khazid'hea felt a wall of surprisingly stubborn resistance every time it hinted about Obould. The orc, all the orcs, thought of their leader in terms beyond the norm. It took some time for Khazid'hea to truly appreciate that in compelling the orc to supplant Obould, it was asking the orc to assume the mantle of a god. When that reality sank in, the sentient sword backed away its demands, biding its time, hoping to learn more of the orc army's structure so that it could choose an alternative target.

In those days of mundane labor and boring peace, Khazid'hea heard the whisper of a name it knew well.

"They're saying that the drow elf is Drizzt Do'Urden, friend of King Bruenor," another orc told a group that including the sword's current wielder.

The sentient sword soaked it all in. Apparently, Drizzt and a companion were striking at orc camps in the region, and many had died.

As soon as the sword-wielder left that discussion, Khazid'hea entered its mind.

How great will you be if you bring Drizzt Do'Urden's head to King Obould? the devilish sword asked, and it accompanied the question with a series of images of glory and accolades, of a hacked drow elf lying dead at the orc champion's feet. Of shamans dancing and throwing their praise, and orc females swooning at the mere sight of the conquering champion.

We can kill him, the sword promised when it sensed doubt. *You and I together can defeat Drizzt Do'Urden. I know him well, and know his failings.*

That night, the sword-wielder began to ask more pointed questions of the orc who had relayed the rumors of the murderous dark elf. Where had the attacks occurred? Were they certain that the drow had been involved?

The next day, Khazid'hea in its hand and in its thoughts, the sword-wielder slipped away from its companions and started off across the stony ground, seeking its victim and its glory.

But for Khazid'hea, the search was for a new and very worthy wielder.

27

GROUSING

The audience chamber of Mithral Hall was emptier than it had been in many months, but there could not have been more weight in the room. Four players sat around a circular table, equidistant to each other and all on the diagonal of the room, so that no one would be closer to the raised dais and the symbolic throne.

When the doors banged closed, the last of the escorts departing, King Bruenor spent a moment scrutinizing his peers—or at least, the two he considered to be his peers, and the third, seated directly across from him, whom he realized he had to tolerate. To his left sat the other dwarf, King Emerus Warcrown, his face scrunched in a scowl, his beard neatly trimmed and groomed, but showing a bit more gray, by all accounts. How could Bruenor blame him for that, since Emerus had lost nearly as many dwarves as had Clan Battlehammer, and in an even more sudden and devastating manner?

To Bruenor's right sat another ally, and one he respected greatly. Lady Alustriel of Silverymoon had been a friend to Bruenor and to Mithral Hall for many years. When the dark elves invaded the dwarves' homeland Alustriel had stood strong beside Bruenor and his kin, and at great loss to the people of her city. Many of Alustriel's warriors had died fighting the drow in Keeper's Dale. Alustriel seemed as regal and beautiful as ever. She was dressed in a long gown of rich, deep green, and a silver circlet accentuated her sculpted features and her silvery hair. By all measures, the woman was beautiful, but there was something more about her, a strength and gravity. How many foolish men had underestimated Alustriel, Bruenor wondered, thinking her pretty face the extent of her powers?

Across from the dwarf sat Galen Firth of Nesmé. Dirty and disheveled, carrying several recent scars and scabs, the man had just come from a battlefield, obviously, and had repeatedly expressed his desire to get right back to the fighting. Bruenor could respect that, certainly, but still the dwarf had a hard time in offering too much respect to that man. Bruenor still hadn't forgotten the treatment he and his friends had found in Nesmé, nor the negative reaction of Nesmé to Settlestone, a community of Wulfgar's folk that Bruenor had sponsored.

There was Galen, though, sitting in Mithral Hall as a representative of the town, and brought in by Alustriel as, so she said, a peer.

"Be it known and agreed that I speak not only for Silverymoon, but for Everlund and Sundabar, as well?" Alustriel asked.

"Aye," the other three all answered without debate, for Alustriel had informed them from the beginning that she had been asked to serve as proxy for the other two important cities, and none would doubt the honorable lady's word.

"Then we are all represented," Galen Firth remarked.

"Not all," said Emerus Warcrown, his voice as deep as a boulder's rumble within a mountain cave. "Harbromm's got no voice here."

"Two other dwarves sit at the table," Galen Firth argued. "Two humans for four human kingdoms, but two dwarves do not suffice for only three dwarven mines?"

Bruenor snorted. "Alustriel's getting three votes, and rightly so, since them other two asked her to do their voting here. Why yerself's even getting a voice is something I'm still wondering."

Galen narrowed his eyes, and Bruenor snorted again.

"Not I nor King Bruenor would deign to speak for King Harbromm of Citadel Adbar," Emerus Warcrown added. "King Harbromm has been advised of the situation, and will make his decisions known in time."

"Now is the time to speak!" Galen Firth replied. "Nesmé remains under assault. We have driven the trolls and bog blokes from the town and pushed most back into the Trollmoors, but their leader, a great brute named Proffit, has eluded us. While he lives, Nesmé will not be safe."

"Well, I'll be sending ye all me warriors then, and right off," Bruenor answered. "I'll just tell Obould to hold back his tens of thousands until we're properly ready for greeting him."

The sarcasm made Galen Firth narrow his eyes all the more.

"We will settle nothing about our enemies if we cannot come to civil agreement among ourselves," the ever-diplomatic Alustriel put in. "Bury old grievances, King Bruenor and Galen Firth, I beg of you both. Our enemies press us—press your two peoples most of all—and that must be our paramount concern."

Emerus Warcrown leaned back in his thick wooden chair and crossed his burly arms over his barrel-like chest.

Bruenor regarded his counterpart, and offered an appreciate wink. Emerus was dwarf first, Bruenor understood clearly. The hierarchy of his loyalty placed Bruenor and Harbromm, and their respective clans, at the top of Emerus's concerns.

As it should be.

"All right then, them grievances are buried," Bruenor answered Alustriel. "And know that I lost more than a few good Battlehammers in helping Galen Firth there and his troubled town. And not a thing have we asked in kind."

Galen started to say something, again in that petulant and negative tone of his, but Alustriel interrupted with a sudden and harsh, "Enough!" aimed directly at him.

"We understand the plight of Nesmé," Alustriel went on. "Are not the Knights in Silver doing battle there even now, securing the region so that the tradesmen can rebuild the houses and strengthen the wall? Are not my wizards patrolling those walls, the words of the fireball ready at their lips?"

" 'Tis true, my good lady," Galen admitted, and he settled back in his chair.

"The trolls are on the run, and will be put back in the Trollmoors," Alustriel promised all three of them. "Silverymoon and Everlund will help Nesmé see to this need."

"Good enough, and what's yer timetable?" asked Bruenor. "Will ye have them back afore winter settles in too deep?"

The question seemed all the more urgent since the first snows had begun to accumulate that very day outside of Mithral Hall's eastern door.

"That is our hope, so that the people of Nesmé can return to their homes before the trails grow deep with snow," Alustriel answered.

"And so that yer armies will be ready to fight beside me own when the winter lets go of the land?" Bruenor asked.

Alustriel's face grew very tight. "If King Obould presses his attack on Mithral Hall, he will find Clan Battlehammer bolstered by the forces of Silverymoon, Everlund, and Sundabar, yes."

Bruenor let a long and uncomfortable moment of silence pass before pressing the point: "And if King Obould decides that his advance is done?"

"We have spoken of this before," Alustriel reminded him.

"Speak of it again," Bruenor demanded.

"By the time winter passes, Obould's army will be powerfully entrenched," said Alustriel. "That army was formidable enough when it was marching against defended positions. Your own people know that better than any."

"Bah, but ye're giving up!" King Emerus interrupted. "Ye're all thinking to leave the orc to his gains!"

"The cost in dislodging him will be terrible," Alustriel explained, not disagreeing. "Perhaps too great a price."

"Bah!" Emerus growled. He slammed a fist onto the heavy wooden table—and it was fortunate that the table was built so sturdily, else Emerus's smash would have splintered it to kindling. "Ye're going to fight for Nesmé, but Mithral Hall's not worthy of yer sacrifice?"

"You know me better than to say that, King Emerus."

Alustriel's statement did calm the dwarf, who was far more on his edge than normal after the catastrophe at the river. Earlier that same day, King Emerus had presided over the consecration of the River Surbrin, saying farewell to nearly a thousand good dwarves.

He fell back in his seat, crossed his burly arms again, and gave a great, "Harrumph."

"King Bruenor . . . Bruenor, my friend, you must understand our thinking in this," Alustriel said. "Our desire from Silverymoon to Everlund to Sundabar to rid the land of Obould and his thousands is no less than your own. But I have flown over the occupied lands. I have seen the swarms and their preparations. To go against them would invite disaster on a scale heretofore unknown in the Silver Marches. Mithral Hall is open once more—your path across the Surbrin will be assured. You are now the lone outpost, the last bastion for the goodly folk in all the lands between the Trollmoors and the Spine of the World, the Surbrin and Fell Pass. You are not without friends or support. If Obould comes against you again, he will find the Knights in Silver standing shoulder to shoulder with Clan Battlehammer."

"Waist to shoulder, perhaps," Galen Firth quipped, but the scowls of the two dwarves showed him clearly that his feeble attempt at humor was not appreciated, and Alustriel went on without interruption.

"This piece of ground between your eastern door and the Surbrin will not fall, if all of it is to be covered in layers of the dead from the three cities I represent at this meeting," she said. "We are all agreed on this. Winter's Edge will be expanded as a military encampment, and supplies and soldiers will flow through Silverymoon to that town unabated. We will relieve King Emerus's dwarves here, so that they can return to their work in securing the Underdark route between Felbarr and Mithral Hall. We will offer great wagons and drivers to King Harbromm, so that Citadel Adbar can easily enter the conflicted region as they see fit. We will spare no expense."

"But you will spare yer warriors," Bruenor remarked.

"We will not throw thousands against defended mountains for the sake of nearly barren ground," Alustriel bluntly answered.

Bruenor, wearing the same expression and seated in the same posture as his dwarf counterpart, offered a grim nod in response. He wasn't thrilled with Alustriel's decision; he wanted nothing more than to sweep ugly Obould back to his mountain hole. But Bruenor's people had done battle with the orc king and his legions, and so Bruenor surely understood the reasoning.

"Strengthen Winter's Edge, then," he said. "Work your soldiers in concert. Drill them and practice them. I wish that the Moonwood had chosen to attend this meeting. Hralien, who speaks for them, has promised his support, but from afar. Surely they fear that Obould is as likely to turn against their forest as against Mithral Hall, since they chose to enter the fray. I expect the same loyalty to them, from all o' ye, as ye're offering to Mithral Hall."

"Of course," said Alustriel.

"They saved me a thousand dwarves," Emerus agreed.

Galen Firth sat quietly, but not still, Bruenor noted, the man obviously growing agitated that the discussion had so shifted from the fate of his beloved Nesmé.

"Ye go get yer town put back together," Bruenor said to him. "Ye make it stronger than ever before—I'll be sending caravans full o' the best weapons me smithies can forge. Ye keep them damned trolls in their smelly moor and off o' me back."

The man visibly relaxed, even uncrossing his arms and coming forward as he replied, "Nesmé will not forget the aid that Mithral Hall offered, though Mithral Hall was terribly pressed at the time."

Bruenor responded with a nod, and noted out of the corner of his eye that Alustriel was smiling with approval for his generous offering and words. The King of Mithral Hall wasn't thrilled with the decisions made that day, but he well understood that they all had to stand together.

For if they chose to stand alone, they would fall, one by one, to the swarms of Obould.

"You don't know that," Catti-brie said, trying to be comforting.

"Delly is gone, Colson is gone, and Khazid'hea is gone," Wulfgar replied, and he seemed as if he could hardly stand up while uttering those dreaded words.

He and Catti-brie had sent the news throughout Mithral Hall that Khazid'hea was missing, and had made it quite clear that the sword was not to be handled casually, that it was a weapon of great and dangerous power.

It was obvious that someone had taken it, and few dwarves would be put under the spell of any sentient weapon. That left Delly, or one of the other human refugees who had set out across the river.

It had to be Delly, Catti-brie silently agreed. She had come to Catti-brie's room before, the woman knew. Half-asleep, she had once or twice seen Delly staring at her from the doorway, though out of concern or jealousy, she did not know. Was it possible that Delly had come in to speak with her and had been intercepted by the machinations of a bored and hungry Khazid'hea?

For where had Delly gone? How dare she leave Mithral Hall with Colson, and without ever speaking to Wulfgar?

The mystery had Wulfgar on the very edge of outrage. The man, battered as he had been, should have been resting, but he hadn't gone to his bed in more than a day, ever since the troubling report of Ivan and Pikel Bouldershoulder chasing after a lone figure running off to the north. The dwarves were betting it to be Cottie Cooperson, who was quite out of her mind with grief, but both Catti-brie and Wulfgar held a nagging feeling that someone else might be out of her mind, or at least that someone might have inadvertently let a malignant spirit into her mind.

"Or is it that we have been infiltrated by stealthy allies of Obould?" Wulfgar asked. "Have spies come into Mithral Hall? Have they stolen your sword, and my wife and child?"

"We will sort through all of this," Catti-brie assured him. "We will find Delly's trail soon enough. The storms have lessened and the ferry will soon be running again. Or Alustriel and King Emerus will aid us in our search. When they come out from their meeting with Bruenor, bid them to find the refugees who went across the river. There we will find answers, I'm sure."

Wulfgar's expression showed that perhaps he was afraid of finding those answers.

But there was nothing else to be done. Dozens of dwarves were searching the halls, for the sword, the woman, and the toddler. Cordio and some of his fellow priests were even using divining spells to try to help the search.

So far, there were only questions.

Wulfgar slumped against the wall.

"Obould will be dead in three days," Stormsinger the giant growled. "That was your promise, Princess Gerti, yet Obould is alive and more powerful than ever, and our prizes—pegasus, dark elf, and that magical panther he carries—have flown from our grasp."

"We are better off having Drizzt Do'Urden working toward the same goal as we," Gerti argued, and she had to raise her voice to lift it above the tumult of protest that was rising all around her. Once again the weight of events pressed down on the giantess. It had all seemed so simple just a few tendays past: She would lend a few giants here and a few giants there to throw boulders from afar at settlements the orcs had surrounded, softening up the defenses so that Obould could overrun the towns. She would gain spoils of war for the cost of a few rocks.

So she had thought. The explosion at the ridge, where twenty of her giants had been immolated, had irrevocably changed all of that. The assault into Mithral Hall, where several more had fallen to tricks and traps, had irrevocably changed all of that. The ceremony of Gruumsh, where Obould had seemingly taken on godlike proportions, had irrevocably changed all of that.

Gerti was left just trying to bail out of it all, to let Obould and the dwarves battle it out to the last and leave herself and her kin playing on both sides of the equation so that, whoever proved victorious, the battle would not come to Shining White.

The grumbling around her showed her clearly that her kin weren't holding much faith in her or her curious choices.

If only Drizzt Do'Urden had slaughtered the wretched Obould!

"Drizzt is a formidable opponent," Gerti said, following that notion. "He will find a way to strike hard at Obould."

"And at Shining White?"

Gerti narrowed her eyes and scowled at the petulant Stormsinger. Clearly the large warrior was positioning himself as an alternative to her when the great Jarl Orel finally let go of life. And just as clearly, many of the other giants were beginning to look favorably on that positioning.

"Drizzt will not, by his word, and he will dissuade others from coming against us, should Bruenor defeat Obould."

"It is all a waste," Stormsinger groused. "We have lost friends, all of us, and for what gain? Have we more slaves to serve our needs? Have we more wealth than we knew before we followed King Obould of the orcs? Have we more territory, rich mines or wondrous cities? Have we even a single winged horse, one handed over to us and now handed away?"

"We have . . ." Gerti started to say, but a chorus of complaining rose up in the room. "We have . . ." she said more loudly, and repeated it over and over until at last the din lessened. "We have gained position," she explained. "We could not have avoided this war. If we had not joined with Obould initially, then we would likely find him as an enemy soon enough, if not already. Now that will not happen, for he is indebted to us. And now King Bruenor and all of his allies are indebted to us, despite our waging war on them, because of Drizzt Do'Urden. We have gained position, and in a time as conflicted and confusing as this, that is no small thing!"

She spoke her words with conviction and with the weight of her royal position behind her, and the room did quiet.

But they would stir again, Gerti feared, and Stormsinger, though he did not respond at that time, would not let the matter drop there.

Far from it.

28

THE WAVE OF EMOTION

"Well, that's that, then," Ivan Bouldershoulder said.

He and his brother stood over the woman's body. She was lying on her belly, but with one arm reaching up above her and shoulders turned so that they could clearly see her face.

A couple of inches of snow had gathered around the still form. Pikel bent over and gently brushed some from Delly's cold face, and he tried unsuccessfully to close her eyes.

"Poor Wulfgar," said Ivan.

"Oooo," Pikel agreed.

"But I'm not for seeing her little one anywhere near," said Ivan. "Ye think them damned orcs might've taken the kid?"

Pikel shrugged.

Both dwarves scanned the area. It had been a small camp, obviously, for the remnants of a campfire could be seen in the snow, and a collection of branches that had likely served as a lean-to. Delly's body hadn't been there long—no more than a couple of days, Pikel confirmed for his brother.

Ivan moved around the area, kicking at the snow and poking about every rock or log for some sign of Colson. After many minutes, he finally turned back to his brother, who was standing on the highest ground not so far away, his back to Ivan and looking up at the sky, shielding his eyes with one hand.

"Well, that's that, then," Ivan said again. "Delly Curtie's lost to us, and the little kid's not anywhere to be found. Let's get her wrapped up and take her back to Mithral Hall so Wulfgar can properly say farewell."

Pikel didn't turn around, but began hopping up and down excitedly.

"Come on, then," Ivan called to him, but the green-bearded Pikel only grew more agitated.

"Well, what're ye seein?" Ivan asked, finally catching on. He walked toward his brother. "Sign o' where them stupid orcs might've gone? Are ye thinking that we should go and see if the little kid's a prisoner?"

"Oo oi!" Pikel shouted, hopping anxiously then and pointing off to the north.

"What?" Ivan demanded, and he broke into a trot, coming up beside Pikel.

"Drizzit Dudden!" Pikel squealed.

"What?"

"Drizzit Dudden! Drizzit Dudden!" Pikel shouted, hopping even higher and jabbing his stubby finger out toward the north sky. Ivan squinted, shielded his eyes from the glare, and saw a large flying form. After a few moments, he made it out as a flying horse.

"Pegasus," he muttered. "Might be them elfs from the Moonwood."

"Drizzit Dudden!" Pikel corrected, and Ivan looked at him curiously. He guessed that Pikel was once again using those magical abilities that could grant him attributes of various animals. Ivan had seen Pikel imbue himself with the eyes of an eagle before, eyes that could pick out a field mouse running across a meadow from hundreds of yards away.

"Ye got them bird eyes on, don't ye?" Ivan asked.

"Hee hee hee."

"And ye're telling me that's Drizzt up on that flying horse?"

"Drizzit Dudden!" Pikel confirmed.

Ivan looked back at the far distant pegasus, and shook his hairy head. He glanced back at Delly Curtie. If they left her there, the next snow would bury her, perhaps until the spring thaw.

"Nah, we got to find Drizzt," Ivan said after a moment of weighing the options. "Poor Delly and poor Wulfgar, but many've been left out for the birds since Obould come charging down. Stupid orc."

"Stupit orc," Pikel echoed.

"Drizzt?" Ivan asked.

"Drizzit Dudden," his green-bearded brother answered.

"Well, lead on, ye durned fool doo-dad! If we find them orcs and them orcs got Wulfgar's little one, then who better'n Drizzt Do'Urden to take the kid away from them?"

"Hee hee hee."

The sentient sword had worked its way through five wielders since Delly Curtie. Using its insidious telepathic magic, Khazid'hea invaded the thoughts of each successive owner, prying from it the identity of the nearest orc it feared the most. After that, with a more worthy wielder identified, Khazid'hea had little trouble in instigating a fight among the volatile creatures, and in shaping that fight so that the more worthy warrior proved victorious.

Then news had come that the dark elf friend of Bruenor Battlehammer was working in the area once more, slaughtering orcs, and Khazid'hea found its most lofty goal within apparent reach. Ever since the companions had come to possess the sword, Khazid'hea had longed to be wielded by Drizzt Do'Urden. Catti-brie was worthy enough, but Drizzt, the sword knew, was a warrior quite different. In Drizzt's hands, Khazid'hea would find the promise of victory after victory, and would not be hidden away in a scabbard while the drow warrior fired from afar with a bow.

A bow was a cowardly weapon, to Khazid'hea's thinking.

How great will your glory be, how wonderful the riches, when you bring King Obould the head of Drizzt Do'Urden, the sword told its current wielder, a slender and smallish orc who relied on finesse and speed instead of brute strength, as was usually so with his brutish race.

"The drow is death," the orc said aloud, drawing curious stares from some nearby orcs.

Not when I am in your hands, Khazid'hea promised. *I know this one. I know his movements and his technique. I know how to defeat him.*

Even as the orc started away, heading northwest toward the last reported encounter with the drow and his elf companion, Khazid'hea began to wonder the wisdom of his course. For the ease with which the sentient sword had convinced the orc, had convinced every orc that had picked it up, was no small thing. Drizzt Do'Urden was not a weak-willed orc, Khazid'hea knew. The drow would battle against Khazid'hea's intrusions.

Unless those intrusions only reinforced that which Drizzt already had in mind, and from everything Khazid'hea had learned, the drow was on a killing rampage.

It seemed a perfect fit.

Drizzt rolled off the back of Sunrise as the pegasus set down in a fast trot. Landing nimbly, Drizzt ran along right behind the mount as Sunrise charged through the orc encampment, bowling monsters aside.

In the center of the camp, Drizzt broke out from behind, rushing ahead suddenly to cut down one orc still staggering out of the pegasus's path. Two short strokes sent that orc flying to the ground, and the efficiency of the kill allowed Drizzt to reposition his feet immediately, spinning to meet the charge of a second creature. A right-handed, backhanded downward parry lopped the tip off that second orc's thrusting spear, and while he made the block, Drizzt brought his left arm across his chest. The orc overbalanced when it felt only minimal resistance to its thrust, and Drizzt slashed right to left with that cocked blade, tearing out the creature's throat.

A thud behind the drow had him leaping about, but the threat from there was already ended, the creeping orc cut down by a well-placed elven arrow. With a quick salute to Innovindil and Sunset soaring over the camp, Drizzt moved on in search of his next kill.

He spotted a form in the lower boughs of a thick pine and rushed to the trunk. Without slowing, he leaped against it, planting his foot, then pushed off to the side, climbing higher in the air and landing atop one of the lower branches. Three quick springs brought him near to the cowering orc, and a few quick slashes had the humanoid tumbling to the ground.

Drizzt sprang down to the lowest branch again and did a quick survey. He picked a lone orc at the far end of the camp, then a trio closer and to his left. With a grin, he started for the trio, but stopped almost immediately, his gaze suddenly drawn back to the lone figure approaching from across the way.

His heart went into his throat; he wanted to scream out in denial and rage.

He knew the sword that orc carried.

Drizzt came out of the tree in a wild rush. He held all respect for the devastating weapon set in the orc's grasp, but it didn't matter. He didn't slow and didn't try to measure his opponent. He just rushed in, his scimitars working in a blur of motion, spinning circles over his shoulder, slashing across and stabbing ahead. He cut, he leaped, and he thrust, over and over. Sometimes he heard the ring of metal as he struck the fine blade of Khazid'hea, other times the rush of air cracking over his blades, and other times the softer sound of a blade striking leather or flesh.

He went into a spin around the orc, blades flying wide and level, turning their angle constantly to avoid any feeble parries, though the orc was already past any semblance of defense. The drow stopped in mid-turn and rushed back the other way, right near the orc, blades stabbing, smashing, and slashing. Technique no longer mattered. All that mattered was striking at the orc. All that mattered was cutting that creature who was holding Catti-brie's sword.

Blood flew everywhere, but Drizzt didn't even notice. The orc dropped the blade from its torn arm, but Drizzt didn't even notice. The light went out of the creature's eyes, the strength left it legs, and the only thing holding it upright was the constant barrage of Drizzt's hits.

But Drizzt didn't notice.

The orc finally fell to the dirt and the drow moved over it, smashing away with his deadly blades.

Sunset set down behind him, Innovindil leaping from her seat to rush to his side.

Drizzt didn't even notice.

He slashed and chopped. He hit the orc a dozen times, a score of times, a hundred times, until his sleeves were heavy with orc blood.

"Drizzt!" he finally heard, and from the tone, it registered to him that Innovindil must have been calling him for some time.

He fell to his knees and dropped his bloody blades to the dirt, then grabbed up Khazid'hea, holding it across his open, bloody palms.

"Drizzt?" Innovindil said again, and she crouched beside him.

The drow began to sob.

"What is it?" Innovindil asked, and she gathered him close.

Drizzt stared at Khazid'hea, tears running from his lavender eyes.

"There are other possible explanations," Innovindil said to Drizzt a short while later. They made camp down near the Surbrin, off to the side of a quiet pool that hadn't quite iced over yet so that Drizzt could clean the blood from his hands, his face, his whole body.

Drizzt looked back at her, and at Khazid'hea, lying on a stone on the ground before the elf. Innovindil, too, stared at the sword.

"It was not unexpected," Drizzt said.

"But that didn't lessen the shock."

The drow stared at her for a moment, then looked down. "No," he admitted.

"The orc was paid back in full," Innovindil reminded him. "Catti-brie has been avenged."

"It seems a small comfort."

The elf's smile comforted him somewhat. She started to rise, but stopped and glanced to the side, her expression drawing Drizzt's eyes that way as well, to a small bird sitting on a stone, chattering at them. As they watched, the bird hopped from its perch and fluttered away.

"Curious," said the elf.

"What is it?"

Innovindil looked at him, but did not reply. Her expression remained somewhat confused, though.

Drizzt looked back to the stone, then scanned the sky for any sign of the bird, which was long gone. With a shrug, he went back to his cleaning.

The mystery didn't take long to unfold, for within an hour, as Drizzt and Innovindil brushed Sunrise and Sunset, they heard a curious voice.

"Drizzit Dudden, hee hee hee."

The two turned to see Ivan and Pikel Bouldershoulder coming into view, and they both knew at once that the bird had been one of Pikel's spies.

"Well, ain't yerself the fine sight for a tired dwarf's eyes," Ivan greeted, smiling wide as he moved into the camp.

"Well met, yourself," Drizzt replied, stepping forward to clasp the dwarf's offered hand. "And *curiously* met!"

"Are you not far from the dwarven lines?" Innovindil asked, coming over to similarly greet the brothers. "Or are you, like we two, trapped outside of Mithral Hall?"

"Bah, just come from there," said Ivan. "Ain't no one trapped here—Bruenor busted out to the east and we're holding the ground to the Surbrin."

"Bruenor?" Innovindil asked before Drizzt could.

"Red-bearded dwarf, grumbles a lot?" said Ivan.

"Bruenor fell at Shallows," Drizzt said. "I saw it myself."

"Yeah, he fell, but he bounced," said Ivan. "Priests prayed over him for days and days, but it was Regis that finally woke him up."

"Regis?" Drizzt gasped, and he found it hard to breathe.

"Little one?" Ivan said. "Some call him Rumblebelly."

"Hee hee hee," said Pikel.

"What're ye gone daft, Drizzt?" asked Ivan. "I'm thinking ye're knowing Bruenor and Regis."

Drizzt looked at Innovindil. "This cannot be."

The elf wore a wide smile.

"Ye thought 'em dead, didn't ye?" Ivan asked. "Bah, but where's yer faith then? Nothing dead about them two, I tell ye! Just left them a few days ago." Ivan's face grew suddenly more somber. "But I got some bad news for ye, elf." He looked to the sword and Drizzt's heart sank once more.

"Wulfgar's girl, she took that blade and come out on her own," Ivan explained. "Me and me brother—"

"Me brudder!" Pikel proudly interrupted.

"Me and me brother come out after her, but we found her too late."

"Catti-brie—" Drizzt gasped.

"Nah, not her. *Wulfgar's* girl. Delly. We found her dead a couple o' days back. Then we spotted yerself flying about on that durned winged horse and so we came to find ye. Bruenor and Regis, Catti-brie and Wulfgar been worrying about ye terribly, ye got to know."

Drizzt stood there transfixed as the weight of the words washed over him.

"Wulfgar and Catti-brie, too?" he asked in a whisper.

Innovindil rushed up beside him and hugged him, and he truly needed the support.

"Ye been out here thinking yer friends all dead?" Ivan asked.

"Shallows was overrun," Drizzt said.

"Well, course it was, but me brother—"

"Me brudder!" Pikel cried on cue.

Ivan snickered. "Me brother there built us a statue to fool them orcs, and with Thibbledorf Pwent beside us, we give them the what's-for! We got 'em all out o' Shallows and run back to Mithral Hall. Been killing orcs ever since. Hunnerds o' the dogs."

"We saw the battlefield north of Keeper's Dale," Innovindil remarked. "And the blasted ridgeline."

"Boom!" cried Pikel.

Drizzt stood there shaking his head, overwhelmed by it all. Could it be true? Could his friends be alive? Bruenor, Wulfgar, and Regis? And Cattibrie? Could it be true? He looked to his partner, to find Innovindil smiling warmly back at him.

"I know not what to say," he admitted.

"Just be happy," she said. "For I am happy for you."

Drizzt crushed her in a hug.

"And they'll be happy to see ye, don't ye doubt," Ivan said to Drizzt. "But there's a few tears to be shed for poor Delly. I don't know what possessed the girl to run off like that."

The words hit Drizzt hard, and he jumped back from Innovindil and turned an angry glower over the sentient sword.

"I do," he said and he cursed Khazid'hea under his breath.

"The sword can dominate its wielder?" Innovindil asked.

Drizzt walked over and grabbed the blade, lifting it before his eyes. He sent his questions telepathically to Khazid'hea, feeling the life there and demanding answers.

But then something else occurred to him.

"Get yer flying horses tacked up then," said Ivan. "The sooner we get ye back to Mithral Hall, the better for everyone. Yer friends are missing ye sorely, Drizzt Do'Urden, and I'm thinking that ye're missing them just as much."

The drow wasn't about to argue that, but as he stood there holding the magnificent sword, the sword that cut through just about anything, his thoughts began cascading down a different avenue.

"I can defeat him," he said.

"What's that?" asked Ivan.

"What do you mean?" Innovindil asked.

Drizzt turned to them and said, "I outfought Obould."

"Ye fought him?" an incredulous Ivan spouted.

"I fought him, not so long ago, on a hillock not so far from here," Drizzt explained. "I fought him and I scored hit after hit, but my blades could not penetrate his armor." He brought Khazid'hea up and sent it slashing across in a powerful stroke. "Do you know the well-earned nickname of this blade?" he asked.

"Cutter," he answered when the other three just stared at him. "With this sword, I can defeat Obould."

"It is a fight for another day," Innovindil said to him. "After you are reunited with those who love you and fear you are lost to them."

Drizzt shook his head. "Obould is moving now, hilltop to hilltop. He is confident and so his entourage is small. I can get to him, and with this blade, I can defeat him."

"Your friends deserve to see you, and your friendship demands you attend to that," said Innovindil.

"My service to Bruenor is a service to all the land," Drizzt replied. "The folk of the North deserve to be free of the hold of Obould. I am given that chance now. To avenge Shallows and all the other towns, to avenge the dwarves who fell before the invaders. To avenge Tarathiel—we'll not get this chance again, perhaps."

The mention of Tarathiel seemed to take all the argument out of the elf.

"Ye're going after him now?" Ivan asked.

"I cannot think of a better time."

Ivan considered things for a bit, then began to nod.

"Hee hee hee," Pikel agreed.

"Ye hit the dog for meself, too," Ivan remarked, and his smile erupted with sudden inspiration. He pulled out his hand crossbow, of near-perfect drow design, and tossed it to Drizzt, then pulled the bandolier of explosive darts from over his shoulder and handed them to the drow.

"Pop a couple o' these into the beast and watch him hop!" Ivan declared.

"Hee hee hee."

"Me and me brother . . ." Ivan started to say, then he paused and looked at Pikel, expecting an interruption. Pikel stared back at him in confusion.

Ivan sighed. "Me and me brother—" he started again.

"Me brudder!"

"Yeah, us two'll get back to Mithral Hall and tell yer friends that ye're out here," Ivan offered. "We'll be expecting ye soon enough."

Drizzt turned to his elf friend. "Go with them," he bade her. "Watch over them from above and make sure they arrive safely."

"I am to allow you to go off alone after King Obould?"

Drizzt held up the vicious sword, and the bandolier and crossbow.

"I can defeat him," he promised.

"If you can even get him alone," Innovindil argued. "I can aid in that."

Drizzt shook his head. "I will find him and watch him from afar," he promised. "I will find an opportunity and I will seize it. Obould will fall to this sword in my hand."

"Bah, it's not a job for yerself alone," Ivan argued.

"With Sunrise, I can move swiftly. He'll not catch me unless I choose to be caught. In that event, King Obould will die."

The drow's tone was perfectly even and balanced.

"I will not stay at Mithral Hall," said Innovindil. "I will see the dwarves there, and I will come right back out for you."

"And I will be waiting," Drizzt promised. "Obould's head in hand."

It seemed as if there was nothing more to say, but of course Pikel added, "Hee hee hee."

A DEEP BREATH

"I will grow weary of this travel soon enough," Tos'un Armgo said to his drow companion.

They had been on the move for days and days, finally catching up to Obould many miles north of where they had expected to find him, the western door of Mithral Hall. There too, the fight had not gone well, apparently, and the orc king seemed in little mood for any discussion of it. It was fast becoming apparent that the travels had just begun for the two drow if they meant to remain with Obould. The orc king would not set stakes anywhere, it seemed, even in the increasingly inclement weather.

One bright morning, Tos'un and Kaer'lic awaited his arrival on some flat stones outside of the foundation of a small keep atop a steep-sided hill, their first real chance to speak with Obould since their return. Obould would entertain guests only at the pleasure of Obould. All around the two drow, orcs were hard at work clear-cutting the few trees that grew among the gray stone and dirt of the hillsides, and clearing any boulder tumbles that could offer cover to an approaching enemy.

"He is building his kingdom," Kaer'lic remarked. "He has been hinting at this for so long now, and none of us bothered to listen."

"A few castles hardly make a kingdom," said Tos'un. "Particularly when we are speaking of orcs, who will soon turn their garrisons upon one another."

"You would enjoy that, no doubt," a gruff voice responded.

The two dark elves turned to see the approach of Obould, and that annoying shaman Tsinka. Kaer'lic noted that the female did not seem at all pleased.

"A prediction based upon past behavior," Tos'un said, and he offered a bow. "No insult meant to you, of course."

Obould scowled at him. "Behavior before the coming of Obould-who-is-Gruumsh," he replied. "You continue to lack the vision of my kingdom, drow, to your own detriment."

Kaer'lic found herself taking a slight step back from the imposing and unpredictable orc.

"I had figured that you two had followed your two kin to the side of your Spider Queen," the orc said, and it took a moment for the words to register.

"Donnia and Ad'non?" Kaer'lic asked.

"Slain by yet another drow elf," Obould replied, and if he was bothered in the least by that news, he did not show it.

Kaer'lic looked at Tos'un, and the two just accepted the loss with a shrug.

"I believe that one of the shamans collected Ad'non's head as a trophy," Obould said callously. "I can retrieve it for you, if you would like."

The insincerity of his offer stung Kaer'lic more than she would have expected, but she did well to keep her anger out of her face as she regarded the orc king.

"You kept your army together through a defeat at Mithral Hall," she said, thinking it better to let the other line of conversation fall away. "That is a good sign."

"Defeat?" Tsinka Shinriil shrieked. "What do you know of it?"

"I know that you are not inside Mithral Hall."

"The price was not worth the gain," Obould explained. "We fought them to a standstill in the outer halls. We could have pressed in, but it became apparent to us that our allies had not arrived." He narrowed his eyes, glared at Kaer'lic, and added, "As we had planned."

"The unpredictability and unreliability of trolls. . . ." the drow priestess said with a shrug.

Obould continued to glower, and Kaer'lic knew that he at least suspected that she and Tos'un had played a role in keeping Proffit's trolls from joining in the fight.

"We warned Proffit that his delays could pose problems in the north," Tos'un added. "But he and his wretched trolls smelled human blood, the blood of Nesmians, their hated enemies for so many years. He would not be persuaded to march north to Mithral Hall."

Obould hardly looked convinced.

"And Silverymoon marched upon them," Kaer'lic said, needing to divert attention. "You can expect nothing more from Proffit and his band. Those few who survive."

A low growl issued from between Obould's fangs.

"You knew that Lady Alustriel would come forth," Kaer'lic said. "Take heart that many of her prized warriors now lay dead on those southern bogs. She will not gladly turn her eyes to the north."

"Let her come," Obould growled. "We are preparing, on every mountain and in every pass. Let Silverymoon march forth to the Kingdom of Dark Arrows. Here, they will find only death."

"The Kingdom of Dark Arrows?" Tos'un silently mouthed.

Kaer'lic continued to scrutinize not only Obould, but Tsinka, and she noted that the shaman grimaced at the mention of the supposed kingdom.

A divisive opening, perhaps?

"Proffit is defeated, then," the orc king said. "Is he dead?"

"We know not," Kaer'lic admitted. "In the confusion of the battle, we departed, for it was obvious that the trolls would be forced back into the Trollmoors, and there, I did not wish to go."

"Wish to go?" Obould said. "Did I not instruct you to remain with Proffit?"

"There, I would not go," said Kaer'lic. "Not with Proffit, and not for Obould."

Her brazen attitude brought another fierce scowl, but the orc king made no movement toward her.

"You have accomplished much, King Obould," Kaer'lic offered. "More than I believed possible in so short a time. In honor of your great victories, I have brought you a gift." She nodded to Tos'un as she ended, and the male drow leaped away, skipping down the hillside to the one remaining boulder tumble. He disappeared from sight, then came back out a moment later, pulling along a battered dwarf.

"Our gift to you," said Kaer'lic.

Obould tried to look surprised, but Kaer'lic saw through the facade.

He had spies and lookouts everywhere, and had known of the dwarf before he had ever come out to meet the dark elves.

"Flay his skin and eat him," Tsinka said, her eyes suddenly wild and hungry. "I will prepare the spit!"

"You will shut your mouth," Obould corrected. "He is of Clan Battlehammer?"

"He is," the drow priestess answered.

Obould nodded his approval, then turned to Tsinka and said, "Secure him in the supply wagon. We will keep him close. And do not injure him, on pain of death!"

That elicited a most profound scowl from the shaman, a look Kaer'lic did not miss.

"He will prove valuable to us, perhaps," said Obould. "I expect to be in parlay with the dwarves before the turn of spring."

"Parlay?" Tsinka echoed, her voice rising to a shriek once more.

Obould turned his scowl upon her and she shrank back.

"Take him now and secure him," the orc king said to her, his voice even and threatening.

Tsinka rushed past him to the dwarf, then roughly tugged poor Fender along.

"And injure him not at all!" Obould commanded.

"I had expected you to press into Mithral Hall," Kaer'lic said to the orc king when Tsinka was gone. "In truth, when we returned to Keeper's Dale, we expected to find the orc army scattering back for the Spine of the World."

"Your confidence is inspiring."

"That confidence grows, King Obould," Kaer'lic assured him. "You have shown great restraint and wisdom, I believe."

Obould dismissed the compliment with a snort. "Is there anything else you wish?" he asked. "I have much to do this day."

"Before you move along to the next construction?"

"That is the plan, yes," said Obould.

Kaer'lic bowed low. "Farewell, King of Dark Arrows."

Obould paused just a moment to consider the title, then turned on his heel and marched away.

"One surprise after another," Tos'un remarked when he was gone.

"I am not so surprised anymore," said Kaer'lic. "It was our mistake in underestimating Obould. It will not happen again."

"Let us just go back into the tunnels of the upper Underdark, or find another region in need of our playful cunning."

Kaer'lic's expression did not shift in the least. Eyes narrowed, as if throwing darts at the departing Obould, the priestess mulled over all the information. She thought of her lost companions, then simply let go of them, as was the drow way. She considered Obould's attitude, however, so disrespectful toward the dead drow and toward the Spider Queen. It was not so easy to let go of some things.

"I would speak with Tsinka before we leave," Kaer'lic remarked.

"Tsinka?" came Tos'un's skeptical response. "She is a fool even by orc standards."

"That is how I like my orcs," Kaer'lic answered. "Predictable and stupid."

Later that same day, after casting many spells of creation and imbuing a certain item with a particular dweomer, Kaer'lic sat on a stone opposite the orc priestess. Tsinka regarded her carefully and suspiciously, which she had expected, of course.

"You were not pleased by King Obould's decision to abandon Mithral Hall to the dwarves," Kaer'lic bluntly stated.

"It is not my place to question He-who-is-Gruumsh."

"Is he? Is it the will of Gruumsh to leave dwarves in peace? I am surprised by this."

Tsinka's face twisted in silent frustration and Kaer'lic knew she had hit a nerve here.

"It is often true that when a conqueror makes great gains, he becomes afraid," Kaer'lic explained. "He suddenly has so much more to lose, after all."

"He-who-is-Gruumsh fears nothing!" shrieked the volatile shaman.

Kaer'lic conceded that with a nod. "But likely, King Obould will need more than the prodding of Tsinka to fulfill the will of Gruumsh," the drow said.

The shaman eyed Kaer'lic curiously.

Smiling wickedly, Kaer'lic reached into her belt pouch and pulled forth a small spider-shaped fastener, holding it up before the orc.

"For the straps of a warrior's armor," she explained.

Tsinka seemed both intrigued and afraid.

"Take it," Kaer'lic offered. "Fasten your cloak with it. Or just press it against your skin. You will understand."

Tsinka took the fastener and held it close, and Kaer'lic secretly mouthed a word to release the spells she had placed in contingency upon the fastener.

Tsinka's eyes widened as she felt an infusion of courage and power. She closed her eyes and basked in the warmth of the item, and Kaer'lic used that opportunity to cast another spell upon the orc, an enchantment of friendship that put Tsinka fully at ease.

"The blessing of Lady Lolth," Kaer'lic explained. "She who would see the dwarves routed from Mithral Hall."

Tsinka moved the fastener back out and stared at it curiously. "This will drive He-who-is-Gruumsh back to the dwarven halls to complete the conquest?"

"That alone? Of course not. But I have many of them. And you and I will prod him, for we know that King Obould's greatest glories lay yet before him."

The shaman continued to stare glassy-eyed at the brooch for some time. Then she looked at her new best friend, her smile wide.

Kaer'lic tried hard to make her smile seem reciprocal rather than superior. The drow didn't worry about it too much, though, for Tsinka considered her trustworthy, thought Kaer'lic to be her new best friend.

The drow priestess wondered how Obould might view that friendship.

The walls of Mithral Hall seemed to press in on him as never before. Ivan and Pikel had returned that morning with the news of Delly and of Drizzt, bringing a conflicted spin of emotions to the big man. Wulfgar sat in the candlelight, his back against the stone wall, his eyes unblinking but unseeing as his mind forced him through the memories of the previous months.

He replayed his last conversations with Delly, and saw them in the light of the woman's desperation. How had he missed the clues, the overt cry for help?

He couldn't help but grimace as he considered his responses to Delly's plea that they go to Silverymoon or one of the other great cities. He had so diminished her feelings, brushing them away with a promise of a holiday.

"You cannot blame yourself for this," Catti-brie said from across the room, drawing Wulfgar out of his contemplation.

"She did not wish to stay here," he answered.

Catti-brie walked over and sat on the bed beside him. "Nor did she want to run off into the wild orc lands. It was the sword, and I think myself the fool for leaving it out in the open, where it could catch anyone walking by."

"Delly was leaving," Wulfgar insisted. "She could not tolerate the dark tunnels of dwarves. She came here full of hope for a better life, and found . . ." His voice trailed off in a great sigh.

"So she decided to cross the river with the other folk. And she took your child with her."

"Colson was as much Delly's as my own. Her claim was no less. She took Colson because she thought it would be best for the girl—of that, I have no doubt."

Catti-brie put her hand on Wulfgar's forearm. He appreciated the touch.

"And Drizzt is alive," he said, looking into her eyes and managing a smile. "There is good news, too, this day."

Catti-brie squeezed his forearm and matched his smile.

She didn't know how to respond, Wulfgar realized. She didn't know what to say or what to do. He had lost Delly and she had found Drizzt in a dwarf's single sentence! Sorrow, sympathy, hope, and relief so obviously swirled inside her as they swirled inside him, and she feared that if the balance tilted too positively, she would be minimizing his loss and showing disrespect.

Her concern about his feelings reminded Wulfgar of how great a friend she truly was to him. He put his other hand atop hers and squeezed back, then smiled more sincerely and nodded.

"Drizzt will find Obould and kill him," he said, strength returning to his voice. "Then he will return to us, where he belongs."

"And we're going to find Colson," Catti-brie replied.

Wulfgar took a deep breath, needing it to settle himself before he just melted down hopelessly.

All of Mithral Hall was searching for the toddler in the hopes that Delly had not taken her out. Dwarves had gone down to the Surbrin, despite the freezing rain that was falling in torrents, trying to get a message across the way to the ferry pilots to see if any of them had noted the child.

"The weather will break soon," Catti-brie said. "Then we will go and find your daughter."

"And Drizzt," Wulfgar replied.

Catti-brie grinned and gave a little shrug. "He'll find us long before that, if I'm knowing Drizzt."

"With Obould's head in hand," Wulfgar added.

It was a little bit of hope, at least, on as dark a day as Wulfgar, son of Beornegar, had ever known.

". . . orc-brained, goblin-sniffing son of an ogre and a rock!" Bruenor fumed. He stalked about his audience hall, kicking anything within reach.

"Hee hee hee," said Pikel.

Ivan shot his brother a look and motioned for him to be silent.

"Someone get me armor!" Bruenor roared. "And me axe! Got me a few hunnerd smelly orcs to kill!"

"Hee hee hee."

Ivan cleared his throat to cover his brother's impertinence. They had just informed King Bruenor of Drizzt's intentions, how the drow had taken the magical sword and Ivan's hand crossbow and had gone off after Obould.

Bruenor hadn't taken the news well.

Thrilled as he was that his dear friend was alive, Bruenor couldn't stand his current state of inaction. A storm was whipping up outside, with driving and freezing rain, and heavy snow at the higher elevations, and there was simply no way for Bruenor or anyone else to get out of Mithral Hall. Even if the weather had been clear, Bruenor realized that there would be little he could do to help Drizzt. The drow was astride a flying horse—how could he possibly hope to catch him?

"Durned stupid elf," he muttered and he kicked the edge of his stone dais, then grumbled some more as he limped away.

"Hee hee hee," Pikel snickered.

"You'll only break your foot, and you won't be able to even go out to the walls," said Regis, rushing into the hall to see what was the matter. For word was passing through the complex that Drizzt had been found alive and well, and that King Bruenor was out of sorts.

"Ye heared?"

Regis nodded. "I knew he was alive. It will take more than orcs and frost giants to kill Drizzt."

"He's going after Obould. All by himself," Bruenor growled.

"I would not want to be Obould, then," the halfling said with a grin.

"Bah!" snorted the dwarf. "Durned stupid elf's taking all the fun again!"

"Hee hee hee," said Pikel, and Ivan elbowed him.

Pikel turned fiercely on his brother, his eyes going wild, and he began to waggle his fingers menacingly, all the while uttering birdlike sounds.

Ivan just shook his head.

"Boo," said Pikel, then "hee hee hee," again.

"Will ye just shut up?" Ivan said and he shook his head and turned away, crossing his burly arms over his chest.

He found Regis staring at him and chuckling.

"What?"

King Bruenor stopped, then, and similarly regarded Ivan, and he, too, began to chuckle.

Ivan stared at them both curiously, for unlike the pair, he couldn't see that his brother had just turned his beard as green as Pikel's own.

"They're thinking yerself to be amusing," Ivan said to Pikel.

"Hee hee hee."

Head down, cowl pulled low, Drizzt Do'Urden did not remain under shelter against the storm. North of Mithral Hall, it was all snow, blowing and deepening all around him, but with Sunrise in tow, the drow made his way across the uneven, rocky terrain, moving in the general direction of where he had last seen Obould. As the daylight waned, the drow ranger found a sheltered overhang and settled in, lying right along Sunrise's back to share some of the steed's body heat.

The storm finally broke after sunset, but the wind kicked up even more furiously. Drizzt went out and watched the clouds whip across the sky, stars blinking in and out with their passing. He climbed up over the jag of stone he had used for shelter and scanned the area. Several clusters of campfires were visible from up there, for the region was thick with the remnants of Obould's army. He marked the direction of the largest such cluster, then went back down and forced himself to get some much-needed rest.

He was up and out before the dawn, though, riding Sunrise, and even putting the pegasus up into a series of short, low flights.

A smile spread on the drow's face as he neared the region of the previous night's campfires, for the pennant of Obould soon came into view—the same flag he had seen flying with the orc king's personal caravan. He found a good vantage point and settled in, and soon enough, that same caravan was on the move once more.

Drizzt studied them closely. He spotted Obould among the ranks, growling orders.

The drow nodded and took a wide scan of the region, picking his path so that he could shadow the caravan.

He'd bide his time and await the opportunity.

We will kill them all, the vicious Khazid'hea whispered in his mind.

Drizzt focused his will and simply shut the telepathic intrusion off, then sent his own warning to the sword. *Bother me again and I will feed you to a dragon. You will sit in its treasure piles for a thousand years and more.*

The sword went silent once again.

Drizzt knew that Khazid'hea had sought him out purposely, and knew that the sword had desired him as its wielder for some time. He considered that perhaps he should be more amenable to the sentient blade, should accept its intrusions and even let it believe that it was somewhat in charge.

It didn't matter, he decided, and he kept up his wall of mental defense. Khazid'hea could dominate most people, had even taken Catti-brie by surprise initially and had bent her actions to its will.

But against a warrior as seasoned and disciplined as Drizzt Do'Urden, a warrior who knew well the intrusive nature of the sentient sword, Khazid'hea's willpower seemed no more than a minor inconvenience.

Drizzt considered that for a moment, and realized that he must take no chances. Obould would prove enough of a foe.

"We will kill them all," Drizzt said, and he lifted the blade up before his intense eyes.

He felt Khazid'hea's approval.

30

WHEN GODS ROAR

Kaer'lic Suun Wett nearly fell over when she saw the distinctive form of the winged horse sweeping in from the south. Orcs readied their bows, and Kaer'lic considered a spell, but Obould moved first and fast, and with little ambiguity.

"Hold your shots!" he bellowed, rushing and turning about so that there could be no mistaking him.

As he turned Kaer'lic's way, the drow priestess saw such fires raging in his eyes that they washed away any thoughts she entertained of ignoring his command and throwing some Lolth-granted spell at the pegasus rider.

That only infuriated her more as the winged horse closed and she recognized the black-skinned rider astride the magnificent creature.

"Drizzt Do'Urden," she mouthed.

"He dares approach?" asked Tos'un, who was standing at her side.

The pegasus banked and reared up, stopping its approach and seeming to hover in the air through a few great wing beats.

"Obould!" Drizzt cried, and as he had maneuvered himself upwind, his words were carried to the orcs. "I would speak with you! Alone! We have an unfinished conversation, you and I!"

"He has lost all sensibility," Kaer'lic whispered.

"Or is he in parlay with Obould?" asked Tos'un. "As an emissary of Mithral Hall, perhaps?"

"Destroy him!" Kaer'lic called to Obould. "Send your archers and cut him down or I will do it my—"

"You will hold your spells, or you will discuss this matter with Ad'non and Donnia in short order," Obould replied.

"Kill the ugly beast," Tos'un whispered to her, and Kaer'lic almost launched a magical assault upon the orc king—until good sense overruled her instinctive hatred. She looked from Obould over to Drizzt, who was taking the pegasus down lower onto an adjoining high point, a huge flat rock wedged against the steep hillside, its far end propped by several tall natural stone columns.

Kaer'lic did well to hide her grin as she looked back at the orc king, all adorned in his fine plate mail fastened by spider-shaped buckles. Though she hadn't planned on getting anywhere near to Drizzt Do'Urden, in effect, the scene was playing out exactly as she had hoped. Better than she had hoped, she thought, since she had not expected that Drizzt Do'Urden himself would prove to be the first formidable foe King Obould faced in his "improved" armor. If Drizzt was half as good as Kaer'lic had come to believe, then Obould was in for a very bad surprise.

"You intend to speak with this infidel?" she asked.

"If he speaks for Mithral Hall and they have anything to say that I wish to hear," Obould answered.

"And if not?"

"Then he has come to kill me, no doubt."

"And you will walk out to him?"

"And slaughter him." Obould's look was one of perfect confidence. He seemed almost bored by it all, as if Drizzt was no serious issue.

"You cannot do this," Tsinka said, moving fast behind her god-figure. "There is no reason. Let us destroy him from afar and continue on our way. Or send an emissary—send Kaer'lic, who knows the way of the drow elves!"

The sudden widening of Kaer'lic's red eyes betrayed her terror at that prospect, but she recovered quickly and flashed Tsinka a hateful look. When Tsinka's responding expression became concerned, even deeply wounded, Kaer'lic remembered the enchantment, remembered that she was "best friends" with the pitiful shaman. She managed a smile at the fool orc, then lifted her index finger and waggled it back and forth, bidding Tsinka not to interfere.

Tsinka continued to look at her dear, dear dark elf friend curiously for a moment longer, then happily smiled to indicate that she understood.

"This one is formidable, so I have heard," Kaer'lic said, but only because she knew she would hardly dissuade Obould from his intended course.

"I have battled him before," Obould assured her with a shrug.

"Perhaps it is a trap," Tsinka said, her voice falling away to ineffectiveness as she sheepishly looked at Kaer'lic.

Obould snickered and started to walk away, but stopped and glanced back, his yellow teeth showing behind the mouth slit in his bone-white helmet. Two strides put him past Kaer'lic, and he reached over and grabbed poor Fender by the scruff of his neck, and easily hoisted the dwarf under one arm.

"Never parlay without a counteroffer prepared," he remarked, and he stormed away.

Drizzt was not surprised to see Obould stalking from the far hilltop, though the sight of the dwarf prisoner did catch him off his guard. Other than that squirming prisoner, though, Obould was moving out alone. As he had shadowed Obould looking for the proper terrain, Drizzt had concocted elaborate ambushes, where he and Sunrise might swoop down from behind a shielding high bluff in a fast and deadly attack on Obould. But Drizzt had known those plans to be unnecessary. He had taken a good measure of the orc king in their fight, in more ways than physical. Obould would not run from his challenge, fairly offered.

But what of the dwarf? Drizzt had to find a way to make sure that Obould would not kill the poor fellow. He would refuse the fight unless the orc king guaranteed the prisoner's safety, perhaps. As he watched the approach, the drow became more convinced that he would be able to do just that, that Obould would not kill the dwarf. There was something about Obould, Drizzt was just beginning to see. In a strange way, the orc reminded Drizzt of Artemis Entreri. Single-minded and overly proud, always needing to prove himself—but to whom? To himself, perhaps.

Drizzt had known beyond the slightest bit of doubt that Obould would come out to meet him. He watched the orc king's long strides, noted the other orcs and a pair of drow creeping about in a widening arc behind the solitary figure of the great king. He had his left hand on Icingdeath, and he drew Khazid'hea from a scabbard strapped on Sunrise's side, but put the blade low immediately so as not to offer any overt threat.

We will cut out his heart, the sword started to promise.

You will be silent and remain out of my thoughts, Drizzt answered telepathically. *Distract me but once and I will throw you down the mountainside and rain an avalanche of snow and cold stones upon you.*

So forceful and dominant was the focused drow that the sentient sword went silent.

"He will win, yes? With the magic you put on his armor, Obould will win, yes?" Tsinka babbled as she moved to a closer vantage point beside the two drow.

Kaer'lic ignored her for most of the way, which only made the foolish shaman more insistent and demanding.

Finally the drow priestess turned on her and said, "He is Gruumsh, yes?"

Tsinka stopped short—stopped both walking and babbling.

"Drizzt is a mere drow warrior," said Kaer'lic. "Obould is Gruumsh. Do you fear for Gruumsh?"

Tsinka blanked, her doubts spinning around to reflect a lack of faith.

"So be silent and enjoy the show," said Kaer'lic, and so overpowering was her tone, particularly given the enchantment she still maintained regarding Tsinka, that her effect over the babbling shaman proved no less than Drizzt's dominance over Khazid'hea.

"Say what you must, and be quick," Obould said as he mounted the high flat stone directly across from the drow. Sunrise took a few quick strides and flew off the other way, as Drizzt had instructed.

"Say?" the drow asked.

Obould dropped poor Fender down onto the stone, the dwarf grunting as he hit face first. "You have come with parlay from Mithral Hall?"

"I have not been to Mithral Hall."

A smile widened on Obould's face, barely visible behind that awful skull-like helmet.

"You believe that the dwarves will parlay with you?" Drizzt asked.

"Have they a choice?"

"They will speak with their axes and their bows. They will answer with fury, and nothing more."

"You said that you have not been to Mithral Hall."

"Need I return to a place and people I know so well to anticipate the course of Clan Battlehammer?"

"This is beyond Clan Battlehammer," said Obould, and Drizzt could see that his smile had disappeared. With a growl, the orc king kicked the squirming Fender, sending the dwarf flying off the back side of the stone and bouncing down a short descending path.

The sudden surge of anger caught the drow off guard.

"You wish for a parlay with Mithral Hall?" Drizzt stated as much as asked, and he didn't even try to keep the surprise out of his voice.

Obould stared at him hatefully through the glassy eye-plates.

Questions came at Drizzt from every corner of his mind. If Obould desired a parlay, could it be that the war was at its end? If Drizzt battled the orc king, would he be showing disloyalty to Bruenor and his people, given that he might have just witnessed a sliver of hope that the war could be ended?

"You will return to your mountain homes?" Drizzt blurted, even as the question formulated in his thoughts.

Obould scoffed at him. "Look around you, drow," he said. "This is my home now. My kingdom! When you fly on your pet, you see the greatness of Obould. You see the Kingdom of Dark Arrows. Remember that name for the last minutes of your life. You die in Dark Arrows, Drizzt Do'Urden, and will be eaten by birds on a mountainside in the home of King Obould." He ended with a snarl and lifted his greatsword up before him, beginning a determined approach.

"Who is your second?" Drizzt asked, the unexpected words halting Obould. "For when you are dead, I will need to know. Perhaps that orc will be wiser than Obould and will see that he has no place here, among the dwarves, the elves, and the humans. Or if not, I will kill him, too, and speak with his second."

Drizzt saw Obould's eyes widen behind the glassy plates, and with a roar that shook the stones, Obould leaped ahead, stabbing ferociously with his powerful sword, the blade bursting into flame as he thrust.

Out snapped Icingdeath, in the blink of a drow eye, the enchanted weapon slapping across the greatsword, extinguishing the fires in an angry puff of smoke as Drizzt hopped to the side. He could have struck with Khazid'hea, for Obould, in his supreme confidence, had abandoned all semblance of defense in the assault. But Drizzt held the attack.

The greatsword came slashing across, predictably, forcing the drow into a fast retreat. Had he taken that first opening and struck with his new-found sword, Drizzt would have scored a hit, but nothing substantial.

And in that instance, Obould would have recognized his unanticipated vulnerability.

Obould pressed the attack wildly, slashing and stabbing, rushing ahead, and on the high ground behind and to the side of the flat stone, orcs cheered and shouted in glee.

Drizzt measured every turn and retreat, letting the fury play out, using less energy than his outraged opponent. He wasn't trying to tire Obould, but rather to gain better insight into the orc's turns and movements, that he could better anticipate.

The greatsword flamed to life again with one feinted stab that became a sudden reversal into a downward chop, and had Drizzt not seen a similar distraction tactic used against the elf Tarathiel, he might have found himself caught by surprise. As it was, the descending greatsword met only the slap of Icingdeath, extinguishing the larger weapon's fires.

Obould came on suddenly and wildly, charging straight for the drow, who stepped left, then leaped back right, going into a roll as Obould started one way then threw himself back the other, slashing his sword across. That sword flamed to life again, and the rolling Drizzt felt the heat of those magical fires as the blade cut above him.

Drizzt came up to his feet and spun, then back-stepped and slid off to the side once more as Obould continued to press. Around and around they went, the orcs cheering and howling with every slash of Obould's sword, though he got nowhere close to hitting the elusive drow.

Neither did he show any signs of tiring, though.

Finally, Obould stopped his charge and stood glaring at Drizzt from behind the flames of the upraised greatsword.

"Are you going to fight me?" he asked.

"I thought I was."

Obould growled. "Run away, if that is your course. Cross blades if you are not afraid."

"You grow tired?"

"I grow bored!" Obould roared.

Drizzt smiled and faked a sudden rush, then stopped abruptly and caught everyone by surprise when he simply tossed Icingdeath up into the air. Obould's eyes followed the ascent of the sword.

Drizzt reached his free hand behind his back and brought out the loaded hand crossbow, and as Obould snapped his gaze back upon him—yes, he wanted the orc king to see it coming!—the drow gave a shrug and let fly.

The dart hit Obould's helmet in the left eye then collapsed in on itself and exploded with a burst of angry flame and black smoke. Obould's head snapped back viciously, and the orc king went flying down to the stone, flat on his back, as surely as if a mountain had fallen atop him. He lay very still.

Gasps and silence replaced the wild cheering of all those looking on.

"Impressive," Tos'un quietly remarked.

Beside him, Kaer'lic stood with her jaw hanging open, and beside her, Tsinka whimpered and gasped.

They watched Drizzt snap the hand crossbow back behind him, then casually catch the falling scimitar.

Kaer'lic noticed the approach of the pegasus, and suddenly feared that Drizzt would escape once more—and that, she could not allow.

She began casting a powerful spell, aiming for the flying horse and not the too-lucky drow, when she was interrupted by Tsinka, who grabbed her arm, and screamed, "He moves!"

The drow priestess looked back at Obould, who rocked up onto his shoulders, arching his back and bending his legs, then snapped back the other way, leaping up to his feet.

The orcs screamed in glee.

Drizzt hid his surprise well when Obould was suddenly standing before him once more. He noted the tip of the dart, embedded in the glassteel plate of the helmet, and the black scorch marks showing over the rest of that plate, and partially over the other one as well.

He hadn't expected to kill Obould with the dart, after all, and it was a fortunate thing that the orc king's fall had caught him more by surprise than his sudden return, for Obould howled and attacked once more, slashing with abandon.

But . . .

He couldn't see! Drizzt realized as he stepped aside and Obould continued to press the attack at the empty air before him.

Kill him now! the hungry Khazid'hea implored, and the drow, in complete agreement, didn't even scold the sentient sword.

He stepped in suddenly and drove Khazid'hea at a seam in the orc king's fabulous armor, and the fine blade bit through and slid into Obould's side.

How the great orc howled and leaped, tearing the sword right from Drizzt's grasp. Obould staggered back several steps, blood leaking out beside the sticking blade.

"Treachery!" Obould yelled, and he reached up and yanked the ruined helmet from his head, throwing it over the cliff face. "You cannot beat me fairly, and you cannot beat me unfairly!"

To Drizzt's amazement, he came on again.

"Unbelievable," whispered Tos'un.

"Stubborn," Kaer'lic corrected with a snarl.

"Gruumsh!" howled the gleeful and crying Tsinka, and all the orcs cheered, for if that sword protruding from Obould's side would prove a mortal wound, it did not show at all in the great orc's pressing attacks.

"He doesn't even know when he's dead," Kaer'lic grumbled, and she launched into a spell, then, a calling to magical items she had fastened by the grace of Lady Lolth.

It was time to end the travesty.

Drizzt tried to battle past his incredulity and properly respond to Obould's renewed attacks. It took him several parries and a few last-second dodges to even realize that he should draw out Twinkle to replace his lost sword.

"And what have you gained for all of your treachery, drow?" Obould demanded, pressing forward and slashing away.

"You are without a helmet, and that is no small thing," Drizzt shouted back. "The turtle has come out of its shell."

"Only so that I can look down upon you in the last moments of your life, fool!" Obould assured him. "That you might see the pleasure on my face as your body grows cold!" He ended with a devastating charge, and turned in anticipation even as Drizzt started to jump aside.

The move caught Drizzt off guard, for it was truly an all-or-nothing, victory-or-defeat maneuver. If Obould guessed wrong, turning opposite Drizzt's sudden dodge, then Drizzt would have little trouble in slamming one or both of his scimitars down upon the back of the orc's skull.

But Obould guessed right.

On his heels, corralled and running out of retreating room, Drizzt parried desperately. So fast was Obould's sword-work that Drizzt couldn't even think of launching an effective counter. So furious was the orc king's attack that Drizzt didn't even entertain any thoughts of swinging for his exposed head. Drizzt understood the power behind Obould's swings, and he knew that he could not fend that greatsword. Not the shirt he had taken from the dead dark elf, not even the finest suit of Bruenor's best mithral stock would save him from being cloven in half.

Very simply, Obould had guessed right in his turn and Drizzt understood that he was beaten.

Both his blades slapped against the slashing greatsword, Icingdeath extinguishing the stubborn fires yet again. But the shock of the block sent waves of numbness up the drow's arm, and even with a two-bladed parry, he could not fully deflect the swing. He fell down—that, or he would have been cut in half—and scrambled into a forward roll, but he could not get fully past Obould without taking a hit, a kick at least. He braced himself for the blow.

But it did not fall.

Drizzt came around as he got back to his feet, to see Obould squirming and jerking wildly.

"What?" the orc king growled, and he jolted left then right.

It took Drizzt several seconds to sort it out, to notice that the spider clasps on Obould's armor were animating. Eight-legged creatures scrambled all over the orc, and by Obould's roars and jerking movements, it seemed as if more than a few were stopping to bite him.

As the orc thrashed, pieces of that fabulous armor suit went flying. One vambrace fell to the stone, and he kicked his legs to free himself of the tangle of flapping jambs. His great breastplate fell away, as well as one pauldron and the backplate. The remaining pauldron flapped outward, held in place only by the embedded sword—and how Obould howled whenever that vicious blade moved.

Not understanding, not even caring, Drizzt leaped in for the kill.

And promptly leaped back out, as Obould found his focus and countered with a sudden and well-timed sword thrust. Drizzt winced as he back-stepped, blood staining his enchanted shirt on the side. He stared at his opponent through every inch of his retreat, stunned that Obould had found the clarity to so counter.

Separated and with a moment's respite, Obould straightened. His face twisted into a grimace and he slapped one hand across to splatter a spider that had found a soft spot in his toughened orc hide. He brought his hand across, throwing the arachnid carcass to the ground, then reached over, growled and grimacing, and pulled Khazid'hea free of his side, taking the pauldron with it.

Wield me as your own! the sword screamed at him.

With a feral and explosive roar, Obould threw the annoying sword over the cliff.

"Treachery again!" he roared at Drizzt. "You live up to the sinister reputation of your heritage, drow."

"That was not my doing," Drizzt yelled back. "Speak not to me of treachery, Obould, when you encase yourself in an armor my blades cannot penetrate."

That retort seemed to quiet and calm the orc, who stood more upright and assumed a pensive posture. He even offered a nod of concession to Drizzt on that point, ending with a smile and an invitation: "I wear none now."

Obould held his arms out wide, and brought his greatsword flaming to life, inviting the drow to continue.

Drizzt straightened against the sting in his side, returned the nod, and leaped ahead.

Those watching the fight, drow and orc alike, did not cheer, hoot, or groan over the next few moments. They stood, one and all, transfixed by the sudden fury of the engagement, by the hum of swords, and the dives and leaps of the principals. Blade rang against blade too many times to be heard as distinguishable sounds. Blades missed a killing mark by so narrow a margin, again and again, that the onlookers continually gasped.

The confusion of the battle challenged Drizzt at every level. One moment, he felt as if he was fighting Artemis Entreri, so fluid, fast, and devious were Obould's movements. And the next moment, he was painfully reminded by a shocking wave of reverberating energy flowing up his arm that he might well be battling a mighty giant.

He let go of all his thoughts then, and fell into the Hunter, allowing his rage to rise within him, allowing for perfect focus and fury.

He knew in an instant that the creature he faced was no less intense.

Any traces of her charm spell was gone then, Kaer'lic knew, as Tsinka Shinriil, finding herself deceived by the drow's work on Obould's armor, leaped up beside Kaer'lic and began shrieking at her.

"You cannot defeat him! Even your treachery pales against the power of Obould!" she screamed. "You chose to betray a god, and now you will learn the folly of your ways!"

Truly it seemed a moment of absolute glee for the idiot Tsinka, and that, Kaer'lic could not allow. The drow's hand shot up as she mouthed the last words of a spell, creating a sudden disturbance in the air, a crackling jolt of energy that sent Tsinka flying away and to the ground.

"Kill her," Kaer'lic instructed Tos'un, who moved immediately to see to the enjoyable task.

"Wait," Kaer'lic said. "Let her live a bit longer. Let her witness the death of her god."

"We should just be gone from this place," said Tos'un, clearly intimidated by the spectacle of King Obould, who was matching the skilled drow cut for cut.

Kaer'lic flashed her companion a warning look, then turned her focus back upon that high stone. Her eyes went wild and she began to chant to Lady Lolth, reaching within herself for every ounce of magical strength she could muster for her powerful spell. The very air seemed to gather about her as she moved through the incantation. Her hair bristled and waved, though there was no wind. She grasped at the air with her outstretched hand then brought it in close and reached with the other one. Then she repeated the movements again and again as if she was taking all of the energy around her and bringing it into her torso.

The ground began to tremble beneath them. Kaer'lic began a low growl that increased in tempo and volume, slowly at first, but then more forcefully and quickly as the drow priestess began to reach out toward Drizzt and Obould with both hands.

Thunder rolled all around them. The orcs began to cower, shout, or run away. And the ground began to shake, quick and darting movements at first that grew into great rolling waves of stone. Rock split and crumbled. A crevice appeared before Kaer'lic and charged out toward the unfazed combatants.

And the high rock split apart under the force of Kaer'lic's earthquake. And stones tumbled down in an avalanche. And Obould fell away, roaring in protest.

And Drizzt went right behind him.

31

TO BE AN ELF

Her nose was no more than a misshapen lump of torn flesh, with blood and grime caked all around it and over her left eye. Kaer'lic's spell had broken most of the bones in Tsinka's face, the shaman knew, and Tsinka was glad indeed when she had awakened to find the two drow long gone. Everyone was long gone, it seemed, for the orcs had run away from that terrible earthquake.

For many minutes, Tsinka Shinriil sat and stared at the broken rock across the way, plumes of dust still hanging in the air from the weight of the avalanche. What had Kaer'lic done? Why had Lady Lolth gone against He-Who-Was-Gruumsh? It made no sense to the poor, broken shaman.

Moving against hope, Tsinka pulled herself to her feet and staggered toward the area of disaster. She followed the same path Obould had taken on his approach to the renegade drow. She could still see some of her god's footprints in the snow and dirt before her. Half-blinded by drying blood and streams of tears, Tsinka stumbled along, falling more than once, crying out to her god.

"How did you let this happen?"

She nearly tripped over a form half-buried in the snow and rubble, then recoiled and kicked out at it when she saw it was that ugly little dwarf. He grunted, so she kicked him again and moved along. She pulled herself up on the remains of the flat rock that had served as the battleground. The earthquake had split it in half, and the far half, where both Obould and Drizzt had been standing, had fallen away.

Tsinka wiped her arm across her face and forced herself to stagger forward. She fell to her knees and peered into the area of ruin, into the dust.

And there, only a dozen feet below her, she saw the form of a battered but very much alive dark elf.

"You!" she howled, and she spat at him.

Drizzt looked up at her. Filthy and bruised, bloody on one side and holding one arm in close, the drow had not escaped unharmed. But he had escaped, landing on a small ledge, perched on the very edge of oblivion.

"Where will you run now?" Tsinka shouted at him.

She glanced all around then scrambled to the side, returning a moment later with a rock in each hand. She pegged one down at him and missed, then took more careful aim with the second and whipped it off his upraised, blocking arm.

"Your flying horse is nowhere about, drow!" she shouted, and she hopped around in search of more ammo.

Again she pelted Drizzt with rocks, and there was nothing he could do but lift his arm to block and accept the stinging hits. He had no room to maneuver, and try as he may, he could not find any handholds that would propel him back up to the flat rock.

Every time she threw a stone, Tsinka scanned the skies. The pegasus wouldn't catch her by surprise, she vowed. The drow had played a role in destroying He-Who-Was-Gruumsh, and so the drow would have to die.

He was out of options. There was nothing Drizzt could do against the assault. He still had his scimitars and Ivan's crossbow, but the remaining darts he'd left on Sunrise, who was nowhere to be seen. Sitting on the tiny ledge, Drizzt had hoped that the pegasus would find him before the inevitable return of his enemies.

No such luck, and so all he could do was deflect the stinging stones with his upraised arms.

The orc shaman disappeared for a longer period of time, then, and Drizzt desperately looked around. No pegasus came into view—and in his rational thoughts, he knew that it would be some time before Sunrise would come back to the unstable, devastated area.

"At least Obould is gone," he whispered, and he glanced out over the ledge, where the shifting stones continued to rumble. "Bruenor will win the day."

Whatever hope that notion inspired disappeared in the realization of his mortality, as Drizzt looked back up to see the orc hoist a huge rock over her head in both hands. He glanced to the sides quickly, looking for some place he might leap.

But there was nothing.

The orc snarled at him and moved to throw.

And she lurched and went flying, both her and the rock tumbling out too far, past the surprised drow and down the broken mountainside. On the rock above, hanging over the edge, loomed a hairy and battered face.

"Well met, Drizzt Do'Urden," said Fender. "Think ye might be taking me home?"

"We will go to Gerti and determine what she is about," said Kaer'lic.

"The dwarf is gone and Tsinka is likely plotting our demise," Tos'un replied.

"If the pig-faced shaman even lives," Kaer'lic retorted. "I hope she does, that I might make her death even more unpleasant. Too much have I seen of these wretched and foul-smelling orcs. Too many tendays have we spent in their filthy company, listening to their foolish gibbering, and pretending that anything they might have to say would be of the least bit of interest to us. Gruumsh take Obould, and Lady Lolth take Drizzt, and may they both be tortured until eternity's end!"

So caught up was she in her ranting, that Kaer'lic didn't even notice Tos'un's eyes go so wide that they seemed as if they might just roll out of his face. So full of spit and anger was she that it took her some time to even realize that Tos'un wasn't looking at her, but rather past her.

Kaer'lic froze in place.

Tos'un squealed, turned, and ran away.

Kaer'lic realized she should just follow, without question, but before her mind could command her feet to run, a powerful hand grabbed her by the back of her hair and jerked her head back so violently and forcefully that she felt as if her entire body had been suddenly compacted.

"Do you recognize the foul smell?" Obould Many-Arrows whispered into her ear. He tugged harder with that one hand pulling her down and back, but not letting her fall. "Does my gibbering offend you now?"

Kaer'lic could hardly move, so forceful was that grasp. She saw Obould's greatsword sticking past her, off to the side. She felt his breath, hot against her neck, and stinking as only an orc's breath could. She had to tug back and stretch her jaw muscles so that they could even move against that incredible pull, and she tried futilely to form some words, any words.

"Casting a spell, witch?" Obould asked her. "Sorry, but that I cannot allow."

His face came forward suddenly, his jaw clamping on Kaer'lic's exposed throat. She reached up and grabbed at him and squirmed and thrashed desperately, with all her might.

Obould tore his face away, taking her throat with it. He yanked Kaer'lic back and put his bloody and battered face right before her, then spat her own flesh into her face.

"I am imbued with the blessing of Gruumsh," he said. "Did you truly believe that you could kill me?"

Kaer'lic gasped, her arms flailing wildly and uncontrollably, blood pouring from her torn throat, and bubbling from the air escaping her lungs.

Obould threw her to the ground and let her die slowly.

He scanned the region, and noted some movement on a distant ridge. It wasn't Tsinka, he knew, for he had seen her broken body on the stones as he climbed back up the mountainside.

He'd need to find a new shaman, a new consort who treated him as a god. He'd need to move quickly to reconsolidate his power, to cut short the rumors of his demise. The orcs would be fast to flee, he knew, and only he, imbued with the power of Gruumsh, could stop the retreat.

"Dark Arrows," he said with determination. "My home."

The weather broke, leaving the air fresh and clean, and with a warm south wind blowing. Bruenor and his friends would not stay inside, spending their days along the northern mountain spur, staring off into the north.

Pikel Bouldershoulder's bird scouts were the first to report a pair of winged horses, making all speed for Mithral Hall, and so it was not a surprise, but such a tremendous relief nonetheless, when the distinctive forms finally came into view.

Bruenor and Wulfgar moved a couple of paces out in front of the others, Regis, the Bouldershoulders, Cordio, Stumpet, and Pwent behind them, and Catti-brie in back, leaning heavily on a wooden cane and on the side of the tower.

Sunset set down on the stone before the dwarf king, Innovindil lifted her leg over before her and dropping quickly, turning as she went to support poor Fender through the move. Without that support, the dwarf would surely have tumbled off.

Wulfgar stepped forward and gently hoisted the dwarf from the pegasus, then handed him to Cordio and Stumpet, who hustled him away.

"Obould is gone," Innovindil reported. "The orcs will not hold, and all the northland will be free again."

As she finished, Sunrise landed on the stone.

"A sight for an old dwarf's sore eyes," Bruenor said.

Drizzt slipped down to the ground. He glanced at Bruenor, but his stare remained straight ahead, cutting through the ranks, which parted as surely as if he had shouldered his way through, leaving the line of sight open between the drow and Catti-brie.

"Welcome home," Regis said.

"We never doubted your return," offered Wulfgar.

Drizzt nodded at each, though he never stopped staring ahead. He patted Bruenor as he walked past. He tousled Regis's hair and he grabbed and squeezed Wulfgar's strong forearm.

But he never stopped moving and never stopped staring.

He hit Catti-brie with a great hug, pressing up against her, kissing her and crushing her, lifting her right from the ground.

And he kept walking, carrying her along.

"That is what it is to be an elf, Drizzt Do'Urden," Innovindil whispered as the two moved to, and through, Mithral Hall's new eastern door.

"Well I'll be a bearded gnome," said Bruenor.

"Hee hee hee," said Pikel, and Regis giggled, embarrassed.

They all were fairly amused, it seemed, but Bruenor's mirth disappeared when he glanced across at Wulfgar.

The big man stared at the path Drizzt and Catti-brie had taken, and there was a wince of profound pain to be found behind his mask of stoicism.

EPILOGUE

"She will understand," Drizzt said to Catti-brie, the two of them sitting on the edge of their bed early one morning, nearly two tendays after the drow's return to Mithral Hall.

"She won't, because she'll not have to," Catti-brie argued. "You told her that you would go, and so you shall. On your word."

"Innovindil will understand . . ." Drizzt started to argue, but his voice trailed off under Catti-brie's wilting stare. They had been over it several times already.

"You need to close that chapter of your life," Catti-brie said to him quietly, taking his hands in her own and lifting them up to her lips to kiss them. "Your scimitar cut into your own heart as deeply as it cut into Ellifain. You do not return to her for Innovindil. You owe Innovindil and her people nothing, so yes, they will understand. It's yourself that you owe. You need to return. To put Ellifain to rest and to put Drizzt at peace."

"How can I leave you now?"

"How can you not?" Catti-brie grinned at him. "I do not doubt that you'll return to me, even if your companion on your journey is a beautiful elf.

"Besides," the woman went on, "I'll not be here in any case. I have promised Wulfgar that I will journey with him to Silverymoon and beyond, if necessary."

Drizzt nodded his agreement with that last part. According to the dwarf ferry pilot, Delly Curtie did come near his craft before it set off for the eastern bank with the refugees from the north, and he did recall seeing the woman hand something, perhaps a baby, over to one of the other human women. He couldn't be certain who—they all looked alike to him, so he declared.

Wulfgar wasn't about to wait until spring to set off in pursuit of Colson, and Catti-brie wasn't about to let him go alone.

"You cannot go with us," Catti-brie said. "Your presence will cause too much a stir in those gossiping towns, and will tell whoever has the child that we're in pursuit. So you've your task to perform, and I've mine."

Drizzt didn't argue any longer.

"Regis is staying with Bruenor?" Drizzt asked.

"Someone's got to. He's all out of sorts since word that Obould, or an orc acting in Obould's stead, continues to hold our enemies in cohesion. Bruenor thought they would have begun their retreat by now, but all reports from the north show them continuing their work unabated."

"The Kingdom of Dark Arrows. . . ." Drizzt mouthed, shaking his head. "And Alustriel and all the others will not go against it."

Catti-brie squeezed his hand tighter. "We'll find a way."

Sitting so close to her, Drizzt couldn't believe anything else, couldn't believe that every problem could not be solved.

Drizzt found Bruenor in his audience hall a short while later, Regis sitting beside him and the Bouldershoulder brothers, packed for the road, standing before him.

"Well met again, ye dark one," Ivan greeted the drow. "Me and me brother . . ." Ivan paused.

"Me brudder!" said Pikel.

"Yeah, we're off for home to see if Cadderly can do something about me . . . about Pikel's arm. Won't be much fighting to be found up here for a few tendays, at least. We're thinking to come back and kill a few more orcs." Ivan turned to Bruenor. "If ye'll have us, King Bruenor."

"Would any ruler be so foolish as to refuse the help of the Bouldershoulders?" Bruenor asked graciously, though Drizzt could hear the simmering anger behind Bruenor's every sound.

"Boom!" shouted Pikel.

"Yeah, boom," said Ivan. "Come on, ye green-bearded cousin o'

Cadderly's pet squirrel. Get me home—and no small roots, ye hear?"

"Hee hee hee."

Drizzt watched the pair depart the hall, then turned to Bruenor and asked, "Will your kingdom ever be the same?"

"Good enough folk, them two," said Bruenor. "Green-bearded one scares me, though."

"Boom!" said Regis.

Bruenor eyed him threateningly. "First time ye say 'hee hee hee,' I'm pulling yer eyebrows out."

"The folk o' the towns're going to let them stay, elf," the dwarf said, turning back to Drizzt. "Durned fools're to let the stinking orcs have what they took."

"They see no way around it, and no reason to find one."

"And that's their folly. Obould, or whatever smelly pig-face that's taking his place, ain't to sit there and argue trade routes."

"I do not disagree."

"Can't let them stay."

"Nor can we hope to dislodge them without allies," Drizzt reminded the dwarf.

"And so we're to find them!" Bruenor declared. "Ye heading off with Invo . . . Inno . . . that durned elf?"

"I promised to take her to Ellifain's body, that Ellifain might be properly returned to the Moonwood."

"Good enough then."

"You know that I will return to you."

Bruenor nodded. "Gauntlgrym," he said, and both Drizzt and Regis were caught off guard.

"Gauntlgrym," Bruenor said again. "We three. Me girl if she's ready and me boy if he's back from finding his little girl. We're to find our answers at Gauntlgrym."

"How do you know that?" Regis asked.

"I know that Moradin didn't let me come back to sign a treaty with any stinking, smelly, pig-faced orc," Bruenor replied. "I know that I can't fight him alone and that I ain't yet convinced enough to fight beside me."

"And you believe that you will find answers to your dilemma in a long-buried dwarven kingdom?" asked Drizzt.

"I know it's as good a place to start looking as any. Banak's ready to take control o' the hall in me absence. Already put it in place. Gauntlgrym in the spring, elf."

Drizzt eyed him curiously, not certain whether Bruenor was on to something, or if the dwarf was just typically responding to sitting still by finding a way to get back on the road to adventure. As he considered that, however, Drizzt realized that it didn't much matter which it might be. For he was no less determined than Bruenor to find again the wind on his face.

"Gauntlgrym in the spring," he agreed.

"We'll show them orcs what's what," Bruenor promised.

Beside him, Regis just sighed.

Tos'un Armgo had not been so alone and out of sorts since he had abandoned the Menzoberranzan army after their retreat from Mithral Hall. His three companions were all dead and he knew that if he stayed anywhere in the North, Obould would send him to join them soon enough.

He had found Kaer'lic's body earlier that morning, but it was stripped of anything that might be of use to him. Where was he to go?

He thought of the Underdark's winding ways, and realized that he couldn't likely go back to Menzoberranzan, even if that had been his choice. But neither could he stay on the surface among the orcs.

"Gerti," he decided after considering his course for much of that day, sitting on the same stone where Obould and Drizzt had battled. If he could get to Shining White, he might find allies, and perhaps a refuge.

But that was only *if* he could get there. He slipped down from the rock and started moving down the trail to lower ground, sheltered from the wind and from the eyes of any of Obould's many spies. He found a lower trail and moved along, making his way generally north.

Do not abandon me! he heard, and he stopped.

No, he hadn't actually heard the call, Tos'un realized, but rather he had felt it, deep in his thoughts. Curious, the drow moved around, attuning his senses to his surroundings.

Here! Left of you. Near the stone.

Following the instructions, Tos'un soon came upon the source, and he was grinning for the first time in many days when he lifted a fabulous sword in his hands.

Well met, imparted Khazid'hea.

"Indeed," said Tos'un, as he felt the weapon's extraordinary balance and noted its incredibly sharp blade.

He looked back to where he had found the sword and noted that he had just pulled it from a seam in Obould's supposedly impenetrable armor.

"Indeed. . . ." he said again, thinking that perhaps not all of his adventure had been in vain.

Nor was Khazid'hea complaining, for it didn't take the sentient sword long to understand that it had at last found a wielder not only worthy, but of like mind.

On a clear and crisp winter's morning, Drizzt and Innovindil set out from Mithral Hall, moving southwest. They planned to pass near to Nesmé to see how progress was going on fortifying the city, and cross north of the Trollmoors to the town of Longsaddle, home of the famed wizard family the Harpells. Long allies of King Bruenor, the Harpells would join in the fight, no doubt, when battle finally resumed. And so desperate was Bruenor to find allies—any allies—that he would gladly accept even the help of eccentric wizards who blew each other up nearly as often as they dispatched their enemies.

Drizzt and Innovindil planned to stay along a generally southwesterly route all the way to the sea, hoping for days when they could put their winged mounts up into the sky. Then they'd turn north, hopefully just as winter was loosening its icy grip, and travel back to the ravine and harbor where Ellifain had been laid to rest.

That same morning, the ferry made the difficult journey across the icy Surbrin, bearing Wulfgar and Catti-brie, two friends determined to find Wulfgar's lost girl.

Bruenor and Regis had seen both pairs off, then had returned to the dwarf king's private quarters to begin drawing up plans for their springtime journey.

"Gauntlgrym, Rumblebelly," Bruenor kept reciting, and Regis came to know that as the dwarf's litany against the awful truth of the orc invasion. The mere thought of the Kingdom of Dark Arrows covering the land to his very doorstep had Bruenor in a terrible tizzy.

It was his way of escaping that reality, Regis knew, his way of doing something, anything, to try to fight back.

Regis hadn't seen Bruenor so animated and eager for the road since the journey that had taken them out of Icewind Dale to find Mithral Hall, those many years ago.

They'd all be there, all five—six, counting Guenhwyvar. Perhaps Ivan and Pikel would return before the spring and adventure with them.

Bruenor was too busy with his maps and his lists of supplies to be paying any attention, and so he missed the sound completely when Regis mumbled, "Hee hee hee."